TWELVE DAYS OF CHRISTMAS

Trisha Ashley was born in St Helens, Lancashire, and gave up her fascinating but time-consuming hobbies of house-moving and divorce a few years ago in order to settle in North Wales.

For more information about Trisha please visit www.trishaashley.com

CW00671767

TRISHA ASHLEY

Twelve Days of Christmas

AVON

This novel is entirely a work of fiction.
The names, characters and incidents portrayed in it are
the work of the author's imagination. Any resemblance to
actual persons, living or dead, events or localities is
entirely coincidental.

AVON

A division of HarperCollins*Publishers*
77–85 Fulham Palace Road,
London W6 8JB

www.harpercollins.co.uk

This paperback edition 2011

First published in Great Britain by
HarperCollins*Publishers* 2010

Copyright © Trisha Ashley 2010

Trisha Ashley asserts the moral right to
be identified as the author of this work

A catalogue record for this book is
available from the British Library

ISBN-13: 978-1-84756-337-8

Set in Minion by Palimpsest Book Production Limited,
Falkirk, Stirlingshire

Printed and bound in Great Britain by
Clays Ltd, St Ives plc

Mixed Sources
Product group from well-managed
forests and other controlled sources
www.fsc.org Cert no. SW-COC-001806
© 1996 Forest Stewardship Council

FSC is a non-profit international organisation established to promote the
responsible management of the world's forests. Products carrying the FSC
label are independently certified to assure consumers that they come
from forests that are managed to meet the social, economic and
ecological needs of present and future generations.
Find out more about HarperCollins and the environment at
www.harpercollins.co.uk/green

Acknowledgements

I would like to thank Pauline Sheridan for both her expert advice on Arab horses and the excellent recipe for warm horse mash; and also Carol Weatherill for a little light goat husbandry, especially the toast and treacle!

For my good friends and fellow 500 Club members, Leah Fleming and Elizabeth Gill, with love.

Prologue: The Ghost of Christmas Past

Even though it was barely December, the hospital ward had been decked out with a tiny tree and moulded plastic wall decorations depicting a fat Santa, with bunchy bright scarlet cheeks and dark, almond-shaped eyes. He was offering what looked like a stick of dynamite to Rudolf the very red-nosed reindeer, but I expect you need explosive power to deliver all those presents in one single night.

My defence strategy for the last few years has been to ignore Christmas, shutting the door on memories too painful to deal with; but now, sitting day after day by the bed in which Gran dwindled like snow in summer, there seemed to be no escape.

Gran, who brought me up, would not have approved of all these festive trappings. Not only was she born a Strange Baptist, but had also married a minister in that particularly austere (and now almost extinct) offshoot of the faith. They didn't do Christmas in the way everyone else did – with gifts, gluttony and excess, so as a child, I was always secretly envious of my schoolfriends.

But then I got married and went overboard on the whole idea. Alan egged me on – he never lost touch with his inner child, which is probably why he was such a brilliant primary school teacher. Anyway, he loved the whole thing, excess, gluttony and all.

So I baked and iced spiced gingerbread stars to hang on the

tree, which was always the biggest one we could drag home from the garden centre, together with gay red and white striped candy canes, tiny foil crackers and twinkling fairy lights. Together we constructed miles of paper chains to festoon the ceilings, hung mistletoe (though we never needed an excuse to kiss) and made each other stockings full of odd surprises.

After the first year we decided to forgo a full traditional turkey dinner with all the trimmings in favour of roast duck with home-made bottled Morello cherry sauce, which was to become my signature dish. (I was sous-chef in a local restaurant at the time.) We made our own traditions, blending the old with the new, as I suppose most families do . . .

And we were so *nearly* a family: about to move to a tiny hamlet just outside Merchester, a perfect country setting for the two children (or maybe three, if Alan got his way) that would arrive at neatly-spaced intervals . . .

At this juncture in my thoughts, a trolley rattled sharply somewhere behind the flowered curtains that enclosed the bed, jerking me back to the here and now: I could even hear a faint, tinny rendering of 'The Twelve Days of Christmas' seeming to seep like a seasonal miasma from the walls.

Perhaps Gran could too, for suddenly her clear, light grey eyes, so like my own, opened wide with an expression of delighted surprise that had nothing to do with either my presence or the home-made pot custard I'd brought to tempt her appetite, the nutmeg-sprinkled top browned just the way she liked it.

'*Ned? Ned Martland?*' she whispered, staring at someone only she could see.

I'd never seen her look so lit-up and alive as she did at that moment, which was ironic considering those were her last words – and the words themselves were a bit of a puzzle, since my grandfather's name had been Joseph Bowman!

So who the hell was Ned Martland? If it *had* been Martland, of course, and not Cartland, Hartland, or something similar. But no, I was pretty sure it was Martland – and he'd obviously meant a lot to her at some time. This was fairly amazing: had my grave and deeply reserved grandmother, who had been not so much buttoned up as zipped tightly shut and with a padlock thrust through the fastener for good measure, been keeping a romantic secret all these years? Had she lived her life without the man she truly loved by her side, just as I was living mine?

Perhaps there's a family curse, which would account for why, after Alan's death, she kept going on about the sins of the fathers being visited on the next generations – though actually, as I pointed out to her, that would have meant me rather than my husband. But if there *is* a family curse it looks set to end with me, because I'm the end of the line, the wrong side of thirty-five, and with my fruit in imminent danger of withering on the vine.

I've had too much time to think about that lately, too.

I've no idea what Alan's last words were, if any, because I was still asleep when he went for his early morning jog round the local park before work. When I woke up and went downstairs there was no sign of him and it was all worryingly Marie Celeste. The radio was spilling out some inane Christmas pop song to the empty kitchen and his bag, with its burden of marked exercise books, was on the floor by the door. A used mug and plate and a Tupperware box of sandwiches lay on the table and the kettle was barely warm.

As I stood there, puzzled and feeling the first stirring of unease, the police arrived to break the news that there had been an accident and Alan would never be coming home.

'Don't be silly,' I heard my voice telling them crisply, 'I'm doing duck with some of my bottled Morello cherry sauce for Christmas dinner – it's his favourite.'

Then, for the first and only time in my life, I fainted.

* * *

3

Alan had been trying to rescue a dog that had fallen through the ice on the boating lake. How stupid was that? I mean, if a *dog* fell through, then even a slightly built man like Alan would, too. The dog was evidently *not* a retriever, for it swam through the broken ice created by Alan's fall, scrambled out and ran off.

I was so furious with Alan that at the funeral I positively *hurled* the single red rose someone had handed me into the grave, screaming, '*What were you thinking of, dimwit?*'

And then I slipped on the snowy brink and nearly followed it in, though that was entirely due to the large shot of brandy my friend Laura, who was also Alan's sister, insisted we both drink before we set out. Luckily her husband, Dan, was on my other side and yanked me back at the last minute and then Gran walked around the grave from where she had been standing among a small cluster of elderly Strange Baptist friends and took a firm grip of my other arm, like a wardress.

But by then I was a spent force: grief, fury and guilt (the guilt because I had refused to take up jogging with him) seemed to blend so seamlessly that I didn't know where one ended and another began.

He'd left me on my own, closing the door on the future we had all planned out. How *could* he? I always thought we were yin and yang, two halves of the same person, soulmates destined to stay together forever throughout eternity – if so, I'd have a few choice things to say when I finally caught up with him.

My coping strategy had been to close the door on Alan in return, only allowing my grief full rein on the anniversary of his death in late December and shutting myself away from all reminders of the joyous seasonal festivities he had taught me to love during the all-too-brief years of our marriage.

There's even less reason to celebrate Christmas now . . .

Christmas? Bah, humbug!

Chapter 1: Pregnant Pause

Since Gran had been slipping quietly away from me for years, her death wasn't that much of a shock, to be honest. That was just as well, because I had to dash straight off to one of my house-sitting jobs right after her austere Strange Baptist funeral, though finding her journals in the small tin trunk in which she kept her treasures just before I left was a *very* poignant moment ...

When I'd locked up her little sliver of a terraced house in Merchester (not that there was anything in it worth stealing) I'd taken the trunk home with me: the key was on her keyring with the rest. I already had some idea of what was in it from glimpses caught over the years – postcards of Blackpool, where my grandparents spent their Wakes Week holiday every year, my annual school photographs, certificates and that kind of thing – layers going back in time.

I'd only opened it meaning to add her narrow gold wedding band, but then had lifted up a few of the layers to see what was underneath – and right at the bottom was a thin bundle of small, cheap, school exercise books marked 'Esther Rowan', bound together with withered elastic bands. Opening the first, I found a kind of spasmodic journal about her nursing experiences starting towards the end of the war, since the first entry was dated October 1944, though it began by looking back at earlier experiences:

*I'd started working as a nursing auxiliary at fifteen, which
meant that when war broke out at least I wasn't sent to do
hard, dirty work in the munitions factory, like many
Merchester girls.*

I thought how young they started work back then – and, reading
the following entry, how stoical she was:

*Tom, my childhood sweetheart, enlisted in the navy straight
away, though I begged him to wait until he was called up.
Sure enough, he was killed almost immediately, to the great
grief of myself and his poor, widowed father. After this, I
resolved to put all girlish thoughts of love and marriage
behind me and threw myself into my nursing duties . . .*

That last line struck me as being much like the way I'd moved
house and thrown myself into a new job right after Alan died:
only somehow in my case it didn't seem stoical, more a denial
of those wonderful years we had together.

I knew Gran had eventually gone on to marry the father of
her childhood sweetheart – she had said to me once that they
had felt they could be a comfort and support to one another
– so where this Ned Martland came in was anyone's guess! I was
starting to think I must have imagined the whole thing . . .

Gran seemed to have filled the ensuing pages with a moralising
mini-sermon on the evils of war, so I put the journals back in
the trunk again, to read on my return.

I spent a week in Devon, looking after a cottage for one of my
regular clients, along with two budgerigars called Marilyn and
Monroe, Yoda the Yorkshire terrier and six nameless hens.

It was very soothing and allowed me the space to get a lot of
things straight in my mind – and also to make one large and
potentially life-changing decision – before coming back home

braced and ready to sort out Gran's house, which belonged to a church charity. They were pressing me to clear it out and hand back the keys, so I expect they had a huge waiting list of homeless and desperate clergy widows.

I had a week before my next Homebodies assignment, which I was sure would be more than adequate. And I was quite right, because I'd almost finished and was starting to look forward to escaping to the remote Highland house-sit which would safely take me over Christmas and into New Year, when it was suddenly cancelled.

Ellen, the old schoolfriend (or so she calls herself – Laura and I remember things a little differently) who runs the Homebodies agency, tried to persuade me to cook for a Christmas house-party instead, but she did it with little hope.

'I don't know why she even bothered asking,' I said to Laura, who had popped in to help me sort out the last of Gran's belongings. Well, I say *help*, but since she was heavily pregnant with her fourth baby she was mostly making tea and talking a lot. She's blonde, pretty and petite (my exact opposite), and carried the baby in a small, neat bump under a long, clingy tunic top the same shade of blue as her eyes.

'She asked because you're a brilliant cook and it pays so much better than the house-sitting,' she replied, putting two fresh mugs of tea down on the coffee table. 'Plus, she has all the tact of a bulldozer.'

'But she knows I need a rest from the cooking in winter and I don't do Christmas. I like to get away somewhere remote where no-one knows me and pretend it isn't happening.'

Laura sank down next to me on Gran's hideously uncomfortable cottage sofa. 'She probably hoped you'd got over it a bit and changed your mind – you've been widowed as long as you were married, now. We all still miss Alan dreadfully, especially at this time of year,' she added gently. 'He was the best brother anyone could ever have. But he wouldn't want us to grieve forever, Holly.'

'I know, and you can't say I haven't picked up the pieces and got on with my life,' I said, though I didn't add that even after eight years the grief was still mixed fairly equally with anger. 'But Christmas and the anniversary of the accident always bring things back and I'd much rather spend it quietly on my own.'

'I expect Ellen's forgotten that you weren't brought up to celebrate Christmas in the same way as everyone else, too.'

Laura and I go way back to infant school, so she understands my slightly strange upbringing, but Ellen only came on the scene later, at the comprehensive (and though she denies it now, she tagged on to the group of girls who bullied me because of my height).

'No, the Strange Baptists think the trappings of the season are all pagan manifestations of man's fall from spiritual grace – though Gran could play a mean Christmas hymn on the harmonium.'

Laura looked at the space opposite, where the instrument had always stood against the magnolia blown-vinyl wallpaper. 'I don't know how you managed to fit that harmonium into your tiny cottage, I bet it weighed a ton even though it wasn't very big.'

'It did, but I was determined to have it because it was Gran's pride and joy – the only time she seemed happy was when she was playing it. It *just* fitted into the space under the stairs.'

I hadn't kept a lot, otherwise: the pink satin eiderdown that had covered my narrow bed as a child and two austere cross-stitch samplers sewn by my great-grandmother. One said, 'Strange are the ways of the Lord' and the other, 'That He may do His work, His strange work'. That was about it.

What was left was a motley collection of cheap utility furniture, battered enamel and aluminium saucepans and the like, which were being collected by a house clearance firm.

The house had been immaculate, apart from a little dust, and Gran had never been a hoarder, so there hadn't been that much

8

to sort out. Her clothes had already been packed and collected by a local charity and all that was left now to put in my car was a cardboard box of neatly filed household papers.

'I think I'm just about finished here,' I said, taking a biscuit from the packet Laura had brought, though Garibaldi are not actually my favourite – a bit too crushed-fly looking. 'So, are you going to call this baby Garibaldi, then?'

Now, this was not such a daft question as you might suppose, since during her last pregnancy Laura had been addicted to Mars bars and she had called her baby boy Mars. He should thank his lucky stars it hadn't been Twix or Flake.

She giggled. 'No way! But if it's a girl we might call it Holly after you, even though it will be a very early spring, rather than a Christmas, baby.'

I hated my name (my late mother's choice), but I was quite touched. 'I suppose it *would* be better than Garibaldi,' I conceded, 'especially for a girl.'

I took a sip of the pale, fragrant tea, which was the Earl Grey that Laura had brought with her, rather than the Yorkshire tea that Gran had always made strong enough to stand a spoon in. 'The van will be here any minute, so we've just got the box of papers to stick in my car and we're done. The meter reader came while you were in the kitchen, so I expect the electricity will be turned off any minute now, too.'

As if on cue, the dim bulb in its mottled glass shade went out and left us in the gathering shadows of a December afternoon.

'"*Lead kindly light, amid the encircling gloom,*"' I sang sepulchrally.

'You know a hymn for every occasion.'

'So would you, if you'd been brought up by a Strange Baptist.'

'Still, it's just as well you'd finished sorting out,' Laura said. 'She wasn't a great hoarder, your gran, was she?'

'No, apart from the few mementoes in that tin trunk I took home – and I've been reading a bit more in that sort of diary I told you I'd found. Some of it is fascinating, but you have to wade through lots of Victorian-sounding moralising in between.'

'You could skip those bits?' she suggested.

'I thought about it, then decided I wanted to read it all, because I never felt I really knew her and it might give me some insight into what made her tick.'

'She was certainly very reserved and austere,' Laura agreed, looking round the sparsely furnished room, '*and* frugal: but that was probably her upbringing.'

'Yes, if ever I wanted to buy her a present, she always said she had everything she needed. She could never resist Yardley's lavender soap, though, but that was about as tempted by the lures of the flesh as she ever got.'

'She was very proud of you, having your own house and career.'

'I suppose she was, though she would have preferred me to train to be a teacher, like you and Alan – she didn't consider cooking much above skivvying. And when I left the restaurant and signed up to Homebodies instead, she thought cooking for large house-parties in the summer and looking after people's properties and pets in the winter was just like going into service.'

'It's worked very well though, hasn't it? You get paid so much for the summer jobs that you can take the poorly paid home-sitting ones in the winter.'

'They're more for a change of scene and a rest, so staying rent free in someone else's house suits me fine: I get to see a different bit of the country and they get their house and pets taken care of, so they can enjoy their hols without any worries.'

'But now your next home-sitting job has fallen through, you could spend Christmas Day with us, couldn't you?' she suggested. 'We're going over to Mum and Dad's for dinner and Mum is always saying she hardly sees you any more.'

'Oh no, I *couldn't*!' I said with more haste than tact.

'It would be better than staying home alone – *and* I've just invited my cousin Sam to stay. His divorce has been finalised and he's at a loose end. You got on so well when you met in the summer and went on that date.'

'Laura, that wasn't a date, we just both wanted to see the same film. And he's at least a foot shorter than me.'

'That's a gross exaggeration – a couple of inches, at most! Anyway, he said he liked a woman who knew her own mind and the way you wore your hair made him think of Nefertiti.'

'Did he?' I said doubtfully. My hair is black, thick and straight and I keep it in a sort of long, smooth bob that curves forwards at the sides like wings. 'I expect he was just being kind. Not many men want to go out with someone taller than themselves.'

'They might if you ever gave them the chance, Holly!'

'There's no point: I met my Mr Right and I don't believe in second-best.' Alan had found me beautiful, too, though I had found it hard to believe him at first after all that school bullying about my height and my very untrendy clothes . . .

'It doesn't have to be second-best – I know you and Alan loved each other, but no-one would blame you, least of all me, if you fell in love with someone else now. Alan would be the last man to want you to mourn him forever.'

'I'm not still mourning, I've moved on. It's just . . .' I paused, trying to sum up how I felt. 'It's just that what we had was so perfect that I know I'm not going to find that again.'

'But *was* it so perfect? Is any marriage ever that?' she asked. 'And have you ever thought that you weren't actually married for long enough for the gilt to wear off the gingerbread?'

I looked at her, startled. 'What do you mean?'

'Well, you *were* very happy, but even the best relationships change over time: their little ways start to irritate you and you have to learn a bit of give and take. Alan wasn't perfect and neither are you: none of us are. Look at me and Dan, for instance. *He* can't understand why I need forty-six pairs of shoes and *I*

11

hate coming second in his life to rugby – but we still love each other.'

'Apart from our work, the only thing Alan and I didn't do together was the running – we shared everything else.'

'But one or both of you might have felt that was a bit claustrophobic eventually. Alan was a dreamer too – and he dreamed of writing. You couldn't do that together.'

'Well, I didn't stop him,' I said defensively. 'In fact, I encouraged him, though the teaching took up a lot of his time and energy. And I was going to write a house-party cookbook, so we *did* share that interest too, in a way.'

'Oh yes – I'd forgotten about the cookbook. You haven't mentioned it for ages.'

'It's nearly finished, just one more section to go.'

That was the one dealing with catering for a Christmas house-party, which I had been putting off.

'I do realise the dynamics of the relationship would have changed when we had children, Laura, but we had it all planned. I wish now we hadn't waited so long, though.'

'There you are, then,' she said triumphantly, 'if you find someone else, it's not too late to start a family – look at me!'

'Funnily enough I was thinking about that in Devon, and I decided that although I don't want another man, I *do* want a baby before it's too late. So I thought I'd try artificial insemination. What do you think?'

She stared at me from startled, long-lashed blue eyes. 'Really? Well, I suppose you *could*,' she conceded reluctantly after a minute. 'But wouldn't you prefer to try the natural way first?'

'No,' I said simply. 'I want the baby to be just mine.'

'How would you manage financially? Have you thought it through?'

'I own the cottage,' I pointed out, because I'd paid off the mortgage on our terraced house with the insurance money after Alan died, then moved out to an even smaller cottage in the

12

countryside between Ormskirk and Merchester. 'And I thought I could finish off the cookery book and maybe start doing party catering from home.'

'I'm not sure you've seen all the pitfalls of going it alone with a small child, but I know what you're like when you've made your mind up,' she said resignedly. Then she brightened and added, 'But I could help you and it would be lovely to be able to see more of you.'

'Yes, that would be great and I'll be counting on you for advice if I get pregnant.'

'I must say, you've really surprised me, though.'

'I surprised myself, but something Gran said right at the end made me realise I ought to go out there and get what I want, before it's too late.'

'You mean when she said some man's name you'd never heard of?'

I nodded. 'It was the way she said it – and she could see him, too. I'd never seen her smile like that, so she must have loved and lost him, whoever he was – and perhaps her journal will tell me that eventually. Her face went all soft, and I could see how beautiful she must have been when she was young.'

'Just like you, with the same black hair and light grey eyes.'

'Laura, you can't say *I'm* beautiful! I mean, apart from being the size of a maypole, I've got a big, beaky nose.'

'You're striking, and your nose isn't beaky, it's only got the tiniest hint of a curve in it,' she said loyally. 'Sam's right, you do look like that bust of Nefertiti you see in photographs ... though your hair is a bit more Cleopatra.'

I was flattered but unconvinced. Gran's skin had been peaches and cream and mine was heading towards a warm olive so that I look Mediterranean apart from my light eyes. Gran's mother's family came from Liverpool originally, so I daresay I have some foreign sailor in my ancestry to thank for my colouring – and maybe my height, which has been the bane of my existence.

'I quite liked Sam, because at least he didn't talk to my boobs, like a lot of men do,' I conceded and then immediately regretted it, because she said eagerly, 'So you *will* come to us, if only for Christmas dinner? I promise not to push you together, but it would give you a chance to get to know him a bit and—'

My phone emitted a strangled snatch of Mozart and I grabbed it. Saved by the muzak.

Chapter 2: Little Mumming

At my last hospital I was frequently left in sole command of a children's ward in a separate building, night after night. When the air raid sirens went I took all the children down to a dark and damp cellar, where I had to beat hundreds of cockroaches off the cots and beds before they could be used. Finally, earlier this year, weakened by too many night shifts, lack of sleep (for I found it impossible to sleep during the day), too much responsibility and poor food, my health broke down and I was sent home to recover.

October 1944

I hoped the call wasn't the man from Chris's Clearance saying he'd decided against collecting Gran's fairly worthless sticks of furniture and bric-a-brac, but no, it was Ellen from the Homebodies agency.

'Holly, you know I said there was nothing else on the books over Christmas?' she said in her slightly harsh voice, without any preamble. Ellen doesn't do polite, except to the customers. 'Well, now something's come up and I'm going to ask you to do it for me as a *big, big* favour!'

'A favour?' My spirits lifted. 'You mean a *house-sitting* big favour?'

Laura caught my eye and grimaced, shaking her head and mouthing, 'Don't you dare!'

'Yes, a major crisis has just blown up,' Ellen explained. 'You remember Mo and Jim Chirk?'

'You've mentioned them several times, but I haven't met them. They're one of your longest-serving and most dependable house-sitting couples, aren't they?'

'They *were*,' she said darkly. 'And they were supposed to be house-sitting up on the East Lancashire moors over Christmas – they'd been two or three times and the owner asked for them again – but no sooner had they got there than their daughter had her baby prematurely and they're flying out to Dubai to be with her.'

'You mean, they've already *gone*?'

'They're on their way home to repack and get their passports, then they're booked onto the first flight out. They phoned me just before they left – and so they should, too, because they've dropped me right in it!'

'It doesn't sound as if they could help it, Ellen – it's just one of those things. I hope the baby is all right.'

'Which baby?'

'Their daughter's baby.'

'I have no idea,' she said dismissively, which wasn't any surprise, since where business is concerned she's totally single-minded.

'Look, could you help me out by taking the job on? It should be two people really, because it's a large manor house in its own grounds, and a bit remote and there are a couple of pets to look after, too. Only there's no-one else free on the books apart from you. Could you possibly go? Tomorrow? I'll make sure you get double pay,' she wheedled.

'If there are pets, who's looking after them at the moment?'

'The owner's elderly aunt and uncle live in the lodge and say they will keep an eye on things until you get there, but I don't think they can really be up to it, or presumably Mr Martland wouldn't have needed Homebodies in the first place.'

'*Martland?*' I interrupted.

'Yes, Jude Martland. Have you heard of him? He's quite a well-known sculptor – he did the Iron Horse next to the motorway near Manchester, all welded strips of metal – very modern.'

'Oh yes, I think I have. But actually, I heard that surname recently in another context and it's unusual, that's why I was surprised.'

'Just a coincidence, then – truth is stranger than fiction,' she said, disinterestedly rustling some papers.

'That's true,' I agreed, and of course these Martlands could have no relationship to the Ned Martland Gran had mentioned (assuming I'd even heard the name right): she was a working-class girl and wouldn't have mixed in the same circles as minor gentry from moorland manor houses.

'Anyway, he inherited the pile, which is called Old Place, about a year ago and he's abroad somewhere, but so far we haven't managed to get hold of him to tell him what's happening. He isn't coming back until Twelfth Night.'

I'd turned away from Laura's disappointed face, though I could feel her eyes boring accusingly into my back. I was starting to suspect she'd hastily invited her cousin Sam for Christmas as soon as I'd told her my Christmas job had fallen through – the idea had probably never crossed her mind until then.

'It doesn't sound too arduous,' I said to Ellen. 'I've looked after quite big houses before single-handedly. What are the pets you mentioned?'

'One dog and . . . a horse.'

'*A horse*? You call a horse a *pet*? Ellen, I don't do horses!'

'It's very elderly and you do know a bit about horses, because you went to that riding school with Laura, remember.'

'I only watched her, that hardly qualifies me to look after someone's horse, does it?'

'I expect you picked up more information than you think you

17

did. Mo said she was very easy to look after and all the instructions were written down.'

'Yes, but—'

'I expect the elderly couple in the lodge can advise you if there's any difficulty. And there's a cleaner and a small village nearby with a shop, so it isn't *totally* isolated. What do you say?'

'Well . . . I suppose I could. But I'm a bit worried about the horse. I—'

'Oh, that's *wonderful*!' she broke in quickly. 'I'm sure the horse won't be a problem, it's probably in a field and you only have to look at it once a day, or something. And the good news is, Mo and Jim felt so awful at landing the job on someone else at such short notice that they left all their supplies for Christmas behind for whoever took it on. Though actually, I suppose they could hardly take a turkey and all the trimmings out to Dubai with them!'

'No, but it was a kind thought. Where exactly *is* this place, did you say?'

'I didn't, but I'll email you directions and all the details now. It's a bit off the beaten track, but you usually *like* that.'

'Yes, especially over Christmas. That aspect of it is perfect.'

'I don't know what you'll do up there, because apparently the TV reception is lousy and there's no broadband.'

'I'll be fine – I'll take my radio and lots of books.'

Clicking off the connection, I turned to find Laura looking at me reproachfully. 'Oh, Holly, it would have been such fun to have you here for Christmas!'

'Believe me, it wouldn't: it would have been like having the Grinch. And I'll enjoy myself in my own way. There are only two animals to look after, so I'll have lots of time to experiment with recipes and write that last section of the book. If I'm going to go ahead with the baby idea, I need to get it finished and find a publisher!'

Laura sighed and cast her eyes up in mock resignation, but she knew me too well to try and persuade me out of it.

'Now, what can you remember about horse management?' I asked hopefully.

I printed out Ellen's instructions as soon as I got home and she was right – it was in a remote, upland spot, near a small village I'd never even heard of.

Getting ready that night was all a bit of a scramble, though I couldn't resist continuing my nightly reading of a page or two of Gran's journal, which was getting more interesting again now she wasn't talking about the past, but engrossed by the present. By November of 1944, she was evidently well enough to go back to work:

> *Now I have recovered I have been sent to Ormskirk hospital, which pleases me because it is nearer home and also Tom's widowed father, a sweet, kindly man, is the minister at the Strange Baptist chapel here. But my lodgings are very poor, in a nearby house run by a dour, disagreeable woman. The food is scanty and bad and we sleep dormitory-style, so there is little privacy. The treat of a fresh egg, which was a parting gift from my mother, I gave to my landlady to boil for my breakfast – but it never appeared and my enquiries about it met only with surly grunts.*

I read on a little further as she made new friends and settled in, but really I was way too tired to keep my eyes open and there would be lots of time to read the journals over Christmas – in fact, I would take the whole trunk of papers with me to sort out.

Early next morning I loaded the tin trunk into my car along with everything else I usually take with me on assignments – boxes of herbs, spices and other basic ingredients, general food supplies, a cool box of perishable stuff, vital utensils, cookery books, laptop, house-party recipe book notes and my portable radio . . . It was pretty full even before I added a suitcase, holdall and my wellies.

Laura, resigned now to my decision, had driven over to give me my Christmas present (she's the only person who ever gives me one). In return I gave her a bag of little gifts for the family, some of them home-made and edible.

She also gave me strict instructions to call her daily, too. 'Tell me all about it. Old Place sounds terribly posh, somehow, and I've never even heard of the village – what did you call it again?'

'Little Mumming. It's near Great Mumming, apparently. I'd never heard of it either, but I've found it on the map.'

'It's all been such a rush – are you sure you've got everything you need?'

'Yes, I think so – most of it was still packed up ready to go. And I've put in my wellies, jeans, dog-walking anorak . . .'

'A smart dress, in case the local squire's lady leaves calling cards and you have to return the visit?'

'You need to stop reading Jane Austen,' I said severely. 'And I think this Mr Martland might *be* the Little Mumming equivalent of the local squire, in which case, if there is a lady, he will have taken her away with him, won't he?'

'Unless she's upstairs in Bluebeard's chamber?'

'Thank you for sharing that unnerving thought.'

'You're welcome. But the house can't be that big, can it? Otherwise there would be some live-in help.'

'Not necessarily, these days,' I said, drawing on my long experience of house-party cooking, where sometimes the only live-in staff had been myself and the family nanny. 'Ellen mentioned a daily cleaner. It's big enough to have a lodge though, because the owner's elderly uncle and his wife live there and I'm to call in for the keys on my way up to the house.'

'I can see you're dying to go, but I still don't like to think of you marooned in a remote house all on your own over Christmas,' Laura said. 'Have you got your phone and charger, and enough food and drink in case you're miles from the nearest shop? I mean, the weather report said we were in for a cold snap next week and the odds on a white Christmas are shortening.'

'Oh, come on, Laura, when do they ever get the long-term forecasts right? And come to that, how often does it snow here, especially at Christmas?'

'But it's probably different in East Lancashire, up on the moors.'

'It might be a bit bleaker, but I'll believe in this snow when I see it. And Ellen said Jim and Mo have left me all their food, since they won't need it – they were only stopping at home long enough to fling some clothes in a suitcase and get their passports before they flew out to Dubai. I'm hardly likely to eat my way through a whole turkey and all the trimmings over Christmas, even if I do get snowed in.'

I gave her a hug – but cautiously, because of the very prominent bump. 'I'll be fine, you know me. Give my love to your parents and have a great time and I'll see you on Twelfth Night!'

I climbed into the heavily-laden car and drove off, Laura's small figure waving at me in the rear-view mirror until I turned the corner, realising just how fond of my best friend I was.

Now Gran had gone, was there anyone else in the whole world who *really* cared about me? Or who *I* really cared about? I couldn't think of anyone . . . and it suddenly seemed so terribly sad. I'd had other friends, but mostly they'd been Alan's too, and I'd pushed them out of my life after the accident.

But soon, if my plans for a baby came to fruition, I would have someone else to love, who would love me in return . . .

My spirits lifted as I drove further away from home, just as they always did, for the joy of each assignment was that no-one knew me or my past, or was interested enough to find out: I was just brisk, capable Holly Brown from Homebodies, there to do a job: the Mary Poppins of Merchester.

21

Chapter 3: Weasel Pot

I have made friends with Hilda and Pearl, who have the beds either side of me at the lodging house, and they are showing me the ropes at the new hospital. Like many of the other nurses their chief desire seems to be to marry, preferably to one of the young doctors, and they teased me until I explained that I had lost my sweetheart in the first months of war, so that I now saw nursing as my life's work.

November, 1944

Little Mumming lay in a small valley below one of the beacon hills that run down East Lancashire, where a long chain of fires was once lit as a sort of ancient early warning system.

On the map it hadn't looked far from the motorway, but the poor excuse for a B road endlessly wound up and down, offering me the occasional distant, tantalising glimpse of Snowehill, topped with a squat tower, but never seeming to get any closer.

Finally I arrived at a T-junction that pointed me to Little Mumming and Great Mumming up a precipitous, single-track lane – though rather confusingly, it also pointed to Great Mumming straight ahead, too. All roads must lead to Great Mumming.

I took the sharp left uphill turn, sincerely hoping that I wouldn't meet anything coming in the opposite direction, because although there were occasional passing places, there were also high dry-stone walls on either side, so I wouldn't be able to see them coming round the series of hairpin bends.

I passed a boulder painted with the words 'Weasel Pot Farm' next to a rutted track and shifted down a gear. Was there *ever* going to be any sign of a village?

Then I crossed an old stone humpbacked bridge, turned a last bend past a pair of wrought-iron gates and came to a stop – for ahead of me the road levelled and opened out, revealing Little Mumming in all its wintry glory.

It was a huddled hamlet of grey stone cottages, a pub, and a small church set around an open green on which sheep were wrenching at the grass as if their lives depended on it. Perhaps they did. Winters were presumably a lot bleaker up here.

High above on the hillside a Celtic-looking figure of a horse had been carved out from the dull red earth or sandstone, using just a few flowing lines. It could be an ancient hill marking, or maybe some more recent addition to the landscape.

After a minute I carried on and pulled in by the green, turning off the engine. I needed a moment to unclench my hands from the steering wheel after that ascent.

The village looked as if it had grown organically from the earth, the walls and roofs all lichen-spotted and mossy. There was a raw wind blowing and it was midmorning, so I suppose it wasn't surprising that it was deserted, though I did have the sensation that I was being watched from behind the Nottingham lace curtains . . .

But the only movement was the sign swinging in the wind outside the pub, the Auld Christmas, which depicted a bearded old man in a blue robe, holding a small fir tree and wearing a wreath of greenery round his head. Very odd. The pub advertised morning coffee and ploughman's lunches, which would have been tempting had the journey not taken so much longer than I expected.

The shop Ellen had mentioned was nearby, fronted by sacks

of potatoes and boxes of vegetables, with the Merry Kettle Tearoom next to it, though that looked as if it had closed for the winter. It was probably just seasonal, for walkers.

I consulted my map, started the engine, then continued on past a terraced trio of tiny Gothic cottages and over a second, smaller bridge to yet *another* signpost pointing to Great Mumming up an improbably steep and narrow strip of tarmac.

No wonder all the vehicles parked outside the pub were four-wheel-drive!

After half a mile I turned off through a pair of large stone pillars and came to rest on a stretch of gravel next to a lodge house that had been extended at the back into a sizeable bungalow.

It was very quiet apart from the rushing of water somewhere nearby and the rooks cawing in a stand of tall pine trees that must hide the house itself, for I couldn't see even a chimney stack.

As I got out a little stiffly (I hadn't realised quite how tense that drive up had made me), the lodge door opened a few inches and a tall, stooping, elderly man beckoned me in.

'There you are! Come in quickly, before all the warm air gets out,' he commanded urgently, as if I was a wayward family pet.

I sidled carefully past a large and spiky holly wreath into a long hallway. Once the door was safely shut behind me he turned and came towards me with an odd, slightly crablike gait, holding out his hand.

'Noël Martland. And you must be Holly Brown – lovely name, by the way, very suitable.'

'Oh? For what?'

'Christmas,' he replied, looking vaguely surprised that I needed to be told. He wore a drooping, ex-Air Force style moustache, partially covering the extensive, puckered shiny scars of an old burn.

He caught my eye: 'Plane shot down in the war. Got a bit singed, landed badly.'

24

'Right,' I said, admiring the economy of description of a scene that would have occupied half a film and had you biting your knuckles on the edge of your cinema seat.

'Best to say straight off: people always wonder, but they don't like to ask.'

He took my coat and hung it carefully on a mahogany stand, then ushered me into a small, square, chintzy sitting room that would have been very pleasant had it not been rendered into a hideous Christmas grotto. Festoons of paper chains and Chinese lanterns hung from the ceiling, swags of fake greenery lined the mantelpiece and the tops of all the pictures, and there were snowglobes and porcelain-faced Santas on every flat surface.

In the bow window, fairy lights twinkled among so many baubles on the small fake fir tree that the balding branches drooped wearily under the strain.

Observing my stunned expression with some satisfaction he said, 'Jolly good, isn't it? We like to do things properly in Little Mumming.' Then he suddenly bellowed, 'Tilda! She's here!'

'Coming!' answered a high, brittle voice and with a loud rattling noise a tiny woman pushed a large hostess trolley through a swinging door from what was presumably the kitchen.

'My wife, Tilda,' Noël Martland said. 'This is Holly Brown, m'dear.'

'So I should suppose, unless you've taken to entertaining strange young women,' she said tartly, eyeing me from faded but still sharp blue eyes. Though age had withered her, it had not prevented her from applying a bold coating of turquoise eye shadow to her lids and a generous slick of foundation, powder and glossy scarlet lipstick. Under the white frilly apron she was wearing a peach satin blouse with huge dolman sleeves that finished in tight cuffs at the wrists, and a matching Crimplene pinafore dress. Her matchstick-thin legs in filmy loose stockings ended in pointed shoes with *very* high stiletto heels. I felt glad she had the trolley to hang onto.

25

'The agency said you were coming on your own, though really a couple would have been better. But I suppose we're lucky to get *anyone* at such short notice, over Christmas,' she said, eyeing me critically.

'I am sure you will cope splendidly!' declared her husband.

'That remains to be seen, Noël,' she snapped back. 'Miss or Mrs?' she suddenly demanded, with a glance at my naked left hand.

'Mrs,' I said, 'I'm a widow. I do a lot of cooking, so I've never been much of a one for rings.'

'A widow? Tough luck,' she said, taking the covers off a couple of dishes to reveal plates of pinwheel sandwiches and butterfly sponge cakes.

'You shouldn't have gone to so much trouble,' I protested. 'I really wasn't expecting to be fed, just to pick up the keys!'

'I didn't – we always have an early lunch anyway, so I made extra. My housekeeper has gone home for Christmas as usual, but I do most of the cooking in any case – it's nothing to me. I was a TV chef, you know, in the early days. If I'd known the exact time of your arrival, I could have whipped up a soufflé.'

'This looks lovely,' I said, taking a sandwich. 'Were you a TV cook like Fanny Craddock, then?'

Her face darkened alarmingly and it didn't need Noël's appalled expression and shake of the head to inform me that I had made a faux pas.

'Don't mention That Woman to me,' she snapped. 'She was nothing but a brass-faced amateur!'

'Sorry,' I said quickly.

'I was Tilda Thompson in those days – and much more photo-genic than *she* ever was, all slap and false eyelashes.'

This seemed to me to be a case of the pot calling the kettle black, but I made a vague noise of agreement.

'Coffee?' Noël chipped in brightly, pouring me a cup with a slightly trembling hand.

26

'Thank you.' Having tasted the sandwich I was eager to accept anything that might wash the flavour away . . . whatever it was.

'Did you call Jessica?' Tilda Martland asked her husband.

'On my way to the door, m'dear. But perhaps I had better call again.'

Upstairs a door slammed and footsteps thundered down the stairs like a herd of inebriated rhinos.

'No need,' she said dryly.

Jess was a tall, skinny, dark-haired girl of about twelve or thirteen (not quite as tall as I had been at that age, but even skinnier), dressed entirely in black, from glasses frame to shoes. Anyone less like a Jessica I never saw. She certainly stood out against the chintzy, ornament-laden and over-bedecked sitting room.

'This is our granddaughter, Jessica,' Noël Martland said.

'Jess, Grandpa,' she corrected, in a long-suffering way.

He smiled at her affectionately. 'Jess, this is Mrs Brown who is going to look after Old Place until your Uncle Jude gets back.'

'Please do all call me Holly,' I suggested.

'Then you must call us Tilda and Noël.'

Jess eyed me curiously, in that slightly-shifty adolescent way that generally denotes nothing much except acute self-consciousness. 'I'm only here on my own because my parents are in Antarctica. But now my great-uncle's dead and Jude's gone off somewhere, we can't stay at Old Place over Christmas and New Year like we usually do. It's a drag.'

'Jess's parents are studying pelicans,' Tilda said, unveiling another plate of tiny sandwiches, this time cut into teddy bear shapes.

'Penguins,' corrected Jess. 'Emperor penguins. And how old do you think I am, Granny?'

'Going by your manners, six.'

'Ha, ha,' said Jess, but she took a teddy bear sandwich and,

27

after lifting up the top to examine the innocuous-looking ham filling, ate it.

'It's such a pity that Mo and Jim had to go off suddenly like that, isn't it?' Noël said. 'But it couldn't be helped. I only hope you don't find it too lonely up there – there is a cleaner twice a week, but the couple who used to look after my brother, the Jacksons, retired and my nephew looks after himself when he's home.'

'That cleaning girl is a slut: I don't think she ever does more than whisk a duster about for half an hour and then drink tea and read magazines,' Tilda said. 'But I expect you will soon have everything shipshape again, Holly.'

'I'll certainly make sure the areas of the house I *use* are kept neat and tidy,' I said pointedly, because it was a common misconception that home-sitters would also spring-clean and do all kinds of other little jobs around the house and garden and I often found it as well to make the real position clear from the outset. 'I'm here simply to make sure the house is safe and to look after the animals. I believe there are a dog and a horse?'

'Lady – she was my great-aunt's horse, so she's ancient,' Jess said. 'Me and Grandpa went up in the golf buggy yesterday afternoon and again this morning and I filled her water bucket and haynet, but I couldn't get too close because I'm allergic to horses. I sneeze.'

'That's a pity,' I said sincerely, because I could have done with a knowledgeable, horse-mad child.

'Yes, but I'm all right with dogs as long as I don't brush them, so I took Merlin out for a run.'

'That's something,' I agreed, assuming Merlin to be the dog I'd been told about.

'We left Lady in for the day, with the top of the stable door open, in case you were late arriving – it goes dark so early at this time of year,' Noël said, 'and you wouldn't want to be bringing her in from the paddock in the dark, before you've got your bearings.'

'No indeed,' I said gratefully.

'Jude sets great store by her, because she was his mother's horse,' Noël said, eating one of the strange pinwheel sandwiches with apparent relish. I had tried to swallow the rest of mine without chewing.

'He was happy enough to leave her in the Chirks' care again, but I'm not sure what he will think about someone he has never met taking over,' Tilda said.

'Ellen, who runs Homebodies, has been trying to contact Mr Martland to inform him of what has been happening. Will you please explain, if he calls you?'

'Yes, of course,' said Noël, 'and he is bound to, in the next day or two. He may then call you up, too.'

'I admit, I'll feel happier when he knows there has been a change of house-sitter.'

'Well, it's his own fault for staying away so long,' Tilda said. 'We didn't think he meant it when he suddenly said he didn't intend coming back from his trip to America until after Christmas, did we, Noël?'

'No, m'dear, because normally, as Jess said, we move into Old Place for Christmas and New Year. My sister Becca also stays from Christmas Eve until Boxing Day, too – you probably passed her house on the way here, New Place? Big wrought-iron gates, just the other end of the village.'

'Of course she passed the damned house,' snapped Tilda, 'did you think she was parachuted in?'

'Turn of speech,' he said apologetically, but twinkled at me.

I suddenly wondered if Alan and I would have ended up like this, with me bossing him about and him good-naturedly suffering it? There was no denying that I *was* bossy and organising. But then, *he* had had a stubborn streak, too . . .

'Still, it would have been a bit difficult this year, what with my poor brother passing away last January and then Jude falling out with Guy,' Noël sighed.

'It wasn't Guy's fault, really,' Tilda said dispassionately, 'that girl just got her hooks into him.'

I didn't ask who Guy was because, to be honest, I wasn't terribly interested in people I was never going to meet. I finished my coffee and put down my cup and plate. 'Well, that was unexpected but delicious: thank you so much! And now I'd better get up to the house and settle in.'

'Sharon, the cleaner, should still be there, so get her to show you round before she goes. It might be the most useful thing she's done all year,' Tilda suggested.

'I expect she does her best: it is a large house for one person to clean,' Noël said mildly. 'Not that Jude can make much of a mess, because when he is home he seems to spend most of his time down at the mill, working on his sculptures, or in his little study next to the library.'

'Oh yes, I heard he was a sculptor.'

'He's *very* famous,' Jess said, '*and* very bad tempered. He only cancelled Christmas because he saw that engagement announcement and I think he's *mean*. I bet he didn't even remember that Mum and Dad wouldn't be able to be here this year and I'd be coming on my own.'

'Jess, that will *do*!' commanded Tilda, and she lapsed into sulky silence.

I got up. 'Well, I think I'd better go up to the house while it's still light and settle in.'

Noël also got up and found me a vast bunch of keys, pointing out the largest. 'That's the front door. I expect you will work the rest out for yourself.'

'I could come and show you,' Jess offered quickly.

'Now, Jess, you know you've promised Old Nan you will visit her this afternoon: you'd better go and get ready, you can't disappoint her,' Tilda said. 'She'll have made you a special tea.'

'*More* nursery food!' Jess said disgustedly.

'And change into something that isn't black.'

Jess groaned and stomped off upstairs.

'She's so disappointed not to have Christmas at Old Place,' confided Noël in a whisper, as though he thought we could be overheard from above, 'and whatever she says, she adores Jude. It will be very quiet here for her, I'm afraid. Mo and Jim kindly invited us to share their Christmas dinner and that would have been *something*.' He sighed again. 'I am an expert on Christmas, you know – I've written a book on its history and traditions, so I do like to celebrate *properly*.'

'And so we will! I have a plump little chicken that will do very well for the three of us,' Tilda said stoically.

I suddenly wondered if they were expecting me to offer to cook Christmas dinner instead of the Chirks, even though I hadn't even arrived at Old Place yet, so I said quickly, '*I* don't celebrate Christmas.'

'Not celebrate Christmas?' Noël looked as stunned as if I had admitted to some abhorrent crime.

'No, I was brought up as a Strange Baptist.'

'Oh – right,' he said uncertainly. 'I think I've heard of those . . . And the lady who runs the Homebodies agency – Ellen, is it? – mentioned that you have not long since lost your grandmother, so I don't expect you feel particularly festive this year?'

'No, not at all . . . or any year, in fact.'

'My dear, I am *so* sorry,' Tilda said and added, graciously, 'We quite understand – and if you feel at all in need of company at any time, you are always welcome to call on us.'

'But surely – with a name like Holly – you must have a *birthday* to celebrate during Christmas?' Noël asked suddenly.

'It's Christmas Day, actually, but I don't celebrate that, either.'

'So is mine and I feel *just* the same,' he said understandingly. 'It would simply be too presumptuous to share the Lord's birthday, wouldn't it?'

31

Chapter 4: Rose of Sharon

I was brought up to consider the tawdry trappings of Christmas and the practice of avarice and extreme gluttony to be far removed from the way we should celebrate Christ's birth. And yet, the gaiety of my fellow nurses was heart-warming as they decorated the hospital wards and endeavoured to bring some seasonal cheer to the patients.

December, 1944

Safely back in the car I tried to decide what had been in the pinwheel sandwiches. Whatever it was had tasted like decayed fish paste, but *looked* like black olive pâté. It was a complete mystery to me and I might have to ask Tilda for the recipe, out of sheer curiosity.

The drive went up one side of a steeply-banked stream through the pine wood and then turned away, opening up onto a vista of sheep-nibbled grass across which, beyond a ha-ha, I could see a long, low, Jacobean building. It was rather larger than I had expected, though I suppose the size of the lodge should have given me some idea. The low-slung wintry sun sparkled off the mullioned windows, but there was no sign of life: not even a wisp of smoke from one of the line of four tall chimneys.

I drove over a cattle grid and pulled up on the gravel next to a battered red Ford Fiesta, noting as I did so that the flowerbeds that flanked the substantial front door inside an open porch looked neglected and the doorknocker, in the shape of a Green Man with frondy foliage forming his hair and beard, had not been cleaned for months.

I longed to have a go at it with Brasso. It's not that I love cleaning, because I don't, just that I like things neat, clean and orderly. I really have to fight the urge sometimes in other people's houses; you'd be surprised what a mess they can leave them in.

As I got out of the car, a youngish woman came out, a half-smoked cigarette in one hand. Her magenta hair was scraped back into a ponytail, apart from one long, limp strand that hung over her face like wet seaweed, and she was wearing a salmon-pink velour tracksuit that left a goose-pimpled muffin top of flesh exposed.

'Hello,' I said, holding out my hand. 'You must be the cleaner, Sharon? I'm glad you're still here, I'm late and I thought you might have gone by now.'

'I was just about to when I heard your car,' she said, taking my hand as if she wasn't quite sure what to do with it and then letting it go immediately. 'Call me Shar – and I'm not really a cleaner, I've just been helping Jude out for a bit of extra cash since my Kevin's been laid off. Not that he pays me the going rate, he's too mean.'

'Isn't that illegal?'

'Cash in hand, innit? He's got me over a barrel. You'd better watch out you get your money.'

'Oh, that's okay, the agency pays me.'

'You won't see me no more after today, because I'm starting behind the bar in the pub in Great Mumming after Christmas, a regular job. So Jude Martland can stick his miserly money and his smart-arse comments where the sun don't shine.'

'Right,' I said noncommittally, reeling slightly under this information overload. 'So ... Mr Martland knows you're leaving?'

'I told him I wasn't doing Christmas and no-one works over New Year,' she said sulkily, 'especially if they don't get a bonus.

33

Then he said since he could never tell whether I'd been in to clean or not, I didn't even deserve what he paid me, let alone any extra. He's such a sarky bugger!'

'I see.'

'So if I've took another job, it's his own fault, innit? I'm not bothered.'

'I expect it is.'

'If he rings, you can tell him I've had a better offer.'

'If he should ring, I'll certainly tell him you've resigned from your job,' I agreed. 'Now, before you go, do you have time to quickly show me over the house and where everything is?'

'I don't *know* where everything is, do I? I only vacuum and dust, and that's too much for one person. An old couple used to do the cooking and see to the house and generator, but they retired after the old gent, Jude's dad, died. January, that was.'

'So I've heard . . . and did you say there was a *generator*? I thought the house had mains services.'

'It does, but the electric's always cutting out *and* the phone line is forever coming down between here and the village because the poles need replacing. The TV doesn't work very well either, because there's no Sky dish, though they've got one at the lodge. It's a complete hole, I don't know what you're going to do with yourself.'

'That's all right, I'm not bothered about TV. I've brought my radio with me and lots to read.'

Sharon looked at me as if I was a strange and alien species with three heads. 'There's no mobile phone reception either, unless you walk halfway up Snowehill, or down past the lodge,' she informed me as a clincher.

'Well then, if the phone line goes dead, the exercise will do me good,' I said pleasantly. I have worked in remote places before – the house I should have been minding in Scotland was much more isolated than this – though I had not, admittedly, previously had to cope with a generator. I only hoped the electricity

34

didn't cut out before I found the instructions on how to operate the thing!

I smiled encouragingly at her. 'Now, I'd *really* appreciate it if you could quickly show me round? Normally we try and visit a property beforehand to meet the owners and get the lay of the land, as it were, but obviously in this case it wasn't possible.'

Sharon sullenly and reluctantly agreed and stood back to let me past her into a long stone entrance chamber. It had a row of heavily-burdened coat hooks, a brass stand full of walking sticks and umbrellas, and a battered wooden bench, under which was a miscellaneous collection of wellingtons and walking boots.

'Go through the door at the end,' she directed and I found myself standing in a huge, high-ceilinged sitting room the size of a small barn with an open fireplace practically big enough to roast an ox in. A worn carpet in mellow, warm colours covered most of the stone floor and an assortment of occasional tables, velvet-covered sofas and chairs was grouped on it. A dogleg staircase rose from one corner to a balustraded gallery above, that ran around three sides.

'What a lovely room! It looks as if it started out as a great hall in a much older building?'

'They say this is the really old bit in the middle, the rest was added on later,' she said indifferently. 'There's two wings – the kitchen one is set back, you go through a door behind that wooden screen over there. This other side is bigger, with the family rooms and another staircase. Come on, I'll show you.'

She ushered me briskly through a series of dark-oak-panelled rooms with polished wooden floors. Some had elaborate white-stuccoed ceilings, but they all looked dusty, dull and neglected. There was a small morning room with a TV, a long dining room sporting a spectacular, if incongruous, Venetian mirror over the hearth, and a well-stocked library with a snooker table in the middle of it.

She paused at the door next to it. 'Jude uses this room to work in and he locks it when he's away.' She sniffed. 'You'd think he didn't trust me.'

He probably didn't, though actually I'd found that there were quite often one or two mysterious locked rooms in houses I was looking after: Bluebeard's chambers, as Laura had suggested, though their secrets were probably only of the mundane kind.

But this room revealed its secrets, for the top of the door was glazed – perhaps it had been the land agent's office, or something like that. It held a tilting draughtsman's table, a large wooden easel and several tables bearing a silting of objects, including jars of pencils, brushes and lots of small models, presumably of sculptures. It was hard to make out what they were from that distance. There was also what looked like one of those hideaway computer workstations – but if so, then it must be dial-up, because there was no broadband here and, given the apparent unreliability of the phone lines, being able to connect with the internet must be a matter of luck. But that was okay – Ellen was the only person who ever emailed me much, with details of jobs.

'There's never been anything of value to lock away in Old Place anyway,' Sharon was saying scathingly, though I noticed a wistful look on her face like a child at a sweetshop window. 'Though Jude's that famous now, they're saying that even his little drawings of horses for those weird sculptures of his can fetch hundreds of pounds.' She nodded through the glass door. 'And he just crumples them up and tosses them in that waste-paper basket!'

'Well, that's up to him, isn't it? Presumably he wasn't happy with them.'

'You'd think he'd leave the basket for me to empty, but no, he takes them outside and puts them in the garden incinerator!' She obviously bitterly regretted this potential source of income going up in flames.

'That *does* seem a little excessive,' I agreed, amused.

Apart from a couple of china and linen cupboards, the only

other door from the passage was to a little garden hall with French doors leading outside. The trug of garden tools on the bench looked as if they hadn't been touched for half a century and were waiting for Sleeping Beauty to wake up, don the worn leather gauntlets, and start briskly hacking back the brambles.

'Is that a walled garden out there?' I asked, peering through the gathering gloom.

'Yes, though no-one bothers with most of it since Mrs Martland died . . .' She screwed up her face in recollection. 'That would be ten years ago now, thereabouts.'

'Is there a gardener?'

'An old bloke called Henry comes and grows vegetables in part of it, though he's supposed to have retired. He lives down in Little Mumming, in the almshouses – those three funny little cottages near the bridge.'

'Oh yes, I noticed those. Victorian Gothic.'

'I wouldn't know, I hate old houses,' she said, which I could tell by the state of this one.

There was a little cloakroom off the hall, with a splendid Victorian blue and white porcelain toilet depicting Windsor Castle inside the bowl, and I was just thinking that peeing on one of the Queen's residences must always have seemed a little lese-majesty when Sharon said impatiently, 'Come on: I need to get off home,' and gave me a dig in the back.

We went upstairs by a grander flight of stairs than that in the sitting room, with a stairlift folded back against the wall.

'That was put in for Jude's dad,' she said, hurrying me past a lot of not very good family portraits of fair, soulful women and dark, watchful men, when I would have lingered. 'Six bedrooms if you count the old nursery and the little room off it, plus there's two more in the staff wing.'

She opened and closed doors, allowing me tantalising glimpses of faded grandeur, including one four-poster bed. The nursery, up a further stair, was lovely, with a white-painted wooden bed with a heart cut out in the headboard, a scrap-screen and a big rocking horse.

'There are more rooms on this floor, but they're shut up and not used any more. The heating doesn't go up that far.'

'Oh yes, I noticed there were radiators – all mod cons! I'm impressed.'

'I wouldn't get excited, it never gets hot enough to do more than keep the chill off the place.' She clattered back down the stairs and hared off along the landing. 'Two bathrooms, though Jude's had an en suite shower put into his bedroom since he inherited.'

'That isn't bad for a house of this size,' I said. 'There's the downstairs cloakroom, too.'

'And a little bathroom in the staff wing, where you're sleeping. This is the family wing, of course – your room's in the other, where the old couple who used to look after the place lived.'

Evidently house-sitters ranked with servants in Jude Martland's eyes – but so long as I was warm and comfortable, I didn't mind where my room was.

The bedrooms either opened off the corridor, or the oak-floored balcony, where I stopped to gaze down at the huge sitting room, which looked like a stage set awaiting the entrance of the actors for an Agatha Christie dénouement, until Sharon began to rattle her turquoise nails against the banister in an impatient tattoo.

Once through the door into the other wing the décor turned utilitarian and the bathroom was very basic and ancient, though with an electric shower above the clawfooted bath. The bedroom that was to be mine was plain, comfortable – *and* clean. I expect Mo and Jim did that as soon as they arrived.

As if she could read my thoughts, Sharon said, 'Mo and Jim changed the bed ready for you, but they hadn't time to wash the sheets, so you'll find them in the utility room, I expect. I don't do washing.'

I was tempted to ask her exactly what she *did* do, but managed to repress it: it was none of my business.

We went down the backstairs to the kitchen, a very large room with an electric cooker as well as a huge Aga, a big scrubbed pine table in the middle, a couple of easy chairs and a wicker dog basket. This looked like the place where the owner did most of his living – it was certainly warmer than the rest of the house.

'The Aga's oil-fired – the tank's in one of the outhouses – and it runs the central heating, but you don't have to cook with it because there's a perfectly good stove over there.'

'Oh, I like using an Aga,' I said, and she gave me another of her 'you're barking mad' looks, then glanced at her watch.

'Come on. Through here there's the utility, larder, cloakroom, scullery, cellar . . .'

She flung open a door to reveal two enormous white chest freezers. 'The nearest one's full of Mo and Jim's food and so are the cupboards, fridge and larder.'

'Yes, they said they were leaving it for me, which was kind of them.'

She closed it again and led me on. 'That's the cellar door and there's firewood down there as well as the boiler. This by the back door is sort of a tackroom, it's got feed and harness and stuff in it for the horse.'

Something had been puzzling me. 'Right – but where's the dog?'

'In the yard, I don't want him under my feet when I'm cleaning, do I?'

'Isn't it a bit cold out there?' I asked and she gave me a look before wrenching the back door open. A large and venerable grey lurcher, who had been huddled on the step, got up and walked in stiffly, sniffed at me politely, and then plodded past in the direction of the kitchen.

'That's Merlin. He's past it, should be put down.'

I said nothing and she added, leading the way across to a

small barn on the other side of the cobbled yard, 'Like the horse – it was Jude's mother's and it's way past its three score years and ten, if you ask me. But he won't hear of it.'

There was something familiar but very spiteful about her tone when she mentioned Jude Martland's name that made me suspect a touch of the woman scorned. Maybe she had taken the job hoping for a bit more from him than a weekly pay-packet?

Now she looked at me sideways, slyly. 'You single?'

'Well, yes – widowed.'

'Don't get your hopes up, then – he goes for skinny blondes, does our Jude – though his brother stole his last one.'

'I'm not remotely interested in what he goes for and anyway, I won't meet him: he'll return after I've left, on Twelfth Night.'

'Oh – Twelfth Night! You want to watch yourself in Little Mumming if you're still here on Twelfth Night! Did you ever see that old film, *The Wicker Man*?' And she laughed unpleasantly.

'Well, I'll just have to take my chance, won't I?' I said cheerfully, since she was obviously trying to put the wind up me. Sure enough, she was talking about ghosts and haunting a minute later as she slid back the bolt and opened a barn door.

I've cooked in some of the most haunted houses in the country and all I can say is, the kitchen and the servants' bedrooms are *not* where they generally hang out.

Failing to get a rise out of me, she said, 'Your instructions for looking after the horse are on the kitchen table in that big folder thing. He's a great one for instructions, is Jude Martland.' She gestured inside the barn. 'The horse is down the other end.'

I could see a couple of looseboxes and a pale equine shape in one of them, but I didn't disturb it: time enough when I had read the instructions!

'Well, that's it then,' Sharon said, bolting the door again and leading the way back into the kitchen, where she pulled on a red coat that clashed with the magenta streaks in her hair and picked up her bag. 'I'm off. I expect the old people at the lodge will tell you anything I've forgot and you won't starve, at any rate, because there was enough food here to withstand a siege even before Mo and Jim brought all their stuff.'

When she drove off I was more than glad to see the last of her. I think the old dog was, too, because when I went back into the kitchen carrying the first load of stuff from my car, he wagged his tail and grinned in that engaging way that lurchers have, with a very knowing look in his amber eyes.

'Well, Merlin, it's just you and me, kid,' I told him, in my best Humphrey Bogart voice.

Chapter 5: Hot Mash

Hilda gave me a bar of good soap, which I was very glad of, and Pearl a lovely purple felt pansy she had made to pin to my coat. Luckily Mr Bowman – Tom's father and the minister at the chapel here – had recently presented me with several very pretty old bookmarks with Biblical texts and silk tassels, so that I had something by me to give them in return.

Christmas 1944

By the time I had brought all my stuff in, put the perishable food in the fridge and taken my bags up to the bedroom allocated to me, I was more than ready to sit down at the kitchen table with a cup of coffee and the Homebodies file, which Ellen gives to all the clients to fill in with essential information and emergency phone numbers. Jude Martland's was crammed with printed pages, mostly relating to the care of the dog and horse.

First I read the note that Mo and Jim had left tucked inside it, for a bit of inside information, and learned that the owner was more than happy for the house-sitters to help themselves to any of the food in the house, including the fish and game in the larger of the two freezers. '*But not the alcohol, since the wine cellar is locked*' had been added, which was okay by me, because I wasn't much of a drinker. Other than that, the TV reception was lousy and mobile phones worked best if you stood in the ear of the horse on the hill, or ten paces down the lane from the lodge and two steps right. (I expect finding that out kept Jim occupied for *hours*.)

I glanced at the generator instructions and discovered it was in an outbuilding and was automatic, so should in theory look after itself, and then made sure I knew where the main water stopcock was and the fuse box. The latter I found in the tack-room, with a working torch next to it on a shelf, together with a couple of candle lanterns and a wind-up storm lamp.

I was starting to form a picture of Jude Martland, who was clearly quite practical and obviously cared about the animals . . . And yet, he paid his cleaner a pittance and neglected his lovely house, so he was either broke or mean – maybe both. Or perhaps those with an artistic temperament simply don't notice muck?

I went back in the kitchen, poured another cup of coffee, and checked out the animal care instructions. Merlin, who was now leaning heavily against my leg with his head on my knee, was easy: two meals a day, with a pill for his arthritis crushed into the breakfast one, and he needed daily walks to help prevent him stiffening up.

Well, didn't we all?

I'd already spotted his brush, food, biscuits and a supply of rawhide chews in a cupboard in the scullery, next to a hook with a dog lead and a large brown pawprint-patterned towel helpfully marked 'DOG', in case I had found it a struggle to make the connection.

The horse was an Arab mare called Lady, which I would have thought a delicate breed for an exposed, upland place like this. She was twenty-five years old and that sounded quite an age for a horse too. But then, what do *I* know?

She had a paddock with a field shelter behind the house, where she spent the day unless the weather was extremely bad, though he had omitted to define what 'really bad' entailed. I should ensure the water in the trough was not frozen over and that a

43

filled haynet was hung on the paddock fence. Billy would go out with her.

Who, I wondered, was Billy? I puzzled over that for a moment and then read on.

She was brought into the stables at night and this would need mucking out and the water replenishing every day, a process I vaguely remembered from Laura's brief horse-mad phase. She was to keep her rug on all the time, except when it was removed daily for grooming and to check for rubbing.

In the evening she had a warm mash cooked up from ingredients to be found in metal bins in the tackroom and liberally spiced with a medication called Equiflex . . .

Good heavens! I was starting to think that Lady was going to take up most of my time and be a lot trickier to care for than I'd hoped, and I admit I was getting slight cold feet about it. So I thought I'd better take a proper look at her before the light totally vanished and Merlin, seeing me put my coat on, was determined to accompany me, even though I thought he ought to stay in the warm.

Along one side of the cobbled yard were the outbuildings that I knew contained the woodshed, generator and the extremely large oil tank that supplied both that and the central heating – but exploring those would have to wait for the next day.

Merlin and I went into the barn and I found a light switch by the door. Lady put her head over curiously and I saw that she was not much bigger than the ponies Laura had ridden and had a gentle expression and big, liquid dark eyes. Emboldened, I opened the door of the loosebox and slipped in to check her water and hay, and the fastenings of her rug . . . and I was just stooping over the bucket when the straw rustled and then something butted me hard in the legs: it was a small, black goat.

Billy? Obviously. But someone might have mentioned it! Luckily it had no horns, but it was now staring at me with light, slightly-mad-looking eyes.

I topped up the water bucket from the tap just outside the loosebox, foiling Billy's attempt to get out, because I wasn't sure how easy he would be to get back in again.

There was plenty of hay, both up in a net out of Billy's reach and in a hayrack lower down. Lady's warmly-lined rug was secure and she looked comfortable, so I left them to it for the moment.

I'd taken Merlin's lead out with me and now attached it to his collar: I wasn't sure if he was likely to run away, but I have learned through long experience that it's better to be safe than sorry. We went out of the side gate and followed the track alongside the paddock towards the hill. We didn't go far, though, just enough to stretch Merlin's poor old legs and mine. By the time we turned back I needed the torch I'd put in my pocket, and the lights in the courtyard looked bright and beckoning.

The wind was biting, so the threatened cold spell might actually be coming and I think we were both glad to get back into the warmth of the kitchen. I was feeling really weary by now, but there was one last task to be performed before I could settle down there: Lady must have her hot mash.

I followed the recipe to the letter: one scoop of quick-soak dried beet, steeped in boiling water for ten minutes, one scoop of chopped alfalfa, two scoops of pony nuts and a handful of linseed cake. Then I left it to cool a bit before stirring in the Equiflex.

It smelled quite nice, considering.

Merlin would have come out to the stables again with me, except that I thought he had had enough of the cold for one day and so shut him in, despite his reproachful expression.

Lady was eager to get her head in the bucket, though I had to hold off Billy, who wanted to share. Even little goats, I found, were surprisingly strong. I'd taken a handful of biscuit-shaped things from a container marked with his name that I'd spotted in the tackroom, but he was more interested in the mash.

Horses give off a surprising amount of heat, don't they?

* * *

45

Merlin greeted my return with huge relief, as if I'd been gone a week, so I expect the poor old thing was feeling terribly confused.

When I'd thawed out I phoned Laura, but only for long enough to give her the number here to ring me back: clients don't appreciate you running up huge phone bills, but obviously using my mobile was going to be tricky. I only hoped Sharon was exaggerating the frequency of the phone lines going down . . .

'How are you getting on?' Laura asked. 'What are the animals like?'

'The dog's an old lurcher, a sweetie called Merlin – he's a bit lost and lonely, I think, because he keeps following me around. The horse is a white Arab.'

'Grey, horses are never white.'

'You can call it grey, but Lady's as white as snow, with huge, dark eyes. She's very old, quiet and gentle, so I don't think looking after her is going to be a problem – except she's living with this little goat no-one mentioned.'

'A *goat*?'

'It was in the loosebox with her, so I suppose it's keeping her company. It's got a bit of the evil eye and it kept trying to eat her hot mash. I had to hold it off, and it was surprisingly strong.'

'Hot mash? You had to cook *dinner* for the horse?'

I described the cordon bleu horse mash and confessed my worry about looking after the elderly, delicate-looking mare, and she made reassuring noises.

'I'll tackle mucking out and grooming tomorrow. I only wish I'd been interested in that sort of thing while you were having riding lessons, though I expect it's just a matter of common sense.'

'You wheelbarrow the old bedding to the manure heap, and then spread a layer of new straw – simple. Mucking out will be good exercise, too.'

'Yes, I expect it will.'

'So, what's the house like?'

'Lovely. I've only had a quick tour around so far but I can see it's mostly Jacobean, though part of it looks much older. The central heating isn't very efficient so I'll probably light a fire in the big inglenook fireplace in the sitting room tomorrow and that should warm the house through. My bedroom isn't too bad, because it's right over the kitchen with the Aga.'

'How big *is* this place?'

'Bigger than I expected, but I've cooked for house-parties in much larger and grander houses. The sitting room is huge and looks like it might have started life as a medieval hall, but then two new wings have been added and lots of dark panelling and moulded ceilings.'

'That sounds pretty grand to me!'

'You could fit the floor space of my entire house in the kitchen wing with room to spare,' I admitted.

'That's a stately home as far as I'm concerned – and you are in sole possession, the lady of the manor.'

'Yes, but I know my place: the hired help's bedroom is in the service wing, though there's a bathroom opposite with a decent electric shower. I expect I'll spend most of my time in the kitchen and just take a quick daily walk round the rest of the house to check everything is all right.'

'Sooner you than me, rattling around alone in a spooky old house in the middle of nowhere.'

I laughed. 'You know I don't believe in ghosts or the super-natural! No, I'll be fine. The cleaner showed me round when I arrived, but she isn't coming back because she's got another job. She won't be any loss, though, because the place is totally filthy and neglected, she can't have been doing anything. Then again, Jude Martland was paying her a pittance, so you can't really blame her for that.'

'So – you'll be entirely alone all the time? It isn't *really* haunted, is it?'

'Sharon – that's the cleaner – tried to put the wind up me,

47

telling me about ghosts and an annual local ceremony on Twelfth Night. She seemed to be implying that the villagers would want to use me as some kind of ceremonial sacrifice, but I wasn't really listening because it was all entirely daft!'

'You won't be there that night anyway, will you?'

'No, I'm leaving that morning, before the client gets back – that was the arrangement Mo and Jim had.'

'Is it very isolated? I can't imagine what you'll do with yourself.'

'Apart from trying to finish off my cookbook, I've brought that tin trunk of Gran's papers to sort and I'm going to carry on reading her journal at bedtime, too. She's been sent to a new hospital and made friends, so it's getting more interesting.'

'Perhaps that Ned Martland she mentioned was one of the doctors and she had a crush on him?' she suggested.

'Maybe,' I agreed. 'I'll tell you if I find out. And I'm not totally isolated here, because the village is only about half a mile away and, if I feel like company, the old couple at the lodge have invited me to drop in any time. But you know me – I like being alone.'

'Sam was really disappointed when I told him you weren't coming for Christmas Day after all,' she hinted, but I just laughed.

By now, it seemed like a week since I had set out for Little Mumming and I decided on an early night.

Merlin and I had our dinner, and then he accompanied me around the ground floor while I checked the doors and windows. We'd returned to the kitchen and I was just about to fill my trusty hot water bottle, when suddenly the phone on the large dresser rang loudly, nearly giving me a heart attack.

'Is that Holly Brown?' demanded a deep voice that seemed to vibrate right down to my feet and back again in a very novel, if slightly disturbing, way.

'Yes, speaking.'

'Jude Martland: I just caught up with my emails and found one from Homebodies saying the Chirks had had to leave and *you* were taking over.'

'That's right, and I'm so glad you've rung, because—'

'No, it's damned-well *not* all right!' he rudely interrupted. 'I've just called my uncle, and apparently you're not only alone in the house, but you've also no experience with horses whatsoever!'

'Look, Mr Martland,' I said soothingly. 'I always house-sit alone and your instructions were very comprehensive – *exhaustive*, even. Well, apart from the goat,' I qualified.

'What?'

'Billy. There was no mention of him.'

'Of course there was – you just didn't bother looking for it! But what really matters is that I left Old Place, Lady and Merlin in safe hands, with people I knew and trusted – then suddenly I hear that someone totally unsuitable has been drafted in, without a by-your-leave!'

'Actually, I'm repeatedly rebooked by the same clients, year after year,' I said evenly. 'You were lucky that my Christmas placement had also fallen through, so that I was free to step into the breach! And thank you, Holly Brown, for coping with the emergency,' I found myself adding acerbically.

There was a pause, then he growled, grudgingly, 'I suppose there was no alternative, but I'm not happy with the arrangement – or that Homebodies went ahead and did this without asking me.'

'Ellen did her best to contact you and, in any case, she knows I'm completely trustworthy and capable.'

'Sending a young woman to look after an isolated house alone, especially over Christmas, can hardly be ideal.'

'Thank you, but I don't celebrate Christmas, I'm not actually that young and I *prefer* isolation.'

'Noël mentioned you didn't celebrate Christmas – and that's another problem, because my aunt and uncle were looking

49

forward to having Christmas dinner with the Chirks and *I* felt better knowing Tilda wouldn't have to cook it. I know she still does most of their cooking, but she's looking quite frail these days.'

'Yes, so she said, but I don't think she's going to attempt the full monty – they're having a roast chicken instead,' I said. 'And I expect her granddaughter will help her.'

'Oh God, I'd entirely forgotten about Jess being there on her own this year!'

'Mmm . . . I'm afraid you don't seem to be her favourite person at the moment, Mr Martland.'

There was a pause, and then he suggested, 'Perhaps you could cook the Christmas dinner instead of the Chirks? You *can* cook?'

'I'm a professional chef, that's what I do during the summer,' I said icily, 'and my charges are *very* high. In winter I prefer to house-sit for a rest. Catering for family dinner parties doesn't come into my current plans and besides, as I've said, I don't celebrate Christmas in any way.'

'But—'

'Mr Martland,' I interrupted firmly, 'while I'm sorry your arrangements have been put out, you can rest assured that I'll keep an eye on your property and look after the animals until your return on Twelfth Night.'

'But how can I be sure of that when I know nothing about you, except that you have no knowledge of horses and—'

'Look,' I said, 'you don't have any alternative! If you think I'm going to drink your gin and fall into a drunken coma over Christmas, neglecting the animals and burning the house down, I suggest you email Ellen for my CV and references. Good *night*, Mr Martland.'

And I slammed down the receiver.

I regretted my lapse into rudeness almost immediately. It must have been tiredness, but also there was something about his manner that rubbed me up the wrong way. While a bit of snappishness might be allowable in a cook of my calibre, provided I produced delicious meals, which I always did, it's not such a good idea with house-sitting clients.

The phone rang again almost immediately. Sighing, I picked it up.

'You hung up on me!' he said incredulously.

'I'm sorry, but the conversation seemed to have run its natural course. Now, it's been a long day and I was just on my way to bed . . . Oh, and by the way,' I added as an afterthought, 'your cleaner has resigned, with effect from today. But going by the filthy state of the house, I daresay you'll hardly notice.'

This time when I put the phone down, he didn't ring back. I filled my hot water bottle, patted Merlin, and took myself off up to bed where, despite my exhaustion, I found myself going over and over the conversation with the irritating and unreasonable Jude Martland. I would be sure to leave *long* before he came home on Twelfth Night!

In the end I switched on the bedside lamp and read a few more entries in Gran's journal until, soothed by the small dramas of the hospital ward and her battles with her awful landlady, I finally fell asleep.

Chapter 6: Horse Sense

A new case has arrived on Pearl's ward – a bad leg wound and they are trying penicillin on it, which seems to be doing the trick. The patient is a young man and apparently a member of a local gentry family. Pearl and the others were whispering and giggling about him and how good looking he was, though I told them it was what was on the inside that mattered, not the outside. But I am ashamed to say that, stirred by curiosity, I peeped in later to see what all the fuss was about and Sister nearly caught me!

January, 1945

After breakfast next morning I checked on Lady and her smelly little companion, fed them a few chunks of carrot, then clipped back the top of the stable door to the courtyard.

They both looked fine, but I thought I would leave them where they were until it was fully light and took Merlin for a walk up Snowehill. He seemed to be moving a little easier this morning and I suspected he'd missed a couple of his pills and regular exercise in the last few days.

The closer we got to the red horse hill figure, the harder it was to make out what it was. It had been cut out of the turf and the earth banked on either side to make a raised edge. The natural red sandstone lay revealed, though it didn't stand out like the white horse ones I'd seen elsewhere and was on a much smaller scale. I wondered if it was ancient, perhaps Celtic? I seemed to recall that Celts were keen on horses. Or perhaps it was a more modern addition to the local scenery?

A track up to the beacon ran right by it and, looking down, I could see that it met the road above Old Place, where there was another farm. It was well trodden, so I expect lots of walkers come here to climb up to the folly. I'd do it myself one day, too, only not this particular one: I had too much to do.

I was just about to go back down when there was a quick spatter of Mozart from my pocket. The ringtone somehow didn't seem quite right for a windswept Lancashire hillside, but I'm not sure what would. Ride of the Valkyries?

'Caught you!' Ellen said triumphantly. 'I tried the house but there was no reply.'

'No, I'm up on the hill behind the house. In fact, the only mobile reception is up here, or down near the village, so you're lucky to have caught me at all.'

'What are you doing on the hill?'

'Walking the dog – and he's old and arthritic so I can't keep him standing about here very long.'

'I only wanted to warn you that I found a flood of emails from Jude Martland in my inbox this morning and he isn't happy about the change of home-sitter, though he should be grateful I could find *anyone* at such short notice!'

'Yes, that's what *I* told him.'

'You mean, you've spoken to him? He didn't mention that . . . or maybe I just haven't got as far as that email yet.'

'He rang last night and he struck me as a very autocratic and disagreeable person – and totally unreasonable! I told him I was perfectly capable and competent, but I'm not sure he believed me.'

'*I* told him much the same, but he still wanted to see your CV and references, so I faxed them. They're all glowing so they'll put his mind at rest.'

'I doubt it, because he seemed more worried about the horse than anything and you have to agree that I've no experience with them at all. But still, the instructions he left were clear enough and I'm sure I can manage. I made her hot mash last night and I'm going to put her in the paddock shortly and have a go at mucking out.'

'Oh, you'll be fine,' she said comfortably, which was easy for her since she wouldn't be the one coping! 'Well, I just wanted to warn you in case you got a phone call, but obviously you've dealt with him. And once he's read your CV I expect he will feel much happier. I told him he was lucky that one of my best house-sitters was free to step into the breach.'

'I hope so, though he may want regular bulletins on the horse and dog. Some pet owners do.'

She agreed and rang off, and Merlin and I went home again. I was dying to have another look around the house, but thought I'd better tackle Lady's stable first. From what I recalled, it was simply a matter of removing the old straw and replacing it with new: how hard could *that* be?

I changed into old jeans, a warm fleece and wellies, girded my loins and went to do the Augean stable bit. Merlin heaved himself up out of his basket with a resigned expression, but I gave him one of the rawhide chews out of the cupboard and left him in the kitchen with it: I needed my full attention on what I was doing.

At least by the New Year I would be able to add looking after horses and goats to my CV if I wanted to, though I wasn't entirely convinced I would ever want to see a goat again.

It was still very cold, though there was a wintry sun shining, and I had no idea whether I should put Lady in the paddock or not. Or perhaps just the cobbled yard, while I tried to sort out her bedding?

The shovel and wheelbarrow were easy to find – and so was the manure heap over the wall in the paddock. There were bales of straw and one or two of hay at the opposite end of the barn to Lady's box, and more in a sort of half-loft overhead, with a rickety wooden ladder. Luckily I can tell straw from hay because guinea pigs, rabbits and chickens have all been previous charges of mine.

I was still debating what to do with Lady and her companion – *especially* her companion – when help arrived unexpectedly in the form of a large, elderly woman on a stocky brown cob. She hailed me from the other side of the gate, then dismounted and led her horse through, shutting it behind her. She was wearing a Burberry check headscarf tied pirate-fashion instead of a riding hat and a hugely-caped wax jacket, so she looked like a slightly eccentric highwayman.

'Hello,' she said in a deep, hearty voice, holding out her hand. 'I'm Becca – Becca Martland, Noël's sister. He told me you'd arrived, so I thought I'd ride this way and see how you were doing.'

We shook hands. She was by no means as tall as me (at six foot, not many women are!) but she made up for it in girth.

'I'm very glad to meet you – especially since I was just about to muck out Lady and I wasn't sure what to do with her while I did it,' I confessed, seeing knowledgeable help was at hand. 'Is it too cold to put her in the paddock, do you think?'

'Not at all, Arabs are tough as old boots and she'll go in the field shelter if it rains, or to get out of the wind. Have you taken her rug off and brushed her?'

'No, though I did check that it was secure last night.'

'We'll do that first, then, because I don't suppose anyone has for a couple of days. You go and open the gate to the paddock, while I tie Nutkin up in the barn out of this cold wind and fetch the brushes from the tackroom.'

We let Billy out while we groomed Lady – Becca assured me he never went far from her side. Indeed, he dithered in the open door until I gave him a quick shove and closed it behind him and then he hung about outside, bleating.

'Lovely creature, Lady,' Becca said, stripping off the rug and then handing me one of the two oval brushes with the concise instruction, 'Firm strokes in the direction of the hair.'

'But she's terribly old, isn't she? I was a bit worried about that when I read Mr Martland's notes.'

'Oh, twenty-five is nothing for an Arab! I'd look after her myself when Jude's away, but it takes me all my time to look after one horse these days. And I'm not taking on the bleeding goat,' she added. 'Noël said you hadn't had much experience with horses?'

'No, to be honest, going to the riding school with my best friend when she had her pony phase was about it,' I explained. 'Mr Martland's instructions are very detailed and I'm sure I can manage perfectly well, but it would be wonderful if I could call on you for anything that puzzled me? It might make Mr Martland feel better too – he rang last night and was fretting about whether I could cope.'

'Oh, did he phone? I don't suppose he said he was coming back for Christmas after all, did he?' she asked hopefully, stopping her brisk brushing and staring at me across Lady's snowy back.

'No, I'm afraid not. Did you think he might change his mind?'

Her face fell. 'Not really, it's just that the Martlands have always celebrated Christmas together, here at Old Place. It doesn't seem right to have the head of the household on the opposite side of the world.'

She put her brush down and showed me how to put the rug back on securely, which was simple enough with Lady, but I should imagine very difficult with a less cooperative horse!

'Jude loves horses and he's particularly attached to Lady,' she said. 'She was his mother's horse, you know, so he's bound to worry about her. But of course you can call me if you're concerned about anything, I'll leave you my phone number. Not that you can always get through, because the lines are hanging loose from the poles like limp spaghetti and a good wind can cut the connection to Old Place for a week or more.'

She said this as if it was the most normal thing in the world.

'Couldn't the lines be repaired?' I would certainly have had it sorted out in no time, if I lived here!

'Apparently all the poles need replacing and they'll get round to it eventually, but there's only Old Place and Hill Farm up this road until you get to Great Mumming, so it's not exactly high on their priority list when it comes to allocating resources.'

'Oh yes, I saw the farm when I walked Merlin up to the red horse earlier and I noticed the sign on the main road pointed two ways to Great Mumming, so presumably it carries on past Hill Farm?'

'That's right, but the road beyond the farm isn't much more than a track with tarmac over it that goes round the side of Snowehill – a bit of ice and you don't even want to *think* about trying it,' she said, then gave a deep laugh. 'One of those SatNav things keeps sending motorists up here as a short cut to the motorway – and it might be, as the crow flies, but not by car!'

Billy's plaintively protesting bleats rose to a crescendo. We let Lady out into the paddock and he followed her, butting against her legs.

Becca picked up a fork. 'Come on – now I'll help you muck out. You bring the barrow.'

She must have been in her seventies, at least, but she could still wield a fork with the best of them and gave me what was essentially a very useful masterclass. Under her direction I trundled the used bedding over to the manure heap, then spread a thick layer of clean straw in the loosebox, padded out at the sides and round the washed and filled bucket.

'You don't need to do this every single day – just pick up the manure and put down a bit of fresh straw if it isn't too bad.'

'How cold does it have to get before I keep her inside during the day?'

'Oh, she can go out even if it snows, but you might need to double-rug her,' she said breezily.

'Right . . .' Jude Martland and his aunt seemed to have two different views on just how fragile Lady was!

I was glowing by the time we'd finished mucking out, and probably steaming gently in the chilly air, just like the replenished manure heap.

'There – that's fine, all ready for bringing her in before it goes dark. Did you manage her warm mash all right last night?'

'Oh yes, it was just a matter of following the recipe. And thank you very much for showing me what to do, it's been invaluable,' I said gratefully.

'I'd better pop back in a day or two and give you a few more pointers,' she suggested.

'That would be great, if you can spare the time.'

'Noël says you're from West Lancs, near Ormskirk? What do you shoot over there?'

'Shoot? I don't shoot anything!'

'Pity – there's not an awful lot up here either, bar the odd rabbit and pigeon,' she commiserated, 'but you'll find some of those, and a few pheasants and the like, in one of the freezers.'

While I've cooked an awful lot of game over the years for house-parties, I think killing something simply for pleasure is a bad thing – but when working I just cook, I don't give opinions!

'I'm a town girl, really, brought up in Merchester,' I admitted, 'though my work usually takes me into the country from late spring to early autumn when I cook for large house-parties. The rest of the year I take home-sitting assignments, like this one.'

'Oh, you cook? It's a pity we can't have a house-party at Old Place over Christmas, then,' Becca said wistfully. 'I call it a bit selfish of Jude to go off like this, even if he has been crossed in love. His brother Guy ran off with his fiancée last Christmas, you know.'

'Your brother did mention something about it,' I admitted. 'He and his wife told me you all usually spend Christmas together and their granddaughter had been looking forward to it, but actually, in winter I like a rest from all the cooking and, besides, I don't celebrate Christmas.'

'Against your religion, I expect,' she said vaguely, with a glance at my black hair and pale olive skin. People are always asking me where I am from and seem surprised when I say Merchester.

'And the old people really look forward to having their Christmas dinner here too,' she went on. 'I don't think they've quite taken in that it isn't going to happen this year.'

'You mean Noël and Tilda?' I ventured. Clearly she wasn't numbering herself among the ranks of the elderly!

'Well, yes, but actually I meant Old Nan and Richard Sampson, who was the vicar here until he retired. They live in the almshouses in Little Mumming. Of course, there's Henry too, but he always goes to his daughter's for his dinner, including Christmas Day. Did you notice the almshouses as you came through the village?'

'The row of three tiny Gothic-looking cottages?'

'Yes, that's where the family stash away the last of the retainers. Old Nan is in her nineties, but bright as a button, and Richard's about eighty, fit as a flea and walks for miles. By the way, Henry still comes up here when the fancy takes him and hangs out in the greenhouse and walled garden – you might suddenly stumble across him.'

She nodded at a small gate set in an arch. 'Through there – small walled garden, Jude's mother loved it, but it's pretty overgrown now apart from the vegetable patch. The greenhouse backs on to the stables and barn and Henry has a little den up at one end with a primus stove to make tea.'

'Right – I'll keep an eye out for him! But I do hope the other two have understood the situation and made other arrangements for Christmas Day?'

'I don't know, old habits are hard to break.' Becca shook her head. 'Like Tilda – she talks as if she still does all the cooking, but really that Edwina of hers does most of it now, with Tilda getting in her way and bossing her about. So it's always been very convenient that they can come here for a week at Christmas while Edwina has a break.'

'Mr Martland's absence does seem to have created quite a lot of disappointment and difficulty,' I said, thinking that since he must have known how all these elderly people relied on him, it was very selfish indeed of him to flounce off abroad like this, even if he *had* been crossed in love.

'Well, it's not *your* fault,' she said briskly.

'Do you have time to come in and have a cup of tea?' I asked. 'I brought a fruit cake with me.'

'Lovely, lead the way!'

She didn't take her scarf off, but removed the wax jacket, revealing a quilted gilet and cord riding breeches of generous and forgiving cut. Merlin hauled himself out of his basket to greet her.

'Hello, old fellow,' she said fondly, stroking his head with a large hand. 'Stayed here in the warm, did you?'

'He's already had a run, I thought he'd be better in,' I said, making tea and taking the cake out of the tin. 'The house seems a little chilly despite the central heating, so I thought I'd light the big fire in the sitting room later.'

'Jolly good idea. There's always been a fire lit there in winter, it's the heart of the house, but Jude's been neglecting the place since the Jacksons retired, though they were getting a bit past it and glad to go once my brother died. Noël told me you'd just lost your grandmother, too – sorry,' she added abruptly, but with sincerity.

'Thank you, yes, it *was* quite recent. She brought me up because my own mother died soon after I was born.'

'Sad,' she said. 'Jude's mother died several years ago now, but he adored her. I think that must have been where he got his arty ways, because there was never anything like *that* in the family before. And I expect that's why he dotes on Lady too – but then, he loves all horses, even if they do sometimes look a bit tortured in those sculptures he makes!'

'I don't think the one I've seen near Manchester looked tortured, just . . . modern. You could still tell what it was.'

'He has a studio in the woods just above the lodge – the old mill house. You'll see a path going off the drive to it, but it'll be locked up, of course.'

There was nothing in the instructions about looking after that as well, thank goodness, though I expected I'd walk down that way with Merlin one day.

Even though the family's disappointment over Christmas was none of my doing, my conscience had been niggling away at me slightly, so when she got up to go I said impulsively, 'You wouldn't like the enormous frozen turkey and giant Christmas pudding the Chirks left, I suppose? Then you, your brother and sister-in-law and Jess could have a proper Christmas dinner together.'

'Oh, *I* can't cook anything more complicated than a boiled egg! So it looks like I'll be eating Tilda's roast chicken dinner at the lodge on Christmas Day and then going home to cheese, cold cuts and pickles.'

That made me feel even more guilty, though why I should when none of these broken arrangements were my fault, I can't imagine! It is all entirely down to the selfishness of Jude Martland!

Chapter 7: The Whole Hog

Sister is a great lump of a woman, big and cold enough to sink the Titanic, though she moves silently enough for all that and caught Pearl sitting on the edge of the new patient's bed, a heinous crime. Now Pearl has been moved to the children's ward and I have taken her place, Sister saying she trusts me not to flirt with the patients! This does not, of course, stop them trying to flirt with me ...

January, 1945

When Becca had gone (with a big wedge of foil-wrapped cake in her coat pocket), I finally had time to take another look around the house, Merlin at my heels. He had taken to following me about so closely now that if I stopped suddenly, his nose ran into the back of my leg. It felt quite cold and damp even through my jeans; generally a healthy sign in a dog, if not a human.

I wanted to familiarise myself with the layout and especially with the position of anything that might be valuable, and make sure that I hadn't missed any windows last night when locking up. I would mainly be living in the kitchen wing, unless the urge suddenly came upon me to watch the TV in the little morning room ... Though actually, I'd really taken to the sitting room, vast though it was, so I might spend some time there once I'd lit a fire.

I can't say I found any valuables, apart from a pair of tarnished silver candlesticks and an engraved tray on the sideboard in the dining room, and a row of silver-framed photographs on the upright piano at the further end of the room.

When I lifted the lid of the piano I was surprised to find it was only slightly out of tune and I wondered who still played it. I picked out the first bit of 'Lead Kindly Light' (a hymn Gran taught me to play on her harmonium), which echoed hollowly around the room. It was a lovely instrument, but in the event of a fire I'd be more inclined to snatch up the silver than heave the piano out of the window.

Closing it, I examined the photographs, most quite old and of family groupings – weddings, picnics, expeditions in huge open-topped cars – all the prewar pleasures of the moneyed classes.

At the end of the row was a more recent colour picture of two tall, dark-haired young men, one much bigger, more thickset and not as handsome as the other, though there was an obvious resemblance. The handsome one was smiling at whoever held the camera, while the other scowled – and if this was Jude Martland and his brother, then I could guess which was which, even after speaking to the man once!

The library held a very mixed selection of books, including a lot of old crime novels of the cosy variety, my favourite. I promised myself a lovely, relaxing time over Christmas, sitting beside a roaring fire with coffee, chocolates and cake to hand, and Merlin and the radio to keep me company.

The one wall free of bookshelves was covered with more old photographs of family and friends – the Martlands were easy to pick out, being mostly tall and dark – but also of men strangely garbed and taking part in some kind of open-air performance. It might have been the Twelfth Night ceremony Sharon mentioned, in which case it looked to me like some innocuous kind of Morris dancing event.

The key to the French doors in the garden hall was on my bunch and I let myself out into the small walled garden, after pulling on an over-large anorak. If this belonged to Jude Martland, then he was a *lot* bigger than me – about the size of a grizzly bear, in fact!

The garden had a schizophrenic personality: half being over-grown and neglected, with roses that had rambled a little too far and encroaching ivy; while the other was a neat array of vegetable and fruit beds. The large, lean-to greenhouse against the back of the barn could have done with a coat of paint, but inside all was neat and tidy, with tools and pots stowed away under benches or hung up on racks, and a little hidey-hole at the end behind a sacking curtain where Henry hung out, though it was currently vacant. He had a little primus stove, kettle, mug and a tin box containing half a packet of slightly limp digestive biscuits and some Yorkshire Tea bags.

I went back indoors, shivering. It was definitely getting colder and if we did get ice and snow, as the forecast for next week had hinted we might, I was sure that the steep road down from the village would quickly become impassable and we'd be cut off. This was a situation that had often befallen me in Scotland, so I wasn't particularly bothered by the idea, though I made a note to check that I had all the supplies in the house that I needed, just in case. I could call in at the lodge and make sure *they* were well prepared too.

Upstairs I wanted to check on the attic, but the door to that was locked and I didn't have the key – which would be unfortunate if the pipes or water tank leaked or froze! But perhaps it had been entrusted to Noël for emergencies and I made a mental note to ask.

I stopped by my bedroom to hang up the rest of my clothes and stack the books I'd brought and my laptop and cookery notes on a marble-topped washstand, ready to take downstairs later. Gran's little tin trunk looked right up here, the sort of thing a servant might once have had . . . I sat on the edge of the bed and flicked through the first journal until I found where I had left off reading last night: the next few entries seemed to increasingly mention the new patient . . .

Firmly resisting the urge to skim, I closed the book: I was enjoying slowly discovering my gran through her journals every evening, a couple of pages at a time, and didn't want to rush that.

'Come on, Merlin,' I said, gathering up my books and stuff for downstairs, and he uncoiled himself from the little braided rug at the end of the bed and followed me.

I dumped everything in the kitchen then checked out the cellar, where I was happy to see a whole wall of dry logs and kindling for the sitting-room fire and the boiler burbling quietly away. The wine cellar door was locked of course, but funnily enough, Jude Martland seemed to have overlooked the drinks cabinet with its decanters of spirits and bottles of liqueur in the dining room, so if the urge *did* uncharacteristically take me to render myself drunk and disorderly, the means were freely to hand.

But this was unlikely: I like to be in control way too much!

By the time we emerged back up into the kitchen, Merlin had begun to heave long-suffering sighs, so I put some dog biscuits from an open packet into his bowl and had a lunch of bread, cheese and rich, chunky apricot chutney from a jar I'd brought with me, before checking up on the provisions.

The kitchen cupboards were well stocked, though some of the food looked as if it hadn't been touched for months. The tall fridge contained butter, eggs, bacon and an awful lot of cheese left by Mo and Jim, plus the few perishable items I'd brought with me. Mo and Jim obviously liked to go the whole hog at Christmas, because as well as the gigantic turkey and a ham joint in the freezer, there was a pudding the size of a small planet, jars and jars of mincemeat and even some of those expensive Chocolate Wishes (like a delicious fortune cookie) that are made in Sticklepond, a village near where I live.

The biggest freezer was packed with game, meat and fish, and the other contained an array of bread, pizza, chilli and a whole stack of instant meals of a sustaining nature: these probably formed the owner's staple diet, in which case gourmet he was *not*. What with those and a very plentiful supply of tea bags, coffee, longlife milk and orange juice, I was starting to get the hang of what Jude Martland lived on when he was home!

I noted down anything I thought I might run out of, which the village shop could probably supply, but I was unlikely to starve to death any time soon.

Merlin, bored, was now fast asleep in his basket by the Aga – sweet!

I chopped up a carrot and took it out to Lady, dropping a bit down for Billy, who was scrabbling at the fence with frantic greed. Lady has lips like softest velvet and, although her coat is snowy white, oddly enough the skin under it is black.

When the carrot had all gone, she and her odoriferous little friend wandered back up the paddock and I went to check the level of oil in the huge tank in the outbuilding (satisfyingly full), and had a look at the generator. This was a dauntingly large piece of machinery but apparently should switch itself on if the mains electricity fails, then back off again when it returns. The Homebodies folder did mention that if it didn't turn on automatically, you had to come out here and do it manually . . .

I was just leaning over it, examining the switches, when a voice suddenly rasped behind me, 'You don't want to mess with that there bit of machinery, gurl!'

I whipped round, startled, to find I had company in the shape of an elderly man, small and thin, with long limp wisps of snuff-coloured hair on either side of his cadaverous face. He was holding a bulging sack in one hand and a slightly threateningly raised stick in the other. I have seen more prepossessing old men.

'Women shouldn't meddle with what they don't understand.'

'You wouldn't be Henry, would you?'

He nodded. 'My daughter ran me up to fetch a few taters and carrots. And you're the gurl has come to look after the place, instead of Jim and Mo?'

The tone of his voice left me in no doubt that this was not, in his opinion, a good exchange. In fact, I was beginning to find Jim and Mo Chirk a hard act to follow: they seemed to have made themselves very popular with everyone in previous visits!

'I haven't been described as a girl for years,' I said pleasantly, 'and I'm actually one of Homebodies' most experienced house-sitters.'

'You're a grand, strapping lass, I'll allow that,' he conceded, 'but all the same, you shouldn't meddle with the generator. I showed Jim the way of it, but I'm not having it messed about by any Tom, Dick or Harry.'

'Thomasina, Richenda or Harriet?' I suggested and he looked at me blankly. 'If the electricity goes off and it doesn't switch itself on, then I'll have to know how to do it, won't I?'

'Nay, you leave it to them as knows what they're doing.'

'Meaning you?'

'That's right.'

'But you might not be around when I need to switch it on – perhaps we'll get snowed in, and then what would I do? But don't worry, Mr Martland left instructions and it looks *perfectly* simple.'

'You don't want to tinker with it,' he insisted obstinately.

We seemed to have reached an impasse. I said calmly and perfectly politely, 'I'm sorry, but it's part of my job to keep the place in good running order, so if I have to run the generator, I will: after all, I can't be expected to sit in the dark in a cold house over the Christmas holidays, can I?'

He gave me a look of deep disfavour, but seemed eventually, after much rumination, to accept the logic of my argument. 'I can see you're a stubborn, determined creature, just like Jude, who always thinks he knows best . . . Well, I suppose I'd better show you the way of it, then, but you're not to touch it unless you can't get hold of me, mind?'

'Certainly,' I agreed, and we shook hands on it, though since he spat into his palm first, it was possibly the most disgusting thing I have ever had to do while maintaining a polite expression.

I couldn't see what all the fuss was about really with the generator, it was quite simple. Then Henry said his daughter was waiting and hobbled off with his sack of booty and I went indoors and washed my hands with bacteria-busting hand gel.

I fully intended raiding his vegetable plot myself, but I would be scrubbing everything well before cooking it, because I wouldn't put it past him to pee on the compost heap like a lot of old gardeners – if not worse.

Once I'd thawed out, I cleaned out the hearth in the sitting room and laid a fire, fetching up kindling and logs from the cellar in an ancient-looking wicker basket. I only hoped the chimney had been recently swept, because setting the place on fire would probably be the end of my home-sitting career. But luckily the smoke drew upwards, rather than billowed out, and no clouds of soot descended.

Once it was going well I set the brass fireguard in front of it, then opened all the unlocked doors in the house to let the warm air circulate through – old houses could quickly get musty if you didn't keep them aired.

I settled down for a nice rest in front of the sitting-room fire once I'd done that, with a good, strong pot of tea and another slice of my slightly depleted fruit cake to hand.

I felt I deserved a break: there was quite a bit to do at Old Place compared to some other house-sits, though I was sure I'd soon fall into a routine with the animals now I'd got the hang of it. Then the rest of the time would be my own . . . except that

I really would have to clean this lovely room if I intended spending much time in here!

I'd been half-expecting Jude Martland to ring again much later in the day, but it was typical of the man I was beginning to know that he should instead call just as I'd finally sat down for a rest! The phone in here was on a round table by the window, too, with only a hard chair next to it.

This time he was fractionally more conciliatory, presumably because he'd read my glowing references from satisfied clients, and I was determined to keep my cool.

'Miss Brown, I don't think I thanked you yesterday for stepping into the breach at such short notice,' he began stiffly.

'Mrs – and of course I understood that you were concerned that your house and animals were being taken care of by a total stranger. But you can rest easy: everything is *perfectly* under control and your Aunt Becca came here and gave me some excellent advice about Lady, as well as her phone number, should anything crop up.'

'Oh good!' He sounded relieved. 'You did put Lady's medicine in her warm mash last night, didn't you?'

'Of course.'

'And kept Billy away from it until she'd eaten it?'

'Naturally,' I said, though it had been quite a tussle to stop Billy diving into the bucket before Lady was finished. 'Lady's fine. And your gardener, Henry, helpfully showed me what to do if the electricity goes off and the generator doesn't come on automatically.'

'*Henry* told you?' he repeated incredulously.

'Of course! He could see the necessity, in case he wasn't available to come to Old Place and deal with it himself. And I mean to walk into Little Mumming tomorrow, so I'll call in to see your aunt and uncle at the lodge to ask them if they need any shopping. So you see, you've nothing to worry about and can enjoy your holiday,' I finished kindly.

69

'It's not entirely a holiday: there was a ceremony to unveil one of my sculptures yesterday.'

'Oh yes, I've seen that horse you did up on a hill near Manchester and it's very nice.'

'*Nice?* Do try not to sound *too* impressed,' he said, seeming a bit miffed. 'I'm supposed to be off to the Hamptons to stay with friends for Christmas tomorrow, but I don't see how I can possibly relax and enjoy it when I know you're alone at Old Place looking after everything – the weather can be bad up there, you know, Little Mumming is often cut off in winter.'

'So I've already been told – and really, the dimmest person would be able to appreciate that if the steep hill down from the village was icy, it would be impassable. But don't worry, I've often been snowed in up Scotland and it's not a problem.'

'You don't mind isolation then?'

'No. In fact, I enjoy it. I have some work I want to finish off too – a book of house-party recipes I'm compiling.'

'Yes, you said you were a cook,' he said thoughtfully. 'Look, I know you said you didn't celebrate Christmas, but I really think you might reconsider—'

I could see he was about to ask me to cook the family Christmas dinner all over again, probably due to a suddenly guilty conscience, so I interrupted him quite firmly before he got going.

'Mr Martland, I try to ignore Christmas as much as I can and also I recently lost the grandmother who brought me up. She was a Strange Baptist, so I wasn't raised to think the worldly trappings of the season of importance in any case.'

'What was strange about her being a Baptist?' he asked, diverted.

'Nothing. Strange Baptists were a breakaway sect at the turn of the century, though there aren't that many of them left.' I glanced out of the window. 'Now, if you'll excuse me, your uncle and niece have just arrived in a golf buggy, so I'd better go and let them in, there's a biting wind out there.'

70

'No, wait,' he ordered, 'go and fetch him to the phone, so I can speak to him. I—'

'Call him yourself later, if you want to,' I interrupted and put the receiver down. Cut off in his prime again. This was getting to be a habit – but he was proving to be a most *irritating* man, especially that deep, rumbling voice: it was as disturbing as distant thunder!

Chapter 8: Deep Freeze

The new patient's leg is answering well to the penicillin but he teases me when I am changing his dressings and tries to make me laugh . . . and sometimes succeeds, despite my best attempts to keep a straight face.

January, 1945

'We thought we would call in and see how you were getting on,' Noël explained, 'though Becca stopped briefly on her way home and said you were doing fine. But I wanted to return some books to the library in any case. Jude doesn't mind my popping in and out, I've always had the run of the place. And Mo and Jim said they didn't mind in the least, either.'

'Of course, it's your family home, so you must come and go as you please,' I assured him.

'Thank you, m'dear,' he said, with his attractively lopsided smile, 'only of course, now I have had to give up driving the car, the golf buggy is very chilly and really not up to winter weather conditions.'

'I drove Grandpa up,' Jess said. 'I was bored and I like driving the buggy; only I'm not allowed to do it on my own.'

Seeing she was looking wistfully at my slice of fruit cake I said, 'Can I get you both some tea and perhaps a slice of cake? Mine has gone cold because your nephew just rang again, so I was going to make a fresh pot anyway.'

'Oh, Jude got through?' he asked. 'What a pity we were not here in time to speak to him.'

'I'm afraid he simply *had* to go. But I expect he'll phone you back later.'

'Very likely . . . but we don't want to disturb you if you are busy,' he said, with a look at the pile of papers next to the easy chair.

'Not at all, I was only going to look at some notes for a recipe book I'm compiling – *Cooking for House-Parties*. I've been collecting recipes and tips for years, but now I'm finally hoping to get it ready to send out to publishers in the New Year.'

'Do people have large house-parties any more? I remember them as a young man, and jolly good fun they were, too!' said Noël a little wistfully.

'Oh yes, you'd be surprised – but probably they're very different from the ones you knew.'

'I know Becca still gets invited to shooting and fishing ones,' he said. 'And the family have always gathered here at Old Place between Christmas and Twelfth Night, so *that* is a house-party too, I suppose.'

'I think your book needs a less boring title than *Cooking for House-Parties*,' Jess said frankly.

'That's just the working title, but if you can think of a better one, let me know.'

'I'm writing a vampire book, with lots of blood,' she confided.

'I expect there would be in a vampire book.'

'There wasn't a great deal, as I recall, in Bram Stoker's *Dracula*,' her grandfather said doubtfully.

'There will be in mine. I'm going to kill off all the girls at school I don't like – *horribly*.'

'Good idea – that sounds immensely satisfying,' I said.

Noël settled comfortably on the sofa in front of the fire. Jess came through to the kitchen with me and, while I brewed a fresh pot of tea and laid the tray with cups and saucers and the remains of my fast-vanishing fruit cake, fetched a carton of long-life orange juice from the lavish supply in the larder and opened it.

'Jude likes this with his breakfast.'

'Going by the ready meals in the freezer, he doesn't do much cooking, does he? There's lots of other food in there, but most of it looks as if it's been there for ages, especially the game.'

'I think he forgets to cook half the time, apart from breakfast. It's Aunt Becca who puts all the game and trout and stuff in the freezers – she's forever visiting friends and coming back with more than she knows what to do with. She gives it to Granny, too. Do you *like* rabbit?'

'When it's cooked properly.'

'I don't. I can't help thinking about how harmless and nice rabbits are.'

'Well, no-one's going to force you to eat one, are they?' I said with a smile. 'I could make you a rabbit you *would* like one day though – a chocolate blancmange one! There's a lovely Victorian glass mould in one of the cupboards and I'm dying to try it. You could come to tea, if your grandparents say it's all right.'

'Oh, they won't mind. What's blancmange?'

'A kind of flavoured milk jelly.'

'Is it like Angel Delight? Granny has some of that in the cupboard.'

'Sort of. You know, someone ought to eat up the game in the freezer, it's such a waste otherwise.'

'As long as it isn't me. Though actually, your cooking might be better than Granny's – her food is all a bit weird.'

'I expect she just cooks like she did early in her career and tastes have changed,' I said tactfully. 'By the way, the black stuff in those pinwheel sandwiches she gave me for lunch . . . I don't suppose you know what that was?'

'It's a heavily guarded secret. I call it minced rancid car tyre.'

'That's a pretty fair description,' I admitted.

'I know Granny carries on as if she does all the cooking herself,

74

but actually Edwina does most of it really,' Jess confided. 'That's the *real* reason why they always move into Old Place when she goes off to her relatives for Christmas and New Year. Goodness knows what Christmas dinner will be like this time!'

I felt another inconvenient pang of conscience, though why I should I can't imagine, since it's Jude Martland who ought to be having them, not me!

'You can help her with the cooking,' I suggested. 'I used to help my gran, that's what started me off thinking I wanted to become a chef.'

'She's very bossy and says she doesn't want little girls in the kitchen under her feet when she's busy, even though I'm nearly thirteen and way taller than she is! I help Grandpa with the washing up, instead.'

The tea was ready and I carried the tray into the sitting room, finding Noël half-asleep before the fire, though he woke up the instant the crockery rattled.

'Lovely to see the fire lit in here again,' he said, 'it seemed so cold and unwelcoming without it.'

'I thought it would air the house out – old houses seem to get dank and musty very quickly, don't they?'

'Yes, indeed. Of course, with only a week to go until Christmas Eve, this room would usually be decorated for Christmas by now, with the tree in the corner by the stairs and a kissing bough . . .' he said regretfully. 'All the decorations are in the attic, though Jude's mother used to make swags of greenery from the garden, she was very good at that sort of thing.'

'The attic is locked, as are one or two other rooms,' I said. 'That's fine, but do you have the keys in case there's an emergency, like a burst water pipe?'

'The attic isn't locked, it's just the door that's very stiff,' Jess said. 'I remember that from playing hide and seek last Christmas. When I went up there, no-one found me for ages.'

'That was because it was supposed to be out of bounds,' Noël

75

reminded her. 'But yes, I do have all the rest of the keys, including the one for the mill studio, just in case.'

'Oh good. I don't suppose for a minute I'll need them, I just like to know. I expect I'll only really use this room, apart from the kitchen wing – it has a lovely warm, homely feel to it, despite being so big.'

'Yes, it was always the heart of the house.' He sighed and his gaze rested on a black and white family group photograph that stood on one of the occasional tables. 'There were five of us children, you know, and now only Becca and I are left. Jacob was the eldest, but he was killed at Dunkirk, poor chap, and another brother, Edward, was badly wounded later. Alex – Jude's father – inherited, though he didn't marry until late in life. But they're all gone now, all gone . . .' He shook his head sadly. 'Alex passed away last January, after a long illness.'

'I noticed the house had some adaptations for an invalid, like the stairlift . . . and excuse me, but did you say one of your brothers was called Edward?' I asked.

'Yes, though we always called him Ned.'

I was startled by the revelation that there had indeed been a Ned Martland, a contemporary of Gran's – but surely this was just one more of those strange coincidences that life throws at you? I couldn't see how their paths could ever have crossed . . .

'He was a bit of a rip, but full of fun and mischief – Jude's younger brother, Guy, reminds me of him.' Noël shook his head with a rueful smile. 'There was no real harm in him, but he *was* the black sheep of the family, I suppose, whereas Guy has settled down very well lately – he's an international banker in London, you know.'

'He's settling down with Uncle Jude's ex-fiancée,' Jess pointed out. 'And *I* don't think Uncle Guy is very nice at all.'

'He is very naughty to tease you,' Noël said, 'but he doesn't mean any harm by it.'

Since Jess was at the age where your main wish in life is to

76

be totally invisible and anyone even *glancing* at you could be an agony, I thought Guy Martland sounded very insensitive and mean indeed! Just as objectionable, in his own way, as his brother Jude, in fact.

'I'm sure it was all for the best that Jude's fiancée broke the engagement, because she can't have been in love with him,' Noël said, 'and I am a firm believer in marriage being for life.'

'Yes, me too – and beyond,' I murmured absently, my mind still on Ned Martland.

'Guy and Coco – that's her silly name – just got engaged,' Jess said. 'It was in the paper and I think that's why Uncle Jude said he wasn't coming back from America until after Christmas.'

'Oh, but he already had the invitation to spend the holidays with friends after the event to mark the installation of his sculpture . . . Though perhaps you are partly right, Jess,' her grandfather conceded. 'I expect Guy would have thought nothing of turning up for a family Christmas despite everything, had Jude stayed at home.'

'They haven't spoken since last Christmas,' Jess explained. 'Jude invited Coco here to meet the family and she and Guy got *very* friendly. Uncle Jude was pretty grim.'

'I expect he would be!' I agreed, though going by the photographs I'd seen, and my brief conversations with him, he was *always* pretty grim.

'Then she and Jude had a big argument and Guy drove her home and that was it.'

'I don't feel that Guy behaved very well in the circumstances, even if there was a mutual attraction between him and Coco,' Noël said, looking troubled. 'It upset my brother, too, that there was a breach between his two sons and Jude thought it hastened his last illness.' He shook his head sadly. 'Not that Alex liked her very much – it was her first visit to Old Place and she made it clear she was expecting a much larger and grander house.'

'It seems pretty large and grand to me,' I said, surprised.

'Still, she won't have to live here if she marries Guy – and Jude will just have to forgive and forget.'

'I don't suppose she'll come here much anyway,' Jess said. 'She didn't seem to like being in the country at all and wouldn't go out except in the car, because she hadn't brought any shoes except stiletto heels, though she could have borrowed some wellies. *And* she's scared of horses and dogs. Granny says she's all fur coat and no knickers, and Guy could do better.'

I swallowed a sip of tea the wrong way and coughed, my eyes watering.

'I don't think you should repeat that phrase, really,' Noël said mildly.

'How on earth did she meet Jude in the first place?' I asked. 'It doesn't sound as if they had a lot in common.'

'She is a model and also, I believe, aspires to be an actress. Someone brought her to Jude's last big retrospective exhibition and introduced her. She's very, very pretty indeed, if your taste runs to fair women.'

'Uncle Jude's must, mustn't it?' Jess said.

'I suppose we do tend to be attracted to our opposites,' I suggested.

'You're very dark, so was *your* husband fair?'

'Jess, you really shouldn't ask people personal questions!'

'I don't mind – and yes, my husband had blond hair and blue eyes. His younger sister is my best friend and has the same colouring – she's *very* pretty too.'

How I'd longed to be small, blonde and cute when I was at school, rather than towering above everyone, even the boys! I'd been thin as a stick too, which had made me even more self-conscious – though actually I wasn't sure it was any better later when I filled out and men started to talk to my boobs instead of me . . . except Alan, of course.

'Well, I think we ought to be going!' Noël said, getting up.

'I'm walking down to the village tomorrow, to explore,' I told

78

him. 'I'll call in at the lodge to see if there's anything you'd like me to bring back from the shop.'

'I'll ask Tilda,' he promised. 'You are very kind!'

It seemed to me that, far from being isolated and alone at Old Place, I was going to be inundated with visitors!

The day had gone by in a flash, so I went to put the dried beet to soak in a bucket for Lady's bedtime mash and then went out with it and some of Billy's goat munchies to lure them back into the stable.

Thanks to a bit of timely advice from Becca, I knew that if I was carrying the bucket then Lady would simply follow me into her loosebox and Billy would come with her, and so it was. Then I shut them both up all cosily for the night.

After my conversation with Noël, I abandoned my cookbook notes and brought down Gran's journal and read on steadily into the evening. I was again tempted to flick forward and see if I could spot any mention of Ned Martland, but I'd been enjoying all the details of Gran's life as she slowly came out of her shell under Hilda and Pearl's influence and I didn't want to rush it: this was a girl whose idea of a night of dissipation was a trip to the cinema!

I finished that journal and read the first page or two of the next in bed before I went to sleep. By then Gran had started referring to the new patient as 'N.M'! It occurred to me that there was a very natural way her path might have crossed with the Old Place Ned Martland – and after what Noël had said about his brother being a black sheep, I'll be really worried for her if it turns out to be him.

But I suppose even if it is, then given Gran's upbringing and nature, it could only have been some kind of *Brief Encounter*!

Chapter 9: Daggers

Hilda and Pearl kindly warned me that N.M. was a flirt and not to take anything he said seriously, but he was very sincere and sweet when I told him about Tom and my intention to devote my life to nursing. He is kind when he is being serious and easy to talk to.

February, 1945

Next morning the wind had died down a bit, but everything was thickly furred with frost. But then, it's been growing steadily colder since I got here and, according to the radio, the odds on it being a white Christmas were getting shorter and shorter by the minute.

The house was already starting to warm through now I'd lit the fire, though, and I was keeping it going by a lavish application of logs from the cellar. The place will soon feel cosy, despite its size.

After breakfast (which I ate with the latest of Gran's journals propped in front of me) I let Lady and Billy out. Billy ignored the open gate and jumped straight over the fence like a . . . well, I was going to say *goat*!

I hung a filled haynet on the rail, high enough so that Lady wouldn't catch her feet in it when it was empty (another bit of advice from the invaluable Becca!) and broke a thin skin of ice on the trough, before tidying up the loosebox.

Merlin had wandered off up the paddock, which I thought was probably exercise enough for the morning, so I went back in and prepared to give the sitting room the sort of cleaning my Gran always referred to as 'a good bottoming', something it clearly hadn't had for quite some time.

It's part of the Homebodies remit that we keep the rooms of the house that we actually use neat and clean, it's just that the houses aren't usually quite on this scale!

I don't enjoy the process of cleaning, but I *do* love a nice clean room, so I suppose you could call that job satisfaction. Although it's not in the same league as providing an excellent dinner for twenty-five people with mixed dietary requirements every day for a fortnight with effortless expertise. Now *that's* satisfying on a creative level, too – I sometimes think cooking is a kind of ephemeral art form.

Anyway, by the time I'd vacuumed the pattern back into existence on the lovely old carpet, mopped the bit of stone floor around the edges, removed spider's webs from every corner and polished the brass fender, fireguard and furniture (and even the front door knocker, while I was about it), it all looked wonderful – and *I* looked a grubby mess and had to go and shower again.

By this time it was late morning, so I put on my warm, down-filled jacket and set out for the village with Merlin, since he was desperate to come with me. The poor old thing seems to have attached himself to me already, but life must have been very confusing for him lately.

As well as exploring, I wanted to see if the shop had the extra supplies I had on my list and anything Tilda might want, so I hoped there would be something to tie Merlin to outside it. I suppose I should have taken the car really, only I like to walk and my rucksack is very roomy.

Noël insisted I went into the lodge for a moment, even though

Merlin seemed to take up a lot of space in the small, cluttered room, and when he wagged his tail he nearly took out the Christmas tree and a snowglobe. I felt a bit like Alice in Wonderland when she'd drunk the get-bigger potion, myself.

Tilda was reclining on the sofa, resplendent today in an orange satin blouse and a long black skirt, though I thought she looked a little tired under the lavish makeup. Jess was sitting on the floor doing a vampire jigsaw on the coffee table, the lid with its gory picture propped up in front of her.

'There aren't enough corners,' she said by way of greeting.

'Life's like that sometimes,' I commiserated. 'Or sometimes there are too many.'

She gave me a look from under her fringe.

'Have you tried the phone up at the house today? Only you'll find it keeps going dead, because of the wind,' Tilda said.

'The wind?'

'Blows the wires about, but it's much worse than usual,' Noël said. 'We hadn't noticed until George Froggat – he owns Hill Farm further up the lane – told us. One of the poles is leaning at an angle between here and the village, so the wire is practically down. He called BT and they say it'll be after Christmas before they can get someone up here to look at it, but those poles have wanted replacing the last two years and more.'

'That's a nuisance,' I said, but thinking that at least it might spare me one or two of Jude Martland's irritating calls!

'It will be if it falls right down and cuts us off completely,' he agreed. 'Jess's mobile works, but not terribly well.'

'And only if I walk down the lane towards the village,' Jess said. 'Uncle Jude phoned when we got back yesterday and the phone was a bit dodgy even then, wasn't it, Grandpa?'

'Very, I could only hear what he was saying intermittently.'

'I suppose he was fretting about Lady again?'

'Her name *did* crop up,' he admitted. 'But then he said something about you coping, so I expect he has realised that everything

82

will be absolutely fine. The line went dead after that and he didn't try and ring back again.'

'Anyone would think we would all fall apart without his lordship home,' Tilda scoffed. 'But even when he is here, he spends most of his time shut up in his studio.'

'Did you want me to get you anything from the village?' I offered.

'George brings us the paper every morning, that's why he stopped by, but you could fetch us a bottle of sherry from the pub,' Tilda said. 'In fact, you should have lunch there; they do a good ploughman's or a pot pie.'

'Do they? That would be nice,' I said, remembering that I hadn't had lunch yet and breakfast seemed an awfully long time ago, 'but I'll have to do it another day because I wouldn't be able to take Merlin in.'

'Oh, the Daggers won't mind.'

'The *who*?'

'Daggers. The Dagger family have always had the Auld Christmas. In fact, Nicholas Dagger plays the part of Auld Man Christmas in the Revels on Twelfth Night,' Noël said. 'Jude is Saint George and I used to be the Dragon, only I've had to hand the part on to a younger man.'

'I'm sure Holly isn't interested in our local customs, you old fool,' Tilda said.

'I think they sound fascinating,' I said politely, though I've never been a great one for Morris dancing and the like, and if this one was all Christmassy too, then that took the icing and the cherry off what was already a quite uninteresting cake.

'It's a pity you will miss it,' Noël said.

'Yes, I'll be leaving that morning, because your nephew will be on his way home from the airport. Now, I'd better get going.'

'Can I come down to the village with you?' asked Jess. 'In fact, can I come to lunch at the pub with you, too?'

'Well, I—' I began, hesitantly, glancing at her grandparents.

'Not if you don't want her to,' Noël told me.

'I'm afraid she is having a very boring holiday here in the lodge this year,' Tilda said, 'but that is no reason why she should impose herself on you if you don't feel like company.'

I didn't really mind and, even if I had, it would have been impossible to say so. I just hoped they were right about the pub letting in dogs. Jess went off to get her coat, which was of course black, and Tilda made her put on a beanie hat and gloves. Then, to her complete disgust, she handed her a wicker basket shaped like a coracle in which reposed three greaseproof-wrapped parcels.

'Cheese straws,' confided Jess once we were walking down the lane. 'Granny keeps making them because they're dead easy, but they don't taste of anything much, especially cheese. They're for the oldies in the almshouses.'

'Oh yes, that's the old Nanny—'

'*Everyone* calls her Old Nan – she's ninety something.'

'And the retired vicar?'

'Richard, Richard Sampson. He's pretty old too, but he walks miles, though he's a bit absent-minded and sometimes forgets to turn around and come back. People phone up Uncle Jude from miles away and he has to go and collect him in the car.'

'Then let's hope the weather keeps him at home until your uncle gets back! The other house is Henry the gardener's isn't it?'

'Yes, but he's pretty active too and although he's retired he's always up at Old Place.'

'Yes, the walled garden and the generator do seem to be his chosen stamping grounds. He sounded a bit territorial about them.'

'His daughter lives in the village and keeps an eye on him – she works in the Weasel Pot farm shop in summer. But Old Nan and Richard haven't got any relatives left, they're *way* too old, so they're used to coming up to the house for Christmas Day dinner. I'm not sure what they're going to do this year – I'm not even sure I've got it into their heads yet that it isn't going to happen.'

I had another of those inconvenient pangs of conscience – which are so unfair, since none of this was my fault in the least!

'Now Jude has gone away I wish Edwina, Granny and Grandpa's housekeeper, were still here, because I think Granny's Christmas lunch will be a major disaster,' Jess said frankly. '*And* she's overdoing things. I don't really think she's up to it.'

'Mr Martland's absence does seem to have made it very diffi-cult: selfishly flouncing off when he must know that everyone depended on him!'

'Yes, he's a selfish pig,' she agreed and sighed. 'Even having Christmas dinner with Mo and Jim was something to look forward to, but now everything is *so* boring I was even glad to see Aunt Becca yesterday.'

'Don't you like her?' I asked, surprised. 'I thought she was very nice.'

'I like her, but all she ever talks about is horses, fishing and shooting things and she didn't even stop more than a couple of minutes because the wind was too cold to leave Nutkin tied up outside.'

'She was a great help telling me what to do with Lady. A horse is quite a responsibility when you're not used to looking after them.'

'She said you were competent and capable and she didn't see why there should be any problems.'

'No, I don't either, though it's good to know I can get hold of someone who knows a lot more about horses than I do if a problem comes up.'

'Aunt Becca said Mo and Jim left you the huge turkey and everything for the Christmas dinner we were having,' Jess remarked with a sideways look at me from under her fringe. 'Couldn't you cook it instead, Holly?'

I was taken aback by her directness. 'You haven't been talking to your Uncle Jude, have you?'

'No, it just seemed like a good idea.'

'Well, it might do to you, but it's not what I bargained for when I agreed to take this job! I do house-sitting so I can have a rest from cooking the rest of the year,' I told her firmly, and her face fell. 'And remember I said that I don't celebrate Christmas anyway? In fact, I do my best to ignore it.'

'Oh, that's right, it's against your religion.'

'Strictly speaking, I don't actually have a religion any more,' I admitted, 'but the grandparents who brought me up only celebrated the religious aspects of it – extra chapel services and readings from the gospels – so it's not something I really miss.'

'You mean when you were little there were no presents, or a Christmas stocking or anything?' she demanded, turning stunned brown eyes up towards me.

'No, there was nothing like that, and no big blow-out special dinner either, though Gran was a good plain cook. Her raised pork pie was *legendary*.'

Jess was unimpressed by pork pies in the face of my other childhood deprivations. 'No tree, or decorations, or Father Christmas . . . ?'

'No, though I secretly used to exchange presents with my best friend, Laura – I did a paper round, so I had some money of my own. But when I got married my husband loved all that side of Christmas, so we celebrated it just like everyone else. We'd buy the biggest tree we could tie on top of the car and load it down with lights and baubles; hang garlands and Chinese lanterns and make each other surprise stockings full of silly bits and pieces . . . it was fun.'

But then, everything I'd done with Alan had been fun . . .

'Then why did you stop?'

'Because he died,' I said shortly. 'It was just before Christmas and there didn't seem any point in celebrating it at all after that.'

'What did he die of?' she asked with the directness of the young. 'And was it ages ago?'

'It was an accident . . . eight years ago on Monday.'

This was an anniversary I usually marked quietly and alone, though the way things were going, that would not be an option here unless I stopped answering the door and took the phone off the hook.

'What sort of accident?'

'He fell through the ice on a frozen lake.'

'I keep thinking my parents are going to fall through the ice in Antarctica and a killer whale or something will eat them,' she confessed.

'Oh, I shouldn't think so, I'm sure they know what they're doing.'

'Yes, but Mum tends to keep walking backwards with the camera.'

That *did* sound a bit dodgy.

'A lion nearly got her once – I saw it. If they're not home during the holidays I usually fly out to wherever they're working, only I couldn't really do that this time.'

'No, I don't think it would be very easy to get to Antarctica,' I agreed. 'By the time you got there it would probably be time to turn around and come back, too. You go to boarding school, don't you?'

'Yes and I quite like it really – I've got lots of friends.'

'I used to get bullied because I never fitted in and I was always taller than my classmates, even the boys. There was a group of girls who made my life a misery – I was really self-conscious about my height.'

'I get that a bit sometimes, but we all have a sixth-form mentor we can talk to and they sort it out for us.'

'Sounds like a good idea. I wish we'd had something like that.'

We'd arrived at the village by now and Jess decided to offload the cheese straws first, starting with Old Nan, who when she

87

answered the door was the size of a gnome and wrapped in a crocheted Afghan shawl. On her feet were fuzzy tartan slippers with pompoms and a turn-over collar that fitted snugly round her ankles.

Jess introduced us and said, 'We're not stopping, Nan, because we're going to the shop and then the pub for lunch, but Granny sent you some more cheese straws.'

Old Nan took the parcel without much enthusiasm. 'A body could do with something a bit tastier from time to time,' she grumbled.

'Well, you should try living at the lodge – it's all lumpy mashed potato, tinned rice pudding and not much else at the moment,' Jess said. 'At least you all get to go over to Great Mumming tomorrow in a minibus for the WI Senior Citizens Christmas dinner so that will be a change, won't it?'

'If the weather holds, because there's snow on the way. Not that it's like dinner up at Old Place anyway. They use those gravy granules and tinned peas, you know.'

'So does Granny. But I hope you're right about the snow, because I've never seen *really* deep snow.'

'Be careful what you wish for. And be off with you, if you won't come in, I'm letting all the warm air out standing here like this.' And she shuffled backwards and closed the door firmly.

'She gets a bit grumpy when her rheumatism is playing up,' Jess explained, stepping over a low dividing wall and knocking on the next door.

The retired vicar, Richard Sampson, was a small, wiry, white-haired man with vague cloud-soft grey eyes and an absent expression. He came to the door with his finger in his book to mark the page, and seemed to struggle to place Jess for a minute, let alone take in her introduction to me. Then a smile of great charm transformed him and he shook hands. Unlike Old Nan, he seemed genuinely pleased about the cheese straws.

'He forgets to eat and I'm sure he hardly ever cooks,' Jess

explained, leading the way to the third and final door. 'He does have something hot in the pub occasionally, though, if Henry calls for him on the way there.'

'Speak of the devil,' I muttered, because the old gardener had presumably heard the knocking next door and come out from curiosity already.

'Afternoon,' he said to me and then added to Jess, 'if those are more of Tilda's blasted burnt offerings, then you can keep them!'

'These aren't burnt,' Jess said. 'And if you don't want them, just give them to Richard, he seems keen on them. Oh, and remind him about the Senior Citizens lunch tomorrow and don't let the minibus go without him.' She thrust the package at him. 'Right, now we've got other things to do. Bye, Henry.'

'Women!' Henry muttered, closing the door.

We passed the little church in its neat graveyard. Next to it was a dark-green painted corrugated iron building, little more than a shed, that according to a sign was the parish hall, but the rest of the village was across a small stone bridge over the stream, where we were nearly flattened by a big, glossy four-wheel-drive vehicle taking it too fast.

It stopped and reversed, nearly getting us again, and the side window slid down to reveal a pair of annoyed, puzzled faces.

'Where's the Great Mumming road?' demanded the driver, who was shaven-headed and seemed to have been designed without a neck, since his chin just ran away into his chest. 'The SatNav says we can turn down to the motorway from there.'

'This little lane can't be it, can it?' said the woman next to him, resting a handful of blue talons along the window. 'We must have missed the turn.'

'No, this is the road to Great Mumming – but only if you're a sheep,' Jess said. 'That's why people keep following their SatNavs.'

'Are you being cheeky?' the man said belligerently.

'No, she's simply being truthful,' I said quickly. 'Apparently it

89

isn't much more than a track so the SatNav has an error. You'd be better off turning round and going back down the way you came.'

'Left at the bottom of the hill and you'll get to Great Mumming,' Jess put in.

'Oh, bollocks, what a total waste of time!' he said.

Without a word of thanks the window slid up, the car shot forward, turned noisily in front of the church, and then streaked past us going the other way again. But we were ready for it and had run across the bridge and onto the pavement.

'Charming,' I said.

'People following the SatNavs *are* just like sheep,' Jess said. 'At least most of the lorry drivers take one look at the lane down by the junction and realise there's a mistake, though once one did turn into it and got stuck on the first bend. They had an awful job getting it out, Grandpa says, and had to rebuild a bit of the dry-stone wall.'

The small shop next to the shuttered Merry Kettle café had overflowed onto the pavement with a stand of fruit and vegetables, bags of potatoes and carrots and netting bags of firewood.

'I love this shop! Mrs Comfort's got everything.'

'It certainly looks like it,' I agreed. 'What shall I do with Merlin?'

'There's a hook in the wall to tie him to and a bowl of water,' she pointed out. 'There, under the table.'

There was, too, and Merlin, tethered, sat down on a piece of flattened cardboard with a look of patient resignation. I think he'd been there before.

Inside, the shop proved to be a Tardis, since it went back quite a way into what had probably originally been the second room of the cottage. In America I think they call this sort of shop a Variety Store and there was certainly an infinite variety of stuff crammed into this one.

Mrs Comfort was plump, with a round face and high

cheekbones that turned her eyes to slits when she smiled – rather attractive, in a Persian cat sort of way. Her straight mouse-brown hair was pulled back tightly and clamped to her head with a large, crystal-studded plastic comb.

'Hi, Mrs Comfort, this is Holly, who's minding Old Place for Uncle Jude over Christmas.'

'I thought that couple were back again, that have been before?' she said, looking at me curiously as I ducked my head to avoid the wellingtons hanging by strings from the beams.

'They had to leave because their daughter had her baby much too early,' I explained.

'Shame – hope the poor little mite is all right?'

'I don't know, they haven't told us.'

'Well now, what can I get you?' she asked, a hopeful glint in her eye.

'Do you have newspapers?'

'There's a *Mail* left, but that's the last. I've had three lots of lost drivers in already, and they've all bought one. That SatNav's good for trade!'

'We just saw another one,' Jess told her, 'but they didn't hang about after we told them they'd gone wrong.'

'I expect there's more of them in the pub – I sometimes think the Daggers must have paid the SatNav people to send cars up here, they do a much better winter trade in coffees and lunches now than they used to.'

'It's an ill wind that blows nobody any good,' I said and she agreed fervently.

She had most of the things on my list, including dried fruit so I could bake another cake to replace the one that had vanished. I bought more flour too, because if I was getting daily visitors, I might as well offer them a seasonal mince pie or two, and the Chirks had left several enormous jars of mincemeat.

While I was buying all this Jess had expended much time and thought over the line of sweet jars and now purchased a supply

91

of Fairy Satins, triangular humbug-shaped sweets in alarmingly bright colours, and a large bag of wine gums.

'And can I see proof that you're over twenty-one, young lady?' asked Mrs Comfort.

'Ha, ha, very funny,' said Jess. 'You know there isn't a drop of alcohol in them.'

'How's the book coming along, dear?' asked Mrs Comfort, weighing out Satins on the scales and tipping them into a paper bag, which she twisted at the corners.

'I'm on Chapter Six now and the vampires are having a midnight feast.'

'That sounds like fun.'

'Not for the girls they're feasting on – but they deserve it,' Jess said.

'Mrs Comfort is a poet,' she confided to me as we left the shop and collected Merlin. 'There are lots of writers here: me, Mrs Comfort, Grandpa with his Christmas book and Granny's cookery books. Richard has written a couple of pamphlets too, on the Revels and the red horse.'

'Little Mumming is clearly a hive of literary activity!' I said, impressed.

Chapter 10: Wrung

*I find myself looking forward to seeing N every day now,
which makes me feel disloyal to Tom's memory, so that I was
hardly able to meet his father's eye when I went to the chapel.
But soon he will be well enough to leave and things will be
as they were.*

February, 1945

The Auld Christmas was a smallish hostelry with a large barn
behind it and a cobbled forecourt on which a few vehicles were
parked. Now I was closer I could see that the old man on the
sign seemed to be wearing a mistletoe and oak-leaf crown and
carrying a club, but it was hard to tell, because the coats of
varnish protecting it had turned it the colour of Brown Windsor
soup.

'Are you sure about the dog?' I asked as we went in.

'Yes, come on,' Jess urged me, pushing open an inner door to
the left of the passage.

We stepped down into a dark cavern, lit at one end by a
roaring open fire and at the other by the dull glow of a fruit
machine. Behind the counter was a buxom, red-haired woman
of about forty-five and a couple of obvious locals were sitting
near the fire, eating bread and cheese. An even more obvious
pair of strangers were eating at a table nearby and they looked
at Merlin with acute disapproval.

'Do you mind the dog?' I asked the woman behind the bar. 'Only Mr Martland said—'

'Oh, we know Merlin, Jude brings him down here all the time and he's better behaved than most of our customers,' she said, then shot a look at the muttering strangers and added loudly, 'and them that don't like it can go in the public bar next door or take themselves off.'

The complaining voices abruptly ceased.

The woman wiped her hand on a pink-spotted, duck-egg blue apron and held it out to me: 'Nancy Dagger. My husband Will's down the cellar, changing kegs and that's his old dad over there near the fire.'

A tiny man with a long, snowy beard suddenly leaned forward out of a hooded chair, the like of which I had never seen before, and said in a high, piping voice, 'That's right – I'm Auld Man Christmas, I am!' Then he laughed wheezily, like a pair of small musical bellows. 'Heh, heh, heh!'

'Take no notice,' Nancy said. 'We know you're looking after Old Place instead of those Chirks what have been here before, Henry told us all about it last night. But I've never known Martlands to be away from Old Place at Christmas before!' And she shook her head. Then she gave me a sharp look and added, 'But then, I suppose you're family?'

'Not at all, I just work for the same agency as Jim and Mo.'

'I thought you had the look of a Martland, being tall and dark and all,' she insisted, eyeing me closely – but then, it *was* gloomy in there.

'No, I'm not related to them – and Mr Martland will definitely be back for Twelfth Night, because I'm due to leave that morning.'

'He should be here now, that's how it's always been,' she said. 'People round here don't much like change.'

'It's because he argued with Guy and didn't want to see him,' Jess told her. 'But I think it's mean of him not to think of the rest of us.'

'Well, talking won't mend matters,' Nancy said. 'What can I get you ladies? Are you having lunch?'

I ordered a hot pot pie and, after much deliberation, so did Jess. 'Pies aren't my favourite thing,' she explained, 'but I'm getting a lot of cold food from Granny, so I might as well have something hot while I can.'

'I expect the old folk will have a bit of a struggle to cope this year, poor things,' Nancy said. 'I can make you a nice cup of drinking chocolate, how about that? Squirty cream on top.'

'Oh yes, that would be lovely, thank you!' Jess said. 'Oh, and Grandpa gave me some money to pay for Holly's lunch, too.'

'That was a kind thought,' I said, touched – and also still feeling uneasily and illogically guilty again after Nancy's remarks.

I did have all the food for Christmas dinner and cooking it wouldn't be a problem . . . so was I now obstinately punishing Noël, Tilda and Jess, simply because Jude had got my back up? Was I being as selfish as he was?

How much of a hardship would it really be, to put my personal inclinations on one side and invite them for one meal?

It was no use, I was simply going to *have* to do it!

I could look on it as research and write that Christmas chapter for my book, after all!

When we got back to the lodge I handed over the sherry, then said, 'I've been thinking things over and you know, it seems such a pity to waste all that lovely Christmas food that the Chirks left behind, because I won't be able to eat it all. So, even though it's very short notice, I wondered if you could possibly all come for dinner on Christmas Day with me anyway?'

'Oh *yes*!' exclaimed Jess, bouncing up and down in her large, black lace-up boots.

'But you don't celebrate Christmas, m'dear, so surely that would be an imposition?' Noël asked doubtfully.

95

'I don't have to *celebrate* it, just *cook* it,' I said brightly. 'Anyway, I'm sure it will make a nice change.'

'Well, in that case . . .' he said, glancing at his wife.

'It's very kind of you,' Tilda said. 'Of course, I *was* fully prepared to do a festive lunch, but I do see your point about not wasting the Chirks' food.'

'Lovely – then that's settled,' I said. 'If Mr Martland gets through to you again on the phone, will you assure him that Lady and Merlin are both fine, if he is still fussing about them, and tell him of the change of plan? He did suggest yesterday that I carried on with the Chirks' invitation, so he can't have any objection.'

'Oh, did he? How kind and thoughtful of the dear boy,' Noël said.

'Yes, wasn't it just?' I replied, slightly sourly.

'Of course it will be a lot more work for you than you bargained for originally,' he said. 'I expect you usually charge quite a lot for cooking, don't you?'

'Yes, but actually you'll be doing me a favour, because I still have to write the chapter on Christmas house-party catering for my book, so it'll be good research.'

'I may well be able to give you some useful tips for your book, too,' Tilda said graciously, and I thanked her.

'I think you *should* be paid a little more – I'll speak to Jude about it,' Noël insisted.

'No, please don't – I'm sure I'll love doing it and of course I'll bill him for any extra food I have to buy.'

Noël rubbed his gnarled hands together gleefully. 'Well, well – a Martland family Christmas celebration after all – how splendid! And I include *you* in the family now, m'dear, because you already feel like one of us.'

'Nancy Dagger thought she was a Martland,' Jess said.

'Only because I'm tall and dark,' I said with a smile. 'It's quite gloomy in the pub, isn't it?'

'I expect that is it,' he agreed, 'and by the way, do call Jude by his first name. There is no need to be formal when we are going to be seeing such a lot of each other.'

'But I'm not going to be seeing anything at all of Jude,' I pointed out. 'Though if the telephone works, I suppose I'll *hear* a lot more.'

'Do call him Jude – he isn't one to stand on formality,' Tilda said. 'The artistic type, you know.'

'Not really, the most artistic I ever get is cake decorating . . . and that's a point, because the Chirks didn't leave a Christmas cake. I'd better get back and start one. Thank goodness I just bought more dried fruit and candied peel!'

'It is too late in the day and it won't taste right,' Tilda objected. 'But I have a Dundee cake in a tin that Old Nan gave us, so I could bring that.'

'No, it's fine, I have a last-minute recipe where you steep the fruit in spirits for a couple of days before making it and it really tastes rather good. If I do that today, it can have a good long soak.'

'Oh great,' said Jess. 'And you were going to make mince pies anyway, you said.'

'Yes, those too. Would you mind if I borrowed this basket, Tilda? Only I bought much more than I expected. Jess was a huge help carrying everything back, though – she had the heavy rucksack.'

'Good girl,' Noël said.

'*And* I'll come and help you put the decorations up,' Jess offered.

'Decorations?' I echoed, not having thought any further than food, drink and the chore of cleaning the dining room for Christmas Day lunch.

'Yes, all the decorations are in the attic, and there's holly and ivy in the woods for the taking.'

'I – hadn't thought that far yet,' I hedged. 'Let me make a start on the baking first.'

'Okay, and then we'll do it,' she persisted. 'There's a couple of trunks of amazing old clothes in the attic you might like to see, too . . . though I'm too old for dressing up now, really.'

'Oh . . . well, we'll see.'

Tilda, suddenly looking much more alert and bright-eyed, swung her legs off the sofa and slid her feet into a pair of improbably tiny black velvet high-heeled slippers, edged with waving fronds of pink marabou. 'Now, what would you like us to bring? We have a lovely big box of luxury crackers – and Noël has the keys to the cellar, of course, so he can find us something decent to drink.'

'If you're sure Mr – I mean *Jude* – won't mind?'

'Not at all, he's the most generous of souls.'

I hadn't seen much sign of anything except selfishness yet, but perhaps, as well as hidden cellars, the unknown Jude had hidden depths too?

But as far as I was concerned, they could stay hidden: I'd never before liked a man less just on the sound of his voice! And now, because of him, instead of spending the anniversary of Alan's death in quiet contemplation, I would be gearing up for a feast.

I got up. 'Well, if you'll excuse me, I'd better get back. I have a lot to do.'

Merlin retired to his basket by the Aga, exhausted, and watched me with his bright amber eyes while I listed all the things I needed to do before Christmas Day.

I'd been working on it all the way up the drive – not only deciding on the menu (traditional), starting a cake and getting the large ham I had spotted out of the freezer to slowly defrost so I could cook it, but also finding the formal cutlery and crockery . . . *and* cleaning the dining room and downstairs cloakroom, too.

At least I'd already done the sitting room!

I would ignore the bit about decorations. Jess could come and put them up, if she really wanted to, though it hardly seemed worth it for one day.

I found a huge mixing bowl in one of the cupboards and into it went the dried fruit and chopped peel I'd bought that day, bulked out with some sultanas and a packet of slivered almonds (only a month out of date) from the store cupboard.

Into the mix went the drained and chopped contents of a jar of cocktail cherries (these, tiny silverskin onions and olives seemed to be well stocked in the larder, among the pickles and preserves), and the brandy from the decanter in the dining room, eked out with a bit of rum.

Then I covered the bowl with cling film and put it on a shelf in the larder, before ticking that task off my increasingly extensive to-do list.

Advance organisation is the absolute *key* to successful catering for large parties – I make that plain on the very first page of my book!

It wasn't a huge surprise to me when Jude rang just after I got in from giving Lady her warm mash and Billy a distracting handful of goat biscuits, and shutting the two of them in for the night. The wind had dropped, letting a few flakes of snow float idly down like feathers, so presumably the floppy phone lines weren't blowing about.

'Jude Martland,' he announced brusquely, as if I hadn't already guessed who it would be.

'Lady's fine – she's just had her mash and she's snugly bolted in for the night with Billy,' I assured him, before he could ask. This time I was determined I wouldn't let his autocratic manner annoy me, but remain my usual calm, professional self. 'And Merlin had his arthritis tablet with his breakfast and I've just given him a good brushing – which he badly needed, by the way.'

'Oh . . . right.' He sounded slightly disconcerted. 'That wasn't actually what I was going to say. I've just spoken to Noël and Tilda – the line was too bad to hear a word earlier.'

'I know, it was a bit windy.'

'I understand you've agreed to do what I asked and cook Christmas lunch for the family?'

'Yes, but only because I was in an impossible situation and there was nothing else I could do. But it was *your* responsibility to look after everyone, not mine to try and pick up the pieces after you'd swanned off in a huff.'

'I did *not* swan off in a huff! And anyway, it's no business of yours why I decided to spend Christmas over here – nor can I see why you're making such a fuss about laying on Christmas dinner, when everything has been provided for you by the Chirks and you're a cook anyway!'

'Chef,' I said icily, though normally I don't mind being called by either title. 'And you obviously have *no* conception of the amount of work involved – not just preparing, cooking and clearing up dinner, but cleaning your filthy dining room and the downstairs cloakroom, which looks as if mud wrestlers have had a bout in there.'

'Then get what's-her-name – Sharon – to help,' he said shortly.

'You've forgotten – she's resigned.'

'Oh yes . . . Well, it's not *that* bad, is it? You're exaggerating! A quick run-over with a duster and the Hoover . . .'

'Look, I'm used to keeping the parts of the house I'm using clean and tidy – though even then they don't usually need a total deep-clean – but that's *all* I'm contracted to do, other than look after the animals! Conversely, when I'm doing house-party cooking, my clients don't expect me to do anything except produce delicious meals – and my charges for that are *extremely* high!'

'Oh, I see! I suppose that's what this is really all about, trying to get a lot more money out of me?'

'No, it isn't – and you couldn't *afford* my prices,' I snapped.

'According to that boss of yours at Homebodies, I'm going to be paying you double house-sitting rates anyway, so at this rate it would probably be cheaper to send them out to a good restaurant in a taxi,' he mused gloomily, 'except that they wouldn't go. They seem to think that you invited them out of the kindness of your heart – they've no idea how very cold and mercenary you are, Mrs Brown.'

'I'm not in the least cold and mercenary, I simply resent being put in the position of picking up the pieces of the mess you left after you walked away from your responsibilities. And what about the elderly people in the almshouses who usually spend the day here, too?'

'I sent them a Christmas hamper each,' he said indignantly. '*And* Henry.'

'Big of you, Mr Martland!'

'You know, I think you could start calling me Jude, now we're on insulting terms,' he suggested. 'Holly certainly suits *you*: spiky!'

'And you're objectionable and overbearing. And don't you think you're making a lot of unfounded assumptions about someone you've never met?'

'Well, aren't you?'

'No, I'm basing my opinion of you on hard evidence. But believe it or not, my only reason for agreeing to do the cooking was that I like your aunt and uncle and Jess and felt sorry for them – Tilda's really too frail to cope alone. But think what you want. Meanwhile I don't think we've anything further to say to each other. Good night – *Jude*.'

'Don't you *dare* put the phone down on me again—' he growled, just as I did exactly that thing.

It rang again almost instantly, but I ignored it and then later, when I was going to ring Laura, it was dead as a dodo.

Chapter 11: Slightly Tarnished

*Today I asked N what his home was like and he said it was
an old house up in the hills – in fact, just below one of the
beacons. So I said, was it Rivington Pike, because I remember
a Sunday school day trip there as a girl but he laughed and
said no, much smaller than that and the little stone tower on
the hill – nothing much to look at.*

February, 1945

Last night I lay in bed reading Gran's journals late into the night
again, more and more convinced that N.M. would turn out to
be the Ned Martland she had loved and lost – and one and the
same as the black sheep of Old Place and therefore closely related
to the obnoxious Jude. The description of his home was the
clincher.

By some amazing coincidence Fate had directed me here – but
then, they say truth is always stranger than fiction.

I could tell she was increasingly fascinated by him (and he had
quickly become simply 'N', so presumably they were now on first-
name terms), but he sounded like a hardened flirt to me. Poor,
innocent, chapel-bred Gran wouldn't have stood a chance . . .

However, since she then spent two sleep-inducing pages on
pious reflections about the state of the world before the next
entries, maybe she would prove entirely unassailable.

There was a light sprinkling of snow when I went out to the

stables, but, remembering what Becca had said, I put Lady and her smelly little friend out in the paddock anyway, where she immediately started to paw the snow from the grass as she grazed.

I am quite getting into a routine now, and soon had the loosebox mucked out and freshly laid with new straw ready for the evening. The exercise made me glow, so I expect it did me good. After that Merlin and I took a little walk up to the red horse, which was actually now white like everything else, though you could still see the bumps and hollows of its outline.

I found a sheltered spot behind some gorse bushes and rang Laura on my mobile. She'd just got back from dropping the children at her mother's house for the day, to give her a rest.

I asked her how she was and she seemed to be blooming, as she always was during pregnancy.

'I hope mine goes as well, when I follow plan A in spring,' I said. 'I thought I could cook all summer to get some money in, and then retire until the baby has arrived. Assuming it works, of course – there's no guarantee it will at my age.'

'Haven't you met any nice men up there? I was hoping you might, and give up the whole mad AI thing,' she asked hopefully.

'Yes – Noël Martland's lovely, but he's ancient and married. And I suppose you could say I've met Jude Martland via the phone, but I'm *so* glad I'll have left before he gets back, because he's selfish, overbearing, autocratic . . . quite horrible! I think all he really cares about are his horse and dog.'

'You seem to have gathered a lot about him from a couple of phone calls,' she said, amused.

'We argue every time – he's quite insufferable. He's got a really deep voice, too, and sort of *rumbles* at me down the phone.'

'What, one of those knicker-quiveringly deep voices?' she asked with interest. 'The kind that vibrate down your spine and back up again?'

'Laura!' I exclaimed, then laughed. 'But, yes, it does and I suppose it *would* be quite sexy if he wasn't being so rude to me. And unfortunately I just can't seem to stop saying horrid things back, which isn't like me at all: normally I manage to keep a professional relationship going, whatever the provocation. But it isn't just his calls that make me dislike him, it's also seeing how his actions have affected everyone here.'

And I told her how he'd abandoned his duty to look after his family and the elderly people in the village and taken himself off in a fit of pique, after he saw the engagement announcement between his brother and his former fiancée.

'I expect he was so upset he didn't think it through,' she suggested.

'Perhaps not, but once he'd had time to think he could have come back, couldn't he? And then he seemed to assume that because the Chirks had invited his aunt and uncle to Christmas dinner, I should be happy to do the same . . . and actually,' I added, 'I am.'

'What, cooking Christmas dinner for his family?'

'Yes, the Chirks left an enormous turkey and Christmas pudding anyway. And then Tilda Martland is so frail I don't think she should even be *trying* to cope with the cooking, especially since she has her granddaughter to stay. Once I realised that, there wasn't anything else to do but invite them.'

'You *are* kind, Holly!'

'I'm not, really – I didn't want to do it. Only then I started to feel that I was being as mean and selfish as Jude.' I sighed. 'So now I'm committed to hosting a family Christmas dinner in a house that doesn't belong to me and which is in need of a damned good clean, using food left by someone else!'

'You'll cope, you always do.'

'We've had some snow too, and I can see that we're likely to get cut off if it carries on – you've never seen such a steep, narrow, bendy road as the one up to the village! Luckily, there's an amazingly well-stocked shop and enough food in the house to last a year, I should think, if you don't mind eating a lot of fish and game.'

'Jude shoots, then?'

'No, it's his Aunt Becca who does that, the horsy one. And she fishes, so she's probably responsible for the trout and salmon – *and* the whole frozen pike.'

'A *pike*? How do you know it's a pike?'

'Everything is labelled. I've never cooked pike before, but they're supposed to be good eating . . . I have a recipe for stuffed pike in my book of old English cookery,' I added thoughtfully.

I always took my favourite recipe books away with me, along with my giant notebook, and it was just as well. It's amazing what I'm asked to cook sometimes!

'Are you serious?'

'Yes, of course. I couldn't eat a whole one myself, it's pretty big, so I would have to ask the Martlands back another time to help me eat it. On Christmas Day it will be turkey and all the trimmings, of course, because that's what they're expecting.'

'It's quite funny, when you think about it, that you ran away from the idea of spending a family Christmas with me, but ended up having to host one yourself!'

'Yes, I know, I can see the irony of it,' I agreed. 'Still, after Christmas Day, things will go quieter and I can relax and get on with my book again. Meanwhile, Jude accused me of trying to squeeze a whole lot of money out of him for cooking for the family, when I don't intend charging for it at all! So I'm going to phone Ellen and tell her that if he calls, she isn't to tell him what I charge for house-party cooking. I told him he couldn't afford me.'

'Isn't he rich? The house sounds very grand!'

'Grand but neglected, with just that useless cleaner coming in, and she told me he paid her half the going rate so he has to be either poor or stingy – or maybe both. But artists don't usually have loads of money, do they?'

'I think he's doing all right, he's quite well known.' She paused.

'It's the weekend – Ellen hates being called then unless it's an emergency, doesn't she?'

'Tough.'

'*And* she's going to be really mad if you go ahead and get pregnant and then hand your notice in! You're her best and most reliable cook, she told me so.'

'Double tough. Laura, you know those wartime journals of Gran's?'

'Yes, they sound fascinating.'

'They're getting even more fascinating,' I said, and described how there seemed to be a romance forming between her and one of the patients – and my growing conviction that the Ned Martland she had once loved was Noël Martland's younger brother.

'It does sound likely, doesn't it?' she agreed. 'It's such a coincidence that you should be there. Really, it's just like a novel!'

'That's what I thought, though I hope it's not a tragedy, because Noël's brother sounds like a bit of a bad lot. I'll have even more reason to dislike Jude Martland if his uncle broke Gran's heart!'

'They say everyone has got a novel in them, don't they? Only I'd have thought your grandmother's would have been a fairly sedate Mrs Gaskell sort of affair.'

'Yes, that's what I'm hoping. And I don't think I've got a novel in *me* but I might just have a recipe book – if I ever have the time to finish it,' I added bitterly.

'How's it going?'

'Not very fast so far, because there's simply been too much to do and a constant stream of visitors. And when I've had a spare minute, Gran's journals have been a bit too fascinating to resist.'

'Well, ring me if you find out anything else interesting!'

I was getting chilly by then and only got Ellen's answering machine when I tried her number, so I left a message on that, before heading for home.

* * *

I gave the fruit soaking in brandy a stir and it was already starting to smell delicious: you really can't fail with that recipe.

Looking at my by now extensive to-do list, I thought I had better gird my loins and start on the rest of the cleaning, on the principle of getting done first what you least want to do.

It was already evident to me that the Jacksons, the elderly couple who had since retired, had really cared for the house. The linen cupboard, where tablecloths, runners and napkins were kept, smelt of lavender sachets and a plentiful supply of cleaning materials lined the utility-room shelves.

I filled a cream enamel housekeeper's bucket with everything I thought I would need and carried it through to the dining room, along with the old upright vacuum cleaner and a long-handled, slightly-moulting brown feather duster.

Always start at the top of a room and work downwards: that was the lesson Gran had taught me. I dealt with the cobwebs and worked my way down the panelling, then vacuumed some of the dust out of the curtains using the extension hosepipe, set on low. I'd polished the furniture and was well into cleaning the floor when Jess suddenly appeared.

I nearly had a heart attack when I caught sight of her dark figure with its pale face standing silently in the doorway. I gave a yelp and she said, 'Did I make you jump? I did knock, but I had Grandpa's key, so when there was no answer, I came in. Granny sent me to see if you needed any help. Not that I *like* housework,' she added mutinously.

'Neither do I, actually, but I *do* like the look and smell of a fresh, clean room. It would be wonderful if you could give me a hand. I've nearly finished in here and I was going to do the garden hall and cloakroom next, so if you could take the feather duster and get rid of all the cobwebs in the corners first, that would be great.'

'Oh – okay,' she said, brightening slightly, presumably because I hadn't immediately handed her the vacuum cleaner.

Merlin followed her out – he didn't seem to like the noise.

I finished off the floor, then took the silver candlesticks and tray through to the utility room to clean later, before going to see how Jess was getting on.

'Merlin eats spiders,' Jess told me. 'I suppose he thinks they're snacks on legs.'

'Good, I hate them.'

Jess's main contribution to the cleaning after that was to entertain me while I worked by telling me the details of the plot of her vampire novel, until finally I straightened my aching back and declared, 'Lunch time, I think.'

'You look very hot and grubby!'

'That's because your uncle has let his house get filthy – he should be ashamed of himself.'

'I don't suppose he even noticed,' Jess said. 'When he's working he doesn't, and he's working most of the time. Even when he isn't you can tell he's still *thinking* about it. What are you having for lunch?'

'Nothing exciting – an omelette probably. What are you having?'

'God knows,' she said gloomily. 'Probably tinned soup – and I'll be the one in charge of heating that up, because Granny's tired today and Grandpa is hopeless.'

She got up. 'I suppose I'd better come back tomorrow and help you make beds. That's why Granny sent me, really, to tell you to make sure the bedrooms are aired.'

'*Beds?*'

'Granny said it would be much more convenient if we all stayed on Christmas night.'

'Convenient for who?' I said, startled. I was sure they'd only been coming for lunch when Mo and Jim were doing the catering and I don't remember any previous mention of staying over . . .

'For you, of course, so you won't have to drive us back to the lodge. And they've told Auntie Becca that Christmas lunch was on again, so she's coming too.'

'What – to *stay*?'

'Yes.' She counted up on her fingers. 'So that's three bedrooms, isn't it?'

'I suppose it is,' I said faintly. 'Oh, joy! And yes, you'd better come back tomorrow and help, because I expect I'll now have to clean the bedrooms before I can make the beds up.'

I'd have to revise my menu plan, too, if I was catering for rather more than just Christmas lunch! It was just as well the warmth from the big log fire in the hall was permeating all the rooms upstairs and airing them – except for the owner's Bluebeard's chamber, of course. If that was damp and dank and chilly when he got back, that would be his own fault.

'Your Uncle Jude called last night, so I assume the phone is working again.'

'Did he? I think he must like you!'

'No, I think it's the opposite, actually.'

'Auntie Becca called back later to say that since Christmas was on as usual, she'd popped down to the village to tell Old Nan and Richard.'

'Oh my God!'

'Is that a problem?'

'Oh no,' I said faintly, 'I mean, after looking forward to a quiet and restful few weeks on my own, I should be delighted that I'm now going to be cook, cleaner and general factotum for a large house-party, where everyone bar you is so elderly they're obviously not going to be a lot of help, shouldn't I? *Whatever* gave you that idea?'

She grinned. 'I know you're joking – and it's going to be much more fun than last year, when Great Uncle Alex was so ill and Guy and Jude fell out over Guy and Coco flirting, though Guy flirts with *everyone*. Aunt Becca said she was surprised when she saw the announcement of his engagement to Coco, because although he always wanted whatever Jude had, he lost interest once he'd got it.'

That seemed very acute of Becca. 'A bit of a Cain and Abel syndrome?' I asked, interested, but she looked blank.

'I hate Guy, he's always winding me up and he never buys me a present either, just gives me money.'

'That *is* a present, it just means he has no idea what you want.'

'Jude usually gives me a present even if sometimes it's a bit weird. But I don't suppose he even thought of it this time, dropping everything and rushing off like that.'

'He said he sent hampers to Old Nan and Richard, so I'm sure he will have remembered.'

'You know,' she said with an air of one making a major discovery, 'I like Jude much better than Guy, even if he is grumpier! If he says he'll do something, he does. And when he's home, he lets me go and mess about in the studio with modelling clay sometimes and he's going to teach me to weld, too.'

'Well, that's certainly a life skill that not a lot of girls your age have.'

She jumped up. 'Look at the time! I'd better go, or Granny will be trying to open that tin herself.'

'I'll bring you some homemade soup down tomorrow,' I promised. 'I usually have a big pot of it permanently on the go and top it up every day, but I just don't seem to have had a minute since I arrived, so there isn't enough at the moment.'

Making more soup and having a good turn-out of the kitchen cupboards occupied most of the rest of the day, and no call from Jude Martland marred my peace . . . until he rang really late, just as I was thinking about bed.

'I emailed your boss at Homebodies and asked her how much you charged for your cooking,' he said without any preamble. 'My God, I don't know who can afford those wages!'

'I expect she gave you the weekly rate, but I told you I was expensive.' Trust Ellen to try and get more money out of a client without even consulting me, too!

'If you add that on top of double house-sitting rates, it's extortionate,' he said. 'And you won't be doing anything millions of women won't be doing for their families for nothing over Christmas.'

'They will be doing it for love – and it makes you think, doesn't it? Christmas is always hard work for women.'

'That's not what I meant . . . though I suppose you have a point,' he agreed grudgingly.

I was about to tell him that I had no intention of charging him for anything other than the house-sitting, and would have a word with Ellen about it, but something seemed to hold me back. He probably wouldn't have believed me anyway.

'Did you want anything else, or did you just ring me to complain about the Homebodies charges?'

'I phoned for the sheer pleasure of hearing your voice,' he said sarcastically and then I was listening to the empty air: he'd gone.

I fell into bed, exhausted and irritated in equal measures and wasn't much soothed by the next few pages of Gran's journal, since I could see ominous signs of where things were heading:

Sister caught me laughing with N this morning and hauled me over the coals for it. I was very upset by this, and was lucky not to be moved from that ward. N was sweet and said he would make it up to me once he is well again, though he didn't say how . . .

Still, at least I might get the chance to find out more about Ned Martland from Noël over Christmas, so every cloud has a silver lining, even if it is slightly tarnished.

Chapter 12: Deeply Fruited

N was discharged from hospital today and sent home to convalesce, but before he left he caught my hand and pleaded with me to meet him on my next half-day. Against my better judgement I eventually agreed, though I stipulated that it must be somewhere out of the way, since I do not wish to be the target of idle gossip among the other nurses.

February, 1945

Yesterday's snow had half-melted by evening, but it froze overnight and then a fresh covering over the top made things pretty treacherous outside. I was worried about Lady on the cobbles and rang Becca to ask if I should still let her out.

'Of course,' she said, and she was quite right, because Lady walked across to the paddock with small, cautious steps as if she'd been doing it all her life – which actually, I expect she had.

Becca had also said she was looking forward to Christmas Day. I seemed to be the only one who wasn't. I'd caught her on the way to church, because apparently the vicar comes over from Great Mumming once a fortnight to hold a service here and today was the day: in fact, I could hear the distant peal of the bell as she rang off.

The brandy-soaked fruit for the Christmas cake smelt intoxicatingly delicious when I fetched the bowl into the kitchen and then began assembling and weighing the rest of the ingredients, which is the most time-consuming bit, along with greasing and lining a cake tin. Luckily there was a good selection of those in all shapes and sizes and I had found a suitably large one in the cupboard yesterday.

Once the cake was safely baking, as well as some mince pies to offer what I now foresaw would be a permanent flow of famished visitors, I had a sit-down with a cup of coffee to brace myself for another bout of the hated cleaning, this time of the bedrooms.

I was getting heartily sick of it – not to mention of Jude Martland, the cause of all this extra work! So when Jess turned up again, this time I was much more remorseless in making her help me.

She told me which rooms her grandparents and Becca usually had and said she herself always slept in the old nursery. The rooms didn't seem to have been used since the previous Christmas, so that apart from a coating of dust and needing the beds made up with lavender-scented linen from the big cupboard at the end of the passage by the stairs, they didn't actually take a huge amount of time to do – much less than I expected.

Jess showed me the cupboard full of old toys in the nursery, though some of them were more recent, mainly miniature instruments of mass destruction that had probably belonged to Guy and Jude. The room was at the back of the house and, like mine and Jude's, afforded an excellent view of the horse figure on the side of the folly-topped Snowehill, which was certainly living up to its name today. The red horse was now white and practically indistinguishable, much like Lady in the paddock below, though Billy was a small dark blob.

By the time we'd finished upstairs, the scent of fruit cake from the slow oven had wafted gently through the house to tantalise our nostrils and I took the cake out and tested it with a skewer while Jess wolfed down the first batch of mince pies I'd made earlier.

She watched me curiously. 'Why are you poking holes in it?'

'One hole, just to see if it's done. If it isn't, the cake mix will stick to the skewer.'

'Oh, right. These mince pies are much nicer than shop ones,' Jess added, with an air of discovery.

'I've made them the way I like them best, with lots of filling and thin pastry, but the shop ones tend to go the other way. There's a box of them in the larder that the Chirks left, but I don't like the look of them.'

'I could take them back with me,' offered Jess. 'Grandpa would probably be glad of them, because they have to be better than anything Granny whips up, even though he always says he enjoys everything she cooks.'

'How is she today?'

'Quite lively – she said she was going to make a batch of rock cakes, though I don't suppose they'll be any nicer than the cheese straws.'

'I'll give you some soup to take back for lunch, I've made a lot more.'

I'd found one of those giant Thermos flasks earlier with a wide mouth for soups and stews, so I scalded it out and ladled the soup into that.

'There, thick enough to stand a spoon in, as my Gran would have said.'

'It smells lovely. I'd better take it back now, because they've probably decided to have rock cakes for lunch and that's not enough to keep them going. Meals at the lodge are getting weirder and weirder by the minute.'

When she'd gone I had a bowl of the soup myself, with a warm, buttered roll (luckily there was a good supply of bread in the freezer too, and also several of those long-life part-baked baguettes in the larder), then I covered the end of the kitchen table with newspaper and sat there with a pot of tea to hand, polishing up the tarnished silver from the dining room.

When I was coming back from replacing them on the side-board, I glanced out of the sitting-room window and spotted a tractor coming up the drive with a snowplough contraption on the front. It swept gratingly around the turning circle in front of the house, narrowly missing my car, then vanished up the side, but not before I'd caught sight of Henry in the passenger seat next to the fair-haired driver.

I presumed he was being dropped off at the back gate and, sure enough, by the time I got to the kitchen he was stumping across the courtyard to the door and I could hear the roar of the tractor departing again.

'Hi, Henry,' I said, 'was that George Froggat, the farmer from up the lane?'

'That's right, Hill Farm. Gave me a lift, he did.'

'That was kind.'

'Nay, he was coming up anyway, seeing the council pays him and his son to plough the lane to the village, and Jude pays him to do this drive and Becca's. He makes a good thing out of it.'

'Oh yes, I think Tilda and Noël mentioned something about that.'

'Saw you at the window, did George. Said you looked a likely lass. I said you were none too bad,' he conceded grudgingly.

'Well . . . thank you,' I said, digesting this unlikely pair of compliments.

'I told him you were a widow, too. He's a widower himself.'

I glanced at him sharply, wondering if he was about to try a spot of rural matchmaking and saw that he looked frozen, despite wearing numerous woolly layers under a tweed jacket obviously built for someone of twice his girth.

'Look, come in and get warm,' I ordered and, despite his protests, I thawed him out in the kitchen with tea and warm mince pies. The first batch had almost gone already, so it was just as well I had loads more baking, which I intended to put in the freezer.

'The weather's turning worse and I might not get back up over Christmas, so I've come to show you where the potatoes are stored, and the beetroot clamp and suchlike, in case you need to fetch any more in,' he said, when he'd drunk his tea and regained a less deathly complexion.

I was touched by this kind thought and we went out to the walled garden, once I'd donned my down-filled parka and gloves.

I returned half an hour later with a basket of potatoes and carrots and a string of onions, leaving Henry to retire to his little den in the greenhouse, though I told him to tell me later when he was leaving. His daughter couldn't fetch him today, so he'd intended walking home, but I would insist on driving him back, however icy the road down was.

The drive *was* slippery, but someone (presumably George) had sprinkled grit over the steepest bit of the lane below the lodge, so we got down that all right.

Going by the leaden sky I thought we might be in for another snow fall, and it was a pity the shop was closed because I would have bought yet more emergency supplies while I had the car with me, especially now I was having lots more visitors!

I pulled up outside the almshouses and Henry clambered out, clutching his usual bulging sack of booty.

'Her at the end's wanting you,' he said with a jerk of his thumb and I saw Old Nan was waving at me from her window with surprising enthusiasm. But this was soon explained when Jess shot out of her cottage, still fastening her coat, and climbed into the passenger seat next to me.

'Great, I thought I was going to have to walk back,' she said, turning round to pat Merlin, who was on the back seat.

'We both might, if the car won't go up the lane – it's pretty icy. What were you doing down here?'

'Granny made about three million rock cakes and they weren't very nice, so I volunteered to bring some for Old Nan and

Richard, just to try and get rid of them quicker. Your soup was good, though.'

I got back up the hill by the skin of my teeth and dropped her at the lodge, but I didn't go in because it was quickly getting dark and even colder by then, and I wanted to bring Lady and Billy in.

I should have left a light on in the porch: it was slightly eerie and silent when I got out of the car, just the scrunch of my boots on the drive and the sudden high-pitched yelp of a fox not far away, which Merlin took with matter-of-fact disinterestedness.

It's odd, growing up in Merchester, I'd had this idea of the countryside as a quiet place, but in its way it's usually just as noisy as the city: foxes scream, hedgehogs grunt, sheep baa, cows moo, birds sing, rooks caw, tractors roar . . . it's a cacophony! A cacophony interspersed with moments of deep silence. This was one of them.

I was glad to get inside and switch on the lights in the sitting room, where the embers of the fire only needed a log or two to spring back into life.

When I checked the phone, I seemed to have missed a call from Jude. What a pity!

I spoke too soon, because when I came back in from the stables he rang again before I could even get my freezing hands around a hot mug. (I'd been tempted to plunge them into Lady's warm mash!)

'You weren't in earlier,' he said accusingly. 'I tried to ring you two or three times.'

'No, I am actually allowed to leave the premises occasionally for a couple of hours under the terms of the Homebodies contract,' I said. 'I'm sure I told you that I was going to the village to do some shopping – and I called in on your aunt and uncle and everything seemed fine. I got them a couple of things they needed from the village, too.'

'Oh? Is that little service going on the bill, too?' he said nastily. 'And I rang *much* earlier too and you weren't there then, either, so—'

'This *was* much earlier. I came back ages ago and then went straight out to bring Billy and Lady in and do her warm mash. *They* are both absolutely fine too – I rang Becca this morning to ask her if it was too cold to put them in the paddock and she said it wasn't. So in fact, the only creature around here that *isn't* fine is me, because I'm tired, freezing cold and hungry,' I added pointedly.

'Well, sorry for disturbing you!'

'That's all right, I have had one or two previous clients who were so neurotic about their pets they called every day. Did you have any particular reason for ringing this time?'

'No, it's simply that the novelty of having my employees insult me hasn't worn off yet.'

'I am not actually your employee,' I pointed out. 'I work for Homebodies. And I return the compliment: my clients tend to praise me rather than insult my integrity.'

I think we might have been neck-and-neck with slamming the phone down that time.

118

Chapter 13: Christmas Spirits

On my half-day I cycled out to meet N at a teashop. One of his brothers dropped him off there, though he did not come in, and was to pick him up later. It was good to see him again and though at first I felt very shy, we were soon as at ease with one another as we had been at the hospital.

February, 1945

I read a bit more of Gran's journal over breakfast. Now that she seemed to be embarking on a clandestine romance with Ned Martland, I was even more tempted to skip forward and discover what went wrong, but restrained myself.

I did wish she wouldn't keep going off into long-winded soliloquies about the state of her conscience and what she thought God's purpose for her was between entries, though.

I kept thinking about her while I did my chores and then took Merlin for a little run, so I called Laura to talk it over when I had gone far enough up the hill to get a good signal.

'How are you feeling?' she asked me.

'Me?' I said, surprised. 'Oh, *I'm* fine, except there is so much to do here. Laura, you know those old journals of Granny's?'

'Mmm, you said you were reading a bit every night and were beginning to suspect that one of the Martlands might have been your Gran's lost love – see, I'm keeping up with the plot,' she said encouragingly.

119

'Yes, that's Edward – Ned – Noël Martland's younger brother and I'm positive he's the N.M. she's nursing back to health in her journal. She seems to be slowly falling for him and they're having clandestine meetings!'

'Well, you already knew she loved him. I wonder what went wrong?'

'I don't know, I just hope he didn't break her heart, because he sounds a bit of a rake. I expect I'll find out a bit more about him over Christmas . . .' I began, but then there was a crash and a wailing noise at her end as one of the children had some minor disaster and she had to ring off quickly.

At least everything is now more or less in hand for Christmas Day. I've taken the fine ham the Chirks left behind out of the freezer and put it in the fridge to defrost slowly, the menu is planned, the cake awaits its marzipan and icing and I have the wherewithal to bake endless mince pies.

But I went quite mad and cleaned through the rest of the house, too – or at least everything that wasn't locked up. Having set my course, there seemed no point in being half-hearted about things just because Jude Martland was so objectionable, and anyway, the clean bits made the rest of it look so much worse . . .

The slightly musty, dusty scent of neglect has given way to the homelier ones of wood fires, beeswax and lavender polish, baking and fresh coffee.

While I was working away I'd been keeping an eye on the weather, for outside large slow flakes of snow were stealthily falling. I saw George snowplough up the drive and turn down again, but this time he was alone. If he gets paid by the council for every trip, I suspect I'll see a lot of him!

By early afternoon the snow was even thicker and showed no sign of letting up, so I decided to bring Lady and Billy in early, then took off Lady's rug and rather inexpertly groomed her. She seemed to enjoy this, though Billy was a nuisance as always, forever butting me in the legs and nibbling the hems of my jeans.

I'd almost finished and was just putting Lady's rug back on, when Jess made one of her silent appearances: I think she must practise them.

'Don't stand there in the snow, come in,' I invited, so she did, with a cautious eye on Lady and then sidled gingerly past Billy.

I think actually she's afraid of horses and has invented an allergy to conceal it, because she never sneezes or shows any other symptoms.

'To what do I owe the honour of this visit?' I asked, but then looked up and saw her pale, anxious face. 'What is it? Is something wrong?'

'Grandpa asked me to walk up and tell you that Granny had a little fall in the kitchen last night.'

I stopped fastening the strap of the rug and turned to stare at her. 'Is she hurt?'

Her lower lip wobbled slightly. 'She bumped her head and knocked herself out, and we weren't sure if she'd broken anything, so we didn't like to move her. I had to ring for an ambulance.'

'Oh, poor Tilda – and poor Jess, too,' I said, giving her a hug. 'But why didn't you ring me?'

'It all happened so fast! Granny had come round a bit by the time the ambulance arrived, but they insisted on taking her to hospital for X-rays and a checkup, so Grandpa and I went too.'

'So, is she still there?'

'No, she refused to stay even though they wanted to keep her in overnight for observation and we came back in a taxi about two this morning. It only just managed to get up the hill!'

'Wow, you *have* been having a time of it! I only wish I'd known.'

'Grandpa didn't want to bother you, but if they had kept her in hospital he was going to ring and ask you if I could move up here for a bit.'

121

'Of course you could, that wouldn't have been a problem. How is your granny this morning?'

'Still in bed and Grandpa's trying to persuade her to stay there. I think she's a bit shaken up and bruised and she's probably going to have a black eye, too. I made us all some toast for breakfast . . . and we don't seem to have got round to lunch,' she said, and then added hopefully, 'I washed the soup Thermos out and brought it back.'

'Good thinking – some nice, hot soup will do them both good.' I gave her another hug and then finished fastening Lady's rug. 'You know, they're really not up to looking after themselves any more, are they? It's a pity their housekeeper had to go away just now, though I'm sure the poor woman is entitled to take Christmas off.'

'She always has the same two weeks, while Granny and Grandpa are happy to move up here for Christmas and New Year and me and Mum and Dad are usually here, too.' She paused and swallowed hard, tears not far away again. 'Grandpa said, just think how awful it would have been if Granny'd been cooking and holding something hot when she fell.'

'God, yes, he's right – it could have been so much worse!'

Jude Martland, you've got a lot to answer for! I thought – swanning off and leaving everyone to cope alone, when he must have seen how frail his elderly relatives were getting.

'Come on,' I said, leading the way out of the loosebox, 'we'll go and phone your Grandpa.'

'You can't, that's why I had to come and tell you. The phone line was a bit iffy this morning when Grandpa called the mobile number Uncle Jude gave him, and just after he'd told him about Granny's accident and her going to hospital, it all went totally dead. I walked down the lane to have a look and one of the poles was right down, so that's it and we're cut off.'

'Oh – then at least your Uncle Jude knows what's happening,' I said, relieved, 'though I don't suppose he said anything remotely useful?'

'I don't think he got the chance,' she said doubtfully.

'He might try and call you back on your mobile?'

'He doesn't know the number . . . and that's not working now either, because I dropped it down the toilet at the hospital.'

'Oh, yuk! I don't even want to know how you managed that,' I said. '*Or* what you did with it afterwards.'

'It's in a plastic bag one of the nurses gave me.' She looked at her watch. 'I'll have to get back soon – Grandpa's very tired and he must be hungry, because *I'm* ravenous and I don't want him to get ill, too.'

She sounded as if the cares of the world were on her small shoulders, poor child.

'Of course, and I'll come with you,' I said, and we set out as soon as I'd put more hot soup in the flask and quickly made cheese and tomato sandwiches.

A worried Noël was obviously deeply relieved to see me. 'It's very kind of you to come, m'dear. I really didn't want to be any more of a nuisance.'

'You're not a nuisance at all. How is Tilda now?'

'Furious with me for getting Jess to call the ambulance but she's still in bed,' he said, lowering his voice. 'Very unlike her, so it must have shaken her up. She says she has a headache too, but insists she will get up later and cook lunch.'

'It's nearly teatime, Noël! But I've brought hot soup, sandwiches and mince pies that you can all have now. And then do you think you ought to call the doctor about Tilda's headache?'

'She won't hear of it – only takes homeopathic remedies, you know. Never lets illness get the better of her!' he added proudly.

But there was no homeopathic cure for the encroaching infirmities of old age, which must overtake us all in the end . . . There seemed to be only one way of preventing Tilda from trying to carry on as usual and hurting herself even more in the process . . .

'You know, I really think it would be best if you all moved up to Old Place this afternoon and stayed, at least until Tilda is better,' I said with resignation.

'Oh *yes!*' said Jess eagerly.

'I had thought of asking, but I really didn't want to burden you with extra work,' Noël said anxiously.

'Not at all: Jess has helped me clean and make the beds already, so it'll be no trouble at all,' I lied.

A huge expression of relief crossed his face. 'If you are sure ... and perhaps you will like the company?' he suggested, brightening. 'Jess and I will help you as much as we can, too.'

'Will Tilda be happy to move up to Old Place?'

'Oh yes, I'm *sure* she will.'

'Then shall I come down in the car in a couple of hours and collect you, when you've packed a few things?'

'No, that's all right, George will call in later with the newspaper, if it has got through to Little Mumming, and I'm sure he won't mind bringing us up in his Land Rover.'

'He seems very obliging and he certainly keeps the drive free of snow!'

'He's a very nice chap, is George. He and his son Liam do a good job of keeping the lane clear, and then the folks at Weasel Pot Farm below the village keep the lane on that side ploughed too, though sometimes they have to give up on the last steep bit down to the main road if the snow is too heavy.' He glanced through the window. 'If this keeps up, we might well be snowed in for a couple of days.'

'Then up at the house will be the best place for you – there's lots of food, it's warm and if the electricity fails, there's the generator.'

'Very true!' Noël was cheering up by the minute, as was Jess. 'Well, this will be fun, won't it? A proper family Christmas at the old home after all!'

'Yes, won't that be great?' I said slightly hollowly.

'Oh, but I was forgetting – you don't celebrate it, m'dear?'

'Not at all, I'm sure it's going to make a *lovely* change,' I said valiantly, and left them to their sandwiches, soup and packing.

As soon as I got home, I started to prepare for my visitors and then George drove them up when it was practically dark in a long-wheelbase Land Rover, together with all their baggage, a carton of perishable foodstuffs, and a huge plastic Santa sack full of wrapped presents.

George Froggat was a tall, well-built, middle-aged man with a mop of pale flaxen hair, a healthily pink face, sky-blue eyes, and an engaging grin. It was just as well that he was built on sturdy lines, because he had to lift Noël down and then he simply scooped Tilda up, carried her in and deposited her on the sofa by the fire in the sitting room.

He came back and shook hands and said he was very pleased to meet me, then helped carry everything else in. He wouldn't stay for a hot drink, but just as he was going, he said, 'Nearly forgot, here's something from me and my family.' Then he hauled out a Christmas tree bound with sacking from the back of the Land Rover and propped it in the porch.

'Gosh, that's almost as tall as I am!' I exclaimed.

'Aye, you're a grand, strapping lass,' he said approvingly, looking me up and down, then got back into the driving seat. 'I'll call in to see how things are going in the morning, or my boy Liam will, when we clear the drive.'

Tilda and Noël were still in the sitting room in front of the fire while Jess, looking martyred, was ferrying luggage upstairs in relays. I could hear the whine of the stairlift, so she wasn't carrying all of it herself.

'Would you like tea?' I asked. 'Or – maybe something stronger?'

'Good idea! There's whisky, gin and brandy in that little cabinet in the dining room, and glasses,' Noël said.

'I'm afraid I've finished off the brandy,' I confessed, 'and the cellar's locked.'

'Not surprised you needed it in this weather,' Noël said. 'And I've got the keys, all right. Jude leaves them with me when he's away and there's plenty more down there.'

'Actually, the brandy was for the Christmas cake, I didn't drink it.'

'*That* should have been made months ago, I told you,' Tilda piped up disapprovingly in her cut-crystal accent, from the depths of a sofa. Shaken up and bruised or not, she was wearing stiletto-heeled shoes and full makeup, despite being dressed only in a warm coat over her nightdress. I expect they made her feel more herself.

'It smelled delicious when Holly took it out of the oven,' Jess said. 'And we hadn't got one at all!'

'I kept thinking Jude wouldn't be away for Christmas, after all,' Tilda said, 'so I put off buying one. But there's the Dundee cake in a tin that Old Nan always gives us at Christmas, I've brought that. Where did you put it, Jess darling?'

'In the kitchen, with the other food and stuff.'

'Really, this quick Christmas cake recipe comes out surprisingly well and I thought Jess might help me ice it later,' I said.

'Wonderful,' Noël said, rubbing his hands together. 'And we can go up into the attic and look out the decorations tomorrow.' Then his face fell. 'But I have forgotten, there is no tree. We put up a little artificial one for Jess, but we didn't think to bring it.'

'It's all right, George left one as a gift in the porch,' I said. 'I thought it would be better left out there for the moment.'

'Oh, jolly good! Is it a big one? That always goes in the corner over there by the stairs.'

'It's *huge*,' I said with resignation. It looked as if I was in for a traditional Christmas whether I wanted one or not, so I might as well just give in right now and go with the flow!

* * *

After tea and mince pies – or whisky and mince pies in Noël's case – Tilda went upstairs to lie down, using the stairlift under protest, though she was obviously still shaky. When I took her a hot water bottle presently, I found her half-asleep already under the flowered satin eiderdown, though that was probably the exhaustion of directing Jess with the unpacking of the suitcases.

Noël stretched out on the sofa for a nap while Jess and I went into the kitchen and had a fun, if messy, time marzipanning and icing the cake and sticking a lot of old decorations on it that we found in a Bluebird Toffee tin in one of the cupboards. There was a complete set of little plaster Eskimos, sledging, skiing or throwing snowballs, and an igloo.

'Didn't you even have a Christmas cake when you were little?' asked Jess, positioning a polar bear menacingly near one of the Eskimos.

'No. My gran often made lovely fruit cakes, but she didn't set out to make a Christmas cake as such.'

'I think it's really sad that you never had a tree, or presents or crackers or anything, until you were grown up.'

'I thought so too, when I was at school,' I said ruefully. 'I so envied all my friends! I expect that's why I went overboard with the whole seasonal gifts, food and decorations thing when I got married. But that isn't really what Christmas should be about, is it?'

'But it's *fun!*' she protested. 'I love everything about Christmas – but not as much as Grandpa. He's an expert, you know, he's written a book about it.'

'Oh yes, I think he mentioned that.'

'It's called *Auld Christmas*, like the pub name, and it's about ancient traditions being absorbed into new ones and stuff like that, and how the Twelfth Night Revels celebrate the rebirth of the new year and goes back way before Christianity.'

'Does it? It sounds like *you're* an expert too,' I said, impressed.

'Oh, Grandpa's forever going on about it, and my parents have always brought me to Old Place for Christmas, so it's just sort of seeped in.' She looked a bit forlorn suddenly. 'I wish they could be here this time, too, but I do understand. They could hardly fly back from Antarctica just for the Christmas holidays, could they?'

'No, but they must be missing you an awful lot.'

'Oh, they'll be so into what they're doing they won't even remember I exist until they get back!' She sounded tolerant rather than aggrieved by this. 'But they did record a DVD wishing me Happy Christmas before they went, a bit like the Queen's message, though Granny says I can't have it until Christmas Day.'

'That's something to look forward to.'

'Yes, and I don't mind them not being here so much now we're staying with you. Christmas is going to be much more fun! You don't really mind if we have a proper one, do you?'

'I suppose not, and it's starting to sound as if I'll have enough of Christmas this year to make up for all the ones I've missed.'

'And presents, too. I make all mine and I've got a wonky one I practised on you can have,' she said generously.

I couldn't imagine what she'd made, but I thanked her anyway. 'I wasn't expecting anything – I wasn't even expecting *Christmas*, come to that! Mind you, I do have one present already, from my best friend.'

'What's she like?'

'She's my husband's younger sister and my opposite in every way: tiny, fair and blue-eyed like he was . . . but she doesn't look like him otherwise.'

'Was your husband short, then? Uncle Jude is a *giant*.'

'He was exactly the same height as me – six foot.'

'That's tall enough to be a model, except they're all skinny.'

'Well, you know what they say: never trust a skinny cook.'

'Do they?' She frowned. 'Oh, I see: it means you don't love food.'

'And won't eat your own cooking!'

When we'd finished and I'd fixed a paper frill (also from the toffee tin) around the cake, I covered it with a large glass dome I'd spotted in one of the old glazed-fronted cupboards that lined one wall of the huge kitchen, then put it in the larder.

'Now, perhaps we'd better make some more tea and you could take it through while I start dinner. Could you pop up and see if your Granny's awake and would like some?'

I'd taken some beef mince out of the freezer as soon as I'd got back earlier and now quickly made a large cottage pie and put it in the oven, then cored baking apples to stuff with dried fruit, brown sugar and cinnamon. There was long-life cream, ice cream and a half-used aerosol can of squirty cream that had come from the lodge with the other perishable food ... and when I counted, there were a total of four and a half aerosol tins of sweetened cream, so it must play a large part in their diet!

Tilda had a tray in bed and the rest of us ate around the big pine table in the kitchen. By the time I'd cleared this away and then gone out for one last check on Lady and to give Merlin a run, I was exhausted.

But I still felt on edge, as if waiting for something – and I realised it was Jude's daily call! In a peculiar way, I sort of missed the adrenaline rush of crossing swords with him, even if he had managed to provoke me into losing my temper on more than one occasion.

Noël had gone to bed and Jess was in the morning room watching something fuzzy and probably highly unsuitable on the TV, half-glazed with sleep. I sent her upstairs, but she made me promise to come and put her light out on my way up in a few minutes. The child in her was only just beneath the surface: I ended up reading her a bit of *The Water Babies* from a book we found on one of the shelves, before tucking her up with her teddy bear and saying good night.

* * *

Tonight I could only focus on the journal entries for long enough to discover that Gran's first meeting outside the hospital with N seemed set to become the first of many.

Then my eyes started to close as if weighted with lead and I switched out the light and sank back on the pillows – only to start awake again a moment later, my heart racing, filled with shocked guilt because for the first time in eight years, I had forgotten the anniversary of Alan's death!

I climbed out of bed and fetched his photograph in its travelling frame from the top of the washstand: and that's how I fell asleep, holding onto my lost love, my face wet with tears.

Chapter 14: Toast and Treacle

I met N again and this time he had borrowed his brother's car, though I am sure he should not yet be using his injured leg so much. When I told him so he laughed and said that he was fine, and would soon be getting his motorbike out of storage, though he needn't think I will get on it!

February, 1945

I was up much earlier than everyone else, seeing to Merlin and double-rugging Lady, as Becca had suggested doing if it got really cold, before letting her and Billy out into the snowy paddock.

It was bitterly icy out there and the wind felt as if it was coming straight off the tundra so, after hanging the haynet on the fence and breaking the ice in the water trough, I was glad to go back in and thaw out. Mucking out would have to wait for later.

By now I'd found a note about the care of Billy, which had come adrift from its place in the file and been pushed into the pocket at the back. However, apart from feeding him some of the goat biscuit things every day, which I had been doing anyway, he seemed to eat much the same as Lady. At the bottom of the typed page, Jude had written: *If Billy gets ill and goes off his food, tempt him with toast and treacle.*

Was he serious?

I got the defrosted ham out of the larder and boiled it, pouring away the water. Then I smeared it with honey and mustard, stuck it with cloves, and put it in to bake.

By the time I'd followed this up by making a blancmange and a quick chocolate cake from a favourite recipe, Noël and Jess had appeared. Tilda was, as I expected, still shaken, bruised and stiff, though she'd apparently announced her intention of coming down later.

When I asked them what they would like for breakfast, Jess said, 'A bacon and egg McMuffin, if you *really* want to know.'

'There are muffins in the freezer, you could have a Holly Muffin instead, if that would do?'

In fact, we all had bacon and egg-filled muffins, including Tilda, though Jess took hers up on a tray along with toast, marmalade, butter and a little fat pot of tea.

Apparently she usually eats a hearty breakfast, though if she got through that lot, then she must eat her own body weight every day, since she's the size of a sparrow!

Fortified by that, Noël and Jess were all set for an expedition to the attic to fetch down the Christmas decorations.

'There are only two days to go before Christmas, so there's no time to waste,' Noël said. They wanted me to go with them, which in my new spirit of drifting with the seasonal flow I agreed to do, just as soon as I'd cleared the breakfast things.

Jess was dispatched to collect her granny's breakfast tray and tell her where we were going to be, in case she thought we'd deserted her. I was just checking the ham when there was a hammering at the back door.

George must have snowploughed up the drive again, for the tractor with the heavy blade on the front was on the other side of the gate and, to judge from the footsteps across the snowy cobbles, he'd already made a couple of trips to and fro. There was a large holdall and a suitcase at his feet, and he was holding an assortment of other stuff, including a lot of greenery.

He gave me his attractive grin over the top of it, his healthy pink face glowing under its shock of white-gold hair and his sky-blue eyes bright.

'Morning! Met the postie in the village and thought I'd save him the trouble of bringing your mail up, seeing I was coming anyway. I've brought the old folks', too, though theirs mostly looks like Christmas cards.'

'That's kind of you.'

'If you take that?' he suggested and I relieved him of a large bundle held together with red elastic bands, two parcels, a hyacinth in a pot and the bunch of holly and mistletoe.

'Henry sent you the hyacinth, and the holly and bit of mistletoe are from me. I'll cut some more and drop it off in the porch later.'

'Oh – how kind of you both,' I said, gingerly holding the prickly bouquet and trying not to drop anything. 'And the bags . . . ?'

He picked them up and heaved them over the threshold.

'Becca's. I cleared as far as New Place and she called to me and asked if I'd drop them off.'

'She did?'

I supposed it made sense, when I came to think about it, since if it carried on snowing she might have to walk up through the snow on Christmas Day. She did seem to need an awful lot of stuff for one night, though!

'We've just finished breakfast – why don't you come in and have a cup of tea?'

'Nay, I haven't time, but I'll carry Becca's bags through for you if you like, one of them's heavy.' He stamped the snow off his boots and came in, shutting the door behind him.

'Is that George?' called Noël from the kitchen. 'Tell him to come through!'

'I can't stop,' George called back, but walked up the passage anyway, while I lingered to put the holly and mistletoe in the utility room together with the hyacinth, until I could find it a saucer to stand on.

133

Despite what he'd said, he was sitting at the kitchen table when I went in and Noël was pouring him a mug of slightly stewed tea.

I put a plate of mince pies in front of him and, sniffing the air as appreciatively as a truffle hound, he said, 'Something smells good in here!'

'That's the ham cooking . . . and maybe the cake I made earlier.'

While he consumed a succession of mince pies he told us what the lane down to the main road was like, which was pretty bad for anything except four-wheel-drive vehicles, especially the last steep, bendy stretch from Weasel Pot Farm.

'Their lad Ben's doing a roaring trade, pulling the SatNav people out of the ditch on the first corner. They get partway up it, then slide down again.'

'You'd think they would take one look and realise the SatNav was wrong,' Noël said.

'More money than sense, buying those things in the first place,' George said.

'But the postman got up it all right?' I asked.

'He's got a Post Office Land Rover and he's used to it,' he explained. 'Did you make these mince pies yourself, flower?'

They were quite small, but even so, I'd never seen anyone put a whole one in their mouth before. I nodded, fascinated.

'They're champion – you're a grand cook as well as a strapping lass,' he said with approval.

Jess giggled and he grinned at her. 'And you'll be another strapping lass too, when you've finished growing.'

Jess blushed, but actually I think she was quite pleased.

'The forecast says more snow is likely on higher ground,' Noël said, 'so I suppose we might get cut off.'

'Maybe, though we usually manage to keep the lane to the village open, don't we? But you couldn't get even the tractor over the Snowehill road to Great Mumming, now.' George consumed the last mince pie on the plate as though he was popping Smarties, then got up. 'Well, I'll be going: the dog's on the tractor and it's bitter out there. I'll drop you more greenery off later, Holly, you'll want it for the decorations – this first lot's more of a token gesture. And maybe you'll have hung the mistletoe up in the porch when I come back,' he added with unmistakable intent, and it was my turn to blush.

'Oh yes, we *must* hang up the mistletoe later,' Noël agreed, 'and have lots of green stuff in the sitting room. We were just about to go up into the attic and bring down the decorations when you arrived.'

'Then I'll leave you to it.'

Noël showed him out, while Jess got the giggles. 'George *fancies* you!'

I carried on sedately stacking the mince pie plate and the mugs in the dishwasher. 'He fancies my cooking, Jess, that's all.'

'Do you think he's nice-looking?'

'Yes, he's very handsome, in a rugged, outdoor kind of way.'

Noël came back in. 'It's bitter out there, isn't it? And what are these two bags he's brought?'

'They're your sister's – I suppose she thought she might as well send her overnight things up with George while she had the chance, in case the weather worsens. Jess, you could help me carry them up to her room while we're going in that direction. Take the overnight bag and I'll have the case.'

'I'll look through our mail later,' Noël said.

'There's already a whole stack for Jude. It's piled on that table in the front hallway,' I told him.

'I'll bring it all in later and sort it out,' he promised. 'A lot of it is probably junk.'

We dumped the bags in the room that had been assigned to Becca and then Noël checked again on Tilda, who was fast asleep, before we carried on up past the nursery.

Jess gave the attic door a good shove and it opened reluctantly with a protesting screech.

'Jude ought to get that fixed, it's always sticking,' Noël said, pressing down a light switch and illuminating a large space, well filled with the abandoned clutter and tat of centuries.

'There's another, smaller attic over the kitchen wing, but there's nothing much in it, as I recall. In the days when there were several servants, I think some of them slept there.'

'I hadn't even noticed a way into it,' I confessed.

'It's in a dark corner of the landing and looks like a cupboard door.'

'That would account for it'.

Noël led the way to a dust-sheeted pile between a large trunk and a miscellany of broken chairs. 'Here we are,' he announced and Jess tore off the sheet eagerly.

'We need all these boxes marked with a large C, and that red metal stand for the Christmas tree,' he began, then noticed he'd lost my attention. 'I see you are admiring the Spanish chest, m'dear?'

'Yes, it looks ancient?'

'Parts of the house are extremely old and the chest has always been here. We think it might be Elizabethan and came into the family when an ancestor married a Spanish bride, or perhaps a few years later. Did I mention that family legend has it that Shakespeare once visited Old Place, too?'

'No,' I said, 'though it doesn't surprise me, since they found those Shakespeare documents over at Sticklepond recently. He seems to have got about a bit, doesn't he? You'd probably be hard-pressed to find any large house in West Lancashire that he wasn't alleged to have visited!'

'Very true!' he acknowledged. 'You know, until recently we used to act out *Twelfth Night* on New Year's Eve: "If music be the food of love, play on . . ."' He sighed wistfully. 'Oh well . . .'

'I'm not allowed to go in that chest for dressing-up things,' Jess said.

136

'No, the mumming costumes for the Revels are in it, though the heads are stored in the hayloft behind the Auld Christmas.'

'The *heads*?' I repeated.

'The Dragon and Red Hoss and the Man-Woman's hat and mask,' he explained, though that didn't make things much clearer: the opposite, if anything.

'You know,' he added, looking at me with a puzzled air, 'you already feel so much like one of the family that I keep forgetting that you are not, and don't know all our little ways and customs. But I *have* mentioned the Revels on Twelfth Night, haven't I?'

I was glad to be thought of as one of the family, even though I was doubling as cook and general factotum, because I was in a strange position: it's easier when I'm on cooking assignments, because then I'm *definitely* staff.

'Is it Morris dancing? I've noticed the photographs, especially in the library.'

'That's right, dancing and a little play-acting – just a simple ceremony . . .' he said vaguely. 'It takes place on the green in front of the Auld Christmas and has been performed for centuries, though of course there have been changes over the years. I'll show you some more photographs after dinner, if you like?'

'Thank you, that would be really interesting,' I agreed, thinking that this might be a way of getting him to tell me more about his brother Ned.

'Oh look – sledges!' Jess said, spotting them leaning against the wall behind the boxes. 'Two of them and they're plastic, so they must have belonged to Uncle Jude and Guy.'

'That's right,' Noël said. 'There are a couple of old wooden ones around somewhere too, that we oldies had when we were children – or maybe they fell apart, I can't remember.'

There was so much clutter; *anything* could be up there, including Santa and all his reindeer. It could do with a jolly good clear-out.

'I think the blue one was Jude's and the red one Guy's, though

I expect they fell out over *that*, too – Guy always wanted what his older brother had and they were forever squabbling.'

'I suppose that's natural,' I said.

'In a child, but perhaps not so allowable in an adult ... though now Guy's getting married and settling down, I expect he will see things differently. There's nothing like having children of your own to give you a new perspective on life.'

'*I* was a mistake,' Jess announced.

'More of a very welcome surprise,' amended her grandfather.

'Would it be all right if I used one of the sledges, Grandpa?'

'Take them both down, m'dear: perfect weather for sledging and perhaps Holly will join you. I wish *my* poor old bones were up to it,' he added wistfully.

Jess carried the sledges downstairs first, then came back up and started ferrying down boxes of decorations to the sitting room. I took the tree stand and a carton marked 'swags and door wreath' while Noël clutched the box containing a precious antique hand-carved wooden Nativity scene. By the time we'd stacked everything in a corner of the sitting room, I had to go and start making lunch.

Tilda stubbornly insisted on coming downstairs and joining us for soup, egg sandwiches and chocolate cake. Apart from a slightly black eye, she looked a little better, though moving very stiffly. Afterwards she established herself on the sofa in the sitting room and exhibited a slight tendency to issue orders to all of us, but especially me, wanting to know exactly how I would be coping with the catering over Christmas. But I didn't really mind that, because when I cook for house-parties I'm used to consulting over the menus, so I sat down with her for a good discussion.

'Luckily the house is extremely well stocked and I always bring my cookery books, recipe notebook and favourite store cupboard ingredients with me, so there should be no problem. There's a shelf of cookery books in the kitchen, too.'

When I'd leafed through one or two well-thumbed-looking ones, I'd found additions pencilled next to the recipes, so someone had been a keen cook: either the last housekeeper or perhaps Jude's mother.

'We might run out of fresh salad, fruit and perishable things if the village is snowed in, but we can get by without them,' I added. 'There's loads of bread in the freezer, and butter, eggs, cheese, long-life juice, milk and cream. We certainly won't starve.'

'And you have everything you need for the traditional Christmas dinner?' she asked.

'Yes, there's no problem there. I cooked the ham this morning and I've taken the turkey out of the freezer and put it in the larder to defrost slowly. What time do you usually have it? Are you a lunch or evening family?'

'About two in the afternoon, then we only need a late supper of sandwiches and cake instead of dinner. We do the same on Boxing Day.'

'Right . . . though perhaps we might like a change from turkey on Boxing Day? I noticed a whole salmon in one of the freezers and thought we could have that instead, then a second roast turkey dinner the next day, before I use up the remains in dishes like curry for the freezer.'

Tilda gave her gracious approval to all my plans, which was just as well, since I would have carried on regardless. I don't let any of my clients interfere with my cooking, with the exception of dietary requirements; although since I smile and nod while listening to them issuing orders, I'm sure they think the resulting wonderful food is all their own idea.

'We have champagne with Christmas dinner,' Noël said, 'but I'll see to the drinks so you needn't worry about that.'

'I'll need some more brandy for the pudding too,' I told him, 'because I used up what was in the decanter.'

'I'll go down and get some now and scout out what else Jude's got in the wine cellar,' he promised.

'There's no rush – let your lunch settle first,' I suggested. 'You've had a busy morning.'

'And now that the main menus have been sorted, I think I'd like cake or scones for afternoon tea, today,' Tilda said autocratically, before going back upstairs to rest.

'Sorry, m'dear, she's a bit bossy and she keeps forgetting you aren't staff,' apologised Noël.

'Well, I suppose I *am* really, since I'm being paid to be here.'

'Edwina doesn't stand any nonsense, she just says to her, "You'll get what you're given, my lady, and like it!"'

I grinned. 'You just can't get the serfs to behave themselves these days, can you?'

'I think of you more and more as one of the family,' he said kindly, 'though since we've made so much more work for you over Christmas, you deserve to be paid for it – and if Jude doesn't do something about it, then we will make it up to you.'

'Oh no, really – I'm enjoying the company and I love cooking,' I insisted, because he is such a sweetie. 'I'm *perfectly* happy with my house-sitting fee!'

Chapter 15: Advent

I meet N whenever I can slip away – I can't help myself. He says we were meant to be together, he knew it from the moment he saw me and I feel the same way, though horribly guilty when I think of poor Tom. I did sincerely love him, just not in the way I now love N . . .

February 1945

The sky, which had earlier been almost as blue as George's eyes, had turned leaden again. Jess took one of the sledges up to the top of the paddock where it sloped quite steeply, while I finally got round to mucking out the loosebox. I'd only just started when the side gate clanged and I looked out to see Becca leading Nutkin through it.

'Hell of a journey!' she greeted me, closing the gate behind her. 'I had to bribe George to bring my bags earlier – have they come? He's making a mint out of the bad weather, the rascal.'

'Yes, he dropped them off after breakfast and we've put them in your room. But I'm surprised to see you, since it isn't very good weather for riding, is it?'

'I led Nutkin on the worst bits, but I couldn't leave him alone at home if there was a chance I'd get snowed in here, could I?' she asked reasonably. 'Weather's closing in again, so I thought I'd better take the chance and come up now, especially with Tilda, Noël and Jess being here already.'

'You mean – you've come to stay, too?'

'That's it,' she agreed. 'One more can't make any difference to you, can it? In fact, it'll be easier, because I can give you a hand with the horses.'

'Great,' I said faintly, though I suppose having an equine expert on hand *would* be a relief if we were snowed in. She put Nutkin in Lady's loosebox and rubbed him down briskly with wisps of hay, then we went in to tell Noël she had arrived. Jess came too, since she said her fingers were freezing and so was her bottom.

Noël, who was snoozing on one of the sofas in the sitting room, woke up and blinked as we all trooped in. 'Becca! This *is* a surprise!'

'Weather's getting worse, so I thought I'd send my bags up and come to stay now. I've brought Nutkin,' she explained succinctly.

'Well, how nice, a jolly family party!' Noël rubbed his hands together. 'It's a pity the boys can't be here too, but there you are.'

'Stopped at the Auld Christmas on the way, to bring a little cheer.' Becca reached into two deep pockets inside her waxed, caped coat and produced a bottle of sherry from each. 'We're all partial to a drop of good sherry . . . which reminds me, where's Tilda?'

'Resting, but she'll be down again later. She says she isn't quite so stiff now the bruises have come out – though she's black and blue, poor old girl!'

'I brought some horse liniment – always does the trick for me.'

'Yes, but it smells disgusting, Becca,' he objected dubiously.

'Nicholas Dagger said to tell you they were all set for Twelfth Night and rehearsed for the dancing.'

'Good, good!' he said. 'Aren't you going to take your coat off?'

'No, I'm going straight back out to see to the horses,' Becca said. 'Lady's loosebox still needs mucking out and I'll have to make the other up for Nutkin.'

142

'But you must be frozen, and I can do that,' I offered.

'Not at all – you've got enough on your plate already. But I'll need Jess to wheel the barrow to the manure heap and fill the buckets.'

'I'm allergic to horses and I'm cold and wet,' Jess said sulkily. 'I'd rather just help Grandpa get the decorations up.'

'You mean you're allergic to hard work,' Becca said severely. 'You don't have to come near Lady or Nutkin. Now, run up to my bedroom and fetch the holdall – it's got Nutkin's rug and headcollar in it.'

Jess gave in, though *not* graciously.

I put on a large casserole to slow-cook for dinner, using some very nice beef from the freezer, home-grown carrots and a good splash of beer from a stash of large bottles I'd discovered on the stone floor of the larder, pushed well back under the bottom shelf. I drank what was left – it was best bitter and I probably needed the iron.

Jess came back in looking limp, so I suggested she go and start putting up the decorations with Noël when she had warmed up a bit.

But Becca, who was still full of energy, borrowed my radio and took it into the tackroom, where she was sitting cleaning Nutkin's saddle when I followed her with a substantial slice of chocolate cake and a cup of tea to keep her energy levels up.

Later she made the hot mash and went out again to get Lady and Billy in, since it was starting to get dark, so she was proving to be worth her weight in pony nuts already.

Jess and I carried in the Christmas tree and managed to angle it into its red metal holder, though the top of it almost brushed the gallery above. Then she and Noël steadied the stepladder while I draped the garlands as they directed, from each corner of the room to the middle of the ceiling, and hung Chinese lanterns and baubles from the wall light fittings.

Then I left them unpacking the Nativity scene and went back to the kitchen, where even sober Radio 4 was intoxicated with the spirit of Christmas.

Luckily, no-one seemed to have any objection to eating meals off the kitchen table, which made life much easier than traipsing to and from the dining room with plates and platters, though we would use it on Christmas Day and Boxing Day, of course.

There was a chocolate blancmange rabbit for dessert, quivering on a bed of chopped green jelly, which proved surprisingly popular with everyone, not just Jess. It vanished right down to its tail and, what with that and the chocolate cake, I was starting to wish I had brought more than one tin of cocoa powder with me!

Tilda hadn't got any at the lodge when I asked her, only Ovaltine, which was not at all the same thing, but she thought the village shop stocked it, so another trip was clearly needed.

After dinner was cleared away (and thank goodness there was a dishwasher! If the electricity did go off, I only hoped the generator was up to running it), we retired to the half-decorated sitting room and Noël, as he had promised earlier, fetched the photograph albums that charted the Revels from the library.

They all seemed to feature the same strangely-dressed and masked figures and, as I had suspected, Morris dancing, though they carried swords. I don't suppose they were *real* ones, though.

One picture of four tall, dark young men standing with a young version of Becca particularly interested me.

'That's me,' Noël said, pointing to a handsome man, little more than a boy, 'and that's Jacob, my eldest brother, but he was killed at Dunkirk, poor chap. Ned was injured too, but later – that's him next to Jacob and then Alexander, Jude's father, who inherited Old Place.'

'And then me,' said Becca.

144

'I recognised you instantly, you haven't changed much,' I told her, and she looked pleased.

'Keep pretty fit, considering,' she said. 'Of course, I'm the youngest.'

I looked again at the photograph. 'So . . . what happened to Edward? You said he was injured?'

'He had a bad leg injury, but they tried penicillin on it and he made a speedy recovery. It seemed he was going to settle down after that, but it wasn't to be . . . and he never played Red Hoss in the Revels again.'

Noël seemed about to drift away into old, and perhaps unhappy, memories so I said, 'Red Hoss? I think you mentioned that character before.'

Noël thumbed forward until he found a photograph of a man wearing a rather scary and fierce horse mask. 'That one – I forget you know little about it,' he said apologetically, 'as I said earlier, I feel we have known you for ever – and you look so like one of the Martlands that you would fit into the family album quite easily. It's a strange coincidence, isn't it?'

'Yes, it certainly is,' I said absently, staring at another photograph of Ned Martland, without the mask, next to it. It was neither large nor clear, but something about his expression reminded me of a framed photograph of my mother that had always had pride of place on top of Gran's harmonium . . . and still did, though it was now in my cottage. But then, when I leaned forward for a better look, I realised it was just a trick of the light.

'And I don't suppose you had ever heard of the Twelfth Night Revels in Little Mumming before, had you?'

'Or about the red horse hill figure,' I agreed.

'We try not to publicise either of them – and actually, these days the Revels are more of a Twelfth Afternoon ceremony. Since the war, you know. But traditionally, a fire was lit on the beacon, as well, and then there was a procession back down from it.'

'I don't suppose you could light fires at night during the war, it'd be way too dangerous.'

'No, it was the blackout, you see. And with most of the young men off at war, some of the older ones who took their places were not really up to climbing the hill. But my father kept the Revels going as well as he could.'

'Wouldn't publicising the Revels bring lots of tourists here?'

'That's the whole point, m'dear. We have plenty of walkers, cyclists and stray drivers from spring to autumn: the pub, the shop and the Merry Kettle do well, the farm shop at Weasel's Pot thrives, and George gives trailer rides behind his tractor up to the beacon: that is enough for us. We don't want the Revels to be taken over by a lot of arty crafty folk who will want the whole thing preserved like a fly in amber, instead of letting it gently evolve as it has done over the centuries.'

'I see what you mean,' I agreed.

'Richard Sampson wrote a short pamphlet about the Revels and the red horse, for private circulation only, and I can look you out the library copy if you are interested?'

'Yes, I'd love to read it. Won't the Revels be snowed off this year if the weather carries on like this? Unless a thaw sets in soon, of course.'

'Oh, we've had heavy snow in January before and it has gone ahead. We all live locally, you see, and it's only half a mile down to the village from here. If the snow hasn't gone by then, Jess can pull me there on the sledge!'

'I might, Grandpa, but I'm not pulling you back up the hill again!' she protested.

'I wasn't serious, m'dear. Your Uncle Jude will be back by then and he will manage something.'

I had been drawn back to studying the prewar photograph of the young Martlands. 'So, Ned recovered from his leg wound? What happened to him after that?'

'It was ironic, really – he was killed in a motorbike accident only a couple of months after the war ended.'

'That's . . . quite tragic,' I said slowly and, since Noël was looking troubled, I didn't press him for more details.

But maybe that's why nothing ever came of Granny's big romance? And if so, it was terribly sad! Noël had implied that his brother Ned was a bit of a black sheep and he *had* sounded like a flirt at first, only now he really appeared to have fallen for Gran, just as she'd fallen head over heels in love with him.

Poor Gran – now I knew that her happiness would be cut short by Ned's accident, it made reading about it that night even more poignant!

> *When I confided in Hilda and Pearl, they said if N really loved me, why did it have to stay a secret that we were seeing each other? So then I asked N when we were going to tell our families that we were courting, and he said there was no hurry, because he didn't want to share the few precious hours we could spend together with anyone else at present.*

He must have had a lot of charm to persuade a girl with her strict upbringing to meet him clandestinely! It seems very odd at this remove in time that they should have felt the need to keep their romance secret, but class differences and the social divide were more important then, I suppose.

Then my eye fell on the next, short entry and I had a total 'Oh, my God!' moment: I think I *seriously* underestimated Ned Martland's charm!

Chapter 16: Comfort

I am too ashamed to go to chapel and look Tom's father in the eye. I am a sinner, a grievous sinner.

March, 1945

I woke up later than usual, heavy-eyed after a night full of strange, uneasy dreams, and lay there thinking about Gran. I still couldn't see any other interpretation for what I'd read but the one I'd originally thought of, and all sorts of possibilities and implications kept going through my head.

Eventually I resolved to try to put it to the back of my mind until I could talk it over with Laura, though that was easier said than done. In the end I decided I'd take the current volume down with me to dip into if I got a quiet moment alone. I could put it on the cookery book shelf in the kitchen, because no-one else ever looked there.

When I drew the curtains it was still almost dark but I could see that there had been a further fall of snow. Becca was obviously an early bird too, because I could see her below me, turning Nutkin into the paddock to join Billy and a well-rugged-up Lady. Her presence here is obviously going to be a huge asset while I am so busy with everything else, though I suppose if Jude knew she'd taken over most of my horse-minding duties, he would want to dock my house-sitting fee!

I still had the care of Merlin, though, and carefully stirred his medicine into his food every morning, though actually he was such a soft, biddable creature he would probably have eaten it straight from my hand. I was getting very attached to him – he was such a lovely, affectionate dog, always pleased to see me.

Becca and I had breakfast together and then she sat on with a mug of tea, listening to the radio and watching me as I soaked trifle sponges I'd found in the cupboard (which were indeed more than a trifle out of date, but well sealed up) in a little sherry purloined from the drinks cabinet in the dining room and then made a pheasant terrine, having defrosted the birds overnight.

'You're very organised!' she commented.

'It's just my job – thinking ahead and knowing what to prepare for the dishes I intend making is second nature. Forward planning.'

'Well, I wish you could stay here and cook permanently.'

I smiled. 'I don't think your nephew would be too pleased about that – we don't seem to get on very well when he rings,' I told her, though oddly enough I had sort of missed our slightly acerbic exchanges ever since the phone had gone dead . . .

When Noël and Jess appeared, Becca had a second breakfast with them but Tilda had hers in bed again, though that seems to be a habit rather than a sign that she's still feeling under the weather.

While they were eating they discussed their plans for the day. Jess and Noël proposed to finish putting up the decorations and then do the Christmas tree, but before they could put that plan into action, Becca dragged Jess out to help with mucking out, buckets and haynets.

Noël fetched Tilda's tray down while I cleared up and checked on the terrine, which was both looking and smelling good. I've always found it a popular dish.

Becca and Jess were not outside long and returned with pink

149

noses and chilly hands just as Noël was making a fresh pot of tea, which seems to be about the extent of his culinary skills.

'George has been up and he says he's left you some more holly and stuff in the porch. I'll help you put it up, once I've thawed out,' Becca promised, 'but one of my favourite old films is on later and I thought I might watch that – *Winter Holiday*. If Tilda is down, she might want to see it, too.'

'She has come down. I just came to get her a cup of tea.'

'Then you can pour me one too, it's bloody nithering out there.'

'I've never heard of *Winter Holiday*,' Jess said, 'and the reception is so bad here you can hardly see anything anyway. I don't know why Uncle Jude hasn't got Sky like Granny and Grandpa. At least at the lodge I could watch something *good*!'

'There's a video and DVD player,' Noël pointed out. 'You brought some DVDs up with you, didn't you?'

'Yes, but I've seen them all a million times. And I can't play computer games because Jude keeps it locked away in the study – and anyway, it's really, really ancient so it's too slow for any of the games I've got. If he wasn't so mean he would have got a new one by now.'

'You shouldn't call him mean,' chided Noël. 'I expect Father Christmas is bringing you a lovely present from him.'

'Oh, *Grandpa*!' She rolled her eyes. 'I'm much too old to believe in Father Christmas *and* I saw that big parcel with American stamps that George brought yesterday. I suppose there are some from Mum and Dad in that big sack of presents you brought up with you?'

Noël tapped the side of his nose and tried to look mysterious, while I suddenly realised that I would be the only one who wasn't giving or receiving presents on Christmas Day . . . like Granny's first Christmas at the new hospital in Ormskirk, when she had nothing to give to her friends in return for their gifts, until she'd thought of the bookmarks . . .

150

I didn't even have bookmarks – and, come to think of it, Jess had said she was going to give me something she had made herself, so presumably I would have one present at least.

As if she could read my mind, Jess piped up just then and said, 'We can put all the presents under the tree when we've finished decorating it. I've nearly finished making all mine, but I've still got to wrap them.'

'Jess is an expert in origami,' Noël said proudly.

'I make origami jewellery and sell it at school,' Jess explained. 'Tiny, fiddly origami.'

'That's very clever,' I said, 'I'd love to see some of it.'

I'd been wondering whether to take a last trek down to the village to stock up on odds and ends that seemed likely to run out, like cocoa powder, and now I thought I ought to get in a supply of small emergency Christmas gifts too, just in case!

'Are you going to help us decorate?' asked Noël. 'You seem to have been very busy already, so perhaps you would rather put your feet up for a bit, m'dear?'

'No, I'm fine. I'll help you for half an hour and then I think I'll walk down to the village. I need a few last things from the shop and to stretch my legs, but I won't take Merlin – it's a bit freezing out there for his arthritis and I'd have to tie him up outside.'

I could see Jess was torn between coming with me and decorating the tree, and added quickly, 'I'd be grateful if you could keep an eye on him while I'm out, Jess? The poor old thing is missing his master and has latched on to me as a substitute, so he isn't going to like my going off without him.'

'Yes, and I'll need you to climb the stepladder while I hold it,' Noël pointed out. 'I can't do it alone and our old Father Christmas needs to go on top of the tree.' He held aloft a brownish figure of moulded paper. 'My brother Jacob bought this with his pocket money when he was about five, so that makes it well over eighty years old,' he said sentimentally.

'He's a venerable Santa,' I said, touched, 'and he's earned his place. And actually, I think if I leaned over the balcony I could put him on top of the tree from there.'

I managed to put quite a lot of small baubles on the top of the tree that way and helped drape the long string of fairy lights around it, so at least when I went out I knew Jess wouldn't be teetering about too high up on the ladder.

'You will be careful while I'm out, won't you?'

'Of course – we're a team, aren't we, Jess?' Noël said. 'The sitting room will be a picture by the time you get back!'

'I'm sure it will,' I said and left them to it while I made a few preparations in the kitchen and then got wrapped up for the walk. (I didn't fancy my chances of getting the car back up the hill this time.)

Merlin was beginning to look anxious, but when I went back into the sitting room Jess stopped unravelling a garland and made a fuss of him.

'I'm just off, but I've left soup in the pan on the back of the stove and sandwiches in the fridge for lunch. There's carrot cake or mince pies for after. You don't need to save anything for me, because I'll have bread and cheese in the pub.'

'I'll sort that out and from the sound of it, I don't think we'll starve while you're gone,' Becca said cheerfully. 'And if you *don't* come back, we'll send out search parties!'

'If I gave you the keys, could you possibly pop into the lodge and just make sure everything is all right?' asked Noël. 'No burst pipes – always a worry at this time of the year.'

'Yes, of course.'

'And if you need anything from the kitchen, just help yourself,' Tilda said graciously from the easy chair where she had placed herself to direct the decorating proceedings.

'Thanks – that would be very useful, especially if you have almond and vanilla essences?'

'I'm sure there are. Bring back what you need.'

'I don't like to ask for yet another favour,' Noël said, 'but if I gave you Jude's mobile phone number, could you try calling him while you are down there, and tell him where we are?'

'I'll give it a go,' I said dubiously, since I'm not in the habit of making transatlantic calls.

'And go and make sure Old Nan and Richard are all right while you are down in the village, too,' ordered Tilda autocratically, though it did show a caring and thoughtful side to her.

'Actually, I've wrapped up half a dozen mince pies each for them already.'

'Good idea.'

'Wine gums,' said Jess suddenly. 'Can you bring me back a big bag?'

'You'll rot your teeth,' said Tilda.

I left Jess hanging onto Merlin's collar and set out, feeling just like one of those tiny figures in a vast snowy Breughel landscape painting. I followed the ploughed track down the driveway (I *thought* I'd heard the roar of the tractor earlier), slipping and sliding a bit on the fresh snow that had half-filled it. It was easier going under the pine trees by the river, where the ground was free of snow, and on impulse I turned up the wide path off it to where I knew Jude's mill studio was.

It was only a few yards until the trees opened out to reveal a tall, narrow building with the remains of a mill race and dark, deep-looking pool below it. I peered through the window and saw that it was open right up to the rafters and full of all kinds of mysterious shapes, most vaguely equine.

It was pretty freezing so I didn't linger, but went on to the lodge, where everything looked fine. The kitchen cupboards didn't reveal much that I hadn't got already, apart from a few flavourings, spices and ground almonds, which I put in my rucksack in case I forgot them on the way back.

The lane down to Little Mumming had been cleared and grit spread on the worst part of the slope, but it was still slippery, so I was grateful when George stopped his long-wheelbase Land Rover and offered me a lift. I had to share the front seat with his slightly smelly sheepdog, but to be honest, by then I was just glad of the warmth.

'You must have been out really early, George! How is the road down beyond the village?'

'Liam was the one out first thing and he said you could still get a four-wheel drive up and down to the main road, but anything else would be in trouble,' he said. 'My lad and Ben from Weasel's Pot are friends, so one ploughs up and the other down and it gives them a chance to meet in the middle and waste time, like.'

I smiled. 'You all seem to work really hard already – you must have plenty to do without all this road clearing.'

'Ah, but farmers have to diversify to make the money these days, and the council pays well for road clearing. Then Jude and one or two others pay me for clearing their drives too, so it all helps.'

'Yes, I suppose it must.'

'And in the summer I hitch up this dinky little trailer with bench seats behind the tractor and take the tourists up the track to the beacon and back. Pays better than the sheep, that does.'

'That's very enterprising,' I said and, as we came down past the church, added, 'you know, I hadn't thought to ask if the shop would even be open today!'

'Oh, Orrie will only close Christmas and Boxing Day and she'll always open in an emergency – she lives above the shop. Yes . . . very obliging, is Orrie,' he added thoughtfully – I could see I had an established love rival!

'She certainly seems to have a wide-ranging stock, doesn't she?'

'Yes, well, she's a general store and gift shop rolled into one, you see – caters for the tourist trade in summer and opens that café of hers for cream teas. Were you wanting anything in particular?'

'Not really, just a few bits and pieces I thought we might run out of, and Tilda wanted me to check up on Old Nan and the Vicar – do you think you could drop me by the almshouses? I've been wondering how they'll get up to Old Place for Christmas dinner. At a push, I expect I could drive them home again in my car, but I'm sure it won't go up this hill. I'd have to leave it down there.'

'Nay, that little car of yours won't be much good on ice! It's a pity Jude took his old Land Rover with him, or you could've used that.'

'But I couldn't use someone else's car and I've never driven a Land Rover before.'

'Well, don't you fret about Christmas Day: our Liam can plough the road to the village and your drive first thing and then one of us will go down and fetch the old folks up for you.'

'Surely you won't be out on the roads on Christmas morning?'

'We're farmers: we'll be out tending the livestock anyway, Christmas morning or not.'

'You're very kind,' I said gratefully.

'My pleasure,' he said, with a quick sideways glance accompanied by his engaging grin.

Some children were making a snowman near the church and it all looked picturebook with its coating of snow . . . until I saw where the children had chosen to stick the carrot.

'Little bleeders,' George said amiably, glancing at them as we passed and circled the green.

'Noël's told me a bit about the Revels. He said there would be a ring of twelve fire braziers as well as the bonfire.'

'That's right. Originally there were twelve small bonfires and one big one, but Jude made some wrought-iron basketwork braziers that spike into the ground, so we use those instead now. It's the same idea, just easier and safer.'

He gave me another sideways look from his sky-blue eyes as he pulled up outside the almshouses. 'Noël doesn't usually say much to strangers about the Revels: none of us do. He must have taken an uncommon shine to you.'

'I think it's because he keeps forgetting I'm not one of the family, since I'm tall and dark, which seems to be usual with Martlands.'

'Yes, the dark side does seem to win out, and you do have a Martland look – I thought so from the first.'

I wasn't sure if that was a compliment or not!

'I'm starting to be sorry I'll miss the Revels. Do you take part in them?'

'Oh yes, there've always been Rappers from Hill Farm,' he said mysteriously as I got out, and added that he was going to see his sister, who lived on the far side of the village, but would look out for me on the way back.

Although Henry was out (I left his foil-wrapped package on a little shelf inside the porch and hoped it would be all right), the other two both seemed pleased to see me and accepted as a matter of course the news that someone from Hill Farm would pick them up and bring them to Old Place on Christmas Day. In fact, Old Nan told me that George wouldn't need to bother, since Jude would come himself, he always did. Clearly she had lost the plot again.

Richard had also lost it, since he addressed me as Miss Martland and told me to inform the family that he would take a midnight carol service on Christmas Eve, since the vicar from Great Mumming was unlikely to make it. 'He usually does an early service here, then goes on to the church in Great Mumming.'

'Won't you be exhausted taking a late service – and in the cold?' I asked.

'I don't sleep much these days, anyway. And there are paraffin heaters in the church, you know – we have to keep the damp out.'

I didn't go in either cottage, or keep them lingering in the cold: I wanted to get on and get my errands done so I could have a quiet lunch . . . and I had Gran's latest journal in the pocket of my rucksack. I had a feeling I was going to be too busy after this to spend much time relaxing.

There was a call box in the village, but it was out of order and goodness knows how much change I would have needed to call a mobile phone in the USA, anyway! I stayed in there out of the cold while I tried the number Noël had given me on my phone, but a disembodied voice told me it was unavailable.

Well, at least I had tried . . . and, since I'd been braced to deal with Jude's brusqueness (especially when I told him I'd be billing him for the call), I now felt strangely deflated!

Mrs Comfort, who was sitting behind the shop counter knitting, perked up and greeted me with enthusiasm, especially when I said I needed a few last-minute presents.

'Gifts are mostly through in the Merry Kettle,' she said, pointing through the open door into the café where the overflow of her goods was displayed, probably to tempt the visitors in summer while they consumed their cream teas.

I could feel her eager, beady eyes boring into my back as I looked around at the limited selection of toys, games and novelties. There was also a large wooden display stand of everything from mugs to dishcloths printed with inspirational thoughts and labelled 'The Words of Comfort Range from Oriel Comfort'.

I was curious more than anything, because I'd already decided to make my emergency gifts myself: I'd noticed a cache of old, clean jam jars, wax discs, labels and cellophane lids in the scullery at Old Place and I intended filling them with sweets.

So I bought lots of the brightly coloured shiny ones that Jess liked, along with wine gums, humbugs, Liquorice Allsorts, mint imperials and coconut mushrooms, then added Sellotape, Christmas tags and a big roll of flimsy, cheerfully garish gift-wrap. I even found some red gingham paper napkins that could be cut into circles to make covers for the jars, too, and a bag of elastic bands to secure them.

As my pile of purchases mounted up on the counter, Mrs Comfort looked cheerier and cheerier and began to make helpful suggestions.

'Noël likes Turkish Delight,' she confided, 'and his missis likes Milk Tray chocolates – he often buys her some. This is the last of the Turkish Delight, you're in luck. And what about these chocolate tree decorations?'

Unbidden, she added them to the heap and then cast her eyes over her stock, obviously wondering what else she could offload onto me.

I whisked out my shopping list. 'There are a few things I need, if you have them, like cocoa powder, icing sugar, jelly . . .'

In fact, there weren't many things she *didn't* have. It felt a bit like watching a magician producing endless doves from a top hat.

'And you'll want the last tins of squirty cream,' she urged me.

'We've already got tons of the stuff!'

'Love it, they do, at the lodge,' she assured me. 'Can't get enough of it.'

I ticked the last thing off (more matches) with a sigh: I was wondering how I would get everything up the hill again, unless George spotted me.

Oriel took a new tack: 'Old Nan, she likes chocolate mints and the vicar is partial to humbugs. Henry's more of an Uncle Joe's Mint Ball man.'

Surely, I thought, I wouldn't need presents for people I'd barely met, who were only coming for dinner? But then, it might be better to be sure than sorry.

'All right,' I capitulated, 'but I ought to leave Henry's now, in case I don't see him again before Christmas.'

'I'll slap a bit of gift-wrap on it for free and take it across later, shall I?' she suggested obligingly.

'If you wouldn't mind, that would be great.'

'Not at all.'

'Well, that *must* be everything!'

But she wasn't about to let me go without a struggle. 'What about Jess's Christmas stocking? Got everything you need for that?'

I stared at her, startled. A stocking on Christmas morning like all my friends had had was the thing I'd most desperately longed for when I was a little girl: but surely Jess was now too old?

'She's nearly thirteen, so I would have thought she was too grown up for one this year? But if she isn't then I suppose her mother or Tilda will have seen to it.'

'Perhaps – perhaps not. And in my experience, you're never too old for a stocking. Perhaps you should take a couple of bits and pieces, just in case they've forgotten about it?'

'Like what? *I've* no idea what she would like!'

'Let me see,' she mused. 'It's a funny age: they're a child one minute, quite grownup the next.'

She took down a jar containing sugar mice with string tails in white, lurid yellow, or pink and prepared to give me a master class in Christmas stocking preparation.

'You need one of these at the bottom, with a tangerine or something like that to start with. When I was a little girl there used to be a handful of nuts, though I never knew why, since you could hardly crack Brazil nuts in bed with your teeth, could you?'

'We've got fruit and nuts, but I don't think Jess would be very excited by finding them in her stocking, since she can help herself any time she likes.'

'It helps to fill it up, but we can put in a packet of Love Hearts instead. Most of my toys are too young for her, but there's a pack of Happy Family cards and a couple of jokes, like the whoopee cushion and the ink blot, that I expect she'd like. And maybe a fluffy toy sheepdog? I keep them for the summer visitors, with the postcards and stuff.'

'Do you think she's a fluffy toy sort of girl?' I asked doubtfully, but she was already delving deep into a large wicker basket and came up with a black, wolfish-looking creature with yellow eyes that had been lurking at the bottom.

'I just remembered – this came in mixed with the last lot of collies, and I never got round to sending it back.'

'Right,' I said, and then on impulse added an elasticated bracelet of polished dark grey stones.

'How about a jigsaw puzzle? I always think a big puzzle is something the whole family can do together on Christmas Day.'

'I'm sure I saw a whole stack of them in the old nursery,' I said quickly.

'This one's got a lovely Christmas scene on the front – and if you return it afterwards with all the pieces, I'll buy it back for half price,' she added enticingly and, my willpower totally sapped by now, I nodded dumbly.

Paying for that lot pretty well cleaned me out of cash, since Mrs Comfort didn't take cards of any kind, and once I'd filled the rucksack I had to buy a big jute bag with one of Oriel's inspirational thoughts on it: *A Loving Heart Keeps You Warm on Winter's Nights.*

It had been a choice between that or *Love Circles – Pass It On*.

You know, when I looked closer, the things on that stand were irresistibly awful!

Chapter 17: Rapping

*N says nothing can be wrong when two people truly love each
other, as we do, but I know what we did should only happen
within the bounds of marriage . . .*

March, 1945

I hauled my purchases over to the church and sat on a stone
bench in the porch out of the wind, to phone Laura on my
mobile. (I did dutifully try Jude's number again, but got the
same message.)

'Oh, good,' she said when she answered, sounding relieved,
'I've been trying to get through to the house and it kept saying
there was a fault on the line.'

'There is – one of the poles holding the phone wires up has
fallen down and taken the next one with it. Is everything okay?
How are you?'

'Oh, *I'm* all right and the baby's kicking like mad. The other
three are so excited about Christmas they're hysterical and Dan's
just helpfully vanished, presumably to buy my present. He's
always so last minute! But how are *you* doing? I'm worried about
you, taking so much on and being so isolated.'

'Isolated is the last way I'd describe Old Place, actually, Laura!'

'You sound a bit worried – which is not like you at all. What
is it, are you finding it too much?'

'Of course not – you know me, I *thrive* on a challenge,' I

assured her, though she didn't yet know quite how *much* of a challenge my current post had become! 'But there's something on my mind I'd like to run past you, to see if you think I'm imagining things.'

'Go on, then, tell me.'

'It's Gran's diaries. Things between her and Ned Martland have hotted up quite a bit and . . . well, I think they had *sex*.'

'Good heavens,' she said mildly, 'I didn't think that was invented until the sixties.'

'It certainly wasn't for good Strange Baptist girls like Gran, that's for sure, especially in 1945! She must have been sure they were going to marry, but obviously that didn't happen – and since I just found out that Ned was killed in an accident I'm hoping that was the reason, not because he abandoned her!'

'Didn't you skip forward and try to find out? I would have!'

'No, because to be honest, so much is happening that I'm exhausted by bedtime and I hardly have a minute to myself during the day, though I did have another quick look while I drank my first cup of coffee this morning.'

'And did you find out what happened?'

'No, she's been wrestling with her conscience for pages and pages, but I'm keeping the current journal in the kitchen and dipping into it whenever I have a minute on my own. But the thing that's worrying me is that Noël implied that Ned was a bad lot as far as women were concerned: charming and lovable, but unreliable. I keep thinking: what if Gran got *pregnant* and relied on him to make an honest woman of her?'

'Aren't you jumping the gun a bit? She hasn't said so, has she?'

'Not so far, but I can't help wondering . . .' I paused. 'Laura, you know I'm not fanciful, but I've felt at home here from the minute I arrived and that I sort of . . . fit in. And the other thing is, I'm constantly being mistaken for one of the family – even Noël forgets that I'm not. The Martlands are all tall and dark, though they don't have light grey eyes like me and Gran.'

'Your Gran wasn't tall, but didn't she have dark hair when she was young?

'Yes, and she told me my colouring came from her side of the family – her ancestors came from Liverpool, a seafaring port and I've always assumed there was a good dose of foreign blood. So I might just be imagining any resemblance to the Martlands . . . My mother was quite tall and had black hair too,' I added, though that proved nothing one way or the other. Unfortunately, I have no idea what my father looked like, because after my mother died soon after giving birth to me, he emigrated to Australia and vanished out of our lives. Gran neatly cut him out of all the wedding photographs.

There were rumours that he'd started a new family over there, so I might have half-siblings somewhere, but although I'd had one try at tracing him (without Gran's knowledge!) I didn't get anywhere.

'I can see where you're going with all this, Holly, but it could still be just a coincidence that you're tall and dark. And with your grandfather being a Strange Baptist minister, I don't suppose he would have married your gran if he knew she was pregnant by another man, would he?'

'It doesn't sound very likely when you put it like that,' I admitted.

'He was much older than she was, wasn't he?'

'Yes, she told me once he was the father of her childhood sweetheart, who was killed in the war, and it seemed natural that they should marry and console each other. I barely remember him, though everyone says he was the nicest, kindest of men.'

'Perhaps you should just carry on reading the journal and not try to join up the dots yet,' Laura suggested.

'I suppose you're right – and besides, I'm way too busy to worry about it, really. But I might just try and discover when Ned's accident was and then check that against the dates Gran got married and my mother was born – I've brought the whole trunk of her papers with me. If it doesn't all match up, then I'll know for sure.'

'That's true,' she said. 'And there's no point in worrying over it, when it's all in the past. I mean, it's not like you're going to claim a stake in the family fortune or anything, is it?'

I laughed. 'I don't think there is one! The house is pretty shabby and Jude Martland didn't hire any live-in staff when the last ones left, plus he seems obsessed with how much money I'm costing him – or he *thinks* I'm costing him. I really should charge him for all the extra work I'll be doing, because things are escalating!'

'So what's happening? I thought you were just having the family from the lodge up for Christmas dinner?'

'I was, only they've moved in already and so has Becca, Noël's sister, so I'm hosting a Christmas family house-party at Old Place. I'm cook, groom, maid and cleaner – though to be fair, Becca seems to have taken over looking after the horses.'

And I told her all about Tilda's accident and how inviting them to move into Old Place immediately was the only possible solution, and then Becca turning up on Nutkin and the discovery that there would also be two more guests for Christmas dinner – the retired vicar and the family's old nanny.

'If Jude Martland doesn't like any of this, it's tough, and he'll have to sort it out with his relatives when he gets back, because I could hardly stop them, could I? And we couldn't consult him first, because of the lines being down.'

'You could call him on your mobile, or from the village?' she suggested.

'I just tried and it said his number was unavailable. It's a relief not having him calling me every day and harassing me, really, because none of my clients have ever done that before!'

'It'll be okay, Holly – I mean, what else could you do? It was really taken out of your hands,' she said, laughing.

'You're right, I couldn't do anything else, even though it means

164

a lot more work – *and* being part of a big family Christmas celebration.'

'You might even find yourself enjoying it,' she suggested.

'At least there's enough food and drink in the house for a twelve-month siege, and Noël has the keys to the cellar, so that's his responsibility.'

'So, even if you are totally snowed in, you can manage?'

'Oh yes, and I've just bought up the village shop, too! There were a few things I was running out of and I suddenly wondered if I needed some presents.'

When I explained about the sweets and then Oriel Comfort's suggestion of a Christmas stocking for Jess, Laura thought *that* was funny too.

'If Jess isn't too old for one, surely her granny or mum will have it in hand?' I said.

'Perhaps, but you can never have too many things in your stocking.'

'I bought a huge jigsaw puzzle of a Christmas scene too, because I thought it would keep everyone occupied if the weather was bad. Oriel says if I take it back afterwards with all the pieces, she'll give me back half the price.'

'She sounds a hoot.'

'She is – and I think she's also my love rival. George, the farmer who gave me a lift down today, is an admirer.'

'Oh? What's *he* like?' she asked, interested. 'Hunky?'

'He's well-built, with white-blond hair, bright blue eyes and a very attractive smile.'

'Sounds lovely!'

'But on the downside, well the wrong side of forty and a widower with an adult son. He said I was a strapping lass and he liked my mince pies, which may constitute an offer of marriage round here, for all I know. Only I think, from something he said, that Oriel was favourite before my mince pies stole his heart.'

'Are you going to fight her for him?'

'No, I think I'll probably retire gracefully from the field . . . though he is nice. I've bought you one of Oriel's pamphlets of inspirational verse for your birthday present, with matching shopping bag.'

'I can't wait! Ring me on Christmas Day if you get a chance, but I know it'll be difficult to get away so I won't worry if you go quiet for a couple of days at some point.'

'I'll do my best. And could you ring Ellen and just update her with the situation for me?' I asked, to cover my back in case the objectionable Jude was miffed at my arrangements. 'And tell her not to bill Jude extra for the cooking and cleaning, because she's sent the list of charges to him and he thinks she is.'

She promised to do that and then she had to go. My bottom had practically frozen to the bench while talking, but I left my bags there while I had a quick look into the unlocked church, which was chilly, but quiet and lovely, with an old stained-glass window at one end showing Noah's ark and all the little animals going in two by two, including a pair that looked like giant slugs. I think Noah should have given those a miss, together with spiders and a few other unlovely things.

Collecting my shopping I trudged through the snow to the Auld Christmas, where I ate delicious crumbly Lancashire cheese, bread and pickles in a snug empty of anyone except old Nicholas Dagger, who was in the same hooded chair by the fire.

I chatted with Nancy a bit and then, perhaps awoken by our voices, Nicholas poked his head around the side of the chair like a strange species of tortoise.

'I'm Auld Man Christmas,' he piped. 'My father was Auld Man Christmas and his father before him, and—'

'Yes, we know, Father,' Nancy said soothingly, adding to me in whispered explanation, 'he gets excited at this time of year.'

'That's all right, Noël Martland told me a little bit about the Revels and then George Froggat did too, on the way down when he kindly gave me a lift.'

166

'They told you, did they, then?' She looked at me thoughtfully.

'Only a bit – I know it's a fairly private ceremony, just for the village. Do you play a part in it, too?'

'Oh no, I only watch. Women have never taken part in it.'

'Isn't that a bit sexist?'

She looked doubtful. 'No, because we don't want to be in it. There's a man dressed up half as a woman, though. I like the Rapping best.'

'You know, George said he joined in the Rapping, but I thought I'd misheard him – it seemed a bit unlikely. They don't breakdance too, do they?'

She giggled. 'No, the Rapping's just dancing with swords.'

'What, on the ground, like Scottish dancing? Rapiers?'

'Rapper dancing is different to that – they weave their swords together to make a sort of knot pattern. Then after the Dragon kills St George, it puts its head in the middle of the knot and they chop it off.'

'It *kills* St George?'

'Yes, but it's only pretend and the Doctor makes him better. Old vicar says it's all deeply symbolic – rebirth and suchlike. It's in his little pamphlet.'

'Noël said he would look for that in the library later, I must read it. So is that the end of the Revels, after the Dragon's head is chopped off?'

'Pretty much. St George gets up and they all dance again and that's it. We open up the pub afterwards, but everyone's usually still full of wassail.'

'Sounds fun.'

'Mrs Jackson, that used to be the cook-housekeeper at Old Place, she used to bring the Revel Cakes, but of course they retired after Jude's father died.'

'Oh? What were they like?'

'Spicy little buns with candied peel on top and lots of saffron

167

to make them yellow. Sort of coiled round like a Cumberland sausage.'

'They sound interesting – I'll look for the recipe. It may be up there somewhere, she left a lot of recipe books. If I find it, and I've got the ingredients, I'll make some before I go and Jude can bring them down with him on the day.'

'Or you could stay for the Revels and bring them yourself?'

'I think Jude is expecting me to have gone by the time he gets back. I'll probably be exhausted by then anyway and ready for a rest! I'm used to cooking for very large house-parties, it's my summer job, but then the food preparation and cooking are all I do. Now I'm cleaning and doing all the rest of it, too.'

'It's a hard time for women anyway, Christmas: nothing but cooking and washing up, cooking and washing up …' She sighed heavily.

'Yes, and you're working in here as well.'

'Well, that's the way of it,' she said with resignation and then she was called into the public bar on the other side, which was getting busier, and I was left to the roaring fire, the snoring Auld Nicholas and the rest of my bread and cheese.

I sat there quietly reading the next few entries in Gran's journal, though without making any further major discoveries other than her desire to get their romance on to an official footing.

As I was about to leave, I remembered that I wanted to buy a half-bottle of brandy for the flaming Christmas pudding, because the stuff Noël had brought up from the cellar looked much too good to use for the purpose. Nancy was just giving me my change when the outer door slammed heavily and a thin, tall blonde staggered into the snug, dragging behind her an enormous glittery pink suitcase on wheels with a vanity case strapped to the top of it.

'It must be one of them SatNavvers,' Nancy whispered. 'Barking mad if she tried to get a car up the lane in this weather!'

Chapter 18: Ice Maiden

Today I accused N of putting off telling his parents about us, because he feared they would not be pleased and think me not good enough, being the daughter of mill workers. He said neither would mine approve of him, since he was not a Strange Baptist or, indeed, any other kind of Baptist.

March, 1945

'Hello?' she said, looking from one to the other of us while pushing back a large, white fur hat that had slipped drunkenly over a face that was still extremely pretty, despite being pink and shiny with cold, exertion and temper. 'Thank *God* there's some sign of life in this hole. I was starting to think everyone had been wiped out by the plague, or something!'

'Did you turn off the main road to get to Great Mumming?' I asked her. 'Only those SatNav things send you the wrong way.'

'No, I *intended* coming here, but my car slid on the ice on the first bend and now it's in the ditch. I need someone to drive me to Old Place.'

Nancy had been eyeing her narrowly. 'Aren't you that model that was engaged to Jude and came here last Christmas, the one that took up with his brother, instead? Arrived with one, and left with the other?'

'I suppose you *could* put it like that. I'm Coco Lanyon. I expect you know me from the Morning Dawn Facial Elixir TV advert.'

'No,' Nancy said simply: I don't suppose she gets a lot of time to watch the telly.

As well as the fur hat, Coco was wearing shocking pink Ugg boots and a long, white quilted coat. Her hair was platinum-pale too, but her face was still almost as pink as her boots.

Her voice, a trifle on the shrill side, must have penetrated Nicholas's ears, because his wizened face suddenly appeared around the side of the chair again and he chipped in, in his own high but sweet, elven tones, 'I'm Auld Man Christmas, you know!'

'We know, Dad,' Nancy said. 'You just sit back and let me see to the customer.'

'I'm not a customer,' Coco snapped. 'I'm merely in search of transport.'

'But why are you going to Old Place?' I asked and she swivelled her ice-blue eyes in my direction and looked down her retroussé nose at me . . . or tried to, because I was inches taller.

'And *you* would be?'

'Holly Brown. I'm looking after Old Place while Jude Martland's away.'

'Oh, right . . . did your husband drive you down? Because if so, you can take me back up with you right now.'

'You're mixing me up with the couple who usually come – I haven't got a husband and I didn't bring my car today, because it would never have got up the hill. In any case, why *do* you want to go there?'

'You mean – Guy hasn't arrived yet?' she demanded, staring at me.

'He hadn't when I left a couple of hours ago and we certainly weren't expecting him – *or* you. Why did you think he might be here?'

'Because this is where he *said* he was going, of course!'

'But . . . surely he wouldn't have come here when he's fallen out with his brother?' I asked, puzzled.

'Oh, but he rang old Noël early last week, so he knew Jude

170

would be in the States right over Christmas and it would be safe to hole up here. But I'm not letting Guy get away with this – he can't throw me over just because I sent the announcement of our engagement to *The Times* and set a date for the wedding! We're going to Mummy and Daddy's for Christmas, too, and they've invited *all* the family to an engagement party on Boxing Day.'

'You didn't tell Guy any of this beforehand?' asked Nancy, clearly fascinated.

'He's a commitment-phobe, he'd have carried on dithering forever,' Coco said shortly. 'He may have dashed up here in a panic, but he'd better have got over it by now, because he's coming straight back to London with me.'

I wouldn't put it past her, either, because even cross and pink-faced she was stunningly beautiful . . . if you liked chilly blondes with ice-chip pale blue eyes, that is, and presumably, both Guy and Jude did.

Still, I certainly didn't want another unexpected visitor, so she could remove him with my blessing. 'I suppose you'd better come back to the house with me, I don't really see what else you can do. Perhaps he's arrived by now – he probably stopped off for lunch on the way, or something.'

I turned to Nancy. 'Would it be all right if we left the luggage here for a bit? I've got all my shopping and I don't suppose Coco can carry much more than the beauty box up with her. That case is *enormous*!'

'What, this little thing?' Coco said, astonished. 'It's only an overnight bag, in case we decided to go back early tomorrow instead of today. And I'm definitely not carrying anything anywhere, because I'm still exhausted from the walk from the car. *You* can go up to the house and tell Guy to come and fetch me. I'll wait here and—'

George stuck his head through the half-open door just at that moment and, spotting me, said, 'I thought you might be in here,

Holly, Orrie said you headed this way. Did you want a lift back up to Old Place? It's snowing again and I'm on my way home.'

'*I* certainly do!' Coco exclaimed and he raised a flaxen eyebrow at her.

'This is—' I paused. 'I'm so sorry, I've forgotten your second name.'

'Coco Lanyon – the model.'

'She was the one that was engaged to Jude last Christmas, and then took up with Guy instead,' Nancy explained helpfully.

'Only they've had a bust up,' Nicholas piped. He was evidently following the intricate plot without difficulty now he was fully awake. 'She thought he was up at Old Place and she's followed him.'

'Ah, that explains it! I thought I just saw that big black Chelsea tractor of Guy's go up the lane, monster that it is,' George said. 'It's well-gritted and he took a run at it, so he probably made it.'

'There, you see?' said Coco. 'He *is* here.'

'Is that your car in the ditch further down?' asked George. 'Ben from Weasel Pot said some madman had tried to get a sports car up the hill.'

'Mad*woman*,' Nancy suggested and Coco gave her a nasty look.

'Yes, it's mine and I'd like it towed out and brought up to Old Place as soon as possible.'

George removed his cap and scratched his head thoughtfully. 'Them from Weasel's Pot'll tow it out for you all right, but it'll cost you. And there's no point them trying to get it up to the house, so they'll probably leave it here in the village. Those little cars are too low down to be any use in the snow – *or* in the country, come to that,' he added disparagingly.

'Whatever,' she said haughtily. 'Now, please take me up to Old Place.'

'If you don't mind, George,' I said apologetically. 'But just as far as the lodge will do, I don't want to put you out any more

172

and we can drop off the bags there. Perhaps Guy will go down and fetch them.'

'Don't be silly, he must take me right up to the house,' Coco insisted. '*You* can walk if you want to.'

'I'll take *you* home gladly, Holly – but I've two sheep in the back now, and the dog's in the front, so I've no room for another passenger.' He raised a fair eyebrow at Coco. '*You'll* have to wait and see if Guy will fetch you, unless you want to try asking young Ben – he went into the public bar.'

'Young Ben?'

'From Weasel's Pot.'

'What is this weasel's pot you all keep rabbiting on about?' she said irritably.

'The farm you passed after turning off the main road,' I told her. 'They have the council contract to plough the lane up to the village, and George here ploughs the lane down.'

'That's right, and you can ask Ben about towing your car out too, while you're at it,' George suggested.

'Look, I'm in a hurry, so *you* get a lift up with this Ben, and tell him to get my car out for me,' Coco said to me. Then she indicated her case to George, clearly expecting him to pick it up. 'Right, I'm ready – but you'll have to put the dog in the back.'

'Sorry, no can do,' he said, not looking sorry at all. 'And I didn't offer *you* a lift in the first place. I'm none too keen on that perfume you're wearing and if it makes my Land Rover reek of musk, it'll unsettle the dogs. They squeeze it out of weasel glands, you know.'

She stared at him. 'Rubbish! This perfume is very, very expensive and they wouldn't use something like that!'

'Isn't it musk rat glands?' I said. 'That sounds more likely.'

'Happen you're right,' he conceded.

'There's an old Lancashire saying about weasels,' piped Auld Nicholas and then declaimed in a thin, singsong voice: '"*If you*

173

see a weasel, pee in its ear. If you see another, tie its bum up with string.'"

'What on earth does that mean?' demanded Coco.

'No idea,' Nicholas said. 'Hee, hee!'

'Senile!' she muttered and, abandoning him, turned a sweetly seductive smile on George. '*Please* do take me up to the house – I'm so cold and tired! I can pay you for your trouble, you know.'

'I've told you already, try your wiles on young Ben, you'll get nowhere with me,' he said shortly and she furiously flounced out in the direction of the public bar.

'Let's hope you get rid of her and Guy tonight,' George said, helping me out to the Land Rover with my million and one purchases. 'If not, she won't be driving that sports car home, because nothing short of a four-wheel drive will make it down to the main road by morning.'

'But Guy's got one of those, you said? So I suppose he'll drive them back tonight and arrange something later about her car,' I suggested hopefully.

The sheepdog obligingly made room for me on the bench seat and we set off, George refusing to stop until he'd taken me right to the front door, where we found a large people-carrier still steaming gently: Guy *had* arrived.

I staggered in with my shopping and found all the family in the sitting room, which someone had now artistically festooned with swags and swathes of artificial greenery, mixed with the real thing that George had brought.

Tilda was sitting in her usual place on the sofa before the fire, Merlin fast asleep on the rug at her feet, while Noël, Becca and Jess were putting final touches to the Christmas tree.

A tall, dark, thin and very handsome man was leaning on the stone mantelpiece watching the proceedings and I would have easily recognised him as Guy from the family photos, even if I hadn't expected to see him.

As I came in and put down the heavy bags I thought the room looked like a stage set, especially the way they all turned to look at me as if they'd been given a cue. Merlin hauled himself to his feet and ambled over, tail wagging furiously.

'Ah, Holly, there you are! We've had an unexpected addition to the family party,' Noël said gaily. 'This is Guy, Jude's younger brother.'

'How do you do?' he said, with a charming smile, shaking hands. 'I've been hearing all about you!'

'That sounds ominous,' I said, bending down to stroke Merlin. 'Actually, I knew you were here because I just ran into your—'

'Have you got anything for *me* in that shopping bag?' interrupted Jess.

'Yes, some chocolate tree decorations.' I rummaged in the hessian bag and found them.

'Oh good, we hadn't got any of those and Uncle Guy didn't think to bring anything at all.'

'I didn't think I'd need to, because I expected to find that couple here Jude usually hires when he's away. And since I knew they'd already invited Tilda, Noël, Becca and Jess for Christmas dinner, I thought one more wouldn't make any difference.'

'And you knew Uncle Jude wasn't here to throw you out on your ear,' Jess said. 'You were sneaky and mean, going off with his girlfriend, even if I didn't like her much!'

'Neither do I now, that's why I'm here,' he drawled, not noticeably put out by this criticism.

'Jess, that was very rude of you,' Tilda said.

'What the child said was true, though: you've always wanted what your brother had, from being a child. Then as soon as you got it, you lost interest,' Becca said bluntly. 'And you had a damned cheek, thinking you could just move in here while he was away and be looked after by the couple house-sitting.'

Guy reddened. 'Part of the reason I came was because I was worried about Noël and Tilda, left to cope on their own. It was

175

thoughtless of old Jude to cancel Christmas and go off in a huff.'

'He was going to New York anyway and we told him not to bother about us – we could manage on our own. In fact, I was quite looking forward to cooking a Christmas dinner again,' said Tilda, 'and I would have done, if I hadn't had that damned fall.'

'I know you would have cooked a wonderful dinner, m'dear,' Noël said soothingly. 'But we're quite happy to be back at the old homestead again now, with Holly in charge, aren't we?'

'I could see that's what everyone wanted and I wouldn't stand in your way,' she said, casting herself into a martyr's role with relish, though she'd clearly been more than relieved to be whisked up here and looked after. 'You behaved very badly, Guy, so we could quite understand why Jude felt like a change this year and wanted to get away – especially when he found out about that engagement announcement.'

'Yes, that's all very well, but Jude is the head of the household now and he has responsibilities, like seeing Old Nan and Richard are looked after,' Becca pointed out, shaking her head. 'He didn't need to invite Guy and that girl, so there would have been no problem.'

'Never mind: thanks to lovely Holly here, it has all worked out well,' Noël said, 'and Jude will be back for Twelfth Night, which is the most important thing.'

'You still haven't told us why you've dashed up here, Guy,' Tilda said. 'Didn't you tell us last week that you were spending Christmas in London with that girl?' She frowned. 'What *was* she called? It was something to do with clowns.'

'Coco,' said Jess. 'Like a bedtime drink. Though it would have been much worse if she'd been called Horlicks, wouldn't it?' she added innocently.

'Different spelling of Coco, I expect, like Coco Chanel,' I said quickly. 'And speaking of Coco—'

'I think Horlicks suits her. I'm going to call her that from now on,' Jess broke in gleefully.

'I would *so* much rather you didn't, darling,' Tilda said.

Guy was grinning. 'Don't be a spoilsport, Tilda! But luckily you won't have to call her anything, Jess, because she isn't here. She never really took to Old Place last Christmas anyway, she's more of a town girl, our Coco.'

'I suppose you got tired of her, like all your other girls?' Tilda said, with a slight note of indulgence. Guy seemed to be a bit of a favourite of hers, though Becca didn't seem too keen. I suppose all that charm can't have the same effect on everybody.

'Let's just say I had a wake-up call,' he admitted. 'Things got a bit rocky when she fired off that engagement announcement to the papers – and then when she told me her parents were organising a big family engagement party on Boxing Day I thought, "no thank you" and bailed out.' He shrugged. 'I'm not ready to tie myself down yet.'

'As I said,' Becca observed dispassionately, 'as soon as you get the prize, you lose interest.'

'Thanks for that quick character analysis, Becca. But actually, she was so easy to poach that I did Jude a favour. If they'd got married, it would never have lasted.'

He gave me a delightful smile – he seemed distinctly profligate with them. 'But I'd *much* rather be here in the bosom of my family instead. You don't mind if I stay, do you, Holly? You wouldn't throw me out into the cold, cold snow?' he wheedled.

He was a bounder, as they would have said in the twenties, as beautiful and untrustworthy as a snake. If he took after his Uncle Ned, then I could understand how poor, innocent, strictly-brought-up Granny had been so quickly swept quite out of her depth!

I looked helplessly at Noël and Tilda. 'I . . . well, everything is snowballing! I only came here to keep an eye on the house and look after the animals – and then suddenly I'm holding a house-party without the owner's permission! And I couldn't get him on the phone either, though I did try.'

'Oh, but Jude won't object, I assure you,' Noël said. 'The dear fellow will understand.'

'I'm not sure he will, Noël, because Mr Martland's girlfriend is—'

'Uncle Jude won't mind in the least about *us*,' Jess interrupted, 'but he will about Uncle Guy!'

'I wish you'd drop the "uncle" bit, sweetheart – it makes me feel terribly old,' he complained.

'You *are* terribly old,' she said witheringly.

'If you think *I'm* old, Mini-Morticia, then your beloved Uncle Jude must be ancient!'

'But I don't think of him as old, because he's fun,' she said, which was a surprise to me, since nothing I'd heard about him so far would have led me to think of him as a fun person. 'You're silly and mean and you're going all wrinkly round the eyes.'

'Laughter lines,' he said, though he turned his head and examined his face anxiously in the cloudy bevelled mirror above the fireplace. 'Yes, laughter lines . . . and is that a car I hear arriving?' he added. 'You're not expecting anyone else, are you?'

'We weren't even expecting *you*,' Becca pointed out.

Jess ran to the window. 'Oh look, it's Ben from Weasel's Pot!' She went all pink, so clearly she has a crush on the young farmer. But then she wailed, 'Oh no, he's driven off without coming in to say hello! But someone got out first – a woman with an enormous suitcase. Who on earth can it be?'

'I've been trying to warn you,' I said desperately, 'it's—'

Jess turned a startled face towards us. 'It's Horlicks, and she looks *really* mad! Shall I lock the door?'

178

Chapter 19: I Should Coco

*N has been discharged from the army by the medical board
and told me he has been offered a job by a friend of his
father's as soon as he is fit enough. I thought he might then
go on to ask me to marry him, now he will soon be in a
situation to support a wife – but he did not . . .*

April, 1945

It was too late to follow Jess's suggestion and Coco didn't even
knock but simply swept in, looking like a slightly grubby and
marked-down ice princess.

I don't suppose she'd realised she'd be finishing her journey
in the cab of a tractor, crammed in with her luggage, which she
now dropped in the doorway with a loud crash. It appeared to
be decidedly the worse for wear, as did Coco: white was not
perhaps the most suitable colour for gruelling journeys. She was
clearly also in a flaming temper, which wasn't improved by her
reception.

'Oh God, what are *you* doing here?' Guy said wearily and
Becca, Tilda and Noël all stared at her in astonished unwelcome.

'What do you mean, what am *I* doing here? Don't think you
can just dump me like that and get away with it just because
you got cold feet at the idea of our wedding. Get over it, because
you're coming back to London with me right now!'

'Like hell I will,' he said. 'You might have consulted me before sending off engagement notices and arranging celebration parties.'

'You *agreed* with me when I said May weddings were the best, but you had to pick your date quickly before they got booked up!'

'I might have done, because I don't listen to half the rubbish you talk. But I certainly never said I wanted to get married in May or any other time!'

'Well, that's why we got engaged, wasn't it?'

He shrugged. 'Lots of people get engaged and it doesn't lead to anything, and you were making a fuss about it. I didn't know you would send an announcement to the bloody newspapers! And finding your parents had organised the family round on Boxing Day to give us the seal of approval was the last straw.'

'They didn't invite them specially, it just seemed a good time to toast our engagement, while the family were all together,' she snapped.

'Well, you go and toast it, then, I'm staying right here.'

'Oh, don't be silly! I've driven all the way up here and my car's ended up in a ditch, all because of you. Of course you're coming back with me.'

She gave a distracted look at Jess, who had set up a low chant of 'Hor-licks, Hor-licks, Hor-licks!'

'Does the child have to make so much noise?' she demanded.

'Jess, darling, that will do,' Tilda said mildly.

'She doesn't like you,' Guy said. 'None of us like you.'

'Now, now, Guy,' Noël said. 'Manners! Coco, come to the fire and get warm. I hope you weren't hurt when your car went in the ditch?'

Coco had had a long and wearisome sort of day and she wasn't listening to Noël. Instead she turned on Guy and unsurprisingly lost her temper completely, saying a few choice and very personal things about him in her shrill voice that I could see Jess storing up for future use.

Nettled, he began to fling barbed comments back so, since a battle royal seemed to be starting, I carried my shopping through into the kitchen, followed by Merlin.

I had to switch all the lights on because it was still snowing heavily and didn't look like stopping any time soon, which was a bit worrying from the point of view of getting rid of my two unwanted visitors . . .

I quickly stowed everything away, hiding the presents I'd bought under a pile of tea towels in the cupboard in case Jess took it into her head to rummage about before I'd had a chance to wrap them.

Then I made a cup of coffee while I wondered whether I could stretch the sausage and mash with mustard sauce that I'd planned to serve for dinner to include two other diners, or if I should defrost more sausages. Dessert could be a sort of Eton Mess, with tinned raspberries and yet more squirty cream from the lodge. Or I could do something with the overripe bananas left by the Chirks . . .

I looked at tomorrow's menu, which was to be grilled trout for the adults – there was a plentiful supply in the freezer – and home-made salmon fishcakes for Jess if she didn't fancy that. And dessert would be whichever of the two choices we didn't have tonight.

I'd just put another quick chocolate cake in the oven and whipped up an easy starter of sardine pâté to have with French toast, when Becca and Jess followed me into the kitchen.

'Tilda and Noël have gone into the morning room to watch TV,' Becca said, 'it's all getting a bit shrill in there – tears before bedtime, I reckon. Guy's just told her he can't drive her anywhere tonight, even if he wanted to, because he had a couple of stiff whiskies after he arrived.'

'Oh dear, did he?' I said helplessly. 'I was hoping he might at least take her to the nearest railway station, since he's got that big four-wheel drive – the weather is closing in and even if her car is all right after being in the ditch, I don't think it's up to these kinds of conditions. George certainly didn't think so.'

'Well, I don't suppose there's a police car sitting in the lane in this weather, waiting to catch drunk drivers,' she said. 'He just didn't want to do it.'

'Did you like the Christmas decorations?' asked Jess.

'Yes, they look lovely; I didn't get a chance to say before. Who did the holly, ivy and mistletoe arrangements? So much more swish than sticking stuff in vases, like I did with that first bunch George gave me!'

'Me – one of the useless things I learned at finishing school,' Becca said.

I gave another distracted glance out of the window. 'It's still snowing – do you think we ought to bring the horses in?'

'Yes, that's why we came out, really. I'll do that and get their hot mash early, too. Jess's going to help me.'

'I'm so glad you're here to see to Lady,' I said gratefully. 'I'm going to be so busy with everything else that knowing you're keeping an eye on her and Billy is a weight off my shoulders.'

'Well, I need to see to Nutkin anyway, so another horse is neither here nor there if I have a willing slave like Jess to do the heavy work and keep that damned goat out of the way.'

Jess gave her a pained look: I don't think mucking out and trundling wheelbarrows about is her favourite pastime, even though she is now resigned to her fate.

'That goat is evil,' she said bitterly. 'I've got bruises all up the back of my legs where he keeps butting me.'

'We took Merlin out for a little run before lunch,' Becca said. 'He was missing you – amazing how quickly he's got attached to you, he's like your shadow.'

'I know, I expect he's pining for his master, that's why,' I said. Merlin, hearing his name, half-wagged his tail, looking up at me with warm amber eyes.

'When we've sorted the horses out I'm going to take the sledge up the paddock again – do you want to come, Holly?' invited Jess. 'You can have the other sledge.'

'I would have loved to, but I need to prep the vegetables for dinner and I want to put the jelly layer on the trifle,' I said. 'Tomorrow though, definitely. And we could bake and ice some gingerbread biscuits to hang on the tree, if you like?'

'Oh yes, that would be fun!'

When they'd gone out I could still hear raised voices from the sitting room, despite the closed door at the end of the passage: the acoustics must be jolly good. I could make out melodramatic lines, like:

'I broke off my engagement to Jude for you!'

'I didn't ask you to – it was just a bit of fun on the side until Jude walked in on us.'

'That's not what you said then – I thought you loved me!'

'I'm not responsible for what you think, thank God.'

After that, I shut the kitchen door, too, and put the radio on.

I didn't really need to start on dinner yet, now the pâté starter was in the fridge, but since it looked as though I would be alone for quite a while I took the opportunity to make my presents.

I scalded the empty jam jars from the utility room and dried them thoroughly, before filling them with sweets and covering each with a circle of cellophane topped with one cut from the red and white gingham paper napkins, held down with a red elastic band. They looked really good.

I wrapped them up and labelled them, except for a couple of extra ones I left blank for unforeseen emergencies. Then I stowed them away in the cupboard under the tea towels again, along with the bits and pieces for Jess's stocking – assuming she was going to have one. I made a note to ask Noël or Tilda about that later.

Becca came back in, snow sparkling in her iron-grey curls. 'It's almost dark and still snowing out there . . . and are the lights flickering, or am I imagining it?'

'No, they do keep doing that. I hope the power isn't going to cut off.'

'Oh well, it does from time to time, but the generator will take over if it does. What's happening with those two?' She jerked her head towards the hall. 'Still arguing?'

'As far as I know – unless one of them has murdered the other and is out there burying the body in the snow.'

'Ha!' she said. She looked around her approvingly: 'It looks different in here since you arrived – cleaner, for a start, and it's good to see the Aga being used again.'

'It looked like Mo had made a start on cleaning in here, but Sharon didn't seem to have touched anything in the house at all. I can't imagine what she did when she was here.'

'No, she was worse than useless. I told Jude he should get another couple in to look after the place, but he said he could look after himself.'

'It's not that easy to find live-in staff anyway these days and very expensive if you do.'

'True, and ones that can cook are like hens' teeth. What's that lovely smell?'

'Just another quick chocolate cake – we seem to get through cake at an amazing rate!'

'Wonderful.' Becca cocked her head, listening for any noise from the sitting room, then said doubtfully, 'It's gone ominously quiet in there.'

'I closed the kitchen door so I couldn't hear.'

She got up and opened it again. 'Oh yes – she's crying hysterically now.'

'Just as well I took more sausages out of the freezer, then,' I said gloomily. 'I don't think either of them are going anywhere tonight.'

'No, the weather's worse out there now, so it wouldn't be advisable until the roads are cleared and gritted in the morning.'

'Unless we're totally snowed in overnight, have you thought of that?'

Tilda tottered in, the heels of her velvet mules clicking on the stone floor, and sat in a wheelback chair. 'That imbecile boy has given Coco a snifter of brandy now, to stop her crying, so there's no getting shut of her until tomorrow!'

'We'd just decided we weren't going to get rid of her before morning anyway,' I said. 'But I suppose we're going to need a couple more beds made up.'

Guy appeared, looking harassed, which was hardly surprising since you could hear the sound of loud, angry weeping and the occasional scream of 'Bastard!' all the way from the sitting room.

'She's got a good pair of lungs on her,' Becca commented.

'Things are a just a *little* tricky,' Guy said, with a wry smile. 'Coco wants to go home, only I'm not risking my car taking her down to see if hers has been towed out of the ditch yet, because it's snowing so hard I'd never get back up again – have you looked outside recently? It's a nuisance Jude took the Land Rover, that would have made it.'

'You could run her back to London in your car in the morning,' I suggested.

'No way: I'd already told her it was all off between us, so it's her own fault if she didn't believe me and came up here on a fool's errand,' he said ungallantly.

'So, what's she going to do?'

'She'll have to stay tonight and then perhaps she can get a lift down to the village tomorrow with George when he ploughs our drive, to see if her car still works.' He shrugged. 'If not, perhaps she can bribe one of the boys to run her to the station instead. So,' he said, flashing a smile of outstanding charm in my direction, 'I wondered if you'd be an angel and make another bed up besides mine, which is the one opposite Jude's?'

'I haven't made yours up,' I said shortly, 'nor am I going to! Presumably you know where the linen cupboard is? I've had the fire in the sitting room going since I got here and all the doors upstairs open to air and warm the rooms.'

He looked taken aback. 'Oh . . . right.'

'I think Coco will have to go in the little bedroom on the nursery floor, next to Jess, which I don't suppose she'll be keen on. Otherwise there's only Jude's room, which is locked, and even Noël doesn't have the key to that.'

Becca said, 'It's almost a full house!'

'There's the other servant's room in this wing too, I'd forgotten that, though it's a bit Spartan and unused looking,' I said.

'She wouldn't like that at all,' Guy said.

'Well then, give her your room and you can have one of the others tonight,' Becca suggested.

'Not me! She can put up with the nursemaid's room.' He paused, eyeing me uncertainly, presumably for signs of weakening. 'Well, I suppose I'd better go and do something about the beds, then,' he said finally.

Becca got up. 'I'll find you the clean sheets, or God knows what you'll be putting on them – tablecloths, probably. But after that you're on your own, because I've already seen to the horses and I'm tired.'

'You told him,' Tilda said to me approvingly when they'd gone out. 'He's a good boy really, but he expects other people to carry him round all the time.'

'I just needed to make my situation plain. I'm not a servant and I'm not going to run around after him.'

'Of course not – we consider you as a guest, almost one of the family,' Tilda said graciously. 'And you are quite a good cook, dear – something smells delicious.'

'It's the chocolate cake,' I explained again. 'I'd better take it out. And if you switch the kettle on, I'll make us some tea in a minute. There are cheese scones, too.'

'Shop ones?' sniffed Tilda, as I took the cake out of the oven and turned it out on the cooling rack.

'No, ones I made myself.'

Becca returned and by unspoken agreement we had our tea

at the kitchen table, leaving Coco as sole occupant of the sitting room, though I did offer her a cup of tea and a scone when I took Noël's through to the parlour, which she rejected with evident loathing.

Tilda asked me what we were having for dinner and approved my choice of sausage and mash.

'Good wholesome winter food!'

'I've made sardine pâté for a starter. I thought we could have that in the sitting room on a tray.'

'And what about dessert?'

'It's either a raspberry Eton Mess, or alternatively there are some overripe bananas that the Chirks left, so I could do cold banana custards or bananas in rum, with cream. What do you think?'

'Oh, custards. With just a teeny sprinkle of nutmeg on each one.'

'If you say so,' I agreed. Along with squirty cream, nutmeg and paprika seemed to feature largely in the foodstuffs Tilda had brought from the lodge to add to the catering supplies. 'In fact, I'd better do those now, so they will be chilled by dinner time.'

While I was making the custard, Tilda helpfully sliced up the bananas and put them in the ramekins, talking about her past glories on TV, especially her wonderful series on canapés, on the subject of which she had enlightened the nation.

'You have no need to worry about canapés while *I* am here,' she said generously.

'Well, that's a huge weight off my mind,' I assured her.

'I'd better call Jess in,' Becca said. 'I'd forgotten she was still sledging and it's pitch black out there, though of course the light bounces off the snow. But she must be cold by now.'

While she went to fetch her in, I asked Tilda whether Jess was having a Christmas stocking or not.

'She had one last year,' Tilda said, 'but Roz – my daughter – didn't mention it to me, though she did leave Jess's presents. She might have forgotten about the stocking, because she is the scattiest creature. Or perhaps Jess is too old?'

'Mrs Comfort said they are never too old, so I got a few things from her to make one up, in case.'

'Oh well – you carry on with that, then,' she ordered autocratically, as Jess came in with red cheeks and covered in snow, and was sent straight back out into the passage to remove her coat and wellies.

Chapter 20: Flickering

I begin to wonder if Hilda and Pearl are right about N, because despite the offer of a job he still has not asked me to marry him. Every time we meet he reassures me that we will always be together, but I can't go on in this clandestine way any more and so have told him that I would not meet him again unless we agreed to tell our parents and get engaged.

April, 1945

Luckily Coco retired to her bedroom once it was ready for her, so everyone could go back into the sitting room for a pre-dinner drink and warm-through by the fire, which got them from underfoot while I cleared and laid the kitchen table for dinner.

Now there were so many of us, I suppose it would have made sense to have used the dining room, but I felt too tired to be traipsing to and fro with hot dishes: no, the kitchen would have to do. And with a bit of luck and perhaps an overnight thaw, maybe I could get rid of Guy and Coco in the morning. Getting Coco safely home again was *his* responsibility, after all, and I didn't want him here either, charm though he might.

He was so not *my* type, but if Ned Martland was anything like Guy, then I could see why poor Gran fell for him, and not surprised that he now seemed to be playing fast and loose with her.

I popped upstairs to apply a little makeup, brush my hair and change my jeans for smarter black crepe trousers and a dark red tunic top with a beaded neckline: last night both Becca and Tilda had come down for dinner in long skirts, though since Noël and Jess hadn't changed at all, that might have been more for comfort than anything.

Of course, I don't bother what I wear when cooking for house-parties, because I don't eat with the clients then, but in the kitchen. However, now we were *all* to eat in the kitchen.

The family were gathered together in the sitting room when I went through with the pâté and French toast starter on a tray. Tilda and Becca were in their long skirts again and Noël was now wearing a Tattersall check shirt under a rubbed dark blue velvet smoking jacket, while Guy, in oatmeal cashmere, looked like an advert for upmarket men's clothing. Jess had an endless supply of black jeans and tops, so it was impossible to tell whether she had changed or not. She was sitting at the table by the window, doing something fiddly with scraps of paper.

'Let me take that for you, it looks terribly heavy,' Noël said, starting to get to his feet as if I was some fragile creature, rather than a six-foot Amazon.

'No – do let me,' offered Guy with a ravishing smile, pre-empting him. He put it down on the coffee table and asked me, 'Would you like a drink? Sherry, gin and tonic? Name your poison.'

'No thanks, I'm not much of a drinker, especially when I'm cooking. Is Miss Lanyon coming down for dinner?'

'Coco – and you must call me Guy, because I feel we're on intimate terms already, now all my dirty washing has been dragged out in front of you.'

'I'm sure we all know much more about your private affairs after today than we ever wanted to,' Tilda said severely. 'So, is your young woman going to grace us with her presence this evening?'

'She's not my young woman, Tilda, and I've no idea.'

'I wouldn't put it past her,' Becca said, 'though I'm sure we are all quite sick of the sight of her. I was actually grateful to you when you went off with her last Christmas, Guy – think how awful it would have been if she'd married Jude and settled here!'

'Actually, I think it was the thought of spending most of the year here that put her off Jude before she even set eyes on me,' Guy said dispassionately. 'She's not a country girl and she has her eyes firmly set on her career.'

'If you can call prancing up and down a catwalk half-naked a *career*,' Tilda commented acidly.

'She's trying to break into acting too,' he said and just at that moment the door swung open and Coco stood revealed, a vision of angularly icy beauty. She is so pretty she is unreal and I'm not at all surprised that Guy and Jude fell for her.

She held her catwalk pose long enough for us all to take in the one-shouldered, slinky, nude-silk trousered garment that she was *almost* wearing. I sincerely hoped the slashed top part was held on with boob tape, because otherwise she would be in serious danger of dangling her little dumplings in the dinner.

'Here you all are,' she said gaily, then directed a dazzling smile at Guy. 'Darling, get me a drink, won't you? You know what I like.'

Clearly she'd regrouped and was now changing tactics to one aimed at luring back her errant lover.

'You're going to catch your death in that outfit,' Becca observed. 'Have you got it on the right way round?'

'Of course! It's supposed to look like this,' she said indignantly.

'Then I'd better lend you a cardigan – Tilda's won't be big enough.'

'Oh, I'm quite warm enough, thank you!' Standing close to Guy as she accepted her drink, she laid a hand on his arm and said seductively, 'If not, Guy can warm me up, can't you, darling?'

'Oh yuk! Horlicks is getting soppy,' Jess said disgustedly.

'Do all help yourselves to the starter and I'll call you through into the kitchen when dinner's ready,' I said, making a neat exit.

'Aren't we eating in the dining room?' I heard Coco ask piercingly as I went out again. 'Why do we have to eat in the kitchen, with the help?'

That comment hardly endeared her to me and nor did her announcement, once we were seated at the table, that she didn't eat carbs.

'Or any kind of processed food,' she added, looking at the dish of sausages with something akin to horror.

'These are extremely good sausages I found in the freezer,' I said. 'I'm afraid if you want something else, you'll have to cook it yourself.'

Coco looked at me with dropped jaw. 'Me? Why can't *you* do it? That's what you're here for, isn't it?'

'No, it isn't!' Becca told her.

'That's right, Holly isn't our resident housekeeper and cook, you know, she only came here to look after the house and animals while Jude was away,' Noël said gently. 'She isn't employed to cook or look after his family as well, and is only doing it from the kindness of her heart. And we are all very grateful.' He gave me one of his charming, lopsided smiles.

'Not at all, I'm sure we're going to have a lovely Christmas,' I lied. 'Much more fun than being on my own.'

'And this food is wonderful,' Guy said, tucking into his mustard mash with gusto. 'You can cook as well as look stunning, so you're everything I ever wanted in a woman: will you marry me?'

Jess giggled but Coco shot daggers at both of us, even though he was just playing the fool.

'On your past track record, no.'

'That told him,' Becca said.

'I must say, you have cooked this very nicely,' Tilda said. 'And the pâté was lovely too – simple but good.'

'Hearty plain food is the best,' agreed Becca. 'I'll eat Coco's sausages and mash if she doesn't want them.'

'Not if I get there first,' Guy told her with a grin.

'Or perhaps Jess should have them: she needs to keep her strength up if she's helping me with the horses,' Becca suggested. 'Luckily, she appears to have outgrown her allergy to them.'

Jess gave her a dirty look, but she seemed to be putting away her dinner without any difficulty, even though I'd spotted a crumpled scatter of silvery chocolate tree decoration wrappers on the table where she'd been doing her origami earlier.

'I have to eat *something*,' Coco said sulkily and helped herself to one sausage, a bare teaspoon of mash, and a microscopically small fragment of carrot.

The room went dark again, just for an instant.

'Why do the lights keep doing that? The electricity isn't going to go off, is it?' Coco asked nervously. 'I'd hate that, because I'm sure this house is haunted.'

'Don't worry, if it does the generator will take over,' I said soothingly. 'And if it doesn't, the gardener showed me how to switch it on manually.'

'*Henry* did?' said Noël, opening his eyes wide. 'He has never let me anywhere near it.'

'Or me,' said Guy. 'Not that I want to, I'm not at all mechanically minded, unlike Jude.'

'You're the kiss of death to all machinery,' Tilda told her husband. 'Look what you did to the Magimix.'

'I did fly aeroplanes during the war, m'dear, so you can't say I am hopeless with *all* machinery.'

'That was entirely different,' she snapped and I could see she was tired out and hoped she would go to bed right after dinner. I think the fall must have shaken her up much more than she was letting on, though at least her eye was now only faintly rimmed with a yellow and blue bruise.

Predictably, Coco spurned the banana custards I'd made for

dessert and said she would go and smoke a cigarette in the sitting room until we came through with coffee.

'I'm sorry, I'm afraid this is a no-smoking household: it said so clearly in the owner's information folder,' I said apologetically.

'Oh, don't be silly,' she snapped, 'and anyway, Jude isn't here to see!'

'That's immaterial: I'm responsible for the house until he returns and must follow his instructions.'

'Yes, and we agree with Jude, so you'll have to do it in the porch like last Christmas,' Tilda told her.

'But I'll freeze!'

'You certainly will in that garment,' agreed Becca. 'I'd go and put something more sensible on, first.'

'I haven't got anything sensible,' she said sulkily.

'Well, the coat and hat you arrived in, then.'

'Yes, and that's another thing – my white coat cost me a fortune and after being in that tractor it's never going to come clean again!'

She flounced out and I think we breathed a collective sigh of relief.

'I expect she will just go and smoke in her room instead, she's that kind of person,' Becca said. 'Really, Guy, we could have done without her here, she is *such* a drag. I don't know what you and Jude ever saw in her.'

'Apart from being stunningly beautiful, she can also be fun, believe it or not,' he said dispassionately. 'But she's shallow as a puddle and totally self-centred.'

'You have lots in common then,' Tilda said tartly. 'I can't think why you broke up.'

'I think you are tired, m'dear,' Noël said gently. 'Wouldn't you like to go to bed and I will bring you a hot drink up?'

'Perhaps that would be a good idea,' Tilda conceded. 'The child could do with an early night, too.'

194

'I'm not a child,' Jess protested, 'and I want to finish making the last present before I go up.'

'Half an hour, then,' Tilda said firmly.

The others went into the sitting room and I took the coffee tray through and then retired to the kitchen to clear away and look over tomorrow's menu, sincerely hoping that I wouldn't have two extra mouths to feed after breakfast!

Guy brought the tray back. 'Still at it? Only everyone else has called it a day and gone to bed. What are you doing?'

'Putting the jelly layer on this trifle and then I'm going to let Merlin out for a last run and check on the horses before I go to bed.'

And I would take the journal back upstairs with me too, because, however weary I felt, I was sure I could manage to read another page or two. It kept drawing me like a moth to the flame – I'd been dipping into it at every opportunity.

The light flickered off and then, with extreme reluctance, back on again.

'The horses will be fine. Put Merlin out and then come and have a nightcap with me,' he suggested.

'No, thank you.'

'Pity. Still, we'll have lots of time to get to know each other so much better over Christmas.'

'I hope not – I'm expecting you and Coco to leave in the morning.'

'Well, Coco's certainly going, even if I have to bribe one of the farmer's boys to take her all the way to London in the tractor. But *I'm* staying.'

'That's very unchivalrous of you!'

'Not entirely: she's such a crap driver I certainly wouldn't let her drive herself back to London in these conditions, even if they do get her car out of the ditch.'

'I still think you should take her yourself,' I said. 'Jude won't want you staying here and I would much prefer it if you left, too.'

'You don't mean that *really*,' he said, but finally, getting no response to his flirting, he took himself and his amazingly effulgent aftershave off to bed.

I put the trifle in the fridge and then, accompanied by Merlin, went through and banked up the fire in the sitting room, set the guard safely round it and tidied up. Apart from the usual creakings and sighing of an old house all was quiet and peaceful.

'Last run, Merlin?' I asked, shrugging into my down-filled jacket and picking up my big, rubber-cased torch, because whatever Guy said, I knew my duty. But we'd only just got to the back door when the lights went out – and this time stayed out.

The generator and I were about to get better acquainted.

Chapter 21: Loathe at First Sight

I have heard nothing from N since my ultimatum and I am missing him dreadfully. The others talk of little except the Victory celebrations tomorrow but though I am so very glad this awful war is over, I cannot wholeheartedly lose myself in the excitement of it all as they do.

May, 1945

When I opened the back door the snow was still falling in big, fluffy flakes, and had banked up so I had to wade through it practically up to the top of my wellingtons.

Merlin turned around almost immediately and asked to go back in, which I couldn't blame him for in the least, even if I would have preferred his company.

I don't think I'd quite appreciated how pitch black it would be out there without the yard lights on and the moon hidden behind clouds. The wind was clanking something against the metal gate, but otherwise the snow seemed to have a deadening effect on the usual country night noises. It's lucky I'm not of a nervous disposition.

I switched on my torch and trudged across to the barn, with its sweet smell of hay and warm horse. Nutkin was hanging his head drowsily and barely flickered his ears at me when I shone the beam at him, but I couldn't see Lady at first. This threw me into a panic until I found her lying down very comfortably in the warm straw, with Billy next to her.

I went quietly out again and bolted the door, then made my way across to the generator room and into the silent darkness. It was just as cold in there as it was outside, since the back wall was slatted for ventilation.

It all looked subtly different in the dim light but, according to Henry, all I had to do was flick a couple of switches to turn the generator on manually – and then, if that had no effect, startle the machine with a quick and underhand thump to a vital bit of its anatomy.

This, he'd assured me, *never* failed.

I'd just pressed down the switches (with no discernible result) when I sensed rather than heard a slight movement in the doorway behind me and knew I was no longer alone.

'What the hell are you doing in here?' demanded a deep, rumbling and ominously familiar voice, which then added more urgently, 'And don't *touch* that—'

But he was too late, because after the first heart-stopping second, logic had told me I was in no danger from that quarter – so I'd ignored him and dealt the generator a sudden blow. This had the desired result: it burst instantly into roaring, throbbing noise.

Then I turned round and said calmly, 'Why don't you put on the light now it's working again, and introduce yourself?'

But unfortunately, when he did, I decided I'd liked him much better in the dark. To say he was a large man was like saying that grizzlies are quite big bears, for he was not only extremely tall, but broad across the shoulders too. A pair of red-rimmed, deep-set dark eyes looked out of a face that only the words 'grim' and 'rugged' seemed to describe, framed by the fur-edged hood of a giant parka.

'My God, it's the abominable snowman!' I heard my voice say rudely, though in my defence it has to be admitted that I'd had a long and very trying day. 'That's *all* we need!'

He covered the expanse of floor between us in two quick strides, pushing back the hood to reveal a lot of short dark hair, all standing on end, and looked down at me (which was not something I was used to) with a heavy frown furrowing his forehead.

Those new theories about us all having a bit of Neanderthal DNA might be true, then.

'Holly Brown, I presume?'

'Yes – and you don't have to tell me who you are, because it's obvious now I can see you better: Jude Martland. I thought you were in America?'

'I was,' he said shortly. 'But the last I heard from Noël was that Tilda had had an accident and been rushed off to hospital, so I didn't know what the hell was happening! I've been travelling ever since.'

Well, that would account for the red-rimmed eyes and the dark stubble, at least, though the bad-tempered expression was probably a permanent feature on a face that could only be described, even by his loved ones, as rugged rather than handsome.

'You were so concerned you came straight back?'

I must have sounded incredulous, because a spark of anger glowed in his eyes and he snapped back, 'Of course I did! With a mercenary witch in charge of my house, I didn't hold out much hope that anyone would be rallying round.'

'Thanks. If I sounded surprised, it's because you didn't strike me as someone who would care enough about any of your family to fly back straight away.'

'I can't imagine where you got that idea . . .' He paused, still glaring at me. 'Do I *know* you from somewhere?'

'No, I'm glad to say I've never met you before in my life.' I rather wished it had stayed that way.

'You look vaguely familiar. But never mind that – where are Noël and Tilda? There was no sign of life at the lodge.'

'Here, of course! They moved in with Jess on the afternoon after the accident, and your Aunt Becca came the next day, so she's here too. I did try and call your mobile to tell you what was happening.'

'I was probably over the Atlantic by then.' He looked at me thoughtfully. 'So, who else had you already invited to stay with you, some friend or other? There were two cars by the gate, though the snow's drifted over them.'

'Of course I didn't invite a visitor!' I snapped. 'I wouldn't *dream* of doing such a thing while looking after a house, unless I had prior permission from the owner.'

'Then whose is the second car?'

'The small one is mine, but the other—'

'A plaintive voice from the cold outer darkness broke in. 'Excuse m-me,' it said through chattering teeth, 'd-do you think you c-could p-possibly c-continue this c-conversation indoors? Only I th-think I've got hypothermia.'

Jude Martland moved to one side, revealing his companion to be a smaller, fair man. He seemed to have several layers of clothes on, though going by the outer one, a light raincoat, none of them was terribly suitable for trekking through snowdrifts in arctic conditions.

'I'd forgotten about you!' Jude said, then turned to me: 'Look, I'm going to bring the Land Rover into the shelter of the yard. You take him into the kitchen and thaw him out.'

'Yeah, and what did your last one die of?' I muttered, but he was running his hands over the gently throbbing generator and didn't hear me. Honestly, men and their toys!

'It's fine,' I assured him. 'Henry showed me what to do if it wouldn't start automatically. There's no mechanical skill involved that I can see.'

'There is if it goes wrong,' he said, then turned and strode off.

'Well, do come into the house,' I invited the shivering stranger and he followed me in gratefully. I made him take his soggy

200

shoes and outer layers off in the passage and put them in the utility room to dry off, along with mine.

Now I could see him better, he was very handsome, in a thin, fair way – chilled but perfectly preserved. 'I'm M-Michael Whiston,' he said, holding out a hand like a frozen blue fish.

'Holly Brown – come on through, it's warmer in the kitchen. And never mind the dog, Merlin is harmless.'

Merlin didn't seem terribly interested in the stranger, except in a polite sort of way, but at the roar of the Land Rover's engine outside and then a pair of heavy thuds – presumably as baggage was tossed through the back door – he uttered a low bark and began to wag his tail.

'Just as well someone's glad to see him,' I muttered. I pulled up a chair next to the Aga for Michael and then fetched a picnic rug from the utility room and draped it around him. He smiled gratefully.

I'd put the kettle on and was making tea by the time Jude came in, in stockinged feet and drying his hair on Merlin's towel. He tossed it aside and bent to fondle the old dog's ears.

'I looked in on Lady – she seems fine,' he said grudgingly.

'Of course she's fine, I kept telling you she was. And Becca's keeping an eye on her now, too.' I handed him a mug. 'Give your friend this, he's got hypothermia. I've put brandy in it.'

'Not the good brandy from the dining room, I trust?'

'No, I used that up in the cake. This is some cheap stuff I got from the pub.'

'You put my Armagnac in the cake?' he asked with disbelief.

'I had to make a Christmas cake in a hurry and I assumed it wasn't much good or you would have locked it in the cellar with the rest of the booze. Mo and Jim wouldn't have touched it anyway and neither would I – all the Homebodies staff are vetted for honesty, soberness and reliability.'

'I forgot about it until too late, but it was Sharon I didn't trust, not Mo and Jim.' He stared at me. 'I'd never have thought

201

of anyone putting the last of my father's good brandy in a cake, though!'

'It's not the last, Noël found another bottle in the cellar. And anyway, the cake is for your family and it smells delicious. Now, for goodness sake, give the tea to your friend before it goes cold!'

'Michael isn't my friend, I'd never met him before tonight. He's just another fool who got his car stuck on the lower road trying to take a shortcut.'

'The SatNav sent me down there,' the man said, gratefully clamping both shaking hands around the mug, though at least his teeth seemed to have stopped chattering. 'But the snow got too bad and I couldn't go any further.'

'I had to bring him with me, I couldn't leave him to freeze to death in his car. I'll be surprised if even the snowplough gets through in the morning, if it carries on like this.'

'*I'm* astonished you got up here at all if it's that bad, because George Froggat said the bottom end of the lane often gets impassable in snow and ice and the weather's much worse now. But I sincerely hope you're wrong, and it thaws out a bit by morning.'

'I had chains for the tyres in the back of the Land Rover, so I stopped and put them on as soon as I left the motorway. But no-one in their right mind would drive up narrow country lanes in this weather without them.' He gave the other man a look of scorn.

'Well, thank you for rescuing me, anyway,' Michael said, with an attempt at a smile. 'And for making me put on half the clothes in my suitcase, too!'

I sat down at the table with my tea and Merlin immediately abandoned his master and came and sat down, leaning against my leg as he usually does, his head on my knees. Jude gave him one of the frowning looks he'd been bestowing on me earlier, though slightly puzzled, too.

Now I'd got over the surprise, I'd started to wonder how Jude's arrival would affect me: after all, I was only here to house-sit and he wouldn't need me now. Still, time to sort that out in the morning. I'd pray for a sudden thaw!

'I'll have to give Michael a bed for the night,' Jude said.

'Then I'm afraid it will either have to be yours or the little servant's room next to mine in this wing.'

He had been pushing back his unruly dark hair, which was trying to curl damply, but now stopped and stared at me with his treacle toffee-coloured eyes. 'Why? What's the matter with the others? I mean, only three of them can be occupied, apart from yours?'

'Actually, no, all the rooms in that wing are in use tonight: your brother Guy arrived earlier and his fiancée – or ex-fiancée I should say, since they've had a falling-out – followed him. I've put her in the nursemaid's room next to Jess, since Guy wouldn't give up his room for her and we couldn't put her in yours, because it was locked and even Noël didn't have the key.'

'What, Guy and Coco are here?' he demanded, missing most of the explanation and going straight to the nub of the matter.

'Yes, Coco managed to run her car off the road and I have no idea where it is now, but the other car outside is your brother's.'

'Guy's got a nerve, coming up here while I'm away!' Anger sparked in his eyes.

'He certainly has: he seemed to think he could simply turn up and the Chirks would feed and look after him!'

'And I suppose you let him bamboozle you into letting him stay?'

'Look,' I said shortly, 'I got back from a shopping trip to the village and he was here already, with your aunt and uncle, in his family home. How do you think I, the house-sitter, was supposed to eject him? Oh, and he'd had a couple of drinks by then, too, so there was no way he could have driven anywhere.'

'I suppose not,' he agreed reluctantly. 'You said Coco had an accident? Is she all right? Where is everyone?'

'Coco's fine, apart from some exhausting hysterics after arguing with your brother when she arrived, but it's been a bit of a day, and they've all gone to bed. I was just about to as well, once I'd checked on Lady and Nutkin, but then the electricity went off and the generator obviously wasn't going to start up on its own.'

'I hope you've been keeping the heating on all the time at a low level, like I said in the instructions?'

'I don't think it has any temperature other than low, does it? But I haven't touched it and I've also kept the fire going in the sitting room day and night and opened all the upstairs bedroom doors to let the warm air circulate and air them, luckily.'

'Except mine, presumably?'

I shrugged. 'Unless any air sneaked in through the key-hole.'

'I don't mind where you put me, I'm just grateful you've taken me in,' Michael offered, sounding much better.

'The only bedroom left used to be a servant's one and is a bit Spartan, but it's warm and comfortable enough and I'll make your bed up and put a hot water bottle in it,' I told him.

'You're very kind: bed with a hot water bottle sounds like bliss.' He gave me that charming smile again and I found myself smiling back.

'That's all right. You'll have to share my bathroom, which is just opposite – in fact, you'd better have a hot bath before you turn in. Come on.'

'What about *my* bed, aren't you going to make that, too?' asked Jude sardonically.

'No – and if your room is chilly and musty, it's your own fault for locking it.'

I led Michael up the backstairs, first collecting his two expensive-looking bags from the hall, where Jude had dumped them in a puddle of melting snow with his own. I put out towels and ran a bath while he unpacked his night gear, then while he was in there I made his bed up.

I heard Jude climb the backstairs and walk along the passage, heading for his own wing, and apart from Merlin the kitchen was deserted when I fetched the hot water bottle.

Hoping Michael wouldn't fall asleep in the bath, I went up to my own bed after washing up the mugs and saying good night to Merlin. Luckily the bathroom was now empty and, in fact, the whole house seemed quiet when I cautiously opened the door to the gallery a crack and listened: a brooding silence reigned.

I had a feeling it wouldn't be quite so tranquil in the morning . . .

By now, I was at that stage beyond exhaustion where you're looking at everything through thick glass, so I climbed into bed and picked up Gran's latest journal, saying aloud, '*Please* let me have jumped to all the wrong conclusions so there's no possibility I'm related to that objectionable man!'

Chapter 22: Outcomes

I have been feeling ill, especially in the mornings, and although it is still early to tell, I am sure I am expecting. I sent a note to N asking him to meet me urgently and intend to slip out very late this evening. Pearl and Hilda, who are in my confidence and very anxious to know the outcome, will wait up to let me back in again.

May, 1945

I woke very early, before it was light, and lay there for a little while thinking about poor Granny, for whom the outcome I had feared seemed to have come about. She didn't marry Ned Martland in the end, but I don't know if this was because he abandoned her (which looks horribly likely) or because he was killed before it could happen.

And here I was, landed in the middle of a Christmas house-party (the very thing I had tried to avoid), for the family of the man who seduced poor Gran – it's bizarre!

But I suppose everything at Old Place might be about to change with the arrival of the master of the house, because presumably I was now redundant – surplus to requirements. Assuming, that was, that Jude knew how to cook?

And it was at that inconvenient moment that I suddenly realised that before the arrival of Guy, Coco and the objectionable Jude, I'd actually begun to *enjoy* all the Christmas preparations and would be sorry to leave!

But if they clear the roads I expect Jude will send Coco and his brother packing back to London, and expect me to leave too. He might want to count the silver first, since he seemed to have a very nasty, suspicious mind.

Up to that point, though, I knew my duty and would carry on as usual, so I got up and showered, then dressed in sensible jeans and jumper and went downstairs to let Merlin out and give the horses a bit of carrot.

It was still pretty dark, but I could see that the snow had drifted up one side of the yard and not the other, where the Land Rover stood. I didn't think it seemed worse than the previous night though, just crunchier underfoot.

I cleaned out the ashes and stoked up the embers of the sitting-room fire, got everything out ready for breakfast and laid Tilda's tray.

While I was busy, the radio kept announcing that it was Christmas Eve, as if I might have the five-minute memory of a goldfish, but somehow these reminders didn't seem to hurt quite so much as they usually did, possibly because I had so much else on my mind at the moment.

Perhaps, at last, I was starting to relinquish the past and move on. A fresh start in the New Year – and maybe a fresh new life to go with it. Thank goodness nowadays having babies out of wedlock was totally acceptable, unlike in Gran's day!

Merlin was eating his breakfast, liberally sprinkled with his medicine, and I had made giblet stock and a bowl of stuffing for tomorrow and was putting a batch of biscuits in the oven, when Michael came diffidently into the kitchen. He looked a different man to the frozen one of the night before – very hand-some in a slightly haggard way, with fine features, light brown hair and hazel eyes. He was wearing a pale cashmere jumper to rival Guy's, over cream chinos, which was about as practical an outfit for the country as any of Coco's.

'Good morning! I heard you moving about down here, so I hoped you wouldn't mind my coming down for a cup of coffee? I'm a bit of an addict – and *something* smells delicious!' he added, sniffing the air appreciatively.

'Spiced biscuits for the tree,' I explained. 'Would you like cereal or a full cooked breakfast?'

'Well, bacon and eggs and toast would be perfect – but I could do it if you're busy?'

'No, that's fine, this is the last batch of biscuits. No-one else seemed awake, so I thought I'd get them done, because I promised Jess – that's Jude's niece – that we could ice them together this morning,' I said, touched by his thoughtfulness. 'But there's a cafetière over there and coffee in the cupboard above it, so you could make us both some while I'm cooking?'

We chatted while he was eating his breakfast and I was washing up those things I'd used for the biscuits that wouldn't go in the dishwasher, like the old metal pastry cutters shaped like Christmas trees, bells, stars and all kinds of other things. I told him how I did cooking and house-sitting for a living and in return he confessed, with a modest air, that he was an actor.

'Oh really? I expect you're terribly distinguished and I should have recognised you, only I rarely have time to watch TV or go to the cinema.'

'Not really famous – I'm mostly stage, except that I had a part in a film last year and made a bit of a success of it – *The Darkling Hours*. Sort of Harry Potter crossed with Tolkien and a dash of C.S. Lewis, but it went down well and I've had a few high-profile cameo roles since.'

'Oh yes, that was a huge success! I haven't seen it, but I've heard about it. You were in that?' I was impressed.

'It certainly put me on the radar.' He smiled rather sadly. 'But while we were filming, my wife had an affair with one of the other actors and we've broken up.'

'Oh, I'm so sorry.'

'We had . . . irreconcilable differences. The marriage hadn't really been working out. Debbie's taken our little girl, Rosie, to spend Christmas with her parents in Liverpool, so I called in to visit her and take some presents on the way up to stay with my Yorkshire friends. But after that, taking the SatNav's short cut led to my downfall.'

'Well, it could be worse – at least you saw your little girl *before* you got stuck. How old is she?'

'Two – and I think she's already forgetting me,' he said sadly. 'At first Debbie said she'd rather I didn't see her at all, but I want to stay in her life if I possibly can and I think we can stay friends if we work at it, for Rosie's sake.'

'Yes, of course you do and I'm sure Debbie will come round.'

He smiled at me. 'I do feel better for talking it through, so getting myself stuck in the snow has had one good result! But my friends are going to be wondering what on earth has happened to me. I tried ringing them from my car last night, but they were out and I had to leave a message. And this morning I can't get a signal at all!'

'No, the phone reception here is lousy. You either have to walk down the drive just past the lodge or up the hill behind the house, before you can get a signal.'

'It doesn't really look like hiking weather out there, does it?' he said, glancing out at the winter wonderland. 'I wonder if it would be all right if I made a brief call from the house phone?'

'I expect it would have been, only the poles have come down, so *that* isn't working either, though there is a call box in the village, about half a mile away.'

'Oh well, that's that. I'm hoping I'll be able to get off a bit later today anyway, if it's stopped snowing and they clear the roads.'

209

'I don't *think* there's been more snow since last night, but it's a bit hard to tell, because it's drifted and there's been a freeze overnight – it's all crunchy underfoot.'

'It'll probably thaw out once the sun comes up properly,' he suggested optimistically.

'A local farmer snowploughs the drive and the road to the village with his tractor, so he'll be up later this morning and can tell us what it's like out there,' I told him. 'If it's passable, then I should think Jude's brother and his girlfriend will be leaving too, so they could probably give you a lift down to your car. Or *I* could, because I'll be leaving myself, though I'll probably have to dig my car out. I hope it starts: I haven't moved it for days.'

He looked up, surprised. 'But – I was a bit too out of it last night, so I might have misunderstood – but aren't you here to look after the house and do the cooking for Jude's elderly relatives?'

'No, actually this was only supposed to be one of my house-sitting jobs, to look after the empty house and the animals over Christmas.'

I'd made some fresh coffee and now sat down with him while he ate toast and marmalade, and explained what had happened. And as I was talking, I began to see everything that had led to this moment as a series of unfortunate events, a bit like the *Lemony Snicket* film, and actually some of it was quite funny. In fact, by the time Guy walked in on us, we were getting along as if we'd known each other for years.

He looked taken aback to see a stranger there and instantly demanded, 'Who the hell is this?'

Coco drifted half-awake through the door after him, ethereally pretty in a diaphanous pink dressing gown and no makeup. Then she too spotted the visitor and jerked wide-awake, exclaiming, 'Michael – *darling*!'

He put down his cup hastily and got up. 'Er . . . Carla?' he ventured uncertainly.

She threw herself at him like a rose-tinted flying squirrel and kissed him with a *mwah! mwah!* noise on both cheeks. 'I haven't seen you for ages! You remember me, don't you – Coco Lanyon?'

'Of course,' he assured her, though I deduced from his expression that he didn't. But he *was* an actor, so he returned the embrace, told her how wonderful she looked, and asked her what she was doing just now, and she told him about her Morning Dawn Facial Elixir TV advert.

'This is Michael Whiston, he's a well-known actor,' I explained to Guy while all this luvviness was taking place.

He helped himself to coffee. 'A friend of yours?'

'No, I never met him before last night. He took a wrong turn when his SatNav told him to and—'

I broke off because Noël, in dressing gown and slippers, and Becca and Jess, who were dressed for mucking out, arrived to find the stranger in their midst and general introductions and explanations ensued.

'Michael and Jude arrived late last night, when I was switching on the generator – the electricity went off and the automatic switchover didn't happen,' I explained succinctly.

'You mean, *Jude* is here?' Guy demanded, getting straight to the crux of the matter.

Coco went white – though actually she was pretty pale to start with, a translucent Nordic fairness. 'Oh God, he's not, is he?'

'Oh, shut up, Horlicks,' Jess said. 'I'm glad Uncle Jude's here! Do you think he's brought me a present, Holly? Can I go and wake him up?'

'The poor boy must have jet lag, to have got here so quickly,' Noël suggested. 'Let him sleep.'

'No, I'm sure he's fine,' I said heartlessly, 'you can wake him in a minute, Jess. But first, could you take this tray up to your granny?'

I'd been buttering toast and soft-boiling an egg while all the

211

explanations were going on and now I added a little pot of tea to the tray. 'There. If you take that, I can get on with everyone else's breakfast.'

'But Guy – Jude is here!' Coco wailed, looking terrified. 'What are we going to do? Oh, I *wish* I'd never come.'

'Don't we all,' muttered Becca.

'Oh, I don't think he'll throw *me* out into the cold, cold snow – not his baby brother,' Guy said easily. 'I can't guarantee he won't throw you out though, Coco.'

'Don't be silly, no-one will be leaving until the roads have been cleared,' I said.

'And of course Jude won't throw you out anyway, m'dear,' Noël reassured her.

'Now, does everyone want a cooked breakfast?' I asked briskly.

Coco shuddered even more. 'An omelette made with egg whites for me,' she ordered. 'Black coffee.'

'You could put the kettle on and make a fresh pot,' I suggested. 'And there are lots of eggs if you want to do your own thing. I'm cooking fried eggs, grilled bacon, tomatoes and toast.'

'And very good it was too,' Michael said, giving me a warm smile and seeming not to notice that Coco was looking outraged. 'I'll make the fresh coffee. Since I'm the unexpected visitor I'd like to make myself useful and you wouldn't let me cook.'

'Well, Noël and I are useless in the kitchen, so *we'll* just keep out of the way,' Becca said.

But to my surprise Guy also made himself useful by buttering the toast, while I fried the eggs and grilled bacon and halved tomatoes brushed with olive oil.

Jess returned, reporting that Jude was now getting up. 'He won't say if he's brought me a present, so he probably has. And I told Granny about Jude being home and *she's* pleased too,' she announced. 'She said she expected he would send you packing,

212

Horlicks, and Guy would have to drive you back in his car, so we could get rid of both of you and have a lovely Christmas.'

'You horrible child,' Guy said dispassionately and then pulled ghastly faces at her until she giggled. Suddenly, despite not wanting to in the least, I found myself liking him a bit, despite his being so horrid to Coco.

'Are those biscuits for the Christmas tree?' Jess asked, spotting them cooling on the rack. 'When did you make them?'

'Early this morning, while most of you were still asleep. I thought we could ice them later, and put ribbon through ready to hang them on the tree. We've got icing sugar and I brought natural food colourings with me.'

'Oh, great.' She slid onto a chair next to Noël and helped herself to toast and jam. 'Horlicks, you shouldn't play with your food,' she said severely.

Coco, who had taken a fried egg and was engaged in cutting out the yolk, looked at her with disfavour. 'I don't know why you keep calling me that, but I wish you'd stop!'

'Yes, it's very rude,' said Becca, but without any great conviction.

Coco ate one mouthful of egg white and then pushed the plate away, though since she had the look of one who retired to sick up her meals immediately after eating them, it probably saved time. Or maybe she was just naturally all bones and angles?

'I need a ciggy.'

'Well, you're not smoking it in *my* house,' Jude's deep voice said from behind her and the huge kitchen seemed to shrink with his entrance. Guy paled slightly for all his bravado and Coco looked frankly petrified.

'Oh, look, it's the Brother Grimm,' I said involuntarily, looking at his set jaw – though to be fair, with one like that it would be hard for him to look soft and pleasant. And I can't imagine why these kind of remarks keep slipping out when he's there, because normally I keep a firm rein on my rebellious tongue with clients!

'Good morning to you, too,' he said to me sarcastically, then took his place in the large wheelback chair at the head of the table as if it was his by right – which, come to think of it, it was. 'I don't suppose there's any breakfast left?'

'Yes, of course, I did extra bacon when I knew you were getting up and I'll fry you a fresh egg. Guy, would you stick a bit more toast in?'

'We seem to have quite the extended family party, don't we?' Jude said, looking round the table. 'Odd, I don't remember inviting any of you – though Noël, Tilda and Becca are always welcome, of course.'

'And me,' said Jess.

'Not when you wake me up at the crack of dawn by hitting me with a pillow,' he said gravely. Then he raised an eyebrow at Coco and Guy. 'Congratulations! I saw the notice in *The Times*. When's the wedding?'

'There isn't a wedding, or even a proper engagement,' Guy said. 'Coco was jumping the gun.' He picked up his piece of toast and added, nonchalantly, 'Come to think of it, there wasn't even a gun – I've been trying to get rid of her for weeks.'

'That's a lie,' Coco exclaimed. 'Everything was fine! I can't think what's got into you suddenly, Guy!'

'Sanity?'

'He's fickle, m'dear – takes after his Uncle Ned,' explained Noël kindly, which was definitely not the sort of thing I wanted to hear about Ned Martland just then!

'Was Ned Martland *really* fickle?' I couldn't resist asking Noël.

'Yes, m'dear, but he genuinely fell in love with them. Heart soft as butter – but he couldn't marry 'em all, could he?'

'There you are, Coco,' Guy said easily. 'I can't help it, it's in my genes. I'm moving on to the next woman already.' He blew me a kiss.

'Oh, rubbish,' she snapped, then with an effort she rallied, got up and kissed Jude's unresponsive (and unshaven) cheek, twining

214

her arms girlishly around his neck. 'Jude, darling, Guy and I had a misunderstanding and he's still cross, so that's why he's being silly, but I know you'll be happy for us, about the engagement.'

'There is no *us*, I kept trying to tell you,' Guy interrupted. 'Sending an engagement notice to *The Times* without telling me doesn't actually constitute one.'

Coco burst into tears. 'You are so cruel to me!' she sobbed. Looking around for sympathy she did the flying squirrel thing at Michael again. 'Please take me away from these horrible people – this terrible, terrible place!'

'That's an awful line and you used it with me last Christmas,' Guy remarked critically, 'right after Jude found us together. And you're never going to make it as an actress because the delivery was terrible.'

Coco's sobs began to verge on the hysterical and Michael patted her gingerly, while making a face at me over her head.

'Poor child,' Noël said. 'I really don't think you've treated her well, Guy.'

'Oh, just fill the big jug with cold water and throw it on her,' suggested Becca, which was probably also something they had taught her at finishing school.

Coco hastily removed herself from Michael's shoulder, to his evident relief, and, declaring that she was going to dress and pack, flounced out of the room. I supposed I ought to do the same really – the packing bit, not the flouncing – though the thought was not terribly inviting. But then, neither was the idea of spending Christmas under the same roof as Jude Martland.

Noël rose from his chair, saying to Jude, 'Glad to have you back, my boy. I'll go and see if Tilda is getting up.'

'How is she doing?'

'Almost herself again,' he assured him. 'You'll see for yourself, shortly.'

'It was kind of you to rescue me,' Michael told Jude, 'but I hope to leave later too, just as soon as we know the roads have been cleared. Perhaps you can give me a lift down to my car?' he suggested to Guy. 'Or Holly says I might be able to get the local farmer to take me on his tractor?'

'Yes, George Froggat, who has the farm up the lane, will clear the road and our drive some time this morning, and he'll tell us what the road's like. I'd certainly love to see Guy and Coco on their way, and I expect you're keen to get off as well, but I can't very well turn you all out if it's impassable,' Jude said, though he looked as if he'd like to.

'Glad to hear it, though a couple more days of Coco's hysterics and we might change our minds about turning *her* out into the snow,' Guy said. 'But I'm prepared to pay George good money to take her away, so all is not yet lost. In fact, I'll take my coffee into the sitting room and watch out for him.'

'So long as he takes *you* away, too,' Jude called after him.

'You wouldn't throw your little brother out into the cold, cold snow, would you?' Guy said plaintively, turning in the doorway and clutching a melodramatic hand to his chest.

'Yes, I would,' Jude said uncompromisingly. 'And Coco's your responsibility now, so it's up to you to see she gets home safely.'

'There's a good fire in the sitting room, if you would like to go through with Guy,' I suggested to Michael.

'And it's time we saw to the horses, Jess,' Becca said. 'It's getting late.'

'Oh, but I'm going to ice the biscuits with Holly!' she protested.

'I need to clear up the kitchen and do one or two other things first,' I told her. 'We'll do it when you come back in. And it's so bitterly cold out there that I'm not sure they should go out today, even double-rugged.'

'So, who made you an equine expert suddenly?' Jude said rudely.

'Oh, you only have to explain something to Holly once, and

she's got it,' Becca said. 'But the horses can probably go out for a couple of hours. They've got the field shelter.'

When they went out Jude got up too, narrowly missing his head on the lamp that hung over the table.

'Could we have a word?' I asked.

'Later. I want to have a look at Lady in the daylight myself without her rug, and make sure she hasn't lost any condition. *And* check on the generator – which, by the way, you needn't go near now I'm back. After that I'll be in my room next to the library, catching up with the mail.'

'Yes, but—'

'Later!' he snapped again and went out before I could point out that there probably wasn't going to be any post for a while and also that, if he meant his email, the phone was off, making a dial-up connection impossible.

And before I could mention my urgent desire to remove myself from under his roof.

Chapter 23: Pieced Together

At my news N went quite pale with shock, though he quickly recovered and took me in his arms, repeatedly reassuring me that everything would be all right. He was so much his old, loving, sweet self that I went back to my lodgings feeling very much better.

May, 1945

A little later the generator stopped roaring suddenly as the mains electricity came back on. According to Noël, in winter it flickers on and off more often than the fairy lights on the tree. Still, at least the generator had switched itself off, as it was supposed to.

By late morning we were all gathered in the sitting room over elevenses of tea, coffee and, by Tilda's request, the Dundee cake that was Old Nan's annual gift to them.

'Then we can say how much we enjoyed it, when we see her,' she pointed out.

'*Are* we seeing her?' asked Guy.

'Oh yes, she and Richard will be here for dinner as usual tomorrow.'

Jess and I had water-iced the biscuits in bright colours and were hanging them on the tree with loops of embroidery silk that she had found in an old Victorian sewing box from the morning room, for want of ribbon. Becca was steadying the ladder while I reached up to do the higher branches.

Tilda was on the sofa in front of the fire, with Merlin on the rug at her feet, and Noël, Michael and Guy were at the table in the window, trying to finish piecing together one edge of the jigsaw that I'd bought at Oriel Comfort's shop, with Coco restlessly watching them from the window seat. There is something very compulsive about a jigsaw puzzle, although it didn't seem to have that effect on Coco; but then, that was probably nicotine deprivation.

Jude had retired to his little studio office next to the library, though he must have heard Coco's screech when she finally saw George's tractor coming up the drive pushing aside the fresh snow like an icebreaker, because he was there when I came back from letting him in.

I expect I must have looked a little bit pink and ruffled, but I regained my composure while George got over his surprise at finding Jude back from America.

'Never mind that,' interrupted Coco from the window seat. 'What I want to know is, has the road been cleared, so we can get away?'

'I hope by "we" you mean you and Michael,' Guy said.

'If you are going to be so mean and I can't get my car out, then I'm sure Michael would drop me at a railway station.'

George took off his battered felt hat and ran his fingers through his thick thatch of silver-fair hair so that it stood on end. 'Hold your horses! Liam had a hell of a job clearing the lane down to the village this morning, the old snow's ridged into ice underneath the fresh stuff. And young Ben from Weasel's Pot was at the pub, and he told him the lane below the farm is impassable and nothing's moving down on the main Great Mumming road either.'

'But that's ridiculous! Surely, if Jude got up here last night, it's possible to drive down again?' Coco exclaimed.

'It hadn't frozen over with all this fresh snow on top last night,' George said, looking her over dispassionately, as if she was a rather poor heifer.

'And I only just made it up the hill to Weasel Pot with chains on the wheels,' Jude put in.

'Yes, and though I don't doubt you could get down to the village and back, it would be pointless going further, you'd just get stuck,' George agreed.

'But you or someone else with a tractor could get me out of here, couldn't you?' wheedled Coco in a little-girl voice. 'Me will pay you wots and wots of money!'

'Excuse me while I throw up,' I muttered.

George shook his head. 'I told you, it's impassable.'

'But presumably the council will be out clearing the main road by now, won't they?' suggested Michael. 'Might it be possible later today?'

'You can't have been listening to the weather forecast or watched the news – the snow's wreaked havoc all over the country. The council won't bother with the little roads either, when it's all they can do to clear the main ones.'

'Guy!' Coco said, turning to him. '*Do* something!'

'Don't look at me, I can't perform miracles,' he said and she gave an angry sob.

'It's your fault I'm here in the first place! Mummy and Daddy will be wondering where on earth I am, and they've invited the whole family round on Boxing Day to meet you because we're engaged *and* bought champagne to toast us. And—'

'Oh God, she's going hysterical again,' Becca said disgustedly. 'Shall I throw some cold water on her? *Please* let me do it this time – I'd feel so much better!'

'Now, Becca,' Noël chided. 'The poor child's just a little overset.'

But Coco was not so far gone that she hadn't heard this implied threat. She retreated to sob quietly on a sofa as far removed from Becca as possible and Michael followed her after a minute and sat next to her, talking quietly and patting her hand.

'I'll be off then,' said George, looking hopefully at me, but I avoided his eye and let Guy see him out this time.

'It looks as if I'm stuck with all of you over Christmas, unless some miraculous thaw takes place, which seems unlikely,' Jude said with resignation when Guy came back.

'We might as well make the most of it, then,' Guy said. 'Coco, do stop making that noise.'

'I c-can't help it – I want to go home!' she wailed.

'It's not looking very likely at the moment.'

'I'm sorry to put you out like this,' Michael apologised to Jude.

'Oh, *you're* the least of my worries. Don't give it a thought.'

'Perhaps someone will help me dig out my car, just in case it does thaw out this afternoon?' I asked. Jude turned and looked at me from his treacle-dark eyes and snapped, 'Why, where the hell do you think *you're* going?'

'Home, if I can get out. But if not, I thought perhaps the pub might do rooms . . . I mean, now you're back, the job I was hired for is finished, isn't it?'

'Not so fast,' he said, 'you invited a houseful of people here and promised to cook for them, so you can't just take off like that.'

'Actually, I only invited half of them.'

'But, Holly, you can't go,' wailed Jess, 'it won't be as much fun without you! And what's more, Uncle Jude can't cook!'

'There is that,' he admitted. 'Though of course, Tilda can.'

'Tilda can't cope with the cooking, not after her fall,' Noël said. 'She's still recovering.'

'Load of old fusspots – I'm fine,' Tilda insisted. 'Though why spoil things when Holly and I have everything organised between us?'

Jude turned his dark eyes forbiddingly in my direction. 'Anyway, when did I say I wanted *you* to leave? And, by the way, the pub *doesn't* let rooms.'

'You *didn't* say you wanted me to. But now you're here, the job I was engaged for is ended and I'm sure you would rather I went, so—'

'The job damned-well isn't ended!' he interrupted. 'I'm paying you at great expense to do the cooking for my family over Christmas and you're going to stay and earn your money, every last penny of it!'

'Oh, no, you're quite wrong, Jude,' Noël told him, looking surprised. 'Holly refuses to charge us any extra, though I have told her she should be paid for all her extra trouble, when she was expecting to have a peaceful couple of weeks on her own.'

'I don't find cooking for you any trouble,' I assured him.

'Of course she doesn't,' said Tilda. 'And very good she is, too.'

'Thank you,' I said, touched by this unexpected tribute.

'Not as good as me, obviously, but very good,' she qualified.

'Loth though I am to disillusion you both,' Jude said to them, 'I am in fact going to be paying Homebodies through the nose for Holly's services.'

'No, you're not,' I corrected him. 'It's your own fault if you assumed I would do anything you wanted if you offered me enough money, but I've already told Ellen that I'll only be putting in a bill for house-sitting and any extra groceries I've had to buy.'

I smiled at Tilda and Noël. 'I was enjoying myself, actually.'

'And of course you must stay, Holly, we wouldn't dream of letting you do anything else!' Noël insisted. 'In any case, if she can't get out, what is she supposed to do, camp out alone in the lodge until she can leave?'

'I'd be very happy to stay at the lodge, if you didn't mind?'

'No, no, of course you are staying here, m'dear!'

'Yes, for we've decided the menus right through to Twelfth Night!' said Tilda.

'And Holly's not only a brilliant cook, she's *fun*,' Jess told her uncle. 'Merlin loves her too,' she added as a clincher.

Indeed Merlin, deducing from his master's voice that he was angry with me, now clambered onto my lap and was facing him protectively, all long, dangling limbs and rough fur.

'He does seem to be her shadow, I can't think what's got into him,' Jude said, staring at his dog. 'So, Holly Brown, you've wormed your way into the heart of the family in a very short space of time, haven't you? You seem to be a very dangerous, Becky Sharp sort of woman to me. And I'm *still* positive I know you from somewhere.'

Having read *Vanity Fair*, I wasn't too keen on being likened to Becky Sharp – and I certainly wasn't a fortune hunter out to marry him!

'We all thought she looked familiar too,' Noël said, 'but I expect it's only that she has the Martland look – the dark hair, height and light olive skin. So not only does she feel like a member of the family already, she also looks like one and fits right in!'

'I suppose that could be it,' Jude agreed.

'But I get my light grey eyes and dark hair from my grandmother,' I put in quickly. 'In fact, apart from being tall and dark, I don't *really* look like any of you.'

'You're much prettier than Jude, that's for sure,' said Guy, eyeing me thoughtfully. 'Though *pretty* isn't really the right word – you're beautiful, in an unusual way.'

'What, me?' I said, astonished. After years of bullying about my height and looks, not to mention Gran's repeated assertion that I had no reason to be vain, I found this hard to believe.

'Yes – even George looked smitten with you – and if he didn't kiss you under that handy bunch of mistletoe in the porch before you brought him in, why were you blushing?'

'It was nothing, he just took me by surprise. I hadn't even noticed the mistletoe hung in the porch until he grabbed me.' I could feel myself going pink again, because there was no mistaking that George fancied me!

'Becca and I hung that up,' Noël explained. 'There's always a bunch of mistletoe there.'

Behind me, Coco's piercing voice could be heard saying to

Michael, 'Guy said that housekeeper woman was beautiful – but she's not, is she? And I mean, she might be tall enough to be a model, but she's *way* too fat!'

I turned round and snapped, 'If you think being a healthy weight is fat, then you're sick! In any case, I'd rather be fat than so skinny I rattled when I walked! Excuse me: if no-one's leaving, I'd better go and do something about lunch.'

I went out to the kitchen since clearly I hadn't got much option but to stay, unless the roads miraculously cleared and this now seemed unlikely. Lunch was only going to be soup and sandwiches and I would lay it in the sitting room. I was getting tired of having so many people underfoot in my kitchen. There were some nice pale blue two-handled soup cups with saucers and stacks of paper napkins. I'd found a stash of real linen ones in the downstairs cupboard, but as far as I was concerned they could stay there until Jude had managed to find a handy skivvy willing to wash and iron them for her lord and master after use.

A few minutes later Jude followed me in and closed the door, then stood there with his arms folded, looking at me in a frowning, puzzled sort of way. I ignored him, as much as you could ignore something that size glowering at you, while I put the soup on the stove and got out some little oval tins of expensive game pâté I'd discovered in one of the cupboards. The use-by date was the end of December, so they needed eating.

'I wish you'd sit down and stop looming about,' I snapped eventually. 'Cooking isn't a spectator sport, you know.'

He pulled out the sturdiest of the wheelback chairs and sat on it and it protested, but weakly: I think it knew its place.

'My mother liked to cook and I loved to watch her,' he said unexpectedly.

'I envy you that, because I never knew mine: she died when I was born. Gran told me lots about her, but it's not the same thing,' I said, softened by this picture of him as a child, hard

224

though it was to imagine now. 'Perhaps some of the cookery books on the shelf are hers?'

'I expect they are, but she was just an amateur, while you, as you told me on the phone, are a highly-paid cook.'

'Chef.'

'Whatever.' He fixed his treacle-dark eyes on me and I noticed for the first time that they had disconcertingly mesmerising flecks of gold in them . . .

I wrenched my gaze away with an effort and carried on with what I was doing and he said, 'Look, Holly, I don't understand what game you're playing, though it's pretty clear you're up to *something*; but since we need your help over Christmas, I'll pay you whatever you want. It seems as if you're going to be stuck here with us, anyway.'

'Unless I go and stay in the lodge? But I'm not *up* to anything and nor did I offer to look after your family for money. I did it because I felt sorry you'd spoilt their Christmas – and also, I *really* like them.'

'So, are you saying you were just winding me up when you told me your charges were astronomical and that I couldn't afford them?' He scowled blackly at me.

'My cooking charges *are* astronomical, but I didn't actually say I was going to bill you for them at any point, did I? I told Ellen not to.'

'You let me assume you were!'

'Only because you annoyed me by assuming I was totally mercenary.'

'I don't know what's the matter with you – I got on fine with Jim and Mo! And surely you can't be this rude to all your clients?'

'I only give back as good as I get! In fact, I'm a perfectly calm, competent and reasonable person.'

'Oh yes, *perfectly* reasonable: after all, you only implied I'd neglected my elderly relatives and then got me so worried that you wouldn't look after them properly that I got on the first plane back from America. *Then* I found you'd filled my house full of people.'

'*I* filled your house? Whose family, ghastly ex-fiancée, free-loading brother and refugee actor are they anyway, may I ask?' I demanded. 'And did anyone ask *me* if I wanted to double the number of people I was cooking for? *Or* offer to help me – apart from Michael, who isn't part of your family at all!'

We glared at each other. He was looking a bit rough, which was probably equal parts bad temper and jet lag . . . or maybe he always looked like that?

'If your uncle and aunt wouldn't mind, perhaps it *would* be best if I removed myself down to the lodge,' I said after a minute. 'I'll leave you detailed instructions for cooking dinner tomorrow and tonight's is really quite simple. I can show you the menu plans and Tilda will tell you—'

'Just stop right there!' he snarled, then wearily rubbed a hand across his tired face and gave a long sigh. 'Look, Holly, I think perhaps we've simply got off on the wrong foot. Couldn't we put the past behind us and start again? If I apologise in fifteen different positions and not mention money, will you *please* stay over Christmas and do the cooking?'

There was a slight element of gritted teeth about this apology and proposal and I said suspiciously, 'What, as general skivvy?'

'As a house guest who has kindly offered to do the cooking.'

'I'll think about it,' I said, 'perhaps you are right, and we should let bygones be bygones and start over again. But meanwhile, if your vacuous ex-fiancée demands another egg-white omelette, I might just oblige and then rub her silly face in it.'

He grinned suddenly with genuine amusement and I blinked at the transformation: he looked younger – perhaps not much older than me – and if he wasn't handsome, he was still interestingly attractive . . . if you liked the strong-featured, hard-jawed type, that is.

'She has elderly parents who've spoiled her rotten, but she's not usually quite this bad.' He paused and added, 'Was it my imagination or was she turning the charm on me at breakfast?'

'Only in a general way, I think,' I said, considering this. 'She's all over Michael like a rash, of course, but then, he's apparently a well-known actor and she's met him before, so it isn't really surprising.'

'I got the impression he was just soothing her down, because it's *you* he seems to be getting on with like a house on fire. In fact, if you've been snogging George as well, you seem to have managed to get off with two total strangers in no time at all.'

'I wasn't snogging George and I haven't "got off", as you put it, with either of them,' I said with dignity. 'They're just both very nice men.'

'Well, my brother isn't and he seemed to be eyeing you up a bit, too.'

'What, saying I was beautiful?' I laughed. 'Oh, that's silly, he was just winding Coco up. I think he's being a bit cruel to her, because he must have led her on to think they were going to get married, or she wouldn't have sent off the announcement and told her parents, would she?'

'You've met her now: *you* tell *me*.' He got up, narrowly missing the lamp suspended over the kitchen table. 'So, do we have an agreement? You'll stay and do the cooking?'

'I suppose so,' I agreed reluctantly. 'But I'm doing it for Jess, Noël, Tilda and Becca – and for Old Nan and Richard.'

'Richard?' He raised a thick dark eyebrow. 'Another man you're on first-name terms with already?'

'Don't be so daft, you great streak of nowt,' I said crisply, which had been one of my grandmother's favourite put-downs to uppity men, and he grinned again and got up, clearly taking my agreement for granted.

But by then I'd realised that flouncing off to the lodge and being a hermit really wasn't an option anyway, not when there was a Christmas dinner to cook, and people I was fond of who would be disappointed if it wasn't right.

'I'll stay until after Boxing Day, at least, then see what the roads are like. But until then, this is *my* kitchen and I won't have any interference with my cooking – is that understood?'

'I can't guarantee that from Tilda,' he said dubiously.

'That's all right, she doesn't interfere, just *suggests*.'

'Then it's a bargain,' he said gravely and offered me a shapely, long-fingered hand the size of a bunch of bananas. At least, unlike Henry, he didn't spit in his palm first.

Chapter 24: Birkin Mad

Hilda and Pearl said N should have asked me to marry him right away, but I am positive he will when we meet again on Thursday and then all will be well.

May, 1945

After lunch it was pretty clear that the weather wasn't going to change: in fact, the sky was ominously pewter-coloured again. Coco still didn't seem to grasp that some way couldn't be found to get her home and in the end said that if no-one would help her, then she was going to walk to the village and possibly even down to the main road, where her phone would work and she could summon help.

'Who from?' asked Guy interestedly.

'The AA? The police? *Someone* to take me back to civilisation!'

'Look, it's not going to happen, much though we wish it would,' Jude said impatiently.

'No, nothing short of a helicopter could do the trick, I'm afraid,' Noël told her. 'But I'm sure we will all have a fun Christmas together,' he added optimistically.

'A helicopter!' She seized on the idea avidly. 'The air-sea rescue people could—'

'Oh, don't be so stupid,' Jude snapped. 'You can't ask the emergency services to helicopter you out, just because you want to go home!'

'I don't think there's really anywhere flat enough for them to land anyway,' Noël said, considering it. 'Only the green, and the houses are all a bit too close to that. Of course, they can winch people up.'

'Well then, Jude could take me down to the main road where there is bound to be somewhere flat enough. I can phone Mummy and Daddy and get them to arrange something. Or you can lend your Land Rover to Guy and we could both—'

'Nothing doing,' said Guy. 'Give it up.'

'You're all so horrible to me, except Noël and Michael! I want to talk to Mummy and Daddy,' she whined.

'If you start that howling again, I'm going to slap you,' Becca said uncompromisingly, which seemed to work just as well as threatening her with a drenching.

'Look, Coco,' said Michael kindly, 'I ought to phone my friends and let them know what's happened to me, so why don't you and I walk down towards the village together until we can get mobile signals? It'll give us a chance to see what conditions are really like, too.'

'All right,' she agreed sulkily, 'but if I can find someone who can get me out of here, I'm not coming back!'

'We'd better find you both something more practical to wear before you set out, then,' Tilda observed. 'You won't get very far dressed like that.'

Becca rooted out old wellingtons and waxed coats that more or less fitted and they set off down the drive, Coco's rather Dr Zhivago white fur hat striking a strange note. They walked through the virgin snow at the side of the drive, so where the tractor had ploughed must have been too slippery.

'I hope they're going to be all right and Coco doesn't do anything stupid,' I said, watching them from the sitting-room window until they disappeared into the pine trees above the lodge.

'Michael seems a sensible chap, so I'll be surprised if they

230

go very far,' Jude said, 'and even Coco will be able to see that it's impossible to get out. Not that I want her or Guy here, of course, but I'm prepared to put up with them under the circumstances.'

'Thanks,' said Guy dryly.

Jude looked measuringly at his brother. 'Don't think I've forgotten how you behaved last Christmas, though, and how much it all upset Father, when he was so ill,' he said evenly.

Guy looked slightly shamefaced. 'No, well – look, I'm really sorry about that! It's just that as soon as I set eyes on Coco I fell madly in love – she's so stunningly pretty.'

'You did? I thought you just took her away because she was my fiancée!'

'No,' Guy said wryly, 'I fell for her, hook, line and sinker. But then I fell out of love with her quite suddenly, just after she sent that engagement notice to the papers. It was quite a wake-up call. What about you?'

'*Me?*' Jude said. 'Oh, the minute I saw her again. In fact, in retrospect, you might have done me a favour by breaking up our engagement, because I don't think I'd grasped before quite how silly she is! I must have been blinded by her looks.'

'Me too,' agreed Guy. 'It's strange how when I thought I was in love with her, everything she said seemed funny and endearing, whereas now it's intensely irritating.'

'Still, that's not her fault – but it *is* yours that we're landed with her for Christmas,' Jude said. 'You'll have to look after her and see she doesn't make a huge nuisance of herself until we can get her out of here – and also has a bit of fun, too.'

'That's a tall order – but Michael might do the trick. He's a good-looking guy and a well-known actor and she seems to be turning her sights on him a bit, did you notice?'

Jude nodded. 'Yes, she was wittering on about acting and some TV commercial she'd been in. Okay, let's foist her onto him, that should keep her happy and occupied.'

231

'That's so unfair – Michael's way too nice for Coco!' I exclaimed unguardedly and they both looked at me.

'Have *you* got your eye on him too? You'll have to work fast if you don't want Coco to cut you out,' advised Guy. 'You haven't seen her when she swings into action!'

'Don't be silly, I barely know the man,' I snapped. 'But I *can* see he's good-natured and kind, which is more than can be said of you two!'

'Attagirl,' commended Tilda drowsily from the sofa. Then she swung her tiny feet off it and slid them into her marabou and velvet mules. 'Well, I'm glad you two boys are friends again.'

'I wouldn't go quite that far,' Jude said, but when she insisted on them shaking hands he did so and even allowed a relieved Guy to thump him affectionately on the back.

'Pax?' Guy said hopefully.

'Pax,' Jude agreed.

'Have I missed something?' asked Noël, who had been snoring away on his own sofa like a small buzz-saw for the last ten minutes.

'The boys are friends again, Noël, and I think I will go and have a little rest on my bed now,' Tilda said. 'What are the rest of you going to do this afternoon?'

'I'm going down to the studio for an hour or two,' Jude said. 'Make sure everything is all right.'

'You could have walked down there with Michael and Coco,' Noël pointed out.

'I could, but I didn't want to.'

'Can I come with you, Uncle Jude?' asked Jess.

'Yes, if you wrap up warmly.'

'And Holly, too?'

'Oh no,' I said quickly, 'I'll be glad of some time to myself in the kitchen, there's lots to do.'

'You never stop,' Becca commented. 'Cooking seems to me to be very hard work!'

232

'It is, and especially hard on the feet: that's why I usually have a rest from it over the winter. But I do like cooking and I've never catered for a large Christmas house-party before, so all this is a novelty and a challenge.'

Jess said, 'Holly's writing a cookery book, but she hasn't thought of a good title yet.'

'We could have a brainstorming session later,' suggested Guy.

'Thanks, but I'll storm my own brain in due course,' I replied and retired to the comforting ambience of the kitchen. Merlin went with me, though he did cast a 'my loyalties are divided' look back at Jude. He's so much happier when we're in the same room – and I'm starting to get the feeling that Jess is, too!

I added more vegetables to the soup pot and put it on the Aga, then did a bit of food prepping for later, including bringing the turkey into the kitchen to come to room temperature for tomorrow. But really what I wanted to do was search among the recipe books on the shelf to see if I could find anything like the Revel Cakes that Nancy at the pub had described. And the very first book on the shelf, the big, fat, red hardback copy of *Mrs Beeton*, turned out instead to be a box, full of handwritten recipes and cuttings from magazines and newspapers: quite fascinating! This kind of thing is like treasure trove to a keen cook.

The Revel Cake recipe was in there, written in a faded copper-plate hand on thick cream paper. I copied it out into my own notebook and put the original back into the box. It seemed to be a spicy bun mixture, with one or two additions, like saffron and a sprinkle of chopped candied peel on top, and I expect it evolved into that over centuries from something very much plainer. You pulled the dough into a long roll and then made little concentric coils, like fossil ammonites. If I was here long enough and had the time, I could make and freeze batches to leave for Twelfth Night. I wondered how many would be needed?

The house seemed to have gone pleasantly peaceful and when I put my head through the sitting room door it was empty, apart from Becca, stretched out asleep on the largest of the sofas. There must be something naturally soporific oozing out of the walls.

I could hear the TV from the morning room, some kind of sport, going by the roars, so Guy was probably in there with Noël.

I threw another log on the fire and then retired to the kitchen again, this time to read a bit more of Gran's latest journal. Now I'd met Jude Martland and his attractively untrustworthy brother, I even more urgently wanted to discover if Gran really had been pregnant and, if so, whether Ned was going to offer to do the right thing by her. I can't say it was looking very promising at the moment and if Guy is really like his uncle, then Ned can't have had any staying power whatsoever. And in that case, I really wouldn't want to find I was even *distantly* related to his family!

But if my mother *was* Ned Martland's daughter, then my grandfather was the brother of Jude and Guy's father, which would make us cousins – removed cousins it's true, though not, if Ned abandoned Gran, far enough for my liking!

Then I thought of dear Noël, Becca, Jess and even Tilda, who I am growing fond of despite her being such an old toot, and realised that I wouldn't mind being related to *them* at all.

I restrained the urge to skim forward in the journal, but settled down with my fingers crossed, hoping that maybe Gran wasn't pregnant after all, broke up with the untrustworthy-sounding Ned, and married my grandfather instead.

Unfortunately, everything in the journal pointed to a different conclusion – as did my mother's birth certificate when I went upstairs and had a rummage in the trunk and found it. This was probably why I was a bit short with Jude when he and Jess came back, bringing a breath of chilly air with them.

Jess said she'd made a snowman while Jude had been messing

about in his studio, and that the mill pond was almost completely frozen over.

I shivered: 'You didn't go on the ice, did you?'

'No, I wanted to, but Uncle Jude told me not to.'

'What's the delicious smell? And are those scones?' Jude asked hungrily.

'It's just the soup – I like to keep a big pot going in winter. And the scones are cheese ones for tea. I was just about to take them through to the sitting room. I thought Tilda might be down by now.'

'Whatever I ought to be paying you, you'd be worth it,' he said sincerely, taking the tray I'd set out.

'And as I keep telling you: you couldn't afford me.'

He looked down at me curiously. 'I don't know why you're so convinced I'm penniless.'

'Oh, I'm sure you're not *entirely* penniless, but you're an artist with a neglected house and no live-in staff, so clearly you aren't exactly rolling in it.'

'It's a lifestyle choice.'

'What, the grubby, neglected house?'

'No, I meant not having any staff living in. Actually,' he added, 'I hadn't realised the house *was* getting in a mess until I came back and saw how much better it looked now.'

'You shouldn't have been so stingy and paid Sharon a bit more, then. She wasn't exactly going to bust a gut for half the minimum wage, was she?'

'Is that what she told you I paid her?'

'Yes, and no Christmas bonus either. Do you mean – it wasn't true?'

He laughed. 'No – and so much for trying to do a good turn! When I advertised the job she came to me with a sob story about her husband being unemployed and being so angry he was taking it out on her. I felt so sorry for her I took her on – and paid her double.'

'Double?'

'Yes, believe it or not. Then I realised how useless she was *and* caught her trying to steal some of my sketches from the wastepaper basket in the study. I really wanted to get rid of her, I just didn't know how.'

'Oh . . . then I'm sorry. I thought you were mean as well as poor,' I apologised.

'Uncle Jude's got lots of money, Holly,' Jess said. 'Mummy says his sculptures sell for ridiculous amounts and he's rolling in it.'

Jude gave me the strangely attractive smile that softened the hard line of his mouth and quirked it up at one corner. 'You didn't think Coco wanted me for my good looks alone, did you? So yes, whatever your charges are, I could pay them. But since you won't accept that, I'm under an obligation to you.'

'You needn't be, because I'm not doing it for you.'

'I know, but I still feel under an obligation. I'll just have to find another way to pay you.'

I discovered I was still staring up (a novelty in itself) into his gold-flecked dark eyes and hastily looked away. 'Did you see Coco and Michael?'

'No, but everyone else is in the sitting room. I thought they'd be back by now, but they must have gone on to the village.'

'I hope Coco doesn't try anything silly.'

'Michael seems the sensible kind, I don't suppose he'd let her.'

'What are we having for dinner tonight?' asked Jess, getting on to something she considered more important.

'Pheasant pie with redcurrant jelly and winter vegetables. I'm making great inroads into the frozen pheasants. And we'll have the trifle for pudding, if you help me whip the cream and sprinkle hundreds and thousands on it later.'

'Or we can use squirty cream, that's my favourite.'

'Yes, I noticed and I got the last of Mrs Comfort's stock, so you can use as much as you want to.'

'Cool! But I don't know if I like pheasant pie.'

'You can try it and see, and if not, I'm bringing the ham through as well so we can take the first cut at that: it's a monster and should last for days.'

Eventually the remains would turn into pea and ham soup, *my* favourite – if I was here long enough to make it.

I slipped out of the back door later and made for the track up the hill to call Laura, but the snow had drifted across it quite deeply in places and the signal was still poor when I had to stop. Then we kept getting cut off, which was frustrating.

I managed to tell her about the ghastly Coco and the handsome love-rat Guy landing on me. 'And if Guy is like Ned Martland, as they keep telling me he is, then I can understand why poor Gran fell for him, though it's looking more and more as though he got her pregnant and then abandoned her, just as I feared.'

I lost the signal then, but when I got her back I dropped the final bombshell: 'But the icing on the cupcake of life is that Jude Martland turned up late last night, too!'

'But he was supposed to be in America, wasn't he?'

'Yes, but he thought I was a cold-hearted, money-grubbing bitch who wouldn't look after his aunt and uncle after Tilda had her accident!' I said indignantly. 'So he just got on the first plane home. *And* I like him even less in person than I did on the phone, if that's possible.'

'Hasn't he got any redeeming features?'

'He might have one or two,' I admitted reluctantly, 'but the annoying parts outweigh them.'

'So, why aren't you on your way home, then?'

'We seem to be snowed in and none of us can escape, unless we get a sudden thaw.'

'Sounds like a fun house-party, then!'

'Yes, I agreed glumly. 'The only good thing is that Jude brought an actor called Michael Whiston with him.'

'Oh, I've heard of him, he's very attractive!'

'Yes he is, and also a really nice man and – oh, damn!' The connection had cut for the third time, so when I got her back I said, 'This is hopeless, so I'll give up and try again tomorrow. Give my love to the family.'

'And Sam?' she asked hopefully, but then the signal symbol vanished once more and I shoved the phone back into my pocket and trudged back down the hill, where no-one except Merlin had noticed my absence.

The afternoon was beginning to grow dark and I, at least, was getting worried about Michael and Coco, when the familiar tractor appeared up the drive, this time with a gritting trailer behind it and a youth at the wheel who I guessed from his silver-gilt hair to be George's son, Liam.

Crammed into the cab with him were our two missing refugees. By the time I'd opened the door, Liam was helping a drunk, tearstained and dishevelled Coco out of the cab, followed by Michael, who was looking long-suffering and carrying one of Oriel Comfort's inspirational hessian bags: *Raindrops Are God's Tears of Joy*.

Liam gave me a wink and a knowing grin that I found hard to interpret – or perhaps didn't *wish* to interpret – then jumped back into the cab and roared off, spraying a generous flourish of grit as he went.

'I see you found the shop open?' I said to Michael, with a nod at the bag, and he smiled.

'Once I'd seen the state of the roads it occurred to me that since we were clearly going nowhere for Christmas, I ought to contribute a bit to the festivities here. Then once I was in the shop, something came over me.'

'You mean Oriel Comfort came over you: she's *very* persuasive. You should see what I bought last time! But come in, you both look freezing.'

Since Coco seemed likely to remain drooping there like a half-melted candle, Michael took her arm and towed her in after him. 'We're not too cold, actually – we were freezing when we got to the village, of course, but I left Coco in the pub to phone her parents and thaw out while I was in the shop.'

'So I see,' I closed the front door and surveyed her. She swayed slightly and blearily focused her ice-chip eyes on me.

'Mummy said Daddy had the flu, so Christmas and our engagement party were cancelled anyway! She said there was no point in my rushing back, I should stay here – but they never liked Guy anyway.'

'Right . . .' I said soothingly, removing her waxed coat and hanging it up on a peg, then pushing her down and pulling off her wellingtons, while Michael divested himself of his own borrowings.

'And when I said what about my presents, because I was *so* looking forward to finally getting a Birkin bag, she said, "What Birkin bag?" Coco continued in a high-pitched whine. 'Can you believe it? I told her months ago to get on the list for one, because it was what I wanted for Christmas, and the stupid cow forgot!'

'I don't think you should call your mother a stupid cow,' I said, any feelings of faint sympathy vanishing abruptly. Coco had all the warmth and emotional depth of a winter puddle: how on earth could seemingly intelligent men like Jude and Guy ever have fallen for her?

She gave me another bleary look and said rudely, 'Who cares what *you* think?' Then she heaved herself up. 'I'm going to have a hot bath.'

'Let's hope she doesn't fall unconscious and drown in it,' Michael said, though not with any great concern, so she must have tried even his good nature and patience to the limit. 'I think I'll go up and follow suit, if that's all right?'

'Yes, good idea. Come on, I'll make you a hot drink to take with you. Did you have any lunch?'

'Yes, bread and cheese in the pub, though Coco's lunch was entirely liquid, as you see. Her parents should have christened her Vodka, not Coco.'

As his contribution to the festivities, Michael had very thoughtfully bought two large boxes of chocolates and three bottles of the special sherry from the pub that Nancy had told him the older members of the party favoured.

'Oh good,' I said, relieved. 'Becca brought some, but the way they knock it back, it wasn't going to last. And the chocolates will go down well, too.'

'I've also got a small gift for everyone,' he admitted, 'from Mrs Comfort's *Sunbeams are God's Thoughts* range.'

'I bought a few things too, but mine are mostly edible gifts. I'm going to put them under the tree later.'

'I'll do the same, then, and I've bought wrapping paper, but if you have a roll of Sellotape I could borrow, that would be great.'

He's such a nice, kind, thoughtful man and I really like him! I'm going to give him one of the extra jars of sweets I've already wrapped. I suppose I should give one to Coco, too, but she isn't going to want sweets, I wouldn't have thought: too full of sugar.

And nothing, in her eyes, will compare to her longed-for Birkin bag, anyway.

Chapter 25: Christmas Carol

I waited and waited in our usual place and N did not come.
What am I to think? Surely something must have happened
to prevent him coming and I will get a message soon? Or is
this some terrible kind of retribution for my sins?

May, 1945

Jude and Jess did the horses together to give Becca a rest and
then Guy, all charm, offered to lay the dining table (we were
dining more formally tonight, it being Christmas Eve) and help
me in any other way, and I took him up on it. He and Michael
(who had come back down with his wrapped gifts and put them
under the tree), did all the donkey work and carried things
through for me.

When everything was under control in the kitchen and
everyone was in the sitting room, including a sullen and still not
entirely sober Coco dressed in something scarlet and scanty, I
took in a tray of filo pastry savoury starters and stayed for a
drink.

Michael had presented his sherry and chocolates to Tilda,
presumably as titular presiding lady of the house, the alpha
female of our wolf pack. He was now so much in favour that
when everyone else had gone through to the dining room and
he was helping me to carry through the main course, he told
me he felt just like an invited house guest and that he thought

Christmas at Old Place would probably be more fun than with the friends he was intending to stay with.

'It's certainly going to be different to any Christmas *I've* ever had,' I said, and told him a little about my Strange Baptist upbringing and how I had only really celebrated Christmas in a religious way, apart from the all too brief years of my marriage.

'And then my husband died in an accident at this time of year, and my mother too – and now my gran, who brought me up: so you see, celebrating Christmas doesn't come naturally to me!'

'No, I can see why you would much rather have ignored the whole thing,' he agreed, and then gave me a kind hug. 'Poor Holly!'

Jude, who had just come into the kitchen, stopped dead on the threshold. 'I came to see if you wanted me to do anything for you – but Michael seems to have got that covered,' he said rather surlily and went out again, closing the door with a near slam.

'What's biting him?' I exclaimed.

'I expect he thinks we're getting a bit too friendly,' Michael said with a grin. 'He's probably jealous.'

'Don't be daft, he doesn't like me, so why should he be jealous? Maybe he disapproves of the help getting matey with the guests?'

'But Coco seems to be the only one who thinks of you as staff.'

'She appears to be transferring her affections from Guy to you, have you noticed? You'd better watch your step, Michael!'

'I will, but I expect it's only because she thinks I can help her into acting – which I can't, of course, even if she can act, which I doubt very much.'

'No, I should think she can only play one part: Coco,' I agreed.

The dining table looked lovely, with a red damask cloth and red candles in the silver holders.

Coco remained silent and sullen for most of dinner, eating little and drinking too much and Jude had gone quite morose too, though he doesn't appear to be a laugh a minute person anyway. But everyone else seemed in good form even though Jess was clearly over excited about the approach of Christmas Day.

Tilda even complimented me on the pheasant pie and said she couldn't have done it better herself, though I noticed that Coco merely scraped a little of the middle out of her piece and ate it with about a teaspoon of vegetables. Then she reacted with loathing when offered trifle.

'But it's lovely! I did the cream and decorated it, didn't I, Holly?' Jess said.

'Yes, you made it look beautiful. How about an apple or clementine, then, Coco? Or a little cheese?'

'Cheese is full of fat and I hate fruit.'

'So what do you usually eat at home?' I asked curiously.

'If anything,' Jude said, *sotto voce*.

'Steamed fish and edamame beans,' Guy said with a grimace.

'Oh, there's lots of fish in the freezer, Coco – in fact, we're having a whole salmon on Boxing Day. But there aren't any edamame beans.'

'I don't even know what they are,' Jess said.

'They've only really got popular lately – stars seem to eat them a lot. I don't know why, because I don't find them very exciting,' I said.

'I'm sure *Michael* knows what they are,' Coco said, her intimate smile clearly meant to show that they inhabited the same, more sophisticated, world. Now she'd had another glass of wine she'd perked up again, unfortunately, and was turning the full battery of her charm on Michael. He began to look a little nervous.

She said she was sorry she'd been upset earlier, but knew he would understand the artistic temperament. Then she told him all about the facial elixir advert all over again, and how her agent

243

was going to send her for an important role in a new film, and kept on and on, even when Jess sighed loudly and said, 'We know all about that already, Horlicks!'

But this slightly febrile cheerfulness waned a little when we went back into the sitting room and she spotted the heap of gifts under the tree, because they reminded her that she wasn't going to get her Birkin bag.

Jess, who had been lovingly fondling the ones with her name on, said, 'You have got some presents, at least three, Horlicks.'

'I can't imagine why you keep calling me by that silly name,' she said, but looked slightly mollified, though I didn't imagine that she was going to be delirious with pleasure to receive Michael's Oriel Comfort-inspired gift, or the jar of bath scrub I'd hastily whipped up in the kitchen from sea salt, olive oil and essential lavender oil.

I didn't know what the third one was, though going by the rather slapdash wrapping, Jess had put it there. I hoped it wasn't something horrid.

Jude insisted on making the coffee and bringing it through to the sitting room while I relaxed, which was unexpectedly thoughtful of him, though the gesture was spoiled because he also brought the petits fours I'd intended for Boxing Day. Now I'd have to make some more.

The coffee was good, so he's not entirely devoid of kitchen talents. He certainly seemed to like marzipan . . .

'Do you happen to have any more ground almonds at the lodge if I run out?' I asked Tilda.

'Oh yes, I'm sure we have – Edwina uses them a lot. Do go down and rummage in the kitchen and fetch anything you need,' she said graciously.

The men went to play snooker in the library and Coco drifted aimlessly after them.

'Do you think she's anorexic?' Becca said. She was puzzling over the big jigsaw, which hadn't got very far yet. I leaned over her shoulder and moved some pieces of the edge from one side to the other: it was pretty obvious where they went from my angle.

'She does seem to vanish for ages after every meal,' Tilda said. 'Not that she eats much anyway. Maybe she's throwing it back up?'

'She eats loads of laxatives,' Jess said unexpectedly. 'That's weird, isn't it?'

'How do you know?' I asked, surprised.

'I saw her eating what looked like a handful of sweets when she thought she was alone, so I had a look in her handbag and it's stuffed with packets of Fruity-Go. Her bedside table drawer is, too, and she's forever going to the loo.'

'Jess, darling, you really shouldn't root about in other people's rooms,' Tilda said mildly. 'But no wonder she spends ages in the bathroom!'

'That must be how she stays as thin as a tapeworm,' Becca agreed. She and Jess helped carry out the coffee things and then went to play Monopoly with Tilda while I stacked the dishwasher, cleared up the kitchen and fed Merlin.

When I went back into the sitting room, everyone had returned and Guy, Michael and a bored Coco were grouped around the jigsaw puzzle. Jude, Tilda and Jess were finishing a game of Monopoly which Tilda won, a veritable property tycoon.

Noël seemed to be waiting for me. 'Ah, there you are, m'dear – just in time for a Martland family tradition.' He picked up a leather-bound copy of Charles Dickens's *A Christmas Carol*, and began to read aloud, rather beautifully.

Even Coco stopped her restless movements and fixed her eyes on him, though when he reached the part with the ghosts she kept casting nervous glances over her shoulder, as if one might be standing right behind her.

We all applauded at the end and Noël stood up to take a

modest bow. 'Thank you! We used to read a few scenes from *Twelfth Night*, too – but on New Year's Eve.'

Coco came alive and avidly seized on this. '*Twelfth Night*? I know that, we had to do it at school. There are lots of boring bits that are supposed to be funny, but quite a lot of mixed-up love scenes, too.'

'I've played Sebastian in the past, at Stratford,' admitted Michael.

'Then perhaps we should revive the tradition and you could take the part again?' suggested Noël.

'Assuming you're still here by New Year's Eve,' Guy said.

'We could do it earlier if the roads thaw and it looks like we can get away, can't we?' Coco said, and then enthused, 'And why can't we *act* out the parts, not just read them?'

'I suppose we could, if you want to,' Noël said. 'We have several printed copies of the scenes we used to use in the library.'

'You can be Sebastian, Michael, and I will be the fair Olivia,' Coco said, striking a pose. 'Guy, you can be Orsino and I suppose Holly had better be Viola, seeing she's Sebastian's twin and she can look like a man.'

'Thanks,' I said. 'But that doesn't work really, does it? Sebastian and Viola are supposed to be very like each other.'

'The audience will just have to use their imaginations, then,' she snapped, and I could see she was angling to do her love scenes with Michael. However, from what I recalled of the play, that left me to fall for Orsino.

'I hate acting,' Guy said. 'I don't even perform in the Revels, so it'll have to be Jude. Noël will link the scenes as usual and prompt, and I'll be your admiring audience with Tilda, Jess and Becca.'

'I'm not much of an actor either,' Jude said.

'Or me,' I put in hastily.

'Well then, you and Holly can just read the parts, okay?' Coco said impatiently.

She was the only person really keen on doing any acting, presumably to show off her skills to Michael and, perhaps, to get a little closer to him. However, no-one put up much of a protest and Noël said he would find the printed parts the next day.

I expect we were all too relieved that Coco had found something to occupy herself with to object and she became quite animated while talking with Michael about rehearsing.

But still, I thought we would be long gone by New Year's Eve, and she would abandon the play like a shot if she could get away!

Tilda decided to go to bed and ordered Jess upstairs too, though she didn't want to go.

'I'm too excited, I'll never sleep.'

'Then Father Christmas won't come,' Tilda told her.

'Oh, Granny! The presents are all here, and I know it was Mummy who did the stocking last year, because it was so awful. I'm not even hanging one up this time.' But she trailed off after her.

'It's very late, but it's been a pleasant evening,' Becca said and Noël agreed, 'Yes, best get off to bed myself too, I think.'

Even Coco seemed ready to go up – all that emotion and alcohol must have been exhausting, though I noticed she lingered long enough to look at her presents under the tree, which was sort of *slightly* endearing: twenty-four going on five.

Saying good night, the party broke up and vanished one by one, except for Jude, who went to let Merlin out for a last run and check on the horses. I banked the fire up and collected a couple of abandoned sherry glasses and was in the kitchen washing them up when he came back in. Snow flecked his dark hair, so it must have been coming down thick and fast.

Merlin greeted me as if he hadn't seen me for a month instead of a few minutes and Jude regarded him with disfavour. 'That creature must have gone senile in my absence, I think he's forgotten who he belongs to!'

247

'That reminds me, I must wrap his present up when he's not looking.'

'You got my dog a present?'

'Just a large rawhide bone from Oriel Comfort's shop. She really does stock everything, doesn't she?'

'So much so that I expect her shop to suddenly explode under the strain one day,' he agreed. 'I don't suppose you've some spare Christmas wrapping paper? Only I got a few things in the airport on the way home, when I had time to kill between flights.'

'Yes, Mrs Comfort only had huge rolls of the stuff so there's plenty left, even though Michael's had a bit, too,' I said, getting the paper out of the cupboard.

He muttered something that sounded suspiciously like, 'I bet he has!' then headed out, stopping on the threshold to ask, 'You *are* going to bed now?'

'Yes, I just have one or two last things to do down here first.'

He looked at his watch. 'I almost forgot – it's nearly midnight and, snow or not, Richard will be at the church. Come on!'

Grabbing my hand, he towed me through the silent house to the front door, which he unlocked and threw open. A flurry of snow touched my face and faintly on the breeze I heard the distant, magical sound of church bells in the valley below.

'Merry Christmas!' Jude said as they stopped. Above our heads the bunch of mistletoe revolved in the breeze and he stood very still, looking down into my face. Then, as if driven by some compulsion he would have preferred to have resisted, he bent his head and quickly brushed his lips against mine.

I shivered, but the surprise made me acquiescent, and I was still standing in the open doorway, snow whirling round my head and my face tilted up to his, when he just as suddenly turned on his heel and went off without another word.

Men!

*   *   *

I transferred the sausage and bacon rolls, stuffing and bread sauce from the freezer to the fridge before I went upstairs to my room.

I'd hidden all the items that were to go into Jess's Christmas stocking in my wardrobe, so when I'd changed into the unexciting long white cotton nightdress and robe that Gran had made for me to the archaic pattern she favoured herself, I laid everything out on the bed next to a large sock. A *very* large sock.

I put a clementine in the toe, since it was a satisfying shape, but had decided against the nuts. Then everything else I'd bought went in, pushed well down, with the yellow-eyed wolf sticking its head out of the top.

After that, I sat reading Gran's journal until I thought Jude would have gone to bed – and *poor* Gran, my guesses had been quite right and her big romance was all going pear-shaped.

Because I'd arrived at that stage of tiredness where you feel spaced-out but entirely awake, I read on for longer than I intended. But at least when I did finally pick up the stocking and tiptoe quietly (apart from some odd rustlings from the stocking) across the gallery and along the west wing passage towards the nursery, the house was silent and everyone was fast asleep . . .

Or so I thought, right up to the moment when Jude's door swung silently open like something from a fairground House of Horrors and he grabbed me and pulled me into his room, closing the door behind us. I gave a strangled yelp and pushed him off, my hands meeting the bare skin of a well-muscled chest . . . an *extremely* well-muscled chest.

'Shhh!' he said, switching the light on, which was possibly even scarier, since he was towering over me wearing only loosely-tied pyjama bottoms. His dark hair was standing on end and I wouldn't be surprised if mine was, too. I dropped my hands as though they'd been burnt and took a step back as he released my arm.

'What on earth were you doing, sneaking round the house at

this time? Where were you going?' he demanded suspiciously in a menacing rumble.

'I *wasn't* sneaking,' I hissed furiously back, 'and you nearly gave me a heart attack, grabbing me like that, you total imbecile! It's just as well I'm not easily frightened.'

His dark eyes wandered down my thin white cotton robe to my bare feet and back again. 'Miss Havisham, I presume?' he said sarcastically. Then he spotted the bulging stocking I was holding. 'Or wait – it must be Mother Christmas! And isn't that one of *my* socks?'

'Yes, if you left it stuffed into a pair of wellies in the garden hall. I washed it yesterday and sewed this bit of ribbon on to hang it from the end of her bed by – it's for Jess.'

'I didn't think you were doing it for me. But isn't Jess too old for that kind of thing?'

'Not according to Mrs Comfort, she says they're never too old. I wouldn't know, I never had one as a child. But Jess did say that last year's was a huge disappointment and she thought her mother only remembered at the last minute.'

'She's a bit scatty, is my cousin Roz. Shoved in a small chocolate selection box and a clementine.' He frowned down at me. 'And what did you mean, you never had a stocking?'

'I was brought up by my grandparents – my gran mostly, because my grandfather was much older than she was. But they were Strange Baptists – he was a minister in the church.'

I waited for him to ask me what was strange about them again, but instead he said, 'Oh yes – I think you mentioned that as the reason you don't usually celebrate Christmas. A bit like the Plymouth Brethren?'

'I suppose so, in some ways: they certainly only celebrated the religious aspects of Christmas.'

I hadn't put my slippers on, because I thought I would be quieter without them and now I realised my feet were blocks of ice and it was more than time to go.

'Fascinating as it is to discuss my childhood and religion with you in the middle of the night, Jude, if you'll excuse me, I'd better get on.'

I tried to push past him, but he was still blocking the way, an inscrutable expression on his face. 'You know, I still find you very hard to read, Holly Brown!'

'Well, don't rack your brains over it,' I said sweetly, 'I'm an open book. Now, I'd like to get this done because I've had to set my alarm *really* early so I can put that enormous turkey in the oven, and if I don't go to bed soon it won't be worth it. What a monster!'

I think he was unsure if I was applying the epithet to him or the turkey, but he finally shifted to one side and I made my escape. But unfortunately, just as I emerged into the passage, I came face to face with Noël, who must have been returning from the bathroom.

However, he merely smiled in an avuncular and unsurprised way and murmured, 'Ah, getting to know each other better, I see? Good, good!' with no apparent innuendo intended, and carried on.

I got a touch of the Cocos and had to clamp my hand across my mouth to keep a hysterical giggle in, while behind me, Jude said, sounding amused, 'We can only hope he was sleepwalking and will have forgotten he saw us in such compromising circumstances by morning.'

I turned to look back coldly at him and in return he gave me an enigmatic smile that I would have quite liked to have smacked off his face. Then he retreated, closing his door silently behind him.

I mouthed a very rude word then tiptoed off up the nursery stairs, turned the handle and crept in. Jess was dimly illuminated by a moon-shaped nightlight, curled up in bed with one arm around her teddy bear, looking angelic and very much younger. I hung the stocking on the end of her bed and sneaked out again.

I only hoped it wasn't a huge disappointment to her, though surely after last year's it had to be an improvement?

This time I walked on the far side of the passage as I passed Jude's room – but my precaution was needless.

Chapter 26: Socked

There is still no word – can he really have abandoned me with so little compunction? I now see how truly I have fallen from grace and I feel the baby is my punishment for it. I do not know what to do . . . where to turn. Hilda and Pearl are my only support – and how I wish now I had heeded their warnings!

May, 1945

I went downstairs very early in jeans and jumper, ready for cooking, not using the backstairs but the dogleg ones from the gallery. Descending slowly into the dark sitting room, I inhaled the strangely exciting mingled scents of woodsmoke and pine needles, which instantly brought to mind past Christmas mornings with Alan, all the more poignant for being happy memories.

I stoked the fire and plumped up the cushions, stuck a few pieces of jigsaw into the last remaining places round the edge (a compulsion too hard to resist), then switched on the tree's fairy lights. They twinkled in the dark corner under the stairs, reflecting off the gift-wrapped pile beneath. It seemed to have grown since I last looked, with an added layer of parcels inexpertly wrapped in the paper I'd bought.

Suddenly I spotted my name on one, written in a bold hand I recognised from all those handwritten additions to the

Homebodies manual. I was just about to pick it up when I firmly stopped myself, because I wasn't a child like Jess, unable to keep from fondling my presents!

I cast the ash from the fire onto the icy patch outside the back door, just as Gran used to, and let Merlin out into the still-dark world. At least it seemed to have stopped snowing, though it had frozen hard again overnight.

In the stable both horses were still half-asleep, but Billy bleated plaintively at me. I gave them all extra Christmas chunks of carrot, then left them for Becca to do later, as she had told me she would. It was bitterly cold out there, the icy wind holding a threat of snow, so perhaps it would be better if they stayed indoors today. I worried even more about Lady now I'd grown to love her, and I was even getting attached to Billy. Still, that was a decision I could safely leave to Becca and Jude now.

Merlin and I were both glad to get back indoors again, though even as I was kicking off the snow from my boots and giving him his breakfast, I was thinking about the day's cooking.

There was breakfast to prepare too and everyone would come down at intervals, getting under my feet if I wasn't careful. I couldn't serve it in the dining room, since I wanted to lay the table for Christmas dinner, so I decided to put a cloth on the small round table in the sitting room and put the toast rack, butter, marmalade and jam on that, then people could collect Holly Muffins like the ones I'd made at Jess's request the other day and take them in there to eat.

But first things first: the monstrous turkey was stuffed, foil-covered and stowed in the biggest of the ovens, with a lordly antique blue and white dish to receive it when it was finally roasted, which had matching gravy boats and lidded vegetable dishes.

The previous night I'd taken the chipolata sausages wrapped in bacon, sage and thyme stuffing, giblet stock for gravy and bread sauce out of the freezer ('here's some I made earlier!'), and now I prepared the sprouts and put them in a plastic bag in the fridge. The parsnips and potatoes were soon peeled and sitting in cold water and the pudding provided by the Chirks could go in Jude's industrial-sized microwave . . .

When that was all done I lifted tomorrow's salmon out of the freezer, along with the last packet of filo pastry I'd brought and a packet of prawns to make today's starter, and left them on a stone shelf in the larder to defrost slowly, the fridge now being a little full.

Once I'd emptied the dishwasher I checked my list and time-table and I seemed to have everything well in hand. As it was *still* extremely early, I sat down with a well-earned cup of coffee for a few quiet minutes before starting breakfast.

A few minutes was literally all I had, because then Jess suddenly appeared, still in her pyjamas and dressing gown, bringing her stocking with her to show me what she'd got. She laid it on the kitchen table and began pulling out the contents.

'I woke Uncle Jude up first and he said it was *his* sock and he'd like it back when I'd finished with it, only without the pink ribbon.'

'It has to be his, really, no-one else has feet that big.'

'He said he wasn't Father Christmas when I asked him and I think I've seen some of the things in Mrs Comfort's shop, so maybe Mummy actually *remembered* this year and asked Granny to make me one?'

'She must have done, there's no other explanation. What did you like best?'

'Oh . . . the wolf, I think. Or maybe the bracelet . . . When do you think I can open the rest of my presents?'

'When everyone else has come downstairs and had breakfast, I expect.'

'Uncle Jude said he was getting up, he might as well, now I'd woken him.'

255

'You can give Merlin his present now, if you like?' I suggested, as a slight sop.

'Oh yes!' She jumped up eagerly. 'You know, sometimes I think giving presents can be nearly as good as getting them.'

'Definitely!'

Merlin was suitably gratified and, after nosing off the loosely-wrapped paper, retired to his basket by the Aga, where he could be heard chomping away at one end of the rawhide bone while I was cooking bacon and eggs for two sustaining breakfast muffins each. Then I sent Jess upstairs to put some clothes on.

'Granny likes me to wear a dress on Christmas Day,' she said disgustedly.

'Oh, do we dress up a bit?' I asked. 'I don't often wear a dress in winter either, if it makes you feel any better, but perhaps I should go and change later.'

'It would feel fairer if you had to do it, too.'

'Okay, but you'd better put your jeans on now and give Becca a hand with the horses, if you wouldn't mind? That would be a great help.'

'Unless Uncle Jude's down first and does it,' she said hopefully.

'If he is, then perhaps you could help me lay the dining-room table, instead.'

But by the time she reappeared Becca was in the kitchen finishing her breakfast and there was still no sign of Jude. When they'd wrapped up warmly and gone out to the stables, I fetched the last packets of muffins from the freezer: I'd underestimated how hungry everyone would be this morning and we'd already eaten two apiece. There was still plenty of other bread, both loaves and buns and several of those long-life part-baked baguettes so we wouldn't run short. I might make soda bread one day for a change, too.

No-one else appeared, so after pottering round a bit more, ticking things off my list, I went upstairs and changed into a

256

dark-red velvet dress and flat, soft, black leather ballerina slippers. Cooks spend so much time on their feet that they tend to prefer comfort above style – and anyway, killer heels would have made me a giantess. Though here I wouldn't have stood out quite so much, because Coco is only two or three inches shorter than I am and Jude positively *towers* over me.

The colour of the dress flattered my light-olive skin and dark hair, which swung smoothly against my neck. That's the only advantage of having thick, straight hair: it obligingly hangs where you put it, like a heavy curtain. I added a little makeup and then, remembering Sam's comment, a slightly Nefertiti-ish dark line around my eyes and a bit of lippy (I'm not exactly high maintenance). Then I tried looking mysterious in the mirror, but I can't say it really came off.

I put in the garnet earrings that were Alan's last present (I found them hidden, gift-wrapped, weeks after his death), with feelings of sadness and regret, rather than my usual mixture of grief and anger. And I suddenly realised, with a pang of loss, that since I had arrived at Old Place I no longer had the comforting sense that he was walking beside me. I suspected he had gone for good, leaving me to go on entirely alone . . .

It was just as well my eyeliner was waterproof. I dabbed my eyes with a tissue and then ran down to the kitchen and wrapped a big white apron from the drawer over my dress. I cooked lots of bacon and eggs, which I'd just put on a hot, covered dish ready for the next Holly Muffins, when Jude finally arrived, his dark hair still wet and curling slightly from the shower. He was wearing a loose blue chambray shirt with a T-shirt under it and jeans, which was a lot more than he'd been wearing the night before . . . I felt my face going hot, but hoped he didn't notice.

'Sorry I'm so late, but I fell asleep again after Jess woke me up and—' He broke off and examined me critically. 'Have you been crying?'

'No, chopping onions – I wept buckets.'

'Right,' he said uncertainly. 'I meant to be down early to see to the fire and get more wood up from the cellar, as well as do the horses so you and Becca didn't have to, but I'm afraid I dozed off again.'

'I expect you're still jet lagged, but I'd be grateful if you fetched more wood up because I haven't got round to that yet and the log basket's almost empty. Becca and Jess are doing the horses now, so they should be in soon – we've already had our breakfast.'

'I think the smell of the bacon is what finally woke me up and got me down here,' he confessed.

'I'm doing bacon and egg muffins, and toast too if anyone wants it, but they'll have to eat it in the sitting room, because I don't want you all under my feet while I'm cooking the Christmas dinner.' I stood poised over the cooker, spatula and warm plate in hand. 'Do you want one muffin or two?'

'Two, at least. Do you want *me* from under your feet as well? Only you might want some help, even unskilled labour.'

'I have it pretty well in hand, thanks – I'm very organised, you know.'

'Yes, I'd noticed that,' he said gravely, with a glance at the menu charts and timed to-do lists I'd pinned to the kitchen corkboard.

'Michael's also offered his help as skivvy and he's very handy around the kitchen.'

'I'm also handy . . . even if I don't know much about cooking. I'd like to learn some time.'

'What, you'd like to learn to cook?'

'A man gets tired of ready meals,' he admitted.

'Well . . . I suppose you *could* help a bit.'

As the rest of the party straggled down, I ushered them firmly back out of the kitchen while Jude ferried tea, coffee and muffins to the sitting room.

'Noël's the last,' he said, coming back in with a tray, 'he said he just wanted one.'

'Just as well, we're on to the very last muffin after that. I don't suppose Coco ate one?'

He grinned. 'She did, actually, but then she dashed out to the downstairs cloakroom, so I hope she isn't sicking the whole thing back again.'

'I think she uses alternative methods to control her weight,' I said and he looked slightly baffled.

'Laxatives – I don't suppose the muffin will even touch the sides going down. What a waste of good food!'

He looked startled. 'Really? I'd no idea, I just thought she didn't eat enough.'

'She's so painfully thin that maybe we should lock her in the dining room after lunch without her handbag, until she's digested something?' I suggested.

'Is that where she keeps them?'

'It is, according to Jess.' I swiftly assembled the last muffin and put it on a tray with a little pot of tea. 'Could you take Tilda's tray up? Then I expect she'll come down. She'd better, because I can hear Jess and Becca coming back in, and Jess is so desperate to open her presents she'll probably *explode* if she has to wait much longer!'

'She was really excited about that stocking you did,' he said and looked thoughtfully at me. 'She thought her mother had asked Tilda to do it – it was really kind of you to think of it.'

'It was Mrs Comfort's idea really – and don't tell Jess it wasn't her mother,' I warned, just as Jess burst through the door.

'Uncle Jude, Uncle Jude, can I open all my presents now?' she yelled, flinging herself at him.

'By the time you've washed your hands and changed, you'll be able to, because your granny will be down,' I said. 'I've put my dress on, so you need to keep your end of the bargain.'

She pulled a face and rushed out again and off up the back-stairs like a herd of clog-dancing baby elephants.

'You look very nice in your red dress, Holly,' Jude said, as if the compliment had been drawn out of him with hot pincers, and then took himself off.

Since most of me was covered with a Victorian frilled apron, I expect he was just being polite to make up for nearly scaring me to death last night . . . Though come to think of it, he hadn't *seemed* terribly repentant at the time.

Men are so weird.

If you're terribly organised you can easily spare time for other things even while cooking the Christmas dinner, so when I was called into the sitting room for an orgy of present unwrapping everything was fine to be left, though I remembered to take my pinny off first. Merlin, his rawhide chew firmly clenched in his jaws, came with me.

Jess was in charge of ferrying the presents to their recipients and, to my surprise, I ended up with quite a pile, though they included Laura's, which I'd brought down with me when I changed earlier.

'There's another one here for Merlin,' Jess said.

'You'd better unwrap that one for him,' Jude suggested, so I knew the rubber ball inside was from him. Merlin retired under the nearest table with his booty, where the occasional squeak of rubber as he clamped his teeth on his ball, or the squidgy squish of rawhide chewed soft, could be heard during any pause in the conversation.

While Jess ripped the paper off her presents as fast as she could, the rest of us started on ours with a little more restraint. I decided to open Laura's first, which was a lovely emerald green pashmina scarf wrapped around a well-thumbed book that I immediately recognised: her copy of *The Complete Guide to Pregnancy and Childbirth*. Inside she'd written:

Happy Christmas, Holly! I know what you're like once
you've made your mind up so, since I'm calling it a day
after number four, I'm handing this on. But I can't help
hoping that you might just be snowed up with a nice man
– that George sounded as if he had possibilities – and
change your mind about going it alone!
  Love, Laura

I took a quick look round but no-one seemed to be looking in
my direction except Jude, who I hoped was too far away to make
out what the book was. I quickly wrapped the scarf around it
again.

Jude had already sent presents to Tilda, Noël and Jess when
he thought he would be away for Christmas, but on some impulse
(probably to fill in time between flights, since he can't have
known that the family party was about to double in size) he
seemed to have bought up half an airport gift shop as well. There
were giant foil-wrapped chocolate pennies and those chocolate
bars that look like gold ingots, small teddy bears dressed as
Beefeaters and London bus keyrings. These items seemed to have
been labelled randomly, but we all got at least one. I had a penny
and a bear. Coco, who was again inclined to be tearful about the
Birkin bag that never was, got an ingot and a keyring.

Unlike Michael, who had thoughtfully bought and wrapped
a small article of Comfort for each person present (pens
and notebooks inscribed with Oriel's *Sunbeams are God's
Thoughts* line) Coco only received, she didn't give – not even
thanks.

As well as my booty from Jude's spending spree and Michael's
gift, Tilda and Noël gave me a copy of Tilda Thompson's *Party
Pieces* recipe book, printed in 1958, all about the art of the
canapé. I was delighted and I kissed them both gratefully.

'You didn't kiss me for *my* presents,' observed Jude, and since
I wasn't sure if he was serious or not, I did kiss his cheek, though

I had to stand on tiptoe to do it, which was a novelty – as was his very unusual, and extremely masculine, aftershave. Then, in the interests of fairness, I kissed Michael, too.

'Thanks, Michael – I love my *Sunbeams* pen and notebook!'

'Hey, what about me?' asked Guy. 'Where's my kiss?'

'You didn't give me a present,' I pointed out. Guy, who like Jude had already sent presents to the lodge, hadn't felt the need to do anything further.

'*I* didn't give anyone a present,' Becca said. 'I never do. Just money to Jess, so she can get what she likes.'

'You brought us two bottles of very fine sherry, m'dear,' said Noël.

'I thought *you* were going to give me a ring for Christmas, Guy,' Coco said, with an accusing look. 'I thought this Christmas was going to be *really* special!'

'You thought wrong,' he said flippantly. 'But you might find one in your cracker at dinner.'

'Oh yes, they're very good crackers – *we* brought them,' said Noël. 'There's no saying what you might find in them!'

'Why don't you open the rest of your presents, Coco?' I said hastily.

My jars of sweets and chocolates had gone down well, though Coco was unexcited by her homemade bath scrub and Michael's offering, dropping them onto the sofa next to her, half-unwrapped. But then she opened Jess's gift and seemed, at last, to be genuinely pleased with the necklace of origami beads on knotted silk cord inside.

'Yours was my first experiment, Horlicks, and it's a bit wonky so I thought you might as well have it,' Jess said. 'I just had time to make one for Holly, or she would have got it instead.'

Becca, Tilda and I had lovely necklaces, too.

'They're all gorgeous,' I said admiringly. 'You are clever, it must be very fiddly making the little paper beads.'

'It is, a bit, but I'm really good at it now,' she said modestly. 'I get orders for them at school, I've got quite a good thing going. I'm going to branch out into earrings, too.'

'And mine is dark red, just like my dress – how amazing a coincidence is that?' I said, putting it round my neck and squinting down at it.

'It's not: I looked in your wardrobe and there was only one dress in there, so I made it to match.'

'Jess, you really shouldn't snoop in people's bedrooms, we've told you before,' Becca said severely.

'I didn't, I just *looked*. There was a pile of notebooks on the chest of drawers and I accidentally knocked them off . . .' she added innocently, looking at me through her thick black fringe. 'One fell open and it looked like a sort of diary?'

'Yes it is, but not mine, just a journal my gran kept, a very interesting one about nursing during the war. I found it in a box of her papers I'm sorting out.'

Jess lost interest immediately and changed tack. 'Uncle Jude, Holly looks pretty in dark red, doesn't she?'

'Holly looks lovely in everything,' Guy said, with one of his charming smiles, 'Anyone with her looks who can also cook deserves my total adoration.'

'Oh, don't be so daft,' I said uncomfortably, unused to this sort of teasing, though I noticed that Jude hadn't said anything one way or the other this time, even out of politeness – in fact, he seemed to be back to the suspicious stare again. 'I know I'm nothing to write home about.'

'Get on with you, m'dear!' said Noël gallantly.

'Has anyone ever told you you look like that head of Nefertiti?' asked Guy with an air of originality.

'Yes – my best friend's cousin Sam did, though I couldn't see it myself.'

'Who's Nefertiti?' asked Jess.

'An ancient queen of Egypt, noted for her beauty,' Noël said.

'There's a photo in one of the books in the library, I will fetch it later and show you. And speaking of photographs . . .'

He whipped out a little camera and his family all groaned in a resigned sort of way.

'Another Martland Christmas must be recorded for posterity!'

Chapter 27: Knitting

Today one of the nurses showed me an old society magazine that she had been given by a patient, saying that there was a picture in it of N and his fiancée, the daughter of a lord, and asked me hadn't I been sweet on him when he was a patient there? She is a spiteful creature and hoped to hurt me, but she could not have known how this news pierced me to the heart and destroyed all my faith in the man I loved! All the time I thought we were courting, he'd been engaged to another girl – and one of his own social standing.

May, 1945

Noël insisted on taking several pictures for the family album although, as Michael pointed out, some of those present were not actually family.

'But all friends,' he said merrily. I'd already noticed that he, Tilda and Becca could put away a tidy amount of sherry between them, but Christmas Day seemed to have given them licence to start on it right after breakfast.

'I was in last year's photographs,' Coco said sulkily, 'and look where it got me!'

'That was because you dumped Jude and went off with Guy instead,' Tilda said acidly. 'So if you have in turn been dumped by Guy, it serves you right.'

'Yes . . . well, that's all water under the bridge now, m'dear, isn't it?' Noël said hastily and then marshalled us all into various groupings, whether we liked it or not. Coco automatically fell into languid model poses at the click of a camera. She was wearing a tunic like a gold satin flour bag over mustard leggings and clumpy shoe-boots, but it looked quite good on her.

'There, that will do until we can get one with Old Nan and Richard in, too,' Noël said finally. Then he smiled at me and added, 'Now *you* will be in the family albums for posterity, too!'

'Did she want to be?' asked Jude, eyeing me narrowly again.

'We've been looking at the old albums, especially the pictures of past Revels,' Noël explained. 'And very fascinated you were too, m'dear, weren't you?'

'Totally,' I said, seizing the moment to try and find out a little more, 'especially in that lovely one of you with your brothers and Becca at the Revels, taken just before the war.'

Becca said sadly, 'Oh, yes, that was the last one when we were all together. Jacob was killed at Dunkirk and Ned died in that accident not long after the war . . . and now poor Alex is gone, too.'

'Well, there's no need to go all maudlin,' Tilda said crisply.

'No, you're right,' she agreed. 'Better to remember how much fun we had – we were all so young in that picture!'

'Noël said Ned was the black sheep of the family?' I prodded her.

'Yes, though he wasn't really *bad*, poor fellow, just weak-willed where women were concerned. But he was handsome and charming, very charming . . . Poor Ned. Guy is very like him.'

'Thanks,' Guy said dryly.

'You've had more girlfriends than I've had hot dinners,' Becca said forthrightly.

'But at least he never got any of them pregnant,' Tilda pointed out. 'Or not that we know of, anyway.'

'You mean – Ned *did*?' I asked, startled but schooling my face to an expression, I hoped, of polite interest.

266

Noël, looking troubled, nodded. 'A little mill girl – or at least, I think she was a mill girl, I can't quite remember after this space of time. He came running back home and told our parents and they were horrified – not just because they thought she was unsuitable, but because he was already engaged to the younger daughter of Lord Lennerton and was about to start working for him. They had hoped he was going to settle down at last.'

'Well, you can't say that's like me,' Guy said indignantly. 'I hold down a responsible job and I've never got a girl into trouble. I haven't,' he said with a darkling look at Coco, 'even got *engaged*!'

He'd wandered over to the jigsaw and was now staring down at it. 'Someone has put the missing edge pieces in that we couldn't find last night!'

'That was me early this morning, they just sort of fell into place as I was passing,' I said apologetically, then hauled the conversation back to where I wanted it: 'So what happened after Ned came clean to his parents about . . . the little mill girl?'

'Nothing, because he was killed soon after that,' Becca said.

'He always drove a little too fast and recklessly,' Noël explained. 'He misjudged a bend and that was it. Tragic – very tragic.'

I was just thinking that the whole affair was even more tragic for my grandmother, when Jude suddenly said to me, 'You're very interested in the family, and especially in my Uncle Ned?'

'Not at all, I simply find old family photographs fascinating,' I said lightly, meeting his dark, suspicious gaze with limpid innocence. 'I brought a boxful of my gran's that I'm sifting through at the moment – papers and photographs all mixed up.'

'Ah, yes, didn't you tell us that she was the wife of a Baptist minister?' asked Tilda.

'Strange Baptist,' said Jude, and Coco asked predictably, 'Why, what was strange about them?'

'Nothing, it was just what they were called,' I explained patiently. 'They took their name from a Bible quotation, "Strange are the ways of the Lord", though someone told me once that

that was a mistranslation and it only appeared in one version of the Bible.'

'And is this the same box of papers where you found your gran's wartime nursing journal?' asked Jude acutely.

'Yes,' I said shortly, then got up. 'Excuse me, I need to get back to the kitchen.'

'Can I do anything to help?' asked Michael, Guy and Jude almost simultaneously.

'Yes, lay the dining room table for me. There was a long Christmas runner for down the middle of the table in the linen cupboard – it's on the sideboard with the box of crackers Tilda and Noël brought. And, Jude, could you sort out the drinks? I don't drink much, so I've no idea what you want with it.'

'Jess and I are going to help, too,' announced Tilda, hauling herself upright and inserting her feet into her marabou-edged mules. 'We're going to make a hedgehog.'

'A hedgehog?' Maybe that's what had been in those awful pinwheel sandwiches on the day I arrived – roadkill!

'Yes – you know, chunks of cheese and onions on cocktail sticks, stuck into half a grapefruit,' Jess explained, as they followed me into the kitchen. 'Granny gives them little eyes and a nose with cloves.'

'Oh, of course – how lovely!' I said. 'But I'm afraid I haven't any grapefruit. Would half a large potato do, if I scrub it first?'

'Yes, but Jess will scrub it,' Tilda said. 'I'm sure you have lots else to do.'

'I just need to pop these filo pastry spicy prawn parcels in the oven, they won't take long. Those and the hedgehog should be more than enough to hold everyone while I finish off the dinner.'

When the hedgehog was made, Jess, together with Noël, Tilda and Becca, went into the parlour later to watch the Christmas message her parents had recorded on DVD for her. Then she came and insisted I went and watched it too, which luckily was at a moment when I had ten spare minutes between things.

I thought her parents looked quite mad – they were both dressed as Father Christmas, even down to the white cotton-wool beards, for a start – but in a fun way. Roz is another tall, dark-haired Martland.

Liam, George's son, brought Old Nan and Richard up to the house at about one, and by arrangement was to call for them again later. I was busy in the kitchen when they arrived and by the time I carried the tray of starters through they were already drinking sherry before the fire, so it was just as well Michael bought some more!

'Me and Granny made the cheese and pickle hedgehog,' Jess pointed out proudly. 'It's crumbly Lancashire cheese and silver-skin onions, but we had to use half a scrubbed potato to put the sticks in, we haven't got any grapefruit.'

'It looks lovely,' Noël said, as Michael helpfully passed round plates and the red paper napkins covered in reindeer that I'd got from Oriel Comfort's.

'Are there carbs in cocktail onions?' asked Coco doubtfully. She must have spurned the sherry because she was holding a glass of something dark green instead, though I couldn't imagine what *that* was. Crème de menthe, maybe? There were all sorts of odds and ends in the drinks cabinet in the dining room.

'No calories at all, and the cheese is almost fat-free too,' I lied, and she perked up a bit and selected the cocktail stick with the smallest chunk on it.

'More sherry, vicar?' asked Guy, winking at me.

Old Nan, unasked, held out her glass too and smiled at me over the top of it, all blindingly white false teeth and deeply-netted wrinkles. 'Where on the family tree did you say you came in, dear? I've forgotten,' she said amiably. 'One of the distant cousins, of course, but which . . . ?'

'I'm not a member of the family at all, I'm just looking after the house,' I told her and she looked at me severely and declared obstinately, 'Oh yes you are – you can't fool Old Nan!'

'She gets confused,' Becca whispered to me. 'Just agree with her, it will save lots of trouble.'

'I've brought you a present anyway,' Old Nan said and, after a quick scrabble in her oversized knitting bag, she pulled out several small tissue-covered parcels and thrust one of them at me. 'Come and get yours, the rest of you!'

'What a lovely hat,' I said, unwrapping a ribbed and bobbled creation in electric blue and candy-pink stripes. 'Thank you so much!'

Jude unexpectedly plumped down on the sofa next to me, which made a protesting squeak – and *I* probably did too, because the cushions tilted and practically slid me into his lap.

He examined my gift critically. 'Actually, I think yours is a tea cosy, because it has a hole each side. *Mine's* a hat.'

'They might be for my ears?'

'No, because your ears would get frostbite, which would defeat the whole point of wearing a warm hat, wouldn't it?'

'Yours *is* the tea cosy,' Old Nan said to me.

'Thank you, I'll treasure it forever.'

Old Nan liberally distributed her knitted offerings so that everyone, including Michael and Coco, had a hat, scarf or tea cosy – or, in Jess's case, a knitted mouse with a long yarn tail and whiskers.

'Of course, Tilda and Noël have already had their *real* present,' Old Nan said in a pointed sort of way.

'Oh yes, the Dundee cake – and I'm afraid we have already eaten it,' Noël confessed, 'and very delicious it was too.'

Her wrinkled face dropped with disappointment. '*All* of it?'

'Yes, but there is a very fine Christmas cake uncut, that Holly has made for us.'

'Lavishly using the best brandy, the last of the stock my father laid down,' Jude said darkly.

'That's all right, then,' Old Nan said brightly, then gave Coco, who was sitting next to Michael, a hard stare.

Michael had evinced genuine delight with his magenta-and-pink-striped scarf and wound it round his neck, but Coco was still fingering her lime-green bobble hat with a blank expression. Though actually, her complete repertoire of expressions only seemed to encompass blank or sulky, which didn't bode well for her acting aspirations.

'Isn't that the flibbertigibbet Jude was engaged to last Christmas, the one that ran off with Guy, instead?' Old Nan asked Becca in a piercing whisper.

'I didn't run off with anyone,' Coco snapped, overhearing. 'In fact, Guy made all the running!'

Richard smiled benignly around. 'But now the past is forgiven and forgotten and here we all are together again for Christmas. Coco and Guy are engaged to each other, Nan.'

'No-one is engaged to anyone,' Guy said firmly.

'But then, if you're not engaged, what is *she* doing up here?' demanded Old Nan querulously. 'I didn't like her last time!'

'And back at you!' Coco said rudely.

'Old Nan is my invited guest,' Jude pointed out to her, 'while *you* are not, so you'd better mind your manners.'

Jess suddenly jumped up, exclaiming, 'Oh, I nearly forgot – Liam brought a present from his dad for you, Holly! I left it in the hall while I was hanging the coats up.'

She ran to get it and I asked hopefully, 'Did everybody get one?'

'No, just you,' Becca said with a grin.

Jess returned with a long parcel that could only be a stick – and it was, with a beautifully carved ram's head handle.

'You *are* honoured to have one of those,' Jude said, taking it from me and examining the carving. 'He's renowned for them, but he usually sells them and rarely gives one away.'

271

'He *loves* you, he wants to *marry* you!' chanted Jess, dancing round me like an evil sprite.

'No such thing,' I said with composure, though I might have blushed slightly since they were all staring at me.

'Then why did he give you a special present?'

'Jess, don't tease her,' Tilda said.

'But who can blame old George for being smitten?' asked Guy, raising an eyebrow. 'He's a widower you know, Holly, with his own farm – a bit of a catch. You could do worse.'

'Uncle Jude is a widower, too,' Jess said, 'and he's got Old Place and lots of money because his statues sell for *squillions*.'

'That's a slight exaggeration of my eligibility,' Jude said, unembarrassed.

'I didn't know you'd been married,' I said, turning to him in surprise.

'*We* forget, because it was such a long time ago and she died young, a bit like that film – what was it called?' said Becca. '*Love Story*, that was the one.'

'It was nothing like *Love Story*,' Jude said shortly, his face going all shuttered, so it was still clearly a painful memory even after all this time.

'And he isn't Holly's suitor, either, so it doesn't matter, does it?' said Coco with a brittle laugh. 'I can't see why everyone is getting so excited, just because an old farmer has given the cook a walking stick.'

'He's not actually all that old, just a bit weathered,' Becca pointed out. 'Late forties, at the most.'

'That *is* pretty old,' Jess said. 'Uncle Jude is only thirty-eight.'

She seemed to think this was a matter for congratulation.

'And I'm a mere thirty-six,' Guy said, bestowing one of his ravishing smiles on me, though to no effect: unlike Gran, I wasn't going to be taken in by a handsome, womanising Martland.

I was sure he didn't *really* fancy me, he just probably automatically flirted with any woman around.

'And I'm a very successful investment banker, too,' he added as a clincher.

'Change the B for a W and that's more like it,' Jude muttered rudely next to me, surprising me into a snort of laughter.

'Don't listen to him,' Guy said. 'Anyway, you'll find I'm much more fun than George: he spends most of his days talking to sheep.'

I wasn't used to this kind of flirting, however insincere, and I didn't know how to play the game, so it was a relief to escape back into the kitchen.

And I only hoped Jess hadn't got it into her head to try and matchmake me with her beloved Uncle Jude, because it was an idea doomed by our mutual antipathy from the start!

Noël welcomed us into the dining room with a lively rendering of *The Twelve Days of Christmas*, accompanying himself on the piano and Tilda joined in the last verse with a brittle and slightly wavery soprano.

And the Christmas dinner, if I may say so myself without sounding too immodest, was cooked to a turn.

The golden-roasted turkey and chipolatas wrapped in bacon, the bread sauce, the crispy roast potatoes and parsnips, the firm, small sprouts from Henry's garden and good Lancashire gravy so thick you could almost stand a spoon up in it . . . *all* were perfection.

Once everyone was well lubricated with alcohol to a state of reasonable bonhomie, we pulled crackers, shared the mottos and wore the silver cardboard crowns (which, oddly enough, suited Jude best – with his broad brow, thick straight nose and strong jaw, he looked like a rugged prince fresh off the battlefield). Then we set to, and even Coco, with an air of reckless abandon probably engendered by whatever the green drink was she had had earlier, ate at least a teaspoon of everything.

I only hoped it would stay in her system long enough to do her some good, and although I was considering hiding her supply of laxatives when I had an opportunity, I wasn't sure quite what the effect of going cold turkey on the Fruity-Go would have on her . . .

Finally Jude ignited the brandy over the large, domed pudding and carried it into the specially darkened room, the blue flames dancing. Michael brought up the rear, carrying the brandy butter and white sauce.

At the end of the meal Jude opened champagne and everyone toasted my cooking, which was very gratifying. Then he proposed a second one to Noël's birthday.

'And Holly's, too,' Noël said, raising his glass to me, 'we share the same birthday.'

Then they all retired to the sitting room, totally stuffed, though Jude, Jess and Michael helped me clear the table first.

I loaded as much into the dishwasher as it would take and joined them, after sneaking a bit of turkey into Merlin's bowl and giving him a Christmas kiss on the top of his rough grey head.

Old Nan and Tilda had fallen asleep at either end of the big sofa, their feet up on the cushions, and Noël reclined on the smaller one: but the rest of the party were playing Monopoly at one of the tables, even Coco, though she kept laughing a lot for no particular reason and declaring that she was only going to buy *pink* properties.

I drifted over to the jigsaw (they irritate me until they are finished, because I like everything neat and tidy) and immediately spotted that one piece was upside down. When that was righted, after carefully examining the picture on the box, I completed a whole corner of sky.

But then, I've found in life that it always pays to scrutinise the packaging.

Chapter 28: Christmas Present

In the end I had to face up to the inescapable truth that my lover had abandoned me. There was no help for it: in desperation I went home and told my parents of my plight. The scene that followed was worse by far than ever I could have imagined.

May, 1945

Liam duly appeared in the big farm Land Rover with chains on the wheels, ready to take the guests home. Both were carrying care parcels of cake, sausage rolls and turkey and stuffing sandwiches, to keep them going once the dinner wore off, though personally I felt like a python that had swallowed a goat, and might not have to eat for a month.

I gave Liam another hastily-packed jam jar full of sweets as a reciprocal present for his father, though I'd also done one for him, so the gesture wouldn't seem *too* particular – I was feeling flattered but cautious! I'd now run out of my stockpile of goodies and Liam's were the Jelly Babies (my particular weakness) that I'd bought for myself.

'Could I hitch a ride with you as far as the lodge?' I asked. 'I can get a mobile signal there and I want to phone my friend to wish her Happy Christmas. But I'll walk back, I need the exercise.'

'It's going to be dark soon,' Guy pointed out.

'I can hardly miss my way back though, can I? And I'll take

Merlin with me for company, if that's all right with you, Liam? I won't be long.'

'We'll see to the horses while you're out,' Becca said, 'won't we, Jess?'

'Or I can do it, Becca, if you'd like a rest?' Jude offered.

'No, that's all right – you can do it in the morning and give us both a lie-in!'

'I'll give you the key to the lodge, if you wouldn't mind just checking that everything is fine again?' asked Noël.

'Of course, and perhaps I could collect one or two things that we've nearly run out of from the kitchen while I'm there?' I wasn't quite sure what he thought might go wrong at the lodge, apart from a burst pipe or the abominable snowman taking up residence ... which he wouldn't be doing, because he was already living here, at Old Place!

And as that thought crossed my mind, my eyes met Jude's dark ones, disconcertingly and broodingly fixed on me again with his brow furrowed. Perhaps he thought I might ransack the lodge for family silver while there?

I had to wear my long winter coat instead of the warm hooded anorak I would have preferred: one of the penalties of putting on a dress in winter. But it was that or risk frostbite in my extremities.

Richard and Old Nan were temporarily revived by air so cold that you could feel it penetrating right into all the little branchy bits of your lungs, like extreme Mentholyptus inhalation, but they'd dozed off again by the time Liam dropped me and Merlin at the lodge.

Everything was fine and I ransacked the kitchen cupboards and filled my rucksack with more ground almonds, dried fruit and other odds and ends that I might need if the Big Freeze continued. Then I locked up carefully and walked a few yards down the side of the road, my feet scrunching on virgin snow, until the signal showed strongly on my mobile.

It took quite a while for Laura to answer, probably because the noisy family party going on in the background made it hard for her to hear her phone, but when she did, she said she was fine.

'Stone cold sober, of course – oh, the joys of pregnancy! Just you wait.'

'Yes – speaking of pregnancy, I unwrapped that book you gave me right in front of everyone else this morning!'

She laughed. 'Sorry about that, but I forgot you wouldn't be alone. Did they see it? They'll think you've got a bun in your oven if they did!'

'I hid it quickly and only Jude seemed to be looking at me at the time. He was right the other side of the room, though, so he'd need eyes like a hawk to read the title. He *has* been giving me some funny looks ever since but that's nothing new: a brooding stare seems to be his natural fall-back expression.'

'Ah yes, how is the lord and master, apart from the brooding, Heathcliff stare and deep, sexy voice?'

'We've sort of come to a bit of a truce, but he's still wary and he seemed very suspicious when I was asking Noël a few questions about Ned Martland earlier. Just because I'm tall and dark, like most of the Martlands, I think he might have started to worry that I'm a family by-blow, wanting a share of the inheritance. And come to that, I might *be* a family by-blow, or the daughter of one, but I don't *want* to be.'

'I take it you haven't got far enough in the journals to find out for sure, yet?'

'No, though it's not exactly looking promising.'

'Well, let me know. And I *hoped* Jude would turn out to be nicer than you thought and you'd get to really like each other,' she said optimistically. 'Is he good-looking?'

I considered this. 'He's dark, but not handsome like his brother Guy, because his face is too rugged and he has a square jaw that makes him look a bit grim. But he does have a very attractive smile, when he bothers to use it.'

277

'He must have used it, or you wouldn't know! And isn't he tall as well as dark? Handsome isn't everything!'

'Yes, he must be a good six-foot-six tall and very broad across the shoulders, though he tapers right down to really slim hips – in fact, he's pretty fit without his clothes on!' I added teasingly.

'*Holly!*'

'Don't get excited, I just ran into him on my way to hang up Jess's stocking last night and he was only wearing pyjama bottoms.'

'He sounds to me as if he has a lot going for him, if you can get past your first dislike. I mean, if he's way taller than you are, that has to be good, right?'

'But I'm not used to a man towering over me and making me feel small, so I'm finding it a bit disconcerting, to be honest. He kissed me under the mistletoe too, even though he doesn't like me – but it was something and nothing, so I don't know why he bothered. Men are so odd!'

'Hmmm . . .' she said thoughtfully. 'How about the other men?'

'I'm getting to really like Michael Whiston, he's such a nice man and he also likes to cook, but I'm not attracted to Guy the love-rat in the least, because apparently he bears a huge resemblance to his Uncle Ned.'

'And also, presumably, because you know he's a love-rat?'

'There is that, though I do find myself quite liking him sometimes against my better judgement: he has a lot of charm. He and Jude have made up their argument, but he's still clearly jealous of his brother, which isn't a nice trait, and he's been totally fickle and heartless with Coco. I'm starting to feel a bit sorry for her, actually,' I added.

'But I thought you loathed her at first sight?'

'I did. But the thing is, she's twenty-four going on five years old and has clearly been Mummy and Daddy's little princess all her life, so she can't seem to cope with not getting her way in everything. She bursts into tears, or sulks. Michael and Noël are the only ones who've been really kind to her, because they're both very soft-hearted. But now she's showing signs of setting her sights on Michael, so he probably wishes he hadn't been so nice!'

'Oh?' she said interestedly. 'Does he fancy you instead, then?'

I laughed. 'No, not at all – and I'm sure Guy doesn't either, though he tries to flirt with me. But Michael and I are getting to be good friends.'

She sighed. 'All these men and you don't fancy a single one of them, not even a *tiny* bit?'

'Don't forget my *real* admirer, George.'

'George?'

'The slightly-weatherbeaten blond hunk of a farmer. He sent me a present today, a beautifully carved walking stick. Apparently it's a great honour to be given one, though I suspect from something Liam let slip while driving me down to the lodge that he also hedged his bets by giving one to Oriel Comfort at the village shop, too.'

'Do you *really* fancy him, then, Holly?'

'A bit . . . he's very attractive in his way, but I can't see myself as a farmer's wife. Or *anyone's* wife – not again. Been there, done that, and I'm not looking to find another husband, I'm just going to go it alone, as planned.'

'You won't *be* alone if you go ahead with the AI and it works,' she pointed out. 'Look, why not give it six months first, Holly? Go out with a few men and —'

'I went out with Sam, and that didn't work.'

She sighed again. 'Once, which is hardly giving it a chance, and you haven't been out with anyone else, have you? If men show any interest, you back off.'

'But not many of them do, or they're not serious, like Guy, so you might as well give me up as a lost cause. I met my soulmate and losing him hurt too much to want to try again, even if I believed there was another Mr Right out there, which I don't.'

'You're hopeless!' she said, but affectionately. 'The children loved their presents, by the way.'

'So they should, when you told me exactly what they wanted!'

'But I didn't tell you what *I* wanted, and *that* was lovely too.'

'Easy! I remembered when the saleswoman in Debenhams sprayed that perfume on your wrist and I thought you were never going to wash your arm again! And I adore my scarf, by the way – I'm wearing it now. Light but very warm.'

'The family send their love and wish you were here with us.'

'It's probably better that I'm not, I'd only be a reminder that Alan wasn't there.'

'Don't be daft, you know he's always in our thoughts anyway, especially around this time of year. But we've accepted what happened and moved on with our lives, even though we miss him terribly – and since your gran died, I'm getting the feeling that you're finally beginning to do the same.'

'Yes, I realised I'd dealt with Alan's death by closing the door on it, rather than properly grieving. But now I keep thinking of him and remembering the happy times we had, especially at Christmas.'

'You were twice as brisk and bossy once you'd moved to the country and started working for Ellen, but now you sound much more like the old Holly, though with a bit of extra bite.'

'Thanks.'

'I expect being pitchforked into having to cope with Christmas has done you a power of good.'

'You're probably right, but I still feel guilty about forgetting the anniversary of Alan's death.'

'No, that was a very healthy sign and you shouldn't feel guilty in the least.'

'There's so much to do every day at Old Place that I hardly have a minute to myself and certainly no time to brood over the past – or if I do, it's over Gran's past, because I'm dying to find out what happened.'

'But if there's loads to do, then even if the roads thaw, Jude might want you to stay on?' she suggested.

'Actually, I *have* agreed to stay and cook right over Christmas – there weren't really a lot of alternatives. After that, we'll see. At least there are other people now to look after the horses and sort out the generator if our electricity goes off again.'

'That "*our*" sounds very proprietary!'

'I've put in so much hard work on Old Place, I feel I have an interest in it,' I said. 'I've got really attached to Merlin, too – and Lady is a sweetie. She makes this blowing noise down her nose whenever she sees me, but that might be because I keep giving her chunks of carrot. Actually, I'm rather missing helping to look after her now that Becca has taken over,' I admitted. 'She used to shove her nose down the back of my neck when I was mucking her out and it was all velvety.'

'What, Becca?'

'No, you imbecile, Lady!'

By now it was quite dark and really too bitterly cold to stand there much longer. My feet seemed to have turned to ice despite having Merlin sitting on them (he's not daft), so I said my goodbyes and headed for home.

Chapter 29: Abominable

My father sat there as if poleaxed for several minutes, then told me very coldly that I was no daughter of his and I was to leave his house and never return. My mother, though she cried, did not go against him. He told her to pack the rest of my things and send them on to me.

May, 1945

I was just trudging back up the drive through the dark stand of trees above the lodge when a huge menacing figure suddenly stepped right out in front of me.

The adrenaline was pumping and I had my heavy, rubber-coated torch raised ready in my hand to defend myself with, by the time it occurred to me that Merlin wasn't in the least alarmed. I upended it and clicked on the beam, following him as he bounded forward and greeted Jude, who must have been lurking at the end of the path that led to his studio.

'Hello, you fickle old fool,' he said, fondling Merlin's ears, then he looked up apologetically, squinting into the light in a way that did little to aid his beauty. 'Sorry, did I startle you? I felt like some fresh air and thought I might as well go down to the mill and maybe walk back with you. I didn't like the idea of you wandering about alone in the dark and snow.'

'Actually, I wasn't at all nervous until you suddenly loomed up. I have a perfectly good torch, as you see.'

'Yes, I've noticed – and taking the beam out of my eyes would be a kindness,' he said acidly.

I lowered it slightly.

'Thanks, it felt like I was being interrogated under a search-light. It must be a *big* torch?'

'All the better to hit you with, if you'd turned out to be an assailant,' I explained. 'Rubber casing, though, so it would only have concussed you, at worst. Or best.'

'No chance, you couldn't have reached up that far!'

'I might have had to go for a different, softer target,' I admitted and he winced. 'Generally, though, most muggers wouldn't be much taller than me.'

'I suppose not,' he said, falling into step beside me as I headed past him up the drive. Merlin took up his position with his nose pressed to the back of my leg – or rather, the back of my long winter coat.

There was no snow under the thick stand of pines, though it glimmered ahead where the wood opened up to the snowy turf in front of the house. Somewhere away to the left was the faint rushing noise of the stream, mingling with the sound of the bitter wind stirring the treetops.

'Christmas dinner was wonderful,' he said finally, breaking the silence. 'Did I tell you?'

'Yes, you even proposed a toast to my cooking. And I loved my presents – thank you. They were a surprise, because I wasn't expecting any except Jess's necklace, which she'd been hinting about.'

'That's okay, I'm just glad I had that mad moment in the airport shop and bought the place up. But you must be tired – you've barely stopped since early morning.'

'No, not really, I'm used to cooking for house-parties, though I don't usually do anything else *but* prep, cook and clear. Tonight we're only having sandwiches, sausage rolls, cake, mince pies and trifle for supper, which I'll put out in the sitting room – that

283

should do it. Or people can take a tray into the morning room if they want to eat and watch TV.'

'You know, I really am grateful that you took Tilda and Noël up to Old Place after Tilda's accident,' he said. 'It's made me realise just how frail they are – I think seeing them every day must have blinded me to it. I just took everything Tilda said about doing the cooking at face value.'

'In her head, Tilda is still capable of doing everything she used to and she seems to have deluded herself and Noël that she still does most of the cooking at home, though according to Jess it's their housekeeper that actually does it.'

'I think Noël knows, but he always goes along with whatever she says for a peaceful life. She tries to boss you about, too, I've noticed.'

'I don't mind, it's a head-chef sort of bossing – I had to take a lot of that when I first started my career in a restaurant in Merchester. I ended up being head-chef there myself before . . . well, before I left and joined Homebodies instead.'

'Was that after your husband died?'

We were now out of the trees and crunching through the crusty snow up the side of the drive, where it was less slippery. 'Yes, I wanted a complete change.'

If he was asking personal questions, then I didn't see why I shouldn't, too, so I said, 'I hadn't realised until today that you were a widower?'

'Yes, I met Kate at art college, we married while still students and then, as you probably gathered, she died of leukaemia a few months later.'

'That was tragically young. What was she like?'

'Sweet, talented, funny . . . brave, especially towards the end,' he said, remembered pain in his voice. 'I felt guilty just for being healthy when she was literally fading away before my eyes. Coco looks a bit like her – I think that must have been what attracted me to her, though she's nothing like Kate in character.'

284

'I'm *so* sorry: I shouldn't have reminded you of her.'

'It doesn't matter – it's better to face your demons, isn't it?'

'That's the conclusion I've come to,' I agreed, 'but it's taken me some time.'

'But your loss is much more recent than mine: I lost Kate such a long time ago that mostly she's just a sad, distant memory . . . though I knew I never wanted to feel pain again like I did when I lost her,' he added in a low voice, more to himself, it seemed to me, than for my ears.

'I was married for eight years and my best friend is my husband's sister, so I'd known Alan most of my life. We were *very* happy.'

'I expect he liked being bossed about, then,' he suggested outrageously; back to normal Jude mode, just as I was feeling much more in sympathy with him.

I was about to vehemently deny this suggestion when the words stuck to my tongue, because it was perfectly true, even if Alan didn't actually mind. 'It wasn't like that,' I explained. 'He was easy-going, but stubborn, too – if he made up his mind to something, I couldn't change it.'

Like taking up jogging, for instance, which led to his death . . .

'He was killed in an accident, Jess said?'

'Yes, just before Christmas – another reason why I've never celebrated it since. In fact, I usually spend the anniversary of his death somewhere quiet, where no-one knows me.'

'Then—' he stopped. 'Oh, *now* I see what made you so reluctant to do what I wanted at first! I'm sorry if you were forced into a celebration you didn't want!'

'That's okay, I've started to think all this enforced festivity is actually good for me. And Alan was a sensitive, quiet man with a strong sense of humour – he wouldn't have wanted me to become a hermit on his account, even once a year.'

'No, not if he loved you, he wouldn't,' he agreed. 'Have you been out with anyone since . . . ?'

'His cousin, Sam.' I didn't say that it wasn't a real date at all, since I didn't want to sound totally unsought after. 'What about you?' I didn't see why he should ask all the intimate questions!

'Oh, loads of girls, but nothing serious until Coco: there was something … vulnerable about her. I thought she needed looking after. And she's stunningly pretty too, of course.'

'True,' I said, feeling oversized, ugly and capable, none of them terribly attractive traits. 'There is something of the little girl lost about her, isn't there? But it would be like living with a petulant toddler forever.'

I hoped that didn't sound sour-grapes.

We crunched on a bit towards the house and then out of the blue he asked, 'The grandmother who brought you up – is that the same one whose diaries you're reading?'

'Yes,' I admitted reluctantly, 'though it's not so much a diary as jottings about her nursing career during the war. My mother died giving birth to me, which sounds a bit Dickensian, but she had acute liver failure. And my grandfather was much older than my gran, so I only just remember him.'

'Your life seems to have been a succession of tragedies!'

'Not really, not much more than most people's are. And yours doesn't sound much better either, when you think about it, because you lost first your wife, then your mother and father.'

'Well, let's not wallow in it,' he said more briskly. 'At least, thanks to Noël, Christmas at Old Place has always been a high spot of the year, whatever happens – he does love the whole thing. And so do I, really – deciding to stay away this year was a stupid idea. I feel guilty for forgetting that Jess's parents weren't going to be at the lodge for the holidays, too.'

'You do seem to be her favourite uncle.'

'She's taken a shine to you, too,' he said and added point-edly, 'like Merlin. Have you been putting something in their food?'

'Only goodness,' I said. 'Noël seems to have unlimited enthusiasm for the Revels too, doesn't he?'

'Local people appear to have been telling you an awful lot about them, which we don't do usually,' he said thoughtfully. 'They must forget you're a stranger, probably because, as Noël said, you're tall and dark like the Martlands.'

There seemed to be a slight questioning note in his voice, so I thought I would get things straight (or as straight as I was absolutely certain of, to date!): 'Until a couple of weeks ago, I hadn't even heard of you,' I said, which was true enough. 'I take after my gran's side of the family, who came from Liverpool originally. Gran always thought there was a foreign sailor ancestor in the mix somewhere.'

'Oh? Well, the Martland colouring dates back to a long-ago Spanish bride and the darkness genes seem to win out, more often than not, over centuries of fair brides. Becca's hair was dark before she went grey, too, though her skin was always peaches and cream, not sallow like mine and Guy's. She was quite a beauty in her day, was Becca.'

'Since first Alan's cousin and then Guy thought I looked like Nefertiti, maybe I have Egyptian blood and should get regressed and find out?' I said dryly.

'I wouldn't take anything my brother says too seriously.'

'I think I'm quite smart enough to work that out for myself, thanks, and anyway, he isn't my type.'

'What exactly *is* your type?' he asked curiously. 'What was your husband like?'

'Same height as me but slim, fair, blue eyes . . .'

'Sounds like Michael.'

'I suppose it does, really. *He's* a really nice man too, like Alan, very kind and thoughtful,' I said warmly and we were silent after that until we reached the house.

We went round through the courtyard so Jude could go and have a look at Lady and I could go and towel-dry Merlin before letting him loose in the house. His shaggy coat was hung with icy droplets, so that he looked as if he was covered in Swarovski crystals: but he was already a precious object to me.

At Coco's insistence, Noël had found the printed excerpts from *Twelfth Night*, so she could practise her scenes with Michael. This seemed to me more of a ruse to retire with him to a dark corner, though he firmly declined to go into a quieter room where they could be on their own.

Noël said the rest of us could read through our parts tomorrow, which would be soon enough, since we were not going to act them out.

'Though I daresay you could all perform, even if you don't memorise the words and have to *read* your parts,' he said, 'it would make a pleasant change?'

It all seemed to me, as the Bard would have put it, much ado about nothing, but if it kept Coco relatively quiet and occupied I was prepared to put up with almost anything!

'Do you like Uncle Jude now?' asked Jess when, at her insistence, I went up to say goodnight.

'Well, I—'

'Only he keeps looking at you, so I think *he* likes *you*.'

'I think he's just still sizing me up, that's all.'

'He's much younger and richer than George.'

'That's very true, but I'm not actually searching for a rich, young, new husband, Jess, so—'

'I think he really *does* like you,' she insisted.

'You're wrong, Jess – I'm not his type, or he mine,' I assured her, though I did feel a bit more sympathetic towards him since our conversation on the walk back earlier. 'Funnily enough, he asked me what my husband was like earlier and I told him fair and blue-eyed.'

'Uncle Jude's wife was blonde too, I've seen her picture.'

'Yes, like Coco: opposites often do attract.'

'But not always?'

'No, not always.' I looked down at her, tucked into the little white-painted bed, along with her worn teddy bear, the wolf and a Beefeater bear and said, 'But in the case of your Uncle Jude and me, it ain't gonna happen, baby!'

She looked disbelieving, but let it drop . . . for the present, though she did seem horribly taken with the idea.

'I'll tell you a secret,' she said, 'Horlicks snores!'

Back in my room, I picked up Gran's journal, which earlier I'd been dying to get back to, only now the words seemed to be dancing about on the page so I didn't get very far.

But my heart was absolutely wrung for her and I positively *hated* Ned Martland!

Chapter 30: A Bit of a Poser

When I left my parents' house my eyes were blinded with tears so that I could hardly see where I was going. I made my way to an old weir, deep in dark woodland, and I admit that it was in the back of my mind to end it all. However, as I stood there, a single beam of sunlight pierced the trees and I seemed to hear a gentle voice telling me that I must go on. I had transgressed, it was true, but it appeared that God still had a purpose for me.

May, 1945

Waking early as usual on Boxing Day, I reread the entry in Gran's journal and cried over it, despite knowing that she really wouldn't drown herself like the heroine of a Victorian melodrama, but in the end marry and keep the child – my mother.

Poor Gran sounded *so* racked with guilt and desperation!

I still can't help but feel fond of Noël, Tilda and Becca, but their acceptance of Noël's casual dismissal of Gran as 'a little mill girl in trouble' does not reflect well on them. Evidently none of them ever wondered what had happened to her after Ned abandoned her!

But I'll have to accept that I'm part of this family, whether I want to be or not, though at least now there's a rational explanation for the pull of attraction to both the people (or some of them) and Old Place that I've felt since I arrived here.

The house was still totally silent when I got up and let Merlin out into the darkness of the courtyard, then cleaned out the grate in the sitting room and scattered the ashes outside the back door as usual – in fact, by now I had gritted quite a decent path halfway to the stables!

Merlin followed me back in, shaking off flecks of snow from his wiry dark grey coat, and ate his arthritis-pill-laced breakfast with gusto, while I slipped back out to Lady's stall with a morning gift of Henry's home-grown carrots for her, Nutkin and Billy.

I clipped back the top of the stable door to the courtyard and I was in the stall, standing with one arm across Lady's warm back while she nuzzled carrot chunks from my hand, when Jude looked in. I knew who it was, because his enormous frame eclipsed all the light from the courtyard, until he shifted slightly to one side.

'Hello – did you forget that I said I'd come down early and do the horses instead of Becca and Jess this morning?'

'No, but I only came out to give Lady a bit of carrot, that's all. I haven't got time to see to her and everything else!' I snapped. It might be totally irrational, but I felt angry with him because it was his uncle who had put poor Gran in such a harrowing plight!

'That's okay, I'll do it,' he said, sounding mildly surprised – but then, we had seemed to have come to a better understanding of each other yesterday so I don't suppose he expected to have his head bitten off.

'And I was going to clean out the fireplace in the sitting room, too. Just leave all that for me, now I'm back.'

'I like to get things sorted early – but someone should run the vacuum cleaner over the sitting-room floor later, if you *really* want to be helpful,' I said and he gave me a puzzled look from his deep-set dark eyes.

Lady, having eaten her carrot, turned her head and vigorously rubbed her nose up and down my arm, the muscles of her neck rippling and Jude suddenly said urgently, 'Stay *exactly* like that!'

I had no time to wonder if the command was meant for me or Lady before he'd whipped out a small camera and flashed it right in my eyes.

'What on earth . . . ?' I began indignantly, but he ignored me and kept snapping away. Lady seemed quite blasé about it: if anything, she held the pose better than I did.

Nutkin, who had closed his eyes and dozed off after his share of the carrot, opened them and stared at us with mild astonishment through the barred partition dividing the boxes.

'Right, now stay like that while I fetch a sketch pad,' Jude said, putting the camera back in his pocket.

'I can't, I've things to do in the kitchen. And why do you need *me*? I thought you were only interested in horses.'

'They *are* my main subject, but I sculpt all kinds of other things and I often include a human form with my animal sculptures. The way you were standing with one arm across Lady's back while she turned her head towards you was full of lovely, flowing lines,' he said regretfully, as I gave Lady a last pat and unbolted the door to come out past him. 'Oh, well, I suppose it doesn't matter – I have the pictures on film and in my head,' he said, though he still seemed a bit reluctant to move out of my way right until the last minute, looking down at me with those deep-set eyes like dark, peaty, dangerous pools . . .

But right then, that just reminded me of poor Gran again.

Back in the warmth of the kitchen I said to Merlin, 'Your boss is a great, big, surly, autocratic bear!' Though in fact *I'd* been the surly one this time: he had just been bossy. Merlin wagged his tail politely.

I prepped everything ready for lunch, which was actually going to be another early cooked dinner, but dead easy: the whole salmon I'd taken from the freezer the previous morning, Duchesse potatoes, petits pois and a piquant sauce.

Jude stayed outside so long I'd forgotten about him. By the time he came back in, Michael had also come downstairs and we were laughing together over something silly as I cooked bacon for breakfast and he laid the table.

Jude, who I could now see in the clearer light of the kitchen, was sporting so much black stubble along his formidable jawline that he looked like an overgrown Mexican bandit, glowered darkly at us and went on through without a word. Perhaps he's not really a morning person? Or *any* time of day person?

He did reappear later, washed, shaved and smelling faintly of the wholesomely attractive aftershave that was presumably designed for rugged men, and put away an impressive amount of breakfast. But he didn't really join in the conversation with the others, though he probably wouldn't have got much out of Coco, anyway. She drifted silently in, wearing her diaphanous pink negligee, like some species of attenuated jellyfish, and then communed silently with a cup of black coffee until I cut the yolk out of a fried egg and plonked the remains down in front of her. She shuddered.

'Eat it!' I ordered and she gave me a slightly alarmed look and picked up her knife and fork.

Jude seemed increasingly abstracted and soon disappeared into his little study/studio next to the library. Perhaps a lot of his taciturnity is actually artistic temperament and he simply vanishes into a new idea? I get a bit withdrawn when I'm working out a new recipe, only without the rattiness, of course . . . or usually without the rattiness. I did feel I had been a bit mean to him earlier, taking something out on him that wasn't his fault.

Everyone else (except Coco) had talked around him as they ate, as though he were the elephant – or Yeti – in the room that all saw but no-one mentioned, so presumably they are quite used to his moods.

Jess made me promise I'd go out as soon as I'd finished clearing up in the kitchen and join her in sledging down the sloping paddock with Guy and Michael – and even Coco ventured out eventually, in borrowed wellingtons and her grubby once-white quilted coat.

I'd been sledging before of course, though using a flattened cardboard carton to sit on, but I'd never made snow angels until Jess and Guy showed me how, by falling backwards into the virgin whiteness and waving my arms up and down to make wing shapes. The horses and Billy were astonished.

It was great fun and so was the snowballing . . . until I got one down the back of my neck. I wasn't so keen on the icy trickle down the spine as it melted.

We were all freezing and wet by the time we went in to dry off and change, but healthily glowing too. And everyone glowed even more when Guy concocted mulled wine in a jam pan on the small electric stove, demanding cinnamon sticks and other ingredients while I was busy putting the salmon in the larger Aga oven, wrapped in a loose parcel of foil with butter and bay leaves.

He left the pan and all the mess for me to clear, of course – but then, that's typical of most men when they cook anything, isn't it?

I didn't drink the small glass of wine he gave me, beyond a token sip to see what it tasted like (surprisingly nice).

Michael came back long after everyone else, because he'd trudged up the hill in the snow to phone his little girl, but this time his ex-wife wouldn't let him speak to her.

'Debbie said it would just upset her, because since my last call she keeps asking for Da-da and she's been unsettled.'

He was so upset that I gave him a comforting hug – and just at that moment Jude wandered in, cast us a look that was hard to read, silently poured himself some coffee from the freshly-made pot, and went out again.

He does choose his moments to appear! And I expect he's drawn *entirely* the wrong conclusions – if he noticed at all, that is, because he did look *very* abstracted.

I gave Michael the remains of my mulled wine: that seemed to cheer him up a bit.

We had a starter of little savoury tomato and cheese tartlets I'd made and frozen a couple of days ago. Becca took a plate of the tartlets to Jude in his study and said he was working, but he still hadn't emerged by the time we were in the dining room, sitting down to the perfectly-cooked salmon (adorned with the very last bit of cucumber, sliced to transparency), so I went to call him.

He was leaning back in his chair, his long legs in old denim jeans stretched out, and the crumb-strewn plate by his elbow. The desk and the corkboard behind it were covered with line drawings and photographs of me and Lady, so he must have one of those instant digital printer things and possibly an instant digital memory, too.

'Dinner – it's on the table,' I announced loudly, but when he finally looked up at me it took his eyes a couple of minutes to focus. Then he smiled seemingly involuntarily – and with such unexpected charm and sweetness that I found myself responding. Then the smile vanished as suddenly as if it had never been, leaving only the memory of it hanging in the air like the Cheshire Cat's grin.

'Dinner?' I repeated, and finally he got up and followed me obediently to the dining room, though he didn't seem to notice what he was eating, even when Tilda pointed out that the capers in the piquant sauce had been her idea. It was sheer luck he didn't choke on a salmon bone, really. (But I can do the Heimlich manoeuvre, I would have saved him.)

Before dessert, which was a choice between the very last scrapings of the trifle and Christmas cake, he abruptly got up, declaring that he was going down to work in the mill studio for a couple of hours.

'Can I go with you again, Uncle Jude?' asked Jess eagerly. 'You promised to show me how to weld.'

'Not today – another time,' he told her and her face fell. 'Holly – you come down to the studio in about half an hour or so, I want you to pose for me.'

'Me? Not *nude*?' I blurted, horrified, then felt myself go pink as they all looked at me.

'Not if you don't want to, though I'll have had the big Calor heaters on for a bit by then, so the place will have warmed up,' he said, his mouth quirking slightly at one side. I *thought* he was joking, but I wasn't quite sure.

'Absolutely not,' I said firmly. 'I've got some black velvet leggings and a fairly clinging tunic jumper I can change into, if you like, but that's as figure-revealing as I'm prepared to go.'

'I'll settle for that,' he said gravely.

'*I* certainly like the sound of it! Can I come and watch?' asked Guy cheekily.

'Or maybe *I* should go, as chaperone?' Michael suggested, twinkling at me.

Jude scowled at them both, his sudden burst of good humour vanishing. 'Unnecessary!' he snapped and went out. We heard the front door slam a few minutes later.

'The dear boy does spend most days down at the studio when he is at home,' Noël said. 'He works very hard.'

'Edwina usually takes him a flask of coffee and sandwiches for lunch,' Tilda said, 'she dotes on him and I am sure he would starve if she didn't, because he forgets the time when he is down there.'

'Does jolly good sculptures, especially the horses,' Becca said. 'Look like mangled metal up close, then step away – and there they are! Seems like you're going to *be* in one, Holly.'

'I don't know why he wants *you* as a model when he could have had *me*,' Coco said, inclined to be even sulkier than Jess.

'Oh, but anyone can have you,' Guy said ambiguously, though luckily Coco didn't seem to have caught the double meaning.

'It's because you'd be two-dimensional, Horlicks,' Jess said.

'That was quite good, Jess,' Tilda said impartially, 'if a trifle rude.'

'It was only that he saw me with Lady this morning and liked the way I was standing with my arm across her,' I explained. 'I expect if it had been Becca he'd seen, he'd have asked her instead.'

'Oh, I don't think so!' Becca said, with one of her deep barks of laughter. 'Face that sank a thousand ships.'

'It seemed to be lines rather than features he was interested in.'

'Well, I've certainly got a lot more of those than you have.'

'I still think he's really mean,' Jess complained. 'He promised to teach me how to weld and there's lots of modelling clay in the studio, too. I'm *bored*.'

'I don't see how you can possibly be bored, with the amount of presents you got yesterday, young lady,' Tilda observed. 'Go and play with that wee-wee thing your poor, misguided parents bought you.'

'Wii, Granny!' Jess said.

'I hope you and Jude aren't going to be down there long, because I thought we could all read through our parts in the play later this afternoon, now we've had a look at them,' Coco said, which was optimistic as far as Jude and I were concerned at least, since we both had other interests to keep us occupied already.

'I'll be busy when I get back, it might have to be after supper,' I said and her face fell.

'I'm not sure that Viola isn't a better part for me, with Michael as Orsino, now I've read it,' she said. 'We might have to re-cast.'

'Oh? I thought Olivia was the big romantic lead?' I said.

'Viola seems to get the better lines and I have to pretend to fall in love with her for most of it!'

'Do you?' I said, surprised. I really would have to find time to read it!

'It's a comedy of errors, with two entwined romances,' Michael explained. 'But I see myself more as a Sebastian than an Orsino, and I already know the part.'

'I suppose I'd better stick with Olivia then,' she said reluctantly. 'We could practise our scenes on our own somewhere, Michael, if the others are busy?'

She bestowed on him an intimately promising smile and a fleeting expression of horror crossed his mobile face. Then, with huge aplomb inspired by the instinct of self-preservation, he tossed a big fat truffle of a diversion in front of her: 'Noël, didn't you mention that there were costumes somewhere in the attic we might use, if we really wanted to get into our parts?'

'Oh – costumes!' breathed Coco, avidly taking the bait.

'I know where they are – the dressing-up box!' Jess said, brightening up instantly too. 'I could show you!'

'Perhaps I'd better go with you,' Noël said anxiously. 'It's not the big chest at the front – that has the Twelfth Night Revels costumes in it, though of course the heads are stored with the swords in the barn behind the pub. No, it's the cabin trunk further back.'

Actually, I'd much rather have explored the dressing-up box with them than trudge down through the snow to pose for Mr Bossy-Boots Martland, but I had a feeling that if I didn't show up he would come back and carry me off by brute force anyway: he was quite capable of it.

'I think you should *all* dress up for your parts,' Jess said. 'Don't worry, Holly, I'll find something nice for your big love scene with Uncle Jude.'

'*Which* big love scene?'

'Haven't you read the play yet?' asked Coco.

'Yes, at school, but I've forgotten about it; it was a long time ago. And I haven't even had time to read through those printed

298

scenes you gave us all. But I thought the central love affair was between Sebastian and Olivia?'

'There's a sort of double love tangle going on,' Noël explained. 'The play has its roots in mumming, with lots of cross-dressing and characters not really being who they appear to be – a bit like the Revels!'

I really *must* try and glance through my helpfully-highlighted printout and find out *exactly* what I've let myself in for!

Chapter 31: Fool's Gold

I felt guided by this voice to visit the father of my childhood sweetheart, the Strange Baptist minister of the chapel in Ormskirk. I had been avoiding Mr Bowman ever since my fall from grace, which must have both puzzled and hurt him.

May, 1945

I changed into my black velvet leggings and dark green tunic jumper, which is an outfit I usually only wear for relaxing in when I am on my own, since it's all very clingy, especially in the bum and twin peaks areas.

When I knocked on the studio door there was no reply, but I went in anyway: it was too cold to hang about outside like an unwanted carol singer.

Jude barely looked up from what he was doing, which was hauling out thick metal rods and wire from a large plastic bin, and grunted at me, but I don't speak pig, so I left my snowy wellies just inside the door and had a wander around in my socks until he became a little less *Animal Farm*.

The building had once had two floors, though now the upper one had been removed and skylights set into the roof to make a large, well-lit space. The walls were painted a creamy white and it smelt of a complicated, but not unpleasant, mingling of Calor gas heater, damp sacking and hot metal. Jude's aftershave might have been based on it.

There were enormous double doors let into one wall, presumably for the removal of finished sculptures . . . and come to think of it, that must be why the path up from the drive was wide and rutted, because they probably had to reverse large vehicles right up it to the studio.

It was furnished with a large, raised wooden model's dais, like a mini-stage, a smaller door that presumably gave on to a storage area for materials, a small furnace of some kind, easels, tables, large metal and wooden stands, a tilting draughtsman's desk and workbenches covered in a clutter of sketches, tubs of brushes, modelling tools and pencils, bits of clay, little models of sculptures and fragments of twisted metal. It all looked in need of a good sort and dust to me, but I expect he preferred it like that.

Dotted about on what remained of the floor space were finished sculptures in various mediums, most mounted on bases, plinths or stands of one kind or another. The biggest – life-size, in fact – was unmistakably Lady, even if it *was* composed of metal triangles, but Becca was right and from close to it looked like a heap of junk. Another was just a series of fluid lines in bent tubular metal that were equally unmistakably the Celtic red horse up on the hill.

He'd been telling the truth about it being reasonably warm down there once the heaters got going, but nothing would have induced me to strip down to the buff, though I did finally take my anorak off and hang it up. That was as far as I was prepared to go.

When I turned round, I found Jude was looking at me assessingly, one corner of his straight mouth quirking up in a way that seemed to denote private amusement.

'*Very* dryad.'

I am a little on the large side for ditsy dancing in the woods, so I ignored this as sarcasm and asked, 'What did you want me for?'

'To try and capture the way you were standing this morning,

301

with your arm across Lady's back and her head turned towards you. The whole thing looked as if you were fused into one . . . though it would have been better if she hadn't been wearing her rug. Still, I've got loads of photographs, sketches and models of her already, like this one.' He indicated the finished life-sized sculpture. 'If you stand next to it, in the same pose, I could get some ideas down of the scale and how it will go, even if the horse isn't in the right position.'

He seemed serious, so I climbed onto the rectangular block the sculpture was sitting on and draped an arm across it as directed, while he pulled an easel up at an angle and stuck a large sketchbook on it.

'Is this one sold somewhere?' I asked. 'Don't you always work to commission?'

'Only sometimes, I generally just do what I feel like and then sell it – or not, if I don't want to. I decided to keep that one. Turn slightly to face her head . . . No, just *your* head, not your whole body!' he exclaimed, then with two impatient strides he seized me and actually *manhandled* me into the position he wanted, which felt *really* weird.

Then he went back to his easel and studied me minutely, as if I was a slightly dodgy car he was thinking of buying, for want of anything better, before swiftly making sketch after sketch, using big sticks of charcoal. These he then simply dropped on the floor around his feet.

At first I was disconcerted by the way he barely took his brooding, deep-set dark eyes off me, his brow furrowed with concentration, but I slowly relaxed as I realised it was an impartial and remote scrutiny: it wasn't me as a *person* he was seeing at all!

From time to time he dragged the easel into a different position, so he could draw me from all angles and presumably get some concept of me in the round. It seemed to take him ages – but then, I do have a *lot* of round.

'I wish I had Lady here,' he said at one point, and then later murmured, as if to himself, 'and I *wish* you would take your clothes off!'

'I bet you do, but it ain't gonna happen! Look, Jude, I've gone numb down one side, so can I move now? I must have been standing here for hours.'

'Oh . . . yes, I suppose you have,' he said, blinking at me as if he'd forgotten I was an animate object, with a voice and a lot of opinions. 'I think I've got enough to make a start.'

'On a sculpture?' I climbed down slightly stiffly and fetched the flask of coffee I'd had the foresight to bring with me.

'Yes, but I'll make a maquette or two, first.'

'Maquette?'

'A small three-dimensional study, exploring ideas.'

'Right.'

'We'll see if Lady will oblige with the same pose without the rug when she comes in later and then I can take a few more pictures. And I'll need you down here again tomorrow.'

He came and sat next to me on the wooden edge of the model's dais and I handed him a plastic mug of coffee and a mince pie from a plastic box.

'I can hardly wait,' I said politely.

'It wasn't so bad, was it?' he asked, sounding surprised. He was close enough so I could see all the fascinating little specks of gold – probably fool's gold – suspended in his molasses-dark eyes.

'Well, no . . .' I admitted, 'though I thought you were only going to do one or two quick sketches, not dozens.'

'You're going to be immortalised in brazed and welded steel for posterity,' he promised, which has to be the best offer of any kind I've had for a long, long time – and certainly one up on the popcorn and Coke Sam bought me the time we went to the pictures.

'Where's Merlin?' he asked.

'I left him up at the house. I wasn't sure if he was allowed in the studio or not.'

'Yes, he always comes with me, unless lured away by visiting dryads,' he said wryly and then we sat there silently, but fairly companionably, drinking our coffee and eating mince pies.

'Sorry I bit your head off earlier, I was upset about something,' I said eventually.

'That's okay – anything you want to share?'

I looked away from his enquiring eyes and shook my head firmly. 'The others have gone into the attic to look for costumes for the play,' I said, changing the subject. 'The way Coco's carrying on, we'll end up having to act out *our* parts too, though in my case I'll have to read the lines, because I won't have time to learn them by heart.'

'I don't know them by heart either: it used to be Becca, Tilda and Noël who did most of the reading. At least it doesn't take long, because not only is it quite a short play, but Noël's edited out all the slapstick and Malvolio stuff and filled in with a brief linking summary,' he said, then glanced at me from under his heavy dark brows and added, his already thrillingly deep voice going even lower, 'But if we act them out, then I expect I can manage a few *appropriate* actions.'

The corner of his straight mouth quirked up again, but I wasn't quite sure what he meant by that, since most of his actions towards me so far have been highly *inappropriate*, like dragging me into his bedroom on Christmas Eve!

Jude came back to the house with me and we went round through the stableyard, where we found that Becca had just brought the horses in and started grooming Nutkin.

'I was playing hide and seek with the others, but me and Tilda got spotted first, behind the sitting-room curtains,' she said. 'One of my feet was sticking out. They'd found everyone except Coco when I thought I'd better do the horses, so I left them to it. She's so skinny, she probably slipped between a crack in the floorboards.'

'That's a slight exaggeration, but she is worryingly thin now,' Jude said.

'I'm thinking about confiscating her laxatives,' I confessed. 'I don't want her to waste away while I'm doing the cooking and have her on my conscience.'

'Even if you do, she'll probably just go back to them when she leaves,' he pointed out.

'Perhaps, but at least I'll have tried.'

Jude removed Lady's rug and took some more pictures of me standing with her, though I declined to take my wellies off this time, even if I did reluctantly part with my anorak. He even drew a couple of quick sketches, though the light wasn't exactly brilliant in there and Lady kept trying to nibble the edges of the paper.

'You're a muse now,' Becca said, pausing in her steady brush-strokes. 'I've read about artists and their muses, you need to watch yourself!' And she laughed heartily.

Luckily I don't think Jude took in what she'd said, because he seemed to have mentally retired to his own little Planet Zog again, closing his sketchbook and walking off to the house without another word to either of us.

We exchanged a look and then I put my anorak back on and started to groom Lady, which has to be one of the best arm-toning exercises going.

When I went into the house a little while later, Coco was still missing and they were getting anxious about her.

'I can't think where she's got to,' Guy said. 'We've even looked in the attic, which was supposed to be out of bounds, but there's no sign of her anywhere.'

'Did you check to see if her coat and hat were missing? She might have gone outside,' I suggested.

'Yes, I thought of that,' Michael said, 'but they're still there. I don't think she'd have stayed out very long anyway, it's too cold. And she's not exactly the hillwalking type, so she won't have got lost.'

'No, I just thought she might have had a sudden impulse to set out for the village, but obviously not.'

'Did you look in all the chests and trunks?' asked Tilda from the sofa, where she was comfortably reclining while watching the hunt. 'Only I suddenly remembered that story about the bride playing hide and seek on her wedding day and vanishing, only for them to find her skeleton in a chest years later.'

Noël looked very struck by this. 'Of course! It's just the sort of silly thing she would do – and there are two or three in the attic, as well as the sandalwood chest on the landing.'

Guy, Jude and Michael dashed upstairs, but I couldn't myself see Coco squeezing herself into a trunk. 'Did you check the cellars?' I asked Jess.

'Yes, and the utility room and everywhere else I could think of. Come on, let's go up the backstairs and see if they've found her yet.'

I followed her upstairs, stopping to check the wardrobe in my room and Michael's and the linen cupboard between them. And then suddenly I remembered Noël telling me there was another door at the top of the staircase, leading to a stairway to the unused servants' rooms in the smaller attic over this wing. It was in a dark corner, easy to miss, but from behind it came a faint scrabbling and a wavering cry of, 'Help! Heeelp!'

'Coco? It's all right, we'll have you out of there in a minute,' I called, tugging at the handle, which wouldn't budge. 'Quick, Jess, go and get your Uncle Jude and the others, I can't shift this.'

Jude could, though, and with one mighty wrench it creaked open, revealing a tearstained, pallid figure huddled on the bottom stairs.

He picked her up as if she weighed nothing and she clung to

306

him whimpering, 'I thought no-one would ever find me and I was going to be there forever! And I went upstairs to see if there was another way out and something big and white flapped at me!'

Shuddering she turned her face into his shoulder as he stroked her hair and said gently, 'It's all right, Coco, I've got you now.'

At that moment I felt a sudden pang of something that I feared might be jealousy: *I* had never been held so tenderly in someone's arms as if I was feather-light and fragile! (Alan would have fallen over, had he tried.)

'You'd better put her on her bed,' Guy suggested. 'Come on, Coco, you're safe now and we would have found you eventually.'

'I hadn't even noticed that door was there,' Michael said.

'Noël told me about it and I suddenly remembered. But Guy's right and she ought to go and lie down for a bit. Someone make her a hot drink and I'll sit with her.'

'Guy can do that while I check for the mysterious ghostly thing,' Michael said. 'If I vanish, you know where I am!'

I followed after Jude, who had laid Coco down on her bed and was now attempting to detach her arms from their death grip around his neck.

'Oh, there you are,' he said to me with some relief.

'Guy's making her a hot drink and Michael's gone to see what frightened her in the attic.'

'Oh, it was horrible, swooping at me out of the darkness!' Coco shuddered, reaching for Jude again, though he was now out of reach.

Guy brought a mug of tea and said, 'I've told the others we've found her and Michael says there was a pigeon up there – one of the windows is broken – so that must be what flew at you.'

Coco sat up and took the mug, pleased if anything with all the attention she was getting and starting to look a lot better. 'Is there sugar in this?' she asked after a sip.

'Sweetener,' Guy said, though I was sure he was lying. He exchanged a look with Jude and they both made their escape, while I seized the moment to give Coco a good lecture on the danger to her health from guzzling laxatives like sweets. She took it like a chided little girl and I felt about a century older and quite mean by the time I'd finished.

Then I removed her stash of Fruity-Go from the bedside table. 'I know you've got more in your handbag, but I suggest you ration yourself to a normal dose every day until you run out, then stop them altogether. If you eat small, sensible meals, you'll be fine, you really don't need them.'

'And you won't tell Mummy, will you?' she asked, since I had used this as a threat, without any intention of carrying it out. 'Only she'll have me locked up in some ghastly addiction clinic!'

I agreed that no, I wouldn't do that, before carrying away my spoils and flushing them straight down the nearest loo. It took several flushes before they all vanished.

Coco came down later in a slightly chastened and quiet frame of mind, but soon showed signs of reviving since everyone was being nice to her, in their own way. She'd brought her handbag with her and kept a firm grip on it at all times, so she was obviously afraid I would change my mind and empty that of laxatives, too!

After supper, Jess showed me the long satin dress she'd picked out for me, which was not only a fairly sickly shade of salmon pink, but about twelve inches too short, though apparently for most of the play I would be disguised as a man anyway.

Coco had appropriated a white dress in which she looked like an emaciated bride and Jess herself wore a crown made of papier-mâché and glass jewels. She'd been wearing it to supper, too.

'I just like it,' she explained. 'I don't have to have a real costume since I'm only Props, though Michael said that's one of the most important jobs in the theatre. I have to make sure everyone is dressed for their parts at the right time, with all the things they need.'

'I think *you'd* better wear a man's overcoat until the end of the play, where you're revealed as Sebastian's sister – there's one hanging up in the hall. Your boobs are *way* too big,' Coco said to me, making me immediately sorry I'd been kind to her earlier – but I expect now she was feeling better she was getting a bit of her own back about the Fruity-Go.

'I find myself unable to second that opinion,' Guy said and I gave him a cold look.

'Holly's in perfect proportion,' Jude said. 'I should know, because I've spent most of the afternoon drawing her.'

I wasn't sure whether to be embarrassed about having my figure discussed in this way, or take this remark as a compliment.

'She's too tall though, even for a model,' Coco objected.

Jude looked slightly surprised. 'Do you think so? She seems about the right height to me.'

'*I* am perfect, all the top designers say so,' Coco said.

'Well, it's a strange world and it takes all sorts!' Noël said cheerfully. 'Now, what did we find for Jude to wear in the play?'

'Just this dark blue velvet cloak,' Jess said. 'And a sword and moustache.'

'I don't mind wearing the cloak, but I draw the line at stick-on moustaches,' Jude said firmly.

'I daresay he could grow one by tomorrow if you insisted on it,' Tilda remarked from the sofa in front of the fire. I think that might have been a *slight* exaggeration . . . maybe *two* days.

Guy went back to the half-finished jigsaw, though going by his expression, it annoyed him that I had stuck a couple more pieces in earlier. He gave me a suspicious stare that reminded me strongly of his brother.

We pulled chairs into a half-circle near the Christmas tree, ready to read through our parts for the first time, but first Noël gave us a brief run-down of the plot and the characters we would be playing.

'Orsino, Duke of Illyria – that's you, Jude – is in love with Olivia, played by Coco.'

'"If music be the food of love, play on. Give me excess of it; that, surfeiting, the appetite may sicken and so die,"' declaimed Tilda thrillingly from the sofa.

'Precisely, m'dear,' Noël said. 'Now, Sebastian and his twin sister Viola – you and Michael, Holly – are shipwrecked. Viola thinks her brother is dead, so she disguises herself as a man, and takes service with Orsino, as Cesario.'

'All this cross-dressing must have been even stranger in Shakespeare's time, when Viola would have been played by a young boy, playing a woman, disguised as a man,' Michael said, with a grin.

'I'm glad *I* don't have to pretend to be a man, I'd never pull it off,' Coco said. 'Olivia is a ravishingly beautiful countess, but she doesn't fancy Orsino.'

'That's one interpretation,' Jude said. 'But she's certainly not very bright, because when Orsino sends Viola/Cesario to woo her, dressed as a man, she falls in love with her.'

I was feeling confused already and Coco frowned, 'I'm not too keen on that bit, can't we change it?'

'I think we ought to leave it as the Bard put it, m'dear,' Noël said, 'it's integral to the plot. So basically,' he continued, 'Viola falls in love with Orsino, who thinks she is a boy. Olivia falls in love with Viola, ditto, Orsino thinks he loves Olivia, and Sebastian isn't really dead, he's on his way there with his friend Antonio.'

'Then it all comes to a head with lots of misunderstandings and mistaken identities, until finally Sebastian is married to Olivia and Orsino decides he'll settle for Viola.'

'But only if she looks good in a dress,' Jude remarked, with a sideways look at me, but I didn't rise to the bait.

We read it through aloud, with a bit of good-natured heckling by Becca and Tilda. Luckily, I didn't seem to have too many soppy things to say to or about Jude/Orsino, since he doesn't know Viola isn't a boy until right near the end. It was a bit embarrassing when Coco had to pretend she was in love with me as Cesario, though . . .

Michael's scenes with Olivia were also towards the end, when all the tangles get cut, but she still seemed dead set on getting him alone on the pretext of rehearsing them, a move he was clearly determined to resist to the death! I couldn't work out if Coco had fallen for Michael (which wouldn't be a surprise, since he's very handsome, in a slightly drawn and haggard way), or simply saw him as a stepping stone to an acting career; but she'd certainly abandoned any claim on Guy and was going all out on a charm offensive.

Meanwhile Guy still persisted in trying to flirt with me and the fact that he wasn't getting anywhere increasingly appeared to puzzle him. He followed me into the kitchen later when I went to make cocoa for those who wanted it, which was just me, Jude and Jess, because the rest of the party were hitting the sherry or the hard stuff again.

'You know, I really like you, Holly,' he said, 'and I want to get to know you better. But let's face it, I'm getting nowhere, am I? Why is that – am I too shallow, or don't you like the colour of my socks?'

'You simply aren't my type.' I was clattering pans and cutlery into the dishwasher for one final go of the day.

'No? That's strange, because I've always considered myself a universally appealing one-size-fits-all type,' he said modestly.

'Not as far as *I'm* concerned: and my gran would have said you were all mouth and trousers.'

'Is that good?'

'No. Don't forget that I've seen first-hand that you're a total love-rat, too – *and* everyone says you're just like your Uncle Ned, who abandoned one poor girl when she was pregnant because he was already engaged to another at the time,' I said acidly. 'So no, I don't think you'd be much of a proposition, even if I believed you were serious and not just being daft.'

He sighed. 'You've got me all wrong . . . but I'll change your mind. Till then, couldn't you *try* and like me?'

'I do a bit, sometimes,' I admitted. 'You can be quite funny.'

'I'm not sure if that's good or not. But the right woman would be the making of me, Tilda says so – and *you* look a bit of all right to me.'

'I wouldn't have thought anything short of a frontal lobotomy would change you,' I said dubiously, 'but then, she knows you better than I do.'

He laughed. 'I wish now I hadn't let Jude take my place as Orsino. He's going to get all the hands-on action.'

'There won't *be* any hands-on action and I only agreed to do this stupid play to keep your wretched girlfriend in good humour, so she didn't ruin Christmas for everyone else . . . and to cheer her up a bit, because I felt sorry for her.'

'She's not my girlfriend anymore and she's already got her sights on Michael to fill the vacancy. He's proving surprisingly resistant to her charms, though, just as you are to mine.'

'Yes, that's because *he's* not daft, either.'

'Or perhaps because he's got other interests?'

I looked at him with surprise and then laughed. 'Do you mean me? Michael and I are becoming good friends, but there's no attraction between us of any other kind. Strange as it may seem to you, I'm perfectly happy single.'

'Me too,' Michael said, coming in just in time to overhear the last sentence. 'I wish someone would tell Coco that!'

Guy grinned and went back to the others and I said to Michael, 'I think it's mean how Jude and Guy keep throwing you and Coco together, just because they're tired of her. They hope chasing you will keep her amused.'

He shrugged. 'I've been pursued before, not to sound too

immodest – and she's not my type. But I'm looking on it as a sort of price to be paid for being made so welcome here over Christmas, the unexpected guest.'

'I wouldn't say *Jude* seems to be making you very welcome!'

'I think he has his reasons,' Michael said with a smile. 'Just as I suspect Guy is flirting with you partly to wind his brother up – though that's not to say that he doesn't find you attractive, too, because I can tell he does.'

'I can't see why Jude would care if Guy *did* get off with me. But it isn't going to happen, even if Guy is under the delusion he can twist me round his little finger if he turns on the charm enough.'

'We'll just have to keep rescuing each other if we get cornered,' suggested Michael.

'Aren't you two ever coming back into the sitting room?' Jess asked, appearing in the doorway still wearing her jewelled crown. 'I'm bored again!'

'Just finished,' I said, putting the mugs on the tray to carry through, along with some Parmesan twists and little bowls of nuts and olives.

Jess came right into the kitchen and directed an interrogative stare at Michael. 'Michael, do *you* fancy Holly? Only Guy and George and Uncle Jude do.'

'Jess!' I exclaimed.

'No,' he answered gravely, 'I think she's a really nice person and I hope we'll always be good friends, but I don't fancy her in the least.'

'Oh good, that's *exactly* what I thought,' she said, her brow clearing. 'She doesn't really like Uncle Guy that much, I can tell, and George is way, way, too old. So that just leaves Uncle Jude, doesn't it?'

'To do what?' asked Jude, bringing in a tray full of dirty glasses – all lovely old lead crystal ones that would need hand-washing.

313

'Oh, we were only discussing who's got a sweet tooth,' I said quickly. 'Jess, do you want me to show you how to make instant microwave meringues and chocolate cake in a mug?'

'What, *now*?' she asked. 'Isn't it too late?'

'Not really – it only takes a few minutes. Then you can eat them before you go to bed.'

'Great,' she said. 'I wish you were *always* here, Holly – don't you, Uncle Jude?'

'I don't know,' he said, sombrely regarding me. 'She's a bit like an irritating speck of grit in an oyster, and I'm not sure if she's going to turn into a pearl or not.'

If Michael and Jess are right, and Jude *is* a little bit attracted to me, it sounds as if he really doesn't want to be – and I feel exactly the same way about him!

Chapter 32: Puzzle Pieces

Mr Bowman is a sweet, kindly man and, though I knew he would be deeply grieved by my story, I hoped he might also find it in his heart to give me some measure of forgiveness and understanding.

June, 1945

Gran's story has turned terribly sad, but of course I now see where it's all heading and feel so glad that someone as nice as my grandfather rescued her! But no wonder she was so reserved and totally buttoned up after that!

However, though I can guess the outcome, I'm determined not to jump ahead to the last entries, but read it in order, even though after her decision to go and see the minister she spent three more whole pages in examining the state of her conscience and the depth of her guilt in such exhaustive depth it eventually sent me to sleep.

This morning, after I'd let Merlin out and given the horses a bit of carrot each, I came back in to put the kettle on, only to find Jude already in the kitchen dressed in old jeans and a navy sweater ready for action, sitting by the table putting on his socks.

'Do you think you could rescue my other wellie sock from Jess some time and remove the pink ribbon?' he asked, looking up. 'This is my only other pair and they're going through at the heels.'

'Okay, unless you'd prefer me to sew matching ribbon to the other, instead?'

'Perhaps not,' he said and then went off saying he was going to replenish the logs in the cellar from the ones in the wood store outside, because we'd got through an awful lot and the next ones could be drying out.

Later he cleaned the ashes from the sitting-room fire before going back out to see to the horse: these were all the sort of jobs I was only too happy to relinquish to him. Well, except looking after Lady: I enjoy spending time with her now.

When I'd fed Merlin I consulted my menus and schedule for the day, so that by the time he returned from the stables, I was well on the way to getting some turkey and ham pies in the oven.

He proved useful for making cups of tea while I was working and then he sat in a chair by the Aga out of the way with a sketchbook, his eyes following me around the room as I made a tray of mincemeat flapjacks and then cast a few fresh additions into the bubbling soup pot.

Now that I knew the way Jude's eyes followed me round the room was just an impersonal artistic scrutiny, it didn't really bother me at all. In fact, I kept forgetting he was there and carrying on like I always did when alone – talking to Merlin as I tossed him the odd scrap and, I expect, occasionally singing. I suppose I get almost as engrossed in my work as he does in his.

'There we are,' I said eventually, ticking a couple more things off the day's schedule, 'just breakfast to get ready now.'

'Do you get up and go on like this early every morning?' he asked curiously.

'I do when I've got a house-party job. When it's house-sitting, of course, I just see to the pets, or plants, or whatever I'm keeping an eye on, then the day is my own,' I said pointedly. 'When I'm cooking, though, I find it best to plan the menus and schedule in advance to make it all so much easier later.'

'I feel *really* guilty now, especially since you keep saying you won't accept any extra money. I'll have to think of some other way of thanking you for all this hard work.'

'So you said. But don't bother, because I volunteered to do it – though of course, I didn't know it would be double the number of people I originally invited.'

He put his sketchbook away and helped me to cook the breakfast which, as I said to him, seemed to be the one meal he *could* put together without a microwave.

'You obviously haven't found my secret cache of microwave all-in-one all-day frozen breakfasts yet, then,' he said sardonically. 'Though *you* can talk, after teaching Jess how to make microwave desserts last night!'

'I'm not against microwaves, it's just what you do with them. The meringues and cake are a short cut, but also fun. And now they have the Tilda seal of approval.'

'They have my seal of approval too, come to that and, by the way, I expect you down at the studio again after lunch.'

'I thought you'd finished with me yesterday?'

'No, don't you remember? I said I wanted to make a maquette or two next.'

'Yes, but I didn't think you'd need me for that. And it's Sunday, so another early cooked dinner – cold cuts, roast potatoes and vegetables. I must raid Henry's carrot store, I gave the last to the horses. Oh, and pudding will be frozen Arctic Roll, specially requested by Noël. It has to be one of *your* favourites, too, because there are *six* in the freezer.'

'It is,' he admitted, 'but strange as it may seem, I like it with lots of hot custard poured over it.'

'Well, that can be arranged, even if it does seem weird. But then, I suppose Baked Alaska is a bit odd, too.'

'I expect Richard will hold a short church service today, seeing the regular vicar won't be able to get through,' he said thoughtfully. 'Guy can take Becca, Noël and Tilda down in my Land

Rover if they want to go, which they probably will, and stay in the pub until he brings them back. Coco and Michael could go with him, so long as he doesn't let Coco get drunk again.'

'*I'd* quite like to go to the pub,' I said wistfully, 'but I'd better stay here and get dinner ready instead.'

'I'm afraid they're bound to bring Old Nan and Richard back with them,' he said apologetically. 'And did anyone tell you that they always come on New Year's Eve for dinner too? They can be more audience for the revived *Twelfth Night* readings.'

'No-one tells the cook anything. But two more won't put me out unduly. There's soup to start with, loads of turkey and ham, and I'll do a few extra vegetables.'

'I think there's still a jar or two of Mrs Jackson's fruit chutney in the larder,' he said.

'There is and I brought some of my own apricot chutney, too.'

I could hear people stirring in the house now – the clank of the water pipes, the creaking of old floorboards and, not least, the unmistakable thump of Jess's feet as she ran across the landing and galloped down the wooden stairs.

'Everyone's about to appear – and these sausages are done, so I'm off to the studio,' Jude said, handing the tongs to me. 'Tell Guy about church and the Land Rover. I'll see you later – and *I'm* not coming back for lunch so bring me something to eat.'

'Yes, boss,' I said sarcastically, and that totally transforming smile lit his face again for an instant: then one blink and it was gone – and so was he.

Later Guy, Coco and Michael all managed to squeeze into Jude's Land Rover along with the church party, including a mutinous Jess who would rather have gone to the pub. Noël said they would come back up with George, who he was sure wouldn't mind giving them a lift in his larger vehicle, along with Old Nan and the Vicar.

It looked a bit uncomfortably sardine-like, even though Jess and Coco didn't take up much room and Tilda is the size of your average fairy. Becca *is* pretty substantial in the beam end, though. Once they were in, the windows immediately fogged up and Guy leaned across Coco and cranked down the passenger side.

'You can phone your mum and see if your father is feeling better yet, Coco,' I suggested and she looked at me blankly.

'Why? It doesn't matter if he is, because it's too late. My engagement is *totally* over.'

'And not even a Birkin bag to go back to,' Guy commiserated and she flushed angrily.

'I hate you, Guy Martland!'

He ignored her and instead said invitingly to me, 'Sure you won't come? You can sit on my lap.'

'No thanks, I need to sort out early dinner,' I said, though actually, now it came to it, I rather fancied a bit of time to myself, too.

And it was *bliss*. I had a quick tidy through the house, plumping up the cushions in the sitting room and pausing to put a few more pieces in the jigsaw puzzle. I can't imagine why it was taking everyone so long to finish, and I know it annoys Guy when he finds I've had a go, but there's something quite irresistible about a large jigsaw, isn't there? Oriel was right.

After that I retired to the kitchen with my laptop and updated the notes for my cookbook with things that I'd tried and tested over Christmas, talked to Merlin and then went out with him for a little walk up the track.

A skin of ice had formed on the water trough in the paddock, and I broke that into jagged pieces like clear toffee and hooked them out onto the ground, before we left. Lady was pawing the snow to expose the grass beneath, ignoring the haynet, but Billy was up on his hind legs against the fence having a good go at the bottom of it and Nutkin was thoughtfully chewing a mouthful from further up.

There hadn't been any fresh snow for ages, so perhaps the

worst was over and soon it would start to thaw? Then I, and the rest of the uninvited and unwanted members of the party, could leave . . .

Somehow, that was no longer quite such an enticing thought.

The Little Mumming expedition returned in two Land Rovers, the pub party fairly merry, especially Coco. Still, Michael had at least remembered my request to bring back yet more sherry supplies for the elder members of the party, who were getting through it at a surprising rate.

George helped Tilda, Noël and Old Nan out of his Land Rover, though Richard and Becca jumped down unassisted from Guy's, being still pretty spry. Then he rounded them all up and drove them into the house, a bit like a friendly but worried sheepdog.

I took the chance to thank him for his lovely present and he beamed and in turn thanked me for mine.

'Won't you come in?' I asked.

'Only as far as the mistletoe – if you insist!' he said meaningfully, and winked at me – and for a minute, I admit I was quite tempted!

'Oh, it fell down, so we had to put it in a vase,' Jess said very quickly, appearing suddenly by my side like a sombre Jack-in-the-box. Tilda had dragooned her into a short black dress over tights for church, though she'd completed the outfit with big black lace-up boots and a long coat. 'You can't stand under it any more,' she added, 'so it doesn't count.'

'Pity,' he said good-humouredly, though now he was close enough I'd spotted the faint imprint of a perfect lipstick bow on one of his lean, pink cheeks in an odd raspberry shade that reminded me of Oriel, so he'd obviously been spreading his net wide again.

But he didn't go away *totally* disappointed, because I fetched one of the turkey and ham pies from the kitchen wrapped in tinfoil to take home for him and Liam. He opened the corner of the foil to look at it, and I thought he was going to go down on his knees in the snow and propose right there and then.

'What's he got that I haven't?' demanded Guy as he drove off.

'Sincerity?' I suggested.

I'd laid the table for Sunday dinner in the dining room, which was easier than the kitchen for such a large party, and then afterwards I cleared up and left them in the sitting room with coffee, sherry, mincemeat flapjacks and the last remnants of the Christmas cake, while I changed into leggings and tunic jumper and took a Red Riding Hood basket of lunch down to the studio, accompanied by Merlin this time.

I didn't go straight there, though: first I walked on a bit past the lodge so I could update Laura on my suddenly becoming an artist's model.

'It's weird, because he stares at me while he's drawing, but it's sort of impersonal. Not that he doesn't keep looking at me at other times too – Michael and Jess are convinced he fancies me.'

'How do you know he's staring, unless *you* keep looking at *him*?' she asked astutely.

'He *is* a bit hard to ignore when he's in the same room,' I admitted. 'In fact, he's a bit hard to ignore when he's in the same house: the atmosphere sort of changes.'

'Hmmm . . .' she said thoughtfully. 'Perhaps he does fancy you?'

'He might a bit, but having been widowed and then jilted, I don't actually think he wants to – and anyway, he still thinks I'm up to something.'

'You are, in a way – trying to find out the truth about your gran,' she said. 'And I think you're more attracted by Jude than you're admitting, because you're afraid of falling in love again, too!'

'A bit of physical attraction is neither here nor there! He's not my type and, going by Coco, I'm not his! It's really embarrassing playing Viola to Jude's Orsino, though,' I said, and gave her a graphic description of our play-acting.

321

'Michael is Sebastian, my twin brother, so he gets off with Coco as Olivia in the end, but desperately wishes he didn't, poor man. He'd feel *much* safer with me. But at least the play's keeping Coco fairly amused. She managed to lock herself in an attic earlier today and had a panic attack, and I seized the moment to give her a talking to about her laxative consumption and confiscated most of them.'

'Wasn't that a bit high-handed?'

'It was for her own good. If the snow doesn't thaw soon, I might even get a bit of meat on her bones and colour in her cheeks before she goes home.'

'So I take it there's still no chance of escape yet?'

'No, but in any case, I don't think Jude would let me go until he's finished with me.'

'That sounds . . . dodgy. But interesting.'

'As a model in the studio, idiot!'

I'd made Jude a sort of hot chopped-up version of the roast turkey dinner, like giant toddler food, and put it in one of the wide-mouthed Thermos flasks from the kitchen to keep it hot.

One good thing about him is that even with half his mind on his work, he still appreciates my cooking. I shared the flask of coffee, sitting next to him with a certain quiet companionship on the wooden model's dais while he ate it.

Merlin sat between us, alternately leaning first against me, then Jude, then back again, and sighing a lot.

'What's the matter with this stupid dog?' Jude asked eventually, puzzled.

'Conflict of loyalties, I think. He feels he should be with you, but he doesn't really want to leave me. Ideally, he'd like us both to stay in the same place all the time.'

'But I notice when it comes to the crunch, he more often follows *you* than *me*.'

'Yes,' I admitted, 'but he'll forget all about me when I'm gone. I *am* going to really miss him, though!'

I put one arm around Merlin and gave him a hug.

Jude watched me with an absent expression I was becoming familiar with and said, 'Hmmm . . . must do some sketches of you two later. But first, back to work again – I'm making an armature to support the sculpture. The maquettes are on that table over there, if you want to see.'

He got up and went back to constructing something substantial and vaguely horse- and human-shaped in bent metal rods, pushed into a large hollow support on a fixed base.

There were three small models on the bench, one in clay, one seemingly twisted from wire, and one constructed with snippets of tin stuck together with blobs of wax.

Weird.

I went back to sitting on the edge of the dais and watched him for a bit to see if he might want me for anything, since he'd been so insistent I go down; but I think he'd forgotten me again. Maybe he'd just wanted his lunch brought?

He didn't seem to feel the cold at all. Although it wasn't that hot in the studio he'd stripped off his jumper and the thin T-shirt beneath was stretched across an impressive array of muscles I remembered all too clearly from my private viewing of them on Christmas Eve, tapering down to a slim waist and hips . . .

I was just thinking that although he was a giant, he was a very well-proportioned and fit-looking one, when he looked up and gave me one of those dramatically sudden, heart-stoppingly sweet smiles, before going back to work again.

I don't think he realises he's doing it! But I expect it's only an expression of sublime happiness, blissed out in the act of creation.

Now *that* feeling rang a bell in the distant recesses of my memory . . .

From time to time he made a random comment, evidently

323

thinking aloud. Once he said, 'I must arrange a way for Jess to speak to her parents, when we can get out of Little Mumming,' and later he told me my lines were nearly as beautiful as Lady's. I took that as a compliment.

Eventually, when I could see the light outside was starting to go, I got up, and Merlin uncoiled himself to come with me. 'Jude, I'm going now. You won't forget to come back for supper, will you?'

He looked up absently. 'No, okay,' he said, but I wouldn't put money on him remembering, unless his stomach insisted.

When I got back Becca and Jess had long since brought the horses in and Guy had driven Old Nan and Richard home in Jude's Land Rover.

The kitchen was in a bit of a mess because Jess had been showing Tilda how to make microwave meringues and chocolate cake in a mug. I promised to write the meringue recipe down for Tilda. I could imagine endless plates of them appearing at the lodge, garnished with the ubiquitous squirty cream and, perhaps, sliced strawberries in summer.

'We found Coco in your room earlier,' Jess said, 'searching for her Fruity-Go.'

'That's because there are hardly any left in my handbag,' Coco said sulkily. 'I only wanted a few more.'

'I'm afraid I flushed them all away – cutting out the middle woman, as it were,' I confessed and then she slightly hysterically accused me of wanting to ruin her figure, her career and her entire life.

Tilda told her she should be grateful someone cared about her health, but if she found herself constipated she would brew her up a nice dose of senna pods.

That seemed to have a remarkably calming effect.

Jude did remember to come back for supper, which was just sausage rolls, tomatoes (the very last of the salad), smoked salmon

324

sandwiches and more microwave cake and meringues (with swirls of squirty cream, of course). We'll all be as fat as pigs by New Year.

Guy had noticed some additions to the jigsaw and accused me of putting them there, as if it was a crime. When I admitted my guilt, he said pettishly that since I was so good at it I might as well finish the whole thing.

He and Coco have so much in common, it's a pity they didn't make a go of it!

I told him I'd got it for everyone to share and we'd *all* done a bit of it, even Coco (probably the upside-down bits in the wrong place), so he could stop throwing his rattle out of the pram.

'Hear, hear!' said Becca.

Honestly, hurt male pride over something as trivial as a jigsaw? And okay, beating him at snooker and then Scrabble first probably didn't help . . .

I would quite happily have continued playing Monopoly, Scrabble or Cluedo with the others all evening, but no, Coco had us all practising our scenes in the play again, though mainly she just wanted an audience to watch her unintentionally hamming it up with poor Michael. I think it's called overacting.

However, I caught the bug and started hamming it up a bit myself – and then, to my surprise, Jude began playing up to me, so it was not such a drag as it might have been.

Chapter 33: Turning Turkey

Mr Bowman was extremely shocked and grieved by my story, but said though I had done wrong, the fault was not all mine. He offered to seek out N to try and make him see where his duty lay, but I refused, because clearly N has abandoned me and could never have been serious in the first place, since he was already engaged to marry someone else. But then we prayed together for guidance . . .

June, 1945

I fell asleep last night on another of those long, moralising passages from Gran's journal, this time describing what Mr Bowman said in his prayers (which obviously he must have said aloud, since she wasn't telepathic) and how grateful she was that he hadn't turned her away like her parents had.

Then she compared her lot at length to some scene in *The Pilgrim's Progress*, which apparently had a Slough of Despond, though that does seem a *bit* harsh on Slough.

Times were so different then: I still couldn't understand how Ned could have been so heartless as to abandon her.

When I let Merlin out, I saw that it hadn't snowed any more, but nor did the winter wonderland show signs of going away any time soon: it was all deep and crisp and even, as the carol says.

Jude was downstairs again soon after I was, but I don't mind if it becomes a habit, since he doesn't get in my way while I'm making my preparations for the day. In fact, it's handy having someone to ply me with cups of tea or coffee while I'm working, tend the fire and do other odd jobs around the house, though so far he's shown no sign of taking me up on the vacuuming.

Becca was down quite early too, but Jess has now been let off morning horse mucking-out duties, to her huge relief. I expect she's already in training to become nocturnal when she's a teenager.

This morning's first task had been to remove the remaining meat from the turkey carcass and put the bones on the stove to simmer for stock. Then I turned what was left – which was a surprising amount, really – into a good spicy curry to go into the freezer. A few bits of turkey found their way into Merlin, too.

I'd finished this and the kitchen was filled with the aroma of gently simmering stock and rich spices by the time Becca and Jude came back in from the stables, adding a not-unpleasant hint of warm horse and hay to the mix.

'Something smells good,' Jude said appreciatively.

'It's just stock and turkey curry for the freezer.'

'What are you doing now?' asked Becca. 'Isn't that the old mincing machine?'

'Yes, I found it in one of the drawers.' I finished screwing it down firmly on the edge of the kitchen table. 'I'm making mince for burgers – that's what we're having for dinner tonight.'

'What, you're turning my best steaks from the freezer into burgers?' demanded Jude predictably, spotting them on a plate.

'There aren't enough steaks for everyone, but minced up there *is* enough to make burgers – and they'll be delicious, you'll see,' I promised, turning the handle briskly.

327

'I have to believe you,' he said, watching me with that now-familiar quirk of the lips, 'everything else you've cooked so far has been!'

'It certainly has and Jude should offer you a permanent job,' Becca suggested with a grin.

'He couldn't afford me.'

'Yes I could, I can't imagine why you persist in assuming I'm on my uppers.' He paused on his way out, presumably to change and shave, since he was back to the Mexican bandit look. 'Can we have chips with the burgers?'

'You can have my version of them, done in a baking tin in the oven with a little olive oil and a few herbs.'

When he came back, looking about as civilised as a Yeti can get, he helped me to cook breakfast for everyone again before he went off to the studio, reminding me to come down after lunch and bring him something to eat, so clearly the pattern of our days is now going to be like this. Perhaps he just wants me on tap, in case of a sudden urge to check the pose, or something? Or then again, it may be just a cunning ruse to get his lunch delivered daily until Edwina returns to the lodge.

After breakfast Tilda got up and she, Noël and Becca decided to watch an old film on video – they seem to especially love musicals.

Jess and Guy were all for going out with the sledges again, but I think Michael would have been quite happy to carry on sitting at the kitchen table, drinking coffee and discussing recipes with me; except that Coco said that if he wasn't going out they could practise their love scenes together, and he changed his mind. In the end we all went out, though I came in earlier than the rest to make another chocolate blancmange rabbit for later, seeing as the first one hadn't just gone down well with Jess, but had also been a surprise hit with everyone else. Then I set out a nice lunch of turkey and ham pie, warm garlic bread (garlic paste and ready-to-bake baguettes from the larder) and the last of the tinned pâté.

When lunch was cleared I left for the studio with Jude's substantial picnic and the big flask of coffee.

By then Coco had got her way and she and Michael were to practise their parts for the play this afternoon – only not alone, but with Noël helpfully reading mine and Jude's parts and Jess in attendance as Props, wearing her crown.

Jude had finished making the armature and was welding bits of leaf-shaped metal together around it when I went into the studio, though he stopped and gave me a protective visor like the one he was wearing.

'Sparks aren't going to fly as far as the dais, are they?' I asked, though I noticed Merlin had taken one look at his master and retired underneath it.

'No, but the light from the torch is very bright, better to be safe than sorry,' he said, and then went back to work. As yesterday, he just seemed to want to have me around, without actually needing me.

The torch was fuelled by two different sorts of gas cylinders and I thought it all looked a bit dangerous, though he seemed to know exactly what he was doing.

'Are you *really* going to teach Jess to do that?' I asked, pouring him a cup of coffee when he finally stopped to eat his late lunch.

'Yes, why not?' He sat down on the edge of the dais next to me. 'It's safe enough if I watch her all the time – I know what I'm doing. I'd like to leave it until she comes for part of the summer holidays, though, when she'll be thirteen.'

'Does she spend most of the school holidays with Noël and Tilda?'

'It depends – her parents are away a lot. You'll have gathered that Roz and her husband Nick study wildlife and make documentaries, so Jess does end up here with Noël and Tilda quite a bit. But sometimes she gets to fly out to exotic locations, too.'

'You're her favourite uncle, she cheered up no end once you came back.'

'She's seems to have taken a shine to you, too – like Merlin, she's happiest if we are both in the same room!'

'I'm sure I was just your stand-in and you're her real security figure,' I said. 'She does seem surprisingly accepting about her parents being away so much and having to go to boarding school.'

'Actually, she loves it. It's a surprisingly old-fashioned and Enid-Blyton sort of school, where the girls can go riding and keep pets, but after thirteen they have to leave, so that will be difficult for her. It's not how I'd want to bring up *my* children if I had any, would you?' he said, and gave me a swift, sideways glance that I found impossible to interpret. 'I'd want them around, not packed off somewhere away from home.'

'Me too, I can't see the point in having children otherwise,' I agreed and we were silent for a minute. I was thinking about single motherhood, and how different it would be for me, compared to how it would have been for poor Granny – but it was still quite a daunting proposition. Good forward planning is obviously required in that situation, just as in cooking.

Goodness knows what Jude was thinking about.

When he went back to work we exchanged a few sporadic (and sometimes illuminating!) remarks, and then after a bit Merlin and I slipped out and walked home . . . Or back to Old Place, which is somehow starting to *feel* like home.

I beat Guy three times at snooker, and what with that and my having finished a whole section of the jigsaw in an absent moment earlier, when I had gone in to put more logs on the fire, he was a bit huffy.

Oddly, it didn't seem to put him off flirting with me after we'd had yet another read-through of the play scenes. And, do you know, I think Michael was right because Guy only *really* flirts with me when Jude's there! So he must think he's making Jude jealous . . . unless he's misinterpreting Jude's interest in me?

Jude had so far performed no suitable *or* unsuitable actions, apart from twirling an imaginary moustache in a faintly lasciv- ious way at me and tossing his blue velvet cloak over one shoulder. We were getting hammier and hammier in our scenes and it was driving Coco mad, especially when Michael joined in.

'You're not taking it seriously!' she practically screamed when Jude and I were overacting the scene where Orsino says he quite fancies Viola, now he knows she's a woman, only he'd like to see her in a dress. (And I'd thought Jude had been joking about that bit.)

'It's only a family entertainment, after all,' Noël said. 'Why not have fun? I expect that's what Shakespeare intended when he wrote the play.'

'I'm sure Michael would rather we did it seriously,' Coco said.

'No, I do enough serious acting the rest of the time – and really, I'd have preferred a *complete* rest from it.'

She pouted, which is not a good look on someone of four, never mind twenty-four.

'Can she act?' I asked him later, when no-one could overhear. Michael is forever taking refuge from Coco with me in the kitchen, and he's proving very helpful at peeling vegetables and hand-washing anything that won't go in the machine, though he borrows my long rubber gloves to do it. I suppose actors can't really afford to have dishpan hands.

'No, she's as wooden as a log,' he said, with an attractive grin.

'Yes, that's what I thought. Poor Coco!'

'Poor nothing! Her parents are super-rich and have spoilt her rotten, so it's about time she learnt that money can't buy you everything.'

'It's certainly not going to buy her way into acting if she's useless, is it?'

'It isn't going to buy her *me*, either,' he said grimly and I laughed.

'You'll be so glad to get away from here.'

'No, actually, apart from Coco this has been one of the best times of my life! I'm really enjoying it. What about you?'

'Me? Well, it's just work really – another busman's holiday like yours, but . . . well yes, I suppose I *am* enjoying it. Or most of it. It's strange, because I've always felt miserable at Christmas before.'

'That's not surprising, considering how many sad things have happened to you around this time of year,' he said sympathetically.

'Yes, but in retrospect, I can see hiding myself away and going into mourning at the first sound of a Christmas song and a bit of tinsel wasn't the *best* way to go about dealing with it,' I admitted. 'But I think I've now been immunised against fear of Christmas forever.'

'Or immunised *with* it, so you now *have* to celebrate it?' he suggested.

He might just have a point.

Tuesday followed much the same pattern as the preceding days, except that as soon as the sun came out you could see a thaw starting on the courtyard cobbles and the part of the drive where George and Liam had ploughed it clear.

I went down to the village with Guy, Coco and Michael mid-morning, in order to stock up on my depleted food supplies at Oriel's shop, though of course there would be no fresh fruit, bread or vegetables yet, let alone a new consignment of the squirty cream so beloved of Tilda and Jess!

We all went into the shop – I think we felt that we hadn't seen one for months.

'I hear George gave you one of his sticks for a present?' Oriel asked me, stacking up flour, baking powder and tinfoil in front of me on the counter.

'That's right and it's beautifully carved. It was very kind of him,' I replied cautiously.

'Oh yes . . . he's *kind* all right, is George,' she said jealously and I felt a sudden pang of sympathy: I found George very attractive, but I wasn't seriously interested in him and until my advent Mrs Comfort had been without a rival. What if she was in love with him?

'Yes, he's such a nice man that I wish I had a father just like him,' I said firmly and she looked pleased. A broad smile crossed her face.

'A *father*? Would you now? I suppose he *is* a lot older than you.'

He was . . . though not that old! But anyway, it had the desired result and in a flood of bonhomie she presented me with a paper bag of Jelly Babies, free.

I slipped off while the others were still debating their purchases, leaving Oriel telling Coco firmly that no, she couldn't sell her all her remaining stock of laxatives: she was rationing them to one box per customer until new deliveries arrived.

I went to check that Old Nan and Richard were all right and gave them the last slices of the turkey and ham pie and some cake I'd brought with me. Then I rang Laura from the church porch, where it was a little sheltered.

She said Ellen had called her, complaining that she couldn't get hold of me to tell me about the wonderful job she had lined up for me, starting the weekend after Twelfth Night, and how she was sure I wouldn't mind cooking for a Middle Eastern client's huge house-party at a swish London address, now I'd had a nice rest from it.

'I hope you put her right!' I said indignantly. 'I've done nothing but prepare and cook meals since I got here. And she knows I only do home-sitting until Easter.'

'I wound her up by telling her you'd settled in so well that they'd probably pay you a fabulous sum to keep you as permanent cook.'

'Funnily enough, Jude said much the same . . . and *I* said he couldn't afford me. But apparently he really is quite well off, you were right.'

'Of course he is, dimwit! His sculptures go for megabucks, I Googled him!'

'Well, I'm not going to take a permanent position here anyway. I'll just slip quietly out of their lives as soon as it thaws. And providing Jude has stopped needing me to hang around being a muse, too.'

'I think you quite like it!'

'It is sort of thrilling watching him with the torch thing welding metal together,' I admitted. 'He seems to like to have me there, though he's so absorbed he forgets he isn't alone for long stretches. Then he sort of comes to and spots me and smiles and says something.'

'Like what?'

'Oh, all kinds of things: sometimes he asks me about myself, but usually it's whatever's going through his head right at that moment. He likes his food, too, and I take him lunch down in the early afternoon, after we've had ours up at the house.'

'This all sounds as if it's becoming very intimate and cosy!' she teased me. 'Weren't a lot of artists' muses also their mistresses?'

'Maybe, but I'm hardly likely to go that route after Gran's example and with a member of the same family who let her down, am I?' I reminded her. 'I mean, even if I found big, bossy, taciturn men attractive, Jude is almost certainly my cousin.'

'But not even a *first* cousin.'

'No, his father was my grandfather's brother . . . I think,' I said, trying to work it out.

'That's not *terribly* close,' she said encouragingly. 'They can't touch you for it.'

'Oh, *Laura*! You're as bad as Jess.'

'The little girl? Is she matchmaking?'

'She's not actually that little – she's nearly thirteen and she's

334

going to be another tall Martland. But yes, she's trying to push me and Jude together at every opportunity. She adores Jude and we seem to have been cast in the role of surrogate parents, since her parents have to be away. I think she'd like it to be a permanent arrangement, but I've told her it ain't gonna happen!'

'Famous last words,' she said, and I told her she was a hopeless romantic but in this case she might as well give up.

Over at the pub I found Coco drinking vodka and soda and Guy and Michael with pints of beer, talking about football, which is not something I find of any interest. So I had coffee and chatted to Nancy instead, until eventually I had to chivvy the others out, or there would have been no lunch on the table that day.

This made it much later than usual when I took Jude's lunch down to the studio and he was inclined to be a bit narky when I told him why, but I expect hunger pains had stopped the flow of his inspiration, or something.

However, he cheered up once he'd eaten, and while he was working we had quite a few exchanges of companionable conversation – and also several equally companionable silences. I am finding the time spent in the studio strangely relaxing . . .

Jude's good mood lasted for the rest of the day, until just after our next totally unnecessary play rehearsal, when he went all morose and Neanderthal again. I think it was because he came into the kitchen when Michael and I were having a slightly cruel giggle about Coco's acting.

I'd just spoken Olivia's line, in a simpering falsetto, '"Nay come, I prithee: would'st be ruled by me?"' and Michael, as Sebastian, snatched me into his arms, crying passionately, '"Madam, I will!"'

'Excuse *me*!' Jude said and then dropped the tray of glasses down on the table so that one fell over and broke, before going back out and slamming the kitchen door, for good measure.

Michael gave me a knowing look, and I threw the oven glove

at him. Okay, I now admit Jude's jealous: but that still doesn't mean he intends making any move on me which – now I'm pretty sure he's my cousin – is just as well!

When I was cosily tucked up in bed that night and flicking through Gran's last journal to find my place, a tiny black and white photo fluttered out onto the duvet.

It was unmistakably Ned Martland – I knew those features so well now, from the family album. But he looked very young and handsome, standing by a prewar motorbike. On the back he'd written, 'All my love, your Ned.'

Obviously, he hadn't seen fit to mention that she'd only had all his love on a *temporary* basis.

I propped the picture up against my alarm clock so I could study it better, trying to puzzle out his character from his features. And that's how I fell asleep – and plummeted right into a tangle of dreams in which Jude was welding bits of old motorbike together, wearing little more than his protective visor . . .

It was pretty disturbing stuff, I can tell you. I woke up in a muck sweat.

Chapter 34: Slightly Thawed

*Mr Bowman said that had Tom not lost his life in the war
we would have been married with a family by this time and
he felt Tom would want him to help me. There was only one
way that he could think of to do that, which was to give me
the protection of his name, so he asked me to marry him right
away. He is the kindest and most generous person in the world
and, since I could see no alternative, I gratefully accepted.*

June, 1945

Jude came down early again next day, still in a deeply morose
and taciturn mood, which probably wasn't helped by my
inability to look him straight in the eye after last night's red-hot
dreams.

Then he vanished back upstairs as soon as he'd seen to the
horses with Becca, so there was no-one to ply me with tea while
I worked, or help cook the breakfast while passing the odd, quiet
remark . . . and somehow, I missed the companionable silences,
too. It's strange how quickly you get used to something . . . or
some*one*.

Becca asked me on her way through the kitchen if we'd had
a falling out. 'I don't know what's got into the boy this morning!'

'Not that I know of, though he's hardly spoken to me since
last night,' I told her, though I didn't add that I thought he might
have misinterpreted finding me in Michael's arms again, since

that might lead to a whole lot of other questions I didn't even want to think about.

He didn't come back down until Jess and everyone else apart from Tilda were eating breakfast, and even then he didn't sit down, just made himself a thick bacon sandwich and wrapped it in foil to take with him.

'I won't need you today,' he said to me curtly.

'Can I come then, Uncle Jude?' asked Jess eagerly.

'No,' he said and went out and Merlin, for once, followed him – though with a troubled look back at me. Perhaps he was reattaching himself to his master?

'I hate Uncle Jude!' Jess said bitterly.

'I thought it was me you hated, Mini-Morticia?' Guy said.

'Only when you call me Mini-Morticia, *Uncle* Guy,' she said and he winced.

'Never mind Jude, he seems a bit grumpy today for some reason,' I said. 'I don't suppose he was thinking what he was saying. Why don't you start making a snowman out at the front now the thaw seems to be starting, while there's still lots of snow? Then, when I've cleared breakfast away, I'll come and help.'

'I suppose I *could*,' she said sulkily. I hoped some of the others might offer to go with her, but Michael had decided to walk up the track and phone his ex-wife, in the hope she might have relented about letting him speak to his daughter, and no-one else seemed to be terribly keen, though Noël said he would look out later, to see how the snowman was coming along.

But when I went out after about twenty minutes, Jess was nowhere to be seen, and there was no sign of activity other than a shovel stuck upright in a patch of virgin snow and a trail of footprints leading off towards the drive.

Her wellingtons and coat were missing, so I checked the yard and paddock first, and then the house, without result. Michael had come back and he and Guy were playing snooker in the library, but when I asked they said they hadn't seen her.

338

'I entirely forgot to go and see how the snowman was doing,' Noël confessed guiltily when I went back to the sitting room to report her disappearance.

'I bet she's gone down to the studio to plague Jude into letting her mess about with the modelling clay, or something,' Becca suggested.

'Oh yes, that will be it,' Noël said, 'though of course she should have told one of us where she was going first.'

'But then we would have stopped her from disturbing Jude,' Tilda pointed out. 'You know he can be such a bear when an idea strikes him.'

'He can be a bear anyway,' Coco said. She was sitting by the jigsaw puzzle, so I expect she'd rammed a few more pieces into the wrong places. Then she drifted out, probably to feast on the last fluff-covered Fruity-Go from the bottom of her handbag, or to have an illicit cigarette in her room with the window open.

'That girl's a waste of space,' Becca said, then added that someone should go down to the studio and bring Jess back. 'But don't look at me, I think I ate too much breakfast and I want to have a doze in front of the telly. *White Christmas* is on again.'

'Oh, is it? I might join you,' Noël said.

'And I will too, if Holly doesn't need me,' Tilda agreed, though I wasn't about to suggest *she* trekked off down the drive in her high-heeled marabou and velvet slippers to look for Jess.

'I'll walk down and bring her back with me. I can give my friend another ring while I'm down there.'

'Oh, good! Tell Jess she's very naughty and bring her straight back,' Tilda said.

I set off down the snow at the edge of the drive, which was definitely not as crisp as it was yesterday. It didn't seem quite as deep, either, so perhaps was starting to subside from underneath in the way drifts sometimes do, leaving a crystal shell of harder snow on top.

It was more than possible that Jude had sent Jess straight home again, so at any minute I expected to find her dejectedly trudging towards me. And I decided I didn't really need to call Laura again either, since nothing much had happened to report since yesterday, apart from Jude's suspiciously jealous-looking hissy fit.

It occurred to me that there was no-one else in the whole world *except* Laura who genuinely cared about me any more: no family or other friends close enough. Yes, there was a circle of people I'd known from school who all met up occasionally, including Laura and my erstwhile Homebodies boss, Ellen, but that was not the same at all . . .

Laura's family were always kind, but I had distanced myself too much after Alan died and now the breach is unbridgeable. We grieved in different ways – they celebrated his life and I pretended it had never happened. But I'd changed so much in the last couple of weeks . . .

And here at Old Place I was suddenly surrounded by long-lost relatives, even though none of them realised the connection and would probably be highly embarrassed if they did ever know! Jude would immediately believe the worst, that I was out for what I could get, and think he'd been right to be suspicious all along!

Still, since I wasn't going to tell them, it didn't matter.

There was still no sign of Jess when I turned off the drive up the track through the dark pine trees, so I thought Jude must have relented and let her stay. But then, as the trees opened out onto the banks of the stream below the studio, I suddenly spotted her black-clad figure – right in the middle of the frozen mill pond, testing the ice by stamping on it with one booted foot.

It made an odd, high-pitched, singing sound and my blood ran cold: I raced for the bank, calling urgently, 'Jess! Jess! Stop that and come back here this minute!'

She half-turned, startled by my voice – and then there was a horribly loud cracking noise like a small explosion and down

340

she plummeted with a scream and a splash. For a heart-stopping moment she vanished completely . . . and then her head popped up and she was floundering among bobbing shards of ice in the bitterly cold black water.

I didn't stop to think, just ran out onto the frozen pond and flung myself face down, reaching out to her. I managed to grab first one of her cold little hands in a firm grip, and then the other, soaking myself in freezing water to the shoulders in the process.

'It's all r-right,' she said through chattering teeth, though her face looked blue-white, 'I can s-swim.'

But how long would she last in water at that temperature? And the ice beneath *me* was starting to crack too, I could hear it; but I didn't know if I was capable of sliding backwards and pulling her with me – and I certainly wasn't letting go of her.

It was just looking as if I would be joining her – though in that case I thought perhaps I would be able to boost her out onto the ice to go and fetch help – when I heard the slam of the studio door and Jude's deep voice exclaiming, 'What the *hell*?'

Perhaps my shouts had alerted Merlin: I could hear frantic muffled barking.

'I think the ice underneath me is breaking,' I called, as calmly as I could. 'But if it does, I have a plan to get Jess out and you can go for help.'

'I have a better plan: can you keep hold of her if I pull you *both* out?'

'Yes, of course, if you're quick. My hands are starting to go numb.'

He *was* quick: my ankles were seized in a grip like iron and, with a mighty heave, I was sliding back across the ice like a walrus in reverse gear, bringing the sodden dead weight of Jess with me.

'Oh God, Holly, I could have lost you both!' he said, scooping me up into a suffocating bear hug as soon as he'd landed us safely, and then just as suddenly sitting me down in the snow while he did the same to Jess. Then he said grimly, 'Jess, you know you shouldn't mess about by the water on your own, let alone go on the ice!'

'You *w-were* here, I w-wasn't on my own,' she said through chattering teeth.

'But I didn't *know* you were here – and Holly didn't know how deep the water was when she came to your rescue,' he said, pulling off her wellies and tipping out the water. 'You would have frozen to death if you hadn't got out. What if I hadn't heard you, or Holly hadn't come just when she did? How long do you think you would have lasted?'

'You w-would have heard me shouting,' Jess said. 'Or maybe I c-could have climbed back onto the ice.'

'No chance – and Holly would have been in there with you in another few minutes, freezing to death.'

'Never mind all that now, she's going to get pneumonia if she carries on sitting there, soaked to the skin,' I told him.

'*You're* pretty wet and cold too,' he said, frowning at me. 'I'll just switch off things in the studio and get Merlin, then we'll have to run all the way up to the house, there's nothing else for it.'

'*Run?*' I repeated incredulously, because I was starting to feel limp and shaky and as if I'd like a nice lie down in the soft snow.

'It'll warm you up,' he said, then vanished into the studio and came back a minute later with Merlin, who washed our faces with a warm tongue in an excess of relief.

Jude rammed Jess's wellies back on, hauled us both to our feet, and forcibly propelled us back towards the house at a shambling run, slipping and sliding through the snow, only his firm grip on our arms keeping us upright.

I expect it looked quite comic, even if it didn't feel like it.

Luckily Becca saw us coming from the morning-room window and deduced that something was wrong. She capably took charge of Jess, whisking her off for a hot bath.

'And you too,' Jude said to me, divesting me of my boots and wet anorak in the warm kitchen as if I was a helpless toddler . . . which was actually about what I felt like.

'Oh, I'm all right,' I protested, though I was shaking with cold and shock. 'I'll just go and change.'

'No, you won't – you'll have a hot bath too, I'll go and run it for you now,' he insisted. 'Come on, you can get the rest of your things off while I'm running it.'

My fingers were so frozen I had trouble getting out of my jeans, but I managed it and then when I got in the hot bath I got pins and needles as the circulation returned, which was *agony*.

Once that wore off my body felt heavy and limp, even though my mind was churning with painful thoughts: the whole experience had shocked me to the core in more ways than one. Not only might Jess and I have died (though I was still pretty sure I could have got Jess out, if I'd fallen in the water), but it had brought back all the trauma of Alan's death, too.

But I couldn't stay in there forever and Jude must have heard the water running out, because there was a cup of hot, sweet tea laced with whisky on my bedside table when I emerged . . . right next to the photo of Ned I'd left propped up there, though since it seemed to have fallen on its face, I hoped he hadn't noticed.

The tea was disgusting but I drank it anyway, in case he took it into his head to check, which would be just like him. I could feel the unaccustomed whisky thawing some of the internal chill.

When I finally went back down to the kitchen, in one of my warm, comfortable tunic jumpers and dry jeans, Jude was there waiting for me and made me more tea, insisting I sit down next to the Aga.

'But not six spoons of sugar in it this time, or whisky!' I protested weakly.

'Sugar's good for shock and I was worried it might have caused you some lasting harm . . . but maybe I *shouldn't* have put whisky in it?' he added, sounding worried.

'No, I – I think in a way it might have done me good.'

'What is it?' he asked, turning with the mug in his hand and getting a good look at my face. 'You're not feeling *ill*, are you?'

'N-no, I'm fine. It's not that – it's just that my husband, Alan . . . that's how *he* was killed, running onto a frozen lake to save a dog that had fallen through the ice . . . Only it was really deep and he wasn't much of a swimmer, so he died and . . . well, I've only just realised that he couldn't help it!'

The words poured unstoppably out of me and a rush of tears filled my eyes, blinding me. 'I've been so angry with him all these years for being such a fool – leaving me alone the way he did, just to rescue a d-dog – and I would have done exactly the same for Merlin, or any other living creature, let alone Jess!'

And then I was crying in earnest and Jude put down the mug and came and pulled me up into a warm, comforting, enveloping embrace against his broad chest, patting my back with a large and surprisingly gentle hand as I cried.

'He couldn't *help* it!' I sobbed into his shoulder, in a wimpy way I would normally deplore. 'He *couldn't* help it!'

'No, he'd have had an adrenaline rush and his impulses would have taken over on the spur of the moment, just as yours did – and thank goodness you were there, because I might not have heard Jess and I don't think she could have got out alone – she'd have died. And you risked your own life to save her, so I could have lost you *both*.'

I could have pointed out that he'd never had me in the first place, but I was feeling too limply acquiescent and in need of comfort. I fished out my handkerchief, mopped my eyes and blew my nose.

'Feeling better now?' he asked, then as I looked up to reply, that wonderful fleeting smile of his suddenly appeared . . .

And then, I'm not sure how, my arms were around him, too,

and we were kissing as if we would never stop . . . Until he suddenly wrenched his mouth from mine and held me at arm's length.

'I'm so sorry, Holly! I shouldn't have taken advantage of you, when you were so shocked . . . but that took me by surprise too – I really didn't intend to kiss you.'

'It's all right, it doesn't matter – forget it,' I said shakily, recalling all the reasons why that very passionate kiss shouldn't have happened between us. 'I think it must have been the whisky – I'm not used to it.'

'Was it just the whisky, though? I got the feeling you wanted to kiss me as much as I wanted to kiss you,' he said and our eyes, inches apart, met and held for a long moment.

I looked away first. 'Perhaps . . . but it was just a physical thing.'

'Was it, Holly?' he said quietly. 'I think we need to talk when you're feeling better . . . but first, there's something I really need to ask you right now—' he began.

But whatever it was, it would have to wait, because just at that moment Becca popped her head through the door to tell us that Jess seemed to be no worse for her icy plunge and was tucked up under a blanket in front of the sitting-room fire with Tilda, reading a book.

'Feeling okay now?' Becca asked me kindly. 'Jude looking after you?'

'Yes, I'm fine, thank you,' I said, though I knew my eyes must be red, a dead giveaway. 'I'd better do something about lunch, because it's practically dinner time and everyone must be starving.'

'I'll do that,' Jude said.

'No, I can manage.'

'Then manage *me*: you sit next to the Aga and boss me about – you're good at that.'

'It takes one to know one,' I snapped back and he grinned.

345

'There you are, you're feeling better already!'

I gave in and sat down – by now the whisky seemed to have gone to my legs anyway. 'It was only going to be Gentleman's Relish sandwiches and cups of soup, followed by mincemeat flapjacks or the last of the mince pies – I took those out of the freezer earlier.'

'I think even *I* can manage that. And actually, I'm not a *totally* hopeless cook, whatever you might think.'

'Don't forget that I've seen the extent of your ready meal supplies in the freezer.'

We were surprisingly amicable in our bickering, now that the awkwardness of an embrace which had taken both of us by surprise had worn off. But though we might have acknowledged a mutual physical attraction, I expect he was now remembering all the reasons why taking it any further would be a really bad idea, just as I was.

I wondered what on earth he had been going to ask me when Becca came in: maybe if I was a secret pretender to the throne of Old Place?

I felt absolutely fine later and insisted on cooking dinner myself, though I ended up with Michael and Jude, in slightly wary alliance, as assistants. Tilda and Jess made another potato-hedgehog starter with cheese and small pickled onions on cocktail sticks.

But at least Jess and I were excused the final play rehearsal and could loll about watching the others, until ordered off early to bed with hot water bottles by Jude. When I protested that I had things to do in the kitchen first, he said there was nothing that couldn't keep until the morning and also that he was perfectly capable of locking up and all the rest of it himself, pointing out that he had managed to survive perfectly well before my arrival, so I gave in.

He'd been giving me very searching looks all evening, but since they weren't dissimilar to the ones he sent my way when he was drawing me, he was probably just sizing me up for another sculpture: given my watery performance, a Little Mermaid, perhaps?

I was quite happy to go off to bed, really, because I was starting to feel exhausted and strangely light-headed, though calm in an odd sort of way: I suppose the whole experience on the ice had been a very cathartic one, when I came to think about it.

Now I'd accepted that Alan couldn't help the actions that had led to his death, I could finally forgive him, letting go of the anger that had burdened me for the last eight years and enabling me to remember him, quite simply, with love.

And Gran? According to her journal, she seemed to have determined to do much the same:

Yesterday I packed my bags and departed from my lodgings without fuss, and was married that afternoon by special licence, a friend of my husband's in a nearby town officiating. It all seemed like a strange dream, but I now mean to put out of my head all memories of what went before, and make Joseph the best possible wife, even though our relationship will always be only that of loving friends.

June, 1945

Chapter 35: Acted Out

Joseph put a newspaper into my hand this morning, pointing to the report of the death of my lover in a motorbike accident. Then he left me. Later, we prayed together for N. I am so sorry for his family and for his fiancée, if she truly loved him. That chapter of my life is now closed . . . apart from the child I carry.

June, 1945

Jude was downstairs early and back to being quietly helpful, though there was still some awkwardness between us – in my case largely because that passionate kiss had featured largely and rather feverishly in my dreams last night. I knew *he* was thinking about it too – our eyes kept meeting and then we'd both immediately look away.

I felt absolutely fine, with no ill after-effects, as I assured him when he asked, accompanying the question with one of those searching stares from his deep-set dark eyes.

I was glad that we seemed to be friends again and he seemed cheerful enough (probably, in the light of day, deeply relieved that I hadn't taken the kiss seriously!).

He even fell in with Coco's suggestion that we have a quick run-through of our play scenes after breakfast, before he went to the studio, since it was New Year's Eve (which, what with everything else happening, I had managed to forget!) and the final performance was to be later today, in front of an invited audience of Old Nan and Richard.

We played our *Twelfth Night* roles straight and serious, no hamming this time, and then off Jude went, commanding me to bring his lunch to the studio later, so we were back to normal again – or what passed for it.

'Okay,' I agreed, 'but I won't be able to stay long because I've got way too much to do. I want to turn the ham bone into pea and ham soup for tomorrow, for a start, and then I thought I might make some soda bread.'

'Sounds good to me,' he said. 'By the way, Guy, one of us will need to drive down and pick up Old Nan and Richard this afternoon.'

'I'll do that if you like, then,' he offered and then gave me a glinting, flirtatious smile. 'Holly can come with me.'

'Holly will be too busy cooking dinner for eleven people,' I replied pointedly.

'We've discussed the menu: it's all very straightforward,' Tilda said. 'Smoked mackerel mousse on toast triangles – my very own recipe – roast lamb with rosemary and then treacle tart and custard.'

'Lovely,' Becca said. 'I'm not going to want to go home when the roads have thawed. Maybe I could ask Richard to pray for more snow?'

Merlin had stayed with me this morning, but accompanied me down to the studio when I took Jude's lunch.

He was welding, totally absorbed in his work, so I put on the spare visor and sat in my usual place on the dais to watch him until he finally switched off the torch.

'It's coming along, don't you think?' he asked, examining his handiwork critically. Already, what had started out looking like a few linked metal leaves had begun to elongate and swirl into the interlinked forms of horse and woman. It was turning out a bit like one of the maquettes he'd made, so I could see roughly where it was heading.

'Yes, and I believe you now when you say you get paid good money for your sculptures,' I teased him and he grinned.

'You're very good at dampening my pretensions, but my work is much in demand, I'll have you know! "Some are born great, some achieve greatness and some have greatness thrust upon them."'

'Is that from the play? I don't remember that bit.'

'It's in one of the scenes we're not doing,' he said, sitting down next to me. Merlin came out from under the dais and nudged his way between us, leaning his weight affectionately against Jude's shoulder; though that might have been just a keen interest in the sandwiches.

Jude was silent while he ate, his mind clearly on his work rather than anything else, but when he'd finished and I was packing the remains back into the basket, he suddenly said, 'Holly, we need to talk about yesterday, when I—'

'Oh, let's forget all that,' I said brightly. 'We'd both had a shock and it makes you do the strangest things. I feel *much* better now.'

'Yes, but Holly, you—'

I picked up the basket and headed for the door. 'I must go – see you later. I'll be so glad to get this wretched play over with!'

The New Year's Eve audience, well primed by a good roast lamb dinner and a drop or two of sherry, were prepared to watch three rank amateurs and one professional actor massacre scenes from the Bard with equanimity.

In fact, *I* wished I could have watched it instead of acted in it, because it must have been hilariously funny, what with me spending most of the time looking like a waif in Jude's enormous greatcoat, Coco a skeletal Bride of Frankenstein and Jude, resigned but unable to resist slightly hamming it up, in his blue velvet cloak and imaginary moustache.

Michael played it straight, but gave a muted performance, probably to stop the rest of us looking quite so awful: but if so, it didn't really work, especially in the parts that hinged on Sebastian and Viola looking identical: 'An apple, cleft in two, is not more twin than these two creatures: which is Sebastian?'

You couldn't have found two people more *unlike* than Michael and me if you tried, so I couldn't blame the snort of laughter that came from Guy's corner of the room at that point.

However, the rest of the audience applauded each scene enthusiastically, though that might have had something to do with the sherry.

Michael spoke his final lines very well, considering he had the distraction of Coco draped adoringly around him by this point, and then it was Jude's turn to declare his love for me – such as it was:

'Cesario, come – for so you shall be, while you are a man; but, when in other habits you are seen, Orsino's mistress and his fancy's queen.'

To my mind, that line's about as romantic as Prince Charles saying, when asked if he was in love with Diana, 'Yes – whatever *love* means,' even if Jude did accompany the words with a look of smouldering promise. I think I may have underestimated his acting abilities as well as his artistic ones.

There was another round of applause and Old Nan dabbed her eyes with a pink tissue and said sentimentally that it was terribly moving and she loved a happy ending. 'And I'll knit you and Jude a nice Afghan for your wedding present,' she declared, beaming at us.

'We're not really getting married, it was just in the play, Nan,' I explained.

'I don't hold with all this living together out of wedlock,' she said severely. 'Don't think you're getting my Afghan until you tie the knot with this poor lass, Jude Martland!'

'All right, Nan,' he said. 'I'll bear that in mind.'

'Interesting play, isn't it?' the vicar said, allowing Guy to refill his sherry glass. 'Nothing is what it seems right until the end and it must have been even more confusing in Shakespeare's day, when the female parts were played by boys.'

'Yes, so a boy was playing a girl, pretending to be a boy!'

'That's right. It all harks back to mumming and ancient pagan cross-dressing fertility rituals, like the Man-Woman character at the Revels, as you will see.'

'If I'm still here,' I said. 'It does seem to be slowly thawing, so I might have left.'

'Of course you'll be here,' Old Nan snapped tetchily, waking suddenly from a half-doze in time to catch this. 'Where else would you be?'

Quite possibly in a smart house in London cooking falafels, if Ellen got her way, I thought!

Guy ran Old Nan and Richard home again soon after that. To my surprise, no-one seemed interested in staying up until midnight to see the New Year in since, as Noël explained when I asked, Twelfth Night had always been Little Mumming's night of transition from the old year to the new, and that was not likely ever to change.

Everyone went to bed except Jude, who followed me into the kitchen where I was about to wash the sherry glasses.

I thought he was going to let Merlin out and take a last look at the horses, but instead he came and turned me round by the shoulders, staring down at me as if my face was a slightly untrustworthy map he was trying to read, to find a destination he was not sure he wanted to reach.

'What's the matter?' I asked uneasily.

'It's what Richard was saying: because *you're* not really who you say you are either, are you, Holly?'

'What do you mean? Of course I'm Holly Brown!' I hedged.

'Oh, I'm sure that's your *name*, but I've suspected practically from the first moment I set eyes on you that you were related to us, probably on the wrong side of the blanket. Given Ned's nature and the way you seemed to steer the conversation onto him at every opportunity, he seemed the likeliest candidate. Then when I saw that photograph of him on your bedside table, it all clicked into place and I realised that your grandmother must have been the—'

'"Little mill girl" Noël told us about, that Ned got into trouble?' I finished bitterly. 'Yes, she was, but she wasn't a mill girl, she was a nurse.'

'I'm *so* sorry,' he apologised, though it was hardly *his* fault. 'What happened to her?'

'It's all in her diaries, the ones I've been reading since I got here – how he seduced her and then, when she got pregnant, dumped her and ran off home. She found out he'd been engaged to someone else all the time,' I told him, 'and then her parents disowned her too, and she was so desperate she even thought about taking her own life.'

'Oh, God, that's terrible!' he said.

'Yes, but then the local Strange Baptist minister came to her rescue and married her – my grandfather.'

He ran a distracted hand through his dark hair, so that it stood on end. 'I had no idea! It doesn't reflect very well on my Uncle Ned – or my family – does it?'

'No, nobody seemed to care what happened to her.'

'Did she ever know he'd been killed?'

'Yes, but only because she saw it in the local newspaper. It must have been a horrible way to find out.'

'The family really forgot about her and the baby, they never offered her any money for support? I find that so hard to believe!'

'So far as I've got in the journal, she'd heard nothing from them – and anyway, she wouldn't have wanted their money even if she hadn't married my grandfather. And if you think *I* came here hoping to ingratiate myself with the family to get some

353

kind of financial gain out of the connection, then you're *quite* wrong!' I added indignantly.

'The thought *did* cross my mind at first,' he admitted, 'but not for long. I mean, half the time you didn't even seem to like us, especially Guy – which was when I twigged that he was supposed to be just like Ned and started to put two and two together.'

'Believe it or not, I had no idea I was related to you, until I started to read Gran's diaries.'

'You mean, you'd never even heard of the Martlands before?'

'Not until a couple of weeks before I came here.' I described Gran's last words. 'Then Ellen told me the name of the family she wanted me to house-sit for and I thought it was just one of those strange coincidences: there seemed little chance your Martlands could have any connection to my gran. In fact, I was more than half-expecting the lost love of her life to have been one of the doctors at the hospital!'

'I can see why you feel bitter about what happened, but Ned always sounded weak rather than bad, so perhaps if he hadn't been killed, he *would* have supported her?' he suggested.

'I don't think so and nor did Gran, or she wouldn't have felt so abandoned that she thought of killing herself.'

'Well, thank God she didn't,' he said and then added, frowning, 'and I suppose this makes us cousins of a kind, though *not* first cousins, which is probably just as well . . .'

His hands on my shoulders tightened their grip and, seeing his intent, I said hastily, 'Too close for kissing.'

'Have you never heard of kissing cousins?' he said, raising one eyebrow and giving me that brief, intimate and spine-sapping smile.

'I don't think the saying means *that* kind of kissing,' I said, resolutely releasing myself and stepping back. 'We're still too close for that, even if our connection is illegitimate – and anyway, I'm not going to go the way of my grandmother, falling for a Martland!'

'But I'm not remotely like my Uncle Ned!' he said, looking slightly hurt. 'And I don't think the relationship is close enough to matter – if we don't want it to.'

'Look, Jude, there may be a bit of physical attraction between us, but you're really not my type, and I'm *certainly* not yours, so how closely related we are isn't ever going to be an issue. And no-one else needs to know about this: in a couple of days I'll be gone as if I was never here.'

'Yes they do – Noël needs to know,' he said stubbornly. 'He'll be delighted and so will Tilda and Becca, not to mention Jess, because they're fond of you already. I don't think you'll manage to escape us so easily, after that.'

'You're not really going to tell him!'

'Just watch me!' he said, then looked down at me thoughtfully and asked quietly: 'Is there anything else you'd like to tell me about, Holly . . . in confidence?'

'No, nothing at all!' I snapped and he seemed strangely disappointed.

What on earth else can he have expected me to confess to? Being the lost heir of the Romanovs, perhaps?

I escaped to bed after that, where I tried to distract myself from the scene in the kitchen by reading a bit more of the journal, though I wasn't expecting any more revelations: I knew the outcome.

Granny seemed to have stoically thrown herself into the role of minister's wife and if there was some talk in the congregation about the sudden wedding and the disparity in their ages, they seemed to have accepted it.

I was just nodding over another long, long passage about Gran's undeserved good fortune and the mercy of God when I heard a loud yell from Michael's room next door, followed by a loud crash and a more feminine scream and exclamations.

I leapt out of bed and rushed onto the landing and then

paused with my hand on the doorknob to his room, suddenly wondering if I was interrupting something I shouldn't be!

Jude, who was closest, arrived from the other direction and I could see from his expression he'd got the same idea – and that he thought I was coming *out* of Michael's room, not going in!

'Sorry,' he said abruptly. 'I thought I heard a scream.'

'You did, but it wasn't me.'

Michael's door swung open and Coco stormed out, the near-transparent folds of her negligee clutched around her.

'Forget it!' she said viciously over one shoulder.

'Coco?' I heard Michael say, before she slammed the door behind her, cutting him off.

'What?' she said, catching sight of us. 'Look, I was sleepwalking, all right?' And she brushed past Jude and vanished.

He gave me one of his more unfathomable looks and followed her.

Chapter 36: Piked

Joseph asked that he might be moved to a different chapel, since Ormskirk had so many sad memories now and it would give us a chance to start afresh. At my request, he is reading The Pilgrim's Progress *to me in the evenings while I am knitting or sewing, so that my head, heart and hands are all occupied.*

June, 1945

When Jude came down this morning he didn't mention the Coco episode – and neither did I. I was hoping that, on reflection, he would keep his discovery about who I really was to himself, too.

When he came back in from the stables I was just making a stuffing for the pike, to an old English recipe I'd found in one of my books. I'd never cooked one before, but waste not, want not. I'd run out of sausage meat for the stuffing, but had defrosted some of the last of the excellent pork sausages from the freezer and removed the contents, which would do just as well.

Jude must have been warm from mucking out, because he pulled his jumper off and the T-shirt underneath came with it . . . I was still staring at him, slightly mesmerised by the play of muscles across his broad back, when he turned and caught me.

'The thaw seems to have well and truly set in,' I said quickly, concentrating my attention back on what I was doing, though when I risked another glance up he was giving me that intent look from his deep-set eyes under a furrowed brow again, the slightly suspicious one that should have been dispelled now he knew about Gran.

'Holly, I hope you'll remember what I said last night: if you want to confide in someone, you can trust me.'

'Mmm . . .' I said, totally puzzled. Confide *what*, exactly? He already knew all my secrets – even, now, that I fancied him!

'What on earth *is* that you're stuffing?' he asked in a totally different voice.

'It's a pike Becca caught last year and shoved into the bottom of your freezer. I strongly believe that if you kill living creatures, then you should eat them. So we are.'

'I didn't even know it was in there!'

'That's because you never delve deeper than the surface layer of convenience foods.'

'True. By the way, I'll be back for lunch today,' he said, which was a surprise. Perhaps inspiration had flagged?

After breakfast I went out in the snow again with Guy, Jess and Michael, because as Jess pointed out, it might not be around much longer. She was right, too, because it was now subsiding faster than an exuberant soufflé that had overreached itself.

Coco had come down late and in a mood of silent sulkiness, which I put down to a combination of post-performance boredom and the result of whatever happened – or didn't happen – between her and Michael last night. She was certainly giving him the cold shoulder.

Michael snatched a moment to unburden himself while we were climbing to the top of the paddock with the sledges. 'Coco came to my room last night!'

'Yes, I know – and so does Jude. We both heard the screams and yells and came out onto the landing. She said she was sleepwalking!'

'Sleepwalking nothing!' he replied. 'One minute I was fast

asleep, and the next she'd tossed the duvet off and jumped on me, stark naked!'

'No!' I gasped. 'That was pretty brazen.'

'So I yelled – as you do, if someone jumps on you when you're asleep – and automatically threw her off. She landed on the floor and screamed . . . and that really woke me up so I realised what was happening and tried to calm her down.'

'I don't think it worked, Michael!'

'No, especially when she came on to me again and I made it clear I didn't fancy her in the least,' he said ruefully.

'I expect that would make her angry,' I agreed. 'Not many men would have turned her down!'

'Perhaps not . . .' He paused and glanced at me, 'but the thing is, Holly – well, I'm gay,' he confessed. 'That's really why my marriage broke up.'

'Really? Yes, I suppose that would make a bit of an irreconcilable difficulty,' I said, surprised, and he laughed.

We'd reached the top of the paddock now and I put down my sledge. 'But if you don't mind my asking, Michael, why did you get married in the first place?'

'Debbie knew I was gay because she was my best friend and we shared a flat – but then she suddenly changed and thought she could change me, too. I wanted a family, so I think I let her persuade me it would work and we got married and had our little girl.' He smiled sadly. 'For a while I thought we might be able to make a go of it. But then she fell for someone else – and so did I. And I don't know why I'm telling you all this,' he added, sounding surprised. 'My being gay is still a bit of a secret.'

'I expect you haven't really talked it over with anyone before, that's why. And of course I won't mention it to anyone else, but why does your being gay have to be a secret?'

'I usually get the romantic lead roles and I just don't feel audiences would take me seriously if they knew I was openly gay, even though I'm sure most people in the business have a good idea.' He ran a hand through his light brown hair, which ruffled attractively, and smiled ruefully. 'I don't know! I'm just certain that I'm not ready to step *right* out of the closet yet.'

'I understand – and anyway, your private life should be just that. But poor Coco!'

'Poor me, you mean!'

'She's mad with you, though I'd have thought she'd still want to keep on your right side, because of getting into acting.'

'Yes, but she isn't very bright, is she?' He sighed. 'I think she's going to be a real pain now that the play's done and I've turned her down – but maybe with this thaw they'll clear the roads soon?'

'And then we can *all* go home,' I agreed briskly and he gave me a look.

'Not quite *all* of us, I don't think, if Jude has anything to do with it!'

I felt my face going slightly pink. 'If you mean you think there's something going on between Jude and me, then you are quite wrong!'

'No, I'm not: the way you keep catching each other's eye is a dead giveaway, not to mention all those cosy hours alone in his studio, when he made it quite plain he didn't want any other visitors. I can't imagine why you're both in denial.'

'Don't be silly!'

'I'm serious! In fact, I think I'm in imminent danger of having my nose punched if he catches me in anything even *remotely* resembling a compromising situation with you again.'

I remembered Jude's expression of black rage when he'd briefly thought I was coming out of Michael's room last night and shivered. 'There may be a little physical attraction between us—'

'Like the way the air crackles between you whenever you're together?' he said helpfully.

'—but that's all,' I finished. 'In fact, he more or less told me the other day that losing his wife made him never want to fall in love again – and I feel exactly the same way. It hurts too much when you lose them.'

'Aren't you two ever coming down?' called Guy from the bottom of the hill and I climbed onto the red sledge and pushed myself off with such force that I shot down past the astonished horses and nearly went into the fence at the bottom.

I'd made the pea and ham soup and fresh soda bread, so we had that for lunch along with cheese, pickles and chutney. My stocks of staples like cheese and butter were dwindling rapidly, so really it was just as well that the thaw *had* set in.

Despite my coaxing, Coco refused to come into the kitchen with us and eat anything, saying she must have put on pounds over Christmas because of my meanness and she needed to get back in shape for her next modelling assignment, so apart from Michael it was just family . . . of which I was a member, even if it appeared that Jude had thought better of telling the others.

But, hard on the heels of that thought, he suddenly looked around the kitchen table and announced, 'There's something I feel it's important you all know, though Holly doesn't want me to tell you.'

'You're getting married – hurray!' cried Jess and his sallow skin flushed a bit.

'No, it's not that sort of thing, Jess,' he said. 'I'm not starting to announce my engagement on an annual basis. In fact, perhaps you should go somewhere else while we discuss this – it's very personal to Holly.'

'Oh no – I'll be quiet, I promise!'

'If you're going to tell everyone, you might as well include Jess,' I said resignedly.

'Okay,' he agreed. 'Well, Holly's been reading through her gran's diaries while she's been here and discovered that she's the granddaughter of Ned Martland.'

'What, Holly's grandmother is the mill girl Ned—' began Noël, astounded, then stopped suddenly.

'Seduced and abandoned, yes,' I agreed, 'though actually, she nursed him back to health, she wasn't a mill girl.'

'Oh dear,' Tilda said, rather inadequately.

'Understatement of the year, Tilda,' said Becca.

'So you can see why she was a bit reluctant to mention it and claim relationship with a family like ours,' Jude said.

'Not that I blame you for what Ned Martland did,' I said quickly, though of course sometimes I *had* a bit . . .

'I certainly didn't intend to sound disparaging about your grandmother,' Noël apologised. 'And in fact, I am extremely happy to meet you at last, m'dear!' He exchanged a meaningful look with Tilda and continued, 'Many's the time I've said to Tilda that I wished I could have found Ned's girl after he was killed.'

'Then why didn't you?' I asked bluntly.

'Well, the thing is, there was a dreadful fuss when he told my parents about her and the baby, especially since he was engaged to the daughter of Lord Lennerton at the time, who was going to give him a job so he could work his way up to the board. It looked like he was finally about to settle down, so our parents were pleased – which made finding out about your grandmother even more of a blow.'

'But he knuckled down and did what they wanted?'

'Not exactly. We didn't know much about his girl, except that she was from a working-class background – not even her name. But the thing is, my brother Alex and I could see Ned had genuinely fallen in love with her, and we thought he should marry her anyway, not pay her off like our parents wanted him to do.'

'Did he *really* love her?'

'Oh yes, I'm sure he did, though he didn't realise it until he came home and began to miss her. But he was weak-willed so

362

it took him weeks of dithering before he made his mind up and wrote to his fiancée to break it off. Then he went to tell your grandmother that he wanted to marry her.'

'He actually *did*? But he can't have seen her, because she would have said so! She did see the notice of his death in the paper, but she was married to my grandfather by then.'

'He probably found out that she had married someone else, then, and was killed on the way back home. I suppose we will never know precisely what happened. But after that, there seemed no way of finding her.'

'I think we all expected her to turn up,' Becca said. 'Our parents would have felt duty-bound to support her and her child, if she had.'

'I've felt so guilty all these years that she didn't ask for help – and also that it was my doing in persuading him to go back to her, that made Ned take the road that day and led to his death,' Noël said sadly.

'But you didn't know that would be the outcome, and at least he was doing the right thing,' Becca pointed out.

'If he'd discovered she'd married someone else, perhaps he was too upset to concentrate on the way back and that might have caused the accident?' I suggested, softening towards Ned a fraction.

'But he was fast and reckless on that motorbike anyway, wasn't he?' Jude said. 'You've always told me that.'

'And *this* is the uncle you all keep telling me *I'm* like!' said Guy rather bitterly. 'Weak, vacillating . . .'

'Actually, you aren't quite *that* bad, dear,' Tilda allowed.

'Thanks!'

'Well, the past is all water under the bridge now,' Noël said. 'I hope your grandmother was happy in her marriage?'

'Grandpa was the father of her childhood sweetheart, a Strange Baptist minister. I only just remember him, but he was a lovely, sweet-natured man – everyone loved him.'

'Thank God,' Noël said sincerely. He did look as if a burden had been lifted from his shoulders and Tilda, next to him, patted his hand. 'You feel things too much, Noël.'

'Thank you for telling me all that, though,' I said. 'I do feel so much better about Ned now I understand that he did really love her, in his way. And she never forgot him, you know: just before she died she said his name and smiled, and I'm sure she could see him in the room.'

Jess, who'd been obediently silent throughout, now piped up, 'Does that make you my auntie, even if you *don't* marry Uncle Jude, Holly?'

'I suppose I am, in a distant sort of way,' I agreed. 'But there'd be no question of me marrying Jude even if we weren't cousins, so it's all academic.'

'But people do marry their cousins, don't they?' she insisted, but fortunately by then Noël, Becca, Tilda and even Guy had gathered around me to warmly welcome me into the family, the missing Martland come home: a bit like the one ewe-lamb that was lost in the parable Gran used to tell me when I was little.

Jude went off down to the studio and took Jess with him, though she had to promise not to go anywhere near him while he was welding. I hoped he would tell her to drop the whole matchmaking idea, because if he did have any designs on me, they were not likely to be marital but more of the quick-fling variety. He'd made it clear he was not looking for anything more . . . and so had I, come to that.

Still, feeling a flush of sudden warmth towards the world, I made Coco an egg white omelette, which looked vile, and took it through to her with a glass of fizzy water. She was in the morning room huddled miserably in front of the TV, though due to a burst of snowy interference it was hard to tell what she was watching. She actually thanked me for the omelette, though she did say that fizzy mineral water made you fat.

'Spoil yourself,' I said encouragingly, leaving her to it while I went back to the kitchen to study my recipes and whip up a dessert to follow tonight's fatted calf – or fatted pike, in this case.

Chapter 37: Bumps

We have moved to Merchester and today Hilda visited us here for the first time and confessed that N came to look for me on the day of his accident, meaning to ask me to marry him, but she and Pearl told him I had already married someone else . . . They had not wanted to cause me further pain but, after discussing it, thought now that it was important that I knew this.

August, 1945

The drive is now clear of snow, even if it is still banked up on either side of it, and right after breakfast there was a loud tooting of horns and we all poured out to see that Liam and Ben had towed Coco's sports car up to the door.

It was distinctly battered around the rear bumper and they'd gaffer-taped one end of the registration plate to the back to stop it completely falling off.

'Oh my God,' Coco exclaimed, clutching a hastily-snatched waxed coat (how the mighty are fallen!) around her thin shoulders. 'My poor car!'

'Better have it looked at by the garage in Great Mumming, before trying to drive it anywhere very far,' advised Liam.

'Yes, these low sports cars are useless on snow anyway and even if you made it to the motorway, you'd be blinded by spray from other vehicles,' Ben said critically. Then he spotted a bashful Jess and said kindly, 'Hello, we've heard you've taken to swimming in ice holes like they do in Sweden and places!'

She blushed. 'I just fell in. I thought it was completely frozen, but the bit right in the middle wasn't.'

'Done it myself years ago, when we were skating on it,' Ben admitted. 'Do you remember, Liam? Soaked me to the skin and I went home freezing.'

Jess brightened. 'Oh, did you?'

'She still wasn't supposed to be down near the river on her own,' Jude pointed out.

'Well, I don't expect she'll do it again – I didn't,' Ben said.

'How are the roads doing?' asked Jude.

'I don't expect there's any sign of the main one being cleared and my car dug out?' Michael asked hopefully. 'Not that I'm in a hurry to get away, but I don't want to be a burden on you for longer than I can help it, Jude – you've been very kind.'

'*I'm* in a hurry,' Coco said. 'I'm *desperate* to get out of here!'

'We saw the snowplough go through on the Great Mumming road earlier, but no traffic's been through yet. Maybe later today,' Liam said. 'But you can't get down to it anyway yet, because the hill below Weasel Pot is too bad. It might be all right tomorrow, if it keeps thawing like this.'

'Me and Dad walked down first thing and the end of Weasel Pot Lane is one big snowdrift, though it's sinking. You can see the red roof of your car,' Ben added consolingly to Michael, 'so the snowplough didn't run into it by mistake. Often happens, that does.'

'Oh . . . that's good,' Michael said nervously. 'Thank goodness I didn't buy a white car – and I'll certainly never follow SatNav again!'

367

'If the Three Wise Men had had SatNav, goodness knows where they would have ended up,' agreed Noël, who had delayed coming out long enough to wrap himself in his overcoat, deerstalker hat with flaps and scarf.

'If there's a bit more of a thaw tomorrow, we could go down and dig your car right out,' suggested Guy. 'Then it'll be even easier to spot. It's pulled off the road, isn't it?'

'Yes, Jude helped me push it onto the verge . . . or where we thought the verge was, because it was a bit hard to tell at the time.'

'I could come back to London in your car with you when it's clear, couldn't I?' Coco suggested, fluttering her false eyelashes at Michael hopefully, his rebuff clearly forgotten in her eagerness to get away. 'The AA can rescue mine later.'

'I'm going to see the friends I was to visit first – and actually, I'd thought of finding somewhere local to stay so I could watch the Twelfth Night Revels: I've heard so much about them now that I can't bear to leave without being there. Though I won't mention it when I leave, of course.'

'Good man!' Noël said.

'You're one of us,' Becca agreed.

'And naturally you're welcome to stay here for it,' Jude said, though not altogether enthusiastically.

Coco was pouting. '*I* don't want to stay for some stupid Morris dancing that no-one cares about anyway. Guy, you'll just have to drive me home, that's all there is to it. Then I never want to see you ever again.'

'*I'm* not leaving before Twelfth Night either,' Guy said.

'But last year we did!'

'Yes, but that was because I'd just had a punch-up with Jude. I don't have to get back to work until afterwards, so I might as well stay.'

'I think you're all mad – I just want to get home!' she wailed.

'I do think that the least you can do is take Coco back home,

Guy,' Jude said. 'It's your fault she got stuck here after all, and anyway, you never take part in the Revels.'

Guy raised a quizzical dark eyebrow at his brother. 'Are you trying to get rid of me?'

'I certainly feel my days have been enlivened by your company for long enough.'

'We could dig *my* car out tomorrow too, it's sitting in a snow-drift behind the house,' I suggested.

'Why? *You're* not going anywhere yet,' Jude snapped at me rudely, then brushed past into the house, only to reappear a few minutes later ready to go down to the studio. 'I'll expect you after lunch,' he tossed at me in passing.

'Holly is Jude's muse,' Becca explained to the boys, who looked blank.

'*And* she's a distant cousin,' added Noël. 'Isn't that lovely? One of the family.'

'Everyone'd guessed that already,' Liam said.

I did go down to the studio as ordered, but diverted long enough to give Laura a quick update on what had been happening, mostly the edited lowlights, like being outed to the entire family as an illegitimate relative, until I told her about the accident.

'But you could both easily have died!' she exclaimed, horrified. 'Thank goodness Jude heard you! Are you really all right?'

'Fine – but afterwards I fell to pieces, because it made me realise that Alan couldn't have stopped himself running onto the ice to rescue that dog – sheer instinct takes over in that sort of situation and I'd have done just the same for Merlin. It was . . . cathartic. I cried buckets over Jude Martland and he was very comforting.'

'So there you are, he has a kind heart!'

'And then he kissed me. Or I kissed him – he'd put a lot of

whisky in my tea for the shock and I wasn't myself. He could give George lessons,' I added thoughtfully.

'*Holly!*'

'Don't get excited: he was the one who stopped. He said he hadn't meant to take advantage of me when I was upset . . . but he'd probably just thought better of it. I told him it didn't matter, it was just shock and whisky, and we'd forget it.'

'Is that possible?'

'Yes,' I said firmly. 'Apart from him being my cousin, he's already made it plain he's not looking for any long-term commitment and I'm not about to repeat Gran's mistakes with another Martland male, either.'

I didn't dwell on my increasingly confused feelings about Jude, but I'm sure she read between the lines because she knows me too well.

Jude stopped working straight away when I went into the studio and wolfed down his lunch, so he must have been hungry. After that, he feverishly drew sketch after sketch of me with Merlin, almost as if he suspected I might suddenly vanish into thin air, before going back to his welding.

He was stripped to his T-shirt again . . . and it's no use: I may know he's not my type and he's out of bounds because he's my cousin – but my God, I have to admit there's something terribly sexy about him when he's welding!

I was so hot, if I'd gone out and rolled in the snow, it would have hissed.

Maybe I just have cabin fever, after being cooped up here so long? The sooner I get away, the better!

In Gran's journal that night she rambled off into another long soliloquy on the subject of God's plans for her and about loving forgiveness, though not everyone shared her views:

My parents have still not forgiven me, despite my marriage:
perhaps they think I tricked Joseph into it. We have
arranged that I will go to Joseph's sister in Cornwall well
before the baby is expected, which will seem natural
enough: Joseph has told her the truth and she wrote a
wonderfully kind letter to me . . .

I couldn't believe that it was already Sunday again! Where has the time flown to?

Richard had sent word that he was holding another church service, since clearly the official vicar would not be making an appearance. According to Becca he only held services in the village twice a month anyway.

'It's not what it was when Richard was the vicar here, before they joined the two parishes together. He's not part of the community,' she grumbled. 'Though of course, Richard holds a service on the Sundays when he doesn't come, so we don't feel the loss.'

Guy and Michael were to drop them off at the church on their way to dig out Michael's car, but I declined to go with them since I wanted to have a trial run with the Revel Cakes and had steeped some saffron overnight ready. Jude decided to help them instead of going straight to the studio, but Coco, who was hideously bored, elected to give herself some kind of super-duper beauty treatment upstairs.

I didn't tell her I'd put her designer padded coat in the washing machine on hand wash. It looked so filthy, there didn't seem to be anything else to do with it and I thought it would come out okay if I tumbled it on low heat afterwards . . . But then, even if it didn't, she would probably have binned it once she got home, anyway.

'You don't know how to clean a fur hat?' I asked Tilda a couple of hours later when the church party had returned, dropped off by George, and a batch of delicious Revel Cakes were sitting on the wire rack, golden yellow with saffron and crusty with candied peel and sugar.

'Talcum powder and a good brushing might help?' she suggested.

'I thought it would be nice to send Coco off tomorrow looking less like a tramp,' I explained. 'I washed her coat and it's come up quite well. It's in the tumble drier now.'

'It'll be so lovely if we can get rid of her,' she agreed. 'What *is* that delicious smell?'

'Revel Cakes, though really they're more of a fruit-topped bun, aren't they? I found the recipe in a box in the kitchen, but I thought I'd better have a trial run before baking lots of them, because I only had dried yeast and not fresh. Would you like one?'

'I think we'd *all* like one,' Becca said. 'I'm going to miss your cooking when I've gone home – and now the lane down to the village is thawing out, I haven't really got much excuse to stay on, have I?'

'None of us want to outstay our welcome,' Noël said, 'and we've had a truly wonderful Christmas, thanks to you, Holly! But if Edwina manages to get here tomorrow, as she originally planned, *we* will be able to leave, too.'

'Edwina does my shopping with theirs and fills my freezer up with ready meals,' Becca said. 'She's a little powerhouse! Even Jude gives her his shopping list sometimes, too.'

The car-excavation party were late getting back for lunch, but eventually drove up in Michael's red car, though they'd had to jump-start it.

'Ben managed to plough down to the lower road, and there's traffic along it now,' Guy said. 'I wasn't sure Michael's car would get up the hill, but it made it once Ben had spread some grit and put a spare set of chains on the wheels.'

From the way they all talked about it, you'd think they'd just returned from some perilous Arctic expedition, mugged by polar bears at every turn!

'Coco had come down to lunch (or not to lunch), looking much as she did before her beauty treatment, and was told that she could probably leave tomorrow.

'With me driving you – under *extreme* protest,' Guy explained.

'And wearing your lovely white coat,' I said. 'I've washed it and it's come up just like new!'

'You *washed* it?' she exclaimed, staring at me with wide, ice-chip blue eyes.

'It's surprising what will wash on a gentle cycle, and there didn't seem to be anything to be lost. I gave your hat a brush too, but really you need a specialist cleaner for that one.'

Typically, Coco didn't thank me for my efforts, but examined her coat as if incredulous it should have survived my cavalier treatment of it.

Tilda had said she had a packet of saffron at the lodge and I could see I'd need more for the Revel Cakes if I was to do a very big batch. So after lunch was cleared away, Jude and I walked down the drive together, though this was not by any intent on my part: he just happened to be setting off for the studio at the same time.

He was pretty quiet – but then, he often was.

'How many Revel Cakes do you think I'll need to make?' I asked him as we walked down through the pine trees to the lodge, passing the track up to the mill – he'd decided to go to the lodge with me first, for the exercise, though I would have thought digging Michael's car out was enough of that for one day.

He thought about it. 'About forty or fifty? Everyone in the village and from the farms comes and they'll eat at least two of them each, I would have thought. Mrs Jackson used to take a big, flat wicker basket of them down – I think it's still hanging up in the scullery.'

'Well, baking those should take up quite a big chunk of

tomorrow,' I commented, as we got to the lodge and he turned to leave me. It was quite dark in the last shadows cast by the pine trees, and the sun hadn't finished thawing the crazy-paving path to the front door. This was a fact I only *truly* appreciated when I skidded on the half-frozen slush and came crashing down hard on my derrière. After the first moment of shock, it was *really* painful and brought a rush of tears to my eyes.

Jude scooped me up as if I weighed nothing and, taking the key from my hand, carried me into the lodge and deposited me on the sofa.

'My bum's soggy, I'll make the sofa wet,' I protested, getting straight back up again. 'Ouch, that really jarred me all the way up my back!'

'I hope you're going to be all right,' he said, looking at me with surprising anxiety. 'I mean, you should be more careful in your condition and think about the baby, even if it *is* early days yet.'

'Baby, what baby?' I demanded blankly, staring at him wide-eyed and thinking he'd run mad. 'What on earth are you talking about, Jude?'

'Look, Holly, I saw that pregnancy and childcare book you got on Christmas Day, so I know you're expecting.'

'Oh – *that*!'

'I suppose the father's that Sam character you've mentioned a couple of times? And I expect it was another reason why you were so interested in finding out about your real grandfather – it takes a lot of pregnant women that way, I think. Does Michael know?'

'Hello – did I hear my name?' said Michael, putting his head round the door at this inauspicious moment. Then he saw us, inches apart and staring inimically at each other, and looked embarrassed.

'How did *you* get here?' I exclaimed.

'I thought I ought to drive my car up and down the drive

374

for ten minutes to charge the battery up,' he explained, 'and then the door of the lodge was wide open, which seemed a bit weird.'

'Come right in,' invited Jude, looking particularly grim, rather than his everyday version. 'I was just asking Holly if you knew she was pregnant?'

'I beg your pardon?' Michael said.

'Of course he doesn't know, you halfwit – because there *is* no pregnancy,' I snapped.

'You're *not* pregnant?' Jude gave me a searching look. 'But – why the book then?'

'If it's any of your business, which it isn't, I've decided that this spring I'm going to try for a baby, using AI.'

'AI?'

'Artificial insemination.'

'You couldn't do it any other way?' he asked incredulously. 'What's the matter with the men where you live?'

'Of course I could, but I didn't *want* to do it any other way!'

'Won't Michael oblige? After all, you two seem to be thick as thieves – that's why I asked if you'd told him when I thought you were pregnant.'

'Look, Jude,' said Michael patiently. 'Holly and I have become good friends, but that's all there is to it – and all there ever will be. And I'll tell you why: it's because I'm gay. Holly already knows.'

'You're *gay*?'

'Yes, but I'm not officially out,' he qualified, 'only to close friends.'

'But – you were married. You've got a little girl!'

'That was a mistake.'

'Right . . . But then, why the secrecy?'

'I've already explained to Holly: I'd feel weird doing male romantic leads with everyone knowing. I'll come out officially when I'm past it.'

'You're *gay*,' Jude repeated . . . And then one of those sudden smiles transformed his face. 'That's *wonderful*.'

'Thank you for your support,' Michael said dryly.

Jude's smile turned into a wicked grin. 'But poor Coco! Flogging a dead horse.'

'Poor *Michael*, you mean!' I said indignantly. 'You and Guy threw him to the wolves all right.'

'Sorry,' he apologised, not sounding very.

'That's all right,' said Michael. 'Well, I'll leave you two to it and go back to the car – I left the engine running. I can probably get out tomorrow,' he added awkwardly.

'Oh, stay as long as you like,' Jude said expansively, his good humour restored.

'I'll hitch a lift back up to the house with you,' I said quickly. 'I just slipped on the ice and it's painful. I'll probably have some impressive bruises on my backside by morning.'

'Okay,' he said and Jude went off to the studio while I fetched the saffron and then carefully locked the door.

'Phew, I feel so much safer now Jude knows my little secret,' Michael admitted, turning the car and heading for home. 'I thought he was going to spoil my good looks one of these days. Are you *really* going to try AI, Holly?'

'Yes, I made up my mind to go it alone, before I came here,' I explained. 'I knew I wouldn't ever find another man like Alan.'

'Perhaps not, but you might find someone very different, if you looked . . . like Jude,' he suggested.

'He's certainly *different* all right, and he brings out the worst in me.'

'You're attracted to each other, that's a start.'

'That's just a physical thing . . . and anyway, even if it wasn't, I think our family relationship is too close for anything else.'

'Right . . . well.' He gave me another charming sideways smile. 'In that case, there's always me if you want a volunteer donor that you actually know – and I can tell you from my daughter, I make *very* nice babies! Only for God's sake don't tell Jude I volunteered!'

'That's really sweet of you,' I said, touched. 'I'll bear it in mind.'

Chapter 38: Photo-Finish

The baby arrived, thankfully late and quite small, but healthy.
It is a girl and we have called her Anne. She is very precious
to both of us and Joseph dotes on her as if she were his own.
He says she is a gift from God.

January, 1945

Gran's journal slowly peters out soon after the baby – my mother – arrived, but I expect she found other things to occupy her time with and was too busy. I knew she'd been a very active minister's wife.

I was still quite stiff and sore from my fall and my bum was probably black and blue – but also maybe green, from the liniment Becca gave me to put on after a long, hot soak in the bath. She said she swore by it, so I gave it a go even though it smelt very odd and I suspected it was designed for horses. It certainly seemed to take a lot of the soreness out. I ought to try it on my fetlocks after a hard day in the kitchen!

I wasn't quite so quick off the mark as usual going downstairs and I knew Jude had beaten me to it, because I heard him down in the courtyard as I was getting dressed. He'd cleaned out the sitting-room fire, too, when I checked . . . and there was just one small, tantalising corner of the jigsaw left to do. Before I knew it, the pieces were snapped into place, and the Victorian Christmas scene complete.

I'd put saffron in water to steep overnight for the Revel Cakes, and the liquid was a beautiful golden yellow. When I'd made myself a cup of coffee, I got out the biggest mixing bowl, a vast affair with a blue-glazed inside, and made the dough. Kneading it energetically for ten minutes released quite a bit of bottled-up emotion and was probably very therapeutic. Jude came back in while I was pummelling and looked at me with some surprise.

'Revel Cakes,' I explained, 'They're a sort of lightly-fruited spiced bread, really, so the yeast needs to work for two or three hours at least, before I make them.'

I dropped the yeasty yellow mass into the bowl, covered it in cling film and set it near the Aga to rise.

'Sorry I got the wrong end of the stick yesterday,' he apologised, putting the kettle on and making more coffee without being asked, one of his main early morning assets, while I started on my next task, a hearty winter casserole of venison for dinner tonight, which we would have with jacket potatoes from Henry's store, followed by a baked custard. This was apparently Noël's favourite dessert, just as it had been my Gran's.

'You certainly jumped to some strange conclusions about me – but then, you're always doing that!'

'You're right,' he admitted. 'I've misjudged you all along. But this time the truth is even weirder! Holly, I can't believe you're *seriously* going to go it alone and have a baby by AI! You can't have thought—'

'I've thought of *everything*,' I interrupted. 'I have it all planned – and it's none of your business anyway, is it?'

He sighed and ran his fingers through his dark hair, which was starting to curl, being in need of cutting. 'It feels like it is – but we can discuss it later.'

'No, we can't: I'm going to be busy all day and then I'll have to pack.'

'But, Holly, you don't really intend to dash off tomorrow morning if the roads are cleared, do you? Why not stay for the

Revels? It seems silly to miss them now and the family will be *really* disappointed if you aren't there. You could stay one extra night, couldn't you?'

I looked at him and weakened slightly, because I so desperately wanted to see them now I'd heard so much about them . . . especially Jude as Saint George!

'I suppose I *could* . . . But I don't have to stay on, I can pack my car and leave right after it's over, like Michael's doing.'

'But he's only driving as far as his friend's place near Leeds tomorrow night, and you'll have a much longer drive. Anyway, if you leave immediately, you'll miss all the fun.'

'What kind of fun?' I asked suspiciously, remembering Sharon's hints of some kind of Wicker Woman sacrifice.

'Well, the wassail, for a start.'

'Wassail?'

'A sort of hot apple and ale punch that Nancy brews up.'

'Oh yes, I think she did mention that.'

'And Old Nan, Richard and Henry will all expect you to be there too, right to the end with the rest of the family. So you see, you might as well stay over that night.'

That brief but wonderful smile flashed across his face like a rare comet and I felt my willpower dissolving faster than sugar in hot water . . .

One more night couldn't hurt, could it?

'Okay,' I heard myself say.

'Good.' He looked pleased, but that was possibly because he knew he was going to get one extra well-cooked dinner before he was forced back onto his usual diet of convenience foods.

He started off cooking bacon for breakfast while I finished the casserole and put it in the slow oven. The pot custard could go in later, when I baked the Revel Cakes, and possibly a carrot cake – goodness knows, we had enough of those, since Henry was clearly the Carrot King.

For once, everyone else came down for breakfast at more or

380

less the same time, except Coco, who arrived late demanding black coffee – though I made her eat an omelette too – and then went back up to finish her packing. You'd have thought she'd already have done it, if she was so desperate to leave!

Guy set off in his big Chelsea tractor right after breakfast with Coco, her white coat a testament to my laundering skills, but her hat still a trifle manky. She'd made it so unendearingly plain that she couldn't wait to shake the dust of the place off her stilettos that we all gathered outside, prepared to wave her off with *huge* enthusiasm.

'Goodbye, Horlicks!' Jess called gaily, but she pretended she hadn't heard.

Guy kissed everyone goodbye before he got in, including me, and wished me good luck, though I don't know why he thought I would need it more than anyone else.

'And by the way, I forgive you for doing the last bit of jigsaw!' he added.

'It was too tempting and I didn't think you'd have time this morning. But now Jude can take it back to Oriel's shop and get half the price refunded.'

'Thrift is clearly your middle name,' Jude said to me with amusement as we waved goodbye to the vanishing people-carrier. 'Are you going to come down to the studio later?'

'I could walk down with your lunch early, but I won't be able to stop – I'll need to get back and start making fifty fiddly little spiral Revel Cakes. The dough will have risen by then.'

Or at least, I *hoped* it would.

I made my pot custards and the carrot cake, went out to have a long talk over the fence with Lady, then gave Merlin a good brushing in the tackroom, which would be his last before I left.

That thought made me feel sad: I'd become so attached to

him that I would be lost without my faithful shadow following me about. I'd miss Lady, too, and even Billy . . .

We had an early lunch, which Jess didn't eat a lot of, due to her having searched out and devoured every last remaining chocolate decoration on the tree while everyone else was occupied. The older members of the party had been closeted in the morning room with *Road to Rio* and Michael, who is house-trained, had washed, dried and pressed his laundry in the utility room.

I was so busy I should have asked Jess or Michael to take Jude's lunch down to the studio for me, but instead found myself drawn down there one last time, like iron filings to a magnet.

And I was glad I had, because the sculpture was really taking shape! It looked a bit as though a tornado had whirled huge metal leaves into the semblance of a horse and woman, rather than having been purposely constructed: I suppose that was what Jude intended?

He was deeply absorbed in what he was doing and I put the basket down where he would spot it when he returned to Earth and tiptoed away – or as much as you *can* tiptoe when wearing wellies.

Rolling dough into fifty small sausages, winding them into tight spirals and sprinkling them with chopped candied peel and sugar took *forever*.

Just as I was transferring the last lot from an oiled muffin tin to the cooling rack, Noël popped in to tell me that their housekeeper, Edwina, had managed to get through in her small estate car, bringing fresh groceries for both them and Becca, so I made a tray of tea and some of the carrot cake and took it through to the sitting room.

Edwina was a spare, middle-aged woman with severely scraped-back sandy hair and the expression of a martial marmoset. She seemed to have them all organised for their own good, even Tilda, and I could see she was very efficient.

'I found Jude in his studio and he told me what happened and that you were all up here,' she said. 'I've filled your fridge and freezer, Becca, and you owe me fifty-seven pounds and eighty-five pence – the receipt's on the worktop by the microwave.'

'Oh, thank you, Edwina,' Becca said gratefully. 'I'll ride Nutkin home after breakfast tomorrow, and then perhaps someone could drop my bags off later?'

'I expect Jude will,' Noël said.

'Jude suggested you and Tilda stay here tonight and come home in the morning and I said it was a good idea,' Edwina said. 'It'll give me a chance to take down the decorations and have a good clean through.'

'Oh, good,' Noël said. 'Holly's made a custard tart for tonight and I was looking forward to it.'

Dinner being sorted, apart from popping the ready-scrubbed jacket potatoes in the oven, I went up early to change into my red velvet dress: this was, after all, the last family dinner I would have here. I thought I might as well make a bit of effort.

And, hot on the heels of that thought, it suddenly dawned on me that I would be alone at Old Place with Jude tomorrow night – apart from Merlin and Lady and Billy, of course . . . I can't think why I hadn't realised that before! But still, he would be in one wing, and I the other . . .

There was still lots of time, so I started packing a few things together, like my laptop and cookbook notes, and bundling Gran's journals back into the trunk again . . . though first I reread the last entry. And then, for some reason, it occurred to me to turn the page and there I found another tiny black and white photo, fixed in with a sort of gummed paper hinge.

N with his parents, she'd written underneath. *He showed it to me, then must have dropped it, for I found it one day after he had gone then slipped it into my bag and forgot about it.*

On succeeding pages she'd later added one or two more random entries, mainly to mark tragic events – and hadn't she already had enough to bear? The one about my mother made me cry:

> *It was very hard to lose my only child and a cruel blow to Joseph. But he said we must accept God's will and not see it as a punishment for any wrongdoing, for he firmly believed that the Almighty was not a vengeful God.*
>
> *December 1972*

'Holly's staying until the day after tomorrow,' Jude told everyone at dinner.

'Oh, good. And then you will be back again soon, now you have found us, won't you, m'dear?' asked Noël.

'Of course, I'll miss you all,' I said, though there was little likelihood I would ever see them again . . .

'Easter,' he suggested, 'if not before.'

'There isn't an Easter Revel too, is there?'

'No, only a little pace egging, that kind of thing,' he said vaguely. 'But you're one of the family now, you should be here.'

'That reminds me,' I said, picking up the photo, which I'd put inside a folded bit of card next to my plate. 'I found another picture stuck into the last of Gran's journals – it's Ned again, with your parents.'

I handed the photograph to Noël and he nodded. 'Oh, yes – I remember this picture of Ned being taken. It was just after he came to live with us.'

'What do you mean, "live with us"?' asked Jude puzzled. 'Where else would he live?'

'He means after Ned was orphaned,' Becca said helpfully.

'No, I don't know,' Jude exclaimed. 'What on earth are you all talking about?'

'I thought you knew – my parents adopted Ned, who was a

second cousin. He'd have been two or three years younger than Jess at the time,' Noël said.

'So . . . Holly is only the granddaughter of a *connection* of the Martlands?' Jude said, astounded.

'Well, he *was* a Martland all right, anyone could see that, though through the distaff line, and we always thought of him as our brother. But yes – and actually, I suppose that accounts for why Holly looks like him more than anyone else in the family.'

'Seems like it,' said Jude. 'Well, well!'

Jess asked, puzzled, 'So is Holly still my auntie, then?'

'Nominally, but the family connection by blood is so diluted it's transparent,' Jude said cheerfully.

'But she still is, and always will be, a member of this family,' Noël said and then, while I slowly digested the implications of his revelation, he meandered on about the Revels and how my arrival had been the end of one thing and the beginning of something new, just as the Revels symbolised the end of the old year and the start of the next.

'And then next Christmas, we'll all be together again, a new cycle completed,' he said.

'Except Coco, I hope,' Tilda put in acerbically.

'She wasn't so bad in the end, m'dear.'

'Huh!' Tilda said inelegantly.

'And me,' said Michael, who had been interestedly listening, 'I won't be here.'

'Oh, you'll always be welcome, too,' Jude told him, 'I feel you're quite one of the family,' and Michael grinned at him.

'Uncle Jude, if you and Holly aren't really cousins, does that mean—' began Jess, but I hastily diverted her by appealing to her greed.

'Jess, why don't you go and fetch that box of Chocolate Wishes that the Chirks left? I'd forgotten all about them. They're sort of a chocolate fortune cookie.'

'Oh *yes!*' she squealed, running out of the room.

385

The wish inside mine said, *Follow your heart: you are already in the place you were meant to be.*

If the chocolate hadn't already been moulded together, I would have suspected Jess of writing it herself and putting it in there.

'So we're not even kissing cousins any more – or perhaps this means that we *are*?' Jude said, following me into the kitchen later while I was stashing a load of dirty crockery in the dishwasher.

I turned to find him standing too close for comfort and looking down at me very seriously.

'It's good news anyway, because ever since we kissed, I can't stop thinking about you and you're driving me mad!'

'You're driving me mad too, Jude Martland, but *not* in a good way!' I snapped, on the defensive as usual. But this time I knew it was because I didn't want my heart breaking again – and Jude could do just that, if I let him.

That sudden smile appeared. 'Couldn't we try that kiss again? You might change your mind!'

'No! I've had such a rollercoaster of a journey finding out about Gran – and now this, to end it all! I don't know what I think any more about *anything*: I'm *totally* confused.'

'Poor Holly,' he said sympathetically – and just then Jess burst in to ask if either of us wanted the last Chocolate Wish.

'No, I think I just got the answer I wanted from mine,' Jude told her.

Chapter 39: Signs and Portents

Right at the end of her journal, in an entry dated simply 'Christmas 2001', Gran had written very poignantly:

> It is poor Holly's turn to suffer a great loss – that of her husband. But she is still young and I pray that one day she will find long and lasting happiness with someone else.
>
> Just as I once knew, without the shadow of a doubt, that God still had a purpose for me, I am certain that my prayers for Holly will be answered, like a True Cross on the sampler of my life.

I don't think having my heart broken by another Martland is quite what Gran was praying for and Jude certainly didn't fit into the pattern of *my* life sampler. In fact, he was more in the nature of a huge, tangled knot, rather than a True Cross, and I'm sure she herself would have described him as a great streak of nowt – I could hear her saying it now.

What on earth was I thinking of, agreeing to stay on tomorrow, for Twelfth Night?

Becca got up early this morning, which I was grateful for, since it meant I wasn't left alone with Jude. After a largely sleepless night I still felt just as confused about my feelings for him – and about *his* intentions.

When they came back in from the stables, bringing that now-familiar sweet smell of horses with them, Jude didn't linger helpfully in the kitchen, but went off to shower and change and by the time he'd come down again the rest of the party had started to appear, too.

There was that strange last-day-of-the-house-party feel about things that I was familiar with at second-hand: a reluctance to leave, mingled with looking forward to being home. But since I shared it for once, I found it unsettling . . .

'We didn't put the horses out first thing, since Becca and Nutkin are off after breakfast,' Jude said, constructing a giant egg and bacon sandwich using a large, floury bap.

'We thought they might as well spend a little time together in the stable before we go, then Jude can put Lady and Billy out in the paddock,' Becca said. 'I mucked out yesterday, so a bit of a clean-up should do the trick.'

'Yes, I'll do that, then drop your bags off afterwards,' Jude agreed.

'And Edwina will come to fetch us shortly, too,' Noël said.

Tilda had actually come down for breakfast, and I thought that now Edwina was back to look after them, they were quite happy to go home – even if Jess would clearly rather have stayed at Old Place!

'I could stay tonight, at least, couldn't I?' she wheedled. 'It's Holly's *last* night!'

'Of course, if your Uncle Jude agrees,' I said quickly and he gave me one of his more unreadable stares.

'Your Uncle Jude is entitled to a bit of peace occasionally!' he told her.

'Ooh! You want to be alone with Holly!' Jess exclaimed with an air of discovery and I felt myself go pink.

'I do, but I can't imagine how you guessed,' he said sardonically.

'Jess; don't tease,' Tilda said. 'Of course you are coming back to the lodge with us.'

'We'll all be meeting up at the Revels later in the day, anyway,' Noël pointed out. 'I can hardly wait!'

Once they had gone, the house felt strangely empty. I expect Lady and Billy were already missing Nutkin, too.

Jude was busy helping to ferry luggage about and then cleaning out Nutkin's empty loosebox and Michael, who had already packed, kept me company in the kitchen while I was doing a few last-minute jobs.

I decided on some of the turkey curry as an easy dinner for tonight and took that out to defrost, then froze lots of single portions of leftover venison casserole (I'd made a double quantity, especially), with easy heating instructions written on the lids: Jude's diet before I came was *dreadful* and I didn't want him to lapse entirely as soon as I'd gone . . .

It was odd with just the three of us eating lunch in the kitchen at the big table and I think Michael felt a bit of a gooseberry, even though I was glad he was there – and Jude didn't seem to mind at all! In fact, he seemed amazingly cheerful, so perhaps he actually preferred being alone and now couldn't wait to have the place to himself?

'Could you take Holly down to the Revels with you this afternoon, Michael?' Jude asked. 'Only I have to go early to get ready and Edwina will drive Noël, Tilda and Jess there.'

'If you've got room for that enormous basket of Revel Cakes, too?' I said. 'Otherwise I'll take my car.'

'No problem: they can go on the back seat,' he said. 'My bags all fit in the boot.'

'What about Merlin? I presume he stays here?' I asked Jude.

'Yes, he wouldn't like all the noise.'

He vanished after lunch, but came downstairs later with an armful of mumming costumes from the attic, which he stowed carefully in his Land Rover before driving off with a casual, 'See you both later!'

His mind seemed to be elsewhere: but then, with Jude, I have learned that this is *not* unusual.

I changed into my red dress, boots and long winter coat for the occasion, with the bright green scarf Laura had given me . . . in fact, if we got down to the village early enough, I hoped to get a chance to slip away and ring her, because I really *needed* to talk to her!

When I carried the huge basket of Revel Cakes into the snug of the Auld Christmas, Tilda, Noël, Becca and Old Nan were already there in front of the fire, but there was no sign of the usual inhabitant. He was probably off donning his costume.

'Where's Jess?' I asked.

'Gone to fetch Nan's distance glasses, she left them behind,' Tilda explained. 'And Edwina's gone to see Oriel – they are old friends, but she will be back in good time for the start. We old things sit outside, well wrapped up, you know.'

'I wondered who the chairs were for,' Michael said.

'I don't want to sit out: I wish I could still take part,' Noël said wistfully.

'I feel a bit left out, too,' Michael agreed, 'but I expect that's the actor in me!'

Nancy was gathering ingredients by the vast vat in which she intended mixing the wassail and I went to see what she was putting into it.

'I've another panful mixed ready in the kitchen,' she told me. 'It's best to be prepared early.'

'Yes, I've always found that a good plan in life, too,' I said, though the more I thought about it, the less prepared I felt to spend a night alone at Old Place with Jude Martland!

'This thing is insulated,' she said, banging the side of the vast tub with a wooden spoon the size of a small paddle. 'They used to keep the wassail hot by sticking red-hot pokers into it, but times have changed and this is much easier.'

'It smells like a fairly heady mix – what's in it?'

'Ale, cloudy apple juice and a roasted apple or two, cinnamon and nutmeg . . . A baby could drink it,' she assured me. 'But it keeps everyone warm and gives them stamina.'

'Stamina?'

'Yes, for the dancing.'

'Right . . .' I said, thinking that that sounded pretty harmless. 'Well, I'm just slipping across to the church for a few minutes – I want to ring a friend and there's a good signal in the porch.'

'I'd have suggested the barn, you get a pretty good signal there, too, but that's where they're all getting their costumes on. I hope they've remembered to make the circlets: I wonder if *you* will get one this year?' She eyed me thoughtfully.

What circlets? I wondered, as I dashed across to the little church and called Laura's number, hoping desperately that she would answer. When she did, I barely let her get a word in before pouring out the news of my latest discovery.

'Laura, I'm *not* Jude's cousin after all! Well, actually, I suppose I am, but so many times removed I'm probably just as much cousin to half of Little Mumming!'

'What do you mean?'

I explained about Ned, my grandfather, having been adopted by the Martlands and she said, 'Great! So now your little Puritan soul has been satisfied, you're free to lust after Jude?'

'And vice versa – not that the thought that we were related seemed to be holding him back from making a move on me before.'

'There you are then, go for it,' she encouraged me. 'I can tell you want to.'

'Yes,' I admitted, 'only I don't know what he wants!'

'I think I could make a guess,' she said dryly.

'Yes, but he's already made it plain he doesn't want to fall in love again and neither do I. But on the other hand, I'm not a

391

light-affair sort of person, am I, let alone a one-night-stand person? And . . . well, he's *difficult*. There's an attraction between us, there's no denying that, but we argue and snap at each other all the time and although he did say once he'd like me to stay on, I don't know if he wanted me as cook, bottle washer and unpaid artist's model, or *what*!'

'*What*, I should think, by the sound of it,' she said, amused. 'Why not just go with the flow tonight and see what happens? Put your Strange Baptist upbringing and all those carefully-worked-out life plans to one side, and go off-piste.'

'You're advising me to have a night of mad passion?'

'If it pans out that way and you want to. Then you can just walk away tomorrow . . . or not. Go for it!' she encouraged.

'I'm afraid, if I do, I might get hurt,' I confessed.

'That's better than keeping your heart in a block of ice for the rest of your life, isn't it?'

'I think you're quite mad!' I said, though I could feel a bit of a smile trying to drag up the corners of my mouth. 'You know, Gran said she hoped I'd meet another nice man and settle down, it was at the back of her last journal.'

'There you are, then.'

'I'm sure Jude Martland isn't thinking about settling down and anyway, he's not really nice, he's surly and bossy most of the time.'

'Artistic temperament?' she suggested. 'And he sounds as if he has lots of good things going for him too. He loves his animals, for a start.'

'I suppose so,' I conceded reluctantly, and sighed. 'Not only the circumstances but the signs and portents seem to be conspiring against me, too: we had some Chocolate Wishes after dinner last night, and the message in mine implied I'd found what I was looking for.'

'So, what are you waiting for?'

'Ah, but I don't believe in signs and portents.'

'Then perhaps you ought to start!' she told me. 'Where's Jude now?'

'I haven't seen him since after lunch and he was a bit distant: but then, he was probably psyching himself up for his performance later.'

'Sounds promising!'

'His performance in the Revels, I meant, idiot,' I said. 'He's Saint George . . . and speaking of the Revels, I'd better get back: it must be about to start soon.'

'Call me tomorrow, let me know you're okay,' she said more seriously.

'I'll be back tomorrow, so you will be able to see for yourself,' I reminded her.

By now it was mid-afternoon and the light was just starting to fade. People had begun to gather around the green and in front of the pub, where the vat of wassail had been carried out and set on a sturdy table, together with my huge basket of Revel Cakes.

Tilda, Noël and Old Nan were enthroned nearby, wrapped in tartan travelling rugs and fussed over by Edwina, but I went with Becca, Nancy, Jess and Michael to stand on the grass with the other spectators after we'd had a warming beaker of wassail, though by then Jess was sulking because Nancy wouldn't let her have any.

The crowd murmured and then hushed as a torch was put to the big bonfire and carried round to light the circle of twelve braziers spiked into the ground. Now I noticed for the first time that there was also an inner ring of strangely-wrought metal horses' heads, unmistakably Jude's work, to which had been attached bunches of holly, ivy and mistletoe and red bits of cloth that stirred in the breeze: the whole green looked like a barbaric henge of fire.

Then, approaching from the direction of the barn behind the

pub, I heard the sound of a fiddle and Richard appeared, playing a lively air as he walked and dressed in a long green fur-edged velvet robe over (I hoped) lots of warm clothes.

Following him into the circle of light from the braziers jogged six Morris Men dressed in traditional white, with bells jingling and red ribbons flying, but carrying long swords and with painted black masks across their faces, which gave them a strange, slightly sinister look.

'Those are the Rappers,' Becca whispered.

I recognised George Froggat and Nancy's husband, Will, but not the rest. They formed a set and danced, using their swords a bit like staves (so I hoped they were blunt!), and then fell back into two rows, leaving the centre free for the strange figures who now came forward in procession, each introducing himself to the spectators with a short, rhyming couplet.

There was Auld Man Christmas, the diminutive Nicholas Dagger, in a blue velvet robe, an evergreen crown, and carrying a club almost as large as he was; a scary Red Hoss, painted scarlet and with jaws that could open and close with a loud snap; the Dragon, green and leathery, with a fearsome head and long tail that dragged on the ground and the strange Man-Woman figure. From the front he – or perhaps that should be *it* – looked just like the Rappers in white shirt and trousers and straw hat; but then he turned around, revealing a woman's mask over the back of his head and a long skirt.

'That's Liam as the Man-Woman,' giggled Jess, as he began to circle round, handing out circlets of ivy and mistletoe to any woman who seemed to catch his fancy, which included an excited Jess, Nancy and Oriel Comfort. But he didn't give *me* one and I felt quite left out!

Richard stopped playing for long enough to bow and introduce himself to the crowd as the Doctor. And then, finally, Jude in his guise as Saint George walked out of the darkness to large cheers: a huge and strangely fearsome figure, wearing a white surcoat with a red cross and a helmet with a nosepiece. He was carrying an even bigger sword than the Rappers . . . and in his other hand, a gilded, sparkling circlet of ivy and mistletoe. He strode over and placed the circlet on my head, and I was so surprised by this that I expect my jaw fell lower than Red Hoss's (who was Henry, by the way – I'd spotted him inside when he snapped his jaws in my face).

Then Jude walked back to the middle of the circle while Nancy, who was standing nearby, giggled. 'He used to give that to me, not having a lady of his own!'

'*I am St George,*' boomed Jude, '*a bold and brave knight. In Egypt with a dragon, I did fight.*'

'Why Egypt?' I whispered to Becca.

'The Crusades made some of the elements change: other places have Saint George kill a Turkish knight, but we carried on with the Dragon – and here it comes.'

From somewhere inside the great, leathery beast a voice that was unmistakably young Ben's from Weasel Pot shouted, after a couple of opening roars:

'*I am the Dragon*
With a roar I'll slay
And yon bold knight
With his life will pay!'

Then he and Jude rushed at each other and a mock fight ensued – only for the Dragon to kill Saint George. The crowd gave a united groan.

'That shouldn't happen, should it?' I asked Becca worriedly, looking at Jude stretched out on the grass.

'It's all right,' whispered Jess, who had edged up beside me. 'Wait and see!'

Auld Man Christmas, Red Hoss and the Man-Woman, whose roles had so far consisted of working the crowds and scaring small children into fits, now turned inwards to face the tragic scene and said as one:

'*Alas, poor Saint George!*'

The Dragon moved into the middle of the circle, leaving poor Jude lying on the cold half-thawed turf, though fairly near the bonfire, so I hoped he wouldn't entirely freeze to death.

Richard struck up another air on the fiddle and the six Rappers began to dance again, this time their swords weaving together, to form a series of intricate patterns that culminated in a sort of knot with a hole in its centre. The Dragon approached – and then suddenly they lowered the knot of swords over its head, tightened it with a scraping clash of metal – and the Dragon's head flew off, to land with a soggy thump near my feet.

I nearly had a heart attack and it was a huge relief when I realised it was hollow!

The dancers fell back into two rows again, revealing the headless Dragon lying on the ground, and there was a round of applause and some cheers.

Richard swung round on his heel and pointed his violin at the lifeless Saint George, declaiming loudly:

'*I am the Doctor*
Be not affright
With my trusty potion
I'll put all right!'

Then he took a small bottle out of his pocket and pretended to sprinkle something over the recumbent knight. I watched, riveted, as Jude slowly stirred, sat up and then got to his feet and bowed, to more rapturous applause.

'That's it – come on!' Becca said, and she and Jess and everyone else rushed into the circle and joined hands, dragging me with them. Somehow in the crush I found myself with Jude on my left and the Dragon, without his head but with his tail looped over his arm, on my right, as we all joined hands and danced round. I could see Michael, Jess and Becca among the circle of dancers – and George, holding Oriel's hand. She looked flushed and happy, her ivy and mistletoe circlet tipped over one eye.

No-one else seemed to have a gilded one . . . and it was just as well that Jude had pushed it down firmly onto my head, because he suddenly whirled me round and round until I was too breathless to go on.

'It's no use, I'll have to have a rest!' I begged, panting, and he laughed and walked with me over to the pub, his arm still around my waist, though he took his rather scary helmet off first: that was a bit of a relief. We stood talking to Noël, Tilda and Old Nan and I accepted a beaker of the warming punch . . . and then possibly another. In fact, I lost count of how much I'd had, but it tasted innocuously of warm apples and Nancy *had* said you could give it to a baby . . .

My foot started to tap in time to the music and Jude's arm tightened around me a little as Nancy took the beaker from my hand and replaced it with a fresh one.

'Nancy,' I said suspiciously, focusing on her cheerful, flushed face with an effort, 'when you said you could give this to a baby, were you serious?'

'Yes, if you wanted it to go to sleep for a couple of hours. Maybe not, these days though, when they've even taken the alcohol out of gripewater.'

Richard played the music for what looked like a final mad bout of strip-the-willow, then handed his fiddle on to someone else and joined us.

Michael, who'd followed him, said, 'It's been really fascinating to watch. It's such an interesting mixture of pagan fertility ceremony and miracle play.'

'That's very astute of you,' said Richard. 'The red ribbons, holly, ivy and especially the mistletoe wreaths the women are given *are* all to do with rebirth and fertility.'

'And the triumph of good over evil, that's what the Saint George and the dragon part signifies,' Noël put in.

'Doesn't the pagan element bother you, Vicar?' Michael asked.

'Oh no,' he said cheerfully, his white hair blowing in the breeze.

It was certainly now starting to unsettle *me*, despite the soothing effects of large quantities of punch!

We waved Michael off, and then the actors in the Revels went to the barn to remove their costumes, reappearing in normal guise. By then, the last of the wassail and the Revel Cakes had been consumed and people started to disperse: some home, and some into the Auld Christmas. Edwina dragooned Tilda, Jess and Noël into the car and drove them back to the lodge, but Becca walked off home, a Revel Cake wrapped in a paper napkin in her pocket for later.

'They're supposed to be a lucky talisman if you keep it for the year,' she'd told me, 'but I think I'd rather eat it.' Then she'd looked at me and added, 'And perhaps you'd better eat something as soon as Jude gets you home, too: that wassail packs a lot more punch than you think.'

'That's because it *is* punch,' I said, and giggled.

'I'll look after her,' Jude promised, putting his arm around me again, probably because I was swaying slightly.

'Yes, *that's* what's worrying me,' Becca said grimly, and he laughed.

Chapter 40: Twelfth Night

Driving back with Jude I felt warm and cosy, but also strangely limp and boneless too.

'That was lovely,' I said dreamily.

Then the phone in my pocket rang, waking me slightly. 'Can you stop here? Only I'll lose the signal if you go past the lodge and it must be Laura.'

'Or Sam?' he snapped suspiciously, pulling in to the side of the lane.

'Why on earth would it be Sam?' I blinked at him, trying to focus. 'He doesn't even have my number.' I'd managed to dig out the phone by now and said, 'Hello?'

'Holly, are you there?' demanded a strident voice.

'Oh, it's you,' I sighed. 'Yes, I'm here, Ellen . . . but I'm not *entirely* with it.'

'Why, you're not ill, are you? Did Laura tell you about the London job? Only it's next week and I have to know now if you'll do it. You will, won't you?'

'Next week?' I murmured, drifting back off into a warm and sleepy haze.

Jude removed the phone from my limp grasp and demanded rudely, 'What do you want?'

I could hear Ellen quacking loudly.

'No,' he growled, 'she *can't* go and cook anywhere – she's

staying here.' And he clicked the phone off, shoved it back into my pocket, and started the engine again.

'That was a bit cavalier,' I protested, reviving slightly, 'and I'm *not* staying.'

'You can phone her back tomorrow if you want to, when you're fit to make decisions.'

Back at the house we went straight through to the kitchen, where Merlin was delighted to see us. Under the bright lights, Jude took me by the shoulders and stared worriedly down at me.

'I think I should sober you up with coffee, you're not used to our wassail. Or maybe you should just go to bed?'

'Yes, that's exactly what Laura said we should do,' I agreed dreamily.

'I'm getting to like the sound of this friend of yours more and more.' The corner of his mouth quirked up slightly.

'Are you? She's prettier than I am – small and blonde.'

'She might be pretty, but you're *beautiful* – and you're just the right height.'

'Only to a giant.'

'Lucky you've got one to hand then, isn't it?'

'And I don't need sobering, because I'm not drunk,' I told him. 'I just feel . . . good. Relaxed.' In fact, I relaxed right there and then against his broad chest and he sighed deeply and put his arms around me, leaning his cheek against my hair.

'That's nice,' I said, snuggling in a bit closer. 'Jude, when you keep saying you don't want me to go . . . are we talking permanent employment here? Or a quick fling? Only I don't—'

He gave me a slight shake and my mouth snapped shut. 'I'm talking marriage, you idiot! You, me – and children, too, if we're lucky. Which we *should* be after tonight.' The corner of his mouth quirked up with amusement. 'Saint George's wreath never fails – ask Nancy! She's had three of them, nine months to the day after a Revels.'

This dispelled the clouds of wassail slightly and I indignantly tried to push him away. 'You mean you and *Nancy*—'

'No, you idiot, Nancy and her *husband*.'

'Oh.' I relaxed against him again and he wrapped his arms closely around me. 'Did you mean that, about getting married?'

'Old Nan had another word with me about that Afghan she's knitting for us tonight – but anyway, I'm a marrying man and I fell in love with you the minute I set eyes on you. Only I didn't want to admit it, especially when I thought you were up to no good!'

'Well, I wasn't.'

'I know now, but I loved you anyway, though it might have made me a bit bad-tempered.'

'Just a bit – but perhaps trying to pretend to myself that I wasn't falling in love with you made *me* a little grumpy, too! But if we married, we'd fight all the time, wouldn't we?'

'Yes, I'm looking forward to it.'

'I haven't said yes, yet,' I pointed out. 'But I might, if only because I can't bear to be parted from Lady and Merlin.'

'You'd better,' he muttered, kissing me, and it quickly became clear that our last scorching kiss had been little more than a preliminary warm-up.

But when I came up for air, I tried to release myself. 'I'd better put the dinner in the oven, Jude: it's all ready, apart from cooking the rice and—'

'Forget it, you're not putting anything in the oven tonight,' he said, not letting go of me. 'But *I* might, if you tempt me too much.'

'That was *very* rude!' I told him seriously and he grinned.

'I only really want you for your cooking – and your lovely, poseable body,' he said, running his hands over it appreciatively. Then he kissed me again and I completely lost any interest in anything else, even food.

* * *

Later – much later, cosily snuggled up against him in his four-poster bed, I said severely, 'I can't think what I'm doing here! Falling for you was definitely *not* in my life-plan.'

'Then plan me into your schedule and write yourself a recipe with me as the main course,' he suggested.

'Just don't think I'll always play a meek Viola to your Orsino!' I warned him.

'You never did do that. But okay – I think our play is done.'

'Or maybe only the first act?' I said seriously. 'I'm starting to see a pattern here, with the end of one thing becoming the beginning of the next, just like Richard was saying earlier . . . Do you think that's mad?'

'No, but it might be the aftereffects of the wassail.'

He pulled me back into a crushing embrace and asked, hopefully, 'Time for a bit more Revelling?'

Read on for some delicious
recipes from Trisha

Recipes

Wassail
A very old punch of ale, apples and spices. It was popular throughout Christmas, especially on Twelfth Night. This will make about six small glasses: increase quantities as desired.

Ingredients:
1 pint of ale (500ml)
⅓ pint of apple juice
Juice and zest of an unwaxed lemon
1 tablespoon honey
¼ teaspoon each of ground ginger, nutmeg, cloves and cinnamon

Method:
Simmer the lemon juice and zest, apple juice and spices gently in a pan for about ten minutes, without letting it boil.

Add the ale and honey, stirring to dissolve, and heat through: again, be careful not to let it boil.

This is drunk warm and you can add a lemon slice to each glass/cup.

Ginger and Spice Christmas Tree Biscuits

These make a thin biscuit that will retain its crispness for quite a while on the tree; though if you make a double batch, you can keep some to nibble at in the biscuit tin, too!

Ingredients:

4oz (100g) butter
8oz (225g) plain flour
6oz (175g) soft brown sugar
1 small egg, beaten
1 level teaspoon of ground ginger
½ level teaspoon ground cinnamon
¼ teaspoon ground cloves (optional)

Method:

Sieve the flour and spices into a bowl and then add the butter, chopped into bits. Rub it into the flour between your thumb and fingers (as you do with shortcrust pastry).

When you have a mix like fine breadcrumbs, add the sugar and most of the egg, then knead lightly into a firm dough. Add the rest of the egg if necessary.

Put the dough in a bowl, cover with cling film and place in the fridge for at least half an hour. (This makes it easier to roll out and cut.)

Heat the oven to 190°C, 375°F, gas mark 5. Grease a couple of baking trays.

Roll the dough out fairly thinly on a lightly floured board, then cut out shapes as desired: you can get Christmas cutters, but gingerbread men also look good on the tree. If you just want round biscuits, then roll the dough into a long cylinder shape and slice thinly.

Pierce each biscuit so it can be hung from a thread or ribbon (I use a chopstick), then place on the baking tray, well spaced.

Bake for about ten minutes, until light golden brown at the edges – but keep an eye on them!

Remove and place on wire racks to cool.

I ice mine by mixing a little icing sugar and water with natural food colouring in egg cups (add water in drips, it needs to be quite thick) and then I use a small nylon paintbrush I keep just for this purpose (wash new ones before use) to blob, trickle and write on the biscuits. This is the fun bit . . . Allow to go hard.

Revel Cakes

Despite the name, these are actually a lightly fruited and spiced little bread roll. Holly soaked saffron in some of the water overnight to give them a yellow colour, though this is not vital. (But if you do, you will need to warm the water again next day before using.) She also added some chopped mixed peel to the dough.

Ingredients (for about twelve small buns – it can be doubled for a larger quantity):
13oz (375g) strong white flour
1 teaspoon caster sugar
7½ fl oz warm water (soak a couple of good pinches of saffron in 5 fl oz of it overnight if using)
1 teaspoon salt
¾ oz butter
½ teaspoon mixed spice
¾ sachet of fast dried yeast
3 oz (75g) chopped mixed peel

Method:
In a bowl or jug, mix the sugar, 2½ fl oz warm water and the yeast and allow to stand for five minutes or until frothy.

Sift the flour and salt into a large mixing bowl together with the spice. Rub in the butter, then make a well in the middle of the flour and pour in the yeast mixture and most of the rest of the warm water. Mix to a dough, using more water if needed.

Knead for ten minutes, then put the dough in a large oiled bowl, cover with cling film, and leave somewhere warm for approximately two hours, until it has at least doubled in size.

Put on a floured board and give it a quick thump or two to let out trapped air, then knead for two or three minutes. If using chopped peel, at this stage stretch the dough gently into a thick square and sprinkle the fruit into the middle. Fold the dough in over it, then knead as before for a couple of minutes.

Put it back in the bowl for ten minutes. Meanwhile, preheat the oven to 220°C, 425°F, gas mark 7. Grease baking trays or muffin tins.

On a floured surface, roll the dough into cylinders about six inches long and wind them round in spirals to make buns the way Holly did, then bake in muffin tins. Alternatively, form into small balls for ordinary rolls and place on a baking tray.

Cover trays with a tea towel and put in a warm place for half an hour, or until they have doubled in size. Bake for about fifteen minutes. When cooked they will be pale golden brown, feel lighter and sound slightly hollow when tapped underneath.

Transfer to a wire rack to cool.

A WINTER'S TALE

Trisha Ashley was born in St Helens, Lancashire, and gave up her fascinating but time-consuming hobbies of house-moving and divorce a few years ago in order to settle in North Wales. As research for this novel, Trisha spent time working for the National Trust – and quickly found that running a stately home is not all cream teas and croquet on the lawn!

Trisha is currently working on her next novel, *Wedding Tiers*, to be published by AVON in 2009. For more information about Trisha please visit www.trishaashley.com and go to www.BookArmy.co.uk for exclusive updates.

Praise for Trisha Ashley:

'Trisha Ashley writes with remarkable wit and originality – one of the best writers around!' Katie Fforde

'Full of comedy and wit.' *Closer*

'Trisha Ashley . . . makes for enjoyable reading.' *The Times*

By the same author:

Sowing Secrets

TRISHA ASHLEY

A Winter's Tale

AVON

AVON

A division of HarperCollins*Publishers*
77–85 Fulham Palace Road,
London W6 8JB

www.harpercollins.co.uk

This paperback edition 2011

1

First published in Great Britain by
HarperCollins*Publishers* 2008

Copyright © Trisha Ashley 2008

Trisha Ashley asserts the moral right to
be identified as the author of this work

A catalogue record for this book is
available from the British Library

ISBN-13: 978-1-84756-338-5

Set in Minion by Palimpsest Book Production Limited,
Grangemouth, Stirlingshire

Printed and bound in Great Britain by
Clays Ltd, St Ives plc

Mixed Sources
Product group from well-managed
forests and other controlled sources
www.fsc.org   Cert no. SW-COC-1806
© 1996 Forest Stewardship Council
FSC

FSC is a non-profit international organisation established
to promote the responsible management of the world's forests.
Products carrying the FSC label are independently certified
to assure consumers that they come from forests that are managed
to meet the social, economic and ecological needs
of present and future generations.

Find out more about HarperCollins and the environment at
www.harpercollins.co.uk/green

I would like to take this long-overdue opportunity to thank
Diane Pearson, the President of the Romantic Novelists' Association,
for first introducing me to my wonderful agent, Judith Murdoch –
and I only hope Judith feels the same way, after enduring
my sense of humour for several years.

For Margaret James, a friend for all seasons.

Prologue: The Dream

*Mother, what did you foretell, when you held my hand
so tightly and wept, then said that the future could not
be altered and I must go to the manor of Wynter's End
in your stead?*

From the journal of Alys Bezzard, 1580

No house as ancient as Winter's End was ever entirely silent:
even at eight years old, Sophy Winter knew that. Crouched
on the floor of the gallery, she felt like Jonah sitting in the
belly of the whale, surrounded by creaks and sighing,
feeling, rather than hearing, the heavy heartbeat of a distant
long-case clock and the sharply flatulent rattling of the
water pipes.

She peered through the wooden banisters, down into the
depths of the stone-flagged Great Hall where her grandfather's King Charles spaniels lay in a tangled, snoring,
comatose heap on a rag rug before the log fire.

Nothing stirred in the darker shadows beyond. Satisfied,
she ran to the end of the gallery and climbed onto a curved
stair rail that seemed to have been designed for little fingers
to grip; then, clinging on for dear life, she slid with an exhilarating, rushing *swoosh!* of cold air, right to the bottom.

Slowing down was always tricky. Fetching up with a
thump against a newel post bearing a carved cherub's head,

1

she lost her grip and would have fallen off, had she not been caught and rather roughly set on her feet.

In the ensuing silence, a moth-eaten stag's head dropped off the wall and landed with a clatter, glassy eyes vacantly staring at the intricately plastered ceiling.

Sophy looked up and her impish, round-cheeked face, framed in dark curls, not unlike the carved cherub's behind her, became instantly serious. Grandfather didn't like her to use the front stairs, let alone slide down the banisters. In fact, Grandfather didn't seem to *like* her at all, and it was somehow Mummy's fault – and where *was* Mummy? If Sophy hadn't been sitting on the gallery floor watching for her for so long, she wouldn't have been tempted to slide down the banisters in the first place.

Grandfather stared back at her, ferocious bushy brows drawn together over a formidable nose and an arrested expression in his eyes. 'A Pharamond, that's who *your* father was,' he said slowly, 'from over Middlemoss way. Why didn't I see that before? But which one . . . ?'

Nervously Sophy began slowly to back away, ready to make a run for the safety of the kitchen wing.

'Hebe!' he shouted suddenly, making Sophy jump and all the spaniels start awake and rush over, yapping.

'What are you bellowing for? You sound like a cross between the Last Trump and a cow in labour,' Great-Aunt Hebe snapped, appearing suddenly round the carved screen. Her fine, pale, red-gold hair stood out around her head in a flossy halo and she brandished a large wooden spoon that dripped a glutinous splat onto the flagged floor. One of the spaniels licked it tentatively: you never knew quite what Hebe was cooking up.

Sophy gave a little nervous giggle – Grandfather *was* loud enough to wake the dead slumbering in the grave-yard, and since that was her least favourite of Aunt Hebe's biblical bedtime stories she found the idea slightly worrying . . .

'Aunt Hebe,' she said urgently, running to her and grabbing a handful of slightly tacky cotton apron, 'the dead people won't climb out and walk round the graveyard in their bones, will they?'

'No, they'll all wait for the end of the world,' Hebe said. 'It was just a figure of speech.'

She looked over her head at her brother. 'What's up?'

'The child was sliding down the banisters again.'

'Well, she *is* a child. You did it, I did it, Ottie did it . . . we all did it! Now, let me get back to my stillroom. Come on, Sophy, you can give me a hand.'

'Wait,' he said. 'Take a look at her and tell me which family round here has black, curly hair? I don't know why I didn't realise it before: she's a Pharamond.'

'What, from the Mosses?' Hebe held Sophy away and stared at her. 'What nonsense! There's been the occasional dark-haired Winters ever since Alys Blezzard married into the family in the sixteenth century – and anyway, all the Pharamonds *I've* ever met have had dark blue eyes, not hazel, and narrow, aquiline noses. If anything, Sophy's nose turns up.'

'She's got the look,' he insisted.

'I don't think so – and does it matter anyway?'

'Of course it bloody matters! They're all mad as hatters in Middlemoss!'

'Sophy isn't mad.'

'Oh, no? What about her imaginary playmate?'

Aunt Hebe shrugged. 'Lots of children have invisible friends.'

'Alys isn't *always* invisible,' Sophy said in a small voice, but Grandfather didn't seem to hear her.

'I'm sure I'm right,' he said, 'and why wouldn't Susan say

3

who the father was, unless he was a married man? God knows where she's been the last few days, but if she doesn't mend her ways, she'll find herself out on her ear.'

At this inopportune moment Susan Winter slid in through the great oak door, setting down a colourful carpetbag on the floor; tall, fair, slender and pretty in a long, floaty dress with little bells that chimed softly as she moved, smelling of sandalwood and patchouli. Like a fairy, Sophy always thought, not a dark little hobgoblin like herself.

'So you're back, then? Where have you been?' Grandfather demanded, switching that fierce gaze to a new victim. 'And, more to the point, *who* have you been with? Another married man?'

Susan, who had been smiling vaguely at the group, her blue eyes unfocused, flinched and took a step backwards. 'W-what do you mean? Some friends took me to the Reading Festival to see Genesis, that's all, Daddy!'

'Friends! I know the riffraff you call friends! Layabouts and hippie scum! I'm telling you, Susan, I won't tolerate any more of your loose behaviour, so if you want me to house you and your bas—'

'*Not* in front of the child!' protested Hebe, and Sophy was suddenly snatched off her feet and carried away through the baize-lined door to the kitchen wing. It slammed behind them, cutting off the escalating sound of shouting and weeping.

'What's Mummy done now?' Sophy asked, as she was set back down again. 'Is it my fault, for making Grandfather angry? Aunt Hebe, what has Mummy—'

'Quickly!' Aunt Hebe said, flapping her apron and shooing her through the kitchen past Mrs Lark, like a reluctant hen into the coop.

The cook, who was single-mindedly pounding steaks with a sort of knobbly wooden mallet, looked up long

4

enough to remark, 'Bile pills, that's what *he'll* be needing, before the night's out,' before resuming her assault.

'Deadly nightshade, more like,' muttered Aunt Hebe. 'Come on, Sophy, into the stillroom – I've got rose conserve on the stove, and I don't want it spoiled. And you should know by now that your grandfather is all bark and no bite.'

Although Aunt Hebe was tall and rangy and not at all cosy, she always smelled of roses, which was safe and somehow comforting, unlike Mummy's patchouli, which made Sophy feel excited but vaguely unsettled, much like Mummy herself did.

And after Mummy took her away late that night, leaving behind Winter's End, Aunt Hebe, the little dogs, and everything loved and familiar, she always did find the scent of roses a comfort in an alien world, long after she had forgotten the reason why.

Chapter One: There Must Be an Angel

Despite my fears I found Wynter's End most delightfully situated above a river, with terraces of sweet-scented knots. Sir Ralph was greatly pleased to see mee – but not so the mistress. Mary Wynter is Sir Ralph's second wife and I perceived from the moment she set eyes on mee that she was mine extreame enemy, though I know not why unless she hateth every woman of less years than herself.

From the journal of Alys Blezzard, 1580

No matter how many times I dreamed of the terrible day that culminated in my mother taking me away from Winter's End for ever, I still woke up with my face wet with tears and a sense of anguish – *and* guilt.

Was the final argument that precipitated our flight *my* fault for provoking Grandfather once too often? I had been a mischievous child, always getting into trouble.

My mind groped desperately after the disappearing echoes of once-familiar voices, the last lingering fragrance of Gallica roses ... but as always they slipped away, leaving me with only the fragmented memories of my early childhood to take out and examine, one by one, like faded treasures.

Since my grandfather's brief visit earlier this year everything had been stirred up again and old wounds had

7

reopened. But surely it shouldn't still hurt so much. It was so long ago, that settled time before my mother and I, cast out of Eden, had moved around the country from squat to travellers' van to commune. Eventually, like random jetsam, we'd washed up at a remote little Scottish commune, where we'd run out of road. And then later my poor feckless mother had *literally* run out of road . . . but as Marlowe said, that was in another country: and besides, the wench is dead.

Dead and gone.

It was still dark and I reached for the bedside lamp, only to find that it wasn't there. Then, with a sickening jolt under the ribcage, I remembered that it was already packed away – and why.

I had to pad across the cold, bare floorboards to switch on the ceiling light before climbing back into bed. The white candlewick coverlet, with its raised diamond pattern and central flower motifs, suddenly reminded me of the intricately moulded plaster ceilings of Winter's End. Strange that I hadn't thought of that before, but perhaps, subconsciously, that had been why I bought it.

Yet I barely ever allowed myself to think of Winter's End – not with my conscious mind, anyway – for that was the past, with the door forever shut, and the present had to be dealt with.

And what a present! That day I would be moving out of the tied cottage where Lucy and I had lived for over twenty years, because my elderly employer recently suffered a bad fall and the consequence was that my job had come to an abrupt end.

At first I thought everything would work out fine, especially when Lady Betty's nephew arrived to look after things until she recovered enough to come home. Conor was a chubby, balding man who always reminded me of an amiable frog, though unfortunately he turned out to be a complete toad.

On previous visits to Blackwalls he had seemed fond of Lady Betty and otherwise entirely harmless (apart from a slight tendency to invade my personal space and squeeze my arm with his plump white fingers, while telling me how grateful he was to me for looking after his aunt). That opinion lasted right up to the point where he got power of attorney and had poor Lady Betty, confused but weakly protesting, whipped straight from the hospital to an expensive retirement home. Personally, I don't see that keeping fourteen cats, and telling visitors to your stately ruin that you are the reincarnation of Ramses the First, is anything *like* enough reason to be declared incompetent to manage your affairs. She'd managed them perfectly well for years, with a little assistance from her faithful staff, and she *never* wore the headdress and robe in public.

I think Conor's betrayal was a much greater shock to her than the fall, which I told him straight the day I found out about it – and then he had the gall to come round to the cottage that very evening, well tanked up, to try to exercise some kind of medieval droit de seigneur, insinuating that keeping my home and my job depended entirely on how 'friendly' I was.

I had an instinctive knee-jerk reaction and droited his seigneur until his eyes watered. Pity Lady Betty hadn't been able to do the same, once he had charmed and weaselled the 'temporary' power of attorney out of her and showed his true colours.

The upshot was that Conor gave me immediate notice and put my cottage and other assets up for sale – and of course without a job I couldn't get a mortgage to buy it myself. In any case, I couldn't match the price the people

9

buying it as a weekend cottage were prepared to pay. Let's face it, I couldn't even raise the deposit.

When my husband, Rory, did his vanishing trick and left me holding the baby over twenty years ago, I took the job of Lady Betty's general factotum and moved to a remote little Northumbrian village with Lucy, mainly because it offered a cottage as well as a small salary. There weren't many applicants, or I don't suppose I would have got the job at my age and with a small child, despite having had lots of relevant experience working for the mistress of a small Scottish castle ever since I left school.

But the minute we arrived at the village I knew it was *meant* to be, because I recognised the place. My mad mother and I (and her man of the moment) had once set up home in our vans in a lay-by just outside it, and for several days no one had tried to move us on. That was exceptional, since normally we seemed to be as welcome as a bad smell.

So you see, serendipity brought us here, and Lady Betty loved children and was quite happy for me to fit my work around Lucy's needs. But my pay wasn't huge, so I'd staggered from one financial crisis to another over the years, with never quite enough money to make ends meet, juggling bills and later helping Lucy out at university when her student loan and part-time job weren't quite enough.

If only the interest wasn't so high on that small loan I took out . . . and if only I hadn't had to increase it further still to cover nearly two thousand pounds of vet's bills for poor Daisy! And all in vain, though of course I had had to *try* because she was Lucy's dog too, and we both loved her. And if only I hadn't economised the month before she got ill by letting her pet insurance lapse, it would have been perfectly all right.

If only . . .

Why did everything have to go pear-shaped at once? My

life was like a volcano: it lay dormant for long enough to let me think it was acquiescent, and then suddenly tossed out hot rocks.

My mother would have said, 'Accept your karma and go with the flow, darling,' but just look where doing that got her. She flowed over the Atlantic, over California and down a rather steep canyon. And then, since she still had her old passport, they returned her to Winter's End for burial: a toss of the dice and right down the snake to where you started out, though perhaps not in quite the same pristine condition.

But it was not in my nature to be miserable for long, and soon fingers of silvery sunlight began to gleam around the edges of the black cloud of despondency. I knew something good was coming, even if not precisely what, because I have a touch of the second sight from my witch ancestor, Alys Blezzard.

And after all, there were hours yet before I had to hand over the keys of Spiggs Cottage to strangers and always, *always* in the past something had happened to avert calamity at the last minute ... though perhaps calamity had never been on such a grand, overwhelming scale before. I mean, I'd put down roots here at last, shallow and tentative though they might be, and it was the only home Lucy had ever known. I'd been so determined that Lucy would have the secure and settled upbringing I hadn't had myself once Mum had torn me away from Winter's End.

I sat up, hugging my knees. It wasn't too late to save the cottage – the contract wouldn't be exchanged until later that morning. There was still time for the cavalry to come riding over the hill to rescue me, bugles blowing and flags flying, just as they always had.

I was filled with a sudden glow of unfounded optimism. Getting up, I sprayed on a liberal, fortifying blast of

11

Penhaligon's Elisabethan Rose perfume (the only extravagance in my life, unless you counted Lucy), pulled on a red jumper and jeans that clung to my abundant curves, and ruthlessly dragged a hairbrush through wildly curling dark hair.

Then I went to make coffee and await the arrival of the postman. The last post . . .

No, I wouldn't think like that! The postman would bring *good* news – a reprieve. Maybe I'd won the lottery (despite never buying a ticket) or the Pools. Or perhaps Conor had metamorphosed overnight from a cockroach into a human being and, repentant, he would refuse to sell the cottage and instead beg me to stay there rent free for ever (no droit de seigneur included).

My best friend, Anya, who believes our guardian angels watch over us twenty-four seven, would say that she heard the hushing whisper of mine's wings as she (or should that be *it*?) rushed to the rescue.

I only hoped my very own Personal Celestial Being wouldn't collide on the doorstep with the cavalry or there would be feathers everywhere.

Chapter Two: Distant Connections

I applied all the cures and simples my mother taught mee so well, and young Thomas Wynter's suffering is much alleviated, though it is clear to mee that he will not make old bones.

From the journal of Alys Blezzard, 1580

I'd been so *positive* I could hear those hoofbeats and the *swoosh!* of angel's wings coming to the rescue – but either I was mistaken or they took a wrong turn, for Spiggs Cottage was lost to me.

I couldn't understand it . . . and even several days later, I still couldn't quite believe it. My life had gone full circle so that I'd have to start all over again, twenty years older but still with no money, qualifications or assets other than a vintage Volkswagen camper van with about twice the world's circumference on the clock, inherited, by rather permanent default, from my mother.

Lucy and I had always used it to travel about with friends in the holidays, but it began to look as though I would have to live in it again permanently, until someone in the village came to the rescue with the offer of a big static caravan for the winter.

Though grateful for any temporary roof over my head, there was nothing quite so freezing as a caravan out of season. The cold pierced from all directions, like living in an ice cube. I wouldn't have been surprised to find a shivering polar bear at the door asking to be let out.

But at least it was a roof over my head until the site reopened in March, and it was far larger than either the van or the cottage. This was just as well, since the materials for the little round silk and satin crazy-patchwork cushions I made and sold mail order took up quite a bit of space.

My cushions, each feather-stitched patch embroidered and embellished, were *very* upmarket. Luckily the buyers couldn't see the raggle-taggle gypsy making them, or the charity shops and jumble sales where I bought the old clothes to cut up for pieces!

I blew on my frozen fingers and read over the letter I had written, breaking the news that we were homeless to Lucy, so very far away teaching English in Japan.

Darling Lucy,

My job at Blackwalls has finished rather suddenly. Poor Lady Betty was making a good recovery from her fall, but her nephew got power of attorney and took charge of things, with disastrous results. Do you remember Conor? You said when you met him once that he was a slimy little creep, and you were quite right – he has put Lady Betty into a home and now seems to be selling up the whole estate.

In fact, he's sold our cottage already, but though it was sad to leave it I am ready to have a change of scene and a new job. Meanwhile, Dana – you remember her from the Pleasurefields camping site? – is letting me live in one of her static caravans rent free, which is very kind of her. I'm making a special cushion as a thank-you.

Don't worry, I packed up everything in your room very carefully, and the contents of the cottage are stored

14

in the next-door caravan. I can stay until they open up again in March, but I don't suppose I will be here very long. There are one or two nice-looking jobs advertised in *The Lady* magazine, with accommodation included, so I've written off with my totally impressive CV. You can't say I haven't had a lifetime's experience of looking after ancestral piles, even if I've only ever really been a glorified cleaner-cum-tour guide.

I'll let you know when I hear anything and hope to have a lovely new home for you to come back to when you return.

Love, Mum xxx

Who was I fooling? Lucy would be on the phone to me two minutes after she got the letter ... which was why, I suppose, I was taking the cowardly way out and posting her the news.

I hoped, by the time she got hold of me, to have a new job and a new life lined up somewhere else. The applications lay on the table, ready to post except for stamps – and then I suddenly remembered it was the post office's half-day and the clock was hurtling towards twelve.

Leaping up, I dragged on my jacket and flung open the door – then teetered perilously on the brink, gazing down into a pair of eyes of a truly celestial blue, but even colder than the caravan. Missing my footing entirely, I fell down the two metal steps into the surprised arms of an angry angel.

Maybe Anya was right after all, I thought, as he fielded me neatly – except that angels are presumably asexual, while this one was undoubtedly male, even if his short, ruffled hair was of corniest gold. He smelled heavenly too, *and* expensive. I think it was the same aftershave that Conor used, at about a million pounds a molecule, but it smelled *so* much better on my visitor.

He set me back on my feet, stared down at me in a puzzled sort of way, then said, 'I'm looking for Sophy Winter – I was told she was staying here.'

'She is – you've found her.'

'*You're* Sophy Winter?'

'Well, I was last time I checked in the mirror,' I said tartly.

'But you can't be! You don't look like—' he began, then broke off to give me a comprehensive once-over, checking off my minus points on some mental list: dark hair – check; hazel eyes – check; unfashionably generous hourglass figure – check; supermarket jeans and jumble-sale jumper – check. Number of Winter attributes scored: nil.

'Right . . .' he said doubtfully, 'then you must have been expecting me. I'm your cousin, Jack – Jack Lewis.'

'But I haven't got any cousins,' I protested. I certainly didn't recall any . . . and surely even my mother would have mentioned them if I had.

'I'm a very *distant* cousin and since I didn't go to live at Winter's End until shortly after you and your mother had left, you wouldn't remember me. But I'm sure you've heard of me?'

'No I haven't,' I began – and then the full import of what he had just said sank in, shaking me to the core. I exclaimed incredulously, 'What do you mean, *you* lived at Winter's End?'

I'd always imagined Winter's End and Grandfather and the twin aunts and the little dogs and *everything* just going on for ever, like a scene securely enclosed in a snowglobe. Even if I could never get back into that closed world again, at least I had been able to take it out and give it a shake occasionally . . . But now it seemed that this stranger had almost immediately taken my place there!

He misread my amazement as suspicious disbelief and flushed crossly. 'If you must know, my mother was your grandfather's cousin and we lived in New Zealand. She died

16

when I was five, and when my father remarried I was sent back home.'

'Oh,' I said uncertainly, because despite his hair not having the true red-gold Winter tint he *did* have a look of my mother, now I came to consider it – or how she would have looked in a rage, if she'd ever had one. While 'feckless' and 'stoned' would have been the two words that summed my mother up best, she was good-natured to the point where it was a serious handicap in life. 'But why are you here? And why did you think I would be expecting you?'

I must have sounded as genuinely bewildered as I felt for the anger in his eyes slowly thawed and was replaced by something like speculation. 'You mean you don't know anything about me? And you haven't heard the news yet?'

'No! And what news?'

'That William Winter is dead, for a start,' he said bluntly.

'Grandfather's *dead*?' Things seemed to blur dizzily around me and I sank down onto the top step of the caravan.

'Dead for months. And while I, as the last male descendant of the Winters, get the title, I don't suppose you will be surprised to learn that he left Winter's End and everything else to *you*.'

My vision cleared and I looked up to see that he was eyeing me narrowly.

'W-Winter's End? *Me*? You're mad or . . . or there's some mistake!' I stammered. 'He's only seen me once since we left, and he didn't seem to like me any more then than he did when I was a little girl!'

'*Once*?' It must have been obvious that I was telling the truth, for his expression slowly altered to a rueful smile of singular and quite dazzling charm, exuding such warmth that, despite my state of numb shock, I found myself returning it.

'Sorry, I seem to have got hold of the wrong end of the stick. I've made all the wrong assumptions! What on earth

17

must you think of me? Look, let's start again, shall we?' He took my hands and pulled me to my feet. 'Sophy, I'm *delighted* to meet you at last!'

Then, enfolding me in his arms, he kissed me on each cheek before taking my hands again and stepping back to look at me with what appeared to be genuine admiration.

But do not think I was entirely inactive during this embrace – no, I was actively inert and acquiescent. I hadn't had my hands on such a gorgeous man within living memory, even one with a dodgy temper who had just told me things I didn't want to hear – *and* some I couldn't believe.

You try dating in a small village, while juggling a low-paid and exhausting job and turning your hobby into a little business on the side, all under the critical and jealous eyes of your daughter. None of my potential suitors had made it past first base. If I actually managed to find a babysitter and got out of the house with a man, you could bet your bottom dollar Lucy would be running a high fever or throwing out interesting symptoms before I reached the end of the street.

And I hadn't had much more luck since she went off to university. All the men in my age bracket seemed to be looking for skinny young blondes. That, or they had a serious impediment they forgot to mention, like a wife.

So now, enfolded in softest cashmere and anaesthetised by Amouage Gold Pour Homme, if I had any conscious thought at all it was along the lines of, Yes! Bring it on!

Ten minutes later we were sitting in my icebox of a caravan drinking coffee and talking like old friends.

'So you see,' Jack was explaining, 'we didn't even know old William had found you until the will was read. He'd tried and failed to discover where you and your mother were in the past, of course. Then when your mother . . .' he searched for a tactful phrase, 'when your mother was brought

18

home, he tried again to trace you – but on the wrong side of the Atlantic, since we assumed you would have been in America with her. After that we thought he'd given up, until we discovered he'd secretly left you Winter's End and,' he shrugged and smiled charmingly, 'we thought *you* must have finally got in touch with *him* and managed to persuade him into leaving you everything.'

'No, he traced me through an advert for cushions I put in a magazine, and a few months ago he simply turned up out of the blue. And although it was lovely to know he'd never stopped trying to find me, I don't know why he bothered, because he spent most of the time lecturing me about where I'd gone wrong in life and which decisions I could have made better. He'd hired a private eye to dig into my past, so he even knew things I'd forgotten. He didn't look much different from how I remembered him, either . . . except he seemed frailer and his hair was white, of course.'

I looked back at my early memories of him: a tall figure with the Winter pale red-gold hair, bright blue eyes and the beard of a biblical prophet. (The only one of those attributes I don't regret not inheriting is the beard.)

'So that's the only time you saw him?' Jack asked, accepting another refill but declining anything to eat. I'd laid out before him everything I had in the way of refreshments – two cherry-topped coconut pyramids and a carob-covered rice cake – but going by his expression, I don't think he recognised them as food.

I took the rice cake myself, the pyramids, crumbly and sticky, being a bit hard to eat neatly in company. 'Yes, he just turned up one afternoon on my one day off – but of course the private eye would have told him when I'd be in. Lucy was home and she is *so* defensive that she and Grandfather spent most of the time trying to score points off each other.' I shuddered. 'They actually seemed to enjoy it, but

I hate arguments and fights. He didn't suggest we visit Winter's End, either – he said it was too late and would just stir things up.'

At the time that had hurt and I had wondered why he had gone to the trouble of finding us at all, but then he had added that he wasn't in the best of health and had just wanted to assure himself that we were all right.

Which we were, of course – totally penniless, but all right.

'Who's Lucy?' Jack asked.

'My daughter. She's twenty-two, and out in Japan teaching English for a year . . . at least, I hope it's only a year, because I miss her terribly.' I cupped my hands around my own mug and stared down into it. 'But you did say that Grandfather left me Winter's End, didn't you? I didn't imagine that? Only I'm sure you *can't* be right because – I mean – why on earth would he? It's too incredible to be true! And in any case, surely I would have been told about it by now if he had?'

'You haven't, because the solicitor had strict instructions from my uncle to wait until the estate was settled before contacting you – or telling the family where you were. He knew there would be a fuss because, you see, I was brought up expecting to take on Winter's End as the next *legitimate* heir . . . even if you turned up again, which of course you didn't. But it wasn't entailed on the next male descendant, so he was free to leave the estate to who he liked.'

'So, why did he do it?' I asked, ignoring this slur on my birth.

'My uncle and I didn't see eye to eye about some things: he just couldn't understand modern business methods, for a start. And he'd been draining the money that should have gone to keep the house in good repair into his garden restoration schemes instead, but when I remonstrated with him, he flew right off the handle.'

20

'So when the will was read you naturally assumed I'd schemed to get him to leave Winter's End to me?'

'Yes – sorry about that! But you can understand how I felt, can't you? The old man must have been senile to do such a thing – I love the place and I'd grown up believing it would one day be mine, that's what made me so unreasonably angry. As soon as I managed to find out where you lived I thought I'd come up here and make you an offer for Winter's End, but temper got the better of me!'

'Make me an offer?' I'd started to be convinced I was in some strange dream and would wake up again any minute. 'You mean, you want me to *sell* Winter's End to you?'

'Yes, just that. I could challenge the will because William was clearly unhinged when he wrote it – but this way seems more civilised.' He leaned forward and took my hand in his, looking down into my eyes in a way that made the caravan seem suddenly very much warmer. 'Listen, Sophy, it's the only practical thing you *can* do, because I'm afraid you've inherited a total white elephant and all the liabilities that go with it. Winter's End is falling down and has been for years, because of all the income being diverted into the garden restoration. He even took out a bank loan against the house to fund the final stages. It's got wet rot, dry rot, woodworm … you name it, and it's got it. And there aren't even any major assets you could sell off. There was one decent painting, a Stubbs, but William arranged for it to go to the nation in lieu of death duties.'

Despite the mesmerising effect his nearness and those devastating blue eyes were having on me, it occurred to me that Grandfather seemed to have had it all worked out – not the actions of a senile man.

'But *you* still want Winter's End?' I asked him curiously.

'Yes, it's my family home, after all, where I was brought up … I love it. And I'm a property developer, a very successful one, so I know what needs to be done and I can afford to do it.'

'I understand. I was just starting to feel the same way about my cottage, even though it didn't belong to me.'

He looked seriously at me, his eyes frank and earnest: 'Please let me buy it back, Sophy! I'll even pay well over the market value – how about that? It can't mean anything to you, can it, since you left it when you were a small child? And I don't suppose you could afford the upkeep, anyway.'

I said slowly, 'No, I – no, how *can* it mean anything to me? I was eight when I last saw it.'

'*Liar!*' said a voice in my head – Alys's voice, tenuous and far away, as if speaking down a very bad telephone line, but instantly familiar to me even after all these years.

Alys, are you back again?

But if she was, she was now silent. Maybe my subconscious had simply ascribed her voice to my innermost thoughts? For of course I did long for Winter's End – but the Winter's End of my childhood, before Jack took my place and everything changed – and there was no way back to that.

'You could come and visit whenever you liked anyway,' he offered, with another one of those glorious smiles. 'We're family, aren't we? And now I've found you, I've no intention of letting you get away again!'

I sighed and shook my head. 'You know, it's *so* ironic! I was waiting for an angel to come to the rescue – but now it's too late. Only a week ago I'd have jumped at the chance without a second thought, because I could have bought my cottage and not had to move out.'

He looked puzzled, so I explained what had happened, and then he suggested I could still make the new owners of the cottage an offer they couldn't refuse.

'I could, but they are rich City types who've bought it for a holiday home and I don't think they would be likely

22

to sell it even at more than its value. They're busy ripping out every original feature and tossing the cottage's entrails into a skip, so all the things I loved about it have already gone. If there is one thing my early life has taught me, it's that when everything changes, you move on – and you can never go back and expect things to be the same.'

Not even at Winter's End, except in my dreams . . .

'But you could buy somewhere new?' he suggested. 'I expect you've got friends here?'

'Not really. I know a lot of people but I've only got one *real* friend, from way back, and she tends to move around a lot.'

In fact, she moved around permanently; but Anya, with her dreadlocked red hair and her home made from an old ambulance, was probably a world away from the sort of people my cousin Jack knew.

'Well, now you've got me,' he said, giving my hand another squeeze and then letting it go. 'Whatever you decide, we'll always be friends as well as distant cousins, I hope. But I know, when you have thought it over, you'll realise that the right thing to do is to sell Winter's End to me, to keep it in the family.'

'I expect so, but – well, none of this seems real at all yet. I need time to think – and hear the news officially from a solicitor, too, before it sinks in properly and I start to believe it!'

'You will. Hobbs is the family solicitor, though he is semi-retired, and he said he was going to call in and see you personally on his way up to Scotland. I expect he's hard on my heels. Oh, by the way,' he added casually, 'I promised Aunt Hebe that I'd ask you if you had the book, and if you have, take it back with me.'

'The . . . *book*?' I stared at him blankly while the clanging of alarm bells sounded in my head. 'Do you mean that

23

Victorian children's book of gruesome stories from the Bible that Aunt Hebe used to read to me? I did take that away with me – still got it, in fact, though I didn't inflict it on Lucy. It used to give me nightmares, but I was horribly fascinated by it!'

'No, she meant Alys Blezzard's household book, a little, really ancient notebook of recipes. It's a priceless bit of family history, and it's been missing since your mother ran off. They just sort of assumed she took it with her.'

I shook my head. 'No, sorry. Mum told me all about Alys – she liked the idea that she was descended from a family notorious for witchcraft – but she never mentioned any book.'

'Are you *sure* it wasn't among her things?' he pressed me. 'It's quite an heirloom, so Hebe's always been upset that it's missing.'

'She didn't leave a lot of possessions behind when she went to America, so I'd have noticed something like that.'

'And she wouldn't have taken it with her?'

'No, I'm sure she didn't. I helped her decide what to take and did the packing. We had to buy a suitcase especially, because we didn't think her old carpetbag would stand up to aeroplane baggage handlers.'

'Then Aunt Hebe *will* be disappointed!' He stood and pulled out a slim gold case from his pocket. 'Look, I'll have to be off now, but here's my card – ring me when you've seen Hobbs and had a think about my offer. Selling Winter's End is the only sensible option, you know . . . and remember, whatever *anyone* says, I love the place and only want the best for it.'

'OK,' I said, slightly puzzled, and he put his arm around me and gave me a squeeze. He seemed a very hands-on kind of person, when he wasn't miffed. But I understood how he felt about Winter's End because I, too, had loved my little cottage.

'And at least you have inherited something I, a mere female, can't – the title,' I pointed out. 'Sir Jack!'

'Very true. And of course there *is* a long family tradition of intermarriage in the family, especially when a girl is the heiress . . . much like now, I suppose,' he said, with a teasing smile. 'Keeps the title and the property together.'

'I – yes, I suppose it does,' I agreed, slightly taken aback.

'Oh, Sir Jack, this is so sudden!' he said in a mock-modest falsetto, and I laughed.

'But seriously, Sophy, I don't intend letting you go out of my life five minutes after I've found you, whatever you decide,' he said, and kissed me again before he left, this time in a less than cousinly way. But that's OK – he *is* something less than a cousin, after all.

After he'd gone everything seemed a bit leached of colour and lifeless, including me. I drank about a gallon of Rescue Remedy, then went out to the VW and fetched a wooden box from the ingenious special hiding place that one of my mother's friends had made for it (and her stash) long ago.

It was rectangular, quite deep and surprisingly heavy, and when I opened the lid the delicious aroma of ancient books wafted out. I should know that smell, I've dusted libraries full of them in my time. Anyway, I adore books. That's where I acquired most of my education. The scent of old leather bindings promised escape into another, comforting world, much as the scent of roses once reassured me that Winter's End still existed just as I left it.

Carefully I lifted out *A Little Child's Warning: A Treasury of Bible Stories* with its faded gilt edges and the cover depiction of a small child praying, eyes cast up to heaven, but my icy hands fumbled and almost dropped the book.

A positive cascade of pressed roses fell out, with the papery whispering of old ghosts.

Chapter Three: Diamond Cut

They have given mee a chamber in the solar to be near Thomas. I spend much time there – or in the stillroom, which is sadly neglected, Lady Wynter having no interest in those arts in which it should be her pride to be accomplished. I walk in the gardens when I can spare the time and pick herbs. The plants I need that grow wild in the woods and pastures are harder to obtain and some must be picked by the light of the moon . . . To slip out here unseen is difficult.

From the journal of Alys Blezzard, 1580

'Anya!' I said, when I finally managed to reach her. 'My guardian angel is a golden Lucifer – diabolically handsome and slightly sulphurous round the edges. He's hot – and I think I'm in love!'

'How do you know?' she said, sounding as if she was standing in a metal oil drum (which she might have been – you never know with Anya).

'That I'm in love?'

'No, that your guardian angel is a Lucifer.'

'Oh – because he visited me yesterday,' I said. 'He's sort of a cousin – a very distant cousin.' Then I told her all about my grandfather's death, my inheritance – and Jack's offer.

'And he was furious when he first turned up, because he

26

thought I'd somehow managed to brainwash Grandfather into leaving Winter's End to me. Once he realised I hadn't he was really, really nice.'

'I bet he was,' she said, sounding unconvinced. 'But after all you've told me about your childhood at Winter's End and how you feel about the place, I can't understand why you don't sound delirious with pleasure.'

'Well, for one thing I'm still stunned and wondering why on earth Grandfather did it; and for another, it isn't the Winter's End I remember, because it's clear that Jack took my place soon after I left,' I said slowly. 'Apparently the house is really run down and there is a big outstanding bank loan against it too, which Grandfather took out to pay for his garden restoration.'

'What were you expecting, a Shangri-La that always stayed the same?'

'It *did* always stay the same, in my imagination – and part of me thinks it's better left like that, and I should never try to go back there.'

'Well, they always say, be careful what you wish for,' Anya said breezily, 'but actually, I always thought the only reason you started working in stately homes was because you were trying to recreate a bit of what you once had – and just think how useful all that experience will be now! Doesn't the thought of doing such a major clean-up get your juices flowing?'

She knows me only too well.

'I wish *my* angels would conjure something up like that, Sophy. I'm getting a bit tired of wandering around now,' she confessed to my surprise, because she has been on the road since she was eighteen and left the commune. We did this sort of role-reversal thing. When I arrived at the commune I was tired of moving about and just wanted to settle down, while she was fed up with the whole thing and attracted to the kind of life I'd had with Mum.

27

'I think when Guy gets a job I might settle somewhere near him,' she added thoughtfully. 'He's got lots of interviews.'

'I'm not surprised; he got a first-class degree.'

Guy is Anya's son, a year younger than Lucy, and was always bright – and very determined. When he was eleven he insisted on staying with his grandmother in Scotland during the school terms and got grade A *everything*.

'How is Lucy doing?' Anya asked.

'She seems fine, but I wish she wasn't so far away. And some man keeps pestering her, which I find worrying. She says he seems fascinated by her being so tall and blonde. There have been a couple of cases of British women being stalked and even murdered in Japan.'

'But Lucy is very sensible, Sophy. I'm sure she wouldn't put herself at risk.'

'Perhaps not, but if I *did* sell Winter's End to Jack, she could come home and I would be able to pay off her student loan and buy a cottage somewhere. Then maybe we could start up a business together and—'

'Don't you do anything hasty,' she warned me, 'especially with this relative of yours. He doesn't sound like any kind of angel to me, but he *does* sound the kind of clever, tricky, devious man you always seem to go for.'

'I don't know what you mean by "always". I can count on one hand the number of men I've been out with since Rory left me,' I said with dignity and some modesty, leaving one or two of my brief encounters with absolute no-hopers out of the reckoning. 'And I can't imagine what I've said to make you think that about Jack! He's a really genuine, lovely person – and what's more, he's *family*. Anyway, I can't do anything at all until the solicitor turns up. I'm still trying to take it all in, but I'm worried that Grandfather might have changed his will on impulse after arguing with Jack about spending too much on the garden, and then died before he could change it back. It *does* seem unfair that he should leave the house to me. Anya—'

There was a plaintive bleeping. 'Blow – my phone's almost dead,' she said, and was cut off.

My belated rescue turned out to be a very belt-and-braces affair, for next day the cavalry, in the sober and suited form of the family solicitor, turned up too.

You see, I knew good things were on the way. My second sight was just a bit dodgy about *when*.

Mr Hobbs said he had already written to tell me he was coming to see me today 'on a matter to my advantage', but of course I haven't had the heart to go back to Spiggs Cottage and collect my mail since I left. The new owners are probably putting it straight into the skip, anyway.

Any more strange men visiting my caravan and, as far as the village is concerned, I might as well hang a red lamp over the door, even if this one looked so old and desiccated that strong winds could have blown him away. I've learned the hard way that a divorced woman is always seen as a sexual predator, after everyone else's menfolk (which is why, I suppose, I haven't made many friends here and hardly ever get asked to dinner parties).

But I invited Mr Hobbs in, and he was surprised to find I already knew of the legacy, until I told him about Jack's visit and his offer to buy Winter's End. Then, over tea and rather overdone rock cakes (the caravan stove is a bit temperamental), I asked him if he knew exactly *why* my grandfather hadn't left the estate to Jack.

'After all, he was the obvious heir, wasn't he, even if they had had one or two disagreements? It does seem unfair.'

'He had his reasons,' he said cagily. I suppose it was only natural that he should side with my grandfather – they were of an age and had probably been friends. 'Jack is the only son of his cousin Louisa, now deceased, and was born in New Zealand. When his father remarried he was sent back here to school, about a year after you and your mother left . . . and of course he spent the holidays at Winter's End and looked on it as his home. He is divorced with no children – another disappointment to your grandfather – and has a house in London. You know he is a property developer?'

'He did mention that. Presumably a successful one, if he could afford to buy me out?'

'Yes indeed: one cannot say that he hasn't risen by his own endeavours. His father purchased a small house for him to live in when he was at Oxford, and then later he renovated it and sold it at a profit and bought two more on the proceeds . . . and so it went on. I suppose his enterprise is quite remarkable. *Nowadays* he specialises in buying large period properties cheaply and converting them into extremely upmarket and expensive apartments,' he added meaningfully.

I stared at him. 'But surely you don't think he would do that to Winter's End? He said he loved the place and wanted to restore it to its former glory – and he seemed so sincere.'

'I am sure he did: his sincerity must be one of his greatest business assets,' Mr Hobbs said drily. 'And of course he *has* restored the houses he has purchased, which might otherwise have fallen into irreversible decay. They were all, like Winter's End, within an easy commuting distance of thriving major cities.'

'Oh,' I said, digesting this. 'But in the case of Winter's End, that could be just a coincidence?'

'Of course, that may be so. However, in his eagerness to persuade you to sell your inheritance, he may have been perhaps a little *selective* in the information he imparted to you. For instance, did he touch upon the various responsibilities that come with the legacy?'

'I . . . no, *what* responsibilities?'

'Apart from your grandfather charging you to complete a garden restoration scheme that has, in my opinion – and I have to say in all fairness, Jack's – nearly brought the house to ruin, the livelihoods of several people working for the Winter's End estate depends on your decision. You might also want to consider that Winter's End has been your Great-Aunt Hebe's home for all her life, though she does, of course, have some means of her own, as does her twin sister, Ottilie, who resides for part of the year in the coach house.'

I felt responsibility settle round my shoulders like a lead cape. 'But I know nothing about managing an estate! How could I possibly take it on?'

'But you *do* have relevant experience in looking after old properties, Ms Winter. Sir William thought you were just what Winter's End needed.'

'He did? But I've no experience of running one, only doing the donkey work and passing on orders to the other staff. And do call me Sophy – I have a feeling we are likely to see a lot of each other.'

His face broke into a smile like a rather jolly tortoise. 'Or one of my sons – I am semi-retired, you know, though I like to keep my brain active by retaining one or two clients. But to get back to business, Sophy, Winter's End is not a large house, although the gardens are extensive and take quite some keeping up, especially the yew maze and all the box hedges and topiary. Do you remember the spiral maze?'

I nodded. 'At the front of the house.' I felt a sudden pang for the small, mischievous Sophy who used to run through it with Grandfather's pack of miniature spaniels chasing after her, yapping madly – and who would then usually have to go back and rescue one or two of them who had got lost among the labyrinthine turns. 'It was quite low, wasn't it? Most tall adults would be able to see over the top of the hedges.'

31

'That's right, and all those curves and rounded edges take a good deal of clipping. Then there is a considerable area of woodland on the opposite side of the valley to the house and one tenanted farm. Are you interested in gardening at all?'

'I had enough of mulching and digging in all weathers when I lived in the Scottish commune to cure me of wanting to be a hands-on gardener, but I do love the frivolity of gardens made just to *look* at.'

'Quite,' he said. 'And Sir William told me that you have considerable expertise in caring for old houses and their contents from your previous employment, do you not?'

'Oh, yes, I left school at sixteen and my first job was in a Scottish castle. The Mistress saw to it that I learned the correct way to clean it and all the valuable things it contained.'

'The *Mistress*?'

'That's how she liked to be addressed by her staff,' I explained, 'which I was, until I ran off and married her cousin Rory. Then after I had Lucy I got the job here at Blackwalls with Lady Betty, keeping everything clean and in good repair, passing on her orders to the other staff, taking guided tours around the house on open days, being her PA . . . you name it, I did it. Lady Betty didn't pay me a lot, but she was very kind to me and Lucy, and I was fond of her.'

I touched the little gold, enamel and crystal bee brooch I wore. 'She gave me this as a keepsake when I visited her in the hospital, because she said she had a premonition she wasn't going to see Blackwalls again. And she was quite right, because once she signed the power of attorney, her nephew had her moved to an upmarket old people's home and she just lost the will to live. The last time I visited her she didn't really recognise me.'

32

I fished a tissue out of the box and blew my nose, while Mr Hobbs looked away tactfully.

'After he had been up here to see you, your grandfather said, and I quote his very words, "It seems to me the women of the family have always run things behind the scenes here at Winter's End, so one might as well take over as head of the family and have done with it." He thought you would make a better job of it than Jack ever would, especially with Lucy to help you. Yes . . .' he added thoughtfully, 'he was particularly taken with your daughter.'

'He *was*? But they quarrelled the whole time he was here!'

'He said she had the typical Winter temperament, allied with an almost masculine sense of business.'

'Well, I suppose he meant that as a compliment,' I conceded. 'She *is* very bossy and argumentative, though it's called assertiveness these days, and she did business studies and English at university.'

'Those would be considerable assets in running the estate. Sir William also said that, although so unlike your mother in character, in appearance Lucy reminded him very much of how Susan had been at the same age.'

'Yes, she's tall, slender and has that lovely red-gold hair – nothing like me. I don't look like a Winter at all. Even Jack, who is only a cousin several times removed, looks more like a Winter than I do!'

'Oh, there are the occasional darker Winters,' he assured me. 'Sir William told me that he was deeply sorry that he had not seen you grow up, but I believe he *would* have discovered your whereabouts much earlier had your mother not changed her name to all intents and purposes, to –' he looked down at his papers – 'Sukie Starchild.'

'I know. Dreadful, isn't it? She wanted to call me Skye, but I stuck to Sophy. I did have to use the surname Starchild on the few occasions when we stayed somewhere long enough for me to go to school, though, so Grandfather couldn't find us. She *said* she was afraid I would be taken away from her, but I often wondered if there was something else making her so paranoid about it.'

'There was,' Mr Hobbs said. 'Sir William did tell Susan that he would cut off her allowance and have her declared an unfit mother if she didn't change her ways, but those were merely empty threats that he had no intention of carrying out, for he often said things in temper that he afterwards regretted.'

'But my mother obviously believed he meant them that time?'

'That is so, but when she left she also took with her a diamond necklace that was not actually hers to dispose of – a family heirloom, in fact. He circulated its description, so he would have been notified if it came up for sale, but when it didn't he assumed it had been broken up and the stones recut.'

'I *wondered* how she bought the van in the first place!' I exclaimed. 'And she did have some very dodgy friends when I was very small and we were living in squats in London.'

'Sir William assumed she would return when the money ran out, so by the time he realised she wasn't going to, and began to try to trace you both, you had vanished.'

'She was terrified of him finding her, and I suppose that explains why – but she never could stand anger and loud voices; she was such a gentle person.'

'He never quite gave up hope that you would both be found, Sophy – and then, of course, he discovered that your mother had died in an accident. You know that her body was repatriated, and is buried in the family plot in the Sticklepond graveyard?'

I nodded. 'Though I didn't find out until much later what had happened.'

'Your grandfather assumed you had been in America with her, so that is where he searched again for you, without result.'

'No, I was fourteen by then, and I'd had enough of travelling. I didn't like my mother's new boyfriend much, either, so I didn't want to go to California with them. We'd been living in a commune in Scotland and my best friend's mother offered to look after me if I stayed, so I did until I got a live-in job at the castle, when I was sixteen.'

'And stayed lost until someone pointed out the unusual name "Sophy Winter" in a magazine advert,' Mr Hobbs said, 'when, on making enquiries, Sir William discovered that you were indeed his granddaughter.'

'Yes, I reverted to my real name after my mother died. I always felt ridiculous as a Starchild – *so* old hippie. And I didn't change my name when I married Lucy's father, I just stayed a Winter. I was only married for five minutes anyway.'

Actually, that was a slight exaggeration: it was five weeks, just long enough for me to fall pregnant and for commitment-phobe Rory to get such cold feet that he went away to find himself. So far as I know, he's still looking.

'Yes, that did worry your grandfather a little – but at least you *had* got married.'

'Unlike my mother?'

He ignored that, smoothing out the papers in front of him with a dry, wrinkled finger. 'You have no contact with your former husband?'

'No, none. He was a cousin of the owner of the castle I was working in, a diver working on the oilrigs – you know, six weeks on, six off. He was ten years older than me, but we fell in love and married in Gretna Green – very romantic – and then settled down in a rented cottage. Then he supposedly went off back to work and instead vanished.'

I had waited and waited for him, sure he would come

35

back, until I finally realised that he'd taken everything he valued with him and never meant to return at all. With hindsight I could see that I had been the one in love with the idea of marriage and domesticity, the family I yearned for, and he had simply gone along with it in a moment of madness, or frustrated lust, or . . . something.'

'And that is the last you saw of him?' Mr Hobbs prompted gently. 'He never contacted you again?'

'No, though I'm sure his family knew where he was. But they wouldn't have anything to do with me, of course, because they were horrified when he married the help. I've heard that he has been working abroad ever since, and I divorced him eventually. There hasn't been anyone serious in my life since then. I don't need anyone really; I've usually got a dog.'

'Quite,' he said, though looking slightly perplexed. 'That does, however, simplify matters. I would most earnestly advise you *not* to consider selling the property at this juncture, and certainly not without visiting it first. Indeed, they are all expecting you to take over the reins as soon as possible.'

'*All?*' I said, startled. 'How many people are we actually talking about here?'

'Well, your twin great-aunts – though of course they were provided for under the terms of your great-grandfather's will. Ottilie leases the coach house, which she converted into a studio with living accommodation soon after your mother left. You *do* remember her?'

'Yes, though I saw much less of her than Aunt Hebe. She didn't come to Winter's End much when I lived there – isn't she a sculptor?'

'Indeed, a very well-known one. She made something of a misalliance in her brother's eyes when she was in her forties by marrying his last head gardener, though I believe

36

Sir William was more grieved at the thought of losing his right-hand man than at the marriage itself. But as it transpired he did not, since Rufus Greenwood was as passionate about restoring the Winter's End gardens as he was himself. He stayed on and Ottilie had the old coach house converted so she could divide her time between her husband at Winter's End and her studio in Cornwall. Still does, though she is now widowed.'

'So, who else is there? I remember a cook-housekeeper . . .'

'Yes, Mrs Lark and her husband, Jonah, are the only live-in staff now. There are three gardeners – four, if you include the head gardener . . .' He ruffled the papers a little, seemed about to say something, and then thought better of it. 'Ye-es. There is a daily cleaner . . . and Mr Yatton, the estate manager, who like myself is semi-retired, but he comes in most mornings to the office in the solar tower.'

'Four gardeners and only one cleaner? For a place that size?' I exclaimed, amazed, because if there is one thing I do know about, it is the upkeep of old houses.

'At first a cleaning firm was brought in occasionally, but I don't think that has happened for three or four years now.'

'A specialist firm? One used to dealing with the contents of historic buildings?' I asked hopefully.

'No, a local agency called Dolly Mops. They are very thorough – my wife uses them.'

I winced, thinking of all the damage a well-meaning but untrained cleaner might have inflicted on the fabric and contents of Winter's End.

'Then, of course, there are the Friends,' Mr Hobbs added.

'The . . . friends?'

'The Friends of Winter's End, a local group of history enthusiasts, who volunteer to come in on the summer opening days to sell tickets, and look after those rooms open to the public – the Great Hall and gallery. The house and gardens are open two afternoons a week, from May to the end of August.'

'I understand from Jack that the house is in very poor condition and there isn't enough money to restore it. Is that so?'

'While it is true that your grandfather diverted most of his income into renovating the gardens, he did not touch the capital, which is securely invested – though of course, no investments bring the returns they used to, and an old house like Winter's End needs a considerable amount of keeping up. And unfortunately, he took out a bank loan when he started to restore the maze and the terraces, secured against the property, which is a drain on the estate.'

'Jack mentioned that. How big a bank loan?' I asked hesitantly. I wasn't sure I really wanted to know.

'I believe there is still twenty thousand pounds outstanding.'

'Good heavens!'

'Yes, indeed – it is all *quite* a responsibility.'

The 'r' word again – and although I had pretty well run Blackwalls for Lady Betty, having the ultimate responsibility for my own stately pile was still a scary prospect. On the other hand, the thought of having a whole neglected house to put right sort of appealed . . . OK, I admit it, it drew me like a magnet, especially if this time the house I would be working in would actually be *mine*!

But I now had two rather differing views of my inheritance to compare – three, if you counted the letter from my grandfather that Mr Hobbs now handed to me, though actually it was more of a brief note scrawled in thin, spidery writing, urging me to complete the garden restoration project – his 'Memorial to Posterity' as he put it. It was abundantly clear that I needed to see Winter's End for myself before deciding what to do, and the sooner the better: I would be upping sticks and decamping to rural west Lancashire as soon as I could get my act together.

Besides, I was beginning to feel a strong, almost fearful tug of attraction, as though some connecting umbilical cord stretched almost to invisibility had suddenly twitched, reminding me of its existence.

Mr Hobbs must have drawn his own conclusions from the expression on my face, for he seemed to relax and, with a satisfied smile, said, 'So, I may inform the family that you will be arriving shortly?' He looked around at the cluttered caravan. 'It would seem you do not have a home or employment to keep you here.'

'Very true,' I agreed. 'No, there is nothing to keep me here – so I'll go to Winter's End and then make my own mind up what will be the best thing to do.'

'Spoken like a Winter,' he said approvingly.

'Yes, but Jack might not be pleased about it,' I said, suddenly remembering my handsome cousin's existence (be still my beating heart!). 'He told me that he'd decided, before he met me, that if I wouldn't sell Winter's End back to him he would challenge the will. If he has a strong case, is there really any point in my going to Winter's End?'

'Oh, that's an empty threat, my dear,' Mr Hobbs assured me. 'Your grandfather was perfectly *compos mentis* when he made the will: only look at the way he left instructions for everything to be settled before you were informed of your inheritance, so you could step right in and pick up the reins. I am sure Jack has already taken legal advice and been told the same thing.'

He stood up and began to gather his papers back into his briefcase, declining my offer of more tea and rock cakes with every sign of polite revulsion. There's no accounting for tastes.

39

Chapter Four: The Moving Mollusc

Now Thomas is somewhat recovered it is pleasant to have such a sweet-natured companion little older than myself, for he is not yet twenty. We play at Glecko in the evenings, or I read to him. In truth, I read better than hee, for my mother's father was a great scholar and taught her well, and in turn she has taught mee. Other skills she had from her own mother, and though some may whisper of black arts, she does only good, not ill.

From the journal of Alys Blezzard, 1580

When Mr Hobbs had gone I tore up the letter to Lucy, which was still lying unposted on the table and, blowing the expense, phoned her.

I was then under orders to give her every minute detail from the moment I got to Winter's End, and not make *any* major decisions without consulting her. She also, like Anya, said Jack sounded clever, devious but attractive – just my type, in fact – and I was not to promise him *anything* until she got home and OK'd it.

I didn't know why either of them should jump to conclusions about poor Jack like that – nor did I know why my daughter turned out to be such a bossy little cow. She even tried to organise my life for me, just as I did for my own feckless mother, only with much less justification . . .

'Great-Grandfather left Winter's End to *you*, not Jack,' she said, 'so there must be a reason. The least you owe him is to go back and look at the place.'

'Yes, I know, and I feel quite differently about him now that I know he never really gave up looking for your granny and me. And Mr Hobbs said he took quite a shine to you, Lucy, and thought you would be great for Winter's End.'

'Well, I rather liked *him*, too,' she said, then, changing the subject, enquired in a bored voice that didn't fool me in the least, 'How is Anya? And I suppose Guy has sent me all kinds of messages?'

'Actually, no, he hasn't, though Anya was asking after you. He's on the road with her at the moment, now he's finished his degree, but he's job-hunting.'

'I suppose that accounts for why he hasn't emailed me for ages,' she said, sounding a bit miffed, 'though there *are* internet cafés.'

'I expect he's been busy and he will catch up with you later. Anyway, you always said he emailed too much and he should get a life,' I pointed out mildly.

'Well, he's such a nerdy little geek – but he's still one of my oldest friends.'

'You haven't actually seen him for a couple of years, Lucy – you were both always off doing things in the university holidays whenever Anya and I met up. But take it from me, he doesn't look remotely like a nerdy little geek any more. He's all grown up.'

'I'll believe that when I see it,' she said.

I only wished she could see it right then, and all my maternal urges were telling me to send her some cash and tell her to get on the next plane home . . . except that I hadn't got any money, of course. But Jack had, and I was sure if I accepted his offer to buy Winter's End he would advance some to me straight away, when he knew what it was for.

41

But I simply couldn't rush into a decision that would affect many more lives than mine, even though I realised that if I was mad enough to take on Winter's End I would still have the same money problems I'd always had, only on a much, *much* grander scale.

It took me a while to think what to say to Jack, but in the end I only got his answering service. I left my mobile number and a message telling him that, now I had spoken to the solicitor and read my grandfather's letter, I felt a responsibility to at least *go* to Winter's End and see how things were for myself, and I hoped he would understand.

But if he did, he didn't tell me so . . . unless that was the series of phantom text messages on my phone? I usually manage to delete them before reading them. They just slip through my fingers and vanish.

I have a disease called Technological Ineptitude; I'm some kind of throwback to the Stone Age, but I'm not proud of it.

I managed to lose three more text messages before Jack got the idea and phoned me instead. He has a voice like melted Swiss milk chocolate – smooth, rich and creamy; my knees went quite weak. He was so sweet too, and said he quite understood.

'That's such a relief. I thought you might be cross!' I blurted out, and he laughed.

'Now, why should I be cross? In fact, I'll come down myself and show you what needs urgently doing to the house, and I'm quite sure that when you've seen the scale of the problems – not to mention the sheer costs of running a place like that, and paying back the bank loan – you'll be more than happy to let me buy it. After all, it will still be your family home, where you will always be sure of a welcome, but without all the expense and hassle of trying to keep it from falling into a ruin,' he pointed out reasonably. 'You'd be in a win/win situation.'

'I expect you're right,' I said, feeling a warm glow at the thought of being part of the extended family again. Since he was being so nice about it, I asked, 'Do you think it would be OK if I had our belongings sent down there to store? Only, whatever happens I don't think I will be coming back here to live, and it will be easier to pack them up now.'

'Of course – there's loads of room. Give Hebe a ring and tell her when your stuff is arriving – unless you've already spoken to her?'

'No, I will do, of course, but I am feeling a bit nervous about it. I don't know why, because she was always very kind to me, in her way.'

'Oh, old Hebe's all right – you give her a ring,' he said cheerfully, then added, his voice going deeper and sort of furry, 'I'm *really* looking forward to seeing you again, Sophy! I haven't been able to stop thinking about you since we met,' and my insides turned to a mass of quivering jelly. I was rather looking forward to seeing him again too.

Our meagre possessions, including a few small bits of good furniture culled from local auctions or given to me by Lady Betty, were dispatched to Winter's End as a part-load with a furniture removal firm. I just don't seem to accumulate things like most people do, except books, which I buy second-hand like other people buy sweets. I keep my absolute favourites in a little shelf unit built into the camper van because, deep down, I think I'm always expecting to move on. In fact, I keep *all* my treasures in the van.

I didn't know what Aunt Hebe would do with our stuff when it arrived; when I nervously rang her to warn her of its imminent appearance, I suggested she stack it all in an outhouse somewhere for me to sort out.

'Oh, I expect Jonah will find somewhere,' she said vaguely.

'You don't mind my coming back to Winter's End, do you, Aunt Hebe?'

'Not at all, for how else can things be settled satisfactorily? And I'm sure we're very *happy* to welcome you back to the fold, Sophy,' she added, in a voice that suggested that she was anything but, 'though of course I always thought Winter's End would go to Jack, and it's very hard on the poor boy—'

Then she broke off and said again that I would be very welcome, but it was clear that as far as she was concerned, my advent was a very mixed blessing.

When I spoke about Lucy, I feared my own voice had the very same doting tone in it as Aunt Hebe's when she uttered Jack's name: bewitched, besotted and bewildered. But that didn't stop me feeling slightly jealous. I had always thought that she was fond of me, in her way, yet evidently my absence had been more than compensated for by Jack's arrival, the cuckoo who'd taken my place in both the nest and her affections.

When I finally managed to see Lady Betty before I left for Lancashire, it was clear that she had all but forgotten me too.

I had been to the stiff and starchy care home once before, and the same white-overalled woman was on the reception desk. She asked me for my name and then checked a list while I undid my coat. It was hot in there and smelled of air freshener and surgical spirit.

'I'm afraid you are not on the list of permitted visitors,' she said, pursing her lips, 'though you have been before, haven't you? I recognise that funny little brooch you're wearing.'

'My bee?' I said, taken aback but thinking fast. 'Yes, it is unusual, isn't it? Lady Betty gave it to me – and I won't be on the list of visitors because I'm just an employee. Mr Conor Darfield asked me to bring in a few things that she wanted.' I lifted the carrier bag to show her.

'Oh, right,' she said, 'perhaps if you leave—' She broke off as an elderly gentleman, who had been shuffling about the foyer in a desultory sort of way, suddenly made a determined, if hobbling, sprint for the front door.

'No, no, Colonel Browne, come back!' she called – but too late, he'd gone. 'Oh, blow – I'd better catch him before he vanishes,' she said distractedly, lifting up the flap in the counter and coming out.

'That's all right,' I assured her, sincerely hoping the poor colonel made it to wherever he was going, 'I know where Lady Betty's room is – I'll just pop up.' I don't know if she heard me because she was off in pursuit, but I seized the opportunity to run upstairs.

I tapped gently on the door of Lady Betty's room before going in, finding her in bed. As soon as I saw her I realised that this would be our last goodbye, for she seemed suddenly to have grown smaller, as if she was already shrinking away into death, and there was no recognition in her clouded eyes.

I sat quietly with her for ten minutes, feeding her bits of ratafia biscuits and sips of whisky and water from the supplies I had smuggled in (both of which she had always loved), and she took them with greedy eagerness, opening her mouth like a baby bird. She seemed to become slightly more alert then, and I talked to her, trying to raise some spark of recognition, but there was only one brief moment when her eyes focused on my face and she said my name and smiled. Then she closed her eyes and to all intents and purposes went to sleep.

I left the remainder of the biscuits in the bedside cabinet, but took the whisky bottle away with me. I had a feeling that anything remotely pleasurable would be banned in this sterile place.

The receptionist, looking distracted, was on the phone and only acknowledged my departure with a wave of the hand. 'Yes,' she was saying, 'he's gone again. Must have had a taxi waiting outside – and God knows which pub he's gone to this time . . .'

I only hoped the colonel had a good time before they caught up with him.

The exterior of the VW was painted in time-faded psyche-delic flowers, just as it was when my mother drove it, but I had made the interior over to my own tastes. Now, it was more like an old-fashioned gypsy caravan than a camper – deep, glowing colours, brightened with lace and patch-work and painted tables, ingenious shelves and cupboards, all sparklingly clean and smelling of roses.

There was a place in it for every item that was essential to me, so I felt as reassured as a snail in its shell once I was driving down to Lancashire, even though I was nervous about actually *arriving*.

But after all, if I got cold feet, I could always just get in my van and vanish again, couldn't I? Though come to think of it, that's what my mother always did, and that's really not a pattern I want to repeat.

It's a long way from Northumberland to west Lancashire, especially when you don't drive at much more than forty miles an hour, and since my heater wasn't working very well my fingers were frozen to the wheel most of the time. But the autumn colours were very pretty coming over the Pennines, and I noticed that, as I dropped back down towards Brough, all the bushes were covered with scarlet berries – supposed to be a sure sign of a hard winter to follow.

I made one overnight stop soon after that, near a village with a wonderful bakery, and then set out early next morning on the final leg.

It was just as well that Mr Hobbs had given me directions to Winter's End, for I was lost as soon as I took the Ormskirk turn off the motorway and then drove into a maze of small, hedged lanes. And although as I reached the large village of Sticklepond everything looked vaguely familiar (except that the general shop had turned into a Spar and the village school into a house), I don't think I would have easily found the right narrow road leading off the green.

I paused to consult the Post-it note I'd attached to the dashboard: 'Half a mile up Neat's Bank take the first right turn into a private road, by the white sign to Winter's End. Fifty yards along it, you will see a car park on your left and the main entrance gates to your right . . .'

The tarmacked road had a ridge of grass growing up the middle and the walls seemed to be closing in on me. Surely they couldn't get coaches up there?

I slowed right down and, sure enough, here was the sign and an arrow – but set back into a sort of clipped niche in the hedge so as to be almost invisible unless you were opposite it. I'd overshot a bit, so I reversed slightly and started to turn – then slammed the brakes on to avoid the tall man who leaped athletically down from the bank right in front of me and then stood there, blocking my way.

The engine stalled, and while we stared at each other through the windscreen a bird dropped a long series of sweet, high notes like smooth pebbles into the pool of silence.

The tall man had eyes the cool green of good jade, deeply set in a bony, tanned face with a cleft chin, a straight nose and an uncompromising mouth. His floppy, raven-black hair looked as if he'd impatiently pushed it straight back from his face with both hands and his brows were drawn together in a fierce scowl.

If he wasn't exactly handsome he was certainly striking, and I had a nagging feeling that I'd seen him somewhere before . . . *especially* that scowl. A warning dream perhaps, half-forgotten?

Since he showed no sign of moving I reluctantly wound down the side window and, leaning out, said politely, 'Excuse me, do you think you could let me past?'

'No way,' he said belligerently, folding his arms across a broad chest clad in disintegrating layers of jumpers, each hole showing a tantalising glimpse of the other strata beneath. 'And you can go right back and tell the rest of them that they're not welcome here. This is private property.'

'The rest of them? Who?' I asked, tearing my eyes away from counting woolly layers with some difficulty.

'The other New-Age travellers. I've had trouble with your kind before, setting up camp on land I'd cleared for a knot and making an unholy mess.'

A *knot*? Wasn't he a bit big to be a Boy Scout?

'Look,' I said patiently, 'I'm not a New-Age traveller and—'

'Pull the other one, it's got bells on,' he said rudely. 'You're not welcome here, so if you're trying to scout out a good spot for the others you'd better turn right around. Tell them the car park's locked up for the winter and patrolled by dogs, and if they come up the drive they'll be run off!'

'Now see here!' I said, losing patience, 'I don't know who you are, but I've had a long journey and I'm too tired for all of this. My name is Sophy Winter and—'

'*What!*'

He took an impetuous stride forward and I started

48

nervously, banging my head on the top of the window frame. 'Sophy Winter and—'

'Good God!' he interrupted, staring at me in something like horror, then added unexpectedly, in his deep voice with its once-familiar Lancashire accent, 'Blessed are the New-Age travellers, for they shall inherit the earth!'

'I'm *not* a New-Age traveller,' I began crossly. 'I keep telling you and—'

But he still wasn't listening. With a last, muttered, 'Behold, the end is nigh!' he strode off without a backward look. I know, because I watched him in the wing mirror. His jeans-clad rear view was quite pleasant for a scoutmaster, but I still hoped he'd get knotted.

49

Chapter Five: Pleached Walks

Today to my great grief and sorrow came the news of
my mother's death and the babe with her. But I already
knew the very moment of her passing: it was as if all
my mother's arts flew to mee on the moment of her quit-
ting this earth and my eyes were opened to a terrible
pre-knowledge of destiny that moved like dark shadows
around mee, step for step.

From the journal of Alys Blezzard, 1580

Slightly shaken, I restarted the engine and crawled up the
lane between grassy banks and sad, autumnal brown hedges,
feeling that this first encounter did not bode well. I only
hoped he wasn't tying knots anywhere close by . . .

And then it occurred to me that since he looked a bit
son-of-the-soil, he could even be one of my inherited three
gardeners, though maybe not. Greeting his future
employer like that was hardly the way to achieving lasting
job security.

A wide, gated and padlocked opening on the left declared
itself to be Winter's End visitors' car park, well and truly
shut for the winter. Opposite was a matched pair of sandstone lodges linked by an arched chamber set with a
weathered shield, carved with a crest that looked exactly
like a whippet with a black pudding in its mouth. An

immaculate half-moon of turf in front of each had been bordered with box hedging torturously clipped to form the words 'WINTER'S' on one side, and 'END' on the other – a strangely municipal and time-consuming labour of love that contrasted strangely with the once-splendid iron gates. For goodness' sake! Had they never heard of wire wool and Cure-rust?

The gates were open, but, in their present state, looked more like the jaws of a trap than a welcome. I turned cautiously between them onto a drive that ran through a dark tunnel of trees, slowing to wait for my eyes to adjust after the bright autumnal sunshine.

This was a lucky move, as it turned out, because a large grey horse was advancing to meet me – if you can call it an advance when it was going backwards rather fast. I stamped on the brakes for the second time in five minutes, and the creature briefly slammed its fat rump into the front of my van before whirling round, snorting down two red, foam-flecked nostrils, its eyes wildly rolling. The rider, almost unseated, was clinging on like a monkey.

Two thoughts about the matter crossed my punch-drunk mind from opposite directions and collided in the middle. One was that the woman seemed to have no control over her mount whatsoever; and the second (rather regretfully), was that *I* would never look so good in riding clothes: too big, too curvy, too *bouncy*.

Imagine Helen of Troy in tight cream breeches and a velvet hat.

She spared me a fleeting glance from curiously light brown eyes and called, 'Sorry about that!' very casually, considering there was probably a horse's-bottom-shaped dent in the front of the VW. Then, with some inelegant flapping of the reins, she urged her mount off down the road at a clattering trot.

'Idiotic creatures, horses,' said a voice in my ear, and I jumped again. 'Saw me dressed in white and ran off – though it's a holy colour, I always wear it to go to church and I'm off to do the flowers later. But she was a Christopher before she married, and none of them ride well. I suppose she thought Jack was here – though you never know, because she's never been what you might call fussy where men are concerned.'

I might have tried to explore this interesting statement further had I not had other things on my mind, for I would have known my great-aunt Hebe instantly anywhere: tall, bony, aquiline of nose like a slightly fuzzy Edith Sitwell, with her shock of fine hair, now white rather than red-gold, partially secured into a high knot with a chiffon scrunchie.

If I *hadn't* recognised her I would probably have been running after the horse, due to the polar-bear-crossed-with-Miss-Havisham style of her apparel. A floating, ivory-coloured, crystal- and sequin-dotted chiffon dress, layered for warmth with a yellowing fake-fur coat and fluffy scarves, and worn over white wellington boots of the sort only usually seen in hospitals and clinics, made for a striking ensemble.

There was a lump in my throat. 'Hello, Aunt Hebe,' I said, slightly unsteadily.

She regarded me severely, then leaned in through the still-open window and kissed me, though the silver pentacle and golden cross that hung around her neck on separate chains swung forward and bashed me on the nose first. Evidently Aunt Hebe still liked to hedge her bets, a family tradition.

'You're late! We expected you over an hour ago, so I thought I would walk down and see if there was any sign of you. I'd better get in.' She opened the passenger door and, clambering up with some difficulty, arranged her skirts. The familiar scent of crushed rose petals came in with her, and I felt eight again . . .

'Off you go,' she said briskly, and I realised I'd been staring at her, waiting for some sign that my return held real meaning for her. Maybe I hadn't quite expected bunting, banners and a fatted calf, but a little more than a peck on the cheek and a ticking off – but then, there had never been much in the way of maternal softness about Aunt Hebe.

Obediently I moved off again up the dark driveway – and then nearly went off the road as something beat a sudden tattoo on the roof. It was definitely one surprise too many in a very eventful day.

'Nuts,' said Aunt Hebe, unfazed.

'Right . . ?' I said uncertainly, my heart still racing away at twice the normal speed. 'There certainly are!'

She gave me a sharp, sideways look and I managed to get a grip on myself. 'I didn't know I was expected any particular time, Aunt Hebe. In fact, I nearly stopped to get something for lunch in the village. I've been thinking about Pimblett's hot pies all the way down here – didn't Mum sometimes buy me one on the way home from school?'

'I dare say, but lunch is being prepared for you up at the manor,' she said reprovingly, 'and I believe it *is* hotpot pies. Everyone is waiting to meet you first, though.'

'*Everyone?*' I echoed, then added, perhaps too eagerly, 'Is Jack here already?'

She gave me another sidelong glance. 'Jack sent his apologies, but business matters prevent him from welcoming you home until the weekend. He's probably putting it off, for he'll find it difficult, seeing someone else in his place – but there, what's done is done, and the obvious solution is in his own hands.'

53

I supposed she knew all about his offer to buy Winter's End and there was no question about where Aunt Hebe's loyalties lay.

'You've turned out not too badly, considering,' she added, turning her beaky head to study me.

'Thanks.'

'Though you appear to have no dress sense. Jeans are *so* unflattering on women of a certain age.'

'I don't know, they hold me in where I need holding in, like a twenty-first-century corset. Exactly *who* did you say was waiting to meet me?'

'*Everyone*,' she repeated as we came out of the darkness under the trees. 'Everyone that matters, anyway.'

And there was the house sitting in a puddle of autumn sunshine, the light dully glittering off the mullioned windows, a shabbily organic hotchpotch of black and white Tudor and local red sandstone, with the finger of an ancient tower poking triumphantly upwards above the rest.

It looked as if it had grown there, like some exotic fungus – but a ripe fungus on the point of decaying back into the earth it had sprung from. Before the porch a distant double row of miscellaneous figures waited, like the guard of honour at a low-budget wedding and, as if on cue, a small, fluffy pewter cloud let loose a confetti of snowflakes.

'Oh, yes – I see them now,' I croaked nervously, crunching slowly up the gravel. To my left stretched the curving, billowing shapes of yew that formed the maze, the gilded roof of the little pagoda in the centre visible in the distance. My feet would know the way to it blindfold . . .

'The maze has been extended at *huge* expense back to the dimensions of the old plan, and the pagoda regilded, since your time,' Aunt Hebe informed me, so maybe I *wouldn't* find my way into it so easily – and I suspect a lot of the bank loan went on restoring it.

'Most of the rest of the garden has been extensively restored, too, since you were last here. It became quite a *mania* with William.'

Everything in the garden looked pleached, parterred, bosketted and pruned to within an inch of its life. A mere glance showed me that there were still abundant examples of all four garden features here, but the immaculately manicured grounds only served to make the house look the more neglected, like a dull, dirty jewel in an ornate and polished setting.

I circled my incongruous vehicle left around a convoluted pattern of box hedges and little trees clipped into spirals, and the fountain at its heart sprinkled me with silver drops like a benediction as I came to a halt.

We climbed out to a thin scatter of applause and a voice quavering out: 'Hurrah!'

Hebe rearranged her collection of white angora scarves around her neck and, taking me by the elbow, drew me forward and began making introductions.

'You remember Mrs Lark, our cook – Beulah Johnson as was? And her husband, Jonah?'

'Welcome back, love,' Mrs Lark said, her twinkling eyes set in a broad, good-humoured face so stippled with brown freckles she looked like a deeply wrinkled Russet apple. 'Me and Jonah are glad to see you home again.'

'That's right,' Jonah agreed, baring his three remaining teeth in a wide grin. He had mutton-chop whiskers and looked like a friendly water vole.

'I certainly do remember you, Mrs Lark!' I said, basking in the genuine warmth of their welcome. 'You used to make me gingerbread men with currant eyes.'

'Fancy remembering that, after all this time! Well, I'll make some for your tea this very day – and some sticky ginger parkin too, that you used to love.'

Hebe urged me onwards by means of a small push between the shoulder blades. 'This is Grace from the village, our daily cleaner.'

'But no heavy stuff, me knees won't take it no more,' piped Grace reedily, who indeed looked even more steeped in the depths of antiquity than Mrs Lark, and was about the size of the average elf.

'And Derek, the under-gardener, and Bob and Hal . . .' Aunt Hebe said more briskly, towing me onwards before I could register any more than that Derek was a morose-looking man whose ears stuck out like old-fashioned car indicators, Bob was the one wearing a battered felt hat with a pink plastic daisy in the band, and Hal's large front teeth had a gap between them you could drive a bus through.

Aunt Hebe made a tut-tutting noise. '*No* sign of Seth. I expect he forgot all about it.'

'Who's Seth?' I said, irrationally feeling faintly aggrieved that one unknown man was missing from my royal reception committee.

'Seth Greenwood, the . . . well, I suppose he's the head gardener. But he's a bit of a law unto himself.'

'Oh, right!' I said, comprehending, because head gardeners *could* be tricky. They often seemed to think they owned the garden and did it their way regardless of what the owners wanted. Though according to Mr Hobbs, in this case he and my grandfather had been two minds with but one single thought.

'My sister, Ottilie, *married* the last head gardener,' Hebe started, in a tone that made it clear that she had committed a major *faux pas*, 'and so Seth—' She broke off and added curtly, 'Here *is* Ottie.'

A tall figure in jeans and a chambray shirt over a polonecked jumper strode round the corner of the house, smoking a long, thin cheroot. This she flicked into a bed

56

of late-flowering pansies and then embraced me vigorously, thumping me on the back. 'Glad to have you back, Sophy: you should have come sooner.'

'Thank you, Aunt Ottie,' I said, coughing slightly. Even now, in her eighties, Ottie seemed to be twice as alive as her twin; she crackled with energy.

'Just call me Ottie, everyone does. Clear off, you lot,' she said to the staff. 'You've only come out of curiosity and you've all got jobs to get to.'

'That's a fine way to talk,' Mrs Lark said good-humouredly, 'but I do need to see to my split pea and ham soup for tonight's dinner. There'll be lunch in the breakfast room in fifteen minutes.'

'I'll see you later,' Ottie said, 'settle in. Tell that vacant sister of mine to show you your room. You don't want to be hanging about out here in the cold.'

'Perhaps you would like to follow me?' Hebe said without looking at her, and it became obvious that my aunts were not speaking to each other. 'I expect my sister wants to get back to making mud pies in the coach house.'

'I'm just finishing the last figure in a major sculptural commission,' Ottie said pointedly. 'You must come and see it before it goes to be cast, Sophy.'

Then her eyes caught sight of something behind me and opened wide in surprise. 'Look, it's *Charlie*!'

Turning, I found the final resident of Winter's End on the top step, staring at me with slightly bulging eyes set in a pansy-shaped face – one of those tiny, black and white spaniels that you see so often in old paintings.

'Oh, of course, Grandfather always had several King Charles spaniels, didn't he? Though *this* can't be one of the ones I remember.'

'No, this is the last one my brother had. He's only five, and— Good heavens!' Aunt Hebe exclaimed, as Charlie descended the steps slightly shakily and bustled up to me in the manner of all small spaniels, tail rotating like a propeller.

He skirmished around me, whining, until I sank down and stroked him. Then he attempted to climb into my lap and I fell over backwards onto the gravel, laughing, while he tried to lick my face. Finally I got up with him in my arms.

'Well!' Hebe said, sounding surprisingly disapproving. 'He's been pining after William for *weeks*, but he certainly seems to have taken to you!'

'Poor old Charlie,' I said, holding him close. He felt like little more than skin and bone, and smelled like a dirty old carpet. I didn't think anyone could have brushed him since my grandfather died and, like the house, he was in serious need of some TLC.

'My sister is a sentimentalist and would probably have preferred him to howl on the grave permanently, like Greyfriars Bobby,' Ottie said with a grin, then walked off, her shirttails flapping and the black bootlace that held back her long grey hair starting to slide off.

'Perhaps you would like to go to your room before lunch?' Hebe suggested.

Everyone else had vanished. Still carrying Charlie, I lugged my carpetbag out of the van with one hand, then followed Hebe through the door from the porch and round a huge, heavy carved screen into a cavernous hall paved with worn stone.

She crossed it without pause and began slowly to ascend the curved staircase towards the balustraded gallery – but I had come to a stop in the middle of the floor under a sky of intricate plasterwork, overwhelmed by a flood of emotion. Suddenly I was fused to the house, wired in: I was Sophy at eight and at the same time Sophy at considerably more than thirty-eight . . . But I was back where I belonged and the house was happy about it, for there was a space in the pattern of Winter's End that only I could fill.

It was an acutely Tara moment: the years when I had been away were gone with the wind. This was *my* house, *my* place on God's good earth, and nothing would ever tear me from it again. I knew I would do anything – *anything* – to keep it.

I had thought I was a piece of insignificant flotsam swept along on the tide of life, but now suddenly I saw that everything I had learned, every single experience that had gone into moulding me, had been leading up to my return.

I was transfixed, translated, transformed . . . trans-*anything* except, ever again, transient.

Tomorrow might be another day, but it certainly wouldn't be the one that saw me signing away my inheritance.

Jack was out of luck.

Chapter Six: Unravelled

Father still hath not sent for mee, nor any word, so I asked leave to return home. But Thomas Wynter hath suddenly set his heart on marrying mee, despite his family's opposition – and mine, for I feel for him as though he were a brother, no more than that. They do not like the match, yet he is Sir Ralph's onlie child and he will denie him nothing . . .

From the journal of Alys Blezzard, 1580

I did a slow turn, arms spread wide to embrace the house, letting my long-suppressed memories of Winter's End rise to the surface at last like slow, iridescent bubbles.

The Great Hall and the cross passage, which was partly hidden by the enormous carved wooden screen, separated the family part of the house from the service wing, the area I seemed to recall best. Over there was the door to the kitchen with its huge black Aga, Mrs Lark's domain and the source of comfort, warmth and treats. Then came the stillroom, where Aunt Hebe held sway, brewing up potions and lotions, and receiving mysterious late visitors to the side door for whispered, urgent consultations. Beyond that again, a maze of stone-flagged, utilitarian rooms and the cellar steps.

Here in the hall there was no longer a fire in the cavernous hearth, only cold grey embers, but ancient cast-iron radiators were dotted about as though dropped randomly into place and a hollow, metallic clunking indicated that they were working, a fact that wasn't immediately obvious from the chill air. A powerful energy ran up from the soles of my feet to the crown of my head, filling me to the brim with a life force compounded of the vital essence of Winter's End and of my ancestors who had loved it before me – the alleged witch, Alys Blezzard, among them.

From the dark shadows behind me I heard the once-familiar echo of her light, serious young voice whispering, *'Welcome – welcome home, at last!'*

'There you are,' I murmured.

'Of course – I never left.'

'I missed you, Alys.'

Aunt Hebe's face, an elderly Juliet, appeared like a waning moon over the balustrade high above and she called, slightly querulously, 'Aren't you coming, Sophy?'

'Yes, of course!' I came back to earth with a start, and ran up the stairs to the gallery with Charlie, who had been sitting watching me, at my heels.

She looked at him with disfavour. 'The dogs have *never* been allowed upstairs.'

'But he's so sad and lonely at the moment, Aunt Hebe. I'd really like to keep him with me.'

'You can do as you wish, of course – for the present. *Fill* the house with dogs if you want to, though I expect Grace will complain about the hairs.'

'I think one dog will do to be going on with, and he won't shed so much hair once I have given him a good brushing.' That was an experience neither of us was going to enjoy, because currently he was just one big tangled knot and a pair of bright eyes.

Following her through a door at the back of the gallery I found myself in the Long Room, which was exactly what it said on the packet – a narrow, wooden-floored chamber running from one wing to the other, jutting out at the back of the house above the terraced gardens.

The wooden shutters were all partly closed over diamond-paned windows yellowed with grime, so that we walked in a soupy half-light past paintings so dirty it was hard to tell the subject matter. Even so, I noticed that nothing above shoulder height had been cleaned within living memory, and cobwebs formed tattered silk drapery across the ceiling. Some of them brushed Aunt Hebe's head, but she seemed oblivious.

Lower down everything had been given a rough once-over, the legs of the furniture showing evidence of repeated violent batterings with a Hoover nozzle.

'Grace surely can't be the *only* cleaner?' I said, itching to get my hands on a duster. 'It must be too much for one person to cope with, especially since she's getting on a bit.'

'She does what she can, and my brother occasionally got a team in from an agency to give the place a good spring clean until a couple of years ago, when he said it had got too expensive. The Friends of Winter's dust the Great Hall and the minstrels' gallery when we open to the public. Those are the only parts of the house the visitors are allowed into, you know. It's mainly the gardens they come to see.'

Clearly she'd never considered lifting a duster herself, and the house was *desperate* for some TLC. Poor tiny, ancient Grace could never hope to manage it all herself, for while the house was not some enormous mansion, it was low and rambling, with lots of panelling and wooden floors and ups and downs.

I was yearning to make a start on it . . . but maybe five minutes after I arrived wouldn't be tactful. With an effort I managed to restrain myself, thinking it was ironic that I had spent all my life learning the art of cleaning other people's stately piles, not knowing those skills would one day be necessary to transform my own. Again, I had that strange sense of fitting into some preordained pattern, the vital bit of missing jigsaw.

They say everyone has some skill or talent and mine just happens to be cleaning. Not romantic or exciting, perhaps, but there it is – and exactly what was needed here. Now a missionary fervour was invading my heart, filling me with the longing to convert the dirt.

As we walked along I noticed lighter patches on the walls where pictures had been removed – perhaps when Grandfather was searching for something to pay death duties with. How odd to think of him here, planning the implications of his impending death on the Inland Revenue, making sure everything was settled before I was even told he had gone.

'Are the missing paintings still away being cleaned and valued?' I asked.

'No, they have been returned. They're stacked in the Blue Bedroom waiting to be rehung.'

At the end we turned left past a suit of armour made for a short, fat gentleman and went through a door into the West Wing, down two steps, round a corner, and up one step to a passage.

'This is the Blue Bedroom,' Hebe said, indicating a door, 'then my room and a bathroom. The Red Bedroom will be Jack's when he arrives. Of course, he should have had my brother's room, only,' she added resentfully, walking on and throwing open another door, 'Ottie *insisted* that you should have it.'

'But really, I don't mind at all if Jack has Grandfather's room,' I protested. (Especially if Grandfather actually died there!) 'I thought perhaps my old room on the nursery floor . . .'

My voice petered out: someone had lit an incongruous little gas heater in the magnificent fireplace and the red glow reflected off a great mahogany bed covered with the kind of jewel-coloured crazy patchwork that I make myself. The curtains were of the same soft, faded gold velvet as the bed hangings and, like the Long Room, the oriole windows jutted out over the terraces at the rear of the house, with a distant glimpse of the river at the bottom and the wood across the valley.

'What a lovely room! You know, I don't think I ever came in here when I was a child,' I said, pulling back the drapes. Below were laid out the intricate, lacy shapes of terraced knot gardens, though the lowest level looked to be still very much a work in progress.

'I'm so happy to be back, Aunt Hebe!' I said spontaneously, turning to smile at her. 'I haven't forgotten how kind you always were to me, telling me bedtime bible stories and giving me rose fondants when I hurt myself.'

She softened slightly. 'Couldn't have you growing up a *complete* heathen. We missed you when Susan took you away, but we thought she'd be back again eventually, when the money ran out. And of course you were only a *girl*. It would have been different if you had been a boy.'

'Sorry about that,' I said drily, though her casual dismissal hurt.

'My brother hoped that Susan would come to her senses and get married, and there would be more children – a son,' she added, rubbing it in. But I'd already got the message: to Aunt Hebe, girls didn't count, and illegitimate girls counted even less.

'But then my cousin Louisa died and eventually Jack was sent back to school in England, and spent all his holidays here.'

'Well, I'm sure that made everything right as rain, then,' I said sourly. I mean, I liked Jack, but much more of this kind of thing and I would start to go off him rapidly.

'It should have done, but I'm afraid Jack was a disappointment to my brother. Their characters were just too dissimilar, though Jack did try, by taking an interest in the architecture of the house and the family history. Then

64

William somehow got the idea that Jack was thinking of marrying Melinda Seldon – or Christopher, as she has been calling herself again since her husband died. But if he *had* been, which I personally very much doubt, he gave it up once William made it clear he disapproved of the match. He never liked her, though of course she's very wealthy now and, goodness knows, Winter's End could do with a rich heiress marrying into the family.'

'Was she the blonde woman on the grey horse that ran into my car?' I asked, thinking rather despondently that the equestrian Helen of Troy and Jack would have made a wonderful couple – but also that Jack hadn't seemed the kind of man who would meekly give up the woman he loved just to please his grandfather.

'Yes, that was Melinda. She was widowed last year and moved back here to live with her mother, who is one of my oldest friends. Naturally, she and Jack saw a lot of each other. For one thing, they have lots of friends in common, but also he had entered into a business arrangement with her to develop the property she inherited from her late husband.'

'She is very beautiful,' I said wistfully.

'She is, but also a great flirt – as a girl she played all the local boys off against each other quite shamelessly – but if Jack was tempted after she was widowed, then I expect he thought better of it, even before William mentioned the matter. He had already made one misalliance, you see, soon after he left university – a short-lived affair.'

'So was mine, though in my case it was my husband's family who thought he'd made a misalliance.'

'Oh no, dear, nobody marrying a Winter could possibly think that,' Aunt Hebe assured me – but then, she had never met the Mistress.

'Things did seem to improve between Jack and William until they had that last ghastly argument . . .' She shuddered.

'Oh? What was that about, Aunt Hebe?'

'Jack had long wanted William to transfer ownership of Winter's End to him, to try and avoid death duties, but he wouldn't hear of it. This time Jack told his uncle that if he didn't divert some of his income into keeping the house standing, he would have nothing but a garden to inherit anyway.'

'Well, goodness knows, he was right about the house. Another couple of years of neglect and possibly it would have passed the point of no return.'

'Yes, but my brother took it badly and told Jack he shouldn't count his chickens before they hatched. And then, to top it all, he'd heard about one of Jack's business deals – such a *clever* boy – and accused him of only wanting to get his hands on Winter's End so he could turn it into an apartment block. I told him he was being absurd, because Jack wouldn't dream of doing anything of the kind to his ancestral home.'

'No, I'm sure he wouldn't,' I agreed.

She smiled approvingly. 'I'm sure my brother would have seen sense if he hadn't suddenly discovered where *you* were and made that disastrous will. I can't think what got into him.'

'Sickening for you and Jack,' I agreed, fascinated despite myself by this one-viewpoint argument, because it had obviously never occurred to either of them that I had any kind of right to inherit Winter's End.

'Yes – you do understand, don't you? William didn't even tell us he had found you, so the will came as a complete shock. And although Mr Hobbs says he was in his right mind and the will can't be challenged, he can't have been, really.'

'He seemed to be all there with his cough drops when I met him,' I assured her. 'He spent most of his visit arguing with Lucy and it perked him up no end.'

'Lucy?'

'My daughter.'

'Oh, yes, I'd forgotten.' Clearly, yet another girl was not

of great interest. 'Didn't Jack say she was working abroad somewhere?'

'Japan – teaching English, but only for a year to make some money. The wages are good, and they run up such huge debts these days with the student loans, don't they?'

'Jack didn't. In fact, that's when he started his property renovation business.'

With an effort I refrained from remarking that Lucy had not had a rich parent to buy her a house when she went to university.

'So you see,' Aunt Hebe said insistently, turning her finely lined, hawk-nosed profile towards me, 'Winter's End should have been Jack's. You *do* see that, don't you? But he says he is going to buy it from you, so everything will be right again.'

'He *did* offer to buy it when he visited me in Northumberland,' I agreed, and again that overwhelming burst of feeling for Winter's End ran through my veins like liquid fire, 'but of course I hadn't seen it then. I – I didn't realise . . .'

'No, I suppose you barely remember it. It can't mean to you what it means to Jack.'

'Until I got here I only had a few random memories . . . and dreams. I used to dream about Winter's End,' I said. 'But from the moment I stepped into the house it felt like . . . like *home*.'

She was looking at me sharply now, seeing a little of what I felt in my face. 'Of course – and it is your home. Dear Jack said that you would always be welcome to visit Winter's End. We're very happy to have you back in the family circle again.'

'That's very kind of you, Aunt Hebe,' I said, then took a deep breath and added, 'but actually . . . well, I think it is going to be the other way around. *Jack* will always be welcome to visit Winter's End, but I'm not parting with it, even to him!'

Her mouth dropped open. 'But Jack said you *would* – he's had the documents drawn up and everything – and now I have explained it all to you, you *must* see that it is Jack's by right!'

'No, it's not – it's mine. Grandfather trusted me to look after Winter's End and his dependants, and that's what I'm going to do. The house *needs* me. I'm sorry if Jack is disappointed, but that is my final decision. Here I am, and here I'll stay – whatever it takes!'

She stared at me. 'You looked just like my brother when you said that! Strange, for you are so dark you could be a changeling in the family. But you are quite attractive, in your way,' she added in a non-sequitur, 'and possibly not too old to give Winter's End an heir.'

'I already have – Lucy,' I pointed out, 'and I wasn't planning to have any more.'

She shrugged off Lucy and changed tack. 'Jack is coming down this weekend. He is *very* handsome, isn't he?'

To my annoyance I felt myself grow pink. 'Very.'

'And very persuasive,' she added, and smiled slightly acidly. 'I am sure you will soon see sense once he has explained things to you in person. He sent you the bouquet over there, by the way, with a very nice message.'

One of those arrangements of out-of-season, sterile-looking blooms in an incongruously modern vase filled with what looked like (and possibly was) frogspawn, stood on a side table, a white card propped up against it: but shouldn't my message have been sealed in a little envelope?

'We won't discuss it any more at the moment, because I am sure things will work out for the best in the end,' Aunt Hebe said, seemingly more to herself than to me. 'Right will prevail, one way or the other.'

I could see which way her mind was now heading – and whose rights she was concerned about – but I no longer knew quite what to think of Jack. For one thing, I'd like to know if my grandfather's suspicions were correct and something had been going on between him and this Melinda Christopher, who would be a rather hard act to follow . . . I was just about to try a bit of delicate – or indelicate – probing on the matter, when I saw that Aunt Hebe was staring fixedly at the shabby carpetbag I'd dumped on the bed.

'Wasn't that your mother's?'

'Yes. She had very few possessions because she was always travelling about, and she tended to give her stuff away. But this she hung on to.'

'But the book – Alys Blezzard's household book – Jack said you hadn't got it? You don't think your mother would have given *that* away or . . . or lost it? We assumed, when we discovered that it was missing, that she took it with her.'

I looked directly, and slightly accusingly, at her. 'Mum did tell me about Alys Blezzard's book, and that the original was kept locked away. But just how did Jack know about it? I thought it was supposed to be a secret, passed down only through the women of the family?'

She shifted a little, guiltily evading my gaze. 'Oh, Jack thinks it's only an old book of household hints and recipes – which it *is*, really. He's terribly interested in anything to do with the history of Winter's End – and anyway, it isn't *truly* secret because copies of the recipes have been passed on by generations of Winter women, especially daughters leaving to get married – but not all of it, of course, just the useful bits. We always assumed your mother took it with her, but I suppose she could simply have hidden it somewhere before she left.'

'If you thought she took it, you probably haven't had a real search for it. I expect it'll turn up,' I suggested, noticing for the first time that Charlie had managed to scramble on the bed and now had his head inside the carpetbag.

So *that's* where I had put the Eccles cakes.

Chapter Seven: Cold Embers

Father hath ridden over and hastily closed with the bargain, not seeking my wishes in the matter, though it is contrary to my will. I hear rumours that he too is to wed again, not a month after my mother and the babe departed this life . . .

From the journal of Alys Blezzard, 1580

After she had gone I let Charlie finish the Eccles cake, since he clearly needed feeding up – but on the floor, not the ancient and quite beautiful patchwork quilt.

It obviously refreshed him, because afterwards he started to chase invisible mice around the room, energetically leaping and pouncing.

There was an antiquated little bathroom through what looked like a cupboard door in the panelling, but I had little time to do more than splash my face with tepid water and shove my snarled hair behind my ears before I heard someone beat merry hell out of a gong, down in the depths of the house.

'Now, where do you think lunch is?' I asked Charlie, who wagged his tail but showed no sign of guiding me there, though he did follow me out when I called him.

I retraced my steps to the minstrels' gallery and luckily spotted Jonah crossing the Great Hall. He was wearing a stiff brown linen apron and staggering under the weight of a huge tray, on which reposed several covered serving dishes and a large squeezy bottle of scarlet ketchup.

Quickly I ran downstairs and followed him through the door into the West Wing and then into the breakfast room.

'*There* you are,' said Aunt Hebe, a spooky figure in the Stygian gloom. 'We always eat in here when it is just family – so much cosier and more convenient than the dining room, I always think.'

While I wouldn't have called a room that was a ten-minute hike from the kitchens convenient, I supposed it was all relative. Once my eyes had adjusted to the darkness I did have vague recollections of the room, with its sturdy Victorian table, carved wooden fire surround and the faded hearth rug on which Charlie immediately curled, in front of the dead grate. But if only someone had taken the trouble to wipe the grime of years from the windows, things would have looked a lot better.

Or maybe they would have looked worse? For, while there was some evidence of a little low-level duster activity, the wainscoting and furniture didn't exactly gleam with beeswax and love, and whole colonies of spiders seemed to have taken up residence in the dirty chandelier. Did no one in this house ever look up?

The table had been reduced to a cosy ten feet or so in length by removing several leaves, which were stacked against the wall. Two places had been set.

Hebe indicated that I should sit at the head of the table. 'William's chair, of course, and though it should be Jack's place now, since my poor misguided brother made it perfectly clear that *you* were to be the head of the household, so be it – until poor dear Jack can take his rightful place.'

Jonah, who had been clattering things about on a side table, now plonked a warm plate down in front of each of us. Then, removing tarnished silver covers from the serving dishes with a flourish, he handed round two pastry-crusted hotpot pies, some mushy peas and a generous helping of pickled red cabbage.

'You've forgotten the water,' Aunt Hebe reminded him.

'I've only got one pair of hands, missis, haven't I?' he grumbled, adding cloudy tumblers and a large jug of dubious-looking fluid to the table. Then he stood back and said benevolently, 'There you are, then – and your semolina pud's on the hotplate yonder when you're ready for it, with the blackcurrant jam.'

'Thank you, Jonah.'

'Yes, thank you,' I echoed, looking down at my plate, on which the violent red of the pickled cabbage had begun to seep its vinegary way into the green of the mushy peas. I put out my hand for my napkin, then hesitated, for it had been crisply folded into the shape of a white waterlily and it seemed a shame to open it.

Jonah leaned over my shoulder and poked it with one not altogether pristine finger. 'Nice, ain't it? It'd be easier with paper serviettes, though, like they have at the evening class down at the village hall. It'll be swans next week.'

'Will it? Won't the necks be difficult?'

'*Thank* you, Jonah,' Aunt Hebe said again with slightly more emphasis, before he could reply, and he ambled off, grinning. Charlie hauled himself up and followed him, and I hoped Mrs Lark would give him something to eat. I was so starving I'd rather not share my hotpot pie, and I didn't think he would fancy mushy peas or pickled cabbage.

Mind you, my last dog ate orange peel, so you just never know.

'We generally find our own lunch and tea in the kitchen, but Mrs Lark wanted to give you something hot today. Though there is usually soup –' she looked around as if surprised at its absence – 'and we just have fruit for dessert.

72

But today there's semolina, which is apparently your favourite pudding.'

'It might have been once . . . I can't remember.' I hoped Mrs Lark wasn't going to feed me exclusively on the type of nursery diet I ate as a child. My tastes have changed a little over the years.

Mind you, when I stirred a generous dollop of home-made blackcurrant jam into my semolina and it went a strange purple-grey colour, it did all sort of come back to me why I had liked it – stodgy puds are nearly as comforting as chocolate.

When we had finished, and Jonah had brought coffee in mismatched cups and saucers, Aunt Hebe said that she would give me a brief tour of the house. 'Just enough to remind you of the layout, for I am sure you will want a more detailed survey as soon as you have time,' she said shrewdly.

She was quite right, I was already mentally compiling a mammoth shopping list of cleaning materials, some of them only obtainable from specialist suppliers. It was lucky I already knew a good one, called Stately Solutions, wasn't it? Serendipity again, you see.

'After that, I am afraid I must go out,' she said, glancing down at the watch pinned to her cardigan. 'I am closely involved in the work of the Church, and it is my turn to do the flowers.'

She fingered the heavy chased gold cross that swung against her bony chest – and I remembered I had seen the small silver pentacle on its chain around her neck earlier that day, the two symbols in incongruous proximity. Perhaps they summed up the conflicting sides of her heritage – the old religion hidden against her skin, the new for outward show?

With the brisk, detached air of a tour guide running late (which of course I recognised, having been one), she took me round the major rooms of the house. 'Dining room, drawing room, morning room, library, cloakroom . . . Mr Yatton's office is here, in the solar tower, and of course at Winter's End he is always called the steward, rather than estate manager.'

'Like on a cruise ship?'

'I know nothing of cruise ships: the appellation is a tradition here,' she said dampeningly.

This part of the house was only vaguely familiar, for my allotted domain as a child had been the nursery, kitchen wing and garden. Stumbling after her through such a warren of dark passages that I half-expected a giant rabbit to bound around the corner at any minute, I thought that each room seemed dingier and more neglected than the last. But I suppose once the sun vanished and the day started to fade it was bound to look worse, especially since the lights weren't switched on.

'This is Lady Anne's parlour.' She cracked open a door a few measly inches, then prepared to shut it again.

'Lady Anne? You don't mean Alys Blezzard's daughter, do you?' I asked, sticking my head under her arm and peering round the door into a small chamber, whose furnishings and decoration, like that of the rest of the house, were an eclectic mix of several centuries.

'Yes, did Susan tell you about her? This was her favourite room and, so it is said, her mother's before her. She was the heiress, of course, and married a cousin, so she remained Anne Winter and stayed on at Winter's End. Over there in the alcove is the wooden coffer that Alys Blezzard's household book was always kept in. We discovered both the book and key had vanished soon after your mother left, and so drew the obvious conclusion . . . but then, being the elder of us, Ottie had charge of the key after your grandmother died, and she is so careless, even with important things.'

The box was about two feet long and perhaps thirteen or fourteen inches high, with two narrow bands of carved flowers and foliage to the front. The sturdy strap-work hinges and lock plate were of decorative pierced metal.

'It's quite plain, isn't it?' I said, feeling slightly disappointed. 'Somehow I expected it to be more ornate – and bigger.'

'This one is a *very* unusual design for the late sixteenth century,' she corrected me, with a look of severe disapproval. 'Not only is the inside heavily carved instead of the outside, it also has a drop front and is fitted out with compartments. Family legend has it that Alys Blezzard's husband, Thomas, gave it to her as a bridal gift, since he was afraid that she might be suspected of witchcraft if she left her book and some of the ingredients she used to make her various charms and potions lying around.'

'So she really *was* a witch?'

'Only a white witch – little more than what we today would call a herbalist,' Aunt Hebe said defensively, and her long bony fingers curled around her gold cross.

I turned back to the box. 'So, how did you know the book was missing, if you hadn't got the key, Aunt Hebe?'

'The box was lighter, and nothing moved inside it when it was tilted.'

'Of course – though if it had been one of those huge heavy affairs with a complicated locking mechanism, which I thought it would be, I don't suppose you would have known it had gone.'

'Actually, there *is* one of those in the estate office, full of old family papers, which I expect Mr Yatton will show you, if you are interested. That's where my brother discovered the original plans for both the terrace gardens and the maze, rolled up in a bundle of later documents. Smaller boxes like this one were probably intended to keep precious things like spices under lock and key originally, but Alys locked away her mother's household book instead.'

'Which became known as Alys Blezzard's book – even though she was really Alys Winter after she married Thomas?'

'Yes. When she received the book after her mother's death,

she continued to add to it, as women did then, often passing them on for several generations. But at the front she still signed herself as Alys Blezzard, so I don't think she ever really considered herself to be a Winter. She was the last of that particular branch of the Blezzards too; her father married three times, but had no more children.'

Like a curse, I thought, shivering. I noticed that Charlie was looking fixedly at a point behind me, his tail wagging, but when I turned there was nobody there – or nobody visible.

'I keep having the feeling that there's someone standing right behind me, Aunt Hebe. Is the house haunted? I mean, apart from Alys.'

'Oh, yes. When you were a little girl you called your imaginary friend Alys – I had forgotten. And you were quite convinced that she talked to you! But of course she *does* haunt the house, because of her tragically early death, and there are several other ghosts including the robed figure of a man from about the same time. They say the family was hiding a Catholic priest who was taking gold back to the Continent, to further the work of the Church, but he was betrayed and is still searching for his treasure.'

'You'd think if he hid it he would know where it was, wouldn't you?'

'Well, yes, I suppose so, though each generation has made major alterations to Winter's End so he might be a trifle confused. There are several other legends too, for of course there had been a dwelling on this site for many centuries before Winter's End was built. If you are interested in such things, there is a book in the library called *Hidden Hoards of the North-West* . . . unless Jack still has it. He's been fascinated by the idea of hidden treasure since he was a little boy,' she added indulgently, 'and I had to read to him from that book at bedtime every night.'

That caused me another unworthy pang of jealousy. 'You

used to read to *me* from a scary Victorian book of bible stories, Aunt Hebe!'

'But you were an ungodly child,' she said severely, 'born of sin.'

I didn't think I had been particularly wayward, just mischievous, but I let it go. 'Have *you* seen any of the ghosts?'

'I thought I saw a Saxon in the garden once, at dusk, looking for the hoard he had hidden before a battle. But it was probably just one of the gardeners.'

The windows of Lady Anne's parlour looked out over the terraces at the back of the house and were curtained in a predominantly coral-coloured William Morris fabric. The walls above the inevitable dark wainscoting had been painted the same shade, and coral tones softly echoed in the faded, but still beautiful, carpet.

I felt as though the room was casting an aura of welcome around me and I could see myself sitting there in the evening, piecing together my crazy cushions. 'Aunt Hebe, would you mind if I used this room? It's lovely, and I'll need somewhere to make my patchwork.'

'I can't say I ever much cared for sitting in here,' she said, looking slightly surprised, 'and though Mother was a skilled needlewoman and used to embroider beautifully, she did it in the drawing room after dinner. The firescreen in the study is her work.'

'I'll look out for it. Where do *you* like to sit in the evening, Aunt Hebe?'

'Sometimes one place, sometimes another . . .' she said vaguely, like an elderly Titania – which indeed, she resembled. 'Though I often work in the stillroom until late, or go out – I am on several village committees. There is a TV in the library, but I also have one in my room, for William and I tended to live *very* separate lives.'

'We didn't have a TV in the commune and I've never really felt the need for one since, but we always had a radio when I worked at Lady Betty's. I like to listen to Radio 4 when I'm sewing. You can't really watch something and sew properly, can you?'

'I don't know, I've never tried.' She looked at her watch and then shooed me out along a tapestry-hung passage and up some spiral stairs. The door at the top opened between my bedroom and the arch leading to the upper level of the tower, which was a complete surprise – I'd noticed it, but thought it was another cupboard.

'I don't remember these stairs at all!'

'That is because you were not allowed to use them. William insisted you were confined to the nursery and the kitchens, though we were forever finding you sliding down the Great Hall banisters. There are the stairs to the attic nursery floor over there, which you will recall, so we won't bother going up – the rest of the roof space is now entirely given up to storage. I keep the door to that side locked, otherwise Grace sneaks off up there and smokes.'

She turned on her white, wellington-booted heel and sped off, appearing to be losing interest in the tour fast. 'You know this bedroom floor already,' she tossed over her shoulder. 'There are six bedrooms – eight if you include the nursery suite – but the Rose Room is never used.'

I fell down some ill-lit steps and bumped into her round the corner as she came to an abrupt stop.

'Turn left and you enter the Long Room again, at the end of which is the door to the East Wing where there are further bedchambers, the Larks' living quarters, and the backstairs to the kitchens. This one takes us onto the landing, of course, commonly called the minstrels' gallery, and, since it projects over the hall, I expect they did sometimes have musicians there when they were entertaining. When Ottie and I were girls we had parties with dancing in the Great Hall, and the band sat up here and played.'

That must have been quite a sight – the tall, slim, blue-eyed Miss Winters, their red-gold hair floating as they danced the night away with their dinner-jacketed partners . . .

'What sort of music did you dance to?' I asked curiously, and would have loved to have known if she had a favourite partner too, had she been in the mood for reminiscence, but the past clearly held no fascination for Aunt Hebe. Ignoring my question as though I had never asked it, she carried on with her tour. 'The Great Hall and the solar are much older than the rest of the house, but the Winters were forever knocking bits down and rebuilding them. You can see from the blocked fireplace halfway up the wall that the hall was once single storey with rooms over it, and then the height was increased and the ceiling plastered, leaving only the minstrels' gallery.'

She clomped off and I could feel the gallery floorboards bouncing under my feet. 'Most of the lesser family portraits are hung here, and on open days the visitors can come up. We lock the door at the end, but the family can still reach either wing of the house by way of the Long Room if they wish, without meeting a member of the public.'

'It's very dark; you can hardly make the portraits out. Does anyone actually want to come up here?'

'Oh, yes, for Shakespeare is rumoured to have visited Winter's End, and if so presumably would have stood on this very spot – if he came at all. But show me an old manor house in this part of Lancashire where he *isn't* supposed to have been!'

'Really?' I said, interested. 'I didn't know that.'

She shrugged bony shoulders impatiently. 'There is a theory that he spent the Lost Years here in Lancashire, in the employment of various local families, especially the

Hoghtons – and he is supposed to have a particular connection with Rufford Old Hall, near Ormskirk, which is now, of course, a National Trust property. There is a book about it in the library, I believe.'

'Really? I'll look for it later, along with that hidden treasures one.'

It was beginning to look as if I would have plenty of bedtime reading for the foreseeable future!

Aunt Hebe was losing interest in Shakespeare. 'One of the volunteer stewards, the Friends of Winter's End, stands at either end of the gallery, and they have a fund of anecdotes concerning his apocryphal visit and stories about Alys Blezzard. That portrait in the middle is supposed to be her, but it is some dreadful affair painted by a jobbing artist, from the look of it, more used to depicting prize bulls and sheep.'

'Hard to tell,' I agreed, peering at it. 'It looks as if it has been dipped in Brown Windsor soup. In fact, most of the paintings I've seen seem in want of a cleaning.'

'Only a few in the Long Room were cleaned when your grandfather was searching for something to pay the death duties with. But once they found the Stubbs, that sufficed.'

She started to descend the stairs, but I paused and ran my hand over the curved banister, remembering the small Sophy who used to climb up onto it, clinging on for dear life as she swooshed down . . .

The Great Hall looked dark and yawningly empty below me, but not half as big as I recalled – *nothing* was. The house, which had seemed so huge in my childhood memories, had in reality shrunk to quite modest proportions, though it would still be a worryingly monumental task to restore it to its former glory.

'Do you ever light the fire now?' I asked, joining her at the bottom of the stairs.

'The fire?' She turned to look at it, as if, by magic, flames would appear. 'We always used to – but I suppose no one has given the orders since William died.'

She pointed at a stack of screens against one wall. 'On open days all these are set out into a display of the history of the house, the supposed Shakespeare connection – and Alys Blezzard's story, of course. You know the legend is she was distantly related through her mother to the Nutters, who were known witches?'

'Yes, Mum told me all about that. She said Alys really *was* a witch.'

'Yes ... Susan was always a fanciful child,' Aunt Hebe said dismissively. 'A knowledge of simple herbs and their curative effects does not mean one is versed in the black arts and in league with the devil.' She pulled out the corner of a screen: 'This one is the history of Winter's End and the Winter family. Then there is the story of how the original Elizabethan plans for the terrace were discovered and the restoration begun – and about the missing part for the lower terrace.'

'Missing?'

'Yes, torn off and not anywhere to be found. William and Seth were still arguing about what *might* have been on the lower terrace right up until the end. Indeed, the arguments kept William's spirits up amazingly.'

'Seth?'

'The head gardener – so called.'

'Oh, yes, I'd forgotten, though his name's pretty apt for a gardener, isn't it? Sort of *Cold Comfort Farm*. I only hope there isn't something nasty in the woodshed.'

'Only wood,' she said seriously, 'and spiders – did you mean spiders? I am not fond of them myself, but freshly gathered cobwebs make an excellent poultice for wounds.'

The tour ended in the kitchen, where Mrs Lark was sitting

in a rocking chair in front of the Aga knitting, with the radio on. Charlie lay in a position of blissful abandon on a rag rug at her feet. His stomach, as round as if he'd swallowed a small football, rose and fell to his stertorous breathing.

Aunt Hebe again consulted the watch attached to her flat bosom by a bow-shaped golden brooch. 'Time to go – but before I do, I will be happy to pass you these.'

And she literally *did* pass me the most enormous bunch of keys, some of them museum pieces in their own right. 'But Aunt Hebe, I can't take these from you!' I protested.

'There is no reason why not, for this bunch is mainly symbolic. We hardly ever lock anything away – except the Book, when we had it, and a fat lot of good that did us. Indeed, I have no idea what half of the keys are for, and in any case I was only ever nominal housekeeper, for Mrs Lark does it all. No, my business is the walled garden – which that Seth Greenwood is forbidden to touch! I grow practically all the fruit and vegetables for the house and I have bees and chickens. And of course, the stillroom through there is for my use only. You may look at both,' she added grandly, 'but not poke and pry and stick your fingers into what doesn't concern you!'

'Yes, Aunt Hebe,' I said meekly, hearing the echo of the same words in the voice of an eight-year-old, curious to know what her witchy ancient relative was cooking up.

'I expect Mrs Lark will show you her apartment herself, though perhaps after your long journey you might wish to put off any further inspections of your *realm* until another day,' she said slightly acidly, and departed back through the swinging, baize-lined door to the hall.

She left a snail trail of silver sequins behind her: she must have caught a loose thread on something.

Chapter Eight: Sovereign Remedies

Sir Ralph asked mee whether I was of the Old Religion and I said I was. I swore to it, and he was well pleased. I know them to be Catholics like Father, despite their outward show of compliance to the new faith; they do not know that the old religion I swore to is not the same as theirs . . .

From the journal of Alys Blezzard, 1581

Mrs Lark said, 'Don't you worry about her – she never took any interest in the housekeeping, but she's kept us in fruit and vegetables for years – and honey, chickens and eggs too. Now, do you want me to show you our rooms? Up the backstairs, they are.'

'I would – but not today, if you don't mind, Mrs Lark. So much needs doing that I think I need to go round in daylight with a notebook and write down a list of priorities,' I said, though actually, what I really wanted to do was run about the house shrieking, 'It's mine, mine – all mine!' at the top of my lungs, now that Aunt Hebe was no longer there to depress my pretensions.

'The whole house is falling to pieces and that filthy I'm ashamed of it,' Mrs Lark said forthrightly. 'I clean my own rooms, but though poor Grace does her best with the rest of it all, it's too much for her. And I do the cooking and ordering, but further than that I don't go – not at my time of life.'

'Of course not. You shouldn't have to do anything else. It isn't your job.'

'That's right,' she agreed, less defensively. 'My Jonah, he's butler, valet, handyman – whatever's wanted – though he started out as groom when Mr William used to hunt. But he's a man, so he doesn't notice what wants doing, never has – you have to tell him.'

That explained the lack of a fire in the Great Hall then: it was merely that no one had thought to give the orders! I mooted the point.

'I'll tell him when he comes in,' she said. 'September to March it's always kept lit, because it takes the chill off the whole place.'

'What do we usually burn?'

'Logs. The gardeners cut and stack them in the old stables – there's always plenty. Ecologically sustainable,' she added conscientiously, 'from our own woodland.'

'Oh, good,' I said. 'How often does Grace come in?'

'Weekday mornings generally, unless there's a party or visitors. She does the beds and towels Wednesdays and Fridays – they go to the laundry, though there's a machine out through the back, if you want it. Grace does any other washing as required, and the ironing. Other than that, when she's vacuumed through and done the kitchen floor and the bathrooms, she's no time for anything else. In fact, I reckon it's all getting a bit much for her; she's not as fast as she used to be.'

'I think it's amazing she does so much!'

'She's not as old as she looks. I keep telling her all them cigarettes she smokes make her look like a living mummy and wheeze like a piano accordion. I've never smoked and we're the same age, but *I've* got the complexion and figure I had at thirty to show for it.'

Leaving Mrs Lark knitting and Charlie sleeping, I took a quick look at the stillroom, Aunt Hebe's domain, where racks and bunches of anonymous vegetation hung everywhere and the scent of attar of roses and rush matting vied with other, stranger, odours.

A small table with a chair each side stood near the side door to the shrubbery: Aunt Hebe's consulting desk for furtive evening customers?

Gingerly (and guiltily!) opening a cupboard, I found myself nose to nose with a row of glass-stoppered jars and bottles, all bearing labels written in a spiky black gothic hand: 'ORRIS ROOT', 'HOLY WATER (Lourdes)', 'FULLER'S EARTH,' 'POWDERED GINGER', 'GROUND BARN OWL BONES (Roadkill 1996)'.

Ground owl bones?

'LIQUORICE EXTRACT', 'POWDERED AMBERGRIS', 'DRIED BAT WINGS'.

I shut the door hastily, deciding not to open any more cupboards – then immediately did, thinking it was the way out. This one contained shelf after shelf of much smaller bottles and jars with fancier labels. Pinned to the inside of the door was a hand-written price list. 'Number 2 Essence: A sovereign remedy for restoring the joys of marriage,' I read, 'Two pounds fifty.'

After all these years without even a word from Rory, it would take more than an essence to restore *my* marriage! The next remedy was clearly aimed at all those exhausted wives with priapic elderly husbands, pepped up on Viagra: 'Number 5 Essence: The tired wife's friend. Two drops in any liquid given to the husband near bedtime will ensure an unbroken night's rest. (Do not exceed dose.) Three pounds.'

It looked like Aunt Hebe had gone into production on a large scale.

I popped my head back through the kitchen door. 'Mrs Lark, do Aunt Hebe's remedies actually work?'

She looked up. 'Well, no one's ever asked for their money back to my knowledge.' She cast on a couple more stitches and added, 'Or died from them, either.'

'That's a relief,' I said, and went back to my tour, though I hesitated before opening any more doors. But luckily the next one merely gave on to a passage with the narrow backstairs going up from it and the cellar entrance. There was a warren of rooms beyond it, many of them unused except for storage (one of them was stacked practically floor to ceiling with what looked like empty florist's boxes), but this area looked very familiar to me. I had been allowed to play here and to ride my red tricycle up and down the flagged floors. How I'd loved that trike! The chipped skirting boards were probably my doing.

Feeling nostalgic I wandered on until I came to another passage, across which a fairly new-looking door had been installed. It was unlocked and when I passed through I saw that it had a sign on the other side saying: 'PRIVATE! NO ADMITTANCE BEYOND THIS POINT.'

Here, by removing the door between two rooms and throwing out a little glassed-in conservatory overlooking the top terrace at the back of the house, a tearoom of kinds had been created. There was a counter topped with a glass food display cabinet adorned with dust and dead flies, and a collection of mismatched pine tables and chairs, varnished to the deep orange shade of a cheap instant suntan.

It all looked terribly half-hearted and uninviting, though perhaps in summer when they opened they gussied the place up a bit with bright tablecloths and flowers.

The visitors' loos were off the further room and a brief glance told me were of Victorian servants' quality, though

I suppose at the time it was the height of luxury for the staff to have indoor toilets at all.

I retraced my steps to the warm kitchen, where Mrs Lark ceased knitting long enough to look up and smile at me. Charlie didn't appear to have moved an inch since I left.

'Did you remember your way around, lovey? You played out there all the time when the weather was bad, making dens out of old cardboard cartons, or riding that little trike of yours, though in the summer you were always outside. You used to run round and round the maze like a mad thing, with your granddad's spaniels all chasing after you, barking their heads off.'

'It's all coming back to me – I remembered my way around this wing perfectly, despite a few changes. What are all those empty boxes in one of the rooms for?'

'Mistletoe. Winter's End is noted for it. But I don't suppose you remember the mistletoe harvests before Christmas, when the gardeners gather it and it's packed off to London?'

I shook my head.

'Perhaps you were kept away, for the berries are poisonous. The boxes used to be stored in a shed, but the mice got at them.'

'I suppose they would,' I agreed. 'The tearoom is a bit rough and ready, isn't it? And the toilet is inadequate, I should have thought, especially if there's a coach party.'

'It was the staff toilet until Sir William put in that nice cloakroom under the backstairs, and the teashop used to be the laundry and brewhouse. But we don't need a laundry now we've got the utility room, and the only brewing is what Miss Hebe does next door, and better not to ask about most of *that*,' she said darkly.

'Definitely not,' I agreed. 'When we're open, who does the teas?'

'The Friends serve them, but I cook the pastries and scones.'

'That must make a lot of work for you?'

'I like to do a big bake, and Grace comes in extra and cuts the sandwiches, but we don't get so many visitors.'

'I'm surprised you get any, because there isn't much of the house open to see, is there?'

'No, but they come for the garden mostly. It's a picture in summer, though Seth says the terraces are still a work in progress. Gardening clubs and so on – they like to keep coming year after year to see how it's going on.'

'Surely it must be nearly finished by now? They've been at it for years, from what Mr Hobbs was saying!'

'Oh, yes, I think there's only the bottom terrace to do, though it seems to me they spend as much time maintaining the garden as they did making the thing in the first place – all these grown men snipping and clipping! Miss Hebe seems able to manage the whole walled garden on her own, apart from getting one of the gardeners to do the heavy digging, or clean out the hens, which makes Seth mad. He thinks of nothing but his blessed restoration scheme and your granddad was just the same.'

'I'll look round the garden as soon as I've got the chance, but it sounds as if it's had enough time and money expended on it and getting the house back in good order will be what's important now. Things are going to change.'

'I'm glad to hear it. When we heard how Sir William had left things, we did wonder if you would come back or just sell the place.'

'I wondered too, at first, but once I'd seen Winter's End again I knew I was back for good,' I said firmly, though somewhere inside I was quaking at the thought of explaining that to Jack . . .

Charlie gave a sudden snort and opened his eyes, then

88

got to his feet and ambled over, tail wagging. I bent down to stroke his matted head. 'Do you know where Charlie's brushes are?'

'The cleaning room, two doors down the passage on the left. I doubt you'll get a brush through that mess, though, but I'll tell Jonah to give it a go, shall I?'

'No, I think you might be right about not being able to get a brush through it. He'll have to be clipped, and I'd say from the way he's walking that his claws need cutting too. He can't have been getting out and about enough to wear them down, while he's been moping. In fact,' I decided, 'what I *really* need is a dog grooming parlour!'

'Milly's Mutt-Mobile,' Mrs Lark said.

'What?'

'Jonah's sister's husband's brother's girl. She has a mobile dog parlour. Shall I ring her?'

'Oh, *would* you? Ask her if she could come up and do something with Charlie as soon as she has time.'

'I'll be glad to. I feel that bad for neglecting the poor little thing, though I kept trying to coax him to eat, and Miss Hebe tried one or two of her potions on him. But he's just had a huge dinner now, so he's on the mend.'

Yes . . . Aunt Hebe's household-book-derived potions.

'Mrs Lark,' I said, sitting on the wooden settle facing her, 'I expect you know about Alys Blezzard's book, don't you?'

'Oh, yes, there've always been copies of what you might call the *everyday* recipes in circulation, and they were used in the kitchens here, but of course not nowadays . . . though come to think of it, I do still use the one for medlar cheese. Your aunt got her recipes for the lotions and potions and stuff she brews up from the original, though they're not Christian to my way of thinking, because it's well known that Alys Blezzard and her mother were both witches. Lots of people locally, they come up here of nights and buy

89

them. I use the rose face cream and hand cream myself,' she added reluctantly. 'There's no harm in *them*.'

'My mother always said Alys was a witch. She liked to think she took after her, brewing up charms and spells, but she didn't really. It was just a pose.'

'Alys Blezzard was distantly related to the Nutters through her mother, and *they* were witches,' Mrs Lark said. 'Some of them were burned for it, I think, a lot later. Alys was took – betrayed by the family, some say.'

'Took?'

'Gaoled her for questioning, but she died before they could do anything. Just as well, though Seth says she probably wouldn't have been burned as a witch back then; the burnings was later. But ducking would likely have been just as fatal, especially in the wintertime, if they got carried away.'

I shivered. 'What a horrible thought! And didn't they sometimes tie suspected witches up and throw them in the water, and if they sank they were innocent, but if they floated they were guilty? They had no chance, did they?'

'Before she died Alys entrusted the book to a servant, to give to her daughter when she was old enough,' she said, with a bright-eyed look at me. 'I overheard Miss Hebe saying so to Jack – and that it was full of treasures. Alys had said so herself on the flyleaf.'

'She told *Jack* that!' I exclaimed, because Mum had definitely led me to understand that the ancient, handwritten book with all its recipes, was some great and precious secret handed down only to the women of the family – and if there was one thing certain, it was that Jack wasn't one of those.

'Of course, that was enough to get him going, seeing the way he's been treasure-hunt mad from a little lad – and he turned the place upside down looking for the book in case your mum hadn't taken it after all.'

'But the treasures are just the recipes!'

She shrugged her plump shoulders. 'Miss Hebe couldn't even remember properly what Alys had written in the book because it was Ottie that had charge of the key to the box, and she'd rarely let her look at it. And when Ottie found out she'd told Jack, she was right mad! They haven't spoken since – but then they were forever falling out, so that's nothing new. When Ottie married the gardener they didn't speak for five years, Hebe was that disgusted – only it was probably all down to jealousy because he was a fine figure of a man, though she'd never of married him herself, of course.'

'You know, I *thought* they weren't speaking. But how did Ottie find out that Hebe had talked to Jack about it in the first place?'

'Because he tried pumping her about the book and got a right flea in his ear for his trouble. Ottie told him straight it was nothing to do with *him.*'

'That explains a lot. I was surprised Jack knew about the book at all, when he came up to see me in Northumberland, but I can see now that of course its existence was bound to be generally known about within the family and copies of some of the recipes in circulation. But Aunt Ottie was right – the rest is no business of Jack's.'

I got up. 'I think I'll just bring the rest of my bags in, then move the van round the back. It lowers the tone of the place, standing out there.'

'You can park it in the courtyard or the barn, if you like,' she said. 'Leave your bags in the hall and Jonah will take them up for you. Your other stuff that came, we stored it in the attic nearest your old nursery. You remember where that is?'

'Yes, Aunt Hebe showed me, but more and more is coming back to me anyway.'

'Your mother's things that were returned with her, they're all in her old room – the Rose Bedroom. Mr William

91

wouldn't let us change a thing in there after you both ran off. It's just the same as the day she left and it's never been used for visitors.'

This was unexpected of Grandfather, and rather touching. And I'd never given a thought to what had happened to any of the luggage Mum took to America with her – but of course it would have been returned to Winter's End.

'I expect you'll want to go down to the graveyard in a day or two, pay your respects,' Mrs Lark suggested. 'It's got a nice stone angel – looks a bit like your mum did the last time I saw her. Mr William had fresh flowers sent down every week.'

'Yes, I'll do that,' I said, getting up. 'Thank you, Mrs Lark.'

'Come back for a bit of tea later, if you want. If I'm not here, there's parkin and gingerbread men I made special – they're over there cooling on the rack.'

I ate one right there, hot and bendy though it was, and then, with Charlie still following me like a small shadow, I brought in the rest of my bags and piled them at the bottom of the staircase. Then I drove round the back, past the tower and through an arch into a flagged courtyard. A pair of doors opened onto a barn that already contained a battered sports car that I somehow knew was Ottie's, and the Volvo estate that had been Grandfather's. But there was still plenty of room, so I put the van in there and then walked out into the yard again.

One side of the courtyard was formed by the old coach house, now transformed into a home and studio in which, through a large glazed door standing ajar, despite the cold wind, I could see Aunt Ottie standing motionless in front of some monstrous shape, smoking a cheroot, her back to me.

I pushed open the door and went in. Without turning, she said: 'Well, Sophy, what do you think?'

Chapter Nine: Lost in Translation

Tomorrow I will be marryed. Fond though I am of Thomas, to embrace him will be to embrace death itself – yet there is no escape. I look to the future and see only dark shadows closing in on mee.

I asked one bride gift only – that my mother's maid, Joan, be sent for, since my father hath turned her off, and this boon was granted to mee. Though seemingly a simple creature, she is of our old ways and was devoted to my mother. She brought with her my mother's household book, which I mean to continue with, and some other things I have hid to be safe.

From the journal of Alys Blezzard, 1581

I wasn't surprised that Ottie knew who was there without turning round, because I can often do that myself. I think it's a Winter thing – like the way I frequently have a flash of foreknowledge that something good or bad is heading in my direction. That was partly why I didn't go to America with my mother, though it turned out that the dark shadows were gathering for her, not me.

I examined what looked like a cross between a cow and a giant bat, the clay seemingly slapped on over the armature with a giant paddle, and said cautiously, 'It's a very interesting interpretation.'

I mean, what do *I* know of modern sculpture? My knowledge of art comes from dusting several miles of old pictures in a freezing Scottish loch-side castle, or Lady Betty's collection of pseudo-antique Egyptian relics; and if I never see another washy watercolour of Highland cattle, or crumbling alabaster Canopic jar, it won't cause me any grief whatsoever.

'Interpretation of what, exactly?' Ottie enquired with interest.

'I have absolutely no idea,' I confessed, and she laughed.

'Good – I hate humbug.' She regarded her monstrous creation with complacency. 'It's called *Folded: 25* and it's the final one for an installation in Swindon. This could be the most exciting thing that's ever happened to the place.'

She turned her bright blue eyes on me and asked, 'Settling in all right?'

'Yes, thanks. I've just unloaded the van and put it in the barn, and Aunt Hebe gave me a quick tour of the house to remind me of the layout, before she had to go down to the church. Aunt Ottie . . .'

'Just call me Ottie, everyone does.'

'Ottie,' I said firmly, since she had seemingly lost interest in me again and gone back to contemplating her sculpture through a haze of sweet blue smoke, 'Aunt Hebe appears to have told Jack all about Alys Blezzard's book and now he thinks it might hold a clue to finding a hidden treasure.'

That regained her attention. 'My sister's a fool – always was, always will be. She said she thought he ought to know, since there were no female Winters left after us. But of course there were – you! And I knew you would come back one day, because I've got a dose of the family second sight, while Hebe just inherited the skills to whip up potions and charms.' She looked at me sharply. 'You're like me, I think?'

'A bit. Not so much second sight as more of a vague sense of good or bad coming my way – either as a light on the horizon and my spirits lifting, or dark shadows closing in on me.'

'Hmm,' she said. 'You'll probably get a stronger dose when I've popped my clogs. That's what happened to *me* when my grandmother died. I suppose it's only the Winter tendency to marry second or third cousins that has kept it so strong in the family all these centuries.'

I remembered Jack's joke about that and also, guiltily, that he was still entirely unaware of my transition from reluctant heiress to Homecoming Queen. I had an uncomfortable suspicion that 'consort' wasn't in his vocabulary . . .

Ottie ground the stub of her cheroot out under the heel of her boot. 'That Hebe's daft as a brush, wittering on about things she knows very well she shouldn't, and putting ideas into Jack's head. Not that there aren't enough twisty little cunning ideas in there already,' she warned, with a sharp look at me.

'Is that why you and Hebe aren't speaking to each other?'

'Partly. I suppose Susan told *you* all about the book?'

'Yes, and everything that *her* mother told her, but she thought you knew more than she did.'

'William's wife was giddy, like Susan – sweet, but no substance to her – and she died young. It put me in a bit of a dilemma, to be frank, though I had great hopes of you. Did you ever see that series on TV, *Buffy the Vampire Slayer*?' she added, with disconcerting abruptness. '"Into every generation a vampire slayer is born"?'

'No, we never had a TV. And where do vampires come in?' I asked uneasily.

'They don't – but into each generation or so of Winter women is born one to be trusted to keep Alys Blezzard's secrets safe, and pass them on to the next, like an endless game of tag down the centuries. There have been Regency belles, disapproving Victorian misses and twenties flappers,

but they've all kept the faith. I'm the Buffy for *my* generation – but there seems to have been a slight glitch with the
next two. However,' she added more cheerfully, 'since I also
had a bit of the magic about me, I knew it would all come
right in the end! You're here, and here to stay, aren't you?'

'Well . . . yes – but I have absolutely no idea how I'm
going to manage it!'

'You'll find a way,' she said confidently.

I would have to. Losing Winter's End again simply wasn't
an option. I went back to what Ottie had been saying. 'So
Mum *was* right and you do know something more – and
maybe Alys's references to treasures mean more than *I*
thought, too?'

'The book is itself a rare treasure – a household manuscript of that age, written by a woman,' she said evasively.
'There have always been copies of the more useful, everyday
recipes circulating within the family, but when Hebe showed
an interest in the more esoteric side, I let her go through
the original book to look for others – more fool me! Now
she's blabbed about things she had no right to, and Jack's
been creeping about searching the place like something out
of a Secret Seven novel, looking for buried gold. Seth found
him using a metal detector in the grounds just after William
died and threatened to wrap it round his neck if he caught
him digging holes in the beds again. Then I told him he
needed the permission of the owner to do it anyway, which
made him even more furious, of course.'

'I suppose it would, since apparently he's been brought
up to think himself the heir all these years,' I pointed out.
'It's a difficult situation for him. But I can't understand why
Hebe told Jack in the first place.'

'She doted on the child from the moment he came back
from New Zealand and spoiled him to death, so I suppose
it was on the cards that she would tell him everything she

knew eventually. But goodness knows why, because he isn't showing any sign of getting married again, so there's no wife to take the secret on to the next generation.'

'Oh? I saw Melinda Christopher this morning as I was arriving – her horse tried to sit on my car. Aunt Hebe said Grandfather thought she and Jack seemed to be getting close when she first moved back here, until he showed that he disapproved.'

Ottie thought that one over. 'I don't think so. They are just old friends and move in the same circles. But she's a rich widow, so now William isn't here to put his oar in, perhaps Jack will see her in a different light. He's always found money powerfully attractive. He and Melinda have got *that* in common.'

I returned to our original subject with an effort. 'I still don't see why Aunt Hebe had to tell Jack anything.'

'Nor me. She just said she thought he ought to know, now he was the last of the Winters.'

'Only the last of the *male* Winters, and he's not actually a Winter at all unless he takes the name by deed poll, is he? Still, all he seems to know is that Alys mentions secret treasures on the flyleaf of the original book.'

'That's right, and luckily she couldn't even remember the exact wording of that. In fact, there's only me who knows *everything* now – custodian of the family secrets, as you might say.' She paused. 'When I realised Hebe had blabbed, though, it did make me wonder if *I* should confide in someone, too. Especially someone who could keep an eye on Jack's treasure-hunting when I wasn't here.'

She looked at me and away again. 'You see, I knew you were going to come back, and since the key and the book vanished when your mother did, I assumed you had them. I mean, you *have* got them, haven't you? It would be terrible if the book was lost for ever!'

I ignored that, staring at her, aghast. 'Ottie, are you saying that *you* told someone else the family secrets too?'

'Well, I'm no spring chicken any more,' she replied defensively. 'I knew you would return, but not *when*. What if you came back too late? So I told someone I trusted exactly what Hebe had told Jack, and left a letter with the solicitor to be given to you when you turned up, telling you the rest.'

'Ottie, *who* did you tell?'

There was the sound of heavy, rapidly approaching footsteps, and then a tall, broad-shouldered shape blotted out the light. 'Ma?' a familiar deep, Lancashire-accented voice demanded. 'Ma, are you there? I think old William must have been off his head! He's only gone and left the place to a spaced-out New-Age traveller and she—'

He stopped dead when he suddenly saw me and his mouth closed like a trap. Charlie, who had been sitting on my feet, got up and wagged his tail. That dog has no discrimination whatsoever.

I turned incredulously to Ottie. '*Ma?*'

She looked self-conscious. 'Yes, this is my stepson and your head gardener, Seth Greenwood. Have you met?'

'*Your* stepson is *my* so-called head gardener?'

'Yes.' She looked away and fiddled with a metal modelling tool while I put two and two together fast: 'Don't tell me your tit-for-tat retaliation for Hebe's indiscretion was to tell *him*?' I jerked a finger at the gardener, who glowered at me. 'At least Jack was *family*!'

'Well, so is Seth – by marriage. And at least he can be trusted to do what is best for Winter's End, while Jack's just out to line his pockets in any way he can,' she said defensively. 'If he'd inherited, the place would have been converted into some kind of upmarket apartment block and slapped on the market five minutes after probate was granted.'

'I think you are wrong – and I don't know why you're

so against Jack. He seems to me to care deeply about Winter's End! But that's beside the point, because *neither* of them should know anything about it at all.'

'Someone needs to keep an eye on Jack, Sophy, you take it from me – and I'm not always here.'

'But now *I* will always be here.'

'Yes, and Jack's going to be pressing you to show him the book the minute he realises you have it, after all – which you do, don't you?' she asked again, slightly anxiously.

'If I have, then it is mine by right – and in any case, I refuse to discuss it any further in front of *him*. Or, in fact, at all! I think you and Hebe have both betrayed a sacred trust.'

I turned and for the first time spoke directly to Seth, who was lounging in the doorway with his arms folded across a broad expanse of holey jumper and an evil look in his green eyes, like a villainous but worryingly attractive character in a B movie. That elusive memory stirred again . . .

'Just bear in mind, Seth Greenwood, that I am not about to have my property searched by you, or anyone else, for a treasure that doesn't exist. If you want to keep your job, and Jack wants to keep his visiting rights, then you'd both better consider that!'

He straightened up suddenly and said furiously, 'Now just you look here—'

But Ottie broke into a great peal of laughter, drowning him out. 'That's it, Sophy, you tell him straight!'

'I will,' I said, 'especially now I've remembered where I met your stepson before!'

'Not a happy meeting?' she asked interestedly.

'No!'

'I *thought* I recognised that van,' he said coolly, making it clear that *I* certainly wasn't memorable enough to stick in his mind. 'Didn't I move you and your New-Age traveller friends on a couple of years ago, over near Rivington?'

'You certainly *tried* to move us on, even after we'd explained that we'd had to stop because Sandy's baby was coming early.'

'I'd heard that sort of story before.' He rubbed his straight nose and then added grudgingly, 'Though that time it turned out to be true, I admit. You know, I thought women in childbirth only screamed like that in films.'

'Sandy believed in letting out the pain.'

'She did that all right. They could hear her up at the house.'

'That's a gross exaggeration. And we left as soon as we could, didn't we, without doing any damage?'

'No, you didn't – you made a mess of the ground I'd had cleared for a knot garden.'

From the way he said 'knot garden' you would think we had desecrated a sacred site, but it gave me the opening to hit him where it hurt.

'Well, bear in mind that now Winter's End is mine I can invite *hordes* of New-Age travellers to camp here any time I want to,' I said nastily and out I marched, though I wasn't entirely convinced that Seth was going to move aside and let me through until the very last minute.

He towered over me and out of the corner of my eye I noticed that his mouth was twitching, which was probably either temper or a nervous tic. After his remarks earlier in the day I sincerely hoped he hadn't got religious mania too.

Mrs Lark consoled me in the kitchen with tea and very gingery parkin. She also confirmed my suspicion that my aunts had immediately divided into two opposing camps once Jack had arrived and then Ottie married Seth's father, the new head gardener.

'Jack looked like an angel, but he was mischievous, and Seth always ended up getting the blame for his pranks until Ottie stepped in. He was a stoical little boy and I don't suppose

100

he would have said anything, but she said she wouldn't stand by and see him being punished for things he hadn't done.'

'No, I don't suppose she would,' I agreed, digesting this new insight into what had gone on during my absence from Winter's End. Maybe if I had remained there it would have been *me* who would have got all the blame, bottom of the pecking order?

Mrs Lark suggested I should go and change for dinner, but she didn't say into what – a giant moth, maybe? If I carried on eating at the current rate I'd certainly be changing into something bigger, but not necessarily better, though I did take the hint and put on a long plum-coloured crinkle-cotton skirt and flat Chinese silk slippers.

When I went down I found Ottie and Hebe studiously ignoring each other in the drawing room, both looking defensive and sheepish. Ottie was still in clay-smeared jeans, though she had removed the outsize man's plaid lumberjack shirt she had been wearing in the studio as an overall. Hebe, abandoning her whites, was arrayed in a long, dark green velvet dress that was bald on both elbows and the seat.

'There you are,' Aunt Hebe said. 'I've poured you a glass of sherry. My sister seemed to think you wouldn't like it, but then, she has very depraved tastes. It comes of living as a bohemian for most of her life and only pleasing herself.'

I took the glass, though actually Ottie was right and I don't really like it much.

'In fact, I don't know why my sister is here at all,' Hebe added. 'Perhaps you ought to ask her.'

'William liked the family together for dinner,' Ottie said. 'I always come over when I'm home, unless I'm working late. Then Mrs Lark sends it over. Saves cooking for just me too. Do you mind, Sophy?'

'Not at all. In fact, I like it, but I'd like it even more if you two would speak to each other! I'll find it very wearing being a sort of conversational conduit, and so far as I can see, you have both betrayed a trust, so the honours – or dishonours – are even.'

'Huh!' said Ottie, and she and Hebe exchanged wary sideways glances from identical bright blue eyes.

Then Jonah beat the gong and we trooped into the breakfast parlour. Dinner was the split pea and ham soup that Mrs Lark had mentioned earlier, giant Yorkshire puddings filled with roast beef, carrots, peas and gravy, and apple tart and cream, washed down with a glass of red wine from a dusty bottle. The room began to slowly waver like something seen through bull's-eye glass: it had been a very long and tiring day.

We had coffee in the library, and then Ottie left for the coach house and Hebe vanished upstairs. Jonah, when he came in for the tray, said she was addicted to soaps, which she recorded on video and watched in the privacy of her own room, my grandfather having been scathing about them.

By then I was really fit for nothing except the long, satiated sleep of the python that ate the goat – and if this sort of food appeared in front of me every day, I thought, my waist would vanish and my figure would not even resemble an extreme hour glass, but a fishing float.

'I'm going to my room too, Jonah,' I said, yawning hugely. 'I'm so tired I'm starting to feel as if I'm underwater with my ears about to pop. It's been a long and eventful day.'

'If you want a nightcap, it's in the drinks cabinet over there,' he offered.

'That *would* finish me off!'

'Breakfast's at eight, Miss Sophy.'

'Just call me Sophy,' I said, getting up wearily. I'd noticed that Mrs Lark, as befitted her important position as cook, was always addressed as such, and everyone called my aunt Miss Hebe, but other than that there was precious little formality between the family and staff, which suited me.

102

'I'm more used to being the hired help than the lady of the manor, Jonah, and, goodness knows, you've known me since I was a little girl. I remember you leading me round on one of Grandfather's hunters!'

'Kingpin, that was – a gentle giant. It was a sad day when Sir William sold up the horses, but there, his hip was giving him the gyp, so he had to do it.'

His words were starting to come and go . . . as was the room. 'Well, good night, Jonah,' I managed, then added, remembering, 'Oh, and could you light the fire in the Great Hall tomorrow morning and every morning after that?'

'Yes, Mrs Lark's already said you wanted it lit. The logs are ready and I'll put a match to it first thing tomorrow. And she says to tell you Milly from the dog parlour will be here right after breakfast to sort Charlie out.'

'Oh, good,' I said, thinking that it was odd, but strangely pleasant, to have people do things for me for a change, rather than the other way round! Charlie, his days of looking and smelling like a small unwashed rag rug so nearly at an end, heaved himself up from in front of the fire and followed me out, but showed no signs of coming upstairs. 'Where does Charlie usually sleep?'

'In the kitchen. The Aga stays warm all night and Mrs Lark's got a nice bone for him, she's that pleased to see him eating again. I'll let him out first, though, before I lock up.'

I think even Charlie's limited vocabulary included the word 'bone' – or maybe he just felt that everything was back to normal again, for he followed Jonah off across the hall without another glance back, tail waving hopefully.

I have vague recollections of shedding my clothes, dragging on a nightdress and climbing into the big mahogany bed, where I sank deep into feathers and unconsciousness.

I didn't need to dream about Winter's End any more – I was there.

Chapter Ten: Clipped Edges

Lady Wynter taunts mee much, saying how is it that I can read and write so well, yet it is well known that my mother's family was lowborn and tainted with rumours of witchcraft? I return soft answers – that my mother's father was a scholar and she in turn taught mee everything she knows – such cures and salves as anyone versed in such things might know. She is curious about this little book, but I keep it about my person.

From the journal of Alys Blezzard, 1581

There was a chill in my bedroom next morning that the small gas fire and one lukewarm radiator did little to dispel. I showered hastily under an antique contraption over the claw-footed bath and then went downstairs to the Great Hall – to find it quite transformed!

My instructions to Jonah had been obeyed and now a log fire blazed and crackled on the wide hearth, throwing out a fierce heat that made the huge, dark and dusty chamber almost cosy. Heat rises, so over the next few days my arctic bedroom and the upper regions of the house might, with a bit of luck, begin to thaw out.

Reluctantly tearing myself away from the fire I headed for the breakfast parlour, where I half-expected what I found – a lavish spread of cooked dishes on hotplates, including (as though Mrs Lark had purposely chosen all the foods starting with 'k') kippers, kidneys and kedgeree, plus a line of Tupperware boxes of cereals, a bowl of prunes and a jug of orange juice.

I don't usually eat a cooked breakfast, but of course any resistance was useless once I'd smelled the bacon.

'That's the way,' Jonah said approvingly, coming in with a fresh pot of coffee while I was demolishing an indecently large plateful. 'You're a grand, strapping lass, not one of these skinny Minnies with stick arms and bosoms like two fried—'

'*Thank* you, Jonah,' Aunt Hebe said firmly, looking up from a well-thumbed garden catalogue, 'we have got everything we want now.'

She was dressed today in workman-like brown corduroy trousers and a green-patterned Liberty lawn shirt under a quilted gilet, and was breakfasting frugally on toast and a poached egg.

'I normally just have porridge or cereal,' I said, 'but it was too tempting to resist, all laid out there.'

'Yes, you must watch your figure,' she said, looking at me thoughtfully. 'Most men these days, Jack included, seem to prefer the svelte woman, like Melinda Christopher.'

'I've seen bigger stick insects than Melinda Christopher,' I retorted, hurt. 'I'm not overweight, I just naturally have big boobs and wide hips. My waist measurement is quite small.'

'You are not at all a typical Winter – it is such a pity.'

'Neither was Alys Blezzard, if that painting upstairs is a true portrait. But I would much rather not have so much temptation at breakfast. I'm sure there's enough food here for at least ten hearty eaters – and I don't know about you, but I wouldn't eat kidneys any time of day, and though I love both kedgeree and kippers, *not* first thing in the morning.'

105

'William liked a good choice – and anyway, Jack is partial to a full English breakfast. Men are, aren't they?'

'I can't remember, it's too long since I lived with one. But Jack's not here all the time and when he is, I don't suppose he would find having just bacon and eggs too much of a hardship, would he? Do we really need all the rest of it?'

'Perhaps you had better discuss it with him when he comes down at the weekend?'

'Perhaps,' I agreed, refraining from saying that it wasn't actually going to be any of his business now. I *must* stop being such a coward and break the news to him that I'm not going to sell Winter's End (even if I still have only the vaguest of ideas on how to generate enough income to keep it), or Hebe will get in first. In any case, since I hoped he would still consider Winter's End his home and help me to get it back on its feet again, it might be tactful at least to make a show of asking his advice occasionally!

But I made a mental note to do something about the lavish catering because there must be such a lot of waste, though I expect some of it goes into Charlie, now he is eating again. He had greeted me effusively when I came downstairs, but was currently shadowing Jonah, who now popped his head through the door to tell me that Milly had arrived and wanted to know what she was to do with Charlie.

'And Mr Yatton is in the office,' he said, with a jerk of the head in the direction of the solar tower, 'but no hurry, Mrs Lark always gives him a bacon and egg bap and a cup of coffee to keep his strength up. His sister, Effie, does for him at home, and she doesn't let him have anything like that – rabbit food he gets, there.'

Milly, a fresh-faced girl in jeans and jumper, was waiting in the Great Hall with an unsuspecting Charlie, who looked like a giant, unappetising furball. 'What,' she said, looking at him slightly despairingly, 'would you like me to do with him?'

'I think the only thing you *can* do is clip his coat short, then give him a bath. And I'm sure his toenails are too long, because he hasn't been having walks, so could you do those, too?'

'OK – and had you better buy him a coat until his fur gets longer again? Only he'll be cold when he's out, otherwise.'

'Yes, I suppose I had, you're right.'

'I've got some in the van, nice red tartan ones, with matching leads and doggy-doo holders.'

'Er – lovely,' I said weakly, 'could you put it on the bill?'

She took the unsuspecting victim out to her van while I went off to the estate office.

Mr Yatton, my steward, was small, slight and handsome, with silvery hair and a finely lined face – and, at a guess, the wrong side of seventy. To my huge relief he seemed to handle all the financial side of running the house and estate, right down to paying the staff wages, balancing the books and sorting out the accountant. He had the whole thing literally at his fingertips for, apart from the office desktop computer, he had a laptop of his own and a plethora of electronic gadgets, and so was not so much a silver surfer as a silver technobabe.

'I am here weekday mornings and Sir William used to come in at some point every day to discuss matters, give any orders, sign cheques . . . that sort of thing. That is his desk,' he indicated an oak roll-top, 'now yours. Though you may, of course, prefer the computer desk?'

'No – I mean, I do email and so on, but I don't use the computer much.'

Mr Yatton, looking quite as shocked as if I'd admitted to being illiterate, discoursed enthusiastically about the advantages of the computing age for fully ten minutes, before recalling the true reason for our meeting and proceeding to outline for me the complicated financial affairs of Winter's End.

He was very patient, considering how hard I find it to grasp financial details, but I *longed* for Lucy, who had the sort of brain that could make sense of all this *and* think it was fun, like Mr Yatton.

The annual outgoings were of nightmare proportions and ranged from those I had expected, like the staff wages and fuel bills for heating the house, to things that had never even crossed my mind, like Public Liability Insurance ... and that bank loan. How could I have forgotten about that even for one second?

It was scary to try to take in everything at once, but eventually I began to see a kind of pattern emerging. 'So, basically you are saying that before Grandfather took out that bank loan, there was just about enough income coming in from various sources, including investments, to keep Winter's End in a reasonable state of repair – except that for many years the lion's share of it has been diverted into the escalating cost of restoring and maintaining the gardens?'

'Yes, in a nutshell, though of course costs rise and income may fluctuate,' he pointed out. 'The bank loan was spent entirely on the garden – large yew trees to extend the maze to its original size did not come cheaply – and the repayments are now a heavy drain on the estate on top of all the other expenses.'

'Oh God!' I said, closing my eyes briefly. 'Well, given all that, and with four gardeners but only one cleaner, the house was bound to deteriorate to the point where there's a huge amount of work to do to get it back into good order. I only hope it's structurally sound, because there's no contingency fund in these figures, is there?'

'No, I am afraid not, though one of the other paintings

Sir William had cleaned proved to be a Herring – a horse painting, though not, of course, in the same league as the Stubbs. He put it to one side.'

'I'll look for it later. I don't really want to sell off more heirlooms than I absolutely have to, though clearing that bank loan has to be a priority. But on the other hand, it would be pointless doing that if the house then fell down about my ears, wouldn't it? Jack seems to think Winter's End needs a lot of expensive repair work.'

'Oh, I should doubt that very much,' he exclaimed, shocked. 'Sir William may have been, if I may say so, blinkered by his fanatical ambition to fully restore the gardens to their previous glory, but he would not have let the fabric of the house disintegrate to that extent.'

'Let's hope you're right; it will make things so much easier. Did you know I'd spent my working life in stately homes, Mr Yatton? I expect I know as much about the best way to clean a marble floor, or get the dust out of a carved overmantel, as any professionally trained conservator, though applying those techniques here will be a bit like shutting the stable door after the horse has bolted. I'm going to do my best to conserve what's left, but to do that I'll need help – and without increasing the staffing bills.'

'Do I deduce, therefore, that you will be reducing the garden staff and increasing the indoor?' he guessed intelligently.

'Not *exactly*, because I couldn't possibly fire any of the people working for Winter's End. They all seem to have been here for years and years! But obviously I can't afford to take on more until I find a way of drastically increasing the revenue, so –' I sat back – 'it looks like I will just have to reallocate some of the gardeners to help around the house when needed, won't I?'

'I suppose that would be the logical solution,' he agreed after a moment, 'but of course Seth won't be pleased, with the garden restoration scheme finally being so close to completion. The last stage is the lower terrace, for which the original plan is missing. We found most of it in that chest over there, mixed up with all sorts of papers, though the bottom had been ripped off. But even when finished, the gardens will take quite a bit of maintenance.'

'But not so much in the winter.'

'No, there is that, though of course a lot of woodland maintenance takes place then, and there is the mistletoe harvest.'

'Exactly how much do I pay Seth Greenwood for his services?' I asked curiously, realising I hadn't seen any mention of his salary among all the figures.

'Nothing at all, though he lives in the lodge rent free. Sir William treated him as one of the family, since he is also your great-aunt Ottilie's stepson. Seth agreed to come back and oversee the remainder of the restoration after his father died, as nominal head gardener, with the proviso that he was free to do his own work whenever he pleased.'

'His own work being . . . ?'

'Designing and restoring knot gardens and parterres – that is his speciality, you know. He writes books and articles, too. Indeed, he is also the author of the little pamphlet on the history of Winter's End that we sell on open days.'

'He's a man of many talents,' I said, curiously put out to find I was getting his services for free. 'Renaissance Man, in fact!'

'Sir William was very fond of him and treated him almost like a son – though, of course, he couldn't have left him Winter's End, since there was no relationship other than through marriage.'

'*And* there was Jack, the obvious heir,' I pointed out, wondering if Jack had felt jealous that Seth had claimed his rightful place in Grandfather's affections, just as *he* had claimed mine in Hebe's? This nest had had two rival cuckoos jostling for position . . .

'Er – yes, though he never really entered into your grandfather's passion for gardening. Are you fond of gardening, Sophy?'

'I love walking in gardens, or sitting in one with a drink in my hand; but I had enough of grubbing about in the soil in all weathers when I lived in a commune in Scotland.'

I contemplated the knotty problem that was Seth Greenwood, and concluded that there wasn't really any way I could get rid of him if he was working for nothing *and* Ottie's stepson – though of course, he might leave in high dudgeon when I radically cut the garden budget . . .

'I do intend completing the restoration, but perhaps not as quickly as my grandfather would have liked, since the house must take priority now. And to fund anything that needs more than simple hard work and elbow grease, I'll need to increase the revenue from Winter's End in some way.'

'The woodland is already well managed and the tenancy terms for Brockbank Farm are very fair,' Mr Yatton said doubtfully.

'Yes, I expect they are, but I was thinking more about increasing *visitor* numbers. Opening Winter's End to the public seems to have been a bit half-hearted and I'm sure there must be lots of opportunity there to generate income.'

'Sir William hated opening the house at all, though the family side was shut off and so quite unaffected by the visitors. But certainly you *could* open for more days, if you wished.'

'I'll give it some serious thought and perhaps, meanwhile, I should harden my heart, sell the Herring and use the money to renovate the visitor facilities? We could enhance our existing assets, like having Alys Blezzard's portrait cleaned and making more of the witchcraft angle, and the legend that Shakespeare might have visited Winter's End could be turned into a major draw too . . . Bigged-up, as they say.'

I was starting to feel hopeful and enthused – washed over by one of those golden glows of unfoundedly optimistic second sight. 'We could have a shop as well as a better tearoom, and sell all kinds of merchandise.'

He looked dubious. 'Sir William hated anything commercial.'

'Commerce is what kept a roof on the last house I worked in, *and* the Scottish castle where I was before that. I know what visitors want,' I said confidently. In fact, in the past I'd frequently wondered why half of them even bothered going round the buildings at all, and didn't just have lunch and then buy souvenirs.

He had been scribbling onto a notepad while we had been talking and now came to a halt and looked up. 'So, your initial idea is to redirect most of what income there is away from the garden and into restoring the house. Then, secondly, to generate new income from increased visitor numbers. Any work needing to be carried out to enhance visitor attractions is to be funded in the first instance by the sale of the Herring painting.'

'Yes . . . that's it so far. That way we should be able to keep repaying the loan and still have some profit left over. I haven't really had much time to work on the finer details, because until I got here I thought I would probably sell the estate to Jack.'

'Oh, no, that wasn't at all what Sir William intended,' he said, looking shocked. 'He expected you to take on the running of the estate and thought that your daughter, Lucy, had a good head for business and perhaps could replace me when I retire.'

I stared at him. 'He did? But he only met her once!'

'Sir William was extremely good at summing up character and – excuse me! – from the sound of it, their encounter seemed to have been a case of like meeting like.'

I cast my mind back to Grandfather's visit and had to concede that he was right. 'They clashed, but they did both seem to enjoy it. And I am sure she will be invaluable in running Winter's End, though she's in Japan at the moment, you know, teaching English on a year's contract. I'd like to get her home, because she's being stalked and there have been all those horrible cases in the newspapers lately.'

'You could send for her now, if you are worried,' he suggested.

'No I can't, because for one thing I'd have to buy her a plane ticket, which would be horrendously expensive, and for another, she's dead stubborn and took this job to try and pay off some of her student loan debts, so I'd have to have something to offer her.'

'If you explain to her that you need her help, then give me her email address so I can start sending her figures, spreadsheets, and an outline of what I do, she may well become so involved and interested that she will agree to come back early,' he suggested craftily.

'You know, Mr Yatton, you may just be right? You're a genius!' I kissed him, which made him go slightly pink and flustered.

Then Jonah came in with coffee and butterfly sponge cakes, after which, fortified, Mr Yatton took me off in an ancient Land Rover to meet the tenant farmer, bumping down the back drive behind the coach house, past a slightly neglected tennis court.

He dropped me off at the door a couple of hours later, by which time I was exhausted, my head buzzing. *He* seemed enlivened, if anything, by the whole thing and clattered off

113

with a cheery wave, saying he had to go and collect his sister, Effie, since it was the Sticklepond teadance club tonight down at the village hall and they were dining at the pub first.

'Tell Miss Hebe that she must save me a jive,' he said, on departing.

A *jive*?

Charlie, looking faintly aggrieved, was sitting on the doorstep, a vision of short black and white fur and lurid tartan coat, a small bone-shaped device under his chin holding, I discovered, a couple of matching red doggy bags. Very tasteful. He kept shaking his head, so it seemed to be annoying him – but then, King Charles spaniels don't have a lot of chin. Perhaps it would be better clipped to his lead, instead?

'Milly said poor Charlie's claws were so long they were going into his pads,' Mrs Lark told me when I went into the kitchen. 'She's going to pop out and give him a going-over once a month, if you like.'

'Yes, I think she'd better,' I agreed, though here was yet another expense.

'Do you want a sandwich? You've missed your lunch and it's gone teatime. I've just made one for Miss Hebe and taken it through into the stillroom. She's been in the garden all day, and if you don't remind her to eat or put it in front of her she'd be no wider than a piece of knotted string.'

'Is she in there now?' I asked, looking at the closed door.

'Yes, brewing something heathenish up for a customer – I didn't ask what. Now, about that sandwich?'

'Oh, no, thanks,' I said with a shudder. 'I've just been out to the tenanted farm, and I'm full of strong tea, fruitcake and Lancashire Crumbly.'

I took Charlie out for a quick walk down the drive and back in the wintry late afternoon gloom, then took his coat off and hung it up in the kitchen with his lead. I left Mrs Lark feeding him and went upstairs to change.

I'd left my mobile behind and there were two voicemail messages: one from Anya, asking how the bloated pluto-crat was feeling today, and the other in Jack's smoothly spine-tingling tones, saying he hoped I'd liked my flowers, and he looked forward to seeing me on Saturday.

So, Aunt Hebe hadn't told him about my decision to keep Winter's End yet? Maybe she thought that I would change my mind when I realised the enormity of the task – or that Jack, when he arrived, would change it for me? Or even that restoring Winter's End would quickly become a joint venture.

I did keep imagining what it would be like if Jack accepted my decision with good grace and then helped me restore Winter's End. It was going to be enjoyable, but also very hard work, and it would be fun to share that with someone else . . .

I still had the phone in my hand when it rang, making me jump, but this time it was Lucy.

'Hi, Mum.'

'That was good timing, darling. I've just come in from spending the most exhausting day, being given a crash course in estate management! I thought I had the estate manager for that – or steward, as Mr Yatton calls himself – but I suppose I ought to try and get my head round it, if only to understand how much I've got – or not got – to keep the place running. That bank loan is *crippling* and since we've only just repaid the interest and started on the capital, there would be nothing to be gained by paying it off early even if we could . . .' I tailed off. 'But, Lucy, just wait until you see Winter's End! I only hope you love it as much as I do.'

'Actually, Mum, I already have.'

'Have what?' I said, puzzled.

'Seen Winter's End. After Great-Grandfather visited us I was curious. You'd always made Winter's End sound like some lost Eden, the Shangri-La of Lancashire, so I thought I'd have a look.'

'But no one has mentioned—'

'No one *knew*,' she interrupted. 'You always said I had the Winter colouring, so I disguised myself with a beanie hat and dark shades and just came on an open day. I saw Great-Grandfather on one of the lower terraces, talking to a gardener, but he didn't see me. He looked ill – much frailer than when he visited us.'

'You could have told me.'

'I thought it might upset you. You always said you could never go back, though I didn't see why not.'

'Because my mother always said—' I stopped. Susan had said a lot of things, not always the exact truth – more an embellished retelling of old stories that grew and changed in time. But somehow her fear of going back to Winter's End had infected me, so that even long after she had died and I was an adult with my own child, it had never occurred to me to return.

Perhaps it was partly because I had loved it so much and felt secure there that I feared to go back and find it all changed. I didn't want the memories tarnished by reality. Just as well too – I'd have been devastated to find Jack had taken my place in Hebe's affections, and Seth in Ottie's and Grandfather's. Not that I think I had ever featured much in either of the latter's, since Ottie was the most unmaternal woman I had ever met and Grandfather had seemed at the time to regard me merely as an irritating blot on the family escutcheon.

'What did you think of it, Lucy?'

'Well, I only saw the gardens and the Great Hall, really,

though the maze was . . . well, amazing! The house looked pretty shabby and the catering facilities were tea and buns in this sort of outhouse at the back. But it . . . I don't know, as soon as I started up the drive I knew it was one of those magic spots that seem to be in a time warp of their own. Do you know what I mean? Like when we took the van up to the Roman fort at Vindolanda, that was a magical place too. You felt you'd stepped out of time.'

'That's interesting, because I feel the same way, and I just *can't* let Winter's End go. Mind you, I can't really afford to keep it, either, because the house has been terribly neglected. All the money for its upkeep has been poured into the gardens and no one even took an interest in keeping the place properly clean. It's disgustingly dirty!'

'Oh, Mum!' Lucy sighed. 'Handing you a big neglected house of your own is like the best present ever! What have you cleaned so far?'

'Only the dog. There's a little spaniel called Charlie, and he was all matted and dirty. But I didn't do it myself – he was beyond that. I had someone come out to clip and bath him and do his toenails.'

'Bet you are dying to get on with sorting everything out, though?'

'Yes, I am, but I had to have this session with Mr Yatton, today first – and apparently the solicitor, the accountant and even my personal bank accounts manager are going to visit me too, in the next few days. I wish you were here, Lucy. You are so much better at business and figures and stuff than me.'

'I should be; that's what I did my degree in.'

'Yes, and amazingly enough, Grandfather seems to have sussed that out. He suggested to Mr Yatton that you could learn to be the steward when you came back, and take over from him when he retires. I don't know how you feel about

117

that? If you like the idea, Mr Yatton said he could start sending you figures and spreadsheets (whatever they are) by email right now. I gave him your address. Is that OK?'

'He emails?'

'The estate office has a computer, but he has a swish laptop too – he's a silver surfer.'

'Cool.'

'So, what do you think? He said he could teach you quite a lot of it by email.'

'Why not? He can send me the figures over and keep me up to date, and I can discuss it with you, or send him emails to show to you – and we'll see how it goes when I get back. But it would be a job, wouldn't it?'

'Yes, a proper job – though the salary might not be huge, to start with. But if we can keep Winter's End going, then one day it will be yours.'

'That's a really, really odd thought . . . though Winter's End sort of got to me, and I keep thinking about it . . .' She added more briskly, 'Don't do anything sudden without asking me first, especially involving men. You know you always go for the wrong sort.'

'I don't! In fact, I've hardly had a chance to go for *any* sort, and it's not my fault that when I started dating again only the dregs of humanity were left over.'

'Jack sounds to me like the wrong sort, or why wouldn't Great-Grandfather have left Winter's End to him? Bet he's a snake in the grass. Don't be too trusting.'

'He is not a snake in the grass and I am not too—'

'I'll have to go. Love you lots. Byee . . .'

I stared at the phone, feeling aggrieved. Lucy had managed to get rid of the few boyfriends I had acquired while she was growing up, and by the time she left for university the pool of available men in my age group had shrunk to a very dubious puddle. I washed and changed, then flaked out on the bed until Jonah beat the gong for another gargantuan dinner, which Hebe, after her day spent in the garden and stillroom, fell on with huge gusto. She ate Ottie's share too, since she was in Manchester at the opening of someone's exhibition. How can she put away so much food and stay so thin?

She was wearing a forties-style dance dress and her hair in a roll with a butterfly hairpin, and after dinner left me to my solitary coffee and went off to the dance.

I spent a happy and productive couple of hours in the cleaning room, checking off and reorganising the supplies, and adding to my shopping list.

I had a feeling that it might take some time to teach Grace new ways of doing things – if it was possible at all. But then, I could just confine her activities to the floors, the bathrooms, changing the beds and doing the laundry, where she couldn't really do that much more damage.

Charlie got bored watching me after a while and vanished, and on my way to bed I found him fast asleep and blissfully snoring in his basket next to the Aga.

Chapter Eleven: O Mother, Where Art Thou?

Thomas in his great kindness has given mee a wooden coffer such as I have never seen before, carved prettily inside and out, and fitted with ingenious drawers and compartments. There is a sturdy lock – he says he fears for mee, and I should keep my secrets therein and the key close.

From the journal of Alys Blezzard, 1581

Breakfast was, if possible, even more indecently lavish than the day before. Recalling Mr Yatton's final words of advice, which had been to the effect that I should take control straight away and start as I meant to go on, I decided to make my very first economy. It might save my figure, as well as some money.

'Aunt Hebe, you know when I said yesterday that cooking this much food was such a huge waste?' I began cautiously, gesturing to the hotplates groaning under the weight of enough calories to keep an entire rugby team happy. 'Well, I've decided to ask Mrs Lark not to do it any more.'

She looked up from her toast, which she was consuming while reading a new gardening magazine that had been left by her plate, presumably by Jonah. 'But I always eat a full cooked breakfast on Sundays, Sophy, and I like a poached egg most days too – and occasionally a bit of bacon.'

'That's fine, then – we can still have bacon and eggs every day, but the full monty just on Sundays, as a special treat.'

'Jack won't like that in the least,' she protested, shaking her head. 'He often brings friends for the weekend too, and they all have good appetites.'

'I'm quite sure Jack will have the good manners to be happy with whatever he's offered – as will his friends. We simply can't afford to go on wasting food on this scale, and it would make less work for Mrs Lark.'

'But she's the *cook* – that's what she *does*.' Aunt Hebe looked at me blankly.

'Yes, and she does it very well too,' I said patiently, 'but she's no spring chicken, is she? Cutting down her workload wouldn't hurt.'

'I suppose you will make what changes you like, Sophy, but I think you are unwise to start without consulting Jack, for you may well find yourself having to put things right back again to how they were before.'

I mentally counted up to ten. 'Of course, I'll always be glad to hear any of Jack's suggestions, Aunt Hebe, and I will always value his advice. But this is only the first of many economies and changes I'll have to make if I'm to turn Winter's End back into the beautiful place it used to be, rather than the shabby, neglected creature it is now.'

'That is a very odd way of putting it! You make it sound as though the house were alive.'

'It is, to me.'

She looked at me strangely, then put down the magazine, drained her cup of tea, and rose to her feet. 'Well, I must get off to feed the hens – but I warn you, any changes to my walled garden will be done over my dead body!'

'Of course, Aunt Hebe – I wouldn't dream of it. But I'm

going to tour the grounds later and I hope you'll at least show me the walled garden and the hens?'

'Certainly,' she said grandly. 'What are you going to do this morning?'

I indicated the embroidered fabric bag slung over the back of my chair. 'Mr Yatton gave me a big notebook and I'm going to go round the house again, this time writing down what needs to be done in order of urgency, and adding to my shopping list. I did a stock-check of the cleaning room last night, while you were out.'

'Oh? Perhaps you should just get the agency in for a sort of late spring clean,' she suggested vaguely. 'What were they called? Ah, yes – Dolly Mops.'

'I'll see,' I said tactfully, because I hated to think of the damage a domestic cleaning agency had already unwittingly wreaked on Winter's End, not to mention Grace's casual attentions over the years.

'Jonah,' I said, as he came into the room and started loading a vast brass tray with crockery and unused dishes of hot food, 'I'm going around the gardens this afternoon – could you send word to Seth Greenwood? Tell him he can come with me himself if he wants to, or delegate it to one of the other gardeners. About two o'clock.'

'I'll do that,' he said, and I followed him back into the kitchen, where I proposed the revolutionary idea of reducing the number and style of breakfast dishes to Mrs Lark.

She looked even more incredulous than Aunt Hebe. 'But we've *always* done it like that!'

'I know, but times change and no one is eating most of it, so it's such a waste.'

'As to that, I make sure Mr Yatton has something in his stomach to start the day with, other than the rabbit food his sister gives him, and then what's not eaten in the kitchen, Jonah makes into swill for the pigs out at the back of the courtyard. All our bacon and ham comes from pigs reared at Winter's End.'

I resolved to avoid the pigsty since I didn't want to meet my future breakfasts face to face. 'It's a pity to cook lovely food just for the pigs, Mrs Lark, but of course you can still cook bacon and eggs every day – just not the kippers, kedgeree, kidneys and all the rest of it.'

'I *suppose* so,' she reluctantly conceded, 'and you'll still want all the trimmings, of course, like tomatoes and mushrooms. Then, on Sundays, you can have a *proper* breakfast.' The thought of pulling out the culinary stops at least once a week seemed to cheer her. 'We could have an extra high tea every day too, to make up!'

'I'm trying to make less work for you, not more,' I protested.

'Now, Sophy love, you've got to keep your strength up – and so has Miss Hebe, what with all the work she does in her garden.'

We seemed to have reached an impasse, so I gave up the battle at this point and changed the subject. 'Mrs Lark, I wanted to ask you a favour.'

'Ask away.'

'I thought I'd invite all the indoor and outdoor staff – that sounds terribly grand, but you know what I mean – to a meeting in the Great Hall on Saturday morning at about ten, to tell them my plans for the future of Winter's End. I should think everyone has been in limbo long enough, wondering what's going to happen. I wondered if you could provide refreshments? Tea and coffee and biscuits, or something?'

'You leave it to me – and do you want me to make sure everyone knows? The Friends too, they had better be there.'

'Friends?' I said, absently.

'Friends of Winter's End.'

'Oh yes, I'd forgotten all about them and they are going to be a really important part of my plans!'

'There are about a dozen Friends, but I only need to tell one and then it's like in that film *Village of the Damned*.'

'Film?' I said, baffled.

'Yes, you tell one of them and then they *all* know. Faster than the speed of gossip – uncanny it is, sometimes. Mr Yatton's sister, Effie's, one.'

'I'll bear that in mind, Mrs Lark.'

'All the gardeners pop into my kitchen during the day for a bite of cake to have with their tea, so I can spread the word then. Grace's here now. She's just washed all Charlie's bedding – said since he was so clean, his blankets ought to be too.'

'That was kind of her.'

'Loves dogs, does Grace. Charlie's in the laundry room with her now; he took his bone.'

So that accounted for his vanishing act after breakfast.

'This meeting ... some of the gardeners said Mr Jack seemed to assume he would still be running the place, the last time he was down,' she suggested. 'He told them Winter's End would be too much for you to run, so you'd sell the place to him. But I said, "No, that can't be right – Miss Sophy's here to stay."'

'Yes I am, and I want Winter's End to be clean, beautiful and whole again, just the way I remember it. It seems to have gone to the dogs since Mum and I left.'

'Sir William threw himself into his plans for the garden even more when your mother took you away,' she agreed, 'to distract himself, I suppose, until you came back – which he was convinced you would, at first.' She sighed. 'Oh, well, it's all water under the bridge now, isn't it?'

'Yes, and now we will all have to pull together to save Winter's End, which will mean some big changes. That can be hard when people are set in their ways.'

I took the notebook and a pen out of my bag. 'I might as well start making my list of things to make, mend and order. I'll do the rest of the house first and then come back to this wing. Perhaps you wouldn't mind just giving me a glimpse of your rooms then?'

'Certainly.'

'And if there's anything, either in the kitchens or your rooms, that you'd like changing or replacing, note it down for me, would you?'

'I'll do that,' she agreed. 'The weekly shopping list is pinned to the inside of that cupboard door there, and Grace puts any cleaning stuff that we're running out of on it.'

'Good. I did an inventory of the cleaning room last night, so I'll add a few everyday things to that, but I'll also have to order some specialist products. Luckily I know a good supplier. Stately Solutions will have everything that I need.'

The entertainment of watching his bedding go round must have palled, for Charlie nudged open the door and came in carrying the remains of a large bone, which he tenderly deposited in his basket. From the smell that wafted in with him, Jonah was boiling up pigswill out at the back somewhere.

'I think we'll have a nice jam roly-poly pudding to follow the salmon and Duchesse potatoes tonight,' Mrs Lark said, absently thumbing through a battered notebook – she appeared to have her own household book. 'Cream or custard?'

'Custard,' I said decidedly, and went out with Charlie at my heels.

All this comforting stodge was lovely in the winter, but I had a feeling that by spring I'd have started to long for a good salad and a big bowl of fresh fruit – and goodness knew what would have happened to my figure by then!

* * *

125

I'd written three pages of notes before I even got out of the Great Hall.

It had always been the heart of the house, the room where everyone's paths crossed repeatedly in a complex minuet of daily living, and now the fire once again glowed in the vast hearth it was much more welcoming.

It was also the place where Alys Blezzard seemed to be most with me – and where I felt positively wired in to Winter's End itself. Standing in the middle of the Great Hall was like recharging my batteries, and filled me with energy and the unfounded golden glow of optimism that reassured me that everything would turn out all right . . . in the end.

There *were* a few shadows drifting like dark smoke in the corners of my consciousness – but then, what life doesn't have its share of shadows?

I looked around me, noticing for the first time that the lime mortar between the stones of the hall floor needed attention and the old rag rug in front of the fire was now so grey and stiff with dirt that it blended into the colour of the floor. I would bet good money on Grace mopping it over every time she washed the floor in here – probably with bleach in her bucket too! But we could try soaking it in mild soap and warm water and see what happened.

The stuffed stag's head on the wall looked ghastly. It was not only balding, but had lost an eye. I guiltily remembered the last time I slid down the banisters and knocked it off – perhaps that had loosened it?

Jonah, coming through the West Wing door with a tray of crockery, said, 'Your grandfather got that head at a sale. A great one for buying junk at auctions, he used to be, before he got so caught up in the gardening. The eye's in that bowl of potpourri on the mantelpiece.'

'Thanks, Jonah,' I said, glad he'd told me before I'd looked in the pot. An eye staring back at me from the dried rose petals would have been a bit of a shock.

'If you like, I can Superglue it back in.'

'Yes, please – and give the head a good brushing while you're at it, will you? I'll try and find something nicer to replace it with later on, when I've got time.'

'I'll do that,' he said, going off whistling.

Half the candle light bulbs in the wheel-shaped holder suspended from the ceiling were dead when I flicked the switch, as were those in the wall lights – muscular naked bronze arms holding out what looked like frosted glass whirly ice-cream cornets.

Humming the tune to the Cornetto ice-cream advert, I slowly turned, taking everything in. The tops of the windows were draped with spider-spun silk, and most of the assorted chairs, settles and benches that furnished the room looked dull and unpolished, except for the tops, where the application of countless bottoms over the centuries had rubbed them up to a fine gloss.

Grace must have gone up the backstairs, because there was a zooming noise from the dimly lit minstrels' gallery way above me, and I could just see the top of her head as she pushed the Hoover to and fro. Then it stopped, and she started working backwards down the stairs with a dustpan and brush.

A hand-held vacuum cleaner would be easier for that, and I made a memo to unpack mine from its box in the attic – if I could remember which one I'd put it in. On the end of the growing list at the back of the notebook I added foam tubing to pad the end of the vacuum cleaner hose, which would stop any more chips being knocked out of the furniture.

Going into the family wing, I popped my head in the steward's office to say good morning to Mr Yatton and tell him what I was up to today, and where he could find me if he wanted me.

'Very good – and Lucy and I have made contact already,' he said. 'I emailed some figures, and she sent me a list of very pertinent questions right back.'

I could imagine – she would shortly be running his affairs much as she tries to do mine. A mobile phone like a thin silvery clam played a snatch of waltz music and, as he picked it up, I smiled at him and returned to my inventory.

In the passage abutting the solar tower a cupboard had been cut into the wall, which was now filled with dull silver and the sad, cracked relics of several valuable tea services. Mum had told me that there had once been an emergency trapdoor exit down into it from the priest's hole above, but after Alys Blezzard's death the family had forsworn the Catholic faith and the priest's hole had fallen into disuse. I couldn't see any trace of it in the cupboard ceiling, but it was pretty dark in there.

The library was quite cosy and, since presumably William had used it a lot, relatively clean and tidy. Even the books, including many very ancient gardening tomes behind glass, looked as if they had been dusted within living memory, and all the lights worked. There was a billiard table at one end, a small TV and video, and a wind-up gramophone with a stack of old 78s in cardboard covers next to it, all humorous monologues.

The top one was 'Albert and the Lion'. I put it on and wound the handle and, as the crackling monologue played, I tried to square this evidence of my grandfather's sense of humour with what I remembered of him. It wasn't easy. After a while I gave up and carried on with my survey.

Like the library, the drawing room was in reasonably good order, though the chairs and sofas were still wearing grubby summer chintz covers, which should have long since been taken off and washed. I wondered if there was a winter set, too? Grace or Mrs Lark would probably know.

Aunt Hebe had staked a claim to a comfortable chair and Berlin-work footstool, next to a table loaded with gardening magazines and catalogues, plus an overflowing bundle of knitting that was the rather snotty green of mushy peas. I sincerely hoped it was intended as a gift for Jack and not some kind of welcome-home present for me.

Not, so far, that there had been much evidence from Aunt Hebe of any real pleasure in my return . . .

The dining room was grandly dingy, with a splendid chandelier that tinkled in the draught from the door, and I noted the threadbare but rather beautiful rug that would have to be professionally cleaned, if I could ever afford it. Goodness knows what state the tapestries hanging in the corridors were in. It was probably just as well that it was too dark to see, and at least the gloom meant they had been protected from much light damage.

I'd left the room I most longed to look at, Lady Anne's parlour, until last . . . and strictly speaking, of course, that should be Lady Winter's parlour, though it doesn't sound quite so cosy.

It was strange that although it was a lovely light room with a door on to the terrace, if felt unused, unloved and neglected.

The dark, dull panelling that covered the lower half of the walls looked seventeenth century, but at some point the plaster above had been painted a deep, coral colour. The shade was echoed in the pattern of the curtains that hung at the windows and over the door to the terrace, and though they were a little faded they had been well lined.

'*Alys Blezzard scratched her initials on the windowpane in the little parlour at the back of the house, in the left-hand corner, and so did her daughter,*' I could hear my mother's

129

voice saying in my head. And when I pulled aside the drapes and looked, there they were, a tangible link to the past – the faint spidery tracery of '*AB*' and '*AW*'.

Maybe I would add '*SW*', for this would now be Sophy's parlour, somewhere I could sit and sew my crazy patchwork and dream. There was even a needlework table, a Victorian pedestal affair with clawed feet like a lion ... which for some odd reason made me think of the head gardener. It wouldn't surprise me if he had big clawed feet inside those sturdy boots and maybe he even turned into a big black cat – something pantherish – when the moon was full?

I shook off this rather disturbing image and turned to the alcove where the ancient wooden coffer in which Alys had kept her secrets stood. I had got over my first disappointment at its outward plainness now and could see that it was a thing of beauty in itself – as was the key, which Mum gave to me as a gift on my fourteenth birthday, just before she made her final, fatal trip. Why hadn't I known the dark omens were gathering for her, not me? And, even if I had warned her, would she have listened?

Shaking off old memories I looked thoughtfully at the box and then at a substantial cupboard built into one corner of the room, with glazed upper doors. If I moved a rather funereal arrangement of wax flowers under a dome of glass and some dubious Egyptian funerary ushabti up a shelf, I thought the box would fit on the lower one. An extra line of defence for Alys's secrets – if they were returned home.

Did they really need defending? Was Jack that keen to find clues to some treasure that, if it ever existed, would have been long discovered and gone? But even if he was, I was certain he wouldn't go to such extreme lengths as breaking open an antique and valuable box to get at the book ... or would he? I had now heard so many opinions of Jack, his character and intentions that I wasn't sure what to believe any more.

But then, how could I possibly doubt the sincerity I'd heard in his voice when he told me how much he loved Winter's End and how pleased he was to meet me at last? I wasn't looking forward in the least to telling him that I wasn't going to sell the place to him, after all, and dashing all his hopes.

I couldn't find a key that fitted the cupboard on my ring, until I thought to open the door below and discovered it hanging inside on a small brass cup hook. I moved everything up a shelf, then slipped out of the door to the terrace (locked, but this time there was a key on the ring) and round the house to my secret cache in the van, returning with the weight of the fabric bag dragging at my shoulder.

I lifted the chest onto the bergère sofa and managed to undo the lock and hasp. Inside, it was as Aunt Hebe had described, completely carved with flowers and foliage and smelling faintly spicy, fitted out with little drawers and compartments. There seemed to be nothing in there, apart from the powdery residue of what might once have been dried herbs until, in a space behind a false drawer front, I discovered a strange polished stone with a hole in it and a rotting velvet bag full of small yellowed bits of bone or ivory scratched with symbols that I thought might be runes. Whatever they were, clearly they had once held some kind of magical significance.

There was a rectangular central compartment that had room and to spare for the little book of bible stories I placed in it – one of my childhood treasures safely returned, at least, even if not the one the box was intended for . . .

'*Alys?*' I looked up, searching the dark corners but seeing nothing, and it occurred to me that perhaps, now I was an adult, I never would. For a moment I wondered if she ever

131

really existed, except in my imagination . . . until, as I locked the chest away behind the glazed cupboard doors, I caught sight of her dim reflection in the dingy glass before she slowly dissolved into the shadows. I could have *sworn* she winked at me.

I left the little room guarding its secrets and went up the stairs that wound round the solar tower. The upper storey had once been a bedchamber, with the ex-priest's hole converted to a powdering closet, but it was now an empty and long-neglected schoolroom. I suppose my aunts must have been taught there, but I went to the village infants' school.

I took a quick, guilty look into Aunt Hebe's bedroom, which was cluttered and cosy, with a sort of kitchen corner by the sink where she could brew cocoa or whatever her favoured bedtime drink was, a La-Z-Boy chair and a giant TV screen. I didn't linger there but wandered through the rest of the bedrooms, including the one where the cleaned pictures were stacked, finding little that a good clean wouldn't fix.

I came at last to more familiar territory – the bedroom that had once been my mother's. I remembered the wallpaper with its plethora of pink roses and the brass four-poster bed, fit for a princess. The frilled muslin curtains were pulled back to reveal a French poodle nightdress case, its topknot tied with red satin ribbon, reclining on the glazed pink chintz eiderdown. It was all the same – and yet, in the cruel light of day, a faded and dusty travesty of how I remembered it.

In one corner of the room lay a battered suitcase, the one we had bought specially for her trip to America. The locks were broken and it had been tied up with twine, which now lay loosened and unknotted around it, and a trapped and limp cotton flounce stuck out of the side of the case like a dead thing.

Suddenly I felt angry: whoever had searched my mother's possessions should have put it all back again neatly. Who could it have been? Grandfather, searching for traces of his lost daughter? Hebe, perhaps, or even Jack, looking for the book?

A handbag rested against the case, but there wasn't much in there, except a wallet containing a picture of me as an awkward teenager with an unfortunate hairstyle, a few dollars, and a dried-out rose-pink lipstick.

In the wardrobe, long cheesecloth dresses swayed like old ghosts and the familiar disturbing scent of patchouli still lingered, reaching out to invade the room.

I hastily closed the door and left. It might be touching that my grandfather had ordered that my mother's room should remain as it was when she ran away, but this was *not* how I wanted to remember her. The room needed exorcising of the past, but for now it could wait.

And so could visiting her grave. She wasn't in either of those places, but with me. For, oddly enough, I had begun to feel closer to my strangely elusive mother once she was dead than I had ever been when she was alive.

Chapter Twelve: Foxed

*I have taken over the preparation of household remedies
and simples and of the making of preserves, fruits and
sweetmeats, Lady Wynter having little interest in such
things, other than the lotion of roses that I made to clear
her complexion. Sir Ralph is in thrall to his young wife,
despite her barrenness, yet he continues in gratitude to
mee that his only son and heir still lives.*

From the journal of Alys Blezzard, 1581

Upstairs, under the eaves, the old nursery lay cold and
neglected and the narrow sleigh bed was stripped and
dustsheeted. I stood looking down at it, remembering the
last time I had slept there . . .

It had been the night we left Winter's End, and Alys had
woken me in the small hours, shaking her head sorrowfully
before fading away at the first faint sound of my mother's
tiptoeing steps.

I'd had time to snatch the book of bible stories from
under my pillow, but very little else before I was whisked
away . . .

All the familiar playthings and books had been put away
in the cupboards, along with some I didn't recognise, which
must have been Jack's. He seemed to have had a penchant
for weapons of mass destruction.

I unlocked the door to the rest of the attic space and found a light switch, but the warren of disused rooms stretching ahead was only patchily lit, a depressingly cluttered vista of anonymous shrouded shapes. I could see why they kept the door locked, though, because if Grace did smoke up there, it would be a major fire hazard.

My own and Lucy's belongings were stacked in one corner of the first room. A quick look through the others didn't reveal anything terribly ominous, like daylight shining through missing tiles, or pools of water on the floorboards, which was a relief. But a better examination would have to wait for when someone (probably me) had swept away all the hanging cobwebs and their occupants. I was sure there would be woodworm, too – what old house doesn't have woodworm? – though I knew that few actually fall down from it.

Sorting the attics would be a huge task, but also a sort of treasure hunt too, for goodness knows what I might find! I would save it as a treat for when I had the rest of the house clean and tidy.

Locking the attic door behind me, I went back down and took a look at the minor family portraits hanging in the gloom of the minstrels' gallery, including that supposed to be Alys, then checked out the Long Room. You could see the light patches on the wall where the paintings that were stacked in the Blue Bedroom and the Stubbs had once hung, but I didn't think any of the other pictures and engravings that were left looked to be of any great value – though if they were, at least the very dirty windows had served to keep most of the sunlight out of the room. I added blinds to my list, but until that could be managed the shutters ought to be completely closed in here when the light was full on the back of the house to prevent any further fading. The furnishings were a mix of chairs in various periods, a love seat and two glass-topped curio tables, containing an assortment of items, including a couple of rather amateur miniatures, a porcelain snuffbox, three carved whale teeth, a bit of netsuke carving and a glass perfume bottle shaped like the Eiffel Tower.

Flanking the door at the far end were two horrid plinths of reddish mottled stone, looking like cheap salami. On one was a marble bust of a hawk-nosed man wearing a lace collar and with his hair in a shoulder-length bob, and on the other reposed a gruesomely detailed small hand carved in alabaster, probably Victorian. I had watched an old black-and-white horror film in the servants' sitting room at Blackwalls once, about someone's chopped-off hand that had run about strangling people, all on its own. I wished now that I hadn't, and I was just wondering which dark corner of the house I could banish the hand to, when Mrs Lark suddenly popped her curly grey head out of the door to the East Wing.

'Thought I heard you! Do you want to come through now and take a peek at our rooms?'

The Larks' suite was immaculately clean, but very shabby, and seemed to have been furnished with old cast-offs from the main house, though a personal touch was supplied by hundreds of cat figurines in every possible pose, and an awful lot of crocheted tablemats.

'Are you a cat lover, Mrs Lark? I don't remember seeing one in the house.'

'I am that! But Sir William couldn't stand them, so we've never had one at Winter's End,' she said sadly.

'Really? Well, *I've* no objection, except that I'm not keen on them in kitchens, walking around on the worktops and table. Would you like to get one?' I asked, and her face lit up.

'Oh, I'd *love* to, Sophy, if you're sure you don't mind? I'll make sure it doesn't go anywhere it shouldn't.'

136

'That's OK then. I like cats, I'm just more of a dog person, myself.'

'I'll get Jonah to take me to the animal rescue centre and pick out a nice kitten as soon as I've got a minute,' she said happily, and then showed me through the rest of their little flatlet, which included a rather Spartan bathroom.

'So, is there anything that you would like that you haven't got?' I asked.

'A shower over the bath and one of them heated towel rails,' she suggested hopefully.

I made a note of it. 'I'll have them installed as soon as I can afford it. Anything else? Painting and decorating, perhaps?'

'That would be lovely. Jonah put all the wallpaper up himself, but that's years ago now.'

'If you'd like to choose the paint and paper, and let me know, we should be able to get on and have that done quite quickly.'

'I'll do that. I've seen some nice wallpaper in *Good Housekeeping* magazine that would look lovely in the bedroom – big pink chrysanthemums. I'll go and see if I can find it.'

'It sounds lovely,' I said, though to be honest, while I could picture rosy, freckled Mrs Lark in such a flowery bower of a bedroom, Jonah, who resembled nothing so much as an amiable rodent, would look quite incongruous. Leaving her searching, I went down the backstairs, meeting Grace on her way up again.

'We're nearly out of Harpic,' she said, by way of greeting. 'I'll be making Mr Jack's bed up now, ready for Saturday.'

'Thanks, Grace,' I said and, feeling the now-familiar *frisson* of nerves, guilt and excitement run through me at the thought of seeing Jack again, carried on down the stairs.

At the bottom I paused, then decided to leave the teashop area for another day. Nor did I need to bother much at this

137

point with the rest of the rooms downstairs in the East Wing, though I did glance in the cellars. They were dry and whitewashed (though in need of a new coat), with the boiler ticking away in one, and another filled with half-empty wine racks and shelves of dusty bottles.

In the kitchen Aunt Hebe had just come in and was washing her earthy hands at the sink, and she asked me, slightly acidly, how my inventory was progressing.

'Fine. Mostly the place is just in need of a really good clean through,' I replied, adding Harpic to the huge list in the notebook while I remembered. 'I can't wait to start!'

'Then your zeal is admirable and should be encouraged, to which end I will give you a big jar of my own beeswax polish. A little goes a long way, with a bit of elbow grease. I'll put some out on the cleaning-room table. Oh, and I've just seen Seth,' she added, in tones that led me to believe she had not enjoyed the encounter. 'He says he is coming at two to show you round the garden.'

I wiped a grubby hand across my face and glanced at the clock, amazed at the time. 'I'd better have a quick wash, then, and have something to eat before he does.'

But just as I reached my room Anya phoned, and by the time I'd updated her on what was happening, washed off the outer layer of filth and returned to the kitchen, Seth was already sitting there, wolfing down ham sandwiches from a platter in the middle of the table.

He seemed to be arguing with Aunt Hebe, for she was saying tartly, '*William* never minded if I took one of the gardeners off for a couple of hours to clean out the hens or do some heavy lifting and digging, and I'm sure dear Jack would have no objection.'

Mrs Lark smiled at me and placed an empty plate opposite Seth, so I sat and helped myself to a sandwich. It was good thick ham, with English mustard that made my eyes water slightly, just the way I like it.

'I wouldn't mind either, if you told me *when* you wanted them and didn't just hijack them when they are doing something else!' Seth snapped. 'We're in the middle of filling in the lily pond on the bottom terrace and Derek's about to start rebuilding the collapsed retaining wall, and we need to get on with it while the weather is good.'

I put in my four penn'orth. 'Losing one of the gardeners for an hour or so occasionally isn't going to cause the whole thing to grind to a halt, is it?'

'That's perfectly true,' Aunt Hebe said, looking at me with approval.

'In fact . . .' I took another bite, chewed and swallowed, feeling Seth's green eyes resting on me coldly, 'in fact, we are all going to have to work as one team from now on, and multitask – as you will find out if you come to the meeting in the Great Hall the day after tomorrow.'

He pushed his plate away and leaned back, folding his arms. 'I see. The old order changeth . . .'

'Yes . . . this meeting, Sophy,' Aunt Hebe said doubtfully, 'shouldn't you wait until Jack arrives and get his approval, before you make any changes?'

'There's no time to waste and I've already had the benefit of the solicitor's advice and then Mr Yatton's – *and* Lucy's.'

'Lucy?' Seth questioned.

'My daughter,' I said shortly, because I was getting tired of having to explain who she was, though that certainly wouldn't be a problem once she got here and made her presence felt. 'She's in Japan, but Mr Yatton has been emailing her. She has much more of a head for figures than I have and she's amazingly practical. I'm hoping she'll come home soon.'

'Sir William told me about her, after he'd been up to see

139

you,' Mrs Lark chipped in unexpectedly. 'He said she'd turned out just the way he'd hoped Jack would and it was wasted on a girl. But then, he was a bit of a mis . . . what's the word?'

'Misogynist?' I suggested, though what she had just told me had made me think more kindly of Grandfather.

'That's the one.'

'You mean, you knew my brother had found Sophy and you never mentioned it to me?' demanded Aunt Hebe, gazing at her with acute disapproval.

'Sir William told me in confidence, Miss Hebe. Some of us don't go blabbing about things we shouldn't to them as shouldn't know!'

Aunt Hebe coloured slightly.

'It sounds to me as if Winter's End is going to suffer from an overdose of managing women,' Seth said gloomily, so maybe *he* was another misogynist.

Draining the contents of a giant blue and white striped china mug, Seth rose to his feet – and I had forgotten quite how tall he was until he was towering over me. 'If you want to see the gardens in the daylight, we'd better get going right now.'

'OK, I'll get a coat,' I said, quelling an irrational urge to challenge everything he said, just for the hell of it. Apart from trying to throw me off the premises when I first arrived, aiding and abetting Grandfather to spend money he couldn't afford on the garden and knowing more about Alys Blezzard's book than he should, nothing was actually *his* fault, was it?

'Do you want to come, Charlie?' I asked. 'Walkies?' But he was now lying on the braided mat in front of the Aga and didn't stir apart from thumping his tail a couple of times, so I left him there.

Outside there was an icy wind blowing that Seth, clad

in what looked like the same multi-holed layers of old jumpers as before, didn't seem to feel. He waited impatiently while I wrapped my scarf around my neck and fastened up my duffel coat, before shoving my hands in my pockets in lieu of gloves.

'We'll start at the front and work round,' he said, as we stood in the entrance porch. 'We have one seventeenth-century engraving of the front garden, when it was set out pretty much as you see it now, though we had to replant part of the maze that had been grassed over, and also restored some of the parterres. The hedging has changed. The maze was hornbeam originally, but now it's yew, and most of the parterres and knots are edged in box – it's longer-lived and easier to manage.'

I followed him down the steps, lingering to look through a clipped arch of variegated holly. 'What's through here? I looks a bit bare.'

'It's the new rose garden – still a work in progress. Do you want me to show you the way round the maze?'

'No, I used to play in there all the time when I was a little girl and I remember the trick of it, which is probably the same even now it is much bigger. I'll find my own way later.'

'Right,' he said shortly, giving me the impression that he wouldn't care if I got lost in there and never found my way out, and off he strode. I trotted after him down gravelled paths between intricately shaped box-edged parterres, sometimes with trees clipped into cones, balls or pyramids at the corners or centres, until finally he halted at a wicket gate set in a long yew hedge that billowed like a satiated green python.

'On open days, this is as far as the public can come. We put a "No Entry" sign on the gate, and ropes across the other paths. Through here is the wilderness and the fern grotto, which I expect you remember? This is a later part of the garden, of course, but Sir William liked it as it was.'

'And the dogs' graveyard is somewhere over here, isn't it?'

'Yes.' He opened the gate for me and then was off again.

We finally came out of the wilderness onto the rear drive behind the coach house, within smelling distance of the pigsty. I was glad to stop for a minute, and catch my breath.

'Over there's the tennis court,' he said. 'Another complete waste of time, in my opinion, taking the gardeners off their work to mow the grass and paint lines, especially since it's only ever used when Jack brings his friends down for the weekends in summer.'

'*You* don't play tennis?'

'No, I already get enough hot, sweaty exercise.'

My mind was suddenly and disconcertingly full of rather wild and earthy speculation, some of which must have shown on my face, because he explained, after a pause, 'Gardening.'

'Of course . . .' I said, my cheeks burning. 'I've never played tennis, but I do enjoy a game of croquet,' I babbled, hastening to change the subject. 'Lady Betty – my last employer – taught me. She swung a mean mallet when she'd had a gin or two.'

'It would be a lot easier to maintain a croquet lawn than a tennis court,' he hinted.

'I expect it would – and look nicer too. We could have a neat, low trellis fence around it, instead of this tattered netting . . . and perhaps a little gazebo in the corner to keep the hoops and stuff in. And a rose growing up it . . . what kind of rose?'

'A Falstaff – dark crimson, with a lovely scent.'

I had an enticing vision of cold drinks set out in the shade, the thunk of mallets on wooden balls and the smell of new-mown grass and roses – though goodness knew when I thought I'd have time for all that, with so much to be done!

Seth was looking at me with a glimmer of approval that would probably wither on the vine as soon as he'd heard what I had to say on Saturday. 'Come along,' he said, and led me into the walled garden that was Hebe's domain, though there was no sign of her.

Again, I remembered it quite clearly from my childhood – full of roses and herbs, fruit bushes, hens, beehives and lean-to greenhouses. Aunt Hebe's hard work out here made us pretty well self-sufficient in fruit, vegetables, eggs, honey and chickens. It was no longer a surprise that she hadn't taken the housekeeping in hand, too!

'I have the greenhouses abutting the other side of the wall,' Seth said as we emerged, 'and the nursery garden. There's a big wooden building where we keep the tools and the gardeners brew tea and eat their lunch. There's a phone extension there, so you can ring down from the estate office in the house if you want one of us for anything. Behind that is the old orchard. Most of the apple trees bear little fruit, but they are valuable for the mistletoe that grows on them. Do you know about that?'

'Yes, Mrs Lark told me about it.'

'It grows wild in the woods too, mainly on the oaks, and the sale of it is increasingly lucrative, in season.'

He didn't offer to show me, but instead walked around the solar tower to the terraces at the back of the house. 'On visitors' days those trellis dividers are pulled out to block off the top terrace to the left of the cross-passage door, so visitors can't look in the windows of the family wing.'

He came to a halt and surveyed the three descending terraces proudly. 'This is what I *really* wanted you to see – the restoration of the knot gardens to the original sixteenth-century design and planting, a very early scheme

– though as I said, we are mainly using box edging, since it's easier. We're on to the lower one now, the last phase. We found all but that part of the plan, so your grandfather and I were trying to come up with a scheme that would be in keeping with the rest.'

I looked down at the terraces, with below them again the river, dammed off to make a small lake and cascade. On the far side, over a humped stone bridge, woodland covered the hillside. The roof of a half-hidden summerhouse could just be seen above the trees.

'It's so pretty!'

'Well, it will be eventually. Jack wanted me just to rebuild the wall and turf the bottom terrace, and leave it at that, but Mr Hobbs said to carry on as before until you arrived and decided what you wanted to do.'

We went down to the second terrace, where he began to wax lyrical about the uniqueness of the restoration at Winter's End and, as I listened to him, I began to appreciate truly that the completion of the gardens was something he wanted passionately, not only as a monument to both his father and my grandfather, but for his own satisfaction.

Strangely, he seemed unable to see that leaving the lovely old house at its heart to rot would leave a hole in the fabric of his beautiful landscape, but I suddenly found this blinkered viewpoint rather endearing. He'd entirely forgotten who he was with and was talking with a single-minded passion about what was evidently the love of his life. Strands of blue-black hair blew around his strong face and his eyes glowed an otherworldly green as he regarded his handiwork.

I shivered suddenly, but it wasn't the cold.

'The central knot of the middle terrace is in the shape of a rose, as you can see if you look down on it from the Long Room – a very unusual design,' he enthused, 'especially for the time.' Then his eyes slowly refocused on my face and took on a warier but still hopeful expression. 'You can see now how important it is to finish the scheme, can't you, Sophy? We're so close, and there will be absolutely nothing like it in the whole country!'

He didn't wait for my answer, but took my elbow and steered me down another flight of stone steps to the lowest level, which was, quite frankly, a muddy mess.

'So far we've started rebuilding the footings of the retaining wall – all the stones are numbered and charted as we remove them. And we've taken out the late Victorian lily pond, which had a ghastly fountain totally out of keeping with the rest of the garden.'

'Oh? What have you done with it?' I asked. 'Even if you didn't like it, it's probably valuable.'

'It's in one of the stables. Some kind of water nymph, I think, with a big bird.'

'Leda?'

'Possibly, though it looks more like a duck than a swan.'

I looked around the stretch of mangled turf, heaps of stones and muddy holes. 'So, had you and Grandfather come to any decision about what to have here?'

His eyes lost that creature-from-another-planet glow and he grinned, making him look all at once younger and more approachable – *and* worryingly attractive too.

'No, we couldn't agree on it at all. Sir William wanted to repeat the design of the top terrace, but I thought it would be better to create a different sixteenth-century knot, this time using the sort of edging plants they would have used before box became so popular, like winter savory, hyssop, thyme and rosemary.'

The otherworldly glimmer again lit his eyes as he turned back to me. 'It might be harder work to maintain, but it would be an interesting variation and could be infilled with plants available at the time too, perhaps repeated in borders at the back near the wall. But not at the front of the terrace, because the view over the lake and river below is enough.'

'Yes, it's lovely,' I agreed, walking over to the low stone balustrade, the frozen grass crunching beneath my feet, and looking down at the waterfall below.

'Planting anything there would simply be gilding the lily,' he said, following me, 'and— *Don't lean on it!*' he yelled suddenly. Flinging his arms around me, he hauled me backwards with a jerk that made my teeth rattle and I found myself, feet dangling above the ground, crushed against a broad expanse of unravelling Aran jumper.

'I – I think mending that might be a priority?' I said weakly, clutching at him as the stone I had been leaning on wobbled a bit and then settled back into place.

'Yes, straight after we've rebuilt the retaining wall,' he agreed, setting me back on my feet and releasing me, then added grimly, 'providing you don't let your aunt take my gardeners away to clean out hens and dig vegetable beds whenever she pleases.'

'I don't think an hour or two here and there is going to make that much of a difference,' I said, still slightly shakily. Then I gazed up at the shabby house with its dull, dirty windows and it seemed to be looking back at me with the hopeful expectancy of an overgrown puppy. 'The tourists come to see the terraces on open days, don't they?'

'Yes, though obviously they are not allowed down to this level yet. We rope it off. When they've seen the Great Hall and minstrels' gallery, they come out through the cross-passage door onto the top terrace and down to the second. Then they usually go back up to the tearoom.'

'Mmm. It all seems pretty amateur at the moment, but higher visitor numbers would increase the Winter's End revenue, especially if we charged a lot more for entrance.'

'You sound as if you've done this before?' he asked curiously. 'I thought you were just some kind of New-Age traveller.'

'I haven't *lived* on the road for years,' I said patiently. 'My mother and I settled in a commune and ever since I left school I've worked in stately homes, doing everything from cleaning the floors to running guided tours. So I know that to entice more visitors, we need to enhance the attractions, and one obvious thing we could do is promote the possible Shakespeare connection more vigorously, both in the house and out. After all, that would fit in with the date of the knot gardens, wouldn't it?'

He nodded, looking cautious. 'I've read the theories that he spent the Lost Years in Lancashire – but he would have been just a teenager for most of them.'

'Well, we don't have to *prove* he was here, just suggest it. I saw a garden once that was entirely planted with things Shakespeare had mentioned in his plays,' I mused. 'Is there any reason why we couldn't do that on the lower terrace?'

'There *are* Shakespeare gardens,' Seth conceded, obviously turning the idea over in his head. 'It probably wouldn't be much different to my original suggestion of keeping the planting on this level purely late sixteenth century.'

'No, as long as the shrubs and plants were mentioned in one of the plays, you could have what you liked.'

'Easy then,' he said drily.

'Well, Hebe did tell me you did your degree dissertation on garden history, so it shouldn't be too hard. You probably know it all already.'

'I'll think about it,' he said, but the embers of that glow were sparking up again in his eyes.

'Is Jack interested in the garden?' I asked suddenly.

'Not particularly. Jack's only interested in Jack and money.'

'That's a bit harsh. Don't you get on?'

He shrugged. 'We don't have a lot in common these days, and I'm not too keen on some of his business methods either, but we used to get on OK in the holidays when he was home from his posh school – I went to the local grammar. But we didn't see much of each other once we left university, until I came back after my father died, to finish what he started. Jack was against the whole restoration scheme and he wanted me to stop once Sir William died, even though we are so close to finishing.'

'Well, you can hardly blame him, when it has been draining the estate for years,' I said, and, seeing his face set into obstinate thundercloud mode added quickly, 'Mr Yatton told me about your working arrangement with my grandfather.'

'It suits me at the moment. I can still run my own business, while keeping an eye on Winter's End.'

'You design knot gardens, don't you?'

'Yes – "Greenwood's Knots. Topiary, Parterres and Knot Gardens a Speciality".'

'That doesn't exactly roll off the tongue, does it? You could have called yourself something more exciting, like "Get Knotted",' I suggested.

His brow knitted, so he looked quite Neanderthal. 'No, I couldn't. No one would have taken me seriously.'

I don't think anyone had ever teased him before, but if he was going to be so serious then he had better get used to it, because I was finding the temptation to wind him up irresistible.

He looked at me for a minute in a slightly baffled way, then said challengingly, 'So, are *you* going to let me finish what my father and Sir William started?'

'Oh, yes. I think my grandfather would come back and haunt me if didn't! But you may as well resign yourself to it taking longer than you anticipated, because getting the house and its finances back in good order again has to be the priority now.'

'No, it's the gardens that attract the visitors, so they need to be completed first,' he insisted stubbornly.

I glared at him. 'Haven't you been listening to *anything* I've been saying? The house is *equally* important – or will be when it is restored. And I intend to see that it is.' I turned and started up the steps, while he followed behind me in brooding silence.

'That box hedge looks pretty ratty,' I said critically as we reached the top again, just to wind him up.

'It's foxes,' he said shortly.

'*Foxes?*'

'A fox, anyway. It seemed to like the scent. Sir William saw it from the windows rubbing itself against the hedges until they wore away. But it's not a problem any longer.'

I turned and stared at him. 'You *killed* it?'

'No, we found it dead on the tennis court. Natural causes, nothing to do with us – unless it overdosed on box, of course.' Before I could decide if that was a joke, he added abruptly, 'I've got things to do.' And off he strode as though he was wearing seven-league boots.

I stared after him, thinking some extremely random thoughts about the way that his silky black hair was just a bit too long at the back and how the width of his shoulders made him seem incredibly slim-hipped . . . And I was pretty sure the bottom layer of his holey, ratty jumpers was a pink T-shirt with some kind of slogan on it.

Then I came to with a start and went in through the unlocked cross-passage door.

Security seemed just a little lax at Winter's End.

149

Chapter Thirteen: Grave Affairs

> *Joan says that in her last hours my mother foretold that I would remain a Blezzard and my child after mee; but my children's children would be Wynters. I do not see how this can be, but it is true that I continue to think myself Alys Blezzard and not Alys Wynter.*
>
> From the journal of Alys Blezzard, 1581

There was something I couldn't put off any longer, even though, with the light fading and the temperature dropping, it wasn't the best time for what I had in mind.

I collected Charlie from the kitchen as company, first inserting him into his garish tartan coat, then drove off in the VW down the back drive, which would lead me, I knew, into the village by the churchyard. I parked in the lane and went in through the unlocked mossy lych-gate, though I felt doubtful about taking Charlie into a churchyard. But there was no one about, so I decided to risk it.

'Don't do anything you shouldn't,' I warned him, and he wagged his tail amiably.

The family plot was easy to find – or perhaps that should be *plots*, since centuries of Winters had filled the original enclosure with weathered stone figures of knights reclining comfortably on top of their tombs amid plainer, lichen-encrusted stones, and spawned whole new enclaves around it. Space had been made for William in one of these, his name and dates added to the splendid, polished slate obelisk at the back. It was topped with the same family emblem that I'd already noticed on the arch over the drive, which really *couldn't* be a whippet with a black pudding in its mouth . . . could it?

My mother's grave was nearby – a simple rectangle edged with clipped rosemary for remembrance, with a small marble angel at its head that reminded me very much of my mother: it was standing on tiptoe in a whirl of curls and draperies, seemingly about to take wing, while casually dropping a half-furled inscribed scroll.

'Well, Mum,' I said, 'here we are, back at Winter's End.' The angel regarded me with blank eyes and a slightly spaced-out smile. Either the sculptor knew my mother or had been shown photographs. 'Did you *believe* all those stories you told me when we ran away?'

She'd certainly been the Scheherazade of the family, though of course no one had been trying to kill her, apart from Fate. And diamonds had literally been a girl's best friend, since she must have been selling them one by one to be permanently stoned for so many years.

'*And* you wrenched me out of my setting too, did you know that?' I told her, slightly bitterly, though maybe I had not been so much a diamond as a rather dark, uncut garnet. 'Winter's End is where I belong – where I should have stayed.'

But then, in her casually affectionate way she *had* loved me, even if she had been happy to let Aunt Hebe and Mrs Lark take over most of the childcare. Perhaps she simply couldn't bear to leave me behind, just as I could never have even contemplated a separation from Lucy? Or maybe she feared that if she left me behind Grandfather would have had me taken into care?

From what I have learned of him since my return, I am very sure he would not – just as I am also sure that Grandfather loved Mum, in his own way. It was just that with typical male obtuseness he had expected more of her than she was capable of giving.

If she *had* left me behind at Winter's End, I wondered what it would have been like, once Jack had arrived. The new fledgeling would certainly have pushed me out of being the main focus of Hebe's affections, even if not entirely out of the nest . . .

I remained lost in thought for ages, until I slowly became aware of voices somewhere nearby, coming from behind the little church, I thought. Charlie heard them too: he got up from the slab he'd been irreverently sitting on and trotted purposefully off, like a small round tartan bagpipe on legs.

'Charlie!' I hissed, chasing after him. 'Come here!'

I managed to snatch him up just as he was about to round the corner of the church, then cautiously stuck my head around, to see who else had chosen this god-forsaken hour to visit the dearly departed.

It was lucky I was partially hidden by a rose bush, for there, not fifteen feet away, were Seth Greenwood and Sticklepond's answer to Helen of Troy, Melinda Christopher.

Seth was staring down at the ground as if he found it really, really interesting and she was gazing at him with those strange, caramel-coloured eyes as if she'd like to eat him, boots and all.

Considering he was looking like a cross between Mr Rochester and Heathcliff in their gloomier moments, I suppose this was hardly surprising.

'Yes, you *have* been avoiding me lately, Seth, and I'd like to know why!' she snapped.

'Actually, I haven't. I didn't even know you were looking for me.'

'I keep coming up to Winter's End, doesn't anyone ever tell you?'

He shrugged. 'I thought you were looking for Jack. I don't know why you two fell out just before Sir William died, but don't expect me to fill in the gap until it's kiss-and-make-up time.'

'Don't be silly, there's nothing going on between Jack and me – and you weren't so unwelcoming when I first moved back here, darling, were you?' she said silkily. 'In fact, I got the distinct impression you were pleased to see me.'

'That was before Jack turned up again and I realised where your real interests lay,' he said coolly. '*Lay* being the operative word.'

'Come on, Seth, you know very well Jack and I are just in partnership to knock down that hideous house Clive left me and redevelop the land, though getting planning permission is taking *for ever.*' She lowered her voice to a seductive purr, so that I had to strain my ears to hear what she said, and added, 'But you and I are old friends too – and much *more* than old friends – aren't we?'

'I don't think we were ever friends, Mel. And, as I told you when you got me down to Surrey on the pretext of designing a garden while you were still married to Seldon, my price is way out of your league.'

She flicked his ragamuffin clothes a disdainful glance. 'You can't be that expensive – and anyway, I've got money. I'm a *very* rich widow.'

'Congratulations, then you've got everything you ever wanted. I hope you and your money are very happy together.'

She moved towards him and laid a hand on his arm, a wistful smile on her lovely face. 'Yes, I've got everything – except *you*. When I married Clive I was just so tired of scrimping and saving, trying to keep up with the crowd and look well dressed on a pittance – it seemed so important then. But I missed you so much and you wouldn't even *look* at me after I got married, just like you're not looking at me *now*,' she snapped pettishly.

He cast her a brooding look and said flatly, 'Look, Mel, twenty years ago you played me and Jack off against each other, then you suddenly chose to marry a man nearly old enough to be your grandfather. Perhaps you thought you could have your cake and eat it, but I never fancied playing Mellors to your Lady Chatterley then – or,' he added bluntly, '*now*, if you marry Jack.'

'Oh – Jack!' she said, with a little laugh. 'Forget Jack. Perhaps I did flirt with him a bit when I first came back, but he's not the marrying kind, though you were – once.' She laid a hand on his sleeve and looked up at him appealingly. 'Do you remember proposing to me?'

'I remember a lot of things I'd much rather not – like begging you to marry me instead of Seldon, before it finally dawned on me that you would never marry a gardener's son with no position or money. I was fine for a bit of a fling, wasn't I? But you wanted more.'

'Don't be bitter, darling, that's all water under the bridge. Now I'm widowed, there's no reason why I can't have my cake *and* eat it too, is there? In fact, I could eat you up right now,' she said huskily, sliding her hands up his arms and looping them around his neck.

In the half-light she looked ethereally fair and lovely and I didn't see that he could possibly resist her. My head was whirling with revelations and speculation – and, it has to be said, with a feeling of relief that my handsome cousin didn't seem to have fallen for her all over again.

Seth was the one she had really set her sights on, and if she flirted a bit with Jack, then ... well, I expect *femmes fatales* just do it automatically when an attractive man comes within reach; that, or it was intended to make Seth jealous, though I didn't think he had the kind of temper that would take very well to that kind of tactic.

'Woof!' said Charlie, as if agreeing with my thoughts, and I quickly clamped a hand around his muzzle and dodged back behind the church. Then I ran back to my mother's grave and set him down, holding on to his collar.

'Ssh!' I warned him, and he waved his tail.

I sat down on a tabletop tomb half-hidden in the grass and waited. A few moments later the throaty roar of a sports car came from somewhere in the village, which I thought was probably Melinda leaving. I was just thinking that Seth must have gone out by the other gate too, when I heard a heavy tread approaching.

A large pair of boots entered my pensively downcast view and I looked up with (I hope) an expression of innocent surprise. And actually, he *had* still startled me, because from my position he looked about seven feet tall and rather forbidding, with his eyebrows knitted above suspicious jade eyes and the chilly breeze flipping his silky black hair about: the Demon Lover in person.

'Oh, it's you, Seth! What are you doing here?'

'Visiting my father's grave – it's the anniversary of his death,' he said shortly, looking surprisingly grim considering he had just had the most beautiful woman I have ever seen in my life practically fling herself at him. 'I like to come and update him on what's happening to his garden – or is *likely* to happen to his garden.'

'Isn't the conversation a bit one-sided?'

'Not necessarily. He was never much of a conversationalist even when he was alive. Anyway, don't *you* feel the channels of communication between the past and the present never quite close?' he asked, to my surprise, because I hadn't had him down as any kind of fey.

'Maybe . . .' I admitted, 'and a definite yes when it comes

155

to Alys Blezzard. But wherever my mother is, she isn't communicating with me in any meaningful way, any more than she did when she was alive, though I can *feel* her close by sometimes, since I got here . . . and I understand her a bit more, I think.'

'She wasn't a good mother? I thought the story was that she snatched you and ran because she was afraid of losing you.'

'Oh, she loved me in her way. I suppose that's why she took me with her. But she was also light-hearted, good-natured, restless, easily bored, and permanently stoned – *and* she was convinced she was a white witch and could do spells and read the crystal ball, which she couldn't.'

I smiled ruefully. 'She was like a will-of-the-wisp – you just couldn't take hold of her at all, because she was always off after some new craze. That's what she was doing in America when she died, going off with a new man to a new place. Only that time I'd had enough and stayed put in the commune in northern Scotland where we'd been staying, though right up to the moment she got on the plane, I didn't believe that she would really leave me . . . and I don't know *why* I'm telling you this!' I added, surprised.

'Oh, graveyards at dusk,' he said, shrugging broad shoulders. 'And at least you knew your mother. I barely remember mine; she died when I was four. Then my father married Ottie, possibly the least maternal woman in the world. Or maybe it was the other way round – Ottie decided to marry my father.'

'But she is fond of you, I could tell.'

'Oh, yes, and I'm fond of her. When Jack and I were children and got into trouble for pranks, he always looked so angelic that he would have got off scot free if she hadn't weighed in on my side. Of course, Hebe always insisted it was me leading her blue-eyed boy astray, so that never went down well. But it was later that we fell out.'

I could imagine *who* they had fallen out over too, but thought I had better change the subject. 'I don't even know who *my* father is,' I confessed. 'Mum always said he was a gypsy she met at a fairground – but then, she said a lot of things, and most of them weren't true.' I sighed. 'But I loved her anyway.'

Seth looked down at the small angel guarding the grave. 'There are snowdrops and crocus and those little tête-à-tête daffodils in spring.'

'Did you plant them, and the rosemary?'

He nodded. 'I'm not keen on cut flowers on graves, though Sir William insisted on having some sent down every week. I don't know whether you want that continued?'

'No, I don't want cut flowers either. It's fine as it is, thank you. What have you planted on your father's grave?'

'Come and see.' He turned and led the way back round the church, Charlie and I following in his wake.

It was a simple stone carved with spade, fork and watering can, and I liked the wording: 'Rufus Greenwood, perennially bedded here'. The grave was a rectangular knot of low box that must have been trimmed with nail scissors.

It was growing dark and the chilly gloom descended on us like a pall slowly lowered from the sky – not a comfortable thought, even in the nicest of country graveyards.

I shivered. 'I'd better get back home. I've got the van with me – do you want a lift?'

'No, I'll walk back, thanks. I want to think.'

I bet he did. At some point he might want to wipe the pink lipstick off his face too.

Chapter Fourteen: Twisted Wires

Lady Wynter doth question mee closely about the marriage bed and whether I am not yet to bear a child. I too wish it, since I foresee that all my arts will not cause my husband to survive another harsh winter, and a babe would be security for my future here. But I fear there is little likelihood of it coming to pass. When I recall my mother's words on her deathbed – that I would remain a Blezzard, and my child after mee, though my children's children would be Wynters – it puzzles mee much.

From the journal of Alys Blezzard, 1581

Next morning, after a night mostly spent fine-tuning my plans for Winter's End, I had eyes as dark-ringed as a racoon.

After breakfast my very own personal bank accounts manager came to the house with papers for me to sign, which was a novelty in itself. The last time I tried to increase my overdraft by a measly thousand pounds nobody wanted to know me, but now it seemed the world was my oyster. But I wasn't about to use Winter's End either as a cash cow or collateral. It was *my* pearl and I would never risk losing it.

That sorted, I went out to the stables to look for the Victorian fountain Seth had banished there from the lower terrace – and he was right, it *was* truly hideous: a malformed nymph doing something dubious with a long-necked duck.

Mind you, there's a market for everything, so I asked Mr Yatton if it was all right for me to try to sell it.

'Oh, yes, you can do what you like with it,' he agreed, 'with any of your property, in fact, now probate has been granted.'

'Oh, good. I thought I'd phone up one or two architectural salvage places and get them to come out and give me an estimate. Although it's revolting, I might still get enough to send Lucy the money for a ticket home *and* do one or two other things. I'd like to have Alys Blezzard's portrait cleaned, for a start, and I've also promised to have the Larks' rooms redecorated.'

'Lucy is sending me several emails a day with *suggestions*,' Mr Yatton said, 'and lots of very intelligent questions. Though actually I think our today is tomorrow in Japan, isn't it? Oh dear, I do find these time differences quite confusing.'

'So do I, but I think Japan *is* several hours ahead. Lucy isn't trying to tell you how to run the place yet, is she?'

His eyes twinkled. 'Not quite, but she does sound very much like Sir William – straight to the point.'

'Oh, I *do* wish she was here, even if she often drives me mad,' I sighed. 'And I'm sure she's still being pestered by that man. I told you one of her mature students had a fixation about her, didn't I? He keeps following her about and trying to get her to go out with him.'

'Yes indeed, very worrying,' he agreed. 'I'll warn her to be careful when I next email, but I am sure she is sensible enough not to take any risks – and let us hope we will soon have her home again.'

'Perhaps even in time for Christmas! That would be so good, because we've never had one apart,' I agreed, feeling happier.

'If you like, I will phone up suitable architectural salvage firms about the fountain,' he offered. 'In fact, I could go out first and take photographs, then email them together with the dimensions. They might even make you an offer without coming out to see it.'

'That would be a great help, if you would,' I said, then settled down to discuss with him just what I was planning to say at the meeting tomorrow. The thought of giving my maiden speech was giving me acute cold feet . . . as was the idea of facing Jack, though in his case there was also a flutter of excitement in my stomach.

'I don't know if Jack will arrive in time for it, because I haven't managed to get him on the phone yet and he hasn't got back to my messages. He doesn't even know that I'm definitely *not* going to sell Winter's End to him and I do feel bad about that, because I led him to believe I might.'

'I'm sure everyone else will be happy with your decision, since the main worry was that if Jack inherited the property he might decide to develop it and sell it off piecemeal, as he did to the home of the widow of one of Sir William's old friends. I don't know the ins and outs of it, but it caused quite a rift between them and I suspect was the crucial factor in Sir William's decision to leave Winter's End and all his property outright to you.'

'You don't really think he would do that to Winter's End, do you?' I asked bluntly. 'Mr Hobbs does, I know – he as much as said so when he came to see me in Northumberland – but I am sure Jack loves the place and has no intention of doing any such thing!'

'He has certainly never shown much interest in running the estate. His life is in London, so that he tends to use Winter's End as a weekend retreat, frequently bringing friends,' Mr Yatton said cautiously. 'Sir William often said he seemed to think Winter's End was a country hotel.'

'Well, not any longer,' I said firmly. 'This is Jack's home and he will always be welcome here, but any future visitors will have to earn their keep. I can't afford freeloaders and there's lots to do.'

Then I got Mr Yatton to help me surf the internet and find out what sort of plants and shrubs appeared in Shakespeare's works, so I could impress Seth with my knowledge at our next encounter. And actually, it was really fascinating. The Bard had to have been interested in gardening to have mentioned so many. I had no idea what some of them were, but they sounded lovely – bachelor's-buttons, columbine and gillyflowers. But there were lots of more familiar flowers too, like daffodils, pansies and honeysuckle.

When he had printed it all out for me I asked him what state the Royal Purse was in before ringing up Stately Solutions and placing my order for the specialist cleaning materials, and then dispatching Jonah to the nearest ironmongers with a list of more everyday stuff.

After that I went to the library and looked for the book about treasure that Aunt Hebe had mentioned, which proved to be a slim and well-thumbed paperback called *Hidden Treasure Hoards of North-West Lancashire*, shoved in with a lot of local history books near the door.

It was all very interesting, though oral tradition is like Chinese whispers, so what you end up with probably bears little resemblance to the original tale. But Winter's End and its immediate environs seemed to have attracted more than one legend, so it was only surprising that Seth wasn't constantly repelling a positive Klondike of metal-detector enthusiasts.

The vicar called after lunch, which was something I thought only happened within the pages of Agatha Christie novels. She was a brisk, pleasant woman of about fifty and we had

161

a ladylike chat over tea and biscuits in the drawing room, during which I found myself agreeing that next year's annual village fête could be held, as usual, on the car-parking field.

The rest of the afternoon I enjoyably spent cleaning out the corner cupboard in Lady Anne's parlour, first carefully laying the contents out on a side table covered with an old picnic rug.

But apart from the Elizabethan chest there wasn't much else in there of any value – just the display of wax flowers under a glass dome, a couple of dead spiders, the almost-certainly fake ushabti figures, and a cheap and hideous Japanese teaset messily painted with dragons.

Once the cupboard was clean inside and out, I dusted off the little wooden coffer with a new hogshair brush I had borrowed from Ottie. It still looked dull and homely, but I decided to wait for the specialist (and expensive) Renaissance wax I had ordered to arrive, rather than use Aunt Hebe's beeswax polish on it.

Then I washed and dried the glass dome and teaset before gingerly replacing everything, so that when I finally stepped back to admire my handiwork, the china sent out subtle gleams of red and gold from the dark depths of the cupboard and the wax flowers glimmered palely like spectral coral.

I was so unbelievably filthy after just doing that one corner that I had to go and take a long shower before dinner. It was obviously going to take me hours to clean the whole room to the point where I could start making my patch-work cushions in there, but I was dying to get on with the rest of it.

Call me a sad person if you like, but cleaning is such *fun*!

Before I went down for dinner I tried ringing Jack's mobile yet again, not expecting him to actually answer – so that when he did the sound of his warm, caressing voice imme-diately threw me into a panic.

We'd barely exchanged civilised greetings before I was confessing, in a rush, 'Jack, there's something I *have* to tell you! I'm terribly, terribly sorry – but the instant I arrived back at Winter's End, I realised I couldn't possibly ever sell it, even to you.'

There was a small silence and then he said, reasonably, 'But, darling, you wouldn't be so much selling it as helping to keep it in the family. It will cost a small fortune to put the place right and even the everyday expenditure just to keep the place running is huge – way beyond your means. You have no idea!'

'Well actually, Jack, I *do*. The costs *will* be huge, you are right, but I've worked out a plan, and I think if we all pull together as a team we can do it, even if it is a bit of a gamble. I'm going to sell the Herring horse portrait, but instead of paying off that horrible bank loan with the money, I'm going to use it to upgrade the visitor facilities, with the aim of greatly increasing revenue from opening the house. I'm having a staff meeting tomorrow morning, to tell them about it and get them on board – and I really hope *you* will be there too, to support me, Jack.'

'Hebe mentioned something about a staff meeting, and I've no objection to you taking control of the housekeeping and putting the place to rights, Sophy, because goodness knows it needs it! And it *is* your home too, after all,' he said magnanimously. 'I hope it always will be.'

'Gee, thanks,' I said, the sarcasm just slipping out. Hadn't he been listening to me? 'Look Jack, you don't understand! I'm going to—'

'Don't worry your head about revenue or selling things, darling, just mobilise the troops for a spring clean and leave the rest to me. We'll work something out. See you tomorrow!' he added, and was gone.

163

I was so unnerved by this exchange that I immediately rang Anya and told her all about it.

'Jack sounds to me like the sort of spoiled brat who hasn't grown out of thinking that he can have whatever he wants,' she said thoughtfully. 'It will never enter his head that he can't charm you into seeing things his way – and maybe he can, because you're a sucker for that kind of man.'

'He could charm the birds down from the trees,' I agreed ruefully, 'but really, Anya, I'm not such a soft touch – or not where Winter's End is concerned, anyway.'

'Well, watch out. That kind of man can turn quite nasty if you cross them.'

'Jack's not "that kind of man", he's really warm and lovely and interesting,' I said, with more assurance than I actually felt. I mean, he was a bit scary that time he turned up at the caravan, until he realised I hadn't persuaded Grandfather into leaving Winter's End to me, though I suppose that was perfectly understandable. I might have added that he was also cloth-eared and obtuse – but affectionate . . . 'It's only that he does seem to feel that Winter's End is his by right – only now, unfortunately, so do I!'

'Sounds to me like he hasn't grasped that at all, Sophy. He just thinks he's got a gullible free housekeeper,' she commented bluntly.

'Well, he hasn't, as he will find out tomorrow if he arrives in time for the meeting! But don't think the idea of selling it to him and just being the housekeeper didn't sound tempting. I mean, I could stay here always, looking after Winter's End, without any of the responsibilities and financial worries!'

'You're not serious?'

'No, it was only a moment's weakness when I was feeling overwhelmed by it all. Oh, and about Seth – you know, the head gardener? He's having a fling with the local beauty, a rich and very beautiful widow!' I told her what I'd heard and seen in the graveyard.

'Pity. He sounded like he had more possibilities than Jack.'

'He has no possibilities – what gave you that idea?'

'Oh, I don't know. Maybe it was when you described him as very tall, dark, green-eyed and bad-tempered. But if this local beauty has got her claws into him, obviously that's that.' Then she told me the good news – that Guy had got a job near Manchester, so she was going to come down this way, once he was settled.

I was dying to see her and show her Winter's End – *and* see Seth's face when she rolled up in her converted ambulance. I wouldn't warn him she's coming, because that would spoil the element of surprise.

I wondered if there would be any fireworks from Seth at the meeting tomorrow . . . but perhaps not, because he should have picked up some idea of my intentions from our conversation while he was showing me the gardens. But then again, like with Jack, I was not sure he was really taking in what I was saying.

But if they didn't take me seriously, that was their problem . . . And whatever Aunt Hebe, Anya, or anyone else thought, there was no way Jack could charm Winter's End out of me: it was mine, all mine. Though if he actually *did* feel about it the way I did, then I was sorry for him and I'd be more than happy if he wanted to spend lots of time here, helping me get the place up and running.

What with the thought of all the morrow's ordeals – giving a speech of sorts, trying to second-guess everyone's reactions and convincing Jack that I meant what I said – I tossed and turned restlessly for the second night in a row and only fell asleep with the dawn, waking very much later than I ought to have.

Downstairs Jonah brought me fresh coffee and informed me that Aunt Hebe had breakfasted early and was now rearranging the seating in the Great Hall. 'This bacon's dried out – shall I get Mrs Lark to cook you up some fresh?'

'Oh, no thanks, Jonah. There isn't time. You can clear that away now, if you want to.' I just gulped down my coffee and then ran back up the solar stairs for my notes and to take a few deep breaths, before going stealthily along to the minstrels' gallery and peering over the rail.

Aunt Hebe had evidently grouped the chairs by the fire to her satisfaction, and was now sitting there, together with Ottie, Mr Yatton, and Mrs Lark, who was crocheting something lacy.

Seth, a finger of wintry sunshine haloing his very unangelic dark head, was seated on one of the ancient cast-iron radiators, morosely whittling something. I hoped it was up to his weight, but since the radiators never seemed to rise to much above lukewarm at least he was unlikely to burn his extremities.

That Mel Christopher might, though.

The rest of the staff and several total strangers were standing about talking, but went silent when I came slowly down the stairs, pausing at the bottom. To my relief I noticed that the stag now had two eyes, even if he was hung aslant, so that he seemed to be looking at me with sideways suspicion – but then, so were half the people present.

In fact, there seemed to be an awful lot of staring eyes in the room, but I soon realised that the occasion had become an extended family outing, with an impromptu mother and toddler group set up in one corner and a senior citizens' day centre on the window seats.

There was no sign of Jack: I didn't know whether to feel disappointed or relieved.

'Here she is,' Ottie remarked loudly. 'I'd stand two steps

up and talk from there, Sophy, otherwise we won't be able to see you, let alone hear you. This lot are the Friends of Winter's, by the way.' She gestured to a dozen or so elderly strangers, who all nodded at me and then sat down in two rows on the benches behind the chairs, like a jury.

I did as Ottie suggested, looking down into a circle of expectant faces and feeling hideously self-conscious. 'I've called you all together,' I began – then stopped, horrified to find my voice coming out in a much higher pitch than usual. I coughed and started again: 'I've called you together today to explain to you how things stand. I'm sure you must all be anxious to know what my future plans are for Winter's End.'

Seth raised his head and I looked away from his direction hastily. 'What I would *like* to do is make my home here at Winter's End, as my grandfather intended, and for it to go on as before so that you all keep your jobs. But if this is to happen, then the estate *must* start to pay its way.'

'That's right,' Jonah agreed with absent heartiness: he was cleaning his fingernails out with a pocketknife, which was something I wished he'd done before serving breakfast.

'The house has been allowed to fall into a state of neglect and disrepair over the last few years – through no fault of the staff, I hasten to add. For too long, the money that should have gone into its upkeep has been entirely diverted into restoring the gardens, an imbalance that must now be redressed.'

Out of the corner of my eye I could see the three gardeners, Derek, Bob and Hal, turn as one man and look nervously at Seth, whose green eyes were fixed on me in a way I was coming to recognise meant trouble.

I looked down at my notes quickly. 'The garden is nearing completion in any case, and so now the first priority must be to refurbish the house. Additional funding for this will be raised by increased visitor numbers, with an extended season, a larger entrance fee, improved refreshment facilities and the sale of Winter's End-related merchandise.'

'You mean a *shop*?' Aunt Hebe said after a minute, in a very Lady Bracknell way.

'Yes, the existing tearooms could be turned into a sort of giftshop-cum-café area. I've seen it work very well elsewhere, because when visitors are sitting having tea surrounded by things to buy, they very often *do*. The temptation is too much for them. We could even sell a range of your rose-based products, if you wanted to, Aunt Hebe,' I added with low cunning. 'With a cut going to Winter's End, of course.'

She sat up a bit straighter. 'What percentage?'

'My sister was always mercenary at heart,' Ottie commented to the room at large.

'That's easy for someone to say who only has to slap a bit of wet clay onto twisted wire to rake in a fortune,' Hebe snapped.

'We can discuss percentages later.' I turned back to the rest of the room. 'So, the situation at the moment is that there's a huge amount of work to be done in the house, where we have very little assistance, but much less in the garden, where we have a larger staff. Clearly that needs addressing and, while I certainly don't want to *lose* any gardeners, you all need to be aware that you'll have to become multitaskers, helping with any jobs around the house as and when asked – such as cleaning all the outside windows, for a start. That will take two of you, and I'd like it done on Monday, please, weather permitting. Perhaps you could decide among yourselves who will do that?'

'I'm up for it,' Bob said, the pink daisy in his hat bobbing. 'Make a change from all the eternal tree clipping! I'm cutting box spirals in my sleep, these days.'

'Do they lean sideways like the ones you do when you're awake, Bob?' asked Hal, and they all laughed.

'Thanks, Bob,' I said. 'After that, I'd like a start made on rubbing down the front gates by the lodge, ready for repainting. Rusting gates aren't exactly the image we want to give our visitors when they first arrive, are they?'

I looked around at the sea of faces. 'Well, that's about it, really. The goalpost we're all aiming for is a grand, pre-season opening day to get publicity going before the season starts in earnest at Easter – say Valentine's Day, February the fourteenth. Given the amount of work that needs doing, that doesn't leave us a lot of time.'

Seth stood up suddenly. 'No, it doesn't – and it's the gardens that bring in most of the visitors, so you can't just take the men away and tell them to clean windows, or anything else that isn't their job, whenever you feel like it!'

'Yes I can,' I said mildly, 'and clearly *they* understand why.'

'But the restoration is so near completion – it would be madness to stop now!'

'We're *not* stopping,' I said patiently. 'Weren't you listening? I'm not taking the gardeners away entirely, just asking them to help with things they wouldn't normally do, when necessary, especially in the run-up to the visitor season. If we don't all pull together as a team my plans won't work, I'll have to sell Winter's End – and that will be an end of it.'

'What about Jack?' Hebe asked doubtfully. 'Have you discussed all this with him?'

'Well, I've certainly told him all my plans,' I said with perfect truth. I swept a glance over the rest of the room. 'So, what do you all say?'

'Hear, hear,' Mrs Lark called. 'You're a sensible lass and your grandfather would be proud of you.'

'He wouldn't be too happy about delaying the garden scheme,' Seth snapped, 'especially rebuilding the retaining wall of the lower terrace. I think you're making a big mistake. Old manor houses are two a penny, but the garden scheme is *unique*.'

'William may have been as blinkered on the subject as you, Seth,' Ottie informed him crisply, 'but it's more than just an old manor house to Sophy, and I think you've met your match. She's as passionate about it as you are about the garden. It won't hurt for you to lend a hand and *I'll* certainly do what I can to help.'

'Like what?' Seth demanded sarcastically. 'Don't tell me you're going to start cleaning the windows or polishing the furniture?'

'No, I'm going to make a sculpture for the garden,' she said simply.

'Oh, *that'll* get the crowds in!'

'It'll certainly get a different crowd in from the usual visitors,' she agreed, '*and* help with publicity about Winter's End. And if times get really hard, Sophy can flog it.'

'Thank you very much, Ottie,' I said, grateful for the thought even if unsure how one of her very modern sculptures would fit into the garden. From the look on Seth's face, the same thought had just struck him too.

'A mixture of verdigris green and shining copper, I think . . .' she mused, her eyes going distant.

'Regarding the lower terrace, Seth,' I said boldly, encouraged by Ottie's stance, 'and our discussion about it, since we're going to create a Shakespeare garden, I thought it would be an interesting idea to have some of the stones in the rebuilt retaining wall inscribed with short quotations from the bard.'

This was a brilliant idea that had come to me in the unsleeping night watches, probably due to looking up all those Shakespearean plants.

I was about to add a joke about a bard in the hand, but after a glance at Seth's face, thought better of it.

There was a horribly silent pause vibrating with tension and leashed energy, of the kind that you get before a thunderstorm. Then one of the toddlers burst into noisy tears, shattering the silence, and Seth raised his voice above the yelling and said shortly, 'Sir William didn't want anything out of keeping with the sixteenth-century design of the other terraces. I think that would look incredibly naff, anyway.'

'Not if they're carved into the original stones that you're rebuilding the wall with,' Ottie put in thoughtfully. 'I didn't know you were having a Shakespeare garden, Sophy? I've visited one in the States – Boston, I think.'

'Now, just hold on a second! Nothing has been definitely decided yet about that and—' began Seth.

Ottie talked over him. 'I think it's a great idea and the inscriptions are too: and I know a young stonemason who could do them. We'll all have to think of our favourite quotes.'

'"The truth is out there somewhere",' suggested Jonah.

'I'm not entirely sure that's Shakespeare,' I said doubtfully.

'"Abandon hope, all ye who enter here"!' Grace piped up suddenly from the darkest corner.

'That's more like it,' Seth remarked gloomily.

The rest of the gardeners, who had been in a huddle talking in low voices, now said they were agreeable to lending a hand with anything needed, especially if it was that or Winter's End having to be sold up and their jobs going, and also if there was a possibility of any overtime, they were up for a bit of extra money.

'I don't think *I* could do much more cleaning than I'm doing now, love,' Grace said. 'Five mornings and a bit of extra help when visitors come round.'

'No, that's fine, Grace, I wasn't expecting you to do more. So, what do you all say?' I waited expectantly.

'They say yes, of course,' Aunt Hebe said feudally, giving them the cold blue eye. Agree with my plans or not, she certainly wasn't having any dissension in the ranks. And maybe the thought of cashing in by selling her potions and lotions in the shop might have helped swing the balance, too – that and my having deviously given her to believe that Jack knew all about my plans. (And if he didn't, it was his own fault.)

A chorus of ragged 'that's rights' came from most throats, except Seth's. He turned on his heel and walked out.

As if this was some kind of signal, Mrs Lark folded up her crocheting and rose to her feet, then she, Jonah and Grace began serving tea and three sorts of cake from a trestle at the back of the hall, while Charlie walked around hoovering up dropped crumbs. The children, released from their corner, ran about shrieking. A good time seemed to be being had by all and I was so relieved it was over that I'd eaten two giant rum truffle cakes before I realised it.

'I'll have to put my whole stillroom operation on a more professional basis,' Hebe said, appearing at my side.

'What?' I said, swallowing a mouthful of truffle.

'I'll need to produce a line of basic products with nice jars and labels – have to put my prices up too, because of the bigger overheads. Shall we say two per cent of the profit goes to Winter's End?'

'Shall we say twenty?' I countered, which I thought was moderate considering she was growing most of the ingredients in *my* garden, and producing it, rent free, on the premises.

In the end we settled on ten. I thought I'd been done.

Then the Friends of Winter's, who also seemed to be

172

friends of Hebe, surrounded me and promised their support.

'We will discuss it among ourselves at our regular meetings – we're a historical re-enactment society too, you know – and then talk it over with you at the Christmas gathering,' said Mr Yatton's sister, Effie, who looked just like him.

'*Which* Christmas gathering?' I asked blankly.

'Have you forgotten?' Aunt Hebe asked. 'The staff, tenants, Friends and all their families – *anyone* connected with Winter's End – come here on the morning of Christmas Eve.'

Into my head came a sudden memory of Father Christmas sitting by the fire handing out presents . . . the smell of fir trees, mulled wine and mince pies in the air. 'Yes . . . I think I *do* remember.' And come to think of it, Christmas now wasn't that far away – weeks, rather than months – and I really hadn't given it a thought until now.

Soon people started to drift away home, though some stayed to give Mrs Lark and Jonah a hand to clear the plates and urns back to the kitchen. Ottie returned to her studio and when Hebe vanished in the direction of her stillroom, I picked up the last of the piles of crockery and followed her towards the kitchen door.

I'd barely nudged it an inch open with my shoulder when the sound of voices in discussion stopped me in my tracks, even though I know that eavesdroppers rarely hear any good of themselves.

One of the gardeners – it sounded like Derek, the morose one – was saying: 'But Jack said he would either overturn the will or buy out the new owner, and when he did all our jobs would be safe.'

'Ah, but he says a lot of things, does Jack, and it's mostly hot air,' Hal said. 'Who knows what would happen? I heard him trying to order Seth to just shore up the wall on the

173

bottom terrace and leave it at that – not that Seth took any notice. But it doesn't sound to me like he means to finish what Sir William started. No, I reckon Sophy's ideas are worth a go, at any rate.'

'Seth isn't going to like it. He's like a bear with a sore head.'

'Looks like Seth will have to lump it, then.'

'Sophy's got some odd ideas in *her* head,' Mrs Lark said, 'like wanting me to cook less food. But her heart's in the right place. She's letting me have a kitten, which is something Sir William didn't hold with.'

'And she said she didn't expect me to work more hours than I do now,' fluted Grace.

'That's right,' Jonah agreed. 'I think we should wait and see. And she didn't say she *wasn't* going to let Seth finish the garden, just that it would be slower than he wanted, so I expect he'll come round. And if it all works out, things at Winter's will go on pretty much as they always have, it seems to me, only better.'

'You're not going to do less baking, are you, Mrs Lark?' said another voice, which was probably Bob's, though it was hard to tell because he sounded as if he had his mouth full.

'No, don't be daft! There'll always be a scone or a bite of cake for anyone who wants it in *my* kitchen, and Sophy's got as hearty an appetite as any of you.'

I felt myself blushing hotly and vowed to stop being such a pig. If I carried on eating at this rate they would be able to roll me down the hill on pace-egg day.

'Haven't any of you lot got homes to go to?' said Aunt Hebe's voice suddenly – she must have opened the still-room door.

'Just giving Mrs Lark a hand with the crockery, Miss Hebe,' Derek said, 'but we'll be on our way now.'

I took a couple of quick backwards steps into the passage, so it looked like I was just coming round the screen as they came out, wished them goodbye, and went into the kitchen thoughtfully.

Jonah had begun to stack things into the dishwasher in a slapdash sort of way.

'It's only plain stuff. I don't put the fancy china in there,' Mrs Lark explained, 'or the good glasses. Jonah or Grace do those by hand.'

'I think that went quite well, don't you?' I said, suddenly filled with the euphoria of having got something tricky over with and, after all, what I had just overheard had been *mostly* positive. 'I'm going up to change, then show by example and start cleaning again, but first I'll just take Charlie for a quick walk round the wilderness, or he'll be getting too fat now he's got his appetite back.' I could do with some fresh air too – what with the crowd of people and the roaring fire, the Great Hall had become overheated and stuffy.

'All those things you sent Jonah to the shops for, he put in the cleaning room,' Mrs Lark said.

'Great. Everything else should come by delivery van next week, and can be put in there for me to sort out. I'll explain it all to Grace later. Come on, Charlie!' I added, dangling the lead before his little black nose.

Charlie would much rather have slept off his cake in front of the kitchen fire, so it was more of a quick drag than a walk until he gave in and condescended to trot by my side.

In the orchard a chilly, woodsmoke-scented wind was tossing the piles of dead brown leaves about like an invisible hand, though the bare-branched apple trees were covered with the surprisingly fresh spring green of mistletoe.

It was too cold to linger. Cutting back to the house

through the courtyard I came across a spectacular red sports car, which could only be Jack's. My heart did a quick little hop, skip and jump.

Chapter Fifteen: Boxing

There is a priest in the house. They do not yet trust mee with such secrets, despite my father having entertained these dangerous guests. But I have observed their comings and goings and know it to be near where I often sit in the solar.

From the journal of Alys Blezzard, 1581

After leaving Charlie in the kitchen I went through the West Wing looking for Jack, but finding no sign of him, climbed the steep, winding solar stairs to my bedroom.

I had my hand on the doorknob when the floorboards suddenly creaked heavily overhead, and my first thought was that it was Grace – until I remembered that it was Saturday and she would have gone straight home after the meeting, not upstairs for a sneaky smoke. I ran up the narrow stairs and reached the upper landing just as the door to the attics opened and Jack stepped out, a canvas bag in one hand.

He stopped dead, looking totally taken aback and guiltily thrusting the holdall behind him, but he made a quick recovery, dropping it on the worn cord drugget so he could take me into a warm embrace and kiss first my cheek and then my lips before smiling warmly down at me. 'Hi, Sophy, how great to see you again – and even prettier than I remembered!'

'There you are,' I said inanely, thinking dazedly that he

was twice as handsome as I remembered – if that was possible. My lips had gone all tingly and my knees weak just from one fleeting kiss . . . but with an effort, I managed to get a grip. 'I just saw your car, Jack. Did you arrive while I was talking to everyone in the hall?'

'Yes, and I didn't want to disturb you so I came up the backstairs and listened from the gallery long enough to get the "all hands to the pumps or the ship will sink" message, then popped up to the attic. I've still got some stuff stored up here,' he explained, closing the door behind him and leading the way back down the stairs. 'Must sort it out sometime, because I don't suppose you want my childhood junk cluttering up the place if you are having a big clear-out.'

'I don't mind,' I replied, wondering what he had kept up there that was so embarrassing his first impulse had been to hide the bag behind his back. Old girlie mags, maybe? 'Some of my and Lucy's things are up there too, because it's where Jonah put them when I sent them down. You'll have to point out to me what's yours eventually, but it'll take ages to get the rest of the house in order before I even *think* about sorting out the attic floor and—'

'I can see you want to clean the place up, Sophy,' he interrupted me, 'and as I've said, I'm all for that – but I did suggest you ought to defer any major plans until we've had the roof and timbers looked at, got some estimates, and discussed it all.'

I noted the 'we' with a sinking heart and turned to face him squarely as we reached the corridor outside my room. 'Jack, I did mean it when I said on the phone to you that I couldn't bear to give up Winter's End, you know. I simply *can't* sell it, even to you.'

'But, darling,' he said in his lovely, mesmerising voice, his blue eyes hurt, 'I know it's early days yet, but I thought you felt the same as me and – well, that you wouldn't so much be *selling* Winter's End as *transferring* it back to its rightful owner, before we settle down here for ever – the perfect partnership! I want this always to be your home, too.' He put his arm around me and looked down into my bemused face. 'You know it's the only thing to do, Sophy – the right thing to do?'

One little part of my brain – the everyday, sane, Sophy bit – was jaw-droppingly stunned, wondering what exactly he'd meant by a 'partnership'; the rest of me was drowning in the deep, sincere, cerulean depths of his eyes. His soft voice lapped over me like warm waves, my heart was thumping away like mad and I was starting to go dizzy.

Then suddenly it felt as though someone had poured a bucket of iced ectoplasm down my back and Alys's translucent face materialised, palely glimmering, from the darkness behind Jack.

'I *wish* you wouldn't do that!' I said, with a gasp.

Alys shook her head, more in sorrow than in anger, before fading away, leaving me shivering violently.

The spell was well and truly broken, but Jack had clearly felt nothing, for he was still looking down at me expectantly. 'Do what?'

I pulled back gently. 'Jack, it's so wonderful to find family I never knew I had, and you know you'll always be welcome here, because it's just as much your home as mine. But I didn't realise how deeply I cared about Winter's End until I came back, and now I feel that control of it simply *has* to stay in my hands. It's what my grandfather wanted, what I want – and what the *house* wants too.'

I might have added that it also seemed to be what Alys Blezzard wanted, but thought that might be an assertion too far for him to take in at present.

'I know just how you feel,' he said, though going by his confident smile, I still didn't really think he'd grasped what I was saying in the least. In fact, he looked like a man who'd always known he could have anything he wanted, whenever he wanted it – including me. 'But you couldn't possibly take it on alone, with no resources, because it needs an awful lot of money spending on it. I'll show you later. There's woodworm up in the attics for a start – and probably worse.'

'*Worse?* What do you mean?'

He shrugged. 'Wet rot, dry rot . . . maybe even deathwatch beetle . . .'

I stared at him with horror. 'Surely not?'

'It may not be as bad as it looks,' he assured me.

'Oh God! Look, just let me change into my jeans and you can show me now.'

'Sorry, didn't I say? I'm going out to lunch.'

'*Out?* But you've only just got here!'

'I've got lots of friends locally, and we like to catch up when I'm here,' he explained, and I immediately felt like Billy-no-mates, especially since he didn't invite me to go with him. 'I thought I'd get it out of the way, so we can spend the rest of the weekend together.'

'Of course,' I agreed, wondering if the friends included the luscious Melinda. 'And actually, I'd decided to make a proper start on the cleaning today anyway. I'd better get on with it.'

He raised a quizzical eyebrow. 'Not on your own, surely? Aren't you going to get people in to help?'

'No, rough cleaning has already done too much damage and I want to conserve what's left. I'll do it one inch at a time and get there in the end – you'll see. I've got industrial-sized amounts of cleaning materials arriving early next week and Hebe has given me beeswax polish and bushels of rose potpourri.'

He looked at me strangely. 'You look excited about *cleaning* the place!'

'Oh, I am, I'm dying to see what a bit of TLC and elbow grease can do. Another pair of hands would be really useful, though, and there are one or two things you could help me with while you're here if—' I had begun enthusiastically, when he glanced at his Rolex and exclaimed at the time.

'Must dash!' He kissed my cheek in a cloud of that delicious aftershave and dashed off, tossing gaily over his shoulder, 'See you at dinner.'

Dinner? Was he going to be out to lunch all afternoon?

Only after he'd removed his effulgent presence from before my dazzled eyes did I start to wonder how he'd got into the locked attic in the first place. At least, I was pretty sure I'd locked it . . . hadn't I? I went back up and, opening the door, switched on the light. In the first room my and Lucy's boxes and bags and sticks of furniture were stacked up, and I noticed that the top cartons were untaped.

Had they been like that before? I couldn't remember – but maybe Aunt Hebe had been curious enough to come up here and rummage round when they arrived. Or perhaps neither she nor Jack had believed that I hadn't got Alys's book and one or both of them had searched my possessions for it?

It was not a comfortable thought. I could imagine Aunt Hebe thinking she had the right to do it, but I found it hard to believe that Jack would poke and pry into my personal possessions. He seemed such a sincere person, whatever everyone else said about him, though I suppose there must be a touch of ruthlessness about him where business is concerned, as both Mr Hobbs and Mr Yatton had implied, or he wouldn't be a successful entrepreneur.

Alys didn't seem to trust him either – did she know something about him I didn't? Maybe I should buy a Ouija board and ask her.

I had a quick early lunch alone in the kitchen, helping myself from a vat of cockieleekie soup pushed to the back of the Aga, and then decided to start on Lady Anne's parlour in earnest. I felt drawn to the room, but also I wanted to start

181

making my patchwork cushions in there in the evenings. They're not just a lucrative sideline, they're an addiction.

It was lucky I hadn't advertised for a while, and so had completed what orders I had had before I moved here. Now I could start making a stock of cushions to sell in the brand-new gift shop-cum-tearoom instead, perhaps with the family crest embroidered on each one.

But first things first. I removed the grubby chintz covers from the furniture, revealing a rather nice bergère suite with faded red velvet cushions, a ladylike pair of small Victorian armchairs in a dull, mossy green and a padded tapestry rocking chair. I took the huge armful of dusty-smelling fabric through to the utility room and loaded the first batch into the washing machine on a cool cycle, hoping they wouldn't shrink, before collecting a stepladder and cleaning materials.

'I'll be glad when everything else I ordered arrives,' I said, finding Mrs Lark in the kitchen as I was on the way back, loaded down and shadowed by Charlie. 'I need the proper solutions – *and* Renaissance wax.'

She popped a piece of rather chewy Dundee cake in my mouth, as though she were feeding a baby bird. 'Grace'd love a Dyson. She says that old Hoover's more blow than suck.'

I chewed and swallowed. 'Good idea – and ideally we should have one upstairs and one down. I'll put them on my list when I've got my hands free.'

I'd taken to wearing my little embroidered bag with the notebook, pen and big bunch of keys, permanently slung across my ample chest, messenger style, and the list was now assuming the proportions of a short novel. As soon as I crossed one thing off, ten others took its place.

A few hours later I stepped back and looked at the parlour, brushing strands of hair from my face with one grimy hand, hot despite having opened one of the windows to let in the chilly breeze.

What had looked like a century's worth of cobwebs were gone from the ceiling and light fittings, and I had taken the worst of the dust off everything, though careful washing and polishing remained to be done.

Using the stepladders I'd managed to unhook all but one of the heavy curtains, which now lay bundled on the floor, ready to be sent to the cleaners. I only hoped they would survive the experience. I was just struggling with the last one when Seth's dark head suddenly popped in at the open window.

You know that bit in *Jurassic Park* where the velociraptors are chasing the children round the kitchens? Well, it felt just like that. My heart stopped dead and I nearly fell off the ladder.

He shot out one large hand and steadied it as I wobbled precariously, then regarded first me, and then the room, with mild surprise. "'And beauty making beautiful . . .'" he quoted unexpectedly, adding complacently, 'Shakespeare – one of the sonnets. I forget which.'

I blushed even though I wasn't sure if he was being sarcastic or offering an olive branch, in his own fashion. 'I'm in a beautiful state of filth, that's for sure! And the room still has a long way to go.'

'A bit of dirt never hurt anyone. *I* revel in dirt,' he said amiably.

I looked at him cautiously, wondering what had brought on this sudden friendliness. He must have seen my surprise, because he explained. 'Ottie's given me a rocket. As she pointed out, it would have been even worse if Jack inherited Winter's End because there's a good chance he'd sell it. That's probably why he's been urging me to turf the bottom terrace and leave the garden restoration at that, since Sir William died – he doesn't want any more money spent on it.'

'I know you don't think a lot of Jack, but this is his family home and he wouldn't sell it. You are quite wrong about that,' I said hotly.

'You really don't know him that well yet, do you? No, Ottie's probably right, so now I'm not allowed to be anything other than complaisant and helpful ... even if I *do* still think that taking my gardeners off their own work, when we're so near completing the lower terrace, is a bit arbitrary, to say the least.'

'I haven't entirely, they just have to help out with the house now too,' I said patiently. 'You must see that I need help and I can't afford to employ more people in the house, so unless you want to lose a gardener or two entirely, this is the only solution.'

He looked around at my handiwork and had to agree. 'I suppose you're at least putting your money where your mouth is – you've already single-handedly transformed this room.'

I grinned. 'Actually, I *adore* cleaning and have been dying to make a start. It's my one skill. I've spent all my life mucking out minor stately homes. It's something I know all about – that, and doing the tour guide thing.' I turned on the stepladder and began to try to unjam the stiff brass curtain hooks again, and he pushed the window further open and climbed in over the sill.

'Come down from there!' he ordered. 'Those curtains are too heavy. You should have got someone to help you.'

'I managed fine, it's just this last one that's stiff.'

But I was glad to let him wrest the hooks into submission, and when the last curtain was down, asked, 'Would you mind helping me to bundle them up for the cleaners, too?'

'Will they survive it?' he said doubtfully.

'They've got two chances – but they're heavy William Morris fabric, so probably. But if not, I know you can still get the same pattern, at a price. I rather like it, don't you? It's Victorian, of course, but the furnishings and décor at Winter's End are such an eclectic hotchpotch of ages and styles that they somehow blend together and I want to keep it that way.'

Charlie had been sneezing at the dust and getting in our way while we were folding curtains, but as the door swung open he turned and barked wheezily at Jack, not stopping until I picked him up.

'That animal hates me,' Jack said disgustedly. 'It has no discrimination. Hi, Seth, how's the trug and trowel trade?'

Seth sighed deeply, so I guessed he'd heard that line a million times before. 'Fine,' he said, putting the bundle of folded curtain down on the floor with the others. 'See you later,' he added, turning on his heel and going out by the terrace door, but whether he was talking to Jack or me I wasn't sure. The room felt suddenly chilly and full of portents, and I was shivering.

Alys has a cold way of expressing her feelings.

'What on earth are you doing?' Jack asked, surveying me with amusement, and I felt suddenly aware of my dishevelled and filthy appearance. Unlike Seth, Jack clearly didn't revel in dirt.

'Making a start on the cleaning, like I said. I'm just about to do the windows, if you'd like to give me a hand?'

I knew it was a silly thing to say even before he glanced down at his immaculate pale blue cashmere sweater and said, 'There isn't time – or not if you want to wash and change for dinner.'

'It's not *that* late, is it?' I looked at my watch. 'Oh God, it is. I'd better dash.'

I left all the cleaning stuff where it was, but I did close the door, the window and then all the shutters, leaving Alys ensconced in slightly cleaner darkness.

Chapter Sixteen: Polite Expressions

It being Mary Wynter's birthday and she a connection of theirs, tonight the Hoghtons sent over some of their company to entertain us with music and poetry and such like amusements. One of them, they say, came north to escape punishment for the writing of scurrilous verse. He was a very comely youth, perhaps a year older than myself, dark-eyed and with a smile that melted my heart. I could not help myself . . . I gave my husband a draught to sleep deep that night, and had Joan bring Master S to mee . . . For good or ill, this was meant to happen – it was my destiny, I know it.

From the journal of Alys Blezzard, 1581

Quickly I showered off the patina of filth, then brushed my wet hair as flat as possible, even though I knew it wouldn't last. Water just seems to encourage it to curl even more dementedly.

Then I changed into my favourite outfit of midnight-blue velvet jeans and a pretty top in the same colour, sprinkled with tiny silver stars, blasted myself with Elisabethan Rose, slung my embroidered bag over my shoulder and was ready.

And yes, all this effort *was* entirely for Jack's benefit, though I completely forgot about makeup until I was halfway downstairs and it was too late to go back.

There was no sign of Charlie, who had headed off determinedly in the direction of the kitchen earlier, but Hebe and Jack were already in the drawing room and Ottie wandered in just after me. She was wearing a knitted striped wrap over a knee-length caftan and silk harem pants, with lots of clunky amber jewellery – you could hear her coming five minutes before she arrived.

Jack pressed us to try some strange cocktail of his own invention, and though I knew by now that Hebe was a sherry drinker, she accepted a glass of the strange absinthe-and-God-knew-what concoction without more than a half-hearted protest, then sipped it gingerly.

Me too. I'm not much of a drinker at all, but I was powerless to resist that bad-boy smile on his handsome face.

Only Ottie was immune to his charm and, firmly declining, poured herself a whisky. I soon wished I'd had her willpower, because the cocktail not only made my head spin, but also scoured my sinuses like caustic soda. (Not that I have ever put caustic soda or anything else up my nose, you understand, but if I had, I would have expected the effect to be much the same.)

'I hope poor Mrs Lark hasn't done something that will not divide into four, like soufflés,' Hebe observed as the gong rang out, looking sideways at her sister.

'If Mrs Lark has cooked something that won't divide, I'll eat my hat – or bread and cheese,' Ottie replied calmly. 'I come over most nights when I'm up here, so why wouldn't she expect me? Sophy doesn't mind my coming over for dinner any more than William did, do you, Sophy?'

'Not at all, you're very welcome. I noticed there's always an extra place set for you anyway,' I said, as I followed her into the breakfast parlour where Jonah was clattering the serving dishes. Then a thought struck me. 'Does Seth . . . ?'

'Mostly caters for himself, or goes down to the pub,

though he's generally here for Sunday lunch. William liked the whole family together, and it's served early, so Mrs Lark can have the afternoon and evening off.'

'That's right – we go to church and visit the family,' Jonah said. 'Now come and get sat down, before your dinner goes cold!' He placed a platter of salmon and dishes of vegetables in the centre of the table, amid a flotilla of crisply folded paper napkin swans (which seemed to be purely for decoration, since we all had linen ones at our places, as usual), and then went out.

'Not that Seth is really *family*,' Hebe said, seating herself, but carrying on the previous conversation. 'Unlike dear Jack.'

Jack grinned and blew her a kiss.

'He's my stepson, which is family enough – and anyway, William was fond of him,' Ottie said. 'So am I, come to that. He's never been the least trouble, even as a child. Always off doing his own thing. Still is.'

I thought of the lonely, motherless little boy, suddenly presented with a brilliant but totally unmaternal stepmother. It was perhaps not surprising that Seth seemed defensive, verging on surly, though today he *had* shown an unexpected charm. And when he smiled, he looked so totally transformed that suddenly it had been all too easy to see why Melinda had been trying to reel him back in . . .

'Penny for them,' Jack said to me, and I went so pink that I'm sure he thought I'd been daydreaming over him.

'Oh, I was just thinking about family relationships – you and Seth growing up here together,' I said hastily.

'I wasn't actually here much except in the school holidays. I went to Rugby, Seth went to the grammar school.'

'I thought he might like to go to boarding school too,' Ottie explained, 'but he just refused. Said he wasn't going to leave his friends and he was happy where he was. Always had his own mind, did Seth . . .'

Jack shrugged. 'We've always got on well enough, but we've got our own friends and interests.'

'You didn't get on when Seth found you digging holes in the garden with that metal detector,' Ottie said. 'Treasure-hunting – and William not dead a week!'

'A slight disagreement,' Jack said, smiling at me. 'I'd just got it, and wanted to try it out, but I only dug where the earth was already disturbed. Seth is a bit hasty, sometimes, where the garden is concerned.'

'I've heard all about your treasure-hunting – in fact, I've read that hidden treasures book in the library,' I told him. '*And* I saw all the Enid Blyton adventure books in the nursery, so I think maybe she has a lot to do with this mania of yours too.'

He flushed. 'Hardly a mania, Sophy – just a little hobby. Don't you think it is exciting that there might be something valuable hidden here at Winter's?'

Before I could reply, Ottie chipped in, going back to what we had been previously discussing with an air of spurious innocence, though her eyes were sparkling maliciously. 'Actually, Jack, you and Seth do have *one* friend in common – Mel Christopher.'

'Now, Ottie,' Jack said with easy good humour, 'you know very well we were all children together, so of course I saw a lot of Mel when she first moved back here – and *before* she moved back here too, for I was the first person she called when she was deciding what to do with that ghastly house Seldon left her. But if she and Seth have something more going on between them now, that's their business and good luck to them.'

He smiled at me across the table and added, 'I've got other interests.'

'Sophy, *you* used to play with Melinda occasionally, when you were a little girl,' put in Aunt Hebe, 'but she was a year or two younger.'

189

'I *did*?' I cast my mind back and said, doubtfully, 'I do remember a little girl, but I'm sure she wasn't called Melinda. She was a complete pain, always worried about getting her clothes in a mess.'

'Yes, that was her – her mother called her Lindy.'

'And little Lindy was stringing both Jack and Seth along before she upped and married Clive Seldon,' Ottie explained helpfully to me. 'And you can't tell me she married a man old enough to be her grandfather for any reason except money.'

'I am afraid she was always a trifle mercenary,' Hebe agreed, shaking her head sadly, 'though I hate to say so, since her mother is one of my oldest friends. The Christophers are poor as church mice, of course, but Mel is a wealthy widow now, so I suppose she can afford to marry anyone she wants to. I'm glad you can see that she's not the girl for you, Jack. I knew William was quite wrong about that – and it's just as well, as things turned out.' She smiled meaningfully at me and I felt myself go scarlet.

Jack's veneer of affability was showing signs of cracking. 'Mel's just an old friend – don't listen to these two being catty about her, Sophy! Just because she's beautiful and married an older man—'

'More than thirty years older,' interjected Ottie, with relish. 'Even her stepchildren were older than she was.'

'– *doesn't* make her mercenary,' Jack finished determinedly. 'And I can't think how we got onto the subject anyway, because I'm sure we weren't discussing Mel, but Seth, whose horticultural obsessions I find quite boring, to be totally frank.'

Actually, I'd found Seth's enthusiasm and passion worryingly attractive . . .

'You find anything not concerned with making instant money boring,' Ottie said.

'That's not fair,' Hebe defended her ewe lamb hotly. 'Jack

190

loves Winter's End and cares deeply about all of it, including the gardens!'

'Or does he just care for anything that enhances the *value* of Winter's End?' Ottie said, and Jack smiled sweetly at her from across the table, his good humour seemingly regained.

'No, I just want – as Sophy wants – to see my home restored to the beautiful place it used to be.'

'*My* home', I noted, not 'our' or even 'the family home' . . . and I was feeling increasingly Gollum-like in my obsession with Winter's End. It was *my* Precious, and no one else's! A potent combination of irritation and the absinthe cocktail made me decide to throw a conversational spanner into the works.

'By the way, I actually *do* have Alys Blezzard's household book,' I said recklessly, helping myself to more salmon and cucumber.

Hebe dropped her fish fork with a clatter.

Jack's was suspended somewhere between his plate and his lips, while his bright blue eyes were fixed keenly on me. 'The real one, not a copy?'

'Yes, the original. Mum did have it, but she entrusted it to me before she left for America. She said Alys appeared to her in a dream and told her to. So now it's returned to its rightful place.'

'I thought you must have it,' Ottie said, but she looked relieved all the same. 'I hope you have locked it back in the box?'

'Oh, yes. And the box itself is now locked into the corner cupboard in the parlour, for extra security.'

Hebe was staring at me indignantly. 'But you told Jack you didn't *have* the book!'

'Of course I did, because according to what Mum had always told me, Jack shouldn't have known anything about it in the first place. I needed time to think and to see what the situation was like when I got here.'

'Ottie always had charge of the key and the book until Susan took them,' Hebe said, 'and although she didn't look after the key very well, I suppose she should have it back again.'

'No, I think Sophy should keep it now,' Ottie said, unconcernedly carrying on with her dinner. 'What she does with it is entirely up to her. I'm passing on my responsibility.'

'I'm so relieved to know the book is safe,' Jack said, 'and I don't mind admitting I'd *love* to see it! Since it isn't a secret any more, won't you show it to me, Sophy?'

He gave me the sort of intense, butter-rich smile that makes you quiver from head to foot like a plucked violin string, but I hardened my heart – with an effort. 'No, I won't. And I know why you want to see it, Jack. You're cherishing the mad idea that Alys wrote down a clue to the whereabouts of treasure. But she didn't and you'll have to take my word for it that the only treasures are the recipes. If you think about it sensibly, you'll see that she hadn't anything else to leave – how could she have? She wasn't an heiress and could have had nothing to conceal of any value.'

'You don't know that!' began Jack eagerly. 'It's rumoured that the family was hiding a priest in the house around the time she was imprisoned, and he had gold plate with him that he was taking to the Continent for—'

'Just an old legend with no proof,' I interrupted firmly, 'and Mum said she was sure the house had been searched from attic to cellar several times over the centuries on the strength of it.'

'I expect you're right, but if I could just *look* . . .' he wheedled.

'No way, it stays under lock and key – and *I* have the key. And what's more,' I stated firmly, 'I won't stand for you, or anyone else, going on any more half-arsed treasure hunts in or out of the house!'

Hebe said primly, 'That is hardly a polite expression to use, Sophy!'

'Don't be such an old spinster. And the girl is quite right, the place must have been searched so many times over the centuries that if there was anything to find, they would have,' Ottie said. 'And *didn't* Sophy sound just like William!'

'Yes, she did,' Jack said, eyeing me thoughtfully. 'Look, Sophy, I admit I'd like to find something valuable, and I'm still convinced there is something to find. But my only motive is to help keep Winter's End in the family. It will take much more money to return it to its former glory and pay for its upkeep than you have any conception of.'

'Yes I have, and I've got a plan,' I said indignantly. 'I keep telling you!'

'A few extra visitors?' He shook his head. 'That isn't going to make a significant difference.'

'Perhaps not, but a vastly increased number of visitors over a longer opening season, all paying more to come in, and spending money while they're here – that *will* make a difference. But first we need to enhance the attractions within the house, like working the Shakespeare and witchcraft angles more, and upgrading the café, so that the gardens aren't the only draw.'

'Using *what* for money?' put in Jack smoothly, hitting the nail on the head because I knew spending the Herring money on upgrading the facilities in order to attract greater numbers of visitors was, to continue the fishy analogy, using a sprat to catch a mackerel.

'Oh, I think we are all going to be very surprised by what Sophy will achieve,' Ottie told him. 'Just wait and see.'

I hoped she was right – and I also hoped that, before too long, *she* would surprise *me* with whatever part of the family secret my mother hadn't been able to tell me.

Chapter Seventeen: Pressed

Today a messenger came for Sir Ralph and later privily gave mee a small packet. Inside were some lines of verse to my dark beauty, though ye mirror tells mee that Master S is more than generous in his praise . . . I sent no reply, nor if he come again will I see him, but make some excuse of illness, for that way danger lies. I am like a butterfly that hath had her one day of dancing and pleasure and must now pay with death . . . though not yet mine. The shadows have left mee to gather around Thomas, who daily weakens before mine eyes, despite all my endevors.

From the journal of Alys Blezzard, 1581

After dinner we all went into the library, where Hebe watched fondly as Jack thrashed me at billiards, and then not so fondly as Ottie wiped the floor with him.

Jack was not, I noticed, a very good loser, which was a bit worrying. I mean, if he went all tight-lipped and threw his cue about just because he lost a game of billiards, what was he going to be like when it finally dawned on him that he wasn't going to get possession of Winter's End? And, whatever he meant by a 'partnership' between us, was that likely to be one of equals?

Somehow, I had begun to suspect not.

Ottie went back to the coach house after Jonah brought the coffee in, and Aunt Hebe got up and started to gather her knitting and garden magazines together.

'I am rather tired, Jack, so I think I will retire and leave you to amuse Sophy – and I expect you have arranged to meet your friends later anyway, haven't you?'

Since he'd already met up with them at lunchtime *and* said he was going to devote the rest of the weekend to me, I confidently expected him to deny any such intention. So I felt a bit stunned and, if truth be told, somewhat chagrined, when he agreed. 'Yes, I did think I'd pop down to the pub for an hour or so and see who's about. If only you hadn't exhausted yourself with all that cleaning, Sophy, I would have suggested you come too, but I can see you're all in.'

'Oh, I'm not *that* tired,' I protested, then gave the words the lie by yawning hugely, though that was probably just the power of suggestion.

He laughed. 'You need an early night – and then tomorrow morning, right after breakfast, we can have a good discussion about everything,' he promised. 'There should be plenty of time before I go.'

'*Go?*'

'Yes, of course.' He looked surprised. 'I'm just closing a deal on a property in Shropshire. But don't worry, I'm not leaving until after lunch.'

I was starting to see what Grandfather had meant about Jack using Winter's End like a hotel. The disappointment must have shown on my face, for Aunt Hebe said kindly, 'Jack is terribly busy, you know, Sophy. It was kind of him to take the time to come this weekend especially to give you the benefit of his advice – and of course he knows *all* about renovating old properties.'

'I'm just sorry I wasn't able to be here when Sophy arrived,' Jack said, smiling warmly at me.

'That's all right – you did send me the lovely bouquet, after all,' I said grudgingly, though still feeling annoyed and short-changed.

'I *am* exceptionally busy at the moment, darling, but *you* can get me any time you like on my mobile,' he assured me. 'And be prepared to see a lot more of me in the future too, because I'm used to popping in and out without warning.'

'We're always happy to see you, when you can get away,' Aunt Hebe said fondly.

'I'm told you often bring friends to stay for the weekend too?' I said, still feeling ratty.

'Yes, of course, in the summer. William never minded who I invited.'

'Neither do I. In fact, the more the merrier, since from now on, all my visitors will have to come prepared to work hard for their keep,' I said firmly, deciding to make my position plain from the outset. I wasn't running a country house hotel and there was no slack in my budget for free-loaders – except Jack, I suppose, who had so far proved to be ornamental rather than useful.

'*Work?*' he said, as though it was an alien concept.

'Cleaning, polishing, painting and decorating – helping to get the place straight again. And if they're here when the house is open to the public, they might even find them-selves selling tickets or helping in the tearoom.'

'One doesn't generally expect to work when invited for a country house weekend visit, dear,' Aunt Hebe pointed out. 'You go for walks and play tennis and that kind of thing.'

'Things change, Aunt Hebe.'

Like the tennis court, soon to be transformed into a croquet lawn . . . I'd noticed that Seth had taken down the netting already, though apparently no one else had.

'Right . . .' Jack said, looking thoughtfully at me. 'But you know, I always hated the idea of my home being open to anyone with the price of a ticket, so I really hope you will think better of that idea. It's not going to bring in the kind of income you need to keep a place of this size running.' He rose to his feet. 'But we can discuss it tomorrow – and perhaps, if you are really not too tired, you wouldn't mind running me down to the pub before you go to bed? I'll probably get a lift back.'

He would need to. While I had drunk only one (fairly lethal) cocktail and a lot of water, he had also demolished most of a bottle of wine, and then chased his coffee down with a stiff whisky.

'Yes of course, and I'll come in for a quick drink too, Jack. It's early, after all. But after that, I'll leave you to it and come home.'

For a moment I thought Jack looked almost disconcerted, but I must have imagined it because he said warmly, 'That's even better, Sophy!' and Aunt Hebe beamed on us.

The Green Man was large, full, warm and noisy, though when I walked in with Jack right behind me, there was a sudden lull and every head turned in our direction, as though the film had stuck in one of those old Westerns when the hero enters the saloon. But before I had time to feel paranoid they all looked away again and the babble resumed.

There were familiar faces – Seth and a group including a couple of the gardeners were playing darts at the far end of the L-shaped room, and Grace was perched on a tall stool in front of the mahogany bar, her little strapped shoes dangling way above the brass foot rail. She flapped her hand at me in greeting.

A voice from behind us, very loud and county, bellowed, 'Over here, Jack – and bring your new filly with you!'

'This filly, Freddie, is my lovely cousin Sophy,' Jack said, putting a proprietorial arm around my waist. 'Be nice!'

Freddie had a red face, straw-coloured hair and a tendency to talk to my breasts. He was sitting with several other people, who Jack introduced me to in dizzyingly quick succession. I didn't really take in their names, except to notice that the women's included a China and an India – and, for all I knew, a Tasmania and an Outer Mongolia.

They were all eyeing me appraisingly, but I suppose, being Jack's friends, they *would* be interested in the usurper – and *I* was equally interested in seeing the crowd Jack would rather hang out with than be with me. After all, that had been the main reason I'd suggested coming in for a drink in the first place – sheer curiosity.

There was a curious similarity about the women, who were all skinny and wearing skimpy tops and jeans that they hadn't picked up at a supermarket with the weekly shop. Some of them were probably as old as me, but it was impossible to tell because they had all Botoxed, Pilated and face-lifted their way to the same toned and smooth-skinned blankness.

I immediately felt fat, overdressed and cheap – but then, as one of the gardeners at Blackwalls used to say, a weed is just a flower growing in the wrong place. The dartboard end of the room, where Seth seemed to hang out, was *much* more my kind of ambience, and Seth, who had exchanged his usual layers of ratty jumpers for a black fleece and jeans, much more my usual kind of man . . .

Well, apart from the instant antipathy and his bad temper, that is.

Some of the women reluctantly shifted up and made room for me to sit on the curved bench seat, by moving their enormous, baggy leather handbags onto the shelf behind; but the body language was making it very clear that never in a month of Sundays would I be accepted as one of *this* crowd.

Jack went to the bar to get drinks and the group, ignoring me, resumed a desultory conversation about things and people I didn't know that seemed designed to show me just how much of a fish-out-of-water I was. I mean, as far as I'm concerned Polo means a mint with a hole in it, and my one experience of London life was a weekend trip with the WI to see *Miss Saigon* and the wonders of Harrods (mostly the perfume department – they had to prise me out, laden with sample cards).

I thought it would be better when Jack came back, but apart from putting his arm around me again and giving me one of his dazzling smiles, he joined right in. I sat there sipping a Coke and contemplating my exit strategies.

Ten minutes seemed plenty long enough – in fact, if I hadn't been checking the clock over the bar I would have thought it was more like an hour. I was just about to plead exhaustion and make my escape, when a hush fell on the room for the second time that evening.

Thankfully, this time it wasn't me but Melinda Christopher who had provoked the silence, and for a minute or two she just stood there smiling like the Snow Queen in all her shimmering, icy beauty, and let them look at her. The smile brightened when she spotted our group ... Then her light brown eyes rested on Jack sitting close to me, and narrowed, though I don't know why because she turned on her stiletto heels and made for Seth like an arrow flying to its target.

He didn't seem noticeably welcoming, but he certainly got the full treatment – the kiss on the cheek, the hand on the arm, the earnest gaze up into his face as she stood close to him – all performed with little glances over his shoulder to where we were sitting so that I started to wonder if this was for Jack's benefit?

And if so, was Jack aware of it? Was that the reason why he suddenly remembered my existence and began to flirt with me, or did I have a nasty, suspicious mind? His technique was just as good as Melinda's: his head close to mine, his voice low and intimate ... The aftershave alone was enough to render me semi-conscious.

Whatever his motives were I was, I have to admit, starting to enjoy it, when a crisp voice said, right behind me, 'Aren't you going to introduce me to your new *friend*, Jack?'

The Ice Queen cometh.

'Budge up, everyone, and let Mel sit on the other side of Jack,' Freddie shouted gaily. 'Make it a clean fight, girls!'

'Shut up, Freddie,' Jack said, looking embarrassed, but he didn't object when Mel squeezed in on his other side. In fact, he made room for her, which left me practically hanging off the end of the bench seat. 'This is Sophy, Mel – a cousin of sorts. I told you about her.'

I leaned forward, so it didn't look as if I was hiding behind Jack. 'Actually, we've already met, in a manner of speaking. Your horse tried to sit on my van, the day I arrived here.'

'Oh?' She gave me a blank, bored stare, though I had the feeling she knew exactly who I was. 'I don't remember – but hi, anyway.' Then she added something in a low voice, so *I* couldn't hear, but everyone else did, because they all laughed.

'Your mother used to bring you over to play with me sometimes when we were little girls too,' I said more loudly. 'Aunt Hebe reminded me. I'd forgotten, but it's all come back to me now.'

'Oh, I don't think so. I can't have been more than a baby when you were last at Winter's End,' she said icily.

'Come off it, *Lindy* – you're only a year younger than me. Don't you remember how I used to call you toffee-eyes, and you would start crying?' I said helpfully.

'You're thinking of someone else.' She glared at me, then

200

turned her thin back and started to tell the others some terribly long and involved story, which they all seemed to find highly amusing. She kept drawing Jack in for corroboration and after a while he withdrew his arm from behind me and half-turned away, so I would say that Mel had won that round – and probably any other round she decided to engage in. But I came to the conclusion this was merely a demonstration of power that was also intended to make Seth, her real target, jealous, because she was constantly checking the effect her flirting was having on him.

It didn't seem to be putting him off his darts, so she can't have got much satisfaction from that. But then, I have a feeling that sort of tactic simply wouldn't work with a man like Seth.

I decided it was time to go.

The plump, curly-haired woman behind the bar caught my eye and waved at me, smiling. I got up, murmuring, 'Excuse me, Jack, I think I see an old friend,' but I'm not sure he, or any of the others, registered I'd gone. I wasn't out of sight, but I was certainly already out of mind.

But before I could make a hasty exit from the pub, the woman who had waved beckoned me over. 'It's Sophy, isn't it? I thought you'd remember me! Val? We were in the infants' school together.'

She looked vaguely familiar . . . and then it all came back to me. 'Hi, Val! Of *course* I remember you – and especially the day that horrible little boy put frogspawn down the back of your neck!'

She shuddered. 'It's given me frog phobia for life.'

'Wasn't he vile! What was his name?'

'Josh Priestly.'

'I wonder what happened to him? No good, I expect!'

'Well, actually, I'm married to him – he's the landlord, the man at the other end of the bar.'

'Oh,' I said weakly, 'how lovely!' I managed to smile when he waved at me. I hoped he had grown out of practical jokes and nasty surprises.

Val gave me a drink on the house, which I couldn't very well refuse, so I slid onto a vacant barstool. I glanced over my shoulder at the table in the corner, but there was no sign anyone had noticed my absence.

'Cheers!' said the small, rotund man on the stool next to me, catching my eye and lifting his glass in salute. 'And welcome back to Winter's End.'

Thanks,' I said, deciding that he looked harmless. He was middle-aged, yet had an air of puckish boyishness about him that owed a lot to the bright curiosity in his eyes.

'You won't know me – George Turnbull. I only moved into the area a few years ago, but I've heard all about you, of course. The whole place was buzzing after news of the will got out. I heard your cousin's nose was right out of joint.' The grin that went with this remark took away any offence.

'He's not really a cousin – well, I suppose he is, but a very, very distant one, and he's taking it very well,' I assured him, which was no more than the truth, even if I had a strong feeling that the reason for that was because Jack was still convinced he would get Winter's End back, one way or another.

'Someone told me you'd been working as a cleaner, just a single mother trying to scrape a living. Then – *wham* – heiress of Winter's End! It's romantic, that, just like a fairy story.'

I wondered who he'd been talking to, but agreed that yes, it *was* like a fairy story. He was both sympathetic and funny, asking me whether things had changed much since I'd lived here as a little girl, and telling me quite scurrilous gossip about some of the new people who had moved into Sticklepond since I left.

We'd been chatting for several minutes when Seth's dark head suddenly came between us and he said quietly, 'So, has your new friend told you he's a newspaper reporter?'

'*What?*' I said, turning startled eyes on my companion.

George grinned unrepentantly. 'Even a reporter is entitled to his evening off, Seth, though the whole rags-to-riches thing might make a good story. I've heard you've got ambitious plans for extending the visitor facilities at Winter's End, Miss Winter, so you never know when you might need a bit of publicity.'

'I suppose not,' I agreed, sliding off the stool into the small area of floor space next to it not already occupied by Seth's big boots, 'but the right kind of publicity! I'd really hate to see my private life in the newspapers, George.'

'You might change your mind – here's my card. But you'll usually find me here in the evenings, if you want me.'

'I'll bear it in mind,' I said, 'but now I must go – it's been a long day. Excuse me, Seth, I can't get past you.'

But Seth, frowning, was gazing beyond me to where Mel and Jack were now deep in a serious, heads-together discussion of some passion – though of what kind I wasn't sure, except that it didn't seem entirely amicable.

Suddenly I felt amazingly annoyed with Seth for being stupid enough to fall for that kind of woman *and* angry with myself for minding about the way she flirted with Jack.

I certainly didn't feel I needed to say goodbye to either of them and nudged Seth sharply in the ribs.

'You're blocking my way – I want to go. If you're leaving too I could give you a lift?'

The green eyes suddenly refocused on me. 'Why not? There's nothing to stay for.'

He didn't say much on the journey back, except to remark

203

morosely that now I'd told my life story to George I could expect to see it splashed all over the *Sticklepond and District Gazette*.

'I didn't have to tell him my life story because he already knew most of it. I can't imagine who gave him all the details.'

'Well, it wasn't me . . . though it might have been Grace. She was in earlier and they were talking when I arrived.' He shook his head. 'A half of Guinness and she's anybody's.'

'You don't really think he'd use it, do you? I don't think my story is *that* interesting.'

'Depends how short of news they are. But the circulation's very small, there is that,' he said, and lapsed into silence again until I dropped him off.

That was gratitude, considering I'd gone all the way round to take him to the lodge. I should have made him walk from the house.

Chapter Eighteen: Friendly Relations

*My poor husband is no more. Last night he could not
get his breath and though I tried everything in my power,
he left this life at midnight. At the last, to ease his passing,
I whispered to him my good news and he squeezed my
hand and smiled.*

From the journal of Alys Blezzard, 1581

When I got home I didn't feel sleepy any more – too full
of confused emotions and edgy irritation. So, with reckless
extravagance, I rang Lucy from the telephone extension in
my room, which made me feel terribly guilty, even if settling
the phone bills was now entirely my responsibility. I didn't
stop to calculate the time difference between Winter's End
and Japan either (which I usually get wrong anyway), but
luckily she picked up.

'Lucy, I wish you were here. Can't you come home?'

'Maybe . . .' she said, showing slight signs of weakening
for the very first time, 'though I'd have to pay for my own
ticket if I left before the end of my contract.'

'I can find the money for that, somehow. I really do need
you here to help me.'

'That's true – goodness knows what you've been doing
without me to keep an eye on you!'

'Nothing really, except getting organised for Operation

Save Winter's End,' I said, and updated her on the meeting and how my plans had gone down.

She gave gracious approval. 'But don't *totally* alienate that gardener. He's free, for one thing; and for another, he's sort of family.'

'Only by marriage to your great-aunt Ottie . . . or is that great-great?'

'Whatever. Seth sounds interesting, though, and you still need him to sort out the bottom terrace, don't you?'

'I suppose so,' I conceded. 'And he did sort of apologise later . . . or at least, I think it was meant as an apology – he quoted Shakespeare at me, then helped me take down the parlour curtains. Tomorrow we'll both have to be polite, because apparently all the family, including Seth, gathers round the table for the Sunday roast. Considering Ottie and Hebe are barely on speaking terms, that must be a riot.'

'Why aren't they speaking?'

'It's to do with Alys Blezzard's book.' I had lowered my voice despite the several inches of solid oak between any eavesdropper and me.

'Our witchy ancestor? How can they fall out over a book? Anyway, you've got it.'

'Yes, but Hebe's read it and remembered enough of what Alys said in the foreword to blab to Jack, and now he seems to think there's a hidden treasure at Winter's End!'

'And is there?' she asked, interested. 'I thought that bit in the flyleaf was about the recipes, especially the rose ones?'

I had brought Lucy up to know about Alys, as my mother had done with me, making the book an exciting secret between us. I suppose, through the centuries, that was always how it was . . .

'Reputedly there are at least *three* treasures hidden at Winter's End, including a Saxon hoard somewhere in the grounds. But all old houses have these stories, and generations of Winters have probably sifted every inch – when they weren't busy rebuilding, panelling or stuccoing. The place is a total architectural hotchpotch.'

'I noticed that when I visited. Maybe Alys did hide something, though I don't think it would be any kind of valuable thing in the money sense, would you, Mum? Perhaps just her more incriminatingly witchy recipes, and a few scraps of parchment or paper would be easy to conceal.'

'Yes, that's quite possible. Your grandmother always thought there was something else that only Ottie knew about.' I spared her the information that her great-aunt also thought she was Buffy the Vampire Slayer.

'Or it might be some scandalous titbit of family history,' suggested Lucy, still turning over the possibilities. 'Perhaps the King popped in and showed Alys a right royal good time?'

'I think it was Queen Elizabeth then, and she didn't seem to be inclined that way,' I said doubtfully, because my grasp on history is not brilliant. 'Still, whatever it is, I expect Ottie will tell me in her own good time.'

'Oh, I *do* want to come back and search now, Mum, just in case. It's all so Famous Five! And if either of the great-aunts has any secrets, I bet *I* could winkle them out. You know I can twist little old ladies round my fingers.'

'It's your golden curls and blue eyes that get them every time. But not these two old ladies,' I assured her. 'Anyway, Jack has the same advantages, plus that of being male, and Hebe adores him. He's here at the moment, though he missed most of my speech.'

'Have you told him you're not selling Winter's End yet?'

'I've certainly *tried*, but he just doesn't seem to take it in. I'm sure he's convinced I'm just playing Lady of the Manor and will be sweet-talked into selling eventually. He says he has the money to maintain it, but I could still make Winter's End my home, so I'd be in a win/win situation.'

'Big of him,' Lucy commented.

'Yes . . .' I added after a pause, because I still wasn't entirely sure on exactly what terms Jack envisaged us both living at Winter's End. 'I went to the local pub with him tonight and met some of his friends.'

'Oh? Did you have a nice time? I'm not sure being wined and dined by Jack is a good idea. You're so susceptible to that kind of man.'

'I had an *interesting* time – and I'm not susceptible to *any* kind of man,' I said with dignity, 'I've learned my lesson. If it makes you feel better, Jack didn't wine and dine me, either, just bought me a Coke, let his rich friends snub me, then lost interest in me entirely once one of his old flames came in.'

'Oh, Mum, it sounds horrible!'

'It was. I left early and came back with Seth Greenwood instead.'

'That's more like it. I do like the sound of *him*.'

'I can't imagine why. He's rude, overbearing and obsessed with finishing the garden to the point where he doesn't see anything else. And don't get your hopes up, because he just wanted a lift. Jack's old flame is Seth's, too. I think they fell out over her years ago. But now she's back, she seems to have a thing going with Seth and the flirting with Jack was just intended to whip him back into line. She played the field before she married and, so far as I can see, she's reverted to type now she's widowed.' I sighed. 'She's called Melinda Christopher and she is *stunningly* beautiful in an unusual way – silvery blonde hair and these strange, very light brown eyes.'

'You're beautiful too,' she assured me, loyally but inaccurately, 'and just think of the money you would save by marrying the head gardener!'

'Lucy, apart from the fact that he's having a second-time-round torrid fling with Melinda, I don't even *like* him,'

I said patiently, 'and he doesn't like me, especially since I told him completing the garden didn't have priority any more. The only reason he's being even marginally polite to me is because Ottie's insisting on it. And we aren't actually paying him any wages.'

'Oh, no, I'd forgotten that. Still, at least he is useful, which is more than Jack seems to be.'

'Well, not so far, but he is going to take me round the house tomorrow morning and show me some of the more major things that want fixing, which will be really helpful. He was even hinting at deathwatch beetle earlier, though I think he's exaggerating a bit, because I had a look around myself, and apart from all the superficial neglect, structurally it doesn't look bad at all.'

'I'd trust your gut instinct then, Mum, rather than what Jack says.'

'I don't know why you say that. You haven't even met Jack yet! He's genuinely glad to have me back in the family circle, and he's very sincere, open and affectionate and—'

'Wants Winter's End, one way or another? Yeah, I've got the message.' She sighed. 'I wish I was there to judge for myself. And you will need someone full time to manage the business side, especially when Winter's End is open again. I could do that as well as learning about running the estate from Laurence.'

'Laurence?'

'Mr Yatton. He's *so* sweet.'

It appeared that Lucy and Mr Yatton were such kindred spirits that they were now emailing each other constantly. I thought they were in love. I only hoped they were both in love with the same thing, i.e., Winter's End, computers and the joy of numbers, otherwise their romance was doomed to be short-lived, since he must have about a fifty-year start on her.

*　　*　　*

209

At breakfast Hebe was clad in shades of white from head to foot, presumably in deference to it being Sunday.

I hadn't taken Jack for an early riser, but there he was with his nose in the trough already. Mrs Lark, unleashed from weekday economy, had outdone herself, and the side table and hotplates looked like a lavish, blow-the-budget page from Mrs Beeton.

They both looked up from their loaded plates long enough to wish me good morning, though my reply to Jack was naturally a bit on the chilly side. Arctic, even.

He seemed to be a black pudding and devilled kidney man, though I wouldn't have eaten either if you'd paid me, especially at breakfast. But I couldn't resist bacon, sausage, eggs, tomatoes, mushrooms and hash browns.

When I sat down at the table I discovered a late, deep crimson rose by my place. Jack, sitting opposite, bestowed his most ravishing smile on me, just as if he hadn't entirely forgotten my existence the night before at the pub once Melinda got a grip on him.

'If Seth sees that rose, you're a dead man,' Jonah told Jack, coming in with fresh toast. 'Protective about the new rose garden, he is.'

'Well, he won't see it, will he? Anyway, I think the family are entitled to cut their own roses, if they want to,' Jack said good-humouredly. 'A rose for a rose!'

'Did you pick it this morning?' I fingered a red damask petal, wondering if it was meant to be some kind of apology.

'Yes, while the dew was still on it. It's a sure charm for softening the heart of a loved one, isn't it, Hebe?'

'Get on with you!' she said fondly. 'I'm sure Sophy's very fond of you already. Her heart doesn't need softening.'

'That's not dew anyway, it's frost melting.' Jonah was determined to be grumpy. 'It's probably full of earwigs, too. Shall I take it away?'

210

'You could ask Mrs Lark if she can find a bud vase for it,' I suggested, and he went out holding it at arm's length, as if it might blow up.

Aunt Hebe and I are not chatty early morning types and had quickly fallen into the habit of eating our breakfast for the most part in amicable silence. Jack was quite the opposite, and I soon found his cheery bounciness, plus the way he talked through enormous mouthfuls of food, rather trying.

Finding me unresponsive, he started to give me hurt glances and, once Aunt Hebe had ordered Jonah to bring her little white Mini car round to the front of the house and gone off to get ready for church, Jack said tentatively, 'You seem very quiet this morning, Sophy?'

'I'm quiet every morning. It's just the way I am,' I said shortly, draining the last of my coffee.

'Oh, good. I thought you might be cross because I didn't see you home last night. You did say you would slip off early, but one minute you were there, and the next you'd vanished.'

'I'm not surprised you didn't notice. You and Mel Christopher seemed to have a lot to discuss,' I said pointedly.

'Just business – nothing personal, darling,' he assured me. 'We've been trying to get planning permission to knock down her house in Surrey, and it's been dragging on for months. It's a dreadful place, like a cross between a hacienda and the Parthenon: you'd think they would be *begging* me to demolish it and put something better in its place.'

He pushed back his chair and got up. 'Come on – let's go and inspect the stately pile! And you'd better get your coat, because I thought we would start with the outside.'

We walked down the drive in the crisp autumnal sunshine, our breath hanging in white clouds on the icy air, then stopped and turned to face the house at the point where it divided to circle the knot garden in front of the porch.

'There,' Jack said, standing behind me with one hand on

my shoulder and the other pointing at an area of the roof, 'if you look carefully, you can see all the lead flashing needs replacing. That's enormously expensive, for a start. *And* the chimneys are all in danger of coming down, so they need repointing at the very least, and possibly rebuilding. And see that damp area on the wall over there? That's where a gutter is blocked.'

Seth suddenly popped up in the middle of the round knot garden with all the speed and surprise of a pantomime demon through a trapdoor. He must have been grubbing about bent double behind the fountain, because there was nothing else big enough to hide him.

'You're probably right about the gutter, Jack, but not the rest. Remember, Sir William had the whole roof surveyed and repaired the year before last, after that big storm,' he said mildly. 'Said he didn't want the place falling down about his ears.'

Jack looked disconcerted. 'Yes, but he wouldn't have spent any more money than he could help on the house, so it was probably just patched and it's deteriorated since then.' He gave Seth a dirty look, then took my hand in his and headed back towards the porch. 'Come on, Sophy, I've got something else to show you.'

When the something turned out to be in his bedroom I had a moment of doubt, because Jack was clearly a fast worker, but it proved to be just an old book in a plastic bag. 'You know I brought some of my things down out of the attic yesterday? Well, when I started looking through them I found –' he took the ancient tome out of the bag and flipped it open dramatically – '*this*!'

Inside, neatly snuggled into a tunnel chewed from the book's pages, lay a revolting, fat white grub.

'Oh, *yuk*!' I said, recoiling. 'What is it?'

'Deathwatch beetle.'

'Oh my God – are you sure? I thought they ate wood.' I leaned forward for a better look.

'Books *are* made of wood, Sophy. Probably just the thing for a light snack. But you do see, don't you, that if they're in the *contents* of the attic, they'll already be in the timbers and would cost a fortune to eradicate. This is *really* serious.'

He carefully placed the book back into its polythene bag and we went up to the attics so he could show me where he found it. Then he pointed out what he said were spots of rot or loose tiles letting in damp, and more evidence of beetle infestation – fresh-looking holes and wood dust.

But it all smelled perfectly dry, if dusty; and, as someone who used to go up into the attics at Lady Betty's every time it rained, to adjust all the receptacles under the various leaks in the roof, I couldn't in truth see anything much amiss with it. It was quiet too: aren't deathwatch beetles supposed to make a ticking noise?

It occurred to me, not for the first time, that in his eagerness to get the house Jack might be over-egging the pudding . . . and was what Seth had just said in the garden intended as a sort of warning, meant to put me on my guard?

But then, there was that horrible grub. There was no getting away from *that* bit of evidence.

'You may think you can afford to renovate the place and make it pay its way, just by getting a few extra visitors to Winter's End,' Jack was saying when I broke out of my trance. 'But you have no idea what sort of problems can arise in houses of this age. The sheer daily running costs alone would horrify you.'

'Actually I *do* know, Jack,' I said patiently. 'I mean, apart from having had a few sessions with Mr Yatton, you're forgetting I've worked in historic buildings before, and on a much larger scale than this.'

His eyes widened. 'But I thought you were just a cleaner,'

he said, unintentionally making it sound only one step above prostitution. 'Didn't you tell me that? Or maybe it was Hebe.'

'Yes, I *started out* as a cleaner in a castle in Scotland when I left school, but often had to double up and show visitors round at weekends during the season, or sell the tickets. My last job was at a fortified manor house, Blackwalls, in Northumberland, and I did anything and everything – cleaning, tour guide, ticket seller, housekeeping, passing orders on to the gardeners, cutting and arranging flowers, acting as Lady Betty's PA – you name it, I did it. I may not be terribly good at the accounting and number-crunching side of things, but everything else I'm pretty clued up on.'

'Oh,' he said, rather blankly.

'So you see, I do know what I'm doing, and I'm determined to make it work, whatever problems Winter's End has – even deathwatch beetle. I'm sorry if I led you to believe I might sell it at first, but I had no idea how I would feel when I got back.' I looked at him nervously. 'You've been so kind, Jack, and I hate to disappoint you, but there's simply no way I could do it.'

'But, Sophy,' he said softly, sliding an arm around my waist and looking down at me with a tender, teasing smile, 'it really doesn't matter which of us inherits in the end, does it? Don't you see that by leaving Winter's End to you, William was just trying to bring us two together?'

'*What?*'

'Yes, I'm sure he thought you would be a steadying influence on me, and that leaving you the place would bring you back here – and the rest would follow as the night the day. As it has . . . as it *will*.' He bent his golden head and brushed my mouth lingeringly with his.

At first sheer surprise held me still under the gentle pressure of his lips. But as he gathered me closer to his broad chest I decided to go with the moment, closed my eyes, and kissed him back, even though a little imp of common sense was telling me I'd regret it.

If there had been any windows where we were standing, they would have steamed up.

'I see you and me and Winter's End going on into the future *together*,' he murmured, raising his head at last, 'don't you, Sophy?'

'I – I don't know,' I said breathlessly, hardly taking in what he was saying, since he was still punctuating his words with little kisses. I'd never played with fire before but – my God! – I could get to like it. This couldn't be me, Sophy Winter . . . I felt as though I had stepped into the central role in a chick-flick, but I didn't know the part.

Jack, at least, knew his role perfectly. 'Yes, you do! You, me, Winter's End – it was *meant* to be.' He abruptly stopped kissing me and held me slightly away from him. 'But William wasn't as clever as he thought he was, because he left one vital thing out of the reckoning.'

'What was that?' I asked, dazedly opening my eyes and blinking.

'Pride. *I* should have inherited Winter's End and instead all I've got is the title. One day I'd like to invite the woman I love to share *my* home with *me*, not the other way around . . . and that's why I'd really like you to sell the house to me now, or sign it over at least, Sophy,' he said earnestly. 'That's not unreasonable, is it? Then we can turn it into a true family home.'

He tried to kiss me again, but as his words slowly sank in, my state of boneless bliss began to dissipate slightly and I pulled back.

He looked tall, gloriously handsome and rather hurt. 'Darling! I don't want to rush things, but you *do* feel the same way too, don't you? That we have a future here, together, once this is sorted out?'

'But I hardly know you yet, Jack,' I began, feeling rushed, flushed and confused.

He laid one finger over my lips. (His other hand was running lightly up and down my spine in a rather distracting way.) 'Come on, Sophy, you know you feel just the way I do, admit it! And you said yourself that William should have left Winter's End to me.'

'Did I?' I couldn't remember saying that, but I suppose I might have done – *before* I came back and fell under the house's spell again.

'Yes you did, and all you have to do to make things right is sign the place over to me. All your problems will then be mine to resolve, with no need to turn the place into some kind of Shakespearean theme park. In fact, we won't need to open to the public at all, this can just be our home.'

My legs might have gone a bit weak while he was kissing me, but my brain, such as it was, hadn't entirely turned to mush. Sign over my inheritance? Cancel all my lovely, exciting plans?

At this not entirely inopportune moment the air stirred icily around me in a now-familiar way, and I heard a thready whisper: '*Don't do it – Winter's End belongs to you and only you.*'

I stared around wildly, but there was no sign of Alys.

'What's the matter, darling?' Jack asked tenderly. 'Are you shivering?' He took off his jacket and slung it around my shoulders, the silk lining still warm from his body.

'It's nothing,' I said, wondering if this time I had only imagined those words of warning, that chilly presence? I shivered, but this time not from the thrill of Jack's nearness. In fact, I discovered to my astonishment that although I found him very attractive, the idea of marrying him held no charm whatsoever – if that was what he (and not just Hebe) had in mind. I mean, even if I had been as mad about him as he evidently thought I was, did I want to spend my life watching him forget my existence every time Mel Christopher, or any other beautiful woman, walked into the room? Or spend even another minute with his boring, hideous friends? I don't *think* so.

Anyway, I was getting really excited about *my* plans for the estate!

I stole a glance at him: he was looking as icily angry as he had the first time we'd met, like an irate Lucifer who turned out to be my guardian angel instead, though actually Alys's shade seems to have taken on that role now.

'Jack, can't you see that your solution would put *me* in the position you say you find unbearable?' I pointed out gently.

Letting me go abruptly, he turned to stare out of the window.

'I'm sorry, Jack,' I said, miserably aware that I had led him on a bit . . . or maybe that should be a *lot*, 'but that's how I feel. I'm just being *honest* with you.'

Sophy Winter, now eligible for Slut of the Year.

To my relief, when he turned he was smiling again, albeit ruefully. 'I'll just have to change your mind then, won't I? I expect people have been telling stories, prejudicing you against me, that's what's making you so cautious. But you *can* trust me – and once you really get to know me you'll realise we both want the same thing for Winter's End, and I hope we want each other too. Now, are you going to come and see me off?'

'*Off*? I thought you were staying for lunch?' I said, following him downstairs.

'Afraid I can't after all. I'm already packed and Jonah should have brought the car round to the front and put my bags into it by now. You'll have to say goodbye to old Hebe for me.'

I fetched my duffel coat and gave him back his jacket

before we went outside, where the long, lean shape of his sports car was indeed sitting in front of the porch. Beyond it, Seth was leaning over with one large hand braced against a spouting dolphin, picking dead leaves out of the fountain.

There was no escaping Jack's final, lingering kiss, though this time it did absolutely nothing for me, not even a slight tremble around the kneecaps. This might have had something to do with the fact that Seth watched our embrace rather sardonically – which I know because I kept my eyes open this time.

Still, Jack seemed satisfied enough with my wooden response and drove off, tooting his horn triumphantly. Maybe Obtuse and Optimist are his middle names – but then, he is warm, affectionate, tall, rich, handsome, charming and right out of my league, so why should it ever enter his head that I could refuse him anything he asked?

Chapter Nineteen: Suitable for Bedding

*The baby is darker than the Wynters . . . but so am I,
taking after my mother in such things. It was beyond
disappointment to them that it was a female child, but
already they are planning one day to marry her to her
cousin and so the line will go on . . .*

*Another Wynter – I think often of my mother's words
and am comforted in my grief and guilt, for surely these
things are ordained and the pattern cannot be changed?*
From the journal of Alys Blezzard, 1581

Seth had gone back to his leaf picking, but I walked round
the knot until I was facing him. 'Was any of that true, what
Jack said about the roof?'

He straightened and rubbed his straight nose reflectively.
'I don't think so. The house is structurally sound, just shabby
and neglected – a fact I seem not to have noticed until you
came along. So maybe Ottie's right about my being blinkered about the garden, after all – only it is so frustratingly
close to completion!'

It was a partial capitulation, but I had more important
things on my mind at the moment. 'The house is in a worse
state than you think: Jack just showed me a deathwatch beetle
grub he found in an old book in the attic and he says it's rife
up there, plus wet rot, dry rot and goodness knows what else.'

'Does he?' Seth said sceptically. 'Strange – I could count the number of times I've ever seen Jack voluntarily open a book on the fingers of one hand.'

'He *said* he found the grub while he was collecting some of his belongings from the attic.'

'You can take it from me, books weren't part of them. Look, Sophy, perhaps I'm being a bit unfair to Jack, but I would tend to take anything he says with a pinch of salt. I know he can be very persuasive.'

'I'm not so easily taken in,' I said defensively, though I knew I had blushed. Maybe he would think it was the cold air making me pink-cheeked?

'I'm glad to hear it.' Seth had turned and was looking thoughtfully at the neglected façade. 'Sir William told me he wanted *you* to have the place, and Lucy after you. The house may be down at heel, grubby and shabby, but he wouldn't have let it fall into total disrepair, because he loved it – he just loved the garden more.'

'As you do.'

'Yes,' he said simply.

I frowned. 'So, are you implying Jack brought the grub with him? But surely he wouldn't do something like that just to scare me into selling Winter's End to him, especially if he seems to think he can get it for nothing, just by—' I stopped dead and this time went totally scarlet.

Seth raised one eyebrow. 'Jonah tells me Jack took one of the Danse du Feu roses to give to you this morning – very romantic.'

'The snitch.'

'Come with me to the rose garden,' he said abruptly. 'I've been thinking about the Shakespeare angle and I think we could follow it through a bit there . . . It's still a work in progress, as you can see. Once William had put in all those beds of shrub roses along the drive, he thought we might as well go the whole hog and have a rose garden proper. This space wasn't really doing anything.'

It wasn't doing much now, either. It still looked rather bare and forlorn. 'If it makes you feel any happier, I would much rather Jack had left the rose on the bush,' I said. 'It must have been the last flower left in the garden.'

'Just about, though I've known the old moss roses to have the odd bud even at Christmas.' He shrugged. 'Anyway, I just got some new rose catalogues and when I was flicking through I found a very attractive crimson William Shakespeare *and* there's a Dark Lady, an Ophelia, a Thisbe, a Falstaff – lots of roses with Shakespeare connotations. And a Sophy's Rose, too – described as suitable for bedding,' he added gravely, though I was pretty sure he was laughing at me.

I looked at him suspiciously. 'There aren't any Sophys in Shakespeare, are there?'

'Perhaps not, I can't think of any – but it would look good in this back border.'

'A Shakespeare rose garden would be lovely,' I said thoughtfully. 'He mentions musk roses too – we ought to have some of those.'

'Yes, and now would be a good time to order new roses, ready for bare root planting.'

And mean yet more expense. Winter's End seemed to need constant drip-feeding with money. 'If you let me have a list of what you want to order, I'll see what I can do,' I conceded.

'I've got some short Shakespeare quotes for the wall too. Ottie and I had a brainstorming session,' he said. 'Ottie says to tell you she will have them carved as a gift to you and Winter's End.'

'That's very generous of her!'

'Oh, you can't fault her generosity and *she* seems to think it's a good idea. But as soon as the engraving is done, I'll need *all* the gardeners back to get that wall rebuilt,' he added firmly. 'We can't start on the last knot and the beds properly until then.'

'I expect they'll have finished most of the major tasks I wanted done by then anyway,' I said. 'After that I'll just need them for odd jobs as they crop up.'

He was about to say something – and probably a fairly *terse* something – when a tall, stringy man with a camera in one hand walked through the arch.

'Hello! I thought I heard voices. Would you by any chance be Sophy Winter?' he asked me.

'Yes, I am. But who—'

He whipped up the camera and took several shots in quick succession and then, as Seth started towards him, took to his heels and ran. A motorbike roared into life on the drive a second later.

'Gone. He must have wheeled it up here, or we'd have heard him,' Seth said, coming back. 'You do realise what this means, don't you?'

'That you have pathetically desperate paparazzi in Lancashire?'

'No, that it's a slow news week in the *Sticklepond and District Gazette*, and you're about to make the centre spread.'

After that, I made Seth go up to the attics with me to see the evidence of rot and infestation that Jack had pointed out, even though he protested that he was no expert at anything except knots.

'*And* I was going to go back and change for lunch. Your aunt Hebe will give me the fishy eye if I turn up like this.'

He had a point. He was wearing the usual layers of jumpers that looked as if they had been ravaged by a giant moth and the outermost one was unravelling at the hem. But I dragged him up there anyway.

He walked after me through the attics in silence but, when I pressed him, said that it was odd the way all the places that showed signs of infestation were near a working light bulb. 'And the woodworm holes are regular, almost as if they've been drilled. They're all new too – there don't seem to be any old ones nearby – and this powdering of sawdust underneath looks fresh.'

'Jack said he came up here to get some of his old things, but everything is covered in thick, undisturbed dust, except for my belongings in the first room,' I said reluctantly. It's not that I *wanted* galloping woodworm, wet rot and death-watch beetle in the attics, it's more that I didn't want Jack to be proved to be so devious as to plant the evidence of them. 'He was carrying a holdall when he came out too.'

'To bring out the book in, naturally,' Seth said drily. 'I can't see anything up here that looks as if it belongs to Jack, and if there are any more books, they're packed away in boxes, not lying about.'

'Yes, OK,' I snapped. 'I think I've got the message loud and clear! He *does* want me to sell Winter's End to him, but you are wrong about his motives because he sees us running it together as a family home.'

'I see,' Seth said. 'But there was no need to bite my nose off for pointing out the obvious. You made me come up here, after all!'

I knew it was unfair of me, but after all, he had made me wonder just how devious Jack was. I didn't want to believe he was using his considerable amatory technique simply to get me to part with Winter's End, even though I knew a man like him could have pretty well anyone he wanted . . . and probably had. No, I was sure Jack was sincere – but that wouldn't stop the businessman in him trying to get it for less!

It hadn't worked anyway – the merest suggestion that I

223

signed over Winter's End and I went all Gollum, even without Alys putting her oar in. I thought we had reached an impasse in our relationship . . .

Seth and I were still glaring at each other when the gong rang, so that we arrived for Sunday lunch late, cross and cobwebby.

'What a pity Jack had to rush off like that, Sophy, just when you were getting on so well,' Aunt Hebe said, anointing her roast beef with a generous libation of horseradish sauce. 'I am so glad, it will be the perfect solution.'

'What will?' Ottie asked, looking up from her plate. 'Solution to what?'

Hebe ignored her. 'Poor Jack was terribly hurt that William didn't leave Winter's End to him, and he hates the idea of it being commercialised and spoiled when there is no need for it. It should be his – and, of course, if he and Sophy make a match of it, then it *will* be!'

I nearly choked on my roast parsnip.

'We're not going to make a match of it, Aunt Hebe,' I said firmly. 'Fond though I am of him, of course, we won't be traipsing together down the aisle together any time soon.'

'Yes, aren't you going a bit fast?' Ottie demanded crisply. 'Sophy hardly knows the man! And she hasn't so far struck me as being *entirely* stupid either, even if Jack has been turning on the charm.'

'I expect you are worried that Melinda is still around such a lot, Sophy,' Aunt Hebe said kindly, 'since she is so terribly attractive *and* wealthy. But Jack has assured me that it isn't *him* she comes to Winter's End to see, but Seth, so there is no need to be jealous.'

'I'm not jealous,' I said flatly and rather untruthfully.

Seth, who had been quietly but methodically demolishing roast beef and Yorkshire pudding, looked up. 'Mel loves the

224

thrill of the chase, so I expect she's trying to use me to make Jack fall back into line with the rest of her numerous admirers.'

Going by what I had seen and heard in the graveyard, I thought Seth was seriously underestimating her interest in him.

'Oh, no, Seth,' Aunt Hebe said, 'Jack isn't interested in Melinda in the least, he told me so. *You* were the one who was devastated when she married Seldon. I remember William saying that you had sworn never to marry anyone else. And you haven't, have you?'

He coloured slightly under his tan. 'That was an awfully long time ago!'

'Yes, and even though he hasn't married, he hasn't exactly lived like a monk for the last twenty years, pining for his lost love,' Ottie pointed out. 'Far from it!'

'Thanks, Ottie,' he said, deadpan.

'And when she came back and the unattainable became the opposite, I expect you quickly got her out of your system,' she said kindly.

'Look, could we leave my personal life out of this? Mel was just a youthful folly and I think we're all entitled to at least one of those,' he said, looking as embarrassed as any teenager being quizzed by his elders about his love life.

'I'd agree with that,' I said, thinking of my brief marriage, 'and I'm not about to commit any more, youthful or otherwise. I'm sorry, Aunt Hebe, but though I'm already very fond of Jack, it's just in a sisterly sort of way.'

Ottie nodded agreement, but Seth was looking so sceptical that I would have thrown my dinner at him, had I not somehow managed to clear the plate while we were talking.

It was clear from Aunt Hebe's expression that she didn't really believe I could resist Jack's charms either, however much I protested.

And unfortunately, I feared, neither did Jack.

*   *   *

225

I tossed and turned all night, going over and over everything, so I was bleary-eyed by the time I reached the estate office that morning. You'd think I would fall into a stupor of exhaustion every time I climbed into my gorgeous antique bed – but no, I am Sleepless in Sticklepond, which doesn't sound quite as romantic as Seattle . . .

Mr Yatton, who had enough energy for both of us, had already made more appointments for me with the accountant and Mr Hobbs.

By mid-morning, after some lively bargaining in the stables, he had also closed the deal on the fountain for more money than I thought anyone would be prepared to pay for a limp stone girl with a deformed duck, and started looking into the price of airline tickets back from Japan on the internet, just in case.

I did some calculations with what was left of the money and decided to have Alys Blezzard's portrait sent away for cleaning, buy Grace the Dysons of her dreams, Seth his rose bushes (as a sweetener to his temper), and have the Larks' rooms redecorated and a shower installed . . . And that would probably be it, apart from a small contingency fund.

'The next step is to sell the Herring painting,' Mr Yatton said, 'which should fetch enough for you to begin upgrading the visitor facilities. Would you like me to contact the auction house?'

I'd brought the painting down to the office that morning, and it was really rather nice . . . but the house was nicer, so it would have to be sacrificed for the greater good. 'Yes, please.'

Jonah popped his head in and said, 'Sophy, there's a delivery van just been from an outfit called Stately Solutions. Where do you want all the boxes put?'

'In the cleaning room. I'll come in a minute and sort it out. Thanks, Jonah.'

Mr Yatton supplied me with sticky labels and a marker pen, and Mrs Lark some large empty jam jars, and I went off to unpack everything. When it was labelled and stowed away, I called Grace in for a little chat.

She looked around the room curiously. 'Well, you have been busy!'

'Yes, as you see, Grace, I'm making one or two changes, though it shouldn't affect you too much. I'm very happy with your work and I don't want to change your routine. I still want you to change the beds and do the bathrooms on your regular days, sort out the laundry, and clean all the floors. But you won't need to worry about any further cleaning, dusting, or polishing, because I intend doing the rest of it myself.'

'You mean I'll have *less* to do?' she asked doubtfully. 'Do you want me to come in fewer days, then?'

'No, exactly the same as you do now.'

She knitted her brows. 'So you want me to do less work in the same hours?'

'Yes, that's right.'

'For the same money?' She clearly thought I was quite mad.

'Yes. Now, there are just a couple of things I'd like to change about the way you clean. First, I'm going to buy two Dyson cleaners, one to be kept upstairs in the housemaid's cupboard, and one down here.'

Her eyes lit up. 'That'll make a difference!'

'I hope so. Now, see these little foam rubber cylinders? They fit onto the end of vacuum cleaner hoses, so that when you're cleaning around furniture and into corners with the nozzle, things don't get banged and scratched.'

I demonstrated with the end of the old Hoover. 'Could you remember to start doing that right away?'

'All right,' she said absently. I think her mind was full of Dyson dreams.

'The other major change is that all floor washing is to be done with this special solution.' I showed her the container. 'You need only this capful in your bucket; a little goes a long way.'

'Can I put a bit of bleach in with that?' she asked doubtfully.

'Absolutely not. You need only this stuff, nothing else.'

'I always put a bit of bleach in,' she said stubbornly, 'especially in the bathrooms.'

'It will be best if you clean everything with the solution from now on, including the bathroom floors, otherwise you would have to keep a separate bucket and mop for bleach because you couldn't use the same one for both. Now, do you think you could do those things for me?'

'If you like. When will I be getting the Dysons, then? Mrs Lark's got an Argos catalogue in the kitchen; they've got them in that.'

'Perhaps you could get the catalogue and show it to Mr Yatton? We might be able to order them this week, but in the meantime, don't forget to put the foam on the end of the old Hoover, will you?'

'All right,' she agreed, obviously humouring me. She glanced over the room again. 'It looks different in here – what're all these little brushes in the jars for, and the white cotton gloves and stuff?'

'I want to try and preserve everything in the house, and the best way is to keep special brushes, dusters and cotton gloves for cleaning and handling specific things. See,' I said, showing her a label on the shelf, 'this is the Silver Dip, and the brushes, dusters and cotton gloves are only for that purpose. The brass and copper have their own. Over here are cobweb brushes, and this is a banister brush – you might want to use this when you do the stairs, but nowhere else. Don't mix things up or use anything for other than its real purpose.'

'You've put tape and foam around everything, even the metal bits on the paintbrushes?'

'Yes, to stop any scratching. I'm not aiming for perfect conservation, because I'm no expert. Besides, Winter's End is a family home rather than a stately pile, so I'll just do my best. I'll still use feather dusters and window wipes, when it suits me! Oh, and this is my own hand-held vacuum cleaner – it will be handy for cleaning fixed furnishing fabrics.'

'I saw the parlour curtains all bundled up in the laundry room,' she said, 'and the chair covers hanging on the drying rack. Do you want me to put another load of them in, and then iron the dry ones?'

'That would be great, if you have time, Grace. I'll put them back on myself later, when I've cleaned the chairs – unless there's a set of winter covers?'

'There is for the drawing room, I think,' Grace said. 'Maybe I've seen them in the linen cupboard.'

'I'll have a look later, but now I must phone up and get the parlour curtains collected. They are old, they'll have to go to a specialist cleaner.'

'Right, I'll get on with me floors, then.'

I handed her one of the foam tubes. 'Thanks, Grace – and there's your bucket over there, with a new mop. You do understand why I'm doing all this, don't you?'

'Yes,' she said, 'and I'll whiz through everything, once I've got me Dyson!'

When I went back later to see how Mr Yatton was getting on, Grace had already taken him the catalogue with a big cross next to her preferred model.

He was arranging the packing and collection of the Herring and the portrait of Alys, but I phoned up about the curtains myself, using a firm Lady Betty had favoured, who collected and delivered.

The rest of the day passed happily or, in my case, blissfully. Upstairs, Grace sang as she cleaned and Mrs Lark, rosy with excitement, had made her arrangements and was planning an afternoon visit to a cat rescue home to look for a kitten.

I'd set Jonah the task of soaking the rag rug from the Great Hall in an old tin bath of mild soap solution, and on my way to and from the cleaning room I heard him singing to rival Grace, only more discordantly. I put my head round the laundry-room door and discovered he was walking up and down on the rug in the bath in his bare feet, trousers rolled, as though he were treading grapes. Going by the colour of the water, the method seemed to be working.

Bob and Hal were outside cleaning the windows, rattling the long ladders as they extended them, with lots of shouting and many breaks for cups of tea and cake in the kitchen.

And I – well, I was in my element, cleaning and polishing the parlour until the panelling and furniture softly gleamed and the windows lost their soupy murk.

Chapter Twenty: Having Kittens

The baby thrives in Joan's care, and she is such a simple creature seemingly that they have accepted her into the household as they never have myself. Sir Ralph dotes on the child, but I can see my Lady wishes mee gone . . .
From the journal of Alys Blezzard, 1582

Seth obviously believed in striking while the iron was hot, because he came up after dinner with some rose catalogues.

Since Hebe was dispensing her dark arts in the stillroom, he found me alone in the parlour carefully cleaning the chairs with the little hand-held vacuum, through a net cover to protect the fabric.

Charlie was keeping me company, mostly by lying on my feet whenever I stopped moving, and sighing deeply. His nose was well and truly out of joint because of the fuss being made over the new kitten in the kitchens, but I expected he would get used to it.

I didn't hear Seth come in, what with the noise of the vacuum cleaner and having the radio on, so my heart gave a great *thump* when I looked up and caught sight of him. Mind you, it seems to do that anyway whenever I see him unexpectedly.

He took in the room with an expression of astonishment. 'It looks so different in here – what a transformation!'

'It's getting there, and it'll look even better when the curtains come back. Now I just have to do the same to the rest of the house!'

'Without the full-time assistance of Hal and Bob, I hope. I presume they *have* finished cleaning the windows? I haven't seen them all day.'

'Yes, they finished and they worked really hard.' I didn't mention the frequent refreshment breaks. I seemed to have fallen over one or other of them every time I passed through the kitchen.

'So I can have them back again tomorrow, then?'

'Well, yes ... though I do want the front gates rubbed down and repainted while the weather is dry. But I suppose they could do that as overtime,' I conceded.

'That would be much better, because this mild weather is good for working on the lower terrace too.'

'I *have* asked Bob to come tomorrow morning and help Jonah to clean all the inside windows,' I confessed quickly, feeling strangely guilty. 'It'll be much quicker than doing the outside, so you should have him back by afternoon. I don't want Jonah climbing any ladders, at his age.'

Seeing his expression grow a little thunderous, I suggested hastily, 'Let's move into the drawing room – there's a fire there, and we can have a drink.'

He gloomily and silently followed me, but mellowed once he had a glass of good single-malt whisky in his hands and we were poring over the lovely catalogues and deciding what roses to order.

Charlie sat between us on the sofa, and nudged the catalogues from underneath from time to time whenever I stopped stroking him to write something down. This was quite often, actually, because I'd never seen so many lovely roses. It would have been so easy to get carried away, except that I knew my budget would only stretch so far.

232

After a while Mrs Lark sent Jonah in with a three-tiered orange Bakelite cake stand laden with cheese puffs and ratafia biscuits, plus news of what the kitten was up to. I could see that the Adventures of Gingernut were likely to become hourly bulletins.

'She's taken it upstairs now and she's going to pop a hot-water bottle wrapped in a blanket in the basket with it, in case it's missing its mother.'

'Mrs Lark's got a kitten,' I explained, handing the cake stand to Seth. 'Have a ratafia biscuit? They were my last employer's favourites. I took her some last time I saw her.'

'You were fond of her?' he asked, taking one.

'Yes, Lady Betty was always very kind. In fact, she gave me this little brooch that I always wear, when she was in hospital after a fall. She had a premonition she would never see her home again, though I told her she was wrong, and I'd give the brooch back the day she returned to Blackwalls . . . Only she never did, she went to a nursing home instead. I've rung to see how she is a couple of times, but they won't tell me.'

'Couldn't you phone up the family?'

'No, there's only the nephew, and he's a toad,' I said shortly. 'But I've written to the cook, so I should get some news soon, I hope.'

I brought my mind back to the present. 'Well, I think those are all the roses we can afford at the moment, Seth.'

'There will be enough to make a difference, and we can list the varieties in the Winter's End guidebook, which I suppose you will want to update anyway?'

'Yes . . . I've been thinking about that, and I'd like it to be more a glossy brochure than a pamphlet, and with more emphasis on Alys the witch and the Shakespeare-was-here angle.'

'Ottie seems to be having second thoughts about using Shakespeare to reel in the tourists, for some reason,' Seth commented, 'maybe because it's so apocryphal? Mind you, we don't have a lot of concrete evidence about Alys the supposed witch, either.'

'But that's why she was imprisoned, wasn't it? And she was born, got married and died, so those dates must be recorded.'

'Oh, yes, I made a few discoveries when I was researching for the pamphlet. That's how we came to find the original plan for the planting on the terraces, while Sir William and I were turning out the Spanish chest in the estate office in search of Alys's records. Alys Blezzard's maternal grandmother was quite lowborn, from a family that became notorious a century or two later for witchcraft, the Nutters. But her grandfather was a scholar, so she married above her station. And then Alys's mother married a Blezzard, who were minor gentry.'

'I'd heard about the Nutter connection. And I suppose when Alys married Thomas Winter, that was a step up again?'

'Yes, though she seems to have come here in the first place because she had been well versed in healing by her mother. She nursed the heir to Winter's End back to health, then he insisted on marrying her. She had one child, a daughter, was arrested for witchcraft fairly soon after that and died while in custody.'

'That's all so terribly sad!'

'It's even sadder when you think that she was only about seventeen when she died.'

'Good heavens! How old can she have been when she married?'

'Perhaps fifteen – it wasn't unusual then.'

'So young? Poor Alys . . . and no wonder she's still here!'

He gave me an odd look and I said hastily, 'I didn't see her grave in the churchyard – where is she buried?'

'Since they thought she was a witch and her mysteriously

sudden death might be suicide, they wouldn't have put her in hallowed ground. Legend has it she's buried somewhere on the estate – and when I was cutting back some of the undergrowth last year, not far from the pets' graveyard, I found a large plain slab of dressed local stone. I *suspect* that might be it, but I'm not going to disturb it and find out.'

'Definitely not! But I know she loved Winter's End, so she will be happy to be buried in the grounds.'

He didn't ask me *how* I knew.

'I'd better have another look at the pamphlet, Seth. I haven't really read it properly yet.'

'You won't find anything very sensational in there – more facts than legend.'

'We'll have to change that – spice it up! Then it'll sell like hot cakes.'

'You seem very mercenary and cynical for the child of a hippie,' he said, looking at me curiously.

'*Because* I'm the child of a hippie – one of us had to be practical. But I'm prepared to do anything to keep Winter's End going – *anything*!'

'Then marrying Jack might be counterproductive,' he commented drily. 'At best you'd find yourself living in one wing, with the rest of the estate divided up and sold off piecemeal as swanky country homes.'

'Who's cynical now?' I said tartly. 'Couldn't he just love the place like I do, and only want it so that he can preserve it? And anyway, as I said earlier, I have absolutely no intention of marrying him, whatever wishful thinking Hebe's indulging in.'

'From what she was saying at dinner, Jack's indulging in it too – but then, he's always been prepared to go the extra mile to get his way.'

'So, you're implying that he would only want to marry

235

me to get Winter's End?' I said indignantly. 'Thanks a bunch!'

I don't know why it made me so cross, since the same suspicious thought had already entered my own head. That Jack was falling for me was something that seemed believable only when he was there in person, telling me so . . .

'Look, that's not what I meant,' Seth began to protest. 'I just wanted to warn you that—'

'Yes it was,' I broke in hotly, 'but whatever his reasons were, it wouldn't work out anyway. I've already told him how I feel.'

I suppose, since he had seen Jack kiss me before he drove off, I couldn't blame Seth for looking sceptical – or for abruptly changing the subject to something less fraught with pitfalls.

'Ottie and I found a few good Shakespeare quotes that seemed relevant when we had our brainstorming session,' he said, handing me a list, 'or relevant to gardening, anyway.'

'"This knot intrinsicate of life . . ." *Antony and Cleopatra*,' I read out. 'That's good.'

'"And Adam was a gardener", from *Henry VI* – we must have that,' he said. 'And I like the *Othello* one: "O thou weed!"'

'I raided the book of quotations in the library before dinner myself, and found one or two of my own. A bit more general than yours, like "Alas! poor ghost."'

He looked at me, one eyebrow raised. 'Any particular ghost?'

'Yes, Alys, of course. Aunt Hebe was right about her walking,' I confessed. 'Though so far she's proved more of a guardian angel than a ghost.'

He seemed unsurprised by my revelation. 'In what way?'

'Oh, just turning up and . . . well, never mind, you'll think I'm mad – which brings me nicely to my next quote, also from *Hamlet*, "O my prophetic soul!"'

'Well, I suppose they don't all have to be about gardening. Would your ghost approve of "What's past is prologue"?'

'Probably. Where's it from?'

'*The Tempest*. That's my favourite Shakespeare play, because, as it says in *Macbeth*, it's like much of life, "full of sound and fury, signifying nothing".'

I think he must have meant his love-life.

I went and fetched the book of quotations from the library and we added a few more, then we started discussing what plants to have in the Shakespeare garden on the lower terrace, and turned to the 'I know a bank' speech from *A Midsummer Night's Dream*.

'Musk roses again, of course,' I suggested.

'Yes, and for the rest, we have lots of shrubs and plants to choose from: the list is endless, from thyme, balm and bay, to carnations, columbine, daisies and daffodils.'

'And bilberries, burdock, bay and burnet,' I said, throwing in a few I remembered from my research. 'I Googled it.'

Seth looked unimpressed. 'Shakespeare mentions so many plants that he must have been interested in gardening.'

'Maybe that's what he was doing in Lancashire during the Lost Years, working as a gardener,' I said flippantly, and he gave me a withering look.

Out in the passageway the grandfather clock started to chime and didn't look like stopping any time soon. The evening had simply flown by and the cake stand was empty, though I had no recollection of eating anything. There wasn't even a crumb left, except those caught in Charlie's whiskers.

The central chandelier was suddenly switched on, flooding the room with dazzlingly bright light.

'Are you still up?' Hebe said, then she caught sight of Seth sitting next to me on the sofa and looked at us with acute disapproval.

'We were discussing the planting scheme for the Shakespeare garden, Aunt Hebe,' I explained, feeling like a guilty teenager, 'and the quotations for the wall. I didn't realise it was getting late.'

Seth drained the last of his whisky and got up. 'Yes, I think we have enough ideas to be going on with, for now at any rate.'

Aunt Hebe lingered behind in the study while I escorted Seth to the front door and locked it behind him. She re-emerged just as I'd washed up our glasses and the cake stand, and settled Charlie in his basket in the kitchen, then followed me upstairs, as though she suspected I might double back and let Seth in again if she didn't. She would probably have liked to lock me into my bedroom, but had to content herself with frostily wishing me good night.

I'd left my mobile phone in my room again, and found I'd missed three calls from Jack, but nothing from Anya or Lucy. I missed another one from Jack while I was in the bathroom, going through the motions of cleaning my teeth in a haze of sudden exhaustion. Then, just as I got into bed, he rang me *again*.

'Hello? Sophy?' he said, in a warm, intimate voice. 'At last – don't you *ever* carry your phone around with you?'

I propped myself up against the pillows sleepily. 'Yes, but sometimes I forget. But I've been in the house most of the day, except for walking Charlie, so you could have got me on the house phone if it was urgent.'

'Well, I've got you now, darling. Sorry I had to dash off like that yesterday, but business is business and I've got three properties I want to complete on, before Christmas.'

'Oh? I thought you did them up one at a time,' I said sleepily. 'You've already bought Melinda's old house, haven't you? That'll make four.'

'Mel's house is so ugly that I bought it just for the land

238

it's standing on. She gets a percentage when I sell it on for a housing development, but I'm still waiting for permission to knock the main building down. It's taking ten times longer than I bargained for.'

'So it isn't a nice house?'

'No, it's a ghastly sixties concrete monstrosity, by some Dutch architect who only built a couple of them over here. But never mind that. I hope you've been thinking about me and what I said to you?'

The truth was, that apart from that brisk exchange with Seth on the subject, before we settled down to the exciting task of choosing roses, the day had gone by in such a flash that I'd hardly thought of him at all for hours. Before I could stop myself, my blunt tongue had said so.

There was a hurt pause. 'You seem to have been making a late night of it. Hebe just called me, quite upset because you spent the evening with Seth. I hope you aren't harbouring any hopes in that direction, because he's involved with Mel.'

That must have been what Hebe was doing while I was letting Seth out. The devious old witch!

'Look, he brought some catalogues up so we could choose roses for the garden,' I snapped. 'I don't even *like* the man, but he *is* my head gardener, in case you'd forgotten! And anyway, I'm not accountable for how I spend my time – to you or to anyone else.'

'Of course not,' he said quickly. 'I just wished it was me you'd spent the evening with, that's all.'

'Jack, you had every opportunity of spending an evening with me when you were here at the weekend,' I pointed out. 'You decided to go to the pub instead, to be with your friends.'

'Oh, I see!' he said, with an air of discovery. 'This is all still because of Mel. You're jealous of her, aren't you? But really, there's no need to be – she's *very* old news as far as *I'm* concerned – just a friend.'

'I am *not* in the least jealous of Melinda and I don't care what sort of news she is,' I snapped and he laughed infuriatingly.

'Good night, darling, sweet dreams – of me!'

I said something unprintable but he'd already gone, cocooned in smug delusion. Paradoxically, the more I saw how irresistibly gorgeous *he* thought he was, the less attractive I seemed to find him.

And as for Seth, if he was stupid enough to fall for someone like Mel, and let her give him the run-around all over again, then he deserved all he got!

Chapter Twenty-one: Ghost Lace

*There has been another priest hidden in the house
these three days, but he is to leave as soon as it is dark
tonight – the house has been searched once and it is
feared they mean to search again. Joan says there is a
rumour abroad that he is carrying gold from Lord R.
back to France with him, but I do not know the truth
of this.*

*Sir Ralph is much scolded by his wife for putting them
in such danger and I overheard him promise that they
should no more profess the Catholic faith but instead
throw in their lot with the new religion, though he is in
fear for his immortal soul.*

From the journal of Alys Blezzard, 1582

Ottie retired to her house and studio in Cornwall until
Christmas, though I couldn't imagine anywhere more
inspiring than Winter's End.

Each morning the view across the valley from my
bedroom window changed quite magically as autumn firmly
advanced towards winter, stripping the last of the bronze
leaves from the trees and picking out the knots and bushes
on the terraces below with frost.

Indoors, Jonah kept roaring fires going in the Great Hall,
helping to dispel the chilly dankness of the rest of the house,

and I embarked on an exhausting but enjoyable flurry of frenzied cleaning.

The days flew by as Winter's End began to emerge like a butterfly from a rather dingy chrysalis. I was happy as a pig in clover and so, it seemed, was just about everyone else.

Grace swooped about the house with her new vacuum cleaners, singing shrilly. Whenever I had the gardeners into the house to help, Jonah followed them around, telling them how *he* would have done everything had he been twenty years younger, which seemed to give him great satisfaction. And as for Mrs Lark, she was so grateful at being allowed to have the kitten that she seemed to feel the need to stuff food into me at every turn.

'If I wasn't burning off so many calories with the cleaning, I'd simply have burst out of my clothes like the Incredible Hulk by now,' I told Anya on the phone. 'I might have burst altogether. I wonder if our *insides* are green?'

'I shouldn't think they're a pretty sight, whatever colour they are, so let's not go there. Tell me everything that's been happening instead, because it's like *Upstairs, Downstairs* from both viewpoints at once.'

'Nothing terribly exciting,' I said doubtfully. 'I've met my accountant and one or two other people Mr Yatton thought I ought to, and signed loads of papers that gave me acute headaches to get my head around . . . I've removed yards of cobwebs and dispossessed some of the biggest spiders I've ever seen in my life, and I've polished so much panelling I'm doing it in my sleep.'

'Go on, what else?' she prompted.

'Two of the gardeners have been helping me to move heavy furniture and roll rugs, and luckily one of them, Hal, is a dab hand with the paste pot and brushes, so I've arranged for him to redecorate the Larks' rooms. The other one, Bob, is concentrating on repainting the front gates.'

'And how is the Gorgeous Gardener taking that?' she enquired with interest.

'He's not so much gorgeous as grumpy. He tends to go off the deep end even if I just borrow one of them for an hour and it took me *ages* to get it through his thick skull that Hal and Bob were going to do most of the extra work as overtime. He's *obsessed* with finishing the lower terrace – but even when we had a cold snap and the ground was too frozen, he was up in the woodland, chopping down dead trees.'

'So, does your aunt Hebe still think you two have got a thing going on?'

'No, not now she's seen the way we argue all the time, and I'm sure Jack never believed it at all; he's too confident of his own attractions. He's taken to phoning me up late every night, schmoozing me.' I sighed. 'You know, it's only a few weeks since I would have thought that was wonderful, but now I just wish he wouldn't, because I'm shattered by bedtime. But I have to answer it, in case it's Lucy.'

'At least you don't seem to be besotted with him any more, that's one good thing. You had me quite worried there.'

'I was never besotted,' I replied with dignity, 'just dazzled. You wait until you see him, then you'll understand why I found it hard to think straight when he was there! And I am growing fond of him – just not in any relationship kind of way any more, and certainly not handing over Winter's End fond!'

'I expect he'll get the message eventually.'

'I hope so, but Aunt Hebe's also driving me crackers by constantly telling me how wonderful he is and what a great husband he would make – which perhaps he might, but not mine, even if he asked me – which he hasn't, directly, just hinted. It'll be difficult when it does finally dawn on both of them that I really *am* here to stay, and Winter's

End is going to open to the public with a bang next year, whether Jack likes it or not.'

'I'm looking forward to seeing it, at last,' Anya said, for now that Guy had got the job near Manchester she was working her way down, via a string of autumn craft fairs, to visit him and then drop in on me.

I wasn't sure what Aunt Hebe would make of my best friend, with her red dreadlocks and nose ring . . .

'How are you and your aunt getting on, apart from the campaigning on Jack's behalf?' Anya asked, as if reading my mind.

'Oh, we're settling down into a routine. She has her own preoccupations and I have mine, so we live pretty separate lives; probably much as she did with Grandfather. Neither of us is a great talker at breakfast, thank God. That was the worst thing about Jack: he was too damned cheerful at dawn! And we aren't often in the kitchen at the same time for lunch. But we have a genteel chat about our respective days over a glass of sherry every evening, before dining together, followed by coffee in the drawing room while she knits.'

'Very civilised. What's she knitting?'

'I think it may be some sort of jumper or cardigan,' I said dubiously. 'It's snotty green and quite big, so I hope whatever it is, it's meant for Jack.'

'And what do you do? You must be tired with all the cleaning by the evening.'

'I sit in the parlour with Charlie, listening to Radio 4 and sewing my cushions.'

With a glowing wealth of bright silk and satin scraps scattered across the polished top of the needlework table, a fake but cheerful electric coal-effect fire in the grate, and Charlie at my feet (or even *on* my feet), I was perfectly happy.

And if sometimes the presence of Alys Blezzard in the

room was so real that I spoke aloud to her – well, there was no one else there to hear me and think me mad.

Apart from Charlie, of course, and *he* was aware of her too.

I was still awaiting the return of the parlour curtains (preferably in one piece), and though the windows had wooden shutters, that night I had left them open because the terraces looked so pretty with the knot gardens frosted and palely gleaming under a full moon.

I was engrossed in embroidering a rose onto an ivory silk patch, when a sudden sharp rapping at the terrace door nearly gave me a heart attack – and all I could see was this hulking great shape lurking outside, a pallid face pressed to the glass.

But it was the sheer size of the monster that gave its identity away, after one long, ghastly moment when I remembered every horror story I'd ever read – especially one particularly scary one where a drowned man was summoned back from the sea . . .

I let my breath out in a great sigh and nudged Charlie off my feet so I could get up. He was still snoring – some guard dog.

'Did you *have* to knock suddenly like that?' I demanded, turning the key and letting Seth in, along with a chilly breeze. 'My heart's still racing!'

'Sorry, I didn't think. I often walk around this way when I'm going to the pub, then take the short cut through the shrubbery, and I saw you through the window looking very domestic and cosy. In fact, the whole house is starting to look different, and I can see all the hard work you've put into it,' he said, which I think was as close to an apology for his grumpiness as he could get.

He walked over to the table and examined my sewing. 'What are you making?'

'Crazy patchwork cushions. I used to make them as a

little business, but I thought I would get some ready for our gift shop before I advertise again. My friend Anya makes jewellery, and Aunt Hebe is going into production on a line of rose-based creams and lotions, so it's going to be a very upmarket little shop. But we will still stock all the usual bits and pieces visitors like too – pens, pencils, rubbers, teatowels, mugs . . . all kinds of things.'

'So you still intend combining it with the teashop?'

'I think so, but I need to give that whole area more thought, because it could be a real moneyspinner.'

'You could stock my book too. It will be out by then,' he suggested.

'Which book? I mean, I knew you'd written one or two, but no one told me you had a new one coming out.'

'Yes, *The Artful Knot*. It's a short history of the knot garden in this country.'

'That sounds perfect for the shop. You'll have to give me the details so we can order some in – and sign them too.'

'I'll do that,' he said, and bestowed one of his rare – and, if truth be told, devastating – smiles on me. He wasn't wearing his layers of jumpers tonight, just one the colour of butterscotch under a soft, natural leather jacket and his shoes were beautiful. His silky black hair was brushed straight back from his forehead . . .

I was just thinking that when he scrubbed up he made a *very* good job of it, when he said, 'Well, I'd better be off – but why don't you come with me?'

'To the pub – tonight – me?' I began, then stopped, because actually, there was no real reason why I shouldn't, and suddenly I *wanted* to. 'I'm a bit tired but it would be lovely to get out,' I agreed. 'OK – just let me get a coat and put Charlie in the kitchen. I'll leave a note on the table for Jonah too, for when he comes downstairs to lock up.'

*　　*　　*

246

It was so bitterly cold that the breath hung in front of our faces like white clouds and I was glad I'd brought my warm scarf and gloves, but the sky overhead was a magical dark velvety blue sprinkled with stars.

Seth was silent until we'd crossed the top terrace and rounded the corner of the house, where he switched on a torch to light our way. Then he said:

'The stone mason has started lettering the first stones for the retaining wall. He's going to bring them back in batches as he does them, so I can start on rebuilding it at the end of this week.'

'That's fast!'

'Yes, but I suppose it makes a change from gravestones.'

'Is that what he does, memorial carving? I thought he was a sculptor and that's how Ottie knew him.'

'He's that too, he just makes his living from doing the other stuff. So,' Seth added, giving me one of his more minatory sideways glances, 'we'll have the wall rebuilt quite quickly – if you leave my gardeners alone.'

'I always leave you Derek,' I pointed out, 'your right-hand man.'

'Just as well, since he's the only one of us with the skills and experience to rebuild the wall and he'll be in charge of it. But he can't do it alone.'

'He won't have to. Bob's going to finish off the front gates at weekends and Hal's redecorating the Larks' apartment as overtime too. So unless I suddenly think of something else they can help me with, you can have them,' I added provocatively.

'You're just trying to wind me up,' he said gloomily.

'Yes,' I admitted, 'and actually, I'm really starting to look forward to seeing the wall finished and a start made on landscaping the terrace, because that wooden shuttering looks really ugly and it's such a muddy mess down there. Have you decided on the design for the central knot yet?'

'Yes,' he said, but didn't offer to show it to me, so I assumed he was sulking.

I'd been half afraid that Jack's friends would be in the pub, but it was much quieter than last time, with no sign of them or of Mel Christopher, so I expect most of them live in London and only come home for weekends – that, or they usually meet at a more upmarket pub somewhere. I couldn't tell if Seth was disappointed by Mel's absence or not, but then, I don't suppose he would have invited me to go with him if he had had an assignation there with his lady-love.

Grace waggled her fingers at me from the fireplace corner where she was sitting with the journalist, George. I only hoped she wasn't telling him any more of my life history – if there was any left to tell – but since nothing about me had appeared in the local paper, not even the photograph, I expect he had given up on me as way too boring.

I drank Guinness and played darts with Seth, Bob, Hal and the community policeman, Mike, who was a displaced Liverpudlian. After a bit Val came out from behind the bar and took a turn too.

I felt relaxed and happy when I walked back later with Seth, in companionable silence, our footsteps sounding loud in the cold darkness.

As we passed the graveyard I could see the glimmering whiteness of my mother's angel in a swirl of movement – but whether landing or taking off I wasn't sure.

Chapter Twenty-two: On the Rails

*Last night my Lady told mee to put on a dark cloak
and lead the priest from the house by the woodland
path beyond the walled garden, to set him on his way
to a safer house. This I did, but I feared for the poor
old man, though he was calm and resolute enough. He
blessed mee before he left, though he will have heard
the rumours of witchcraft that Mary Wynter hath put
about so assiduously.*

From the journal of Alys Blezzard, 1582

The local newspaper came out again, thankfully without
any mention of me in it, so I decided I could stop worrying.
Even in Sticklepond and the surrounding villages, there had
to be a lot more exciting stories than 'Mrs Mop inherits
manor house'.

Life was fast becoming a near rural idyll – that is, if I
managed not to think about running costs, income tax
demands, the costs of accountancy firms, solicitors, public
liability insurance and the like, fortunately all the things
that Lucy and Mr Yatton seemed to find both comprehen-
sible *and* exciting.

My financial troubles might now be on a truly magnificent scale, but they didn't seem to feel as insurmountable,
probably because I was not struggling alone any more. And

with my best friend now making her leisurely way down from Scotland in her converted ambulance, I just needed to gather Lucy back into the fold to feel totally happy. All I ever really wanted from life was a settled home and a family around me – could that really now be within my grasp?

Slowly I settled into a pleasant routine, the whole house starting to glow and come alive as the reek of dust, damp and neglect was replaced by the mingled scents of beeswax, lavender, rose potpourri and love. Aunt Hebe had taken to saying approvingly that one day I would make Winter's End an excellent mistress, so I didn't know what she thought I was doing now – playing house?

In the early afternoons I generally took a break and walked with Charlie down the terraces and over the little bridge, climbing up through the woods on the other side of the valley to the summerhouse perched among the trees, which gave me a whole new perspective on Winter's End.

It was weathered and half-rotted, as Seth had pointed out to me when I started using it, but the wooden pillars holding up the lintel and roof seemed firm enough and the bench seat inside was dry. From there, I could see the gardeners all toiling away on the lower terrace, with Seth easy to spot, since he was much taller than the rest. The wall was coming along in leaps and bounds, since, as Seth pointed out, I wasn't hijacking his workforce quite so much, even if they were all tired out from doing other jobs around the house in their free time.

Seth was a hard taskmaster. If they were not working on the terrace or in the woodland, then they were kept busy elsewhere in the garden and greenhouses.

He'd taken to dropping into the parlour most evenings, though, via the terrace, so we could discuss progress – or rather, if I were honest, bicker in comfort. We seemed perfectly capable of arguing over *anything*, fighting our way to each truce.

Currently, he was reluctantly incorporating some sensational material I had written into the Winter's End guidebook, but in return I was letting him design a separate garden guide, though I did stipulate that he should include a Shakespeare Trail.

The lower terrace wouldn't be finished until the guidebook went to print but at least Seth seemed perfectly happy about the design now. I was sure that, with typical male forgetfulness, he had entirely forgotten that the best suggestions were mine.

Seth and I also managed to disagree over what was to go on the revamped display boards in the Great Hall, whether the 'William Shakeshafte' mentioned in local documents was actually William Shakespeare, practically all my ideas for Winter's End merchandise – and anything and everything else. In fact, a few times we argued our way down to the Green Man, all through a game of darts and a couple of drinks (with Hal and Bob grinning behind their beer mugs, and Mike the policeman cheerfully refereeing), and back again.

I never saw Jack's friends there, so I concluded they only came to meet up with him . . . and maybe Mel did too, for there was no sign of her either. When I asked Val, she said she rarely came in, so if she and Seth *were* having an affair (and how could he resist her?), then they met up elsewhere.

I wouldn't know – he never mentioned her at all.

One morning after breakfast, when I was up in the minstrels' gallery polishing the wooden balustrade, something came over me – second childhood, unfortunately.

Putting down my soft cloth and jar of beeswax polish, I swung myself astride the wooden banister, my fingers automatically slipping into the groove that ran down beneath, as if carved for the purpose. I hesitated for barely one second, looking over my shoulder down into the depths of the hall, then let go.

It was fast – far faster than I remembered – *scarily* fast. My fingers, slippery with polish, were not slowing me down and I realised my back was going to hit the carved post at the bottom with a thump likely to break one or both of us . . .

They say your life passes before your eyes at moments like this, but all that passed before mine was a brief recollection of the last time I'd slid down the rails like this . . . when, as now, two large, strong hands stopped my progress just in the nick of time.

Eyes still tight shut with terror, I was hauled off and held upright on trembling legs that wouldn't take my weight. For a moment I was eight again and, when I opened my eyes and looked upward with fearful reluctance, I half-expected to see my grandfather's angry face.

Instead, it was Seth, who held me in a grip of iron, white-faced and furious.

'What on earth were you doing?' he demanded, giving me a shake. 'You could have seriously injured yourself if you'd slammed into the post!'

My knees gave and the room whirled dizzyingly around but his arms closed around me, holding me upright. It felt wonderfully comforting.

'Oh, Seth!' I whispered, clinging to him like a drowning woman to a rock, and we stared into each other's eyes from a couple of inches away, united in the horror of what might have happened, had he not been there. His eyes were like a green sea you could drown in . . .

Then the stag's head fell with a clatter onto the stone flags and broke the spell. *Déjà vu.* I took a deep breath. 'Th-thanks for catching me! I used to slide down the banisters all the time when I was a child, but this time it seemed so much faster. I had beeswax on my hands so perhaps I just didn't have the same grip.'

252

'It certainly wouldn't help,' he agreed, but at least he wasn't looking angry any more. In any case, I'd quickly realised that the anger had been because I might have hurt myself ... and looking back, I'm sure that was why Grandfather had been so furious with me too.

'Last time I did it, Grandfather caught me just like you did,' I told him. 'In fact, that's the last time I saw him, and for ages I thought it was all my fault we had to go away, because I'd been naughty.'

'You were only eight, weren't you? So nothing was your fault, Sophy. And your colour's coming back – you looked white as a ghost,' he added with relief.

'I'm all right,' I assured him, though my hands were still clutching the outer layers of his ratty wool jumpers – and come to that, his arms were still around me. I felt safe like that ...

'Good, I wouldn't want anything to happen to you, Sophy,' he said seriously.

'Only because you know that Jack inheriting the place would be even worse. He'd be digging treasure-hunting pits all over the garden, for a start,' I said, rallying, and he grinned.

'No, because your *daughter* would inherit, and she sounds like hell on wheels.'

I began to say indignantly, 'Lucy is *not*—' when a cool voice broke in.

'Am I interrupting something, Sophy? Only the front door was unlocked, so I just walked in – but I'll go away again if you want to get all hands-on with the help. I suppose like calls to like.'

Mel was standing by the carved screen, immaculate in a quilted jacket and tight cream jodhpurs, her light brown eyes cold and furious.

I loosed my grip on Seth's jumper and his arms slowly released me, his face going all shuttered.

'I fell off the – the chair,' I explained quickly, not wanting to mention that I was doing something as childish as sliding down the banisters. 'Luckily, Seth caught me.'

'Oh?' She looked at the nearest chair, which was a knobbly triangular neo-Gothic affair some feet away, and raised a thin brow. 'Jack suggested I should call in and see if I could give you any advice – new kid on the block and all that – but it doesn't look to me as if you need it. I'd certainly recommend Seth for emergencies, though – and if you can get him away from his knots, he's brilliant at all kinds of bedding too, aren't you, Seth?'

She took out a packet of cigarettes and started to root about in her pockets, presumably for a lighter.

'Thanks for the recommendation,' Seth said evenly, though he was white-lipped and clearly furious, 'but I agree that no advice *you* could give her would do Sophy any good.'

Her manner changed in an instant and she smiled at him, a full beam job a bit like Jack's best efforts, exerting a force field of personal attraction. 'I was going to come and look for you afterwards, Seth,' she said caressingly. She spared me a casual, dismissive glance. 'If you've quite finished with him, you don't mind if I borrow him for an hour or so, do you? There's a little something he can help me with.'

I thought the old-fashioned seduction technique was dated, but I didn't bother looking at Seth to see how it was going down: I could guess. 'His time is his own,' I said shortly. 'And by the way, you can't smoke in my house.'

She'd found her lighter and stuck the cigarette in her mouth, but now paused. 'Oh, well, we'll go out then. Coming, Seth?'

But Seth's gaze had gone to the window and hardened into a lethal glare. 'Only to see you off the premises. You've tied your bloody horse to one of the topiary trees, and it's practically got it up by the roots!'

I watched from the porch while Mel ran to retrieve her

horse. It was tossing its head and jerking at the tree, which was trimmed into three balls of box in decreasing size. Before she could grab the reins her velvet hat, which was perched on the topmost one, was suddenly catapulted off and landed in the basin of the fountain, where it floated upside down.

Seth stamped the tree back down into the ground, then retrieved her hat, shaking the water off it. I couldn't hear what they were saying, but I could see Mel was trying to get round him, with one hand laid on his sleeve, smiling that surely irresistible smile up at him – but she was impeded by her horse, who had had enough of standing about in the cold.

It seemed to like going backwards and after a moment Seth took the reins from her and turned and walked off down the drive and, after looking briefly over her shoulder in my direction in what was surely triumph, Mel hurried to catch up.

That was a very neat demonstration of 'this is my property, so hands off' – so it *must* be Seth she was really interested in, not Jack. Presumably that night at the pub she just automatically swung into her usual routine to show me that she could also have Jack – or any other man – any time she wanted to. At least, for Seth's sake, if he was keen on the woman, I *hoped* so.

Climbing the steps back up to the gallery, I wondered what Seth had come to find me for, but I didn't see him again for the rest of that afternoon to ask him – I was just grateful he had been there at the right time.

I polished like a Fury, though. Every surface in the gallery was like glass by the time I'd finished with it.

Then afterwards, feeling strangely unsettled and needing to be alone, I took Charlie and drove to the sea near Southport in the Volkswagen and we had a walk along a cold, blowy beach, followed by a brew-up on the stove – and except for Lucy not being there, it was just like old times.

255

Chapter Twenty-three: Lost Treasures

I was seen, returning to the house – or at any rate, the cloaked figure of a woman – and they suspect us of aiding a priest to escape so come to question us tomorrow . . . I have made such preparations as I can, if it go ill with mee, charging Joan with the care of my child, that she may know my secrets when she is old enough.

From the journal of Alys Blezzard, 1582

Aunt Hebe told me over dinner that the bare-root roses we had ordered had arrived. She'd seen Derek unloading them while Seth checked them over, so it seemed that he hadn't spent the entire afternoon helping Mel with her bedding, after all.

Not that it was any of my business anyway, unless it affected his work – but I couldn't imagine any woman ever becoming more important than the garden, even one as beautiful as Mel.

By a strange coincidence, that evening Jonah had removed the flotilla of paper-napkin swans and replaced them with red ones folded into roses. He'd laid a separate one, with a stem of green florist's wire, by my plate.

'Thanks, Jonah,' I said. 'The roses are really pretty – you are clever!'

'Seth won't mind about that one, and no earwigs neither,'

Jonah said, grinning. 'The kitten ate one that dropped on the floor and it went through the poor little thing like a dose of salts. If I hadn't caught him with the last bit of red paper, I'd have been that worried, because the litter tray—'

'Jonah,' Aunt Hebe interrupted firmly, 'I can see lamb chops, but are we to have no mint sauce?'

Later, as I sat sewing in the parlour, I reflected that roses seemed to be a recurring theme at Winter's End for, once I started to notice them, I discovered they were everywhere. Briar roses were carved on pillars and panelling, and the ancient rose of Lancaster cut into stone corbels. They appeared in tapestries and embroideries, formed the design of the knot garden on the middle terrace and even featured (along with the family whippet-and-black-pudding crest) in the stained-glass quarries set among the plain diamonds of the Long Room windows.

According to Mr Yatton, the crest is a hound holding a black gauntlet, rather than a black pudding, though I am not convinced. But it's quite jolly, so I intend having it printed on lots of things for the gift shop, from pencils to tote bags. There will be two or three different ranges of items, something to suit all tastes, I hope, from roses and Shakespeare to witchcraft. I just keep jotting ideas down as they come to me.

Jack said (and keeps saying in his phone calls, *ad nauseam*) that he hates the idea of Winter's End being 'commercialised' and I should forget about opening the house and just concentrate on getting it back in order again. But if sharing such a beautiful place with other people generates enough income to keep it running, why not? Luckily Seth seems to feel the same way about the gardens as I do, and actually *wants* lots of people to see them, because we don't want a glowering gardener among the vegetation.

But above all, I was quite sure that Alys approved of all the changes I was making. In fact, that evening she felt especially close, so I actually *asked* her if she would mind if I copied out one or two charms from her household book and had them printed on postcards to make money for Winter's End? Call me mad, but I got the distinct impression that she didn't in the least. She might not have lived here long, but I knew she loved it as much as I did.

Still does, come to that.

Tonight Hebe was occupied with her furtive customers in the stillroom and anyway, rarely came into the parlour, which she didn't seem to like. It was too late for Seth to call (not that I ever *expected* him, because he was probably frequently otherwise engaged), and the Larks were settled in for the evening upstairs in their quarters, with Gingernut the kitten and the telly, until it was time for Jonah to do his last rounds of the house.

So I fetched Alys's book from its hiding place and, using a pair of clean white cotton gloves, even though centuries of sweaty Winter fingers had turned the pages already, mine included, I opened it at the front, where there were inscriptions in two different hands – for, of course, this had originally been her mother's book, passed on to Alys at her death.

Alys's writing was still clearly legible, firm and bold, if a little over embellished with loops and curls for current tastes, and hard to decipher:

Herein are many household receipts and hints, which I had from my mother, for the use of simples to cure divers ailments, some that the superstitious would call witchcraft in these sorry times. I have continued to add to the book, as I hope my daughter, Anne, will do after mee, and onward down the generations in the female line for we women know better how to value such things and keep them safe. The treasures within are both my mother's legacy and my own, and the rose lies at their heart. I charge you to use them well.

Alys Blezzard, 1582

Well, that was clear enough – the treasures were the recipes in the book, especially the rose-based ones. I don't think even the Famous Five could conjure a mystery out of that, so Lucy would be disappointed.

And perhaps my mother thought she should have been the keeper of the secret, rather than Ottie, and took the book away with her so she could pass it on to me, her only legacy – apart from the camper van, of course.

But it should never have left Winter's End – even my dotty, spaced-out mother must have known that!

I copied out a couple of recipes that I thought would be suitable for postcards without poisoning anyone who tried them, one for rose tea and another for a sort of universal salve. Aunt Hebe was probably already using them, and Mrs Lark seemed to think she hadn't managed to dose anyone to death yet.

I flicked through the rest of the book, thinking that despite Alys's defence, some of her mother's potions sounded very Dark Arts to me. And so did some of Alys's own additions at the end of the book, interspersed among innocent instructions about which herbs to use to sweeten wooden floors, and how to make sops-in-wine.

Unfortunately, there weren't any recipes for discouraging a persistent lover, and Jack continued his schmoozy evening phone calls to ask how my day had gone, and whether I missed him – which, though fond of him, I hadn't really. It was hard to pinpoint the moment when I had passed from a state of dazzled infatuation to a sisterly – if slightly exasperated – affection, but it wasn't his fault that I'd recovered from the fever so quickly.

He apologised for not being able to get to Winter's End more often. 'I'll make up for it at Christmas, and I'll try to get down for lunch one day soon – I'll let you know when. Just concentrate on getting the house looking wonderful. We'll work out our future plans at Christmas, darling.'

'I've already worked mine out. You should have listened to *all* my speech to the staff,' I said drily, and though he laughed, I thought I had started to detect a note of impatience in his voice.

Perhaps it was at last dawning on him that I hadn't so much got a toehold on Winter's End, as captured the castle.

I finally received an answer to the letter I wrote ages ago to Mrs Dukes, the Blackwalls cook, asking if she knew how Lady Betty was.

It had taken some time for my letter to be passed on because she resigned after she, too, was denied permission to visit her mistress in the nursing home. She said she thought Conor had treated his aunt disgracefully, especially in isolating her from her friends and staff.

I had no other way of finding out what was happening, but by a strange coincidence I received an official missive from a solicitor only a day or two later, giving me the sad but not unexpected news that Lady Betty had died.

Conor hadn't thought fit to inform me of it, but I would have travelled up for the funeral, had I known.

Mind you, I didn't leave him a forwarding address, though Tanya at the caravan site was kindly sending on my mail, which is how I got the solicitor's letter. But Conor did have my mobile phone number, from when I worked there.

I admit that I had a little weep for Lady Betty, so it was a few minutes before I read on and discovered that under the terms of her will, all the permanent household staff would receive a keepsake, which she had personally chosen. Picking them out must have given her hours of pleasure!

Mine was an Egyptian artefact, and the author of the letter enquired if I would I like the solicitor to arrange to have it packed and delivered to me. I wondered which item, from Lady Betty's mainly bogus Egyptian collection, she had left to me. I only hoped it was not the stone sarcophagus, though when I told Seth while I was helping him plant the new rose bushes, he said that it would make quite a good display, planted up – so long as the mummy wasn't still in it.

I knew him well enough now to recognise when he was joking, even though he kept his face straight. It was a good sign, because he'd been a bit gloomy and preoccupied since the day Mel found us in that unfortunately compromising-looking clinch in the Great Hall. And though he still dropped into the parlour sometimes in the evening, his heart didn't always seem to be in our arguments any more.

I didn't think Mel was good news as far as Seth was concerned. Can you have your heart broken twice by the same person? He could be infuriating, but I found I didn't want him to be deeply unhappy, which I suspected was because I was starting to think of him as family, too.

Mr Yatton was to write to the solicitor to arrange delivery of my Mystery Parcel from Lady Betty. I'd treasure it, what-ever it was. Lucy said she hoped it was a mummified cat, a ghoulishly strange desire that would gain no endorse-ment from Mrs Lark, that's for sure, and Gingernut, who seemed to have no respect for other people's property, let alone his own ancient ancestors, would probably eat it.

I wouldn't like to see the mess *that* would make in his litter tray.

*   *   *

Apart from the sad but not entirely unexpected news of my former employer, there were no flies in my balm of bliss until the end of the week.

Then the local rag came out again – and to my horror there I was, after all this time, headlined in the *Sticklepond and District Gazette*.

'WINTER'S END FOR MRS MOP!' it said in huge capitals, followed in slightly smaller type by 'MYSTERY HEIRESS FOUND'.

The meagre and unexciting facts of my inheritance had been used to support a huge edifice of speculation and possibility ... a bit like what I was doing with the guidebook and display boards, come to think of it. Maybe I should have been a journalist.

It was all very sensational, and accompanied by the photo of Seth and me that had been taken in the new rose garden. I looked startled and fat, as did Charlie – but then, he usually does. Underneath it they'd put, 'To the manor born – the new Lady Winter with one of her gardeners at Winter's End,' and then quoted Seth as saying, 'The new mistress doesn't know her a** from her antirrhinum,' which I imagine he might well have done in the first flush of fury after I arrived, though he says not. (And I'm *not* Lady Winter. Unless I married Jack, I would never be Lady *anything*.)

Seth was furious, but I think it was mostly wounded male vanity, because he said the article and picture made him sound and look like a bucolic half-wit. Mind you, it was true that I didn't know what an antirrhinum was, so I asked him and he said it was like a snapdragon.

That should be his middle name – Seth Snapdragon Greenwood.

The day after the horrible article appeared, Jack called in for lunch on his way somewhere. Though he'd let us know he was coming, he arrived much earlier than I expected, so that I was down on the lower terrace getting some air after a morning spent cleaning the furniture in the Chinese bedroom.

Also, the footings for the retaining wall were in, and a couple of plain courses laid, and Seth insisted I put the first of the engraved stones into place.

The stone was a lot heavier than it looked so he had to help, standing right behind me with my hands over his as he carefully manoeuvred 'I like of each thing that in season grows' into place.

I turned in his encircling arms and smiled up at him as the other three gardeners clapped, probably more to restore some circulation to their cold hands than for any other reason, but his answering smile was surprisingly short-lived – then he moved away as if I was suddenly contagious.

A familiar voice hailed me peremptorily from above. 'Sophy!'

It was Jack, standing at the top of the steps looking like an advert for smart men's dressing. Then he ran quickly down, took a couple of strides and kissed me, though I turned my head at the last minute so that it landed on my cheek rather than my lips. It was instinctive, but I felt ungrateful. It wasn't that long since any signs of affection from a dazzlingly handsome man, with no obvious defects or hang-ups, would have been received with loud cries of joy – and now here I was taking evasive action.

'There you are, Sophy – and how nice to see you and Seth getting so *close*,' he said lightly, but with an undercurrent of such unmistakable anger in his voice that it made me flush guiltily even though he'd misread the situation. 'I've been looking all over for you. What's so engrossing about a wall that made you forget *I* was coming?'

'I hadn't forgotten, Jack. You're early. And this isn't any

old wall – some of the stones have got quotations from Shakespeare carved on them, to add to the whole theme of the garden,' I explained enthusiastically. 'I've just officially laid the first one.'

'Isn't that an unnecessary expense?'

'Ma's paying,' Seth said briefly, looking up from sorting the next stones ready to hand to Derek, when he had finished fiddling with his plumb line.

'Oh? I didn't think Ottie was interested in gardens, any more than Sophy was.'

'I *love* the garden,' I protested, as Jack put a familiar and rather possessive arm around my waist and gave me a squeeze. 'I just love the house more, even though I know they complement each other.'

'Well, you can see them any time, but *I'm* only here for an hour, so come on, Sophy – I'm famished and it seems ages since I saw you.'

To my relief he dropped his arm, so we wouldn't have to make our way awkwardly back up the steps like conjoined twins, and instead took my hand.

In the Great Hall the fire burned brightly, casting a rosy glow onto the subtle, faded colours of the newly washed rag rug and gleaming off the polished wooden furniture.

Jonah was sitting on one of the settles in front of the fire, buffing up a pair of halberds, like small axe heads on very long shafts, with Renaissance wax. I'd found them and their wooden mount in the attic, and the battered stag was about to be banished up there instead. The kitten, a ball of fluff the colour of a gingernut biscuit (hence his name), was curled up on a cushion at his side and Charlie was stretched out on the rug. I hoped this meant he was getting used to the usurper at last. At the sound of our footsteps on the stone floor he lifted his head high enough to see Jack, then emitted an indignant bark or two of disapproval without bothering to get up.

'The place looks different,' Jack said, 'I noticed as soon as I came in. And it smells different too!'

'I think it just smells clean and well-aired rather than musty, that's what it is,' I shrugged. 'Come on, let's go and find that lunch, if you're hungry and in a hurry.'

We were eating lunch of minestrone soup, accompanied by garlic bread and the cheeseboard in the breakfast parlour, rather than the kitchen, in Jack's honour. Aunt Hebe was already there, ready to fall on her blue-eyed boy with all kinds of questions and anxious enquiries.

Aunt Hebe indignantly told Jack all about the newspaper article, but he thought no one would take any notice of such a little local rag. He was bright and cheerful, especially on the subject of his wonderful self, telling us about some major property killing he had just made.

But when I started telling him all about what *I'd* been doing at Winter's End, he just shook his head sadly. 'Cosmetic changes are all very well, Sophy, and you've worked wonders, but the place needs the sort of overhaul only money can buy.'

The inference was clear: he had the money and I had the enthusiasm, so that together we would make a beautiful partnership. Aunt Hebe beamed on us benevolently.

'Oh, I don't think there's much wrong with the house, Jack, and anything expensive will just have to wait until funds start to come in and the place pays its own way. And I'm sure that will be quite soon, once we get the visitor numbers rising steadily,' I said with more optimism than I felt, because it was all going to be a huge gamble. 'I'm going to open Winter's End four days a week, from Easter until the end of September.'

'Yes, and I will have much to do if my range of products is going to be ready to sell in the shop by then,' Hebe said.

He frowned. 'I thought we'd agreed that we would discuss our plans for Winter's End at Christmas? You know how I feel about opening it to the public, Sophy. I'd much rather just keep it as our family home and—'

His phone, which he had laid next to his plate on the table, buzzed like a dying fly with an incoming text and he snatched it up, though it didn't seem to be the message he wanted.

'Where was I?' he asked.

'Eating cheese,' I said diplomatically, passing him the board – my favourite one, with a china mouse attached to the cheese wire. 'Your phone's buzzing again.'

'It doesn't matter,' he said, and ignored it after that, even though it went off about every ten minutes.

When lunch was over he accepted, with every sign of delight, the completed snot-green knitted garment that an excited Hebe presented to him.

It wasn't just good manners – his acting was *superb*, which was quite an eye-opener and really made me think. I mean, he is caressing and affectionate and had given every appearance of falling in love with me – but frankly I am not *that* gorgeous; more of a penny plain than a tuppence coloured.

When Hebe, with monumental tact and immense self-sacrifice, reluctantly tore herself away on some pretext, leaving us to have coffee together, he gave me his wonderful smile and said persuasively, 'You really *won't* make any more plans to open Winter's End until we can discuss it properly at Christmas, will you, Sophy?'

'I think I've probably already made most of them, actually, Jack. And you exaggerated the problems with Winter's End, especially the deathwatch beetle, so I would sell it to you at a low price, didn't you?'

He actually laughed, as though he had done something clever. 'Of course I did, darling, though it really *could* do with a bucket of money poured into it. But you don't have to sell it to me if you don't want to, because I meant it when I said I wanted us to live here together, happy ever after – and I suspect you're a traditionalist, so we'll get married eventually, if only to keep Aunt Hebe sweet. So, what's mine will be yours and vice versa, won't it?'

I closed my eyes, but when I opened them again he was still there with that confident smile on his handsome face.

'But, Jack, that's *never* going to happen. I'm not going to sell Winter's End, enter into any kind of partnership, or sign it over to you – and I'm certainly not going to marry you! I've quickly grown very fond of you, but I'm not in love with you and I don't think I ever will be,' I said frankly. 'But I *am* growing to love you like a brother.'

He looked absolutely flabbergasted, but that may have been the unintentionally Victorian sentiment of my last sentence, which just slipped out. Or perhaps he'd never even seriously considered it was possible that I could, in the end, refuse him anything. How could I resist him?

Indeed, I thought, looking at him again – tall, athletically built, golden-haired, blue-eyed and reeking with charm and subtly expensive aftershave – how *had* I managed to fall for him and then un-fall, so quickly? I mean, what exactly was I *looking* for in a man?

He still couldn't take what I'd said seriously, but he was shaken a bit, I think, though he rallied. 'I've rushed you, that's what it is, and I think you're still jealous of Mel, even though it's Seth she's got her claws into, not me, as I keep telling you. She just flirts the way other people breathe.'

I wished she would stop doing both – but maybe that was a bit mean.

I told him that I was not at all jealous of Mel, which unfortunately seemed to encourage him to think I just needed a little more time and persuasion. I was glad when he and his buzzing phone departed, though this time he managed to plant a kiss full on my mouth before dashing off in his sports car.

After he'd gone I felt a bit restless and irritable, so I collected Charlie and went out into the crisp autumnal air, and we were just walking through the wilderness towards the rear drive when I heard a female voice, pitched rather high – Mel.

Charlie and I seemed to have an unerring nose for her assignations and, like last time, I scooped him up and clamped his muzzle shut before he could emit any of his wheezy little barks. His tail flapped – he would much rather be carried than walk, any day.

I supposed it would be Seth she was meeting, but instead of turning away I crept forward until I could see her big grey horse, tied to one of the posts of the stone shelter where the milk churns were once left.

She was standing in the little clearing behind it, talking to Jack. I could see the bright red paintwork of his car further on through the trees, pulled off the drive. Was this a fortuitous meeting, or had they arranged it?

'Did you have to keep texting me all through lunch, Mel? You knew where I was,' I heard him say testily.

'Just reminding you of my existence, in case other distractions made you forget me and our little business arrangements.'

'That's not very likely is it?' he said bitterly. 'And you shouldn't keep coming up here. It could make it awkward. I don't want Sophy to think there's something between us.'

'Why should she think that? There are other attractions at Winter's End, you know. Seth is always glad to see me, even if you're not.'

'Look, Mel,' Jack began angrily, 'I don't know—'

She stopped his words with a kiss, one that went on and

on, with her brown eyes wide open, looking in my direction. I don't know if she saw me or not.

Jack didn't seem to be putting up much resistance. But then, I expect few men would. Did it mean anything? It didn't really matter to me now, but it would, I was sure, to Seth . . .

Then Jack suddenly pushed her away and stood there glaring at her and breathing heavily, so maybe he, at least, wasn't entirely putty in her hands.

I backed away slowly until I couldn't see them any more, not bothering too much about the noise.

I circled the maze aimlessly for quite a while with Charlie, before going back to the house. There was no sign of Seth on the terrace, or in the kitchen, where Mrs Lark said she hadn't seen him that day, so I wondered if he too had slipped away to meet Mel. If so, she might be a little late . . .

But he knew what sort of woman she was; it was his own stupid fault if he had fallen for her all over again!

To Mrs Lark's delight I ate four chocolate brownies, then played with the kitten before finally going off to finish cleaning the Chinese bedroom.

At dinner Hebe remarked that she had seen Mel's horse tethered behind the lodge that afternoon, when she was looking for fungi in the dark trees that surrounded it. (No, don't ask what she wanted them for.)

'So you see, it *is* Seth that she comes to visit. Ottie was quite wrong about things. Jack and Mel are simply friends now.'

'I'm sure they are. She seems a *very* friendly type,' I agreed, and something in my voice made her give me a sharp look.

'You and Jack haven't fallen out, have you? I thought you were getting on really well at lunch.'

'We were, Aunt Hebe, and I love him like a brother, warts and all.'

'Jack hasn't got warts!' she said indignantly. 'There isn't a blemish on his body!'

'Just a turn of phrase. I can see he is perfection personified.'

I sat and sewed in the parlour that evening, as usual, but there was no sign of Seth. He probably had other fish to fry.

But I wasn't entirely alone, because apart from Charlie snoring on my feet, I once or twice looked up to glimpse Alys in the convex mirror on the opposite wall. It made her appear all nose – not a good look.

Chapter Twenty-four: Stunned

Mary Wynter hath told the officers that they were true churchgoers and would not harbour a priest, but that it was well known that I was tainted by witchcraft and would leave the house stealthily by night to attend blasphemous sabbats . . . Her face was filled with spite and I saw her true intentions written there. Yet I could not say the truth, for that would condemn mee equally – perhaps more so, and be greatly detrimental to the family and so also to my sweet babe.

From the journal of Alys Blezzard, 1582

'You're famous, our Sophy,' Jonah said, putting a national tabloid down in front of me at breakfast the following Tuesday, folded to reveal a grainy blow-up of the *Sticklepond Gazette* photograph and an embellished rehash of the article.

'Bloody hell!' I exclaimed. I mean, I hadn't thought my story exciting enough to make even the local paper, let alone be syndicated to a daily.

Aunt Hebe, her attention wrested away from the less sensational pages of *The Times*, said disapprovingly, 'Language!' Then she twitched the newspaper from my trembling hands and read it herself, her silvery eyebrows going up and down and her lips moving with silent outrage.

'This is beyond a joke!' she said at last. 'And half of it is not true anyway – sheer sensationalism! They are just trying to make a rags-to-riches story out of it.'

'But it *is* a rags-to-relative-riches story, I suppose, Aunt Hebe, and I don't think they've actually said anything blatantly untrue, just implied things.' I scanned the article again and noticed something I'd missed the first time under the subtitle 'BARONET BUMPED OUT OF INHERITANCE'.

'This quote from Jack wasn't in the last article – listen to this! "Jack Lewis, now Sir Jack, said today, 'Of course it was a shock, but Sophy and I have become very close and I couldn't be happier for her.' But he wouldn't be drawn about rumours of an engagement between them."'

'I'm sure Jack wouldn't talk to the press,' Aunt Hebe said positively. 'Though he might well put an announcement of your engagement in *The Times*.'

'There is no engagement, Aunt Hebe,' I said wearily, 'there never will be. It's simply a figment of the journalist's imagination.'

And maybe Jack's.

Mr Yatton commiserated with me over the article, though he said nothing could be done about it. But I was still so steaming with anger that I went down to the terraces to look for someone else to pick a fight with, preferably Seth, who could be almost guaranteed to give back as good as he got.

Derek and Hal were sorting out the next layer of stones for the retaining wall, which was rising with amazing speed, while Seth and Bob were removing what remained of the turf and digging over the ground.

It was a chilly, dank sort of day, perfumed with the scent of wet woodsmoke, but it must have been hot work because both men had stripped down to their T-shirts. Bob's was yellow with a smiley sun on it, but Seth's was the pink one I had occasionally glimpsed through the strata of holey

272

jumpers. Now I could see that it had 'Gardeners like to get down and dirty' printed across the front.

'Nice T-shirt,' I said, momentarily distracted.

'Present from Ma,' he said, stopping digging and leaning on his spade. Then he added shortly, with a glance at the newspaper in my hand, 'Congratulations on the engagement. When's the happy day?'

I supposed everyone within ten miles had seen the newspaper.

'Oh, don't be daft,' I said crisply. 'You know very well that there isn't going to be one. The journalist was just trying to add a bit of romance to a boring story. And I'm sure Jack never said anything to imply that we were going to get married.'

'Are you?'

'No, of course he wouldn't, or say all this other stuff about my sad life of drudgery. It makes me sound like a half-witted Mrs Mop,' I said, perhaps more positively than I felt. 'Do you think that's it now, and interest will die down?'

'I expect so, unless you do something newsworthy to keep it going – but we could turn the publicity to your advantage when we have the grand reopening of Winter's End,' he suggested. 'Angled to suit ourselves this time, of course.'

Somehow, when Seth used the royal 'we', it didn't annoy me half as much as when Jack did it. I supposed it was because I felt that, despite our battles, Seth and I were working towards the same end, while I had begun to have a sneaky feeling that Jack had an agenda of his own.

I turned Seth's suggestion over in my mind, though. 'You mean something like, "Heiress saves family home from disintegrating into dust. Hanging Gardens of Sticklepond the Eighth Wonder of the World"? Yes, I see what you mean.'

He grinned, and his sudden smiles are possibly the *ninth*

wonder of the world, because it was amazing how they took the forbidding aspect away from his rather formidable face.

I found I was smiling back and feeling better about things. 'And the hanging gardens are coming along well, aren't they? The front gates look almost finished too, Bob – well done.'

'Yes, we're getting there. It was fiddly work, but I spent all last weekend on them, so now there's only the gold highlights to put on.' Bob stopped digging and looked at me hopefully, fanning his hot, ruddy face with his hat so that the pink plastic tulip in the band nodded up and down. 'Would you like me to go and do it now?'

Seth's relatively benign expression swiftly switched to thundercloud mode, so I said hastily, 'No, there's too much dampness in the air. It's not a good day for painting.'

'I'll finish it off on Saturday as overtime then, shall I?'

'Yes, if the weather's right. Thanks, Bob.'

With all the extra expenses of things like overtime, I was going to need a sudden rush of money to the bank account fast. But Christie's would be putting my Herring painting up for auction before Christmas, and since Mr Yatton managed to find some provenance for it among the family papers, showing that it was commissioned by the baronet of that time to portray his favourite hunter, I hoped it would fetch a very good price. Even so, I needed to keep enough in reserve to repay the instalments on the bank loan until the gate money started to roll in.

There wasn't a single day when I didn't feel thankful for Mr Yatton: what on earth would I have done without him?

Seth hadn't called by the parlour since the day Jack came to lunch, and I'd missed the cut and thrust of our often lively discussions, so I was actually quite pleased when he turned up that evening, even though he seemed rather gloomy. I expect that was the Mel effect. I often glimpsed her horse or her distinctive low, silver car, near the lodge house. I could have banned her from the estate, of course – and don't think I wouldn't have loved to do it. But of course, it was impossible without a better reason than simply disliking her.

Seth tersely informed me that he was going away for a few days. 'I've got a commission to design a small knot garden for a manor house in Devon. I'll be off tomorrow.'

'That's a bit short notice! What about the wall and the lower terrace you were so determined to finish?'

'Derek's the expert where the wall is concerned, he'll be in charge until I get back.'

Derek seemed to be a very hard worker, so I didn't suppose the rebuilding would slow down much, even without Seth's eagle eye on it, but I felt unaccountably cross anyway.

'I haven't seen much of you lately and there are a few things we need to discuss.'

'I've been busy,' he said shortly.

I could imagine what, or maybe that should be *who*, with.

He spotted the huge vase of roses on a side table and, since they were a flagrantly passionate scarlet, it would be a bit hard to miss them, and said jokingly (I hoped), 'From your fiancé?'

'They *are* from Jack, and they must have cost a fortune. I wish I knew a tactful way of telling him that if he *must* send me something, I'd much rather have a rosebush.'

'But I suppose sending a bare-rooted bush wouldn't rank as quite the same flamboyantly romantic gesture?'

'I don't want romantic gestures,' I said curtly, which I didn't – or not from Jack, anyway. 'I'd much rather fill the gaps in the rose garden.'

Somehow it was odd without unexpected glimpses of Seth about the place; not to see him striding about in the distance, up a ladder clipping something, snatching lunch in the kitchen, or the top of his dark head on the terrace below . . .

And I had no one to argue with either except, occasionally, Lucy. She now seemed to have stopped wavering and decided to work right to the end of her contract anyway, even though I knew she was dying to come back and get to grips properly with the business side of Winter's End. She was so stubborn!

To my relief the man following her turned out to be a harmless computer nerd half her size, who simply wanted private English lessons. 'I told him I would, but only in a café near where I'm living – so no need to worry about it any more, Mum.'

But I *did* still worry – illogically, I suppose, since harm could come to her anywhere, including here . . . and I had a worrying awareness of some dark shadows coming, gathering on the edge of my consciousness again . . .

I hoped that whatever danger they foretold, it threatened me and not my child.

A couple of days after Seth left for Devon I took what had become my usual afternoon walk up to the summerhouse in the woods with Charlie, since it was one of those sad, dead-leaf-scented, end-of-autumn days when you want to consider life, the universe and everything. Up in my ramshackle eyrie was as good a place as anywhere.

I paused before going in, to see what was making Charlie lag behind. But of course, as soon as I turned he sat down on the path – never stand when you can sit is his motto. 'Come on, you wimp! I'm not picking you up, we're there,' I told him, and going up the steps strode into the shadowy interior.

As the wooden floor bounced under my feet, making the whole thing tremble like a stage set, I noticed a strange but

276

not entirely unfamiliar scent on the air. Then something caught sharply at my legs and the whole world caved in on me as I went flying headlong into dark oblivion.

I awoke in my bed at Winter's End, with a pounding head and a doctor asking me if I could see double. And for a minute I could – there seemed to be two Charlies, who had somehow got upstairs and onto the bed. Then my vision cleared and we were back to just one.

'Charlie is my darling,' I said idiotically, and he thumped his tail.

'She's delirious,' Aunt Hebe's voice said.

'No I'm not,' I assured her. 'I've got a headache though. What happened?' I frowned. 'Wasn't I up at the summerhouse in the woods?'

The doctor, who had been holding my wrist, let it go. 'I'm afraid you had a bit of an accident, Miss Winter. The building collapsed on top of you, and your head took a glancing blow. But it could have been much worse. It was a lucky escape.'

'I didn't think the building was in that poor a condition,' I said, trying in vain to remember what had happened, 'though Seth did warn me that he thought it was getting to the point of collapse. But I loved sitting up there. I wonder if he can repair it?'

'It's probably beyond it, but don't worry about that now,' Aunt Hebe said, laying a lavender-scented flannel on my forehead. 'You know, I do believe that you are going to have a black eye.'

'Great,' I said morosely. 'How did you find me?'

'The gardeners on the terrace heard Charlie barking and noticed that the summerhouse roof was at an odd angle, so they went to investigate and found you out cold. Charlie was sitting faithfully next to you in the rubble, still barking, and he has refused to leave your side ever since,' Aunt Hebe said. 'He is quite the hero of the hour!'

'Just as well for you,' the doctor said, packing things back into his bag again, 'or you could have been lying there in the cold for hours.'

'Well, dinnertime, at least,' I agreed. 'Everyone would have known it wasn't like me to miss a meal. Good dog, Charlie!'

'I'll leave you some painkillers for the headache, and I'd like you to stay in bed for a couple of days. If you have any other symptoms, including double vision, phone me immediately.' He must have seen my mutinous expression, because he added, 'If you don't stay in bed and rest, you won't recover as quickly. The bang on the head was nasty.'

So I had to stay in bed like an invalid, black eye and all.

Seth was still away, so I suppose he wouldn't hear a thing about it until he got back, but as soon as Jack got the news from Hebe he paid me a flying visit, bringing a little hamper of Fortnum and Mason goodies and a big box of Godiva chocolates, just as if my strength needed building up, which it certainly doesn't.

Mrs Lark was rather miffed about the foodstuffs, since she said there was nothing in there that she couldn't do better, though I felt that producing caviar from the virgin sturgeon might be a feat even beyond her capabilities. Mind you, I found it so weird that I gave most of it to Charlie, thinking the fishiness might do something for what brain cells he possessed.

But it was thoughtful of Jack, and he was so concerned, quiet and kind, that I let him hold my hand and waffle on about our future together in his lovely, mesmerising voice, which just about sent me to sleep.

This time I simply wasn't up to arguing, just glad *someone* seemed to care.

Chapter Twenty-five: Follies

I am imprisoned, though Sir Ralph has seen to it that I am housed separately, in a chamber near the gaoler's lodging. I am afraid – I fear the Wynters wish to be rid of mee, and are taking this opportunity of doing so. Yet punishments for such wrongdoings are seldom harsh – my mother's distant connections, the Nutters, have frequently been accused of witchcraft and escaped with little more than imprisonment or a ducking . . . but others they have hanged, it is true. I have written to my father, to beg his aid, for I have a very great fear of hanging . . .
From the journal of Alys Blezzard, 1582

As soon as I was allowed up and about, Mr Hobbs reminded me that I hadn't yet made a will – a suggestion that cheered me up no end, as you can imagine.

But actually, once the headache vanished I felt totally rejuvenated, so perhaps a couple of days' enforced rest did me good. I threw myself back into the cleaning, sorting, polishing and rearranging with renewed vigour.

Since Seth wasn't there to complain, I had Bob and Hal move the two glass-topped curio tables from the Long Room into the gallery, either side of a column sprouting yet another of those strange light fittings in the form of a naked arm holding an ice-cream cone.

I thought the odd collection of curios would interest the visitors, though I would have to identify and label some of the stranger ones. I was still up there writing a list, with descriptions and little drawings, when my mobile phone rang. For once I hadn't left it in my bedroom.

'Sophy?' a familiar, high-pitched voice said. 'This is Conor Darfield.'

'Hello, Conor!' I said, surprised that he had actually had the grace to phone me about his aunt, rather late in the day though it was. 'I had the solicitor's letter a few days ago and I can't tell you how sorry I was to hear of Lady Betty's death. It must—'

'Never mind that,' he interrupted rudely. 'That isn't why I called. It might interest you to know that I have been going through the will and checking the insurance inventory.'

'I bet you have.' That sounded much more like the Conor I knew and loathed.

He ignored my comment. 'I have been checking items off, and there are two pieces of my aunt's jewellery missing, one of them a brooch. In the form of a *bee*,' he added meaningfully, and my fingers unconsciously curled protectively around it.

'*Then* my attention was called to a picture of you in the tabloids – and what do I see?' He paused dramatically.

'Well, you didn't see a bee – and you're starting to sound like a Dr Seuss book,' I said shortly.

'Your coat is open in the photograph and I am positive that you are wearing—'

'Look, Conor,' I broke in, 'if I was wearing the crown jewels, you couldn't tell from that photograph. But if you *really* want to know, there's no secret about it: Lady Betty *gave* me her little crystal and enamel bee brooch, and I treasure it.'

'I knew it! But when? *When* did she give it to you?' he

demanded. 'There is no record of it, and I'm told she was wearing it the day she had her fall and went into hospital – and the necklace.'

'Of course she was, she always wore them – they were her favourites. But when I went to visit her in hospital, with Mrs Dukes, she suddenly decided to give them away and wouldn't be swayed.'

'Mrs Dukes? Who is Mrs Dukes?'

'The cook who worked for your aunt for thirty years, remember? You know, the one you fired recently?' I didn't mention that Lady Betty had given *her* the string of lapis lazuli beads. Neither item was of any great value, except to us for sentiment's sake; and in any case it was none of Conor's business.

'The cook was impertinent,' he said stiffly. 'So, are you alleging that my aunt gave you the jewellery while she was in hospital? In that case, it may interest you to learn that the receptionist at the nursing home is certain she saw Lady Betty wearing both items when she arrived there! She also noticed that *you* were wearing that very distinctive brooch on a later occasion, so perhaps you took them when you managed, despite my instructions, to get in to see her?'

'I'm not alleging anything,' I snapped. 'The receptionist is either vindictive or a fantasist, and it happened as I said. Lady Betty said she felt that it was time to hand the pieces on, and I was deeply touched.'

'So you say, but I intend to investigate the matter further so, if you wish to escape prosecution, I suggest you immediately return the missing items to me. My aunt was clearly in no fit state to give away her property and, in any case, could not do so because *I* had the power of attorney. Do you und—'

'Conor,' I said, cutting him off again in mid-diatribe, 'what I understand is that you are a greedy little windbag

281

and I wouldn't give you the time of day, let alone something of such huge sentimental value to myself! Good*bye*!'

I was trembling with anger, even though I was sure his accusations had been all hot air.

Afterwards I wondered if I should write and tell Mrs Dukes of Conor's threats? But then, it would only upset her and there was no way Conor could claim back either the brooch or the necklace. It was just pure greed that had led him to try.

Since I'd recovered from my accident (apart from the black eye, which was only just starting to fade), Charlie and I had been redirecting our walks down the drive, just as far as the lodge and then back through the parterres and the yew maze. This gentle amble suited both of us at the moment, though at some point I would have to go up and look at the sad remains of the summerhouse.

That afternoon, as we rounded the bend through the trees, I could see that the lights were on in the large windows at the back of the lodge where the building had been extended.

Seth was back.

It felt oddly right to have him home again, but I couldn't stand like a stalker among the dark trees indefinitely, so after a while I nudged Charlie off my feet and we turned back for home.

Winter's End had been a Mel-free zone since his departure. I wondered how long it would take her to learn he was back?

Someone must have told Seth about my accident, because he inspected the remains of the summerhouse very early next morning, and then after breakfast came to find me and insisted I go back up there with him.

'I haven't had the heart to look at it since the accident.'

'You'd better come now, if only to assess the damage. Nice black eye,' he added.

'Thanks. I'm getting to quite like the yellow and blue shades myself.'

I was panting by the time I got up there, partly because I found it hard to keep up with Seth's long, impatient strides, and partly because Charlie went on strike and I had to carry him most of the way.

What was left of the summerhouse looked even more desolate than I thought it would, for it was not only wrecked, but also slightly charred. 'What happened?' I asked, puzzled. 'Did lightning strike it?'

'No, I think someone tried to set fire to the place, only of course it's all too damp to catch at the moment. Do you remember how it came to fall on you?'

'Not really, only walking up here.' I looked sadly at the wreckage. 'You were quite right when you said it was getting unsafe, Seth. If I'd listened to you, it would still be standing.'

'It would probably have fallen down eventually, but I think it fell on you because it was booby-trapped. Hal thought he spotted a bit of broken twine tied to one of the doorposts, but by the time they had got you back to the house and he came back to look for it, it was gone.'

'He never mentioned that to me!'

'He wasn't sure about it, so he waited until I got back. And I think he was probably right. Look at this.'

He showed me one of the wooden posts that had held up the lintel, which had a groove cut into the soft, powdery wood halfway up. 'I'd say that had had something thin, like baler twine, tied round it and across the doorway to the other one. The two posts already moved when you walked on the boards between them, didn't they? So it wouldn't take much to bring them down.'

'You mean – someone did it on purpose? To hurt me?'

'I don't suppose whoever did it expected the building to collapse, just that you would have a nasty fall.'

'But who do you think could have done it?'

He stopped prowling around the debris and turned his green eyes on me. He looked angry, but that was probably because the summerhouse was now ruined beyond repair. 'Perhaps it was aimed at you personally? You're a creature of habit; you came up here most afternoons with Charlie.'

He turned away and contemplated the ruins again, adding gruffly, 'That lintel is heavy – it could have killed you.'

'Are you implying someone at *Winter's End* rigged it up?'

He shrugged. 'Not necessarily, but maybe someone with connections here – and perhaps a grudge. Though probably it was meant as a malicious trick, not a serious attempt to injure you.'

'Well, that's OK then,' I said drily. 'I can't imagine who would want to hurt me anyway, so you're probably wrong.'

'Can't you?' he said, looking searchingly at me.

'You aren't thinking it was *Jack*, are you?' I asked incredulously. 'I'm sure he wouldn't – and in any case, why should he?'

'No, I wasn't thinking of Jack. He's only ruthless in business – and I don't think he's quite that stupid either, because if anything happened to you, I suppose Winter's End would go straight to Lucy, wouldn't it?'

I nodded. 'According to Mr Hobbs, but he's drawing up a will for me anyway; says it makes things easier.'

'Of course, he might have thought that with Lucy being so young, it would be much easier to persuade her into selling the place,' he said thoughtfully

'He hasn't met Lucy yet,' I added fairly, 'so he wouldn't know she's far from a sweet, malleable young thing.'

'But as I said, violence is very much *not* Jack's thing.'

'Of course it isn't. He was so kind and concerned when he visited me after the accident.'

'Maybe you should tell the police? You could just have a quiet word with Mike.'

'No, I really don't want to do that,' I said quickly. 'I'm sure it must have been local youths larking around, not personal at all. We'll have to keep a closer eye on the grounds.'

'It's your property – and your head.'

I surveyed the wreckage with a sigh. 'It was very pretty . . . do you think we could rebuild it to the same design?'

'I expect so. There are photographs of it. But it will have to wait its turn. I'll get the boys up here later, though, and we'll salvage what we can of the original and stack it in one of the empty stables.'

We descended the woodland path, slippery with a mulch of slimy dead leaves, then crossed the bridge to the lower terrace. Bob and Hal suddenly started working with renewed energy, though Derek seemed capable of carrying steadily on at the same pace for ever, like an android.

'It's coming along really fast,' I said admiringly. 'Just as well, if it is going to be finished by Valentine's Day. You know, it occurred to me the other day that I don't even know where they sell the tickets from on open days! There's so much still to find out.'

'The ticket office is the lodge on the other side of the arch from mine,' said Seth. 'The side window has been turned into a stable door, so they open just the top of that. Do you want to see it? We could walk down and look now, if you like.'

'All right,' I agreed, though Charlie made it clear when we passed the house that he wanted to stay behind, and I had to detour and let him in. I came back out with chunks of warm ginger parkin, which we ate while cutting through the rose

285

garden. It looked a lot less bare now, even though the new bushes were just sitting in the wintry soil not doing much.

It was odd that I hadn't noticed the little stable door in the side of the lodge before, but then it was usually dark and shadowy under the archway.

'Believe it or not, a whole family lived in each lodge once, even though the buildings were tiny. Mine was extended out at the back when I moved in, but this side is still the basic model.'

Seth had a key to the door and flicked on a light switch, revealing a small square room with a flagged floor and a fireplace. A wooden counter top had been fixed to the wall at one side.

'There's the cash box – they need a float at the start of the day, so they have change, like at the tearoom. The tickets will be in the estate office, but you'll need to have new ones done anyway, if you are changing the prices. They have guidebooks here – and they can sell the garden leaflets too, if we get them done in time.'

'We will,' I said firmly, 'if not on Valentine's Day, then for the Easter opening. I think the maze and the Shakespeare Trail will rope them in in droves.'

'One of the Friends in the Great Hall checks the tickets again when they go in,' he said. 'The visitors can't get to the terraces any other way, because the paths at the side of the house are roped off. We can't entirely stop people sneaking in up the back drive, or over the wall, but we can stop them coming into the house unless they've paid.'

'What about the coach parties, do they all have tickets?'

'Yes, a special colour. They have to book in advance, because we can't fit more than one party into the house or tearoom at a time.'

'What puzzles me is how on earth the coaches get up the little lane into the car park,' I confessed.

'They don't. There's a bottom gate on to the main road and they park down there. It's just cars at the top. Hal and Bob take it in turns to check up on the car park, to see everything is OK.'

'I haven't noticed any facilities for disabled visitors.'

'I think Sir William said that since it's a private house, you don't have to have them, and in any case it would be almost impossible to adapt a house of this age. He allowed pushchairs and wheelchairs through the house, but not those enormous baby buggies or electric scooters. And of course they have to get up and down the steps at either end to get in and out.'

'Perhaps we can put wooden ramps at the front and back doors when we are open. And you know the golf buggy Grandfather used in his last months to get around the gardens, the one that's still in the stables?'

He nodded.

'It's a big one, so I thought someone could go up and down the drive on open days picking up and dropping off any visitors who have trouble walking.'

'Why do I have the feeling there goes another gardener?' he groaned.

'Oh, I don't know. I think one of the Friends might enjoy driving it. I'll discuss it with them at this Christmas party I'm supposed to be organising.'

He locked the ticket-office door behind us and then invited me into his side for a cup of coffee and, since I was desperately curious to see his home, I agreed.

We went straight into a comfortable small sitting room and through into a large, untidy, light and airy studio at the back. There was no evidence of Mel's presence here, not even a photograph or a lingering trace of the mingled fragrance of horse and Arpège that was particularly her own. But there were shelves and shelves of books, a workbench

287

and a drawing board with a half-completed diagram of a knot on it. There was also a leather sofa that I arranged myself on, trying to look as if I hadn't been nosily poking about, before Seth came back with the coffee.

While we drank the coffee he told me all about the knot he had been designing down in Devon and I told him about all the weird things in the curio cabinets that I hadn't yet identified. He was just promising to come and have a look at them, when we heard a vehicle pull up outside and the sound of voices, and went out to investigate.

There, with its nose under the arch, was a large, elderly ambulance, painted a fetching sky blue with fluffy clouds drifting up the sides. Facing it, planted firmly in the centre of the drive with his hand held up, was policeman Mike.

A woman was leaning out of the window, her long red dreadlocks swinging, and neither of them noticed us: she and Mike were too busy staring at each other.

Then suddenly Mike's face split into a great grin and she smiled back.

Beside me, Seth assumed an expression of resignation. 'Don't tell me,' he said, 'it's a friend of yours, isn't it?'

Anya had arrived.

Chapter Twenty-six: First Impressions

*I have received word from my father who says that he knew
I would come to a bad end and that he washes his hands
of mee. No one it seems will say anything in my defence
and several near Wynter's End have now come forward to
say I have cursed them ill . . . Mary Wynter will not let my
baby come to mee, but Joan is to bring mee any necessities.
My chamber is damp and dark and my cough worsens.*

From the journal of Alys Blezzard, 1582

'Oh, Anya, it's so good to see you!' I said, as I sat beside
her in the van. Looking in the wing mirror I could see the
two men standing on the drive gazing after us. Mike, looking
dazed, raised one hand and flapped it.

'I think Mike's waving at you.'

'Is that what he's called? He's not your run-of-the mill
fuzz, is he? And he's cheeky, too. When I stopped he said,
"Stand and deliver – your money or your life." I'm sure
that's not in the policeman's handbook.'

'He's from Liverpool, he can't help it,' I explained.
'Scousers are all like that. Did he say anything else?'

'Yes, he asked me if I had a ring on my finger as well as
through my nose. Then he said he didn't think he could
arrest me for anything just yet, but he would work on it,
and was I a friend of yours?'

'You certainly seemed to make an impression on him *and* on Seth too, though since I think he was half expecting a whole convoy of New-Age travellers to turn up, he wasn't as horrified as I expected.'

'Seth being the handsome gardener?'

'Oh, Seth's not really handsome, or not the way Jack is. He's stunning!'

'Attractive, then, if you want to nit-pick. He looked pretty good to me.'

'He *is* attractive when he's all glowing and enthusiastic about his knot gardens,' I conceded.

'And Mike's not bad either. In fact, you seem to be entirely surrounded by tasty men. Are there any more lurking in the undergrowth?'

'Wait until you see Jonah, he's the best of the bunch,' I promised her. 'Carry on left here at the front of the house. You can leave the van in the courtyard at the back and we'll bring the rest of your things in later.'

'Not if that's the house.' She had come almost to a stop and was staring at Winter's End aghast. 'I'd much, much rather stay in the van.'

'Don't be such an inverted snob! If *I* can live in Winter's End, my friends can too. It isn't that grand.'

'This from someone who lived in a two up, two down, tied cottage with an outside toilet – or even in a static caravan for a short while? No, thanks, and I'll hide the van out of the way somewhere. What's through that arch over the other side?'

'The pigsty and the rear drive. You can get back into the village that way.'

'The pigsty sounds much more my scene.'

She drove through and parked neatly behind the coach house, half-hidden by bushes, then gave me a little tissue-wrapped parcel. 'It's a sorry-you-got-banged-on-the-head present,' she explained. 'Though the black eye is a bit of a disappointment – it's practically gone.'

'It was a cracker while it lasted.' I eagerly unwrapped the paper to reveal a pair of earrings that she had made herself, from snipped tin and appliquéd chocolate bar wrappers.

'Oooh, wonderful! Let me put them on.' I admired myself in the rear-view mirror. 'You are clever! Come on, let's take your bags and I'll show you round the house. I'm sure you'll change your mind about not wanting to stay there. I've got the Chinese bedroom ready for you, and you'll love it.'

She looked doubtful, but I took her in by way of the kitchen and introduced her to the Larks first, before springing the rest of the house on her. She immediately endeared herself to them by playing with the kitten and eating four large, sugar-sifted warm doughnuts, one after the other, which was two more than even I could manage.

Mrs Lark admired my earrings. 'I don't think I've ever seen anything quite like them. Are those KitKat wrappers?'

'Yes – Anya made them. She makes jewellery from things people throw away, like tin cans and chocolate wrappers. Just like a Womble.'

'I'll make you a pair of earrings too, Mrs Lark,' promised Anya.

'I'm hoping to sell Anya's jewellery in our shop,' I said, getting up and wiping jam and sugar off my chin. 'Well, come on and I'll show you round the rest of the house.'

'You were right, Jonah *is* a dish,' she said when we were in the Great Hall with the heavy kitchen door shut behind us. 'It's the mutton-chop whiskers that do it for me.'

'If elderly men float your boat, I also have a vintage but *very* handsome estate manager – my steward, Mr Yatton. But he's only here weekday mornings and you might have to compete with Lucy when she gets home.'

'Has she said when she's coming back?'

'Not yet. I thought she was on the point of giving in her notice, but now she's gone back to saying she must see out her contract to the end.' I sighed. 'Well, never mind. Do you want to do the guided tour now?'

'Love it!' she said promptly.

Charlie had followed us out of the kitchen and now lay stretched out on the rag rug in front of the fire, instantly asleep. We left Anya's bags at the bottom of the stairs and I took her all over Winter's End, telling her my plans, until we ended up, ages later, in the dismal excuse for a tearoom.

'I haven't really started on this area yet, except for deciding what sort of basic stock we should have – you know, mementoes of Winter's End. I want it to be a craft shop and gallery as well as a tearoom. I've already got Aunt Hebe on my side about opening the house by offering to sell her lotions and potions in the shop.'

Anya looked around assessingly. 'You have two very good-sized rooms here, plus that little conservatory thing – you can probably seat as many as forty people.' She flung open a door, revealing an empty room with a channel down one side of the stone floor and some metal shelving. 'What's this?'

'I think it might have been the brewery once, and now they use it to store stuff in for the tearoom.'

'I'm sure there are lots of other storage rooms doing nothing, and you could fit this out as a proper shop.' She turned on her heel, and waved a hand at the rest of the place. 'I mean, hang paintings around the café, and have narrow shelves out there filled with things to sell, by all means, but have the till and most of the stock in here.'

'I see what you mean . . .' I said thoughtfully. 'But we'd have to have more lighting in here, and an electric socket or two.'

'I think it would be ideal. What were you thinking of

doing with the tearoom part, Sophy? It looks depressingly dreary at the moment.'

'Paint the walls a warm cream colour, for a start, and then have all the tables and drop-in chair seats covered in the same material . . . something lively.'

'A large gingham check would look good. You can get PVC tablecloth material in that too, which would save laundering,' Anya suggested. 'What kind of food do they serve?'

'Just cakes, scones, sandwiches, with tea or coffee. I suppose they have cold drinks too.'

'Well, that's all right if you don't want to provide full meals, though you could quite easily have hot soup and rolls and maybe salads? Plus, there's plenty of room for a freezer for lollies and ice cream, plus a tall chiller cabinet over there by the wall, so people could collect their cold drinks first and put them on their trays while queuing for food.'

'That sounds a lot more practical – and professional,' I agreed. 'But the teashop is manned by my volunteers, and I'm not too sure yet how they will take to change.'

'I've worked in both teashops and craft centres, don't forget,' she said. 'I could help you set it all up and get it running.'

'I did think of asking you, but would you actually *like* a permanent job? I know you said you'd like to settle down near Guy, but I wasn't sure if you were serious. And the salary wouldn't be very high, especially at first.'

'Yes, I'm serious, though I'm pretty sure I'd still want to travel in the van every winter for a month or two, and sell my jewellery at craft fairs. I don't need much money and I'll be selling my jewellery in the shop too, won't I? I could even set up a workshop area at the back and make it there when it is quiet, so people can watch me.'

I smiled at her ideas. 'Oh, Anya, it would be even more fun if you were here too!'

'Yes, I think it *would* be fun, with the bonus of being

able to see more of Guy – though not too much, because he won't want his mother popping in every five minutes.'

'How is he settling in?' I asked, because she had been to see him before coming here.

'Fine. He's renting a flat and enjoying his job, but he finished with his girlfriend just a couple of weeks ago, so he's a bit down about that. Maybe he'll find someone new where he's working – it's some sort of research lab, not much more than thirty miles from here. It's odd how conveniently things have worked out.'

'I wish Lucy were only thirty miles away too, and maybe I wouldn't worry quite so much.'

'Lucy's the most sensible, capable, kick-ass girl I've ever met in my life, so don't worry, Sophy.'

'I can't help it. Mr Yatton hatched a cunning plan to lure her back home again by getting her involved in running the estate. He emails her all the time with figures and spreadsheets and stuff, but although she's fascinated, it hasn't worked yet.'

'It probably will with a bit more time, because she loves number-crunching and paperwork, doesn't she? And she's a born manager.'

'She's a bossy-boots,' I agreed.

'Well, just don't let her rule your life again when she does get back. Guy sends both of you his love, by the way.'

'I'll tell her. She keeps asking after him.' I had a sudden idea. 'Look, why don't you and Guy come here for Christmas? It would be lovely to have you, and we could make a start on sorting the shop and café out then, too.'

'Sounds good.'

It was getting late, so I persuaded her into taking her bags up to the newly cleaned and polished Chinese bedroom, which Grace had made ready for her. 'The bathroom's across the hall. When you hear the gong, dinner's ready.'

'You'll come and get me before you go down, won't you?' she asked nervously. 'Your great-aunt sounds scary!'

'She isn't . . . really. But we'll go down together and it will just be the three of us tonight. My other aunt is in Cornwall and Jack's not likely to drop in.'

'Pity,' she said, 'I'd like to have a look at *him*.'

'He's not your type, Anya.'

'I don't think he sounds like *anyone's* type. He's probably in love with his own reflection,' she said unkindly.

Once Aunt Hebe had got over the surprise of Anya's large nose ring and red dreadlocks they got on surprisingly well.

When I told her that Anya was to reorganise the shop and tearoom she informed her that her range of rose-based products *must* have the best position.

'Of course,' Anya said tactfully. 'I'm sure they'll be our best-sellers.'

She admired the central table display of paper napkins, which tonight featured both roses as well as the flotilla of paper swans, which seemed to be appearing as a centrepiece to every meal now.

'Nice swans,' she said, picking one up to examine it closer.

Aunt Hebe gave a sniff and, shaking out her linen napkin, spread it across her lap.

'Jonah makes them. He's learning how to do it at evening class. The paper ones are just for decoration but he does it with the linen ones too, sometimes.'

'I'll make you a special one, if you like them,' Jonah promised, overhearing from the side table where he was clattering dishes. She thanked him and said she, in turn, would show him how to make a decent duck later.

Speaking of which, we had savoury ducks for dinner, a delicacy I had forgotten about while up in the frozen far north, and which had absolutely nothing to do with ducks

295

or, in fact, any kind of fowl. In some areas they were called faggots, which was just as puzzling.

I'm not sure Anya had ever even seen a savoury duck before, but after staring at it suspiciously for a moment, she ate it, along with the accompanying onion gravy, colcannon and caramelised carrots.

'It's Guy Fawkes night tomorrow, Aunt Hebe, and we're going over to the bonfire at Middlemoss. Seth says he'll drive us in the estate car – would you like to come?'

'Oh, no, thank you, dear. It's the omnibus of *Cotton Common* tomorrow on the TV and I want to catch up, but you go and have a nice time. What a pity poor Jack is so busy just now. He would have gone with you.'

'Yes, he does seem to be frantically trying to close deals on several properties at once, doesn't he?' I said. 'And all before the New Year, for some reason.'

'I hope he isn't overstretching himself,' Aunt Hebe said worriedly. 'I know he still hasn't got planning permission to knock down that house of Melinda's yet, to sell the land for building. Apparently it's a Kinkerhoogen.'

'Kinkerhoogen?'

'He was an architect in the sixties and this is one of the few houses he designed over here. Although it is very ugly, Jack says they might try and put a preservation order on it, so I hope he doesn't do anything hasty.'

'I'm sure he won't,' I said soothingly, though I had no idea what she meant. I mean, what *could* he do – kneecap the council until they gave him planning permission?

We had coffee after dinner in the drawing room as usual, and then Aunt Hebe flitted off to flog potions to the desperate.

Anya and I then walked down to the Green Man, where she beat a clearly smitten Mike at dominoes, whilst I told

Seth all about our plans and that Anya would soon be a permanent fixture about the place. I thought he took it remarkably well.

Walking back through the crisp, cold darkness, I teased Anya about Mike and she retaliated by saying she thought Seth and I made a perfect couple.

'Perfectly mismatched,' I said, astounded. 'Are you quite mad? He's the exact opposite of my kind of man, and we're always arguing. In any case, I'm sure he's still having a torrid affair with this Mel Christopher I told you about, and she's absolutely gorgeous.'

'She sounds more like a match for the equally beautiful Jack, then,' she pointed out.

'Yes . . . and sometimes I've wondered which of them she really wants. Maybe it's both. She's certainly *had* both. But no . . . really, I'm sure Seth is her main target. Not that it matters to me, of course,' I added quickly.

'Of course not,' Anya agreed, 'or not now you've come to your senses about Jack, anyway.'

'You just wait until you see him, at Christmas! You'll fall for him and poor Mike will never get a look-in again.'

'Not me. My guardian angel has warned me about him already.'

'Did she say anything about tall, dark policemen?'

'Mind your own business,' she said with a grin.

Chapter Twenty-seven: Infernal Knots

Joan brought mee a lock of my baby's hair – but also some-thing of my mother's brewing that she entrusted to her, saying that one day I would be in dire straits and need it. I think she foresaw this moment, for now they talk of putting mee to trial, which I may not be able to bear. I have given her my keepsake and must soon give her this book, for though I conceal it, yet its discovery would go ill for mee.
From the journal of Alys Blezzard, 1582

Next morning we were turning out the cupboard that was once the escape route from the priest's hole, when Jonah appeared, bearing the tray holding the remains of Mr Yatton's breakfast.

'There you are then, Sophy. There's a call from a man who says he's your husband. Mr Yatton told him you hadn't got one, but he's pretty insistent, so he says, do you want it putting through, or will he get rid of him?'

'Must be some crank who's spotted that stupid news-paper article,' I said, carefully putting a Sèvres teacup down on the seventies marbled Formica hostess trolley, which we were using to transfer what was left of the delicate china to the kitchens for washing.

'Mr Yatton says he's got a slight Scottish accent,' Jonah said helpfully. 'Name of Lang.'

Startled, Anya and I stared at each other.

'OK, Jonah, tell Mr Yatton to switch it through to the parlour,' I said, feeling as if someone had punched me in the solar plexus, and he went back off down the corridor, rattling crockery.

'Come on, Anya – whoever it is, ex-husband or some crank, I may need moral support. But it *can't* be Rory, can it?'

As I nervously picked up the phone Mr Yatton said, 'Putting it through.' Then there was a click as he replaced the receiver at the other end.

Into the slightly crackling silence a ghost from the past, in the form of a rather posh voice with the faintest hint of a Scottish lilt, demanded, 'Sophy, is that you? Sophy, are you there?'

'*Rory?*'

'It *is* Rory?' Anya whispered, her eyes wide. 'Are you sure?'

I nodded, my heart racing. It might have been over twenty years since I last heard it, but it's hard to forget your only husband's voice. For a brief moment I was transported back to feeling like the naïve young girl, desperate for a home and family of her own, who had been agonisingly in love with a handsome, charming older man . . .

'Sophy, *darling,*' he said, his voice going all furry and warm, 'I've found you at last! I can hardly believe it!'

He couldn't believe it? My heart stopped pounding and the power of speech returned with a rush.

'What on earth do you mean, Rory Lang, you've *found* me at last? You could have done that any time you wanted to these last twenty-two years. Where the hell have you been?'

'I had a bit of a breakdown—'

'So did our marriage!' I snapped.

'I couldn't help it,' he said in an aggrieved tone. 'I was actually quite ill – hardly knew what I was doing. And

299

afterwards I went abroad. I've been running a diving school in the Caribbean, but please believe me when I say that every time I came home, I searched for you.'

'Lying bastard!' muttered Anya, who now had her dreadlocked head pressed to the other side of the phone and was scowling horribly.

'You can't have searched very hard, because your cousin at the castle would have told you where I was. I wrote to her after Lucy was born.'

'Lucy?' he echoed.

'You haven't forgotten I was expecting a baby when you did a runner?'

'Of course not, I just didn't know that you'd had a girl or what you'd called her – and my cousin never told me she knew where you were. And I truly *did* search for you every time I came back, but with no success at all until I happened to see your picture in the paper recently.'

Anya, who had known him during our whirlwind courtship and the few brief weeks of our married life afterwards, couldn't contain herself any longer and snatched the phone from my hand.

'You lying louse! You abandoned Sophy and the baby totally, and *never* tried to find them until now. If you'd really wanted to, you know very well that all you had to do was go to the commune and my mother would have told you where she was. You're only getting in touch now because you think there's something in it for you.'

'Who is that?' he demanded sharply. 'Put Sophy back on the line.'

'It's Anya. Remember me? I remember *you* all right.'

I removed the phone from her grasp. 'Look, Rory, Anya's right, you could have found me and Lucy any time you wanted to. I don't know why you've decided to contact me now, but we're divorced, nothing to do with each other.'

'*I* never agreed to a divorce.'

'You weren't there to ask, were you? And you didn't have to agree, because I divorced you for desertion. So we've nothing to say to each other and—'

'My daughter! I have a right to see my daughter,' he said hastily.

'Then you'll have to travel a long way. She's in Japan,' I snapped, and put the phone down, my legs going trembly. His voice had all the persuasive charm I remembered – much like Jack's, which made me think that maybe Anya was right and I have a history of falling for smooth-tongued snakes ... though actually, Jack hadn't done anything *terribly* dreadful other than try to trick me into selling Winter's End at a reduced price.

I dialled Mr Yatton. 'That *was* my ex-husband, but if he phones again, I'm not home.'

'Very well,' he agreed, obviously bursting with curiosity but too well-mannered to say anything. But neither Anya nor I thought that Rory would phone again now that he had opportunistically dipped his toe in the water and found it too hot for comfort.

By the time we'd talked it out and then spent another hour or two finishing cleaning the cupboard, and carefully washing and drying the remains of several very pretty old dinner services, I was quite calm again.

We both had to go and shower off the filth afterwards – it's a wonder I haven't washed myself away since I came here. But then, I suppose if it weren't for all the activity, the good food would have made me the size of a hippo by now.

I did mention salads to Mrs Lark once, but she pointed out that they were not in season, in a very final way, so I expect they will make their appearance in spring when it is too late to save my figure.

* * *

After dinner Seth drove me, Anya and (not altogether to my surprise) Mike over to the village of Middlemoss, where they always have a large bonfire, though they have the strange tradition of burning Oliver Cromwell instead of Guy Fawkes.

In fact, from what Seth was telling us on the way over, they have their own rather odd way of doing *everything* in Middlemoss, including performing a weird-sounding mystery play every New Year.

There would be a charity snack stall and, as our contribution, Mrs Lark had made two trays of black treacle toffee, which Jonah smashed to bits with a little metal hammer and put in greaseproof paper cones, though we all sneakily ate some of it on the way over. I suspect we had black teeth afterwards, but luckily it was too dark to tell.

When we got there we handed over what was left of it and then all got hot punch or coffee and roast chestnuts. Anya and Mike wandered off together after a while but, knowing no one else, I stuck to Seth's side.

He seemed to know lots of people there, especially women ... or maybe they were just smiling at him because he looked devilishly impressive in the firelight, all tall, dark and brooding? But he had competition – there was another tall, dark man there who was pretty tasty too.

He knew Seth and came over to speak to us, and it turned out he was Nick Pharamond, one of the family from the local big house. He told Seth that his wife hadn't come because she had gone right off fireworks after a nasty incident.

A few minutes later I knew just how she felt, because a particularly loud bang seemed to set off a sort of chain reaction in my head and I grabbed Seth's arm excitedly. 'I've just remembered something about the day I had the accident. As I went into the summerhouse I could smell perfume and—'

I stopped dead, because there was only one woman I knew who wore that particular combination of hot horse and Arpège.

Seth was looking down at me, frowning. 'Are you sure?'

'Yes . . . or at least, I think I am. But perhaps I imagined it, and it doesn't get us any further anyway, does it?' I said hastily. 'Forget it!'

I found I was still holding on to his arm and he'd put one of his large hands over mine in a very comforting sort of way. 'If I knew who did it . . .' he began menacingly, but the rest was perhaps fortunately drowned out by a series of loud flashes and bangs.

'I think that was the grand finale,' Anya said, appearing out of the darkness with her knitted hat jammed down right over her dreadlocks and her coat collar turned up, Mike right behind her. 'We're a bit sticky because we've been eating candyfloss – that's not something you usually get at bonfire parties, is it?'

'It is in Middlemoss,' Seth said, and then suggested we all call in at the Green Man on the way home. He entirely forgot to let go of my hand until we got back to the car, but I expect his mind was on something else, like one of his infernal knots.

It occurred to me suddenly, right out of the blue, that I'd had more fun since I got to Winter's End than I had done in the last twenty years, precious moments with Lucy excepted.

We were late getting back to Winter's End. The fire in the Great Hall was banked down, with the guard in front of it, Charlie was snoozing in his basket in the kitchen and Aunt Hebe and the Larks long gone to bed.

I'd left my phone behind again and missed three calls from Jack. I hoped he'd given up for the evening, but no, he called again just as I was climbing into bed, which was really annoying because I'd plugged the mobile into the charger on the other side of the room.

'Sophy? Where've you been?' he demanded.

'Out celebrating Bonfire Night. My friend Anya's staying here for a couple of days and we drove over to Middlemoss with Seth and Mike – do you know Mike? He's the local bobby.'

'No,' he said shortly.

'We had a great time. But funnily enough, it seemed to kick-start my memory, and I remembered something I'd noticed, just before my accident in the summerhouse.'

'Oh? Well, it wasn't *me* lurking about in the undergrowth, darling.'

'I know that, it was nothing to do with you – unless you've started wearing Arpège perfume, that is?'

He sighed. 'Mel? Actually, I suspected as much, though I'm sure she didn't mean you any real harm.'

'But why would she want to hurt me at all?' I asked, trying to imagine the elegant Mel being that vindictive . . . which actually wasn't hard.

'Because she's jealous of you, of course.'

'Jealous of *me*?'

'Yes, because of Seth. She's crazy about him, and not only did she find him in a clinch with you in the Great Hall that time, he also seems to be spending more and more time with you. Like tonight, for instance,' he added smoothly.

'Me and two other people! And Seth's not interested in me that way, so she has no reason to feel jealous.'

'Perhaps if you weren't seen out and about with him so much . . . ?' he suggested.

'He's my head gardener – of course I'm going to be seen with him! *And* he's family. But the point is, she could have killed me, and she might have hurt Charlie too. It was sheer luck he was OK!'

'I'm sure she didn't mean anything except to give you a warning scare,' he said easily. 'She thinks you're invading her territory.'

'Oh, yes? And this would be the woman I saw snogging you in the shrubbery when you came here for lunch recently?'

There was a small pause. 'Oh, come on, darling, that was nothing! Mel still likes to think she could get me back if she wanted to, though I've made it clear that I'm only interested in you. That's annoyed her, but not half as much as thinking you're moving in on Seth too.'

'Well, I'm not,' I said shortly.

'I'm glad to hear that,' he said softly. 'It seems ages since I saw you, but I'll be down for Christmas, of course, and I'm looking forward to spending lots of time with you then – *and* afterwards, because I have an invitation to pass on to you.'

'An invitation? For me?'

'Yes, I always go out to Barbados to stay with friends the day after Boxing Day, and when I told them about you, they said they would love to have you too.'

'What, *me*? The Caribbean?' I exclaimed, all tiredness suddenly dispelled by thoughts of coral beaches and palm trees.

'Yes, you!' He sounded amused. 'I assume you've got a passport?'

'Well, yes, I won a weekend in Paris a few years ago. But—'

'We'll have a great time, Sophy, and really have a chance to get to know one another – three weeks in paradise. They have a lovely house with a pool, and we'll go snorkelling and water ski. And they throw wonderful parties – everyone comes, you'll love it. It'll be romantic, too . . . imagine you and me in the evenings, walking along a coral beach.'

'But, Jack, I can't possibly go away after Christmas,' I said blankly, 'there's too much to do organising everything in time for the Valentine's Day opening, for a start!'

'Oh, come on, Sophy, it'll be much more fun than playing Lady of the Manor! It's time you scrapped these mad ideas and let me take care of all your worries. I promise you, you'll feel totally differently by the time we get back from Barbados.'

'I'm not the one with mad ideas, *you* are!' I snapped, now wide-awake but exhausted enough after an eventful day to be ratty. 'I won't feel differently because I'm not going to Barbados – I'm enjoying planning everything here at Winter's End and there's loads to do.'

'Check your passport is still current, darling,' he said, blithely ignoring most of what I'd just said, 'because I'm very sure I can change your mind over Christmas!'

I said something so rude that Aunt Hebe would have been scrubbing my mouth out with disinfectant, but it was too late – he'd gone. I had to content myself with waking Anya up and pouring what he'd said, word for word, into her reluctant ears.

I was *so* going to miss her when she left next day – and I was already missing Alys, who hadn't seemed to have been around lately. Perhaps she'd return when I was alone?

Heading back down the dimly lit corridor to my bedroom, I whispered experimentally: 'And where was my guardian angel when the summerhouse fell on me, Alys?' but there was no reply, not even a chill breeze round the extremities.

306

Chapter Twenty-eight: Vixens

*Sir Ralph came to mee and said his conscience was sore
troubled, as well it might be, but begged mee not to tell
the truth in the matter of his hiding the priest, since it
would bring disaster upon the house. I told him I would
not, for my child's sake, but nor would I admit to practising the dark arts for the same reason. Then I began
to cough and could not stop, to his alarm, for I have the
same malady that affected my husband and the days of
my life would soon run through my fingers like sand
even were I not imprisoned here.*

From the journal of Alys Blezzard, 1582

I awoke one morning to find a fluffy white blanket over
the landscape, and after breakfast I went out to the top
terrace to admire my very own winter wonderland.

Below, with his broad back to me, stood Seth, brooding
over the fact that he would get no work on the terrace done
that day.

It was just too much to resist . . .

My first snowball landed with a *flump!* right between his
shoulder blades and the second skimmed the top of his dark
head. Then I dodged down behind the balustrade, but too
late – he'd seen me.

'Come out, Sophy! I know it's you,' he called up.

I should have had better sense than to stand up, because I was instantly almost knocked off my feet by his return shot. Snow got in my hood and melted, trickling icily down my back.

He was grinned triumphantly.

'I'll get you for that, Seth Greenwood!' I yelled, and for the next few minutes we pelted each other, though since I was higher up I think I had the advantage . . . though maybe he was the better shot.

Anyway, honours were about even by the time Aunt Hebe popped her head out of the door and demanded to know what on earth I was doing.

'Nothing,' I replied innocently, just as a parting shot from below almost propelled me into her arms.

I just hoped Seth was as cold and wet as I was.

'Your voice sounds odd,' Anya said, ringing me from somewhere near Coventry, where she was doing a Christmas craft fair. 'Where are you?'

'I *was* inside a packing crate,' I said, picking bits of straw and polystyrene beads out of my hair. 'Lady Betty's legacy has arrived, and it's rather large, to say the least.'

'What's she left you?'

'It looks like a stone statue of a hippopotamus.' I glanced at the head, which was the only bit unwrapped, and it looked back in a fairly amiable way. 'There were at least two Egyptian gods who sometimes appeared in that form, but if it looks pregnant when I've unpacked it, then it's Tawaret. I don't know if it's really old or not. It looks pretty authentic, but a lot of her collection was fake. She had no eye for antiquities at all.'

'Have you decided where you're going to put it?'

'Yes, there's an empty alcove in the Long Room and I've already moved two ushabti from the parlour up there, so

I can have an Egyptian antiquities corner. It's so big that it's going to take all the gardeners, including Seth, to carry it upstairs. But it shouldn't take long, so I don't think he'll mind *very* much.'

'Oh, the Gorgeous Gardener might protest a lot, but I suspect he's really putty in your hands, Sophy.'

'Don't be daft,' I said, amazed. 'I have to fight him over every little thing. He might be putty in *someone's* hands, but they're certainly not mine. Are you doing well at the craft fairs?'

'Fine. I'm hoping to be sold out by Christmas. How are things your end?'

'We've had a cold snap and it snowed. The garden looks so magical that Mr Yatton's taken lots of photographs and we're going to use one or two for postcards. He and Lucy are currently sourcing stock for the shop on the internet – you know, the sort of place who will print what we want on everything. When I told Lucy you and Guy were going to be here for Christmas I could tell she was dying to come home – but no, she has to be Little Miss Honourable and stick it out to the end of her contract.'

'That's Lucy for you,' Anya commiserated, 'though it would have been lovely to see her again, of course. Have you had time to do any more to the shop and tearoom?'

'Yes, Grace helped me to clean the place out and I've bought the material for the curtains and chair cushions – bright red gingham in a big check – which someone in the village is going to make up. Mr Yatton found me a supplier of a matching PVC table covering by the metre on the internet, but we can cut that to fit the tables ourselves. I'll get the electrician in to install a couple more electric sockets and better lighting later, when the Herring painting is sold and I've got a bit of money. I simply daren't do anything expensive at the moment.'

'Well, that's a start,' she agreed. 'You've been pretty busy!'

'I don't think I'm going to do much more to it before the New Year, except hijack Bob and Hal to paint the rooms when Seth isn't looking – not that there's a huge amount to do in a garden at this time of year anyway. But I need to keep him sweet because he's designing the new garden guide and helping me put the last touches to the guidebook. They're almost ready to go to press.'

'He's worth his weight in visitor tickets, that man. You need to hang on to him,' Anya said. 'And you're not even paying him anything!'

'Actually, I'd arrived at much the same conclusion myself,' I confessed, 'though if he comes with Mel permanently attached, the price of having him around might be too high.'

'Perhaps he's got over her now, like a fever?' she suggested optimistically. 'I mean, you said you'd never seen them out together?'

'No, but I see her car, or her horse, near the lodge and in the grounds often enough. She haunts the place when he's here.'

'Maybe, but could you see her living in the lodge, a gardener's wife?'

'No . . . actually, I couldn't.'

'Or Seth wanting to live anywhere except Winter's End?'

'Not really, but it would depend how mad about her he was, wouldn't it? He might be prepared to make the ultimate sacrifice, but we will just have to wait and see.'

'Mike's been keeping in touch,' Anya said casually. 'He phones me for a chat every now and then. His parents originally came from Antigua in the Caribbean and he's hoping to go there on holiday next year. It sounds like paradise!'

Although she deserved to be teased after her comments about Seth, I nobly restrained myself. Mike is very nice, and if something comes of their obvious attraction to each other, it will be another anchor to keep her living near me, which would be lovely.

In fact, everything seemed to be coming together in a very fortuitous way, like a preordained pattern, even if Jack did so far seem incapable of understanding that I was no longer even remotely romantically interested in him.

It's a pity I was all over him like a rash that time he kissed me, or he might have been easier to convince.

But luckily he was still too preoccupied with business to do more than drop by occasionally, and even his late-night phone calls had a rushed air, as if he was always about to dash off and clinch another deal.

Perhaps, if he ever was really attracted to me, I was losing my charm.

It took all four gardeners to get the heavy statue upstairs, with Jonah supervising the operation, though luckily that didn't impede them much.

'What did you say it was?' Seth asked, panting, when it was finally manoeuvred into place.

'It's an Egyptian goddess, Tawaret – she's often depicted as a pregnant hippo standing upright. But maybe it's just fat, in which case it could be *you*.'

'*Me?*' He looked at me as if I had run mad. 'You think I look like a hippo? And I'm *not* fat,' he added with wounded male pride, casting a glance down at his torso, as if he feared his six-pack had suddenly turned into a beer barrel.

'I never said you were, and you don't look anything like a hippo. But the evil brother of Osiris was called Seth or Set, so this could have been your namesake.'

He patted Tawaret on the head. 'I think this one is female, all right.'

'Careful – she's a bit of a fertility symbol,' I warned.

'I think I'm unlikely to get pregnant, Sophy,' he said mildly.

Bob and Hal were grinning and nudging each other until he said, 'Come on, we've wasted enough time – back to work. There's plenty to do.'

'Mrs Lark's been making Chelsea buns this morning; they should be out of the oven by now,' Jonah hinted.

'Go out by way of the kitchen and ask for some to take with you,' I said hastily, seeing Seth's face darkening.

In his own way, he is as driven as Jack. Or me, come to that. I'm pretty single-minded in my determination to make the house beautiful again and paying its way.

Ottie returned from Cornwall via London, where according to Seth she was arranging for a major retrospective exhibition next year and catching up with her friends.

She was preceded a couple of days earlier by a van bearing the unfinished model for *The Spirit of the Garden* sculpture she is making for Winter's End, wrapped in damp sacking.

It was good to have her back again, though once she had admired the changes I had made to the house and seen the progress of the Shakespeare garden, she retired to her studio to work on the sculpture. I could see her at all hours of the day and night when I was passing through the courtyard, working away in one of her oversized, checked lumberjack shirts.

I think I am starting to feel much as Grandfather did about having all the family around me, and though some of them are more annoying than others, I have grown to love them anyway.

Another strand in the fabric of Winter's End was strengthened when the cleaned painting of Alys came back, too. It wasn't a good painting – in fact, it was a very bad one – but without the dark coating of dirt and old varnish I could see that the artist had managed to catch something

312

sad and secretive about her eyes – though I would love to know what Alys thought of the pursed rosebud lips, which she had never possessed, and the simper. But apart from that bit of artistic licence, it was a fairly faithful, if uninspired, catalogue of her features. Dark curls lay on the young girl's long white neck, and her neat nose had the hint of a tilt at the end, just like mine. For the first time I could see that I looked very like her – or how she would have looked, had she lived to my age. After being for so long the atypical dark Winter, I suddenly felt a renewed sense of belonging. Alys's blood ran in my veins and the two opposing strains of Blezzard and Winter were forever united there.

Maybe *I* should wear a pentacle and a cross, like Aunt Hebe, to symbolise this strange union?

One afternoon in December I was sitting contentedly on the bottom step of the flight of stairs down to the lower terrace, watching Derek and Hal lay a herringbone path in Tudor bricks along the new border in front of the rebuilt wall. The weather had taken a slightly milder turn, but it was still chilly. The freshly dug beds were dotted with pots of shrubs ready to plant out and larger, container-grown trees stood about as if simply dropped from the skies. But I knew there was method in this seeming randomness, because I'd seen Seth's planting scheme.

He'd already marked out the central knot before I got there and was now measuring and laying out the designs for two smaller ones at either end, using some kind of red spray. From where I was sitting it looked a bit like a stencilled, boxy Christmas cracker.

When he'd finished Seth came and sat on the step next to me. 'You'll get piles, sitting on cold stone,' he said mildly.

'That's an old wives' tale, like the one that says eating

313

too much sugar gives you worms. Yuk! Anyway, *you're* doing it too.'

We sat there in amicable silence for a moment or two, contemplating the terrace. 'It's odd how suddenly it's all starting to come together,' I mused. 'Now I can imagine what it will be like once it has all settled and grown a bit – but I suppose you could see that in your head right from the start?'

'Yes, though it's changed a bit as we go along. Using that pile of weathered old bricks from behind the pigsties for the path will give it a settled look instantly and then when we put the gravel down, the pattern of the knots will be more defined until the edging shrubs grow together.'

'Didn't you tell me they used several different colours of gravel in the late sixteenth century?'

'Yes, but I'm sticking to one throughout here, because we've already got the contrast between the bricks and the wall, and it all has to blend together. We'll plant up the compartments inside the knots later with flowering plants popular at the time.'

Now I was starting to see it coming to life and colour too. 'Where are you putting the big topiary trees?'

'The pyramid yews are for either end of the terrace and the holly balls for the corners of the central knot. I've got a large spiral for the middle that I've been nurturing for years – but then, topiary takes time. It's the wrong time of year to do all this, but to be ready by next year, we have to push on when we can.'

'It should look pretty good by Valentine's Day, and absolutely *amazing* by the time we open for the season at Easter,' I said optimistically.

'The major work will certainly be finished by February, so when Derek takes over as head gardener he should be able to keep the place up with just Hal and Bob's help.'

Startled, I turned to look at him, but he was gazing off across the valley. 'Why, where are *you* going?'

'Well, you won't want me once it's finished, will you?' he said diffidently. 'I know you're just letting me stay on to complete the scheme.'

I stared at him, astonished – until I remembered that that was pretty much what I *had* thought at first . . . It seemed a long time ago. 'But Seth, I don't want you to leave!' I exclaimed. 'You're family, for one thing, and you *belong* here.'

'I'm only family by marriage, not related at all, really.'

'You *feel* like family.'

'Do I?' He gave me one of his more unfathomable looks.

'Yes, and you have a stake in the garden too. You know you love it.'

'Yes, of course, but—'

'Look, Seth, do you *want* to go?'

'Well, no . . . but—'

'If it suits you to stay here as before, then that's fine by me. I *really* don't want to lose you.' I found I was gripping his arm as if I could hold him at Winter's End by force, and snatched it away, going a bit pink. 'Free gardeners don't grow on trees,' I finished lightly.

'That's what Ottie says, and that the arrangement seems to suit both of us. Have you seen that sculpture yet, the one we're suppose to fit into the garden? I don't know where she thinks we're going to put it!'

'I thought we'd decided on the rose garden. And do you think I should go and look at it? I thought she might not want me to see it until it's finished.'

'She won't mind. In fact, she may not even notice you're there.'

'She *does* seem pretty engrossed – Jonah takes her dinner across to the studio to her every night. The lights seem to

315

be on in the studio day and night, so she must have a very extreme work ethic – or maybe a work addiction.'

'Yes, you can't say she isn't focused.'

'Every time I pass, there she is working away – wearing one of those enormous lumberjack shirts too. She's so elegant, they seem an odd choice of overall.'

'They were my father's,' Seth said shortly. 'I think she's practically worn them to death.'

'Really? I think that's very touching.'

'I suppose it is. They were pretty wrapped up in each other, though my father's passion was the garden and Ottie's her sculpture. I suppose it equalised out.'

'So where did you fit into the scheme of things?'

'Around the edges, mostly. Ottie was always kind to me, and my father loved me in his own way, but neither of them was very good with children. Things got better once I was older.'

'I always longed to be part of a large family,' I confessed, 'or at least to get back to the feeling of family I'd had when I lived here. Of course there was the commune in Scotland, but that felt more like belonging to a tribe. And then, when I did come back here, I found Jack had taken over the place I once had and I was *horribly* jealous.'

'Natural.'

'I suppose so and now I know Jack I don't really mind quite so much, because I'm fond of him too.'

He got to his feet and looked inscrutably down at me. 'Yes, you are, aren't you?'

'It was lovely to find I had a relative I didn't know about,' I explained. 'Oh, well, I'd better go and get on. Mr Yatton has drawn up a list of all the children who will be coming to the party on Christmas Eve, so I'm going to go and buy presents for Father Christmas to hand out. I suppose I'd better get some spares, too.'

'And I'd better get back to work.'

'Yes . . . Seth, there aren't any box trees down here, are there?' I asked tentatively, because something had been puzzling me.

'I was moving a couple of container box spirals on the top terrace earlier – do I reek of it?'

'Yes, you do rather,' I said with a grin. 'It's not the nicest of smells, though you may attract the odd vixen.'

'You can say that again,' he said obscurely, then went off to admire Derek's bricklaying while I took my frozen and numb bottom back to the house.

Later, I did what I had been longing to do and went over to the studio. I could see Ottie standing in her usual contemplative pose in front of the sculpture, back towards me, so I tapped gently on the glass door before opening it.

'Hi, can I come in? I don't want to disturb you,' I said cautiously, though my eyes were irresistibly drawn to the large shape beyond her

'That's all right,' she said, turning and refocusing her bright blue eyes on me with, it seemed, an effort. 'I was just about to make a cup of tea. Want one?'

'Yes, please, but really I wanted to see how the garden sculpture was coming on, if you don't mind?'

'Look all you like – and there's the maquette; that will give you more idea of how the finished thing will look.' She pointed out a small model on the work surface, then plugged in a clay-smeared kettle and got out a battered tin tea caddy decorated with a portrait of Charles and Di on their wedding day.

I looked from the sculpture to the model . . . and back again. There seemed to be a face, half-animal, half-human, at the heart of it, amid a whirlwind of spiky wings – the Spirit of the Garden, presumably? It was masculine and vaguely familiar . . .

Then I got it.

'It's Seth – and he looks like a lion exploding out of a spiky horse chestnut casing!' I said without thinking, but Ottie just grinned and said that that was it in a nutshell.

The tea was Earl Grey, just as it came out of the pot, but after some rummaging about she produced a box of gingernut biscuits, and proceeded to dunk hers.

'I'll be sending *The Spirit* away to be cast soon. Have you decided where to put it, yet?'

'Yes, I thought it might make a good focal point in the rose garden,' I said, following suit and dunking my biscuit. Ginger and Earl Grey make an interesting combination. 'What do you think?'

'That should brighten it up a bit. I find roses so boring. They stand about looking hostile and thorny for months and then suddenly decide to have masses of flowers.'

'I think Hebe would find that idea practically heresy.'

'So would my husband have done too. You know, I thought Seth would want to hide the sculpture away in the wilderness or in the trees on the other side of the valley: he's such a traditionalist.'

'But the rose garden is new; there's no reason why it shouldn't fit there very well. We've planted lots more roses too and winter-flowering hellebores – Christmas roses – so it won't look quite as bare as you remembered.'

'Speaking of hellebores,' she said obscurely, 'are you still managing to resist Jack's untrustworthy but not inconsiderable charms? You had me quite worried at first and Seth is *still* convinced you're in love with him.'

'Then Seth's wrong!' I snapped, nettled. 'I admit I *did* fall for Jack, and I'm still very fond of him, but in a sisterly sort of way. I've tried to tell him, but he's very . . .'

'Vain? Overconfident? Won't take no for an answer?'

I laughed. 'Well, yes – all of those! I keep thinking that

318

'I've finally got through to him how I feel, and also convince him that I'm here to stay at Winter's End, and then the next minute he bounces right back again.'

'So you're not even going to share it with him, married, partnership, or otherwise? Good,' she said with satisfaction, 'because although he's a charming rogue and I'm quite fond of him, he's not good for Winter's End – or you.'

'Seth should stop worrying about *my* love life and think about his own,' I said darkly, his remark still rankling. 'I wouldn't trust Mel as far as I could throw her!'

'Ah, yes – Mel. From what I hear she does seem to have been at Winter's End rather a lot while I've been away.'

'She has, but not up at the house,' I said pointedly, not mentioning the one occasion when she had called in and found Seth and me in a slightly compromising-looking position. 'But she's so beautiful it is hardly surprising if he's fallen for her all over again – and she's a rich widow now, so I suppose that's an added attraction.'

'Not to Seth. He's never been interested in money. Jack's the one who ought to find that irresistibly attractive.'

'But Jack says it's Seth she's mad about . . . though actually, I did see Jack and Mel kissing in the shrubbery once, which made me wonder if he was being entirely truthful.'

'Hmm . . . well, I heard some odd rumours when I was in London and I don't think Mel's husband *did* leave her as well off as everyone assumes. It would make sense, because we were all surprised when she moved back to live with her mother. She picked up with Seth again, then when Jack turned up made a dead set at him, probably because she knew he had money and thought he was William's heir. But then suddenly it was all off and she was all over Seth again.' She shook her head. 'But I'm sure he's got her measure. He knows she'll only marry someone rich, however fascinated by him she is.'

319

'She seems pretty cold-blooded. I hope Seth knows what he's doing.'

'He hasn't been pining away for love of her all these years, you know. I'm sure he quickly realised he already had everything he wanted right here at Winter's End, just as his father did.'

'So have I,' I said, absently gazing at the sculpture.

'I think it's time I told you the last family secret,' Ottie said abruptly – and did so.

When she'd finished I stared at her. 'You can't be serious!' I said, and broke into a peal of laughter. Hyenas had nothing on me. I think Ottie was a bit put out.

Chapter Twenty-nine: Battle Positions

*Sir Ralph came again. I see he now believes that his
wife's jealous imaginings were no more than the truth,
and is afraid of mee. I told him he must swear that
my carved oak chest and all it contains should go to my
daughter, and none other should have it. If he did not
do this, I would curse him through eternity. He said it
would be done.*

From the journal of Alys Blezzard, 1582

Once I'd turned the family secret over in my head for a
while, it occurred to me that, true or not (and how could
it *possibly* be true?) it would make for absolutely marvellous publicity!

Releasing a story like this just before the opening season
would hugely increase visitor numbers and could make all
the difference between financial success and simply making
ends meet.

And even if the story *is* apocryphal – well, lots of families have their legends, don't they? It's only when people
start researching their family history and discover that actually Uncle Bernard had never even set foot in a rowing boat,
let alone gone down with the *Titanic* while playing 'Nearer,
my God, to Thee', that the boring truth is revealed.

Unfortunately, Ottie was adamant that the secret be kept

clutched fast to our bosoms for ever, and a fat lot of good it would do Winter's End like that.

It was frustrating not being able to talk it through with anyone else, but Hebe couldn't be trusted not to tell Jack and I didn't like to discuss it with Lucy over the phone.

I still think the revelation was the funniest thing I'd heard for ages, and somehow the person I most wanted to share it with was Seth, who unfortunately, being a mere man, was forever to be excluded from knowing about our dramatic little skeleton in the family cupboard.

I was still mulling it all over a few days later, but a worrying feeling that something threatening was about to happen had started to distract me from it a bit.

I hoped Mel wasn't planning any more little booby traps – even though Jack assured me he had had it out with her and she had contritely said that she couldn't believe she could have done anything so spiteful and potentially dangerous.

Neither could I – an apology might have been nice.

But it turned out that the gathering shadows threatened Lucy, and when she phoned me up I knew something was wrong the moment I heard her voice.

'Mum, I'm coming home, and so is Kate,' she said abruptly. Kate is the girl she had been sharing a room with, and they had become good friends.

'What, straight away? But has something happened? Are you both all right?'

'Yes, we're fine, Mum – calm down,' she said, though sounding strained. 'We've just had a bit of a scare, that's all, and it's really spooked Kate. She wants to get the first plane out and I don't fancy staying here without her.'

'You'd better tell me what's happened.'

'You know I said the geek following me was just shy, and really he only wanted me to give him extra English

322

conversation lessons? Well, his friend asked Kate too, and since they seemed harmless she persuaded me we should do it together, for some extra money.'

'Oh, Lucy!'

'Come on, Mum, we weren't mad enough to agree to go to a house or anything like that, just meet after work at a nearby café. And at first it was OK, they bought us coffee and said they wanted to chat to improve their English conversation. But then, when Kate went to the loo, I saw the other man put something in her drink, so when she came back I just made some excuse and got us out of there, fast. They followed us out, so we ran all the way back to our digs.'

'But that's terrible! Lucy, what if you hadn't noticed, or you'd both gone to the loo or—'

'Well, we wouldn't,' she said bluntly. 'We always watch each other's drinks or take them with us, and that would have seemed odd with a cup of coffee.'

'Did you report them to the police?'

'No. I mean, how could we? It would be just my word against theirs. I'd no proof. And we are fine, just a bit shaken, especially since they trailed us back and hung around outside for ages. Kate got hysterical and phoned home, and her father told her to get on the next plane, which was easier said than done. I managed to get us two seats eventually, but it's so near Christmas it was a miracle.'

'Thank God,' I said devoutly. 'So, when do you get here?'

'The early hours of the day before Christmas Eve. Kate's family will pick her up in London, but I've booked a connecting flight to Liverpool. Do you think you could meet me, or will you be too busy? It's the Winter's End staff Christmas party the next day, isn't it? I can get a taxi.'

'I *should* really be here . . . but I'd much, much rather come and meet you. Look, leave it with me and I'll sort something out. But I'm so glad you're both coming home. I think it's the sensible thing to do. You will be careful before then, won't you?'

'Kate's such a nervous wreck she doesn't even want to leave the building, but we're going out later with a whole bunch of friends to do some Christmas shopping and have a leaving party – but we're all staying together, don't worry.'

Of course I was worried, but so glad she was coming back! And when I found Seth wolfishly devouring roast beef and horseradish sandwiches in the kitchen later, he offered to drive me to the airport to collect her. This was really kind of him, because I didn't know the way there and was likely to be too nervous and excited to concentrate.

'I think I'll turn my mum's old room into Lucy's. Did you know it hasn't been touched since she ran away, all those years ago? Grandfather wouldn't have it changed in any way, which is quite touching, but now it's time the ghosts were banished and maybe all the rosebuds too. Lucy isn't a terribly *girly* girl, if you know what I mean.'

'I'm starting to get some idea,' he agreed.

'Only there isn't much time between now and Christmas, and I'd like to paint the walls and perhaps move the furniture . . .' I looked hopefully at him.

'*I'll* come in and help you – you leave Hal and Bob alone!'

And he did too. I packed one small trunk of Mum's things for the attic and the rest I sent to a charity shop. We flung open the windows to let out the last ghost of patchouli and let in the chilly, cleansing air, while obliterating trellised rosebuds with two shades of light mulberry emulsion paint.

I had a shopping expedition to St Helens and bought some new fixtures and fittings for the room, then we carried down her boxes of belongings from the attic, so she could unpack and rearrange as she wanted.

When we'd finished it looked lovely and my excitement

must have been contagious, because I even caught Aunt Hebe putting two Coalport potpourri holders full of dried rose petals on the bedroom mantelpiece, as her contribution to the welcome.

Luckily, Lucy had asked me not to send her Christmas presents out there, but save them for when she came home. Now I would be able to make her a Christmas stocking too ... and maybe one for Guy. Is anyone ever too old for a Christmas stocking?

Ghosts banished, the room remembered only the happy hours and, having had a memory like a particularly happy and spaced-out goldfish, I expect my mother had had a lot of those.

It was a bumper mistletoe harvest this year, and for a few days it was all hands to the packing station in one of the big greenhouses, while Mrs Lark came in and out with sandwiches and hot soup.

Jonah, as was apparently the tradition, spent a day down at the lodge selling bunches of it at the gate, and some of it went to local suppliers, but most was dispatched down to London where it would fetch the best price.

It was odd to think that Winter's End mistletoe would be adorning houses all over the south of England this Christmas – and, since it is lucrative, be helping to support the estate too!

There was still plenty left growing wild up in the woods for decorating the house, and also plenty of holly with bright red berries – the sign, usually, of a hard winter, though we'd only had a couple of cold snaps so far.

'Thank you for the Christmas present, Anya,' I said. 'What possessed you, you idiot?'

She giggled down the phone. 'I know someone who

325

breeds peacocks and they seemed just the thing for Winter's End. Did they get there OK?'

'Yes, your friend brought them in a crate on the back of a pick-up, just after Sunday lunch and when Jonah told us there was a delivery of birds we all went out to look. I was just grateful they weren't flamingos or macaws or something! It's lucky I like that sort of plaintive scream they make!'

'What did Seth think?'

'He wasn't too pleased at first, because he said they would make a mess in the garden, but Hebe was surprisingly keen. She had the gardeners wheel the crate round to an empty run in the walled garden until they settle down, and says she will feed them with the hens. She's named them, too.'

'What?'

'Fanny and Johnnie after the Cradocks who used to do cookery shows on TV. Apparently the inspiration was Ottie saying that the male peacock looked henpecked.'

'Nice. I look forward to meeting Fanny and Johnnie at Christmas.'

'Which is practically here. And guess what, Lucy is coming home, after all!' I said, and told her all about it.

Of course she thought it was all arranged by our guardian angels, which I suppose Lucy's might have done, but I'm pretty sure that mine has not left the building, let alone jetted off to Japan. In fact, ever since Ottie did her Last Revelation thing, I have the distinct feeling that whenever I'm in the parlour in the evenings, Alys is trying to tell me something.

Whatever it is, I hope it doesn't take her as long as it took Ottie.

I woke up the day before Christmas Eve more excited than any child on Christmas Day, and all because Lucy was coming home! I just hope she loves Winter's End as much as I do. At least it was now looking its best – warm, clean, inviting and smelling of rich foods and spices because Mrs Lark was cooking up a storm in the kitchen, both for the party tomorrow and Christmas itself.

There was still lots to sort out for the party, but Seth and I had to set out for the airport right after breakfast. I was so glad he was driving, because not only were the roads icy but I was a bundle of nerves, even though I knew everything would be fine once I saw her.

Lucy, looking pale, and with her red-gold hair dishevelled, staggered out onto the airport concourse laden with twice as much baggage as she went with.

She dropped everything and gave me a huge hug. 'Hi, Mum! I'm *sooo* glad to be back – and I'm shattered, haven't slept a wink on the plane. Where have you put the camper?'

'I've brought the estate car instead, and Seth drove me. He's waiting for us in the short-stay car park – come on.'

The cold air woke her enough to give Seth a very serious once-over followed, I was relieved to see, by one of her more delightful smiles.

'Mum's told me all about you, and you're just the way I imagined, only *more* so!'

'Has she? I mean – *am* I?' he replied, startled, and gave me a dubious look. 'Well, you look exactly the way I imagined you would too!'

She nodded. 'I know, apparently I'm a typical Winter and once you've seen one, you've seen them all. Mum, you sit next to Seth,' she ordered, climbing into the back seat. 'Oh – there's a dog in here,' she added, as Charlie woke up and then greeted her like a long-lost friend, all wet tongue and cold nose.

'It's just Charlie. I'd forgotten he'd decided to come with us. Do you want me to have him in the front?'

327

'No, he's fine,' she said, and next time I turned around they were both curled up together fast asleep.

Seth and I comfortably bickered in low voices all the way home, merely because I'd had the audacity to ask Hal to go into the woods and cut me plenty of holly and mistletoe to decorate the Great Hall, without consulting him first.

I felt unspeakably happy.

When we got back, the Great Hall was half transformed ready for the party. I'd left my CD player up in the minstrels' gallery ready for carols, but Mr Yatton must have put one of his own on, for Handel's 'The Arrival of the Queen of Sheba' was majestically unscrolling itself into the spiced air.

It was strangely appropriate, for as we entered, everyone stopped and formed into a smaller, indoor version of the greeting line I had faced on my arrival: Grace, the Larks – even Ottie, who suddenly appeared as if she had divined by a sixth sense that another Winter had returned, gave Lucy a back-thumping embrace and a muttered, 'Chip off the old block!' before vanishing back to her studio again.

I hoped she would remember to come for dinner, though I might have to send Jonah over to fetch her.

As 'The Queen of Sheba' came to a halt, Aunt Hebe, all in spectral white, drifted silently down the dark stairs. After staring at Lucy intently for a moment, a gaze that Lucy returned in full measure, she embraced her and welcomed her home with much more enthusiasm than she had shown me.

But then, they were as alike as two peas in a pod, except that Aunt Hebe's hair was now white instead of red-gold. Somehow, I got the feeling that Lucy's being a despised female wasn't going to enter into the equation any more . . .

'Well, we'd have known you for a Winter anywhere, young Lucy!' Mrs Lark said, stating the obvious.

'That's right,' agreed Jonah. 'Ho, ho, ho!' he added, in a surprisingly deep bass and Lucy cast me a wide-eyed look.

'Don't worry, he's practising his Father Christmas act for tomorrow's party,' I explained. 'Now, I've told you all about everyone, so you only have to put faces to names. This is Mrs Lark and her husband, Jonah, of course – and this is Grace ... and here come two of the gardeners, Hal and Bob, with some holly.'

'So I see,' Seth said, and the two gardeners edged behind me.

'Don't be a grump, Seth. I only want them to help Jonah put the holly and mistletoe up, and then they can go back and do whatever it is they're supposed to be doing.'

'Raking the gravel, and Bob's chopping the logs,' Hal said, without noticeable enthusiasm. I'm sure they would much rather be inside because it was literally freezing out there.

'Well, make sure Jonah doesn't go up the ladder. You know what you're like, Jonah, trying to do it all yourself.'

When I turned back, Hebe and my daughter were arm in arm. 'Oh, it's so good to be home!' Lucy said, her eyes shining. She smiled, the mirror image of every Winter I'd ever met, except the one in my mirror – and Alys, of course. 'I'm so happy to be here – home at Winter's End at last.'

The magic seemed to have worked its trick and another piece of the pattern of Winter's End seamlessly fitted into place.

After a while I showed Lucy to her room, which she loved – especially since it had once been her grandmother's – and then gave her a quick tour of the house to get her bearings, finishing by introducing her to Mr Yatton, who was busily doing something or other in the solar.

In fact, I left them there together in the end as they seemed to have so much to discuss, and went back to the Great Hall to help. Seth and Derek had brought in a huge

Christmas tree while Jonah and Bob had gone up to the attics to bring down the boxes of decorations that were stored there.

By the end of the afternoon, when the sky outside was darkening, the hall looked lovely, and Lucy had slotted so seamlessly into place that I'm sure everyone had already forgotten that she hadn't always been there.

But I wasn't jealous, as I had been with Jack, for one day Winter's End would belong to Lucy and I wanted her to love it too.

The Great Hall looked wonderfully festive, festooned with holly, mistletoe and swags of greenery tied with big bows of wide red ribbon, and the tree sparkling in the corner, which we all helped to decorate.

The trestles, covered with festive tablecloths, stood ready to receive the mounds of food already prepared by Mrs Lark. Portmeirion Christmas serving bowls and dishes were lined up the middle for nuts, sweets and nibbles, and a stack of plates and scarlet paper napkins were at one end.

Charlie lay in the centre of the revived rag rug in front of the fire like a dead dog, exhausted by watching all this activity.

A large, hooded porter's chair was dragged forward nearer to the fire and garlanded, ready for Father Christmas, and the presents for the children arranged in piles on the table behind him.

Then it was ready. I felt an air of toe-tingling excitement and expectation that I hadn't felt for . . . well, *ever*, really.

Jack arrived late. I heard the peal of his rather noisy horn while I was showering after having helped Lucy unpack some of her stuff. He was last down in the drawing room too, not excepting Ottie, who had remembered to come only because she had finally completed the sculpture.

Seth wasn't there. I'd invited him, but he'd said he had something else to do, and I had a pretty good idea what *that* meant.

When Jack walked into the drawing room, with his usual air of expecting to see a fatted calf laid on for him, the first thing that met his eyes was Lucy, seated on the sofa with a great-aunt on either side, like triplets. His face was stunned. I had quite forgotten to tell him that Lucy was coming home, and Aunt Hebe mustn't have mentioned it either.

For once she didn't spring to her feet with loud cries of joy at the sight of her beloved boy, just smiled and said, 'Oh, there you are at last, Jack – and here's Lucy!'

He recovered quickly. I think I was the only one to notice that his nose had been put out of joint, just as mine had when I first returned to Winter's End and found him cock of the walk.

'Well, this *is* a surprise,' he said, coming forward to shake hands and then kiss Lucy's cheek.

Lucy summed him up, and then a smile that I knew from experience to mistrust appeared on her lips. 'It's not a surprise to me. Mum's told me all about you and I knew you were coming for Christmas.'

Watching them, it occurred to me that, next to Lucy, Jack didn't look quite as splendid. His hair was just gold, not the precious fine red-gold that hers was, and his blue eyes seemed to lack the true azure depth of Lucy's. They both had the typical Winter high-bridged nose, but in Lucy's case her features were delicately drawn and her skin so translucently white she looked like porcelain.

'How lovely to have the family all together,' Aunt Hebe said as the gong went. 'Oh, no time for a drink first I'm afraid, Jack. We'd better go through.'

He changed course from the drinks cabinet. 'Of course.'

He smiled delightfully. 'And I hope I will be able to sit next to my newest cousin and get to know her better.'

'Actually, you're so much older than me that I think of you more as an uncle,' Lucy said sweetly. 'A great-uncle.'

Battle seemed to have commenced, but I wasn't quite sure that Jack had yet grasped the nature of his adversary. But by the time we'd eaten our way through potted shrimps with French toast and Jonah had brought in the Beef Wellington and glazed carrots, he was starting to get a glimmer of understanding.

Jonah had excelled himself in the paper napkin department tonight: there was a huge central display of red paper roses nestling in green crepe paper holly leaves. I complimented him on it.

'It's very festive. You are clever, Jonah, thank you.'

'There's nothing to roses, I could make them in me sleep. Of course, since that time the kitten ate one and it went through the poor mite's system like a dose of salts—' he began, but Hebe, who had been staring with vague disapproval at the bright scarlet roses, interrupted him.

'Of course!' she exclaimed. '*Roses! That's* what it said in Alys's foreword to her mother's household book – that the secret was at the heart of the rose . . .' She frowned. 'Or maybe the heart of the rose was the secret?' she added doubtfully.

'Hebe!' Ottie snapped. 'Button it!' But the warning had come too late. Jack was staring intently at his aunt, his knife and fork suspended.

'Oh, sorry, Ottie, I didn't mean to just blurt that out,' began Hebe, flustered. 'It's just – well, forget what I said, everyone, it's nothing.'

'Is that what it says – roses?' Jack said eagerly. I saw his eyes dart from the flowers carved along the top of the panelling to those embroidered on the firescreen, and feared he was about to embark on a whole new treasure hunt, fruitless though I knew it would be.

'She only meant the use of roses in the recipes, Jack – don't get excited,' I said soothingly. 'Now, could I help anyone to some more of this lovely beef?'

After dinner we all retired to the drawing room but Lucy's long journey was catching up on her, Ottie was in a state of exhausted euphoria due to having completed the sculpture, and Hebe and I were shattered after the preparations for the party, so we all decided on an early night.

Jack was the only exception. Suspiciously bright-eyed and bushy-tailed, he said he would watch TV in the library for a bit, though as I was going out he kissed me good night and suggested I stay for a little while. 'I've hardly seen anything of you, darling. We haven't had a minute to ourselves since I got here.'

'Sorry, I'm just too tired, Jack – and if I know Lucy, she'll be waiting for me to come up. We've still got a lot of catching up to do.'

'So have *we*,' he said, 'but I suppose we can make up for it tomorrow.'

'Perhaps, but it's going to be even more hectic than today. My friend Anya is arriving early in time for the Friends meeting, and her son, Guy, is coming later. They're both staying for Christmas – did I say?'

'No, you don't seem to have told me anything!'

'Oh, didn't I? I thought I had. Well, anyway, they're staying, and then there's the meeting and the party, and clearing up afterwards – so tomorrow is going to be busy. I'll be really glad of your help, Jack.'

'I don't know why you decided to carry on with these feudal traditions, Sophy. I told William often enough that it was a waste of time and money.'

'I think it's a lovely thing to do, to thank everyone for all their help over the year,' I said. 'Good night!' and I dodged when he would have kissed me again.

Some instinct – or maybe it was Alys's chilly presence making herself felt in the passageway – made me go and lock the door to the parlour before I went upstairs, which is not a thing I normally do.

'You reek of horrible aftershave,' Lucy said disapprovingly when I walked into my room to find her sitting on the bed.

'Actually, it's lovely, but you probably associate it with Lady Betty's repulsive nephew Conor. It's the same one he always wore and it was *entirely* wasted on him. In fact, it seemed to wear Conor, rather than the other way round, while Jack's made it entirely his own – a part of the whole handsome and expensive package.'

'Yeah, right,' she said, sounding unconvinced.

I sniffed the air. 'Have you been at my Elisabethan Rose?'

'No, it's something Aunt Hebe brewed up, but it does smell similar, I admit. She just gave it to me on the way to bed, as an early Christmas present.'

'You're honoured. Now come on,' I said, climbing onto the bed next to her and giving her a hug, 'you tell me your secrets and I'll tell you mine!'

Chapter Thirty: Rival Attractions

Now it is clear that my relatives will not intercede for mee, they have subjected mee to the indignities of searching my person for such places as might suckle an imp or devil and threaten sterner measures should I not confess my wrongdoing and name my accomplices.
From the journal of Alys Blezzard, 1582

Jack was conspicuously *not* his usual bright-eyed and bushy-tailed self at breakfast. In fact, he looked a little wan, which I expect was entirely due to his having spent a large part of the night up and about – as evidenced by his fingerprints all over every carved, engraved, embossed or stuccoed rose in the house.

He can hardly have had time for much sleep after that either, because when Hebe went out this morning she discovered that he must have been in the walled garden at first light with his metal detector, digging holes among the apothecary roses.

She was furious, though when she tore him off a strip, he tried to laugh it off. 'But all I found was a silver threepenny bit and a few bent nails, Hebe. I hardly touched the garden.'

'There are holes all over the place,' she said crossly.

'I'll come and help you fill them in right after breakfast, Aunt Hebe,' Lucy offered, and Jack gave her a dirty look.

Clearly he was out of favour at the moment, though I was sure it wouldn't last very long.

'Don't forget the Friends are coming at ten thirty for the meeting before the party,' I reminded them. 'Anya should be arriving any minute too. I asked her to try and get here in time for it, since she'll be running the tearoom and gift shop end of things.'

'You aren't *still* determined to turn the place into a Shakespeare theme park, are you?' Jack said. 'We agreed you would wait and discuss it with me at Christmas before finalising anything.'

'*Not* a theme park, Jack,' Aunt Hebe said disapprovingly. 'Just opening as we have done for many years now, only with a very tasteful little shop too.'

'Of course Mum is going to open the house to the public next year. It's the best way of generating income to keep the place going,' Lucy said combatively. 'And I'm sure your products will be our best-sellers, Aunt Hebe.'

'Thank you, dear.'

'But it all needs organising *now*; she can't hang about waiting for your input, Jack,' Lucy went on. 'Anyway, I'm sure she's got a lot more experience at running this kind of thing than you have. She did everything at Blackwalls!'

Battle *had* commenced, and I knew who my money was on to win. 'Everything *is* pretty well finalised already,' I agreed. 'It has to be, though the February open day is a sort of dry run, to see how it all goes. Then we can fine-tune it ready for the start of the season at Easter.'

'Mum's got some brilliant ideas to increase visitor numbers.'

'Why don't you come to the Friends meeting, Jack?' I suggested, but he said tersely that he had other things to do and sloped off to his bedroom, probably to catch up on his sleep and sulk.

Hebe and Lucy headed for the walled garden and I helped

336

Jonah clear away the breakfast things before dashing upstairs to change into a festive red tunic and jingle-bell earrings, because I didn't think I'd have time between the Friends meeting and the party.

I hadn't seen Seth that morning, but when I looked out of my bedroom window he was standing on the middle terrace, looking down at his new knot. I only hoped he wouldn't forget about the party and start messing about with the design, because he wasn't wearing his gardening clothes and also – well, it wouldn't be the same without him looming about the place.

Anya arrived with just enough time to dump her bags in her room and then have a cup of coffee and a slice of pudding cake in the kitchen with the Larks and me. Then Lucy and Aunt Hebe came in, slightly earthy, and joined us.

'We'll have a good catch-up later, Lucy,' Anya said, having given her a rib-crushing hug. 'And Guy is coming shortly too, if he can get that terrible old car of his to start.'

I looked at my watch. 'Come on, it's almost time for the meeting and everyone will be arriving shortly. We'll go into the breakfast parlour, out of Mrs Lark's way.'

'Jonah had better take Gingernut up to our rooms. He keeps getting under my feet and he'll be safer up there,' Mrs Lark said as the kitten made a dive for the hem of her apron. 'And I'll keep Charlie in here when the party starts, so he doesn't get trodden on.'

I was worried about how the Friends would react to my plans, because asking them to voluntarily staff and steward Winter's End for more than twice the number of days next year, and over a longer opening season, was a big ask.

They all came in together and took their seats around the table, which Jonah had extended again by inserting a couple of the leaves. None of the group was young, and some of them already looked familiar, like Mr Yatton's sister, Effie, a spare, wiry woman wearing a tweed skirt and a lilac jumper sewn with pearls, and a pair of elderly men who were so alike they had to be twins. They all cast curious looks at Anya, with her red dreadlocks and nose ring, but Lucy's presence seemed to be not unexpected.

'Welcome to the meeting,' I said nervously. 'I'm afraid I don't know all your names yet, though I hope I soon will. First of all, I'm going to outline my plans for Winter's End and see what you think of them – I'm sure there will be a lot to discuss. But before we start, I'd like you to meet my daughter, Lucy.'

'Hi,' Lucy said, from her seat beside me.

'And my friend, Anya. I've asked Anya to be here because she is going to create a gift shop in part of the tearoom area and will be in overall charge of both operations.'

'You mean, she would run the tearoom too, and be in charge of the money and everything?' Effie asked, and I braced myself for resentment.

'Well, yes, that's the idea. You would be doing the actual catering, of course, but Anya would cash up for you and get change, order stock . . . all that kind of thing.'

'How *wonderful*! That will take a great deal of pressure off you serving wenches, won't it, Pam?' Effie exclaimed, and the others murmured agreement.

Pam, who was a buxom woman with a high colour in her apple cheeks, beamed. 'Oh yes, Effie! I mean, we can take the money and serve the food all right, but when it comes to even adding up the float for next day, we get stuck, let alone totting up the takings!'

This was a good start and they listened to the rest of my plans with interest, seeming fairly enthusiastic about it all – and not terribly surprised. But since they all seemed to be friends of Aunt Hebe, I am sure she had kept them updated on things.

'I intend opening four afternoons a week, so we would be closed from Sunday to Tuesday. I know Sunday would be a good day for visitors, but since so many of the people involved with Winter's End attend church that day, it wouldn't be practical or right. But we *will* open on Bank Holiday Mondays.'

Effie seemed to be the one in charge of the group, arranging the rotas for who did what on which day. It appeared that the Friends liked to do everything in twos, from manning the gatehouse to stewarding the minstrels' gallery. They all like to stick to their particular areas too, though when I said that I proposed having a sort of taxi service from the car park to the front door by golf buggy, for those who had difficulty walking so far, four elderly gentlemen fought a battle over who got to drive it.

'If Winter's End is going to be open four days a week you can take it in turns,' Effie pointed out firmly. 'We always have a few Friends free too,' she said to me, 'so someone can fill in as and when necessary if it is busy, or during tea breaks.'

'Yes – tea breaks,' I said, looking down at my notes. 'From now on, you will all be entitled to a free pastry or sandwich during your break. If the teashop is busy, Mrs Lark doesn't object to your taking it through into the kitchen, though I hope before the end of our first season of working together to make a little Friends staffroom out of one of the disused rooms in the East Wing.'

That idea seemed to go down well.

'Lucy and I will be sort of floating personnel, filling in where needed, so if any of you can't get to the house for a break you can radio for what you want, and one of us will bring it.'

'Meals on wheels,' Pam said.

'Meals by golf buggy, anyway,' I agreed. 'Now, two other changes that I hope will also make your jobs easier are that you will all have radios, so you can contact each other if necessary; and all Friends will be paid travelling expenses.'

'By radios, do you mean walkie-talkies?' asked one elderly man, whose head had been going up and down like a nodding dog throughout the whole meeting.

'Yes – little ones. We had them where I worked before, and they are very useful.'

An excited buzz of conversation broke out. Effie held her hand up. 'I think I can speak for all of us when I say that that is all very acceptable and shows you value our input into preserving Winter's future.'

'I certainly do. I don't think Winter's End would *have* a future, without you,' I said sincerely. 'None of my plans would work without your help.'

Pam, the buxom lady, nudged Effie and said something in a low voice. 'Ah yes,' Effie said. 'There is just one thing that I wished to ask, on behalf of us all.'

'Ask away,' I said lightly, though my heart sank, wondering whether it would be something that would scupper my whole plan.

'It is this: the Friends originally started as a re-enactment society, which we still are, really.'

'Effie and I started it up,' Aunt Hebe put in, 'though these days I have so many other commitments that I can't always attend the meetings.'

'Oh?' I said, interested. 'What historical period do you re-enact?'

'Elizabethan England,' Effie said.

'Well, that's very interesting,' I began, not quite seeing where the question lay.

'The thing is,' Effie added in a rush, 'that what we would all really like is to be in costume when we are working at Winter's End.'

'You *would*? All of you?' I looked around the ring of faces, astonished.

'Oh yes,' they all chorused.

'Cool,' Lucy said. I could see she was wondering how she would look in a farthingale and ruff.

'Each of us has our own preferences. We take on parts from all walks of life,' Pam said, 'but we serving wenches prefer working in the teashop, appropriately enough!'

'And we're yeomen,' said one of the twin brothers. 'We collect the entrance money at the gatehouse.'

'Well, I think that would be a lovely idea,' I said, 'if that's what you really want to do. And it would certainly fit in with the increased emphasis on the Shakespearean connections of Winter's End and the late sixteenth-century knot gardens. But won't the costumes be uncomfortable, especially in summer?'

'Oh, no, we're used to them,' Effie said, 'and we would welcome the opportunity to wear them more often.'

'I did ask William once,' Aunt Hebe put in, 'but he didn't like the idea.'

'What part do you play?' I asked her.

'Queen Elizabeth, of course,' she replied, as if I should have known. And I suppose I should have guessed, since apart from her hair being no longer red, she bore a striking resemblance to portraits of the Virgin Queen.

'I also would have no objection to donning my costume for an hour or so on visitor days, and walking about the house and grounds with my courtiers.' She bestowed a regal smile on Mr Yatton. 'But I won't have time for more than that – there is much too much to do in my garden and stillroom.'

'That would certainly be an added attraction. Thanks, Aunt Hebe.'

'You must be guest of honour at our next meeting, which will be in the New Year,' Effie suggested. 'Costume optional.'

'Thank you, that would be lovely.' I looked around the table. 'Well, that was certainly a surprise – but a nice one.

I was already thinking of having quiet sixteenth- and early seventeenth-century music playing in the Great Hall, so to have everyone in period dress too will really add to the whole experience.'

'If you don't mind, *I'll* stay as I am,' Anya said.

'Oh, yes, we don't all need to dress up,' I agreed. And it was just as well, because Seth in a doublet and hose could be an attraction to rival Aunt Hebe's Gloriana – I mean, visitors could be killed in the rush.

We had thrashed out lots of details by the time Jonah popped his head around the door.

'People are gathering on the drive, Sophy,' he announced, 'so I'm off to put me Father Christmas suit on.'

'We'd better adjourn the meeting, then,' Aunt Hebe said, getting up. 'Have you mixed the punch, Jonah? Not too strong, I hope.'

'Ottie's doing it now – the usual mixture, that wouldn't hurt a lamb.'

'It had better not,' she said. 'Several of them are driving.'

We all went through to the Great Hall, which smelled of pine and looked magical, with the decorations, sparkling tree and the leaping flames from the fire in the enormous hearth. Anya and Lucy went to help with the food, and Seth came out of the kitchen door backwards, carrying an enormous punch bowl hung with little cups, followed by Ottie bearing a tray full of glasses and cloudy lemonade in a huge glass jug.

There were already big bottles of dandelion and burdock and Vimto at one end of the table, next to a stack of festive paper cups. I helped peel the cling film off the plates of sandwiches, party pies and sausage rolls, helping myself to one or two as I did so. It felt like a long time since breakfast.

'Where's Jack?' Hebe asked. 'He should be here!'

'Perhaps he's still asleep. Maybe someone should go and knock on his door?' I suggested. 'He'll miss all the fun.'

'No, I won't – I'm here,' he called from above, and ran lightly down the stairs, a vision in a silky, open-necked shirt, his golden hair attractively ruffled. 'All ready to hand out alcohol and good cheer to the masses, as usual.'

Clearly his batteries were now fully recharged, which was just as well, for Aunt Hebe sent him straight back upstairs to switch on the CD player.

Good humour unabated, he returned to the sound of 'Good King Wenceslas' and started filling cups with punch for the Friends. Then Jonah appeared from the kitchen, unrecognisable in a totally bogus cotton-wool beard, red suit and black wellies. He arranged himself in the hooded chair while Grace, who had flitted in after him like a wizened Tinkerbell in silver stilettos and a spangly handkerchief-hem dress, prepared to assist in finding the right presents.

'Ready, Miss Hebe,' he said.

'I can hear people crunching about on the gravel outside, Aunt Hebe,' I said nervously, as we took up our positions in front of the door, ready to regally receive our visitors. 'Why haven't any of them knocked?'

'They are waiting for the door to be opened, of course. Seth – could you do the honours?'

Seth, who had been leaning on the fireplace with one booted foot up on the fender, looking rather broodingly into the fire like a mislaid extra from a romantic drama, said, 'Of course.'

Then he cast a handful of pine cones onto the flames, which changed colour like a magic trick. 'Let the festivities commence!'

343

Chapter Thirty-one: Lord of Misrule

They have not let mee sleep these three days, so that I
grow dizzy, and have little time alone in which to think
– which I must suppose is their intention. I have ink
and paper for letters, so may still write, but it becomes
harder to conceal my book. I must ask them to send Joan
to mee soon, and let her take it away.

From the journal of Alys Blezzard, 1582

By the time Aunt Hebe finally let me relinquish my place
at the door, my hand had been shaken so many times it
felt twice the size it usually did, and slightly numb.

The Great Hall was full, hot and noisy, and I didn't
remember seeing half the people there come in. Many of them
were total strangers, but there were lots of familiar faces too,
like Mike, off duty and in jeans and sweatshirt, talking to
Anya, Milly from the mobile dog parlour, the tenant farmer,
the gardeners, the Friends . . . *and* all their families right down
to grandchildren and, for all I knew, great-grandchildren.

No wonder my Christmas gift list had been a long one!

And thank goodness I had wrapped up a few extra presents too, because an excited queue of children still waited
for their turn with Santa. The adults had found their own
(mainly food and drink) gifts on one of the trestles, and
they also seemed to have found the punch bowl . . .

In fact, there must have been a run on it, because it looked as though Jack was mixing a fresh batch. As if feeling my gaze he looked up and smiled at me, then abandoned his post and brought me a glass over.

'Drink this – you look as though you need it!' he said, slipping a friendly arm around me and giving me a squeeze. 'Enjoying your first Winter's End party?'

'Actually, I don't think it *is* my first,' I said, sipping the spicy mixture cautiously. Lady Betty had always mixed a mean bowl of punch, but although it caught at the back of my throat in a familiar way, this tasted nothing like it. 'I vaguely remember them from when I was a small child, especially Santa. It's odd how things keep coming back to me that I'd totally forgotten about.'

'Ho, ho, ho!' bellowed Santa suddenly, his eyes glittering and his cheeks flushed above the white beard. A small child burst into tears, snatched her present and scuttled off, and Jonah took a long drink out of a small tankard. I hoped it contained lemonade or something else entirely innocuous, but rather doubted it.

'There's hardly any alcohol in this punch, is there, Jack? Only Jonah looks a bit flushed and . . . well, lots of people seem to be getting very noisy and a bit excited.'

He shrugged. 'That's parties for you, darling – the punch is harmless, about one part brandy to a hundred of the other stuff.'

'*Wassail!*' yelled Bob in my ear, almost unrecognisable without his hat, clinked glasses with me and then ambled off, grinning. Someone had stuck a 'this way up' sticker on his back that I remembered from the hippo crate.

I took another, more suspicious, sip of my drink and rolled it around my tongue. My eyes watered. 'Jack, I'm sure this—' I began, when to my astonishment I spotted Mel Christopher making her way into the hall, supporting a small, silver-haired woman with black eyebrows and red lipstick.

'What's *she* doing here?' I exclaimed.

Jack turned and looked where I pointed. 'Mel's mother's an old friend of Hebe's but her health isn't good, so I haven't seen her about for quite a while.'

'I think Mel's got a damned cheek, showing her face here after booby-trapping my summerhouse!'

'Well, even so, I don't think you can very well throw her out without causing a scene, if Hebe invited her mother. But let's not worry about *her*,' he added, and I realised he had been quietly edging me into the darkest corner, near the pushed-back screens, without my noticing. 'Now, darling, let's talk about you and me and Barbados—'

'Jack Lewis!' said a voice pitched to shatter glass. 'I've got a bone to pick with you!'

'Er – hi, Mel,' he said weakly, letting go of me suddenly. 'Happy Christmas!'

Her eyes flashed with fury. 'Balls to that! I've just discovered you've knocked my house down without even bothering to mention it to me – *and* without permission from the council either.'

He looked taken aback. 'I told the boys to do it after Christmas when I was away! And I was *going* to tell you, Mel. We're partners, remember?'

'But there'll be a swingeing fine for knocking it down without permission. I didn't expect to be partners in *that*,' she snapped.

'The fine's nothing, when you think how much we will make from selling the land for development,' he assured her. 'They can't make us rebuild the house so we're bound to get the planning permission eventually.'

'And you were going to tell me this *when*, precisely?'

'Before it happened, obviously, Mel.' He tried out a

charming, placatory smile, but it didn't seem to be having much effect.

Her cold brown eyes fell on me. 'Something else seems to have slipped your mind too – like telling me you were off to Barbados with Ben's crowd by private jet right after Christmas – and taking *her* with you.'

'A private jet?' I squeaked.

'Of course. How else do you think I could get you on a flight at a moment's notice?' he said, glancing at me impatiently. 'Now, look, Mel—'

'Look nothing! I found out when I ran into Ben in London and he asked me too. He said I could take anyone I wanted with me.' She looked around and gave a ravishing smile at Seth, who was standing nearby, his clouded jade eyes fixed sombrely on her lovely face. 'Seth's coming – so that's going to be cosy, isn't it? Love Island!'

I suddenly felt unbearably sad, which was probably due to having inadvertently drained the whole large glass of punch. I could feel it burning its way down into my innards. Innocuous, my foot!

'Actually, it won't be that cosy, Mel, because I won't be going. I've got too much to do here,' I said, 'but I hope you three have a lovely time.'

Jack stopped being placatory and shot daggers at Mel. 'Sophy, darling—' he began, but I quickly put as many people between us as possible, though I hadn't realised that Seth had followed me until he said, practically in my ear, 'I wouldn't have any more punch, if I were you. I think Jack's spiked it.'

'I thought as much and there's practically none left now. But there's loads of lemonade and other soft drinks, so perhaps they'll drink that instead and it will dilute it.' I looked up at him. 'Shouldn't you be at home, packing your Bermuda shorts and sun lotion?'

'Shouldn't you be restringing your bikini?' he countered.

'I haven't got a bikini, and you must have heard me say I'm not going. I'd already told Jack when he first invited me, but nothing seems to get through his thick skull once he's got an idea lodged in there. It didn't sound like my idea of fun even if I hadn't got too much to do here already – and I've only just got Lucy back again, so I couldn't possibly go off right now.'

'Neither could I,' he agreed. 'It's not my scene either.'

'Mel seems to think—'

'Mel thinks I'm a dog that can be whistled up any time she likes. She hasn't even asked me – that was the first I'd heard of it.'

'Oh,' I said, suddenly feeling a bit happier – but that was probably the effect of the glass of punch. Just as well I'd only had the one.

A strange figure emerged from behind the huge carved screen and did a bit of languid cavorting in a very take-it-or-leave-it way. 'Is that Derek? Why is he wearing antlers and greenery?'

'Because he's the Lord of Misrule.'

'The *what*?'

He shrugged. 'Lord of Misrule. There's always one and nowadays it's usually Derek.'

He took the empty punchbowl back to the kitchen, while I sipped cold lemonade and watched Derek's antics. They consisted mainly of jogging half-heartedly across the room from time to time and holding what looked like a mistletoe-draped bladder on a stick over the heads of some unlikely couple, until they kissed.

I found this quite amusing until Jack resurfaced, having managed to shed Mel, and Derek shambled across and held his stick over our heads. Jack grabbed me and tried to comply a little too enthusiastically, his aftershave almost entirely extinguished by the smell of brandy – so not *all* of it had gone in the punch.

I was just thinking that it didn't so much feel like being kissed as attacked by a leech, when a grave voice in my ear said, 'Hello, Sophy.'

'Guy!' I exclaimed, repulsing Jack with more force than politeness, and hugged Guy warmly. 'How lovely to see you.'

It was several months since I'd last set eyes on him and he was even more handsome than before – dark auburn hair and the same dark-ringed grey eyes as Anya.

He returned the hug. 'There are six Morris dancers outside, Sophy, and they say you have to go and officially invite them in.'

'Lucy is going to be *so* pleased to see you! How long is it since you last met – about two years? She had such a bad time in Japan, but now she's back—'

'The Morris dancers,' he reminded me patiently. 'It's brass monkeys out there. Don't bother about me, because I'll sort out who's who after the party. And there *is* Lucy . . .' He trailed off, staring across the room at her. She was handing round mince pies, wearing a crown of twisted silver tinsel on her head and a pair of white fairy wings.

Lucy glanced in our direction, caught Guy's eye, did a double take and stared at him incredulously, though she'd known he was coming. But then, he had changed a bit in the last couple of years . . .

Guy was staring back, his face serious, then they began to move slowly towards each other through the throng, like sleepwalkers.

'Funny, I thought they'd be pleased to see each other,' I muttered.

Just as Lucy came to a halt a bare couple of inches from Guy, Derek capered up and practically beat them over the head with the mistletoe stick.

They were still kissing when Seth came to remind me about the group of now shivering Morris men and we had to take the poor things into the kitchen to thaw out. But after a drink or two they warmed up with a brisk measure in the middle of the Great Hall.

Then the fiddler with the Morris men started playing a catchy tune and suddenly everyone was dancing, including me and Seth, and it didn't matter that I didn't know how, because the fiddler called instructions out as he played. We all circled and hopped and swung around until we were hot and breathless.

I tell you, I'm not used to going it like that in the *evening*, let alone late morning.

I didn't see Mel or Jack dancing, though Santa got up and danced with Mrs Lark, and Anya and Mike, Lucy and Guy and most of the Friends joined in. I saw Ottie sweep past with Bob, and Aunt Hebe tripped a very stately measure with Mr Yatton. In the end there were so many dancing that you could do little more than jig up and down, which I found myself doing, nose to nose with Seth. Or maybe, since he is a lot taller than me, that should be nose to chest.

When the music stopped he grabbed me and kissed me right on the lips, so Derek must have popped up even though I didn't see him that time. Then he looked down gravely and said, 'Happy Christmas, Sophy.'

I stared up into his green eyes. 'Happy Christmas, Seth.'

His arms tightened around me. 'Sophy—'

'I'd put her down, you don't know where she's been,' Melinda slurred, grabbing his arm – but more to stop herself falling over than possessiveness this time, I think, so maybe Jack had been keeping her quiet with his brandy stash.

'This one's mine,' she said to me. 'You might as well make do with Jack, if you can get him.'

'I think perhaps it's time you left, Lindy,' I said coldly.

'In fact, you've got a nerve even coming here, after rigging that accident up for me in the summerhouse!'

Her lovely face went blank, so clearly she'd entirely forgotten about it. 'That was ages ago . . . and it was just a *joke*,' she muttered, looking away.

'You told me that you had nothing to do with it,' Seth said, turning to look at her with a frown.

'Well, it's over, let's not rake it up,' she slurred. 'And I don't see why I shouldn't be here, because Jack and I are old friends and anyway, Seth wanted me to come, didn't you, Seth?'

'No,' he said uncompromisingly.

'Liar.' The smile was supposed to captivate him, but was lopsidedly tipsy. She looked back at me and said spitefully, 'Do you think Jack would want you if you didn't have Winter's End? You don't even know who your father is – but he was probably some gypsy from the look of you.'

'I do know, actually – and you're quite right, he was a gypsy.'

'No, he wasn't,' Ottie said unexpectedly from behind me, where she was standing with Hebe and Mr Yatton. 'Is that what Susan told you?'

'Well, it was *one* of the versions,' I confessed, 'but it seemed the most likely one. Do you mean it wasn't true?'

'Certainly not, it was one of the Pharamonds, from over at Middlemoss.'

'That's what William thought,' Hebe chipped in doubtfully, 'but apart from the dark colouring, she doesn't really look like them, does she?'

'No, but I saw them together once and Susan admitted it to me – but I'm not saying which one, because he was married then, and he's dead now. Sophy, we'll talk about it later, OK?'

'OK,' I said a bit numbly, having found and lost my real

351

father inside a couple of minutes. I thought about Nick Pharamond at the Middlemoss bonfire, who presumably was some kind of relation to me . . .

'It doesn't really matter who her father was anyway – Sophy's a Winter, *that's* the important thing,' Aunt Hebe declared.

Lucy broke through the interested circle that had formed around us and linked her arm in mine. 'What's going on?'

'Nothing, darling – and here comes the coffee, everyone!' I called, as Mrs Lark and Grace trundled a trolley in.

Mel looked as if it would take more than a cup of coffee to revive her. She was now in a state of almost total collapse, supported only by Seth, whose face was inscrutable.

'Chloe!' called Aunt Hebe in her crystal-clear tones, head and shoulders above most of the crowd. 'Melinda has had too much to drink – you'd better take her home!'

Between us we loaded Mel into the passenger seat of their car, though we had to pry her fingers off Seth first. Then Chloe drove gingerly off, sitting bolt upright behind the steering wheel.

'Perhaps someone should have taken them home?' I said doubtfully.

'Don't look at me,' Seth said. 'I had some punch too, don't forget.'

'It's Chloe's car, she'll be all right,' Aunt Hebe assured me.

The appearance of the coffee urns had been a signal that the end of the festivities – and the unexpected entertainment – was nigh. Now people began to leave, laden with leftovers because, as Ottie put it, we didn't want to be faced with party pies and limp crackers at every meal for the entire festive season.

'Or even for dinner tonight,' she added.

'It's Lancashire hotpot,' Mrs Lark said, offended. 'It's all ready, it just needs warming up.'

'You must be exhausted, Mrs Lark,' I said, 'after all that.'

'Not me – but I'll put me feet up for a bit after everything's cleared away.'

'You do that now – *we'll* clear up,' Lucy offered, 'won't we, Guy?'

'We'll all help. It won't take long that way,' I suggested, which it didn't, especially since Mike had stayed to help too. Jack seemed to have vanished totally.

Mrs Lark must have let the kitten out, for I found it curled up asleep with Charlie on the rag rug by the fire. From the way Charlie's stomach was distended, he'd been fed at least one mince pie too many by the children when I wasn't looking.

Chapter Thirty-two: Touched

They talk of putting mee to the water next, and the thought of the icy river chills mee to the bone. The gaoler says there is so much evidence against mee now that unless someone in high position speaks for mee, I may yet hang – unless I drown or die of the cold first, I suppose.
From the journal of Alys Blezzard, 1582

When everything was cleared away, Lucy said she was going to help Guy take his things up to his room and then show him the rest of the house – and goodness knows what else, because they had been more or less permanently entwined since setting eyes on each other.

The aunts had gone off on their own affairs and I discovered Jack fast asleep on the drawing-room sofa, with the whisky decanter next to it, snoring with his mouth open. Not a pretty sight.

So that left just me, Seth, Anya and Mike, and since Mike was on duty that night and had to go home, the rest of us decided to walk into the village with him for some air. I made Charlie come, too – he needed to burn off some of those mince pies and other unsuitable titbits. So did I, come to that, but also I needed to clear my head and think about things. It had been an eventful day. Although the snow of a few days earlier had quickly vanished, it was very, very cold, especially after the warmth of the Great Hall. There was still ice on the puddles in places where the sun couldn't reach and leaves crunched crisply under our feet.

At first we weren't very talkative on the way down and Seth looked rather brooding – as well he might, with his lover trying to play him off against Jack. But he revived slightly when I remarked, on passing through the rusted rear gates of Winter's End, that rubbing down and repainting *those* was another important job for the New Year.

'Are you serious? It's *low* priority,' he insisted. 'The visitors aren't going to see them, so they can wait. There are other, more urgent things to do first.'

'They may rust away entirely in the meantime, and they're lovely gates,' I said, noting that he had lost the brooding, abstracted air and that the glint of battle was back in his eyes.

We were still bickering about it when we got to Sticklepond, where Anya elected to stop off at Mike's house for a bit and then make her own way back up to Winter's End.

Seth, Charlie and I carried on through the village and up the lane past the Winter's End car park.

'See how nice the front gates look now they're repainted and gilded,' I pointed out as we came within sight of them. 'And the rear gates are smaller and less fiddly, so it wouldn't take Bob so long to do . . .'

I tailed off as we spotted the familiar shape of Mel's large grey horse tied up behind the lodge house.

Could she possibly have sobered up that quickly? It was only a couple of hours since we'd poured her into the car and seen her off with feelings of profound relief! Pity we hadn't come across her earlier, so Mike could have arrested her for being drunk in charge of a horse.

Seth's face had gone all tight-lipped and brooding again.

'I see you've got company,' I said coolly. 'See you later. Come on, Charlie, nearly home.'

Seth grabbed my arm. 'Sophy, I—'

The lodge door began to open. 'Oh, damn!' he said, letting go of me suddenly and striding off.

I left him to it. I had a call I wanted to make anyway. I needed to ask Ottie one or two questions about what she'd said about my father. I found her in the studio as usual, though she wasn't wearing her working overall of plaid shirt and streaks of clay, but slim black jeans and a cream silk shirt.

'Hi, Sophy. I was expecting you to drop in. Have a glass of champagne?'

'Are you celebrating something?'

'Yes, finishing the sculpture – and one or two other things,' she said, handing me a glass, and though after the glass of punch earlier I'd rather gone off the idea of alcohol, I took it.

'Ottie, was that true what you said earlier – my father *was* one of the Pharamond family?'

'Yes. I assumed Susan had told you.'

'She told me so many different versions, but never the real one. Are you sure?'

'Quite sure. His name was Leo Pharamond and he was married at the time – and he is dead now. He was charming, but he certainly put it about a bit – like Jack, come to think of it.'

'Oh? Well, it's good to know, even though I can't very well make myself known to the family, can I? But I have a family of my own now, so it doesn't really matter any more.'

'Yes, and it is remarkable how like that portrait of Alys you are. It's much more evident now you've had it cleaned.'

'There are one or two dark-haired Winters among the portraits, though perhaps not quite as dark as me, so my colouring isn't entirely due to the Pharamond genes.'

'Mmm . . .' Ottie, the subject explored, seemed to be losing

356

interest and, glass in one hand and cheroot in the other, was regarding her finished sculpture fondly. '*The Spirit of the Garden* can go to be cast right after Christmas.'

'It's very generous of you to give us a sculpture, Ottie. I'm sure lots of people will want to come and see it. Seth showed me that small biography of you they did at the time of your last big exhibition, *Ottilie Winter: Cast Lives*. I thought we could stock copies of that in the shop, and perhaps have postcards done of the sculpture too.'

'You could have postcards made of the sketches for it as well, if you like?' she offered. 'In fact, you can *have* the sketches. You could hang them in the café to give the punters something to look at with their tea.'

'Thanks, Ottie,' I said gratefully, though I thought that even sketches by my celebrated aunt might be too valuable to risk on open display.

'And remember, if push comes to shove and you look like losing the house, you can sell the sculpture.'

I sincerely hoped it wouldn't come to that, but she was right – it did give me a valuable asset. But it also might prove a visitor attraction.

'Seth not come back with you?' she asked. 'And where's that nice friend of yours got to?'

'Anya's gone to Mike's house for tea. He's coming for Christmas dinner. I left Seth at the lodge because he had a . . . visitor.'

'Not Mel? Don't tell me she sobered up *that* quickly,' Ottie said in amazement.

'Perhaps she's come to persuade him to go to Barbados with her after all.'

'Well, he won't,' Ottie said confidently. 'Even if he'd wanted to, which I'm sure he doesn't, he wouldn't leave his beloved knots for that long, would he?'

'Probably not,' I conceded.

'What about you, though? Doesn't the idea of joining the jet set in the sun appeal?'

'No, not in the least. I'd much rather be here, getting Winter's End ready to open.'

'You know, you and Seth have *so* much in common,' she mused.

'Unfortunately, we have even more *not* in common,' I assured her.

I'd left my bag containing my bunch of keys and notebook upstairs in my room that morning, though tucked out of sight at the back of the wardrobe. They were still there, but so too was a familiar, lingering trace of Amouage Gold.

I flew downstairs to the parlour, which was empty apart from more aromatic evidence that Jack had been there. Could he *really* have been so unscrupulous as to take my keys and look for the household book in my absence, or did I have a nasty, suspicious mind? I hated the thought that he might have even touched Alys's coffer . . . though if he had opened it, he would have been disappointed to find only a Victorian book of bible stories inside.

While I was still standing there, undecided, the man himself startled me by sticking his head round the door. 'There you are, darling! I've been looking for you. I hoped you would come back alone.'

'Have you already been in here today?' I asked him sharply.

'Yes, of course – upstairs, downstairs and in my lady's chamber,' he said, smiling innocently.

'Oh,' I said lamely, wondering if I'd misjudged him. 'Why were you looking for me, Jack?'

'To apologise for putting brandy in the punch – but honestly, it was only a smidgen out of my hip flask to liven it up, not much at all. I've already apologised to Aunt Hebe and she's forgiven me,' he said virtuously. 'We've kissed and made up, and I think you and I should kiss and make up too, Sophy, after all those horrid scenes.'

'It doesn't matter,' I said, which was no more than the truth.

'Yes, it does. Mel is such a bitch! She'll say – or do – anything when she's in one of her jealous rages. But just because we had a quick fling years ago, it doesn't mean I can't fall for someone else now, does it? She just can't bear to let any man go.'

'True, I think she's mending her bridges with Seth right now,' I agreed. 'But, Jack—'

'Come and sit here on the sofa with me, Sophy, I want to talk to you,' he said, looking very serious.

I did, but as far away from him as possible, poised for a fast flight if he started to get smoochy. Alys's warning presence was so evident that I was surprised he wasn't aware of the sudden chill in the atmosphere.

'We've got to know each other very well, haven't we? I knew practically from the first minute I saw you that you were the one for me, and I could tell that you felt the same. Maybe I rushed you a bit too much, but—'

'Jack,' I interrupted, 'please don't!'

He shuffled along sideways like a parrot up a perch and took my hand. 'I know I got things wrong at the start, maybe let pride stand in my way, but now – well, now I see things more clearly. I love you, Sophy!'

To my horror he got down on one knee and presented me with a ring, a huge, flashing diamond. 'Marry me, Sophy. You can open the house if you must, do exactly what you like – just say you will marry me. We'll have a long engagement and—'

'No, Jack,' I began, trying to snatch my hand away as he pushed the ring onto my finger. 'I've been telling you for weeks that I don't feel that way about you.'

'Perhaps you still can't quite believe that I love you, but

359

by the time we get back from the Caribbean you'll be as mad about me as I am about you,' he said confidently. 'I've even sent the notice of our engagement to *The Times* already – *that's* how serious I am.'

I was tugging at the ring, trying to get it off, and starting to feel angry. 'For goodness' sake, Jack! I really don't feel like that about you in the least and I don't want to marry you!'

He attempted to take me in his arms just as Charlie, alarmed by my raised voice, sank his teeth into his ankle.

'Bloody hell!' Jack roared, and letting go of me, kicked him away.

Charlie yelped, and I swept him up into my arms and kissed the top of his silky, indignant head. 'Darling, are you all right?'

Lucy burst in. 'What on earth is happening? It sounded like a massacre in here! Is Charlie hurt?'

Then she noticed the blinding flash of the ring still on my finger. It would be a bit hard to miss – vulgar simply wasn't in it. '*Mum!*'

'It's not how it looks,' I said hastily. 'I just can't get it off. I think it will take soap.'

'Oh, come on, Sophy, we can tell her – we're engaged,' he announced to Lucy.

'No we're not! I keep telling you, Jack, I'm not marrying you. I'm not even going to Barbados with you. Not, not, *not*.'

'She doesn't love you that way,' Lucy explained to him kindly. '*I* could have told you that.'

'And you'd better take that announcement out of the paper again,' I said. 'Honestly, to think you could do that without asking me first!'

'I did ask you, and you said you just needed a bit more time to get to know me,' he protested.

'No, that's what *you* said.'

He'd thought he could sweep me off my feet, but I could see it was finally and belatedly dawning on him that it wasn't going to work.

'Could you leave us alone?' he asked Lucy and she looked at me doubtfully.

I nodded at her.

'OK – but I'm just next door if you want me. Come on, Charlie.'

When she'd gone, he said discontentedly, 'I can't believe you really mean it.'

'I do. Sorry, Jack, I'm not in love with you and I never will be.'

'Is it Seth? Mel thought you were getting too close. But she's determined to have him – and what Mel wants, she gets.'

'No, of course it's not Seth – it isn't anyone. I simply don't want to marry again, and I don't need to. Winter's End will always be your home, too, but you must stop all this.'

'You can't blame me for thinking you were in love with me. You led me on,' he said crossly.

'I know I did at first, and I'm sorry,' I said contritely. 'I soon realised I didn't feel that way about you, though I am very fond of you, Jack.'

'That's not good enough! Winter's End should be mine. That's what William really wanted – for us to get together. That's why I borrowed money on my expectations – and now I'm overstretched and it's all your fault. If you won't marry me, the least you can do is help me out.'

I looked at him, puzzled. 'What do you mean?'

'Increase the loan against Winter's End to bail me out, until my company's back in profit again,' he said sulkily.

'Absolutely not!'

'Look, it's just a temporary fix I'm in – but it's your fault that I need the money. It's not fair!'

'I'm sorry,' I said finally and, looking furious, he slammed out of the room.

Lucy came back in, carrying Charlie. 'Seth is so much nicer than Jack. I don't know what you ever saw in him.'

'Nice Seth is at this moment shacked up in the lodge with Nasty Mel and, for all I know, will be jetting off to Barbados with her after Christmas.'

'I'm sure he won't. Anyway, we need him, there's lots to do.'

'Tell me about it!' I snapped, sinking down onto the sofa.

'There's no need to be ratty with *me*, just because you made a mess of things,' she said, hurt.

'Sorry, darling, it's just been a bit of a day, to say the least.'

'Hebe told me what Ottie said about your father being one of the Pharamonds,' she said, plumping down next to me on the sofa.

'Yes, I've just been to see her and it's true. It's nice to know for sure, but I'm not going to approach the family. They know nothing about it, so there's no point in raking it all up.'

'It doesn't matter to me,' Lucy said. 'Mum,' she added, having gone into a trance for quite five minutes, 'Guy has to go back to work on Tuesday, so I thought I would go back over there with him for a couple of days, if you don't mind. We have a lot of catching up to do.' She sighed. 'I hadn't realised how much he'd changed . . .'

'No, that's fine,' I said, though feeling a bit hurt that she was leaving me so soon.

'He'll probably come back here with me at the weekend, if that's all right?'

'He's always welcome here. We'll keep the old nursery bedroom ready just for him, if you like, then he can come and go as he pleases.'

'Thanks, Mum!' she said, giving me a hug.

'Where is Guy at the moment?'

'In the stillroom with Aunt Hebe. When she found out he was a biochemist, she said she had one or two things he could help her with.'

'Oh?' I wasn't sure if that sounded ominous or not. 'Anya's off to Scotland for the New Year, but she'll be back well before Valentine's Day, though she says she won't stay in the house, she'll live in her van somewhere on the estate.'

'She seems to have got on well with that policeman – Mike, is it?' Lucy said, interested. 'He's nice – maybe she will stay with *him*!'

'Maybe. You can never predict what Anya will do, so we'll have to wait and see.' I made up my mind, since the day had been one of confessions and revelations, to add one more.

'Lucy, there's something I have to talk to you about,' I said, and told her about her father making contact. 'I didn't want anything to do with him, but perhaps I should have asked you how you felt before telling him to get lost?'

'I don't want anything to do with him, either. We've managed fine without him up until now, haven't we? And I don't believe all that stuff about not finding us was true, do you, Mum?'

'No, to be honest. I think he must be hard up and when he spotted the article in the paper thought I'd come into money. I don't suppose we'll hear from him again.'

'Good,' Lucy said. She got up. 'I'll go and make some tea and bring it through. You look as if you need it!'

Jack had slammed his way right out of the house and didn't reappear for dinner, though Mel's mother, Chloe, phoned later to say that he was dining there.

That was another surprise – I thought Seth would be too preoccupied with Mel to turn up, but no, he suddenly

363

appeared in the kitchen while I was trying to get that damned ring off. Mrs Lark had suggested immersing my hand in icy water for ten minutes and then applying soft soap, and I had just succeeded in finally wrenching it over my knuckles when he came into the kitchen. In fact, the ring shot off and landed at his feet, shining with soapy iridescence.

'There, that's off,' Mrs Lark said with satisfaction. 'Jack gave it to her, Seth, only it was too small and her finger was swelling up.'

Seth, expressionless, picked it up and handed it back. 'Should I congratulate you?'

'No,' I said shortly, but felt in no mood for explanations. He wasn't looking in the best of tempers himself, so things mustn't have gone well between him and Mel. But then, it was his own stupid fault for having an affair with her in the first place.

Aunt Hebe was upset that Jack was not at dinner, presuming, correctly, that he and I had had an argument. But apart from that the meal went quite well. Lucy and Guy were in good spirits, Anya was cheery, and even I was reviving with the relief of actually having got it through Jack's thick skull at last that I wasn't going to marry him.

Ottie was in an expansive mood, due to having finished the sculpture, and then downed a bottle or so of champagne. In fact, she insisted on sending Jonah down to the cellars to fetch a couple of bottles up, and got the Larks in to have a glass while toasting many Happy Christmases to come.

Only Seth remained quiet and gloomy.

Chapter Thirty-three: Dodgy Dealings

Joan has brought my household book as I requested, so that I might add some words to it, directed to my precious child. I must be guarded in what I say: she will take it with this, my journal and lock them away.

From the journal of Alys Blezzard, 1582

Jack reappeared at breakfast on Christmas morning, chastened, ingratiating and apologetic, though he tended to avoid my eye and I knew he was still feeling furious and aggrieved.

For the sake of Aunt Hebe we all pretended nothing had happened, even though everyone knew by now that he and I had had a row, and about the ring.

Come to that, my finger was still sore and swollen.

Like me, Anya is not a chatty person early in the day and once Jack had got his normal bounce back again and gone all cheery, I could see her wanting to kill him.

Lucy and Guy were the last to come down, and too wrapped up in each other to notice much at all, so I hoped this was True Love. I know Anya felt exactly the same – we just never thought it would happen.

Lucy was wearing a jewelled crown that had been in her Christmas stocking, and Guy a pirate scarf. Aunt Hebe gave them a slightly puzzled look, but said nothing. She probably thought they were the latest fashions.

We indulged in an orgy of unwrapping in the drawing room, while Charlie disembowelled a doggie stocking of treats on the priceless, if threadbare, rug.

The gifts ranged from the mundane (Jack had bought everyone a box of chocolates, though apparently he and Seth exchange a bottle of whisky every year, in some pointless male ritual), through the unusual (Anya's recycled tin and paper jewellery and my little patchwork lavender hearts), to the bizarre (Ottie gave everyone a decorative hen, made in Africa from strips of old plastic packaging and twisted wire).

Seth's, which he'd delivered to the house earlier in a trug, were all small potted plants – except mine, which was a single moss rosebud tied up with a sprig of greenery.

'He's cut one of his roses – for *me*?' I said, amazed.

'Strictly speaking, he's cut one of *your* roses, for you,' Ottie said with a grin. 'One of the old moss roses does sometimes have a flower or two at Christmas, though it's not like him to sacrifice it.'

'No, it isn't!' I agreed, stroking the closed petals with one finger to check it was real. 'What's this green stuff?'

'Myrtle,' Aunt Hebe said, giving me a strange look. 'Moss roses and myrtle . . .'

I went to fill a bud vase with water for my rose, which I carried up to my bedroom.

Downstairs everyone was still unwrapping and exclaiming, so I took the opportunity to quietly hand the ring back to Jack. 'I hope you can get a refund. It looks valuable,' I whispered, embarrassed. 'I got soap all over it, but I washed it off.'

'Thanks,' he said shortly, pocketing it, then noticing Aunt Hebe's eye upon us, kissed my cheek and said with a falsely bright smile, 'Happy Christmas, Sophy!'

He adjusted the blue cashmere scarf that Aunt Hebe had

given him around his neck with a flourish and announced, 'Now I'm going to take my favourite aunt out for a drive! Come on, Hebe – a bit of fresh air will give us an appetite for dinner.'

'But it's starting to snow,' I pointed out, for though the day had started off clear but freezing, leaden clouds had been gathering and the first flakes had begun to fall.

'Oh, it won't come to anything,' he said confidently, 'the forecast said a light scattering at the most,' and Aunt Hebe allowed herself to be persuaded.

After they had gone, I slipped away and went out to the camper van, checking no one was watching me. It had occurred to me that now Jack had checked Alys's coffer, he wouldn't bother again, so I could safely return her book to its rightful place – which is what I was longing to do. I just felt it was like putting the last piece of the jigsaw together, the vital bit.

And Alys must have felt the same, for as I locked her treasure away I felt her presence and a soft, satisfied sigh echo through the room.

The other book I replaced in the van. It would be a dead giveaway if Jack saw it lying around the house!

Seth arrived with Mike, and I thanked him for his present and said what a lovely gesture I thought it was. 'But you shouldn't have cut one of the roses off, just for me.'

'It was that or dig the whole bush up,' he said obscurely, then smiled. 'But I'm glad you like it.'

Lucy and Anya had found some games in the cupboard next to the drawing-room fireplace, and we'd all been happily playing Cluedo for ages when Jack and Hebe came back and put a damper on things. I could see from Hebe's expression when she saw me that he had been giving her his version of events, but she also looked worried and upset, so he'd probably spilled the beans about his financial problems too.

Actually, I did feel a little guilty about those, even though it wasn't my fault he'd got into such difficulties. But certainly not guilty enough to risk losing Winter's End by bailing him out.

Ottie glanced at her sister with a worried expression and Seth and Jack didn't look at each other at all: suddenly, there weren't so much hidden undercurrents in the room as hidden rip tides. It was quite a relief when Jonah came in to say that dinner was ready.

The table in the morning room had been extended and covered with a crimson cloth, and there were crackers and linen napkins folded into crisp stars by every place setting.

Lucy, Guy and Seth helped to bring the food to the table, and then Jonah and Mrs Lark sat down with us to eat it.

It's amazing how much good humour can be restored with a turkey dinner, a couple of glasses of good wine, crackers and silly hats.

Anya and I offered to clear away the remains afterwards, while the Larks left for their usual visit to relatives, and Mike and Seth gave us a hand.

Afterwards I took coffee and mince pies through to the library, where Hebe and Ottie were watching television in unusual amity and Lucy and Guy had started to lay out the pieces of an enormous jigsaw on the billiard table, but there was no sign of Jack.

'He's gone round to visit friends; he thought it would cheer him up,' Hebe explained, looking at me reproachfully. 'And luckily he was right about the snow – the merest sprinkling.'

'But very pretty, and I'm so stuffed with food I think I need a walk,' I said quickly, before Ottie asked why Jack should need cheering up. I could see the question was hovering on her lips.

'Good idea,' said Anya, and Mike and Seth said they would come too, though I hadn't the heart to wake Charlie up and drag him out with us, he looked so blissfully rotund and replete.

We started off down the drive together, the crystalline snow squeaking beneath our boots, but had soon split into two pairs, since Anya and Mike lagged behind us.

Seth and I were silent for quite a while, but after a bit we did start to talk. Well, I say *talk*, but in fact we were soon embroiled in one of our more animated discussions over my suggestion that Derek could repair the lime mortar between the stone flags of the Great Hall floor.

'Isn't it enough that you keep borrowing two of my gardeners?' he snapped. 'Now you want Derek, too! And I suppose you'll have them doing anything and everything but gardening, when the house opens to the public.'

'Well, actually, I did think they might take it in turns to check up on the car park and perhaps both go down after everyone's gone to pick up any litter and empty the bins. And what do you think about having the sole entrance for cars and coaches on the main road, where just the coaches come in now? It seems silly having separate entrances, don't you think?'

'I suppose so,' he agreed grudgingly. 'But we'd have to change the access details in the guidebook before it goes to press.'

'Ottie's sculpture will be off to be cast soon. We'll have to make a base for it in the rose garden before it comes back, I suppose.'

'Yes – another job for Derek,' he said gloomily, helping me over a stile.

When I turned to see how far back the others were, I noticed that Mike now had his arm around Anya so that looked promising, anyway.

I skidded a bit on a frozen puddle and Seth took hold of my arm. I was starting to feel a bit *Pride and Prejudice* – and just my luck to be stuck with the tall gloomy one, who wasn't about to declare his passion for anything other than knot gardens and was in love with the female version of Mr Wickham.

Jack left for London early on Boxing Day morning, so I presumed that, in financial straits or not, he still intended to take off for Barbados.

Without him, apart from Ottie and Hebe having one of their spats early in the day on an undisclosed subject, we were all a lot happier, including Alys, who made her presence known more often, in a friendly sort of way.

Lucy went back to Guy's flat with him for a couple of days and Anya and I threw ourselves into sorting out the tearoom and gift shop before she left for New Year in the Highlands. I missed her, but she would soon be settling down nearby for good, which was a nice thought. Seth was again coming up most evenings, because we were finalising the arrangements for the opening day, but since it appears that Mel flew off to Barbados after all, I suppose he had nothing better to do. But he does seem remarkably cheerful about it. I don't know if that is a good sign or not?

Jack phoned Hebe up several times from Barbados, and it turned out that he has persuaded her to sell enough of her stocks and shares to get his firm out of trouble. That's what Ottie suspected and what made her so mad – and me too, when I found out about it, though sort of guilty as well.

How could he do that to her? Hebe said she didn't need the money and he would pay her back anyway, so I hoped he would.

*   *   *

'I'm told by an inside source that Jack will be featuring on a popular TV programme tonight,' Ottie said, popping in as we were finishing breakfast on New Year's Day. 'It's called *Dodgy Dealings* and I think we should all watch it. It's at seven, Sophy. I'll come over.'

'*Dodgy Dealings*?' I stared at her. 'You mean, exposing something he's done, like a rogue traders programme?'

'Something like that, I think.' Ottie, standing by the hotplate, helped herself to a roll and filled it with crisp bacon.

'I'm sure your information is incorrect,' Hebe said with conviction, 'dear Jack wouldn't do anything wrong.'

'Wouldn't he?' said Ottie indistinctly, through a mouthful of food.

'No – I mean, there may have been one or two little tiny misunderstandings in the past, but that is all.'

'We'll see,' said Ottie.

We all foregathered in the library early that evening, including Seth, whom Ottie had insisted come over.

Lucy – now back from Guy's – as though we were about to watch some blockbuster film, had made a huge bowl of popcorn in the kitchen and was passing it around and we each had a glass of sherry or whisky.

The programme started by explaining that they were there to expose people who hadn't, strictly speaking, done anything illegal, but prospered by taking advantage of the elderly and/or desperate.

They had been contacted by someone who had signed over her house to Jack – an elderly lady, frail and pretty in pink cashmere and pearls. Aunt Hebe exchanged a look with her sister.

'That's Clara Cathcart!' she exclaimed.

Clara explained how she had been widowed and found keeping up the family home very difficult on a reduced income, yet she had hated the thought of leaving it. When Jack Lewis came along, offering to buy the property for a good price and promising that, as part of the deal, she would be able to live out her days there rent free, it had seemed the answer to her prayers. She trusted him because he was the nephew of a friend of her late husband . . .

Mrs Cathcart had duly signed, but soon discovered that by not reading the small print of the contract, she was powerless to stop what happened next.

'I was moved into an estate cottage while my house was "repaired", she said. 'But actually, instead it was divided up into luxury apartments. When I understood what was going on and protested, Mr Lewis explained that I *would* eventually be moving back into the house – into a flat on the ground floor, in what had once been the kitchen quarters,' she said indignantly.

'This fulfilled his contract to house me. Most of the contents of the house had gone into storage . . . I now had to sort and sell most of my belongings, which no longer fitted into my much reduced living space.'

'What do you think of your current accommodation, Mrs Cathcart?' asked the interviewer.

'The flat is quite nice, but it is not at all what I bargained for. It would have been better to sell up in the first place and move away, rather than live in a small part of what was once my home, now full of strangers.'

I think the correct term for what happened next is a sting.

The production team had set up an elderly female actress as the supposed owner of a small stately mansion somewhere in Cheshire, who had answered one of Jack's carefully worded advertisements.

We watched film clips of his original visit, where he exuded the sort of charm I already knew he possessed. Then it cut to his second visit, during which he clearly expected to clinch the deal, with the papers all drawn up ready to sign.

But this time the old lady was directed to insist on slowly reading every word of the small print and querying things, and you could see Jack start to get rattled.

'It says here that you will move me out of the house while renovations take place?'

'Of course. We wouldn't want you breathing in all that dust or being disturbed by the noise. But you would return as soon as it was finished,' he assured her.

'That sounds all right,' she said doubtfully.

'You can trust me,' he said, with one of his delightful smiles. 'Now, if you'd just like to sign here and—'

This was the point where the TV team came in and the presenter said, 'I'm Brent Collins of *Dodgy Dealings*, and I think perhaps you forgot to explain to this lady that when she moves back into her home, it will only be to a small flat in part of it.'

Jack looked initially appalled but soon attempted to talk his way out of it, saying he thought the lady understood his proposals and that he had many former customers very happy with their custom-made accommodation, in which they lived rent free. 'And what I am doing is entirely legal!'

'But you *are* misleading vulnerable people into signing documents that they don't understand, with false promises,' said the presenter. 'But this is one property you won't be getting. Perhaps you could explain—'

But Jack had had enough. 'No comment,' he said, pushing roughly past the TV team and the next shot showed him gunning away down the drive in his familiar sports car.

There was a short, stunned silence around the TV. Then Ottie said brightly, 'Well, that *was* interesting, wasn't it? He's going to find it very hard to persuade anyone to sell their

373

house to him after that, and you can kiss your money goodbye, Hebe.'

'I am sure Jack didn't intend to deceive anyone,' Hebe began indignantly. 'It—'

'Oh, come on, Hebe,' Ottie said. 'Of course he did! I've heard he's borrowed on his expectations too. And there are one or two other strange rumours going round – I've asked friends to look into them.'

'I'd heard about Clara Cathcart from Sir William,' Seth admitted, with a worried sideways look at me. 'I told Jack he was sailing a bit close to the wind – we argued about it. And if he's a bit overstretched, then he's going to find it even tougher now, isn't he?'

'This must be why he's been so keen to close all those deals before Christmas. He must have known this programme would be on,' I said. 'He might have warned us – and no wonder he suddenly decamped to Barbados!'

'I think what he did to those elderly people was ethically *totally* evil,' Lucy said. 'I hope he goes bust.'

'Lucy!' said Aunt Hebe, shocked.

'Well, I bet he'd have done the same to Winter's End, if Mum had been spineless enough to sign it over to him.'

'Oh, I'm sure he wouldn't – and Jack is terribly fond of Sophy!'

'It's in much safer hands with Mum, take it from me,' Lucy assured her, but although the programme might have shaken Hebe's faith, she continued to defend him.

Next day the announcement of my engagement to Jack appeared in *The Times* (I had entirely forgotten that he'd said he'd sent it) and I had phone call from a tabloid, though Mr Yatton fielded that one.

I wrested Jack's number in Barbados away from Aunt Hebe and phoned him, telling him we had seen the TV programme and also that he'd forgotten to cancel the engagement announcement.

He sounded relaxed and amused. 'The programme was a big deal about nothing. They can't touch me, I haven't done anything illegal. In fact, I made very nice little apartments for the owners, all mod cons. And I didn't cancel the announcement because I thought it would get my debtors off my back until things are sorted out, if they think I'm about to marry you. Look, just play along with it for a couple of weeks, OK?'

'*Not* OK! Absolutely not!' I said, and slammed down the phone.

I sent an announcement to *The Times*, unengaging myself, despite Hebe's pleadings.

Chapter Thirty-four: Revelations

*Joan promises to teach the child well, to give her the key
to the coffer when she should be of an age to value its
contents and to make known to her the truth.*
                    From the journal of Alys Blezzard, 1582

'It's nice to be just us two again, isn't it?' Lucy said a week
or so later. She was curled up on the parlour sofa with a
book and I was sewing my patchwork. Charlie was lying
on my feet, which had gone numb, though I hadn't got the
heart to move him.

'Yes, it doesn't often happen now, what with Hebe and
Ottie constantly around, not to mention Guy turning up
at the weekends. And you spend every morning with
Mr Yatton.'

'I'm as likely to find you arguing with Seth in here every
evening, or even vanished down to the pub,' she retaliated.
'And at least my mornings with Mr Yatton are productive.
The Winter's End visitor website is up and running and
we've successfully bid on eBay for a chiller cabinet for the
tearoom, and a couple of display cabinets.'

'My arguments with Seth are productive too,' I protested.
'Well, they are if I win them . . . He is so stubborn, sometimes there's just nothing doing with him. But that's head
gardeners for you.'

She cast me an unfathomable look. 'Aunt Hebe said that rose he gave you at Christmas was significant.'

'I don't know what she means by that, but it was certainly a surprise. I didn't think I rated one of his precious roses.'

'Oh, I'm sure he thinks you're worth a rose. Mum, while we are alone, do you think I could look at Alys's book again? It's ages since I've seen it.'

'You're not going to start treasure-hunting like Jack, are you?'

'No, I just want to refresh my memory, and I'm curious to see the box too.'

'All right,' I agreed, but I still made sure the shutters were closed over the windows and locked the doors before I opened the corner cabinet.

I lifted Alys's household book onto the table, while Lucy admired the way the inside of the chest was carved, and the compartments and false drawer fronts.

'This is really cute,' she said. 'What are these little stones?'

'Some sort of runes, I think, but I'm not sure. Put these cotton gloves on if you are going to touch the book. I keep some in here specially.'

She sighed, but did as I asked and then opened the book at the flyleaf, thoughtfully reading the inscriptions.

'I'll go and make us some coffee,' I said. 'Do you want gingerbread? Mrs Lark said she was making it earlier.'

'Mmm . . .' she said, engrossed.

When I came back she had gone back to examining the box, and had not only entirely pulled out the little drawers but was carefully studying the interior, her fair head bent low.

'What are you doing?' I said, setting the tray down a safe distance away from the chest. 'I know the inside is interesting, but not *that* interesting!'

Lucy, a look of concentration on her face, removed an

377

apostle coffee spoon from a saucer and applied the tip of the handle gently downwards . . . There was a small sound: 'There!' she said triumphantly.

'What is it? You haven't damaged it, have you?'

'No, I just had a hunch. There was only one rose carved among all those leaves and flowers, right down inside the central part of the chest where the household book was, so since Alys said the secret lay at the heart of the rose, I wondered if something might happen if I pressed it – and it has. See?'

I leaned over and she demonstrated. 'This bit of wood that looks like part of the carved design slides out at the front and there's a cavity underneath.'

Something lay within. 'It's another book – and hidden right under the first! I wonder what this one is. It's a tight fit,' I added, manoeuvring with the end of the apostle spoon.

'I was thinking the other day, when I read in the new guidebook about how Alys came here in her mother's place to try and heal the heir of Winter's End, that maybe she would have brought some recipes for the remedies she would need, written down. So I bet it's Alys's *own* household book.'

'Let's see if you're right,' I said, opening the slender volume with great care. On the first page was written, in faded ink and a difficult-to-read hand, 'This is Alys Blezzard's book, in her tenth year.'

'You seem to be right – except she began it long before she came to Winter's End.'

Side by side we sat, trying to make out the entries on each page. Most were lists of herbs and plants, with their uses, and recipes, some more esoteric than others. Gently leafing through, eventually we came to an upside-down page. A couple of scraps of loose parchment fell out, one inscribed with the pre-Christian symbol of good fortune called a Chi-rho cross, the other a line or two of verse. I picked it up, read it through, then stared at the scrawled initials on the bottom.

'A poem?' Lucy said, peering at it. 'The ink is more faded than that in the book, isn't it?'

I held it, my heart beating fast, remembering how I had laughed when Ottie had told me the family secret.

But Lucy was more interested in why the middle page of the book was upside down. 'Oh, I see,' she said, turning the whole thing over, 'she wrote something else, starting from the back. It looks like a sort of diary, though there are no dates, just years.'

I tore myself from the scrap of parchment, but not before gently laying it down in the centre of the table, as though it would shiver into dust at the lightest touch.

Lucy was right, it *was* Alys's journal of sorts, her thoughts from the day she was told she was to come to Winter's End in her mother's place and, though the handwriting was difficult to make out, we deciphered most of it.

It took us ages and at some point I heard Jonah try the door on his rounds of locking the house up, pause, and then go on. But we couldn't stop reading until we got to the end, and I know my face was wet with tears when I finished it – it was so sad. Lucy was sniffling, too.

Where it abruptly ended, another hand had added:

Some say they see the ghost of my mother, dressed in grey, beckoning the priest from the house and others say they have seen her shade dance like one abandoned in the oak glade. I feel her presence sometimes when I am in the little parlour where she spent much of her time, or walking in the fine knot garden; and some-times there is a scent of roses where none blooms. She did betray her husband, yet the Wynters in their turn betrayed her. But I feel she is now at peace, believing her actions were preordained and would one day be of use to her descendants here, in the place she loved. Until that day comes, if come it does, her inmost secrets were best concealed from curious eyes. Anne Wynter

'So Anne knew about this book too. But she only passed on Alys's secret orally; she didn't tell anyone else about the existence of a second manuscript . . .' I said slowly. 'Or the little verse.'

'This maid that's mentioned in Alys's journal must have told her how to find it.' Lucy turned a page or two and said, 'Here's where she says that her lover sent her a "line or two of verse, to her dark beauty". Do you think that's the one on the parchment?'

She reached over to pick it up and I said quickly, 'Be careful – I think it may be rather valuable.'

'WS?' she mused, studying the initials.

But I'd spotted another addition on the back of it, in Anne's bolder hand. I read out hollowly, '"These lines were penned by my true father, who was afterwards one of Lord Strange's men and made a name for himself in London with playwriting . . ."'

'Playwriting?' Lucy looked up at my bemused face. 'It's not – it can't be . . . ?'

'Shakespeare? According to Aunt Ottie, yes it is.'

Lucy went off into a peal of laughter, just as I had done when Ottie'd told me.

'No, really, Mum, it can't be true!'

'It all looks pretty authentic to me,' I said soberly. 'You know, it does sound as if Alys expected the truth to come out one day, when it would help Winter's End and her descendants – and there is nothing more likely to put Winter's End on the map than discovering something like this!'

'It certainly would be mega, mega publicity, whether we could prove it was true or not,' Lucy agreed. 'Oh my God – Shakespeare's my ancestor!'

'The only thing is, Ottie was totally against me using our supposed Shakespeare connection even before we found all this, so I am sure she will hate the idea of making it public.'

'We'll have to persuade her,' Lucy said, her eyes shining.

We called Ottie in next day for a secret pow-wow, while Hebe was down in the village for some meeting or other.

When we showed her what we'd found, she was amazed – and, I think, rather miffed that Lucy had been the one to discover the secret of the box, after all her years of custodianship. She was still reluctant to publicise the discovery, yet it was very clear, at least to Lucy and me, that this was the moment that Alys had predicted, when her secret could save Winter's End.

'And we will have to have the finds verified in some way, by experts, I suppose,' she said.

'They mustn't leave the house,' I said quickly. 'Alys wouldn't like that. I suppose we could get the experts to come to us . . . if we swear them to secrecy first.'

'What if they don't authenticate them?' asked Lucy.

'Oh, I should think they will fall out and argue about it for ever,' Ottie said, 'especially if they are not allowed to take them away to London. But that won't matter, will it? That you found them, and what they appear to be, are the two facts that will bring publicity and visitors flocking to Winter's End.'

'I think we are going to have to involve Mr Yatton,' Lucy said. 'We can trust him totally and we'll need his help.'

'And Seth,' I suggested. 'I'll need him to help me word the press release and all kinds of things.' Which was a bit

381

of a turn around from the day when I was so angry to discover that he knew all about Alys's book . . .

'There are other people we could trust to keep it secret too, like Guy and Anya, but perhaps the fewer that know in advance, the better. What are we going to do about Hebe?' Lucy asked. 'She'd tell Jack right away, wouldn't she?'

'Yes, but she will know something is going on,' Ottie said. 'Perhaps we should tell her that we have discovered Alys's secret treasure hidden in the box, and that it is just another, smaller household book that proves irrefutably that she was a witch? Even if she passed that on to Jack, he wouldn't find it very exciting.'

'So,' Lucy said, her eyes sparkling with excitement, 'when do we go public?'

On Tuesday I drove Aunt Hebe, who was attired in the full regalia of Queen Elizabeth I, including farthingale, ruff and red wig, down to the Friends' meeting at the village hall.

When we got there, even familiar faces like Mr Yatton's looked utterly different in Elizabethan dress. In fact, it looked like we had stepped back a few centuries. They wore costumes from every walk of life, but with a preponderance of the gentry, which I suppose is natural; how many of us would choose to be peasants if sent back in time?

After an official welcome I was introduced to one or two Friends who hadn't been at the meeting, including a small, shy man called Mr Glover, a local antiquarian. He had a bald head framed by wisps of hair and large, lustrous brown eyes . . .

I had a brilliant idea. 'Mr Glover, we could really do with someone to walk around on open days in the character of Shakespeare – and you would be perfect!'

He looked horrified and shrank away. 'M-me?'

'Oh, yes,' Effie agreed, 'what a good idea! And Mr Glover is a poet, too, you know – he would fit the part so well.'

'The odd slim volume,' Mr Glover said modestly, trying to edge away.

Aunt Hebe blocked his escape. 'Come along, Terence, we all have to do our bit.'

'What would I have to do?' he enquired nervously.

'Just wander about the place, holding a quill pen and a roll of parchment, looking for inspiration. You don't have to talk to anyone if you don't want to, you can remain mysteriously silent,' I said encouragingly.

'You might be quite inspired by the experience?' suggested Effie and, in the end, he allowed himself to be persuaded.

'Well, that's that sorted,' Aunt Hebe said, 'so gather round and let's get on with the meeting.'

It appeared that much manoeuvring for favourite jobs had been going on, but an equal sharing had been arrived at – probably by my aunt performing some sort of Judgement of Solomon on anyone reluctant to capitulate.

We had tea and biscuits while the Friends' roles were fine tuned, and then I was escorted to a sort of tissue-paper bower (something to do with the Brownies' activities) where I was to sit and watch the Friends trip a few stately measures.

Some of the serving wenches' blouses barely contained their ample bosoms during the livelier passages, which made Mr Yatton look even happier and poor Terence Glover even more petrified.

In the car going home Aunt Hebe said, 'Well, I think that went very well!' Then she took her wig and crown off, because she said her head was hot.

I caught Lucy in the kitchen this afternoon teaching Mrs Lark how to make sushi. She has given her one or two other recipes too, and apparently our starter tonight will be taramasalata with carrot batons. Wonders will never cease.

I am not sure what Aunt Hebe is going to make of that.

Jack returned from Barbados and paid us a flying visit, greeted by Hebe like a repentant prodigal son, though Ottie took him into the library and gave him a tongue-lashing for borrowing Hebe's money that we could hear from every corner of the house.

He emerged looking hurt and misunderstood, but promised he would pay Hebe back, with interest, when planning permission was granted for the site of Mel's house and he could sell it to developers. He also apologised to me for *The Times* announcement – but then he kissed me and said he would marry me tomorrow if I'd changed my mind, so he is quite irrepressible. But I do think he is genuinely starting to grow fond of me, as I am of him, despite all his devious machinations.

Seth, who was passing through the Great Hall at the time, gave us one of his sardonic looks, but since I saw Mel's grey horse tied up outside the lodge earlier that day, he had no need to talk.

He didn't say whether he found her repentant or not, but the visit did not seem to improve his increasingly dodgy temper and she soon took herself off to London.

Two elderly Shakespeare scholars were practically coming to blows in the parlour (under vows of strict secrecy – I told Hebe they were paper conservation experts), and the rest of the house and grounds resembled an ants' nest that had been stirred with a stick, as the weeks shortened before Valentine's Day.

Seth had finished planting out the lower terrace and was now practically manicuring the rest of the garden with his harried assistants, and Guy was here every weekend, allowing Lucy to boss him into doing all kinds of jobs or vanishing into the stillroom, where he was helping Hebe with her production line.

Anya came back – and quickly moved in with Mike! I heard it was the talk of the village, but I expected they would get over it. She was up here every day, setting up the shop and the stands, arranging stock, getting Lucy to chase up late orders, and making jewellery in the little workshop area she had set up.

There was so much to do and so little time – but there was an air of expectancy and excitement building up at Winter's End that united us all – including Alys. She was happy too, I knew.

One night, a few days before the Grand Opening, I went down to the Green Man with Seth.

As I thought, the journalist, George, was sitting in the corner, reading the paper and drinking a pint of bitter. I went and sat down opposite him, uninvited, and he looked at me warily over the top of his paper.

'George,' I said, 'how would you like me to give you a *huge* scoop, a story that the daily papers would fight to publish?'

'A scoop?'

'Yes, a shocking and amazing family secret handed down through the generations.'

He looked at me cautiously. 'What's the catch?'

'No catch – except that I don't want the story to come out until Valentine's Day. So, you would have to promise to keep it to yourself until the very last minute. Are you on?'

Naturally he couldn't resist the bait, but when I told him all, I thought he might have a heart attack before he wrote the story and had to buy him a double brandy before he got his colour back.

I agreed to let him photograph some of the evidence too – well, facsimiles of some of the evidence, to be honest – for while the real things could never leave the house, I intended to put it about that they were safely locked away in a bank vault.

The article duly appeared in a major daily paper on the morning of Valentine's Day:

> *THE WITCH WHO PUT A SPELL ON THE BARD!*
> *Recently found documents suggest that Alys Wynter, the notorious local witch, was Shakespeare's Dark Lady. If so – even more astoundingly – could the present-day Winter family of Winter's End, near Sticklepond, be the playwright's direct descendants?*

George had made quite a sensational job of it, and the phone began to ring and ring from dawn – but all they got was the estate office answering machine, telling them, 'Winter's End will be opened to the public from one p.m. today. If you are calling about the Shakespeare connection, then no further information will be given at present, though press handouts will be released.'

We were all too busy anyway – busy *and* nervous. The stage was set, the players were in place – lights, camera, *action!*

Chapter Thirty-five: Much Ado

*I am not yet seventeen – how brief was my day of dancing
in the sunlight! Yet there is enough of my mother in mee
to foretell that my child will have a happier life and that
all that happened to mee was meant to be. I have laid
up a treasure for her descendants. That must console mee.*

Alys Blezzard, 1582

I was up on Valentine's Day in time to watch the dawn rise,
which it did with serene promise. For once the weather
reports were right and it was going to be my favourite sort
of weather – bright, sunny and cool.

A late-home fox in the woods on the other side of the
valley gave a sharp, short cry, and far below I could see
the convoluted pattern of the new knot on the lower terrace
outlined with baby box trees, like dark running stitch against
the lighter gravel.

The butterflies in my stomach that I'd had all the
previous day were totally vanished. I examined the future
for portents, and found only the vaguest of darkness around
the edges, wispy and insubstantial, no great threats. I wore
flat boots, a cord skirt and a fitted mock sheepskin jacket
with a broad belt around my waist – Anya said I looked
faintly Cossack. The bee brooch, my lucky charm, was
pinned to the collar.

Aunt Hebe, still somewhat miffed at not being told about the discovery in advance, was trying to pretend that it was just another day, and said that once the opening ceremony was over she intended seeing to her walled garden, the hens and hives, as usual, though she *might* pop in to see if her line of rose-based items was selling later . . . all in full Queen Elizabeth I dress, of course.

The post brought me a big Valentine's card in Jack's unmistakable handwriting, and it occurred to me that he would probably have read the papers by now too . . .

Everyone was in place. The press and at least two TV crews were assembled in a special area near where I would be cutting the ceremonial ribbon across the drive, and behind me were my VIP guests.

Beyond the red ribbon were massing the public, many clutching copies of the glossy guidebook that had been delivered in the nick of time.

The sun was shining weakly and, as the clock in the stable tower chimed the hour, Fanny and Johnnie tried to upstage me by walking to and fro across the gravel emitting the occasional lost-soul cry. But they vanished the instant the first small child ducked under the ribbon and tried to grab them and I launched into my short speech.

'A hearty welcome, all of you, to the first open day of the year at Winter's End Manor. As you know, our unique garden restoration scheme is nearing completion – a fitting memorial both to my grandfather and the previous head gardener, Rufus Greenwood.'

'Hear, hear!' shouted Hal and Bob.

'Rufus Greenwood's son, Seth, is our present head gardener, and has worked wonders to complete the last part of the restoration in time.' I smiled across at Seth, whom I was pleased to see was not wearing his layers of ratty jumpers, though you still couldn't have mistaken him for anything else except a gardener.

'Now, some of you will have seen the papers this morning and read about our exciting discovery. Many old houses and families have secrets, and Winter's End and the Winters have more than their fair share. I'm afraid I'm going to go a bit *Da Vinci Code* here, but there has been a family tradition handed down among the women of the family, that the present day Winters are direct descendants of William Shakespeare, through a sixteenth-century ancestor, Alys – better known locally as Alys Blezzard, the witch.'

There was a buzz of comment, some of it from the press enclosure. I held up my hand.

'When this secret was revealed to me, I thought it was too incredible to be true. However, we recently discovered both Alys Blezzard's original journal and evidence that this legend was, in fact, true – I believe incontrovertibly, though I expect the experts will fight over it for years to come. You will find a small display, including some facsimiles of the documents, in the Great Hall, and you can also follow the Shakespeare Trail round the grounds. Winter's End is still a work in progress, and I hope that when the house reopens at Easter, you will all come back to visit us again.'

I stepped forward and Seth handed me a pair of large scissors. 'I would now like to declare Winter's End open!'

As soon as the ribbon fell to the ground a great stream of people started to rush past me, rather like the start of a marathon.

'How do you think that went?' I asked Seth, as he leaned over to switch off the mike.

'Fine. But brace yourself, here come the press,' he warned, as they converged on me.

* * *

'That went very well, I think,' Mr Hobbs remarked, when most of the assorted reporters and camera crews had rushed off into the house, or were standing about with their phones to their ears. To my embarrassment, I had been interviewed on TV – as had Aunt Hebe, in full farthingale.

'Miss Hebe looked magnificent, didn't she?' he added, but I had spotted a latecomer, a small, frog-faced man, plodding up the drive.

'Excuse me, Mr Hobbs, but I can see a very unwelcome visitor arriving. Do you remember when I consulted you about the phone call from the nephew of my old employer? Don't go away for a moment, will you?'

I stepped forward as he pushed through the VIPs to get at me. 'Conor, what are you doing here? I'm in the middle of opening the house to the public.'

'Brazenly wearing a stolen piece of jewellery to do it!' he said loudly, practically spitting with rage. 'And I had to purchase a ticket before they would let me through the gate!'

Guy, who was right behind him, said apologetically, 'I didn't like to radio ahead to warn you, in case you were still speaking, but I thought he looked a bit deranged so I followed him.'

'Thanks, Guy. And I do know him – unfortunately.'

'Yes – you know me well enough to realise that I meant it when I said that your theft would not go unpunished, if you refused to return my aunt's possessions—'

He broke off, for Aunt Hebe had reappeared, escaped from her own bevy of excited photographers, in time to hear his last sentence. She was a truly magnificent and, it has to be said, slightly scary sight, in full Queen Elizabeth mode, including red-gold wig and a sceptre.

Conor's mouth dropped open.

'Who is this man accusing my great-niece of theft?' she demanded. 'A *Winter*! How dare he!'

I thought that was a bit rich, since family connections had been well and truly tarnished on national TV by Jack's revelations. Unfortunately, Conor had also seen the programme, for he rallied and said, 'Ha! That would be the Winter family related to the Lewises, who defraud elderly widows out of their houses, would it?'

'Well, you should know, Conor,' I said tartly. 'It's just what you did to Lady Betty, only worse – you killed her.'

'He *murdered* her?' Hebe exclaimed.

'Just about. He got her to sign a power of attorney while she was in hospital after a fall, then he had her put into a nursing home and wouldn't let her back. He took over completely.'

'Rubbish!' he blustered. 'My great-aunt lost her mental faculties after a fall. And in any case, it is beside the point. Sophy persuaded her to hand over two items of valuable jewellery – a brooch and a necklace – and I want them back.'

Aunt Hebe turned to me. 'Do you indeed have these items?'

'She's wearing one. That bee brooch there is mine!'

'Lady Betty did give me this brooch, but I don't have the necklace, she gave that to someone else at the same time, while she was first in hospital and fully in possession of her faculties.'

'Rubbish. The receptionist at the nursing home says she had it when she arrived there, and *then* saw you wearing it after your last visit!'

'She's lying.'

'Prove it!'

Mr Hobbs, who had looking on as if watching a puzzling play, said, 'My dear sir, before making this kind of allegation, you should check your facts properly. There is indeed proof that Miss Winter is speaking the truth and I have verified it.'

I dug into my bag and produced a folded sheet of paper. 'I think Lady Betty had already begun to suspect your motivation when she gave me the brooch, and the cook, Mrs Dukes, the necklace. She insisted on signing a statement saying what she had done and had it witnessed by the vicar, who had known her for over thirty years. So you see, you're not going to get them back.'

His mouth opened and closed. 'Forged,' he said at last. 'You've discovered how valuable they are and—'

He yelped as Aunt Hebe smote him across the head with her sceptre. It was only plastic, fortunately, but it still made him stagger about, clutching his ear.

'I'll have the police on you! Assault – theft—'

'Actually, I *am* the police,' said Mike, who must have arrived while I was distracted.

'Then I wish to charge this woman with assault and—' began Conor.

'*I* didn't see any assault,' Mike said. 'Did anyone else?'

'No,' we all chorused.

'And if you attempt to charge my client with the theft of a brooch to which she has a perfect right, we will countersue for defamation of character,' said Mr Hobbs.

Conor glared around impotently at the circle of hostile faces. 'You ought at least to pay me the value of it. The yellow diamonds alone are worth—'

I squinted down at it. 'Diamonds? I thought they were crystals! But whatever it is made of, it doesn't matter. I love it because Lady Betty gave it to me, not for any other reason, and I'm still not giving it up.'

'I am afraid you haven't got a leg to stand on, Mr Darfield,' Mr Hobbs told him with finality. 'I would advise you to leave now, before charges against you are pressed.'

'Yes, perhaps I should escort you to the gate,' suggested Mike. 'It's time I was off, in any case.'

As they vanished down the drive I said, 'Thank you, Mr Hobbs – and Aunt Hebe, you were magnificent.'

'I know how to deal with *his* sort,' she said regally. 'Now, if you will excuse me, I want to see how my products are selling in the shop, and then change and get back to the garden.'

'Why don't you go and have tea with Mr Hobbs first, before the rush starts? I should think most people are still outside yet.'

'I suppose I could,' she agreed.

'And I had better go and do the rounds, see how everything is going on,' I said absently as a tall figure came into view in the distance, a giant among a family of Japanese tourists. Seth seemed to be directing them into the maze, and I just hoped he would rescue them later if they got lost, for I was sure they would not be able to see over the top of the hedges.

Mr Glover, ruffed and carrying his quill and furled parchment, scurried furtively along a distant path, shadowed at a respectful distance by several visitors. He turned his domed bald head in my direction briefly, then was gone.

When it all got too much for him, I had given him directions to hide in the fern grotto, which was out of bounds to the public. I made a mental note to have a tray of refreshments taken down there later. The poor man would have earned it.

It was late afternoon before things started to quieten down, and I managed to snatch a break, sitting on a bench on the top terrace with Ottie and Hebe (now attired in more mundane cord trousers and a padded gilet).

In fact I was feeling exhausted but very happy, when two things happened to make it rain on my parade: Jack suddenly appeared from the house, and then I spotted Mel

Christopher and Seth talking together below. She looked up, then headed towards the steps, trailed by Seth.

'Jack, dear boy!' Aunt Hebe said. 'We didn't know you were coming! Didn't you tell me you wouldn't be able to make it?'

'That was before I read the newspaper this morning!' he said, and I could see he was furious. 'Didn't any of you think to share your fascinating little discovery with *me*?'

'I didn't know either until this morning,' Hebe said. 'They kept me in the dark too – but it is quite wonderful, isn't it?'

'You'll certainly be raking the money in now, Sophy. And this poem, or whatever it is, will be worth a fortune!'

'It doesn't matter what it's worth, we won't be selling it,' Ottie said. 'But it certainly won't do visitor numbers any harm!'

'And don't you think you should give *me* a share in all this?' he demanded angrily.

'Share in what?' asked Mel from behind him. 'Jack, I thought you might be here. I want a word with you!'

'Not now, Mel,' he said impatiently.

'It's never now – and things are getting a little *urgent*,' she snapped.

'You know, I had an interesting phone call from an old friend the other day,' Ottie said conversationally, but in carrying tones. 'I'd asked her to check some rumours out for me – and guess what? Jack and Melinda are married.'

'Married?' I gasped, turning to stare at Jack, the man who had been professing love and pressing me to marry him, all this time. 'Are you *sure*? I mean—'

'Yes, they married quietly in London, a short time before William died. Presumably they kept it quiet because he disapproved of Mel.'

Hebe paled. 'Surely there is some error? Jack—'

But he was looking at me, blue eyes earnest. 'We soon realised it was a mistake, Sophy! When I went down to make her an offer for the house . . . well, one thing led to the other. But we're getting divorced.'

'And you owe *me*, for agreeing to keep quiet about it, all this time!' Mel snapped.

'Oh? And does poor old Seth know anything about it – or that he's been replaced by your rich new lover in London?' Jack said nastily.

I was so stunned by all this that I had entirely forgotten that Seth had followed Mel, until he took two hasty strides forward and felled Jack with a single blow. Then he stood back, breathing heavily.

Jack got up slowly and warily. 'I suppose I deserved that.'

Seth frowned and examined his skinned knuckles. 'Actually, I'm not sure you do. Maybe you deserve an apology instead, since I'd no idea Mel was married to you when she came back here or I wouldn't have—'

He broke off and turned on Mel. 'You lied to me.'

'It was always you I loved, Seth,' she said nervously, taking a step back.

'I can't imagine why you and Jack got married in the first place,' Ottie said frankly, 'except that you are both shallow, grasping types. I suppose like called to like.'

'Thanks, Ottie,' Jack said, with a glimmer of humour.

'Jack thought I was a hugely rich widow,' Mel said sweetly, 'but actually, Clive tied all his money up in his children, without telling me, the bastard. All he left *me* was that monstrosity of a house and a small annuity. But then it turned out that Jack wasn't rich either and he didn't even get Winter's End. I always rather fancied living here, a Lady.'

'You'd never be a lady, because you can't make a silk purse out of a sow's ear,' Ottie said frankly. 'So you fell out when you discovered each other's lack of cash?'

Mel nodded sulkily. 'Jack said if I kept quiet about the wedding, he'd pay me off when Sophy signed Winter's End over to him and I could have money *and* you, Seth. I always loved you!'

Seth's arms were folded across his broad chest, probably to stop him hitting anyone again. 'I don't think you know the meaning of the word.'

'Actually, you have made a slight error of judgement, Mel, because Seth is by no means penniless and he will be *very* well off one day,' Ottie said. 'I've been raking in the money for my sculptures for years, plus my investments have done rather better than Hebe's, and I've left everything to him. He's as close to a son as I've got.'

'*What?*' Melinda looked from one to the other. 'I thought you would leave everything to Sophy!'

'I've given her a sculpture – if she gets desperate she can flog it. Mind you, if Seth is daft enough to marry you once you've divorced Jack, I might be tempted to change my will.'

'I won't be,' he said. 'Her new, rich lover in London can have her.' And, turning on his heel, he walked away.

'Seth!' wailed Mel, running after him and catching at his arm, but he shook her off. She looked back at us and then trailed away.

'So everything you said to me was just a sham, Jack?' I said sadly. 'I never really believed you were in love with me, but to find you'd been trying to cheat Winter's End out of me like that . . .' I shook my head, tears welling.

'Sophy darling,' he said, hurt, 'of course I love you! I meant every word, and we'd have been married the minute my divorce came through. We still can be, if—'

'Oh, shut up!' I said shortly, the tears popping right back into my ducts. 'You wouldn't know the truth if it bit you on the ear.'

396

His smile became more genuine. 'I do love you, Sophy – you're so *acerbic*!'

'Well, come to that, I suppose I still love you, in a way – warts and all. But like a brother.'

'I don't know why you keep saying that Jack has warts,' Hebe said, rallying from her state of stunned stupor. 'I am sure everything has been a frightful mistake and if we go back to the house and talk things over . . .'

'I don't think there's very much left to discuss, Aunt Hebe, and I've got things to do – excuse me.'

Suddenly I wanted to be alone and made for the private side of the garden, where I sank down onto a rustic bench in the wilderness and burst into tears.

'Don't, Sophy,' Seth said, behind me. 'I can't bear to see you cry.'

'Well, go away then!' I snapped, fishing out a tissue and blowing my nose.

Instead he came to sit next to me, looking troubled and sad. 'Jack's not worth crying over, you know – but I suppose there's no point in telling you that. I'm so sorry.'

I stopped sniffling and stared at him. 'I'm not crying over him, you idiot. It's just, well, it's all come as such a shock and I don't know what's real and what's not any more. And I know *you* loved Mel, so to hear all that must have been just as bad for you. But maybe Mel does still love you, in her way, so—'

'I don't think she even understands what the word means. Once I realised that, I knew that a beautiful face just wasn't enough any more.'

'But you've been having an affair with her all this time, so you must care for her and—'

'No, I haven't! I'm ashamed to say I *did* succumb briefly – but that was before I met you. She never gave up trying to get me back, even though she could see I was falling for you.'

397

'For *me*?' I said incredulously.

'Practically from the moment I met you. But it's all right – I've always known you were in love with Jack, even if you couldn't quite bring yourself to trust him completely,' he said gloomily. 'I knew he was an untrustworthy character with a dodgy set of ethics – and that he and Mel had been having an on-off relationship since she was widowed – but I couldn't say so, could I, while you were head over heels in love with him?'

'But I've *never* loved Jack,' I protested.

He looked up. 'Never?'

'Well, admittedly, I was dazzled by him a bit at first, as you were by Mel, though it soon wore off. How could you possibly think I was in love with him?'

'I haven't been able to think properly at all since you arrived and started turning my life and my plans upside down,' he said, sounding more like his old, argumentative self. 'And I was jealous of Jack.'

I met his eyes and discovered that otherworldly glow in them – this time for me. 'I've been jealous of Mel too, and I knew she was still involved with Jack to some extent because I saw them kissing in the shrubbery once. But I just didn't want to admit to myself that I'd fallen for a big, stupid, argumentative—'

He cut my words off by grabbing me and kissing me hard. Being a perfectionist, his kiss was perfectly planted.

Someone in my head was singing 'Sowing the Seeds of Love'.

Later, walking back to the house, his arm around me, he said, 'Did you never notice that I made a true lover's knot for you in the Shakespeare garden? Or that the moss rose I gave you for Christmas meant my heart was yours? Is there *no* romance in your soul?'

I sighed happily. 'No – and this is never going to work, you know. We're like chalk and cheese, we argue all the time.'

'Yes, but I think we'll make a good partnership now we've both come to realise that the house and the gardens are equal in worth – that, like the two of us, the one is nothing without the other.'

'Perhaps you're right, Seth. After all, if *I* love the house best and *you* love the garden, that balances perfectly. The jewel and the setting – that's what Alys said to me once.'

'Alys? You still think she's talking to you?'

'I *know* she is. And she's currently saying the sixteenth-century equivalent of "What took you so long, dimwits?"'

'It's been a comedy of errors,' he agreed, taking me in his arms again. Then he said, punctuating the words with kisses, 'Shall I compare thee to a summer's day? Thou art more lovely . . .'

He broke off as Lucy came through the arch near the maze. She smiled on us benignly.

'There you are, Mum. Ottie just told me what happened with Mel and Jack, and I wondered if you were all right.' She grinned. 'But I see you are *more* than all right.'

'Yes, but you look a bit pale, darling – are you exhausted?'

'No, I'm angry. I just met my father for the first time, at the gate – drunk,' she added in disgust. 'Guy radioed me when he turned up and said who he was, but I wouldn't have known him from that old photo you've got.'

'Your *father*?' Seth said.

'Don't worry, Mum hasn't seen him for over twenty years,' Lucy said to him kindly.

'My ex,' I explained. 'I'm sorry you had to meet him like that, Lucy.'

'He called me his "wee lassie" in a terribly bogus accent and tried to kiss me, but I told him I knew all about him and didn't want anything to do with him, and that you didn't want to see him, either. Then he got angry and said maybe the papers would want to know some of the things he could tell them.'

'I can't imagine what he *could* tell them, unless he makes something up.'

'I told him to get lost. What a sleaze bag!' she said disgustedly. 'Let's hope that's the last time he turns up.'

I looked at my watch. 'Come on, it's nearly time to close up and we've been away for ages.'

'Relax, Mum. Guy and I have sorted everything out and everyone's coped really well – no crises at all, except Charlie got out of the kitchen at one point and some children fed him cake until he threw up. But he's all right now.'

Everything, in fact, seemed to be all right now . . .

Chapter Thirty-six: Endpapers

*This proof of what my mother said should lie hidden,
for it would go ill if it were discovered, even though she
believed it would one day ensure the fortunes of her
descendants and their continuance at Wynter's End. I
pray it may be so, but do not see how that might ever
come to pass.*

Anne Wynter, 1602

One of the newspapers paid Rory money for some lurid
stories about my past but, as I pointed out to them when
they asked me for my version of events, I was too young
when I married him to have had one. I told them all about
my struggles as a suddenly single mother instead. The paper
ran our two stories side by side and apparently Rory left
the country soon after that.

Not surprisingly, I didn't hear from Conor again after
Hebe hit him on the head with her plastic sceptre.

Hebe grew reconciled to our marriage, and for her sake
Seth and Jack declared a truce. He may be a complete
rogue, but I couldn't help but still be fond of my handsome cousin . . .

The Shakespeare scholars continue to argue over the
evidence and don't look like coming to a conclusion
any time soon, but Seth and I kept the story going by

judiciously feeding titbits to the press, through the medium of George.

By May, it was clear that Winter's End had become a top visitor attraction, and we were accepting coach bookings months in advance. My gamble had paid off.

Foreign tourists hung around for hours, cameras at the ready, awaiting Hebe's appearances as the Virgin Queen or to take photographs of each other arm-in-arm with the bashful Bard – if they could catch him.

But then, all the Friends, in their colourful costumes, were a big hit – especially the silent young woman with the curly dark hair who seemed to appear practically out of nowhere when visitors were admiring the paintings in the minstrels' gallery, even though she only smiles and shakes her head when they ask her questions . . .

One fine Sunday, a few days before our wedding in May, Seth and I were looking down at the lower terrace, which had begun to grow together and showed promise of being the most beautiful of the three.

The house was closed, but faint shouts were borne on the breeze as Derek, Hal and Bob earned some overtime, helping to install *The Spirit of the Garden* among the roses.

'I never thought everything could turn out this happily,' I sighed, but Seth, who had that familiar faraway look in his eyes, was obviously turning over some knotty garden problem in his head and didn't reply, except to tighten his arm around me a bit.

'Guy and Lucy will move into the lodge together, when we've had it done up a bit . . . Mike is trying to persuade Anya to tie the knot with him, too . . . And it even looks as if Ottie will manage to badger Jack into repaying Hebe's money, now he's sold the site of Mel's property to developers.'

And there would be no conflict in sharing Winter's End

402

with Seth, because the house is my passion, the garden his. We complement each other in every way . . .

It was Alys who had made all this possible and I knew she approved of what I was about to do.

I gave Seth a dig in the ribs with my elbow and he grunted indignantly. 'What was that for?'

'You're not listening to me, and there's something I want to show you.'

'Oh God – it's not another design for a replacement summerhouse, is it?'

'No, it's a sort of wedding present, from Alys.'

I fished in my by now battered embroidered bag and produced a card folder containing a slip of torn parchment between two pieces of acid-free tissue. 'Here you are. It's another thing we discovered with the hidden cache, but we didn't tell anyone about it.'

He examined it with interest. 'I recognise that symbol. It's an ancient one, the Chi-rho. And while it's nice of Alys to want to share her magical symbols with me, I don't quite see—'

'Turn it over,' I said patiently. 'She reused a bit of some other document.'

He did and suddenly went still and silent.

'It *is* the lost bit of the garden plan, isn't it?' I asked. 'And though it's pretty faded, can you see what's in the middle of the lower terrace?'

He lifted his head, his green eyes glowing in the way that always made me feel oddly breathless. 'Yes – it's a true lovers' knot,' he said softly, then pulled me into his arms and thanked me in the way I'd hoped he would – while safely holding the precious scrap of parchment well out of harm's reach, of course.

You could never take the gardener out of this man and that, luckily enough, turned out to be just the way I liked it.

Which season are you?
Take our fun quiz and find out!

1. If you won £5000 on the Lottery what would you spend it on?

    A – You would immediately whisk yourself and your loved ones away on a fantastic beach holiday, no expense spared!

    B – You would do that home improvement that you've always dreamed of – a swanky new bathroom or an extension to the kitchen.

2. When surfing the net, which are your most visited websites?

    A – Your first click is always something that lets you know what's going on in your area – sites like *Time Out* or *Daily Candy*.

    B – You are a dedicated Facebooker, and love spending your lunch breaks (or sneaky ten minutes when the boss isn't looking!) catching up with old friends.

3. What kind of food do you most like to cook?

    A – You're adventurous in the kitchen, and love to try complicated South-East Asian dishes with unpronounceable ingredients.

    B – You're a big fan of comfort food – yummy favourites like mashed potatoes or overflowing bowls of pasta.

4. When it comes to taking time off, what's your ideal way to spend your holiday?

A – Holidays to you mean two weeks of total relaxation, lying on a warm beach with a good book in one hand and a long, cool drink in the other . . .

B – Your ideal break is cultural as well as recreational and you always prefer far-flung destinations to package deals. You're not fulfilled unless you have to get vaccinations before your trip!

MOSTLY A's – Spring/Summer Suzy

Like a lizard, you love the heat and like to be out and about between March and September. You're never happier than when you're lazing on a beach, enjoying an alfresco drink in a pub garden or wielding the tongs at a BBQ!

MOSTLY B's – Autumn/Winter Annie

You love everything about the winter months, whether it's making rib-sticking puddings to insulate you from the cold, wrapping the family's Christmas presents or crunching through piles of autumnal leaves!

LAST CHRISTMAS

Julia Williams grew up in North London, one of eight children, including her twin. Coming from a large family, Christmas was usually a chaotic affair, and her earliest memories of the festive season include tales of her parents' drinking sherry with the milkman at four in the morning, that deliciously exciting sound of rustling paper in the dark, always wishing for snow and never getting it, the inevitable satsuma in the stocking, watching *The Wizard of Oz* – again – and fighting for the last chocolate in the Quality Street tin. Since she's grown up and had a family of her own, she wonders with awe how her parents managed to always make Christmas so much fun without any apparent signs of stress . . .

To find out more about Julia go to her website at www.juliawilliamsauthor.com or visit her blog at www.maniacmum.blogspot.com.

By the same author:

Pastures New
Strictly Love

JULIA WILLIAMS

Last Christmas

AVON

This novel is entirely a work of fiction.
The names, characters and incidents portrayed in it are
the work of the author's imagination. Any resemblance to
actual persons, living or dead, events or localities is
entirely coincidental.

AVON
A division of HarperCollins*Publishers*
77–85 Fulham Palace Road,
London W6 8JB

www.harpercollins.co.uk

This paperback edition 2011

1

A catalogue record for this book is
available from the British Library

ISBN-13: 978-1-84756-339-2

Set in Minion by Palimpsest Book Production Limited,
Grangemouth, Stirlingshire

Printed and bound in Great Britain by
Clays Ltd, St Ives plc

Mixed Sources

Product group from well-managed
forests and other controlled sources
www.fsc.org Cert no. SW-COC-1806
© 1996 Forest Stewardship Council

FSC is a non-profit international organization established to promote the
responsible management of the world's forests. Products carrying
the FSC label are independently certified to assure consumers that they
come from forests that are managed to meet the social, economic
and ecological needs of present and future generations.

Find out more about HarperCollins and the environment at
www.harpercollins.co.uk/green

For Ann Moffatt and Rosemarie Williams,
Granny Dreamboats both.

Prologue

Marianne sat back in the comfort of Luke's brand new BMW M5. Every inch of its sleek leather interior screamed luxury, while the latest technogizmos pronounced its top-of-the-range, worthy-of-praise-from-Jeremy-Clarkson status. She glanced at Luke, who oozed confidence with practised ease as he drove with one hand on the wheel. Marianne sighed happily . . .

'What?' he said, laughing at her.

'Just pinching myself,' she replied. 'I still can't believe all this is real.'

'You are daft,' said Luke grinning, before he accelerated into the wind.

It wasn't the first time she'd had to pinch herself since she and Luke had got together. His charm and looks had entranced her from the start, even though she had felt thoroughly out of his orbit. In fact, Luke was so far removed from the sort of man she tended to fall for, the strength of her feelings had taken her by surprise. But there was something mesmerising about the combination of hazel-brown eyes and fair hair, which swept back off a strong, classical-looking face.

Under normal circumstances Marianne would never have met someone like Luke, but, thanks to Marianne's two rich friends, Carly and Lisa, who still seemed to earn ridiculous amounts of money in the City, even with the credit crunch, she had found herself on a skiing trip during February half term. Her teacher's salary wouldn't usually have stretched to that, but at the last minute Carly had pulled out and generously donated her space to Marianne, who then spent a dizzyingly intoxicating week hitting the slopes and revelling in an après-ski environment she could hardly have imagined being part of in her normal life.

She'd met Luke on the first day when, overcome with nerves, she'd fallen flat on her back in front of a group of more experienced skiers. Their laughter hadn't been unkind, but Marianne was already feeling like a fish out of water in the company of these sophisticated beautiful people. She was so far removed from her own world, and they knew it. Now she felt that she'd proved herself for the ugly-duckling klutz she undoubtedly appeared to them.

Luke was the only one who hadn't laughed. Instead, he'd swept her up in those strong arms and offered to teach her to ski. Throughout that week he'd treated her with tenderness and affection, combined with infinite amounts of patience at her obvious lack of skiing ability. Marianne had been hugely grateful for his kindness. The fact that Luke was incredibly good looking, charming and clearly fancied the pants off her had also been a great help. He made her feel like a graceful swan, even though she knew the ugly duckling was hidden away somewhere, underneath the ski gear. Being with him was a magical, dazzling, life-changing experience.

Since then, Marianne felt like her feet hadn't touched the ground as Luke whisked her into a world so completely alien to her own. He took her to Henley for the Regatta, to Wimbledon for Finals Day, to Silverstone for the Grand Prix, for weekends away in the country at exquisite hotels where she felt like a film star. Every day with Luke was an adventure, but today he had surpassed all her expectations.

He'd rung the previous night. 'Fancy a weekend at my parents' place in the country?' had been his opening gambit. Marianne's heart had leaped with anticipation. With Luke it was always feast or famine – he was either frantically busy at the weekends, or impulsively spiriting her off somewhere exciting. Which was wonderful but sometimes Marianne wished they could put their relationship on a bit more of an even footing.

Did this mean that finally he was going to introduce her to his family? He'd met her parents twice now. She'd been nervous as hell on both occasions, but Luke was his usual charming self, and professed himself delighted by Marianne's rather tame suburban home. Her parents had been charmed, and her mum, who was desperate for grandchildren, had to be restrained on at least one occasion from asking outright when Luke was going to join the family.

Marianne had expected a reciprocal invitation, but so far it had been unforthcoming. Luke, it seemed, was happy to meet her family, but evasive about his own. She knew he'd got money, knew he worked for the family firm in property development – 'building eco towns' was how he put it – but, apart from that, the crumbs of information he'd scattered had been few and far between. Perhaps if she weren't so dazzled by his brightness, she would have asked more questions earlier. Besides, if he wanted to tell her things, she surmised, he would. She didn't want to pry.

They were driving through winding country lanes, the late summer sun warming the car and casting long shadows on fields ripe with corn and bursting with abundance. Cows wandered contentedly through fields, and birds sang in hedgerows. It was the countryside of her dreams. Of her imagination. As a child Marianne had been obsessed with

3

stories about children having adventures in the country-side: The Famous Five, Swallows and Amazons, the Lone Pine Club all seemed to lead much more exciting lives than she did in the dull North London suburb that she called home. Marianne's favourite television programmes, *The Waltons* and *Little House on the Prairie*, provided further confirmation that her ideal future involved a cosy country cottage, being married to a man who adored her, having several rosy-faced children and, of course, heaps of animals. Their square handkerchief of a garden not allowing for pets, Marianne had been determined to make up for that as an adult.

Growing up in a grey London street, Marianne had always felt stifled and hemmed in by the city. She was never happier than when she was out on a long country walk, breathing in the fresh air and feeling at the mercy of the elements. It had long been her dream to live somewhere like this.

'This is fabulous,' Marianne said. 'What a wonderful place to live.'

'It's okay, I suppose,' said Luke dismissively. 'But I get a bit bored being a country bumpkin.'

'Really?' Marianne was incredulous. She couldn't understand why anyone coming from here would ever think about leaving.

'Nearly there now,' said Luke, manoeuvring the car round an incredibly slow tractor, before putting his foot down and racing through the lanes at an exhilarating speed. The wind whipped back her hair and the sun shone bright on her back. It felt fantastic to be alive.

And then, suddenly, there it was. They came round a bend, and there before them, in the middle of a vast lawn – across which *peacocks* were wandering – was an imposing Tudor house, complete with two wings, Elizabethan towers, black and white timbering and pretty gables. Marianne felt her jaw drop. Finally she was seeing Hopesay Manor, home to the Nicholas family for generations, and where Marianne's future might lie.

'*This* is the family home?' she squeaked.

Luke glanced across at her in amusement.

'Didn't I say?'

'Not exactly,' said Marianne. She'd imagined Luke living in a huge house, of course. But she'd thought it would be a rockstar kind of house, with its own pool and tennis court in the back garden. But this, this was a mansion. Vast didn't quite cover it.

'Well, it's not technically where I grew up. My parents have a pad a bit closer to Hope Christmas. Hopesay belongs to my grandfather. Not that he's here much. Silly old sod still insists on globetrotting, even at his age. I don't think he's been back here for more than a day or two for years.'

Luke said this with unaccustomed savagery and Marianne was taken aback by his sudden vehemence.

'Don't you get on with your grandfather?'

Luke smiled. 'Oh, the old bugger's okay, I suppose. He's just a bit blinkered about the way the world works these days. Insists we have duties to our people, as he puts it. He likes to think we live in some bygone feudal age, when everyone doffs their cap to Sir. He can't see the world's changed.'

'What does he think about your eco towns then?'

'He doesn't know anything about them,' admitted Luke. 'I'm the only one interested in the business side of things in this family. My mum and dad are more into playing bridge and drinking G&Ts than anything else. They're pretty shortsighted too. I run the show in his absence. If he doesn't like the way I do things he should turn up at board meetings more.'

He swept the car into the circular gravel drive in front

5

of the house and they got out and crunched their way up the path to the house. The large oak door was about twelve foot high and looked immensely imposing. Marianne could just about make out an inscription carved in stone above the door. Something about being happy and owing it to God.

'What does it say?' she asked, squinting up to try and see better.

'Oh, nothing important.' Luke dismissed her question with a careless wave, and lifted the brass door knocker and banged it really hard. That, too, was unusual, Marianne noted, as it seemed to depict a man – or was it a man? – wearing some kind of long robe and crushing a serpent underneath his feet. Marianne wanted to ask but, put off by Luke's evident lack of interest in anything remotely connected to the house, she fell silent. Luke impatiently banged the knocker again, and eventually a rather dusty-looking retainer, who could have been any age from fifty to a hundred, came and opened the door.

'Ah, Mr Luke, sir,' he said. 'It's been a while.'

'Hello, Humphrey,' said Luke. 'This is my friend, Marianne.' Why doesn't he say girlfriend, Marianne thought, with a disappointed lurch of her heart. 'I just thought I'd show her round the old pad before we go to see the folks.'

Humphrey nodded, and disappeared somewhere into the bowels of the house, while Marianne stood and looked at the vast hallway in awe. Compared to the suburban London semi that she called home, this was massive. The hallway was panelled in dark oak, and pictures of people in old-fashioned dress lined the stairs, which swept upwards to an imposing landing above. The black and white tiled marble floor echoed as she walked on it. She felt fantastically overexposed in such a huge space. Marianne's stomach contracted. This was so different from where she grew up. How could she possibly

6

ever fit in here? Surely now Luke had her on his home territory it was only a matter of time before he saw it too?

'Jeez, it's dark in here,' said Luke, and opened some shutters to let in the evening light. Motes danced in the beams cast by the setting sun, dazzling Marianne as she stood, silently drinking it in.

'Well, what do you think?' said Luke.

'It's fantastic,' murmured Marianne.

He drew her to him, and her heart thumped erratically as he kissed her on the lips. Marianne felt a familiar flutter in her stomach. She had never desired someone as strongly as she desired Luke. It terrified her how much she wanted him. Suppose he didn't want her as much?

'There's a four-poster in the master bedroom,' he said mischievously.

'We can't,' she protested. 'Not here.'

'There's no one here but us,' said Luke. 'Who's to know?'

'Er – your butler?' She went out with a man who had a butler? This felt so surreal. Any minute she was going to wake up.

'He won't say anything. Besides, he's as deaf as a post so you can be as noisy as you like,' said Luke, with a grin on his face that was impossible to resist.

He dragged her giggling by the hand up the stairs, pointing out various ancestors en route: 'The original Ralph Nicholas, went with Richard I to the Holy Land; Gabriel Nicholas, hid in the priest hole under Edward VI and lived to tell the tale; Ralph II saved Charles II at the battle of Worcester, nada, nada, nada . . .'

'How can you be so dismissive?' said Marianne. 'I mean, in my family the height of historical interest is the time when Great Aunt Maud stood next to George VI at Windsor Park. I come from a noble line of labourers and serfs. This is . . . just . . . incredible. I'd love to have this kind of ancestry.'

7

'You wouldn't if you knew my family,' said Luke, with a grimace. 'With power comes responsibility, manners maketh the man. We have a duty of care. We even have a Latin family motto, *Servimus liberi liberi quia diligimus*, which translates as: "Freely we serve, because we freely love". Having that shoved down your throat from birth is pretty stifling.'

'Oh,' exclaimed Marianne. They had come to the landing, and Luke flung open the window shutters to reveal a landscaped lawn complete with fountains, walled gardens and, in the background, a deer park. 'This is amazing. You're so lucky.'

'I *am* lucky – to have found you,' he said, and her heart skipped a sudden beat. *This* was why she was with him. For the way he looked at her as if she was the only woman in the world. For the way he made her feel so incredibly special. All her doubts and anxieties disappeared as Luke took her hand and knelt down. 'I wasn't going to do this now, but seeing you here looking so incredibly sexy, I can't resist.'

Oh my God, Marianne thought, was he going to . . .?

'Hang on, I've forgotten something . . .' Luke ran over to a set of curtains which was lying in a corner and unhooked a curtain ring. He came running back, fell back down on his knee, and said, 'Now, where were we?'

Marianne stood motionless as he kissed her hand, slipped the curtain ring onto her engagement finger, and said, 'Marianne Moore, will you marry me?'

'Yes,' she whispered. She didn't have to think for a second; this was what she'd wanted her whole life, to be with a man she loved and live in a wonderful place like this. 'Yes, of course I will.' And suddenly she was in his arms, and they were running through the house shrieking with delight.

A sudden slam of the door brought them both to their senses.

'What was that?' said Marianne.

A bell rang impatiently from the hall, and they ran to the banisters to look down.

A smallish, elderly, dapper man stood in the hallway looking rather cross.

'Grandfather?' Luke's face was a picture of shock and dismay.

'Luke, my boy, is that you?' the man said. 'I can see I haven't come home a moment too soon.'

Part One

I Gave You My Heart

Last Year

December 22

Sainsbury's was heaving. Catherine, already feeling hypocritical that she was here at all, felt her heart sink as she saw the hordes of people ravaging through the supermarket, frantically grabbing things from the shelves as if they were in the last-chance saloon and they might never have the chance to shop again. For God's sake, she felt like saying, as she saw people staggering past with trolleys full to the brim with hams and turkeys, mince pies and brandy butter, and the inevitable bottles of booze, it's not like we're all going to starve, is it? Then she berated herself. After all, *she* was here too, wasn't she?

But only for the necessary items, things she'd forgotten, like brandy butter and Christmas pud. Mum had promised to make both, but uncharacteristically for her had forgotten, so Catherine was grumpily facing the seething hordes, all of whom looked as miserable as she felt. She wondered if she should give up and try and make them herself. It's what the bloody Happy Homemaker was always telling people to do.

No, Cat, she admonished herself. There were still presents to wrap, a turkey to defrost, vegetables to prepare, a house to make ready for the guests (and one which would unscramble itself as fast as she tidied) – she *really* didn't have time to make a Christmas pudding. Not even that one from her Marguerite Patten cookbook, which could actually be made the day before. The Happy Homemaker could go stuff herself.

'That sounds like an eminently sensible idea to me.' A little old man in his seventies, wearing a smart gabardine coat, doffed his hat to her as he walked past with a basket under his arm.

'I beg your pardon?' Cat looked at the man in astonishment. She must have been wittering on to herself again. She had a bad habit of doing that in supermarkets.

'I was just observing that you could for once let yourself off the hook,' said the man. 'Christmas isn't all about perfection, you know.'

'Oh, but it is,' said Catherine, 'and this is going to be the most *perfect* Christmas ever.'

'Well, I certainly hope so,' said the man. 'I wish you a very happy and peaceful Christmas.' And with that he was gone, disappearing into the crowd while Catherine was left pondering how on earth a complete stranger seemed to know so much about her. How very, very odd.

Catherine took a deep breath and ploughed her trolley into the fray. Christmas muzak was pumping out, presumably to get her into the spirit of the thing. Not much chance of that, when she had felt all Christmassed out for months. Bugger off, she felt like shouting as a particularly cheesy version of 'Have Yourself a Merry Little Christmas' blared out. Look at all these people. Do any of them look bloody merry?

Christmas seemed to start earlier and earlier every year, and, now she had children in three different schools, Catherine had been obliged to sit through as many Christmas performances (one year she really was going to get Noel to come to one of these things if it killed her), which varied from the sweet but haphazard (her four-year-old's star turn

14

as a donkey), through the completely incomprehensible (the seven and nine-year-olds' inclusive Nativity, which had somehow managed to encompass Diwali, Eid and Hanukkah – an impressive feat, she had to admit), to the minimalist and experimental concert put on at the secondary school her eleven-year-old had just started. One of the reasons Catherine had wanted a large family was so she could have the big family Christmas she'd always missed out on by being an only child. Catherine had always imagined that she'd love attending her children's carol concerts, not find them a huge chore. And no one told her how much work it would be preparing Christmas for a family of six, let alone all the hangers-on who always seemed to migrate her way, like so many homing pigeons, on Christmas Day.

'Next year, remind me to emigrate,' Catherine murmured to herself, as she propelled herself through the mince pie section. Bloody hell. Once upon a time people had bought (or most likely made) mince pies. Now Sainsbury's had a whole section devoted to them: luxury mince pies, mince pies with brandy, mince pies with sherry, deep-filled, fat-free, gluten-free, dairy-free, probably mince-free for all she knew. The world had gone mad.

'Me too.' The woman browsing the shelves next to her gave a wry laugh in sympathy. She looked at Catherine curiously. Oh God, no . . .

'Aren't you—?'

'Yes,' sighed Catherine, 'I'm afraid I am.'

'I'm such a huge fan,' said the woman. 'I keep *all* your recipes. I don't know what I'd do without your lemon tart.'

'Thanks so much,' said Catherine, guiltily hoping the woman wouldn't notice what she had in her shopping trolley, otherwise her cover as the provider of all things home-made was going to be well and truly blown. 'I'd love

15

to stop, really I would, but unfortunately I'm in a tearing hurry. Places to go, people to see. I'm sure you'll understand. Have a wonderful Christmas.'

Catherine felt terrible for rushing off. The poor woman had seemed nice and it was churlish of her to react like that. But couldn't she have five minutes' peace just to be herself and not the bloody awful persona who seemed to be taking over her life? She went to join one of the many huge queues that had built up as she'd wandered round the store, and caught sight of the latest version of *Happy Homes* by the tills. There she was resplendent in a Santa costume and hat (why, oh why, had she let herself be persuaded to do that shoot?), next to a headline that bore the legend, 'The Happy Homemaker's Guide to the Perfect Christmas.'

Any minute now someone in the queue was going to make the connection between the Happy Homemaker and the harassed woman standing behind them, and realise she was a big fat fraud. Catherine didn't think she could stand it. She glanced over at the serve yourself tills, where the queues looked even more horrendous, and people were indulging in supermarket rage as the computers overloaded and spat out incorrect answers or added up the bills wrong.

Catherine looked in her trolley. She had been in Sainsbury's for half an hour and all she had to show for it were two packets of mince pies, a bag of sugar, a Christmas pudding, and no brandy butter. At this rate she would be queuing for at least half an hour before she got served, by which time every sod in Sainsbury's would probably discover her alter ego.

Furtively looking each way up the shop, Catherine pushed her trolley to the side of an aisle and, feeling rather as she had done aged fourteen when she used to bunk off to smoke behind the bike sheds, she abandoned it. They could manage without brandy butter for once. And no one liked Christmas puddings anyway.

As she fled the supermarket, 'Have Yourself a Merry Little Christmas' was still pumping out. Bah humbug, she thought to herself.

Gabriel sat in the lounge, head in his hands. The fire had long gone out and, as the wintry evening drew in, dark shadows were springing from every corner of the normally cosy room. He should make up the fire again. Warm up the place before he went to pick up Stephen. Never had his family home felt so cold and barren.

Stephen.

Oh God. What was he going to tell Stephen? Thank goodness he'd been at the rehearsal for the Village Nativity all afternoon. Thank goodness he hadn't witnessed the latest painful scene between his parents. Gabriel had tried to protect Stephen from the truth about his mother for the best part of seven years, but even he would have had difficulty today.

'You don't understand. You've never understood,' Eve had said, her eyes hard and brittle with unshed tears, her face contorted with pain. It was true. He didn't understand. How could he understand the pain she went through every day, the mental anguish of feeling forever out of sorts with the world and unable to deal with the reality of it?

It was her very fragility that had drawn him to her in the first place. Eve had always seemed to Gabriel like a wounded bird, and from the moment he'd met her all he wanted to do was to care and protect her. It had taken him years to see that, whatever he did, he couldn't protect her from herself. Or from the painful places her mind journeyed to.

'Please let me try,' Gabriel had pleaded. 'If you always shut me out, how can I help you?'

Eve had stood in the house that she had always hated with her bags packed and ready – she'd have been gone without a scene if he hadn't popped back because he'd forgotten to tell her that he was taking Stephen round to his cousins' house after the rehearsal for the Village Nativity, to help decorate their tree – and looked at him blankly.

'You can't,' she said simply. She went up to him and lightly stroked his cheek. 'You've never got that, have you? All this,' she gestured to her home, 'and you. And Stephen. It isn't enough for me. And I can't go on pretending it is. I'm sorry.'

Tears had pricked his own eyes then. He knew she was right, but he wanted her to be wrong. For Stephen's sake as well as his own. Gabriel had spent so many years trying to reach Eve, it was a default way of being. He hadn't wanted to face the truth. There were no more excuses. He was never going to be able to give Eve what she needed. She was a world away from him, and always had been.

'What should I tell Stephen?'

Eve stifled something that sounded like a sob.

'You're a good man, Gabe,' she said. 'Too good for me. You deserve better.'

She kissed him on the cheek, and fled the house towards the waiting taxi, while Gabriel stood in stunned silence. He'd known this moment had been coming from the minute he took her under his wing. She was a wild bird, and he'd always felt that eventually she would fly away and leave him. But not like this. Not now. Not just before Christmas.

Gabriel had lost track of the time while he sat alone in the gathering gloom. It was only now that he was beginning to notice how cold it had suddenly got. How cold it was always going to be now that Eve had gone. He wondered what he was going to do. Whether he'd ever see her again. And what the hell he was going to say to their son . . .

Noel Tinsall stood nursing a pint at the bar in the tacky nightclub the firm had booked for this year's Christmas party, listening to Paul McCartney blasting out what a wonderful Christmas time he was having. Noel was glad someone was. He wondered idly when it would be decent to leave. Probably not wise to go before Gerry Cowley, the CEO, who was strutting his deeply unfunky stuff on the dance floor, leering at all the secretaries. It was only eight o'clock. The party was barely started yet, and already he could see some of the junior staff had drunk more than was good for them. He wouldn't be surprised to find a variety of embarrassing photos doing the rounds on the Internet in the next few days. What was it about the office Christmas party that made people behave so idiotically? Bacchanalian excess was all very well when you didn't have to face your demons at the water cooler the next day.

'Hey, Noel, you sexy beast, come on and dance.' It was his secretary, Julie. Or rather, not his secretary anymore. Not since that jumped-up toerag Matt Duncan had got his promotion. Now Noel had to share a secretary. A further subtle means of making him feel his previous high standing in the office was being eroded. Time was, when people jumped to his beat. Now they jumped to Matt's. Perhaps it was time to get a new job.

Noel hated dancing, but also found it nearly impossible to be rude to people, so before long he found himself in the middle of the dance floor, surrounded by sweaty, writhing bodies, and unable to escape the feeling that everyone was laughing at him.

'You're dead sexy, you know,' Julie was shimmying up

to him, and grabbing his tie. 'Much more than that silly tosser Matt.'

No, no, no! They had always had such a professional relationship, but she was clearly pissed and coming on to him. Not that she wasn't incredibly attractive or anything. And not that Noel wasn't sorely tempted for a moment. Would Cat even know or care if he were unfaithful? Sometimes he didn't think so. Julie was lovely, uncomplicated and she was available. It would be so easy . . .

What on earth was he thinking? Noel shook his head. Definitely time to go.

'Sorry, Julie, I've got to get back,' Noel said. 'Catherine needs me. Kids. You know how it is.' Catherine probably wouldn't care if he were there or not, judging by the notice she took of him these days, but Julie didn't need to know that.

Ducking her alcohol-fumed kiss, Noel made his way out of the club, and into the welcome crisp air of a London December evening. It was still early enough for the third cab he hailed to be miraculously free, and before long he was speeding his way towards Clapton, secure in the knowledge that, despite the amount he'd imbibed, he'd got away without making an idiot of himself.

The cab drew up outside his house, an imposing Edwardian semi down a surprisingly leafy street. The Christmas lights he'd put up with the kids the previous evening flickered maniacally. One of them had no doubt changed the settings again. He bounded up the steps and let himself in to a scene of chaos.

'I hate you.' Melanie, his eldest daughter, came blasting past him and flung herself up the stairs in floods of tears, followed swiftly by his son, James, who shouted, 'I so hate you too!'

'Nobody hates anyone round here, I hope,' he said, but

he was ignored and the house rang to the sound of two slamming doors.

'Don't want to go to bed. Don't WANT to!' his youngest daughter Ruby was wailing as Magda, their latest inefficient au pair, tried to cajole her off the floor of the playroom where she lay kicking and screaming. Noel noted with a sigh that the bookshelf had fallen down *again*. He wasn't quite sure he was up to dealing with that, so he poked his head in the lounge and found Paige, his middle daughter, surreptitiously scoffing chocolate decorations from the tree.

'Where's your mother?' he asked.

'She's on the bloody blog,' said Paige calmly, trying to hide the evidence of her crime.

'Don't say bloody,' said Noel automatically.

'That's what Mummy calls it,' said Paige.

'And don't steal chocolate from the tree,' added Noel.

'I'm not,' said Paige, 'Magda said I could.'

'Did she now?' Catherine came down the stairs looking frazzled. 'Come on, it's your bedtime.'

She kissed Noel absent-mindedly on the cheek before going into the playroom to calm down not only the howling Ruby, but also a semi-hysterical Magda, who was wailing that these children were like 'devils from hell'.

Noel stomped downstairs to the kitchen, got himself a beer, and sat disconsolately in front of the TV. Sometimes he felt like a ghost in his own home.

'Angels! I need angels!' Diana Carew, formidable representative of the Parish Council, flapped about like a giant beached whale. It was hard to see how someone so large could actually squeeze through the tiny door of the room allocated for the children to sit in while they awaited their turn to go on stage, but somehow she managed it.

Marianne suppressed the thought as being bitchy, but it was hard to take her eyes from Diana's enormous bosoms. Marianne had never seen anything so large. And it gave her something to smile about while she sat freezing her arse off in this godforsaken tiny village hall watching the Hope Christmas Nativity taking shape, knowing damned well that any input from her was not actually required. In the weeks leading up to the nativity, Marianne had become grimly aware that she was only on the team because every other sane member of the village, including her colleagues at the village school, had already opted out.

Everyone, that was, apart from the very lovely and immensely supportive Philippa (or Pippa to her friends). Marianne had only got to know Pippa in recent weeks, since she'd been co-opted into helping on the Nativity, but she was fast becoming Marianne's closest friend in Hope Christmas and one of the many reasons she was loving living here. Pippa was bearing down on her now with a welcome cup of tea and a barely suppressed grin. Together they watched Diana practically shove three reluctant angels on the stage, where they joined a donkey, two shepherds, some lambs, Father Christmas and some elves, who were busy singing 'Have Yourself a Merry Little Christmas' as they placed gifts at Mary and Joseph's feet.

'I have to confess,' Marianne murmured, 'this is a rather, erm, *unusual* retelling of the Nativity. I can't recall elves from the Bible.'

Pippa snorted into her tea.

'I'm afraid the elves are here to stay,' said Pippa. 'Diana does a slightly altered version every year, but the elves always feature. It dates back to when she ran the preschool in the village. And it's kind of stuck. Everyone's too frightened of her to tell her to do it differently.'

'Are there actually any carols involved in this?' Marianne

asked. So far, on the previous rehearsals she'd been roped into, the only thing remotely carol-like had been 'Little Donkey'.

'Probably not. At least this year she's dropped "Frosty the Snowman", said Pippa. 'Mind you, it took the Parish Council about three years to persuade her that really, it didn't *actually* snow in Bethlehem on Christmas Day. She loved that snow machine.'

Marianne hooted with laughter, then quietened down when Diana hushed her, before continuing to marshal the children into order and berate them when they'd got it wrong. She was quite formidable. And her version of the Nativity was sweet in its way. It was just . . . so long. And had so little to do with the actual Nativity. Marianne liked her festive season – well, festive. There was a purity about the Christmas story that seemed to be lacking in everyday life. It was a shame Diana couldn't be persuaded to capture some of that.

The natives were getting incredibly restive and parents were beginning to arrive to pick their offspring up. Diana looked as if she might go on all night, till Pippa gently persuaded her that they still had the dress rehearsal to have another run-through of everything.

Marianne quickly helped sort the children out of costumes and into coats and scarves. The wind had turned chill and there was the promise of snow in the air. Perhaps she might get a white Christmas. Her first in Hope Christmas, with which she was falling rapidly in love. Her first as an engaged woman. This time next year she would be married . . .

Nearly all the children had been picked up, but there was one small boy sitting looking lonely in a corner. Stephen, she thought his name was, and she had a feeling he was related to Pippa somehow. Marianne hadn't been in the village long enough to work out all the various

23

interconnections between the different families, many of whom had been here for generations. Marianne didn't teach him, but the village school was small enough that she'd got to know most of the children by sight at least.

'Is your mummy coming for you?' she asked.

The little boy looked up and gave her a look that pierced her heart.

'My mummy never comes,' he said. 'But my daddy does. He should be here.'

Poor little mite, thought Marianne. Presumably his parents had split up. He couldn't have been more than six or seven. Perhaps she should go and let Pippa know he was still here.

Just then she heard a voice outside the door. A tall man entered, wearing a long trenchcoat over jeans and a white cable-knit jumper. A thick stripy scarf was wound round his neck. This must be Stephen's dad.

'Daddy!' Stephen leapt into his dad's arms.

'Woah,' said the man. He turned to Marianne and looked at her with deep brown eyes. Soulful eyes. She shivered suddenly. There was such pain in those eyes. She felt she'd had a sudden glimpse of his soul. She looked away, feeling slightly uncomfortable.

'Sorry I'm so late,' he said. 'Something came up.'

There was something about the way he said it that made Marianne feel desperately sorry for him. He looked as if he had the weight of the world on his shoulders.

'Is everything all right?' Marianne nodded at Stephen who was clinging to his dad's side for dear life.

Stephen's dad stared at her, with that same piercingly sad look his son had.

'Not really,' he said. 'But it's nothing I can't handle. Come on, Steve, I'll race you to your cousins'. I think it's going to snow tonight.'

24

'Can we build a snowman?'

'Of course,' said his dad. He turned back to Marianne. 'Thanks again for looking after him.'

'No problem,' said Marianne, and watched them go. She wondered what was troubling them so deeply, then dismissed it from her mind. Whatever their problem was, it was no business of hers.

This Year

Chapter One

Marianne stood in the kitchen fiddling with her drink, looking around at the shiny happy people spilling into Pippa's cosy farmhouse, an old redbrick building with a slate roof, oozing tradition and country charm. Marianne had fallen in love with this kitchen and its wooden beams, battered old oak table and quarry-tiled floor. It was all so different from the pristine newness of her family home, and exactly the sort of house she'd hoped she and Luke would live in when they were married. *When they were married*. What a distant dream that now seemed.

If it wasn't for Pippa, who had been like a rock to her this last week, she'd never have come. She wondered how soon she'd be able to leave. It was strange how numb she felt, as if she was detached somehow from those around her. There was ice running through her veins. The life she had hoped for and looked forward to had fizzled away to nothing. She had no right to be here, no right to join with these happy relaxed people. Her new year wasn't a new start but a reminder of everything she'd lost. How could her life have altered so abruptly – so brutally – in just a week? She should be in Antigua with Luke right now, just like they'd planned. Instead . . .

Don't. Go. There. Marianne had been determined not to

cry tonight. She knew she was the subject of a great deal of gossip. How could she not be in such a small place? It was the downside to country living of course, and one she didn't relish now. But Pippa had persuaded her to hold her head up high and come out tonight to her and Dan's annual New Year's bash. So come she had. She wouldn't have done it for anyone but Pippa, but the way she was feeling right now, Pippa was the only good thing left about living in Hope Christmas. Not that she was going to stay here much longer. Not after what had happened. As soon as school started next week, she'd look for a new job and go back to London where she belonged.

Marianne watched the crowds surging in and out of the comfortable farmhouse, which seemed Tardis-like. Pippa and Dan had the enviable knack of making everyone feel welcome – Dan was on hand pouring bubbly for all the guests while Pippa worked the room, making sure that the grumpy and irascible (Miss Woods, the formidable ex-head teacher of Hope Christmas primary, who had stomped in with her wooden stick, declaring her antipathy towards New Year: 'Never liked it, never will,') were mollified with mulled wine; the shy and retiring (Miss Campion, who ran the post office, and Mr Edwards, who played the organ in church) were encouraged to fraternise; and the party animals (including Diana Carew, those enormous bosoms taking on a life of their own on the dance floor) had room and space to throw some shapes in Pippa and Dan's new conservatory.

'More fizz?' Dan was suddenly at her side refilling her glass. Was that her third? Or fourth? She probably should eat something. She hadn't eaten properly all week, and the bubbles were going straight to her head. She was starting to get a slightly surreal floating feeling. Perhaps she was going to be all right after all. No one had paid her any attention yet, so perhaps she wasn't the hot topic of discussion she imagined.

Or maybe not. Marianne wandered into the hall, where three people in animated conversation suddenly went silent as she approached. Feeling uncomfortable, she left, only to hear one of them cattily hissing, 'Well, to be honest, it was never going to work was it, the lord of the manor and the teacher?'

Blinking back tears, Marianne knocked back her champagne and grabbed a bottle from Dan, who looked rather taken aback. Marching up to Pippa, she said, 'Fancy getting absolutely bladdered?'

'Are you sure that's such a good idea?' said Pippa cautiously.

'Never been surer,' said Marianne as the strains of 'Girls Just Wanna Have Fun' filled the room. 'My mum always says hold your head up high and sod the consequences. Come on, let's dance.'

An hour later, all danced out, and having moved on from champagne to vodka and orange, Marianne's emotions had lurched from deep misery to a wild ecstasy that bordered on the unhinged. So what if her engagement was over? She was young, free and single again, it was time she took control of things. There must be *some* decent men at this party.

Having worked her way around the entire confines of Pippa's house and discovering that, no, there really weren't any decent men there, Marianne's cunning plan to start the New Year was beginning to look a little shaky. Perhaps it was time for plan A – an early night. Marianne was heading for the hall when the doorbell rang. No one appeared to be taking any notice, so she went to answer it. Standing there was a dark-haired man who looked vaguely familiar. He had the most amazing brown eyes.

'You'll do,' said Marianne, grabbing him by the hand and dragging him into the conservatory.

'Er, I'd better just tell Pippa and Dan I'm here,' he said, before she could get him onto the dance floor.

A wave of sobriety suddenly hit Marianne. What was she doing? She never ever behaved like this. What must this stranger have thought of her? But a more reckless side of her said, so what? It was New Year and her life was in tatters. She quickly brushed her embarrassment to one side, grabbed herself another vodka and orange and started dancing wildly to 'I Will Survive'.

Someone shouted, 'It's nearly midnight.' Suddenly, without warning, her sense of joyous abandon deserted her. Midnight. The countdown to New Year. Everyone singing 'Auld Lang Syne'. Suddenly Marianne couldn't bear it. She stumbled out into the garden, barely noticing that the temperature was below freezing. The alcohol coursing through her veins was keeping her warm. She sat down on a bench, and stared up at an unforgiving moon. The Shropshire hills loured out of the darkness at her, appearing gloomy and oppressive for the first time since she'd been here. She looked back into Pippa's warm, friendly house, full of bright lights and cheerful people. Everyone was having such a good time and she was out here in the cold on her own, sobbing her heart out.

The back door opened and a shadowy figure came towards her.

'Anything I can do?' it said.

'10, 9, 8 . . .'

'Nothing,' sobbed Marianne. 'My life is a disaster, that's all.'

'7, 6, 5 . . .'

'Well, if you're sure. Only . . . you seemed . . . sorry, forgive me. None of my business. I'd better go in. You know.'

'4, 3, 2, 1 . . . HAPPY NEW YEAR!' Screams and shouts came from inside. Marianne suddenly felt hatred for all these people she didn't know who were having such a good time, and suddenly she couldn't bear this stranger's kindness. She didn't want kindness. She just wanted Luke.

'Yes, you'd better,' she spat out.

'Oh.' The man looked slightly put out.

'I hate everything,' said Marianne, attempting to stand up, before falling back in the rose bushes. Her unlikely hero came to help her up. She sat up, looked into his deeply attractive brown eyes, and promptly threw up on his feet.

Noel sat at his desk wading through emails, most of which were completely irrelevant to him. Did he *really* need to be on the Health and Safety Committee's minutes list? There were emails about three leaving parties at the end of January, he noted, people yet again leaving for 'personal reasons'. The credit crunch was hitting his industry hard; building was always the first thing to go. And without anyone buying all those shiny flats in city centres, there wouldn't be any need for new eco-friendly heating systems designed by the likes of him either. Gerry Cowley had been muttering under his collar for weeks before Christmas about the business needing to be leaner and trimmer. In the past, Noel felt he could have relied on his reputation as the brightest engineer GRB had ever employed, but then Matt had joined the firm. Matt, with his lack of dependants, bright-eyed young-man's energy, and brown-nosing abilities. There was someone heading for the top if ever anyone was. And Noel had a nasty feeling that it would be at his expense.

No point thinking about what might never happen. Noel could almost hear his mother's voice. It had been her favourite phrase when he was growing up. Way back when they'd had some kind of relationship, before she'd turned into the mother-in-law from hell and, according to the kids, Granny Nightmare. Not that he'd ever had an easy relationship with his mother. Noel had spent most of his childhood feeling that somehow he'd disappointed her. Particularly after his younger sister was born, who apparently could do no wrong. He envied Cat her relaxed relationship with her mother, Louise, who was Granny Dreamboat in every way possible.

Cat. Something was happening to them. He felt like the sands were shifting beneath him, and the world was changing without him. Ever since Cat had started the blog, and the Happy Homemaker thing had taken off, Noel felt Cat had had less and less time for him. All she seemed to focus on was her work and the children. The money it brought in was undoubtedly welcome, particularly when his own job was looking increasingly dodgy. But when a whole week had gone by and he'd barely seen Cat, let alone spoken to her, he wondered if it was all worth it. Sometimes Noel wondered if there was any place in Cat's heart left for him anymore. And, after the way he'd behaved on Christmas Day, he wasn't sure he blamed her.

This was no bloody good. Time he pulled himself together and got on with some work. Noel started to check through the plans he'd drawn up before Christmas for the air-con system at a nearby leisure centre and sighed as he saw the notes from the architects querying why he couldn't match their exact specifications. When would they learn that the real world didn't operate in shiny boxes and out of plush offices but in the mathematical parameters that physical laws allowed you?

A head popped round the corner. Matt Duncan, looking mighty chipper with himself.

'Have you heard?'

'Heard what?'

'Davy Chambers has copped it.' Matt drew a finger underneath his throat, with barely concealed glee.

Shit. Dave Chambers was going? Dave was part of the furniture at GRB. If he was going, *no one* was safe.

Noel shivered. January seemed to have set in both chill and drear. He had a feeling a cold wind was blowing over the horizon.

So, Christmas over, turkey stuffed, cooked and eaten, house full of plastic toys – mainly broken – children back at school. It's time for a spring clean. Yes, I know, technically we're still in winter, but post-Christmas, full of New Year's Resolutions, is as good a time as any to clear out the rubbish and it's always good to start the year as you mean to go on . . .

Catherine stopped typing and looked idly out from her eyrie-like study at the top of the house as a half-starved crow flapped and flopped its way across the frosty attic roof. Bloody blog. Bloody Happy Homemaker. Some days she wished she'd never started it. It had begun as a piece of fun, posted between Ruby's feeds, something to keep her sane while she worked out what to do about her career.

Catherine, whose idea of domesticity involved the minimum amount of cleaning compatible with reasonable hygiene requirements, had struck on the idea of an ironic take on the life of the twenty-first-century housewife – or homemaker, a term Catherine utterly loathed. She'd sat down and typed sarcastically:

So, here you are, once a busy, successful businesswoman,

tied to the home with a squawling baby and a stroppy toddler.
Is it possible to be a twenty-first-century homemaker and
survive, sanity intact? By applying the same management
skills to your home life that you did to your work, I believe
that not only can you survive, but that you can actually
embrace the challenges being at home throws you. A happy
home is one organised with military precision, which is why
every Sunday evening we sit down as a family and work out
our timetable for the week. A colour-coded copy sits on the
freezer, so I can keep track of Kumon lessons and French club
and when the baby needs her next set of jabs. I've even
perfected my own clocking-in system. It works for me. It can
work for you.

So had the Happy Homemaker been born and, to her
astonishment, had been an instant hit. Unfortunately a
lot of her readers failed to get the irony and took her far
too seriously. Somehow she had stumbled into some kind
of zeitgeisty thing where women appeared to be sitting
at home with their offspring, willing to be lectured at by
a complete stranger about how to run their homes. Soon
she was getting several hundred hits a day, and achieving
a massive following. Her blog became so popular it even
got mentioned in the broadsheets, much to Cat's wry
amusement.

Before she knew it, she was doling out domestic advice
on a near daily basis, and soon the Happy Homemaker was
attracting attention in the wider world, not least from Bev,
her old boss from *Citygirl* magazine, where she'd been
features editor till the arrival of Ruby had finally convinced
her that her home/work balance was all wrong. Bev rang
her one day and offered her a regular feature at *Happy
Homes* magazine, which involved both time in the office
and at home. Coming as it had at a moment when Catherine
had been worn out with the demands of a toddler and

going stir crazy on the school run, she had jumped at the chance. She'd organised herself an au pair, an office at the top of the house, and had looked forward to reclaiming part of her old life.

If only things were that simple. No one else at *Happy Homes*, including Bev, had the domestic ties she did. A couple of the girls had one kid certainly, but four? No one she knew apart from her and Noel had four children. They must have been quite insane.

Initially Cat had thought that going back to work now that the kids were older was going to be a piece of cake. But as the success of the Happy Homemaker grew, so did the pressures. She was constantly in demand in the media, writing articles for the broadsheets, appearing on radio shows, and even making the odd TV appearance. If she had no domestic ties this wouldn't matter. But while she enjoyed the attention her newfound success was bringing her, not to mention the cash, particularly after years of feeling like a second-class citizen who got pocket money, Cat was struggling with balancing it against her family responsibilities, and was particularly conscious that she was giving Noel a lot less attention than he deserved.

And although the kids were older now, they seemed to need her more than ever, particularly Mel, who was struggling to make the transition from primary to secondary school, and Ruby who had started her first day at school without her mum holding her hand – that bloody Christmas edition photo shoot had put paid to that. Catherine had always managed to take her children on the first day of school, but in Ruby's case she'd failed. In fact, she felt she was failing Ruby a great deal. She never had time to read with her (though, thankfully, Paige was a good substitute) and she'd only just scraped into her (admittedly dreadful) Nativity just before Christmas. When she worked late, she missed Ruby's bedtime. Her children were growing up and, at the moment, it felt like they were doing it without her.

And in the meantime she lectured others on how to run their homes, bring up their children and generally cope with day-to-day living. How ironic that she couldn't manage to retain the slightest bit of control over her own situation . . .

Gabriel held Stephen's hand as they walked down the frosty lane on a crisp clear January morning.

'Look, Daddy, a robin!' said Stephen excitedly. Their breath blew hot and steamy in the cold sharp air. It was a shock to the system to emerge from the warm cocoon of family and friends that Pippa and Dan had been providing him with for the last fortnight. He would have been lost without them. Gabriel's parents, who were his default support network when trouble brewed with Eve, had set off on a much anticipated round-the-world trip to celebrate their retirement. Ironically their retiring had been what had brought him back to Hope Christmas, to take over the farm and try to expand the business with Dan and Pippa who were setting up a service to provide organic farm produce. And it was coming to live in Hope Christmas that appeared to have triggered Eve's latest depression.

Gabriel sighed. He still didn't know how he was going to face the future, but he supposed it was a good thing to be forced back into the real world now that Christmas was finally over. Not that sheep were always that accommodating about the Christmas season. He and Stephen had spent a large proportion of the previous week checking on the pregnant ewes. Luckily Stephen saw going out in the snow as an adventure, and being busy had given Gabriel less time to brood.

Gabriel sincerely hoped that going back to school would be a good thing. Eve hadn't contacted them now for nearly a fortnight and, though Stephen had stopped mentioning it, he knew by the way that he would sigh sometimes, or wander off in the middle of a game, that his son was hurting deeply. He only wished there was something he could do beyond the practical to make it better.

'He's got you,' Pippa had said. 'And us. He knows his mother isn't steady, but he also knows you *are*. So long as you can provide security and love, he'll be fine.'

Wise, wonderful Pippa, with more than enough troubles of her own to cope with, but always there to catch you when you fell. Gabriel would have cracked under the strain if it hadn't been for the support of his favourite cousin. Although Pippa was more like a sibling than a cousin, growing up as they had on neighbouring farms, spending a blissful childhood scrumping and fighting and fording streams together. Pippa, a year older, had always been the grown-up, there to bandage his wounds or salve his wounded pride when he'd come off the worse in a playground fight. And she was still doing the same thing. He'd be lost without her.

The robin hopped away and Stephen ran on ahead down the lane, pretending he was an aeroplane. It was good to see him so carefree for once. He was far too solemn usually, and Gabriel continually worried about the effect that events would have on him. Whatever Pippa said, it wasn't going to be easy for him coping without his mother. Flaky and all as Eve was, she did love Stephen, and it was clear that he missed her badly.

As indeed Gabriel did. He felt a sudden constriction in his throat. If only he could have done more for her. If only she'd let him. If only ... But one of the things he was coming to realise with painful clarity was that, however much he loved her, it wasn't enough, it was never going to be enough. Eve's problems were too big for him to mend. Sometimes if you loved someone, you just had to let them go.

Chapter Two

The Saturday before school had started, Marianne walked with a heavy heart from the little cottage she rented at the south end of the village, down Hope Christmas High Street. Even passing Diana Carew's house wasn't enough to cheer her up. Diana's garden was filled with a huge plastic Santa and several gnomes, and her house was a blaze of flashing reindeer even during the daytime. Marianne turned the letter in her hand over and over again. It was the means by which she could flee Hope Christmas, go back to her old life. A life that didn't include Luke. Was that what she wanted? Could she *really* bear that? Once she left, there would be no turning back. But the thought of never seeing him, never touching him, never hearing him laugh or seeing him turn on that dazzling smile that had made her feel like a million dollars. Never to do any of that again. How could she stay here and be reminded every day of what she'd lost?

Part of her wanted to run home to her mum and escape the pain of walking down the High Street every day and risking bumping into Luke or running into his mother on the rare occasions she strayed into Hope Christmas to visit the beauty salon. All Marianne had to do was post this job application to the primary school in Hendon, where a teaching friend from her London days assured her they were crying out for good staff, and then she could look forward to being back home where she belonged. She had to accept it. Luke had been a mistake. Moving to Hope Christmas an even bigger one.

It was a grey dull day. The clear skies of late December had given way to a glowering gloomy January, with dark snow clouds obscuring the hills for most of the day completely, in keeping with her mood. Marianne had never felt so cold in her life. It was a cold that sapped her strength and seemed to reach somewhere into the core of her being. Even the sight of Miss Woods, the erstwhile head of Hope Christmas primary, whizzing precariously down the High Street on her mobile scooter, flag flapping in the breeze, failed to amuse. Although watching Miss Woods hit a corner too fast and oversteer to compensate, causing the large plastic canopy that covered her mean machine to wobble alarmingly, did draw a small smile. There *would* be things to miss in Hope Christmas, and the eccentricity of characters like Miss Woods was one of them.

Vera Campion at the post office was another. Always there with a ready smile behind the counter, offering hope and cheer to all the inhabitants of the village, especially the elderly, her shy kindly nature – not to mention her shortsightedness – reminded Marianne of a mole. One who was a force of great good for the whole village.

'Marianne, how lovely to see you,' Vera greeted her, but her smile didn't look quite as genuine as normal. 'What can I do for you today?'

'A book of first-class stamps, please, Vera.' Marianne handed over the money and looked at Vera again. She seemed very agitated. Marianne wasn't normally one to interfere in other people's lives, but Vera had been immensely kind to her since she'd come to Hope Christmas, and Marianne didn't like to see her like this. 'Vera, I hope you don't mind me prying, but are you okay?'

'Oh dear,' said Vera. 'Is it that obvious? I've just heard that they want to close me down. It's a government initiative, they say. We're not profitable enough apparently. From the summer all postal services are to be moved to Ludlow.'

'But that's terrible!' exclaimed Marianne. 'How will all your old folk get their pensions?'

Vera's 'old folk' formed the core of her customers, and she protected their interests with the fierceness of a mother hen.

'Exactly,' replied Vera. 'And what about the village as a whole? Along with the pub, the post office is the centre of our community. Without it we'll be lost. But they say that with the building of the eco town, which is nearer to Ludlow, people won't want to come here for their post, they'll just get in their cars and drive instead.'

'Very eco friendly,' remarked Marianne. 'Isn't there anything you can do?'

'I don't know,' said Vera. 'But I do know I'm not going down without a fight. Mr Edwards said I should start a campaign.'

Vera blushed at the mention of Mr Edwards. It was not a very well kept secret in Hope Christmas that she nurtured feelings for the church organist but whether he was the only person in the village not to know, or whether he was too shy to approach her, so far Vera's passion remained unrequited.

'That's a great idea,' said Marianne.

'Perhaps you could help?'

'Oh, I'd love to,' stammered Marianne. 'But I'm not sure how much longer I'm going to be here.'

'Are you leaving us then?' Vera looked disappointed and Marianne felt a pang that someone actually cared. Despite what had happened with Luke, she had started to put down roots here. Luke hadn't been the only draw for coming to the country. From the moment Marianne had first come to Hope Christmas she'd fallen in love. The village, with its quaint high street with pretty little shops full of knick-knacks and fabulous old-fashioned bookshop, its square complete with farmers' market, and its tumbledown workers' cottages was everything she'd hoped for from living in the country. The friendliness, the warmth of the school she taught in, the kids she taught – and Pippa, she would miss Pippa. And the longer she'd stayed the more she loved it. It *would* be hard to tear herself away.

'Maybe,' said Marianne, trying to sound vague. The post office wasn't just the hub of the village, it was the main source of gossip. She didn't really want the whole world to be discussing her business.

Making a hurried excuse, Marianne rushed out of the shop, meaning to march straight to the post box and post her well-worn envelope.

'Oh—' Someone was coming in as she was coming out. And they got rather entangled.

'Marianne, my dear, how lovely to see you.'

Oh lord. Did Luke's grandfather *have* to walk by just now? A reminder that getting out of Hope Christmas was going to be essential for her sanity if she was ever to get over Luke.

'Er, hello.' Marianne still hadn't quite figured out how she should address her erstwhile grandfather-in-law – wasn't he a lord or something? – and now they weren't to be related by marriage, she felt even more awkward.

'How are you, my dear?' The kindness in Ralph Nicholas' voice took her by surprise.

'Not too bad, thanks,' said Marianne.

'If it's any consolation, which I know it won't be,' Ralph continued, 'I think my grandson is an utter fool for letting you go, and I've said so.'

41

'Erm, thanks.' Blimey. That was unexpected. Luke's mum, who had always looked as though she were sucking lemons when she met Marianne, couldn't have appeared more relieved by the turn of events if she'd tried.

'I hope the actions of one Nicholas won't be enough to drive you out of town,' Ralph was continuing. 'I think the school would struggle to replace such a talented teacher as you. I thought that you wanted to make a difference.'

Now he'd touched a nerve. Marianne had got so fed up teaching in London schools where the class sizes had seemed impossibly large. Coming to teach in Hope Christmas village school had been a joy. For the first time in her teaching career she really felt she had the time to do the job she loved properly.

'I did – I do,' said Marianne. 'Actually, I *was* thinking of moving on. I've got a job application to post.'

'Pity,' said Ralph. 'I think you could do a lot of good in this village. Not least by helping poor Vera out. Still, if you're determined to leave . . .'

He looked at her so directly and clearly, she almost felt he was stripping her soul bare. Which was absurd as she barely knew him. But she felt her resolve crumble a little. She did like it here. Maybe she shouldn't rush off home the minute something went wrong. That's what her mum always expected her to do.

As if mirroring her thoughts, Ralph added, 'And don't you think it would be better to face out the situation, rather than running away from it? After all, *you're* not the one who's done anything wrong.'

He smiled at her and doffed his hat, before continuing into the post office and greeting Vera. 'Ah, Vera, a packet of your finest Werther's Originals if you please.'

Marianne stared after him open mouthed. Perhaps Ralph

was right. Perhaps she should stay. Help Vera with the campaign. Keep teaching the kids she loved. Pay Pippa back for being such a good friend. Show Luke what he was missing . . .

She turned the envelope over once more, then crumpled it up and stuffed it back in her pocket. She still hadn't quite made up her mind, but maybe Hope Christmas deserved another chance. And, maybe, so did she.

'Cat, are you in?' Noel walked through the door on Friday night and was met by an eerie silence. The hall light was on, but the rest of the house was dark. Odd. He didn't recall Cat saying that the kids were doing anything tonight. Mind you, she was always accusing him of not paying any attention to their activities, so perhaps she *had* mentioned it and he'd forgotten.

He went down the stairs to the basement kitchen, turning on lights as he went. The house was as quiet as the grave without the children. Much as the constant noise and chaos grated on him sometimes, it was better than this funereal silence. Where was everyone?

There was a note on the kitchen table in Cat's writing.

Noel,
    I tried you on your mobile but it was switched off again. (Funny how such a simple sentence could bristle with so much hidden antagonism. Cat was always on at him to turn his mobile on, but he hated being in constant communication with the world, so turned it off unless forced not to. And, whenever he did ring, Cat always seemed to be engaged so he'd long given up trying.) *Magda cut her finger chopping up vegetables* – Noel's eye was suddenly drawn to a pool of blood on the floor by the sink – *so I've taken her to hospital.*

43

Mel on sleepover, Regina has everyone else. Back as soon
as I can get away.
Love Cat
x

Right. So now, instead of settling down with a well earned
beer and a rerun of *Top Gear* on Dave, Noel was going to
have to drag the kids away from Regina, their saintly and
wonderful neighbour, probably feed them, put them to bed,
then wait on his tod till Cat and Magda made it back from
Homerton, which from their many experiences of family
trips to Casualty could be anything up to several hours.
He'd been looking forward to curling up with Cat on the
sofa. Magda was normally out with her disreputable Russian
boyfriend, Sergei, whom Noel darkly suspected was part of
the Russian mafia. Bloody Magda. She ruined everything.
Her life seemed to be one perpetual crisis – if she wasn't
homesick, she'd had a row with the boyfriend. She had to
be the most useless (and sulky) au pair they'd ever had.

Noel left a message on Cat's mobile and then went next
door to round up his children.

'Noel,' said Regina warmly, letting him in, 'do you fancy
a drink? The kids are all fed, and Ali's just come home.'

'Regina, you are an angel sent from heaven, thank you
so much,' said Noel. 'It's been a hell of a week.'

He poked his head into Regina's playroom where two of
his offspring were sharing a sofa with Regina's two youngest,
watching *MI High*.

'James?' he asked.

'With Joel on the Wii,' said Regina.

Satisfied that everyone was quite happy he made his way
down to the basement kitchen, which was a mirror image
of his own and Cat's, and sat down with his neighbours,
reflecting how lucky he and Cat were to have such good

44

mates on their doorstep. Life with four children and a working wife would be impossible otherwise.

'Thanks for this, you two,' he said, as he sipped his beer. 'And sorry to dump on you. *Again*. I don't know what we pay Magda for. It's certainly not to look after the kids. She's more of a liability than all of ours put together.'

'No problem,' said Regina. 'Cat's helped me out more times than I care to mention. It's what friends are for.'

Noel stayed for one more beer, before regretfully deciding he'd better get his charges home. It took him half an hour to round everyone up, and Ruby was only persuaded to go if he promised piggyback rides, but eventually they were through their own front door. Noel made a unilateral decision to dispense with baths that night, and packed the little ones off to bed while he went to prepare something for Cat, Magda and himself to eat.

Top Gear was over by the time he'd finished cooking and cleaning up the mess Magda had left behind. He felt a smidgeon of guilt at the thought that she might actually have hurt herself, but quickly put it away. Magda had cried wolf on so many occasions, he doubted very much that it would turn out to be more than a scratch. He chased James up to bed and turned over to *Have I Got News For You*. There was still no word from Cat. How long did it take to stitch up a finger?

He rang Cat's mobile again but got no reply. In the end, he ate alone in front of the news. He had just dozed off when the phone rang.

'Sorry, I only just got your message,' said Cat. 'We've been stuck in A&E forever and Magda was so hysterical I couldn't leave. But she's being bandaged now, so I hope we won't be too much longer.'

'Oh, okay,' said Noel, feeling somewhat disappointed. 'Your dinner's in the oven.'

'Thanks. I'm really sorry about this.'

'It's not your fault,' said Noel. 'Bloody Magda.'

'Very bloody at the moment as it happens,' said Cat. 'I've never seen so much, in fact.'

'That's not fair. Now I feel guilty,' said Noel. 'Is she going to be okay?'

'Don't,' said Cat. 'She's going to be fine. I, on the other hand, am going completely bonkers. I'll try not to be too much longer.'

'I'll try to stay up without falling asleep,' said Noel. A depressing feature of his mid forties was his uncanny ability to nod off on the sofa. He barely ever saw the end of films anymore.

'If I'm not back in half an hour, go to bed,' said Cat.

'I'll keep it warm for you,' he replied.

'You'd better,' she laughed, and the phone went dead.

Noel breathed a heavy sigh. All thoughts of a cosy evening were gone forever. It was nearly eleven, he may as well go to bed right now, otherwise he definitely would be asleep on the sofa by the time she got in.

Cat went back inside the brightly lit A&E department and sat down on the incredibly hard chair she had spent most of the evening on. Did the person in the NHS responsible for chairs have a particularly sadistic streak, she wondered? Every chair she had ever sat on, in every hospital she'd ever been in, had been incredibly uncomfortable, and usually she'd had to sit on it for hours. She glanced at her watch. It was gone ten thirty. What a waste of a bloody evening. She'd been planning to spend it cuddled up with Noel on the sofa, conscious she'd spent far too many evenings glued to the computer of late.

Trust Magda to manage to slice her finger to the bone. Cat hadn't realised any of her knives were sharp enough.

If it had been anyone else, anyone at all, Cat would have felt sorry for her, but Magda's litany of woes and trauma had left her all empathised out, and, while she had felt duty-bound to sit her down and wrap up the finger after Magda had come round from fainting at the sight of her own blood, Cat had taken her to the hospital while gritting her teeth. It was the only decent thing to do, but for once Cat wished she didn't always feel obliged to do the decent thing and had the audacity to tell Magda to either get useless Sergei to take her in his shiny motor, or send her off in a taxi. In the end, Magda's look of woe, and the sudden flash-forward she'd had to Mel in a few years time, hurt and alone in a foreign country, had been enough to make her rearrange her life at lightning speed. Sometimes having a conscience was a damned inconvenience.

Twenty minutes later Magda emerged, her finger bandaged thickly, her arm in a sling, milking the moment for all it was worth by flirting outrageously with the house officer who'd been unfortunate enough to be assigned to her. He looked so completely overwhelmed, Cat immediately felt sorry for him. Magda was a force to be reckoned with.

'Doctor says I must not work for week,' announced Magda. 'Very bad for finger. Cleaning. Ironing. I must not do.'

'I bet he does,' murmured Cat, thinking frantically ahead to the next week. How many meetings did she have? And could she cancel any of them? She had a feeling Magda's poorly finger was going to prevent her from doing anything remotely like the job Cat had been paying her to do for the last six months. She wished she had the nerve to sack Magda, but trying to find a replacement at short notice was going to be nigh on impossible. Cat was having enough trouble juggling all the demands on her with the cookery book she

47

was working on, as well as the blog and the regular column. She simply couldn't afford to lose Magda – even a useless au pair was better than no au pair. She'd just have to bite her lip and put up with it.

Cat drove silently through the drably dark inner-London streets, not having the energy to strike up a conversation. Even at this late hour it was hideously busy. Cat screamed to a halt behind a night bus disgorging revellers who'd obviously been living it up in town, reminding her of how her life used to be when she wasn't weighed down with the cares of the world. How she envied those young men and women spilling out onto the streets, living their carefree lives of partying and a kebab before bedtime.

Once that had been the way her weekend was too. Once a lifetime ago. Now it was reduced to trips to Casualty with useless au pairs and returning to find the house in darkness. Magda declined the offer of the food Noel had prepared for them and disappeared to her room to hold excitable conversations in Latvian.

Cat sighed. She didn't feel all that hungry now. She put Noel's cold offerings in the fridge, and made her way upstairs. Deep snoring from her bedroom indicated that Noel was already in the land of nod. They had so little time together. And now they'd lost another precious evening. Sometimes Cat worried they would end up having nothing to say to each other by the time the children eventually left home.

She went into the children's rooms, picking up toys, smoothing over duvets and, in Ruby's case, planting a kiss on her cheek. Paige and James both thought they were too big for kisses, and, though once or twice she'd stealthily managed to sneak kisses on them when they were asleep, James had a tendency to roll over and shout 'Gerroff!' and Paige had been known to sit up in a semi-wakeful state and balefully declare, 'You do not kiss me, *ever*!' before falling back to sleep again. Cat stood and looked at them and allowed a blissful contentment to steal over her. Despite the stresses of her day, the sight of her children asleep could never fail to lighten her heart. As an only child she'd always longed for the hustle and bustle of a big family. At moments like this it actually felt worth it.

Satisfied that her children were all well, she snuck back to her husband and undressed silently in the darkness. Noel's snoring had slowed down to more rhythmic breathing. She knew from past experience that he was so deeply asleep he'd need a bomb to wake him up. The feelings of contentment dissipated as she climbed into bed next to him. Noel moved towards her in his sleep, but otherwise didn't stir. Cat shut her eyes feeling defeated and lost. One day her life would run on an even keel. One day . . .

Gabriel strode through the frosty fields that clung around the edges of the hills surrounding Hope Christmas, a cold wind whipping through him. One of his sheep had gone missing and he'd been up early looking for her. Pippa, as ever, had stepped into the breach with Stephen but, having found his errant sheep stuck flat on her back in a ditch, her pregnancy making it difficult for her to get up, Gabriel was now in a hurry to get back so he could at least take Stephen to school. Some days he found the weight of responsibility so crushing he didn't know how much longer he could stagger under it.

'If you still had a proper job . . .' Eve had been wont to cry. She never fully understood what had prompted him to 'drop everything', as she put it, and leave his comfortable job as a marketing consultant, which he had loathed, to retrain at agricultural college so he could take over the running of the farm from his father. How to explain that it was in his blood? He'd grown up farming sheep and had only left it behind because his parents feared for the future of their industry and had wanted him to have a job with more security. But Gabriel had never really taken to city life and had always known that one day he'd go back. When his parents announced their retirement it seemed like the perfect time to do so. He'd loved it from the first, but Eve had never settled.

'If you could be a proper wife . . .' had often been on his lips, but he'd never been cruel enough to say it. Eve, his poor little Evie, couldn't help who or what she was. She'd never been cut out for country living and found the life oppressive. Everyone had warned him he couldn't change her, but Gabriel had been too stubborn to listen, and now he was paying the price.

Where was she? How was she managing without him? He hadn't heard from her in weeks and the sense of loss was still so raw that the pain caught him short sometimes, and he'd find himself blinking away sudden tears that came when he least expected them. Shit. He had to be stronger about this. Stephen needed him. Gabriel couldn't afford to let him down.

Mind you, sometimes his son showed such astonishing strength, Gabriel had to pinch himself to work out who was the child and who was the parent. Stephen seemed to have a knack for knowing just when Gabriel was hurting most, and would sometimes come up and hold his hand, and say, 'It's okay, Dad' in a way that tore at Gabriel's heart. It was at such moments Gabriel's sympathies for Eve's suffering would evaporate and be replaced with cold, harsh fury. How could she have done this to them?

The fury returned briefly as Gabriel strode across the frozen wastes of the land thinking of the life that he'd so badly wanted to share with her. It didn't seem fair. None of it did.

'I think you'll find life isn't very fair,' a voice greeted Gabriel, as he approached the stile leading to the lane that ran down the side of his house.

'What?' Gabriel jerked himself back to the real world to find himself staring into the welcoming smile of Ralph Nicholas, out walking his dog. Where had he sprung from so suddenly and silently?

'Jeez. I must be going mad,' said Gabriel. 'I'm talking to myself now. Sorry.'

'No matter,' said Ralph. 'I know you have a lot to deal with.'

'How?' Gabriel was a little more belligerent than he meant to be. He was uncomfortably aware that his family situation was the talk of the town and hated being the centre of attention. He'd barely ever spoken to Ralph Nicholas, who hardly spent any time in Hope Christmas anymore. How on earth did he know what was going on in Gabriel's life?

'There's not much that happens in this village that I don't know about,' said Ralph. 'Incidentally, do you think it unfair when a fox gets one of your sheep?'

'No,' said Gabriel, 'because I do everything I can to prevent that. If a fox catches a sheep, it's usually bad luck.'

'And if you've done everything you can to help your wife,' said Ralph, 'don't you think you should just accept there's nothing you can do for her? Some people cannot, or will not, be helped. It's just bad luck.'

Gabriel looked at Ralph in astonishment. How had this relative stranger plumbed the depths of his heart so conclusively? He'd never even talked to Pippa about how he really felt about Eve.

'I feel I've failed her,' said Gabriel slowly. 'I wanted to look after her and I couldn't.'

51

'But you can look after your son,' pointed out Ralph. 'I've always found a new hobby very helpful for a broken heart.'

'I don't have time for hobbies,' said Gabriel.

'Well, maybe it's not a hobby you need,' said Ralph. 'But perhaps you could use the considerable talents you have for protection into something that you *can* do something about.'

'What do you mean?'

'Look around you,' said Ralph, encompassing Gabriel's fields and the hills they bordered with a sweep of his arm. 'We take all this for granted. Assume the immutability of it all. But nothing stays the same forever. In case you hadn't noticed, Hope Christmas is under threat. There are moves afoot to change all this.'

'What's that got to do with me?' said Gabriel. 'What can I do?'

'I'd say the post office is as good a place to start as any,' said Ralph. He whistled loudly and his dog, a grey wolfhound, came lolloping up to them. 'Best be off then,' he said.

Gabriel walked on down the lane, shaking his head. He'd heard Ralph Nicholas was eccentric, but not that he was so utterly barking. What did that mad old man know anyway? No one was planning to do anything to Hope Christmas. Why would anyone want to destroy something as beautiful as this? Ralph Nicholas must have got it wrong. And, even if he hadn't, Gabriel had enough problems right now without worrying about the future of his village.

Gabriel strode on down the lane to Pippa's house, where Stephen was contentedly munching his Cheerios.

'Shall I take them in today for you?' he asked his cousin, who was looking distinctly harassed.

'Would you?' she said. 'Lucy isn't too well today. It would be a great help.'

'It's my pleasure,' said Gabriel, and it was. He chased

Stephen and his cousins down the lane to school, whooping and laughing as he pretended to be a monster chasing after them, and a pale weak winter sun emerged from behind the cold grey clouds. It gave him heart somehow. Maybe his future wasn't so bleak after all.

Chapter Three

'Ah, Mrs Tinsall. Thank you for taking the trouble to ring me back.' The voice of the school secretary boomed down the phone, bristling with disapproval that she was speaking to a mother who actually went out to work. Cat had taken advantage of a break in proceedings during the discussion of the cover design for the June issue of *Happy Homes* to check on her messages and clocked to her dismay that she'd missed a call from school. It always panicked her when the school rang.

'No problem,' said Cat, her heart racing. Why was the school ringing her at 3.45? Mum had offered to go and get the kids for her so that she could go to the meeting, Magda claiming her injured finger prevented her from carrying bags and holding the children's hands to cross the road. 'Is dangerous, Cat-er-ine,' she'd said in the annoying singsong voice she always used when she wanted to get out of something. 'I do not want to be danger to the children.'

'I have your children sitting in my office,' said the secretary, 'and I was just wondering if someone was planning to come and pick them up any time soon.'

'*What?*' Cat went cold all over. It was her worst nightmare. It would take her at least an hour to get back, even if Bev (who was gesturing to her to wind up the call) let her go.

54

'I'm so sorry,' she was gabbling now. 'My mother was supposed to come. Oh God. Erm. I'll try and ring her. See where she is.'

'I'd appreciate it if you did,' said the secretary, not noted for her diplomatic skills, 'I'm not paid to babysit your children.'

Cat put the phone down and said to Bev, 'I'm really sorry, this won't take a minute, can you excuse me?'

Bev rolled her eyes. 'Don't be long.'

Cat went into the corridor and punched in her mum's number. She was shaking like a leaf. Suppose Mum was ill? Or had had a fall? She was normally fit and healthy, but Cat had to remind herself from time to time that her capable mother was now seventy-three. Something *must* have happened to prevent her from picking the children up. She never made mistakes like that.

On the third ring, her mother picked up. 'Hello,' she said.

'Mum, are you okay?'

'Well, of course I am,' said Mum. 'Why wouldn't I be?'

'I was worried about you,' said Cat, trying to remain calm. 'You haven't picked the kids up from school.'

'*What?*' said Mum. 'That was today? I thought you wanted me to do it tomorrow.'

'No, Mum,' sighed Cat, 'I rang last night and said today.'

'You said tomorrow,' replied Mum tetchily.

'I did?' said Cat, convinced that she hadn't got it wrong.

'Yes, you definitely said it was tomorrow,' said Mum. 'I even wrote it down.'

'Sorry, my mistake then,' said Cat, trying to make light of it, but seething inside. She felt guilty about feeling so cross with Mum, who rarely let her down, but panic was making her agitated. 'Can you get there now? The school are pretty frantic and I'm stuck in a meeting.'

'I'll be there in ten minutes,' her mother promised.

Cat rang back the school, mollified the secretary, and went back to her meeting with relief. It was hard enough juggling work and home commitments without disasters like that befalling her. Thank goodness it was so rare, otherwise she'd *really* be in trouble.

'Glad to see you're more cheerful.' Pippa walked into Gabriel's kitchen pushing Lucy's buggy, followed by Stephen and her two boys, Nathan and George. She'd offered to return his favour from the morning and pick the kids up from school. Gabriel had accepted gratefully as he'd spent the morning fence-mending and had got seriously behind on his domestic chores.

Gabriel paused from whistling 'Always Look on the Bright Side of Life' and realised with a jolt that since his meeting with Ralph Nicholas that morning he had been feeling a lot more chipper. He'd gone to work with a will and being out in the fresh frosty air had invigorated him. Even coming back to an untidy, silent house hadn't caused him as much internal wrestling as it normally did. He'd got down to tracking down the socks that always mysteriously vanished under Stephen's bed with an enthusiasm he hadn't felt for ages. Maybe Ralph was right. He just needed to focus on the stuff he *could* do.

'Good day at school?' he asked his son, who nodded his assent before running off to watch TV with his cousins.

'Cup of tea?' he asked his cousin. 'You look tuckered out.'

'I am a bit,' said Pippa. 'Lucy's a lot better now, but we did have a bad night with her.'

'I don't know how you cope with three of them,' said Gabriel.

'Well, what else am I going to do?' said Pippa laughing. 'Slit my wrists? By the way, have you seen this?'

She shoved a leaflet in his hand.

STOP POST OFFICE CLOSURES NOW!!
SAVE OUR VILLAGE!!
PUBLIC MEETING THURSDAY 7.30pm

'Oh, *that's* what he was talking about,' exclaimed Gabriel.
   'Who?'
   'Ralph Nicholas,' he replied. 'I met him this morning and he was wittering on that I should try and do something about the things I can do something about, not get hung up on trying to help Eve.'
   'He's right,' said Pippa. 'I'm going to the meeting. Poor old Vera's beside herself. They want to close her down and move the postal services to Ludlow.'
   'But that will be a disaster,' said Gabriel. 'How will people get there? There's only one bus a day.'
   'Exactly. You should have heard Miss Woods going on about it today. They could probably hear her in Ludlow.'
   Gabriel laughed. Pippa was such good company. It did him good to be around her.
   'So, what do you think? I could get Mum to come and babysit for my lot and Stephen could stay over if you like?'
   'We-ell . . .'
   'Oh, come on, Gabe, it's hardly like you've got a busy hectic social calendar now, is it?' teased his cousin. 'You need to get stuck into something else for a change. It'd help take you out of yourself. Plus it is important. Just think how this place will change without its post office.'
   Gabriel stared out of his kitchen window at the bird table Eve had been insistent they'd bought. It had started off, like so many of her interests, as a burning enthusiasm and she went out every day for several weeks to show Stephen the different varieties of birds that were attracted to the garden. But, after a while, she lost interest, and though Gabriel still left food out, it was as if the birds knew she

57

wasn't there any longer. Apart from a lone robin who was pecking at some crumbs, very few of them now came to the garden. But it was time he stopped dwelling on stuff like this and got on with the business of living. Ralph and Pippa were both right. He needed an outside interest.

'Okay,' he said, 'you've twisted my arm. Where do I need to go?'

'Noel, you haven't forgotten your mum's coming on Sunday, have you?' Catherine said before yelling up the stairs to Mel: 'I haven't finished talking to you, young lady!'

Noel walked in on Wednesday evening to the usual chaos. The little ones were arguing over the DVD control, Magda was sobbing hysterically in the corner because Sergei had ditched her – again – James was hardwired into his Playstation and looked like he wasn't going anywhere any day soon, and, as Noel opened the door, he'd heard the telltale thumping of feet on the stairs and slamming of a bedroom door that indicated that Mel was in another of her moods. Though, as Cat often said to him, when wasn't she these days? He couldn't remember the advent of going to secondary school causing the amount of trauma it was evidently causing his eldest but, as his wife frequently pointed out to him, It's Different Now.

'Yes, I had actually. Damn, can't we put her off?'

Cat gave him a withering look.

'You know we can't. I've been making excuses to her since Christmas.'

'Oh, bugger,' grumbled Noel.

'It would be nice if *you* talked to her for once in a while,' said Cat. 'She is your mother, not mine.'

'Yeah, well, you got the lucky straw in that department,' said Noel, unknotting his tie. 'I'd trade Granny Dreamboat for Granny Nightmare any day of the week.'

'Hmm. I'm not so sure of that,' said Cat. 'Granny Dreamboat didn't pick up the children from school today.'

'You're joking,' Noel was stunned. His mother-in-law was always so reliable.

'I'm not,' said Catherine. 'She got the dates mixed up apparently.'

'That's not like her,' said Noel.

'No, it isn't,' said Catherine, frowning slightly. 'Oh, well, no harm done, I suppose.'

A sudden crash from the playroom and a wail had them scurrying.

'That damned bookshelf—' Every week Noel mended the bookshelf and every week someone managed to make it collapse again.

'Can you deal with that?' Cat asked. 'I need to sort Mel out.'

'Oh?'

'Girl talk,' said Cat firmly.

'Right,' said Noel. 'Yes. Bookshelves it is.'

Of late Mel had spent a lot of time huddled with her mother having sobbing fits. It always seemed to be related to women's things. Noel didn't like to ask, or think about that. To him, Mel was still his little girl. The thought that she might be growing up made him very uneasy. His daughter was becoming a woman, and he was feeling tired and old. Sometimes it felt as though the best part of his life was over.

Marianne ducked into the back of the village hall, panting a little. One of the things that had annoyed Luke about her when they were together was how she never managed to get anywhere on time. He did have a point. Since she'd arrived in Hope Christmas, Marianne found it nigh on impossible to walk down the High Street without finding someone to chat to, so she was generally late everywhere. She felt a smidgeon of guilt when she saw Pippa already in the front row. How did she do that? There she was with her three children and much more frantic life than Marianne had, and *she* was never late. Marianne felt a familiar downturn in her emotions. Luke had had a way of criticising her that made her feel pathetic and useless. Could she never get anything right?

There were two empty seats at the back, so she sat down on one of them and hoped that the formidable Miss Woods and Diana Carew wouldn't be taking notes as to who was there or not. Diana Carew, who had of course taken charge, her reading glasses hung about her neck and perched on top of her enormous bosoms, was booming down the microphone about the need to fight back for the sake of their community. Vera, looking more than ever like a frightened mole, got up to speak while Mr Edwards (did anyone ever call him by his first name?) shot her encouraging looks.

'Thank you all so much for coming,' Vera squeaked. 'I've been looking into our options and it seems that we might be able to take our case to the courts and try and stall things for a while. We could also try and diversify. That seems to have worked well in other communities. They've combined their pub with the village shop and post office. That's something we could consider. Thanks to Mr Edwards—' Vera blushed, 'we now have a website, which you can find at www.soshopechristmaspostoffice.com, and I believe he's also set up a petition on the Number 10 Downing Street website, so please do tell all your friends. Miss Woods has kindly drafted us a letter that you can send both to our local MP, the council and the Post Office. We have copies at the front here, or you can download them from the website.'

Vera sat down to a roar of applause, before Diana threw things open to the floor and a lively debate ensued.

'I'm not sure that we really need to go chain ourselves outside the Houses of Parliament—' Diana was saying to a rather enthusiastic teenager, who'd clearly just learnt about the suffragette movement, when the door opened and someone sidled in and grabbed the seat next to Marianne.

'Is this seat taken?'

Of all the seats in the room, why did he have to pick the one next to hers? Marianne stared up into the eyes of the very same stranger whose feet she'd been sick on at New Year.

61

Chapter Four

'Have I missed anything?' Gabriel whispered. He felt incredibly awkward. He knew the new reception teacher from school, of course he did, but he'd barely spoken to her till New Year's Eve. When first she'd flirted with him, and then she'd thrown up on his feet. He could only imagine how mortified she must be feeling right now. Probably best if he didn't mention any of that.

'Not much,' Marianne whispered back, blushing a little. On their previous encounter he hadn't noticed how pretty she was. Her dark curls fell down her back and her bright blue eyes were alive with intelligence. He felt a pinprick of interest in her, which took him by surprise. 'They've set up a website now and have asked us all to write letters to our MP and the Post Office and so on. That's about it. And now we're getting to the point in the evening where we enter a circular debate in which nothing gets resolved.'

Gabriel sat back to listen and had to conclude that Marianne was right. There seemed to be a division already forming between one group – led by a rather forthright Miss Woods – who seemed to think direct action was called for – 'I'll travel down the motorway on my scooter if I have to!' she declared – and another led by Diana Carew, who felt that it would be unseemly to be campaigning in such a public way. 'We don't want Hope Christmas to become synonymous with thugs,' she kept saying, which elicited a harrumphing response from Miss Woods.

Seeing things seemed to be getting out of control, Mr Edwards took the opportunity to leap to his feet and announce that that wrapped it up for now, but that a steering committee was being formed to tackle the issues head on and anyone who wanted to join it was welcome to sign up.

The meeting ended in noisy confusion as people broke off to chat in animated groups.

'So, are you going to join up?' Gabriel nodded towards the front of the hall where a small crowd, including Pippa and Dan, had gathered.

'Not sure,' said Marianne, who looked ill at ease. 'I'm not much of a committee person . . .'

'You shouldn't have chosen to come to live in a village like Hope Christmas then,' said Gabriel, grinning.

'That was clearly my first mistake,' said Marianne, smiling.

She was relieved to see Pippa come bounding up to them both. 'Come on you two, we need some voices of reason on this committee if it's not going to develop into a mad bunfight between Diana and Miss Woods.'

'Pippa, you are a bugger,' said Gabriel. 'I said I'd come along, I didn't say I'd get involved.'

'Now you know that's not the attitude, cousin of mine,' cajoled Pippa.

'Oh my God. You two are related?' Marianne was utterly mortified.

'Didn't you know?' said Pippa. 'I thought you two knew each other. Marianne, my cousin, Gabriel. Gabe, this is Marianne, she teaches reception at the school.'

'We've met,' said Gabriel.

'Have you?' Pippa looked puzzled.

Marianne was now the colour of a tomato.

'New Year's Eve, your house,' she muttered. 'I was sick on Gabriel's feet.'

Pippa roared with laughter. 'Oh my God. Gabe, you never said!'

Gabriel felt almost as embarrassed as Marianne. 'I didn't think it was polite to, and I think you're embarrassing your friend.'

'Oh, Marianne, I didn't mean to offend you. Come on. Let's go to the pub, so you two can get to know each other properly. Honestly, he doesn't bite.'

It's a kind of magic ... That's what I always think about baking. You take four simple ingredients, flour, eggs, butter, sugar, and look what you can achieve with them, anything from fancy cakes to shortbread. And when I was a kid, watching my mother bake was also somehow quite magical ...

Catherine paused from what she was typing and sighed. How was it that the words in her head, which seemed so magnificent, always seemed so dull when transferred to the page? Maybe it would be better if she wrote the recipes first and added the linking bits in later? She pulled a sheaf of material out. Granny Dreamboat's Perfect Victoria Sponge, Auntie Eileen's Fabulous Fairy Cakes ... she'd stolen recipes from around the family and planned them all for this book, which was meant to be a celebration of basic good, honest home-baked cooking, aimed at the generation of women who'd always been too busy for the kitchen.

It was also in part meant to be a homage to her own mother, a way of saying thank you for all the help and support. Ever since she was tiny, Cat could remember her mum cooking in the kitchen, and following her round, eager to learn how to cook herself. It had only been the two of them, when Cat was growing up, and they had bound their love in the kitchen preparing pastry and roast dinners. So it had seemed appropriate to write a cookbook based on her mother's recipes. Catherine paused for a moment. Was it her imagination, or was Mum being rather tetchy of late? It was unlike her to make mistakes, and she'd been quite vociferous in blaming Cat about the day she hadn't picked the kids up. Yet when Cat had sneakily peeked in Mum's calendar she saw Mum *had* written the right day down. Cat had also spotted a pile of unpaid bills in the kitchen, but, when pressed, Mum had insisted she was up to date on all that stuff. The episode had left her with a slight feeling of unease.

She was probably worrying unnecessarily. Noel certainly thought she was. Maybe Mum had just got a bit behind with her bills. Catherine turned back to the screen, her mind utterly blank. Funny that. It was always so easy writing a blog post or an article for *Happy Homes*. But this? This was like panning for gold in a river where you knew you were only ever going to find lead.

It didn't help that she'd only come up here to start working at nine, and she was absolutely knackered. Mel and James needed to be chased into bed so much later now. She'd practically had to prise them away from watching Dave. Magda, who had reluctantly agreed she was fit enough to cope with childcare duties once more, was out with the boyfriend – the bust-up as usual only lasting as long as it took to send a reconciliatory text message. Noel was out at yet another leaving do. From what he was saying about work, which wasn't much, there seemed to be an awful lot of redundancies at the moment. Reading between the lines, Catherine could tell he was worried. She wished he'd talk to her about it, but he seemed unwilling to, and she didn't like to push it.

Sometimes it felt as if a vast chasm was growing between

them. Cat worried that Noel didn't seem to be as pleased with her success as she might have hoped. She even thought he might resent it slightly. But then he'd come home, muck about with the kids, give her a hand with the tea and it was as if there was no division at all. Maybe it was like that for everyone when they had kids, but sometimes (and she felt guilty for even thinking it) Cat longed for the days before they'd had children, when they only had themselves to please. Life had seemed so much simpler then.

Nowadays she was so exhausted coping with the various needs of the children, the demands of Magda, and the difficulties of her job, she had very little left to give Noel. He deserved better from her, she knew that. But it was so hard to give of yourself, when you had nothing left to give.

How she wished her life was as easy and straightforward as the Happy Homemaker's. *She* wouldn't be reduced to trying to write a cookery book late at night, when the children were in bed. Oh no. The sodding Happy Homemaker would have been up at six to do the housework or prepare that day's dinner. She'd have sorted out reliable childcare so she wouldn't spend her days fretting about arrangements she wasn't sure would be met. She'd be able to effortlessly organise her work life so it didn't impinge on her home life, and no doubt *she'd* always be up for dynamic sex in exciting new positions with her husband at any time of the day or night.

There were times when Catherine really hated her creation, and increasingly she was becoming drawn to the idea that she should actually kill the Happy Homemaker off. The only thing stopping her was the financial reward that her alter ego brought them. If Noel's job *was* in jeopardy, Cat couldn't really do her in. Even if, as Cat sometimes suspected from the bitchy comments that occasionally got left on her blog by people who clearly didn't get the joke, thousands of women up and down the country would rejoice to know the *true* state of affairs chez the Happy Homemaker . . .

Marianne settled down in the corner of the Hopesay Arms feeling completely idiotic. How come she hadn't picked up that Gabriel was Pippa's cousin? She'd been so embarrassed about what had happened on New Year's Eve she hadn't told anyone about it. She rather liked the fact that Gabriel hadn't told anyone either. Well, she would like it once she got over the embarrassment. In the meantime, she was squeezed at the end of a large table, feeling out of place and awkward, listening to Vera talking to Mr Edwards in a pink and enthusiastic manner. It was so crashingly obvious that Mr Edwards had the hots for her as well. Marianne had never seen a couple so well suited and yet so shy of each other. She felt almost voyeuristic. But she'd rather be cramped down here than sitting anywhere near Gabriel, whose mere presence made her feel like a prat.

'You are *so* not going to hide in the corner.' Pippa came marching over and dragged Marianne up to their end of the table. Marianne was about to protest but, realising that Vera and Mr Edwards were oblivious to her departure, decided there was no point.

'I can't talk to Gabriel,' protested Marianne. 'I was sick all over his feet.'

'I wondered what had happened to you on New Year's Eve,' said Pippa. 'The trouble was, I was so pissed by the end of the night, I couldn't remember anything about it. Though I do recall Gabe saying something about having sick on his shoes, I just thought it was his.'

'Yes, well, now you know,' said Marianne, 'and you've embarrassed me enough for one evening. So I think I need to go home *right* now.'

'What you need,' said Pippa, 'is to lighten up and meet

67

new people. Coincidentally, my lovely cousin needs to do exactly the same thing. So you are going to get to know him and find out that he isn't at all ogrish, and thinks it's quite funny that you threw up on him.'

Pippa pushed Marianne into the seat next to Gabriel before disappearing to the bar. This was excruciatingly awful.

'I'm sorry about this,' Marianne said, thinking it couldn't get any more awkward. 'I had no idea Pippa was so bossy. She seems to have decided we need to bond or something. But it's quite all right, we don't. After the last time we met, I can quite see that you wouldn't be at all interested in talking to me, so I'll just finish my drink and head on home.'

'Don't do that,' Gabriel said. He looked at her with those lovely brown eyes and Marianne had to swallow hard. 'I once went back to a girl's room and did the very same thing. We've all done something silly under the influence.'

'In my defence,' said Marianne. 'It was a bit of an intense night. I hadn't meant to get so drunk, and I certainly didn't mean to come on to you like that. I was on the rebound.'

'I'll try not to take that as an insult,' laughed Gabriel.

'Oh God, sorry, I didn't mean it like that,' gabbled Marianne. 'It's not that you're not attractive or anything—'

'Glad to hear it,' said Gabriel with a grin.

'—but I was feeling a bit desperate and so was behaving quite out of character. It's just not me to be like that.'

'I know,' said Gabriel. 'And I do understand. I've been there too. I'm sorry to hear about you and Luke Nicholas.'

Marianne suddenly glimpsed the pain she'd seen in his eyes at Christmas. She wasn't one for village gossip but she had picked up that Stephen's mum had left them. She felt a burst of solidarity with him. Things hadn't worked out the way they'd hoped for either of them.

'And I'm sorry to hear about your wife,' she replied.

'Probably for the best,' mumbled Gabriel.

'I don't believe that,' said Marianne. 'As a fellow member of the Lonely Hearts Club, I can tell you're lying.'

'And you'd be right,' said Gabriel. He raised his glass. 'Here's to being friends and Lonely Hearts together.'

'To friends and Lonely Hearts,' echoed Marianne and clinked her glass against his. 'To never falling in love again and a pox on heartbreakers everywhere.'

Noel put his key in the lock, and turned it. Damn. Didn't seem to be working. He blinked myopically down at his keyring, which mysteriously had found itself a twin. Oh. Hang on.

'Wrong key,' Noel slurred. 'That's it.' He stood swaying on the doorstep, got the key in the lock, turned, and hey presto.

'Ssssh,' he said to the wall as he fell against it. 'Mustn't wake everyone up.' Cat had been most insistent on that point, after he'd come home from someone's leaving do the previous week and sung 'Pinball Wizard' so that the whole house had heard. He couldn't help it if the DJ had been a *Tommy* fan.

Noel reached out for the light but the bulb popped. Bugger. He fumbled his way down the corridor towards the stairs that led down to the kitchen. There was usually a stash of new bulbs in one of the kitchen drawers.

As he got there he heard a noise. He paused at the top of the stairs.

There was a bang and a muffled shout.

There was definitely someone down there.

Noel crept back to the family room and rooted round in the dark for a suitable implement. He grabbed something long and hard. That would do.

Taking a deep breath and feeling emboldened by the

alcohol firing through his veins, he crept back down the stairs again.

Nothing. There was no one there. He must have imagined it.

Noel was about to head upstairs again when he heard the dustbins crash outside. Noel paused, his heart in his mouth. Now what was he supposed to do? It was all very well coming over all Neanderthal and protecting your family in theory. He wasn't quite so sure that he'd really like to put it into practice. Particularly now, when he'd started sobering up rather fast.

He crouched tensely in the dark. There were muffled sounds coming from outside. It clearly wasn't a cat. Then he heard the kitchen window opening. Feeling sick to the pit of his stomach, Noel flung himself into the larder. Some hero he'd turned out to be.

Suddenly there was a loud crash and lots of shouting.

Noel came roaring out of the cupboard with his weapon held aloft.

Light flooded the kitchen.

Cat was standing sleepily in the doorway. 'What the—?'

Noel sheepishly put down his weapon – a plastic cricket bat – to see Magda and her boyfriend sitting helplessly on the floor.

Chapter Five

'What the bloody hell is going on?' Catherine stood in her dressing gown feeling a combination of bewilderment, fury and embarrassment. Sergei and Magda were arguing frantically in Russian and Noel was standing waving a plastic cricket bat in the air.

'I thought we were being burgled,' said Noel.

'I sorry, Cat-er-ine,' – God, that singsong whine again, how Cat hated it – 'I forget key. I not want to disturb. So Sergei say, climb in through window.'

'Did he now,' muttered Cat.

Sergei was looking as apologetic as a wannabe Russian mafioso would allow himself to look. 'It was my fault,' he said. He flashed Cat a smile that was clearly meant to be winning, but which reminded her so much of Vladimir Putin, she felt utterly repulsed. 'I didn't want to make Magda trouble.'

Repressing the comment that Magda could make trouble all by herself, Cat grudgingly accepted his apology.

'It's very late,' she said. 'So, Sergei, I think it's time you went home.'

'Oh,' Magda looked stricken. Oh God. *That* Look.

'What's the matter?' said Cat. She glanced at Noel who clearly was having the same horrified thought she was.

'Sergei, he have nowhere to go,' said Magda. 'He fight with landlord, and now he homeless.'

71

'Well, he can't stay here,' said Noel. They'd always been very strict with their au pairs – they could do what they wanted outside the house, so long as they respected Cat and Noel's rules within it.

'Please No-el,' Magda pleaded, 'he has no bed tonight. He can stay here, please?'

Cat looked helplessly at Noel. It was gone midnight and, if Sergei really had nowhere to go, it was a bit harsh to throw him on the streets. She felt herself weakening. Shit, she always weakened in the face of Magda's dogged persistence. The trouble was, if she didn't give in, she was treated to hours of Magda sobbing and right now it was too late and she was too tired to cope with that.

'All right,' she said. 'He can stay, but just for tonight. I want you to promise me you'll find Sergei somewhere to live in the morning.'

'Oh, thank you, thank you, Catherine, you are very nice person,' said Magda, hugging her with such effusiveness Cat began to think that it might have been better to brave the tears.

She and Sergei quickly disappeared upstairs, as if worried that Catherine might change her mind.

'Well done,' said Noel. 'You're always the one saying we should be tough on Magda.'

'Don't,' said Cat. 'It's late, I'm knackered, and I couldn't cope with the thought of Magda's hysterics.'

'Good point,' said Noel, finally putting down the cricket bat and going to shut the kitchen window firmly. 'I can't believe you left this unlocked.'

'I didn't,' protested Cat. 'I'm sure I locked it after tea, before Magda went out . . . Oh, bloody hell, you don't think she left the window open deliberately so she could sneak Sergei in?'

'I wouldn't put it past her, would you?'

72

'Bugger that girl,' groaned Cat. 'I am damned if she's going to pull the wool over my eyes again.'

'Do you think it's a secret Russian mafia plot to steal all our valuables?' said Noel anxiously. 'Perhaps I should take the bat to bed with us. Just to be on the safe side.'

Cat looked at him.

'Don't be daft,' she said. 'Sergei's harmless enough. I think if he is a villain he's probably a pretty inept one, or he'd have managed to break into the house properly. Come on, let's go to bed.'

They turned out the lights and headed upstairs, Noel pausing to put the bat back.

'I can't believe you thought that a plastic cricket bat would work,' said Cat, giggling as she climbed into bed. Suddenly she could see the funny side, and the vision of her husband defending their home by swinging a kid's toy bat above his head made her feel a sudden burst of affection for him. She cuddled up close to him. 'What were you going to do, hit the burglar over the head saying "Biff, kapow!" like some kind of cartoon superhero?'

'I hadn't thought that far ahead to be honest,' admitted Noel. 'I just grabbed the first thing to hand.'

'Well, Superman, do you fancy grabbing what's to hand right now?' Cat said suggestively.

Noel grinned.

'Okay, Lois. If you insist,' he said.

Marianne was out walking early on Saturday morning. Now she'd finally come to terms with the fact that she was staying in Hope Christmas, she'd taken to exploring the hillside paths around the village at the weekends. The countryside was stunning, and she was constantly discovering new and unexpected valleys as she followed the sheep paths that crisscrossed the countryside. Often she saw no one apart from the sheep and the odd solitary buzzard flying high in the sky. Even on glowering grey days, of which there'd been many of late, Marianne found it exhilarating to walk here. But on a bright sunshiny day like today, there was nothing like a brisk walk to dispel her wintry gloom and brush away the cobwebs. And she found that it stopped her sitting inside and brooding about Luke, who had been spotted in and around Hopesay Manor recently, according to Pippa. There were rumours afloat that his eco town idea was causing some kind of controversy now, and that he wasn't seeing eye to eye with his grandfather about the project. Marianne knew very little about his plans, but Pippa had snorted when she'd told her where the proposed site was, a low-lying valley a couple of miles from Hope Christmas.

'He's got to be bonkers to build out there,' Pippa had said. 'It's known as the Lake District round here. It floods nearly every year. Even if we have a drought year, the ground's always soggy in winter. I wouldn't buy a house there if you paid me.'

Seeing Luke's plans through Pippa's eyes was doing Marianne good. She had been so seduced by his good looks and easy charm, she'd failed to see a certain ruthlessness in Luke. People in Hope Christmas certainly didn't seem to be all that excited by his eco town or even to like Luke very much. Marianne was beginning to think that just maybe she'd had a lucky escape. And ever more so on days like today, when she climbed over a stile at the top of the steep hill she'd climbed and looked down the valley towards Hope Christmas.

The hillside was scattered with sheep baaing gently in the bracken, and a fresh wind whipped at her hair and made her catch her breath. It felt gloriously wonderful to be alive, to be alone here on the hillside, the only person revelling in the beauty of her surroundings, watching a red kite circling up ahead and listening to the chattering of the rooks in the trees behind her. She had a sudden absurd impulse to run down the hillside, like Laura in *Little House on the Prairie*. It felt like a long time since she'd been so content.

Deciding, in the end, that she was more likely to catch her foot in a pothole and break her neck, Marianne instead made her way down the hill in a sedate manner. Recent rain had made the ground muddy, so she'd probably been wise not to run. She'd just rounded a bend in the path when a black and white collie came bounding up towards her, panting and barking. It came up to her and submitted to her petting. A minute later a little boy came running up. 'Benjy!' he called, 'I've got your stick.' He was followed by Gabriel.

'Oh, hi,' said Marianne, feeling suddenly shy.

'Hi yourself,' said Gabriel. 'You know Stephen, and this is our dog, Benjy. We're out checking on the pregnant sheep. It'll be lambing time before I know it, and I need to start thinking about getting them inside.'

'Don't they lamb on the hillside?' asked Marianne.

'They can do,' said Gabriel, 'I just prefer to get mine indoors.'

'How big's your flock?' said Marianne.

'Not that big,' said Gabriel. 'I've recently taken over my parents' farm. Since the foot and mouth outbreak they'd really downsized and had half the flock they used to. Pippa, Dan and I are planning to expand the business and produce our own beef and lamb and sell that along with the vegetables we grow locally. Dan farms the cattle and I farm the sheep.'

'It sounds lovely,' said Marianne. 'I'm such a townie, I know nothing about farming.'

'Well, maybe I should show you,' offered Gabriel.

75

'Maybe you should,' said Marianne, smiling.

'Da-ad, come on,' said Stephen, 'I want to go looking for monsters.'

'Oh, and that's the other thing we're doing,' said Gabriel. 'Going on a monster hunt is about the only way I can get Stephen out sometimes. Pippa's brilliant, but I can't always rely on her as a babysitter.'

'It must be tough,' said Marianne with sympathy.

Gabriel gave her that familiar sad look.

'We manage,' he said.

'Da-ad.' Stephen was clearly getting impatient.

'Right, I'd better . . .'

'Yes, of course.' Marianne waved them goodbye and set off down the hill, a small smile playing on her lips. Of all the reasons to stay in Hope Christmas, getting to know Gabriel North better was probably as good as any . . .

'Mum. Let me take your coat,' Noel greeted his mother with a perfunctory kiss. As usual, a feeling of dread came over him when she walked through his front door. Would the kids behave themselves? Would Magda do something shocking? (On her previous visit at Christmas his mother had gone on and on about the horror of meeting Magda in the bathroom exposing her bare midriff.) Would he show her yet again how much he'd failed her in the son department?

Mum hadn't always been so bitter. She'd always had a sharp tongue, true, and Noel and his brother, Joe, had been left in no doubt that their sister, Kay, was the favourite, but when his dad died things had started to go badly wrong. It hadn't been Noel's fault that Dad being ill had coincided with Cat's first pregnancy. He'd done his best to balance the two sets of demands, but it had been incredibly hard being in London and his parents being in Stevenage, and Noel was conscious at times he hadn't been the conscientious son he'd wanted to be. The only comfort at the time had been presenting his mum with her first grandchild, but, instead of taking the event as a positive, she'd turned it into a negative in a way that only she knew how. From the first, Cat had dubbed her Granny Nightmare. She'd barely stayed five minutes to look at her new grandchild, she never offered to babysit when she came to stay and, when the others had arrived in quick succession, had made sarcastic comments about living beyond your means. If it weren't for Cat's incredible generosity and insistence that he should keep on good terms with his mother, Noel might have been tempted to cut her out of his life altogether.

Noel knew from Kay that his mother had felt let down that he hadn't been around more to help sort out his dad's estate, but at the time he'd been the only member of the family tied down with children of his own. Besides, he hadn't expected her to sell up and move out of the family home so quickly. In his darker moments he thought Kay had engineered things so that their mum would give her some cash as a down payment on her first flat, but Cat had accused him of being paranoid.

The final nail in the coffin had been the discovery that, in his mother's determination to cut loose and start again, she'd got rid of all Dad's war memorabilia – including his medals – without telling him or Joe. How she could have done that was beyond him. Noel had always been aware that his parents didn't enjoy the happiest of marriages, but that seemed spiteful beyond belief. The resulting row when he'd told her so had taken several years to recover from. And it was only now (mainly at Cat's insistence) that he was beginning to see a bit more of his mother again. Every time she came, he hoped she wasn't going to stay long. But, for someone who exuded displeasure at her surroundings from every pore, Granny Nighmare also seemed quite happy to ensconce herself *in situ* for days and sometimes weeks at a time.

'I see you've still not mended that shelf,' were his mother's first words on entering the playroom. One day he really would get round to fixing it.

'I'm afraid it's not really a priority at the moment,' said Noel between gritted teeth. 'Why don't you go down to the kitchen and see Cat, while I put your bags upstairs?'

He knew it was a copout, that he was being unfair to Cat, but somehow her toleration of his mother outreached his own and, within seconds of seeing her, she'd already got him riled.

He dug the children out of their respective foxholes – instinctively they'd all vanished when their grandmother arrived – and went to put his mother's things in the spare room. Cat had spent hours cleaning it, and had even found a vase to put daffodils in, but Noel knew from bitter experience there was bound to be something wrong with the room. The only thing his mother seemed to tolerate about coming here was Ruby. Which was ironic as, being the youngest, she was also the most hard work and the one most likely to have a tantrum.

Noel made his way downstairs with a heavy heart. He could already hear his mother quizzing poor Melanie about her school grades (not, as it happened, as good as they should have been, but she'd had problems settling into her new school), and picking on James for not being sporty like his Uncle Joe. It was going to be a very long week.

'I saved you a seat,' Gabriel whispered to Marianne as she snuck in at the back of the second public meeting about the post office campaign. Impressively, Vera had managed to inveigle the MP for South Salop to come and speak on their behalf. He'd given an impassioned speech about the future of rural post offices and promised to raise the matter in the House. Gabriel had his doubts as to whether Mr Silent, a backbench Lib Dem, could actually make any impact, but at least he'd turned up, which was more than the MP from the neighbouring constituency had done – but then it was his government's policies which were leading to such closures, so he probably wouldn't be seen anywhere near a meeting like this.

No one from the Post Office had come either, which was no surprise. To Gabriel's amusement, Vera had installed a cardboard cutout of Postman Pat. Someone was filming the meeting and planning to put it on YouTube. Very droll.

'Have I missed anything?' Marianne whispered.

'Only John Silent's fight 'em on the beaches speech,' said Gabriel.

Vera had now got up and was thanking them all for coming again.

'I've got good news and bad news,' she began. 'The good news is that we have nearly 15,000 signatures on our Downing Street petition,' (this raised a cheer) 'the bad news is that I can't get hold of anyone from the Post Office to come and meet with us and discuss a compromise. So we've decided to take the issue to them. And we're planning a trip to London to visit the Post Office headquarters, as well as presenting our petition at 10 Downing Street. We'd like as many of you to sign up for this as possible, of course. Thanks to Ralph Nicholas, who has several friends in the media, we're hoping to get some national coverage to raise our campaign further.'

'Blimey,' said Marianne, 'that sounds impressive.'

'Good for Vera,' whispered Gabriel. 'I never knew she had it in her.'

'Well, you know what they always say about the quiet ones,' said Marianne. The room was so packed her and

Gabriel's chairs were so close together their knees were nearly touching. She shifted a little in her seat to move away from him. She didn't want him getting the wrong idea.

The meeting soon broke up, with people going to sign up for the London trip and promising to write more letters of protest. Marianne found herself agreeing to take minutes of the next meeting, while Gabriel, having confessed to an interest in Photoshop, discovered he was now going to be running an entire poster campaign.

'Honestly, this village is hopeless,' said Gabriel. 'Give an inch and they take a mile.'

'That's what public service is all about,' sniffed Miss Woods, as she stumped by with her stick. 'We need more altruism in this world, not less.'

'True,' said Marianne, laughing. She picked up her coat and started heading for the door.

'You're not staying for a drink?' Gabriel felt a sudden stab of disappointment.

'Oh, um,' Marianne looked awkward. 'I hadn't really given it any thought.'

'It doesn't matter if you've got plans,' Gabriel said in a rush. 'It's just everyone else is going and I thought—'

'No, I don't have any other plans,' said Marianne, 'a drink would be lovely.'

They made their way into the Hopesay Arms, the friendly local, which was cram-full of regulars and so busy it was three-deep at the bar.

'I'll get these,' offered Gabriel. 'What's your poison?'

'Half of lager, thanks,' said Marianne. 'I'll look for a table.'

'This is cosy,' said Gabriel when he arrived eventually at the fireside table that Marianne had found.

'Oh, I didn't want you to think . . .' Marianne blushed. 'This was the only place I could find.'

'Here's fine,' said Gabriel. He sipped at his beer, and there was a momentary awkward silence, before he said: 'So, how does Hope Christmas compare to London, then?'

'I love it,' said Marianne. 'Even though I grew up in London, I've never really felt like a city person. From the moment I came here I felt like I'd come home. Does that sound odd to you?'

'Nope,' said Gabriel. 'I moved to London for work originally, then stayed for Eve's sake, but my heart was never there. Not really. I always felt I was living in the wrong place, having the wrong life. Now ...' he paused for a moment.

'Now?' she prompted.

'Well, even though Eve's gone and everything,' said Gabriel, 'at least I feel I'm living the life I'm meant to be living. Does that make sense to you?'

'Perfect sense,' said Marianne.

The evening flew by, and, before Gabriel knew it, it was nearly eleven.

'I'd better go,' he said. 'I've got the teenage daughter of my neighbour babysitting and she's got school in the morning. I'd better let her get home.'

'Oh, I assumed Pippa must be babysitting,' said Marianne.

'She couldn't. She and Dan were meeting a possible new supplier tonight.'

'I'd better be off too,' said Marianne. 'It's way past my bedtime.'

'I'll walk you home,' offered Gabriel.

'There's no need,' protested Marianne. 'Honestly, I'm a big girl.'

'And I'm a gentleman,' said Gabriel. 'And, as your fellow Lonely Heart, I insist on walking you home whether you like it or not. I have to protect you from any potential lotharios out there intent on breaking your vow of chastity.'

'All right then,' said Marianne, 'if you insist.'

They got their coats on and made their way down the High Street towards Marianne's cottage. It was a bright starlit night and the moon was full, the kind of night that was made for lovers, Gabriel suddenly thought. And whereas in the pub the warmth of the fire had led to a kind of cosy intimacy with Marianne, out here in the cold he was suddenly pulled back into the reality of both their situations. They really were two Lonely Hearts offering one another companionship. That was all. They walked the short distance back to her cottage in near silence. The intimacy from the pub seemed to have vanished somehow.

When they got there, Gabriel felt suddenly awkward. Suppose she thought . . . ?

'Must get in, early start and all that,' Marianne gabbled. 'Thanks for a lovely evening.'

She almost dived into her cottage. Gabriel was relieved. She clearly hadn't been expecting anything. Which was good. As he had nothing to offer her. Nothing at all.

Chapter Six

'More wine, Angela?' Catherine waved the bottle in front of her mother-in-law almost with bated breath. So far this was the first meal since her arrival that hadn't been peppered with snide comments and sharp asides to Noel. It helped that Magda had gone out for the day, so Angela couldn't harp on about why Catherine had to work and needed an au pair (especially such a lousy one) anyway. Thankfully, though Sergei had outstayed his welcome by two days, Catherine had managed to chuck him out before her mother-in-law's arrival. Seeing as Angela had yet to forgive Cat and Noel for the year they'd lived in sin, she'd have been horrified to discover Magda cohabiting with her foreign boyfriend in the same house, corrupting her grandchildren, even if she appeared to heartily dislike said grandchildren.

'No, thank you, Catherine,' sniffed Angela. 'I don't like to overindulge in the middle of the day.'

But it doesn't stop you knocking back a bottle of sherry in the evening, thought Catherine uncharitably, and shot Noel a knowing look. He raised his eyes to heaven in the helpless manner he always employed when his mother was around. Cat wished he'd stand up to her more.

'I'll have some more, thank you,' said Cat's mother, whom they'd invited over to help dilute the toxicity of Angela's presence. 'I think I'm past the age where I care about overindulging.' She flashed an understanding smile at her daughter, as if to say, *You're doing fine.* Cat smiled back. Not for the first time she felt incredibly grateful to have such an easygoing, wonderful and utterly generous mother.

The meal continued in silence until Ruby and Paige started kicking each other under the table.

'Stop that you two!' hissed Cat, trying not to draw Angela's attention, whose views on children's behaviour at the dinner table were more than a little Victorian. Luckily, Angela had chosen that moment to quiz James about which school he might be thinking about going to, a thorny subject as Noel and Cat were keen for him to try for a grammar school five miles away, which had a much better reputation than the local boys' school, while James of course wanted to go where his friends were going. They'd already been through this once with Melanie, but her friends had roughly divided in half as to where they went, which had softened the pill of saying goodbye to her best friend somewhat.

'She started it!' said Paige, sticking her tongue out at Ruby.

'Did not!' said Ruby. 'Paige, you're a fucking shit!'

The silence at the other end of the table was so deafening Cat felt as though she'd entered some awful time capsule where things were frozen in perpetuity. *Oh my God.* Where on earth had Ruby learned language like that? She battled the urge to laugh. Really it wasn't funny.

'Ruby! You do not say words like that ever!' Cat shouted as sternly as she could. Great, now Angela would have all her worst fears about how terribly her grandchildren were being brought up confirmed.

'James does,' whined Ruby.

'Don't tell tales,' Cat and Noel said automatically. 'Go to your room at once.'

Ruby stormed out of the room sobbing, while Cat and Noel scolded their son, who took himself off to the lounge, kicking the door as he went, complaining about how unfair the world was.

'Angela, Mum, I'm so sorry about that.' Cat tried and failed to recover her poise. 'I had no idea they even knew words like that. It's so difficult nowadays to stop them learning this stuff. I know it was different when we were young.'

'I have to say I am a bit surprised,' said Cat's mum, with an asperity that was unusual for her. 'I thought rather better of your children.'

'Oh, piffle. It's not as if children have only just learnt to swear,' said Angela. To Cat's utter amazement, she was grinning. 'I seem to remember being called in to Noel's school because he'd been writing rude words in the boys' loos. Do you remember, Noel?'

Noel looked as though his teeth were set on edge.

'I don't think you've ever let me forget it,' he said.

Cat let out the breath she'd been holding without realising. That had been a close call but miraculously – presumably because the guilty party had been Ruby-Who-Could-Do-No-Wrong – Angela didn't seem at all fazed by the incident. So much so that within minutes she was insisting that Ruby came back and sat down again, and even went into the lounge to try and persuade James to come back.

'Wonders will never cease,' Cat remarked to her mother later, as they were loading the dishwasher.

'What's that, dear?' Her mother was looking a little distracted, looking at a teatowel as if she'd never seen one before.

'Angela, earlier,' explained Cat. 'I thought she'd be apoplectic about Ruby swearing like that. I couldn't believe she'd seen the funny side.'

Mum looked at her in a bemused fashion.

'Sorry, when was that?' she said.

Cat looked at her, puzzled.

'You know, earlier on,' she said. 'Ruby said a rude word and we told her off, and then rather than Angela being angry she told a funny story about Noel. Surely you can't have forgotten already?'

'No, no, of course not,' said her mother, but she had a slightly perplexed look on her face. 'Right, where do you want these?'

She lifted the washed plates from the table where Cat had left them.

'In the cupboard they normally go in,' said Cat.

'Which is?'

'That one,' said Cat, pointing to the relevant cupboard. 'Mum, are you all right?'

'Never better, dear,' said Mum brightly. 'Oh, of course, silly me. They go in here, don't they?'

'Yes,' said Cat, with a prickle of unease. Was it her imagination, or was her mother becoming more and more forgetful?

'Have you seen this latest about the new eco town?' Pippa was practically exploding as she sat at her kitchen table reading the local paper.

'No, what?' Gabriel had just dropped by to pick up Stephen. He'd been out in the fields since early that morning, tracking down his flock, ready to bring them indoors for lambing. Most of the farmers round here left their sheep on the hillside, but Gabriel preferred having his under cover: when, as had occasionally happened, he'd bred from different stock, the occasional large lamb was born, causing complications that were more difficult to deal with out on the hillside. A couple of sheep were still missing though. He was going to have to go out again tomorrow.

'That bloody Luke Nicholas,' said Pippa, practically spitting with venom. 'Can't think what Marianne can ever have seen in him.'

'Why, what's he done?'

'Just announced that his eco town is going to have a brand new supermarket up the road, which conveniently his company is also building. I bet some money's changed hands with a dodgy councillor over that. It says here that the supermarket is going to be donating a new leisure centre for the eco town. No wonder they got planning permission.'

'A leisure centre doesn't sound very green and, come to that, nor does a supermarket,' said Gabriel.

'Not unless they harness all the energy from the exercise bikes to power the place,' snorted Pippa. 'The whole thing is mad. We don't need a new town this close to Hope Christmas. Besides, I'm sure that land he's building on used to be designated a flood plain. Do you remember that Christmas a couple of years ago when it rained so heavily? The fields round there were waterlogged for weeks.'

'Doesn't it all still have to be approved, though?' said Gabriel. 'Surely he can't just steamroller the thing through?'

'Why shouldn't he?' said Pippa. 'He's got money and influence, hasn't he? I tell you, that bloody town is going to kill Hope Christmas stone dead. What with that and the post office, I despair, I really do.'

Something stirred inside Gabriel. Something that Ralph Nicholas had said to him weeks ago about keeping hold of the things you loved. He looked out at the hillside, towering over the house in the gathering gloom. Gabriel had lived in Hope Christmas for most of his life, and he realised, somewhat to his surprise, that he loved it with every fibre of his being. He couldn't bear the thought of it being under threat. He'd been so preoccupied with his own personal problems he'd given less thought to those of the people around him. Hope Christmas was built around a community that in many cases just about eked out a living. Losing the post office would be a blow, but the eco town could prove the nail in the coffin.

'Can't we challenge it somehow?' he said. 'I seem to remember reading somewhere that there are a lot of protests about eco towns elsewhere. Maybe we should try and find out a bit more.'

'Ooh, Gabe,' teased Pippa, 'you're becoming quite the environmental campaigner, aren't you?'

'Well,' said Gabriel, 'I think you're right. If we don't act now, it might be too late. Maybe it's time to widen our campaign to saving Hope Christmas itself.'

'What do you propose to do, then?' said Pippa, her interest piqued.

'I'm not sure yet,' said Gabriel. 'But I think I might just pay Ralph Nicholas a visit. I wonder how much he knows about what his grandson is up to.'

Noel sat in the boardroom at a budget meeting feeling something akin to despair. Matt Duncan was doing a great brown-nosing job agreeing with everything that Gerry Cowley was saying, however stupid it might be. It also appeared Noel was more out of the loop than he'd thought, as Matt seemed to have access to figures and documents that Noel hadn't ever seen. That had meant that Noel had been unable to answer half the questions asked about this year's sales projections. He'd looked like a real tit. Which is what Matt was after, presumably. Noel half expected Gerry to morph at any moment into Alan Sugar, point at him and say, 'With regret, my friend, you're fired.' Not that he was getting paranoid or anything, but it was clear the writing was on the wall.

Luckily, for the time being, no one was paying too much

attention to him as Karl Dear, the finance director, was having a row with Alan Thompson about the budget his department had been given. Alan was arguing that without sensible funding he couldn't actually build the new freezer stores that Asda had commissioned, and did GRB really want to lose that account, while Karl was patiently and patronisingly telling Alan that no one was immune to the wintry storms blowing over the economic wastelands left behind by the credit crunch, however big the deal they'd wangled. So he was just going to have to compromise like the rest of the company.

Noel was busy doodling on his sketch pad. One of the projects he'd got involved in recently had been to design the heating systems for a new eco town, up in Shropshire. Eco towns were hot property at the moment and everyone was vying for a piece of the action. The company were hoping that if they could make this one work it would lead to more of the same, so the stakes were very high indeed.

There had been talk originally of creating sustainable housing from old workers' cottages close to the village of Hope Christmas, but that had been eschewed in favour of the brand new shiny eco town that the likes of Matt Duncan were keen to build. Noel had been unfortunate enough to have spent an evening in the company of Matt and Luke Nicholas, who ran the local building firm tasked with creating the new town. Having spent a glorious morning strolling around Hope Christmas, which Noel had instantly fallen in love with, Noel couldn't for the life of him see why an eco town was even needed so close to such a wonderful place.

Hope Christmas was already eco friendly. Its shops and restaurants sourced their produce from the local farmers, who held their own market in the village square every Thursday. There was a fabulous bookshop and a great antiques market, which was a real treasure trove. Why anyone needed to replace it was beyond Noel. The whole thing had seemed like a huge waste of money to Noel, and he hadn't made himself popular by saying so.

Noel still felt sure that the cottage route would have been a better fit for this, but he knew throwing suggestions around like, 'Prince Charles has done a good job of this kind of thing in the Duchy of Cornwall', wouldn't get him anywhere. Prince Charles' vision of sustainable developments that incorporated the notion that keeping the existing communities alive might actually be a good thing didn't cut any ice in Matt's shiny world. He was after the glory and so, suspected Noel, was Luke.

The meeting was breaking up, with nothing very much resolved. It was clear that economic conditions were causing nearly all the company's projects to be scaled down, except for the eco town, as Noel realised when he looked through the figures once again when he was back at his desk. Now why didn't that surprise him?

Marianne felt hesitant as she drove up the drive of Hopesay Manor. She hadn't been back for two months. Not since that dreadful night on Christmas Eve. She'd only glimpsed Luke once in the street since. As usual with Luke, his business seemed to be taking him up and down the country, and it seemed that he was rarely at home, preferring to spend more time in his bachelor pad in London.

Marianne had some stuff of his to return. She could have taken a chance that Luke was away and dropped it round at his place, but she couldn't bear the thought that the blonde bimbo was still hanging about, although Pippa reckoned he'd moved on to the next one by now. On Christmas Day Marianne had toyed with throwing most of his possessions in the lake at the front of Hopesay Manor, but she hadn't quite been able to bring herself to. And then she'd hoped that, by keeping them, maybe Luke would have to call round to pick them up. Pathetic, she knew, but she couldn't help that sneaky little hope that he'd still come back. Terrible thing, hope, it kept you going against all the odds, even against the constant battering that Pippa was prone to giving Luke, who as far as Pippa was concerned was systematically trying to destroy all that was good about Hope Christmas.

It was hope that had brought her here now. Hope that if she gave Luke's things to his lovely charming grandfather, maybe Ralph could smooth the way not only for a meeting, but also for the happy-ever-after reconciliation that Marianne knew she shouldn't be contemplating, but couldn't help thinking about. So, here she was, standing like an idiot in front of that imposing door. The first time she'd come here had been the best day of her life. The last time, the worst. What would happen to her here today?

Taking a deep breath, Marianne lifted the large door knocker. She realised looking at it now that she'd made a mistake before – it wasn't a man squashing a serpent, it was an angel. The wings spread round the circle of the door knocker. How unusual.

The sound of the brass knocker ringing against the door echoed ominously, making Marianne feel more nervous than ever. It seemed aeons before the door opened and Humphrey appeared. His face was implacable and, if he felt any surprise at seeing her, he didn't betray it.

'Erm – is Sir Ralph in?' Marianne was feeling like a total idiot now. What on earth had possessed her to come?

'I'm afraid he isn't, madam,' replied Humphrey. 'Is there anyone else you'd like to see?'

'Oh, er, no, it was nothing, really.' Marianne felt herself floundering. 'I'd better go—'

'Who is it, Humph?'

A familiar voice called from inside the house. God, no. She could picture him at the top of the stairs, just as he'd been that day. Her heart was hammering and she felt vaguely sick. She wanted to leave, but her feet seemed to be rooted firmly to the spot.

'Oh, it's you.' Automatically, her heart skipped a beat, but Luke was standing at the door looking down at her as if she was something unpleasant on his shoe.

'I've brought – I've still got some of your things,' stammered Marianne. 'I thought you might like them back.'

'Put them in the hall,' he said dismissively and turned to go. How could he be so cruel?

'Don't you . . . ?' Marianne was speechless. Part of her was shocked to the quick that he could be so unkind, and another part was furious with him. After what he'd put her through. After the promises he'd broken.

'Will there be anything else?' That charming smile, that mocking look. Once it had entranced her, now it was breaking her heart.

'No, nothing.' The fury had abated, as suddenly as it had come, and Marianne was just feeling incredibly sad and foolish. What had she expected? After the way he'd treated her at Christmas, it was hardly as though Luke was going to welcome her back with open arms, was it?

She dropped the box she was holding onto the marble floor of the porch, and it was with satisfaction that she heard something crack. She hoped it was the very expensive bottle of aftershave he'd left in her bathroom, which she'd wedged next to a couple of shirts Luke liked. Hopefully they were now ruined.

She went to the car and got the other boxes, and left them on the porch. Luke had gone back into the house, and Humphrey slowly picked up the boxes Marianne was dumping one by one. This was it then, she thought as she put the last box down. All her hopes and dreams of the future were now definitely over. She might have made a life for herself in Hope Christmas, but Luke couldn't have made it any clearer that she'd be living it on her own.

As she walked back to her car to go home, an old Land Rover drove up and Ralph got out of it. In a rapid glance he assessed the situation.

'It might seem painful now,' he said, 'but at least you're making a clean break. It will get better in time.'

Marianne looked at him bleakly.

'I know,' she said. 'And I am getting better. But this . . . this was hard.'

'Most things that are worthwhile generally are,' said Ralph, patting her on the arm. 'But this too will pass. You'll see.'

He whistled and his dog jumped out of the car and followed him back into the house.

Marianne turned to take one last look at the house. Her hopes of a life with Luke were dashed. But Ralph was right. This would pass, eventually. Things, after all, could only get better.

Chapter Seven

Noel sat in the first-class carriage of the Virgin train speeding for Shrewsbury opposite Matt Duncan, who was getting carried away on a wave of blue-sky thinking about forward projections by which they could rationalise their objectives. Noel was too polite to suggest he stop bull-shitting and actually do some proper work for once. Besides, he knew that wouldn't get him anywhere. Blue-sky thinkers were the future. Hard-grafting, precise engineers like him used to coming up with plans that actually worked were the past. Never had he felt more like a dinosaur.

Noel sighed and pretended to look at his own laptop, as if it could make this sow's ear of a development into a silk purse. There was something he didn't quite like the smell of here. Whether it was the smarminess of Luke Nicholas, who was meeting them at Shrewsbury to take them on site, or the self-satisfied air that Matt always projected whenever he talked about the eco town, but there was something about the whole project that made Noel uneasy. He dimly recalled seeing a comment in the files from one of the original architects about the suitability of the site, but there had been a falling out with that particular architect and no one seemed to know anything more about it.

'This is us.' Matt gathered his things together as the train slid into Shrewsbury station. They got out and made their way to the entrance where Luke Nicholas was waiting for them. Noel sighed again. A whole day with these two goons. He didn't know how he was going to stand it. At least he'd managed to get out of an overnighter, pleading that Cat needed him at home – which she did, it being half term. Not that he'd be much use to her by the time he got back late this evening, but it was better than nothing. He hated staying away from home at the best of times, but the thought of spending a night in a hotel with Matt Duncan was too much to bear.

'Hi again.' Luke held out his hand to greet them, and was interrupted by a distinguished voice saying, 'Well, Luke, me boy, aren't you going to introduce us?'

Luke said, 'Oh, yes, of course. Matt Duncan, Noel Tinsall, meet Ralph Nicholas, my grandfather. As head of the family firm, he thought he'd like to come along for the ride.'

Noel detected a hint of irritation in Luke's voice but he covered up smoothly. His grandfather tipped his hat, and said, 'Luke, I hope I'm not going to be in your way here, just wanted to see what you're up to.'

'And it's a pleasure to have you, Grandfather,' said Luke in a manner that indicated anything but pleasure. 'Gentlemen, if you please.'

Noel followed them to the car, a faint smile playing on his face. He'd had the distinct impression that Luke's granddad was up to something. This might turn out to be a very interesting day indeed . . .

'So that's that then?' Pippa was helping Marianne stick crêpe flowers onto paper plates for the forthcoming Easter Bonnet Parade. She was using the half-term break to get them ready early, knowing that once school had started she wouldn't have much time. Besides, Easter was early this year, it would be upon them before she knew it. In theory the children were supposed to make their own for a competition but, despite it being her first Easter in Hope Christmas, Marianne had had enough experience of dealing with small children having temper tantrums because they hadn't won, and their parents berating her for the extra stress involved in making the bonnets, to make her take the easy option. There were only twenty children in her reception class and she'd become a dab hand at making crêpe flowers over the years. Besides, she found arts and crafts therapeutic and today, every time she picked up the scissors, she was also viciously imagining what she would do to Luke next time she saw him.

'Yes,' Marianne put down her bits of paper and sighed. 'I know, I know. Don't tell me, I was completely bonkers to even think he'd have me back. You don't have to tell me I've made a fool of myself. I've been kicking myself for being so pathetic ever since.'

'Don't,' said Pippa. 'We've all been there. It's a well known psychological condition known as the Heathcliff effect. However much the bastards kick us when we're down, we can't help creeping back for more.'

'What, even you?' exclaimed Marianne. 'I can't imagine you ever being as pathetic about a bloke as I've been about Luke.'

'Even me,' grinned Pippa. 'In that faraway time before I met Dan, I kissed my fair share of toads. I was just lucky that eventually one of them turned out to be a prince.'

'Oi, who are you calling a toad?' Dan had just come in on his way to take the boys swimming with Stephen. Lucy was sitting quietly in the corner 'making' some Easter bonnets of her own.

'Well, at least I got the most handsome one in the pond,' said Pippa, laughing and kissing Dan smack on the lips. Marianne felt a wistful pang as she watched them. It must be so lovely to have that relaxed, secure relationship with someone. Would it ever happen for her? Since the debacle with Luke, she was beginning to wonder if she even wanted it to. Being alone did also mean being safe from further heartache.

'Right, we're off,' said Dan. 'Come on, boys.'

The boys, who'd been happily playing on the Playstation, leapt up and disappeared in a flurry of excitement.

'It'll happen for you one day,' said Pippa, as if reading her thoughts, as she waved goodbye to her family.

'You think?' said Marianne, feeling sadder and bleaker than she'd done since her break-up with Luke. 'Sometimes I think I'll never meet the right person.'

'Never say never,' said Pippa. 'Besides, I don't just think. I know. Somewhere out there, there's someone for all of us. You just have to believe that one day you'll find him.'

Marianne went back to sticking flowers on paper plates. It was all right for Pippa, it had already happened for her. She stared out of the window as the sun set across the magnificent hills rising from the valley floor, casting vivid oranges, pinks and purples in the sky. It was so wonderful living here. She just wished she wasn't doing it all alone.

Gabriel was driving his flock down the country lane that led past the rain-sodden fields where the proposed eco town was to be built. The land fell sharply to the left and plateaued out into large, flat and very soggy fields through which ran a stream that was usually full in spring. The fields, he'd belatedly realised, bordered the edge of his land. He'd only discovered this in conversation with Ralph Nicholas, who seemed as unenthusiastic about the new proposal as Gabriel did. Gabriel had called into Hopesay Manor to see him and over a glass of whisky Ralph had confided that he had originally planned for there to be renovation work on the cottages at the corner of his estate. Somehow, in his absence, this had escalated into a full-blown new eco town which, far from supporting the community as Ralph had intended, threatened to destroy it.

'Can't you do anything?' Gabriel had asked.

'Unfortunately the board have all got behind this,' Ralph said, 'and though I'm technically its chair they don't actually have to do what I say.'

'So, what can we do?' Gabriel had wanted to know. Which was when Ralph had deemed it wise to show Gabriel his old map collection.

'Useful things, maps,' Ralph had said. 'You never know what they're going to throw up.'

Poring over the old charts, Gabriel had discovered an old bridleway, down which he was now herding his sheep, as was his ancient right from time immemorial, written into the laws of Old Salop. And, if he'd timed it right, his sheep-herding should just about coincide with the arrival of Luke Nicholas and his posh engineering folk from London, whom Ralph had assured him were site-visiting today.

Gabriel turned a corner and saw a car coming towards him. A sleek BMW M5 driven by Luke Nicholas. Good old Ralph. Gabriel watched the car slow to a halt as his herd of pregnant sheep baaed and fought their way round it.

Luke got out of the car looking furious.

'What the bloody hell is going on? This is a private road.'

'I'm sorry,' Gabriel tried to look surprised. 'Since when?'

'Since forever,' said Luke. 'This land and this road has been in my family for generations as I'm sure you well know. Now get your sheep out of here!'

'Well, that's funny,' said Gabriel, emphasising the strength of his Shropshire burr and scratching his head. 'Because my family have been using this as a right of way to herd our sheep for generations. I'm only getting my flock off the hillsides ready for lambing. You can't stop me exercising my ancient rights.'

'Oh, can't I?' Luke was angrier than ever. 'We'll see about that. Oh shit!'

Casting another furious look at Gabriel, Luke tried to wipe the sheep dung from his foot in as dignified a manner as possible. Gabriel did his best to keep a blank look on his face as he whistled to Benjy and shooed his sheep past Luke's car.

Luke was bound to find a way round the ancient right to roam thing, his sort always did. But in the meantime, as Ralph had pointed out to him, they'd bought themselves a little more time, and with any luck put Luke on the wrong footing with his friends from London. Gabriel grinned as he passed Luke's car, from where Ralph directed a broad wink at him, and drove his flock baaing and stumbling their way down the road towards home. If nothing else, it had been worth it to see the look on Luke's face . . .

The secret to a happy half term is organisation . . . trilled the Happy Homemaker into Cat's computer. The Happy Homemaker always trilled. She was that kind of woman. God, how Cat loathed her, particularly as she was listening to the chaos downstairs as Magda screamed, 'James! You must come and tidy your room now. Your mother said!' and she could hear the dulcet tones of Ruby and Paige fighting – again. Melanie was mooching miserably in her room, no doubt texting her friends to say what a terrible life she had, following her parents' inexplicable refusal to let her go and see the latest must-see action adventure film, which, sadly for Melanie, had a 15 certificate. Cat might have relented, but she'd seen a clip of it last time she'd been at the cinema and there'd been a torture scene that had made both her and Noel wince.

If you keep the children organised and busy, you will auto-matically find the days progress smoothly with few fights and arguments. As it is often difficult at this time of year to guar-antee outside activities – Cat shivered and wrapped herself more tightly in her fleece. One day Noel would keep his promise and redo her study with some insulation in it – *try to organise visits indoors. Go to a museum or visit an aquarium or a waxworks museum.* Cat scrubbed the last sentence – she knew it would bring forth the normal response in her comments section about it being all right for people who lived in London, as if living in the capital were some kind of crime. The bloggy world was in the main a benign place, but there were some odd people out there and occasionally they took delight in surfacing on her blog. She wrote instead, *If you aren't lucky enough to have a nearby museum, why not try bowling, or go swimming at your local leisure centre? And, failing all else, you could do worse than spend a rainy afternoon playing games like Scrabble or Monopoly . . .*

'Except, I'm sure in *your* house your children would be well behaved enough not to squabble over every bloody move,' Catherine said out loud. How much easier to live in the world of the Happy Homemaker whose children would always obligingly play games together beautifully, create wonderful art and craft collages, spend hours playing poohsticks in the park . . . Cat had to hand it to herself, she couldn't have created a more perfect and unrealistic picture of parenthood if she'd tried.

The chaos downstairs seemed to have died down, which was a relief, as Cat didn't think she could cope with yet another lecture from Angela about her failings as a parent. Her mother-in-law, despite her stay coinciding with half term, hadn't yet managed to offer to do anything useful with the children, although she had at least taken to going out on a cultural tour of duty of the capital. Somehow Cat didn't think the kids would have been all that wowed by the prospect of visiting the National Gallery – they found Tate Modern or being dragged round the Tower of London enough of a chore.

Cat went back to the Happy Homemaker again. What other pearls of wisdom could she dispense? Were there any about dealing with stroppy teenagers and mums who were losing their marbles? Mum seemed so distracted of late. Recently she'd not only forgotten a recipe for a raspberry cheesecake that Cat had wanted to include in the book and which Mum had made countless times over the years but, to Cat's dismay, she'd nearly had her electricity cut off for not paying her bill.

Mum had made light of it, but Cat was beginning to worry that she was hiding something from her. Maybe she had some kind of financial worry that she was too proud to mention? There was no point trying to talk to Mum about it, though. Knowing her as well as she did, Cat knew that if there was a problem she would be keeping it from Cat so as not to 'worry' her. Maybe Cat should ring Auntie Eileen instead. If anyone knew if Mum was having money worries, it would be her. Cat picked up the phone and dialled the number. It was probably nothing, but at least she could put her mind at rest.

Chapter Eight

Noel stumped his way through a sodden, windswept field and wondered who on earth could have thought this god-forsaken place was a good location for an eco town. As soon as the sheep had gone (which had caused him much silent laughter), and they'd got out of the car to inspect the site, the rain had come down in sheets. Of course, he hadn't thought to bring wellies or a decent overcoat, and he was soaked through. Only Ralph Nicholas seemed prepared in his oilskins and ancient galoshes. It was almost as if he knew it would happen. And yet, no rain had been forecast . . . His grandson and Matt looked even more ridiculous than Noel felt, both of them having eschewed something as sensible as a coat for expensive suits – Luke's probably came from Savile Row – and shiny shoes. At least Noel's had some kind of tread in them, which had so far stopped him from going arse over tit in the mud.

He realised as soon as he stood in the field what the problem the architects had mentioned was, and wondered why Matt hadn't seen fit to comment on it. If, indeed, he even realised what it was. The fields where the proposed town was to be built were in a flat valley surrounded by bleak-looking hills, though Luke had been quick to assure them everything looked different in the sunshine. But most importantly it was a valley, with a river running through it, a river that came off the hillside and sloped downhill towards the fields. They were, if he wasn't mistaken, standing on a flood plain. It was a disastrous place to do any building on.

'Erm, Matt, can I have a word?' Noel found himself shouting over the wind and it took three attempts before Matt heard him.

'Sorry, what's that?' Matt looked as though he were turning blue from the cold.

'I think this is a flood plain,' shouted Noel. 'I'm not sure that anything should be built here, let alone a village.'

Matt looked at him in incomprehension.

'It can't be!' he yelled. 'Luke assured me himself this was perfect building land.'

'Look at it!' Noel said. 'The fields are so wet you could grow rice in them. Would *you* want to live here?'

Matt had no answer for that, and Noel trudged back to the car. This was madness, it could only be Matt's inexperience and determination to look good in front of the CEO that had kept the project going so long.

But when they got back to the posh manor house that Ralph Nicholas apparently owned, and where they were treated to an incredibly lavish three-course meal, Noel discovered to his dismay that Matt had no intention of discussing the issue of the site's suitability. Instead, he and Luke seemed to be formalising plans for work to begin.

'Whoa, don't you think you're jumping the gun a bit?' Noel said as they waited for their puddings. 'I'm not sure that that site is incredibly suitable for building on.'

'Why ever not?' Luke directed a charming smile at him. 'I know you didn't see it at its best today, but every house will have stunning views, with a decent garden, not to forget the magnificent playing fields we're planning and the wonderful leisure centre, which will be the heart of our new community.'

It was clearly a well-practised spiel, but it cut no ice with Noel, who'd heard enough of this kind of guff to last him a lifetime.

'Oh, I'm sure you're right,' said Noel. 'It will be a wonderful development, but you're building it in the wrong place. It's got a sodding great river running through it, which at the moment looks as if it's about to burst its banks. How often does that happen?'

For the first time that day Luke looked slightly uneasy. 'We *have* had an unusual amount of rainfall for the time of year,' he conceded.

'The fields are flooded,' said Noel. 'Is this a common occurrence?'

'Well, er . . . It certainly doesn't happen *every* year . . .'

'Oh, come now, Luke,' said his grandfather, from the far end of the table. 'We both know those fields flood regularly.'

'So it *is* a flood plain?' said Noel. 'In the government draft planning statement it clearly states that eco towns are not to be built in areas where flooding is a problem.'

'No, of course it's not a flood plain,' said Luke, who quite clearly had never read any government guidelines about anything. 'I'd never propose such a thing. There is, I grant you, a problem with flooding from time to time, but we've looked into it and we think by building barriers further upstream, or possibly diverting the river, we can prevent this from recurring. Once the water is pumped out of the ground we should reduce the risk of dampness.'

'Thereby increasing the risk of subsidence,' interrupted Noel. 'It's clay – once it dries out it will crack up. No, I can't accept that this is a decent site to build on. It goes

104

against all the government guidelines. I'm afraid I'm going to recommend to GRB that we don't proceed.'

There was a stunned silence. Noel got up to get his coat. 'Coming, Matt?' he said.

'I think I just need to go over a few things with Luke,' said Matt hurriedly, looking pale.

I bet you do, thought Noel, as he was shown to the lobby where he waited an uncomfortable half an hour before a cab appeared to take him to the station. He had a horrible feeling that he might just have marked his card for good. Despite this being a really bad investment, he'd seen enough dodgy constructions in his time to know this would probably go ahead with or without his intervention. The company couldn't afford in these straitened times to turn down such a potentially lucrative deal. This time he'd *really* blown it.

Marianne was walking in the rain. There was something satisfyingly cleansing about Shropshire rain: even when it was cold, there was an invigorating quality to it that walking through rain-drenched London streets lacked. If she was suffering from the Heathcliff effect, she may as well act like a Brontë heroine and catch consumption or something. She'd always found the idea of that very romantic as a kid, although as an adult it seemed somewhat less appealing. And, given that Luke wasn't exactly likely to rush to her bedside stricken with guilt and laden with red roses, there wasn't much point getting a terminal disease.

But walking in the rain was a good purge of her spirits. Despite her assurances to Pippa that now she'd really accept things were over between her and Luke, Marianne actually felt worse than ever. The way Luke had looked through her, like she meant nothing, nothing at all, had cut her to the quick. He used to look at her as if she set his world on fire.

105

He'd told her that she meant everything to him, that a life without her wasn't worth living. And he hadn't meant one single solitary word. Whereas she had. She'd really believed she and Luke were destined to be together forever. Walking out in the pouring rain, her thoughts churned over and over to no helpful purpose. And she realised with a jolt that she was crying, really crying for the first time in months. Great racking sobs were coming out of her, and she found herself shaking violently. How was she ever going to get over this? It was the greatest betrayal of her life.

She didn't notice at first she'd strayed into the edges of Gabriel's land. Slowly but surely she was beginning to work out the geography of the area and, as she walked down footpaths that meandered through the farms dotted about the hills, she was beginning to know which farms were which, and whose sheep belonged to whom. Gabriel's, she knew, were a medium-sized sheep with black faces known as Shropshires, but only because Pippa had told her. She also recognised the telltale blue brand mark that signified they belonged to Gabriel's farm.

Only not today. She'd been so preoccupied that she'd failed to notice there weren't any sheep on the hillside at all. Where were they all? Ever since she'd been here, a feature of her walks had been the sheep who wandered across her path willy-nilly or fled up the hillside at her approach. She'd been spooked by the sheep at first, as she found the way they suddenly ambled in front of her on the paths a bit unnerving, but had gradually got used to them and now a walk wasn't complete if she hadn't said hello to a few sheep on the way. But today there were none.

A noise caught her attention. A bleating sound that didn't seem quite right. It was coming from a little way down the hill and, as Marianne walked down the steep path that led to the fields, the noise became more urgent and panicky.

Maybe there was a sheep in trouble. She scrambled to the edge of the path, and looked down. In a dip in the hillside was a sheep, bleating frantically. A very pregnant sheep. Somehow it must have fallen over the edge and got stuck. The poor thing kept trying to get up and collapsing again. Hang on . . . Marianne cast her mind back to a nature programme she'd watched a while back, from which she'd learnt that when sheep are about to give birth they keep standing up and sitting down. As if on cue, the sheep stood up and its waters broke. Holy cow. Now what was she supposed to do?

Catherine was sitting down in the lounge with a well-deserved glass of wine by the time Noel got home. She was exhausted. Magda had gone out for the evening and Cat had had a fraught teatime during which Melanie had left the table in tears because Paige had 'looked at her in a nasty way'. The advent of hormones and secondary school had rendered her eldest daughter sensitive in the extreme. Cat didn't know what had got into her, but was struggling to come to terms with the fact that the little girl she loved was approaching womanhood faster than her mother would like. A few more years and she'd be leaving home, her life just beginning, while Cat's would be contracting. She felt an oddly jealous pang when she thought of the future that Mel had before her. Was that normal, she wondered, or was she going to turn into a bitter old hag as her daughter shone young and bright and beautiful in front of her? She hoped not. For the first time in her life when she read Ruby fairy tales, she was starting to sympathise with the wicked stepmother more than the beautiful princess. That couldn't be right.

At least all the fraughtness had stopped her thinking about the rest of her utterly stressful day. It had started badly when she'd turned up to see Mum for a cup of coffee, and been confronted with a furious rant about Cat interfering in her business.

'How dare you ask Auntie Eileen if I had any money worries?' Mum said. 'I'm not a child. I have managed my own finances pretty successfully all these years, you know.'

'I know,' said Cat, 'it was just with you having your electricity cut off, and seeing all those red bills last time I was here, I was worried about you.'

'How dare you spy on me!' Mum was bright red in the face. Cat had never seen her like this before. She backed down at a million miles an hour.

'I'm so sorry, Mum, I didn't mean to pry. I was concerned, that's all.'

'Well, there's no need to be,' retorted Mum. 'I made a mistake. It's not like I can't cope.'

'I've never said you couldn't,' said Cat. 'But are you sure you've got enough money?'

'Of course I have,' Mum looked perplexed. 'You know I have a good pension.'

'So there's nothing wrong?' said Cat.

'Repeat after me, "Everything is fine",' said Mum. 'Cat, you worry too much and you don't need to worry about *me*.'

So that was that. But the niggle of worry remained. She sipped her glass of wine and cuddled up to Noel watching the news. She didn't mention her concerns about Mum, as Noel had already made it clear that he thought she was overreacting. Maybe she was. In every other way her mother was perfectly fine. Cat tried to convince herself that there was nothing to worry about, but the growing knot of anxiety in her stomach told her she hadn't succeeded.

Gabriel was scouring the hillside in the rain. One of his ewes was missing. In the palaver of getting round Luke's car, he hadn't noticed. He only realised his mistake when he got back to the farm and herded the sheep into the shed. She must have wandered off. It was one of the ewes who was close to lambing. Gabriel knew he should have had them all in by now but since Eve had left he had found it increasingly difficult to juggle everything, and now he was cursing himself for his lack of planning. Though there were rarely problems with Shropshire sheep at lambing time, this particular ewe had been rather large and he suspected she was carrying triplets. If something went wrong she might die on that hillside, and he couldn't risk that happening. So now he was out searching for her with all the kit he needed in case she gave birth: rubber gloves, string, Vaseline, were all stowed away in his backpack.

He heard a shout and saw Marianne scrabbling towards him.

'I think one of your sheep might be about to give birth,' she was calling.

Gabriel raced towards Marianne, who showed him where the ewe was stuck. It was an awkward clamber, but Gabriel managed to lower himself down onto the ledge where the sheep was.

'There, there, girl,' he said, patting the sheep on the back. He gently eased his way round behind her and, after putting on his rubber gloves, had a feel to see what was going on.

'Damn,' he said, 'it's a big one, and I think there's a smaller twin. Marianne, there's some string in my backpack, can you get it for me?'

Gabriel felt inside the sheep again and found the lamb's front legs. He pulled them towards him, and looped the string around the legs. Gently he pulled the lamb out in time with the contractions. It slipped back for a moment, and he had to loop the string around its legs again. Eventually he could feel it coming and teased it out of the

109

ewe. It flopped out onto the ground and didn't move. Oh no. Please, not that. This happened sometimes, but not often. Gabriel grabbed some grass and tickled the lamb's nose to try and get it to sneeze. Nothing.

'Is everything all right?' Marianne climbed down beside him, looking worried.

'Wait a sec,' said Gabriel. He picked the lamb up by its hind legs, swinging it gently to try and get it to breathe. Still nothing.

The ewe, sensing something was wrong, bleated her distress. Gabriel patted her again.

'Sorry, old girl, there's nothing I can do,' Gabriel felt her pain. He hated losing lambs. The miracle of birth was one of the most precious moments of his job, and it was heart-breaking when it went wrong.

'Oh, Gabriel,' Marianne looked just as gutted as he was. He was shot through with gratitude that she seemed to understand so instinctively how painful it was. Eve never would have noticed at all.

'It's not over yet. There's still another,' he said, and went back to the sheep, who was moaning in pain. The second lamb was coming out legs first. Damn. He hoped they wouldn't lose this one too.

'It's coming out backwards,' said Gabriel. 'Marianne, I may need some help. Can I brace myself against you? I can't risk turning it around or I might strangle it with the cord.'

Slowly but surely he lined the lamb's legs up and, by dint of gentle rocking and timing the sheep's contractions correctly, he eased the lamb out. He could feel Marianne's breathing keeping pace with his own. As the lamb slid to the floor, he thought, *Oh no, not again* – but this time the lamb bleated loud and strong, and within minutes was sucking at his mother's teat. Elation and relief surged through him and without thinking he flung his arms round Marianne.

'Thanks,' said Gabriel, 'I couldn't have done that without you.'

'I'm just glad I was here,' said Marianne, flushed and grinning. 'I've never seen a lamb being born. That was magic.'

Gabriel looked at her and grinned back. She was so pretty, he thought. It always took him by surprise when he was with her.

'Yes, it was, wasn't it?' he said, but he wasn't just thinking about the lamb. Sharing the experience with Marianne had been magical too. She hadn't batted an eyelid, had reacted calmly in a way he could never have imagined Eve doing.

On impulse he hugged her again.

'You were brilliant,' he said.

Marianne whooped for joy.

'I wouldn't have missed it for the world,' she said. 'It's our special spring surprise.'

They stood looking at the lamb, now suckling from its mother. A red kite soared high above them in the bright blue sky, a gentle breeze blew on the pink and purple heathers. Gabriel squeezed Marianne to him. For the first time in a very long while, he felt that all was right in the world.

Part Two

You Gave it Away

Last Year

December 23

Gabriel could hear the bird's frantic cheeping before he saw it. It was a bright, sunny day and he'd been walking in the woods. He frowned. Hadn't it been snowing earlier?

Suddenly the skies went grey and he was filled with an urgent sense of foreboding. The bird's cries became more frequent and desperate. Gabriel knew it was vitally important that he reach the bird. Had to try and help. But couldn't think why or how.

'Daddy!' A shout came from behind him. What was Stephen doing here? He was meant to be at home tucked up in bed. The anguish in his son's voice tore at Gabriel's heart. He should go to his son.

But the bird . . .

Why was the bird so important?

Couldn't he help them both?

The bird was too far away. He could just about see it now, caught in barbed wire, but he couldn't ignore his son's cries, which were getting louder and more persistent.

'Daddy, Daddy, Daddy!'

Gabriel ran in the direction of Stephen's voice, but the wood seemed different today. Less open, more hostile. Dark twisted trees crouched menacingly above him, small spiteful bushes barred his way. Soon he was lost, and frantic. Where was he? Where was Stephen?

'If you love something, let it go.'

'It can't be—'

Eve was there in front of him, blocking the way towards Stephen.

'Eve!' he called out in anguish. She looked at him with such sadness in her eyes, and then she was gone. But there was Stephen, a small sobbing bundle calling his name . . .

Gabriel woke with a jerk, blearily aware that he was cold and stiff. It was midnight, and his tumbler of whiskey was half full, though the bottle beside it was nearly empty. He had vague memories of sitting drinking it, wallowing in nostalgia, but had no idea how long he'd been asleep. He did know that he had a thumping head. The fire had gone out in the grate and through the gap in the curtains he could see it was still snowing. He should go to bed.

'Daddy.' A small shadow appeared in the doorway.

'Stephen.' Gabriel felt uncomfortable. He didn't want his son to see him in this state. Stephen had seen enough that he shouldn't have already.

'Why aren't you in bed?' said Stephen. 'I had a bad dream, and woke up and couldn't find you.'

'I'm sorry.' Gabriel felt worse than ever. 'I fell asleep down here. Come here.'

Stephen climbed onto Gabriel's lap and snuggled against him.

'You're cold,' he said accusingly.

'You're warm,' said Gabriel. 'You can cuddle me and warm me up if you like.' He held his son tight, and kissed him on the top of his head. Maybe Eve had been right. He couldn't help her, but he could look after their son.

'I wrote a note to Santa, Daddy,' said Stephen.

'You know he might not have enough Wiis to go round, don't you?' Gabriel always made a point of damping down

Stephen's wilder expectations at Christmas, which were usually, it had to be said, generated by random promises that Eve made and never kept, like the time she'd promised him a trip to Disneyland Paris that had never materialised.

'I don't want a Wii anymore,' said Stephen solemnly. 'There's only one thing I want. Do you think if I'm really really good Santa will give it to me?'

Gabriel's heart sank.

'It depends what it is,' Gabriel said carefully.

'Shh, it's a secret,' said Stephen. He held out a crumpled bit of paper. 'Can I put this by the fireplace for Santa?'

'Of course,' said Gabriel. 'Now really, it's time you were back in bed.'

Stephen put his letter by the grate and allowed himself to be carried back to bed.

'I miss Mummy,' he said, as Gabriel tucked him in.

'I know,' said Gabriel. 'I do too.'

Stephen looked at him expectantly. This was the point at which he should say something reassuring like, *It's okay, Mummy will be home soon*, but Gabriel couldn't bring himself to. Painful as this was for his son, how could he lie and promise something that wasn't going to happen?

With a heavy heart, Gabriel went back downstairs to tidy up. He paused in the lounge and picked up the letter Stephen had written.

Dear Santa,
I have been very god. Can my mummy plees come home
for Xmas.
Yours sinserly
Stephen North

Gabriel sat back down on the sofa and wept.

* * *

117

The traffic on the North Circular was predictably dreadful. Magda's flight was at three so Cat had planned to leave at ten, partly to give herself plenty of time, and partly to get rid of her sulky au pair at the earliest possible opportunity. She hadn't, of course, factored in Magda's ability to take three times as long as a normal person to get ready. By the time she had finally emerged from her bedroom with enough bags for half an army, it was nearly ten thirty. Although that still gave them over two hours, Cat wasn't convinced that they'd make it through London in time, but she was getting to the point where she was past caring. At least Magda was out of her hair for Christmas.

Magda had only been with them since September and she was already shaping up to be the worst au pair they'd ever had. If Catherine could see a way to reduce her workload slightly (unlikely since the Happy Homemaker had taken over her life), she might think of dispensing with an au pair again. But she needed Magda, otherwise her working day would be reduced by at least three hours, and she couldn't afford that at the moment.

Nor, for that matter, could she afford to spend the best part of a precious day just before Christmas ferrying her rubbish au pair to the airport. Magda had originally planned to go to her boyfriend, Sergei, for Christmas Day, but that was before a frantic phone call from Latvia from which it transpired that her mother was desperately ill – dying even – and Magda needed to get home. Catherine hated herself for being dubious about how ill Magda's mother really was, but she couldn't help thinking it was incredibly convenient that this mystery illness had arrived just before Christmas, considering that Magda had spent months moaning that she didn't have enough money to get home for the festive season. But, of course, this being

118

a crisis, Cat had felt duty-bound to cough up the money for a plane ticket. She had done it with the strictest of provisos that on her return Magda would be repaying the money out of her wages, but Catherine had the feeling that somehow Magda would wriggle her way out of that one.

Still, at least Magda had opted not to talk on the journey, preferring to sit in the back listening to the Cheeky Girls on her iPod. Mind you, the downside of that was that Cat had to listen to her slightly out-of-tune rendition. Too bloody right she was a cheeky girl.

The traffic started moving again and Cat felt a bit more hopeful. Maybe she'd be back by lunchtime. She didn't trust Noel to get through all the jobs she'd left for him. Magda's bed had to be washed and aired ready for her mother-in-law's arrival and the playroom desperately needed a tidy – the kids were all on tidywatch for that one, though if left to their own devices they would make things worse rather than better.

As she made her way on to the M4, Catherine was busy running through lists in her head: presents for mothers, check; presents for kids, mainly check, but Noel was going to have to go out on a frantic last-minute search to get a Baby Annabel who had mysteriously appeared at the eleventh hour on Ruby's list (being the youngest she generally got hand-me-downs, and Cat felt for once she really ought to get a decent present that she actually wanted); present for the husband, uncheck. She'd drawn a complete blank this year for Noel. Apart from a book she knew he'd like, some socks and a couple of CDs, she'd barely got him anything. Which was most unlike her. But things had been so busy recently and, what with working more or less full time now, she'd had less time to shop than normal. Feeling incredibly guilty, she did a last-minute dash round the shops in Heathrow and came out with a leather manbag, which she wasn't even sure Noel would like and which was far too expensive. But that's what last-minute, desperate Christmas shopping always entailed – buying something hideously expensive that you'd see reduced the next week in the sales. She hoped he'd understand. After all, Christmas was for the kids.

'Your mother doesn't like me.' Marianne was fixing in a pearl earring as she got ready in her cosy little cottage for the Nicholas family annual Christmas lunch, held at Hopesay Manor. This would be only the second time she'd been there, and she hadn't met Luke's grandfather since their embarrassing encounter with him in the summer. She'd endured enough of her prospective mother-in-law's snobbiness over the last few months to be sure that she wasn't being welcomed into the bosom of the family with open arms though.

'Don't be daft.' Luke was staring in the mirror as he adjusted his tie. 'She thinks you're great.'

Marianne's heart gave a little lurch, the way it always did when Luke was near. He was so gorgeous and he was hers. Sometimes she had to pinch herself. And sometimes the insecure part of her worried that it couldn't last, and one day he would leave her. Despite Luke's denials when she raised the subject, she couldn't help the gnawing anxiety within her, which made her feel that she was way out of her depth in his family. After all, how many men really married women their mothers so obviously disapproved of?

'Do I look all right?' Marianne gave a twirl in the little velvet black dress she reserved for all occasions when she didn't know what to wear. She felt rather self-conscious though. Was it too short for Hopesay Manor?

'You look fine,' said Luke, who seemed more interested in making sure his own appearance was okay.

'You barely looked at me.' Marianne gave him a friendly poke.

'You look lovely,' said Luke, kissing her on the top of the head. 'Come on, we should go.'

Marianne followed him into the car, her insecurities rising. She was nervous, couldn't he see that? But it was almost as if he didn't care.

Things got worse when they arrived and she realised her clothes were all wrong. All the other women were wearing twinsets and pearls and she was in a cocktail dress. Luke's mother didn't say anything, but her eyebrows rose to the ceiling when she saw the length of Marianne's skirt.

'My skirt's too short,' she hissed at Luke.

'Not for me,' he said, giving her a lascivious look before diving off to talk with one of the directors of the family firm.

Marianne was left standing on her own in the magnificent drawing room. There were about thirty members of the extended Nicholas clan and their friends, but not one of them came anywhere near her. She was too nervous to start a conversation with any of them, so instead concentrated on looking at the picture above the magnificent fireplace, which featured a rather dashing Cavalier on a horse.

'My ancestor, another Ralph Nicholas.' Luke's grandfather was suddenly standing beside her with his twinkling smile.

'I can see the family resemblance,' said Marianne. It was uncanny how alike the man standing beside her was to this portrait of a man from four centuries ago. 'What happened to him?'

'Oh, family legend has it that he helped Charles II escape, and in gratitude was knighted on his return.'

'You certainly have an interesting family,' said Marianne. 'Mine is quite dull by comparison. Labourers and dock

121

workers back to the time of the Conquest. I don't think we even have a convict who went to Australia to liven things up.'

'I'm glad you think so,' said Ralph. 'It's rather a pity that my grandson can't be persuaded to take more of an interest. But that's the trouble with youth. It's wasted on the young.'

Marianne laughed. She was glad to see her future grand-father-in-law didn't seem to have held the awkwardness of their initial encounter against her.

'Now, we can't have a lovely young thing like you standing all by yourself,' continued Ralph. 'Let me introduce you to the rest of the family.'

He gently steered her in the direction of some younger cousins, who certainly seemed a lot less stuffy and pompous than the rest of the family; but Marianne soon discovered that an inability to talk about trust funds and holidays in Antigua were a bit of a conversational stumbling block, and she was immensely grateful when Luke announced it was time to leave.

'Shall we go and have a festive drink in the pub?' Marianne said when they got back, but Luke looked at her blankly.

'Sorry, babe, I've still got some shit to sort out, no rest for the wicked and all that.'

'Oh.' Marianne felt crestfallen. 'I will see you later though, won't I?'

Luke looked vague.

'I'm not sure about tonight,' he said. 'I'll call you.'

And with that he was gone, leaving Marianne on her own, kicking off her shoes, taking off her pearl earrings and feeling terribly alone.

'Daddy, Daddy, Dadd-eee!!!' It's nearly Christmas!!!' Ruby was jumping on Noel's bed with all the glee of a four-year-old two days before the big day. He would have liked to feel as enthusiastic as she did, but the stonking hangover he'd got from the previous night wasn't helping any.

He looked at the time. Damn. It was nearly eleven thirty. He hadn't meant to go back to bed after Cat had left, but it had been so tempting. Cat had left him a depressingly daunting list of things to do and, knowing how exacting her standards were, he also knew he'd been set up for failure. Living with the sodding Happy Homemaker was a pain in the proverbial sometimes.

Noel climbed out of bed, threw some clothes on and went downstairs to discover the lounge in chaos, with bowls of cereal littered about and three out of four of his children still in their pyjamas watching *Harry Potter*.

'Come on you lot, up and out,' he said. Despite a great deal of moaning, Noel eventually managed to get them into some semblance of order, and got a reasonably good system of teamwork going whereby the little ones searched in all the small gaps under sofas and behind cupboards for missing toys, while the older two sorted everything out into the relevant boxes.

In the meantime, Noel tackled the huge pile of washing that had developed overnight apparently. What were they paying Magda for exactly? He even got the broom out and swept the kitchen, which was a first for him, but he knew Catherine was always moaning about how no one did it apart from her.

'I'm hungry.' James appeared at the kitchen door, looking hopeful.

'You're always hungry,' said Noel. He'd only just started – if they stopped for lunch now he'd never be finished.

'I'm starving,' said Melanie, 'when's lunch?'

'Not yet,' said Noel, 'we've got too much to do.'

'I'll make everyone eggy bread if you like,' offered Melanie.

'Brilliant, yes. That would be great,' said Noel. He carried a load of washing upstairs and dumped it in his and Cat's bedroom and then gingerly went into Magda's room to see how that was looking.

For someone who seemed to have packed most of her possessions to take away with her, Magda's room was surprisingly messy. Where did she get all this stuff? Perhaps he should leave it to Cat, he felt like a dirty old man poking around in here, but his mum was due at four and they had at least to have got clean sheets on the bed.

He stripped Magda's bed, and picked up the three half-empty coffee cups on the floor. He decided to leave the lacy knickers and bra draped across the chair. Funny though, he could have sworn Cat had a set just the same.

He marched downstairs feeling quite triumphant, only to discover the kitchen full of smoke and the children bickering.

Cat, of course, chose that moment to arrive back from the airport and, blithely ignoring all the things he had been doing, immediately started haranguing him about the things he hadn't.

Christmas had barely begun and already he was feeling like Scrooge . . .

This Year

Chapter Nine

'Oh God,' said Marianne as she watched Diana Carew, bursting with self-importance, march down the aisle of the church to the altar to where her reception class were perched precariously, clutching their Easter bonnets, ready to burst into 'All Things Bright and Beautiful' when the vicar gave the nod. 'I didn't realise Diana ran the Easter Bonnet Parade too.'

Pippa, who had helped walk the children up from the school, grimaced. 'Hadn't you worked out by now that Diana runs *everything* in Hope Christmas? Without her the place would fall apart. Don't worry, she doesn't get her hands on this service the way she does the Nativity. You won't be seeing any elves and mice today.'

Marianne stifled a giggle. The memory of last year's Nativity in all its awfulness was still imprinted on her brain.

'Are you sure she doesn't want one of the children to dress up as the Easter Bunny?' grinned Marianne.

'Don't even think about it,' warned Pippa. 'I swear she's telepathic. She'll probably suggest it at the next Parish Council.'

But it turned out that Diana wasn't interested in talking about the Easter service that the Hope Christmas primary school always put on in the last week of the Easter term.

'Ah, Marianne, Philippa, I'm glad to get you two together,

I just wanted to check that you were still all right for the Post Office trip next Wednesday? You weren't at the last meeting so I wanted to make sure.'

Marianne and Pippa both muttered excuses. Diana was incredibly good at wrong-footing people but, ignoring their discomfort, she went on, 'We're going to picket the main sorting office in London and then go on to Downing Street. Dear Ralph Nicholas has found us a TV journalist who's going to film the whole thing. It should be terribly jolly. I do hope we'll be seeing you both?'

'School finishes on Tuesday,' said Marianne, 'so I should be able to get there. I'm going down south to visit my parents anyway.'

'I'll do my best,' said Pippa. 'It just depends on the children.'

'Oh, bring them too,' said Diana. 'The more the merrier. Besides, children are *such* good PR!'

She bustled off in a self-important manner to accost Miss Woods, who had hobbled her way down the church aisle and was grumpily looking for a seat, leaving Marianne and Pippa in fits of giggles, which they had to repress quickly as the reception class was getting restive.

Marianne calmed them down and went through once more with the two eldest members of the class what they were going to say, while reassuring the youngest member, who was having the collywobbles. She turned to face the front as the organ started to play and the vicar came forward to welcome the congregation, mainly made up of parents, grandparents and siblings.

She caught sight of Gabriel, who slipped in from the back and squashed his way onto the end of a pew. She smiled and he gave her a small nod of recognition, which filled her with an immediate warmth. She hadn't seen him since the day they'd delivered the lamb together, but she

126

was pleased to see him now. Seeing him in action on the hilltop had given her an increased respect for him. She was glad that they were becoming friends. In fact, for a moment on the hillside, when he'd hugged her after the lamb was born, she'd experienced a slight fluttering feeling as if their friendship could develop into something else. But she hadn't heard from him since, so maybe she'd been imagining things . . .

'Hi, Mum, I was just checking you're still all right for Friday.' Cat was in the kitchen leaning against a worktop and idly flicking through the calendar. Noel had been invited to a charity do at a posh hotel in London through work. He hadn't been all that keen to go, but Cat, whose life of late seemed to alternate between working and picking up children from school, was determined she wasn't going to miss out on the one chance she'd had in ages to wear a glamorous frock.

'Friday?' her mother sounded a little put out. 'What's happening on Friday?'

'You're babysitting for us,' Cat said. 'Remember? Noel and I are going to a charity ball.'

'You are?' her mother sounded quite dumbfounded. 'Well, I'm sorry, darling, but I won't be able to babysit on Friday. You know it's my bridge evening.'

'I thought that was next week,' said Cat in exasperation.

'No, it's this week,' said Mum firmly. 'I know I told you.'

'Like you knew you had to pick the kids up,' muttered Cat crossly.

'Did you say something?'

'Nothing important,' Cat lied, feeling immediately guilty. Cat was aware they relied on her mother to a huge degree. She couldn't help it if she'd double-booked. Maybe it was Cat who'd got the day muddled up. She had so many balls to

127

juggle, what with work, the kids' activities and Noel's increasingly frequent business trips to deal with the eco town in Shropshire, it was no wonder she dropped one occasionally.

'Well, I'm sorry I can't help, dear,' continued her mother. 'I could do next Friday though.'

'It's all right, Mum, I expect I can get Magda to babysit,' said Cat, trying to repress the irritated thought that there was no bloody use her mum babysitting next Friday when the ball was this week.

At that point Magda came in, sulkily bearing a pile of washing. She made a great show of pushing past Cat as she went to load the washing machine. As always when Cat was working at home she felt like a stranger in her own house. Magda had the knack of making it seem like she, Cat, was the intruder, and a martyred air that said, *If you can find time to talk on the phone, surely you can find time to pick the children up*. She'd been keeping up the sulks ever since Cat and Noel had dictated that under no circumstances was Sergei to move in with them.

Cat put the phone down and offered Magda a placatory cup of coffee. Maybe that, and the offer of some extra cash in hand, would be enough to persuade her to babysit on Friday. Maybe.

Gabriel squeezed into his pew with a sigh of relief. He'd just made it in time. The ewe he'd been lambing had conveniently delivered ten minutes before he was due to leave, and Sam, a local farmer, had offered to keep an eye on mother and baby while Gabriel went to Stephen's Easter service. Stephen's class were deemed too old for Easter bonnets, which was just as well as he'd reacted in horror when teased about it, but he'd been asked to sing a solo after the sermon so Gabriel, who felt ambivalent about going to church at the best of times, had felt duty-bound to turn up.

The service commenced and proved to be Hope Christmas' usual mix of the homely (the reception class duly made everyone go 'aah' when they got up and recited a prayer of their own – Gabriel grinned and gave Marianne the thumbs up when they sat down), the bizarre (Diana Carew bounding in as though she had allegedly nothing to do with proceedings and exhorting everyone to join with her in prayers for the mission in Africa where her sister was currently working – the vicar looked slightly startled, but covered it up admirably), and the dull. The vicar couldn't help having a monotone, Gabriel supposed, but it was damn hard keeping awake when you'd been up all night lambing. And he couldn't help suppressing the odd yawn as Richard (he never wanted you to call him anything else) earnestly exhorted him not to forget the importance of the Paschal season and the sacrifice of the Lamb of God. Gabriel smiled wryly to himself – everything seemed to be about lambs at the moment.

Gabriel was counting down the minutes till Stephen's party piece. He'd been surprised when Miss Peterson had sent a note home to say that Stephen had a solo, having had no idea that his son was even vaguely musical, but one of the very nice, if occasionally misguided things about the village school, was their belief that every child had a talent that should be encouraged. Having witnessed the humiliation of footballers with two left feet, and actors who could barely deliver a line, Gabriel wasn't always sure of the wisdom of this approach. He just hoped Stephen wasn't going to get too upset. He'd been in bits on Mother's Day and refused to do a reading in assembly.

Gabriel suddenly jerked awake, hoping no one had noticed him dozing off in the dying moments of Richard's sermon, and realised that his son had made his way to the microphone at the front of the church. He swallowed nervously, but smiled encouragingly at Stephen, who stared past him in steely determination as if he couldn't focus on anything but the back of the church. Stephen stood with his hands in his pockets looking as if he were about to do anything but sing. Gabriel longed to tell him not to slouch. He hoped this wasn't going to be too dreadful. Marianne, meanwhile, had moved to the piano by the side of the altar and played a single note.

Stephen took his hands out of his pockets, pulled himself straight, and launched into a hymn that Gabriel half remembered from childhood.

'Now the green blade riseth from the buried grain,' Stephen sang. Gabriel was aware his jaw had dropped to the floor. His son had the voice of an angel. How was it that he had never known? The purity of the notes he was hitting was astonishing. Gabriel listened with a lump in his throat, as his son sang poignantly of the wheat that lay in the dark earth and the love that springeth green. The courage of his boy. The joy of him. How could Eve have walked away from that? The hymn was religious, Gabriel knew, but all it reminded him of was the death of his marriage, and the pain his wife had caused them. Tears prickled his eyes as the hymn came to an end.

When our hearts are wintry, grieving, or in pain,
Thy touch can call us back to life again;
Fields of our hearts that dead and bare have been:
Love is come again, like wheat that springeth green.

Stephen sang with a pathos to break the hardest of hearts. There was absolute silence when he'd finished. Gabriel smiled at his son through his tears. He watched Marianne putting her arm around Stephen and giving him a hug as she walked him back to his seat. Maybe hope and love could after all come again.

*   *   *

Noel stood gloomily at the bar, wishing he were anywhere but here. At least Cat was with him at a work do for once. The only reason he'd come at all was because it had been made patently clear to him that everyone who was anyone at GRB was expected to go to the charity ball to raise money for eco towns in The Gambia. ('It's a global village,' had become Gerry Cowley's mantra recently.) Noel suspected it was because if they didn't go en masse, the very lucrative contract that House the World were offering might get snapped up by one of their rivals.

Since his trip to Shropshire, Noel had been expecting to be given his marching orders but, while no one had paid any attention to his suggestion that the site of the eco town was completely wrong, neither had anyone given him a hard time about it. Noel was half convinced that Matt was keeping Noel's feelings about the project under wraps so Noel could do the donkey work on the calculations. It was becoming rapidly clear to Noel that Matt was a shit engineer who flew close to the wind at every available opportunity. But presumably even he had to get the calculations right, so now Noel was feeling even more disempowered as he realised that he had simply become Matt's whipping boy. Was there no end to this downward spiral of humiliation?

Apparently not. As he approached their table with the drinks, he was mortified to see that Matt was cosying up to Cat, who seemed to be lapping up his every word. Noel sat down moodily and sipped his pint. Cat barely seemed to notice his return, though she quickly tucked into the wine he'd bought her.

'Hi, darling,' she said. 'Have you heard this outrageous joke Matt's just told me?'

'No,' muttered Noel ungraciously, but Cat barely seemed to notice, leaning forward to laugh at the next thing Matt said, and drinking far more quickly than she normally did.

'Do you have to drink quite so much?' he hissed in her ear, as she stumbled up to go to the loo.

'Don't be such a killjoy,' said Cat. 'Come on, after the next course they've promised dancing. We haven't been out together in ages, let's have some fun.'

But Noel wasn't in the mood for fun. He hated these charity dos. The endless phoniness of people outdoing each other in their outrageous bids for bits of celebrity tat, the excessive amount of money spent on food and booze, when, particularly in this case, half the money spent on the event could probably build an eco town in The Gambia. Maybe it was time he moved on. Did something else. Got away from all these people he was beginning to hate. Yes, but then what?

'Come on, big boy.' Julie was standing before him, looking resplendent in a far too tight little black number. Little being the operative word. 'You owe me a dance from the Christmas do.'

'I do?' Noel glanced over to where Cat and Matt were still in full flow. She barely seemed to know he was there. Well, two could play at that game.

'Sure do,' said Julie, and dragged him on the dance floor, where she proceeded to throw both of them around wildly. Next thing he knew, Cat was next to him with Matt.

'What are you playing at?' she snapped at him. 'You look ridiculous. She's young enough to be your daughter.'

'No more ridiculous than you with your toyboy,' Noel spat back.

'Oh, for heaven's sake,' Cat sighed. 'It may have escaped your notice but Matt has just disappeared into a corner with one of your secretaries.'

Noel looked over to where Cat was pointing and saw Matt all over a buxom girl from Accounts. He felt wrong-footed but wasn't going to admit it.

132

Meanwhile, Julie seemed to have sensed she wasn't welcome and had disappeared, leaving Cat and Noel glaring at each other. Bryan Ferry was just admonishing them to stick together, when Cat said, 'I've had enough of this. You've been like a bear with a sore head all evening. I want to go home.'

'Good,' said Noel. 'I'll call us a taxi.'

Ten minutes later they were speeding home, neither of them speaking, the atmosphere feeling as poisonous as Noel could ever remember. Why had he ruined a perfectly good evening? He and Cat hadn't been out together for ages. They'd spent a fortune and had a rotten time.

They arrived home in silence and were shocked by the sound of music playing at top volume from their lounge.

'What's that bloody girl doing now?' Noel growled.

'How the hell should I know?' said Cat. 'I'm not her keeper.'

Noel strode into the lounge and flung open the door to tell Magda to turn the music down.

'Oh my God—'

Magda was splayed across the sofa, and Noel was mesmerised by the sight of Sergei's firm buttocks bouncing up and down on top of her.

133

Chapter Ten

Cat moved swiftly to the CD player and turned Amy Winehouse off.

'What the hell do you think you're doing?'

Magda sat up and for once had the grace to look rather sheepish.

'I did not know you would be back so soon,' she said. She pulled her satin slip up to cover the bits Cat would rather she hadn't seen, while Sergei hurriedly zipped up his trousers. Without a word he pushed past Noel and ran out of the front door.

'It's immaterial what time we got back,' said Cat, trying with great restraint to keep her voice steady. 'You shouldn't have been shagging Sergei here anyway.'

Magda rapidly went into an orgy of explanation, which went something along the lines of how difficult it was for her and Sergei to find any privacy now he had nowhere to live. Cat felt tired and fed up. Her evening out with Noel had been an utter disaster and now this. Magda was now sulkily getting dressed and Cat got another flash of her silk camisole, which looked remarkably like one of Cat's . . .

'What gave you the right to steal my clothes?' The bloody cheek of the girl. She'd pinched Cat's underwear! God knows what else she was wearing that belonged to Cat.

'You have so many nice things,' whined Magda. 'I am poor. You do not understand.'

'I understand you're a thief and a liar, and not to be trusted,' said Cat. 'I shall be calling the agency in the morning. And I want you out of here by the afternoon. Is that understood?'

At this Magda let out a great wail.

'But I have nowhere to go. And now I don't have Sergei. He will finish with me for sure. And I need money for my sick mother. Please, you can't sack me.'

Cat felt herself relenting. Magda was after all very young. Perhaps, if she'd been in the same situation in her early twenties she might have taken similar advantage. (No you wouldn't have, her inner voice admonished sternly.) Besides, if she got rid of Magda tomorrow there'd be no back-up plan. She'd be left without childcare. And she had a busy week ahead of her.

Cat looked at Noel, who was still standing in stunned silence.

'Well?' she said.

'Your call,' said Noel. 'But if she really is down on her luck . . .'

Lord, he was such a soft touch, although of course that was one of his most endearing qualities.

Cat turned to Magda.

'Okay,' she said. 'This is your very last chance. You can count tonight as a verbal *and* written warning. I shall be ringing the agency to tell them what has happened, and if there is any repeat of this, I mean ANY at all, you'll be out on your ear.'

'Oh, thank you, Cat-er-ine, thank you,' said Magda effusively, the tears on her face miraculously drying. 'I promise it won't happen again.'

'You bet it won't,' said Noel with feeling.

135

Magda gathered her things and disappeared up to her room, while Cat busied herself putting the room to rights.

'Fancy a nightcap?' said Noel.

'I think I need a triple after that,' said Cat. 'I also feel the need to fumigate the room. Honestly, it could only happen to us.'

She looked at Noel and they both burst out laughing, the tension of the evening dissipating as if by magic.

'Give you something to blog about,' said Noel, as they made their way down to the kitchen.

'I don't think so,' said Cat. 'I'm sure the Happy Homemaker's au pair would *never* behave like that.'

The rain was still coming down in sheets as Gabriel strode across his land. There'd been a storm earlier in the week and one of his fences had come down. It shouldn't take him long to mend, but he was soaked through and just wanted to get home and dry. He'd never known a wetter spring. Gabriel had hoped that if the weather improved he'd be able to get the lambs back out on the hillside, but they were still too small to withstand this onslaught. In fact, though Gabriel was quite hardened to the weather conditions, even he felt like curling up in front of the fire toasting marshmallows and drinking hot chocolate with Stephen while they watched CBBC together. He'd been most envious of Pippa who'd offered to take Stephen for him again, and was busy making hot chocolate as he left.

Still, sooner looked at, sooner sorted, as his dad always said. He put his head against the wind and rain and soldiered on, wishing his parents hadn't chosen this particular time in his life to go and find themselves. He missed his father's wisdom and his mother's comfort. Sometimes, even with all the help Pippa gave him, he felt horribly alone.

It was pretty bleak on the hillside today, so Gabriel was

surprised to see a figure coming towards him. Who on earth would be mad enough to be out in this?

As the person approached he realised it was Marianne. Her cheeks were flushed from the exercise and her dark hair curled softly under her woolly hat. She managed to look lovely even in all-weather gear.

'Hi,' he said. 'What brings you out in this dreadful weather? I don't need any assistance lambing today, you know.'

'I'm not sure,' said Marianne cheerfully, who looked if anything even wetter and muddier then he did. 'Unless it's a ridiculous subconscious desire to end up with pneumonia. It wasn't that bad when I left.'

'Where are you headed?' said Gabriel.

'Well, I was going to nip round to the next valley and then back home,' said Marianne, pointing to the path that stretched behind Gabriel and up the hillside. If you could call it a path – it was more of a boggy stream at present. 'I just wanted to make the most of my last day here before I disappear for a fortnight but, judging by that horrendously muddy path, I think I may just call it a day and go home.'

'You're going away?' Gabriel felt a pang of regret. He'd got used to seeing Marianne about the place.

'Only for Easter,' she said. 'I'm going down to this demo at the Post Office, and then on to my parents' for the Easter weekend. I'll probably visit friends in London as well, but I may come back sooner if I'm bored.'

She smiled at him and his heart gave a sudden lurch. Good lord, could he possibly be feeling what he thought he was feeling? A stab of guilt shot through him. Technically he wasn't free, he shouldn't even be thinking about anyone other than Eve, wherever she was. But Eve wasn't here and Marianne was.

'I'll miss you,' he said simply, and realised for the first

time the truth of it. He would miss her. Marianne was fast becoming a necessary part of his life.

Marianne clambered onto the coach a little breathless and late. She'd overslept, having had a restless night. She couldn't put her finger on why. Part of it was to do with going home for the first time since Luke had dumped her – she'd been putting off dealing with her mother's over-solicitousness – and part of it, she had no doubt, had been to do with her rather unsettling encounter with Gabriel on the hillside yesterday.

Marianne had gone for a walk to blow away the cobwebs, having been cooped up all day with a bunch of over-excited reception children who'd eaten far too many chocolate eggs and been made doubly hyper by being kept in for play by the wet. She'd gone out for one of her usual hikes, setting off in a light drizzle that swiftly became a torrent, and she was soon soaked through. Somehow she didn't mind though. There would be plenty of time to stay indoors in London; right now, right here, she felt elemental, and close to nature. It felt fabulous.

Marianne had been lost in her thoughts when she'd run into Gabriel. He'd appeared over the brow of the hill, looking for all the world like some kind of dashing hero. Mr Rochester, eat your heart out. She'd always preferred him to Darcy.

It was with a jolt that Marianne had realised that just meeting Gabriel like that was having a funny effect on her. Her back had felt all tingly and her legs had turned to jelly. And when he said he'd miss her in that lovely Shropshire burr, her heart had given a springlike leap of joy. Suddenly she'd realised she was going to miss him too.

'Penny for 'em?' Pippa had squeezed into the seat next to Marianne and was doling out food to the children.

'Oh, nothing,' said Marianne, 'just thinking.' She daren't

138

mention Gabriel to Pippa. Dearly as she loved her friend, it was obvious that Pippa was itching for the chance to play matchmaker.

She stared out of the coach window as it left Hope Christmas and everyone cheered. When she'd come here she'd been so much in love with Luke. And then he'd broken her heart. But over the last few months she'd come to love Hope Christmas and the people in it more than she'd ever loved Luke. She wondered how much she could let that include Gabriel. Could she think about a relationship just yet? And more importantly, should she? Gabriel had a lot of baggage, even if he were interested: she wasn't sure it would be wise to get involved. But, then again, Marianne thought, as the coach pulled away from the Shropshire hills and the sun broke out through the clouds, what had wisdom got to do with love?

Noel was cutting through Mount Pleasant on his way back to work after rather more of a liquid lunch than he'd intended with an old school friend, when a demonstration caught his eye. There was a TV crew and a bunch of people holding banners. They appeared to be protesting against post office closures and, weirdly, when he got up close he realised they were holding banners saying 'KEEP HOPE CHRISTMAS ALIVE! HANDS OFF OUR POST OFFICE!'

'That's such a coincidence,' he said out loud.

'No such thing as coincidence.'

To his surprise, Ralph Nicholas was standing to one side of the group, looking on with a mischievous gleam in his eye.

'What are you doing here?'

'Can't have my local post office closing down, can I now?' said Ralph. 'It's bad enough that my beloved grandson and your chums are seeking to destroy what remains of our local environment with their wretched eco town schemes. If the post office goes, Hope Christmas will surely die.'

Noel thought back to the pretty village in which he'd stayed on his various site visits. Every time he went up to Shropshire he'd fallen a little bit more in love. He'd even started fantasising about living there. If only Cat could be persuaded to leave London. If only he could find himself a job up there. If only the grass were greener and there were gold at the end of the rainbow.

'That's a great pity,' said Noel. 'It looks a lovely place to live.'

'It is,' said Ralph. 'You should come and stay properly. See for yourself. Then maybe persuade your company not to get involved in my grandson's harebrained schemes.'

'If I had my way, we wouldn't be building the eco town,' said Noel. 'But sadly my clout isn't what it was. No one wants to listen to me anymore.'

He felt maudlin when he said it. He was approaching his mid forties, washed up, his career going nowhere, his wife paying him little attention. What was there left?

'There's plenty left,' Ralph said briskly, as if somehow he'd read Noel's mind. 'If you do ever decide to come to the country, you can always give me a call. My company could do with a decent engineer.'

'Oh, thanks,' said Noel. He rather liked this eccentric old man. 'Good luck with your campaign by the way.'

'Don't forget to sign our petition,' said Ralph, tipping his hat at Noel before going off to engage the manager sent out by the Post Office to discuss the situation with him.

Noel did as he was asked and then walked back to the office.

Move to Hope Christmas? Get a new job as Ralph's engineer? It was a fantasy and he knew it. Let's face it, he had no more chance of moving than of flying to the moon.

Chapter Eleven

'Okay, peeps, listen up.' Beverley had gathered the troops together for the bi-monthly forward planning meeting. 'I know we're all in Easter Bunny land right now, but it's time to give some thought to the Christmas issue.'

There was a collective groan round the table. Every year, agreeing upon the contents of the Christmas issue seemed to get harder than ever.

'Now, now, folks, that's not what I expect,' said Bev. 'Come on, let's do some brainstorming. I've ordered sandwiches for lunch so we can keep going as long as possible.'

'I could do top ten make-up tips for the party season,' offered Abi, the new fashion editor, who looked to Cat both depressingly young and even more depressingly thin.

'Hmm, we've done that every year since forever,' said Bev, 'as has every other mag out there. Can you come up with a twist?'

'Well, I suppose I could funk it up a little,' said Abi. 'Maybe how to be a Christmas fashion victim with a difference? Marrying clothes and colours you wouldn't normally expect. Your little black dress with some glitz and sparkle perhaps?'

'Now you're talking,' said Bev.

Was she? Really? Cat for the life of her couldn't see the appeal. The more Abi talked about the strange things she wanted to join up together, the more Cat had a vision of what Melanie was likely to wear to the next school disco – Mel and all her friends tending to go for a mix-and-match approach. Still, maybe Abi was right and that's what the fashion brigade were after these days. Presumably, being twenty-something, she was far more in the know than Cat.

'We could do a piece on what celebs are getting up to at Christmas,' said Rosie, the entertainment writer. 'You know, Angelina and Brad are going for the traditional roasting chestnuts round the fire approach, you could do the same.'

'Hmm, might work, depends on the calibre of the celebrities, I guess,' said Bev.

'What about an article on Christmas bling?' offered Abi. 'You know, Swarovksi crystals, black Christmas trees – that kind of thing.'

'Didn't you do something similar last year?' Bev asked Cat.

'I'm afraid I did,' said Cat, still groaning at the memory of having to extol the virtues of glass Santas perched atop a snowy table decoration for the reasonable price of £40. 'But I could do a credit crunch version if you like. Can't afford Swarovski, but still want your Christmas to bling? How about a cheaper alternative?'

'That's a possibility, I suppose, depends how tacky cheap bling is,' said Bev. 'Keep working, people.'

After an hour there were a dozen or more ideas on the table, but nobody felt inspired by any of them.

'It all feels a bit old hat,' said Bev, looking critically through the list. 'We've got our usual fashion list, our usual celebs list, our usual what to buy your husband for Christmas list. It doesn't feel fresh. I want fresh. And different. Cat. We haven't heard much from you today. What's the Happy Homemaker's take on Christmas?'

Cat thought back to her own last disastrous festive season

and repressed a shudder. 'You probably don't want to know,' she said. 'Only, I was thinking . . . Nah. Forget it. It's probably a stupid idea.'

'Forget what?'

'It's just, well, I guess we all remember the Christmases of our childhood, and I don't know . . . they seemed simpler somehow. Look at all the stuff we've got down here. Five different ways to stuff a turkey; fill your home with festive garlands; bring some sparkle to your Christmas table. Doesn't it seem, I don't know, a bit too much? Why do we need a brand new Christmas tablecloth and matching napkins each year?

'Since when has Christmas been spoilt because we couldn't get the requisite number of baubles on the tree? And do the kids really need every single electronic gizmo going? When I was a kid you were just as happy with a board game and a book and a satsuma in your stocking. Why does Christmas have to be such a frenzy of consumerism?

'Couldn't we turn it around and go for a simpler approach? What with us being now officially in recession and all, and people not having so much money to spend, why not get back to the true spirit of Christmas?'

'What, like *A Christmas Carol* type of thing?' smirked Rosie.

'Well, yes, a bit, I suppose,' said Cat. 'I could do a piece on how to do Christmas lunch on a budget, Abi could do one on reviving fashions of yesteryear. Rosie, your celeb piece could be about celebs who keep it simple, maybe?'

'It could work, I suppose,' said Bev. 'Yes, I'm beginning to like this. What else could we have?'

'Could we give something away to the family who achieved the simplest Christmas?' said Abi.

'Or donate some money to charity?' offered Clare, Bev's assistant.

'What about finding the perfect Nativity?' said Cat. 'God knows I've been to some dire ones in my time. Last year, all I wanted to hear was a decent carol. Maybe we could give a prize to the school or parish that comes up with the Nativity play that is closest to the spirit of the season?'

'That's a brilliant idea,' said Bev. 'We'll put it on the front cover. Were you planning a break over the summer holiday? If so, cancel it!'

'What do we want?'
    'To save our Post Office!'
    'When do we want it?'
    'Now!!!'

Diana was doing such a good job directing the action, Marianne felt that the rest of them might as well not be there. She was darting about, geeing everyone up, thrusting leaflets into the faces of every beleaguered soul who was going in or out of Mount Pleasant. Unfortunately, though a representative had come out to politely take their petition, there hadn't been too much interest. The TV crew that had pitched up as they arrived had interviewed Vera (much to Diana's chagrin, Marianne had noticed with amusement), but had pushed off, having received a tip-off that someone famous was about to leave The Ivy.

  People were beginning to mill around aimlessly in the street, not knowing quite what to do.

'I think we should chain ourselves to the Post Office building,' said Miss Woods. 'Someone must have a strawberry-thingy with them to send a message to that film crew, to get them back here again.'

'I'm not sure that's such a good idea,' began Vera tactfully, before being swept out of the way by a self-important Diana, her bosoms going before her like a magnificent ship, clearly enjoying herself hugely.

144

'Right, come on now.' Diana bustled up clapping her hands. 'It's time we were moving on. Next stop Downing Street.'

Within seconds the crowd had been marshalled and cajoled into order. You had to hand it to Diana, Marianne thought. She and her enormous bosoms did manage to get things done.

Marianne and Pippa made their way back to the coach, trying to stop the boys making bunny ears behind Diana, though they were both hard pressed not to dissolve into laughter.

'How lovely to see you looking so cheerful,' Ralph Nicholas said, as Marianne waited to board the bus.

'Well, I can't sit around feeling sorry for myself for the rest of my life, can I?' replied Marianne.

'True,' nodded Ralph. 'I'm pleased to see you getting so involved as well. Much better than festering at home.'

'Well, it's all down to you I'm here,' said Marianne. 'I'm glad you suggested it. And that you persuaded me to stay in Hope Christmas. It's not quite how I planned things, but it's not as bad as I feared.'

'Ah well, as one door closes another one opens,' said Ralph. 'You never know what the future holds, which I always find rather exciting, don't you?'

'I've never looked at it like that before,' confessed Marianne, climbing on the bus. 'But you know, I think you could be right.'

Noel was sitting at his desk looking at the mountain of paperwork he had to deal with, contemplating whether he should commit a slow hara-kiri, when Julie came in looking sombre.

'Gerry wants to see you,' she said.

'Oh?' Noel felt his stomach drop to his boots. The cull

at GRB had been going on for months. He knew his days were numbered – surely the only reason that he hadn't gone by now was his ability to cover up Matt's inadequacies. Presumably now that the eco town was well under way, Matt was going to leave him out in the cold, and it was his turn to discover that GRB were going to dispense with his services. Feeling like a condemned man, and aware that ten pairs of eyes were fixed firmly on his back, Noel got up and took the long walk down the corridor towards Gerry Cowley's office. Noel wasn't given much to empathy, but he knew exactly what all the other buggers were thinking. First off it would be a gleam of sympathy for his plight, rapidly replaced with guilty relief that it wasn't them having to face the music.

He knocked on Gerry's door, feeling like a guilty schoolboy. Crikey, he was forty-four. Far too old to be feeling like this.

'Ah, Neil, sit down, sit down,' Gerry said expansively as Noel walked in.

'It's Noel,' said Noel. How many times over the years had he had to say that? All the bloody work he'd put into this company. All those years. He was a good engineer. Damned good. One of the best GRB had ever had. And now he was being put on the scrap heap. He'd been in the same job for fifteen years. Noel had forgotten how to even look for a job. He didn't even have a CV anymore. What on earth was he going to do?

'As you know, these are difficult economical times,' said Gerry.

Noel felt sick. He'd allowed himself a brief flash of hope when Gerry had invited him to sit down – previous redundancy victims had all reported not being allowed to sit – but the mention of the economy was a sure sign of what was coming next.

'And in these challenging times we all have to cut our cloth to fit,' continued Gerry. He paused. Noel felt like screaming, this was excruciating. 'We have to make sacrifices. Some of them painful.'

Go on, Noel felt like saying, just spit it out, but he remained silent.

'You're our best engineer,' Gerry said abruptly. 'And, from what young Matt says, you're doing a grand job on the eco town.'

Noel grimaced. Was this a good moment to say that the eco town was being built in exactly the wrong place? Five years ago when his stock was high at GRB, he could probably have got away with it, but now? He contented himself with a muttered thank you.

'Well, I'd better not beat around the bush any longer,' said Gerry. 'While I appreciate everything you've done for the company . . .'

'You're going to have to let me go,' finished Noel. Considering how many redundancies Gerry must have doled out this year, he seemed remarkably inept at dishing out the bad news.

'Oh.' Gerry looked surprised. 'Well, I'm not exactly letting you go. But I have to be honest, Neil, we are going to have to make some sacrifices.'

'What kind of sacrifices?' muttered Noel.

'The thing is, though, old boy,' Gerry continued in a conspiratorial manner, as if he was doing Noel a huge favour, 'you cost us too much money. Young Matt isn't a patch on you as an engineer, but he's much much cheaper. We don't want to lose you, naturally, but in order to keep you, I'm afraid to say you're going to have to take a substantial drop in salary.'

Noel went cold all over.

'How substantial?' he said.

Gerry named a figure that left Noel reeling. He resisted the impulse to say he was sorry that his mortgage company couldn't generously offer to lower his mortgage to accommodate GRB's needs, but then Gerry dangled the inevitable carrot.

'Of course, if you do a good job on the eco town, things will probably look very different. Hopesay Holdings have considerable interests around the country and abroad. If this project goes well, GRB could be on to a winner. So, if you deliver, Neil, who knows – there might be a big fat Christmas bonus with your name on it.'

Noel left Gerry's office feeling curiously lightheaded. He'd spent months anticipating losing his job, but what Gerry was offering was worse. He didn't even have golden handcuffs anymore, just very tarnished brass ones. The trouble was, with the job market so uncertain, Noel wasn't in any position to bargain and Gerry knew it. The drop in salary couldn't have come at a worse time for them, with their mortgage rate being fixed while interest rates were tumbling. But at least he was still in a job. For now at least.

'Daddy, Daddy, I think one of the ewes is ill.' Stephen came bursting out of the sheep barn as Gabriel walked up with a barrel of food for his flock. He'd left Stephen there looking at the new lamb who'd been born last night. The mother had seemed a little feverish afterwards, but she had seemed more settled this morning. He hoped so. He couldn't really afford the vet's bill at the moment.

Gabriel followed his son back into the barn, where he saw the mother lying listlessly on her side while her lamb forlornly tried to suckle from her. Gabriel leant down and stroked the sheep. 'There there, old girl,' he said, reaching for a pulse. It was faint, and unsteady. He had a bad feeling about this. Even if the mother recovered, she clearly couldn't feed her lamb at the moment.

'Is she going to be all right?' Stephen looked anxious.

'I don't know.' Gabriel was trying to dress it up as best he could, but growing up with animals had left Stephen no stranger to what could happen to them. There was no point pretending the ewe was going to get better if she wasn't. He felt in his fleece for his mobile. 'I need to call the vet.'

'Daddy, look.' Stephen grabbed Gabriel's arm.

Oh no.

The sheep, who had been breathing erratically and in a laboured way, gave a sudden wheezy gasp, and then her head flopped to the floor. Her lamb, whose distinctive black tail made it instantly recognisable, baaed pitifully, its little wobbly legs making it seem more vulnerable than ever.

'Is she . . . ?'

Gabriel put the phone down. He'd need to ring the vet later, but for now there was nothing more he could do for the ewe.

'I'm sorry, Stephen, but I think she is,' said Gabriel.

Stephen flung himself into Gabriel's arms, sobbing hysterically.

'Woah.' Gabriel held his son tight. How strange, when the boy scarcely mentioned his mother now, that watching the ewe die had caused so much distress.

'Can we look after the lamb?' Stephen raised a tear-stained face to his father. 'Can we?'

Gabriel swallowed. Did he really want the lamb in the house? By rights, he should give it to the ewe who'd lost the twin, she had plenty of milk for both. He looked at Stephen's expectant face. He couldn't let him down.

'Of course,' he said. 'I'll fix a box for it in the kitchen, and you can look after it.'

'Can I?' Stephen's face broke into a huge grin and he hugged his dad even harder. 'Daddy, you're the best.'

Together they prepared a box of hay, and Gabriel gently lifted the lamb into it and carried it back to the house. They settled it down in the kitchen and Gabriel found a baby's bottle he kept for the purpose. Soon Stephen was snuggled up on the sofa giving his new pet a bottle.

'He's just like me,' Stephen declared, 'he hasn't got a mummy either. But I'm going to be his mummy now.'

Gabriel didn't know whether to laugh or cry.

Chapter Twelve

'You're too thin.' Marianne's mother stood in the kitchen, looking her daughter up and down as if she were a prize cow. It was the only about the millionth time she'd said so. Marianne sighed. There was a reason she'd delayed coming home. And, after the first rapturous moments of welcome, the joy of a decent meal she hadn't cooked herself, and the luxury of a bath in water that didn't take three hours to heat up via the ancient immersion heater, she had quickly fallen back into suppressing her irritation at her mother's fussing. She loved her mother dearly but, even though Marianne had left home years ago, somehow her mother still failed to recognise her daughter's ability to be independent. Marianne had found her stifling growing up but, now she was an adult, she rebelled against it even more. She felt so hemmed in at her parents' house, she longed for the freedom of the place she was beginning to think of as home. Back there, in a few short minutes, she could be striding out in the Shropshire hills, whereas here the only place to escape to was the drab local park, with its miserable patch of green, graffitied play area and confining borders. Marianne invariably came back from a stroll around the park feeling worse than when she'd left.

'You'd hate it if she didn't make a fuss,' her father always said, and to a degree it was true. But Marianne felt faintly depressed by the thinly veiled disappointment as another chance for her mother to plan a wedding had disappeared, and the prospect of grandmotherhood seemed to be fast disappearing into the distance. Marianne's only brother was a permanent student who was currently travelling the world finding himself. He was about as likely to procreate as an amoeba, though Marianne frequently teased him about leaving a girl behind in every port.

'I'm not too thin, Mum,' said Marianne. 'I've put on half a stone since Christmas.'

Mum sniffed, as if to say, likely story, and Marianne decided to ignore her. She knew her mother only wanted what was best for her, but it was hard enough coming to terms with a broken heart without feeling that her every emotion was being scrutinised by the maternal equivalent of Sherlock Holmes.

'Leave the girl alone,' said her dad, coming in from the shed. Lord knows what he did in there, but the shed, a shadowy feature of her childhood, seemed to have become his second home since retirement. 'She looks perfectly healthy to me.'

Marianne shot him a grateful look. Dad had always been her champion, and helped deflect delicate situations with her mother. He had far more empathy than his wife did, and always knew just when to speak and when to keep quiet, whereas Mum always seemed to feel a silence was there to be filled.

'So, there's no chance of you getting back with that chap?' Mum said. Nothing like the direct approach.

'No,' said Marianne. 'I think there's *very* little chance of that.'

She thought back to the last few months without Luke. It had been hard but, to her surprise, she suddenly realised that she wasn't now as heartbroken as she had been, and was thinking about him less and less.

'Well, plenty more fish in the sea then,' said Mum. 'Anyone else in mind?'

'Give over, Mum,' protested Marianne. 'I've only just come out of one relationship, I'm in no hurry to rush into another.'

'Hmm,' said her mother in disbelieving tones. 'Well, at your age you should get on with it. No time to lose . . .'

The more Marianne protested, the less her mother seemed to believe her.

But then again, as Marianne went to load the dishwasher, and got a sudden flash of Gabriel's face, perhaps it wasn't altogether true . . .

Cat was on her way home from work. She was running late and feeling guilty because she'd promised to get back and help Mel with some science homework that was proving tricky. Science was really Noel's department, but more and more of late he'd been distracted and she'd found it really hard to get him to engage with the children. Cat suspected there was a problem at work, but Noel seemed very tight-lipped about whatever it was and she'd given up trying to prise the information out of him.

Mel had emailed Cat at work with a panicky 'Mum, Homework. Tonight!!!!' email at lunchtime, and Cat had promised she'd get home in time to help her. An increasingly common feature of their relationship of late, Cat wryly noted, was that Mel expected Cat to drop everything for her. Of course, Cat compounded things by always doing exactly that, but she could still remember the uncertainty of her first year at secondary school and didn't want Mel to feel she couldn't ask for help.

The only trouble was, of course, her work life was rarely accommodating of her home life. Just as she was about to leave, one of the subs had queried a line in her last feature on 'How to Detox Your House', and Bev wanted her urgent opinion on the October cover layout, and suddenly it was gone six and she still hadn't answered her emails. She rang Magda to say she was running late, and tried Noel who, judging by the list of missed calls, had been urgently trying to call her. But when she rang back all she got was a 'This mobile is switched off' message, and his work answerphone was proclaiming he was away from his desk. She was about to leave when her mobile rang. Mum. She'd better answer that.

'Hello?' Cat gathered her bag over her shoulder, and headed for the door. The phone went dead. Odd. She rang back and got a busy tone. Damn. On the way down the corridor she kept trying her mother, and continually got the engaged tone. Well, it can't have been that urgent.

The phone rang again as she headed down the road to the bus stop.

'Catherine, there you are,' her mother sounded a bit flustered. 'I've been trying to ring you for hours.'

'I've been trying to ring you,' said Cat, 'but you were engaged.'

'Because I was trying to ring you,' said her mother.

This was going nowhere. 'Was it anything in particular? I'm just on my way home.'

'Oh, nothing,' said Mum. 'Just. This is a bit daft. Can you remember? Do I need flour or eggs in an apple pie? I've got Auntie Eileen coming for dinner, and I keep looking at the ingredients and they both look wrong.'

Cat frowned. Mum was the best cook Cat knew. How strange that she should have forgotten how to make pastry.

'Well, I've never made pastry with eggs,' she said, trying to laugh it off. 'But you do need flour.'

There was a pause.

'Well, of course you don't use eggs in pastry. At least not if you're making shortcrust pastry. Why on earth did you think you did?'

It was on the tip of Cat's tongue to make an acid remark about why her mother had bothered to ring her then, but she paused. There was something very odd about the tone in her mother's voice. In fact, the whole conversation was very odd.

'Mum, are you all right?'

'Never better, dear,' said her mother. 'I will be seeing you all for lunch on Sunday, won't I?'

'Yes, of course,' said Cat.

'Well, bye then,' said her mother, and put the phone down, leaving Cat feeling unsettled. *Was* there something wrong with her mum? And if so, what, if anything, could she do about it?

The last of the ewes had finally delivered her lambs, twins again, but this time neither had died. Gabriel settled mother and babes and made his way back to the kitchen where a sleepy Stephen was sitting with Pippa as he fed his pet one last time before bed.

'Everything all right?' Pippa nodded in the direction of the barn.

'Fine, thanks,' said Gabriel. 'And thanks for looking after Stephen, again. I feel bad about always asking you.'

'Well, you shouldn't,' said his cousin briskly. 'That's what families are for, to help each other out. Besides, if you hadn't had the kids for me on Saturday, Dan and I wouldn't have been able to get out for that meal.'

'True.' Gabriel felt he did little enough for his cousin, so the least he could manage was the occasional sleepover if it helped her and Dan out. 'Stephen enjoyed it anyway, so it was no hardship.'

'I'd best be off,' said Pippa, gathering her things. 'I don't really like leaving Dan to deal with everyone at bedtime.'

'No, of course not,' said Gabriel. 'Are you going to the Monday Muddle on Easter Monday?'

'Wouldn't miss it for the world,' grinned Pippa. 'Besides, Diana Carew said I could have a stall to showcase our produce, didn't Dan tell you?'

'I don't think so,' said Gabriel. 'Mind you, I've been so busy recently everything's going in one ear and out the other. Still, that's great. The Monday Muddle's a brilliant opportunity to show people what we can offer.'

The Monday Muddle was an annual village event held every Easter Monday, along with a traditional market. Part football match, part free for all, the origins of it were lost way back in the mists of time, but everyone in the village turned out to see a football, reputedly two hundred years old and made of an old leather sack, alleged by some to have covered the head of a notorious highwayman, kicked high in the air. In the ensuing scrum, whoever picked up the ball was meant to run with it as fast as they could, without letting go, to the village pub. Miraculously, the event hadn't yet been cancelled by the health and safety brigade, which was remarkable considering how many people ended up injured in the scrum. The person who managed it was then bought pints by everyone else for the rest of the day. All the village men were supposed to take part, but Gabriel often declined.

'Daddy, you are going to go in for it this year, aren't you?'

Gabriel groaned. Stephen had pressured him into going in for it last year, and he had reluctantly agreed. He had never got over the trauma of doing the event in his teens when he'd been a total lightweight and Dan and all his cronies had inevitably sat on him. Dan in fact was still the undisputed champion of the event, being a broad six-foot-plus rugby player. Gabriel, with his wiry build, was fine on speed, but lacked the brute strength to win at such a physical event.

'No,' he said. 'You know I hate the Monday Muddle. Besides, Uncle Dan will beat me hands down, don't you think?'

'He might not,' said Stephen. 'You don't know if you don't try, do you?'

Raising his eyebrows at Pippa at having one of his constant sayings to his son parroted back at him, Gabriel saw his cousin to the door.

'Go on, give it a try,' she urged. 'You never know, you might even enjoy it.'

'I think you can safely say I won't,' said Gabriel, 'but just for you, I'll think about it.'

'I think Marianne's coming back for it too,' Pippa added slyly.

Gabriel's heart gave an unexpected leap at the thought of Marianne being there. 'I thought Marianne was away for the whole fortnight?'

'She was supposed to be,' said Pippa, 'but she's just texted me to say she's going mad at home, so I rang her and suggested she came back for Monday. She thought it might make the perfect excuse for coming back.'

'Oh right,' said Gabriel. Now he really didn't want to take part. The last person he wanted to see him making a fool of himself was Marianne.

'So now you have to take part, don't you?' teased Pippa.

'What do you mean?' asked Gabriel.

'Well, I told Marianne you would be,' said Pippa. 'And she said she couldn't wait.'

'Pippa, I could kill you sometimes,' sighed Gabriel. 'Don't you ever stop interfering?'

'Nope,' said Pippa. 'But it's for your own good, so one day you'll thank me.'

*　*　*

The pub was heaving. Noel was incredibly touched by how many of his fellow GRB sufferers were prepared to come along to cheer him up once the news spread about his change of circumstances. Feeling that he was in the worst of all possible worlds, Noel had seen no other option than to go to the pub. He'd rung Cat to say he'd be late, but kept getting her work answerphone and her mobile was switched off. So he rang Magda, who sounded utterly disinterested but at least promised to pass the message on to Cat. He tried Cat one last time. Still no answer. Leaving a message to say he was going to the pub, but not feeling able to say why, he snapped his phone shut and went to the bar and ordered another pint.

Four pints and no food later, Noel was feeling more than a little unsteady on his feet. He really should go home.

'Are you coming to eat?' Julie appeared by his side with a couple of her cronies.

'I think I'd better be off,' said Noel, aware that he was swaying and also aware that he was probably looking like an undignified, middle-aged twat.

'No, come with us,' commanded Julie, and suddenly he found himself swept up in a wave of youth, beauty and drunken enthusiasm. He tried to ring Cat again, but her mobile was still switched off, and he was so useless at texting sober he couldn't even begin to think about it drunk.

Hours passed and suddenly it was midnight and he was sitting dishevelled in a dingy nightclub, his tie undone, feeling a complete wreck. Really, it was time to go home.

'Come on, come and dance.' Julie was dragging him to the dance floor.

'I've got to go,' he protested feebly.

'No, you haven't,' said Julie. 'Come on, we're having fun.'

Fun. Yes. Noel remembered that. Last time he'd had any fun had been sometime in the Dark Ages.

He let himself go, for a minute forgetting all his troubles under the bright light dazzling his eyes, finding a strange drunken rhythm to the thumping rap of the dance anthem blaring out from the floor. He moved closer and closer to Julie. She was exceptionally pretty. And she'd always been so nice to him . . .

'I really like you, you know,' Julie shouted in his ear.

'I really like you too,' said Noel. He looked down at her. Julie. Julie, his sexy, sweet little secretary. She looked at him. His mouth suddenly went dry and then they were kissing, passionately, stupidly, frantically, as if there was no one left on earth to kiss.

Oh dear God, what was he doing?

Noel broke away in confusion.

'Sorry,' he said. 'Shouldn't have done that. Sorry.'

'I'm not,' said Julie, looking at him lasciviously.

Oh my God. Time to go. Now.

'Julie, you're lovely, but I can't,' Noel said. 'Sorry. Really I am. I didn't mean to be such a shit.'

He fled the dance floor, and ran out into the cold air. He turned his mobile on. Five missed calls from Cat. He leant against the wall of the nightclub gulping in the cool night air. What on earth had he done?

Chapter Thirteen

Catherine sat staring out into the dark garden, sipping a glass of wine and feeling furious. Noel had promised to come home early. It was a bank holiday. They had planned a family day out the next day. He was clearly in the pub because his mobile had been switched off all evening. She'd given up trying to reach it. The kids had all been riotous when she got home, Magda having apparently given them something with thousands of E-numbers for tea. Mel had forgotten all about the important science project by the time Cat had got in; instead, she was in floods of tears because she'd fallen out with her best friend on MSN. Despite Cat's dire warnings about being careful in online dealings, Mel still hadn't quite worked out that MSN wasn't the best place for sorting out disputes. The resulting hysterics had taken an hour to calm down, by which time it was too late to put Ruby in the bath, and James and Paige had managed to cause chaos in the lounge by setting up a complicated *Dr Who* game, which for some reason had required all of Cat's nicest, plumpest, whitest cushions being stuck end to end on the floor. By the time it had all been tidied away and the children chased to bed, it was gone nine.

She glanced at her watch. It was midnight already. Should she go to bed or wait up for him? It was ages since Noel had stayed out so late. And after last Christmas, when she'd made the mistake of confronting him about his late nights in the pub and been given short shrift, Cat was reluctant to give him a hard time. But really she was furious. Why was it okay for him to go out and have a drink with his mates, without a thought for her or the family, when Cat getting out for the evening involved military-style precision planning? And invariably, if she had managed to organise a night out, Noel would always swan in late, as if to make a point about her abandoning her duties for the evening. Long-held resentments bubbled under the surface. This was no good. She was feeling so cross now they'd be bound to have a huge row when he did get home.

Cat finished her drink, washed her glass up, and made her way up to bed. She was halfway up the stairs, when she heard Noel fumbling with the key in the lock.

She went down to open the front door.

'There's no need to wait up for me, you know.' Noel's tone was belligerent.

'I wasn't,' said Cat, trying not to rise to it. 'I was on my way to bed.'

'Oh.' Noel swayed in the hall. 'What time is it?'

'Late,' said Cat. 'You could have rung me.'

'I did,' said Noel. 'Your phone was switched off.'

'That was earlier,' said Cat. 'Where the hell have you been?'

'Well, that's bloody nice,' said Noel. 'How about a kiss when I come through the door?'

'Noel, it's nearly 1 am, I'm really knackered, you're really drunk. I think it's time for bed.'

'Good idea.'

'No,' said Cat. 'I meant bed as in sleep.'

'Sleep? Sleep?' Noel said. 'How can you talk about going to sleep?'

'Quite easily,' said Cat, turning back up the stairs. 'I'm going to bed, you can do what you like.'

'Oh, that's right, walk away,' Noel spat out with sudden venom, and Cat turned and stared at him in fury.

'What's that supposed to mean?' she said.

'You, you're not even interested in me anymore,' said Noel.

'That's not true,' protested Cat.

'When was the last time we had sex, then?' said Noel.

'I don't know,' said Cat, 'the other week, probably.'

'Two weeks ago,' said Noel. 'That's when it was.'

Cat had had enough. 'Are you keeping some kind of record?' she said incredulously. 'For heaven's sake, Noel, just grow up, will you?'

She was shouting now, much louder than she intended. But really, he was the sodding limit.

'You just don't fancy me anymore, do you? Why don't you say it?' Noel had gone from angry to bitter in a heart-beat.

'Where the hell did that come from?' asked Cat in exasperation. 'There's no point talking to you when you're like this. I'm going to bed.'

'Well it's true,' shouted Noel after her.

'Oh, save it,' said Cat, storming back upstairs. She was damned if she was going to sleep with him tonight. He could spend the night in the spare room.

'Can you two keep it down?' Mel appeared, yawning sleepily on the stairs.

'Sorry,' said Cat. 'Dad and I were just going to bed.'

She went into her bedroom and turned on the light. What was wrong with Noel? Why did he insist on behaving so badly? They had never really talked over what had happened at Christmas, and now here they were again, back in the same mess as before. What on earth was going to happen to them?

*　*　*

Marianne sat in a crowded pub with her oldest school friends, Lisa and Carly, whom she'd met to swap stories about old times and catch up on the new. The trouble was, after a perfunctory conversation about what had gone wrong in Marianne's love life, Lisa and Carly seemed utterly uninterested in anything else she had to say now she no longer had a rich boyfriend. Neither of them was exactly the country type and they couldn't understand why Marianne was still holed up in 'the back of beyond', as Lisa put it. In fact, when Marianne thought about it, they'd never been very interested in her really. Lisa with her big City job and succession of fund-manager boyfriends had always been dismissive of Marianne's life choices. 'What do you want to teach for?' she'd gasped in horror. 'Everyone knows teachers are poor.' Carly's job as a gossip girl about town was enough to keep her firmly wedded to the bright lights, big city. 'While there are parties to crash and drinks to blag, I'm your woman,' she was fond of saying. She, too, had barely asked about Marianne's life in Hope Christmas.

'I helped deliver a lamb, you know,' Marianne butted in on one of Lisa's interminable stories about what the recession was going to mean for her. (If you hadn't racked up so much debt on your three credit cards it mightn't be such a disaster, Marianne felt like cattily saying.)

'What on earth for?' Lisa looked incredulous. 'That sounds disgusting.'

'It wasn't,' said Marianne. 'It was rather wonderful actually. I met a friend of mine when I was out walking. He needed help with one of his ewes, and so I helped deliver the baby. Well, it was two babies, but one of them died.'

'You know a *shepherd*?' Carly broke off into peals of laughter.

'I bet he's called Gabriel,' said Lisa. 'Remember how we

163

all fancied Gabriel Oak when we saw *Far from the Madding Crowd* at school?'

'He is actually,' said Marianne, to hoots of laughter from her friends. 'Well, not a shepherd, but he does farm sheep.'

'Marianne, you never cease to amaze me,' said Carly. 'You'll be going all native on us next.'

'What's wrong with that?' said Marianne. 'Gabriel's nice. Living in the country's nice. I like it.'

'Don't you miss the town at all?' Lisa was utterly incredulous.

'Not much,' admitted Marianne. 'If anything, there I feel like I've come home.'

And, with a jolt, she realised it was true. Despite everything that had happened with Luke, she felt more at home in Hope Christmas than she'd ever felt anywhere in her life before. Marianne was overcome with an overwhelming rush of homesickness. Suddenly, she couldn't wait to go back.

Even though she'd hardly known Pippa any time at all, she'd been more of a friend to Marianne than these two had ever been. She might have spent her whole life in London and never realised what life was all about. Pippa had rung her to say that there was some traditional village football match going on on Monday. Her parents were flying out on holiday early on Sunday morning. Carly and Lisa had a host of wild parties to go to, to which she was invited, but where she knew she wouldn't feel welcome. What on earth was keeping her here?

Making her excuses, Marianne got up and left. Lisa and Carly made token noises about wishing she didn't have to go so soon but, as she left them gossiping over a drink and busily texting friends to find out where to go next, Marianne ruefully realised that they wouldn't really miss her any more than she'd miss them. Somehow, she'd clung onto these two friends from her past long beyond a point at which they really had much in common. It was time to live her life in the way she wanted to. A picture of Gabriel swam suddenly before her eyes. Pippa said he was likely to be taking part in this football match, which, if she was honest, was even more of a reason to go. It had been nice to see her family, but it was time to go back to where her heart now belonged.

Noel woke up with the light streaming in through the open curtain. His head was pounding and his mouth was dry. What was he doing in the spare room? He lifted his head up. Bad idea. The room lurched in a rather alarming fashion and he had a sudden awful thought that he might be sick. Crikey. It was a long time since he'd had a hangover that bad. The events of the previous day came flooding back to him. He'd had a paycut. Had he told Cat he'd had a paycut? Somehow he didn't think so. It didn't matter that it was something that happened to thousands of other people every day. It didn't matter that, as Gerry had told him in that hearty-fellow kind of way, it wasn't 'personal'. He, Noel Tinsall, had been utterly humiliated in the workplace. And at a time when he was feeling that his world was contracting, and there were fewer opportunities for him. Waves of self-pity and guilt swept over Noel. He didn't know where they were coming from, he just felt utterly locked in his misery. What would a woman as beautiful, intelligent and attractive as Cat want with someone as worthless as him? He couldn't blame her for hating him. He'd been an utter sod to her last night. His guilt about what had happened with Julie had made sure of that. God, he was making a mess of things. He was beginning to feel he had less and less to offer Cat. How would she react to the news of his paycut?

Suddenly Noel couldn't face the humiliation of telling

her. From the very first moment he'd seen her standing at the bar in their student hall of residence, Noel had been swept away by her beauty and vivaciousness. Over the years neither had been dimmed, but how did she really feel about him these days? Noel sometimes detected a look of exasperation in her eyes, which never used to be there. Was she losing interest in him? And if she was, how would the news that her previously successful husband was heading for the scrap heap go down?

No, he wouldn't tell her, Noel decided. What Cat didn't know couldn't hurt her after all. And, by the time the eco town project was finished, maybe he'd have found himself something else or, who knows, he might even get that elusive bonus Gerry had promised him.

The door opened and a frosty-looking Cat came in with a cup of tea.

'You are still planning to come out with us for the day, I take it?' she asked. 'Ten minutes and counting.'

Noel raised a smile he didn't feel. What he wanted to do was crawl back into bed and stay there for a very long time, but he'd promised the kids. He felt enough of a heel as it was. He couldn't let them down too.

'Be with you in five,' he said, trying a feeble smile.

'You'd better be,' said Cat, thawing a little.

'And sorry,' he added, 'about last night. Being so late and everything.'

'It's okay,' she said. 'Well, it's not okay, but I don't want it ruining today. Agreed?'

'Agreed,' said Noel. He felt relieved, as if he'd been given a reprieve. But for how long?

'Daddy, can I ring Granny Smith?' Stephen was bouncing on Gabriel's bed on Easter Sunday morning. 'I want to wish her Happy Easter.'

166

'Yes, of course.' Gabriel always questioned the wisdom of allowing his son to ring his maternal grandmother. If she knew where her daughter was she never divulged it, and in her strangely dotty way seemed to think that somehow it was Stephen and Gabriel who had caused Eve's problems, whereas, in fact, Gabriel could see now they had started long before Gabriel had ever met Eve.

'Guilt, that's what it is,' had been Pippa's assertion. 'She knows she cocked Eve's life up, but it's easier to blame you.'

But Gabriel couldn't find it in his heart to condemn his mother-in-law. Whether it really was Joan's fault for abandoning Eve with her own mother every time a suitable new lover came along that had caused Eve to be so needy and fragile, he couldn't say. What he did know was that Joan had suffered for it nearly as much as he had.

'Granny, Granny, the Easter Bunny brought me three Easter eggs,' Stephen was bouncing up and down on the bed, a bit bunnylike himself. How much chocolate had he already had? Gabriel had placed a chocolate embargo till after breakfast, but realised he had probably lost that battle already.

'We're going to church and the vicar said we'll have an Easter Egg hunt.' Stephen was explaining the day's events to his grandmother. 'And then we're going to Auntie Pippa's. Can you come and see us soon?'

Gabriel's heart sank. Stephen always asked this. And the answer was always a negative. But this time his son's face lit up. 'You can? That's brilliant!'

Oh. That was unexpected. But what followed was even more so.

'Who's there?' Stephen suddenly demanded. 'Who wants to talk to me?'

The look of expectation on his face suddenly turned to fury.

'Well, I don't want to talk to her!' He flung the phone on the bed, and ran out of the room crying.

'Stephen?' Gabriel looked at his son helplessly, then picked up the phone. 'Joan, what on earth is going on?'

'Is Stephen still there?' she asked. 'Only I've got his mother here, and she wants to speak to him.'

Chapter Fourteen

Gabriel stood in the bedroom, cradling the phone in shock.

'Eve's there?' He couldn't believe it. All these months with no contact, and suddenly here she was at her mother's. 'I thought you didn't know where she was?'

'I didn't,' said Joan. 'She turned up out of the blue last night.'

'Can I speak to her?' Gabriel asked, and then wished he hadn't. What was he going to say to Eve? How could he speak to her and not let rip the fury that had been building in him all these months since she'd gone? It was only now he was here, an inch away from having a conversation with his absent wife, having seen the devastating effect she was still having on his son, that he realised just how very angry he was. Maybe now wasn't a good time to speak.

'I'm sorry,' said Joan, 'she doesn't want to speak to you.'

'Oh.' Fury turned to disappointment. How was it that Eve could churn him up so much, and make him feel so very confused, and yet still a part of his heart reached out to her, still he wanted to make things right between them? Would he never learn?

'And Stephen doesn't want to speak to her,' said Gabriel. He wasn't entirely sure that this was true. Stephen was in shock and had certainly reacted in childish anger, but Gabriel knew how often his son had sobbed into his

169

pillow at night. Despite everything, he loved Eve. Gabriel suppressed a momentary feeling of unease – did he have the right to stop his son speaking to his mother? But then he thought about what she'd put them both through and anger hardened his heart once more.

'I see,' said Joan. 'And that's nothing to do with anything you've said to him, I suppose?'

'It has everything to do with the fact his mother is a flaky depressive who wouldn't understand commitment if it hit her over the head,' retorted Gabriel, his irritation at Joan's jibe reigniting his fury. 'I have done my very best not to badmouth Eve to Stephen. She's done all that herself.'

'She's very sick,' said Joan.

'I know, I know,' said Gabriel, familiar guilt piercing the anger. 'But I can't help her if she won't help herself. And she can't expect to just walk back into Stephen's life like this. Tell her to stay away. For both of our sakes.'

He put the phone down and walked down the corridor to Stephen's room to find him lying on his bed, sobbing his heart out.

'Was Mummy really there?' Stephen asked. 'Will she hate me for not speaking to her?'

Gabriel looked at his son and, unable to bear the look in his eyes, for the first time in his life, he lied to his son. 'No, sweetheart, Granny was mistaken. Mummy's gone away and she won't be back for a very long time. But I'm here, aren't I? And I think we've got an Easter Egg hunt with your cousins.'

Stephen smiled through his tears and reached out his hand to Gabriel, who closed his own over his son's tiny one, then held him in a fierce tight embrace.

'It's you and me now, Stephen,' he said. 'You and me, against the world.'

*   *   *

'You're early.' Cat's mum greeted them as they came through the front door of the Georgian house in which she'd brought Cat up single-handedly, once Cat's feckless father had left. Nothing much had changed for years. The grandfather clock, inherited from Mum's grandmother, still took pride of place in the hall, the shabby comfy furniture from Cat's childhood still retained its spot in the chintzy lounge, last redecorated circa 1990 – 'I don't care what other people think, *I* like it,' was her mother's response to Cat's frequent pleas to get her to redecorate – and the oak-panelled kitchen, all the rage in 1988, retained its peculiar charm because it was Mum's. Cat had learnt to cook here, on the Aga that stood in the corner. She'd invited friends back for coffee, had sat up having illicit late-night drinks with Noel when they were courting. Cat knew every nook and cranny of this kitchen, every one holding a memory precious to her alone. Despite having long since made a nest of her own, Mum's house would always feel like home to Cat.

'Sorry, Mum,' said Cat, looking at her watch, which proclaimed the time to be 12.30, 'but you did say midday. I thought we were late as usual.'

'Oh,' her mother frowned. 'I must be going mad, I could have sworn I said 1pm.'

'We can go away if you want and come back later,' joshed Noel, giving his mother-in-law a kiss. The children all piled in behind him, squabbling about who was going to get Granny Dreamboat's attention first.

'Now now, enough of that, Noel, I'm sure I can cope,' said Mum. 'Cat, if you could be an angel and just put the kettle on?'

'Mind if I'm terribly anti-social and go and watch the Grand Prix?' Noel asked.

'Get away with you,' said Mum. 'You've been using my

house like a hotel since you first met Cat. Why change the habit of a lifetime?'

Noel laughed and went into the lounge with the children, who made themselves at home, as usual finding the various games and books their granny had thoughtfully got out for them. Cat relaxed visibly. Noel had been like a bear with a sore head all weekend and wouldn't tell her what was wrong. After the events of Christmas Day, she'd been nervous about coming here. But, she reminded herself, *your* mum doesn't wind him up like his does.

'Anything I can do?' said Cat, as she sorted out cups and a teapot, her mother never letting her get away with anything as uncouth as teabags and mugs. She knew the answer would be no – her mother was so capable in the kitchen, Cat barely got a look in. It was quite remarkable she'd ever learnt to cook in the first place.

'You could chop the carrots, if you like,' said her mother. 'I haven't quite got there yet.'

'What, the greatest cook in the history of the universe has got behind?' Cat teased. 'I don't believe it. First you've forgotten how to make pastry, now this. You'll forget your own head next!'

'That is a ridiculous thing to say!' Mum snapped. Cat was completely taken aback.

'Sorry,' she said. 'I was only joking.'

'Well, don't,' said Mum tetchily. 'You seem to forget sometimes how old I am.'

'Only because you do,' laughed Cat, trying to lighten the tone. It was unlike her mother to be so stressed.

'All I'm saying is that you shouldn't be surprised if occasionally I can't quite do everything I used to be able to do,' said Mum. She looked rather wistful as she said this, and Cat had a sudden surge of panic. She did take her mother for granted, perhaps it was time she took care of *her* a bit more.

172

'I'm sorry, Mum,' she said. 'I didn't mean to be thought-less. It's just you're always so capable and in control it never occurs to me that you can't do anything.'

'Who said anything about can't?' said Mum. 'I'm not in my dotage yet.'

'I – never mind,' said Cat, turning away. Sometimes you couldn't do right for saying wrong.

'That was lovely,' said Noel appreciatively, as he passed over his empty plate later. It was so restful at his mother-in-law's, and a relief to get away from the tension he'd been feeling all weekend at home – tension, he didn't have to remind himself, caused by his appalling guilt at his own selfish behaviour on Thursday night.

Louise beamed at him with gratitude.

'I'm so glad you enjoyed it,' she said. 'I have so few people to cook for these days, it's a real treat to cook for you all. Though it's unlike the children to leave things on their plate.'

'The children have rather overindulged on chocolate,' said Cat guiltily. 'Sorry about that.'

'Which is why I didn't buy them any,' said her mother. 'I have devised a Treasure Hunt in the garden, though.'

'Treasure Hunt! Yay! Treasure Hunt!' James and Paige practically leapt from the table, Granny Dreamboat's Easter Treasure Hunt being the highlight of Easter Sunday as far as they were concerned. Ruby had only vague recollections from last year, and was sucking her thumb looking bored, while Mel was trying very hard to pretend that she was far too superior to let herself get carried away with anything so feeble. However, once in the garden, where, following weeks of rain, the spring sunshine was finally forcing its way out, she whooped and hollered with the rest of them.

'Is this all I get?' James came marching up to Cat looking

173

thunderous. Normally Granny Dreamboat was scrupulous in providing prizes that were suitable for her grand-children, but even Noel could see that he was far too old for the Thomas the Tank Engine he'd found with his name on. Even Ruby would probably consider herself too old for that.

'Shh,' said Cat. 'Don't be rude. Granny's gone to a great deal of trouble for you.'

James looked mutinous and was soon joined by Paige, who didn't seem too impressed by her Barbie either. 'Doesn't Granny know I hate Barbie?' she whined, and Mel, who clearly thought that she was much too grown up for the Polly Pocket set that seemed to be hers, at least had the grace not to moan about it in front of her grandmother. Only Ruby seemed to be satisfied with her wooden pull-along duck.

'Oh dear.' Louise looked really put out. 'I seem to have muddled up their ages. How did I manage that?'

'It doesn't matter,' said Cat. 'It's easily done, we're always doing it, aren't we, Noel?'

Noel was staring into space trying not to think about Thursday night. Cat dug him in the ribs and he said, 'Oh, yes, all the time.' He was fond of his mother-in-law and didn't like to see her upset.

'Look, let me give them some money and they can get something more suitable each.' Granny Dreamboat thrust some money into Noel's hands.

'Don't be daft,' he said, 'it's good for the kids to learn disappointment once in a while. It's good for their souls.'

'Is it?' muttered Mel. 'Gee, thanks, Dad.'

'Yes, it is,' said Noel firmly. 'But, as I am such a nice, kind, wonderful father, if you all go and hide in the lounge for five minutes, I might just be able to arrange another Treasure Hunt.'

174

'Dad, you're the best!' Paige threw her arms around his neck and Cat gave him a grateful look.

'Yup, the best,' said Noel, feeling like a fraud. 'That's me.'

'Welcome back.' Pippa hugged Marianne and ushered her into her home. 'Have you had anything to eat? I'm just doing brunch for the sportsmen. You can be the first to try out my special new herby sausages.'

Marianne let herself feel overcome with the warmth and generosity of her friend.

'Oh, it is so good to be back!' she said. 'I love my parents dearly, but they were driving me insane.'

Pippa dragged her into the kitchen where Dan was frying sausages for what appeared to be half the men in the village. Marianne had a surreptitious look to see if Gabriel was amongst them and felt a surge of disappointment when she saw he wasn't.

'I thought you said Gabriel was taking part in this great event?' she asked in as casual a tone as she could muster.

'Gabriel? I tried my best,' snorted Pippa. 'He was persuaded to take part last year, but then Dan accidentally sat on his head. The Monday Muddle isn't his cup of tea. I've been trying very hard to make him change his mind, but I fear I'm wasting my time.'

'Oi, who are you maligning?' Gabriel came strolling in just then, holding Stephen's hand. 'I've decided to give it another go this year.'

Marianne's heart lurched, and she looked up to see Gabriel bearing down on her, his dark hair swept off his face, and his cheerful smile brightening his handsome face. Oh, it was good to see him too. She hadn't realised how much she'd valued seeing him around until she'd been parted from him for a while.

'Well, I'll be cheering for you,' said Marianne, with a

175

smile. God, she hoped it wasn't a girlish smile. Or that Gabriel wouldn't notice how hot and bothered she had suddenly become.

Gabriel smiled back, his whole face lighting up. He was gorgeous. She'd somehow failed to notice before – he was always so serious and intent, but when he smiled he was utterly *gorgeous*.

'Well, that makes two of you,' he said. 'Half-pint here is my other supporter.'

'Go, Daddy,' said Stephen solemnly, waving a flag he'd clearly made.

'Surely you've got more than that?'

'You haven't seen how bad I am at this,' said Gabriel.

'He is truly truly awful,' said Pippa. 'I, on the other hand, am married to the Monday Muddle King, so be warned. This game gets really dirty!'

'Right,' said Marianne. 'Crikey, they don't have anything like this in Cricklewood.'

'Well, you're in the country now, aren't you, my dear?' said Pippa, exaggerating her Shropshire burr. 'It's all differen' here, don't you know?'

Marianne laughed and gladly accepted the sausage bap that Dan shoved in her hand. She was starving.

'I think,' she said, to no one in particular, 'I'm going to enjoy this.'

'I'm not,' said Gabriel with feeling.

'You've only yourself to blame,' Marianne teased him. She leant back on the kitchen worktop: despite her sudden hormonal rush, she felt at ease and relaxed around Gabriel, he was such good company.

'I'm doing it for him,' Gabriel nodded at Stephen, who was in animated discussion with his cousins. 'He was so keen for me to enter this year. And he's had enough upset. I thought I owed it to him to give it a go.'

'No word from his mum still?' Marianne remembered how forlorn Stephen had looked on Mother's Day at church.

Gabriel looked awkward.

'Turns out she's staying with my mother-in-law. Stephen rang his granny yesterday, and Eve wanted to speak to him.'

'What did Stephen do?' Marianne asked, as a sudden cold shockwave hit her. Did this mean Eve was coming back?

'Ran off crying,' said Gabriel miserably. 'He said he didn't want to know her. He seemed so upset – I think I may have done something rather stupid. I have to tell someone or I'll burst.'

'What did you do? It can't be that bad,' encouraged Marianne.

'I think it probably can,' said Gabriel, 'I lied to Stephen and said Eve wasn't there. I was so cross with her for hurting him. At the time it seemed the right thing to do. But now. Now I wonder.'

Marianne looked across at Stephen who was now playing happily with his cousins in the garden.

'I'm sure it was the right thing. Anyone can tell you're a great dad,' she said. She thought back to the cruel way Luke had ditched her. Would she rather he'd carried on lying to her? On some days, indubitably yes. 'And sometimes, well, sometimes the truth hurts too much. Sometimes it's better not to know.'

Chapter Fifteen

Gabriel walked into the throng of men standing in a field on the outskirts of the village, feeling sick to his boots. It was only his feelings of guilt about Stephen that had led him to enter at the last minute. Gabriel had never been much of a sportsman, and had always hated the rough and tumble of the Monday Muddle. Until last year, he hadn't entered for at least a decade and, much as he liked Dan and his cronies, he wasn't looking forward to the inevitable ribbing he was going to get when he made a tit of himself as usual. Worse still, Stephen seemed convinced that he was going to be a hero. The thought of failing his son was worse than taking part. And yet, despite his anxiety, he couldn't also help feeling inspired by the fact that Marianne had said she would be cheering for him. She was so uncomplicated, and spending half an hour with her in Pippa's crowded kitchen had been incredibly soothing.

Gabriel glanced round him. The field was full of gossiping villagers who were wandering through all the craft stalls and, by the looks of things, buying plenty. He could see Pippa doing a roaring trade in home-made chutney, while the local butcher in the stall next to her was nearly sold out of hot dogs already. There were the usual Monday Muddle regulars, plus a few first-timers (village rules stated at eighteen, 'when a lad can buy his first pint', every boy in the village was eligible to enter). There weren't too many newbies this year, but Gabriel spotted one or two youngsters he knew as the sons of various acquaintances. He was pleased to note that most of them looked sicker than he felt. The Monday Muddle also attracted people from neighbouring villages, plus the odd rambler who'd been staying in town over the bank holiday weekend and been persuaded when in his cups to take part.

The field was crowded with well-wishers and supporters. Gabriel glanced over at Pippa's stall again and got a welcome boost from the sight of Marianne, who grinned and gave him the thumbs up. Only five minutes to go till he met his doom. Stephen and his friends had taken prime position on the stone wall at the edge of the field, and Ralph Nicholas was striding across the grass bearing the ancient leather football that, legend had it, had been used in the Monday Muddle for the previous two hundred years. The sun was shining, which made a pleasant change from the weeks of rain, but there was still a nip in the air. Mind you, he wouldn't be feeling that once they all got going.

'Fancy a dram?' Dan came up with a half bottle of Scotch. It was *de rigeur* to have something to keep the cold away before the great event.

'Why not?' said Gabriel. 'I may need something to numb the pain when you bring me crashing to the floor.'

'No hard feelings, mate,' said Dan grinning. 'Hey up, I think we might be ready for the off.'

They looked up to see Ralph Nicholas standing on an old crate and addressing the throng.

'Welcome one and all to this year's Monday Muddle. Right, you all know the rules—'

'There are no rules,' roared back the crowd in a well-worn response.

'When I blow my whistle, the ball will be kicked into the

crowd and then it's every man for himself, and first one to bring it home via the usual route will be declared King of the Muddle.'

A hush descended. Gabriel swallowed hard. Why was he doing this, why?

The whistle blew. The ball flew high in the sky and disappeared into the middle of the scrum. Gabriel hovered around the edges while there was the usual toing and froing and head-stamping, before finally a newcomer from a neighbouring village emerged with the traditional shout of 'Mu-dd-dle!' – and they were off.

'Go for it, Daddy!' Stephen was yelling with all his might as Gabriel set off running down the muddy field. He ran past Marianne and Pippa, who were cheering and wolf-whistling wildly.

'Go, Gabriel, go!' Marianne yelled, and suddenly his heart lifted, and he was swept with a huge adrenaline rush. He ran, busting a gut, towards the front of the crowd, easily outstripping the more lumbering members of the village. Maybe he was going to enjoy this after all . . .

Cat was in the kitchen trying out recipes for her new cookery book. Mel had started off helping her but had quickly lost interest, while James and Paige had gone next door to play. Noel was sitting watching DVDs with Ruby. Really she should get them out in the garden, it was such a lovely day and Noel was going back to work tomorrow, but Cat was enjoying the rare luxury of having the time to cook properly.

While other aspects of domestic duty were an arduous chore for Cat, cooking wasn't one of them. She loved the joy of turning basic ingredients into a tasty meal, the almost sensuous pleasure of kneading pastry, the delight of producing something which the whole family enjoyed. Cat could barely remember a time when she hadn't been able to cook, beginning young and shadowing her mother in the kitchen. Interestingly, of all her children, it was James who showed the same propensity. Maybe he'd be the next Jamie Oliver. Cat associated cooking with peace and harmony, with safety and security. The smell of baking always lifted her spirits, as it did now.

She checked on the scones she was cooking and returned to the beetroot soup she was making partly from memory. It was an old family recipe of her Auntie Eileen's, who'd got it from her Polish mother-in-law. Cat was working her way through various recipes that had been in the family for years. They included her mother's famous apple tart, Auntie Eileen's amazing meringues (which she miraculously made without a whisk, instead using two knifes to whisk the egg yolks), and her own grandmother's tasty Irish Stew.

'How's it going?' Noel walked in. Thankfully he'd got over whatever it was that was eating him on Thursday and was less sulky.

'Okay,' said Cat, testing her soup and pulling a face. 'Damn, I'm going to have to ring Auntie Eileen. I don't think I've done this right.'

'What on earth is it?' said Noel peering into the pan. 'It looks like someone's bled to death in the saucepan.'

'Ha, ha, very funny,' said Cat. 'It's supposed to be beetroot soup. I think I may have added too much paprika. Lucky you grew so much beetroot on the allotment last year as it looks like I may have to scrap this lot and start again.'

She poured away the soup and started washing up pans. She'd be rubbing beetroot stains out of her fingers for days at this rate.

'What's in the oven? That smells nice.'

'Granny Dreamboat's Fabulous Scones,' said Cat, 'and yes, when they're ready, you and Ruby can test some.'

'Ah, well, if it's Granny Dreamboat's recipe, it must be all right,' said Noel.

'Talking of Granny Dreamboat,' said Cat, as she started putting pans away, 'did you think she seemed okay yesterday?'

'What do you mean?'

'Just . . . well, the thing with the Treasure Hunt was a bit odd, wasn't it? She's never got the kids' ages wrong before, but it was as if she was buying them things from a few years back.'

'Well, maybe she was busy and made a mistake,' said Noel.

'Maybe,' said Cat doubtfully. 'It's just unlike her. And then there's little things, like the way she rang me the other day to ask how to make pastry. I mean, my mum, ringing me for cooking advice? Plus there was that business of forgetting to pay her bills. I thought she might be in some kind of financial trouble. But now I'm not so sure. She seems to be terribly forgetful of late.'

'So are you,' laughed Noel, 'you never remember anything I tell you.'

'True,' said Cat, as she took the scones out of the oven and deftly turned them onto a cooling tray.

'It's probably just her getting older,' said Noel. 'It's just because she's so capable you tend to think she's invincible. I think you're worrying unnecessarily. Mmm, these are delicious.'

'You're probably right,' said Cat, unconvinced.

'I know I am,' said Noel, kissing the top of her head and disappearing into the lounge with a plate of scones.

'Yummy, scones!' Mel appeared as if by magic.

'Trust you to come back when it's all cooked,' said Cat,

as she tidied up the kitchen. She'd been cooking so long it was nearly time to prepare tea. She tried to convince herself that Noel was right, that the small worrying lapses in her mum's concentration were just the signs of advancing old age but, deep down, she knew she was kidding herself.

'What happens now?' Marianne asked. The last stragglers of the Monday Muddle were heading off down the hill towards the stream, by which muddy back route the Muddlers would make their way back into town. Most of the onlookers had run off down the field cheering them, and she and Pippa were doing precious little trade now.

'Now we pack this lot up and go and find a suitable spot to cheer them on – the bridge over the brook at the end of Willow Valley is always a good place. Sometimes we pelt them with rotten eggs and flour, but I think the committee has vetoed that this year.'

'Blimey, I had no idea the country was like this,' said Marianne. 'It certainly beats a boring bank holiday in town.'

She didn't say she had particularly enjoyed the sight of Gabriel running swiftly through the crowd, looking rather more athletic than he'd let on. He wouldn't have looked out of place in *Chariots of Fire*.

They called Stephen, Nathan and George, and made their way via the road to the brook, where a crowd was starting to gather.

'When are they coming?' The boys jumped about impatiently.

'Soon,' said Pippa, 'be patient.'

A shout from someone near the stream indicated that the first runner was already on his way. The original catcher of the ball clearly hadn't kept it, as it was now in possession of one of Dan's friends. Dan was in hot pursuit, looking fired up and covered in mud.

'One year they'll do this event in the dry,' said Pippa raising her eyebrows. 'It took me ages to get his stuff clean last year.'

'Dad-dy! Dad-dy!' the boys were chanting and Stephen joined in. Gabriel was making his way down the path, covered in sweat, his shirt sticking to him in a way that made Marianne feel most peculiar, his lean legs spattered with mud. The legs. Oh my God. The legs did it. Marianne couldn't tear her eyes off them. Then suddenly the leader tripped and Dan and his friends leapt on top of him. To shouts and whistles, four men rolled in the mud like a bunch of school kids. The ball escaped down the bank and, swift as anything, Gabriel was down there scrabbling frantically in the water for the ball, which was in danger of heading off downstream.

'Way to go, Gabriel!' Marianne leapt to her feet, cheering. The scrummers belatedly realised they'd lost the ball and set off in pursuit of their prey, but their heavy frames, so useful in the scrum, were no match for Gabriel's fleetness of foot.

'I had no idea it would be this exciting,' said Marianne. 'Where to next?'

'If we hurry we should catch them just as they come into the village at the top end of the High Street,' said Pippa.

'Well, what are we waiting for?' said Marianne. 'I haven't had so much fun in years.'

Gabriel was on a high. He raced down the path like a bat out of hell. This was completely exhilarating. He'd never known the Monday Muddle could be so much fun. No wonder Dan and the boys were so obsessed with it. He'd been vaguely aware of the cheers when he'd grabbed the ball, but then, as he'd scrabbled his way up the bank, he'd heard Marianne screaming his name. Something about that had fired him up beyond anything he could possibly have imagined. Suddenly it became vital that he didn't just win this damned thing for Stephen, but for Marianne as well. He wanted to prove himself to her, to show her that he was different from the rest of the crowd.

He ran on, ignoring the mud and the hammering of his heart, the feeling that it might just burst out of his chest. Never had he pushed himself so hard physically, and never had he felt more joyfully, vividly, brilliantly alive. He was dimly aware of the bluebells in the woods as he ran past, of birdsong and sunshine, but that didn't matter because he was nearly at the gate that led to the High Street. He heard the crowd roar and it inspired him beyond anything he'd ever felt inspired to do before. He vaulted the gate without a thought, fired up by adrenaline and stupidity. He could do anything. Anything at all. Free running? He could be king. He was going to be King of the Muddle.

Or not.

As Gabriel leaped over the gate, his foot caught the top bar and the ground rushed headlong to meet him. The last thing he thought was, *That's going to hurt*, and then everything went black.

Chapter Sixteen

'Gabriel!' Marianne wasn't even aware she'd screamed his name, but she was transfixed at the sight of him coming tumbling over the gate. She ran faster than she knew she could up the hill to reach him. Her heart was pounding. He couldn't be hurt. He mustn't be. Not now—

Now *what?* Hang on a minute? What on earth was she thinking? Marianne paused for a moment, stopped short by the bolt of lightning that had hit her out of the blue. Suddenly it all made sense. Oh my God, she'd fallen for Gabriel, big time, and she hadn't even noticed. The revelation was cut short. Gabriel was hurt and needed her. Please, please, let him be okay.

'Gabriel, can you hear me?' Marianne reached him at last, kneeled down and leant over to check his pulse. Thank God for that first-aid course she'd done last year. She never thought she'd have to put the things she'd learnt into practice so swiftly.

Good, he was breathing. His pulse was racing, but then he had been exerting himself. He didn't look like he was going blue around the lips, but you never could tell. Gabriel was Marianne's first proper patient, she desperately didn't want to cock things up.

'Is there anyone medical here?' Marianne shouted above the rest of the crowd who'd followed her. She couldn't see any of the village GPs.

'I'm okay, I'm okay.' Gabriel was coming round. 'Am I dreaming?' he said, as he looked into Marianne's eyes. 'I think I've just seen an angel.' He lay back and shut his eyes. Marianne swallowed hard.

'No, but I think you're probably concussed,' she said.

'Nonsense,' said Gabriel, sitting up. 'I'm the King of the Middle, I mean, Muddle. And I'm going to win this thing. Have ball, will travel.'

'That's the spirit! Go on, my son!' the crowd roared.

'Get him!' shouted Dan, who was running down the path, followed by two other members of the pack.

'Not bloody likely,' said Gabriel. He stood up, staggered slightly, picked up the ball and, with a herculean effort, ran as fast as he could towards the village pub, followed by a host of besieging onlookers all chanting his name. Luckily it wasn't too far.

'Gabriel, be careful!' shouted Marianne, to no avail. What a bloody idiot. Why did he have to go all testosterone-charged on her? 'This is insane!' she wailed to no one in particular.

'Yup,' said Pippa, who had caught up belatedly, 'but this is perfectly normal for round here. You should see some of the injuries Dan's had over the years.'

They watched as Dan made some headway towards Gabriel who was beginning to stagger slightly. Just as it looked as if Dan was going to reach him, Gabriel put on another spurt of speed and, like a man possessed, roared up to the pub entrance and slammed the ball down on the table.

'I am the man!' he declared, before swaying sideways and toppling straight over.

Noel was reading Ruby a story. It had always been one of his favourite pastimes, reading his children to sleep. He loved the way she cosily curled up next to him as he put on silly voices to *The Gruffalo*. He missed the others being young. Mel was so moody and difficult these days, it was hard to know where to begin. He felt guiltily relieved that she took out all her grumpiness on Cat, but sometimes he wished she'd cuddle up to him on the sofa like she used to when she was little. When James wasn't on the Playstation, he was kicking a football about. (Noel had a sneaking feeling he was a great disappointment in the footballing department, very rarely joining the other dads on the sidelines on Saturday – he usually used work as an excuse, but it was mainly because he couldn't stand the other football dads, or standing round with cold feet – and he and Cat frequently rowed about it.)

More and more, Noel felt like he was superfluous in his older children's lives. Although Paige still demonstrated a pleasing tendency to jump all over him as soon as he walked through the door, the older two frequently acted as if they didn't care if he were there or not. Cat had a different take on things, he knew, extolling the joys of older children, but Noel had a sneaking affection for the muddle and chaos of the early days of parenthood when, despite the lack of sleep, the house had felt cosy and comfortable and he had felt a sense of pride at the home he and Cat were creating. Now it often felt like he was a stranger in his own house, and the jobs he had to do (memo to self, mend that sodding shelf) were a constant reminder that he wasn't matching up to either his or Cat's expectations as a husband and father.

His thoughts strayed to the eco town and the one bright spot in his work landscape. Though the trips up north were growing more frequent, the upside was that Noel got to spend more time in Hope Christmas. He'd taken to staying in the Hopesay Arms, the village pub, which was so much nicer than the Travelodge on the nearest motorway. Noel had even stayed once when technically he could have got home. He'd felt guilty about it, almost as if he were having an affair, but, somehow, Noel just wanted to keep Hope Christmas as his secret.

He just couldn't resist the opportunity to wander the little streets, pottering round the quaint shops with their lopsided walls, low ceilings, and displays of geegaws and trinkets that he found incredibly enticing. The shop that drew him back most often was more of an emporium, being a three-storeyed house, crammed full of antiques – most of them rubbish, though Noel had spotted the occasional gem. He harboured wild fantasies of buying one of the tumbledown old farmhouses he'd spotted on the way out of Hope Christmas, and cramming it full of old knick-knacks purchased from the antiques shop, as well as books he'd acquired from the fabulous bookshop, where the book-sellers were now ordering books especially for him. But, somehow, in his head he could never see Cat and the children there. Cat was far too much of a townie to ever countenance a life in the country. It was a pipe dream, and Noel knew it. Besides, by the time Matt and Luke had finished with the eco town there wasn't likely to be anything left of the Hope Christmas he loved. Noel felt hopelessly guilty about the part he was playing in destroying this particular paradise for the sake of a parking lot, but he couldn't see a way out of it without losing his job. And, in the current economic climate, he could scarcely afford to do that.

Realising Ruby was asleep, he gently kissed the top of her head, put the book away and popped his head into Paige's room, where she had her nose stuck in a Jacqueline Wilson.

'Five minutes till lights out,' he said, before going down-stairs and chasing James off the computer and into bed.

Cat and Mel were watching *Pride and Prejudice*, eating popcorn. He didn't mind period drama, but wasn't quite in the mood, so, ignoring the disappointed look on Cat's face, he headed into the study and went online to see if there were any job opportunities out there. After a fruitless half an hour, he realised he was wasting his time. He'd try some agencies in the morning. He switched off the computer and went back into the lounge in time to witness Darcy whisking Elizabeth off into the sunset. Mel said goodnight and Cat cuddled up to him on the sofa while they watched a repeat of *Little Britain*. Noel was uneasy. He still hadn't got round to telling Cat about the precarious nature of his work situation. Somehow there hadn't been a right moment over the weekend. Perhaps he should tell her now.

'Penny for 'em,' Cat said, tucking into a piece of popcorn. 'You seem very preoccupied.'

'I'm fine,' he lied, 'just a bit tired.'

He'd tell her tomorrow. Maybe.

Gabriel lay on a stretcher in a hospital corridor, feeling woozy. This was ridiculous, he shouldn't be in hospital, he was perfectly fine. Trust Diana Carew to insist on calling an ambulance. The paramedic who had checked him over had decided he needed to go to hospital for observation. The adrenaline rush from earlier had completely deserted Gabriel, and he was now feeling like a total prat.

You are the King of the Muddle though, a sneaky voice in his head said very clearly. 'Yeah, and look where that's landed me!' Gabriel said out loud.

'Do you often talk to yourself?' Marianne was standing over him, looking amused.

'Only when my head hurts,' said Gabriel.

'You've only yourself to blame,' said Marianne. 'What on earth were you thinking?'

'I wasn't, much,' admitted Gabriel. 'I just got a bit carried away.'

'I'll say,' said Marianne. 'How are you feeling?'

'Everything hurts,' said Gabriel. 'Where's Stephen?'

'Down the corridor with Pippa and the other kids,' said Marianne. 'I said I'd come and find out what was happening.'

'I'm really glad you have,' said Gabriel. Despite the pain in his limbs, and the aching of his head, he felt a sudden dizzying sense of joy that she was here with him, right now. All the way down that path, it was a vision of Marianne that had been spurring him on. Suddenly life seemed worth living in a way it hadn't done for months. Suddenly he had a reason to get up in the morning with a spring in his step and joy in his heart. He had forgotten the rushing, intoxicating ecstasy of early love – if indeed it was love that he was feeling. Whatever it was, it was making him feel like jumping in the air and punching the sky. For the first time he imagined a future without Eve. And a future with someone else.

'Even though I think you're an utter pillock,' said Marianne, bursting his bubble, 'I'm glad you're okay.'

'Marianne, you say the nicest things,' said Gabriel with a grin.

'Don't,' said Marianne.

'Don't what?' said Gabriel.

'Look at me like that,' said Marianne.

'Like what?'

'Like that,' said Marianne. 'You're stopping me from being as cross as I want to be with you.'

'Well, don't be then,' said Gabriel. 'At least I won.'

'Yes,' said Marianne, with a sudden grin that sent his heart leaping skywards, 'yes, you certainly did.'

* * *

'Cat-er-ine! Cat-er-ine!' Cat was roused from a deep sleep by the sound of Magda sobbing and shouting hysterically.

'What on earth is going on?' Cat leapt out of bed, crossly noting that as usual a bomb could go off and Noel wouldn't even notice, flung a dressing gown around her and opened the door. Magda was standing before her, doubled up in pain, blood pouring from her stomach. Cat looked down and saw a bloody trail of footprints leading from the bathroom.

'I was at club, with Sergei. We dance,' said Magda, who was swaying alarmingly and looked incredibly pale. 'I had my belly button pierced today. It catch on Sergei's jacket and – oh my God, the pain! – it start to bleed. So I come home. But it won't stop bleeding. I am going to die.'

'You're not going to die,' said Cat firmly. 'Don't be ridiculous. And hold your finger over it to stop the bleeding. Where's Sergei now?'

'He is in kitchen. He not like blood.'

'Oh, does he not?' said Cat. 'Haven't you heard of A&E?'

'What?' Magda was leaning against the wall, panting heavily. Christ, she wasn't about to go into anaphylactic shock, was she?

'Let's have a look, shall we?' Cat gingerly removed Magda's hand from her bare midriff to see a stud hanging off a bit of skin, with blood pumping out. Resisting the urge to gag, Cat shoved Magda's fingers over the hole to attempt to stem the bleeding and took her back into the bathroom. She made her au pair lie on the floor with her legs in the air to stop her fainting and prevent the blood flowing downwards and, remembering a trick her Auntie Eileen (a former nurse) had taught her, she held the two pieces of skin together as tight as possible in the vain hope that they would knit back together again. After ten minutes she cautiously took her fingers away and realised that a clot was beginning to form. Going to the first-aid cupboard, she got some steri strips out and stuck them over the wound, having first cleaned it as best she could with antiseptic wipes, ruthlessly ignoring the feeble moans emanating from Magda.

Sergei, meanwhile, had bravely managed to come up the stairs and see how his girlfriend was getting on. He took one look at Magda's bloodied stomach and promptly threw up.

'You're a fat load of use,' snapped Cat. 'Have you been drinking?'

'We both have,' said Magda.

'Great, just great,' said Cat. 'Right, get in the car, both of you. I'll take you to Casualty.'

Cat drove like a maniac through the darkened London streets, furiously thinking about how she was going to deal with this situation. She was so angry she didn't even care if Magda bled to death in the back of the car, she just wanted her gone. By the time they'd got to the hospital, she'd made up her mind about what she was going to do, even though she blanched at the thought of how she was going to manage it. She drew up outside the casualty department and then turned to them both and said, 'I want you to listen carefully. I am going to say this only once. I'm going to leave you here, but you can make your own way home. And, in the morning, Magda, I am going to ring the agency and tell them your services are no longer required. You can come and pack your things up and then you can go. Do you understand?'

'But Cat-er-ine—' began Magda.

'But Catherine nothing,' said Cat. 'You've had enough warnings. I've had it up to here with you and lover boy over there. I'd rather not have an au pair at all than have to put up with one as useless as you.'

It took Cat an hour by the time she'd got back from the hospital and, when she returned, she had to clean up the mess. The last thing she wanted was for the kids to see all that in the morning.

'What's happening?' Noel appeared in the doorway, looking sleepy.

'Magda nearly bled to death all over the floor, Sergei threw up everywhere and I've now sacked Magda,' said Cat, as she mopped the floor with a will.

'Oh, right,' Noel looked a bit bemused. 'Crikey, how did I manage to miss all that?'

'How indeed?' said Cat.

'Here, let me help,' said Noel, going to get another mop. It took them half an hour, but eventually all the mess was cleared up.

'It could only happen to us,' said Cat, who was so wired up she couldn't face going back to bed again.

'Oh, I don't know,' said Noel. 'I'm sure there must be a house somewhere which is more chaotic than ours.'

'You think?' Cat said, bursting into fits of laughter. 'Oh, crikey. How am I going to cope? I've just sacked the childcare.'

'Something will turn up, Mrs Micawber,' said Noel, going over to her and kissing her on the top of her head. He paused. 'Cat, there's something I've been meaning to tell you—'

'Yes?' Cat looked up at him, and was surprised to see a sombre look on his face.

'Mummy!' A sobbing little voice came from the kitchen door. 'I had a bad dream.'

'Did you, pet?' Cat picked Ruby up, and gave her a cuddle. 'What were you going to say, Noel?'

'It doesn't matter,' said Noel. 'Time for bed.'

Cat carried Ruby back to her room but couldn't settle

her, and inevitably she and Noel had an uncomfortable night with Ruby lying aslant across their bed. By morning they were both shattered. The alarm had just gone off when Cat heard a commotion downstairs. She came down to a bewildering sight. Sergei and Magda were struggling to bring a mattress through the front door.

'What the hell do you think you're doing?' Cat said.

'We make protest,' said Magda. 'This my home, you cannot throw me out. Sergei is coming to live here. He will help with children.'

'He will not,' said Cat. 'If you don't take that mattress out of my house right now, I shall call the police.'

Magda and Sergei ignored her and so Cat, without thinking about it, launched herself at the side of the mattress coming towards her and leant on it for all she was worth.

'Noel!' she called.

'What the—' Noel came flying down the stairs and, seeing what Cat was doing, leant against Cat. The suddenness of his arrival pushed the mattress back a little, but Sergei on the other side was putting renewed vigour into things, and suddenly Cat and Noel both found themselves on the floor.

'What's going on?' James appeared at the top of the stairs.

'We're trying to stop Sergei moving in,' said Noel. 'Come and help.'

'This is fun,' said James, who was swiftly joined by his siblings. For a few moments the mattress teetered back and forth before finally, with one push, they were able to expel it from the door. Now it was Sergei's and Magda's turn to end up flat on their back with the mattress on top of them.

'Now, just so we've got this clear,' said Catherine. 'Magda, I'm sacking you. You may come and pick your belongings up later. On your own. If Sergei comes near the place I shall call the police. Got it?'

'Got it,' said Magda sulkily.

Cat went back inside and high-fived her family. She might be left without childcare, but at least she knew the Tinsalls could be relied on to pull together whatever happened. And she would manage. Because she must. She didn't actually have a choice.

Part Three

To Save Me From Tears

Last Year

December 24

'Christmas Eve, it's Christmas Eve,' Noel could hear Kipper intoning in the children's playroom from his study where he was surfing the net. Ruby was sitting with a blanket, sucking her thumb and watching her favourite programme. Any minute now there would be ructions because Paige wanted to watch *The Snowman*, which was on for the zillionth time. Back in the dawn of time they had had a copy on video, but when James was a toddler he had 'posted' it in the video machine and it had never been the same again.

From the kitchen he could hear carols wafting up the stairs. Cat was peeling the vegetables for tomorrow over a cosy cup of coffee with his mum and, though Noel had offered to help, she claimed to be on top of things. Cat had a way of looking at him when she said that which made him feel like an insignificant worm. She always denied it but sometimes Noel felt there was a great female conspiracy going on against him. In the office he was feeling more and more sidelined, and at home he felt thoroughly useless. The one thing Cat was always nagging him about, namely to mend the shelf in the lounge, was the one thing he never seemed to get round to doing. He couldn't quite explain to himself why that was but being nagged reminded him of his mum, and the more Cat nagged, the less likely he was to do it.

Christmas always seemed to make things worse somehow. Sometimes Noel suspected this Happy Homemaker thing had gone to Cat's head somewhat. It was almost as if she felt she had to live the way her alter ego did. Instead of his real, gorgeous, homely wife, Noel felt he was getting the cardboard-cutout, dressed-in-a-Santa-outfit, slightly deranged version currently gracing the cover of *Happy Homes*. The Christmas lists had started appearing in September and she'd been shopping regularly since then. All the Christmas cards had been posted promptly on 1 December, the presents bought, wrapped and hidden in the loft by the end of November, the turkey ordered from the organic butcher on Clapton High Street three months in advance. She'd made the cake at half term, mince pies in November, and spent the previous week baking sausage rolls. Who on earth made their own sausage rolls anymore? *I do*, had been Cat's firm response. The money she was bringing in was, of course, incredibly helpful, but sometimes Noel wistfully wanted his old wife back.

She'd been such a frightening whirl of efficiency, Noel had felt almost gleeful when he discovered she hadn't managed to make a Christmas pudding. Apparently Cat's mum was supposed to do it but had forgotten. Cat had actually returned from Sainsbury's stressed and empty-handed a couple of days earlier, and hadn't taken kindly to Noel's roar of laughter when he'd heard that she'd abandoned the trolley mid-shop. Maybe there was something he could do. He looked at his watch and saw it was only just midday. Sainsbury's was bound to be a nightmare, but at least if he bought a Christmas pudding he might feel slightly less useless.

Noel went down to the kitchen to find his mother relating some hilarious anecdote from his childhood about him pooing his pants, which Cat clearly found very funny. It riled him how well Cat got on with his mother, who did nothing but find fault with him and the children.

'What's my lovely granddaughter up to?' Another bone of contention. Why did his mother insist on favouring Ruby so obviously? She'd done the same trick with his little sister when he was growing up and it still rankled.

'Watching Kipper,' said Noel, bracing himself for the inevitable comment about how much television the children watched. For once, it didn't come.

'If you don't need me, dear,' Angela said to Cat, 'I'll just go and see if Ruby wants company.'

'No, that's fine,' said Cat. 'I really don't need any help now.'

'So, nothing I can do?' Noel hovered, feeling like a spare part.

'Noel, you know the last time I let you loose in the kitchen it was chaos,' said Cat. 'I think everything's sorted. Apart from the sodding Christmas pud of course.'

'Well, I could hunter gather – like, go out in search of one if you want,' offered Noel.

'I think you'd be wasting your time,' said Cat. 'Besides, I need you here.'

'For what precisely?' Noel's irritation got the better of him. 'I've been hanging around all day. You need me for precisely nothing. I'm going to the pub.'

'I didn't mean—' Cat looked stricken, but Noel was too cross to stop now. He stormed out of the house in a state of ire. Honestly. She was the limit sometimes. It was bloody hard to live with someone who was so sodding perfect. A soothing pint was all he needed to calm his nerves.

The pub was thoroughly miserable. Lots of people had obviously come in on their way home from work and the place was packed. 'Wonderful Christmas Time' was blaring out from the loudspeakers. Yes, wasn't he just having one of those. After a solitary pint squashed between a drunk solicitor, who was attempting to chat up the barmaid, and a couple of brickies, who looked like they were settling in for the rest of the afternoon, guilt kicked in and Noel decided to call it a day. He headed out into the cold December afternoon and decided to wander up to the little minimarket on the corner to see if they happened to have any Christmas puddings. By some happy miracle, there was one small pudding still sitting on the shelf. At least he could do one thing right.

'Elves, this way! Fairies, that!' Diana Carew's voice boomed out across the village hall as half a dozen feverishly excited children rushed out of the changing rooms in costume. Marianne paused from administering face paint to an overexcited three-year-old who was going to be a puppy (since when were there puppies in the stable, she wondered). She had a headache and was not looking forward to the rest of her evening. Luke had refused to come to the Nativity, claiming family duties. She sighed. It would have been nice if he could have supported her in this one small thing. But apparently there was only so much time in his busy life and it didn't extend to attending the Village Nativity play.

Marianne knew the evening was going to be a disaster. Most of her reception class, who were playing a variety of angels, stars and animals, were so hyped up on the chocolate cake that Diana had foolishly provided they were going to be impossible to keep quiet. They were excited enough about Christmas as it was, and were overtired – clearly most of them had been having lots of late nights already – and the hour-and-a-half long performance was going to be beyond them. Lord knows how the preschoolers were going to manage, but that was Pippa's department.

202

She helped out a couple of days a week and had volunteered to look after the littlies, as she called them.

'That's me done,' Marianne said, following her small charge out into the hall.

'Wonderful,' boomed Diana. 'Right, we need our mice up on stage, and everyone else to be backstage. Chop chop. Your parents will be here soon.'

Diana's version of the Nativity had to rate as the most bizarre Marianne had ever seen. It followed the story of a little mouse who on Christmas Eve was sent to his room for not sharing his toys with the poor little mice who lived down the road. The mouse then encountered a magic fairy (with her half a dozen very tiny fairy companions, who did a rather long and baffling dance) who took him on a journey to discover the true meaning of Christmas, by way of Santa's workshop, some selfish children, a poor little matchgirl, Bob Cratchit, various animals, and who eventually found himself in Bethlehem. Mary (an insufferable child who turned out to be Diana's granddaughter) and Joseph got about ten seconds on stage and the only carol Marianne recognised was 'Little Donkey'. Despite various suggestions from the Parish Council to shorten it over the years, according to Pippa, Diana wouldn't be budged. So the Village Nativity was now set in stone as an event to be endured rather than enjoyed.

Marianne and Pippa were in charge of the backstage area, a small anteroom at the back of the hall. The children were herded in like excited puppies and Marianne's headache began to get worse, along with an anxious feeling that was growing in the pit of her stomach. She was going straight from the show to Luke's grandfather's for another Nicholas family gathering.

'So, are you all set for tonight?' Pippa said, while she absent-mindedly replaited a fairy's hair.

Marianne grimaced.

'Not really,' she said. 'I'm not looking forward to it at all. Luke's relatives are all so stiff and ghastly. I'll feel like a fish out of water.'

'Ralph Nicholas can't make you feel like that, surely?' said Pippa. 'He's a sweetheart.'

'Oh, he's fine,' said Marianne. 'It's just Luke's mother I have to contend with.'

'Ah, mothers-in-law,' said Pippa. 'What would we do without them? Actually, that's not fair, Dan's mum is a gem. I couldn't manage at all if she wasn't.'

A call came for the fairies to go on stage and Pippa and Marianne watched from the wings as the children yawned their way through the dance. Despite Diana's best efforts (she stood at the back doing every move with them – 'it's a wonder she doesn't leap on the stage,' snorted Pippa), two of the fairies bumped into each other, one sucked her thumb and another spent the whole time in tears. And there was still over an hour to go.

The play dragged on, a combination of folly and high farce, but eventually, to Marianne's relief, it was finally over.

'One down, one to go,' she said with a grimace, as she and Pippa got the children ready to meet their parents. People were shouting 'Happy Christmas' and there was much merriment about how long the show had taken. 'Even by Diana's standards, that was bad,' said Pippa. 'God knows where she's going to take it next year.'

Eventually all the children had gone and it was time for Marianne to go home and get ready. Pippa had rushed off in a whirl, grabbing her own children and getting ready for festive celebrations with various family members. Marianne envied her. She'd elected to stay here this Christmas rather than go home, but right now she was wishing for her own bed and a cosy family Christmas where she could be who she was without let or hindrance. She made her way down the lane to her cottage. Snow was falling gently. Oh well, at least being in the country she was in for a white Christmas.

Cat was feeling out of sorts. She'd spent all morning cooking in the kitchen with Angela and come out to discover that the children had trashed the house. Before his little strop, Noel seemed to have spent the whole morning on the computer and done little to help. Honestly. He was the limit sometimes. Couldn't he *see* that things needed doing? Why did she always have to point it out? It was that frustration that had spilled over and led her to make the bitchy remark earlier.

She was guiltily aware it wasn't altogether true. It was just that when Noel was in the kitchen, he seemed to fill the space and ruin the peace and tranquillity of her ordered way of working. There were occasions when he'd cracked open a bottle of red, put some music on and insisted on dancing with her as they cooked, when he actually made cooking more fun. But then there was the clearing up afterwards. She should probably lighten up a bit about that, but it was so hard when you always felt you had to take responsibility for managing everything.

It was also frustrating to be the only one to write all the cards (though Noel at least had consented to put them in the post) and he'd shown scant interest in choosing Christmas presents. She'd been so busy with doing the extraneous extra pieces for the family – and his family to boot. Why Great Auntie Priscilla had to have bedsocks, and Cousin Ivy's third grandchild needed a bath toy, Cat didn't know. But she did know that Noel never paid any attention to that kind of thing and it was Expected. So *she* had to do it.

There were also all the presents for the waifs and strays she'd somehow ended up inviting for Christmas: as well as Mum, there was Auntie Eileen and Great Uncle Paddy (who wasn't a real uncle at all but a friend of Cat's grandfather), plus Angela, who generally managed to put people's noses out of joint wherever she went, and Soppy Sarah (so called by the children for the way she went around weeping at the sight of small children and animals), their doolally neighbour for whom Cat felt terribly sorry. The trouble was, Cat could never bear the thought of anyone being on their own for Christmas, so somehow half the neighbourhood was now coming.

She still felt guilty about her rubbish Christmas presents for Noel. Mind you, if he wanted more than a couple of CDs, the latest Terry Pratchett and a manbag, he should give her more time to go shopping. Noel was so bad at presents himself, he probably hadn't got her anything at all. It had been known to happen.

The door opened, and Noel came in looking triumphant.

'I come bearing gifts,' he said, holding a Christmas pudding aloft.

'Fantastic,' said Cat, 'where did you get it?'

'I paid a small fortune for it at the minimarket,' said Noel, 'but I do think it was worth it.'

He kissed her on the top of the head.

'Sorry about earlier,' he said.

'Me too,' said Cat.

'I've got a special Christmas surprise for you later,' said Noel.

'Oh, what?'

'Well, it won't be a surprise if I tell you, will it?' said Noel. 'But I think you'll like it. Now come on, what else is there to do?'

'If you could get the kids cracking on their bedrooms,' said Cat.

'Consider it done,' said Noel, and was off shouting his way round the house, getting the kids fired up in a way that she never could.

She'd been wrong to be so negative. Noel always meant well. She should try and listen more. They were going to have a great Christmas. In fact, she wouldn't be surprised if it was the best one ever.

'Are you sure we're not putting you out?' Gabriel asked Pippa for the hundredth time, as he helped sort out Stephen's made-up bed on the floor of the boys' room. Stephen was bounding about excitedly, holding up his stocking and saying, 'Where can I put this, Auntie Pippa?'

Gabriel had been in two minds about letting Stephen take part in the Nativity, but it had kept him occupied, and now he was so excited about staying with his cousins he seemed, for the moment at least, not to mind too much about his mother's absence. Pippa had pointed out that his mum was so often out or away anyway that maybe it didn't make as much difference as they thought – but Gabriel knew that that didn't matter. Eve might not have been the best of mothers but Stephen missed her terribly. It was heartbreaking to see how much. Which was why Gabriel was determined his son should have a fantastic Christmas and was throwing himself into the spirit of things, even though he didn't feel like it.

'I'm the Ghost of Christmas Past,' he said, throwing a sheet over his head and chasing the boys around the room.

'Careful,' said Pippa. 'I really don't want to end up in Casualty on Christmas Eve.'

'Sorry,' said Gabriel, 'I got a bit carried away.' He felt a curious sense of dislocation, as if his feelings about Eve were on hold, but at the same time he felt almost giddy and intoxicated. He had the awful feeling that if he started laughing he might never stop.

'No worries,' Pippa touched him lightly on the arm. 'You okay?'

'I'll have to be, won't I?' said Gabriel.

'Come on, let's leave these rascals to go to bed and let's get you fed and watered,' Pippa said.

Gabriel followed her down to the cosy kitchen and tried to join in the cheerful patter going on between Pippa, Dan and Dan's sister and husband, who'd come over from a neighbouring village for the evening, but he found he couldn't settle. His mind was constantly on Eve, wondering what she was doing. He kept checking his mobile. Maybe she'd left a message but – despite the numerous texts he'd sent her and messages he'd left on her phone, there was nothing. At least if he knew she was okay, it would be something to tell Stephen.

His phone bleeped suddenly, and he nearly jumped out of his skin. He scrolled through his messages. It was from Eve's mum. Excusing himself, Gabriel put on his coat and went out into the front garden where the reception was better. Then, taking a deep breath, he rang his mother-in-law.

'Hi, it's Gabe,' he said. 'Any news?'

Earlier in the week, Joan had been adamant she'd had no contact with her daughter, but now she was texting him out of the blue.

'I've heard from Eve,' said Joan, 'and she said to tell you she's fine.'

'Where is she?'

'With friends,' said Joan.

'Have you got a number?' Gabriel nearly shouted down the phone.

'I'm sorry, Gabe,' said Joan, 'she expressly asked me not to give it you. She doesn't want to see you.'

It was what he'd been expecting, but Gabriel was unprepared for the sharp searing pain that swept through him.

'What about Stephen?' Gabriel asked. 'Surely she can't

not contact Stephen? It's Christmas Day tomorrow, for fuck's sake.'

'I don't know,' said Joan, 'she didn't say.'

'Please,' said Gabriel. 'I'll understand about not seeing me, but please ask her not to do this to Stephen.'

'I'll try,' said Joan. 'But you know she's not in a good way right now. She's very very ill. I'm not sure I can persuade her of anything.'

Gabriel hung up and stared out at the snowy hills. He looked back at the warm glow from the cottage, the upstairs light indicating that Stephen and his cousins were still wide awake. How were they going to get through tomorrow? For the first time, he had to face up to the truth. Eve had gone. And this time, she really wasn't coming back.

This Year

Chapter Seventeen

The sun shone as Gabriel took his ewes and lambs down the lane and out to pasture. He'd delayed getting them back on the hills because up until Easter Monday the weather had been so dreadful. But spring was definitely sprung, and it was a fine clear morning to be out on the hillside. He whistled as he made his way up the valley. He loved these early mornings here, the freshness of the air, the vast blue arc of sky above him, the gentle sound of sheep baaing, the rooks cawing in their rookeries, and the soft spring of the heather under his feet. And the colours on the hillside never ceased to amaze him, ever changing with the seasons. In summer he knew the soft pinks and purples of the heather would become lost in a blaze of glorious gold and green, and by autumn the hills would be red and orange, before fading to the muted soft greens of winter. He felt lucky to be here, at one with nature, enjoying the view.

And since the Monday Muddle he felt luckier still. Marianne seemed to be slotting into his life in a comfortable and easy way. If Stephen had a late club at school, she often walked home with him and stayed for a cup of tea. The three of them had driven over the hills to an isolated country pub for Sunday lunch and then a long yomp across the fields. It had felt natural and right and, when they'd swung Stephen between them, Gabriel had realised with a jolt that this was what he had always been missing with Eve. Precious family moments had been few and far between, either because Eve couldn't 'cope' with Stephen, so Gabriel had taken him out alone, or because, when she had come with them, invariably something would happen to create tension and he and Stephen would have to be on tenterhooks for the whole day. Gabriel tried and failed to think of a single day spent with his wife and son that had been this easy.

He whistled as he wound his way into the valley near the proposed eco town. He could see that work had started already but was amused to notice that the foundations of the proposed houses were deep in mud, and the new back gardens, which led down to the river, were awash. When would they learn? This was such a bad place to build, any fool could see it. Although the weather had perked up of late, the river banks were swollen, and the last few weeks in March had brought severe flood warnings that so far hadn't come to pass. But if they did, Gabriel was fairly sure the river bank wouldn't hold, and the eco town might get swept away before it had even been built.

A few hours later, Noel was standing in the same muddy field looking round him in dismay. By dint of fudging things so that the bulk of the houses in the eco town would be built on the hillside, while the communal areas would be in the spot where there were potential floods, as per the government guidelines, the project been allowed to go ahead.

Coming as he had from the rural beauty of Hope Christmas, it seemed more shameful to Noel than ever that they were tearing up this beauty spot for what was at best going to be a shiny new town with no heart and soul, and at worst was going to be a disaster, leaving both houses and GRB in a quagmire. The sun was shining but he was standing in a swamp and the river was flowing dangerously fast. Even Matt Duncan had blanched when he'd arrived. The soil was so damp, and had been for weeks, work had ground to a halt on the site, the foreman having pushed his workers off and put them on another job that they could actually finish. Noel didn't blame him. In these financially turbulent times it made sense to get a job done so you could get paid. GRB's finances were probably so precarious at the moment, the chances of the builders getting paid on time were slight to say the least, and any delay meant GRB's credit controllers would be rubbing their hands with glee at the thought they could stall paying someone. Noel always failed to understand how credit controllers operated. Presumably they realised that their counterparts in the customers' firms were playing the same game? Sure, they were saving GRB money, but someone, somewhere, was making sure GRB didn't get paid, which in the end could be the difference between keeping your job or not.

Noel swallowed slightly. He still hadn't told Cat about the precarious nature of his situation, and though his heart wasn't in this eco project at all, he felt duty-bound to give it his best shot. Maybe then his job might be safe? And maybe that promised bonus would materialise. But somehow Noel doubted it. There was a chill wind blowing across the business map these days. If he lost his job, for the first time in his life Noel wasn't certain he'd get another one.

'How's it all going, chaps?' Great. Luke Nicholas came swaggering up in a Barbour and this time, Noel noticed to his amusement, wellingtons, looking every inch the country squire.

'We're having a few difficulties with the builders', explained Noel, seeing that Matt looked like he was going to fudge the issue once more. 'They're saying it's not possible to carry on building in this swamp, so they've downed tools and swanned off to another job.'

Luke's eyes narrowed, and a vein began to throb dangerously on his upper temple. Noel stared at it, fascinated. It seemed to be developing a life of its own.

'Not good enough, people,' he said. 'We have investors to keep happy here. Investors who need reassurance in these difficult times that this particular investment is safe.'

Wondering how on earth anyone was going to guarantee that the houses here would actually be sold now that the world's finances were in such a downturn, Noel simply said, 'What do you suggest we do?'

'Throw money at it,' was the succinct reply. 'Whatever the other job is offering them, double it. We've spent too much on this to back out now. And you two. You're the engineers. Find a solution. Presumably you can find *some* way of drying the earth out so the building can recommence. It can't be that hard, can it?'

'It's not quite as straightforward as that,' began Noel, thinking of the fact that they were building on clay, which was going to lead to subsidence problems anyway once the earth had dried out, but he knew he was wasting his time as soon as Matt chipped in with, 'That's fine, Luke. I'm sure we can work something out, can't we, Noel?'

Noel said nothing. There was no point. But he looked at the swamp again and knew the project was failed. No matter how much money Luke Nicholas thought he could throw at it.

Cat was ostensibly working at home on the Christmas issue but so far this morning she'd managed to put on three loads of washing, clear a space on the floor in the chaos that was Ruby's room and make herself three cups of tea.

213

Cat had forgotten how very difficult it was working from home and trying to juggle the competing demands of seeing what needed to be done in the house with that of an editor screaming for copy yesterday.

Since Magda's departure, Cat had been trying to wangle more and more days at home so that she could at least do the school run without relying too heavily on Regina. Regina had been fabulous, it was true, and would help out at the drop of a hat, but Cat knew it wasn't fair to expect it of her friend. She wasn't often in a position to pay back the favour – having to work like a demon in between sorting tea out and getting the kids to bed, Cat couldn't manage to cope with Regina's mob for tea more than once a week – and she was guiltily aware that in the school-mum-helping-each-other-out bank she was heavily in her friend's debt.

In the first couple of weeks after Magda had gone, Cat had asked her mum to help out, but things hadn't gone according to plan. Mum had needed to be reminded every day she was picking the children up from school and, when she got home, the children had started complaining to Cat that Granny Dreamboat was either paying them no attention, or getting cross with them for no good reason. When quizzed about it, Mum was incredibly vague, and Cat was beginning to realise she couldn't even rely on her mother to cook the children's supper when she got in. Nine times out of ten when she got home, Mum would have been 'just about to' put the tea on, the kids were starving and snappy with each other, and the house was in more chaos than Cat could have thought possible.

It was becoming increasingly clear to her that though her mother continued to be delighted to see her grand-children, and frequently moaned that she didn't see enough of them, the reality was they were exhausting her. And after two more occasions when Mum had simply forgotten to turn up on the school run, Cat reluctantly came to the conclusion that her mother was no longer to be relied on. She pushed away the gnawing ache of worry that that was engendering in her. She had enough to deal with, without thinking too hard about the fact her mother appeared to be losing it. Besides, the thought of something being wrong with her clever, capable mother made her shrivel up inside. She wasn't ready to face it.

Particularly not at a time when both Noel and Mel seemed to be locked in their respective bubbles of misery. Noel had clammed up completely on her. He was taking quite a few days working at home (funnily it never seemed convenient for *him* to do the school run), but, whether at home or work, he seemed silent and morose. She couldn't even get him to row with her, which at least would have shown some spark of something. It was as though Noel had lost interest in her and the children. While Mel, Mel was becoming harder and harder work. Cat knew the transition from primary to secondary school had been difficult for her clever, sensitive daughter, but, whereas the other mothers she knew were reporting their children settling down into their new schools, Mel seemed more and more closed in on herself. It was Cat's secret fear that her daughter was being bullied, and she was keeping a weather eye on Mel's MSN account to make sure nothing untoward had happened. It caught at her heart to see her daughter so very unhappy and be unable to do anything about it.

Cat sighed. Maybe she should blog about Mel's problems. One of the bonuses of the blog, she'd found, was that talking about domestic problems she had (not that the Happy Homemaker often admitted to having problems) usually resulted in a wave of supportive posts from people who had been through similar. She'd do that now and get going on the magazine later. It was important that she keep her blog posts up, they'd become a bit sporadic of late.

It's every mother's nightmare. The thought that your child is being bullied and you can do nothing about it. But how do you know if you're child is being bullied? And what, if anything, can you do to prevent it?

Cat began to type and was soon lost in her words. It was one way to stop herself worrying.

Marianne raced late into the latest Post Office Meeting. Vera had called it at short notice, so Pippa and Gabriel had both said they couldn't make it and she'd agreed to let them know how it went.

How it went was very simple. Vera got up, looking ashen-faced, and said in a straightforward manner, 'I'm really sorry everyone, but our campaign has failed. Despite the petition and the picketing of Mount Pleasant, I heard today that my post office licence is being withdrawn. It's nobody's fault, really, they're just following government guidelines, but there's nothing more any of us can do. I really appreciate the help you've given—'

She stifled a sob and sat down again, looking stricken. Mr Edwards, who was sitting next to her, patted her hand sympathetically and handed her a tissue.

'That's outrageous!' Diana Carew boomed from the back of the hall. 'There must be something we can do.'

'Absolutely.' Miss Woods came up, banging her stick determinedly into the ground in a way only she knew how. 'Never say die, that's my motto. Can't we use the interweb a bit more? Set up a Spacebook account or something?'

'I couldn't agree more,' said Diana, and Marianne smiled at the sight of the two of them, for once on the same side, though really she didn't feel like smiling at all.

'Why don't we run our own community post office?' said

Miss Woods. 'I've been skiing the interweb and discovered all sorts of places where communities have kept their post offices alive by working together. We could move it here, to the village hall, and work together with the village farmers to sell some of their local produce. Pippa, you could use it as an outlet for your produce. See, I printed something off about a village in Somerset that did the very same thing.'

'What an excellent idea,' said Diana, who only looked a little put out that she hadn't thought of it herself. 'And what with the new eco town, we might get an injection of new blood into the area, so why don't we suggest to the developers they get involved too?'

Marianne stifled the thought that Luke wouldn't be at all interested in developing anything if it involved the word community. It was a good idea. Maybe it would work.

The meeting broke up in a muddle of excited talk and gloomy harbingers of doom declaring the scheme was doomed to failure. Marianne set off for Pippa's to tell her what had happened, but she paused before she got there and, without questioning herself as to why she was doing it, she walked further up the lane to Gabriel's house. Since the incident at the Monday Muddle she'd been seeing him regularly but, despite her epiphany, to her disappointment nothing had yet happened between them. Gabriel was an inscrutable kind of character, quite hard to read, but she thought he liked her. Trying to calm down her nerves, which were on edge, and her heartbeat, which was so erratic she wondered she hadn't gone into cardiac arrest, she walked down the path and knocked on his cottage door. Maybe she was making a mistake. Perhaps she should have told Pippa what had happened at the meeting and just run into Gabriel in the normal way.

The dark path flooded with light as Gabriel came to the door.

'Marianne, how great to see you.' His warmth seemed genuine.

'I just came—' She hesitated, suddenly feeling like a total idiot. 'I thought you might like to know how the meeting went.'

'And there was me thinking you were coming to see me,' quipped Gabriel.

'I was . . . I am . . . well, both.' Marianne blushed in confusion.

'Good,' said Gabriel. 'Come in and have a drink. I've been meaning to ask you anyway.'

'You have?' Marianne's heart skipped.

'Yes, I have.' Gabriel looked at her semi-solemnly, and then said, 'If only to see you go that spectacular shade of beetroot.'

Marianne felt her cheeks flame even more and her heart went into overdrive on the skipping front. He did like her. He did. She could scarcely breathe, she felt so overcome. From somewhere distant, she realised Gabriel was motioning her into the lounge.

'Stephen's in bed,' he was saying, 'make yourself at home.'

Marianne collapsed onto Gabriel's comfy battered old sofa and let out a sigh of nervous relief. She had the weirdest feeling she'd come home.

Chapter Eighteen

It seemed wrong to be looking up Christmassy stuff at this time of year, but Cat was busy composing an article to go along with the launch of the competition, so she was online, searching through references to Nativity plays of yore, and tracking down more ancient carols to give people a taste of what they were looking for.

Perhaps, she wrote, *in these more difficult times, this Christmas we can return to the simplicity of yesteryear and dispense with too much expense, fuss and nonsense. Perhaps it is time to remember an event, that took place two thousand years ago, in a stable in Bethlehem . . .*

Too corny? Probably, but she knew that was what Bev would want.

Cat glanced at her watch – it was gone nine already. Noel had rung to say that he would be late, his train being delayed at Nuneaton apparently. The little ones were in bed, and James and Mel were playing on the Wii – last Christmas' must-have, over-expensive item, which Cat had felt guilty getting for them at the time. Now, with the credit crunch and the scary amount of borrowing that she and Noel had found themselves embroiled in over the last few years, such purchases were looking self-indulgent to say the least. How had it come to this, she wondered. Cat and Noel had always tried to be careful with money, but then the family had expanded, they'd needed extra space to accommodate the au pair, been unable to move thanks to the craziness of house prices, and ended up borrowing a shedload of money to pay for the loft conversion they required. They'd borrowed it on the strength of the partnership Noel had been promised, but which had yet to materialise. The building trade was bound to be affected by the financial slowdown, and Cat was worried sick about Noel losing his job but, if he shared her concerns, then he was keeping things very close to his chest. Not that he seemed to want to share all that much with her nowadays.

Cat saved the document she was working on and went downstairs to chase James into bed. He and Mel were in the middle of a row because James had won at tennis again.

'He always beats me, it's not fair!' burst out Mel, before rushing off in floods of tears.

'She's such a bad loser,' sulked James, about to throw his nunchuck on the floor – but one glance from his mother stopped him.

'Yeah, well, maybe she is,' said Cat, 'but I don't suppose it helps you rubbing her face in it.' James was generally very self-satisfied when he won and Cat found it most annoying when she played him. With Mel in the sensitive state she was in, he was bound to wind her up.

'You could go easy on her,' said Cat. 'She's having a tough time of it at the moment.'

'I know,' said James in disgusted tones. 'Hormones.'

James had recently had his puberty talk at school and was now apparently the expert on all things hormonal.

'Yup,' said Cat, 'so you have to feel sorry for her really. Now apologise and get to bed.'

Cat followed her son up the stairs and heard him dart in and mumble a feeble apology to Mel before darting out again. Taking a deep breath, she knocked on the door. She was never sure how Mel would react these days.

'May I come in?' she said.

'Suppose,' was the sullen reply.

Mel was sitting against the wall, red-eyed, playing with her mobile phone.

'Anything in particular bring that on, or just everything?' said Cat, squashing up next to her daughter.

'No, nothing. Oh, everything!' burst out Mel. 'I hate being eleven. It sucks.'

'Sure does,' said Cat, 'but twelve will be better, you'll see.'

'It might be worse,' said Mel.

'What, worse than this?' laughed Cat. 'Surely not.'

This elicited a small smile from her daughter and soon Cat had her giggling away as if nothing had happened.

'There's nothing really wrong though, is there, Mel?' Cat asked gently.

'NOoo,' said Mel disparagingly. 'You always ask that, and I always say no.'

'It's only because I worry about you,' said Cat.

'Well, don't,' said Mel, closing in on herself again. 'I'm fine. I just want to be left alone.'

'Okay,' said Cat, 'but get straight into bed and no reading, it's late.'

She paused at the door, looking at her daughter, who looked so vulnerable sitting there. Vulnerable but belligerent.

'You can tell me if something's wrong,' she said.

'There isn't anything wrong,' said Mel, 'except that I want you to go away so I can get undressed.'

Cat laughed, that was a bit more like it. She just hoped that Mel wasn't hiding anything from her. She sighed. Such a short time ago, she'd been terrified by the responsibility of having a newborn baby. Now she worried about her almost teenage daughter being bullied. It was just as well no one had ever told her what being a parent was really like, otherwise she might never have done it.

The last person Gabriel had expected to see when he went to answer the door was Marianne. He'd assumed it would be Dan, who sometimes called in at this time in the evening for a beer. It was automatic for him to ask her in. Gabriel had inherited a welcoming gene from his mother and not to have done so would have felt unnatural. One bonus he was discovering from Eve's departure was that he could invite friends round again. Eve had been wary of people and hated entertaining, so over the years Gabriel had suppressed the welcoming side of his nature. He went into the kitchen to sort out drinks while Marianne browsed through his CD collection. It seemed natural and right that she was here. Gabriel was very glad she'd come.

'What would you like to drink?' he called from the kitchen. 'Wine or beer?'

'Actually, would you mind if I had something soft?' said Marianne. 'I hate going to work with a heavy head. You wouldn't believe how bad it is trying to teach a bunch of five-year-olds with a hangover.'

'Yes, checking on the sheep early in the morning is equally unforgiving,' said Gabriel as he came into the lounge, scouring it for dirty mugs. 'Sorry about the mess. I try hard not to, but it's all too easy to slide into bachelor-pad chaos.'

'It's neater than my place,' said Marianne, laughing as she put down a KT Tunstall CD. 'Can I put this on?'

'Be my guest,' said Gabriel. 'Tea or coffee?'

'Coffee would be great, thanks,' said Marianne as she put the CD on.

'So, how did the meeting go?' said Gabriel as he sat down opposite her. The light from the lamps cast shadows across her face, but he could see from here the way her eyes lit up as she talked, and the natural spontaneity of her manner. Marianne was like a breath of fresh air in his cobweb-filled life. She was bringing light and dance back into the unparalleled gloom he'd been living in since – since, well, forever. Gabriel had never liked to analyse it too much, but now, with a bit of distance between him and Eve, he was beginning to see just how unhealthy their relationship had been.

'Not great,' said Marianne. 'Apparently the post office has got to go, but Miss Woods and Diana Carew are planning to join forces to set it up in the village hall instead. I have no idea if that is feasible or not but, hey ho, it will keep them happy.'

'Miss Woods and Diana agreed on something? Wonders will never cease,' said Gabriel.

'My sentiments exactly,' said Marianne. 'But joking aside, I do hope it will work. It would break Vera's heart to lose the post office. Not to mention causing a huge blow to the village community.'

'You really like it here, don't you?' Gabriel said. 'Don't you miss the city at all?'

'Sometimes,' said Marianne. 'But I fell in love with this place from the moment I arrived. I love its peace and tranquillity and the fact that I can go walking on the hills in all weathers. I feel hemmed in in the city. Here I feel free and alive and, well, happy, I suppose. I'm glad I was persuaded to stay.'

'I'm glad too,' Gabriel smiled at her shyly. He was glad, very glad. That Marianne had come into his life. That she was here now. He still didn't know quite where this was leading, but he was enjoying the newness, the uncertainty, and the sheer joy of getting to know someone as uncomplicated as Marianne appeared to be. Yes, after Eve, she was definitely a breath of fresh air.

* * *

Marianne was enjoying herself too. After her initial anxiety that Gabriel might not want her here, he had put her so much at her ease, she was relaxing into their normal cosy friendship again. She had never been this relaxed with Luke. Never. The whole time she'd been with him, Marianne realised with a jolt, she'd been on tenterhooks in case she said the wrong thing, did the wrong thing, or generally didn't live up to expectations. That was no way to live your life.

'Penny for 'em?' Gabriel's voice intruded into her thoughts.

'Just thinking about Luke, and realising I had a lucky escape,' said Marianne. 'Oh dear, does that mean I'm no longer a member of the Lonely Hearts Club?'

'You can be an honorary member,' said Gabriel. 'So what's changed your mind about Luke?'

'It's taken me a while,' said Marianne, 'but it's recently dawned on me that I was never ever going to fit in in his world. I can't believe I was so stupid as to think I could.'

'Yes, well, we all make mistakes,' said Gabriel. He looked incredibly sad when he said this, and Marianne noticed the quick glance towards the photo on the mantelpiece.

'Is that your wife?' she asked. She was treading carefully, but this seemed the moment for confidences somehow.

Gabriel walked slowly to the fireplace and picked up the picture.

'That's me, Eve and Stephen when Stephen was first born,' he said.

Marianne looked at the smiling couple, a small baby between them. It was hard to imagine that things could have gone so wrong.

'You look really happy there,' said Marianne. 'She's very beautiful.'

'Eve was high as a kite on diazepam when that picture

was taken,' said Gabriel. 'And two weeks later she was in hospital, having taken an overdose.'

'What on earth happened?' Marianne asked, shocked. 'Sorry. I didn't mean to pry. You don't have to say if you don't want to.'

'No, it's probably good for me to talk,' said Gabriel. He rubbed his stubble with his hands and put the picture back on the shelf. 'She was – is – lovely, Eve. But she's fragile. Very fragile. Her home life wasn't exactly stable and I knew she was prone to getting a bit down about things before I married her. I thought I could help her, you see.'

'And you couldn't?' Marianne prompted.

'It's like dealing with an alcoholic. You can't solve their problems, only they can do that.' Gabriel sighed, and looked as if he was in some very far-off, dark place. 'It was different when we met, of course. I was in London, earning good money in marketing. Eve was a secretary in the same company, and we just seemed to hit it off. She was so lively and vivacious and fun. It never dawned on me that anything was wrong.'

'What changed?' prompted Marianne.

'It was a while after we married when I realised she had a problem sticking at anything. I'd stayed with the same firm for five years during which time Eve had had six jobs. Then it was her mood swings. One minute she'd be on top of the world and then she'd be down in the dumps. I thought it was my fault, of course. I did everything I could to make her happy, but eventually she came clean and told me how bad her depression actually was. So we went to the doctor and she got some happy pills and she seemed all right for a while . . .'

'And then?'

'And then we had Stephen. I discovered afterwards that an event like that can trigger a psychotic episode in someone like Eve, but I didn't know that at the time. Eve seemed morbidly depressed that something would go wrong with the baby and was crying all the time. I couldn't leave her alone with him for a minute as I didn't know what she would do. One day I came into the room and she was holding a pillow over his face. She kept crying and saying it was all for the best, this world was too cruel, that it would have been better if he hadn't been born. I took her back to the doctor, got her on stronger medication, and then a week later she tricked me into taking Stephen for a walk. When I got back I found her unconscious next to a suicide note.'

'That's terrible, oh, Gabriel, I'm so sorry,' said Marianne.

'It was,' said Gabriel. 'Eve was in hospital for months after that. Without my parents, who came down to stay with me, I don't know what I'd have done. Eventually she came home, and over time things got better. After a while I thought about coming back here. Mum and Dad were finding the farm too much and Eve had always raved about how wonderful it was up here. I thought she'd like it. I went back to agricultural college, sold our house and we moved back.'

'And did she like it?'

Gabriel sighed.

'At first Eve seemed better here, but she never settled to being a proper mother to Stephen. And I couldn't trust her with him . . .'

Marianne could see Gabriel was close to tears. Instinctively, she moved towards him and held his hand. He closed his own around hers and continued, 'We staggered along like that for years. Never going out because Eve didn't like difficult social situations. Never having people round because Eve couldn't cope. I was constantly on edge in case she did something dangerous, either to herself or Stephen. Of late, I had thought she was getting better.

226

But last winter, she lost the little job she'd had in the village shop and suddenly she hit a downward spiral. I was on the verge of suggesting she go back to the doctor when she walked out.'

'Where is she now?' Marianne asked.

'I have no idea,' said Gabriel. 'She was with her mother at Easter, but she wouldn't talk to me then.'

'What a terrible story,' said Marianne. 'So sad for all of you.'

'Worse for Stephen than me,' said Gabriel. 'At least I can understand Eve's ill, even if I hate it, but Stephen still doesn't get why his mother is so different from other mums. For a long time he didn't want to go to school because he was being picked on. In a way, it's been better for him since she left.'

'At least he's got you and Pippa,' said Marianne. 'That will stand him in good stead.'

'Do you think?' said Gabriel. 'I have to be both mother and father to him. And sometimes it's really hard.'

Marianne squeezed his hand tightly.

'Well, I think you're doing a fantastic job. He's lucky to have you.' She smiled at Gabriel, and suddenly he gave her the most dazzling smile back.

'Thanks,' he said. 'I can't tell you how much it's helping having you in my life.'

Marianne's heart did a sudden lurch. Did he – was it possible that he could – feel the same way as she did?

For a moment they sat looking at each other as if someone had pressed the pause button, then Gabriel moved as if to . . .

'Daddy!' A small voice was shouting from the top of the stairs. Oh my God. Marianne had forgotten for a moment about Stephen.

'I'd better go,' said Gabriel. Was it her imagination, or was he tearing himself away reluctantly?

'Me too,' said Marianne in some confusion. 'I'll let myself out.'

'Thanks for the chat,' said Gabriel. 'It really helped.'

He bounded up the stairs shouting to Stephen, 'What is it, you little rascal? You were supposed to be asleep hours ago.' Halfway up he paused, turned those deep brown eyes on her, and said, 'Call me.'

'Okay,' said Marianne as casually as she could muster but, as she walked down the garden path, her heart was singing.

Noel let himself into a house that seemed worryingly quiet. Since Magda had gone the noise levels had halved, it was true. (When she had been there, if she wasn't on the phone arguing with Sergei in excited Russian, she was playing her 1980s thrash metal music way too loud.) But he was still used to so much noise all the time the silence was slightly unnerving. The lights were all turned off so he switched on the hall light and poked his head in the lounge. No sign of Cat there. Nor in the family room. As he left it, he heard the familiar sound of books sliding off the shelf. That damned bookshelf. It seemed to sum up his life somehow. In his fantasy farmhouse the shelves were always intact, and everything he made fitted perfectly. How he wished he was there and not in this draughty London house with its poky little garden: it was a financial millstone around his neck.

Cat wasn't in the kitchen either. Noel went to the fridge and got out a can of lager. He looked around to see if Cat had left him something to eat. He'd planned to eat on the train, but the buffet car had been shut, and, while he would have liked to have had a beer, he and Matt had instead been trying to thrash out a solution to their mud problem, without much luck. If he thought there was any chance of getting a job somewhere, anywhere, else, Noel would hand in his notice tomorrow, before he finally got pushed.

Cat must be working. He went upstairs, pausing to look at the little ones, who were fast asleep. A light swiftly went off in James' room as Noel entered. He ruffled his son's hair and said, 'I saw you, you monkey. Sleep. Now.'

'Night, night, Daddy,' said James, looking sleepy. Hard to remember he was a nine-year-old, testosterone-filled boy during the day. James always looked angelic at bedtime.

Mel was definitely still awake, lying in bed listening to her iPod and immersed in a Darren Shan book.

'Sleep,' said Noel, 'otherwise you'll never get up in the morning. Where's your mother?'

'On the computer,' said Mel. 'She's been there all evening.'

'Right,' said Noel. 'I'd better go and chase her off then.'

He climbed up the stairs to the top of the house. Cat was crouched in the dark over a computer screen – the only light in the room coming from that and her desklamp.

'Oh, hello,' she said. 'I didn't hear you come in. I was just finishing this off.'

Cat barely looked at him when she said this, she was so deep in concentration. Sometimes he felt like she hardly noticed him.

'Right, I'll just go downstairs and get myself something to eat then,' said Noel.

Cat looked up, frowning.

'Haven't you eaten?' she said. 'I thought you were going to eat on the train.'

'I was,' said Noel, 'but the buffet car on the train was shut. What have you had?'

'I only fancied beans on toast,' said Cat.

No wonder Cat was so skinny, she ate like a bird these days.

'Oh, right,' said Noel. 'I'll just sort myself out something then.'

'I won't be long,' said Cat.

Noel went downstairs with a heavy heart. He'd been planning to tell Cat about his work situation tonight but she seemed so distracted, and he felt so shattered, now probably wasn't the best moment.

And when Cat did eventually come downstairs, she sat next to him for all of ten minutes on the sofa, before declaring herself too tired to stay up a moment longer and going to bed.

Noel cracked open another can of lager, and switched to ITV3 where an old Sly Stallone film was showing. When Noel was young, he'd imagined that hitting middle age would be a point in his life when he had all the answers. So how was it he was sitting here alone, worrying about the future and feeling more uncertain about life than ever?

Chapter Nineteen

Call me.

Marianne was on one of her periodic yomps through the hills. Now that spring was here she was enjoying these walks more than ever. The sight of lambs gambolling in the fresh green fields couldn't help but lighten the spirits and the blustery breezes when, after a determined scramble, she'd finally reached the top of the hill, made her feel gloriously, wonderfully alive. She looked back down the valley towards Hope Christmas. The houses looked like miniature dolls' houses nestling in the hills, which brimmed with purple and pink heathers. It was so beautiful. She was so happy here now, but perhaps she could be even happier.

Marianne knew she hadn't mistaken the look in Gabriel's eyes the other night. She knew that she hadn't imagined it, that he was feeling the way she was feeling. But, and it was a big but, should she, could she, take things further? Marianne would have liked to have been bold enough to proposition a man like Lisa and Carly would – their ability to pick up men never failed to astonish her. They had frequently admonished her in the past to live like a twenty-first-century woman, not like a nineteenth-century heroine, waiting 'like a lapdog', as Carly always put it, for some handsome swain to turn up. But Marianne couldn't help it. She

231

liked the sensation of being courted. She wanted the romance of it. It wasn't her fault that nineteenth-century fictional heroes always seemed so much better than the real thing. No wonder she'd been such a soft touch for Luke. What a sap.

But now, here was Gabriel putting her off her stride, asking her to take the initiative. There was certainly a bit – what was she talking about, a lot – of her wanting to do so, but she was conscious that he wasn't free and that the situation with Stephen was delicate to say the least. She wasn't entirely sure that she wanted the responsibility of children just yet. Particularly that of a child with so many issues. As a teacher, Marianne had seen enough of the stresses caused by family break-up to know that taking on Stephen was not something she should do lightly. But all that aside, maybe she didn't have the courage to take that first step anyway. And then again, suppose she was wrong and he was only after friendship? She'd feel a total fool if that were the case.

'You won't know if you don't try,' she declared loudly, as she came over a ridge of the hill and started her descent into the next valley.

'That you won't.' Ralph Nicholas, who was coming up over the other side of the hill with his dog. For someone apparently so old, he was remarkably not out of breath. 'Which is precisely what I think about stopping that monstrosity my grandson seems intent on inflicting on us.'

He waved his hand behind him and Marianne saw for the very first time what her erstwhile fiancé had been up to over the last few months. She didn't normally walk out this way. The excavation work for the eco town was clearly under way. It was a scene of utter devastation. The ground was all churned up, trees had been torn down, and it looked like something from *The Lord of the Rings*.

'I had no idea it would be so destructive,' said Marianne. 'I thought eco towns were all about preservation, not destruction.'

'My thoughts exactly,' said Ralph.

'You know the Post Office Committee was planning to talk to Luke about encouraging prospective buyers of eco town property to support us, don't you?' Marianne said.

'Sadly, I fear, they'll be wasting their time,' said Ralph. 'Luke hasn't a sentimental bone in his body. He must take after his father.'

'They neither of them take after you, that's for sure,' said Marianne.

'Ah, well, that's because I adopted Luke's father,' said Ralph. 'I live in hope that it will turn out well in the end.'

'It may yet,' said Marianne. 'You never know. Luke might realise the error of his ways.'

'He might,' said Ralph, 'but I doubt it.' He whistled to his dog, who came bounding up covered in mud. 'I think you may find a friend of yours in the valley. There are an awful lot of sheep to keep track of on the hills this time of year, don't you know?'

He walked off whistling to himself with what Marianne could only describe as a twinkle in his eye. How could he possibly know what she was thinking?

Noel was sitting at home, working on the kids' computer in the playroom. He'd given Cat some guff about the pressures of an office move (depressingly he was going to end his days at GRB hot-desking) making it impossible to work in the office. Really it was that there wasn't enough work to keep him there. Although there was a second computer in Cat's office, she'd made it clear that she hadn't welcomed his intrusion into her workspace, so he'd come downstairs to the kids' computer, ostensibly to draw up the plans for the heating system for the proposed community centre, which was apparently going to be the hub of the eco town.

Having spent a very happy morning mooching about Hope Christmas on his last visit, Noel was now convinced that the designers of the town had utterly missed the point. There was a living, breathing community already there. People had begun to recognise him. The man who ran the antiques shop had taken to joking that Noel always came in yet never bought, and the woman in the estate agents', having seen him mooching outside looking at the pictures, had dragged him in and shown him a whole variety of properties, all of which he coveted. When Noel was in Hope Christmas he bought organic meat at the butcher's (he told Cat he'd got it in Smithfield Market), Shropshire honey that he pretended he'd picked up in Oxford Street, far too many books from the tiny bookshop with its informative and friendly booksellers, and used the internet facilities in Aunty Betty's Coffee Shop, where he had met an ancient crone who had got him to show her how to surf.

Noel had fallen in love with Hope Christmas, and yet he had barely mentioned it to Cat. He couldn't even explain to himself why he didn't want to talk to her about it, but it was like he was having a fantasy life, far removed from his normal stresses and strains. And, for now, he just wanted to keep it secret.

From what he had seen of the place, it seemed like the perfect place to live already, so who needed to create a new town so close by? The prices were going to be out of the range of most of the young people in the surrounding villages, even in these uncertain times. Noel wished more than ever that someone at GRB had listened to his suggestions about utilising existing buildings to create sustainable and affordable housing. Every time he visited the building site, he felt sick. A perfectly beautiful valley was being destroyed. And for what? Just so that Luke Nicholas and his cronies could line their pockets.

'Can you do the school run today?' Cat had crept up on him unawares. 'I've got a really urgent feature to finish by five.'

Noel pulled a face. He hated the school run, always feeling out of place among the mums comparing notes about PTA committee meetings and children's tummy bugs.

'I've got a fair bit on myself,' he began to protest.

'Yes, I noticed,' Cat said drily, nodding at the screen, which was displaying the fact that he'd just lost his third game of Spider Solitaire.

'I was only taking a break,' said Noel. 'Didn't you ask your mum?'

This time it was Cat's turn to pull a face.

'I just can't risk it, Noel,' she said. 'She's become so unreliable. I don't know what's wrong with her. But I daren't ask her to pick them up again in case she forgets. Last time it happened she was so upset, I decided neither of us could go through that again.'

Noel frowned. Cat had been mentioning problems with Louise for weeks – he felt guilty for not realising how bad things had got.

'Have you tried to talk to her about it?' he asked.

'You know Mum,' said Cat. 'She would never admit something was wrong. I tried to get her to go to the doctor, but she wouldn't. She says she feels fine, and I'm making a fuss about nothing.'

'She's probably right,' said Noel. 'Don't forget she is in her seventies now.'

'Seventy-three isn't that old,' said Cat, 'and, as she keeps telling me, she isn't senile yet. She never forgot anything till recently, but now it's really hard to get her to remember the simplest things. Yet when you talk to her about the war, she remembers everything, from collecting shrapnel in the streets to having lessons in the air raid shelters. Weird.'

'Very,' said Noel. 'It might just be a phase, you never know.'

'Yeah, it might,' said Cat, looking unconvinced and rather sad. It wasn't like her to make a fuss. Normally she did deal with all the domestic stuff. As he were here, perhaps he should pull his weight a little more.

'Okay. I'll go and pick the kids up, but can you do tea?'

'It's a deal,' said Cat.

She went back upstairs and Noel started another game of Spider Solitaire. He lost. Any more of this and he was going to end up feeling completely emasculated.

Gabriel was tacking a fence post in. Someone driving a digger from the worksite had accidentally run it into his property. Gabriel wanted to make sure the fence was back in place again before he lost any sheep. It was a lovely clear day and he was enjoying his work. He never felt lonely here, out on the hills, but was very much at home and in his element. If it weren't for Stephen, he'd be tempted to occasionally sleep the night in the old shepherd's croft on the top of the hill. Especially in summer. As a young man, he'd often spent time up here on his own with the sheep. He still missed that. Stephen loved being out here too, but he was still young enough to get bored after too long, so this morning Gabriel had left him with his cousins.

'Hello there.' Gabriel looked up from his tacking and swallowed hard. Marianne was standing before him, the sun playing through her dark curls, the wind ruffling them. He'd been an inch away from kissing her the other night. He wondered if she knew. She hadn't called him, so Gabriel had assumed she either didn't know how he felt or was avoiding him.

'Hi,' he said. 'I'm just mending this fence.'

'Yes, I can see that,' said Marianne. 'Do you need any help?'

'That's what I like about you,' said Gabriel, handing her a hammer, 'you're a doer not a chatterer.'

'Oh, I can chat,' said Marianne, 'but I can't help having a strong streak of practicality. My dad was most insistent that I learnt how to fend for myself in the DIY department from an early age.'

'Here, can you bang that post in?' said Gabriel.

They worked in silence for a little while and then Gabriel found himself unable to keep quiet any longer.

'You didn't call,' he said.

'I was going to,' said Marianne.

'I sense a but here,' said Gabriel.

'It's only, well – look, I'm going to be very honest.' Marianne's words came out in a babbling rush. 'I like you – a lot – but there's Stephen and Eve. What if she comes back? What if she doesn't? Does Stephen even want a stepmum? Do I want a stepson? And you've both been through so much—'

'You can stop right there,' said Gabriel. 'I think maybe it's time we both put the past behind us and said goodbye to the Lonely Hearts Club, don't you?' He flung down his tools and, pulling her into his arms with joyous abandon, he kissed her firmly on the mouth. 'Now, does that answer your question?'

'What question?' said Marianne, looking stunned.

'The one you were going to ask about whether or not you could put me through this. And the answer is, yes, you most definitely can.'

Cat was just typing the last words of her feature on 'How to Make the Most of Your Time' (honestly, why had she

237

created an alter ego who was so bossy?) when the phone rang. Cursing, she answered it. Didn't anyone understand about the pressure of deadlines?

'Is there a Mrs Tinsall there?' a voice with a strong Jamaican accent said. 'My name's PC Josephs, and I think I may have your mother here. She seems a little upset.'

Forgetting instantly all about deadlines, Cat said, 'Oh my God, is she all right? She hasn't hurt herself or anything, has she?'

'No, nothing like that,' said the voice, 'but one of her neighbours called us. She was found half an hour ago wandering up and down the street in her nightie. She didn't seem to know where she lived. Luckily her neighbour had a key, so we've got her back home and we're having a nice cup of tea. She's rather distressed though, and is asking for you.'

'I'm on my way,' said Cat, ice chilling her bones. All the fear and anxiety she'd been feeling for months was coming together in a hideous rush. She couldn't let herself think too much about it though, otherwise she'd be sick. Shaking like a leaf, she typed the last sentence and, ever the professional, sent it to Bev with a quick note to say she'd been called away urgently. She rang Noel who, typically, had his mobile switched off, and left him a message, then she got in the car and drove like a maniac to Mum's, trying to suppress the panic bubbling up inside her.

'I really don't know what all the fuss is about,' said Mum when she arrived, looking almost cross that Cat was there. 'I was just a little confused, that's all.'

'Mum, it's the middle of the afternoon,' said Cat, 'and you're wearing your nightie.'

'I felt like a little nap,' said her mother. 'And then I got up and forgot I was wearing it. I only went to the shop to get some milk.' She frowned. 'But then, it was very strange.

238

Like a shutter going down or something. I couldn't quite remember where I was. Luckily this kind young gentleman has been looking after me.'

'Oh, Mum,' said Cat. 'What are you like?' She tried to make a joke, but she'd never felt less like joking. There was no pretending anymore. Something was very very badly wrong.

Cat saw PC Josephs to the door, having prevented Mum from giving him a tip, and thanked him profusely.

'Don't you worry, love,' he said, 'it's my job. Can't have a nice lady like that meeting a mugger, can we?'

Cat laughed and shut the door. She leant against it heavily and took a deep breath. Time to tackle Mum and finally get her to admit they had a very big problem.

Chapter Twenty

'You know, there's really no need for you to come with me,' Mum said crossly as Cat came to pick her up. 'I'm quite capable of getting to the doctor's on my own.'

'Yes, but I think it would be a good idea to have someone to sit with you,' said Cat. 'Sometimes there's a lot to take in when you see a doctor. I know it helped me when I was pregnant having Noel there, there was always something I'd forget to ask.'

Mum still looked mutinous, but at least she got in the car.

'Now, have you got your keys?' said Cat.

'Of course I have my keys. Don't fuss,' said Mum. 'Why wouldn't I have them?'

Why indeed, thought Cat. One of the hardest things she was discovering about dealing with her mother lately was that she was so adamant about things, and so forgetful, that she really had no idea that there had been a problem in the first place.

They reached the surgery in good time and, having signed themselves in, sat in the large modern airy waiting room among young mums and babies – it was evidently baby clinic today. Cat thought back with a pang to how helpful Mum had been when Mel was born. She'd come in every day doling out tea and sympathy and taking over on baby duties when she noticed Cat drooping. How things had changed. These days Mum required nearly as much parenting as any one of Cat's children, and there was no one to prop her up when she drooped. Cat was ever more conscious of a baton being passed to her and it was one that she didn't want to pick up.

'Louise Carpenter.' Dr Miles' voice came over the tannoy.

Cat and her mum gathered up their things and went into the doctor's surgery.

'Hello, Mrs Carpenter, and what can I do for you today?' Dr Miles smiled at them both.

'Well, I feel a bit of a fraud really,' Cat's mum said, turning on a charm offensive. 'I don't think there's anything wrong with me really, apart from that I'm a bit forgetful. Only Cat would insist on me coming.'

'And how does this forgetfulness manifest itself?' said Dr Miles.

'It's nothing, really,' Mum said. 'Nothing at all. Just that I sometimes can't remember where I've put things. I'm sure it's quite normal at my age.'

Cat interposed quickly, 'Come on, Mum, it's a little more than that. You rang me up recently because you couldn't remember how to make pastry.'

'Did I?' Her mother looked doubtful. 'I find that most unlikely. Anyway, I'm sure it's nothing, and we're wasting the doctor's time. I'm sure she has really sick people to see.'

'No, of course you're not wasting my time,' said Dr Miles. 'Let's just run through some points about your general health and take your blood pressure, shall we?'

Cat admired the deftness with which Dr Miles teasingly pulled the story out of Mum, clearly not at all bamboozled by the 'I'm perfectly fine' approach. When it got to the description of what had happened the previous day, she paused and looked at Cat.

241

'Thank you, that's very helpful, Mrs Carpenter,' she said. 'I think I've got enough to build a good picture of what's happening now.'

'I'm sure I'm wasting your time,' muttered Mum, 'there's nothing wrong with me.'

'I'm sorry, Mrs Carpenter, but I think there does appear to be a problem,' said Dr Miles gently. 'Something seems to be going wrong with the hard-wiring in your brain, which is leading to these lapses of concentration. It may be that you are having TIAs – little strokes – which are shutting off the blood vessels in part of the brain, or it may be something else altogether. I need to run some tests to find out.'

'Oh?' said Cat, alarmed. 'What kind of tests?'

'They're nothing to worry about. Just a blood test and an MRI scan to find out if we can get to the bottom of what's happening,' said Dr Miles. 'I just want to make sure we've covered all the possibilities. Like I say, the most likely cause of your mother's problems is that she's having TIAs. But it's perfectly normal at her age, and I'm sure we can sort everything out.' She smiled reassuringly at Cat, who smiled back with a confidence she didn't feel. Whatever was wrong with her mother, Cat knew it wasn't going to be sorted out that easily.

'This feels a bit strange,' Marianne said as Gabriel ushered her out of the car and into the lobby of the country pub where he was taking her for a meal. It was ten miles from Hope Christmas. They'd both agreed that for Stephen's sake they should take things slowly, and, for the time being, secret. Marianne hadn't even said anything to Pippa about it, though she was dying to.

'What is?' asked Gabriel.

'It's really strange coming on a first date when I feel

I know you already so well,' said Marianne. 'I don't think I've ever done that before. I almost feel like I'm dating my brother.'

'Thanks a bunch,' said Gabriel.

'My brother isn't nearly as good looking as you,' said Marianne. 'It's just – well, this will take some getting used to.'

'In a nice way, I hope?' Gabriel said, giving her a little thrill as he took her hand.

'The nicest possible,' said Marianne.

They were ushered into a small lobby area with dark oak panels and a fire burning in the hearth. The early spring weather had turned cold and heavy rain was forecast for that evening. The friendly owner came over and gave them menus, and they ordered their drinks.

Marianne, feeling a little nervous, ordered a G&T, but Gabriel, who was driving, ordered a Coke. They perused their menus in silence before Gabriel declared he'd have the dover sole and Marianne plumped for duck.

'It's lovely here,' she said. 'I've never been before.'

'It's a well kept secret to all but the locals,' said Gabriel. 'Can't have outsiders coming here, can we now?'

'Oh, stop it,' said Marianne. 'Don't tell me I need to have lived in Hope Christmas for three generations before I'll be accepted properly.'

'Five at least,' said Gabriel solemnly. Marianne threw a beer mat at him.

'Cripes, we'd better duck,' said Gabriel. 'There's Miss Woods and, good lord, is that Ralph Nicholas with her?'

Miss Woods was indeed being helped up from her seat by Ralph Nicholas.

'This is a bit cloak and dagger, isn't it?' said Marianne, giggling from behind her menu.

'You still haven't cottoned on to how a small village works

yet, have you?' said Gabriel. 'By the time they're back in Hope Christmas, everyone will know we've had dinner together. And I'd rather Stephen found it out from me than from the village gossips.' Miss Woods had her coat on and was leaving the restaurant. 'Phew, I think we got away with it,' continued Gabriel.

'It's all right,' said a twinkling voice over their heads. 'I won't tell if you won't.'

Marianne wanted the ground to swallow her up. What would Luke's grandfather think of her?

'I think,' said Ralph, uncannily reading her thoughts again, 'you've made a much better choice this time around.' With that he doffed his hat to them, winked and was gone.

'Blimey,' said Marianne, 'I've gone weak at the knees.'

'And you haven't even had your entrée yet,' grinned Gabriel.

'Oh, do shut up,' said Marianne, laughing. Her nerves had vanished. She was with Gabriel, and there was nowhere else she'd rather be.

'How did it go with your mum?' Noel had gone out for the day, purportedly to work but, while he had gone into the office, there had been so little to do, he'd left fairly quickly, particularly when he spotted Julie making a beeline towards him. He'd wandered down Oxford Street and done some desultory window shopping but, despite the temptation to spend, had decided now really wasn't the time to inform Cat they'd just got a new LCD TV, and so eventually found himself in the pub. He'd rung up a couple of ex work colleagues, but they were all busy and had only been able to have a couple of pints each before shooting off, which only served to make Noel feel even more despondent than before.

'Tell you later,' said Cat, who was standing in the kitchen

folding the washing while simultaneously reciting the eight times table with Paige. He marvelled at her ability to do that. It was all he could do to get the washing out of the machine, let alone do maths homework at the same time. Something was bubbling on the stove.

'Something smells good,' said Noel.

'Shit, I nearly forgot about that,' said Cat, rescuing the pan before it boiled over. 'It's only spag bol. Mel!' She called up the stairs. 'Your turn to set the table.'

'Do I absolutely have to?' Mel clumped heavily down the stairs, looking for all the world as if she'd been asked to walk over hot coals.

'Yes, you absolutely do,' said Cat. 'Your littlest sister has done it three nights running.'

'It's so unfair,' sulked Mel, but a look from Noel stopped the rebellion in its tracks. Even Mel knew when not to push it.

'Crikey, you stink of booze, Dad,' she said.

'You've been to the pub?' Cat looked incredulous. 'It's all right for some.'

Noel looked away. How to say that he'd been in the pub because his job was dwindling away to nothing? How to let her know she was married to a man who was worse than useless? Who very soon might not be able to provide for their children? How to begin to say all that?

'So, how did it go?' Noel chose a quiet moment when Mel had gone off to call the others for tea and Paige had gone to put her books away.

'Okay, I suppose,' said Cat. She looked a little teary before saying, 'Dr Miles thinks she may have had a minor stroke, but she's going to run some tests to make sure. I just don't know how serious it is, or how worried I should be.'

'Oh, Cat.' Noel gave her a hug. 'Try not to worry. It might not be anything to worry about.'

245

'No, it might not be,' said Cat, but she didn't look convinced.

She pulled away from him wiping her tears away as the children thundered down the stairs for their tea.

Noel stared out of the kitchen window. It seemed there was never going to be a good time to come clean.

It was chucking it down as Gabriel and Marianne left the Feathers. The pathetic excuse for an umbrella that Gabriel had taken out with him had turned inside out in the wild wind that was whipping furiously across the car park, so Gabriel abandoned it and they ran giggling through the rain like a pair of school kids.

They were soaked through by the time they climbed into Gabriel's ratty old Land Rover, but he rooted around in the rucksack he kept in there for emergencies and soon produced a towel to dry them off slightly.

'Sorry it's a bit rough and ready,' he said.

'No sweat,' said Marianne, who genuinely didn't seem to mind the shabbiness of the interior, or the fact that it smelt of dog.

The rain was coming down so heavily, the windscreen wipers were barely making any difference. Flick, flack, flick, flack they went, making little impact on the sheets of rain pouring down the windscreen. Soon the windows were all steamed up despite Gabriel having the blower on full pelt. It felt oddly spooky in the car, driving down the dark road, barely able to see the white lines thanks to the huge puddles that lined their route. Gabriel slowed down to a steady thirty.

'Sorry, it's going to be a slow old drive home,' Gabriel said. 'The road to Hope Christmas is a bit hairy at the best of times but in these conditions it's going to be lethal. I'm sorry, I hadn't realised quite how bad it was going to be.'

'Do you want to ring Pippa, to let her know we're on our way?' said Marianne.

'Good idea,' said Gabriel, but just then the phone rang. 'Oh, that's her now,' he said. 'Great minds think alike. Pippa . . . you what? Are you all okay? We'll be there as soon as we can.'

'What's the matter?' said Marianne.

'The river's burst its banks and Hope Christmas is flooding. Pippa's got water coming through the front door. Bloody hell. They're closer to the stream than we are, but for all I know my house is flooding too, and Benjy's inside on his own. I know they issued flood warnings, but nothing like this has happened in living memory. I bet it's something do with that sodding eco town. They've been dumping silt into the river for weeks now. Damn. I daren't drive any faster than this. It's going to take ages to get home.'

The rain was showing no signs of letting up and soon Gabriel found himself slowing down to twenty. They passed an abandoned Land Rover at one point, but there were no other signs of life on the road. A few minutes later, a deer ran out in front of them, gave a a startled look into Gabriel's headlights, and ran off into the dark.

Neither he or Marianne spoke as they inched their way further towards Hope Christmas. Why had he decided to come out to the Feathers tonight of all evenings? Gabriel was cursing himself for not realising how bad the rain was going to be. But who could have predicted this? As he drove through Ash Bourton, the village before Hope Christmas, he could see the roads there were awash and people were sandbagging like crazy. A policeman put out his hand to slow him down.

'Where are you trying to get to?' he asked.

'Hope Christmas,' said Gabriel. 'How's the road?'

'You'll be lucky if you make it all the way,' said the policeman. 'They're telling me the High Street's flooded.'

'Well, we have to get back,' said Gabriel. 'I have a son . . .'

'Take it easy then, sir,' said the policeman, and waved them on their way.

'You okay?' Marianne gave Gabriel's hand a quick squeeze.

'I just want to get back,' said Gabriel. His stomach was a ball of tension and he realised he was gripping the wheel harder than it warranted. It was just as well he was, because a car coming in the opposite direction lost its grip on the road and was spinning towards them. Instinctively Gabriel swerved into the bank to avoid it, narrowly missing a tree. The Land Rover came to a juddering halt and he and Marianne were flung forward with the impact. Quickly establishing that everyone had escaped uninjured, Gabriel got going again. They were now a mile from Hope Christmas, but the distance seemed interminable. The rain continued to teem down and, as Gabriel crouched over the wheel, concentrating as hard as he could on what little he could see of the road ahead, he had the most peculiar feeling that he and Marianne were the only two people left on the planet.

Eventually, to his relief, the sign for Hope Christmas flashed up, and the road bent round to the left towards the High Street. Nothing could have prepared them for the sight that greeted them.

'Oh my God.' Marianne was stunned. 'What's – what's happened to the High Street?'

As they came down the valley into what should have been the High Street, all they could see was a torrent of water sweeping through the town. Half the cottages were submerged in water and where the village hall had been destroyed. A police officer was standing helplessly watching the devastation and talking urgently into his walkie talkie.

'I'm sorry, sir,' he said, 'you can't go on. As you can see, the road's impassable.'

'But my son – he's on the other side of the village with

his aunt, I have to get to him.' Gabriel couldn't see anything beyond his frantic need to get to Stephen.

'I'm sorry, sir, truly I am,' said the police officer. 'It all happened so fast, see. The river burst its banks and suddenly we had a flash flood. The emergency services were totally unprepared. But help is on its way. I might be able to get you across when they bring the boats in.'

'Is there anything we can do?' said Marianne.

'Maybe, when the water subsides, you can help me get people out,' said the policeman dubiously. 'But I don't know where they're going to go, because the village hall was swept away.'

Gabriel rang Pippa again and was relieved to hear that everyone was all right, although she and Dan were now bailing out their hall.

They waited for what seemed like forever before the firemen arrived with a boat. Gabriel put on his wellingtons, also handily stowed in the back of the Land Rover, and passed an old pair of Eve's to Marianne, before climbing into the boat and rowing across with the firemen. The firemen quickly established who was in need of rescue and who wasn't – several of the town's oldest inhabitants lived in the cottages – before taking them what was now in effect upstream to the lane leading to Gabriel's house.

They got to Pippa's house to discover Pippa and Dan bailing out for all they were worth.

'Christ,' said Gabriel. 'Are the kids okay?'

'All asleep upstairs,' said Pippa. She was wrapped in an old mac over her pyjamas and looked totally shell-shocked.

'Do you mind if I just check how things are at home?' said Gabriel. 'I left Benjy in the kitchen and I don't want him to be frightened. I'll try not to be too long.'

'No problem,' said Pippa. 'I don't think we're going anywhere for a while.'

'I'll stay,' said Marianne, wading across the muddy water to help Pippa.

Gabriel walked as fast as he was able to his house where he found to his relief that, while the flood waters were swirling round his porch, they hadn't made it into the house. He opened the door and called to Benjy who was barking wildly in the kitchen.

'Here boy.' Gabriel went to comfort his dog, but suddenly Benjy's ears pricked up. Above the wind and the rain came the sound of a lamb in trouble. Benjy barked again and, following his instinct, he shot off into the darkness to rescue it.

'No! Benjy, no!' Gabriel could only watch in horror as his sheepdog disappeared into the gloom.

Chapter Twenty-One

Marianne paddled her way towards Pippa, who was frantically filling buckets with foul-smelling water and pouring them out of the back of the house. Like Gabriel's cottage, Pippa's house was on a slight slope so the water was at least pouring through into the back garden. But the speed at which it was coming meant that, however fast she bailed out, it wasn't fast enough. Dan was in the back of the house trying to rescue as much stuff from the lounge as he could.

'Leave that,' he said to Pippa. 'It's a waste of time. I think we've got to go into damage limitation mode now.'

'If we just kept going—' Pippa's normal composure appeared to be cracking.

'Come on, love,' Dan put his arm around her, 'we can't do anything against this, we just have to save what we can.'

'Dan's right,' said Marianne. 'Come on, let me help.'

Soon they'd formed a human chain and were passing things up the stairs to the boys, who found the whole thing terribly exciting. Lucy, fortunately, had remained asleep.

They worked into the early hours of the morning, when eventually the flood subsided a little, leaving them with a house full of swirling, filthy water.

'I can't even offer you a cup of tea,' said Pippa, sinking exhaustedly onto the stairs. 'I daren't use the electrics.'

'Don't worry about that,' said Marianne. 'Where are you all going to sleep? You can't stay here.'

'There's room at my place.' Gabriel appeared, looking exhausted and dishevelled. 'I only got a bit of rainwater in the hall. Pippa, you and Dan can have my bed, I'll go on the sofa in the lounge. The boys can share with Stephen and Lucy can have the spare room.' He paused and looked at Marianne in a nonchalant kind of way. 'You can have the sofa bed in the conservatory if you'd like.'

Marianne kicked herself for even thinking about what she'd been thinking in such stressful circumstances, but knew he was right. This was hardly the time to announce their relationship to the world.

'I could try and get home,' said Marianne.

'Don't be daft,' said Gabriel, 'there's a river running through the High Street, remember?'

'Oh, yes,' Marianne had almost forgotten the difficulty they'd had in getting over here. Her little rented cottage was on the other side of the High Street. She had no idea whether it had been affected or not.

Pippa gave her a sideways look as if to enquire what was going on, but Marianne chose to ignore it. There would be plenty of time for explanations later.

'Right, let's get everyone out of here,' she said brightly in her best teacherish manner – Pippa was looking too stunned by events to make a decision.

'Yes, right,' said Pippa at last. 'You go ahead with the boys. Dan and I will come on with Lucy.'

Having sorted the boys out with appropriate waterproofs, Marianne and Gabriel trudged off up the path. The rain was still coming down in sheets, and the wind was tearing across the valley in eddying bursts that took their breath away. Gabriel was very quiet but, when they got into the house, he suddenly turned to Marianne. 'Don't say anything

252

to Stephen just yet, but Benjy ran off in the dark. I spent about an hour searching for him, but it's no good. I think I've lost him.'

He looked so desolate, Marianne gave him a hug.

'Maybe he's sheltering somewhere,' she said. 'Come on, let's get these kids inside. We'll all feel better for a hot drink. I know Pippa and Dan certainly deserve one.'

Gabriel gave her a small smile. 'I hope you're right. We've had Benjy since Stephen was a baby. He'll be broken-hearted if anything's happened to him.'

'No use worrying about what hasn't happened yet,' said Marianne, trying to be more cheerful than she felt.

Once Pippa and Dan arrived, she helped Pippa sort the kids out, then they all went downstairs and Marianne made hot drinks for everyone.

'I think I need something stronger in mine,' said Pippa with feeling, so Gabriel produced a bottle of his finest malt and added a generous glug to everyone's coffee. Pippa and Dan soon retired to bed, but Gabriel and Marianne sat close to each other on the sofa, but not so close that anyone who walked in would notice anything untoward, and mulled over the events of the evening, as they listened to the interminable pounding of the rain on the conservatory roof and the whistling of the wind down the chimney.

Eventually, noticing Marianne shivering, Gabriel brought a duvet downstairs and, past caring whether anyone would see them, they cuddled up together underneath it, chatting softly and getting drowsier and drowsier.

'I should move,' said Marianne dozily.

'In a minute,' said Gabriel, pulling her closer to him.

She nuzzled up against him, thinking how long it was since she'd felt this comfortable. Really, she should get up in a minute. They didn't want Stephen to find them like that in the morning. But it was so cosy, listening to the fire crackling in the grate, and the last throes of the winds, which were finally dying down. The last thought Marianne had as she drifted off to sleep, leaning on Gabriel's shoulder, was that he smelt of pine cones and smoke, and how comforting that was.

Despite the late night, Gabriel woke early the next morning with the sun streaming through the lounge window. Typical. The storm had blown past and now it was so calm outside it was almost impossible to imagine that nature could be so destructive. Marianne was already up making tea in the kitchen.

'Couldn't sleep,' she said, coming over to him and giving him a kiss. He allowed himself the swift luxury of taking her in his arms. It felt so comforting after the events of the previous night to hold her there. He felt like he never wanted to let go.

'I'd best be out looking for Benjy,' he said. 'And I need to check all the sheep are okay. I think they were on high enough ground, but it was such a sudden storm, some of them might not have had time to get away.'

'I'll come with you,' offered Marianne.

They set off up the valley, which was incredibly muddy. Looking back down the lane, they could see the flood waters were starting to subside.

'Pippa and Dan are going to have their work cut out,' said Marianne. 'I'll have to go and help them later.'

'What about your place?' said Gabriel.

'With any luck the other side of the village isn't affected,' said Marianne. 'It didn't look so bad when we came in from that side last night. Anyway, it's not as if I own the place, is it? And I haven't really been there long enough to accumulate much stuff. If I was flooded, I doubt I've lost anything of major value.'

'I'm not sure I'd be so sanguine about it,' said Gabriel.

'They're only things,' said Marianne. 'They can be replaced.'

They carried on walking, calling out for Benjy, but there was no response. Gabriel found most of his flock, huddled together for shelter in a little dip near the top of a hill. Apart from a little dampness, they seemed fine. But there was no sign of Benjy anywhere.

They were on the verge of giving up, when they heard some frantic baaing near the spot where they'd helped the ewe give birth.

Gabriel went scrambling over the slippery rock face, with Marianne following behind.

'Oh, no.' Gabriel stopped short at the ledge on which Marianne had found the pregnant ewe trembling and bleating piteously.

'What?' said Marianne, who couldn't see what Gabriel was looking at.

'There,' said Gabriel.

Below the ledge, there appeared to have been a mudslide. At the bottom of it lay the body of a dead ewe, and beside her lay Benjy, his neck clearly broken.

'Have you seen the news?' Cat was standing watching BBC News 24 with a steaming cup of tea in her hand.

'No, why?' Noel came downstairs, still knotting his tie. He didn't feel much like going into the office today, but he couldn't face another day fudging things with Cat at home.

The newscaster was talking about flooding up north. There had been warnings issued the previous night, but apparently it had been much worse than was predicted.

'Isn't Hope Christmas where you've been doing your eco town thing?' Cat said.

'Oh my God.' Noel stared in horror at the screen showing

a river running through Hope Christmas High Street. It was a scene of utter devastation. Noel felt like someone had ripped a hole out of him. The damage would take months to repair. The reporter cut to an interview with a local resident.

'We're lucky to have with us Ralph Nicholas, who owns a large estate here. I understand that you've been putting locals washed out of their homes up in your manor house?' the reporter was saying.

'Yes, indeed,' said Ralph. 'It was the least I could do. Unfortunately we lost our community hall in the flood, so people had nowhere to go. Luckily my house is on a hill and I have plenty of room.'

'And from what I gather, people were out till all hours helping rescue elderly folk trapped in their houses.'

'We're a close-knit community here,' Ralph was saying. 'Folk do tend to help one another. Although not everyone wants rescuing.'

The report then cut to a picture of an old woman leaning out of the top of her house, waving her stick at some firemen who were asking if she needed help.

'Hitler didn't bomb me out of this house, so a little rainwater isn't going to hurt me.'

'When I'm old I want to be like her,' said Cat. She turned the TV off. 'What's this going to mean for your project?'

'A lot of money and a big clear-up operation, I expect,' said Noel. 'That's terrible. Hope Christmas is a lovely place. You'd love it.' It was the first time Noel had ever mentioned what he thought of it, and he felt a spasm of guilt. His mobile rang. Great. Matt Duncan. Ever the harbinger of doom.

'Yes, I've just seen it,' said Noel. 'I doubt very much there's any point us going up there today. From what I've seen on the news, the place looks a complete mess.'

'Luke Nicholas is adamant we have to get up there as

soon as we can. I think he's worried someone might blame the excavation work we've been doing.'

'Well, I'm no expert on the causes of flash floods, but there was a lot of silt dumped in the river, and diverting part of it probably hasn't helped,' said Noel. He wasn't at all happy about the destruction he'd seen on the TV, but part of him couldn't help cheering at the thought that some of Luke Nicholas' chickens might be coming home to roost at last.

'So we may need to do some damage limitation then,' said Matt. 'I need your arse over here right now, so we can start trawling through the files. I do not want any of this coming back to GRB.'

Noel, who rather hoped some of it would come back to Matt, promised to be in the office as soon as he could.

He grabbed a bit of toast, kissed Cat and left. Every cloud had a silver lining. Maybe now Gerry Cowell would see Matt for the bullshitter he really was.

Cat dropped the kids off at school, checked her watch to see if she had time to quickly nip into Mum's before her monthly schedule meeting with Bev and, deciding she did, drove round like a demon to her mother's house.

'What are you doing here?' Her mother looked distinctly displeased to see her.

'I just thought I'd pop in to see how you were,' said Cat.

'I am not an invalid,' said her mother with dignity. 'I am just having a little trouble with my memory at the moment. I'm sure I'll be better soon.'

'I'm sure you will too,' Cat said diplomatically. She didn't want to distress her mother. Of late, any kind of disagreement seemed to set off a reaction. 'But can't a daughter come and have tea with her old mum anyway?'

'Less of the old,' said her mother. That was more like it – this was the mum she knew and loved.

But then she was gone again. Walking into the kitchen, her mother paused, looked perplexed, and stood staring blankly into space. It was as though for a moment the lights had all gone out. Cat didn't know much about strokes, but she wasn't sure this was how they manifested themselves. She had a ghastly insight into what the future might hold.

'Mum,' she said, and then Mum was back.

'Oh, Cat, dear,' she said, 'how nice of you to call in. Would you like a cup of tea?'

'I'd love one.' Cat sank into a seat at the kitchen table. This was terrifying. She was losing her mother before her eyes.

For the next half an hour though, it was as though nothing was wrong. Mum asked after the children and Noel. She talked about the flooding that she'd seen on TV. Everything seemed as normal as could be.

'I'd better go,' said Cat eventually, getting up. 'I've got a meeting at work.'

'Cat—' Mum sat looking incredibly sad and wistful.

'What?' Cat was gathering her bag and surreptitiously clocking her watch. She was going to be late if she wasn't careful.

'Thank you for taking me to the doctor yesterday,' said Mum. 'You're right. I do forget things. I forget things a lot. I have been for a long long time. I just didn't want to admit it to myself.'

Cat sat down again and held her mother's hands.

'Oh, Mum,' she said. 'We'll get through this, whatever it is. I promise.'

'You're a good girl, Cat,' said Mum. 'You always have been.' She paused, and Cat suddenly realised her mother was very afraid, and very vulnerable. 'We need to think about the future, Cat. I don't know how much longer I can be trusted to run my own affairs. So I want you and Noel to have power of attorney.'

258

'We can talk about all that later,' said Cat, tears pricking her eyes.

'I may not have later,' said Mum. 'I've got the forms here. You take them and talk it over with Noel.'

'Whatever happens, Mum,' said Cat, 'I won't leave you.'

'I know,' said Mum, patting her daughter's hand. 'But you must promise me that if I get really bad, you'll sell this place and put me in a home.'

'I could never do that,' said Cat, horrified.

'Never say never,' said Mum sadly. 'My mother started out like this and ended up with dementia. I couldn't cope. You won't be able to either.'

'You never said.' Cat was incredulous.

'It was a long time before you were born,' said Mum, 'and, to be honest, it was something that absolutely terrified me before. So I couldn't talk about it. But now, I'm going to have to.'

'It might not be dementia,' Cat said. 'The doctor never said you had dementia.'

'She didn't have to,' said Mum. 'I know something's wrong. And I don't think I'm having strokes. It's like a blank screen comes over me, and I can't remember where I am or what I'm supposed to be doing. It was just the same with my mum. It's a terrible, terrible disease, but we have to face what's going to happen to me.'

'I don't want to,' said Cat, the tears now flowing freely.

'I know,' said Mum, tears shining bright in her own eyes. 'And I don't want you to have to go through this either. But we can't all have what we want. So come on, chin up. You've got a meeting to get to.'

Mum saw Cat to the door, and they hugged fiercely.

'You promise?' Mum said, as they said goodbye.

'I promise,' said Cat.

259

Chapter Twenty-Two

Gabriel was still feeling shell-shocked about Benjy when he and Marianne got back to his cottage. They'd had to leave the bodies there for the time being. He needed to go back with the Land Rover and get them at some point, but for now he had to work out what to say to his son. Stephen was going to be devastated.

The opportunity wasn't going to come straightaway, somewhat to Gabriel's relief, because he and Marianne walked back into bedlam. The boys were all whooping about like lunatics, and Lucy was sobbing because they'd been teasing her. Even calm Pippa was having trouble keeping control.

'Where's Dan?' Gabriel asked.

'He went down to inspect the damage at our place. You wouldn't believe it, but everything was peaceful till about five minutes ago.'

Gabriel quickly had the boys sitting down in front of the TV, made Pippa a much needed cup of tea, and then sat down next to Lucy. He was immensely fond of his godchild, and he could usually raise a smile.

'What's my favourite girl doing down in the dumps?' he said, and then proceeded to pull funny faces at her till she was giggling away happily.

'That was amazing,' said Marianne. 'You've a real gift with children.'

Gabriel shrugged, and gave her a rather sad smile, 'Looking after people seems to be something of a speciality of mine. Talking of which . . . I really need to find some time with Stephen to explain about Benjy.'

'Do you need any help?' He was touched by Marianne's concern. When Eve had been around she always left all the difficult stuff to him.

'I think this is something I need to tackle alone,' he said. 'But God knows what I'm going to say.'

The office was buzzing when Noel got there. He noticed to his satisfaction that even Matt's smooth exterior had been ruffled by events up north.

'Thank God you're here,' he said. 'I've had Luke Nicholas on the blower five times already. *Five* times. What does he think I can do from here? Work a bloody miracle?'

Noel muttered something placatory and then got to work to find out what the damage was on the site. According to the site foreman, half the foundations were now so water-logged it was going to take weeks – possibly months – before building work could resume. It wasn't as if they'd been dry to begin with. But the local authorities were pumping water out of Hope Christmas, so there was a possibility that the pumps could be borrowed, ensuring the worst of the water could be got rid of. Quite how they were going to dry everything out to meet the incredibly demanding schedule, Noel wasn't quite sure.

He went back through the files and dug out his original plans for revitalising the buildings on the Hopesay Manor Estate. He looked through them again. He felt suddenly angry that the building work had gone ahead despite his objections. He couldn't prove that the flood was a result of the silt being dumped in the river, but given that, according to the reports, Hope Christmas itself hadn't

261

flooded for a hundred years, Noel couldn't help feeling that somehow the work they'd been carrying out was partly responsible. Apart from being morally wrong, it was a flagrant breaking of the stringent government guidelines for the building of eco towns. Matt should really get it in the neck for this.

He printed off the plans, wrote a quick report on the situation in Hope Christmas, promising to visit the site next week for an update, and left both on Gerry Cowley's desk. You never know, maybe Gerry would have a change of heart now. Surely even he would see that pursuing the eco town option now was throwing good money after bad?

'Oh my word.' Marianne and Pippa gingerly entered her farmhouse to see filthy water still swirling through the house and out of the back door. Dan had gone back to Gabriel's place to take over with the kids and start making the inevitable phone calls to insurers. The flood waters had receded somewhat, leaving a muddy, gloopy mess on the floor, but carpets were ruined, the wiring was sodden, the plaster was peeling off the walls, and the skirting boards were warped.

'It's so much worse than I thought,' Pippa said bleakly. 'I know it's stupid to be so upset, but look at it. That's our life. In tatters.'

She wandered desolately through to the lounge, where she picked up a broken photo frame and showed it to Marianne.

'Our wedding day,' she said simply.

'Oh, Pippa,' Marianne hugged her friend hard. Why did the worst things happen to the nicest people? 'Soonest done, soonest mended. As my granny used to say.'

'Has your granny got a phrase for every occasion?' said Pippa with a weak grin.

'Pretty much,' said Marianne. 'Look, why don't I carry

on here for a bit? It's mayhem at Gabe's place and the kids need you.'

'"Gabe"? I knew it! I knew it!' Pippa was practically dancing in delight. 'Now that has really cheered me up. I thought there was something going on between you last night, but I didn't like to ask.'

'Yes, well, last night was hardly the moment for confidences,' said Marianne. 'And now isn't the moment either. We've just found Benjy's body in the valley. Gabriel's devastated and he doesn't know how Stephen's going to react.'

'Oh my God, poor, poor Stephen,' said Pippa, forgetting her own troubles for an instant. 'He's had so much to deal with as it is. He doesn't need this.'

'What's she like?' Marianne said hesitantly, as she gathered up some soggy bits of carpet, ready to dump outside. She wasn't sure she really wanted to talk about Eve but she couldn't contain her curiosity . . .

'Who, Eve?' Pippa rolled her eyes. 'She's pretty, very pretty. And when she's on form, she's funny and lively and inventive. I can see why Gabe was attracted to her, but she's always been flaky as hell. Not at all cut out to be a farmer's wife. I've never met anyone so sensitive.'

'Gabe said as much,' Marianne said. 'I gather she had a lot of problems.'

'And then some,' said Pippa. 'You do have to feel sorry for her. Life hasn't been kind to Eve at all. Her dad left when she was small and, from what I can gather, her mum had a series of boyfriends and didn't show her the slightest interest. You could say she has security issues. Gabe's been amazing, considering all she's put him through. But in the end, it's better all round that she's gone. It wasn't doing Stephen any good, Eve sometimes at the school gate, sometimes not. I can't tell you the number of times I've had to pick that child up at the last minute because Eve was having a funny turn and couldn't come. It broke my heart to see how sad he was. I hope she can sort her head out, but equally I hope she doesn't come back and mess about with Stephen's anymore. That kid's been through enough.'

Marianne felt her original worries about getting involved with Gabriel resurfacing. Was she biting off more than she could chew here? Suppose she just added to Stephen's problems? To take her mind off things, she picked up a broom Pippa had brought in from the kitchen and started sweeping the remnants of sludge and slimy water towards the patio doors.

As if sensing her thoughts, Pippa said hurriedly, 'Oh my God, I hope I haven't put you off.' She scooped the muddy debris up with a dustpan and brush and started chucking it out into her swamp of a garden. 'I think the best thing that could possibly happen to Stephen is to have some kind of stability in his life. I'm sure you being around can only help.'

'If he can cope with it,' said Marianne, working away with a will. 'And that's a very big if. And now's probably not the time to go there. Anyway. You need to get back to the kids. I'll carry on here.'

'Haven't you got stuff to do?'

'Not really,' said Marianne. 'School's closed and I'm sure my cottage is fine, I may as well stay and help you out.'

'I don't know how I can ever repay you,' said Pippa, as she put the dustpan and brush down. 'You're a star.'

Marianne rolled her eyes.

'Ever since I came to this village, you've looked after me. This is the least I can do.' She waved the broom at Pippa. 'Now get away with you, before I sweep you away with this broom.'

Cat logged onto the blog. The post about bullying had evidently hit home. There was a flood of sympathetic messages offering advice and helpful comments. On the increasingly frequent occasions she considered giving up the blog on the grounds that, as well as hating the persona she'd created, it took too much of her time and energy, Cat would often have a response like this to a post and it made it all worthwhile. Sure there were some nutters out there (one or two frequently left annoying messages in her comments section, but she usually ignored them), but in the main she'd found the blogosphere a friendly place. Sometimes it felt like being part of a warm and cosy family, far removed from the messy domestic situation in her real life. There were times, in fact, when she felt that a virtual life might be more satisfying than an actual one. Certainly at the moment she could do with living the fantasy.

She scrolled down through the comments. 'Talk to your daughter, let her know she has nothing to fear from confiding in you,' opined *MommyintheUSA*, while *TwoKidsNoHusband* advised, 'Get in touch with the school. The sooner they know, the sooner they can nip it in the bud.' All good, sound, helpful advice. The only trouble was it was hard to get Mel to talk – she clammed up at the slightest hint of a question about school. Cat was about to sign off, when a new message popped up. *Anonymous*. Hmm. That didn't always mean trouble, but people who wanted to cause trouble in the blogging world weren't usually too keen to leave their names.

'Your daughter is a lying bitch and so are you.' Nice. Where did these people get off on such nastiness? Cat deleted the comment and closed down the blog. She concentrated on writing her recipe for Granny Dreamboat's Winter Warmer, a beef stew replete with winter vegetables and pearl barley. Even in summer, writing this gave her a warm and tingly feeling. Not that it felt like summer, the storm from up north having made its way southwards. It had rained so much today, it was a wonder there was any more rain left in the sky.

Cat looked at her watch. Nearly school pickup time. She started tidying things away when an instant message pinged up on the screen.

One of Mel's friends no doubt. Perhaps on a day off sick and bored trying to instant message her friends.

She opened the message, to a stream of abuse. 'I saw what you wrote on my Bebo page. You are a lying bitch and so is your mum.'

There was a picture of a rather tarty-looking twelve-year-old whose MSN legend bore *Inyourfacebitch*. How very very unpleasant.

With a sinking heart, Cat typed back: 'This is Melanie's mother, who are you?'

'Go away bitch,' was the charming response.

'Does your mother know what you are doing?' Cat typed back.

Her erstwhile correspondent beat a hasty retreat out of cyberspace.

What the hell had that been all about? Cat went into Mel's Bebo account. She had been most reluctant to allow Mel to set one up and had only done so on the condition she had full access to it at all times. She was horrified by what she saw. Her daughter apparently considered a girl at school called Juliette (nicknamed by Mel as 'Screwliette') a lying bitch, and everyone should apparently know what a slag she was. Reeling with shock at the language her eleven-year-old was using, Cat sat back absolutely stunned. There she'd been assuming that Mel was being bullied, but it now looked very much as if her daughter was the one doing the bullying.

Chapter Twenty-Three

Marianne walked down the High Street a week after the flood on her way to the dentist's. People were slowly trying to get back to normal, but it was going to take weeks, if not months, for the cottages on the High Street to dry out again. She walked past Miss Woods' house to see the ex-head of Hope Christmas primary berating the workmen who'd come to clear out her ground floor. In front of the house was a pile of what looked like junk, an ancient fridge-freezer, an old sofa, an aged TV set, but, Marianne thought sadly, it probably wasn't junk to Miss Woods. That detritus was her life. It was shocking to realise just how destructive nature could be.

'I'm sorry about your house, Miss Woods,' Marianne said, narrowly avoiding the stick that was waving at a poor workman who hadn't put a bit of old carpet properly in the skip.

'Don't be,' said Miss Woods. 'It's all old junk anyway. Now I can get myself a new plasma screen on the insurance. And a better computer for surfboarding the interweb. My dial up connection was just so slow. I fancy going Hi Fi.' She paused to tell the workmen off. 'Just what do you think you are doing with that sideboard? It's not to go in the skip, it belonged to my grandmother.'

'What do you think will happen about the village hall?' asked Marianne. Now that the floods had subsided, the true extent of the damage was revealed. The doors were smashed in, one half of a wall had collapsed, and at least two of the windows had been swept away in the flood.

'I expect we'll have to have Parish Council meetings at Diana Carew's place, God help us,' said Miss Woods. 'But at least it might mean the Nativity will get cancelled.'

Marianne grinned. Last year's Nativity still gave her nightmares, and Diana had already begun dropping big hints about how invaluable her help had been, and would she possibly like to get involved in this year's.

'Do you think Diana will ever let that happen?' said Marianne. 'It seems like the Nativity is her baby.'

Miss Woods sniffed. 'Well, high time someone else took it over, I say. I don't think I can stand another year of hearing those bloody elves singing "Wonderful Christmas Time".'

'I don't blame you,' laughed Marianne. 'You should have tried getting them to rehearse it.'

'Perhaps you could take over?' suggested Miss Woods. 'In the old days we used to have a Nativity based on an old Shropshire mystery play, but sadly Diana is too much of a philistine to know what a mystery play is.'

'I don't dare even think about suggesting it,' was Marianne's firm response. No way was she getting embroiled in a feud between the two women. She made her excuses and left, marvelling at the small ways the community of Hope Christmas was pulling together in the crisis. At the butcher's, three burly farmers who supplied him with their meat were helping gut the shop floor, which had been ruined; at the small Parish Centre next to the church, a notice declared free hot meals for anyone affected by the floods till their kitchens were back in order; and, passing the post office, Marianne noticed Mr Edwards helping load Vera Campion's worldly belongings into his van.

'Mr Edwards has very kindly offered me lodgings,' Vera explained pinkly. 'With the post office closing anyway, I didn't have anywhere else to go. And at least this way the insurance is going to give me a bit of a breather while I decide what to do next.'

'It's the least I can do, Vera,' said Mr Edwards. 'I can't have my favourite girl struggling alone now, can I?'

'Oh, Albert.' Vera blushed bright crimson. Feeling like she was spying on them, Marianne went on her way.

By the time she'd reached the dentist's, conveniently placed at the top end of the village so it had escaped the flood, Marianne felt as though she'd said hello to half the inhabitants of Hope Christmas. As she went to sit down in the waiting area, she spotted Ralph Nicholas.

'Ah, my dear, how are you?' he said warmly. 'Didn't lose too much in the flood?'

'No, I was incredibly lucky,' said Marianne. 'I feel so sorry for everyone who's been affected.'

'It's going to take a long time for the village to recover, it's true,' said Ralph, 'but every cloud has a silver lining, I generally find.'

'Oh?'

The receptionist called Ralph's name. Tapping his nose, he smiled at Marianne and said, 'I'd take a look at page 43 in this month's *Happy Homes* if I were you.' And with that he was gone.

Marianne saw the magazine on the table. Idly she picked it up and it fell conveniently open at page 43.

Fed up with the commercialisation of Christmas? Longing for a return to simpler days? Then enter our competition to find the Nation's best Nativity. A prize of £10,000 to the community or school that puts in the best suggestion.

Marianne laughed out loud. Perhaps she should suggest it to Diana Carew. She could only imagine how well *that* would go down.

'Can you explain to me what all this is about?' Cat hadn't confronted Melanie with the evidence of her misdoings straightaway. She'd been so shocked by what she'd found and had needed time to mull it over. Besides, the last thing she wanted to do was accuse her daughter unnecessarily. Maybe, as Noel had pointed out to her, there might be some rational explanation. It could just be a schoolgirl prank that had got out of hand. Perhaps. After a long chat over a coffee with Regina, she'd decided to tackle the problem head on. So, with the rest of her offspring in bed and Noel away in Hope Christmas, trying to sort out the disaster that was the eco town, now seemed as good a time as any.

'Where did you get this?' Mel blushed a furious red and snatched the offending bits of paper out of her mother's hands.

'Your charming friend Juliette left an offensive message on my blog, and sent you some nasty comments on your MSN account,' said Cat. 'She told me you'd written some stuff about her on your Bebo page. I couldn't believe it when I found this. What on earth are you playing at? I didn't even know you knew language like that. After all the things I've told you about being careful about what you say online.'

'She deserved it.' Melanie looked mutinous.

'What did she do?' said Cat. 'It must have been pretty bad for you to have written all this stuff. Come on, Mel, this isn't like you. What's going on?'

Mel said nothing for a moment and then she burst out: 'It's all your fault!'

'My fault? Why on earth is it my fault?' Honestly, the logic of children.

'Why did you have to write on the bloody blog about my training bra?'

'What's that got to do with anything?' Months ago, Cat had written a jolly little piece about the traumas of dealing with preteens and, in this specific instance, the sheer embarrassment for Mel engendered by buying her first training bra. The Happy Homemaker blog was peppered with such stories of domestic life, it was one of the reasons people seemed to like it. But Cat had always been very careful not to mention her children by name – Mel's moniker on the blog was the Mean Teen (James was the Token Boy, Paige the Drama Queen and Ruby the Wild Child).

'Juliette's mum reads your blog all the time,' said Mel. 'All my friends' mums do. And then Juliette read it too, and printed it off and showed everyone in the class. It was so humiliating.'

Cat felt a cold bucket of water wash over her. Never in a million years had it occurred to her that one of Mel's friends might read the Happy Homemaker and make the connection with her. 'I am so, so sorry, Mel. Really, truly I am. I never ever meant for this to happen. But you should have said.'

'I didn't know what to say,' said Mel. 'I was too angry.'

'You do know that this,' Cat pointed to the paperwork in Mel's hand, 'isn't the way to deal with it though, don't you?'

'I suppose,' said Mel sulkily.

'So, what we're going to do is ring Juliette's mum up and you are going to go round there and apologise.'

'Do I have to?' Mel looked horrified.

'Yes, sweetheart, I'm afraid you do,' said Cat. 'It was wrong of me to mention the training bra on the blog, and I am very very sorry. But I will not tolerate a child of mine behaving like this. Got it?'

'Got it,' mumbled Mel.

'Now give us a hug, and we'll say no more about it,' said Cat. She kissed her daughter on the top of her head. 'And can you forgive your old mum? Sometimes grown-ups get it wrong too.'

'I suppose,' said Mel and slunk off up to her room to do whatever it was she did there when she was having an emotional crisis.

Cat went down to the kitchen and poured herself a large glass of red. Bloody hell. How could she have been so stupid? Cat had tossed off that little blog piece in a moment of light frivolity, never thinking for one moment about the repercussions for Mel. It was a lesson to her to be a bit more careful on the blog from now on. If indeed she should even carry it on. Somehow Cat felt she'd reached a turning point. The Happy Homemaker was starting to ruin her home life. She had a feeling that the days of her alter ego were numbered.

Noel was attending a bad-tempered meeting at Hopesay Manor. He'd come up to Hope Christmas the night before, but thanks to the flooding hadn't been able to stay in the cheerful pub he favoured. Instead he and Matt had been holed up in a faceless Travelodge on the outskirts of Ludlow where, remarkably, there was no evidence of flooding at all.

They'd gone to visit the building site first thing, and even Matt had been shocked by the devastation. The pumps had been utilised and the worst of the water had gone but the grey-brown sludge that had been left behind needed to be cleaned out, and the stench was foul. A couple of dead sheep had been swept down the valley, their corpses left in the mud. Noel, having taken numerous photographs and measurements, couldn't imagine how anyone could conceive that this was still a viable concern.

Luke Nicholas apparently could.

'I'm sure this is a problem we can resolve,' he was saying smoothly, several shareholders having expressed concern about the company's liabilities. 'Our investors are really keen to carry on with the project, and accept that this is a little local problem that can easily be sorted out.'

'You've built on a flood plain!' Noel said in exasperation. 'Your little local problem will be repeated if you don't do something to sort it out.'

'I think we have a solution to that,' Luke turned to Matt, 'don't we?'

'There is a way, if we divert the river away from the eco town, that, should the situation arise again – which let's face it is extremely unlikely, there hasn't been a flood this severe in over a hundred years – the village will be safe. I don't see why we can't proceed as normal.'

'Apart from being contrary to government guidelines, which clearly state you shouldn't do anything to create flooding elsewhere, which diverting the river is highly likely to do. This is mad,' said Noel. Several shareholders seemed to agree, but they were overruled by Luke's suave assurances that everything would be done to meet government requirements, and that in the end all would be well. Noel left the meeting feeling more disgruntled than ever. How could he carry on working like this? It was sapping all his strength and integrity.

He left the meeting in an angry mood and walked out of the office buildings on the edge of the estate where the Nicholas family organised their day-to-day business, passing as he did so the small tumbledown cottages that he had hoped to persuade GRB to invest in.

'Now *they'd* make proper sustainable housing, don't you think?' Ralph Nicholas was striding towards him with his grey wolfhound following on behind.

'I said as much the first time I came here,' said Noel gloomily, 'but no one wants to listen to me.'

'I'll listen,' said Ralph. 'Here, take my card. Show me some decent plans, and who knows? Maybe I can persuade my daft grandson and his cronies to change their minds.'

'Maybe,' said Noel, 'but I doubt you'll get anyone at GRB to see sense.'

'You know,' said Ralph Nicholas, 'it's a big wide world out there. I could use a decent engineer if you ever thought about decamping to the country.'

Noel looked at him incredulously. 'Are you serious?'

'Never been more serious,' said Ralph. 'This isn't my only property in the area. And I'd like to invest in decent homes for the people who live round here. Particularly after the flood. Would you be interested?'

'I'd come like a shot, but I doubt I could get my wife to move,' said Noel. 'She's a real townie.'

'Pity,' said Ralph. 'But if you ever change your mind . . .'

'You'll be the first to know,' said Noel. It was so tempting. He'd love to come up here, buy that fantasy farmhouse and start again. It would be a much better life for the kids too. Noel wasn't keen on the thought of James in particular going to the local comp, where stabbings seemed to be the norm. But how could he ever persuade Cat to leave the bright lights and big city? It was never going to happen and he knew it.

Gabriel poured the last bit of earth onto Benjy's grave, and placed the small wooden cross Stephen had made on top of the mound of earth. Stephen had insisted they bury Benjy in the garden, so 'he would feel at home'.

Stephen stepped forward, looking a little self-conscious in front of his cousins and aunt, whom he'd insisted on coming. Gabriel had thought about asking Marianne too, but as he still hadn't divulged the nature of his relationship with her to his son, he decided in the end that it might spell trouble.

'To Benjy,' read Stephen. 'You always came when I threw you sticks. You were always up to tricks. You were my friend and we had fun. Now it seems your days are run. I'll always miss you.'

He wiped a tear away from his eye, and Nathan giggled. Pippa punched him in the ribs and he shut up. Then, one by one, the children solemnly put a handful of earth on Benjy's grave.

'Do you think dogs go to heaven?' Stephen asked.

'Of course they do,' said Pippa, giving him a hug. 'There's a special doggie heaven where they get to chase sticks, and hide bones, and munch on treats every day. Isn't that right, Daddy?'

'Absolutely,' said Gabriel. He was relieved to see that, for the moment, Stephen was happy enough with that explanation. But later, when he was tucking his son up in bed, Stephen said to him sadly, 'Why do so many sad things happen? First Mummy left and now Benjy's died. Do you think it's my fault? Maybe I'm too naughty.'

'Oh, Stephen,' Gabriel gave his son a hug. 'Of course it's not your fault. Who told you that?'

'Nathan,' said Stephen.

'Well, I shall box Nathan's ears next time I see him,' said Gabriel. 'Don't you ever listen to such nonsense again.'

'Why did Mummy leave then?' said Stephen.

'Mummy's very sick,' said Gabriel. 'It makes her sad sometimes and she can't help it. I wanted to help her, but I couldn't either. Sometimes sad things just happen. But good things happen too.'

'Like what?' said Stephen.

'Like I saw Shaun today and he's growing into a fine

big sheep and it will be time to shear him soon,' said Gabriel.

They'd christened the sheep they'd rescued Shaun, and let him out on the hills when he'd grown strong enough. Gabriel often spotted him on account of his black tail.

'Oh, yes, that's good,' said Stephen sleepily. 'But I think it would be really good if Mummy came back.'

'That may not happen,' said Gabriel, and hesitated. Was now the moment to mention Marianne?

'But it might,' continued Stephen. 'I shall make a wish on a star tonight and every night for Mummy to come back home.'

Now was evidently not the time. Gabriel drew the curtains with a heavy heart and kissed his son goodnight. How was he going to prevent Stephen from facing heartbreak all over again?

Chapter Twenty-Four

Cat was in a lunchtime meeting, discussing the layout of the Christmas edition over sandwiches and sparkling water. The plan was to announce the winner of the Nativity competition the first week in December and to print the article about the Nativity in the January issue.

'Come on, people, I've got a really good vibe about this,' Bev was saying as they pored over layouts.

Even Cat had to admit, unenthusiastic as she felt about Christmas given that it was the middle of July (*and* she still had the summer holidays to get through without a family holiday as their finances were so stretched), that it was looking good.

The phone in the meeting room rang and Bev picked it up, 'Yes, she's here,' she said. 'Cat, it's for you.'

Cat picked up the phone. 'Hello, Catherine Tinsall here,' she said.

'Mrs Tinsall? Staff Nurse Tully from Homerton Hospital here. No need to be alarmed but I'm afraid I've got some bad news,' said the impersonal voice at the other end of the phone. 'Your mother's had a fall and is in hospital.'

Cat felt the colour drain from her face. She felt dizzy and sick. She sat down and asked, 'Is it serious?'

'We don't know yet,' said the woman on the other end, 'but she is very distressed and asking for you.'

'Of course, I'll be there right away,' said Cat. She put the phone down, and turned to Bev. 'I'm really sorry, but I'm going to have to go. My mother's in hospital.'

'I'm so sorry,' said Bev, putting a sympathetic arm on her shoulder. 'Yes, off you go, scoot.'

Cat ran to get her things and rushed out of the building, ringing Regina to ask her if she'd mind picking the kids up as an emergency. She had no idea how long she'd be.

By the time she got to the hospital, Mum was asleep. Her face was bruised, and her ribs were cracked but otherwise the cheerful doctor, who looked about ten, declared her to be fit as a fiddle.

'Though, of course, with her medical condition being what it is,' he continued, 'she's very unlikely to be able to continue in her own home. You're going to have to consider an alternative.'

'What do you mean?' So far no one had actually told her what was wrong with her mother, only that they were waiting for the test results.

'Well, as I'm sure you are aware, the fact that your mother is suffering from dementia is probably one of the reasons she fell.'

'It's definite then?' Cat's voice came out in a squeak. 'Mum has Alzheimer's?'

The doctor looked stricken. He was obviously quite junior and not used to having to break this kind of news.

'I'm so sorry,' he said. 'I assumed you knew.'

'Suspected,' said Cat, 'but no one's told us for definite. We hadn't had any test results.'

'Well, technically, there are no tests to diagnose Alzheimer's,' said the doctor. 'It's more a case of ruling things out. The MRI scan shows your mother has suffered from one or two TIAs but her other symptoms clearly point to

Alzheimer's. I wish I could have something more positive to say.'

'It's all right, Doctor,' said Cat. 'In a way it's a relief. At least we know now.'

And now the axe had fallen, she could start planning for the future. She shivered at the thought.

'What do you think will happen now?' she asked.

'It depends how quickly the disease progresses,' said the doctor. 'Realistically, you are going to have to brace yourself for more of this kind of thing. The memory loss and mood changes are likely to get worse, and your mother will be less and less able to manage. I'm so sorry, but it can only go downhill from here.'

Marianne was feeling rather nervous. At Diana Carew's insistence, she'd been dragged into the first meeting of the year for the Village Nativity. Quite why they needed to get on with it in July, she wasn't clear, but Diana had been most insistent that the sooner they started the better.

'Christmas will soon be upon us, you know,' said Diana, 'and, with all the chaos this year, we can't afford to get behind.'

As the village hall was still out of action, the meeting had been called at Diana's house. Fortunately she had a large house situated in a road just off the High Street, halfway up a hill, with a massive lounge that had splendid views of the Shropshire hills. It was a balmy evening so Diana had thrown her patio doors open, letting in the sounds of distant baaing and the odd car. It felt extremely odd to be sitting here discussing the Nativity.

'Right, first things first,' said Diana. 'Here's this year's script, hot off the press from my own fair hand or, should I say, computer.'

She solemnly passed round the scripts. Pippa, who was

279

sitting next to Marianne, whispered mischievously, 'Bet it's exactly the same as last year's.'

When the scripts arrived on Marianne's lap she realised with a groan that Pippa was right. Apart from a few updates to mention the credit crunch and the flood, the script was word for word the same as last year's, right down to the pesky elves.

'I think you're forgetting something very important,' Miss Woods said huffily.

'And that is?'

'As we don't currently have a village hall, where exactly are you planning to put on your great oeuvre?'

Diana shot a poison-dagger look at Miss Woods, before declaring: 'The Vicar has kindly said we can use the Parish Centre. Moving swiftly on—'

'It's too small,' said Miss Woods bluntly. 'You know how packed the Nativity gets. The Parish Centre's all right for your average Sunday when three people and his dog turn up. It cannot possibly cope with all the grannies and aunties and uncles and cousins who come out to watch the Nativity on Christmas Eve.'

'Well . . .' Diana looked utterly flummoxed for once.

'I've got a suggestion,' said Marianne shyly. 'Why don't we use the chapel at Hopesay Manor? It's beautiful, very simple, and probably the perfect place for a Nativity.'

Diana, looking disconcerted that someone else had made a suggestion, let alone someone as new to the village and as young as Marianne, looked on the verge of pooh-poohing the idea. But Pippa jumped in with, 'I think that would be wonderful', and Miss Woods said, 'I'm sure Ralph would be delighted to host it.' The rest of the committee nodded their agreement, so Diana had to reluctantly concede to Marianne's suggestion.

Emboldened by her success, Marianne ventured, 'I've got

another idea. Which might help us all. Has anyone seen this?' She produced the issue of *Happy Homes* that featured the Nativity competition. 'I thought we could enter it and, if we win, put the money towards a new village hall, which could become our community centre too, from where we could run the post office and shop. What does anyone else think?'

'That's an excellent idea,' said Diana, snatching the magazine out of Marianne's hand. 'The Parish Committee are already thinking we need the village hall to offer services for the elderly as well as being a meeting place. I shall look into it straightaway. Luckily we already have our script in place. I'm sure that will steal a march on our competitors.'

'That wasn't quite what I meant—' muttered Marianne. She felt as if she'd been steamrollered by an enormous truck. Whatever chance Hope Christmas might have had in the competition, they didn't stand a chance of winning it now.

'So, as you can see from the pictures I've taken,' Noel was concluding his presentation to the GRB board 'the eco town is not a sensible way forward. And in the current economic climate, I would venture to add that it would be an economic disaster to continue on this path. May I remind you of the original plans I made for sustainable housing on the Hopesay Manor Estate? There is lots of potential for this kind of development in the area, which would fit much better with the local community and provide a long-term plan that we could feel proud of being involved in.'

'Let me just stop you there, Noel,' said Gerry Cowley. 'I think we've seen enough. Matt, have you anything to add?'

'Yes, I have,' said Matt, 'I think Noel is painting far too gloomy a picture of the situation. From what I understand from Luke Nicholas, his investors are perfectly happy to stay on board with the current project, so long as we go ahead with plans to divert the river. I'm doing a feasibility study on that as we speak, and it's looking like the best solution. Given how much money we've already invested in this project, it seems utterly foolhardy to leave it now. I think it offers the best solution currently, as well as in the long term. There are many residents of Hope Christmas whose houses have been affected by the flood. Some of them may well be interested in investing in property with state-of-the-art flood defences. We are currently looking into ways we can make the option more attractive for them.'

Noel knew he'd been wasting his time, even before Matt started speaking. He turned over the card in his pocket that Ralph Nicholas had given him. Did he dare go freelance? Could he afford to do that to his family?

'Noel, a word,' said Gerry as the meeting broke up. Noel stayed where he was, wondering what was going to come next.

'I think we can safely say the Hope Christmas project hasn't been working out as planned,' said Gerry. 'So I've come to my decision. With regret, Noel, I can't keep carrying you any longer. This time I'm going to have to let you go.'

Gabriel and Dan were in the barns shearing sheep. Stephen loved nothing more than coming home from school and leaning over the pens, watching his dad and Dan at work. Gabriel enjoyed it too. He loved the feel of the wool coming off the sheep's back and watching the ridiculous expressions on their faces as they wobbled off, looking distinctly spooked about being naked.

Stephen had seemed much happier over the last week and, though he clearly missed Benjy, as Gabriel did, he had come to terms with his loss remarkably quickly. Gabriel wished he could accept it so readily. He needed to get a new dog soon, a sheep farmer was useless without one, but

Benjy had felt like so much a part of him, he couldn't quite bear the thought of a replacement yet.

He'd also been so busy helping out at Pippa and Dan's, shearing sheep, and taking this year's lambs to market, he and Marianne had had scarcely any time alone. Probably just as well really, he reflected, as he still hadn't quite worked out how to tell his son, following Stephen's revelations. Pippa assured him it would only be a matter of time before Stephen finally accepted that his mother wasn't coming back, but Gabriel wasn't so sure. For all her flakiness, Eve had always shown Stephen great tenderness in the times when she'd been well enough to. And Stephen was an incredibly loyal child. Gabriel had the feeling that, whatever she threw at him, Stephen would always accept her back. He still felt a twinge of guilt for not having told Stephen his mum had been with his grandmother at Easter. Maybe that hadn't been the right thing to do after all.

'Right, all done for today,' said Gabriel, as the last sheep ran off to join her naked friends, baaing indignantly. 'Want a cuppa?' he asked Dan.

'Not today,' said Dan. 'I still need to get rid of the rotten floorboards in the lounge. It's going to be months before we're straight again.'

Luckily for Dan and Pippa, her parents had a large farmhouse on the outskirts of Hope Christmas, so the whole family were currently ensconced there, but the clear-up operation was likely to take, as Dan had said, months. Gabriel had had a lucky escape.

He said goodbye to Dan and he and Stephen headed home. When they got in, Gabriel ran a bath and jumped into it while Stephen watched TV. He was having a rare moment of relaxation when he heard the doorbell ring. Damn. Stephen was under strict instructions never to open the door to strangers. Gabriel leapt out of the bath and, searching for any clothes that weren't filthy and smelling of sheep and finding there were none, he threw a towel round his waist and went down to answer the door. Maybe it was Marianne, she'd said she would call.

'Well, aren't you a sight for sore eyes and no mistake.' Standing in front of him, looking remarkably cheerful and even prettier than he remembered, was Eve.

'Aren't you going to invite me in?' she said.

Part Four

Someone Special

Last Year

December 24/25

Marianne took a deep breath and looked around her. The hall at Hopesay Manor was thronged with people sipping champagne and eating canapés. By the staircase stood the most massive Christmas tree Marianne had ever seen, sparkling with white lights that segued through the colours of the rainbow and back to white in a way that would have looked tacky if they'd been attached to the outside of a council house in Peckham, but here looked immensely graceful. Marianne found herself mesmerised by them. At least it gave her the pretence of something to do. After a perfunctory introduction to half a dozen people Marianne had never met before, Luke had deserted her. Establishing incredibly quickly that she had absolutely nothing in common with the two women he'd left her with (Clarissa, who cared for nothing except her horses, and Stella, who wanted only to talk about hedge funds), Marianne had made her excuses and disappeared into the crowd.

She'd wandered about forlornly before hiding herself by the fire in the corner of the vast drawing room, trying not to look too much like a wallflower, wishing that Luke wasn't proving so elusive. The tight knot of worry that had been building in her since yesterday's disastrous family lunch was getting bigger by the minute. For some reason, she suddenly had a very bad feeling about this evening. Luke seemed so on edge around her and, if she hadn't known better, she might have thought he was avoiding her.

'My rogue of a grandson not looking after you again?' Ralph Nicholas had appeared at her side. He had an uncanny knack of doing that.

'Oh, I expect he's got lots of people to catch up with.' Marianne felt utterly feeble for trying to excuse the inexcusable, but she couldn't bear to admit to this kind man how desolate and abandoned she was feeling. To make herself look slightly less pathetic, she turned her attention to the impressive stone fireplace that dominated the room and pretended that she was concentrating on a detail in it. It was carved out with fleurs-de-lys, and cherubs flew from the corners of the mantelpiece. Above the fireplace hung a massive oval mirror with gilt edges and, above that, carved into the stonework, was a coat of arms with a Latin motto.

'What's the writing above the fireplace?' she asked, squinting at it.

'It's our family motto,' said Ralph. '*Servimus liberi liberi quia diligimus.*'

'What does it mean?' said Marianne. 'I never studied Latin.'

'Freely we serve, because we freely love,' said Ralph. 'It's a code I've always tried to live by.'

'Freely we serve, because we freely love,' Marianne repeated slowly. She vaguely remembered Luke quoting it at her, on her first trip to Hopesay Manor. 'I rather like that.'

There was a pause, during which Marianne wondered how soon she could politely make her excuses, when Ralph suddenly asked, 'Has Luke ever shown you round the place properly?'

'Well, only that first time, when we met you,' said Marianne.

'Let me give you the guided tour, then,' said Ralph.

'What about your guests?' enquired Marianne.

'Do you think they'll even notice if I've gone?' said Ralph.

Marianne laughed and followed Ralph through the house back to the hallway with its amazing oak staircase. It was even more magnificent than she remembered. She remembered the black and white marble paving in the hallway, but had forgotten just how ornate the carvings in the ceilings were. More flying cherubs graced the corners of the room, and the ceiling high above them was dominated by a painting of the world on which an angel stood, plunging a giant sword into a writhing serpent.

'St Michael casting Lucifer out of heaven,' said Ralph.

Ralph led her upstairs and guided her through various bedchambers, many of which had four-poster beds made of oak.

'They're so small,' marvelled Marianne. 'Were people dwarves in the olden days or something?'

'Ah, a common misconception,' said Ralph. 'People in the sixteenth century discovered by trial and error that if they didn't sit up in bed they were likely to suffocate with the smoke as their fires went out, so they slept sitting upright in bed.'

'Well, I'd never have thought of that,' said Marianne, marvelling at the rich tapestries on the walls depicting hunting scenes, mythological creatures and pastoral idylls. Ralph was a wonderful guide and took the trouble to explain every detail.

The connecting corridors between the rooms were often low and panelled in oak, and round every corner there seemed to be a new surprise as Ralph took her past nooks and crannies, and then, to her delight . . .

'We have at least three, but I've only found two,' said Ralph, as he took her into a smallish, rather Spartan-looking room with a wooden seat and small table in one corner. 'Just lean on that panel there for me, would you?'

Marianne duly leaned on the panel and suddenly there was a click and the whole thing swung open to reveal a tiny little chapel.

'It's a priest hole,' she cried in delight.

'Indeed it is,' said Ralph. 'This is where my ancestors used to have mass said by their priest during Elizabeth I's time.'

'This house and everything, it's so amazing,' said Marianne as she followed Ralph back down the corridor to a minstrels' gallery above the Great Hall where the party guests were thronging.

'Glad you appreciate it,' said Ralph. 'But my absolutely favourite part of the house is here.'

They came down the main stairs back to the hall, and he led her down a dark side passage. He opened a small wooden door and Marianne gasped. They were in a wonderful little chapel, where the organist from the village, Mr Edwards, she thought his name was, was playing 'Silent Night'.

'Sorry, Ralph,' he said. 'I couldn't resist.'

'Carry on, carry on,' insisted Ralph.

The chapel was very plain, with whitewashed walls and a simple altar underneath a stained glass window. It was lit with candles and the pews were dark oak. In the furthest corner she could make out the tomb of a mediaeval knight. 'One of my ancestors,' said Ralph, 'he was a Templar. His father's buried in the Temple Church in London.'

'It's wonderful,' said Marianne, looking round her in awe. 'So simple, yet beautiful. How old is it?'

'There's been a chapel of some sort here since mediaeval times,' said Ralph. 'I'm glad you like it.'

'I love it. Thanks so much for showing me,' said Marianne.

'My pleasure,' said Ralph.

Marianne stood in silence, drinking it in as Mr Edwards played the haunting notes of the 'Coventry Carol'. It was the perfect setting for such ancient music, which seemed to hang in the air somehow, and Marianne was momentarily transported to another place, another time. In her mind's eye she could see Ralph's ancestors standing here in this very same chapel, listening to the same ancient song of praise. The carol came to an end and Marianne shook herself from her reverie, before glancing at her watch.

'Oh my goodness, is that the time? I'd better see where Luke's got to.'

'Of course,' said Ralph. 'Don't let an old duffer like me stop you having fun.' He stopped to chat to Mr Edwards, while Marianne made her way back to the party. Luke would be wondering where she was by now. She was heading back for the hall when she heard whispers and giggling round the corner. Was that Luke's voice? Who on earth was he with?

Marianne walked down the corridor with a sinking heart. She turned the corner, to see her fiancé with his tongue stuck firmly down Clarissa's throat.

'That's it.' Cat kneeled back on her heels. She'd sorted all the presents into piles of those to go under the tree and those to go into stockings. James, who'd been up and down the stairs like a yo-yo, had been sent back to bed with stern warnings that if he came down one more time Santa certainly would not be coming. Paige, who had just woken up, burst into tears when she heard her brother declare loudly that there was no such thing as Santa, but Cat had managed to pacify her in the end.

'Drink and one present before bed?' Noel came into the lounge proffering a bottle.

'What a good idea,' sighed Cat.

She leaned back into the sofa and snuggled up next to Noel, grateful that Angela had gone to bed hours earlier.

'Happy Christmas, sweetheart,' she said, 'and thanks for all your help today.'

'I didn't do anything,' protested Noel.

'Yes you did,' said Cat. 'I wouldn't have got anything done without you.'

'Right, presents,' said Noel, putting his glass down.

'Mine aren't desperately exciting, I'm afraid,' said Cat.

Noel got up, went over to the Christmas tree and picked up one of his to give to her, and Cat scrabbled under the Christmas tree for something halfway decent. She found him a couple of CDs she knew he'd like.

'Great, thanks,' he said and kissed her on the top of her head. 'Go on, open yours. You're going to love it.'

Cat ripped open the gossamer-thin paper wrapped round what looked like – was – an envelope. She opened it curiously. Noel clearly was expecting her to like it as he was jumping up and down like a demented chicken.

'A day at the Sanctuary? Noel, that's fabulous! But can we afford it?' said Cat.

'Shh,' said Noel putting his finger to her lips. 'You never do anything for yourself. I think you deserve a treat.'

'I feel terrible, none of your presents are nearly that generous,' said Cat.

'I know a way you can make up for it,' said Noel mischievously.

'We've got to do the kids' stockings first,' warned Cat.

Noel went up first to check everyone was finally asleep and, giggling like schoolchildren, they went round the house putting presents in stockings. This was the best bit of Christmas Eve as far as Cat was concerned. She loved the sound of rustling presents, and the sight of the children

292

softly asleep, knowing how excited they were going to be when they woke up. It took her right back to her own childhood.

They tumbled into bed and made gloriously satisfying love. Cat went to sleep with a smile on her face, and woke up a few hours later with one too. This was going to be the perfect Christmas. The best ever.

The morning didn't start quite smoothly though.

'Don't you have any muesli?' Angela asked querulously at breakfast. 'You know I always have it for breakfast.'

Actually Cat hadn't known. Angela had been insisting on prunes for breakfast since she'd arrived, and to Cat's knowledge had never had muesli when staying with them in her life.

Ruby turned pale at the sight of breakfast and promptly threw up. At which point Cat discovered she'd eaten every single piece of chocolate that Santa had left in the selection box in her stocking. Cat had been planning for the whole family to go to the nine thirty Family Service, but Noel used Ruby being sick as an excuse not to go, and Angela cried off too, leaving Cat with the other three who moaned all the way. Cat had only gone for the carols, and was disappointed not to get any, apart from 'Hark the Herald Angels Sing' at the end. It didn't feel like Christmas at all.

By the time they got home, Mum had arrived with Great Uncle Paddy, who demanded that they find him a straight-backed chair to sit in then complained because it was too uncomfortable. In the end Noel brought down his office chair and shoved a cushion behind it, which seemed to do the trick, but the tone was already set.

Then Auntie Eileen arrived to provide some festive cheer in the shape of gin, which she insisted on everyone sharing. Cat suspected Auntie Eileen had already imbibed a fair bit before she arrived. Her red nose was worthy of Rudolph.

Finally Soppy Sarah turned up late, flustered and apologetically twittering about how long the vicar went on today. She took one look at Ruby dressed in the Santa outfit she'd got for Christmas, pronounced her 'totally adorable', and promptly burst into tears. Cat had to kick both James and Mel in the shins to stop them laughing out loud. They ran off up the stairs in fits of hysterics. Cat rubbed her forehead, where the glimmerings of a headache were beginning to form. She had a feeling it was going to be a very long day. At least she could escape to the kitchen.

Noel, who appeared to have taken Auntie Eileen's offers of gin as a good enough reason to start drinking rather earlier than Cat would have liked, was clearly being driven insane by his mother as he kept coming into the kitchen and annoying her.

'Will you get back out there with our guests?' she hissed.

'You invited them all,' said Noel, 'you go.'

'No-el,' said Cat warningly.

'Okay, okay, I'm gone,' said Noel.

Lunch was eventually served about an hour after she'd intended, as always seemed to be the case on Christmas Day. By now Auntie Eileen had really lost the plot and was humming Christmas carols out loud, which of course was too much for Mel and James who, despite Cat's warning looks, spent most of lunch in fits of hysterics. Meanwhile Soppy Sarah and Great Uncle Paddy had made the mistake of talking politics. As Sarah was the most liberal of wets and Great Uncle Paddy the most right-wing of fascists, this was not going down too well. Thankfully Granny Dreamboat was doing a sterling job of playing referee.

Angela took advantage of this to spend the whole meal quietly needling Noel about his job.

'Is it going to survive this credit crunch, do you think?' she kept asking, till even Cat was sick of it.

'Mum, will you just leave it,' Noel ended up exploding. 'I don't want to talk about work on Christmas Day.'

At that, Angela got up and rushed off in floods of tears, so Cat felt duty-bound to follow her.

'Way to go, Noel,' she said, wondering why, when it was always Noel who made his mother cry, it was she who picked up the pieces.

'How are you doing, cuz?' Pippa found Gabriel in the garden, once again fruitlessly sending a text message to Eve. 'Do you know, if you're not careful, I'm going to smash that phone up and throw it in the midden.'

'You'd probably be doing me a favour,' said Gabriel ruefully. 'You're right. I'm wasting my time. I just keep hoping. It's bad enough for me, but how can she do that to Stephen?'

'I think,' said Pippa carefully, 'that Eve's been in a very very dark place for a long time, and I don't think you can judge her actions right now the way you can a normal person's. And in a way, she may have done the best thing by leaving.'

'How can it be the best thing?' said Gabriel, shivering in the cold. There was still a smattering of snow on the ground, and though the sun was bright in the sky it was hardly warm.

'Don't take this the wrong way, Gabe,' said Pippa, 'but I don't think you help her. I know, I know. You want to. And you've cared for her brilliantly all these years. It's your special skill, that, caring for others. But sometimes people need to stand on their own two feet.'

'And you think Eve is better off without me?' Gabriel knew in his heart that Pippa was right. All his caring for Eve had been useless. He couldn't get inside her head and sort it out, only she could do that.

'In a way, yes. She's just like all those birds with broken wings you tended when we were kids,' said Pippa. 'Only you've never let her have the opportunity to fly. Maybe if you do, she'll come back better, and you three can move forward towards some kind of normal life. You couldn't have carried on the way you were.'

'I know,' Gabriel kicked a toe against the ground. It broke his heart to say it, but Pippa was right. 'I've known for years that things weren't working. I just wanted it so badly to be okay, for all of our sakes. But especially for Stephen's.'

'He's got you,' said Pippa, 'and us. Stephen will be all right. We'll make sure of it.'

Gabriel gave his cousin a grin. 'I'm not the only one in the family with a weakness for lame ducks,' he said. 'Thanks, Pippa. For everything. At least Stephen's had a halfway decent Christmas. He'd have had a rotten time with just me.'

'You are not a lame duck, Gabriel North,' said Pippa sternly. 'Now let's get inside before we freeze to death. I think it's time we started on the mulled wine, don't you?'

The turkey eaten, the Christmas pudding burnt, this should be the time on Christmas Day when Noel should have been feeling at one with the world. But he most definitely wasn't. It was partly because his mother had been nagging him so much. She never knew when to stop, and then always made things worse by crying. He felt lousy that he'd made her cry, but didn't know how to make it better. He'd never known how to do that, so always left it to Cat.

There'd been a brief moment last night, when Noel actually thought they might have something approaching a decent Christmas. But, despite feeling petty about it, he'd had to admit that he was disappointed by the minimalist nature of her present. It was as though she'd used up all her energy on everyone else and had no time for him. This feeling was exacerbated when, in the orgy of present-giving after lunch, he'd variously opened a couple of books, some socks, a shirt, a jumper and . . .

'Good God, Cat, what on earth have you given me a manbag for?' Noel's voice was sharper than he intended.

'I thought you'd like it,' Cat looked stricken, and he immediately felt like a toad. Great. Now he'd made *her* cry. Two for the price of one. Happy bloody Christmas. He grumpily helped himself to another drink and got into bad-tempered conversation with Cat's Great Uncle Paddy about the rights and wrongs of the Iraq war.

Cat started to gather up the table things, helped by her mother, who as usual was quietly going about her business, keeping people happy and entertained and smoothing over rough edges. What would they do without her? For a shameful minute or two Noel was swept with a burning resentment that he got Granny Nightmare for a mother while Cat got the Dreamboat. It didn't seem fair.

The kids had all escaped to the lounge to watch their new DVDs and the oldies, as Cat called them, all seemed to be set for the day chatting about the Good Old Days. Noel went into the kitchen to see if Cat needed some help.

'I'm sorry about the bag,' she said, but she was crashing the crockery round so much, he could tell she didn't mean it.

'Sounds like it,' said Noel.

'What's that supposed to mean?' Cat flung back at him.

'Oh, come on, Cat, I can see how little time you spent choosing presents for me,' said Noel. 'Everyone else got just exactly what they wanted and I, I got precisely zilch.'

'Oh, for God's sake grow up, Noel,' said Cat between clenched teeth. They were conducting the argument in whispers so as not to alert their guests, but anyone walking in the room right now could have cut the atmosphere with a knife.

'If I behave like a child maybe you'll pay me some attention,' said Noel, 'you pay the kids enough.'

'For heaven's sake,' said Cat, 'they're children. You're a grown-up. Don't tell me you're jealous of them?'

Realising that she was right and he sounded ridiculous, but having too much pride to apologise, Noel grabbed his coat, stormed up the stairs and out of the house. 'Where are you going?' Cat shouted after him.

'Out,' said Noel, slamming the door.

It was freezing cold, and for a moment he thought about turning back, but he was so furious – he just wasn't sure exactly with who or what. It wasn't just Cat. It was everything. His work. His mum. The feeling that he was superfluous to requirements.

Inevitably he found himself walking on Walthamstow Marshes, by the river. They often went there for Sunday walks as a family, particularly when the children were smaller. It was the one place he could usually find contentment. But not today. He walked for about an hour, feeling melancholy and out of sorts, before making his way back through the little park that he and Cat took the kids to sometimes. He sat down on a bench and stared disconsolately across the marshes. A low sun was setting, casting golden shadows across a sullen wintry grey sky. Noel felt more out of sorts than he'd ever done in his life before, and at a loss to understand why. What was happening to him? He felt like everything he held dear was slipping through his fingers.

Noel sat there for so long, his feet went numb. At some point he was going to have to go home, but he didn't know whether he was ready to.

'I thought I'd find you here.' Cat stood behind him,

dangling the car keys. 'Come on. This is silly. It's Christmas Day and you're sitting out here freezing to death. I'm really sorry about my crap presents. I didn't know you were going to buy me such a nice one.'

She came over and sat down next to him and put her arm round him.

'What's happening to us?' she said. 'I feel like we're falling apart.'

'It's nothing,' said Noel, 'I'm just out of sorts and grumpy.'

'So you forgive me, then?'

'Nothing to forgive.' Noel reached out to Cat and squeezed her hand. Then getting up, they walked back to the car. Cat was right. It was Christmas Day. The least he could do was try and enjoy it.

This Year

Chapter Twenty-Five

'Eve,' Gabriel swallowed hard. This was so completely unexpected. 'I don't know what to say.'

'You could invite me in,' said Eve.

Gabriel stood uncertainly in the corridor, wishing that he had something more substantial than a towel wrapped round him. Familiar feelings of tenderness, exasperation and incredulity at Eve's behaviour were churning up with pleasure at seeing her again, and a deep white fury that he had been suppressing for months.

'I could,' he said stiffly. 'Or I could tell you to bugger off.'

'I wouldn't blame you if you did,' said Eve, turning her piercing blue eyes on him, bright with unshed tears. 'If I say I'm sorry, I know it's not enough, but I was in a bad way back then.'

He'd forgotten her fragility, and the breathtaking beauty of her porcelain skin, the vulnerability that she barely concealed. It tugged at his heart and he was fighting to resist the urge to comfort her, to look after her, as he always had.

'Stephen didn't deserve that,' said Gabriel, reining in his emotions. However much he cared about Eve, he couldn't forgive her yet for what she'd done to their son.

'I know,' said Eve. 'And I know I probably don't deserve a second chance—'

'You don't,' said Gabriel flatly.

'—but I do want to see our son.'

'What if he doesn't want to see you?' Gabriel knew it was cruel, but he couldn't resist the impulse to wound.

'What are you going to do?' taunted Eve. 'Pretend I haven't been here?'

Gabriel paused. He'd lied to Stephen once about Eve. He didn't think he could do it again.

'How do I know you won't hurt him again?' he said.

'I won't,' said Eve. 'I promise I won't, not this time.'

Gabriel leant heavily against the door.

'I can't be sure of that,' said Gabriel, 'you've let him down so many times before.'

'This time it's different.' Eve was pleading now, and he felt himself weaken as he saw the tears shining in her eyes. 'I know I've not always been there for Stephen, but I am his mum. And he needs me.'

Eve looked so lost and forlorn as she said this, Gabriel felt his resolve crumble, and the old urge to look after and protect her shot right through him. She was right. Whatever Eve had done to him and Stephen, she was still Stephen's mother, and he knew Stephen was capable of a great deal of forgiveness.

'Daddy, who is it?' Stephen had obviously got bored with what was on the TV and had come out to the hall. Gabriel had been shielding the door with his body and talking in low whispers.

But now Eve pushed the door open. 'Stephen?' she said tentatively. Gabriel's wavering emotions immediately veered towards protection. He knew Eve deserved Stephen's rejection, but he wasn't sure he could bear to watch if his son didn't want to see his mother.

Stephen stood uncertainly in the hallway, as if not quite sure what he was seeing.

301

Gabriel tensed.

'Mummy?' Stephen whispered. 'Mummy, is that you?'

'Yes,' said Eve, the tears falling now. 'I've come back to say sorry.'

'Are you really back?' Stephen said, as if he dared not believe it.

'I'm back, and I'm not going anywhere ever again,' said Eve.

Stephen ran down the hall and flung himself in her arms, and Gabriel leant back in relief that Stephen had accepted his mother's return, but felt a gnawing worry about where they went from here. For months all he'd wanted was for Eve to come back and for them to be a family again. But that was before Marianne. If he chose to have Eve back he was going to have to hurt Marianne. But if he chose Marianne, he wasn't sure his son would ever forgive him.

Noel was on his way home when Cat called with the news about her mother. Suddenly his anxieties about telling her he'd lost his job seemed meaningless. Cat sounded tearful and upset, not at all like her calm, controlled self. Noel wanted to go straight to her but knew that, first things first, he had to check how the children were.

Regina was cooking tea and organising homework when he arrived.

'Get along with you,' she said, when Noel suggested taking the children home. 'I'm fine here for another couple of hours. I think Cat needs you right now.'

Noel protested, but Regina wouldn't hear a word of it. 'Come on,' she said, 'remember the time when I'd had my Caesarean when Ollie was born, and Cat took the kids to school for me for weeks? *Weeks.* That's what we do, Noel. We help each other out when we can.'

'I'll give my mum a ring and see if she can come round,'

said Noel. 'That way at least we won't be imposing on you for too long.'

Noel dreaded ringing his mum. Normally he let Cat do it and have one of those mysterious female chats that went on for hours and which involved nothing more important than swapping recipes (he had a feeling some of Granny Nightmare's favourites were going in the cookbook, though Cat had sworn she wasn't going to call her that), or discussing *The X Factor*. If Noel ever did ring his mother, he kept it as short and sweet as possible so she couldn't start telling him about how wonderful his sister and her offspring were and how inadequate he and his were by comparison. On a normal day, he'd never have rung her, particularly when he'd just lost his job. But today wasn't a normal day. Noel loved Louise and couldn't bear the thought of her becoming ill and old. He'd been so caught up in his own problems of late, he'd thought Cat might be exaggerating the nature of her mother's illness, and now he felt ashamed of the thought.

'Hi, Mum,' he said as his mother picked up the phone. 'It's Noel.'

'I've already packed my bag, and I'll be on the first train tomorrow,' said his mother.

'Sorry?' Noel was taken aback.

'Catherine rang me from the hospital to tell me what happened,' said his mother crisply. 'You two are going to need a lot of help while Catherine's mother is in hospital. And Catherine doesn't need to have to worry about the children right now, so I'm coming to stay till you're straight again. It's all agreed.'

'Oh,' said Noel. He'd been gearing himself up for an argument about how she wasn't at his beck and call, and here she was all ready to drop everything to come down. 'That's very good of you, Mum. We both appreciate it.'

'That's what families are for,' said Mum. 'If you can't turn to me in a crisis, who can you turn to?'

Noel was still mulling over the unexpectedness of this when he got to the hospital. He found Cat by her mother's bed, holding her hand.

Louise smiled when she saw him, but seemed a bit confused. 'Catherine, you haven't introduced me to this nice young man,' she said.

'Come on, Mum, you know who this is,' said Cat. 'It's Noel. We've been married for fifteen years.'

'Of course,' said Cat's mum. 'Yes. Noel. That's who it is.' But she looked unconvinced and, by the time the nurse was calling for visiting time to be over, she seemed to have forgotten who he was again.

'I'll be in to see you tomorrow, Mum,' said Cat. 'And I'll go and get you some things from home.'

'Oh, thank you, sweetheart,' said Louise. She looked tired and unsettled. Noel found it very disconcerting to see his energetic mother-in-law looking so frail and, well, *old*, lying in the bed. How could a fall have effected such a dramatic change?

'The doctor thinks the bang on the head may have disorientated her,' Cat said as they left the hospital. 'And her blood sugar is incredibly low. She's barely been eating apparently, which can lead to confusion. I'll have to go round to sort out her place tomorrow. I don't think she'll be going back there for a while. If at all.'

'Where will she stay, then?' Noel hadn't really thought this one through.

'With us of course,' said Cat, 'where else can she go?'

'Cat,' Noel said carefully, 'I know this has been an enormous shock to you, but are you really sure this is a good idea? You've got enough on your plate as it is.'

'Are you saying you don't want to look after my mother?' Cat flared up.

'No,' said Noel. 'I'm just saying think about it carefully. Maybe she'd be better off in a home.'

'There's nothing to think about,' said Cat. 'She's my mum. And we're all she's got. I can't let her go into a home.'

Noel backed off. Now was not the time to have this argument. He put his arm around her and kissed her on the head. 'You never know,' he said, 'it might not come to that. I'm sure we'll work something out.' Though quite what, he had no idea.

Marianne was walking to school, pondering the Nativity problem, and wondering if there was any way she could wrest control of it away from Diana. Miss Woods had been immensely helpful in providing information about the old traditional Shropshire Nativity that had been handed down from mediaeval times and been played in barns and village churches right up to the turn of the last century.

'It's a derivation from an old mystery play,' Miss Woods had explained. 'I can remember taking part in it as a very young girl.'

It seemed so much more appropriate to take that traditional route somehow, particularly now they'd been given the go-ahead to use Hopesay Manor Chapel. The play itself was very simple and therefore suitable for children and, with the judicious use of some sixteenth-century carols, and the beautiful setting, Marianne felt sure they had a very good chance of winning the competition. If only she could somehow persuade Diana Carew.

'Marianne.' She heard her name being called and, turning round, saw Gabriel running up the hill after her. They'd not seen each other for a couple of days, Gabriel having been tied up with sheep shearing and Marianne having given every spare minute to helping Pippa. Even when Gabriel had been helping out at Pippa's they'd not had a lot of time

305

to spend together, and since Benjy'd died Gabriel had been warier of letting Stephen know what was going on between them. She hoped that wasn't an excuse and he wasn't getting cold feet. On the night of the flood, Marianne had really felt they were beginning to establish something together. She didn't want to see their fledgling relationship wither and die before it had even properly got going.

'Gabriel!' she said gladly. She'd have loved to have given him a peck on the cheek, but was aware that hundreds of eyes were probably twitching behind the curtains as it was. Miss Woods and her cronies never missed a trick in Hope Christmas, even when their houses were recovering from flooding.

Marianne waved as Miss Woods went whizzing past. She'd noticed earlier, to her amusement, Miss Woods was taking her electric buggy out again. Since the flood they'd seen less of it than normal as the roads had been too slippery and dangerous.

'Is it just me,' said Marianne, 'or does she get faster on that thing?'

'She's probably gearing up for next year's Grand Prix season,' grinned Gabriel. 'Marianne, I wanted you to hear this from me before anyone else told you—'

'Sorry, what were you saying?' Marianne was distracted for a moment as she saw Miss Woods' buggy topple sideways slightly, before she righted it. 'For a minute there I thought she was going to have it over.'

Gabriel looked incredibly nervous. Suddenly Marianne's heart was in her boots. She had the panicky thought he was about to tell her it was all over. Marianne felt a cold rush of reality flood over her. The most lovely man she'd met in her life, and she'd stalled at the first corner. When was she ever going to get this love thing sorted?

'Marianne,' Gabriel said clearing his throat.

There was a sudden screech of brakes, a thud, and a lot of shouting.

Marianne began to run to the top of the hill, and stared in horror over the other side. Miss Woods' vehicle was lying on its side; she was emerging from it grumpily waving her stick.

'Didn't you see me?' she demanded of a rather woebegone-looking Diana Carew, who was sitting on the floor nursing her shoulder.

'Well, if I'd seen you, I'd not be sitting here like this, would I?' was the acerbic reply.

Marianne and Gabriel went to see what they could do, but Diana waved them away.

'I'm fine,' she said tetchily. 'No thanks to that ridiculous woman.'

'It was an accident,' said Miss Woods to no one in particular. 'If people will not look where they are going . . .'

Stifling a grin, Marianne tried to make Diana more comfortable till medical help arrived, which luckily it did in the form of the local GP who happened to be passing. Breathing sighs of relief, Marianne and Gabriel beat a hasty retreat, as their presence clearly wasn't needed.

'What was it you wanted to say to me?' said Marianne, not entirely sure she wanted to know the answer.

Gabriel swallowed hard.

'There's no easy way to tell you this,' he said, 'but Eve's back. And I think she wants to come home.'

Cat stared in dismay at her mother's kitchen. Noel had offered to do the school run so Cat could go and get some things for Mum. While she was there, Cat had thought she might as well see if Mum had any food she could take in to the hospital. Louise's kitchen, like the rest of her home, was normally pristine. One of the constants in Cat's life had been that calm, orderly home, always a haven of peace where she would come and recharge her batteries. It had been like that her whole life.

Now there was days-old washing-up in the sink, and a nasty smell coming from the dishwasher. Cat went into the cupboard under the sink for some dishwasher tablets, and found Mum had put the salt there, but no tabs were to be found. Rootling around in the other cupboards, Cat discovered Mum had for some inexplicable reason been storing up tins of cat food, though she hadn't owned a cat in years.

Eventually Cat discovered the dishwasher tablets in the cupboard where her mum kept the flour, but not before uncovering everything in a state of complete and utter disorder. Not only that, half the contents of the cupboards were past their sell-by date, and by the time Cat dared venture into the fridge, she wasn't at all surprised to see it covered in mould, with cheese and ham dating from weeks back, and at least two pints of milk that gone off. There could be no more poignant display of her mother's infirmity. Cat wanted to weep for what had been lost.

Memories of her childhood years poured over her in a torrent. Cat sitting at this very kitchen table drinking milk while her mother listened to the radio, making Christmas decorations, doing her homework, while Mum pottered around her. So much of her life had been spent in this kitchen. All of her life spent knowing there was one solid certainty in it. That, whatever happened, however rough things got, there was one person who would never let her down. Whenever she fell her mother had been there to pick her up. And now that certainty had gone forever. From now on she'd have no one to pick her up but herself. She was overcome with an irrevocable sense of loss. Nothing was ever going to be the same again.

This would never do. Cat felt compelled to do something,

anything, to take her mind away from the hopelessness of the situation. Her mother had looked after her for her whole life, and now it was Cat's turn to return the favour. First things first, she could begin to sort this chaos out. Cat set off on a frenzy of cleaning. She cleared out the entire contents of the freezer; she cleaned the fridge; swept the floor; rearranged cupboards; and only when she'd done all that did she sit down and put her head in her hands. Mum had clearly been hiding the extent of her problems from Cat and Noel for months. There was going to be no way she could come back here. She'd have to come to them.

Noel hadn't seemed enthusiastic about the idea, it was true. Cat frowned – surely he couldn't really believe Mum should go into a home? He must see it as she did. Mum had done so much for them, now it was time to look after her.

'But you must promise me that if I get really bad, you'll sell this place and put me in a home.' A sudden vision of Mum swam before her eyes, the last time they'd sat in this kitchen together. Her mother was very stubborn, Cat knew, but Cat could be stubborn too. She sat surrounded by memories of growing up in this place, of coming home with scraped knees, and reading books. Her mother had always been there, an oasis of calm in her turbulent world. Her mother *had* been her world growing up. Cat looked round the kitchen once more. Whatever happened now, however much Mum and Noel might think it was a bad idea, Cat had no intention of abandoning her mum. No intention at all.

Chapter Twenty-Six

'So Eve's back for good?' Pippa whistled sympathetically. Marianne hadn't bothered to go home after work. She couldn't bear the thought of being alone in the little house that had seen so many tears when Luke left her. She knew it wasn't Gabriel's fault. She understood why he was doing this. Why he had to at least give it a go for Stephen's sake. But there was a part of her that was reacting like a child in the playground, stamping her feet and saying, 'It's not fair!'

'Excuse the chaos by the way,' said Pippa, who was folding laundry in the old-fashioned farm kitchen. 'My parents are wonderful to have us here, but there isn't a lot of room. Thankfully now they're retired they do like going off to Spain periodically, so we've got the place to ourselves for a bit.'

Marianne could hear the boys whooping wildly in the haybarn.

'It certainly gives me a break,' she said, wiping her eyes. 'I can't wait for us to get straight again. Living out of bags is so exhausting.'

Marianne felt a pang of guilt. Here she was, wittering on about her paltry problems, when Pippa had so much more to deal with than she did.

'I'm sorry,' she said. 'I've been going on too much.'

'Don't be,' said Pippa. 'Come on, have a cup of tea, and we can put the world to rights. You can tell me all about Diana Carew. Is she going to be all right?'

'I think so,' said Marianne. 'Apparently she's put her shoulder out, though. I shouldn't laugh really, but it was a funny sight seeing Miss Woods take off like that.'

'I bet,' said Pippa. 'If I was more suspicious, I might think she'd done it on purpose.'

'Oh, I can't think she'd do that, would she?' Marianne stifled a giggle at the thought. 'I mean, I know they don't see eye to eye, but that's a bit drastic.'

'It will certainly make it difficult for Diana to run the Nativity,' said Pippa.

'Maybe that's why Miss Woods did it.'

'Pippa, you are a wicked, wicked woman,' said Marianne, laughing. 'Still, you've done me some good, I can face going home now.'

'You never know, Eve might not hang about,' said Pippa, as she saw Marianne out.

'Gabriel seemed to think she would,' said Marianne. 'She says she's much better apparently. She's been undergoing some kind of therapy and now she wants to sort out the relationships in her life, whatever that means.'

Pippa snorted. 'I think staying away would be the best way to do that.'

'Actually, I think she is doing the best thing,' said Marianne. 'This way, Gabriel gets to have some kind of closure if it goes wrong again. At least I think she is . . .'

'I sense a but here,' said Pippa.

'Why the bloody hell did Eve have to turn up now, just when things were going so well with me and Gabe?' Marianne burst out. 'I do understand they've got stuff to sort out, and I'm really trying to be generous. But bloody hell. It's going to get so messy. I'm not sure

311

I want to or even should get involved. Perhaps I should just back off.'

'Don't do that,' said Pippa, 'I know Gabe really likes you. I can't see that he'd go back to Eve now.'

'Yes, but what about Stephen?' said Marianne. 'It all boils down to what's best for him in the end, doesn't it? And let's face it, we all know what's best for him is his mum coming home. I can't ever compete with that.'

'I think that's very altruistic of you,' said Pippa. 'In your shoes I'd be tempted to claw Eve's eyes out.'

'What good would that do?' said Marianne. 'I can't make Gabriel choose me. And I don't want to if it's a question of Stephen's happiness. I just have to wait and see what happens. And hope that somehow, miraculously, everything will work out for the best.'

'Thanks so much for all your help,' Cat said to her mother-in-law with gratitude. 'I really don't know what we'd have done without you.'

'I'm glad to help,' said Angela. 'I always felt bad that I couldn't do more when the children were small. I was too wrapped up in myself after Bill died to think about anyone else.'

'Oh, right.' That was unexpected. 'Maybe you could tell Noel that sometime.'

'Do you think he'd want me to tell him that?' Angela looked so genuinely puzzled that Cat nearly burst out laughing. How was it that Angela and Noel were so incapable of understanding one another?

'I know he would,' said Cat. 'Anyway, that's in the past, you're here now and we're both incredibly grateful.'

It had been two days now since her mother's fall, and Angela had moved in with a vengeance. But, for once, Cat was thankful for the forceful personality, which

312

ensured that things got done. The kids were far more in awe of Granny Nightmare than they were of Mum and Dad, and Cat was amazed at the difference in their attitudes towards room tidying. Angela had even prevailed on Mel and James to help out with household chores, and during the day when everyone was at home, she'd taken it upon herself to give the whole house a spring clean. Under normal circumstances, Cat would have bristled at this invasion of her house but, right now, she was so exhausted and shocked by the rapidity of what was happening to her mother, she was just grateful to come back to a house that was tidy and to a meal that she hadn't cooked. Soon she was going to have to check her emails and see how things were at work, but she hadn't quite got the energy for that.

'It's a pleasure,' said Angela. 'Your trouble is you take on too much. You don't have to be Superwoman, you know.'

Cat sighed 'It's quite a hard habit to break,' she said. 'Once you're used to doing things, it's difficult not to keep feeling you *should* do them.'

'Any news on your mother?' Angela asked. Again, her quiet sympathy had been much appreciated. All these years of moaning about her, and Angela was turning out to be a great support in Cat's hour of need. Better even than Noel, who seemed to be in some mental slump and unable to cope with anything. Cat knew they were both under pressure, but living with Noel at the moment was like walking on eggshells. Although he'd taken a couple of days off, he was now saying he was needed in the office. Which was fair enough, Cat supposed. It wasn't Noel's mum who was ill, and she knew they both couldn't take time off indefinitely, but she just wanted him to be around, to feel that, if she needed to, she could howl on his shoulder. The worst thing about the collapse of her mother was the sudden realisation that her days of being mothered were over. Now it was up Cat to take care of everyone else.

'They're holding a case conference later in the week,' said Cat. 'It turns out she has had a couple of TIAs on top of the Alzheimer's, and they think she can't really manage at home anymore. And I think that too, if I'm honest. I'd hate her to burn the place down or something.'

'So what will you do?' asked Angela.

'She'll come here, of course,' said Cat, shocked that Angela could even think there was another option.

'Oh.' Angela looked disconcerted by this news, and Cat geared herself up for the inevitable lecture. 'I really meant for the long term. She can't stay here indefinitely.'

'Why not?' Cat said. 'She's my mother, and I'm all she's got. I'm going to look after her as long as I'm able to.'

Angela looked gently at her daughter-in-law.

'Cat, I know you think that now. But believe me, I've seen how hard it is for families caring for Alzheimer's patients. You think you'll cope, but it's going to put a strain on everyone. On the children. On Noel. But most of all on you. Do you think that's really fair? You should really think about that, you know.'

'I have thought about it,' said Cat, 'and there's no way my mum is going into a home. She's coming home with us and that's that.'

Noel was meeting a former colleague in a pub in town, who claimed to have some work for him. Now that GRB had finally given him the push, Noel decided he might as well try and get some consultancy work. But his colleague, a lanky engineer called Will, was pessimistic about Noel's chances of success.

'A year ago, yes,' he said. 'You'd have been calling all the shots and been in high demand. But now, with the down-turn in the economy . . .'

He didn't need to spell it out. Noel had been a young engineer fresh out of uni in the early nineties. His first job had lasted eighteen months and, as he was last in, he'd been first out that time. It had taken him another year to find permanent work. But that was before Cat, and the children. He'd been on his own with no family to support. It hadn't mattered that much if Noel didn't work for a bit. Like Mr Micawber, he'd felt something would always turn up.

Noel sank his pint with something akin to despair. In his youth, he'd had that happy-go-lucky feeling that things would work out for the best somehow. More and more he now had the feeling that they *wouldn't*. He knew his outlook was becoming increasingly pessimistic, but it was as if a malaise had taken over his soul. All those years of working so hard to achieve a home of his own, to be able to provide for his family, and now he'd lost his job, and wasn't at all sure of getting another one. Although his redundancy money had given him a cushion, Noel was also worried about their financial situation, which was going to be looking distinctly dodgy if he didn't get another job soon.

He was conscious also that Cat needed him at the moment and yet he found he couldn't be the support to her that she deserved. Noel despised himself for his inability to help her, but yet he seemed powerless to prevent it. If only he could articulate some of what he was feeling, but Noel wasn't good at that at the best of times. This wasn't how he'd planned his life. He felt that everything was shrinking, becoming less. And he was becoming less with it.

Will had to get back to work, promising to give Noel a call 'if anything came up', but they both knew it was mean-ingless. Noel went for an aimless wander round town, before heading home on the bus. No point looking at electronic gadgetry on Tottenham Court Road when you didn't have any money to buy anything.

He felt in his pocket for change for the bus. His season ticket had just run out, and he wouldn't be renewing it in a hurry. Noel still hadn't told Cat about his change in circumstances. With the situation with her mother so tricky, it still didn't feel like the right time. He found a card in his pocket, and pulled it out to look at it.

Ralph Nicholas
Hopesay Manor
Hope Christmas
Shropshire

There was a phone number and an email address. He thought back to their conversation and picked up his mobile.

'So, how do we do this?' Gabriel said, as he sat in the kitchen with Eve, feeling awkward. 'We haven't had any communication for six months, and I'm not sure where to even start. I know you've been very very ill but, Eve, I can't help feeling angry about what you put us through. You have to know that. If we're going to have a future together, I think we need to clear the air.'

Eve sat in silence for a moment.

'You're right,' she said eventually. 'But I can't undo what I've done. I left because I felt you were suffocating me with your love.'

Gabriel bristled.

'I know, I know, that sounds harsh, but it's true. All the time I was with you, I wasn't getting any better. Because you wouldn't allow me to.'

It was Gabriel's turn to fall silent. He found himself

chipping away at a splinter in the old kitchen table that had sat in his parents' farm when he was growing up. Pippa had said more or less the same thing to him. And in recent months, he couldn't deny it had felt like a huge relief, not to have to think about Eve and what she was doing every waking minute of the day.

'And are you better now?' He didn't look at her when he said this and his voice came out tinny and harsh.

'I think so,' said Eve. 'The therapy has certainly helped. I've realised that I have a lot of security issues relating to my mother, which I can't do anything about. But I also realise that I can change things for the future. So I want to make some big changes in my life. Starting right here.'

'Such as?'

'Gabe, I don't know how to say this.' Eve did look very distressed, but Gabriel knew of old that she was good at putting on emotions to get her own way. 'But whatever you might have thought, I'm not here to ask to come back. I think I've realised that that part of my life is over. I'm sorry. You deserve so much better than me. I wish I could have been the farmer's wife you wanted, but I can't, and it was killing me. And coming back here and staying in that damp cottage I'm renting has confirmed I'm really not cut out for country living.'

'Oh.' A wave of pain washed over Gabriel. Despite it all, there had been a forlorn hope that somehow they could put the past behind them and move on, but she'd killed even that. Stephen was going to be devastated. *But you're free to be with Marianne,* a voice whispered in his head, and suddenly he knew that whatever else happened it was okay. Eve had hurt him for the last time. She had no power over him anymore.

'However, there is something else,' said Eve. 'I realise that at times I've not been the best mother to Stephen, but I am his mother.'

317

'I would never stop you seeing him,' said Gabriel. 'You left him, remember?'

'And it was a dreadful mistake,' said Eve. 'Of all the things I've learnt in the last few months, I know that for sure. Stephen is my son. And I want him back. And you can't stop me getting him. Which is why I'm going to be suing for custody.'

Chapter Twenty-Seven

'Can she actually do that?' Pippa demanded a few days later, when Gabriel came round to tell her what had happened.

'Apparently she can,' said Gabriel as he sat down heavily in Pippa's cosy kitchen. 'I don't know what to do, Pippa. What if Eve takes Stephen away from me?'

'But would she be granted custody with her mental health history?' said Pippa.

'I'd have to bring that up,' said Gabriel. 'I don't know that I want to do that. I don't even want it to go to court. It wouldn't do Stephen any good to think we were wrangling over him like two dogs with a bone. Particularly as Eve seems determined to dwell on the fact that I wouldn't let Stephen speak to her at Easter. God, I wish I hadn't done that.'

'What does Stephen think?' Pippa asked.

Gabriel looked out of the window and sighed.

'I haven't figured out a way of talking to him about it yet,' he admitted. 'He's so excited his mum is home, I can't bear to tell him he might have to choose between us.'

'He might not have to,' said Pippa.

'Eve seemed pretty determined to get him back,' sighed Gabriel. 'She says she really wants to make it up to him for the times she's let him down.'

'But is that wise?' argued Pippa. 'Eve is so fragile, who's to say she won't have another relapse?'

'She does seem much better,' said Gabriel. 'I think she was probably right, I didn't help her. She's got herself a job and a flat in London, and has been seeing a therapist who seems to be helping.'

'What?' Pippa looked at him in horror. 'You don't mean she's planning to take Stephen back to London with her?'

'I do,' sighed Gabriel. 'But if he wants to go, what can I do? She's his mum after all. I can't stand between them. Besides, Stephen's pretty cross with me right now. He found out that Eve was at her mum's at Easter when I told him she wasn't. He's saying that he wants to go and live with her and not me.'

'Gabriel North, sometimes you're too soft,' said Pippa. 'Sure Stephen's cross with you, and rightly so, but you can't just let Eve waltz back in and take him back. You have to fight. Have you talked to a lawyer yet?'

'No,' said Gabriel. 'I keep hoping it won't have to come to that. I just wish we could find a way of solving things so that we're all happy. But most of all, I don't want Stephen to suffer any more than he has already. Ultimately, it's up to him. If he wants to go and live with Eve, I won't stop him.'

'There you are, Mum,' Cat led her mother into the lounge and sat her down. 'Let's get you a nice cup of tea.'

'I want to go home,' Mum looked determined – a look Cat was coming to know well.

'Mum, you know that's not possible right now,' said Cat soothingly. 'We talked about this in the hospital, remember?' Why was she even saying that, she knew her mother wouldn't remember. The speed at which the memory loss was progressing was frightening. Although sometimes it

320

seemed as if Mum was totally *compos mentis*, an hour spent in her company was enough to make Cat realise how ill-equipped she was now to look after herself. After a while the conversation would become circular, and Mum would repeat whatever they'd been talking about earlier, as if it had never been mentioned before. Or she would stare off into the distance. But then, weirdly, she'd launch into a tale from Cat's childhood with the clearest of detail. It was as though parts of her brain had just shut down, like a power plant running on the spare generator.

'But I want to go home,' Mum was starting to get agitated. 'I don't like it here. Why won't they let me go home?'

At that point Noel came in. He looked unkempt. Cat had been aware that he had been up half the night tossing and turning, and he'd muttered something about not feeling too great this morning so hadn't gone into work. But she'd been so tied up with Mum, she hadn't got to the bottom of his misery. Making a mental note that she really really must spend some more time with her husband, Cat smiled more brightly than she felt and said, 'But we want you to be here with us, don't we, Noel?'

'Of course we do,' Noel said with a smile, which somehow didn't reach his eyes. He seemed awkward and ill at ease and Cat, remembering how unenthusiastic he'd been about Mum coming to stay with them, suddenly had a panicky feeling that he wasn't as supportive of her as she wanted him to be.

But then he moved round swiftly helping Mum with her coat off, and sitting her down and making her a cup of tea, and charming her in a way only he could. Noel had always loved Mum, and she him. Cat felt a warm rush of gratitude and love for her husband. Not everyone would cope so well with this difficult situation. Soon Mum

321

was much calmer, and had forgotten all about going home.

'Do you want me to do the school run?' Noel asked.

'Crikey, is that the time?' Cat looked at her watch in dismay. Just getting Mum home and settled down had taken the best part of an hour. How on earth were they going to manage every day?

You manage because you must, Mum's mantra from her early childhood popped into her head. It's what she always said when people asked her how she'd coped being left on her own with Cat when her father had left.

'That would be wonderful, thanks, Noel.' She shot him a grateful look and, as he went to get his coat, got up and gave him a hug and a kiss. It felt like ages since she'd been so spontaneous with him. She needed to make more time for Noel. That was a given. And how would they manage with everything? Well, they would, because there was no other choice.

Marianne was scouring the Internet, looking for a decent modern translation of the Shropshire Nativity play. Miss Woods had given her a version that was rather too full of mediaeval Shropshire dialect, which no one was going to understand.

'Aha! Gotcha,' she said as a search engine took her to a site based on mediaeval Mystery Plays. Here it was. *A Shropshire Nativity* translated by Professor A. Middleton. Perfect. Just what she needed.

Marianne printed off the copy that she'd found and started to pull together a list of carols. She'd found a CD of old-fashioned carols, and listening to 'I syng of a Mayden' had brought tears to her eyes, as had the beautiful 'Balulalow' by Britten. She wondered if Gabriel would object to Stephen singing it as a solo. He had such a beautiful voice. She'd also listed the 'Sussex Carol', the 'Coventry Carol', 'Silent Night' and 'It Came Upon the Midnight Clear' and Christina Rossetti's achingly beautiful 'In the Bleak Midwinter'. What she was after was simplicity and purity, and all of those carols fitted the bill perfectly. She just hoped the committee would be as enthusiastic as she was. Marianne knew that here was an opportunity to put on a very special Nativity play and maybe if they were lucky enough to win the competition, give something back to the village that had helped her over the last year.

She started reading through what she'd printed off and making notes, and then decided to go and see Miss Woods, whose knowledge of this kind of stuff was not only encyclo-paedic but, being Shropshire born and bred, was very likely to know more about how to put on something like this. In fact, it was Miss Woods talking about how there had been a mediaeval mystery play at Hopesay Manor in her youth that had first put the idea in her head.

Gathering her things and putting her jacket on, she made her way into the village.

She was coming up to Miss Woods' house, when she saw – oh my God, it couldn't be . . . There was Luke pinning up a notice outside the Parish Centre. She hadn't seen him in months, and annoyingly she felt a little knot of inner tension form as she approached her former fiancé.

'Luke,' she said stiffly, 'it's not often we see you in the village.'

'Marianne,' that dazzling smile again. 'You look lovely as ever.'

'Thanks,' said Marianne feeling wrong-footed. Luke was being much friendlier than the last time they'd met. 'What's that you're putting up?'

'I'm inviting people to a public meeting,' Luke said. 'The vicar's kindly let me use the Parish Centre. I wanted to explain

323

to people about the opportunities afforded to them by the eco town. Now that Hope Christmas appears to be in danger of flooding regularly, I thought people might like to know about the alternatives offered by living somewhere that is both environmentally friendly and capable of dealing with nature's extremities.'

'But I thought your village is on a flood plain?' Marianne frowned. Pippa and Gabriel had been most vocal about that.

'Not anymore,' said Luke. 'Our engineers are looking at ways of diverting the river. You'd be surprised what can be achieved nowadays.'

'But won't that be at the expense of something else?' said Marianne.

'Not a bit of it,' said Luke. 'We're just sending the water in a different direction over the hillside, and providing people with a better class of home. I mean, look at this place.' His arm swept across the High Street, which still looked distinctly dirty and shabby. 'Why would anyone want to live in one of these old damp houses, when they could have the convenience of the latest gadgets, a brand new leisure centre and a new hypermarket on their doorstep?'

'Why indeed?' said Marianne drily.

'So, can I expect to see you at the meeting?' he asked.

'I doubt it,' said Marianne.

'Pity,' said Luke. 'We're offering great rates for first-time buyers, and for key workers. You never know, you could qualify for a great discount.'

Marianne smiled at the thought that Luke might actually be doing something altruistic for once. 'I'll bear it in mind,' she said. Discounts for key workers. She loved Hope Christmas, but she was never going to be able to afford to buy here. Suddenly living in the eco town seemed a more tempting prospect. She dismissed the thought almost as soon as it entered her head with a wry smile – anything Luke was involved in was bound to have a catch in it.

Noel stood in the school playground freezing his backside off. It was the sort of grey damp wintry day where the cold got into your bones and the gloom of winter rotted your soul. He had a sudden desperate urge to be in Hope Christmas, which he instinctively knew would be cosy and cheerful at this time of year. He missed his trips up there so much that he'd eventually plucked up courage to ring the number Ralph had given him, but, when the phone was answered by Luke Nicholas, Noel had lost his nerve and hung up. Maybe Ralph was just being polite. Noel couldn't quite muster his courage to ring again.

He stamped his feet to try and get them warm. Why did they always let them out late on cold days? He hated doing the school run at the best of times. Though it was true that there were a few more dads in the playground than when Mel had first started school, there was something about being surrounded by the Mum mafia that made him feel very nervous. Luckily he spotted Regina standing by Ruby's classroom, so went over to say hello.

'Am I glad to see you,' he said. 'I was just trying to keep a low profile and hoping no one was going to accuse me of being the pervert in the playground.'

'Oh, come on,' said Regina, 'they do know you by now.'

'I know,' said Noel. 'I just always feel as though all the mums I don't know are looking at me as if I'm some kind of paedophile.'

'The times we live in,' said Regina, shaking her head. 'No work today?'

'No,' Noel hesitated. He'd spent most of the last week getting up, putting on a suit, and pretending to go to work

325

as normal. He knew he couldn't go on doing that, but he didn't now know how to tell Cat.

'The thing is,' he said, 'Cat doesn't know this yet, but actually I've lost my job.'

'You what?' said Regina. 'Oh, Noel, I'm so sorry. But why on earth haven't you told Cat?'

Noel shrugged.

'I was going to, but what with her mum and everything, it's been difficult.'

'You can't keep it a secret anymore,' said Regina. 'For heaven's sake, Noel, she needs to know the truth. She deserves the truth.'

'I know,' said Noel. He couldn't explain the apathy that seemed to be afflicting him of late, or the sheer unmitigated terror the thought of telling Cat was causing him. He knew it wasn't rational, but he hadn't felt rational for months. 'And I will. Soon.'

'Soon?' Regina said. 'You should tell her now, really you should.'

'Yes, you're right,' said Noel, turning to greet Ruby who'd come running out shouting 'Daddy!' excitedly. A definite bonus of the school run was the delight with which his children greeted him.

'Tell who what?' Ruby asked as Noel swung her in the air.

'No one anything, you nosy thing,' he said, kissing her on the nose.

As he walked home with the children, making small talk with Regina, Noel was wrestling with his conscience. Regina was right. Sooner was much better than later.

He walked in to find Cat cooking while her mother was dozing in the lounge. The children dropped coats, bags and lunch boxes and proceeded to badger their mother with accounts of their day. Eventually Noel managed to shoo them all into the family room, from where Paige called, 'The shelf's fallen down again', before settling into watching *Tracy Beaker*.

Taking a deep breath, and feeling sicker than he'd ever felt in his life, Noel went over to Cat and took her in his arms.

'There's something I've been meaning to tell you,' he said.

Chapter Twenty-Eight

Cat was flicking through entries for the Nativity competition. They'd had so many Bev had decided to split them into batches for everyone to sort through. Cat was busy putting hers into piles of no hopers, possibles and definite maybes. The pile of no hopers was depressingly large, and she had a sneaky feeling that the possibles pile had grown larger over the last hour or so as a sense of desperation crept in. She only had three choices on the definite maybes.

The trouble was that most of the entrants hadn't followed the brief properly. They hadn't asked for a Nativity with bling (roughly a third of the no hopers were Nativity plays awash with bright lights and flashing Santas), nor for the PC ecumenical versions favoured by the sort of schools Cat's children went to (she'd read some entries that lacked a single mention of the baby Jesus). Cat was ambivalent about religion, but surely the whole point of the thing was that you had to mention the birth of the Son of God. Didn't you?

The three that Cat had picked off the pile hadn't exactly filled her with excitement – the one from the Cornish village of Treadlightly had sounded quite sweet on a first read, but now she was feeling dubious about the thought of watching a Nativity outside in a barn, complete with animals and newborn baby (provided one was helpfully born in the village that week). Hadn't they heard the old adage about working with children and animals? Still, it sounded better than the Clevedon Preschool calypso version, which had only caught her eye because it sounded lively, or the rather po-faced traditional (she had wanted tradition, Cat reminded herself) Nativity offered by the straight-laced sounding Arlington School for Girls. Cat told herself off for allowing a prejudice against public schooling to prevent her accepting that they might actually come up with the goods.

None of them inspired her enormously. What was it she'd been after exactly? Cat cast her mind back to last Christmas and thought about that moment in Sainsbury's when she'd suddenly been heartily sick of it all. What Christmas was missing these days was simplicity. Simplicity and any sense of the spiritual. It was all about greed and excess now.

Feeling rather depressed, Cat got up and headed out for an early lunch, and the chance to do some Christmas shopping. She'd never been so behind at Christmas before, but what with Mum's illness, and now Noel losing his job, Cat was finding it hard to summon up any enthusiasm whatsoever for the festive season. She was still reeling from the fact that Noel had been unable to tell her about his job. Since last Christmas it felt like their lives were unravelling, and now he'd shut her out at a time when he had needed her most. Cat felt powerless to help Noel, but somewhere deep in his soul she feared there was a terrible problem.

Cat mooched miserably down Oxford Street, wandering into shop after busy shop piled high with tat, blaring out 'I Wish It Could Be Christmas Every Day'. The streets were packed, people spilling off the pavements, till Cat felt sure it was only a matter of time before someone went under a bus. At Oxford Circus there was the inevitable bomb scare, rendering the tube station shut and an influx of yet more people into an already overcrowded area. Giving up in disgust, Cat returned empty-handed to the office. As she was about to go through the revolving glass doors, an elderly man who looked vaguely familiar appeared as if from nowhere and tapped her on the shoulder. He was clutching a brown envelope in his hand.

'Catherine Tinsall, I believe,' he said.

'Yes,' said Cat with a frown. 'How did you know?'

'I make it my business to know everything,' said the man, touching his nose. 'I believe you're looking for entries to a Nativity competition.'

'That's right,' said Cat cautiously.

'Of course you want to know why I ask,' said the man. 'Quite right too. Here's our entry. The Parish Committee was terribly worried about the Christmas post, so as I was coming to London, I said I'd hand-deliver it.'

'Well, thank you very much,'

'My pleasure,' said the strange man. He doffed his cap to her and vanished into the crowd as mysteriously as he'd appeared. One minute he was there, and then he was gone.

Cat went back into the office, made herself a cup of tea, and sat down to read the entry. It could hardly be any worse than anything she'd seen so far. It was from a village called Hope Christmas. Appropriate, she thought, smiling, trying to work out where she'd heard the name before. The accompanying letter was from a Marianne Moore, who was a teacher at the village school. Hope Christmas? The name was familiar. It was only when she got to the end of the letter and discovered that, if Hope Christmas won the competition, they were planning to rebuild their village hall, which had been destroyed in the recent floods, that the penny dropped. *Of course.* It was near where Noel's company had been building the eco town. The letter ended with an eloquent plea citing the importance of the village hall, which was at the heart of the community, especially now the village was losing its post office.

Cat turned to the accompanying script. It was laid out professionally – typed with double spacing as requested, which made a change. As she read it, Cat nearly punched the air with delight. Here at last was a simple retelling of the Christmas story. Marianne had gone back to an original Nativity from an early version of a Shropshire mystery play. She'd included a funny scene where Joseph sought out two midwives to attend the labour, and a charming moment with dancing shepherds who were unsure how to take the angels' news. Cat liked the sound of Marianne. But the moment when the baby was born was pure and simple and just what she'd been looking for. Accompanying the script was a carefully selected set of carols, some of which Cat was unfamiliar with but others, like the 'Coventry Carol', were guaranteed to bring a tear to the eye. This was perfect.

She rang home to ask if Noel knew anything about the suggested location, a small chapel to the side of Hopesay Manor, clearly a local stately home.

'Hopesay Manor?' said Noel. 'Yes, I've been there. I don't know about the chapel, but the estate itself is fantastic. I wanted to revitalise the old houses on the estate but was overruled. Remember?'

Cat guiltily cast her mind back to something Noel had been moaning about months ago. She felt constantly guilty around him these days. In the fortnight since he'd come clean about his job, he'd been so tense and unhappy Cat never knew what mood he was going to be in. The only good thing about the current state of affairs was at least he could help keep an eye on Mum, though she felt guilty about that too. It didn't seem fair to impose that on Noel. But she

331

was constantly feeling torn between the responsibilities of the workplace and those of her home. One day she might even work the balance out right.

'Can you come home soon?' Noel said. 'Your mum's getting agitated again and I can't calm her down.'

'I'll try,' promised Cat. Maybe Bev, whose patience with Cat's domestic arrangements was reaching its limit, might be a little more tolerant when she knew Cat had found their Nativity. Maybe. Cat had a horrible feeling that a moment of reckoning was drawing near. She was facing some tough choices but, with Noel out of work, she couldn't possibly think of quitting her job.

'Stephen, what's the matter?' Gabriel had come in from checking on the ewes, who were about to be bred for spring lambing, to find his son sobbing uncontrollably while Eve looked helplessly on. They'd spent the last few weeks cautiously dancing round the issue of what was to happen next. Eve had gone back to London for a little while, apparently to consult a solicitor. Gabriel still hadn't been able to bring himself to find one. He kept hoping that they could resolve this another way. Until then, he had pleaded with Eve not to let Stephen know what was happening, but clearly she'd been unable to keep it secret any longer.

'I thought he'd be pleased,' she kept saying. 'I thought he'd want to come and live with me. All I want is to put things right.' She paced the kitchen, getting ever more frantic. Gabriel recognised this behaviour of old. In a minute, she was going to sit down and start shredding a beer mat or whatever else was to hand. Gently, he sat her at the table, uttering soothing noises, but inside he was seething. Why did she always have to be so destructive? Then he went to their son.

'I don't want to live with her,' Stephen spat out, between sobs. 'I don't have to, do I?'

'You don't have to do anything you don't want to do,' said Gabriel. 'I'm sure we can find a way of working this out.'

'But you said Mummy was back, Daddy.' Stephen raised a tear-stained face and Gabriel's pain shot through his heart. His inaction over the last few weeks had led to him betraying his son yet again. 'I thought we were all going to be together again.'

'I thought so too,' began Gabriel. 'But Mummy and I, well, we've been talking and we don't think we can live together anymore. So we're trying to find a way that you can live with us both. I know it's not ideal, but we think it's for the best, don't we, Mummy?'

Eve was sitting rocking back and forth saying, 'Why do I always get it wrong? I just wanted to make up to him. Why does he hate me?'

'Eve, have you taken your medication?' Gabriel was seriously alarmed. This was the worst he'd seen her for a while.

'No, no, you're right, I should,' Eve looked confused for a moment, and then got up and went to her bag, and found some pills.

'And you lied to me, Daddy.' Stephen said suddenly.

'Stephen, we've already been through this, I didn't lie—' began Gabriel.

'You told me Mummy wasn't at Granny's house when she was,' said Stephen.

'I know I did,' said Gabriel, 'and I've already told you how sorry I am. I just didn't want you to be upset.'

'That's not true,' said Stephen. 'You're a big fat liar and I don't want to live with you either. I want to go and live with Auntie Pippa.'

With that he pushed Gabriel aside and ran upstairs in floods of tears. Gabriel sat back in dismay. Eve seemed to be calming down a bit but was totally unaware of the chaos she had caused. How on earth were they ever going to resolve this?

'Crikey, it feels good to be home,' said Pippa, as Marianne helped her pull the last bit of furniture back into place. She and Dan were moving back in at the weekend, and Marianne had popped in after school to help her sort the house out while the children stayed with Pippa's parents.

'What's the long-term damage?' Marianne asked.

'I think we've been very lucky,' said Pippa. 'These houses are pretty solid and, fortunately for us, the flood swept through quite quickly, and subsided fairly smartly too. It was worse for the houses on the High Street.'

'Do you think those places will recover?' said Marianne.

'Hard to tell, isn't it,' said Pippa. 'Some of them are very badly damaged, and it will be hard now for those properties to get insurance.'

'So you're not tempted by Luke's offers of new housing?' said Marianne.

'Not a bit of it,' said Pippa. 'I know you were going to marry him, but I don't trust that man as far as I can throw him. I'm sure that eco town will still flood, whatever he says.'

'They're offering some pretty good deals,' said Marianne wistfully. 'Even I could afford one.'

'Marianne, please tell me you haven't,' said Pippa.

'No, no, I haven't done anything,' said Marianne. 'I did go and look at the mocked up showhome. And it is very nice. But the ground is very damp still. It would be like living in a bog. I can't see that changing in a hurry. It's just that I'll never afford to buy around here otherwise.'

'I'm sorry,' said Pippa. 'That was insensitive of me. I'm

lucky, I don't need an eco house. But if I did, I can see where you're coming from. Maybe he has really sorted things out.'

'Oh, yes,' said Marianne. 'Maybe he has.'

They both looked at each other and laughed.

'On the other hand,' said Pippa, 'leopards don't change their spots.'

'How's Gabe?' Marianne had been trying very hard not to probe, but it was impossible not to at least ask Pippa how he was. She'd barely seen him since Eve had come back. Only fleeting glances and nods down the High Street. Gabriel always looked pleased to see her when she said hello, but Marianne felt so shut out of his life now, she wasn't sure if he meant it or not.

'Fine, I think,' said Pippa. 'To be honest, I haven't seen that much of him myself. I've been so busy sorting every-thing out here. And I know he and Dan have been working all hours tupping the ewes and getting the winter feed sorted out. None of us has had a moment.'

'Yes, of course,' said Marianne. 'Silly of me.'

'You could phone him,' said Pippa. 'I'm sure he'd be glad to see you.'

'I'll think about it,' said Marianne, but she knew she wouldn't. This was just too complicated and painful. It was better if she stayed away.

Noel sat at his keyboard and stared into space. He was meant to be tarting up his CV, which was why he was actu-ally playing Minesweeper. Like so many things these days, it felt like a huge effort. Just the thought of getting on the Internet and starting to look at jobs was filling him with despair. He had managed to sign on at a job agency but, as Will had predicted, work was very lean. He thought again about Ralph Nicholas' offer. It was wildly impractical.

335

So long as Cat's mum was with them, he couldn't even contemplate a job that took him out of London. He couldn't see what was going to happen, or how they were going to manage. All that he knew was, while the present was uncertain, the future was on hold.

'Noel!' His mother-in-law called plaintively from the lounge. Noel sighed. What did she want now? Noel could feel all his good will towards Louise leaching away as she became more and more dependent on him and Cat. Cat had no idea of how incredibly difficult it was being here in the day with her. No, that wasn't true, Cat did know, because as soon as she came in, she took over, and she was arranging work as much as possible to be at home as often as she could. But one of them had to go to work.

He went into the lounge and his heart sank as he realised that his mother-in-law had had another accident. They'd said it was likely to happen, and now it was happening more and more frequently. She was still just (thankfully) thought Noel, capable of sorting herself out enough for him not to have to clean her up, but these daily incidents were mortifying for both of them.

Cat chose that moment to return from work. He'd called her earlier when her mother had got agitated, but then she'd calmed down, so Noel had phoned back to say it was okay. Cat evidently had decided to come back anyway.

'Oh God, not again,' she groaned, when she saw what had happened. 'It's all right, Noel, I'll deal with this.'

Noel retreated thankfully into the study, and tried to concentrate again on his CV.

A sudden shout pulled him out of himself.

He raced to the bathroom, where he found Cat hysterically screaming at her mother. 'Why can't you just get dressed? It's so simple. Why can't you do it?'

Noel stood looking at Cat in shock. His normally calm

wife was totally out of control, while his mother-in-law stood in her underwear, crying and saying, 'Please don't be angry with me, please don't be angry.'

Cat's face suddenly crumpled and she ran out of the bathroom. Noel grabbed a dressing gown hanging on the side of the bathroom, wrapped it gently round his mother-in-law, and eased her into her bedroom.

Then he went to find Cat who was sitting bleakly on the end of their bed.

'I know, I know,' she said heavily. 'Any more of this and I'm going to end up as a parent abuser.'

Noel sat down next to her and put his arm tentatively round her shoulder.

'You do know we can't go on like this, don't you?' he said.

'I feel like I've failed her,' Cat whispered.

'You haven't failed her,' said Noel. 'Alzheimer's is a ghastly disease. You just have to accept you can't beat it. You're going to hate me for saying this, but I don't think this is working. Your mum needs to go into a home.'

Catherine leant against him and wept.

Chapter Twenty-Nine

Marianne entered the Parish Centre where an impromptu meeting of the Save the Post Office Campaign was being held. The news that the post office was going to shut had been followed swiftly by the flood and the campaign had faltered, only to come back with a vengeance now. Marianne had missed the last couple of meetings, but she'd gathered from Pippa that the idea to have a One Stop Village Shop, which would be manned in part by volunteers from the village and would sell Pippa's, Dan's and Gabriel's local produce, as well as offering post office services, was gaining ground, as was a distinct groundswell of opinion against the eco town. Luke's attempts to win the villagers over had backfired badly and, as far as Marianne was aware, he had yet to sell a single house to an inhabitant of Hope Christmas. That didn't mean he wasn't going to be able to sell them to incomers, but word on the street was that, with recession beginning to really bite, those urban dwellers looking for a good life in the country were somewhat more reluctant to bite the bullet than they had hitherto been. It was beginning to look as if Luke had a huge white elephant on his hands.

'So we're agreed that the next task is to start fundraising for the village hall and shop?' Vera Campion was saying. 'Albert has already drawn up a battle plan.' She blushed when she said this. It was not a very well kept secret that since the flood she and Mr Edwards had finally become an item.

'I've got some really good news about that,' Marianne stood up waving an envelope she'd brought with her. She came to the front of the room. 'I believe some of you already know this, but I entered Hope Christmas for a competition to find the perfect Nativity in *Happy Homes*. And, I found out today that, incredibly, we've won. So this Christmas, a team from the magazine are coming up to photograph the Nativity, and write a feature on us. We may even get on TV. But the best bit is the prize money is ten thousand pounds, which I'm sure you'll agree will help the campaign enormously.'

'That's fantastic,' said Vera, leading the applause. 'I think I speak for us all when I say how grateful we are to you, Marianne.'

'Miss Woods was a great help,' said Marianne, acknowledging the old school teacher who nodded graciously, 'and without Sir Ralph promising to let us have the chapel at Hopesay, I'm not sure we would have won it.'

'I hope you are going to direct it yourself,' said Miss Woods, 'as Diana Carew sadly won't be able to help this year.'

Diana Carew was still out of action as her shoulder had been dislocated in the accident. Even she had realised that it was going to be impossible for her to run things this year, and she was grumpily ensconced at home discovering the wonders of the shopping channel.

'I'd love to,' said Marianne. She looked around her at the excited, enthusiastic faces. Luke didn't understand anything about the community here. No wonder his houses hadn't sold. People didn't want to live a lifestyle, they wanted to live a life. For the very first time since he left her, Marianne felt truly glad he had.

*   *   *

339

'Each of our guests is treated to the best care possible,' the smartly dressed owner of the Marchmont Rest Home was saying as she showed Cat and Noel around. The place was much brighter than Cat had imagined, and a huge step up from the previous two places they'd looked at, neither of which was fit for a dog to live in, let alone her mother. The Marchmont was light and airy, the rooms luxurious, the carpets soft and springy.

'Mum will feel like she's staying in a hotel here,' said Cat. She still felt terrible about what she was doing, but both Noel and Angela had been very firm with her, pointing out the destructive effect Mum's presence was having on their family life. Cat had tried to talk to the children about it and, while they all understood that Granny Dreamboat was very ill, none of them could cope with the fact that their beloved granny kept forgetting who they were, or that she was so fretful and tetchy a lot of the time. Paige and James had been particularly difficult about it and Ruby, being so little, didn't quite understand what was happening. It was only Mel, whom Cat had thought would find it harder, who seemed to have grasped the complexity of the situation with a maturity of which Cat was incredibly proud. She was becoming a great help with Mum, bringing her a cup of tea in the mornings, patiently going over the same crossword puzzle in the evenings. But even so, Cat could see how upsetting it was for them all.

But the clincher had been the conversation she and Mum had had after Cat had screamed at her in such an unseemly fashion. Immediately after the incident, Mum appeared to have forgotten all about it. But a day or so later, she'd suddenly said, as Cat was putting her to bed, 'I'm sorry, sweetheart, for being such a burden to you.'

Cat sat on the edge of the bed and held her mother's hands. When had her skin become so paper-thin?

'Mum, you could never be a burden,' she protested. 'I'm so sorry that I'm not as tolerant as I should be.'

Mum squeezed Cat's hands and said, 'Cat. I know what I am becoming. I know how I can be. It frightens me.'

'Which is why I want to look after you,' said Cat.

'And why you'll end up hating and resenting me,' said Mum. 'I won't let you put yourself through this anymore. I want you to promise me that you will sell my house and find a home for me. I'm not going to be able to make that decision soon, so you have to make it for me.'

'Don't,' said Cat through her tears.

'Cat, you know it's what has to happen,' said Mum. 'We'll manage because we must.'

They'd both cried then, Mum for the loss of independence, Cat for the loss of her mum.

Since that moment, there had been precious few times when Mum had shown such lucidity, and Cat knew that she couldn't put it off any longer. By dint of dropping the price to suit market conditions, her family home had sold so quickly Cat had had to come to terms with yet another blow to her bruised and battered heart.

Clearing out the house had been the worst thing she'd ever had to do. She and Noel had only had a week to pack things up, and in the end were reduced to shoving things in boxes without paying any attention to what was there. In the confusion, Cat belatedly realised she'd accidentally thrown out her mother's favourite earrings, and a family Bible belonging to her grandmother. But the worst of it was the systematic stripping down of everything that she'd known since childhood, of everything that had made her mother the person she was. Somehow it diminished Mum in a way. Apart from the piano on which Cat had bashed out 'Chopsticks' as a child, her mother's battered old furniture had gone to the charity shop; the bed that Cat was

341

born in, so battered and old, had ended up on a skip; the grandfather clock just wouldn't fit in anywhere and had to go to an antiques shop; while the new owners had carelessly and unwittingly poured hot coals on Cat's head by casually talking about getting rid of the Aga ('So 90s,' they'd declared), and putting in a shiny new stainless steel kitchen. Cat knew it had to happen but, as a symbol of the loss of all her memories, it seemed the most potent. Now when she thought of her childhood home, it was tainted with the memory of the way she'd last seen it, stripped bare, and denuded of all comfort.

But at least now they had the money to look after Mum and, of all the homes they'd looked at, the Marchmont was certainly the best they'd seen.

'What do you think?' She was pulled out of her reverie to discover that she was being required to give an opinion. Even now, a part of her wanted there to be another way to solve this. She looked at Noel, who gave her a small grin and the thumbs up.

'You don't have to make a decision straight away,' the owner was saying, 'your mother could come and try it out for a day, see how you all feel.'

Taking a deep breath, Cat said, 'I think that would be perfect. When can we arrange for Mum to come for a visit?'

Gabriel was coming out of the solicitor's office, one of the few buildings on the High Street not affected by the floods. He'd been so angry with Eve that, the day after she'd told Stephen what was happening, he'd immediately booked an appointment with a solicitor. He should have done it months ago, when Eve first left, to consolidate their position, but there was something about his relationship with Eve that had the effect of stultifying him, making it impossible for him to act. With the benefit of distance and hindsight, he was beginning to see how bad they'd both been for each other.

It would be better with Marianne, a voice whispered in his head. Gabriel knew he could have a thoroughly normal relationship with Marianne, had even dared hope that in time Stephen might come round and they could make a fist of a proper family life. But now? He stopped and sighed. Stephen was speaking to him again, but had retreated somewhere deep inside himself. He appeared to have forgiven Eve too and seemed to enjoy the time he spent with her at the cottage she was renting. Gabriel had offered to pay but she declined, making him wonder how she could afford it. True she'd mentioned a job in London, but Eve had been in Hope Christmas a month now, and there was no sign that she was going back to work anytime soon.

Gabriel's solicitor had been confident that he would win custody. 'With your wife's history of mental illness, not to mention the abandonment issue, we have a very strong case,' the lawyer had advised. 'Are you ready to start proceedings?'

Gabriel couldn't give him an answer. Eve's solicitor hadn't written the letter she'd been promising him was on its way. It was like the sword of Damocles hanging over his head. She seemed to him increasingly skittish and erratic, and he was on the verge of suggesting she go back to their doctor, but now he felt in some odd limbo, where he felt he couldn't be so involved.

'Penny for them.' As he walked down the High Street, Marianne was walking up, laden with books. Her eyes were sparkling, her long dark curls tumbling over her shoulders, the cold autumnal air giving her cheeks a healthy glow. It had been weeks since he'd seen her. And suddenly she was there, lovely and natural, and for the moment completely unattainable.

'Marianne,' Gabriel felt suddenly awkward; she must think he'd totally lost interest in her. 'I'm sorry I haven't been in touch.'

'I know it's been tough,' Marianne's ready sympathy was like a balm to his battered soul, but she looked as awkward as he felt. 'Pippa told me what's been happening. Is there anything I can do?'

'Nothing,' said Gabriel. 'But thanks.'

There was an uneasy pause, then he said, 'You've got a lot of books there. I didn't realise teaching reception was so academic.'

'It's not,' laughed Marianne, slightly more at her ease. 'No, these are research. Courtesy of Miss Woods.'

'Research?' Gabriel was puzzled. He'd completely lost touch with what was happening in Hope Christmas over the last few weeks.

'Didn't you hear? We've won a competition to put on the perfect Nativity, and yours truly is running the show.'

'I hope you're going to keep the elves,' said Gabriel, his mood lightening.

'Of course,' said Marianne mock seriously. She paused and then said: 'I realise this might not be the best time to ask this, but do you think Stephen would like to do a solo? He has such a lovely voice, and I thought he'd be perfect to sing "Balulalow".'

Gabriel was suddenly hit by a pain so intense it nearly stopped him breathing. Stephen might not even be with him at Christmas. Besides, he was so fragile, it didn't seem right to put him through that, even if he were here.

'Now's not the best time,' said Gabriel. 'Sorry, the answer's no.'

'But—' Marianne started to protest.

'I said no,' said Gabriel. 'Stephen has enough to cope with.'

'It might help,' said Marianne, 'give him some confidence. You saw how much he enjoyed it at Easter.'

'Marianne, I know you want to help,' said Gabriel stiffly. 'But I can assure you I know what is best for my son. And right now singing in your Nativity isn't. Please let's leave it at that.'

'Fine,' said Marianne equally stiffly. 'But just suppose you're wrong. Stephen has a rare talent. I think it should be encouraged, not stifled.'

'Like I said, he's my son,' said Gabriel. 'Don't ask me again.'

'I think you're being very unfair,' said Marianne, but Gabriel didn't answer, and strode off down the hill, unable to articulate further the rage that was coursing through him, but dimly aware that somehow he'd managed to direct it at entirely the wrong person.

Noel looked at his email inbox. Another slew of rejections to match the ones that seemed to be dropping through his letterbox at a phenomenal rate. He couldn't imagine that he would ever get another job again. Maybe he *could* commute to Hope Christmas and back.

'Cup of tea?' Cat had come in silently. She'd barely spoken all the way back from the visit to the care home. Noel didn't blame her. It was nice as these places go but, however the dedicated staff dressed it up, it was an institution and, judging by the majority of its inmates who had sat rocking silently in chairs in front of the TV, the residents were swiftly institutionalised. It wasn't a fate he'd wish on anyone, not even his mother in her worst moments. Although miraculously of late she seemed to be a lot more helpful than she'd ever been, even turning up today to make sure they could go out together to visit the care home. Cat had told him what she'd said about not helping out before, and for once Noel was prepared to admit that maybe he too had got it wrong, and he'd actually managed to tell her so.

'That's all in the past,' his mother had said to his astonishment. 'For now, Cat needs you,' she'd admonished, and he knew she was right. Cat did need him. Cat was so gorgeous and vivacious, Noel had always felt slightly amazed he'd caught her eye all those years ago when they'd first got together, and now, with his confidence at rock bottom, he wasn't sure that he could keep it.

'Tea would be great,' said Noel. 'How's your mum?'

'Asleep,' said Cat with a sigh. She looked tired and worn out.

'Fancy going out tonight?' he said. 'I mean, my mum's here, we could manage a curry or something.'

'I'd love to,' said Cat, 'but I'm so behind. I've got to write up some Christmas recipes for *Happy Homes*, and work on the book a bit more. My agent thinks she's got someone interested, and she's pushing me to finish it.'

'Oh.' Noel was absurdly disappointed. He knew – thought he knew – she wasn't rejecting him, but she had a way of looking straight through him, as if he wasn't there. It was hard not to take it personally.

'Sorry, Noel,' she said. 'I'm just feeling a bit overwhelmed with everything, what with Mum and you not working. I haven't even started on Christmas yet. Normally I've bought half the presents by October. I just somehow don't have the energy for it this year.'

Noel felt a little bit resentful. Cat had a knack of making him feel like that. *What about me?* He wanted to say, can't you see beyond yourself to me?

'You have had a lot on your plate,' Noel said. 'Why don't you let me help you? After all, I don't have anything else to do with my time.'

346

'I'm not sure I can trust you with the turkey,' Cat said lightly, but it made Noel bristle.

'I'm not a complete idiot, you know,' he snapped.

'I never said you were,' said Cat, looking shocked at the venom in his tone.

'Stop treating me like one, then,' said Noel. 'I am capable of ordering a turkey. You just need to learn to delegate more.'

Cat looked as if she might spit something back, but then thought better of it.

'You're right,' she said, 'and I'm sorry. I am going to need your help. By the looks of things I'm going to have to be up in Hope Christmas on Christmas Eve for this wretched photo shoot. I wish I'd never suggested a sodding Nativity competition.'

'You just leave everything to me,' said Noel, a sudden brilliant thought burgeoning in his mind. 'I think, if you let me, I could sort Christmas out very well indeed.'

Chapter Thirty

'Hello, is that the Woodcote Lodge Hotel?' Noel was enjoying a certain amount of secret squirrelness about his plans for Christmas. It was going to be expensive, he knew, but GRB had at least sorted out a reasonable redundancy package for him and, despite their stretched finances, he was sick to death of being careful. For once he was going to throw caution to the winds. They might not get a chance like this again and, with Cat working herself to the bone at the moment, and all the worry she'd had with her mum, Noel didn't want her to have to think about Christmas at all. So he'd found some hotels offering festive deals in the Hope Christmas area and, to his amazement, the place wasn't booked up.

'Lost a lot of custom because of the flood, see,' the warm Shropshire burr on the other end of the phone informed him, reminding Noel again that he'd love to make his home in such a comforting place. If only they hadn't got Cat's mum ensconced in the Marchmont. There was no way Cat would leave London now. She still felt so guilty about her mother, which was ridiculous as they'd done everything they could for her. She didn't even recognise them anymore. Noel knew it was wrong to think it, but he couldn't help wondering if it would matter if they left. Louise was lost in her own world anyway. They knew she was cared for – would she actually notice they'd gone?

But he couldn't do that to Cat. It would break her heart.

Noel made the booking for all of them to arrive on Christmas Eve and stay for the whole week. They all deserved a holiday. He wasn't sure Cat would go for leaving her mother that long, but he'd had a long chat to the woman who ran the Marchmont and she'd been most insistent that Cat took a break.

'Families always feel guilty,' she said, 'but you can't look after people if your own batteries aren't recharged. Go on, have a good time and we'll make sure that your mother-in-law will have the best Christmas she's ever had.'

Noel doubted that somehow, thinking back to the first Christmases when he and Cat had been married and spending their time in between the two sets of parents. In the end, Cat had felt so guilty about her mother being on her own, they used the excuse of a new baby and a bigger house to have everyone to them. They had been happy years when the children had been small and cuddly and not older and spiky, when he'd felt confident in his job and his marriage. He stared out the window at the greying November sky. Things seemed to have changed so much since then. He still had Cat, it was true, although he felt he only got half of her most of the time. And the children were wonderful, he had to remember that. But he'd lost his job, his father, and now he was losing his wonderful mother-in-law. He felt more weighed down by cares and responsibilities than ever before in his whole life and where once the future had looked rosy, now it simply looked bleak.

This would never do. He turned over the card that Ralph Nicholas had given him all those months ago. Dammit, he would try to ring him again. Maybe there was some way he could do the job and commute. What was the worst that could happen? Ralph could only say no.

*   *   *

Marianne was making a snowman frieze with a bunch of reception children, and trying not to think too much about Gabriel. She hadn't seen him since their disastrous meeting on the High Street and, although she understood that his life was peculiarly difficult right now, she was frustrated at his inability to see that Stephen might be helped by singing in the play. His teachers reported that Stephen, never an outgoing child, was growing more and more withdrawn. Marianne's heart went out to him. It must be so difficult for a child to be caught up in things he didn't understand. And, despite being still cross with Gabriel, her heart went out to him too. Pippa reported that he wasn't eating or sleeping, and that the stress of the situation was making him ratty as hell. Marianne had thought on so many occasions that she should go and comfort him, but didn't know if she'd be welcome.

'Miss Moore,' said Jeremy Boulder, at five years old the eldest and liveliest child in her class. 'Need the toilet, Miss Moore.'

'Off you go then,' said Marianne. She watched him go out of the door at the back of the classroom.

'Miss Moore, look.' Jeremy was jumping up and down and pointing with glee at the glass door opposite her classroom that led to the playground.

'I don't believe it,' Marianne laughed out loud, completely taken aback by what she was witnessing. 'There are sheep in the playground.' She'd never had to deal with *that* in London.

'Where, where?' the children clamoured around her. Marianne led them out onto the corridor. She could see that the fence in the field next to the playground had come down. There'd been high winds last night, presumably that was when the damage had been done. The sheep had strayed across into the grassy area at the far end of the playground,

350

and were now wandering aimlessly on to the concrete area where the children played. They hadn't seemed to work out that they needed to go back the way they came.

'Can we go and look at them, Miss?'

'You'd better not,' said Marianne, thinking of health and safety: then thought, don't be ridiculous, what could sheep do to children?

She called Jenny, her colleague in the next classroom, and together they shooed the sheep back the way they came while the children lined up by the school wall laughing.

The sheep were baaing and running around piteously, but none of them seemed to know where they were going.

'I hadn't realised how much hard work it was being a sheep dog,' Marianne laughed, as she unsuccessfully chased another sheep away from the school entrance where it had stopped to chew the winter pansies Year 3 had planted for Environmental Club.

Suddenly she heard a whistle and a black and white speeding bullet flew across the playground and started rounding the sheep up. She looked up to see Gabriel ordering his dog this way and that until, finally, all the sheep were firmly over the right side of the fence.

'You've got a new dog,' she said.

'Yes, this is Patch,' said Gabriel, 'grandson of Benjy, so even Stephen has taken to him.'

'I hadn't realised it was your sheep in that field,' Marianne added.

'They're not normally. I rotate them during the mating season, so the ewes get enough to eat. They don't breed well if they're too thin. I'm going to have to move them to another field now till I sort out this fencing.'

'Right,' said Marianne, suddenly remembering her class. 'Best get on. Children to teach and that.'

'Marianne,' said Gabriel. He paused, looking awkward. 'I owe you an apology.'

Marianne said nothing, wondering what was coming next.

'I was rude about Stephen and singing the solo,' he said. 'It's just been so hard, and Stephen is so unhappy, and I don't know how to help him.'

'Then let him do this,' Marianne came up and touched Gabriel lightly on the arm. Never had she wanted more to take away someone's pain. 'He's so quiet at school. If he could only do this, I think it would really help bring him out of his shell.'

'Do you? Really?' Gabriel looked at her intently, those dark brown eyes searing into her soul.

'Yes, I do,' said Marianne.

'I'll think about it,' said Gabriel. 'But right now I'd better get these sheep away before you have another invasion.'

'It's given the kids something to giggle about,' laughed Marianne.

'Marianne—' said Gabriel, as she turned to go.

'Yes?' said Marianne.

'Oh, nothing,' Gabriel said abruptly, and turned back to his sheep. Marianne walked back to the classroom feeling crushed. For a moment there, she'd hoped Gabriel was going to ask her to come back. For a moment. But Eve was still here. Nothing had changed. It was foolish of her to expect anything else.

'Hi, Mum, I bought you the paper,' said Cat as she came into her mother's room. Mum was still in her nightie, sitting in her chair rocking back and forth. Cat had come to expect this, and also come to accept any little sign that her mother knew she was there with gratitude. If she didn't, she'd go mad with this. How could it be that her once bright, bubbly mother was reduced to this shell sitting mumbling in a corner?

'That's nice, dear,' her mother said. 'I'm waiting for my daughter. Do you know when she's coming?'

'It's me, Mum,' said Cat, tears springing to her eyes. She still couldn't get used to the fact that Mum didn't recognise her at all anymore but, if she made a fuss about it, Mum only got upset. 'Shall I wash your hair for you?'

The care in the home was patchy. Sometimes Mum was dressed when she came in, sometimes she wasn't. When Rosa was on, Cat always felt relief. Rosa clearly loved Mum and was gentle and tender with her, but then there'd be days when Rosa wasn't there, and the care assistants that Cat referred to as The Lazy Gits would be there instead, sitting down at every opportunity, delighted by Cat's arrival because it relieved them of their responsibility. Cat preferred to wash her mother's hair than let them do it – she'd seen how rough they could be. Though she'd complained to Gemma, the owner of the Marchmont, nothing much seemed to get done. As ever, there was a gnawing guilt about whether she'd done the right thing. But what, as Noel said, was the alternative?

Gently, Cat led her mum to the sink in her bedroom and got her comfy, then ran the water through her mother's hair. Once Mum had done this for her; Cat could still remember the comfort of having her hair washed as a child. Once Cat had done it for Mel, who now wouldn't dream of letting her mum get involved in the ritualistic hairstyling of the preteen. Now, here she was, the child becoming the mother, the mother whose child was needing her less and less. Cat was at a loss to know what her role was anymore. Never had she felt more lost and in need of her mum, and never had the strength of that loss felt more heartbreaking.

She finished washing her mum's hair, and dried it with a towel. Then she sat Mum in front of a mirror, and slowly curled her hair the way she knew she liked it. It was gently soothing to do this task. There was so little she could do for her mother, but she could do this one thing.

When she'd finished, she said, 'There, don't you look nice.'

Mum smiled at her, and patted her hand.

'You're a good girl,' she said. 'Just like my Cat. She's a good girl too, I can't think why she doesn't come.'

It never ever got any easier, but Cat had learnt that repeating that she was there only got Mum more agitated. 'Shall we have a cup of tea?'

'Yes, a nice cup of tea and a biscuit would be lovely,' Mum said. 'I'm glad you're here. You always look after me so nicely. I shall tell Cat when she arrives what a good girl you are.'

Blinking away the tears, Cat went to ask the staff for a cup of tea.

She came back and sat down next to her mother again, taking her hand and squeezing it tightly.

'I'm glad I'm here too,' she said. Even if her mother didn't recognise her, at least she knew she was here to look after her. That was the most she could hope for now.

Gabriel came back to the house to find it in darkness. Eve had taken to picking Stephen up from school every day and taking him home for tea. It was an uneasy arrangement, but so far had worked without incident.

His heart was in his mouth as he turned on the lights, calling Stephen's name. Where were they? Eve hadn't mentioned that she was taking Stephen anywhere.

'In here.' Eve was sitting alone in a darkened kitchen. The last rays of a wintry sun were setting across the valley.

354

'Where's Stephen?' Gabriel had a sudden shocking thought that she might have hurt him in some way.

'He's with Pippa,' Eve was twisting a cup round and round. Suddenly Gabriel had a feeling he knew what she was going to say.

'You shouldn't be sitting here in the dark,' he said gently. 'What's the matter?'

Eve was silent for a moment.

'It's me,' she said, 'it's me that's the matter.'

'What do you mean?' Gabriel felt the need to proceed with caution.

'I've made a mess of everything. Of life with you. Of life without you.' Eve was shaking. 'I've been a lousy mum to Stephen. I am a lousy mum to Stephen.'

'You're not,' said Gabriel. 'He loves you to pieces. It's done him so much good to have you here.'

'Has it?' Eve stared at him with a look of such painful intensity it pierced his soul. 'All I've done is brought him more heartache. I thought I could do it, I really did. But I just can't do this school run thing and being a mum. I do love Stephen. Really I do. I'm just not cut out to be a mother.'

Gabriel sat down next to her and put his arm around her.

'Eve,' he said, 'you've made such great strides. You've done so well. Don't give up on yourself or on Stephen. He needs you, you're his mum.'

'No, he needs you,' said Eve. 'I realise that now. You're mother and father to him in a way I can never be. It was selfish of me to come here and try and take him away from you and I'm sorry.'

'Don't be,' said Gabriel. 'You can't help who you are. But you can help your son. Go if you have to. Don't have him living with you if you don't think you can. But never forget you're his mother. He needs you and you need him. I've seen

355

how happy he's been around you. We can build on that, all of us. Just not in a way that might be terribly conventional.'

'What on earth did I do to you, all those years ago, Gabriel North?' said Eve with the inkling of a smile. 'I bet you wish you'd never met me.'

'If I hadn't, I wouldn't have Stephen,' said Gabriel. 'We might have messed everything else up, but we did that right. If you drop your battle for custody I'll never stop you from seeing him. He needs you in his life.'

'And you need me out of yours,' said Eve. 'I'll explain everything to Stephen this evening. I've booked a train to London tomorrow. But this time I promise I'll come back.'

Gabriel kissed her on the head, and sat back with relief. He was going to keep his son after all.

Chapter Thirty-One

Cat sat down at the computer. She'd barely blogged for weeks now. She had so little time and energy for anything. She'd never been this behind for Christmas. Every time she thought about it a sick feeling entered her stomach, and she felt paralysed. Nothing was going to be ready on time, but for once she didn't care. Dimly she was aware that Noel seemed to be taking it on himself to read through the Christmas lists and bring home bulging bags of goodies from Argos but, for the first time in her life, Cat couldn't get at all enthusiastic about the festive season. She just wanted to curl up in a ball and hibernate till it was all over. She hadn't even managed to rustle up any energy for decorating the Christmas tree, which was normally her greatest pleasure.

Normally, Cat would have found herself blogging amusingly about the varied exploits of her offspring at Christmas: how do you make a camel costume, anyone? But this year, she didn't even have the heart for that. She was heartily sick of the Happy Homemaker. Seeing Mum in the home had made her realise she had to make some changes in her life. It might mean difficult times ahead for her and Noel financially, but they simply couldn't carry on as they were.

I realise I've been a bad blogger of late, she began, *but real life has interfered in a way I could neither foresee or imagine. Some of you may have realised by now, but the Happy Homemaker blog is a façade. It's a cover for my real life and, as I'm sure is the case for a lot of bloggers, it's a carefully constructed edifice – a pretend version of my life, if you like. I hope I'm not going to disappoint any of my readers by saying this, as I'm grateful to you one and all, but I can't keep the façade up any longer.*

Put simply, my life isn't perfect, it never was. I am a mum of four whose domestic life is usually chaotic. I started this blog to stop me going mad when my children were small, and then it ended up taking over my life. Recently, I felt, to the extent that I started forgetting my responsibilities, neglecting my family and in particular not supporting my husband. Events in my life right now have led me to rethink things. My mother has just been diagnosed with Alzheimer's . . .

Cat paused, could she be this honest in her blog? She'd never given away a real thought or emotion before, but somehow the blog seemed to be writing itself. She poured out all her heartache and sadness about the change in her mother, about the way the loss of her mother had made her feel. It was cathartic and necessary. There were no doubt readers who were going to feel cheated about what she'd done, and Bev was going to hit the roof when Cat told her. But Cat didn't care anymore. The Happy Homemaker had to go, and with her, Cat knew her days as features editor at *Happy Homes* were also numbered. She was going to hand in her notice and go freelance. From now on, her family came first.

'Yes, shepherds, if you can dance about like you're cold that will work very well.' Marianne was directing her ten-year-old shepherds, chosen for their comic abilities, as they kept themselves warm waiting for the angels to arrive. She consulted her script. 'Right, then we'll lead into "The Angel Gabriel From Heaven Came", and the angels come in.'

The angels – three fair-haired girls and one brunette (chosen because Marianne felt sorry for her after overhearing her complain she never got to be an angel) – came forward and took their positions.

'We bring glad tidings,' the chief angel said, 'of great joy to all mankind.'

This was going better than she'd expected. Marianne was really enjoying herself. The script that she'd adapted from the mystery play with a little help from Miss Woods (carefully ensconced on a chair in prime position as assistant director) was simple and clear, just as she'd hoped, and the children had all risen to the occasion beautifully. It was less than a week to go till the Nativity. She had a feeling that it was going to be a really special evening.

'Is it too late for Stephen to take part?' Gabriel poked his head around the door just then, looking nervous.

Resisting the urge to run up to him and throw her arms around him, Marianne welcomed them both into the room.

'Stephen, would you like to sing for us?' she said. She'd dropped "Balulalow" in favour of "Away in a Manger" for the crib scene, but she'd happily reinstate it if it meant Stephen singing.

'I've been practising at home,' said Stephen shyly.

'Just sit there for now,' said Marianne, 'and we'll get you to do your piece as soon as we get to the baby being born.'

The rehearsal went on and every fibre of her being was conscious of Gabriel at the back of the room, but she didn't dare look over at him.

'And so it came to pass that Mary gave birth to a son named Jesus,' intoned the narrator, 'and she wrapped him in swaddling clothes and laid him in a manger.'

Mary and Joseph (both chosen by virtue of being the

children of the only two sets of parents who *hadn't* tried to bribe Marianne to give them the role) moved forwards and placed the baby in the crib.

'Wonderful,' said Marianne. 'Now, Stephen, if you just come round to the front. Mr Edwards will give you a note.'

Mr Edwards, who was practising on the ancient piano in the Parish Centre instead of the wonderful organ in the Hopesay Manor chapel that he'd be playing on Christmas Eve, sounded a note. Stephen stepped forward, and began to sing.

'But I sall praise thee evermoir, With sangis sweit unto thy gloir,' Stephen sang and the whole place froze. You could have heard a pin drop as he reached the high notes.

Marianne sat back in delight. She'd been right to get Stephen to sing, she knew it.

'And sing that last rycht Balulalow.' Stephen finished off the last note, which lingered softly in the air.

The cast spontaneously burst into applause. Stephen shyly smiled, and Marianne looked across at Gabriel.

'Thank you,' she mouthed. Now she knew she had the perfect Nativity.

Gabriel waited at the end of the rehearsal for Marianne.

'It's going to be fantastic,' he said. 'You've done brilliantly.'

'Thanks,' said Marianne, 'and I'm glad you brought Stephen. He's going to bring the house down.'

'I have to admit he had me going,' said Gabriel. 'You were right. Singing *is* good for him. I could see how much it's brought him out of himself.'

'I'm glad,' said Marianne. 'He has a rare talent, and it needs to be nurtured.'

There was a pause and Gabriel wondered how to fill it, before suddenly being unable to stop himself from saying: 'So do you.'

'So do I what?' Marianne looked confused.

'Have a rare talent. You've made such a difference to Hope Christmas.' Gabriel paused and looked shyly down at his feet. 'You've made such a difference to me.'

'Oh,' she said, looking stunned.

'Pippa's having mulled wine tonight, I believe,' said Gabriel, looking up at her now, his brown eyes twinkling.

'But what about Eve?' said Marianne. 'Aren't you going with her?'

'Marianne Moore, where have you been? The village hotline must have got the news out by now, surely?'

'What news?' Marianne was puzzled.

'Eve's gone back to London. She's decided she couldn't cope with Stephen and that it's for the best.'

'I'm sorry,' said Marianne. 'I thought you'd be able to work things out.'

'I'm not,' said Gabriel. 'Really, this is for the best. Stephen understands his mother is ill, and he knows we can't be together now. Which means . . .'

He left the rest of the sentence hanging but the broad grin that lit up his face left Marianne in no doubt about his intentions.

'You know you look so much better when you smile,' said Marianne. 'You don't do that nearly enough.'

'I haven't had much to smile about recently,' admitted Gabriel. 'But since I found out Eve's not suing for custody of Stephen, I haven't been able to stop grinning.'

'I bet,' said Marianne. 'And Stephen is really okay about this?'

'Better than I thought he'd be,' said Gabriel. 'He was distraught at the thought of going to London, and I think he understands that Eve can't look after him. Apparently all she ever gave him for tea when he was staying with her was cheese on toast. But she's not going to leave him for good like she did last time. In fact she's coming for Christmas at Pippa's. Weird, I know. But better all round for Stephen.'

'I'm so glad,' said Marianne. 'Really I am.'

'So what about Pippa's and mulled wine then?'

'Yes, right, great idea,' said Marianne. She followed Gabriel and Stephen out of the Parish Centre, down the High Street and to the lane that led to Pippa's house. Snow was gently falling as they entered the lane.

'Magic!' said Stephen and ran up the lane whooping in delight as he tried to catch snowflakes on his tongue.

Marianne linked her arm in Gabriel's. It felt right and natural to have it there. He squeezed it tight.

The short walk to Pippa's was all too brief, and before long Gabriel found himself separated from Marianne in a whirl of Christmas bonhomie. But he was always aware of her presence, following her round the room. Lighting up when he caught her eye.

Eventually they caught up by the mulled wine.

'We must stop meeting like this,' said Gabriel.

'Must we?' The mulled wine had made Marianne flirtatious, and he suddenly had a vivid remembrance of the first time they'd met.

'Well, are you going to kiss her or what?' Stephen appeared next to him with his arms firmly folded, looking very disapproving.

'Um—' Gabriel was totally thrown off his stride. 'Are you saying you wouldn't mind if Marianne and I were together?'

'Duh, *nooo*, of course I wouldn't,' said Stephen. 'Anyone can see you're made for each other. Parents. What are they like?'

Gabriel and Marianne laughed.

'Look, Auntie Pippa even put some mistletoe up there specially for you,' said Stephen. 'Some people are so dense.'

'Happy Christmas, Marianne,' said Gabriel, and bent down and kissed her on the mouth. 'I believe I owe you a drink.'

'I do believe you do,' said Marianne responding more enthusiastically than he would have dared imagine.

'You've done what?' Noel couldn't believe his ears. Cat had just walked in and told him her news. 'Why the hell didn't you ask me about this?'

'You never told me about your redundancy,' Cat said reasonably enough. 'I thought you'd be pleased. In the New Year you can get another job, and I'll go freelance. It will be fine. You'll see.'

'I don't know whether you've noticed,' said Noel, 'but the job offers aren't exactly falling from the trees. Let's face it, I'm a tired, washed-up has-been.'

'Oh, don't be ridiculous, Noel,' said Cat. 'Now you're just feeling sorry for yourself.'

Noel couldn't respond to that because part of him knew it was true. But how could she have handed her notice in without consulting him? It made the Christmas hotel a luxury they could barely afford, let alone the presents he'd bought in a fit of generosity, figuring that he wouldn't have a redundancy package every year and, while Cat was still working, it wouldn't matter if he blew a little of it.

'And why shouldn't I feel sorry for myself?' Noel spat out. 'I've sat here at your beck and call for the last few months feeling like a stranger in my own home. You barely acknowledge me, the kids probably wouldn't care if I was here or not. What is the bloody point of me existing? I barely know anymore.'

'Noel.' Cat looked shocked.

'Daddy, the shelf has fallen down in the family room again.' Ruby bounced in exuberantly. 'Can you mend it?'

'No, I bloody well can't,' said Noel. 'Let your mother mend it. See how well she can do it.'

Ruby burst into tears.

'Noel!' said Cat. 'That was so unkind.'

Appalled at what he'd done, Noel got up and, without a word, picked up his coat and left the house. It was cold out and the wind whipped through him as he walked and walked through the sleet-ridden streets of London, through busy roads bustling with commuters going home to their loved ones, and Christmas revellers sharing the festive spirit. He barely knew where he was going. Only that he had to get away.

Almost without knowing how he'd got there, he found himself on a bus heading into town. His mobile rang. He ignored it. It rang again. So he switched it off. Eventually the bus stopped, and he got off, for a moment unsure of his surroundings. Then he walked for a while until he found himself by Waterloo Bridge. It was brightly lit and on the far side of the river he could see the glow of the National Theatre proclaiming something by Chekhov showing, while below twinkling blue lights gave the trees on the South Bank a festive glow, and the slow ponderous movements of the Millenium Wheel shone out against a dark wintry skyline.

People flitted from one side to the other, full of Christmas cheer, ready to spend a night on the town or go back home to their loved ones. Noel was filled with an overwhelming sense of hatred for them, but it was coupled with a self-loathing he couldn't escape. How could he have been so cruel to Ruby? And to Cat for that matter. She'd been through such a lot lately. Maybe she was right. Perhaps she should be at home more, but how could they manage on her freelance salary and without any income from him? She'd be better off if he were dead. At least the insurance would pay for the house.

He walked over to the side of the bridge. And looked down into the dark whirling waters below. They looked somehow inviting. He'd never contemplated ending it all before, but he'd never been this miserable either.

Cat would be better off without him. Noel had nothing to offer her or the children anymore. He stared into the darkness below. It seemed to call to him. To tease him. To welcome him home.

Chapter Thirty-Two

'Well, go on, if you're going to,' a slightly testy voice came from behind him. 'It's a cold night and I'm not as young as I was. So go on. Do it.'

'Do what?' Noel turned round as the wind whipped his face and stared bemusedly into the twinkling eyes of Ralph Nicholas. 'What on earth are you doing here?'

'First things first,' said Ralph. 'I take it you *were* planning to jump off the bridge, weren't you? So what's stopping you?'

Noel paused. What was stopping him? A minute ago it had seemed like the answer to his prayers. The temptation to end it all had been enormous. But suddenly a picture of Cat swam before his eyes. And a vision of her dressed in black surrounded by the children. Financially she'd be better off without him, but would she *actually* be better off? Wasn't the act he was contemplating supremely selfish?

'My thoughts exactly,' said Ralph. 'Never seen the point of suicide. So unkind to the people left behind. I always make a point of trying to stop them.'

'What do you mean, you always try and stop them?' Noel was reeling, trying to make sense of this.

'Let's just say it's part of my job description,' said Ralph. 'Besides, you can't go topping yourself. Not when I have a job to offer you.'

'What job?'

'Well, I was rather hoping that you'd have the sense to ring me up yourself. I've been waiting for you to, you know. But since the mountain wouldn't come to Mohammed . . .'

'Right,' said Noel, sheepishly. 'But how did you know I'd be here?'

'It's my business to know that kind of thing,' said Ralph, which was about as clear as mud. 'Now, chop chop, I've a few things to show you before you go home.'

Noel found himself following Ralph through the London streets in a daze. For an old man he moved remarkably quickly. Suddenly they were on the Embankment.

'Fancy spending Christmas like them?' he said quietly, pointing to the tramps camped outside Embankment Station.

'No,' said Noel, feeling ashamed of his earlier outburst. How could he feel he had nothing when these people had so little? Normally he walked past the tramps in the street, but now he went up and offered one his coat. Weirdly, he didn't feel cold. In fact, he felt warmer than he'd ever felt in his life.

'Better,' said Ralph approvingly. He led Noel away from the streets into the cloistered seclusion of the Middle Temple, and towards the Temple Church. Noel had been here once before. It was a haven, a sanctuary not far from the hustle and bustle of the London streets. 'Now, shall we go in?'

Noel walked into the back of the church feeling awkward.

'I know, I know, you only come into these places about once a year,' said Ralph. He nodded at the crucifix high above the altar. 'Do you think He minds about stuff like that? Blessed are the pure in heart, theirs is the Kingdom of Heaven. That's what it's all about.'

Noel sank into a pew and stared ahead of him. Candles had been lit and a boys' choir was practising for a carol service. The sound brought tears to his eyes.

'Remind you of anything?' said Ralph.

'When I was a boy, I sang in a choir just like that,' said Noel. He'd forgotten the simplicity and the joy of standing in the choir, belting his heart out. Once his voice had broken, he'd given up.

'See the one on the left?' Noel looked where Ralph was pointing, at a ten-year-old boy who was struggling to sing through his emotions. 'His father died last Christmas. Do you want your son to be feeling like that next Christmas?'

'No,' whispered Noel quietly.

'And see that old woman in the corner?'

Noel looked and saw a bag lady, rocking back and forth against her shopping trolley, muttering to herself slightly madly.

'She used to have a family. Once,' said Ralph. 'But she lost them one by one, and then, eventually, she lost her wits. And now here she is. Every Christmas she comes here because she remembers the carols from her youth. The clergy here give her something to eat, but though they try to set her up in a hostel, she'll never stay. It seems she's forever fated to wander the streets of London.'

Noel looked at the woman, who couldn't have been much older then he was, but her lined face belied her years, and her unkempt appearance betrayed her suffering. Whatever he'd struggled with, was nothing compared to what this poor woman had gone through.

'Still feeling sorry for yourself, are you?' Ralph looked at him kindly. 'Everyone loses their way sometimes. It's whether you can find it again that counts.'

Noel looked back up at the choir.

'I think I want to go home,' he said.

'Excellent idea,' said Ralph. 'I have a feeling your wife might have some very good news for you.'

*   *   *

Gabriel put Stephen to bed and read him a story. It had been a long time since they'd shared a moment like this. Stephen had spent the whole time Eve had been there withdrawing into himself, and somehow they'd got out of the habit of spending time like this together.

'So you're sure you don't mind about Marianne?' he said.

'She's really nice,' said Stephen, looking suddenly shy, 'and, I know this sounds awful, but I have more fun with her than I do with Mummy.'

'You do understand how ill Mummy is, don't you?' Gabriel said with a sigh. 'She loves you, but she can't look after you the way she'd like, or the way you need.'

'I know,' said Stephen, 'but it doesn't matter, because you can do it for her.'

Gabriel kissed his son and went downstairs, where Marianne was waiting for him.

He took her in his arms and kissed her with a long deep sigh of contentment.

'I can't tell you how long I've been wanting to do that,' he said.

'Nearly as long as I have,' said Marianne, with a smile.

'You realise that we'll have to take things slowly, though, don't you?' said Gabriel, 'for Stephen's sake. And for mine.'

'Gabriel North, we can take things as slowly as you like,' said Marianne, 'After all, we've got the rest of our lives to get to know one another better.'

'We have, haven't we?' said Gabriel. He put on a CD, and poured her out a glass of wine. 'Come on, let's dance.'

Marianne burst out laughing as the first words played while they danced slowly in front of the fire.

'"Last Christmas"?' she said. 'I didn't know you had a penchant for cheese.'

'I've always had a soft spot for those Wham boys,' said

Gabriel, pulling her to him. 'But first things first. Do you have plans for Christmas?'

'Well, I was going to my parents', but they've decided to go on a last-minute skiing holiday, so I don't actually have any.'

'Good,' said Gabriel, 'because this year, I want to spend Christmas with someone special, and I'd really like it to be you.'

'What about Eve?' said Marianne.

'She's coming on Christmas Eve to see Stephen sing,' said Gabriel, 'and she'll be there for lunch, but she's not staying. You, on the other hand, I rather think are.'

'I rather think I am,' said Marianne, and fell into his arms.

Cat paced up and down the kitchen, wondering at what point she should call the police. Noel had been gone for hours. She'd dispatched the children to bed, even Mel, who had hovered about uncertainly, till Cat had made up some nonsense about Noel going out with one of his friends for a drink. She wondered whether she should go looking for him, but where to start? And she could hardly ask Regina to have the children in the middle of the night. There were limits to even the strongest of friendships.

This was like Christmas Day all over again. That time Noel had only gone AWOL for an hour. But she'd known how miserable he was. She'd had the feeling for months that he'd been suffering from some kind of depression, and she'd done nothing about it. She'd failed him. And now maybe she'd lost him.

'No, you haven't.' The front door banged shut, she heard footsteps on the stairs and suddenly an old man was standing in her kitchen. There was something familiar about him. 'I hope you don't mind, the door was open, so I let myself in,' he said.

'Who are you?' Cat was astonished by the appearance of this stranger in her kitchen.

'My name's Ralph Nicholas and I'm a friend of your husband's,' said the man, 'and you most emphatically haven't lost Noel. He's on his way back now. By the way, I don't think you've listened to your answerphone messages this evening. One of them is quite illuminating.'

Cat went to the phone and pressed playback.

'Hi, Cat, this is Sophie here.' Cat hadn't heard anything from her agent for a while, she'd almost forgotten about the cookery book. 'Great news. I've got a brilliant offer for you from Collins, they're really keen to do a big number on you, and it looks like we might have a TV series to go with it.'

She named a figure that was staggeringly high – certainly enough to make up for the loss of income from handing in her notice. Cat sat down with a thump. She turned back to Ralph, suddenly realising where she'd seen him before. 'Wait a minute, aren't you—' but she was addressing the empty air. 'What on earth is going on?' she said out loud.

Cat was still sitting there slightly bemused when Noel came back in.

'Cat,' he said hesitantly. 'I'm sorry. I'm so so sorry.'

'No, I am,' Cat ran to him. 'I've been so wrapped up in myself I didn't realise how unhappy you've been.'

'I thought I'd lost you,' said Noel, pulling her close.

'I thought I'd lost you,' said Cat.

'Never,' said Noel. 'Remember that Bryan Ferry song? We should stick together, whatever it takes.'

'I know,' said Cat. 'I know.'

They stood holding each other for a few moments, and then Cat suddenly said, 'Oh, I nearly forgot, I've got some great news. My book's been accepted.'

'That's fantastic,' said Noel. 'Ralph told me you had some good news.'

371

Cat pulled apart and said in puzzlement:

'But that's weird, he was here as well.'

'Who?' It was Noel's turn to look bemused.

'Your friend, he came ahead of you to tell me you were coming home,' said Cat. Come to think of it, she didn't remember him leaving.

'That's odd, he was with me for some of the way home and then I lost him,' said Noel. 'But it's been an odd evening all round.'

'Hasn't it just?' said Cat. She pulled back from Noel, frowning. 'Where's your coat?'

'Uh, I gave it to a tramp,' said Noel.

'Wonders will never cease,' said Cat.

'Yeah, well, like I said, it's been an odd evening,' Noel paused, then said hesitantly, 'Listen, Cat, you can say no to this, but I've been offered a job. The only drawback is that it's up in Shropshire. I know, I know, you won't want to leave your mum, but can we at least think about it? I'm sure we can find her a good home in Hope Christmas. And Ralph tells me there's a lot more support for the elderly up there. In fact, one of his plans is to build a new community centre, where Alzheimer's patients can go and spend time during the day. It would mean your mum might have some kind of life. So what do you think?'

'Six months ago I'd have said go boil your head,' said Cat. 'But I've realised my priorities need to change. Besides, though the Marchmont is doing its best, it's not good enough. So long as we can find Mum a better home in Hope Christmas, I'm up for it. The important thing is we're all together. Nothing else matters.'

Marianne sat in the back of the candlelit chapel as the audience came quietly in. She'd had a flurry of excitement earlier in the day when she'd finally met Catherine Tinsall, aka the

Happy Homemaker. 'Though not for much longer,' Catherine had confessed. 'I've handed in my notice and we're thinking of relocating up here. My husband's been offered a job by Ralph Nicholas renovating some old cottages.'

'I know,' said Marianne grinning. 'The eco town wasn't a popular option round here. Everyone's been buzzing with the new plans.'

Catherine had looked a bit startled that everyone knew her business already, so Marianne added, 'Welcome to village life, you no longer have any privacy . . .'

Luke, it turned out, had been voted off the board once it came to light that he had yet to make a single sale in the eco town. The political tide was turning against the whole idea too and, from what Marianne had heard, he'd departed for sunnier climes in a hissy fit. No doubt he'd soon be selling luxury apartments in the Bahamas.

'Good luck, my dear,' a voice said behind her. She turned gladly to see Ralph Nicholas.

'I don't think I'll need it if you're here,' she said, 'you've brought me nothing but luck this year.'

'All part of the remit,' said Ralph, bowing his head before going to take a seat next to Miss Woods.

The chapel darkened and silence fell, and a little boy got up to sing of a mayden that was makeles. Marianne hadn't been able to resist using Stephen for more than one song and, judging by the rapt atmosphere in the chapel, she knew she'd made the right choice.

The audience were suitably amused by the shepherds' antics, and they sat in silence as the narrator told the ancient tale, and Mary and Joseph came to rest in the stable in Bethlehem as they had done on so many occasions in so many plays throughout history. But none in quite such a magical setting as this, thought Marianne. Stephen's rendition of 'Balulalow' predictably had the women in the audience sobbing into their hankies – even Diana Carew, Marianne was amused to note. Diana had only come along reluctantly at the last moment but, in the end, Marianne suspected, she couldn't quite bring herself to stay away. The wise men, who in rehearsal had kept forgetting their lines, managed to be word-perfect and the whole thing ended with a rousing version of 'Hark the Herald Angels Sing'.

'That was magnificent, thank you so much.' Catherine Tinsall was the first to congratulate her. She was joined by her husband and four children, the youngest of whom was swinging on her dad's arm saying, 'Can we go back to the hotel now, Daddy? I don't want to miss Santa.'

Catherine laughed. 'Be patient, Ruby,' she said. 'It's hours till bedtime.' She turned back to Marianne. 'I'm so glad we chose you, even though I'm not working for the magazine anymore.'

'Well done, my dear, well done.' Diana Carew's bosoms bore down on her. 'I've been saying for years that we needed some new blood to shake things up around here, but no one would listen.'

'I bet,' said Marianne.

'That was wonderful,' said Gabriel, 'but then I knew it would be.'

'Of course it was,' Miss Woods stumped up with her stick. 'She had me to teach her.'

'And I was very grateful for the help,' said Marianne.

'Marvellous effort, my dear.' Ralph Nicholas appeared, as he always did, as if by magic. 'I do hope you're all coming over to the house for mulled wine and mince pies?'

'This is fantastic,' Catherine Tinsall said as they walked from the chapel into the Great Hall, evidently as awed by the fabulous Christmas tree in Hopesay Manor as Marianne

374

had been a year ago. 'Noel never told me how wonderful this place was.'

'So you're staying then?' Marianne asked.

'It looks like it,' said Catherine, grinning at her husband.

'Who's staying?' Gabriel came up and half-inched a mince pie from Marianne's plate.

'Catherine and Noel,' said Marianne, 'this is Gabriel North. Gabriel, meet Hope Christmas' newest inhabitants.'

'Whereas, I, on the other hand, must depart,' Ralph came up to them and smiled enigmatically.

'What do you mean?' Marianne said, 'you're not leaving us?'

'I'm afraid so,' said Ralph. 'My job here is done for the time being. Until the next time, of course.'

'Next time?' Noel looked puzzled.

'There's always a next time,' said Ralph. 'I believe I can leave the renovation of my cottages in your capable hands, Noel. Oh, and if you're interested, I do believe there's a rather fetching old grandfather's clock in the antiques market, which will look perfect in the hallway of that lovely old farmhouse you are going to buy.'

'How did you know?' Noel looked incredulous.

'Haven't you worked out yet that I know everything?' said Ralph with a twinkle. 'But I have to go where I'm needed and, from what I hear, my grandson is causing merry mayhem in Barbados. I live in hope of bringing him on side, but he tries me sorely. But then, of course, as his father is adopted, he's not really a St Nicholas.'

'I thought your name was Nicholas?' said Marianne.

'It is, but we dropped the St because it sounded too pretentious,' said Ralph. 'Now, really, I must be going.'

'Why?' said Marianne, suddenly feeling desolate at the thought that Ralph was leaving.

'Because that's just the way it is,' said Ralph and, in a

familiar gesture, doffed his cap. He walked off down the drive to a waiting taxi, and the snow gently fell on the path.

'St Nicholas?' Noel said. 'You don't suppose – no, I'm being daft.'

'What?' said Catherine.

'It's just occurred to me that Ralph is something of a modern-day St Nicholas, or at the very least a guardian angel. But that's daft. There's no such thing as angels.'

Marianne looked down the drive – the car, and Ralph, had already disappeared into the night.

'Do you know, I'm not sure that it is so daft,' she said, linking arms with Gabriel. 'I think Ralph's been like a guardian angel to me.'

'And to me,' said Catherine. 'Besides, you do know what his name is short for don't you?'

'No.' Marianne looked puzzled.

'He told me his name is Ralph, pronounced Rafe. It's short for Raphael. Which happens to be the name of the angel in Milton's *Paradise Lost* who comes to warn Adam and Eve about Satan.'

'And your point is?' said Noel, puzzled.

'Look above the door,' said Cat. 'I noticed it as soon as I came in. *That thou are hapie, owe to God; That thou continu'st such owe to thyself.* And that Latin inscription, *Servimus liberi liberi quia diligimus—*'

'It means *Freely we serve, because we freely love,*' said Marianne. 'Ralph told me.'

'And they're both quotes from *Paradise Lost,*' said Cat triumphantly. 'From when the angel Raphael comes to warn Adam and Eve about Satan. I know because I did it for A level.'

'And look at all those angels,' Marianne said, with sudden wonder. She pointed above the door, and suddenly they all saw the cherubs flying in the corner, the angel on the door knocker, and remembered all the angel motifs dotted around the house. 'It was right in front of our noses all the time. Ralph *is* an angel.'

'And you know who St Raphael is the patron saint of, don't you?' said Catherine.

'No, I don't,' said Marianne.

'Lovers,' said Cat.

'Whatever he is, I think he's done rather a good job, don't you?' said Gabriel, raising his glass. 'To all of us. Merry Christmas.'

'Merry Christmas' came the instant response, and they chinked glasses to the soft strains of 'God Rest Ye Merry Gentlemen', while they watched the snow fall softly on Hopesay Manor lawn.

Epilogue

A Merry Christmas to my blog readers, one and all. Cat squinted at the screen on her laptop.

'Come to bed,' said Noel plaintively. 'I've got the champagne on ice and everything.'

'Just coming,' said Cat who, thanks to Ralph's generosity, felt she'd probably had enough champagne for one night, but it was Christmas after all.

And thanks to the many readers who've kindly commented on my last post and given me such thoughtful and supportive advice. It reminds me what a powerful thing the Internet is and, at its best, what a positive force for good. I have been hugely touched by the outpouring of emotion my post caused, and am deeply grateful to those of you who've kindly requested that I stay. However, I think enough is enough. As of tonight, this blog is, like a rather famous parrot, no more. Although, never say never and, like Arnie, I may well be back in another form. Who knows? In the meantime, thanks for reading, and I wish you all a very happy and peaceful Christmas. I hope that, like me, you find the peace you deserve.

Cat pressed send, then powered down the computer and climbed into bed where her husband was waiting for her. He presented her with a glass of champagne.

'To us,' Noel said, 'and to our future. Merry Christmas, Cat.'

'Merry Christmas, Noel,' said Cat. 'It's going to be the best one yet.'

In a car speeding off in the darkness, Ralph St Nicholas sat back and smiled.

Acknowledgements

As usual, I have lots of people to thank for the help they gave me when writing this book.

First and foremost, thanks as ever are owed to my brilliant editor, Maxine Hitchcock. When she suggested I write a Christmas book I had no idea how much fun it was going to be. I'd also like to thank Keshini Naidoo and Sammia Rafique at Avon for their continued hard work and enthusiasm on my behalf. Very much appreciated, ladies!

And without the enthusiasm and support of my lovely agent, Dot Lumley, I'd have given up on this writing malarkey years ago, so thank you again for all the help.

Juggling writing and a school-run can be a tricky task. Thanks to my lovely friends, Dawn and Clive Pearce, who picked the children up for weeks while I was writing this book. I can honestly say this book wouldn't exist without their help.

I'd like to say a special thank you to my sisters Paula, Lucy and Virginia for sharing their different experiences of the school-run in town and country, with a particular shout out to Ginia for telling me about the escaping sheep – genius. And my very clever brother John providing me with a Latin translation, which was a much better result than me trying Google translator.

I'd like to thank Nicola Rudd who has been an enthusiastic follower of my blog from the start and whose blogging about Nativity plays was part of the inspiration for this story; all the long-suffering teachers who have put on the many Nativities I've seen over the years; Kate Whalley for enormous help with mental health issues; Chris Montague for helping me out on engineering matters and Heather Choate for giving me background information about Shropshire sheep farming. Any mistakes are entirely my own.

A special thanks goes out to Cath Hicks for sharing her hilarious anecdotes about the pitfalls of having an au pair, although nothing I made up could be nearly as funny as the real thing.

Blogging is something I started to do as a bit of fun, but is now a very necessary part of my online life. I am grateful to Bea Parry Jones for sharing some of the occasional downsides to blogging. However, on the whole I have found blogging to be a positive experience, and over the last year have had much fun, usually David Tennant-related, with the following people: Rob Buckley, Leesa Chapman, Marie Phillips and the elusive but extraordinary Persephone. Thanks guys, it's been a blast. To follow my blog go to http://maniacmum.blogspot.com.

Over twenty years ago, I had a fabulous time taking part in the Chester Mystery Plays Nativity, which was the inspiration for Marianne's play. To all the gang who were there in '87, I bet you never knew then it would end up in a book! Thank you also to the enthusiastic and lovely ladies who run Burway Books in Church Stretton. Quite possibly the best bookshop in the world.

Shropshire has had a hold over my imagination since I was a child and read *The Lone Pine Adventures*. I'm immensely grateful to my parents for choosing to go and live there so I could get to write about it too. Thanks especially to my amazing mother, Ann Moffatt, who told me about Plowden Hall, which is the inspiration for Hopesay Manor, and whose own cooking exploits first got me started in the kitchen.

I'd like to give a special thanks to my former English teachers, Keith Ward and Susan Roache for their inspirational teaching, which in part has led me to where I am today. I had no idea when I was studying *Paradise Lost* all those years ago it would come in so handy!

It seems lucky to have one family you get on with. It seems positively greedy to have two. But that's the fortunate position I find myself in. So for both my families, I'd like to say a big thank you for all the Christmases, past, present and future. Here's to many many more.

Read on for exclusive Christmas Tips from Julia Williams
to help you through the festive season

Christmas Tips

- Defrost the turkey in time.

- Try and buy a few presents every week.

- If you're making a Christmas pudding use Marguerite Patten's recipe, which can be done the day before.

- Try to remain calm. It's only a day.

- Don't invite feuding family members.

- Try and invite only people you like.

- Get those people you like to help you by preparing vegetables.

- Set the table the day before.

- Don't leave present wrapping till Christmas Eve.

- Don't leave present buying till Christmas Eve.

- Ignore any child that wakes up before 7am.

- Try and eat in the evening avoiding early morning putting-on-the-turkey rises.

- Most of all . . .

DO NOT STRESS!!!

Read on for an exclusive extract from Julia Williams's new novel, *The Bridesmaid Pact* coming next year.

It was Doris' idea of course. Everything back then tended to emanate from Doris. She was the glue that bound us all together. She was the sticky stuff that made us all friends. Without Doris we were nothing. And even then we knew it.

'It's on, it's on,' she said, proudly brandishing the new video control of her parents' state of the art Beta Max video machine. Though of course we didn't say state of the art then. Nor did we realise that Doris' parents ahead of the trends as ever, had invested in a bit of technology which was going to be obsolete in a few short years. At eight years old, we were still marvelling at the idea of being able to watch our favourite TV moment of the year, again, and again.

'Go straight to the kiss,' Caz demanded. She was always the most impatient one.

'No, we have to watch it all,' Beth was most emphatic on that point. Her serious little face peeped up from under arms. 'I didn't get to see it because my mum and dad are anti-royalsomething.'

'Royalist,' interjected Doris.

'They don't like the Queen,' said Beth. 'So I wasn't allowed to watch any of it.'

Silently we all marvelled at this. All term we'd talked about nothing but the wedding. About what she'd wear, and who the bridesmaids would be. We'd even had a day

391

off school to watch – Doris' mum and dad had taken her up to London and they'd camped out outside St Paul's Cathedral and watched it on the day – and poor Beth hadn't seen any of it.

'Luckily my mum and dad videoed it then, isn't it?' said Doris. 'Now sssshhh.'

We all settled down on the beanbags and cushions in the room that Doris' American professor dad called the den. Doris' house was like nothing the rest of us had ever seen. It was massive, with huge airy rooms and en-suite bathrooms for every bedroom. Imagine that. Even Doris had one. For me who shared a tiny suburban three bedroomed semi with my parents and three siblings, it seemed like a fairy palace. I still kept pinching myself that Doris had allowed me into her inner sanctum. It would have been easy to hate her, with her little girl ringletted beauty, her film star mother, clever professor father, and amazing house, but somehow, it was impossible to hate Doris. She was kind and generous and dappy and funny, and hid her cleverness (inherited from the professor father) under a carefully cultivated dizzy blondeness – except of course, she wasn't blonde.

The posh voice of the commentator was describing the guests as they arrived, and pointing out Prince Charles waiting with Prince Andrew for Diana to arrive. We all oohed and aahed as the carriages pulled up bearing the Queen and Prince Philip.

'I have to have that dress when I'm a bridesmaid next year,' Doris paused the tape so we could ogle the brides-maids. After some critical discussion, we all agreed that Doris was much prettier then India Knight, and would suit the dress better. It never even occurred to the rest of us to think about any of us wearing the dress—

'Why is it always you?' Caz burst out. Her eyes pinpoint dark, and two bright points of red flaming her cheeks, her attitude as ever, spiky and pugnacious. 'Why can't the rest of us get to wear that dress? Just because you're rich and we're not!'

'That's not fair!' Doris leapt up and shouted. 'Don't I always let you have my stuff and invite you over?'

'So you can feel good,' spat back Caz. 'I know you only have me here because you feel sorry for me.'

'That's not true,' said Beth, ever the peacemaker. 'Caz I think you should say sorry.'

As Caz's best friend, I felt duty bound to take her part, though I didn't think she was being fair either. As the prettiest, richest one of us, and the only one who was going to actually be a bridesmaid, I felt that Doris was quite within her rights to lay first claim to India Knight's dress. After all, even she with all her wealth wasn't going to wear that exact dress.

'Doris, it is true that you always take the lead,' I said reluctantly. Like Beth, I always hated confrontation. And a part of me seethed that just as I'd got to being accepted by Doris, here was Caz trying to muck it up for me again. As she always did. I loved Caz to bits, but why did she have to be so angry all the time? Doris was the one person she didn't need to be angry with.

'Do I?' Doris looked stricken, and I felt even worse. 'I don't mean to. I'm really sorry, Caz, I didn't mean to upset you.'

Seeing her lower lip begin to quiver, and tears dangerously start to wobble down her cheeks, Caz for once softened uncharacteristically. Perhaps even hard as nails Caz couldn't resist Doris' charm.

'It's ok,' she said sulkily. 'I didn't mean to upset you either.'

Relieved that everything had gone back to normal, Doris ran to the huge kitchen and produced ice creams for all of us as we settled down to watch as Diana finally emerged from her carriage, to instant oohs and aahhs and squeals from the four of us.

'Isn't she like a fairy princess,' breathed Beth.

'She's beautiful,' I agreed.

'I'm going to have that dress when I get married,' announced Doris solemnly.

'I think she looks like a marshmallow,' said Caz, who didn't have a romantic bone in her body.

We all threw our ice cream wrappers at her, and settled down in blissful silence to watch as Charles Windsor took Diana Spencer to be his lawful wedded wife—

'To have and to hold, for richer for poorer, in sickness and in health, till death do us part,' we chanted the vows in unison.

'That's so romantic,' said Doris. 'I want to marry a prince when I grow up.'

Caz snorted, so we sat on her. By now we were getting bored of the video, so Doris fast forwarded to the kiss, which we watched over and over again, ecstatically imagining what it would feel like to have a boy kiss you on the lips like that. I thought it must feel very rubbery.

'We should make a pact,' Doris suddenly said. She was like that. Full of odd ideas, that seemed to come from nowhere.

'What kind of pact?' I said.

'We should promise to be friends forever and make a pact that we will be bridesmaids at each other's weddings.'

'I'm never going to get married,' declared Caz firmly.

'You can still be a bridesmaid though,' said Doris. She was impossible to resist, so even Caz was persuaded to stand in a circle. We all raised our hands together and held them up so that we touched.

'We solemnly declare,' intoned Doris, 'that we four will be friends forever.'

We looked at each other and giggled.

'Go on,' she said, 'say it after me.'

So we repeated what Doris had said, and then all four of us said, 'and we promise that when we get married we will only have our three friends as bridesmaids. And we promise that we will be bridesmaids for our friends.'

'From this day forth, forever and ever, shall this vow be binding,' said Doris. And then she made us cut a lock off each of our hair, and bind them together. She put the locks of hair, together with a written copy of the words we'd said, which we all signed, and then put it away in her special box.

'There,' she said, with satisfaction. 'Now we've taken an oath, and we can never ever break it.'

August 1996

Caz

Billy Idol was screaming out it was a nice day for a white wedding, which seemed appropriate in a bar in Las Vegas. I couldn't resist the craving for the next drink, though I knew I needed it like a hole in the head.

'Oi, Charlie boy, gezza another drink,' I was aware vaguely in some dim dark recess of my brain that I'd probably had enough and I was definitely slurring my words. The sensible thing would be to go to bed right now. Call it a day with these very nice and fun-loving work colleagues with whom I'd spent a couple of days bonding in Las Vegas on the first solo photo shoot of my burgeoning career as a make-up artist, and probably the most exciting job I'd had to date. But sense and I didn't go very well together. My sensible head never won over my drunken one.

'What are you on again?' Charlie looked in about as good shape as I was. He had wandered up to the bar. He turned to look at me as he said this, and leaned rather nonchalantly against the bar. He missed, narrowly avoiding smashing his chin on the bar, before righting himself.

'Vodka and coke,' I said, giggling hysterically. Our companions, Charlie's boss Finn, and Sal, the PA to the spoilt model whose photos we'd all been involved in taking for the past couple of days were nuzzling up to each other in one of the deep red heart shaped sofas that littered the bar. It had not been a very well kept secret of the week that they were shagging the pants of each other, despite Finn's heavily pregnant wife at home. I wasn't quite sure how I felt about that. I was no angel it's true, but shagging someone who was hitched with a baby on the way seemed like a complication too far to me. I wondered if he was worth it. Then looked at his rugged, wrinkled face and decided he wasn't. Finn must be nearly twenty years older then Sal. What on earth did she see in him?

Now Charlie on the other hand. He was a bit of alright. Tall, dark, conventionally good looking with a rather fetching quiff that fell over his eye, and which he brushed off with a rather shy movement which I found at once attractive and endearing. Charlie was rather lovely. And might be just the thing to take my mind off the humiliation of being turned down by Steven.

I'd always known Steven would go for Sarah, in the end, despite all his flirting. They always did. Her pretty girl-next-door looks always won them over, even if they were initially attracted to my wildness. My spiky aggressiveness, was in the main too much for most of the men I encountered. Far too toxic, as I'd been told on more then one occasion. They enjoyed the shag, but they never hung around long enough to keep their spare pyjamas in my cupboard.

When we'd met him out drinking in Soho, it was obvious that a cityboy slicker like him would go for Sarah, the safe bet, rather then her more wild and unpredictable friend. Not that it stopped him flirting with me mind, and making lewd suggestions about what he'd like to do with me when Sarah wasn't around. I'd bet a million dollars he never said anything like that to her. I should have been a better friend to her. I should have warned her about what he was like. But annoying prick as he was, Steven also happened to be one of the most gorgeous guys I'd ever met. And when he was flirting, boy did he make you feel good about your-self. And I, despite all my chippiness and bravado, needed a morale boost from time to time. Not that I'd ever admit it to anyone, of course.

So when he finally moved things up a notch, one night when I bumped into him without Sarah, I didn't even think about her and went along with things. And after we'd danced and snogged and gyrated our way round the dance floor, I'd assumed we were going back to his. I was so unprepared for that knockback. I hated the feelings of churned up misery he'd stirred up in me. It made me furious to feel so weak. After that he and Sarah became more of a perman-ent item. And I was left alone. Bruised and sore. And not a little jealous.

Yes, I could do with Charlie to lighten things up. And he seemed to like me . . .

'What time is it?' I jerked awake, and suddenly realised I had dozed off on Charlie's shoulder. There was no sign of the other two. Presumably they'd gone off to consummate their passion. Well good luck to them.

'Three a.m.,' said Charlie, 'but hey, the night's still young. We're in Vegas don't forget. Ever played black jack?'

'No,' I said, 'but there's a first time for everything.'

So suddenly we were out on the streets, when sense dictated we should have been tucked up in bed, running through Vegas like a pair of school kids. It was such an outrageously extravagant place, I felt right at home. I could be anything I wanted here. Anything at all.

It wasn't difficult to find a casino, and soon we were betting money we couldn't afford on a game I barely understood. I was drinking vodka like it was going out of fashion, but here, in this atmosphere, I felt alive in a way I never had, and carried away on a feeling of indulgent recklessness. Charlie was lovely too, really attentive in a way none of the guys I'd ever been with had ever been before. I was enjoying the sensation so much, I let my guard down. And it felt great.

'Hey, look over there,' I nudged Charlie, 'there's a wedding couple.'

'So?' said Charlie, who was looking at his hand trying to work out if he was going to make 21 or have to go bust. His last five dollars were riding on it. I'd had to give up a couple of hands before as I'd run out of money. I wasn't quite reckless enough to go into debt.

'Isn't it cute?' I said, suddenly fascinated with this couple. They seemed to represent something I never thought I'd have. 'I bet there's a little chapel next door where you can get hitched just like that.'

'There is honey,' a Texan blonde with a pink rodeo hat and tassled pink denim jacket next to me, drawled. 'It's called Love Me Tender, and they've got an Elvis impersonator who'll marry you for a few dollars.'

'What a hoot,' I said. I nudged Charlie. 'We should do it.'

'Don't be daft,' said Charlie.

'Come on, where's your sense of adventure?' I said.

'I think marriage should be a bit more serious then that,' said Charlie.

'Oh, don't be so boring,' I said. 'Think what fun we've had tonight. We're made for each other. We'll get married tonight and go home and make a little Las Vegas baby.'

I didn't know what I was saying. I hated babies. I certainly didn't want one now. But somehow, I felt certain of one thing. Charlie and I had connected tonight, in a way I'd never connected with anyone. We should be together.

'You're mad,' said Charlie. He gave me a quizzical look, as if weighing something up. 'Did you mean all that?'

'Course I did,' I said. 'If you win this game, then we get married?'

'Ok,' said Charlie, 'but I don't think I'm going to win.'

Everyone had stuck apart from Charlie. He turned over his hand. Twenty-one. He'd won. Over two hundred dollars. It seemed like a fortune.

'Go on,' I said. 'Now you have to do it. A deal's a deal.'

An hour later, fortified by more vodka and a promise of a singing Elvis – Charlie it turned out was a closet Elvis fan – and we found ourselves in front of the Love Me Tender chapel. The door was heart-shaped, and the outside of the chapel was a sickly pink which reminded me of the terrible blancmanges my grandmother used to make when I was little and Mum was having one of her funny 'turns'. We giggled as we saw it. We'd come armed with our marriage license, which bizarrely in Las Vegas you could buy at any time of the night or day over the weekend, and the sun was just rising above the city, which seemed just as busy now as it had done when we'd embarked on our drinking spree all those hours earlier. I had a moment of panic then. This wasn't how I'd planned my wedding day. I'd always pretended I didn't want to get married, but now I was here, I could admit to myself I wanted the real deal, not this ghastly parody, with a boy I barely knew. I thought of Doris with a pang. She'd be furious with me for not fulfilling her silly pact.

'Come on then,' Charlie grabbed my hand, and pulled me through the door. We were met by an Elvis impersonator who was apparently the official who was going to marry us. It also transpired that he was going to give me away. So I walked down the aisle to the tender strains of *Love Me Do* and then in a few easily spoken words we were hitched. It felt surreal. This wasn't the way I'd ever imagined it was going to be.

We then took a cab out to the desert and held hands as

we watched the sun rise. It was the most romantic moment of a bizarre and weird evening. Charlie kissed me on the lips and said, 'Happy Wedding Day, Mrs Davies. Come on, let's go home.'

We got back to the hotel, and then shyly, I followed him up to his room. It was strange. We'd been behaving so recklessly all evening, and now I felt like a fool. I could legitimately sleep with the guy and suddenly, now I was here, it felt all wrong. In the end, we just stumbled into bed, and collapsed cuddling on the bed from exhaustion and over consumption of alcohol.

I woke at midday. The sun was streaming through the window, and Charlie was still snoring next to me. *Charlie.* I sat bolt upright and looked down at him, the events from the previous night flooding back with sudden and vivid clarity. Oh my god. I'd got married to a guy I barely knew. What on earth had I been thinking? Of all the wreckless things I'd ever done, this had to be the most stupid.

Snapshot: Caz

I knew even as I sat down at the bar with him, I was doing the wrong thing. But a combination of anger at Sarah, and recklessness from having had too much to drink, and a sort of self-hatred which has always been my fatal flaw, led me not to care. Besides. He was here with me. Not with her. I knew it was wrong to want him as much as I did. But I had wanted him from the first time we met. And he chose Sarah, as they always did. I was the one they shagged. Sarah was the one they chose for the long term. And this time, he'd really made it clear he was playing the long game. This time, I'd lost him for good.

Except. Here he was, newly affianced, in a bar with me. Playing footsie under the table, looking at me with lascivious eyes, accidentally touching my hand when there was no need.

I could lie and say I was so drunk I didn't know what I was doing. I could pretend that 'it just happened', like they always say in the problem pages. But it wouldn't be true. These things don't 'just' happen. You have to lose control of the bit of you that's screaming that this is so so wrong, you have to let go of your moral compass and go on a journey into a morass of grubby decisions that you'll later regret. You have to choose all that. It doesn't just happen.

Even at the moment I let him into my flat, I could have just ended it then, after the coffee, before we'd gone too far.

But I was drunk on power, and lust and the feeling I'd got one over on Sarah for once. Besides, I wanted to know what he was like, this golden boy, whom I'd adored for so long.

And once we'd kissed, and cuddled, and got down and dirty, then there was a point, a moment when I could have said, no, this is wrong, we mustn't go any further, but I didn't say it. I didn't try to stop the inevitable, and I could have. Because drunk and all as I was on lust, tantalising as every touch was, I knew exactly what I was doing. But still I continued, carried on a wave of passion into a world where there were no commitments, and I didn't betray the people I loved, and the man I was with loved me for myself, not for the undoubted quick bit of fun I undoubtedly was.

It was only in the morning, when I woke up, and saw him already dressed, already distancing himself from me, that I felt ashamed. I didn't know how I was ever going to face Sarah again. I didn't know how I was ever going to face myself. I felt wrong and dirty and so very, very bad. A sudden vision of my mother, in her worst vengeful mode swam before my eyes. 'You're a dirty little whore,' she hissed in my ear. 'I always knew you'd turn out to be no good.' I turned my face to the wall and wept.

I turned the invitation over and over in my hands, despite the feeling of nausea rising up from the pit of my stomach and the sheer panic that seeing that handwriting for the first time in what, over four years, had engendered in me. You had to hand it to Doris, she certainly knew how to break the ice. Only she could have sent me an invitation to her hen weekend on Mickey Mouse notepaper.

Dorrie and Daz are finally tying the knot, it read, and I snorted with laughter. Trust Doris to make her forthcoming nuptials sound like some kids' TV programme. I was glad she was finally getting hitched to Yakult Man (so called because of his obsession with cleanliness). They were made for each other. *You are invited*, it said, *to Dorrie's extra special hen weekend at Eurodisney. Fab four members only. One for all and all four one* – trust Doris to remember that stupid tag line we'd had as kids. But then, she'd probably been the one to think it up. At the bottom, Doris had scrawled in her unforgettably untidy handwriting (amazing how someone as beautifully presented as Doris could have such terrible writing, but then, that was Doris all over. A mass of impossible contradictions.), *Please come. It won't be the same without you.*

Doris. What a bloody stupid name. How could her parents have been so unkind? She always claimed it was because her mum was a fan of Doris Day, but it seemed like, for once in her impeccably toned and manicured life, Doris' mum had got it wrong and caused a major *faux pas*. Not that Doris seemed to mind. She'd inherited the happy-go-lucky nature of her screen namesake, and took *que sera, sera* as her motto. And because she was just so bloody wonderful, and fabulous, no one ever seemed to even tease her about her name. Now if it had been me . . .

I turned the invitation over in my hands once again. Should I go? It seemed to me, Doris was offering me another chance. Typical of her generosity that. And I didn't deserve it I knew. Last time we'd met, she'd tried to bridge the gap between me and Sarah and guilt and hurt and anger had led me to be unforgivably rude to her. Even Doris had been unable to forgive that for a while. But now it seemed like she had.

But what of the others? Could Beth and Sarah ever forgive me, for what I'd done to them? We grew up in a culture that taught us that redemption is always possible. But I'd been around in the world enough to know that it didn't happen as often as our teachers told us. Besides. You need to earn redemption. To gain forgiveness, you need to be truly, truly sorry. And even now there's a self destructive bit of me which isn't sure that I am . . .

The plane touched down at Charles de Gaulle airport and I took a deep breath. Well, here I was. Finally. It had taken all my courage to come – I'd been tempted by a job in Greece where a famous model was attempting a comeback shoot for M&S. It would have been a great job. Glamorous. In the sun all day, and time in the evenings for some unwinding and Greek dancing in the local tavernas. But Charlie persuaded me otherwise. Charlie was my favourite photographer on the circuit. Down to earth and easy going, he had the most amazing ability to tease the best out of the subjects he shot. Working with Charlie was always a breeze. And he was fun to socialise with too. Not since that mad moment in Las Vegas, that we'd ever been anything other then friends, mind. He was firmly hitched to his live-in girlfriend and attractive as I found him, I wasn't about to go upsetting any apple carts. I'd learnt my lesson too well last time.

I emerged blinking from the airport into the pale March Paris sunshine. I always loved coming to Paris, but it was the cafe culture, museums and walks along the Seine which were the usual attraction for me. Without Dorrie's invite, I doubt I'd ever have visited Disneyland Paris, but here I was on a train out of Paris, bound for Mickey Mouseville. Doris was the only person who could have ever persuaded me to come.

The shuttle service to Marne la Vallee proved surprisingly quick, and I had barely time to get my head together and think what on earth I was going to say to everyone when suddenly there I was, being deposited in front of Woody's Cowboy Ranch – *Toy Story* being Dorrie's favourite

Disney film, she'd insisted we stay here. Suddenly my heart was in my boots, and I was eight-years-old again, being invited for the first time to Dorrie's mansion. It had felt like such a privilege, back then to be entering Dorrie's inner sanctum, and yet in the self-destructive way I have, I'd pretty much blown the chance of making the most of the opportunities being friends with Dorrie and the others had afforded me. I didn't even know if they'd want to see me again, let alone forgive me. Knowing Dorrie, I bet she hadn't told them I was coming.

I checked in at the desk, my nerves making a mash of my school girl French. The unsmiling receptionist responded in perfect English with a look of such sneery disdain, I wanted the ground to swallow me up whole. Giving up on any attempt to speak her language, I said, 'I'm meeting friends, a Doris Bradley?'

'Ah oui, Mademoiselle Bradley is next door to you. I will let her know you have arrived.'

I took my bags and made my way to the third floor, shaking like a leaf. Suppose the others didn't want to see me. Suppose I ended up ruining Dorrie's big weekend? This had been a dreadful mistake. I was wrong to come.

I found room 325, next door to 327. Dorrie's room. I swallowed hard. Should I dump my bags, freshen up, and then go and say hi? Or should I bite the bullet and go straight for it?

The door to 327 flung wide open, and there in the flesh for the first time in years stood Dorrie. Larger then life as ever. Welcoming me in a massive hug. I felt my worries disappear instantly. Dorrie had a way of doing that. It was her special talent.

'Caz! You came, I'm so pleased. Come right in,' she propelled me into the middle of a massive room, complete with double bed and cowboy paraphernalia hanging from the walls.

Lounging on the bed, sipping champagne, were two faces I hadn't seen in a very, very long time. They both looked up at me and registered their shock.

'You never said *she* was coming,' Sarah shot me a look of such venom, I was quite taken aback. God did she really still hate me that much?

'It wouldn't have been the same without her,' said Dorrie firmly.

'Lock up your husbands,' said Sarah. 'Sorry Doz, I know you mean well, but I'm not spending any more time with her then I have to.' She got up and stormed out of the room, pushing past me with evident hatred.

I knew I shouldn't have come.